Mordant's Need

Also by Stephen R. Donaldson:

The Chronicles of Thomas Covenant

Book One: Lord Foul's Bane
Book Two: The Illearth War
Book Three: the Power that Preserves

The Second Chronicles of Thomas Covenant

Book One: The Wounded Land
Book Two: The One Tree
Book Three: White Gold Wielder

The Last Chronicles of Thomas Covenant

Book One: The Runes of the Earth

Daughter of Regals and Other Tales
Mordant's Need

STEPHEN DONALDSON

Mordant's Need

GOLLANCZ

LONDON

The Mirror of Her Dreams copyright © Stephen R. Donaldson 1986
A Man Rides Through copyright © Stephen R. Donaldson 1987
All rights reserved

This edition published in Great Britain in 2007 by
Gollancz
An imprint of the Orion Publishing Group
Orion House, 5 Upper St Martin's Lane, London WC2H 9EA

A CIP catalogue record for this book is
available from the British Library

ISBN-13 9 780 57507 904 5
ISBN-10 0 57507 904 5

Typeset by Deltatype Ltd, Birkenhead, Merseyside

Printed and bound in Great Britain by
Butler and Tanner, Frome

The Orion Publishing Group's policy is to use papers that
are natural, renewable and recyclable products and made
from wood grown in sustainable forests. The logging and
manufacturing processes are expected to conform to the
environmental regulations of the country of origin.

www.orionbooks.co.uk

CONTENTS

Prologue: TERISA AND GERADEN   3

BOOK ONE

One: CALLING   9
Two: THE SOUND OF HORNS   17
Three: TRANSLATION   24
Four: THE OLD DODDERER   33
Five: WARDROBES FULL OF CLOTHES   49
Six: A FEW LESSONS   62
Seven: THE DUNGEONS OF ORISON   79
Eight: VARIOUS ENCOUNTERS   106
Nine: MASTER EREMIS AT PLAY   127
Ten: THE LAST ALEND AMBASSADOR   157
Eleven: A FEW DAYS WITH NOTHING TO DO   180
Twelve: WHAT MEN DO WITH WOMEN   204
Thirteen: FOLLY IN GOOD FAITH   222

BOOK TWO

Fourteen: OUT OF THE RUBBLE   243
Fifteen: ROMANTIC NOTIONS   255
Sixteen: WHO YOUR FRIENDS ARE   274
Seventeen: TERISA TAKES ACTION   286
Eighteen: A LITTLE CONVERSATION   305
Nineteen: THE ADVANTAGES OF AN EARLY THAW   331
Twenty: FAMILY MATTERS   352
Twenty-One: AT LEAST ONE PLOT DISCOVERED   380
Twenty-Two: QUESTIONS ABOUT BEING BESIEGED   396

Twenty-Three: ANTICIPATING DISASTER 416
Twenty-Four: THE BEGINNING OF THE END 434
Twenty-Five: MASTER EREMIS IN EARNEST 452
Twenty-Six: FRATRICIDE 475

BOOK THREE

Twenty-Seven: THE PRINCE'S SIEGE 483
Twenty-Eight: A DAY OF TROUBLE 495
Twenty-Nine: TERISA HAS VISITORS 513
Thirty: ODD CHOICES 528
Thirty-One: HOP-BOARD 539
Thirty-Two: THE BENEFIT OF SONS 556
Thirty-Three: PEACE IN HOUSELDON 583
Thirty-Four: FRUSTRATED STATES 612
Thirty-Five: AN OLD ALLY OF THE KING 634
Thirty-Six: GATHERING SUPPORT 649
Thirty-Seven: POISED FOR VICTORY 680
Thirty-Eight: CONFLICT AT THE GATES 699
Thirty-Nine: THE FINAL PIECE OF BAIT 720

BOOK FOUR

Forty: THE LORD OF LAST RESORT 743
Forty-One: THE USES OF TALENT 751
Forty-Two: UNEXPECTED TRANSLATIONS 765
Forty-Three: THE ONLY REASONABLE THING TO DO 781
Forty-Four: MEN GO FORTH 799
Forty-Five: THE ALEND MONARCH'S GAMBLE 825
Forty-Six: A PLACE OF DEATH 841
Forty-Seven: ON THE VERGE 869
Forty-Eight: THE CONGERY AT WORK 884
Forty-Nine: THE KING'S LAST HOPES 902
Fifty: CAREFUL RISKS 923
Fifty-One: THE THINGS MEN DO WITH MIRRORS 943
Fifty-Two: NO MORE FIGHTING 967

Epilogue: CROWNING THE PIECES 974

To Ross McGuire Donaldson:
        for love,
            laughter
    and just enough dignity

            and

To Perryn Laura Donaldson:
for sunshine and flowers
            whenever you need them
and love
            whenever you want it

THE MIRROR OF HER DREAMS

PROLOGUE

TERISA AND GERADEN

The story of Terisa and Geraden began very much like a fable. She was a princess in a high tower. He was a hero come to rescue her. She was the only daughter of wealth and power. He was the seventh son of the lord of the seventh Care. She was beautiful from the auburn hair that crowned her head to the tips of her white toes. He was handsome and courageous. She was held prisoner by enchantment. He was a fearless breaker of enchantments.

As in all the fables, they were made for each other.

Unfortunately, their lives weren't that simple.

For example, her high tower was a luxury condominium building over on Madison, just a few blocks from the park. She had two bedrooms (one of them a 'guest room,' fully furnished and entirely unused), a spacious living room with an impressive view west, a separate dining room which contained a long, black, polished table on which candles would have gleamed beautifully if she had ever had any reason to light them, and the kind of immaculate modern kitchen displayed in remodeling catalogues.

Her home cost her father what the people she worked with would have called 'a small fortune,' but it was worth every penny to him. The security guards in the lobby and the closed-circuit TV cameras in the elevators kept her safe; and while she was living there she wasn't mooning passively around his house, gazing at him and his business associates and his women with those big brown calf-eyes that seemed too inert, or even too stupid, to intend what he read in them: the awareness of unlove that saw all his pampering and expense as a form of neglect. So he was glad to be rid of her.

And she thought she was glad to be living where she was because the bills were paid, and she could afford to work at the only job she felt herself competent for, the only job in which she thought her life might count for something: she was the secretary for a modern-day almshouse, a mission tucked away in a small ghetto only a fifteen-minute walk from the shining windows and reflected glory of her condo building; and she typed letters of mild explanation and appeal, vaguely desperate letters, for the lost old man who ran the mission.

Also, she thought she was glad to be living where she was because she had been able to decorate her rooms herself. This had been a slow process because she wasn't accustomed to so much freedom, so much control over her environment; but in the end what it came to was that her bedroom, living room, and dining room were decorated completely in mirrors. Mirrors had a seductive beauty which spoke to her – but that wasn't the point. The point was that there was virtually no angle in her apartment from which she couldn't see herself.

That was how she knew she existed.

When she slept, her mind was empty, as devoid of dreams as a plate of glass. And when she was awake, moving through her life, she made no difference of any kind to anybody. Even the men who might have considered her beautiful or desirable seemed not to see her when they passed her on the street, so blind she was to them. Nothing around her, or in her, reflected her back to herself. Without dreams – and without any effect – she had no evidence at all that she was a material being, actually present in her world. Only her mirrors told her that she was *there*: that she had a face capable of expression, with brown eyes round with thwarted softness, a precise nose, and a suggestion of a cleft like a dimple in her chin; that her body was of a type praised in magazines; that both her face and body did what was required of them.

She was completely unaware of the enchantment which held her. It was, after all, nothing more than a habit of mind.

As for Geraden, he was in little better condition.

He was only an Apt to the Congery of Imagers – in other words, an apprentice – and he had been given a task which would have threatened a Master. In fact, the opinion of the Congery was sharply divided about his selection. Some of the Masters insisted this task belonged to him because all their auguring seemed to imply that he was the only possible choice, the only one among them who might succeed. Others argued that he must be given the task because he was the only one of their number who was completely and irredeemably expendable.

Those who claimed that the act of bringing any champion into being was inherently immoral were secretly considered toadies of that old dodderer, King Joyse – and anyway they were only a small minority of the Congery. Apparently, all auguries indicated that the realm couldn't be rescued from its peril without access to a champion brought into being through Imagery. But how that translation should take place – and, indeed, who that champion should be – was less sure.

The Masters who considered Geraden expendable had good reason. After all, he wasn't just the oldest Apt currently serving the Congery: he was the oldest person ever to keep on serving the Congery without becoming skillful enough to be a Master. Though he was only in his mid-twenties, he was old enough to appear ridiculous because he had failed to earn the chasuble of a Master.

He was so ham-handed that he couldn't be trusted to mix sand and tinct without spilling some and destroying the proportions; so fumble-footed that he couldn't walk through the great laborium which had been made out of the converted dungeons of Orison without tripping over the carefully arranged rods, rollers, and apparatus of the Masters. Even rabbity Master Quillon, who had surprised everyone by casting aside his self-effacement and speaking out loudly (as King Joyse might have done, if he weren't asleep half the time) against the immorality of wrenching some champion out of his own existence in order to serve Mordant's need – even Quillon was heard to mutter that if Geraden made the attempt and failed, the Congery would at least gain the advantage of being rid of him.

In truth, this capacity for disaster rendered moot the central ethical point. Normally, the Master who had made that particular glass could simply have opened it and brought the champion into being. But Geraden had again and again shown himself incapable of the simplest translation. He would therefore have to do exactly what King Joyse would have demanded: he would have to go into the glass to meet the champion, to appeal for the champion's help.

His advantages were a willing heart, ready determination, and a quality of loyalty usually ascribed to puppies. His short chestnut hair curled above his strong brow; his face would have well become a king; and the training of being raised with six brothers had left him tough, brave, and little inclined to hold grievances. But his expression was marred by an almost perpetual frown of embarrassment and apology, occasioned by the petty mishaps and knowledge gone awry that harried his heels. His instinctive yearning toward the questions and potential of Imagery was so potent that his unremitting dunderheadedness left a gloom on his spirit which threatened to become permanent until the Congery elected by augury and common sense to send him on the mission to save Mordant's future.

When that happened, he recovered his ebullience. Where he had formerly worked for the Masters with a will, he now labored in fervor, doing the things their art demanded – mixing the sand and tinct with his own hands so that the glass would welcome him, stoking the furnace with wood he cut himself, shaping the mold and reshaping it a dozen times until it exactly matched the one that had made the mirror in which the Masters watched their chosen champion, pouring the hot liquid while blood hammered like prayer in his veins, sprinkling the specially ground and blended powders of the oxidate. At every failure of attention, error, or mischance, he groaned, cursed himself, apologized to everyone in sight – and then threw himself back into the work, hope singing to him while sweat soaked his clothes and all his muscles ached.

He had no more idea than Terisa did that she was under an enchantment. And if he had known, he might not have cared, so consumed was he by the opportunity the Masters had provided – an opportunity which might be a sentence of maiming or even death.

She wasn't the champion the Congery had chosen.

She didn't so much as inhabit the same world as that champion.

In theory, at least, Geraden's mirror would have had to be entirely different.

Book One

ONE

CALLING

The night before Geraden came for her, Terisa Morgan had a dream – one of the few she could ever remember. In it, she heard horns: faint with distance, they reached her through the sharp air over the hills covered with crisp snow like the call for which her heart had always been waiting. They winded again – and while she strained to hear them, again. But they came no closer.

She wanted to go looking for them. Past the wood where she seemed to be sitting or lying as if the cold couldn't touch her, she saw the ridge of the hills: perhaps the horns – and those who sounded them – were on the far side. Yet she didn't move. The dream showed her a scene she had never seen before; but she remained who she had always been.

Then along the snow-clogged skirt of the ridge came charging men on horseback. As the horses fought for speed, their nostrils gusted steam, and their legs churned the snow until the dry, light flakes seemed to boil. She could hear the leather creaking of their tack, the angry panting and muttered curses of their riders: the ridge sent every sound, as edged as a shard of glass, into the wood. She yearned to block out those noises, to hear the horns again, while the three men abruptly swung away from the hills and lashed the snow toward the trees – directly toward her.

As their faces came into focus for her, she saw their fierce hate, the intent of bloodshed. Long swords appeared to flow out of their sheaths into the high hands of the riders. They were going to hack her into the snow where she stood.

She remained motionless, waiting. The air was whetted with cold, as hard as a slap and as penetrating as splinters. In the dream, she wasn't altogether sure that she would mind being killed. It would bring the emptiness of her life to an end. Her only regret was that she would never hear the horns again, never find out why they spoke such a thrill to her heart.

Then from among the black-trunked trees behind her came a man to impose himself between her and the riders. He was unarmed, unarmored – he seemed to be wearing only a voluminous brown jerkin, pants of the same fabric, leather boots – but he didn't hesitate to risk the horses. While the first rider swung his blade, the man made a sidelong leap at the reins of the mount; and the horse was wrenched off balance, spilling its rider in front of her second attacker. Both horse and rider went down, raising clouds of snow as thick as mist.

When a low breeze cleared her sight, she saw that her defender had snatched up the first rider's sword and spitted the second with it. He moved with a desperate awkwardness which showed that he was unfamiliar with fighting; but he didn't falter. In furious assault, he stretched the first rider out against the trunk of a tree before the horseman could strike back with his long poniard.

Watching, Terisa saw the third rider poised above the young man who fought for her – mount firmly positioned, sword hilt gripped high in both fists. Though she understood nothing of what was going on, she knew that she ought to move. In simple decency and gratitude toward her defender, if for no other reason, she should fling herself against the rider. He wasn't looking at her: surely she would be able to reach his belt and pull him out of his saddle before he struck.

But she didn't. In the dream, a small, vexed frown pinched her forehead as she regarded her passivity. It was the story of her life, that mute nothingness – the only quality she could ascribe to her uncertain existence. How could she act? Action was for those who didn't seriously doubt their own presence in the world. During the more than twenty years of her life, her opportunities for action had been so few that she typically hadn't recognized them until they were past. She didn't know how to make her limbs carry her toward the rider.

Yet the man who fought for her did so for no reason she could see except that she was being attacked. And he didn't know his danger: he was still trying to wrest his blade from the body of the rider he had just felled, and his back was turned.

Startling herself and the horseman and the sharp cold, she cried, 'Watch out!'

The effort of the warning jerked her into a sitting position. She was still in bed. Her shout made her throat ache, and an unaccustomed panic pounded through her veins.

She recognized herself in the mirrors of her bedroom. Lit by the night-light plugged into the wall socket behind the bed, she was hardly more than a shadow in the glass all around her; but she was herself, the shadow she had always been.

And yet, while her pulse still labored and a slick of sweat oozed from her face, she thought she heard beyond the comfortless noises of the city a distant calling of horns, too faint to be certain – and too intimate to be ignored.

Of course, nothing was changed. She got up the next morning when her alarm clock went off; and her appearance in her mirrors was as rumpled and wan as usual. Though she studied her face for any sign that it was real enough for men on horseback to hate so fiercely, it seemed as void of meaning as always – so unmarked by experience, decision, or impact that she was dimly surprised to find it still able to cast a reflection. Surely she was fading? Surely she would wake up one morning, look at herself in the mirror, and see nothing? Perhaps, but not today. Today she looked just as she remembered herself – beautifully made, but to no purpose, and slightly tinged with sorrow.

So she showered as usual, dressed herself as usual in the sort of plain skirt and demure sweater her father preferred for her, breakfasted as usual – watching herself in the mirrors between bites of toast – and put on a raincoat before leaving her apartment to go to work. There was nothing out of the ordinary about the way she looked, or about her apartment as she left it, or about the elevator ride down to the lobby of her building. The only thing out of the ordinary was the way she felt.

To herself, so privately that none of it showed on her face, she kept remembering her dream.

Outside, rain fell heavily onto the street, flooding the gutters, hissing like hail off the roofs of the cars, muffling the noises of traffic. Dispirited by the gray air and the wet, she tied a plastic bandana over her head, then walked past the security guard (who ignored her, as usual) and out through the revolving doors into the downpour.

With her head low and her concentration on the sidewalk, she moved in the direction of the mission where she worked.

Without warning, she seemed to hear the horns again.

Involuntarily, she stopped, jerked up her head, looked around her like a frightened woman. They weren't car horns: they were wind instruments such as a hunter or musician might use. The chord of their call was so far away and out of place that she couldn't possibly have heard it, not in that city, in that rain, while rush-hour traffic filled the streets and fought the downpour. And yet the sensation of having heard the sound made everything she saw appear sharper and less dreary, more important. The rain had the force of a determined cleansing; the streaked gray of the buildings looked less like despair, more like the elusive potential of the borderland between day and night; the people jostling past her on the sidewalk were driven by courage and conviction, rather than by disgust at the weather or fear of their employers. Everything around her had a tang of vitality she had never seen before.

Then the sensation faded; and she couldn't possibly have heard rich horns calling to her heart; and the tang was gone.

Baffled and sad, she resumed her sodden walk to work.

At the mission, her day was more full of drudgery than usual. In the administrative office, seated at her desk with the ancient typewriter crouching in front of her like a foul-tempered beast of burden, she found a message from Reverend Thatcher, the old man who ran the mission. It said that the mission's copying costs were too high, so would she please type two hundred fifty copies of the attached letter in addition to her other duties. The letter was aimed at most of the philanthropic organizations in the city, and it contained yet another appeal for money, couched in Reverend Thatcher's customary futility. She could hardly bear to read it as she typed; but of course she had to read it over and over again to get it right.

While she typed, she seemed to feel herself becoming physically less solid, as if she were slowly being dissolved by the pointlessness of what she did. By noon, she had the letter memorized; and she was watching in a state that resembled suspense the line of letters her typewriter made, waiting for each new character because it proved that she was still there and she couldn't honestly say she expected it to appear.

She and Reverend Thatcher usually ate lunch together – by his choice, not hers. Since she was quiet and watched his face attentively, he probably thought she was a sympathetic listener. But most of the time she hardly heard what he said. His talk was like his letters: there was nothing she could do to help. She was quiet because that was the only way she knew how to be; she watched his face because she hoped it would betray some indication of her own reality – some flicker of interest or concentration of notice which might indicate that she was actually present with another person. So she sat with him in one corner of the soup kitchen the mission ran in its basement, and she kept her face turned toward him while he talked.

From a distance, he appeared bald, but that was because his mottled pink skin showed clearly through his fine, pale hair, which he kept cut short. The veins in his temples were prominent and seemed fragile, with the result that whenever he became agitated they looked like they might burst. Today she expected him to rehash his latest letter, which she had already typed nearly two hundred times. That was his usual pattern: while they ate the bland, thin lunch provided by the kitchen, he would tell her things she already knew about his work, his voice quavering whenever he came back to the uselessness of what he was doing. This time, however, he surprised her.

'Miss Morgan,' he said without quite looking at her, 'have I ever told you about my wife?'

In fact, he hadn't, though he referred to her often. But Terisa knew some of his family history from the previous mission secretary, who had given up the job in defeat and disgust. Nevertheless she said, 'No, Reverend Thatcher. You've mentioned her, naturally. But you've never told me about her.'

'She died nearly fifteen years ago,' he said, still wistfully. 'But she was a fine, Christian woman, a strong woman, God rest her soul. Without her, I would have been weak, Miss Morgan – too weak to do what needed doing.'

Though she hadn't considered the question closely, Terisa thought of him as weak. He sounded weak now, even when he wasn't talking about his failure to do better for the mission. But he also sounded fond and saddened.

'I remember the time – oh, it was years ago, long before you were born, Miss Morgan – I was out of seminary' – he smiled past her left shoulder – 'with all kinds of honors, would you believe it? And I had just finished serving an assistant pastorship at one of the best churches in the city.

'At the time, they wanted me to stay on as an associate pastor. With God's help, I had done well there, and they gave me a call to become one of their permanent shepherds. I can tell you, Miss Morgan, that was quite gratifying. But for some reason my heart wasn't quiet about it. I had the feeling God was trying to tell me something. You see, just at that time I had learned that this mission needed a new director. I had no desire for the job. Being a weak man, I was pleased by my position in the church. I was well rewarded for my work, both financially and personally. And yet I couldn't forget the question of this mission. It was true that the church called me to serve them. But what did God call me to do?

'It was Mrs. Thatcher who resolved my dilemma. Putting her hand on her hip, as she always did when she meant to be taken seriously, she said, "Now don't you be a fool, Albert Thatcher. When Our Lord came into the world, he didn't do it to serve the rich. This church is a fine place – but if you leave, they'll have the choice of a hundred fine men to replace you. Not one of those men will consider a call to the mission."

'So I came here,' he concluded. 'Mrs. Thatcher didn't care that we were poor. She only cared that we were doing what we could to serve God. I've done that, Miss Morgan, for forty years.'

Ordinarily, a comment like that would have been a prelude to another of his long discussions of his unending and often fruitless efforts to keep the mission viable. Ordinarily, she could hear those discussions coming and steel herself against them, so that her own unreality in the face of the mission's need and his penury wouldn't overwhelm her.

But this time what she heard was the faraway cry of horns.

They carried the command of the hunt and the appeal of music, two different sounds that formed a chord in her heart, blending together so that she wanted to leap up inside herself and shout an answer. And while she heard them, everything around her changed.

The soup kitchen no longer looked dingy and worn out: it looked well used, a place of single-minded dedication. The grizzled and tattered men and women seated at the tables were no longer reduced to mere hunched human wreckage: now they took in hope and possibility with their soup. Even the edges of the tables were more distinct, more tangible and important, than ordinary formica and tubed steel. And Reverend Thatcher himself was changed. The pulse beating in his temples wasn't the agitation of uselessness: it was the strong rhythm of his determination to do good. There was valor in his pink skin, in the earned lines of his face, and the focus of his eyes was so distant because it was fixed, not on futility, but on God.

The change lasted for only a moment. Then she could no longer hear the horns, even though she yearned for them; and the air of defeat seeped slowly back into her surroundings.

Filled with loss, she thought she would start to weep if Reverend Thatcher began another of his discussions. Fortunately, he didn't. He had some phone calls to make, hoping to catch certain influential people while they were taking their lunch breaks; so he excused himself and left her, unaware that for a moment he had been covered by glamour in her eyes. She returned to her desk almost gratefully; at her typewriter, she would be able to strike the keys and see her existence proven in the black characters she made on paper.

The afternoon passed slowly. Through the one, bare window, she could see the rain still flooding down, drenching everything until even the buildings across the street looked like wet cardboard. The few people hurrying up and down the sidewalks might have been wearing rain gear, or they might not: the downpour seemed to erase the difference. Rain pounded on the outside of the window; gloom soaked in through the glass. Terisa found herself typing the same mistakes over and over again. She wanted to hear horns again – wanted to reexperience the tang and sharpness that came with them. But they had been nothing more than the residue of one of her infrequent dreams. She couldn't recapture them.

13

At quitting time, she put her work away, shrugged her shoulders into her raincoat, and tied her plastic bandana over her head. But when she was ready to go, she hesitated. On impulse, she knocked on the door of the tiny cubicle Reverend Thatcher used as a private office.

At first, she didn't hear anything. Then he answered faintly, 'Come in.'

She opened the door.

There was just room in the cubicle for her and one folding chair between his desk and the wall. His seat at the other side of the desk was so tightly blocked in with file cabinets that when he wanted to leave he could barely squeeze out of his niche. As Terisa entered the room, he was staring blankly at his telephone as if it sucked all his attention and hope away.

'Miss Morgan. Quitting time?'

She nodded.

He didn't seem to notice that she hadn't said anything. 'You know,' he told her distantly, 'I talked to forty-two people today. Thirty-nine of them turned me down.'

If she let the impulse which had brought her here dissipate, she would have that much less reason to believe in her own existence; so she said rather abruptly, 'I'm sorry about Mrs. Thatcher.'

Softly, as if she hadn't changed the subject, he replied, 'I miss her. I need her to tell me I'm doing the right thing.'

Because she wanted to make him look at her, she said, 'You *are* doing the right thing.' As she spoke, she realized she believed it. The memory of horns had changed that for her, if nothing else. 'I wasn't sure before, but I am now.'

His vague gaze remained fixed on the phone, however. 'Maybe if I call her brother,' he muttered to himself. 'He hasn't made a contribution for a year now. Maybe he'll listen to me this time. I'll keep trying.'

While he dialed the number, she left the cubicle and closed the door. She had the impression that she was never going to see him again. But she tried not to let it bother her: she often felt that way.

The walk home was worse than the one to work had been. There was more wind, and it lashed the rain against her legs, through every gap it could find or make in her coat, past the edges of her bandana into her face. In half a block, her shoes were full of water; before she was halfway home, her sweater was sticking, cold and clammy, to her skin. She could hardly see where she was going.

But she knew the way automatically: habit carried her back to her condo building. Its glassy front in the rain looked like a spattered pool of dark water, reflecting nothing except the idea of death in its depths. The security guards saw her coming, but they didn't find her interesting enough to open the doors for her. She pushed her way into the lobby, bringing a gust of wind and a spray of rain with her, and paused for a few moments to catch her breath and wipe the water from her face. Then, without looking up, she headed toward the elevators.

Now that she was no longer walking hard, she began to feel chilled. There was a wall mirror in the elevator: she took off her bandana and studied her face while she rode up to her floor. Her eyes looked especially large and vulnerable against the cold pallor of her skin and the faint blue of her lips. So

14

much of her was real, then: she could be made pale by wind and wet and cold. But the chill went too deep for that reassurance.

As she left the elevator and walked down the carpeted hall to her apartment, she realized she was going to have a bad night.

In her rooms, with the door locked, and the curtains drawn to close out the sensation that she was beneath the surface of the pool she had seen in the windows from the outside, she turned on all the lights and began to strip off her clothes. The mirrors showed her to herself: she was pale everywhere. The dampness on her flesh made it look as pallid as wax.

Candles were made of wax. Some dolls were carved of wax. Wax was used to make molds for castings. Not people.

It was going to be a *very* bad night.

She had never been able to find the proof she needed in her own physical sensations. She could easily believe that a reflection might feel cold, or warmth, or pain; yet it didn't exist. Nevertheless she took a hot shower, trying to drive away the chill. She dried her hair thoroughly and put on a flannel shirt, a pair of thick, soft corduroy pants, and sheepskin moccasins so that she would stay warm. Then, in an effort to hold her trouble back, she forced herself to fix and eat a meal.

But her attempts to take care of herself had as much effect as usual – that is to say, none. A shower, warm clothes, and a hot meal couldn't get the chill out of her heart – a detail she regarded as unimportant. In fact, that was part of the problem: nothing that happened to her mattered at all. If she were to die of pneumonia, it might be an inconvenience to other people – to her father, for example, or to Reverend Thatcher – but to her it would not make the slightest difference.

This was going to be one of those nights when she could feel herself fading out of existence like an inane dream.

If she sat where she was and closed her eyes, it would happen. First she would hear her father talking past her as if she weren't there. Then she would notice the behavior of the servants, who treated her as a figment of her father's imagination, as someone who only lived and breathed because he said she did, rather than as an actual and present individual. And then her mother—

Her mother, who was herself as passive, as nonexistent, as talent, experience, and determination could make her.

In her mind, with her eyes closed, Terisa would be a child again, six or seven years old, and she would hobble into the huge dining room where her parents were entertaining several of her father's business associates in their best clothes – she would go into the dining room because she had fallen on the stairs and scraped her knee and horrified herself with how much she was bleeding, and her mother would look at her without seeing her at all, would look right through her with no more expression on her face than a waxwork figure, and would make everything meaningless. 'Go to your room, child,' she would say in a voice as empty as a hole in her heart. 'Your father and I have guests.' Learn to be like me. Before it's too late.

Terisa had been struggling to believe in herself for years. She didn't close her eyes. Instead, she went into her living room and pulled a chair close to the

15

nearest wall of mirrors. There she seated herself, her knees against the glass, her face so near it that she risked raising a veil of mist between herself and her reflection. In that position, she watched every line and shade and flicker of her image. Perhaps she would be able to keep her reality in one piece. And if she failed, she would at least be able to see herself come to an end.

The last time she had suffered one of these attacks, she had sat and stared at herself until well past midnight, when the sensation that she was evaporating had finally left her. Now she was sure she wouldn't last so long. Last night, she had dreamed – and in the dream she had been as passive as she was now, as unable to do anything except watch. The quiet ache of that recognition weakened her. Already, she thought she could discern the edges of her face blurring out of actuality.

Without warning, she saw a man in the mirror.

He wasn't reflected in the mirror: he was *in* the mirror. He was behind her startled image – and moving forward as if he were floundering through a torrent.

He was a young man, perhaps only a few years older than she was, and he wore a large brown jerkin, brown pants, and leather boots. His face was attractive, though his expression was foolish with surprise and hope.

He was looking straight at her.

For an instant, his mouth stretched soundlessly as if he were trying to shout through the glass. Then his arms flailed. He looked like he was losing his balance; but his movements expressed an authority which had nothing to do with falling.

Instinctively, she dropped her head into her lap, covered it with her arms.

The mirror in front of her made no noise as it shattered.

She felt the glass spray from the wall, felt splinters tug at her shirt as they blew past. Like a flurry of ice, they tinkled against the opposite wall and fell to the carpet. A brief gust of wind as cold as winter puffed at her with the broken glass, then stopped.

When she looked up, she saw the young man stretched headlong on the floor beside her chair. A dusting of glass chips made his hair glitter. From his position, he looked like he had taken a dive into the room through the wall. But his right leg from mid-calf down was missing. At first, she thought it was still in the wall: his calf and his boot seemed to be cut off flat at the plane of the wall. Then she saw that the end of his leg was actually a couple of inches from the wall.

There was no blood. He didn't appear to be in pain.

With a whooshing breath, he pushed himself up from the floor so that he could look at her. His right calf seemed to be stuck where it was; but the rest of him moved normally.

He was frowning intensely. But when she met his gaze, his face broke into a helpless smile.

'I'm Geraden,' he said. 'This isn't where I'm supposed to be.'

TWO

THE SOUND
OF HORNS

Without quite realizing what she was doing, she pushed her chair back and stood up. Involuntarily, she retreated. Her feet in her moccasins made faint crunching noises as they ground slivers of glass into the carpet. The wall where the mirror had been glued was splotched and discolored: it looked diseased. The remaining mirrors echoed her at herself. But she kept her eyes on the man sprawled in front of her.

He was gaping at her in amazement. His smile didn't fade, however, and he made no attempt to get up.

'I've done it again, haven't I,' he murmured. 'I *swear* I did everything right – but any Master can do this kind of translation, and I've gone wrong again somehow.'

She ought to be afraid of him: she understood that distinctly. His appearance there in her living room was violent and impossible. But instead of fear she felt only bafflement and wonder. He seemed to have the strange ability to bypass logic, normalcy. In her dream, she had not been afraid of death—

'How did you get in here?' she asked so softly that she could barely hear herself. 'What do you mean, this isn't where you're supposed to be?'

At once, his expression became contrite. 'I'm sorry. I hope I didn't frighten you.' There was tension in his voice, a fear or excitement of his own. But in spite of the tightness he sounded gentle, even kind. 'I don't know what went wrong. I did everything right, I swear it. I'm not supposed to be here at all. I'm looking for someone—'

Then for the first time he looked away from her.

'—completely different.'

As his gaze scanned the room, his jaw dropped, and his face filled up with alarm. Reflected back at himself from all sides, he recoiled, flinching as though he had been struck. The knotted muscles of his throat strangled a cry. A fundamental panic seemed to overwhelm him; for a second, he cowered on the rug, groveled in front of her.

But then, apparently, he realized that he hadn't been harmed. He lifted his head, and the fear on his features changed to astonishment, awe. He peered at himself in the mirrors as if he were being transformed.

Spellbound by his intense and inexplicable reactions, she watched him and didn't speak.

After a long moment, he fought his attention back to her. With an effort, he cleared his throat. In a tone of constrained and artificial calm, he said, 'I see you use mirrors too.'

A shiver ran through her. 'I don't know what you're talking about,' she said. 'I don't have any idea what you're doing here. How do you know I'm not the right person?'

'Good question.' His grin stretched wider. He looked like he enjoyed the sight of her. 'Of course you can't be. I mean, how is that possible? Unless everyone has misunderstood the augury. Maybe this room pulled me away from where I should be. Did you know I was going to try this?'

Terisa didn't want to repeat herself. Instead of continuing to mention that she had no idea what he meant, she asked, 'Why don't you get up? You look a little silly, lying there on the floor.'

One thing about him pleased her immediately: he seemed to hear her when she spoke, not simply when it happened to suit his train of thought. 'I would like to,' he said somewhat sheepishly, 'but I can't.' He gestured toward his truncated right leg. 'They won't let go of my ankle. They *better* not let go. I would never get back.' His expression echoed the mercurial changes of direction in his mind. 'Although I don't know how I'm going to face them when I do get back. They'll never believe I haven't done it all wrong again.'

Still studying him for some sign that what was happening made sense, she inquired, 'You've had this problem before?'

He nodded glumly, then shook his head. 'Not this exact problem. I've never tried to translate myself before. The fact is, it isn't commonly done. The last one I can remember was when Adept Havelock made himself mad. But that was a special case. He was using a flat glass – trying to translate himself without actually going anywhere, if you see what I mean.'

He looked around again. 'Of course you do. Flat glass,' he breathed as though her mirrors were wonderful. 'It's lovely. And you haven't lost your mind. I haven't lost *my* mind. I had no idea Imagers like you existed.

'At any rate,' he resumed, 'the theory of inter-Image translation is sound, and there are lots of cases recorded. Most people just don't want to take the risk. Since I made the mirror – if I step all the way through, they might not be able to bring me back. Only an Adept can use other people's mirrors – and Havelock is mad.

'But never mind that.' He pushed his digression aside. 'It just looks like I haven't been able to make it work.

'The fact is,' he concluded, 'I've never been able to make anything work. That's why they chose me – part of the reason, anyway. If something went wrong and I didn't get back, they wouldn't lose anybody valuable.'

Baffled as she was by this conversation, her training with Reverend Thatcher came to her aid. He had taught her to ask the questions he expected or wanted. 'Where are you supposed to be?' Again she shivered. 'Who am I supposed to be?'

18

He thought for a moment, chewing his lip. Then he replied, 'I'd better tell you. The augury could have been misinterpreted. An Imager like you might be exactly what we need. And if I'm right—' He shot a gleam at her and began to explain.

'Everyone has studied the augury. Some of what we see in it can't be wrong. It shows over and over again that the only way Mordant can be saved is if someone goes into a mirror and brings back help. For some strange reason, that "someone" is me. Unfortunately, the augury doesn't show me bringing any "help" back. Instead, it shows an immensely powerful man in some kind of armor – a warrior or champion from another world. It doesn't show whether he'll save or destroy Mordant, but he's unmistakable. And about the time of the augury he just happened to arrive in the Image in one of Master Gilbur's mirrors. Judging from what we could see, he was huge – in his armor – and he had enough magic weaponry to tear down mountains. He looked perfect.

'Of course, Master Gilbur could have just translated him to us. Several of the Masters thought we should do that – and defy the King. But the augury is explicit. We're supposed to send me somewhere. Something about me is crucial. Apparently.' He lifted his shoulders. 'There was a lot of argument. Master Quillon said I should go. But Master Eremis said that forcing me to translate myself out of existence was as good as a death sentence – and he isn't usually that serious about anything. That surprised me. I don't like Master Eremis, and I thought he didn't like me. But in the end the Congery decided to let me try.

'So I made the mirror – I made it and *made* it, until we could all see the champion in it perfectly, and the Masters said it was right.' He frowned in bafflement. 'I worked on that so hard. I *swear* it's an exact duplicate of the original. But when I stepped into it' – he met her gaze and shrugged – 'I came here.'

She waited until he was finished; but she already knew what she was supposed to say next. 'So now you think the augury was misinterpreted. It said you had to go get someone. It didn't say who that someone was.'

He nodded slowly, watching her face as if she could make what she was saying true.

'This time the Congery might be wrong.'

He nodded again.

For no good reason, she still wasn't afraid. 'So when you did what the augury showed, you came where you were supposed to be, not where the Congery decided.'

After a moment, he said softly, 'Yes. It doesn't make any sense, does it? It's impossible. A mirror can't translate something it doesn't show. But no matter how badly I foul up, I can't stop thinking things like that. You must have done something. You must have brought me here.' He glanced away, then looked up at her strongly. 'You must have had a reason.'

This remark restored the logical reality of the situation, took away the illusion that she was having a comprehensible conversation. A comprehensible conversation with a man who fell into her living room out of nowhere, shattering one of her mirrors in the process? She wanted to answer him,

None of this has anything to do with me. But she had never learned how to say things like that out loud. Often she felt a quiver of shame and a personal fading when she thought them. Looking for an escape from the dilemma – or at least from the room, so that she could try to pull herself together away from the influence of Geraden's intent brown eyes – she said instead, 'Would you like a cup of tea?'

She had his undivided attention. 'I think I would' – his smile was at once abashed and pleased – 'but unfortunately I don't know what "tea" is.'

'I'll get some,' she said. 'It'll just take a few minutes.' Keeping her relief to herself, she started toward the kitchen.

Before she had gone three steps, he said in a completely different tone – a voice strong and formal, and yet strangely suppliant – 'My lady, will you accompany me to Mordant, to save the realm from destruction?'

In surprise, she stopped and looked back at him.

At once, his expression became contrite and embarrassed. 'I'm sorry,' he said. 'I don't have the right to place demands on you. I just suddenly have the strongest feeling that if you leave this room you won't come back.'

As soon as he spoke, she realized that one reason she wanted to go into the kitchen was to reach the phone. She wanted to call security and tell them there was a crazy man in her apartment babbling about mirrors and translation and champions.

'Do you have these feelings often?' She was stalling while she tried to figure out what to do.

He shrugged; his expression held the shape of his formal question. 'Not often. And they're always wrong. But I trust them anyway. They have to mean *something*.' He hesitated for a moment, then said, 'One of them made me apprentice myself to the Congery. I don't know why – it certainly hasn't done me any good. I've been an Apt for almost ten years, and I never get any further.' His tone was quiet; she heard anger rather than self-pity in it. 'But I still have the strongest feeling that I *must* become a Master. I can't stop trying.'

'But you said you wanted some tea.'

'I didn't know what I was afraid of until you started to leave.'

'I'm not going anywhere,' she responded slowly. 'I'll be back in a few minutes.'

Again, she headed toward the kitchen. She was definitely going to call security. This had gone on too long.

'My lady!' he called immediately. His voice was strong, strangely commanding. 'I beg you.'

She tried to continue, but her steps slowed of their own volition. In the entryway to the kitchen, she halted.

'If I twist and pull suddenly, my lady,' he said quietly, 'I can probably free my ankle. Then I'll be entirely here, with no way to return. And the Masters won't know where I am, since what they see in this mirror is the champion. Then I'll be lost here forever, unless by some chance or miracle they shape a mirror which shows me to them. If, in fact,' he added to himself, 'I *am* anywhere at all, and not lost in the glass itself, as Master Eremis insists.

'But I'll do it,' he went on more intensely, 'before I'll permit you to leave without hearing me.'

For a moment, she remained where she was. She felt herself leaning forward, trying to take the next step which would carry her out of his sight and into the sanctuary of the kitchen. Yet his appeal held her back as if he had a hand on her shoulder.

After all, she asked herself in an effort to think logically, normally, what would happen if she called security? The guards would come and take Geraden away. If they could – if they could wrench his leg free. And then they would have to let him go. He would be free to haunt her life. Unless she pressed charges against him. Then she would have to see him again as his accuser, making herself responsible for what happened to him. Perhaps she would have to see him several times. And she would certainly have to explain him to her father. Either way, she was stuck with him.

She had no desire to stand up in court – or in front of her father – and say that a man she had never seen before had broken into her living room through one of the mirrors and had asked her to save something called 'Mordant.'

Slowly, she turned back to face the young man. For the first time since he had startled her with his unexpected arrival, she was scared. But he was a problem she had to solve, and security wasn't the solution she wanted. Trying to keep her voice level, she said, 'None of this makes any sense to me. What do you want me to hear?'

'My lady—' At once, embarrassment and relief made him look ten years younger. 'I'm sorry,' he said again. 'I've done this all wrong. The way I've been talking, you probably think your mirrors have destroyed my mind. Which is what they should have done. I still don't understand it. But please—'

He had risen to his hands and knees. Now he pulled his torso upright, so that he was kneeling erect among the splinters of glass. Forcing down his confusion and abashment, he achieved a semblance of dignity.

'Please don't judge Mordant by me. The need is real. And it's urgent, my lady. Parts of the realm have already begun to die. People are dying – people who don't have anything to do with Imagery or kings and just want to live their lives in peace. And the threat increases every day. Alend and Cadwal are never exactly quiet. Now they're forming armies. And King Joyse doesn't do anything. The heart has gone out of him. Wise men smell treachery everywhere.

'But the gravest peril doesn't come from the High King of Cadwal or the Alend Monarch. It comes from Imagery.' He gathered passion as he spoke. 'Somewhere in the realm – somewhere where we can't find them – there are renegade Imagers, Masters of mirrors, and they're opening their glasses more and more to every kind of horror and foulness. They're experimenting on Mordant, trying to find in their mirrors those attacks and evils which will be most virulent to the peace, stability, and life that King Joyse forged in his prime. And these Masters seem to have no fear of the chaos that comes from unleashing powers that cannot be controlled.

'Before this winter ends, the realm will begin to crumble. Then there will be war on every hand – war of every kind – and all good things will be in danger.

'My lady,' he said straight to her, 'I don't have any power to compel you. If I did, it would be wrong to use it. And you aren't the champion the Congery expects. I've been such a fumble-foot all my life that my presence here might be just another one of my disasters.

'But I *might* be right. You understand mirrors.' He gestured around the room. 'You might be the help we need. And if you are, we're lost without you.

'Please. Will you come with me?'

She stared at him, her mouth open and her mind dumbfounded. *Dying. War. Every kind of horror and foulness. We're lost without you.* What, me? She had never heard of Mordant – or Cadwal, or Alend. The only countries she knew of that still had kings were thousands of miles away. And nobody anywhere talked about mirrors as though they were doorways into different kinds of reality. *You may be the help we need.* What was he talking about?

As carefully as she could, she said, 'This doesn't make any sense. I know you're trying to explain something, but it isn't working. None of this has anything to do with me.' You don't even know my name. 'I can't help you.'

But Geraden shook his head, dismissed her protest. 'You don't know that for sure. You don't—'

Abruptly, his gaze narrowed as if a new thought had struck him, and he scrutinized her face. 'Are you happy here?'

'Am I—?' The unexpected question made her look away from him, as though he had insulted her – or shamed her. Without warning, her fear was replaced by a desire to cry.

She peered hard into the nearest mirror, trying to reassure herself. Geraden occupied all the reflections, however, although she didn't want to see him. From where she stood, there was no glass or angle that didn't cast his image at her.

In spite of his strangeness, his reflection appeared more real than her own.

'Are you necessary?' he asked.

What a question. She stared deep into her own eyes in the mirror and pinched the bridge of her nose to hold back the tears. She was probably the most replaceable fact of Reverend Thatcher's life. If she evaporated, he would notice her absence immediately; but his concern would last only until he found a new secretary. And days or even weeks might pass before her father became aware that she was gone. Then he would raise an enormous hue and cry, offering rewards, accusing the police of negligence, having security guards fired – but only to disguise the fact that he really didn't care one way or the other what had become of her. And she belonged to no one else.

'Are you—?' He faltered for an instant, then persisted. 'Forgive me. I've got the strongest feeling you aren't happy. You don't *look* happy. And I don't see anyone else here. Are you alone? Are you wedded?' At least he had the decency to sound embarrassed. 'Are you in love?'

She was so surprised – and he was squirming so badly – that she began to laugh. She remained close to tears; but laughing in front of him was an improvement over crying. The fact that she wasn't crying enabled her to turn from her reflection to face him directly.

'I'm sorry.' She had some difficulty suppressing her laughter. 'I guess it's not easy being in your position. You should have had them tie a rope around your waist, instead of holding on to your foot. That way, you would at least be able to stand up.'

'My lady' – again he spoke formally, and again his voice seemed to catch hold of her – 'you are not happy here. You are not needed. You are not loved. Come with me.' He extended a hand toward her. 'You are an Imager. It may be that my glass was formed for you from the pure sand of dreams.'

'I'm not an Imager,' she replied. 'I don't dream very often.'

Her protest was automatic, however, not urgent. She was hardly listening to herself. Because her dreams were so rare, they made powerful impressions on her.

And in her dream she had remained passive and unimportant while three riders had charged forward to kill her and a man she didn't know had risked his life to save her. A man like Geraden. Everything she disliked about herself held her back – her unreality, her fear of her father and punishment, her inability to have any meaningful effect on her own life. But Geraden still held out his hand to her.

She couldn't help noticing that it was nicked and bruised in several places, and one of his fingernails was torn. Still she thought it was a good hand – sturdy and faithful.

It made her think of horns.

Their call carried her fear away.

'But,' she went on, and each word was a surprise to her, conjured by unexpected music out of the ache in her heart, 'I think I would like to find out what's been hiding on the other side of my mirrors all this time.'

In response, his face lit up like a sunrise.

THREE

TRANSLATION

I don't believe it,' Geraden murmured to himself. 'I don't *believe* it.' Then, an instant later, he said excitedly, 'Quick, before you change your mind. Take my hand.'

She didn't believe it either. What was she doing? But his excitement made her want to laugh again. And in her memory the horns called clearly, ringing out over the cold snow despite distance and the intervening hills – called to her.

Quickly, so that she wouldn't have time to change her mind, she moved closer to him and put her hand in his.

At once, she became self-conscious. 'Is that all there is to it?' she asked. 'Don't you have to wave your arms or say magic words or something?'

His grin grew wider and happier as he clasped her hand. 'That's all. The invocations and gestures have already been made. And the ability is born, not made. All you have to do is move with me.' Balancing himself on the knee of his truncated leg, he got his left foot under him. 'And' – his expression sobered slightly – 'watch your step.'

He began to push himself backward, drawing her with him.

As he did so, his right calf disappeared by inches: the flat plane remained stationary, so that as he slid his knee backward more and more of his leg was cut off. He seemed to be using his foot and leg to probe a place behind him – a place that didn't exist.

When his right leg reached far enough, he was able to straighten his knee. Smiling and nodding to Terisa, slowly pulling her after him, he raised himself until he was almost upright. 'You might find it easier,' he said, 'if you close your eyes.' Then he shifted his weight to the other leg.

At that moment, his face went wide with dismay as he lost his balance and started to fall.

His plunge wrenched her forward, toward the wall – toward the plane where first his leg and now his entire body seemed to vanish. Instinctively, she tried to jerk free. But though he flailed for support, his hand held hers in a grip she couldn't break. She tried to cry out, flung up her arm to ward off the impact—

The last thing she saw of her apartment was the splotched plaster where her broken mirror had once been glued. While she was still trying to release the cry of panic trapped in her throat, her marginal grasp on actuality failed, and she faded out of existence.

At once, she passed into a zone of transition where time and distance contradicted themselves. She felt eternity in an instant – or maybe she felt an instant that took forever. Her fall became a vast and elongated plummet down from or up to the heights of the world, even though the plunge carried her no more than half a step foward. She studied the sudden darkness intimately, despite the fact that it was so brief she could hardly have noticed it.

And then, with the same sensation of instantaneous eternity, of huge brevity, she saw Geraden again: he seemed to snap back into existence as though he had been lit to life by the abrupt orange illumination of the lamps and torches.

She recognized it – and immediately forgot it.

He was still falling, his face stretched in consternation; he had misjudged the step behind him. And his hand still gripped hers. She couldn't recover. Even if she had been braced, she might not have been strong enough to stop his collapse toward the gray flagstones.

So she landed on top of him. Because she was trying to get her arms between herself and the impact, she accidentally planted an elbow in his stomach as she hit. His mouth gaped pain, and the breath burst from his lungs. But his body protected her: she flopped onto him and then off again. As a result, she came to rest on her back beside him, her face turned toward the massive old vaulted stone ceiling.

For a moment, the perceptual wrench had the effect of blindness: she stared upward as though she hadn't observed the difference between this place and her apartment. Past her feet, and up two steps from her sprawling position, stood a large mirror in a polished wooden frame. The glass was nearly as tall as she was; it was tinted with a color that only showed at the edges of its surface; instead of being made flat it had been given a faintly rippling curve. On some level, she was aware that what she saw reflected in the mirror wasn't the ceiling above her or the wall behind her. It also wasn't the living room of her apartment. Yet in other ways she was no more conscious of the mirror than she was of the stone on which she lay.

Then, distinctly, she heard someone say, 'Where did you get *her?*'

'You were invisible in the mirror. How did you do that?'

'Where did you go?'

Slowly through her stunned surprise leaked the information that she was stretched on the floor in the center of a circle of men.

What? She thought dumbly, her throat choked with astonishment. A circle of men. *Where?*

There must have been twenty or thirty of them, all staring down at her. At a glance, she saw that some of them were old and others weren't: all of them were older than she was. They wore a variety of cloaks and robes, cassocks and jerkins – warm clothing to compensate for the coolness of the air. Each of them, however, had a chasuble of yellow satin draped around his neck.

25

Some of them peered at her in amazement and horror. She felt that way herself. 'Fool!' one of them rasped. Another muttered, 'This is impossible.'

Others were laughing.

At her side, Geraden gaped for air. A delicate shade of purple spread up from his corded neck over the tight lines of his cheeks.

'Well, Apt,' one of the laughing men said through his mirth, 'here is another fine disaster.' He was tall, strongly built in spite of his leanness. His nose was too big; his cheekbones were too narrow, too flatly sloped toward his ears; his black hair formed an unruly thatch on the back of his skull, leaving his forehead bald. But the humor and intelligence in his pale eyes made him keenly attractive. He was wrapped in a jet cloak, which he wore with an air of insouciance. The ends of his chasuble hung as if he might start twirling them at any moment. 'With all the realm in danger, we send you questing for a champion to save us. But for you this is nothing more than an opportunity for dalliance.

'My lady,' he went on, addressing Terisa, 'it may be that you found young Geraden appealing enough to lure you here. But now that you *are* here, I think you will discover that Mordant has better men to offer.' With a laughing flourish, he bowed over her formally and extended his hand to help her to her feet.

Mordant, she echoed in the same dumb, choked surprise. He did it. He actually brought me to Mordant.

Geraden whooped a breath and began to pull air past the knot in his stomach.

Instinctively, Terisa turned toward him. At the same time, however, one of the men who hadn't been laughing crouched beside Geraden. This man had a face the color and texture of a pine board. His eyebrows were as thick and stiff as bracken, but there was no other hair on his head anywhere. His girth appeared to be nearly as great as his height. 'Shame, Master Eremis,' he muttered, reaching one heavy arm under Geraden's head and shoulders to support the young man as he hacked for breath. 'Find some other cause for amusement. What has happened here is either disaster or miracle. Certainly it is unprecedented. It needs seriousness.'

Master Eremis' smile reached halfway to his ears. 'Master Barsonage, you have no sense of play. What can any man or Master do about Apt Geraden's pratfalls and confusions except laugh?' He turned his attention back to Terisa. His offer of help hadn't wavered. 'My lady?'

'We can weep, Master Eremis,' a guttural voice responded from the circle. 'You have admitted yourself that we are doomed if we do not find the champion augured for us. I care nothing for King Joyse and his petty realm' – at this, the thick man supporting Geraden made a hissing noise through his teeth – 'and I do not care who knows it. Let him sink into senility, and let Alend and Cadwal butcher each other for the right to replace him. But *we* have no other hope, the Congery of Imagers. This blighted Apt has just failed us.'

Terisa wanted to turn to see who had spoken. But she was held by the smile and the eyes and the extended hand of Master Eremis. He was looking at her, *at her*, as if she were real – as if she were really present in this high

26

chamber of cut stone, where the air held a tang of winter and the light came from oil lamps and a few torches; impossibly present here when she had no physical right to be anywhere at all except back in her apartment, staring at herself alone in her mirrors.

The magnetism of his look compelled her. She couldn't refuse him; he gave her the tangible existence she had always doubted. Gazing back at him in surprise and wonder, she let him take her hand and draw her easily to her feet.

'You're wrong,' Geraden coughed. His color was improving. With Master Barsonage's help, he tried to sit up. 'All of you. She's the right one.'

The reaction was loud and immediate: most of the men started talking at once.

'What? A woman? Impossible.'

'Are you blind? Look at her. She isn't even *armed.*'

'This is not the champion you were sent to bring. Do you think we are as foolish as you?'

'But this proves it! Think of the implications. King Joyse and Adept Havelock are right. They *are* alive.'

'Leave the boy alone. I'm sure this was just another accident.'

The guttural voice added, 'What nonsense. Do not be irresponsible. You have made a ruin out of our trust. Do not try to disguise your failure by pretending success.' Terisa saw the speaker now: he was a heavyset man with a crooked back, hands that looked strong enough to break stones, a white beard spattered with flecks of black, and a fleshy scowl etched permanently onto his face. To the other Masters, he concluded, 'I argued and argued that we should not pin our hope on this hapless puppy, but I was outvoted. This' – he pointed a finger as massive as the peen of a hammer at Terisa – 'is the result.'

Master Eremis laughed again and made a placating gesture. But before he could reply, Geraden protested, 'No, Master Gilbur.' Coughing, he struggled out of Master Barsonage's hold and pushed himself to his feet. 'It isn't my fault this time. Think about it—'

Unfortunately, the attempt to stand, talk, and cough simultaneously confused his balance. He stepped on one of his own feet and fell to the side, pitching heavily against two Imagers. They were barely able to catch him. Several men guffawed; this time Terisa could hear their bitterness. They had seen him do things like this before.

When he regained his balance, he was flushed and glowering with embarrassment.

'Apt Geraden,' Master Eremis said kindly, 'you have not had an easy time of this. But what is done is done – and we are no nearer to the champion we need than we were when you began. It might be wiser if you did not vex the Congery further by arguing against the obvious.'

Grimly, Geraden straightened the disarray of his jerkin. 'What's obvious,' he began sourly, 'is that I haven't gone wrong the way you believe. You haven't considered—'

'Boy,' Master Barsonage growled behind him, 'watch your tone. We are Masters here. We are not required to hear the insolence of an Apt.'

At once, chagrin rushed over the anger and embarrassment in Geraden's face. 'I'm sorry. I didn't mean—' He flung a look of misery and contrition at Barsonage. 'But this is so *important.*'

'We are aware of what is important,' rasped the heavyset man, Master Gilbur. 'Credit us with that minimum of intelligence. The rest we will be able to reason for ourselves.'

Terisa was only marginally attentive to what was being said. As soon as Eremis stopped looking *at her,* she was nearly overcome by a sense of unreality. None of this was possible. Where was she really? Was this what happened when her tendency to fade away was pushed to its conclusion? Deliberately, she concentrated on what she could see, trying to convince herself of her surroundings.

She had her back to the mirror on the stone dais: instinctively, she felt that was one glass into which she didn't wish to glance. Master Eremis had positioned her in an almost proprietary way at his side; the rest of the Imagers were clustered around Geraden, Barsonage, and Gilbur. And they all stood near the open center – the dais itself occupied the center – of a large, round chamber with a flagstone floor. Crude-hewn gray granite formed the walls and ceiling. Several huge torches burned in sconces set around the distant walls; but most of the light came from oil lamps hanging from the four thick pillars that supported the high vaults of the ceiling. Within the area marked by the pillars, the center of the chamber was ringed by a carved wooden railing with benches like pews outside it, facing inward. The benches could have seated forty or fifty people.

This, she guessed, was the official meeting hall of the Congery of Imagers. That seemed reasonable – which was good. If it were reasonable, it might also be real.

She would have liked to wander away from the group of men, do a little exploring on her own. But part of her did hear what the Masters were saying. She heard the appeal in Geraden's voice, the weight of sarcasm with which Master Gilbur responded. Though she had only known Geraden for – what was it? ten minutes now? twenty at the most – she felt loyal to him. He had talked and listened to her and smiled as if she actually existed. Meeting the flustered contrite-and-urgent supplication in his eyes, she said to the Masters, 'I think you ought to give him a chance. There must be some reason why I agreed to come with him.'

At once, she winced inwardly and wanted to apologize to Geraden, because Master Eremis let out a peal of laughter. 'There must indeed, my lady,' he chortled. 'I was wrong to speak of dalliance, for that surely was no part of this Apt's appeal. He has many virtues, but grace and wit are not among them. Since we have no reason to believe that you were brought by force, there must indeed be some reason why you are with him.' Several of the Imagers chuckled at Eremis's jest; but Geraden could do nothing except duck his head to hide his misery. 'Well, speak, Geraden,' the Master went on. 'What is it that you believe we have not considered?'

For a moment, Terisa thought that Geraden would refuse to answer. She had watched her father embarrass her mother on any number of occasions, and the only outlet her mother had found for her resentment had been a refusal to speak. But Geraden set aside whatever humiliation he felt. Excitement surged into his gaze, and he took a step forward almost as if he were jumping.

'Master Eremis' – he turned his head – 'Master Gilbur' – again, he faced Eremis, Terisa, and the mirror – 'you know I'm only an Apt, and you laugh because I make a lot of mistakes. But you haven't thought about what she *means*.' He made an open-handed gesture toward Terisa. 'Why is she here? *How* did she get here?

'Master Gilbur, you taught me how to shape that mirror. It's exactly like the one you made. You know they're exactly alike because what you see in this mirror is the same as what your mirror shows. They're the same.

'Master Eremis, have you ever heard of a mirror that could translate things it didn't show?'

This question took several of the Masters aback. Gilbur scowled like the clenching of a fist; Eremis' mouth twisted thoughtfully; Barsonage raised his eyebrows so far that they appeared to grow back over his skull. A small man with a face like a rabbit's nodded vigorously.

Now Geraden was speaking to all the Imagers at once. 'The greatest Masters we know of have never been able to make mirrors that show one thing and translate another. Adept Havelock in his prime couldn't do it. Even the stories about arch-Imager Vagel don't mention any power as strong as that.

'Think about it, Masters. Either I've stumbled by accident onto the greatest achievement in the history of Imagery. Or I'm already the greatest Master since the first mirror was shaped.' Abruptly, he stopped, fixing his gaze squarely on Eremis.

'Or what, Apt?' Master Gilbur growled. 'Surely you do not expect us to stomach either of those alternatives?'

'Or,' Geraden said slowly, still holding Eremis' eyes, 'another power intervened. Maybe it was the same power that shaped the augury. It took me to a place I could not have reached with that mirror. A place where I could find the champion the augury intended instead of the one you chose.'

He was nearly whispering, and his brown eyes shone intently. 'She's the one I should have been sent to bring back. She's the one who can save us.'

For an instant, all the Congery stared in silence at Geraden and his assertion. Then the rabbity Master announced in a high, thin voice, 'I said so. I have said so from the beginning. This proves it. They *are* real.'

'Oh, forsooth,' retorted Gilbur trenchantly. 'The Apt speaks cleverly, but he defies reason. *She* our augured savior? *She* the power to rescue us from Imagery gone mad? Look at her, Masters. What are her powers? How will she fight in our defense? In what way is she superior to the champion we have chosen?'

As he spoke, he aimed a thick forefinger at the glass behind Terisa.

Several of the men shifted their attention there. Even Master Eremis turned and gave the mirror a glance.

Involuntarily, Terisa obeyed Gilbur's pointing.

Her first impression was confirmed: the mirror didn't reflect anything that she could see here – or that she had ever seen.

The tinted and faintly rippled glass showed a scene distant enough to be quite large, but not distant enough to weaken its primary figures. In the middle ground of a stark and alien landscape lit by the scarlet glow of an old, red sun stood a metallic shape which her mind instantly labeled a 'spaceship.' Forming a defensive perimeter around the ship were a number of manlike forms, also metallic: a moment passed before she realized that they actually were men, men in armor. They were under attack; but the destructive beams that chewed pieces off the landscape only glanced from the helmets and chestplates of the defenders. She couldn't see the effect of the fire they returned, but it must have been adequate: they weren't driven back toward their ship.

The central figure of the scene, however, wasn't the ship or one of the fighters. Rather, it was another metal-clad individual who occasionally waved his arms or shifted his attention as though he were directing the battle. He was heavily armed: strange weapons hung on his hips, and strapped to his back was a rifle the size of a small cannon. But more than his armament, it was his stance that conveyed a staggering sense of power through the glass. He stood the alien ground as if he meant to decimate whole populations in order to claim it.

Terisa understood at once that he was the champion, the strong and violent being Geraden had been sent to find.

That was the kind of help Mordant needed? The danger was *that* severe? And Geraden wanted these men to take *her* seriously as an answer to their problem, an augured savior? Suddenly, she realized that Master Gilbur was right. If Geraden considered her a sane answer to a problem of that scope, he was out of his mind.

What kind of lunacy had possessed her to take his hand? She should absolutely have gone to the phone, called security, and accepted the consequences. The strain of having to face her father would have been preferable to the impossibility of where she was now.

It affected her like dizziness. What was she *doing* here? She turned away from the mirror in a blur and seemed to lose her balance. Then she found herself gazing up into Master Eremis' face as if she were asking him for help. Though she didn't know him at all, she felt his intelligence, his strength, his effectiveness. His humor was built on confidence, and it promised results even when he was jesting.

He met her appeal for a moment, and the corners of his eyes crinkled as though he were about to start laughing again. But he didn't. Instead, he let a good-natured frown crease his high forehead. 'Masters,' he said in a musing tone, 'it is a subtle question. We must not dismiss it lightly. Apt Geraden makes a point which deserves consideration.'

Over Master Gilbur's growl of exasperation, Eremis went on, 'That his taste in champions is suspect I grant you. But there is simple truth in his words. Either he has stumbled by chance into a miracle. Or he has secretly made himself greater than us all.' Master Eremis put aside the protests of the Congery with a delicate wave of his fingers. 'Or there is a power at work here which we do not comprehend – and which we must take into account.

'I propose,' he continued promptly, 'that we adjourn for the present. We must have time to think. Mordant's need is urgent, but it does not require foolish haste. What say you? Perhaps tomorrow we will understand these things better.

'Master Barsonage?'

Terisa was faintly surprised to hear him suggest rather than announce an adjournment: she had assumed automatically that he was the leader of the Congery. But that role seemed to belong to the thick, bald man with the eyebrows like scrub and the pine-yellow skin. When Eremis addressed him, he glanced around the Masters for a moment, taking a consensus. After most of them had indicated their assent, he said, 'It is likely a wise idea. I doubt that we will gain much insight into whether Apt Geraden is the victim of accident, genius, or intervention. But we must determine what we will do about it. Those of us who are already weary of argument will need rest before facing that debate.'

Brusquely, he concluded, 'Let us meet again tomorrow.'

Master Eremis grinned his approval. 'Very good.' Then he turned to Terisa and extended his hand. 'My lady, will you accompany me? Someone must offer you the hospitality of Orison. I will see you honorably quartered, as befits a woman of your obvious importance.' He gave the word *importance* a slight, jesting stress, teasing either her or Geraden. 'And there are many things of which I wish to speak with you.'

He was looking squarely at her again, and she doubted that she could have refused his offer even if she had wanted to: his direct attention was seductive and compelling. It seemed to make her throat dry and her knees unsteady. Involuntarily, she reacted to him as if he were the first man who had ever looked at her in that way. As far as she knew, he *was* the first.

But when she raised her hand to take Eremis', Geraden suddenly said, 'My lady, I prefer that you accompany me.' His manner had become formal.

At once, an astonished silence dropped over the Masters; they stared at Geraden as though he had just insulted Eremis. The flush on Geraden's skin betrayed that he was conscious of his audacity. Nevertheless the muscles of his jaw bunched stubbornly, and his eyes didn't flinch.

Master Eremis raised an eyebrow; Terisa felt his concentration shift from her to Geraden. But after a brief flick away his gaze returned to hers. 'Come,' he said in an appealing – and commanding – tone. 'The Apt has played his part in these matters, but now he must leave them to those of greater rank, ability, and experience. You will not complain of my company, I think, my lady.'

She almost went with him. She wanted to – or thought she wanted to – or perhaps she had no idea what she wanted, but if she went with him he might be able to answer that question for her.

The Apt wasn't prepared to let her go, however. 'My lady,' he said, his voice clenched around his anxiety and determination, 'Master Eremis believes that you do not exist.'

His assertion fell into the silence like a personal challenge, as if he were daring the Master to battle.

And a small sting of panic touched Terisa's heart.

Vexation replaced the humor in Eremis' face. He swung scowling away from her; his tall body seemed to poise itself for a scathing retort. But an instant later he drew back a step, his self-control restored.

'That is not properly true, my lady,' he said coldly, without a glance at her. 'I believe that you did not exist until you were translated from the mirror.'

'And therefore,' Geraden went on, 'he believes that you are an object, my lady, an artifact of Imagery – a thing to be used, not a woman to be respected.'

That was too much for Master Eremis. 'Faugh!' he spat. 'I will not debate the meaning of Imagery with a puppy too hapless to earn a chasuble and too witless to respect his betters.' He dismissed Terisa. 'Go with him. He will drive me to distraction if you do not.'

Turning away, he strode through the crowd of Masters. A moment after he disappeared behind one of the pillars, Terisa heard the thud of a heavy wooden door.

Geraden didn't look at her. His gaze was fixed on the flagstones. He was so hot with embarrassment that beads of sweat stood on his forehead.

FOUR

THE OLD
DODDERER

'Arrogance,' one of the Imagers muttered. Another smiled his relish for
Eremis' discomfiture; but most of the Congery felt otherwise. Master Gilbur
gave a heavy shrug of disgust. The rabbity man twitched his nose.

They were glaring at Geraden.

Trembling inside, Terisa studied him too. Softly, hesitantly, she asked,
'What do you mean, he believes I don't exist? Or I didn't exist until I was
translated from the mirror?' That idea hit her too hard, too deeply. Was the
uncertainty of her being so plain that even strangers could see it? 'It doesn't
make any sense. None of this makes any sense. You don't even know who I
am.'

At once, Geraden began to apologize. 'I'm sorry, my lady. I keep treating
you badly, when that's the last thing I want.' He met her gaze with an
expression of brave distress – unhappy about his talent for doing or saying
the wrong thing, but determined to face the consequences. 'I should have let
you go with Master Eremis. I don't know what came over me.'

Before she could protest, That isn't what I meant, Master Barsonage
intervened. 'Apt Geraden,' he said, 'we have little patience for your contrition
just now.'

'I'm sorry,' said Geraden again, reflexively.

'It is a tale,' the Master went on in a tone like a bar of lead, 'we have heard
many times. Silence it, therefore, and heed me instead. I will not command
you not to speak to the King, since I know you would not obey me. I will say
this, however. She is here through your agency. She is your responsibility.
Give her the courtesy of Orison's hospitality as well as the Congery's respect.
She is a mystery to us and must be well treated.

'But' – he clamped a hand onto Geraden's shoulder – 'do not answer her
questions, Apt.'

At that, Geraden's eyes widened. Ignoring Terisa, Barsonage tightened his
grip and his tone. 'As a mystery to us, she is dangerous. Do not betray
Mordant or the Congery to her until we are sure of her.'

Geraden's gaze slid away from the Master's. He studied the stones under Terisa's feet and said nothing.

Very quietly, the thick man asked, 'Do you understand me, Apt? I am the mediator of the Congery. If I dismiss you, you will never again be considered for the chasuble of a Master.'

None of the other Imagers made a sound. Some of them looked vexed; some seemed to be holding their breath. The air in the room was still too cold for comfort.

Geraden's shoulder twisted under the mediator's grasp; then he straightened himself against the pressure. 'I understand you, Master Barsonage.' He sounded faraway and forlorn. 'The lady is my responsibility.'

'In all ways.'

'In all ways.'

Slowly, Master Barsonage released his hand. 'Admirable,' he muttered. 'Good sense becomes you.'

'Ha!' snorted Master Gilbur. 'Admirable, indeed.' He was glaring blackly at Geraden. 'If you believe that he will keep his word, Barsonage, you have become old in your wits.'

At that, Master Barsonage put his hands like barrel staves on his sides. 'Let me caution you against such statements, Master Gilbur. We are little trusted now – and less when you speak with such contempt. Apt Geraden springs from the honest and honorable line of the Domne. The sons of the Domne have always been true.'

Abruptly, then, he turned away from Geraden and Terisa. 'These meetings consume too much time,' he said in a friendly way to no one in particular. 'Again I am late for my noontide meal.' Slapping at his girth, he asked, 'Masters, will you join me?'

Several of the Imagers assented; Gilbur and others declined with varying degrees of courtesy. The Congery began to break up as Masters left the open center of the chamber, moving toward the doors beyond the pillars. After a few backward looks and a murmured comment or two, they left Terisa and Geraden alone.

He continued staring at the stones under her feet as if he were ashamed.

She blinked at him, feeling vaguely stupid. No one was going to answer any of her questions? No one was going to tell her why Master Eremis thought she didn't exist? Surely she had a right to protest?

As a little girl, however, she had occasionally made the mistake of protesting, of trying to stand up for herself. *It isn't fair why do I always have to go to bed you never want me around!* The reactions she had received taught her at an early age the folly of what she was doing. Her parents had wanted her to impinge on their consciousness as little as possible. Her father, in particular, had seldom been gentle when she had called his notice down on herself. Following his example, most of his servants had treated her with bare tolerance. And the numerous private schools to which she had been shuttled at his whim all had specific instructions where she was concerned. A passive child was only dismissed from attention; an assertive one was punished. And it was punishment that had first convinced her that she might not be real.

Over the years, she had learned to let herself feel less and less of the emotions that led to demands and rejection.

So instead of indulging herself in some kind of outcry, she did the next best thing: she watched the flush of Geraden's shame and said nothing.

When he finally raised his head, he looked miserable.

'I'm sorry, my lady. This isn't what I thought was going to happen at all. I knew they would have to be convinced – especially Master Gilbur. But I didn't think they—' He grimaced. 'It isn't fair to drag you into this and then refuse to answer your questions. It just isn't fair. And it's *my* fault again, of course.'

To keep him talking, she asked, 'How is it your fault?'

Glumly, he muttered, 'I didn't tell them about your mirrors.'

There seemed to be no point in reminding him that she couldn't possibly understand what he meant, so she said, 'Why didn't you?'

He shrugged. 'I meant to. But at the last second I had the strongest feeling—' His voice trailed away, then came back more strongly. 'I just don't trust Master Eremis. Or Master Gilbur either, for that matter. I don't want to tell them anything.'

Terisa considered him for a moment. 'But you're still not going to answer my questions.' Thanks to her years of training, her tone betrayed almost no bitterness.

With a wince, he replied, 'No. I can't. You heard him. I think he's wrong, but that doesn't make any difference. He can have me dismissed. I've been trying to become a Master since I was fifteen. I can't give it up.' Again he said, 'I'm sorry.'

Glowering, but unable to meet her gaze, he stopped. His dire expression made him look younger than he was – in fact, younger than she was herself. Unexpectedly, she found that she wasn't angry at him, not even down in the secret places of her heart where she kept her dangerous emotions hidden. He seemed to be upset as much on her behalf as on his own. That was a degree of consideration to which she was unaccustomed.

In response, she surprised herself by inquiring, 'Do you think I exist?'

He looked at her sharply, the glower suddenly gone from his face. 'Well, of course. Isn't it obvious? In fact, you're the proof of what King Joyse and Adept Havelock have been saying all along. Masters like Eremis and Gilbur believe the mirrors create what we see in them. Those things only exist when they're translated out of the glass. But that never made any sense to me. And now it sounds like nonsense – now that I've gone into a mirror for myself and met you.' Excitement improved his appearance considerably. 'That was a shock – when I stepped into the glass expecting to find the champion and found you instead – but it convinced me you're real. Everything in the mirrors is real.'

Then he caught himself; the excitement faded from his face. He became distant and wary, ashamed again. 'But I'm not supposed to answer your questions.'

Terisa almost laughed. Out of nowhere, he made her feel good – better than she had felt for a long time. Already, he had convinced her that if she kept him talking he wouldn't be able to refuse her. He took her too seriously to refuse her. 'Apt Geraden,' she said, 'if I'm real, I must be important. Even if I'm an accident, I must be important. Don't you think it might be a good idea to ask me who I am?'

His eyes went wide: mouth agape, he stared at her. Apparently, he had been so wrapped up in her translation and his argument with the Imagers that he had forgotten the simple courtesy of asking for her name. The realization made him tremble on the brink of more contrition and misery; more apologies.

But an instant later he caught the spirit of her question. His face broke into a grin; he began to laugh. 'Oh, good for you, Geraden,' he said, shaking his head in amused horror. 'You're really doing well today.' Then he took a step backward, assumed a pose of mock dignity, and bowed extravagantly. The effort tripped him; he barely avoided stumbling. 'My lady,' he intoned, 'I prostrate myself before you most humbly. Will you deign to grant me the sublime honor of your name and station?'

'Don't be silly,' she replied, trying to conceal her enjoyment. 'I don't have any "station." My name is Terisa Morgan.'

'My lady Terisa of Morgan,' he continued sententiously, 'you are too kind. I am your most unworthy servant. But if you will accompany me, it will be my great joy to make you acquainted with Joyse, founder of the Congery, lord of the Demesne, and King of Mordant.'

Then he changed back to his normal manner. 'I think it would be a good idea if you met him right away. He needs to know about you, no matter what some of the Masters say. He'll understand how important you are. And he might be willing to tell you what's going on around here.'

When he said this, her mood soured. The reference to 'how important' she was restored her sense of the unreality of the situation. One way or another, she was a mistake: she was the wrong person. In consequence, she felt a sudden, irrational reluctance to meet King Joyse. He might laugh like her father at the idea that she was important.

'Geraden,' she asked awkwardly, 'is there really a reason for all this? You're not just doing an experiment on me, are you? Practicing your translations?'

Somehow, he looked straight into her face and saw what she was feeling. At once, his expression sobered; empathy softened his gaze. 'My lady, I swear to you on my heart that the need is urgent. King Joyse would have the head of any Imager who did frivolously what we've done to you – though there are some,' he digressed momentarily, 'who might attempt it, if they weren't restrained by the Congery.

'In addition, I swear to you,' he went on, 'if your translation is an accident – a mistake of any kind – I'll do everything anybody can do to restore you to your own world.

'And one thing more, my lady.' His tone and his gaze grew sharper. 'I'll find a way to get you back to your own world anyway, if King Joyse or Master Barsonage or *some*body doesn't decide to start treating you better soon.'

Meeting his eyes, Terisa found that she believed him, in spite of herself. The whole idea was secretly amazing – that any man, however accident-prone, would look at her and make promises so seriously. To cover her astonishment, she turned a little away from him. Then, as distantly as she could, she said, 'You'd better call me Terisa. I'm not anybody's "lady." I don't want the King to get the wrong idea.'

She felt rather than saw his approval. 'Thank you. I think you're doing the right thing. I have a good feeling about this.' He put one hand tentatively on her arm. 'Shall we go?'

His attention was focused on her as though he wanted to make more promises. In reply, she gave him the polite, noncommittal smile she had perfected by the time she was a teenager – and groaned to herself because her response to him was so much emptier than his to her. But she went on smiling that way while she nodded her assent.

He gestured past one of the pillars. 'This way, then.'

She was thankful that he let go of her arm as he guided her toward a door.

The door was a massive wooden construction supported with iron struts and bolts: it looked like it had originally been intended to seal people out of this chamber – or seal them in. In, she decided when Geraden opened the door, swinging it outward. But its bolts were arranged so that it could only be locked from the inside.

As he led her through the doorway, they met two guards in the corridor.

The men were both large, rough, poorly shaved veterans with the look of hard service about them. They wore mail shirts and leggings over their leather clothes and close-fitting iron caps on their heads. Each had a longsword at his belt and gripped a pike in his right hand. One of them was marked by an old scar that ran from his hairline down his forehead, between his eyes, and beside his nose almost to his mouth. The other had lost several teeth.

The one whose teeth were missing stared at Terisa in a way she didn't find reassuring; but the other addressed Geraden like a familiar comrade, asking him if there were any Masters remaining in the chamber.

When Geraden shook his head, the guard relaxed his stance. 'Then we're off duty for a while. Listen, Geraden. Argus and I have a small keg of ale waiting. What do you think? Would you and' – he flicked a suggestive glance at Terisa – 'your companion like to join us for a drink?'

'I think, Ribuld,' Geraden replied good-humoredly, 'that you and Argus forgot how to think the day you decided to be soldiers. For your information, my "companion" is the lady Terisa of Morgan, and she isn't likely to spend her time swilling ale with the likes of you. The King is waiting to meet her right now.'

'Too good for us, is she?' muttered Argus. But Ribuld gave him a solid elbow-jab in the ribs, and he stepped back, a look of apoplexy on his face.

Grinning, Geraden drew Terisa on down the passageway.

'Don't let them worry you,' he said softly as they walked. 'Those two look terrible, but they're good men. They trained with my brother Artagel. I'm going to try to get them assigned to keep an eye on you.'

'Why do I need guards?'

'Because—' he began. This time, however, he realized what he was doing right away. 'For the same reason I'm not supposed to answer your questions. Mordant has too many enemies. The Congery has too many enemies. And King Joyse—' Again he stopped, a look of unconscious pain on his face.

'Whether you're here by accident or not, you already have enemies yourself. As long as I'm responsible for you, I want to be sure you also have guards – guards who're going to take you seriously. Ribuld and Argus will do that for me because I'm Artagel's brother.'

After a moment, he muttered, 'Master Barsonage made a big mistake telling me not to answer questions.'

In silence, she walked with him down the corridor.

The corridor was built of the same gray blocks of granite that had formed the walls and ceiling of the Congery's chamber; and it led to several turns, a few doors, a stair, and then into an enormous square hall large enough to be a ballroom.

This place had a smooth floor, the stones closely fitted so that there were no gaps; balconies around the walls, where musicians might sit to play, or from which high lords and ladies might watch the dancing; several huge hearths for warmth. In each corner, broad stairways curved gracefully upward out of sight. But the place was lifeless. It had an atmosphere of disuse, even of neglect: the people and musicians, the excitement and color that might have given it gaiety had gone away. The hearths were cold; and the only light came from narrow windows high above the balcony on one wall, with the result that the hall was full of gloom. The windows permitted a glimpse of sullen clouds.

Terisa shivered as Geraden headed her toward one of the stairways. 'This isn't the direct route,' he commented. 'But we wouldn't be able to get across the courtyard without ruining your clothes.' She was fortunate to be as warmly dressed as she was. What she could see of the sky through the windows looked like winter.

The stairway took them up one level. From there, he led her through a sequence of passages, short stairways, and halls that created a haphazard impression, as if the massive stone pile through which they moved had been constructed randomly, by lumps. But his instinct for mishap didn't include any uncertainty about where he was going: he knew this place intimately.

As they walked, they began to encounter more and more people. Many of them were guards, on duty or on errands; but many more seemed to be the inhabitants of the building. Old men leaned on their brooms in the corridors, stirring small piles of dust with diligent inattention. Girls scurried here and there, carrying linens or buckets or mops. Boys sprinted past, probably pretending that they were involved in something urgent so that no one would stop them and put them to work. As for the men and women—

Terisa found that she could easily estimate their rank by their clothes. Everyone was warmly dressed; but the sweeps and chambermaids wore woolen skirts, wool shawls over their blouses, and heavy clogs, where the ladies had on floor-length gowns of taffeta or satin and supple leather boots, with jewels in their hair or about their necks. The charmen and grooms dressed themselves as Geraden did, in jerkins, pants, and boots, perhaps with a long dagger sheathed at their belts, but the lords wore elaborately woven surcoats over flowing shirts and tight hose, with sabers in ornamented scabbards on their hips. And the intermediate degrees of station could be defined at once by the presence or absence of a sword or a décolletage, by the length of a gown or the embroidery on a surcoat.

In spite of their elegance, however, even the finest lords and ladies didn't look like they had ever been to a ball. Almost without exception, they comported themselves like people who lived under a shadow.

Several of the individuals Terisa and Geraden encountered greeted him, either by name or by title.

All of them stared at Terisa as openly as they dared.

After a while, self-consciousness made her realize that they had probably never seen anyone like her before. The idea was startling – and unsettling.

Shortly, Geraden led her up a series of stairs that doubled back and forth as if they occupied the inside of a tower. They led to a high, carved door with a guard stationed on either side. These men were better kempt than Argus and Ribuld, though they appeared no less experienced and dangerous; but they acknowledged Geraden with the same familiarity.

'This is the lady Terisa of Morgan,' Geraden said. 'Will you announce us? I think the King will want to meet her.'

The guards made halfhearted efforts to conceal the way they ogled her. One of them shrugged: it was his duty to ward the King, but he clearly couldn't think of any reason to believe Geraden was dangerous. The other knocked on the door, let himself into the room beyond, and closed the door behind him.

A moment later, he returned. 'You can go in. But be careful. The King and Adept Havelock are playing hop-board. If the Adept decides you've disturbed his concentration, he might do something unpleasant.'

Geraden gave the man a sour smile. 'I understand.'

His hand lightly touching Terisa's arm, he moved her toward the half-open door.

The room they entered surprised her. It was the first richly appointed chamber she had seen in this place, and although it was about the size of her living room and dining room combined, it was warm. A thick rug, woven in an abstract pattern of lush blues and reds, covered most of the floor. Blond wood paneling had been set over the stone walls, and each panel was elegantly decorated, some with carving, others with fine black inlay-work. Candles burned in brass holders set into the walls; small five-branched candelabra stood on ornamental tables in the corners of the room and on both ends of the mantelpiece above the hearth. Hot coals glowed under the flames in the fireplace.

Two old men sat opposite each other at a small table in the center of the room. One of them wore a purple velvet robe that covered him like a tent. He appeared lost in it, as if it had been made for him when he was young and powerful, and no longer fit him now that his frame had withered. That impression was reinforced by his stark white hair and beard, by the faint blue tint his veins gave his skin, by the arthritic swelling of the knuckles of his hands, and by the watery azure hue of his eyes. A thin circlet of gold held his hair back from his face.

'King Joyse,' Geraden whispered to Terisa.

The other man had lost most of his hair, and what was left of it stuck up from his pate in unruly tufts. His hawk nose gave his face a fierceness which was belied by the constant trembling of his fleshy lips. His eyes seemed to be looking in slightly different directions. He wore a plain, dingy surcoat, which had once been white, with – as far as Terisa could tell – nothing under it. But over his shoulders was draped a yellow chasuble.

'Adept Havelock,' breathed Geraden. 'Some of the Masters call him "the King's Dastard."'

Both men were concentrating intently on a playing board set between them. It was composed of alternating red and black squares, but only the black squares were in use. On them sat small round counters: the King's were white; Havelock's, red. As she noticed the board, Terisa saw Havelock make a move, hopping one of his men over two of the King's and removing them from the board.

They were playing checkers.

A jolt of recognition went through her, upsetting her disproportionately. After all, it was only a minor game – one of the few she had ever played. One of her father's valets had taught it to her in his spare time when she was ten years old; and they had played together at intervals for nearly a year, until he lost his job. He had been a square-cut young man with an odd kindness in his eyes and an infrequent grin. The truth was that she had never really enjoyed the game itself: she had played so eagerly because she had a tremendous crush on him. His attention and his little courtesies to her had charmed her completely. When the man was fired, she had somehow mustered enough courage to ask her father why, but he had refused to give any explanation. 'It's none of your business, Terisa. Go and play. I'm busy.'

Remembering that valet now, she felt an unexpected sense of loss, as if in her small world she had just suffered an important bereavement. The life she was used to had been taken away from her as easily as one of her father's whims, and nobody would tell her why.

The game disturbed her for other reasons as well, however. It was something familiar in a place where nothing was familiar. What was it doing here? What was *she* doing here? Precisely because it was familiar – because it didn't fit – it seemed to make what was happening to her less real.

Geraden took a step forward, but neither King Joyse nor the old Adept looked up from the game. After a moment, he cleared his throat. Still neither of the players took notice of him. He glanced back at Terisa and shrugged, then ventured to call attention to himself.

'My lord King, I've brought the lady Terisa of Morgan to you.' He hesitated briefly before adding, 'I've told her you must meet her.'

Adept Havelock remained hunched over the board, unheeding of everything except his game. But the King raised his head, turned his moist blue gaze toward Geraden and Terisa.

He seemed to take a moment to focus his eyes. Then, slowly, he began to smile.

Terisa thought immediately that he had a wonderful smile. It contained none of the artificial good humor or calculation she might have expected from a ruler. Instead, it lighted his face with a clean, childlike innocence and pleasure: it made him look like a young boy who had unexpectedly found a secret friend. Irrationally, she felt that her entire life would have been different if she had seen anyone smile like that before. She couldn't stop herself from smiling back at him – and didn't want to.

With a slight quaver of age in his voice, he said, 'If you have told her that I must meet her, Geraden, then surely I must. It would be unforgivably discourteous if you spoke anything less than the truth to such a lady – and so it would be equally rude if I failed to make what you have told her true.'

Carefully, he pushed his chair back and rose to his feet. His movements were unsteady; standing, he appeared more than ever lost in his voluminous robe. But his smile remained as pure as sunlight. 'My lady Terisa of Morgan, do you play hop-board?'

Terisa was fixed on King Joyse, but at the edge of her attention she thought she saw Geraden wince.

For the moment, his reactions were irrelevant to her. Buoyed by the King's smile, she replied, 'I haven't played since I was a girl.' That was true – if she didn't count all the games she had played against herself in the years after the valet was fired, games she had played in an effort to be content with her own company. 'We called it checkers. It looks like the same game.'

'"Checkers"?' King Joyse looked thoughtful. 'That seems an odd name.' Then he smiled again. 'But no matter. Perhaps when Havelock has finished giving me his customary drubbing, you will consent to play a game or two with me? I would be delighted to be able to hope – however briefly – for an honest victory.'

'My lord King.' Geraden sounded tense and worried, as if his introduction of Terisa to King Joyse were going seriously wrong. 'I told the lady Terisa you would want to meet her because she came here by translation.'

Geraden's interruption appeared to sadden the King. His smile changed to lines of fatigue and melancholy as he looked toward the Apt. 'I see that, Geraden,' he said quietly. 'I'm not blind, you know.'

'I'm sorry,' Geraden murmured. 'I just meant that she's important. I had to bring her to you.' He was hurrying. 'The Congery sent me into the mirror this morning to try to get the champion they wanted. But I didn't find him. I found her instead. She might be the answer to the auguries.'

Adept Havelock continued to ignore Geraden and Terisa. Scrutinizing the board, he reached out finally and moved one of the King's men, hopping one of his own. Then, triumphantly, he responded by demolishing a whole line of opposing pieces and arriving at the last row, where he crowned himself with severe emphasis.

Grimly, forcing himself to speak in spite of his embarrassment, Geraden went on, 'She proves you've been right all along. The mirrors don't create what we see. The Images really exist.'

King Joyse studied Geraden for a moment. Then he sighed wearily and turned to Terisa. 'My lady,' he said, 'please pardon me. It appears that this urgent young man will not allow us the freedom to play hop-board just now.

'Be reasonable, Geraden,' he continued, shifting his attention back to the Apt. 'You know that I agree with you. But what does her presence here truly prove?' The quaver in his voice persisted: he sounded like he was rehearsing an argument so old that he would no longer have gotten any satisfaction out

41

of winning it. 'Surely it's possible that you found her instead of the champion you sought because of one of your unfortunate mishaps? Or perhaps you've touched on an unsuspected strength in yourself, and you found her instead of the champion because she was what you wished to find? In what way does her translation demonstrate the fundamental nature of Imagery – or of mirrors?'

Geraden looked first startled by the King's argument, then vaguely nauseated. 'But I *saw*—' he protested incoherently. 'It wasn't the same.'

King Joyse watched him mildly and waited for him to pull his thoughts together.

With an effort, Geraden said slowly, 'I made that mirror myself. I saw the champion I was supposed to find in it. He was right there in front of me when I stepped into the glass. But during the translation everything changed. I arrived in a room that was totally different from the Images. *She* is totally different. What you're saying is that I made her up – by some kind of accident, either because I didn't know what I was doing or because I didn't know my own strength. How is that *possible*?'

In reply, the King shrugged – a bit sadly, Terisa thought. 'Who can say? Centuries ago, no one believed that Imagery itself was possible. Even a hundred years ago, no one believed that Imagery might threaten the existence of the very realms which made use of it.

'Geraden,' he said to the pain on the Apt's face, 'I don't claim that she does *not* exist. I only observe that her presence here doesn't settle the question.'

Geraden shook his head and tried again. 'But if you think that way – and you push it far enough – you can't prove *anything* exists. You can't prove I'm here talking to you. You can't prove you're playing hop-board with anybody but yourself. You might not be playing it anywhere except in your own mind.'

At that, the King smiled, then grimaced humorously. 'Unfortunately, I'm confident that my games of hop-board are real – and my opponent as well. The drubbings I receive are too painful for any other explanation.'

'Very wise,' remarked Adept Havelock unexpectedly, without raising his eyes from the board. In lugubrious concentration, he moved two or three of King Joyse's men to other squares; then with his crowned piece he jumped them all, hitting each square emphatically as if to compensate for his wall-eyed vision. 'Only hop-board is real. Ask any philosopher. Nothing else' – he fluttered one hand in dismissal – 'signifies.'

Without meaning to, Terisa smiled at the fond grin King Joyse directed toward Havelock. The Adept's way of playing checkers made it clear that he wasn't in his right mind; nevertheless she found the King's affection for the old Imager catching. Watching them, she forgot for a moment that the present conversation had anything to do with her.

But Geraden was too vexed and unhappy to enjoy the King's playful attitude. 'My lord King, this isn't a joke. The realm is tottering, and all of Mordant is waiting for you to do something about it.' He gathered momentum as he spoke, until his urgency seemed to clear away his smaller uncertainties, contritions, and anxieties. 'I don't know why you haven't, but the Masters finally couldn't wait any longer. They—' He caught himself. '*We*

42

are doing our best to find an answer. And we have. *I* think we have, anyway. The lady Terisa isn't the champion we were expecting – but that probably doesn't matter. There's a reason she's here instead of what we were expecting, and I don't think it has anything to do with accidents. I'm *not* an arch-Imager in disguise. And mirrors don't have minds of their own.'

As she studied his intent expression, Terisa caught a glimpse of what made him so accident-prone. He was too many things at once – a boy, a man, and everything in between – and the differing parts of himself seldom came into balance. She found him attractive in that way. Yet the perception saddened her: she herself wasn't too many things, but too few.

The King was watching Garaden as well; and the lines of his old visage seemed to hint at a sadness of his own. But they also suggested interest and perhaps a kind of pride. 'So much confidence is remarkable,' he commented. The quaver in his voice made his nonchalance sound unsteady, feigned. 'You've spoken of what you've seen, Geraden. Tell me what you've seen that gives you this confidence.'

Geraden hesitated, glancing at Terisa in appeal as though he believed she knew what he was about to say; as though he felt it would be more convincing if it came from her. But of course she had no idea what he had in mind. After a moment, he returned his gaze to King Joyse.

'My lord King,' the Apt said, his own voice shaking with determination and alarm, 'she is a Master of Imagery.'

At that, the King fixed a watery and unreadable look on Terisa – a look which could have indicated surprise or boredom.

Without a glance at the other people in the room, Havelock swept all the men off the board and began to set up a new game.

'I believe,' Geraden went on softly, 'her power pulled my translation away from where I thought I was going.'

The assertion was so absurd that several moments passed before Terisa realized she was expected to answer it. Then, helplessly, she began to blush under the scrutiny of the two men.

Close to panic, she replied, 'No. No, of course not. That's crazy. I don't even know what you're talking about.'

Carefully, Geraden said, 'I found her in a room entirely walled with mirrors.'

'So what?' A distant, self-conscious part of her mind was surprised by how this ludicrous conception frightened her. 'Everybody has mirrors. A lot of people use them for decor. They're just pieces of glass – with something on the back to make them reflect. They don't mean anything.'

In response to her alarm, King Joyse murmured as if he were trying to comfort her, 'Perhaps in your world that is so. Here the truth is otherwise.'

But Geraden was already saying as definitively as he could, 'Each of her mirrors showed her own Image exactly. They showed *my* Image exactly. And she isn't hurt. *I'm* not hurt. I ought to be raving by now. Or my mind should be completely empty. But I'm all right. She's all right.

'They were *her* mirrors.'

An amazed dismay stopped Terisa's mouth. She felt she couldn't understand what was literally being said to her. *Each of her mirrors showed her own Image exactly.* Here that wasn't true. Suddenly, her grasp on the ordinary details of life – the plain facts which showed that she was in contact with reality – was threatened, denied.

And King Joyse peered at her with an intent interest that made everything worse. 'Is this correct, my lady?' he asked as if she had just claimed to be some kind of exotic insect. 'The story is told that an Imager once chanced to form a flat mirror which showed the exact spot on which he stood. Therefore he saw himself in the glass – and was immediately canceled. His body remained where it was until its balance failed, but his spirit had entirely ceased to exist. It was lost in translation. How do the people of your world avoid this fate?'

Groping for sense, she countered, 'That's impossible. Mirrors can't hurt anybody. They just show you what you look like. Except reversed. Like a pool of water. Haven't you ever looked at yourself in a pool of water?'

Both men studied her oddly. In a soft, musing tone, King Joyse said, 'We're taught from childhood to be wary of Images. We don't seek them out.'

Without any particular forewarning, Adept Havelock pounded his fist on the table, then picked up the checkerboard and threw it at the ceiling. The checkers made a sound like wooden rain against the granite of the ceiling and fell back to bounce noiselessly in the blue-and-red rug.

Tottering to his feet, the old Imager roared, 'Horror and ballocks!' His eyes squinted ferociously at both the King and Geraden; patches of scarlet burned on his face; his fat lips shook like wattles. 'She's a *woman!*' He struck a wild gesture in her direction with the back of his hand. 'Are you and every man jack feeble-wit Imager of the Congery *blind?* She is female, fe-fe-*fe*-male.' Saliva sprayed from his mouth. 'Oh, my groin!'

Because she didn't know what else to do, Terisa stood and stared at him.

'Look at you!' Still using the back of his hand, he hit King Joyse across the chest – a blow which was more dramatic in intention than in effect. 'And you!' With his other hand, he struck Geraden. 'Or here!' Awkwardly but quickly, he bobbed toward the floor like a poorly constructed rooster, then pulled himself erect. 'And here!' Another bob. 'And here!' Each time he stood upright again, he brandished a checker in his open palm. 'All *men*, every one! Every one of them!'

But when his hand was full of checkers, he flung them down again. 'By the hoary goat of the arch-Imager,' he shouted as if the three people in front of him had insulted him beyond mortal endurance, '*she is a woman!*'

Moving with an attempt at vehemence which his frail limbs couldn't support, he stamped/shuffled to the outer door of the chamber, jerked it open, and slammed it shut again without leaving. Then, somewhat unsteadily, he retrieved the checkerboard from the floor and set it squarely on the table. Oblivious to everyone else, he took his seat and began to study the empty board as if an intense game were in progress.

King Joyse sighed delicately.

Geraden said, 'I'm sorry.'

Terisa wasn't quite sure why. Her heart pounded as if she had somehow escaped a crisis.

'No matter, my boy,' replied the King, patting Geraden's shoulder absentmindedly, as though the Apt had in fact committed some minor offense. For a moment, his gaze seemed to swim out of focus while he thought about something – or perhaps he was simply taking a quick nap on his feet. Then he nodded to himself. Smiling irrelevantly in Terisa's direction, he said, 'Geraden, it occurs to me to be surprised that the Congery released the lady Terisa in your company. She is here by Imagery – and some of the Masters, I know, are jealous. Also, I suspect that they would always prefer to keep what they do secret from me. Yet here you are. How do you account for that?'

Geraden made an effort to look at the King squarely; but his discomfiture was too strong for him.

'Did you tell the Masters that she may be a Master herself?'

The Apt swallowed thickly. 'No.'

'Ah,' King Joyse said mildly. 'That explains it, then. Of course they let her go, thinking her to be just another of your mishaps. But why didn't you tell them?'

A slow flush spread over Geraden's face. Muscles knotted in his forehead. His embarrassment was so acute that it nearly brought tears to Terisa's eyes. But he clamped his jaws shut and didn't answer.

'My boy, that may have been foolish.' The King's hand still held Geraden's shoulder; his expression was kind. 'You've been trying for – what is it now? ten years? – to become an Imager, a member of the Congery. How can you hope to succeed, if you risk angering the very men who control the knowledge, skill, and position you crave?'

'My lord King.' Geraden forced himself to let the King see the sharp pain in his eyes; and a sudden dignity came to him. 'If I had told them, they would have commanded me to keep all this secret from you. Then I would have been compelled to disobey them directly – and my hope of a chasuble would be lost forever.' There was an undercurrent of bitterness in his voice. 'I can't bear disloyalty to the King of Mordant. I can't give up my dreams. So I act like a fool. They'll believe I didn't notice her mirrors – or didn't understand the significance of what I saw.'

In response, another of the smiles that had first touched Terisa's heart lit the King's face. For a moment, his age, weakness, and uncertainty fell away, and he became simply happy.

'Thank you, Geraden. It pleases me to see such loyalty, especially in a son of my old friend the Domne. I'll try to arrange that you don't suffer for it.

'Now' – his expression grew thoughtful – 'let us consider. How best to do it?

'Tell me.' Slowly, he lowered himself back into his chair across the table from Havelock. His robe settled about him like a tent with the ridgepole cut. 'How did the Masters react to the lady Terisa of Morgan's arrival?'

Relieved by the King's attitude, Geraden relaxed visibly. 'That's easy. You could guess all of it if you wanted to. Everyone was astonished when she came out of the glass. Master Gilbur was furious. I'm sure he thinks I'm criminally perverse instead of' – he grimaced – 'just unlucky. Master Eremis was, well, amused.'

'Among other things, I don't doubt,' the King commented. 'Master

45

Eremis,' he explained to Terisa,' has an eye for loveliness which never fails him.'

Geraden nodded and went on. 'Master Quillon saw her appearance the same way I did, as proof you've been right about Imagery all along. But nobody listened to him.

'Master Barsonage made me responsible for her. He told me to give her all the hospitality and courtesy of Orison. But he told me not to answer any of her questions. Here she is, taken out of her own world for no reason except because I asked her to come, and put down in a place she has no way to understand, and he commanded me not to give her the simple decency of an explanation.'

Terisa hardly heard him. She was wondering. *Is that why he looked at me, looked at me as if I were real?* The idea was so new that it seemed to be full of mysterious importance. *Did he think I was lovely? Do you think I'm lovely? Is that possible?* 'Unless, of course,' the King returned quietly, 'she is a Master Imager and had already chosen us before you met her.'

Geraden scowled. 'What difference does that make? Haven't I been saying all along I think she's an Imager? She still deserves—'

'No.' King Joyse's tone was mild and certain. 'You make an assumption which may be unjustified.

'Master Barsonage's command was not unreasonable. When the Alend Monarch sends his ambassador to negotiate our treaties, and to probe my intentions, he understands much of his world and much of my own. We have that in common. Yet I do not make him privy to everything I know or think or hope, neither for policy nor for courtesy. I do not invite him into the secret places of Orison, or into the secret places of my heart. To do so would be dangerous – too dangerous for any responsible justification. Not knowing his secrets, I could not predict or control the use he made of mine. Still less would I answer any questions which an ambassador from the High King of Cadwal might venture to ask.

'The same reasoning applies to the lady Terisa'– he looked toward her – 'if you will pardon me for speaking of you as if you were absent.' Returning his gaze to Geraden, he continued, 'If, as she says, she comes from a world in which mirrors have no meaning, and is therefore ignorant of us, then it is at best unkind to refuse her answers. But in that case – mark this, Geraden – it is also folly to have brought her here at all. I speak not of morality now, but of the simple question of our practical need. If she is not an Imager, what use can she possibly be to us?'

Geraden held himself still and didn't reply.

Adept Havelock continued to study his blank board, deaf to whatever was being said.

'Conversely, if she *is* an Imager – a Master of mirrors strong enough to wrest your translation away from its apparent Image – then she is here for purposes of her own, which we do not know. She is like an ambassador, similarly to be respected, and similarly dangerous.

'Would you say, my lady,' he asked Terisa unexpectedly, 'that I've summarized the dilemma fairly?'

She stared at him, unable to follow his reasoning. In order to make sense of it, she had first to presuppose the existence of magical mirrors which didn't reflect whatever was in front of them but instead showed alternative worlds or realities. Then she had to take seriously the notion that her own mirrors, the mirrors in her apartment, were like that, giving *her*, Terisa Morgan, power over the reality and even the sanity of other people. The whole argument collapsed into nonsense before it reached the lofty conclusion King Joyse asked her to endorse.

Instinctively, she turned to Geraden. He was her only connection to her own life, with its ordinary facts and limitations. You saw me, she wanted to protest. You saw my apartment. There's nothing magic about it. You didn't lose your mind. None of this has anything to do with me.

His attention was on the King, however. 'But if she's that strong,' he said slowly, 'an Imager more powerful than we can imagine, then it's folly for us to risk offending her. We don't know her purposes – they might be good or bad for us. But they're sure to turn bad if we don't treat her well. We need her friendship, not her anger. We need to be open and decent with her.'

Smiling softly, King Joyse glanced back and forth between the Apt and Terisa as Geraden spoke. When he was done, the King replied, 'Your reasoning has merit. It is fortunate that only rulers are required to make those decisions.'

'My lord King?'

'Apt,' said King Joyse, his tone still mild but now faintly rueful as well, 'here is my command. You are no longer responsible for the lady Terisa of Morgan. Your King thanks you for what you have done – and relieves you of any further interest in the matter. Your duties lie with the Congery, to which you are pledged. You will have no more reason to see or speak with the lady Terisa, and certainly no reason to answer any of her questions.

'You may go. The lady Terisa will remain with me.'

Geraden's face went white: if he had closed his eyes, he would have looked like he was about to faint. But his eyes contradicted his pallor. They flamed with a quick, unflinching anger that seemed to burn all the boyishness out of him.

Softly, he said, 'You consider me unworthy.'

At that, the King's features crumpled into a grimace. He made an abrupt, dismissing gesture. 'Oh, get out.' For the first time since Terisa had met him, he sounded like a querulous old man. 'You're breaking my heart.'

The muscles of Geraden's face twitched. 'Yes, my lord King,' he said between his teeth. Roughly, he turned to Terisa and bowed. 'My lady.'

She had no reply. He was too hurt – and his hurt was too real. She was lost in it. He needed a response from her; but her responses were hidden behind years of silence and passivity.

When he started toward the door, his foot came down on the edge of one of the scattered checkers. His ankle twisted, and he stumbled, nearly fell. Embarrassment darkened his cheeks. His ears were crimson as he made his exit.

Watching the Apt go, Havelock began to giggle in a high, mad voice, as if his mirth were a place where reason or compassion couldn't reach him.

When he subsided, no one spoke for a moment. Then the King said, in an

47

unsteady attempt at nonchalance, 'Well, my lady Terisa of Morgan. We must give some thought to you. You must be made comfortable, with all the hospitality Orison can manage, as befits a guest of your station and importance. And then perhaps you'll consent to a game or two of hop-board? I'm really very tired of Havelock's incessant beatings.'

Geraden had been hurt for nothing. There was no reason for anybody to take precautions against her. To her own astonishment, she heard herself say, 'I'm not your lady. My name is Terisa Morgan, and I'm not anybody's lady. You didn't have to do that to him.'

King Joyse tried to smile, but failed to lift the sadness from his face. 'My lady, I am the King. I will call you by whatever name I choose. And I hope that someday you'll understand.'

With as much sarcasm as she had ever dared use, she returned, 'But you're not going to explain it to me. You don't want to answer any of my questions.'

Instead of replying, King Joyse slowly lowered his frail bones to the floor and started crawling around the room, picking up checkers.

FIVE

WARDROBES FULL
OF CLOTHES

Like a baffled child, Terisa shook her head, blinked her eyes. Unfortunately, nothing changed. Adept Havelock went on peering at his board as if in his mind he were already playing future games. The King continued to collect the scattered checkers, moving on his hands and knees.

The panic which had been gnawing at the back of her mind suddenly got worse. She shouldn't have spoken so sarcastically, so assertively. She was dependent on these people. With one cross word, she could be dismissed from existence. The King could have her thrown into another of those mirrors, and she might end up somewhere even more impossible. The world of the Congery's chosen champion suggested itself to her imagination. Or she might arrive nowhere – might simply dissolve into the gray, unacknowledged, pointless nothing she had feared and fought for most of her life.

I'm sorry, she thought involuntarily, while her alarm increased. Let me stay. I'll be a good girl, I promise.

At that moment, King Joyse braced his arms, levered his legs under him, and tottered to his feet. Moving to the table, he dropped the checkers he had collected in front of Havelock. Then he turned his clean, good smile on Terisa.

'Pardon me, my lady. What have I been thinking about? I'm rude to neglect you in this way. You must be fatigued from your translation, eager for rest and refreshment. Do you have any special requirements in sustenance or comfort? No?' His apology sounded sincere, but his questions were perfunctory. 'Then I'll summon someone to guide you to your rooms and care for you.'

Still smiling, he hunted around him with an increasingly aimless air until he happened to slip one hand into a pocket of his robe, where he found a silver bell with a wooden handle. He rang it vigorously. Almost immediately the outer door opened, and one of the guards stepped into the room.

'My lord King?'

'Ah, thank you.' For an instant, King Joyse appeared confused, as if he had forgotten what he was doing. His damp eyes blinked at the bell in his hand. Then, abruptly, he said, 'A maid for the lady Terisa of Morgan.'

'At once, my lord King.' The guard saluted by tapping his mail shirt with his fist and left the room.

Havelock reset the checkerboard, although King Joyse hadn't retrieved all the pieces.

'Again I ask your pardon,' the King muttered without glancing at Terisa. He scrubbed his hands over his face, sighed, and lowered himself back into his chair. 'My wits aren't what they were.' His smile was gone, replaced by sadness. 'Be honest with me, my lady. Do you have family? Are there those who will be grieved by your absence? They shouldn't be made to suffer for our necessities. I'll command Geraden to find some way to translate a message for them, to reassure them. Poor boy, it will keep him out of trouble. What message would you have sent, my lady?'

'There's—' she began, but her voice caught. There's nobody. She didn't say that, however. She was lost in this situation, and her fear and her ignorance fed on each other. Nevertheless an unfamiliar part of her was almost trembling with anger at the way she was treated. With an effort, she cleared her throat. 'There's only my father.'

'How can he be reached?'

Forced to the truth, she said thinly, 'He'll never notice I'm gone.'

When she said that, the King's gaze flashed at her. For an instant, she couldn't see the white of his hair, the weakness of his stature, the blue tinge of his wrinkled old skin: she saw only the direct strength of his eyes. He was looking at her as though she had somehow moved him.

'Then perhaps' – phlegm made his voice husky – 'you may wish to consider it fortunate that you are here.'

Carefully, trying to keep her panic under control, she said, 'I don't know how to consider it. I don't have enough information. When do you think you might be willing to tell me what's going on?' Then she held her breath in the quick rush of alarm which accompanied temerity.

'Ah, my lady.' King Joyse sighed and spread his hands. His swollen knuckles made the gesture appear at once world-weary and decrepit. 'That surely depends upon yourself. When will you make clear the truth of your origins, your skill in Imagery, your purposes?'

A weakness that felt like vertigo grew in her head. For some reason, it didn't cloud her mind – it simply made her want to lie down. 'You mean,' she said wanly, 'you're not going to tell me anything until I can prove that I exist – that I wasn't created by any mirror – and until I show you everything I know about Imagery – and until I tell you why I pulled Geraden away from what he thought he was doing when he tried to translate that champion' – in fact, all the things she couldn't possibly do in this crazy situation – 'and until I make you believe it.'

Down in the pit of her stomach, she felt a giddy and unexpected desire to laugh.

The King didn't shirk her gaze. Nevertheless the lines of his face became sadder and sadder. She was causing him pain which he didn't choose to explain. After a moment, she had to turn away, unable to go on challenging his peculiar vulnerability. The sound of someone knocking at his door came as a relief to her.

The guard reentered the room, bringing a woman with him.

At the sight of her, King Joyse frowned involuntarily, as if he had made a mistake; but at once he rubbed his expression clear. 'Saddith. Just the one I wanted.'

The woman was shorter than Terisa, with bright eyes, a pert nose, long brunette hair tumbling over her shoulders in natural waves, and a spontaneous smile. She wore a russet skirt that went down to her ankles and a shawl of the same color and material over her shoulders – like the other women Terisa had seen, she was prepared for the cold. But her blouse was open several buttons below the hollow of her throat, and her ripe bosom stretched the fabric. Looking at her, Terisa thought that she must be the kind of woman whom men noticed – the kind who never had any reason to doubt her own reality. The arch of her eyebrows and the angle of her glances suggested that she knew what she was doing.

She scanned Terisa quickly, her eyes wide as she noted Terisa's unfamiliar clothes, a small frown between her brows as she took an inventory of Terisa's face and figure. Then, almost instantly, she shifted her attention. 'My lord King,' she replied, dropping a graceful curtsy. 'You asked for a maid.'

'None better,' he said, making an effort to sound jovial, 'none better. Saddith, this is the lady Terisa of Morgan. She is the guest of Orison. My lady, Saddith will attend upon you as your maid. I'm confident that you'll be pleased with her.'

'My lady,' Saddith murmured, her eyes now downcast. 'I hope that I will serve you well.'

Nonplussed, Terisa fell back on her customary silence. She hadn't expected to be assigned a servant. On the other hand, she luckily had some acquaintance with servants. At least she knew how to live with them – how to spend her time without disturbing the rhythms of their activities, how to keep her requests for actual service to a minimum.

'The lady will be using the peacock rooms,' King Joyse went on. He sounded more and more distant – perhaps because of the distance in Terisa's head, perhaps because his own interest was wandering. 'She'll need a wardrobe. The lady Elega will be able to assist you. Or better the lady Myste – they're more of a size, I think. Whatever food or refreshment she asks, serve her in her rooms.

'My lady' – he had returned his gaze to the board and was studying the checkers – 'we will speak again soon. I look forward to testing your prowess at hop-board.'

The guard held the door open. Saddith looked up at Terisa expectantly. It was obvious that she had been dismissed. But she felt too tired to understand precisely what that meant. The stress of strangeness was wearing her out. And now that she thought about it, she was probably long overdue for some sleep. She had spent a whole day at the mission, typing that letter over and over again, then returned to her apartment for what she had known was going to be a bad night. But she had had no real conception *how* bad—

Fortunately, Saddith came to her rescue. Terisa let the maid's touch on her arm guide her out of the King's chamber.

The guards closed the door behind her.

'This way, my lady.' Saddith gestured down the hall, and Terisa automatically started walking in that direction. The maid moved with her head demurely bowed; but she cast repeated speculative glances at Terisa. As they descended the stairs, she asked, 'Have you made a long journey to Orison, my lady?'

Terisa shook her head. 'I don't know. I came through a mirror – I think.' How far was that? It seemed like forever.

'Imagery!' Saddith responded with polite astonishment. 'Are you a Master, my lady? I have never known a woman who was a Master.'

In spite of her sleepiness, Terisa sensed an opportunity for information. 'Don't women do things like that here?'

'Become Imagers?' The maid laughed delicately. 'I think not, my lady. Men say that the talent for Imagery is inborn, and that only those so born may hope to shape glass or perform translations. They believe, I'll wager, that no woman is born with the talent. But what is the need for it? Why should a woman desire mirrors' – she gave Terisa a coy smile – 'when any man will do what she wishes for her?'

From the stairs, they entered a wing of the immense stone building that Terisa hadn't seen before. Many of the rooms off the long, high halls seemed to be living quarters, and the people moving in and out of them apparently belonged to the middle ranks of the place – merchants, secretaries, ladies-in-waiting, supervisors. Terisa pursued her question with the maid.

'So you don't know anything about mirrors – or Imagery?'

'No, my lady,' replied Saddith. 'I only know that any Master will tell me whatever I wish – if I conceive a wish for something he knows.'

'That must be nice.' Terisa thought she understood what she was hearing; but the idea was too abstract to seem real. No man had ever found her that attractive.

'My lady' – Saddith appraised Terisa's figure again, nodding to herself at what she saw – 'the same is true for you, if you choose to make it so.'

You mean, Terisa thought, if I unbuttoned my shirt King Joyse would tell me whatever I wanted to know? Helpless to stop herself, she started laughing.

'Perhaps,' Saddith said, 'in your world women have no need of that power.' She sounded faintly distressed by the idea: jealous of it? threatened by it?

'I don't know,' Terisa admitted. 'I don't have any experience.'

Saddith looked away quickly; but before her face turned it betrayed a glimpse of mirth or contempt.

After a while, she led Terisa up another series of stairs into what appeared to be another tower. Past a landing at the end of a short hall, they reached a wide door made of polished wood. Saddith opened it and ushered Terisa into her assigned rooms.

It took no great effort of perception to see why they were called the peacock rooms. Their walls were decorated with an ornate profusion of peacock feathers, some hanging like plumes over the dark mahogany tables, others displayed in rich fans where other decorators might have put pictures or tapestries, still others forming a kind of canopy over the large, deep, satin-covered bed. The sizable room Terisa had entered was apparently a sitting room or parlor, its stone floor masked by rugs woven into peacock patterns, its cushioned couch and chairs painted with peacock blue and almost-black purple; but the bedroom could be seen through an arched entryway to her right. A door to the left suggested a bathroom.

The lamps set around the walls were unlit, as were the candles in their holders on the tables; but the rooms were bright with afternoon sunlight which streamed in through several glassed windows in the sitting room and bedroom. That, however, was the only glass to be seen; though she looked for them almost at once, Terisa couldn't discover any mirrors – not above the dressing table in the bedroom, not even in the bathroom.

She shivered. Both the sitting room and the bedroom had substantial fireplaces, but neither was lit. The sunshine on the rugs made their colors burn cheerily, yet outside the windows the sky looked pale, unwarmed. The air in the rooms was too cool for comfort. And the absence of mirrors seemed to have the force of a premonition. How would she be able to tell that she was still here, still real?

'Brrr,' said Saddith. 'Orison did not know of your coming, my lady, and so no one thought to warm these rooms.' She went at once to the sitting room hearth and began setting a fire, using wood and kindling from a firebox close at hand.

Terisa looked around her quarters. In the bathroom, she noticed dully the basin, tub, and bucket (all apparently fashioned of galvanized tin), as well as the cunning arrangement of copper pipes which provided running water (none of it warm). In the sitting room, she tested the cushions of a chair. In the bedroom, she looked into two large wardrobes, which smelled pleasantly of dry cedar but contained nothing. She didn't approach the windows, however. In fact, she refused to glance at them. What she had experienced was already alien enough; she wasn't ready to find out what the world or the weather outside Orison was like.

She had been right the first time: there was nothing in her rooms that she could use for a mirror.

As she returned to the sitting room, the fire was beginning to crackle. Saddith rose to her feet. 'With your permission, my lady, I will leave you now. The King speaks truly. You are near to a size with the lady Myste – although,' she commented with a coy smirk, 'she lacks some of your advantages. I must speak with her about clothing suited to your station. And I am sure that she will be able to make some contribution to the things needed for your toilet.'

She looked at Terisa expectantly.

A moment passed before Terisa realized that Saddith was waiting to be dismissed.

This wasn't how her father's servants had treated her. Surprised, and rather gratified, she mustered her courage to ask, 'Don't you use mirrors for anything except Imagery? They don't have to be made out of glass. How about polished metal?'

Unexpectedly, Saddith shuddered. 'The Masters say the same – but how are we to believe them? Imagers have not always wished other folk well. Perhaps all Images are dangerous. Everyone knows that it is worse than death to see oneself in a glass. Perhaps the danger is not in the glass, but in the Image.' She made a gesture of refusal. 'We do not take the risk.'

'Then how do you see yourself? How do you know what you look like?' How do you know you're real?

At that, the maid chuckled. 'My lady, I see what I need in the eyes of men.'

When Terisa nodded her permission, Saddith moved toward the door. In a moment, she was gone.

Terisa was alone for the first time since she had sat down in front of the mirrors of her apartment.

She was aware that she had some hard thinking to do, but that wasn't what she did. She was overloaded with strangeness, and she wanted to escape. Still avoiding the windows, she went into the bedroom. The air wasn't warm enough yet to encourage her to take off her clothes, so she simply slipped her moccasins from her feet and climbed into bed.

Clutching the coverlet tightly about her shoulders, she curled herself into a ball and went to sleep.

When she awoke, she passed straight from her usual blank slumber into a state of crisis.

There were no mirrors. No mirrors. The walls were decorated with peacock feathers, and she couldn't see herself anywhere. The bed was rumpled, but that had never been enough to tell her who she was – anybody could have rumpled the bed. If she were to see herself now she might bear no resemblance to what she was expecting, that was why she *had* to find some reflection of herself, had to prove somehow that—

The light had dwindled almost to twilight: it was barely enough to bring back her recollection of this place. With an effort of will, she took hold of her fear. Where she was didn't match the way she remembered it. She had an impression of changes – subtle, insidious, vast in implication – of ways in which reality had been rearranged. The dying of the light was the first one she was able to define, and she clung to it because it was reasonable, an indication of nothing more portentous than passing time.

Then she noticed there was a fire in the bedroom hearth.

It hadn't been set recently: the flames were small over a deep bed of coals; the bars of the grate shone with cherry heat; the air was warmer than it had been.

That, too, could be explained, she told herself, insisted to herself. Judging by the light, she had been asleep for several hours. Someone had come in and lit the fire for her while she slept. It was that simple.

But the idea that people had been changing things around her while she slept was too frightening to be simple.

She pushed her feet out of bed and sat up. The soft, woven texture of the rug under her soles reminded her of her moccasins. She put them on, straightened her sleep-creased flannel shirt, and stood up.

Nothing terrible happened. Her body felt normal. The stone and mahogany and feathers showed no signs of dissolution, of translation. Her panic took a few steps backward, and she began to breathe a bit more easily.

All right. Someone had been here while she slept. Probably Saddith. That was easy to check.

Although movement seemed to require an unreasonable amount of courage, she went to the nearest wardrobe and opened it.

It was full of clothes.

At a glance, most of them appeared to be gowns, but she saw robes, skirts, blouses, shawls, and a shelf or two of undergarments. They were the kind of clothes she had seen the ladies of rank wearing around Orison.

The other wardrobe was also full. And on the dressing table she found an impressive array of combs and brushes, fired clay jars containing creams and rouges, crystal vials of perfume.

Her fear actually turned and walked away, though it stopped in the middle distance to keep an eye on her. A little girl who had once enjoyed playing with her mother's dresses and cosmetics gave a small smile. She almost caught herself thinking, This might be fun after all.

But then from the sitting room she heard a woman's giggle, a man's rumbling whisper. As startled as if she had been caught doing something forbidden, she practically ran out of the bedroom.

The woman was Saddith, and Terisa's sudden appearance took her by surprise: an involuntary twitch nearly made her drop the tray she was carrying. 'My lady!' she said, rolling her eyes comically. 'I thought you were still asleep.'

The man was one of the guards Geraden had introduced her to earlier – Ribuld, the one with the scar down the middle of his face. He, too, had been surprised by Terisa's entrance: his hand on Saddith's shoulder, and the disarray of her shawl and hair, suggested that he hadn't been expecting an interruption; had, in fact, been intending to enjoy himself as much as possible while Saddith's hands were trapped by the tray she carried. Nevertheless he promptly showed Terisa a grin which was probably intended to be reassuring.

In the doorway behind Saddith and Ribuld stood Argus, Ribuld's companion. 'Better and better,' he muttered with a gap-toothed leer. 'One for each of us.'

Terisa froze, caught by instinctive alarm.

As soon as Saddith regained her own equilibrium, however, she took pity on Terisa's fright. 'Mend your manners, clods,' she said mildly. 'My lady is not diverted by your sort of humor.' Without apparent effort – or malice – she swung one clogged foot sharply against Ribuld's shin.

Gasping and grimacing, he hopped backward. For an instant, he clutched at his shin with both hands. Then he forced himself to stand upright. A scowl of mingled chagrin, anger, and amusement puckered his scar.

Behind him, Argus sniggered like an adolescent.

'My lady,' Saddith went on primly, 'do not let these louts distress you. They are neither as fierce nor as manly as they would have you think.' Argus faced this remark with open astonishment; Ribuld tried to ignore it. 'And they will not dare to displease you. Though they are plainly dull, between them they possess wit enough to know that if they displease you *I* will be displeased, and then' – she gave the guards an arch smile over her shoulder – 'neither of them will ever walk normally again.'

This time, both men made studious efforts not to react.

'Now, my lady,' continued the maid, 'I have brought some small supper for you, if you care for food. Not knowing how you are accustomed to dine, I thought it best to begin simply. But if this fare is not to your liking, I will gladly bring you whatever I can.'

Saddith's mastery of the situation enabled Terisa to unfreeze. Geraden had told her that he meant to try to have these two men assigned to her, for her protection. So far, he hadn't shown himself to be possessed of especially good judgment. On the other hand, he had been relieved of responsibility for her – which seemed to imply that Argus and Ribuld weren't here at his request? With an effort of concentration, she found her voice. 'What're they doing here?'

'Those two?' Saddith sniffed disdainfully. 'I cannot imagine. That is to say, I know precisely *what* they are doing. But why they have chosen to do it here, I have no idea. Doubtless King Joyse told the guard captain that you should be warded, either for protection or for honor, and the captain displayed his poor sense by assigning those two the duty.'

In his loud whisper, Argus muttered, 'I don't think we should let her talk about us like that, Ribuld. She would sing a different tune if we had her alone.'

'If we had her alone, you overgrown slophog,' Ribuld replied with equal subtlety, 'she wouldn't need to act like this. You wouldn't be scaring the lady Terisa with your lewd attentions.' Then he looked at Terisa and changed his manner to a loose approximation of respect. 'The truth is, my lady, we're not on duty.'

'No?' Saddith was moderately surprised.

'The captain doesn't know we're here – and I'm sure the King doesn't. We're doing this for Geraden. He stopped by the wardroom earlier this afternoon and asked us to look after you. As a personal favor. He didn't say what he was worried about, but he was obviously worried.'

He shrugged his heavy shoulders. 'If you don't want us around, you can tell us to go away. We might do that. But I think we might want you to explain it to Geraden first. He may be the clumsiest man in Mordant, and too young for his age on top of it, but we don't like to disappoint him.'

'You might say,' Argus added with an attempt at formal enunciation and pious sentiment which his missing teeth doomed to failure, 'he comes from a good family.'

This explanation left Terisa groping. She didn't know what to do. Helplessly, she looked to Saddith.

The maid considered Terisa, glanced sardonically over at the two guards, then sighed. 'Oh, let them stay, my lady. There is less harm in them than they might want you to believe. And I doubt that they would willingly insult Geraden by displeasing you. As this lout says' – she indicated Argus with a toss of her head – 'the family of the Domne is well regarded – and especially Artagel, who is said to have the sharpest sword in all Mordant.' She winked knowingly at Terisa. 'Among other things.' Then she resumed, 'Even a brave man might blanch if he insulted Geraden and had to face Artagel in consequence.'

It was Geraden who had wanted to answer her questions, Geraden who had seemed to care what happened to her. Now he had defied – or at least subverted – King Joyse's orders by arranging protection for her. As if she were giving him a vote of confidence, she murmured, 'All right.'

In response, Argus nudged Ribuld and grinned. 'What did I tell you? She wants us. Under those funny clothes, she's got the itch. She's just too fancy my-lady-Terisa to show it yet.'

Saddith turned on him and started to unleash a retort, but Ribuld forestalled her by grabbing Argus' arm and jerking him toward the door, growling, 'Oh, shut up, limpwit. There isn't a woman in Mordant desperate enough to itch for the likes of you.' Argus tried to protest; but Ribuld opened the door and thrust his companion out into the passage. In the doorway, he paused long enough to say over his shoulder, 'We'll be out here all night, my lady' – struggling to sound respectful against his natural inclination – 'if you need us for anything.'

The door cut off Argus' burst of laughter.

Saddith rolled her eyes in affectionate ridicule, then moved to set her tray down on one of the tables. 'As I was saying, my lady, if this fare is not to your liking, you need only tell me. The cooks of Orison are an unruly lot, but I am sure they will attempt to provide whatever you wish.

'First, however,' she went on, 'you must have light.' Briskly, she went to the hearth, found a twig among the kindling, lit it, and used it to begin lighting the candles and lamps.

As the illumination in the room grew, the glow from the windows seemed to fade to darkness almost immediately, closing away any view Terisa might have had of the world outside. Unexpectedly, she felt a mild disappointment. She had missed an opportunity to look out and see what Orison was, where and how it was situated, what kind of environment surrounded it. Earlier, she had shied away from that knowledge; now she wanted it. Her nap must have done her more good than she realized.

That probably also explained why she did seem to be a little hungry. Dismissing the question of the windows, she went to look at the food.

It was familiar and surprising: as familiar as the language spoken by the people of this strange place; as surprising as the fact that these people spoke a language nearly identical to her own. To all appearances, the plate held a thick slice of ham garnished with borage and accompanied by brown bread, Swiss cheese, and string beans; the goblet contained a pale red wine. And, in fact, the ham was unmistakable, as was the bread. Under closer inspection, however, the borage smelled more like thyme, the beans were of a slightly different shape and color than any she had seen before, and in spite of its firm texture the cheese tasted like tofu. The wine carried a gentle tang of cinnamon.

Perhaps she should have feared that the food of this world would make her sick. In view of Geraden's belief that she had enemies, perhaps she should have feared that the food was poisoned. But such considerations seemed entirely unreal. The people she had met looked like normal human beings. They spoke her language. And, as far as she was concerned, she certainly wasn't substantial enough to be an object of malice. With no more hesitation than she had showed walking across the room to look at the food, she sampled the beans and found that they tasted like asparagus. Then she started on the bread and wine.

'Does it please you, my lady?' Saddith had finished lighting the candles and lamps in both the sitting room and the bedroom, and now stood watching Terisa.

'It's very good,' Terisa replied like an obedient girl.

The maid smiled her approval. 'Then I will leave you now, my lady. If you do not wish to rest, and the evening seems long, summon me.' She indicated a bellpull which Terisa hadn't noticed because it was hidden behind one of the peacock feather displays. 'We will find some entertainment for you. Perhaps you will want me to help you try some of your gowns. Several of them will become you nicely, I think. Or perhaps you will want other company. Both the lady Elega and the lady Myste wish to meet you, although they thought to wait until tomorrow so that you could spend tonight recovering from your translation. Both would be fascinated to make the acquaintance of a woman of Imagery.'

Terisa ignored this reference to her purported mastery of mirrors. 'Who are Elega and Myste?'

'They are my lord King's daughters. He has three, of whom Elega and Myste are the eldest and youngest. The second, the lady Torrent, lives with her mother, Queen Madin, in Romish of Fayle. The Queen is the daughter of the Fayle.'

That answered Terisa's question. She didn't know what Romish or Fayle were, any more than she understood Domne or even Orison. But she knew now that she didn't want to meet Elega or Myste tonight. She didn't want to see anybody who would bring her more questions and no answers. She only wanted Geraden – or possibly (a piquant thought) Master Eremis, who may have considered her lovely. Since she couldn't ask Geraden to take any more risks for her, she declined Saddith's offer. 'I think I'll rest tonight.'

'Very good, my lady.' Saddith gave a polite bow and started to leave the room.

But at the door she paused, one hand on the latch. With a roll of her eyes, she indicated Ribuld and Argus. Then she showed Terisa the bolt which locked the door, and pantomimed pushing it home.

Terisa smiled her relief and gratitude. 'Thanks. I'll remember that.'

Saddith replied with her own arch smile and made her exit, closing the door quietly after her.

At once, Terisa went to it and bolted it. Through the heavy wood, she could faintly hear Saddith, Ribuld, and Argus bantering with each other. She was tempted to listen, simply because she didn't understand how any woman could have that kind of relationship with men. Nevertheless she withdrew toward the table where her food waited for her; and in a step or two the laughing voices became inaudible.

She was alone.

In an odd way, she was grateful for the presence of Argus and Ribuld outside her door. They weren't exactly reassuring in themselves, but they – she realized this slowly – were the first people in this impossible situation to reappear after an absence. Geraden had lured her out of her own life into a room full of Masters, but in a short time they had all gone away. He had then taken her to the King, and he had been sent away. Next she had been put in Saddith's charge, and King Joyse and Adept Havelock had fallen into the past. Each new person she met might have been created solely for that meeting; might have ceased to exist as soon as she moved on to someone else.

It was conceivable that none of this was real at all.

Ribuld and Argus, however, spoke of Geraden as though he had a continuous existence of his own, apart from her. They were substantial enough to have a relationship with Saddith which didn't include her, Terisa. Therefore they implied that what was happening to her had continuity, solidity, a dependable fidelity to its own premises and exigencies. They implied that if she were able to retrace her steps she would find the King's suite and the Masters' chamber where she had left them; that Geraden was alive and active somewhere not too far away, trying to do something about his concern for her; that however crazy her circumstances seemed they could be trusted as much as she had ever trusted her own world.

This was rather a large conclusion to draw from a small fact. Nevertheless she accepted it provisionally. It made her a little less afraid.

An entirely unmetaphysical concern impelled her to walk through her rooms again to verify that there were no other entrances. Then she sat down and ate her meal with at least an approximation of pleasure.

By the time she was done eating, the wine had made her slightly drowsy. But she was still too restless to consider going back to bed; so she decided to sample some of the clothes Saddith had brought for her.

Many of them frustrated her: they hooked or laced or buttoned so inconveniently that she couldn't put them on without assistance. Despite that, however, they struck her as finely made and elegant. And the robes and gowns she was able to don for herself made her long for a mirror so that she could see what she looked like. Was it possible that this exposure of breast or slimness of waist, these billowing sleeves or that intricate lace would make her beautiful? Immersed in what she was doing, she didn't notice the passage of time.

She was wearing a floor-length burgundy robe, made of deep velvet, with a wide, black sash and a hood she could have pulled over her head to hide her face, and had just decided to take it off and return to bed for some more sleep, when the wooden backing of the wardrobe in front of which she stood shifted and began to move aside.

Scraping against each other, the back panels opened on a well of darkness.

From the darkness a figure emerged.

If his advance was intended to be silent, it failed significantly: he made bumping and shuffling noises all along the way. Hanging gowns and robes that blocked his path he thrust unceremoniously aside.

She could hear him muttering to himself, 'Softly, softly.' His voice was old and thin, unsteady when he whispered. 'Sneaking into the bedchambers of beautiful women. Hee hee. Oh, you're still a devil, you are. Mirrors are only glass, but lust and lechery last forever.'

Only then did he notice that the front of the wardrobe was open – that Terisa stood staring at him with her hands over her mouth and a look in her eyes which might have been either terror or hilarity.

'What're you doing here?' she breathed. 'What do you want?'

His thick lips shaking, Adept Havelock flinched as if she had threatened to strike him.

In spite of the alarm pounding in her throat, she felt forcibly the conflict between his ascetic nose and sybaritic mouth, the disfocus of his hot eyes. His self-contradictory visage made him look wild – an appearance aggravated by his few remaining tufts of hair. And yet he seemed to be doing his best to calm her. His hands made reassuring gestures; his whole stance was unthreatening, even deferential.

'Luscious,' he said, as though he meant, Forgive me. 'All women are flesh, but you are its perfection.' I didn't mean to frighten you. 'Ha ha, sneaking into bedchambers.' I'm not going to hurt you. 'Lust and lechery.' You can trust me.

He was a madman – that much was unmistakable. Unfortunately, the knowledge wasn't much help. So he was crazy. So what was she going to do about it? She had no idea. Studying him warily, she retreated a step or two to give herself more space. Then she said, 'There are two guards outside my door. They're both big, and they've got longswords. If I shout' – she faltered and almost panicked when she remembered that the door was bolted – 'they'll be here before you can touch me.'

Palms toward her, his hands continued to make placating movements. Parts of his face expressed a fear of which other parts were ignorant: his eyes rolled, and his lower lip drooped, exposing crooked, yellow teeth; but his nose and cheekbones looked too determined to admit fear.

'This winter chills my bones,' he told her as if it were a high secret. 'No one understands hop-board.'

Though they were speaking softly, he put a finger to his lips. Then he turned back toward the wardrobe and beckoned for her to follow.

'You want me to go in there?' Tension made her voice jump like his. The darkness behind the clothes was too deep to be measured. 'Why?'

As persuasively as possible, he replied, 'The King tries to protect his pieces. Individuals. What good are they? Worthless. Wor-r-r-rthless. It's all strategy. Sacrifice the right men to trap your opponent.'

While he spoke, he kept beckoning, urging her toward him.

'No, I'm sorry.' The idea of entering the unknown place behind the wardrobe was even more frightening than the Adept's unexpected appearance. 'I can't go in there.' She was familiar with dark, closed spaces. Despite her best efforts to forget them, she remembered every detail of the times her parents had punished her by locking her into a lightless closet. She had learned a great deal about her own unreality during those times. In that closet she had first started feeling herself fade, drifting out of existence into the effacing black. 'It's too dark.'

'Ho ho ha,' he responded in a tone of supplication. He could only look at her with one eye at a time, and the lines of his face twisted into a plea. 'Dark and lust. We snuff the light so no one will see how we revel. You don't need light to see flesh.'

Reaching into a pocket of his surcoat, he pulled out an irregular piece of glass about the size of his palm. He held it so that she couldn't look into it; but she had the impression it was a small mirror.

He murmured something, passed his hand over the glass, and a beam of warm, yellow light as bright as sunshine shot straight out of the surface.

He shone it around the wardrobe. It showed her that the darkness was a stone passage angling downward inside the wall of the room.

Havelock flashed his light down the passage to demonstrate that it was safe. Then he beckoned to her again vehemently, at once asking and demanding that she go with him.

'No,' she repeated. 'I can't. I don't know what you want. I don't know what you're trying to do to me.' Groping for some response which might penetrate his demented intentions, she asked, 'Does King Joyse know you're here?'

That was evidently the wrong thing to say. At once, Havelock became the furious old man who had thrown his checkers at the ceiling and stormed around the King's chamber. 'Bother Joyse and all his scruples!' the Adept raged, so angry that he was barely able to keep his voice down. His face turned an apoplectic red. And yet he did keep his voice down: he retained that much self-awareness. 'He plays as badly as his daughters! Women and foolishness.'

Flailing his arms, he made gestures that practically shouted, Come with me!

To defend herself, she replied, 'Geraden warned me that the King has enemies. Are you trying to betray him?'

At once, Havelock stopped. He stared at her as though he had been stung. For a second, his whole face expressed nothing but astonishment and dismay.

Then a look of cunning came into his eyes.

She seemed to feel danger pouncing toward her. But it was imprecise: she didn't know how to react. So she stood where she was, helpless as a post, while he raised his glass and shone it directly into her face.

It was as bright as the sun; it made her throw up her hands and reel backward to protect her eyes.

She stumbled against the bed, nearly lost her balance. But before she could either fall or jump aside, Havelock clamped one bony hand around her wrist and jerked her toward the wardrobe.

He wasn't as strong as he seemed. If she could have planted her feet, found some leverage, she would have been able to break his grip. He was too quick for that, however. Keeping her off balance, he impelled her across the floor, into the wardrobe and the opening of the passage.

SIX

A FEW
LESSONS

With her free hand, she clutched for something to hold her back. But suns of blindness exploded back and forth across her vision: she couldn't see anything to grasp. Then she hit the stone of the passage, and cool air breathed up at her out of the unseen depths. Havelock slowed, giving her feet time to fumble for the downward stairs.

Argus and Ribuld would probably have been willing to rescue her from this madman. Unfortunately, her door was locked, and she didn't have time to shout for help.

Her sight cleared quickly, however. Havelock's glass hadn't done her any real damage. In a moment, she stopped bumping against the walls, stopped lurching on the stairs. The Adept pulled her after him as firmly as he could, but now she was able to exert some control over her rate of descent.

His glass revealed all there was to see of where they were and where they were going. The passage was narrow and low: if she had been any taller, she would have been forced to stoop. There were sharp turns and branchings whenever the stair had gone down another ten or fifteen feet. At a guess, the branchings led to other hidden entrances in other suites and chambers. But the main passage continued downward.

The absence of cobwebs and accumulated dust implied that these stone tunnels were used with some frequency.

The air became slowly cooler as Adept Havelock dragged her after him.

Unaccustomed to such exercise, her knees began to tremble. She felt she had been laboring down the stairs for a long time when the Adept arrived at a heavy, ironbound wooden door that blocked his way. It had been left unbolted, but he didn't open it immediately. Instead, he tugged her close to him. Then he released her wrist.

Shining on the door and the stone blocks of the wall, his light cast comic shadows across his face. 'Remember hop-board,' he whispered intensely. 'Nothing else signifies.'

A gesture and a murmur snuffed his glass. In the sudden dark, she heard his surcoat rustle as he returned the small mirror to his pocket. Then he pushed open the door and walked into the lamplight beyond it as if he didn't care whether she followed him or not.

From the doorway, she looked out at a large, square room.

It was furnished – and cluttered – like a study of some sort. A heavy pillar thrust down through the center of the floor, the flagstones of which weren't softened or warmed by any rugs or coverings. Around the pillar, however, stood a number of tables, some of them tilted like an artist's worktable, others flat and piled with papers and rolls of parchment. Stools waited at all the tables, although most of them were being used to hold stacks of old books or layer after layer of loose documents. Under the tables, the floor was furred with dust. Opposite Terisa, an entryway without a door led, apparently, to other rooms. Near the entryway was a rumpled bed, with several blankets tossed haphazardly over the stained gray sheets, and no pillow.

The light came from oil lamps around the walls and the pillar. Their glow showed clearly the two features of the room that most caught Terisa's attention.

Off to one side was a small table with two chairs and a checkerboard. All were at least as richly made as the ones King Joyse used. But there weren't any pieces on the board.

And the walls were lined with doors like the one through which Havelock had just entered the room. They were all bound with iron and heavily bolted. Orison, she realized, must be honeycombed with secrets.

Ignoring her completely now, the Adept moved to the checker table, seated himself with his back to her, and hunched over the board as if he were absorbed in a game.

Terisa cleared her throat to speak, then caught herself. She and Adept Havelock weren't alone. A man whom she had somehow failed to notice at first turned on his stool, leaning his elbow on the desk beside him and propping his cheek against his fist. 'Ah, there you are.' He wore a plain gray robe that looked warm enough to combat the chill in the room (a chill that the Adept didn't appear to feel, in spite of his inadequate garments), and that increased his ability to blend into the background. But over his shoulders was draped the yellow chasuble of a Master.

Looking at him sharply, she realized that she had seen him before. He had a rabbity face with bright eyes, a nose that twitched, and protruding teeth. She wasn't likely to be mistaken about him. He was the one who had agreed with Geraden that her appearance before the Congery proved something.

'Geraden finally condescended to reveal who you are,' he commented, his sarcasm distinct but not severe. 'The lady Terisa of Morgan.' He didn't seem particularly impressed. On the other hand, his tone was polite: he clearly intended no offense. 'I am Master Quillon.

'Adept Havelock—' Master Quillon paused to glance around him. 'Incidentally,' he interpolated, 'these are his rooms, not mine. I believe I would find some way to have them cleaned. Even if I had to do it myself.' Then he returned to what he meant to say. 'Be that as it may, however, he has asked me to tell you a bit about Mordant's history – the background, so to speak, of our present problems.'

When he said that, Terisa's head filled up with air and started to float.

Sudden hope and relief danced together in her chest. At last, somebody was going to tell her what was going on.

A moment later, however, her expectations fell out of the top of her head into the pit of her stomach with a leaden thud. *Havelock* had asked Master Quillon to talk to her? Abruptly, she demanded, 'How?'

The Master looked at her inquiringly. 'How?'

'How did he ask you that? How do you know what he wants?'

Master Quillon twitched his nose and shrugged, his cheek still resting on his fist. 'He has his lucid moments. And you must remember that he has been like this for years. We have had time to become accustomed to him. Occasionally he is capable of making himself understood.'

Well, she thought, that seemed true enough, as far as it went – if dragging people down stairs by main force counted as 'making himself understood.' But as an explanation it didn't suffice. 'Then why?' she asked. 'Assuming that you're right – that you haven't missed what he really wants – why do it? Both Master Barsonage' – she stumbled fractionally over the name – 'and the King told Geraden – no, they *ordered* him not to answer any of my questions.' What she was saying felt increasingly audacious to her, increasingly dangerous. When had she started talking to people like this? But her momentum kept her going. 'Why disobey both of them? Whose side are you on?'

In response, he blinked at her as though the logic of his position were self-evident. Nevertheless he was slow in replying. 'It is not as simple as you make it appear. In spite of his' – the Master glanced at Havelock – 'um, his affliction, Adept Havelock is still the nominal head of the Congery. And there are those among the Imagers who consider his past services to us – and indeed to all Mordant – so great that he continues to deserve gratitude and respect, even compliance. Would you flaunt your father's wishes if he began acting somewhat strangely in his old age?'

Fortunately for Terisa, that was intended as a rhetorical question. Without waiting for an answer, Master Quillon went on, 'In addition, there are times when you must define your loyalties. Master Barsonage is an honorable man who tries to be impartial, but in his heart he stubbornly fears the consequences of any decision or action. As for King Joyse—' He sighed. 'Years have passed since he showed any significant grasp on what happens around him, and his judgment is suspect.'

This didn't satisfy her, but she had pushed her temerity as far as it would go. The old habit of reticence and deference, her emotional protective coloration, reasserted itself and held her back. Master Quillon clearly meant to talk to her, and yet she was irrationally afraid that by speaking she had forfeited what he wanted to tell her, what she needed to know.

Nevertheless her doubts refused to go away. Cautiously, she took a different approach. Indicating the Adept, she asked, 'Why do they call him "the King's dastard"?'

Quillon sighed again and straightened himself on his stool. 'My lady' – he gestured vaguely around him, as if he were suddenly tired of the whole thing – 'will you sit down?'

Obediently, she located a free stool and moved it to the desk nearest him.

She wasn't accustomed to the robe she was wearing – it made her feel awkward climbing onto the high perch of the stool. But when she was seated with her back supported by the edge of the desk, she was steady enough.

Master Quillon began.

'I will assume that you know nothing about us or our troubles.' He still looked like a rabbit, and his nose seemed to twitch whenever he collected his thoughts; but the way he spoke contained a note of dignity. 'If that is untrue, please do not be insulted. There is no other way that I can respect whatever secrets you may have.

'It is difficult to know how or where to begin. We have, in a sense, two histories – that of the kingdoms and that of Imagery – which did not become one until relatively recently – in fact, until King Joyse and Adept Havelock forced them together. You can hardly believe it, I am sure, looking at them now, but in their prime they bestrode Mordant and the rest of our world like heroes, shaking it into a new shape simply because they believed that the job needed to be done.

'Both histories, however, are histories of fragmentation.

'In fact, there was no Mordant – and no Congery, for that matter – until King Joyse created them. Oh, there was a region which went by the name "Mordant," but it was nothing more than a collection of petty princedoms caught between the ancient power of Cadwal to the east and the newer strength of Alend to the north and west. These princedoms were what we now call the Cares – the Care of Armigite, the Care of Perdon, and so on – but they were in reality less substantial than what the Alend Lieges call baronial holdings. They survived only because together they served as a kind of buffer between Alend and Cadwal, which were always at war.

'Alend and Cadwal are actually contiguous along the last eighty miles or so of the Swoll River, but that area is impassable, a swamp to the sea and along the coast—' He started looking around the room as he spoke, and after a moment his explanation trailed off. 'Havelock,' he asked distantly, as though he were talking to himself, or didn't expect an answer, 'do you have a map? There must be one in this chaos somewhere. I ought to show her where these things are in relation to each other.'

Adept Havelock didn't glance up from his board. Concentrating fiercely, he rearranged the pieces he imagined in front of him, and began to study the new configuration.

'Well, never mind,' murmured the Master. Returning his attention to Terisa, he resumed. 'Even without a map, I am sure you will understand the point. Because of the swamp, Cadwal and Alend can only approach each other through Mordant, which is, essentially, a fertile lowland between the Pestil and Vertigon rivers. Alend is too mountainous – Cadwal, too dry. Therefore they have desired Mordant for centuries, both for itself and as a large step toward defeating each other.

'To put the matter simply, the princedoms of Mordant survived by being conquered back and forth, generation after generation – and by always siding with whichever of the two powers happened to be absent at the time. Because Mordant existed in pieces, each piece was easily taken, but hard to hold. Cadwal, for instance, might make itself master of the Care of Perdon, or of

Tor. Alend might take Termigan or Domne. At once, the Perdon – the lord of the Care – or the Tor, the Termigan or the Domne, would swear eternal allegiance to his new prince. At the same time, he would begin looking for ways to betray that prince. So Cadwal would sneak into Termigan, or Alend into Tor, and the people of the Care would be liberated, amid great rejoicing. At once, however, a new prince would replace the old. And so the entire process would begin again, varying only in detail when Cadwal or Alend made a convulsive effort to conquer the whole region. And so the Cares endured.

'Of course, all that bloodshed was terrible. Naturally, a certain number of men voluntarily fought and risked their lives. But they were a small minority of the victims. The peasants of Mordant were constantly being hacked down or conscripted, raped or driven from their land – brutalized in any way the whims of the tyrants suggested. The only reason Mordant was not entirely depopulated was that both Cadwal and Alend needed what they could grow in the fields and on the hills of this lowland, so they were forced to import labor – usually slaves, especially from Cadwal – to replace the lost peasants. These laborers invariably found that life as a peasant was better than life as a slave or a coerced servant, and so they learned loyalty to the Care in which they found themselves. In that way, the population of Mordant was renewed.

'But such things are only bloodshed and tyranny. Mordant's plight was made much worse by Imagery.

'Am I boring you, my lady?'

Terisa was surprised by the realization that she had yawned. The wine, a long day, and reaction after the shock of Havelock's appearance and behavior were making her drowsy. Nevertheless she shook her head. 'I just wonder what all this has to do with me.'

A bit acerbically, the Master retorted, 'It "has to do" with you because you are here. It will affect everything that happens to you while you are among us.'

'I'm sorry. Please go on.'

'Very well,' said Quillon stiffly. His nose twitched for a moment.

'In those days, it seemed that every man of any consequence had in his service, or his employ, an Imager of some kind – or else he served or was employed by an Imager. Cadwal itself was raised to greatness by the first arch-Imager. And as recently as the past century the Alend Monarch used an entire battery of Imagers to bring the Alend Lieges into confederacy.

'Here again the situation was fragmented. The talent which can make an Imager is not common, but neither is it rare. And in times of war, it seems to breed under every hedgerow. As a result, Cadwal has at times mustered armies in which *every* captain was seconded by an Imager. Alend has been nearly as powerful. And of course every lord in Mordant was defended by an Imager who depended on him for support, patronage, or facilities.

'As I am sure you can imagine, the glass which makes mirrors is not something that can simply be poured out in a patch of sand behind some cottage. To study, develop, and use mirrors requires equipment, tinct, furnaces, and much else as well, and so any Imager not born wealthy has always been forced to ally himself with wealth in some way.

'But I digress.

'I wonder, my lady,' he said slowly, 'if you possess the knowledge or experience to imagine the havoc dozens of Imagers can wreak, fighting each other and armies as well as innocent men and women who happen to get in the way. Consider it, if you can. Here stands an Imager whose glass shows a sea of lava. At his word, molten stone floods outward, devouring its own carnage as it moves. There stands an Imager whose glass shows a winged leviathan which can consume cattle whole. At his word, the beast is translated here to rage and ravage until he calls it back – or until some other Imager conceives a means to kill it. And they are only two men. Consider fifty of them, or a hundred, great Imagers and small, all dedicating what mirrors they have to battle and bloodshed.

'Perhaps in your world Imagery is used for other purposes. Perhaps it provides food for the hungry, water against drought, energy and power to better the lot of all men. That has not been our history.

'One consequence' – he sighed – 'is that the knowledge of Imagery – the understanding of what it is, and why it works, and how it might be used – has advanced little from one generation to the next. Imagers have tended to guard their secrets zealously, as protection for their lives, and so the dissemination of new ideas, insights, or techniques has taken decades. In fact, it would not have occurred at all, if the making of mirrors were not sufficiently arduous to require Apts. But each Imager must have help, and so he must teach some youth with the talent how to give that help. In that way, slow progress has been made.

'It is a barbarous history, my lady.' This time, his sarcasm was directed elsewhere. 'We are not traditionally a humane or scrupulous people.

'King Joyse has attempted to change us completely.

'Havelock' – he turned on his stool to face the Adept – 'some wine would be a kindness. All this talk is thirsty work.'

At once, Havelock pushed himself out of his chair and hobbled away to the opposite side of the room, behind the pillar. When he returned, he was carrying a stoneware decanter and a clay goblet. The goblet looked like it hadn't been cleaned any time during the past decade.

Unceremoniously, he thunked the decanter down beside Master Quillon and thrust the goblet into his hands. 'We have a barbarous history,' the Adept said, waggling his eyebrows at Terisa, 'because we drink too much wine. Wine and fornication don't mix.'

Returning to his table, he started playing his invisible game again.

Master Quillon peered morosely into the goblet. Finally, he wiped it out with the sleeve of his robe. Muttering to himself, he poured some of the wine and passed the goblet to Terisa. Then he raised the decanter to his mouth and drank.

She wanted a drink herself. But the dark smear on Quillon's sleeve dissuaded her.

'As I say,' he began again, wiping his lips with the ends of his fingers, 'King Joyse set himself the job of changing everything.

'I can tell you quite simply what he did. First he conquered all the princedoms of Mordant, some by force, some by persuasion. And when he had made Mordant into a separate, sovereign realm, he began waging an odd war against both Alend and Cadwal. In battle after battle, raid after raid, for the better part of two decades, he took no territory, conscripted no soldiers, slaughtered no peasants. In fact, he did nothing to upset the ordinary structures of power in either country. All he did' – the Master rubbed his nose vigorously to make it stop twitching – 'was to take prisoner every Imager he could find and bring his captives here, to Orison. At the same time, he offered universal patronage and safety to every Imager who would surrender voluntarily. In the end, he had collected them all – or we thought he had. From the western mountains of Alend to the eastern deserts of Cadwal, there were no Imagers anywhere but here.

'And when he had them all together, he did not do what Cadwal and Alend desperately feared. He did not try to weld all that talent for Imagery into his personal fighting force. Instead, he created the Congery. And he gave it work to do – peaceful work. Many of his assignments involved the study of specific problems. Could Imagery be used to relieve drought? Could mirrors put out fires? Could Imagers build roads? Quarry granite? Fertilize soil?

'Questions of wealth King Joyse left to Alend and Cadwal.' Master Quillon was digressing again. 'Alend had gold. Cadwal had gems. Mordant did not need them. Crops and cattle, food and fabric and wine, these were Mordant's strength and wealth.

'But overriding such work was another, larger assignment. King Joyse commanded the Congery to define an ethic of Imagery. He commanded the Imagers to answer the great moral question of Imagery: are the beings and forces and things that come out of mirrors created by translation, or do they have a prior existence of their own, from which they are removed by translation?

'All very simple, is it not? Nothing to it.' Quillon took another swig from the decanter, wiped his lips again. 'As you might guess, my lady, I am much harder pressed to explain *how* the King did these things.

'If the reports of him are true, he did it, essentially, by being the kind of man for whom other men – and women as well – were willing to die.

'He was born to the princedom which is now his Demesne, and he became the lord in Orison – though Orison was smaller then – at the age of fifteen, when his father was caught trying to betray the Cadwal tyrant who then held the princedom – was caught and slowly pulled limb from limb by oxen in front of young Joyse and all his family, as if that sort of lesson would teach them loyalty. He was little better than a boy, but already he possessed a quality which made a strong and, um, perhaps wise' – he glanced at Havelock – 'Imager become his faithful friend. What the boy did after that, he and his Imager did together.

'What they did first was to sneak away in the middle of the night, leaving his family to bear the brunt of the Cadwal prince's displeasure.

'Naturally, this did not raise the esteem in which his people held him. So they were rather surprised when he returned at the head of a force from neighboring Tor, threw the Cadwals out, and personally separated the prince from his head.

'Tor had happened to be in a period of independence at the time. And it was somewhat more accustomed to independence than the other princedoms, being situated with the mountains at its back and Perdon, Armigite, Domne, and Termigan around it – therefore difficult to conquer. Young Joyse had insisted to the Tor – who was himself still young enough to be audacious – that the only hope for his people, and for all Mordant, was a union of the Cares against both Alend and Cadwal. And the Tor had liked this idea. He had also liked young Joyse. On the other hand, he had not liked to risk too much of his Care. So he had given Joyse scarcely two hundred men to use against more than two thousand Cadwals.

'Joyse and his Imager and those two hundred men, however, required only three days to free the Demesne. Before sunset of the third day, a new flag flew over Orison – the pennon of Mordant.

'You may wonder how that was done. I can tell you only that King Joyse and his forces made extensive use of the secret passages for which Orison has always been famed. It seems Orison has been a stewpot of plots and counterplots since its first tower was erected,' Master Quillon commented by the way. 'Also, their attacks were directed from the beginning at the Cadwal Imagers rather than at the soldiery. In fact, he spared as many of the soldiers as he could. When he was done, he offered them a choice between service with him or freedom. Those who chose his service became the kernel of the guard which eventually unified Mordant, and which has since successfully defied both Alend and Cadwal for decades.

'At this time, his people reversed their earlier ill opinion of him and became correspondingly enthusiastic.

'With considerably more support now from the Tor, young Joyse set about liberating Perdon. Then the three Cares turned their attention to Armigite, and to Termigan. Domne fell to them almost without effort – it has always been the least of the Cares, though the Demesne is smaller. Finally, in the most savage and costly battle he had yet faced, Joyse freed Fayle from Alend and became King.

'I will not protract this tale with details. You can imagine, I am sure, that all the Cares swore allegiance to King Joyse, but did not all keep their oaths, until he taught them to do so. You can imagine that most of his first success grew from the fact that neither Alend nor Cadwal were expecting what he did, and so the truly cruel wars for Mordant's independence were fought later, when his enemies understood what had happened and rose with all their strength against him. It is enough to say that twenty years passed before our King's hold on Mordant was secure enough to permit him to begin the work of collecting Imagers.

'That was thirty years ago,' murmured the Master, peering into the mouth of the decanter to see how much wine was there. 'For those of us who remember any part of it at all, it was grand. Even young boys, as I was, thought that everything the King touched took on a kind of sanctity, the stature of heroism and mighty deeds.'

The contemplation of his tale – or the effect of the wine – was making him increasingly morose. His jaws chewed indecisively. Perhaps he didn't know how much more he should tell Terisa. Or perhaps he was simply debating another swig from the decanter.

'Go on,' she said quietly. She wanted to learn how the King of Quillon's tale had become the frail old man she had met – a man so ineffective that even people who had worshiped him when they were boys now disobeyed him almost for no reason. 'Tell me what happened.'

Master Quillon made a face. 'Well, of course, with his friend to advise and guide and assist him, the first thing he did was to start collecting Imagers. And the Imagers were so accustomed to hiding their secrets from each other, to looking at everyone else as an enemy, that most of them were reluctant to be collected. In addition, Cadwal and Alend naturally did everything in their power to preserve their access to the resources of Imagery. All three kingdoms existed in an ongoing state of war – undeclared war, but war nonetheless – and at times King Joyse had to hammer at his enemies until they broke. But he also used every possible kind of cunning and stealth. He broadcast bribes. He sent out small bands on lightning raids. He suborned messengers, counselors, captains, anyone who might know the whereabouts of a man he wanted. He even went so far as to kidnap the families of Imagers and hold them hostage until the Imagers surrendered. It was at once more complex and more difficult than the process of forging Mordant out of its separate Cares. It cost him another twenty years.'

Again, he stopped. This time, however, he took an abrupt pull from the decanter and resumed his narration.

'But the bulk of the job had been completed five years earlier. Only one obstacle remained. The Alend Monarch and the High King of Cadwal, it will not surprise you to hear, did not trust King Joyse. They feared what he was doing, even though after each of his raids and battles he left their kingdoms essentially as he had found them. In their eyes, that was insane behavior, and insanity does not inspire confidence in the bosoms of mortal enemies. And, of course, if he had Imagers and they did not they would be defenseless against him.

'The High King of Cadwal, however, was both more prompt and less scrupulous than the Alend Monarch in his response to the threat. High King Festten, who still rules Cadwal from the great coastal city of Carmag, where the minarets rise high above the rocks and the sea, and where every exotic vice known to man is nurtured in the soil of riches and power' – Master Quillon didn't appear to think well of Carmag – 'Festten began collecting Imagers of his own. He formed a force of perhaps thirty men, each of them powerful in Imagery, and set over them the arch-Imager Vagel. In addition, he gave his personal champion of battle, the High King's Monomach, responsibility for the protection of his Imagers. Guarded by the Monomach's incomparable prowess, this cabal dedicated itself solely to the arts of violence, and to the defense of Cadwal, and to the defiance of King Joyse.'

Without warning, Adept Havelock raised his head as if he had suddenly decided to listen to what Master Quillon was saying.

'Five years passed before the King found means to break the cabal,' the Master went on. 'And then most of its members had to be slain. They had become too *acclimatized*,' he muttered sourly, 'to Cadwal's arid morals and lush pleasures. They could not accept transplantation. At the time, it was believed that the arch-Imager had perished also. But now he is thought to be alive – alive and in hiding somewhere, plotting malice.

'The High King's Monomach, of course, was executed for his failure, and another was chosen to take his place.'

With a wide movement of his arm, Havelock wiped his board as though he were sweeping all his men off onto the floor. Then he rose to his feet. Walking over to Terisa and Quillon, he touched her sleeve, leered, and nodded in the direction of the still-open door which had admitted her to this room. When she stared back at him, he rolled his eyes and beckoned determinedly. 'Time and tide wait for no man,' he said as if he were in one of his lucid phases, 'but everybody waits for women.'

'No, Havelock.' Quillon spoke with more firmness than Terisa had expected from him. 'Doubtless you know better than I. But I am going to tell her the rest.'

For an instant, ferocity came over the Adept's face. He clenched one eye closed so that he could scowl murderously at Master Quillon with the other. But Quillon didn't flinch, and Havelock's mood changed almost immediately. His expression relaxed into a fleshy smile.

'Wait for me, Vagel,' he said in a high voice, like a child at play. 'I'm coming. Hee hee. I'm *com*ing.'

Casting a wall-eyed wink at Terisa, he turned away and began rummaging through the clutter on one of his desks.

The Master shrugged. Tilting back his head, he drank what remained of the wine and set the decanter down beside him with a thump. His eyes were starting to look slightly blurred, and two red spots on his cheeks matched the end of his nose.

'That was ten years ago, my lady,' he said in a glum tone. 'For five of those years, we were relatively secure. The defenses King Joyse had created kept us relatively safe. Most of Mordant lived in relative peace. The Congery thrashed out the worst of its conflicts, both of personality and of trust, and became relatively unified, especially as the older generation – the men who remembered fondly what life had been like before King Joyse came along – passed away. By creating the Congery, of course, King Joyse could not control or limit the birth of the talent for Imagery anywhere in the world. But he had control of the *knowledge* of Imagery. Talent could find its outlet only by coming to Orison and accepting the servitude of an Apt.

'Alend and Cadwal were relatively quiet. Most of 'us' – his sarcasm returned – 'were relatively immune to the disorder of the King's domestic affairs. For five years, we did not notice, because we did not want to notice, that his spark was dying out. Perhaps because he had nothing enormous or heroic left to do, he was ceasing to be the man so many of us had loved.

'But eventually we had to notice. Oh, we *had* to.' Master Quillon became more bitter by the moment. 'We could not ignore that there was something evil running loose in Mordant.

'An Imager had begun to translate horrors and abominations out of his mirrors and unleash them to rampage across the land wherever they could find victims.'

In the cool of the room, a sensation of tightening scurried from Terisa's scalp down the length of her spine.

'It is easy to assume that he is Vagel. That is as reasonable a guess as any. He was always expert at finding in his glasses men and monsters and forces of destruction. And he did not trouble his conscience much about the consequences of his translations. But no one knows where he finds the patronage, the resources, to make such mirrors.

'We would also assume that he found them in Alend or Cadwal – but all his Images strike deep into Mordant, and it is inconceivable that such mirrors could be made elsewhere and then brought here across those distances without some word of the matter finally reaching the ears of Orison.

'But if not in Cadwal or Alend, then where? Who in Mordant would level such a threat against the realm? And why does King Joyse do nothing about it?

'Perhaps in the early years of the peril, patience and caution were indicated. After all, the attacks did not come often. Either Cadwal or Alend appeared to be the likely source. It seemed understandable that the King was waiting for his spies or his friends to discover the secret and bring it to him, so that he would know what to do.

'But the attacks grow worse, and no explanation comes. Instead, his spies and friends bring word that Alend and Cadwal have learned what is happening from *their* spies and friends, and are mustering their forces to take advantage of Mordant's danger. Armies gather beyond the Vertigon and Pestil rivers. Raids probe the Cares, testing their defenses. Angry because they are compelled to defend their own without assistance from King Joyse, some of the Cares begin to mutter against him. And still the abominations being translated against us worsen, both in magnitude and in frequency. The arch-Imager, if it *is* he, forms mirrors at an unheard-of rate as well as in perfect secrecy. And still the King does nothing.

'Well, not nothing, exactly,' the Master muttered as if he had acid in his mouth. 'He plays more and more hop-board.

'The Congery, of course, has not been blind to the problem. Even if we did not hear the same reports that reach every ear in Orison, we would have our auguries – and we have learned a great deal about auguring since our efforts were united.

'We can see Mordant dying, my lady, slaughtered by forces which we understand, but which our King, in founding the Congery, has forbidden us to act against. He will not allow us to be a weapon. Though he will do nothing to save Mordant, he is quick enough to march into our laborium and shatter any glass that offers a means of defense. He only permitted us to search for a champion because we agreed, after much squabbling debate, that whatever champion we chose would not be translated involuntarily, but would rather be approached with persuasion and given the opportunity to refuse.

'In short, our King has brought us to the verge of ruin. Unless more men become disloyal – and do it soon – Mordant will return to the days when it was nothing more than a battleground for Alend and Cadwal. And if Vagel is strong enough by then, he will join with one and devour the other, and so will make himself ruler over all the world.'

Brusquely, Master Quillon picked up Terisa's goblet and tossed down the wine she hadn't tasted. Into the goblet, he muttered hollowly, 'I, for one, do not relish the prospect.'

She was listening to him so closely that she didn't notice Adept Havelock until he touched her sleeve.

He was grinning like a satyr.

'I remember,' he whispered. His breath smelled like swamp gas. 'I remember everything.'

'He remembers everything,' growled the Master sardonically. 'Mirrors preserve us.'

'Yes,' Havelock hissed. 'I remember.' His grin was more than lascivious – it was positively bloodthirsty.

Quillon sighed disconsolately. 'You remember, Adept Havelock,' he murmured as though he were playing his part in an especially dull liturgy.

'Everything.'

Abruptly, the Adept gave a capering jump that made his sur-coat flap above his scrawny knees. He followed it with a pirouette, then confronted Terisa again, grinning like murder.

'I remember Vagel.

'He had a glass that poured fire. I had one full of water. He had a glass with a raving beast. But the beast could not breathe water. He had a weapon that fired beams of light which tore down walls and turned flesh to cinders. But the beams only changed water to steam. I *remember*.

'I remember the chamber where I cornered him. Shall I tell you how many candles were lit upon the table? Shall I count for you all the stones in the walls? Shall I measure the way the shadows fell into the corners? Shall I describe everything that I saw in his last mirror?

'It was perfectly flat, but because of its tinct and shape it showed a place among the sharp hills and fells of the Alend Lieges. A high summer sun shone on the meadow grass of the hillside – and on the waterfall, so that it sparkled in the distance. I saw butterflies of a kind which do not come to Mordant, and they danced among the daisies and dandelions. Above the waterfall stood tall fir trees. I saw it all.

'Mark me, my lady.' He glared intensely into Terisa's face, but one eye or the other necessarily scrutinized the pillar behind her. 'I remember Vagel well. I heard his scorn as he laughed at me, and I saw him step into the glass as though he had nothing to fear. I saw first one boot, then the other come down among the grass, crushing the blades. I saw his robe flare ebony under the summer sun. I saw the waterfall blocked from view by his shoulder as he took a stride or two on the hillside.

'Then he turned and beckoned for me to follow him.

'He beckoned to me, my lady.' Havelock's hands made fierce scraping movements, tearing the air in front of Terisa like hungry claws. 'He *beckoned*, and his scorn was still on his face. So I followed him, though every Imager knows that a translation which does not go anywhere is madness.' His voice began to scale upward in pitch. 'Wait for me, Vagel. I'm coming. I'm coming. Ah.' His groan came out strangled, like a scream.

'I'm an Adept. I opened his glass. I stepped into it. But when I did' – his voice was now a high, falsetto croon – 'he plucked the sun down from the sky and drove it into my eyes, and deep inside me everything was made light. Light, my lady, hee hee. Light.' From his throat came sounds like a little girl locked in a closet trying to comfort herself.

Master Quillon coughed. His eyes were red with wine or grief. In a husky voice, he said, 'My lady, you asked why some men call him "the King's dastard." That is because they think him a traitor to his own kind – to other Imagers.

'Well, it is true that he betrayed many Imagers to King Joyse. In his mind, the King's purpose outweighed their right to freedom. But his greatest act of treachery was to the Imagers gathered around Vagel in Carmag. It was he who broke that cabal. Concealing his identity and loyalty, he joined the arch-Imager as simply another crafter of mirrors hungry for power. For three years – his life always in the deadliest jeopardy – he served and studied Vagel, acting the part of an avid disciple, but in truth learning the cabal's defenses and plans. And when he had taught himself how to counter them, he sprang his trap, admitting King Joyse and a squadron of his guard into the keep where the Imagers lived and plotted.

'But the arch-Imager,' Quillon continued sadly, 'had one power which Havelock lacked. He was able – we know this now, though at the time we considered it impossible – to translate himself *within* our world by means of flat glass. When Havelock attempted to follow Vagel, the wrench of a translation which went nowhere cost him his mind, as it has cost the mind of every man but Vagel who has attempted it. For that reason, we believed the arch-Imager dead when Havelock returned raving to King Joyse and no trace of his foe could be found.

'As I say,' the Master sighed, 'Adept Havelock has his lucid moments. But for ten years now the King's chief friend and counselor has been a madman.'

The Adept had been growing increasingly restive during this speech. When Quillon finished, Havelock suddenly flung his arms out violently, as if he were ripping a veil in front of him. Then he grabbed Terisa's arm and dragged her off her stool, pulling her in the direction of the open door. 'Come on, woman!' he roared. 'I can't stand the suspense!'

Suspense? Terisa's thoughts were too full of the things she had just heard. She forgot herself. Apparently, she didn't like being hauled around like a disobedient child. She took a couple of quick steps to catch up with the Adept, then planted her feet and twisted her arm in an effort to break his grasp.

It was easier than she expected. His old fingers slipped from her arm; he nearly fell as he stumbled away from her.

Her heart pounding – not so much at the exertion as at the shock of her own audacity – she turned back to Master Quillon.

He studied her with interest, his head cocked to one side and his nose twitching.

'I want to thank you,' she said before her nerve failed. 'This is a big help. I won't give you away.'

He inclined his head gravely as if her promise were bigger than she realized. 'That would be much appreciated, my lady.'

'I don't know anything about your mirrors,' she went on at once. 'I'm not an Imager. But I think the worlds you see must be real. The place I come from isn't something Geraden and a piece of glass invented by accident.'

Master Quillon shrugged, and his depression returned. 'I hope you are right, my lady. I believe you are. But the arguments on the other side are difficult to refute. If your world is real – and if you are no Imager – then how was it possible for Geraden's translation to go so far awry?'

'I don't know,' she repeated. 'It's all new to me. But' – she was astonished to hear herself say this – 'I'm going to try to find out.'

Perhaps simply to keep herself from saying anything else so much unlike her image of who she was, she yielded to Havelock's dramatically mimed impatience and turned to follow him back into his secret passage.

'Nothing else,' the Adept muttered at her darkly. 'Only hop-board signifies.' When she had entered the passage, he closed the door. In the darkness, he fumbled around for a moment before producing a light from his piece of glass. Then he hurried upward, taking the stairs as rapidly as his old legs could manage.

She found climbing the stairs easier than descending them because she had a better chance to find where she was about to put her feet; but Havelock complicated the ascent by jerking his light from side to side and shining it far ahead of him rather than holding it steady. He was becoming more tense by the moment. His exertions made his breath rattle raggedly in his lungs, but he refused to slow his pace.

'What's the hurry?' she panted after him. The elevators of her apartment building hadn't prepared her to run up stairs.

He paused at an intersection and flashed his light in all directions. Then he squinted down at her for a moment. 'The trouble with women,' he gasped, heaving for breath, 'is that they never shut up.'

As he started upward again, the stone corridor suddenly felt more constricted, narrower. The beat of feet on the stairs seemed like the labor of her heart, reverberating almost subliminally from the walls. The ceiling was leaning down at her. He was crazy; it was crazy how he managed to communicate things he didn't say. Where had this urgency come from, this panic? She didn't understand why she rushed to keep up with him – or why she tried to muffle her breathing at the same time.

Surely they had passed her rooms by now? It wasn't possible that she had been dragged so far down without a better sense of the distance.

She nearly collided with him when he stopped.

'What—?'

At once, his arms flailed furious shushing motions. He stood with his light aimed at his feet and his face in shadow, concentrating hard – listening. In the reflection from the gray stone, she saw that his lips were trembling.

Then she heard it: from somewhere far away, a faint, metallic clashing sound, a dim shout.

Havelock spat a perfectly comprehensible obscenity and threw himself up the stairs, dousing his light as he ran.

For a fraction of a second, she remained frozen as darkness slammed down through the passage. Then she sprang instinctively, as quick as fear, after the Adept, straining desperately to catch him before he left her alone in the dark.

His raw panting loomed ahead of her, almost within reach. She stretched, stretched – and her fingers hooked the fabric of his surcoat.

That was enough. He made a sharp, unexpected turn; she was able to follow, guided by her small grip on his clothes.

His turn took them toward a glow of lamplight, but the illumination came too late. Half a heartbeat after his feet thudded on wooden boards instead of stone, she tripped over the rim of the wardrobe door and sprawled headlong to the floor of her bedroom.

There were peacock feathers everywhere. They floated through the air, swirled in small eddies across the rugs, draped themselves delicately over the edges of the bed. One of them wafted into her face, blinding her while a harsh voice gasped, 'My lady!' and iron rang like a carillon.

The voice sounded like Ribuld's.

She snatched down the feather in time to see him parrying frantically, sparks raining from the length of his longsword.

He and Argus fought with all their strength against a third man who held the entryway to the bedroom, blocking them from her.

The feathers were part of a decoration which this man had torn down to use as a shield.

He wore a cloak and leather armor so black that he was difficult to see: he confused Terisa's sight like a shadow cast on an uneven surface; all his movements looked like the flitting and darting of a shadow. Only his longsword caught and held the light, gleaming evilly as it struck fire from the opposing blades.

He seemed to be at least a hand shorter than Ribuld or Argus, slimmer than either of them. Yet his blows were as strong as theirs.

It was clear that they weren't winning.

Both of them were already badly battered. Argus had a vivid bruise under one eye, and his knuckles were bleeding. Ribuld had sustained a cut to the joining of his neck and shoulder. Notches and tears marked their mail: their opponent had been able to hit them at will.

Now Ribuld reeled away from the force of the attack. Losing his balance took him out of his assailant's reach, but it also fetched him heavily against the side of the fireplace. He stumbled to his knees.

Argus tried to surge forward, his sword hammering for the man's skull. The man was defter, however: his longsword leaped to catch Argus' blow and turn it. Then he smashed his now-tattered shield into Argus' face. Before Argus could counter, the man in black dealt him a kick to the groin which nearly pitched him on his head.

When he hit the floor, he hunched over and began retching.

As smooth as a shadow, the man turned toward Terisa.

Now she saw his face. His eyes shone yellow in the lamplight; he had a nose like the blade of a hatchet; his teeth were bared in a feral grin. She had the indistinct impression that there were scars on his cheeks.

His cloak seemed to billow about his shoulders as he clenched the hilt of his longsword in both hands and raised his blade against her.

'My lady!' shouted Ribuld again.

Charging like a ram, he launched himself at her attacker's back.

She had risen to her hands and knees, but she couldn't move. None of this made any sense. She could only watch as the man in black swung away from her and accepted Ribuld's assault.

Their blades met so hard that she thought she could hear them break. The sound of the iron was the sound of shattering. But this time Ribuld and his longsword held: it was the man in black who was forced to slip the blow past his shoulder and parry the return stroke.

He parried so well, however, that Ribuld had to skip backward to keep his hands intact.

The attacker followed at once, hacking at Ribuld from one side and then the other. Ribuld took the blows with his blade. Sparks spat over his forearms, but he didn't appear to feel the burns. He was retreating again, but under control this time, looking for an opening.

Abruptly, the man jumped away from Ribuld – jumped toward Argus. While Argus gaped horror at him, helpless with pain, the man whirled his sword to lop off Argus' head.

'No!' Desperately, Ribuld tried to catch his opponent in time. But desperation made him reckless. He had no defense when the man in black changed the direction of his stroke. The flat of his blade hit Ribuld in the face and leveled him.

'Now, my lady,' the man said in a voice like silk, 'let us end this.'

With his longsword poised in front of him, he strode into the bedroom.

For some reason, Terisa thought that this time no one would rescue her, that no young man would appear out of her dreams and risk his life to save hers. If she wanted to live, she would have to do something to save herself – shout for help, jump to her feet and flee into the secret passages of Orison, something. Yet she remained lost, unable to understand why anyone would attack her with such hate, unable to move.

Fortunately, at the last moment Adept Havelock hopped out of his hiding place in the wardrobe and fired his glass into her assailant's eyes.

The man gave a roar of pain and recoiled. For an instant, he stood with his forearms crossed over his eyes, his longsword jutting at the ceiling. Then he snarled a curse. Though he plainly couldn't see a thing, he brought his blade down and started forward again, probing the air for someone to strike.

In the other room, Argus heaved himself into a crouch, reached for his sword. 'Now,' he grunted, in sharp pain and ready for murder. 'Now I've got you.'

Terisa's attacker froze. If he could have seen Argus, he would have known that he was safe: Argus was barely able to crawl. But the man couldn't see. He hesitated momentarily while he listened to the sounds Argus made; then he whirled away from Terisa, took an immense, acrobatic leap which carried him over both Argus and Ribuld, and found his way to the door. A second later, he was gone.

Groaning, Argus nudged Ribuld's inert form. 'Go after him, you fool. Don't let him get away.'

Terisa stared about her, too stunned to think in logical sequences. Ribuld and Argus had tried to defend her – and had almost been killed for their pains. The wood of the door was splintered around the bolt. If the man recovered his sight and came back— The Adept was out of his mind, of course, but he understood what took place around him to some extent, at any rate.

'Havelock,' she murmured vaguely, 'did you know this was going to happen?'

He wasn't there. He had already left. The door hidden in the back of the wardrobe was closed.

SEVEN

THE DUNGEONS
OF ORISON

The events of the next half hour had blurred edges and imprecise tones. Her nerves jangled like badly tuned strings, and her pulse refused to slow down. With so much adrenaline in her veins, she should have been more alert, had a better grasp on what was happening. But everything seemed to leak away as soon as she focused her attention on it. Reality had become like sand, trickling through her fingers.

'Get help,' Argus coughed in her direction. He hadn't moved from Ribuld's side; he was hunched there, barely able to hold himself up with his arms. 'If he comes back—'

That was probably intended to mean something. Hadn't she just been thinking the same thing herself? But now she was unsure of it. Her instinct was to simply run away. Use the Adept's secret passage and find her way back to Master Quillon. She wanted warm arms around her. She wanted someone who knew what he was doing to take care of her. Surely Master Quillon would be able to comfort her? So she felt that she was doing the hardest thing she had done in years when she made her way around Ribuld and Argus to the bellpull behind one of the feather displays. From there, she was exposed to the open door. But she didn't know how else to call for help.

She tugged on the satin cord of the pull as hard as she dared. Then she returned to her bedroom.

An impulse she didn't immediately understand made her rearrange the clothes in the wardrobe and then close the door, concealing the secret passage.

Before long – or perhaps after a long time, according to how she happened to feel at the moment – her summons was answered. But not by Saddith. The woman who appeared in the doorway had the look of a chambermaid; she was older than Saddith, however, blowzy with sleep and hasty dressing, and in no good humor. Nevertheless after one glance at Ribuld and Argus, at the scattered feathers and the broken door, she forgot her irritation and fled.

For a moment, she could be heard squalling into the distance, 'Ho, guards! Help!'

'Fool woman,' Argus muttered through his teeth.

Ribuld was stirring. His hands rubbed at his face, then flinched away from his bruised forehead. 'Daughter of a goat,' he groaned. 'Who *was* that bastard?' Weakly, he propped himself up on one elbow and peered around the room. When he saw Terisa, he gave a sigh of relief and sank back to the floor again.

'I'm dying,' Argus whispered thickly. 'Hogswill unmanned me.'

'Forget it,' replied Ribuld in a prostrate tone. 'Won't change your life.'

Shortly, Terisa heard nailed boots hammering the stone of the outer corridor – a lot of boots. Brandishing his longsword, a man dressed like Ribuld and Argus sprang through the doorway. He had five companions behind him, all ready for a fight: they looked clenched for violence, like the three riders in her dream. But there was no fight available. They scanned the rooms quickly, then gathered around Terisa's defenders. 'What happened?' one of them asked, awkwardly jocose. 'Did you two lechers finally meet a woman tougher than you are?'

Before Argus or Ribuld could answer, another man stamped into the room. From his close-cropped, gray-stained hair to his out-thrust jaw, from his swaggering shoulders to his hard strides, he bristled with authority, though he was shorter than Terisa – nearly a foot shorter than any of the men around him. He was dressed as they were, with the addition of a purple sash draped over one shoulder across his mail and a purple band knotted above his stiff, gray eyebrows. His eyes held a perpetual glare, and his mouth snarled as if it had long ago forgotten any other expression.

He scanned the room, assessing the situation, then stalked up to Terisa and gave her a rigid bow. 'My lady,' he said. In spite of its quietness, his voice made her want to flinch. 'I'm Castellan Lebbick, commander of Orison and the guard of Mordant. I'll speak to you in a moment.'

At once, he turned on Argus and Ribuld. Without raising his voice, he made it sound like a lash. 'What's going on here?'

They struggled to their feet. Uncomfortably, they tried to explain the situation. As a personal favor, Apt Geraden had asked them to keep an eye on the lady Terisa of Morgan, in case she got in trouble. He said he didn't know what kind of trouble. But they were off duty, so they decided to do what he asked. Nothing happened for a long time. Then the man in black appeared in the corridor. He walked up to them and told them to let him in, he had business with the lady Terisa. When they asked him what his business was, he snatched out his sword, broke the door open, and tried to kill her. After that, he gave up and ran away.

Listening to them, Terisa realized that neither Argus nor Ribuld knew she had been out of her rooms. In fact, neither of them had seen Adept Havelock. Because of this, they weren't able to account for her attacker's flight. Glancing toward Terisa as if he believed she were responsible, Argus mumbled something about a light, then winced at the way Castellan Lebbick looked at him.

Ignoring her, the Castellan sent the six guards out of the room at a run to rouse the rest of the watch and begin a search for the man in black –

'Although,' he muttered as they left, 'he's probably halfway to oblivion by now.' Then he returned his attention to Ribuld and Argus.

'Let me get this straight. He fought the two of you away from the door long enough to break it open. He got as far as the doorway to the bedroom. He knocked one of you out and disabled the other. Then he panicked and ran away. Doubtless he was terrified by how easily you were overcome. Maybe everybody who serves the King is like you. I'm surprised he didn't die of fright.'

Ribuld and Argus hung their heads.

'My lady?' Lebbick asked grimly.

Terisa didn't answer. Now she understood why she had closed the wardrobe. Havelock had taken the risk of angering both the King and the Congery by providing her with some of Mordant's history, and she didn't mean to betray what he had done for her.

'Very well,' the Castellan growled. 'Let that pass for the moment. Explain this, you ox-headed louts,' he demanded of Argus and Ribuld. 'Why didn't you tell anyone what you were doing here? By the stars, I've spent my life training lumps of dead meat to understand the importance of communications and access to reinforcements. If you believed Geraden enough to think the lady might be in danger, why didn't you take the simple precaution of arranging to be able to call for help?'

The bruise on his forehead gave Ribuld an excuse to raise his hand in front of his face. 'We didn't believe Geraden. You know *him*. We were just doing him a favor. For Artagel's sake.'

'Pigswallow,' retorted Castellan Lebbick. '*I'll* tell you why you didn't tell anyone. If you reported what you were doing to your captain in order to arrange reinforcements, he would report it to me – and *I* would report it to the King. Since the King didn't see fit to command guards for the lady himself, he might have been moved to wonder' – the Castellan's voice sounded capable of drawing blood – 'what *business* it is of yours to meddle in his decisions.'

'We didn't mean any offense,' Argus protested. 'We were just—'

'I know. Spare me your excuses. I'll take care of Geraden. *You* report to your captain. Tell him about this – and count yourselves lucky I don't have you clapped in irons. Go on.'

Argus and Ribuld obeyed, hardly daring to groan. Neither of them looked at Terisa. Carefully – but promptly under the Castellan's glare – they retrieved their swords and hobbled out of the room.

'Now, my lady.' Lebbick rounded on her. 'Maybe we can discuss this matter a bit more openly. I'm sure King Joyse will be relieved to hear you were able to drive off your attacker – alone and unaided – after two of my guards failed. But he might like to know how you did it. And I'm sure he'll want to know what it is about you that brings on that kind of attack in the middle of the night.'

He moved a step closer to her, his chin jutting. 'Who are you, my lady? Oh, I know the story – Orison doesn't keep things like that secret. Apt Geraden brought you here by an accidental translation. But who *are* you?' His eyes held hers, as piercing as awls. 'What game are you trying to play with my King?'

He sounded so angry that she started to tremble.

Another step brought him close to her. If he extended his right fist, pointed his heavy index finger at her, she knew exactly what would happen next. She would begin to babble:

I'm sorry I didn't mean it I won't do it again I promise please don't punish me *I don't know what I did wrong.*

Fortuitously, another guard sprinted into the room at that moment and jerked himself to a halt. He was a young man, and his fear of Castellan Lebbick's temper showed all over him.

'Excuse me, Castellan, sir,' he said in a tumble. 'I didn't mean to interrupt. I have a message from the King.'

Lebbick took a deep breath and closed his eyes as if he were controlling himself with great difficulty. Then he turned his back on Terisa.

The guard swallowed heavily and stared back at the Castellan like a bird caught by a snake.

'A message from the King,' Lebbick rasped venomously. 'You said you had one. Try to remember.'

'Yes, sir, Castellan, sir. A message from the King. He has stopped the search.'

'*What?*' A flick of the whip.

'The King has stopped the search, sir.'

'Well, that makes sense. In times like these, a potential assassin in the castle is a trivial problem. Did he give a *reason* for stopping the search?'

'Yes, sir.' The guard's skin was chalky. 'He said he doesn't like all this running around in the middle of the night.'

For a moment, Castellan Lebbick's shoulders bunched with outrage. Yet he spoke softly. 'Is that all?'

'No, sir. He also said' – the guard looked like he would have been happier if he could have fainted – 'he wants you to leave his guests alone.' And winced involuntarily, as if he expected to be struck.

The Castellan swung his arm, but not to strike the guard. He slapped himself, hard, on the thigh. He growled far back in his throat. He made a loud, spitting noise.

Abruptly, he faced Terisa again.

Like the guard, she winced.

'My lady, be warned,' he said. 'I'm the Castellan of Orison. I'm responsible for many things, but above everything else for the King's safety. He suffers from an unnatural faith in his own immortality. I'm not similarly afflicted.' His jaws chewed the words like gristle. 'I'll obey him as much as I can. Then I'll take matters into my own hands.'

Turning on his heel, he stamped away.

As he passed the guard, he paused long enough to say, 'I want the lady guarded. This time, do it right.' And at the door he stopped again. 'Keep this closed tonight. I'll have the bolt repaired in the morning.'

Then he was gone.

The guard gave Terisa a sheepish shrug – half chagrin at his own timidity, half apology for the Castellan's brusqueness – and followed his commander, pulling the door shut behind him.

As he left, he seemed to take all the courage out of the room with him.

Without warning, everything changed to alarm. Gripping her robe tightly closed, she hurried to the door to listen. She clearly heard the voices of several men outside her room: they were issuing the orders and making the arrangements to have her guarded. Still she felt vulnerable, helpless. A total stranger had tried to kill her. Urgently, she moved a chair to prop it against the door. Then she placed another chair inside her wardrobe to block Havelock's passage.

After that, she didn't know what to do.

For a long time, she couldn't relax or concentrate. High King Festten had had his Monomach executed for failure when Adept Havelock betrayed the arch-Imager's followers. Havelock had lost his mind when he tried to chase Vagel into a flat glass. Master Quillon was willing to tell her stories like these, even though both King Joyse and the Congery prohibited it. For some reason, Castellan Lebbick didn't trust her.

How could all this be happening to her?

But later, unexpectedly, she felt an odd upswelling of joy. Apparently, Geraden had brought her to a place where she *mattered*. The fact that she was here made a difference. Castellan Lebbick took her seriously enough to get angry at her. Master Eremis had *looked* at her. It was even conceivable that he thought she was lovely.

That had never happened to her before.

Eventually, she was able to sleep.

Sunlight from her windows awakened her the next morning. At first, she doubted everything. Wasn't this the bed in her apartment, the place where she belonged? But the light made the rugs on the floors bright, the peacock ornaments of the rooms, the feathers scattered by the man in black. That much of what she remembered was real, at any rate.

The indirect sunshine had the pale color of cold. And the air outside her blankets was chill. She hadn't thought to build up her fires before she went to bed, and they had died down during the night. Holding her breath, she eased out of the warm bedclothes and hurried into the thick velvet robe she had worn the previous night. The stone felt like ice under her bare feet: with a small gasp, she hopped to the nearest rug.

When she looked toward the windows, she hesitated. She wasn't sure that she was ready to see what lay outside. The view might confirm or deny the entire situation.

On the other hand, she felt vaguely foolish for having postponed the question this long. Anybody with a grain of normal human curiosity would have looked outside almost immediately. What was she afraid of?

Unable to define what she was afraid of, she moved to the windows of the bedroom.

The diamond-shaped panes of thick glass – each about the size of her hand – were leaded into their frames. A touch of frost edged the glass wherever the lead seals were imperfect, outlining several of the diamonds. But the glass itself was clear, and it showed her a world full of winter.

From her elevation, she was able to see a considerable distance. Under the colorless sky and the thin sunlight, hills covered with snow rumpled the terrain to the horizon. The snow looked thick – so thick that it seemed to bow the trees, bending them toward the blanketed slumber of the hills. Where the trunks and limbs of the trees showed through the snow, they were black and stark, but so small against the wide white background that they served only as punctuation, making the winter and the cold more articulate.

When she realized how high up she was, however, her view contracted to her more immediate surroundings.

She was indeed in a tower – and near the top of it, judging by her position relative to the other towers she could see. There were four including hers, one arising from each corner of the huge, erratic structure of Orison; and they contrasted with the rest of the castle, as if they had been built at a different time, planned by a different mind. They were all square, all the same height, all rimmed with crenellated parapets – as assertive as fists raised against the sky.

Their blunt regularity made the great bulk of Orison appear haphazard: disorganized, self-absorbed, and unreliable, beset with snares.

In fact, the general shape of the castle was quite regular in its outlines. Orison was rectangular, constructed around an enormous open courtyard. Terisa could see it clearly because her windows faced out over one of the long arms of the rectangle. One end of the courtyard – the end away from her tower – was occupied by what she could only think of as a bazaar: a large conglomeration of shops and sheds, stalls and tents, wagons carrying fodder – all thoroughly chaotic, all shrouded by the smoke of dozens of cookfires.

The other end of the courtyard looked big enough to serve as a parade ground – as long as the parade didn't get out of hand. There men on horseback, children playing, and clusters of people on their way to or from the bazaar churned the mud and snow.

Large as the courtyard was, however, the structure of Orison was high enough to keep it all in shadow at this hour of the morning. The open air must have been bitterly cold: Terisa noticed that even the children didn't stay outside very long.

The other regular feature of the castle was its outward face. Since her window looked over the courtyard, she couldn't see the details of the walls, but she could see that Orison had no outer defenses: it was its own fortification. The whole edifice was built of blunt gray stone, presenting a hard and unadorned face to the external world on all sides.

Within its outlines, however, the castle looked as though it had been designed more for the convenience of its secrets than for the accommodation of its inhabitants. Mismatched slate roofs canted at all angles, pitching their runoff into the courtyard. Dozens of chimneys bearing no resemblance to each other gusted smoke along the breeze. Some sections of the structure were tall and square; others, squat and lumpish. Some parts had balconies instead of windows; others sported poles from which clotheslines hung. She couldn't resist the conclusion that King Joyse had attached the four towers to his ancestral seat, decreed the shape in which Orison was to grow, and then forgotten about it, letting a number of disagreeable builders express themselves willy-nilly.

Now, at least, she understood why she had found Geraden's and Saddith's routes through the castle so confusing. Truncated passages and sudden intersections, unpremeditated stairs and necessary detours were part of Orison's basic construction.

As far as she could make out, the only way into the courtyard from outside was along a road which led through a massive set of gates in the long arm of the rectangle below her. These gates were apparently open, admitting wains pulled by oxen to the courtyard. But her angle of vision didn't let her see whether the gates were guarded.

As she studied the scene, her breath misted the glass. She wiped it clear again with the sleeve of her robe. Then she touched her fingers to one of the panes. The cold spread a little halo of condensed vapor over the glass around each fingertip; a sharp, delicate chill seeped into her skin. That, more than the immense weight of Orison's piled stone, made everything she saw seem tangible, convincing. She was truly *in* this place, wherever it was – and whatever it might mean. She was here.

Shortly, her musing was interrupted by a knock at her sitting room door. Because she didn't want to stand where she was indefinitely, thinking the same thoughts over and over again, she went to answer the knock. On her way to the door, however, she hesitated again. Did she really mean to open that door and admit everything that might be waiting for her? Someone was trying to kill her. He might be outside.

But what choice did she have? None, if she wanted to learn anything more about what was happening to her. Or if she wanted breakfast.

Her heart began to beat more the way it should – more like the heart of a woman whose life was at risk – as she pulled the chair away from the door and opened it.

Two guards she hadn't seen before saluted her.

Saddith was with them, holding a tray with one edge propped on her hip.

A gleam in her eye and a saucy tilt to her head indicated the spirit in which she had been conversing with the guards; her blouse was buttoned to a still lower level, giving out hints of pleasure whenever she moved her shoulders. But as soon as she saw Terisa her expression became contrite and solicitous.

'My lady, are you all right? They said you were, but I did not know whether to believe them. That woman and I traded duties for the night. I did not know that you would be attacked – or that she would be such a goose. She should have stayed with you. I brought your breakfast. I know you are upset, but you ought to eat. Do you think you could try?'

Terisa met the maid's rush of words and blinked. She was relieved to see Saddith again. Saddith was safe; she was real. 'Yes,' Terisa said when Saddith paused for an answer. 'I am hungry. And I'm afraid I've let the fires go out. Please come in.'

With a nod and a wink for the guards, Saddith shifted her tray in front of her and entered the sitting room.

As Terisa closed the door, she heard the guards chuckling together.

Saddith heard the sound as well. 'Those two,' she said in good-natured derision while she pushed aside the supper dishes to clear room for breakfast. 'They doubted me when I told them that the sight of you would make their knees melt – whatever it did to the rest of them. Now they know I told the truth.'

Then she indicated a chair beside the table where she had set her tray. 'Please sit down and eat, my lady. The porridge will warm you while I build up the fires again. Then I think we must find you something better to wear.'

Terisa accepted the chair. Neatly arranged for her delectation, she found grapes, brown bread, a wedge of deep yellow cheese, and a steaming bowl that appeared to contain a cracked-wheat cereal. Remembering the previous night's meal, she began to eat quickly, pausing now and then to relish the combination of the tart cheese and the sweet grapes.

But Saddith didn't stop talking as she worked at the nearest hearth. 'What was he like,' she asked, 'this man in black who attacked you?' She seemed to be excited and pleased about something. 'Orison is full of rumors already. He was taller than Ribuld, and so strong of chest that my arms might not reach around him. He had a hunter's face, and a hunter's glee, with enough power in his hands and thighs to batter Ribuld and Argus as if they were boys.' For a moment, she hugged her breasts. Then she sighed wistfully. 'So the rumor goes. What was he really like, my lady?'

Slowly, unsure of what she was going to say until she said it, Terisa replied, 'He was terrifying.'

'Perhaps if I had not traded duties I might have chanced to see him.' Saddith thought about that for a moment with a quizzical expression on her face. Then she laughed. 'No. I was better where I was.'

Terisa had spent enough time listening to Reverend Thatcher to know a hint when she heard one, so she asked politely, 'Where were you?'

Gaiety sparkled in Saddith's eyes. 'Oh, I should not tell you that.' At once, she strode energetically into the bedroom to rebuild the fire there.

But almost at once she stuck her head past the doorway to ask, 'Do you remember what I said last night, my lady? "Any Master will tell me whatever I wish – if I conceive a wish for something he knows." Perhaps you thought I was boasting.' She disappeared again. For a minute, Terisa heard her working over the fire. Then she came back into the sitting room. 'I will be truthful with you, my lady. I did not trade duties with anyone. I asked that woman you saw to care for you, so that I might have the night to myself – without interruption.

'I assure you that I did not waste the opportunity.' Saddith grinned. 'I spent the night with a Master.'

Terisa had never heard anyone talk like this before; the novelty of the experience made her ask, 'Did he tell you what you wanted to know?'

It was Saddith's turn to be surprised. 'My lady, I did not share his bed because I lacked knowledge.' She giggled at the idea. 'I shared it because he is a Master.'

With a toss of her head, she went back into the bedroom.

Unexpectedly, Terisa found that she couldn't concentrate on breakfast. The maid's frankness disturbed her. It reminded her that she knew next to nothing about men – about the things they did to women; about what pleased them. She had never been an object of desire or tenderness.

Pushing the tray away, she went into the bathroom and made as much use as she could stand of the soap and cold water. Then, her skin tingling under the robe, she joined Saddith in front of the wardrobes to search for appropriate clothing.

Apparently by chance, Saddith chose the wardrobe that didn't contain a chair blocking its back panels. Almost at once, she selected a simple but striking scarlet gown that looked long enough to sweep the floor.

Hesitantly, Terisa said, 'I'm not sure I can wear that color. Wouldn't it be better if I just used my own clothes?'

'Certainly not, my lady,' replied Saddith, firmly but not unkindly. 'I do not know how these things are considered where you come from, but here it is plain that your clothes are not becoming. Also you do not wish to insult the lady Myste, who has been very generous. Here.' She draped the gown in front of Terisa. 'It is not the best of all colors for your eyes,' she commented analytically. 'But it does well with your skin. And it accents your hair to great advantage. Will you try it?'

Feeling at once a little excited and a little foolish, Terisa shrugged.

Saddith showed her the series of hooks and eyes that closed the gown at the back. Then Terisa put aside her robe and pulled the heavy scarlet fabric over her head. It was a snug fit: Saddith's earlier observation that the lady Myste 'has not some of your advantages' seemed to mean she had smaller breasts, which weren't so much exposed by the gown's deep neckline. But it was warm. And it felt flattering in a way that Terisa couldn't define.

She wanted a mirror. She wanted to see herself. The look in Saddith's eyes – half approval, half gauging uncertainty, as if Terisa now appeared more attractive than the maid had intended or wished – that look meant something, but it didn't have the same effect as a mirror.

For Terisa's feet, Saddith produced a pair of fur-lined buskins with firm soles. They didn't exactly complement the gown; but they, too, were warm, and the gown was long enough to hide them.

She was just starting to thank the maid when she heard another knock at her door.

Saddith went to answer it, Terisa following more slowly.

When the door was opened, it revealed Geraden outside.

He had a pinched, white look around his mouth and eyes; a bright red spot marked each cheek, like embarrassment or temerity aggravated by fever. At first glance, he appeared miserable: he must have had a bad night. But when he saw Terisa, his face broke into the helpless, happy smile she remembered from their first meeting.

For a long moment, he gazed at her; and she gazed back; and he grinned like a puppy in love. Then he cleared his throat. 'My lady, you look wonderful.'

Her reaction was more complex. She was glad to see him: partly because, like Saddith, Adept Havelock, and the others, he had come back, demonstrating his capacity for continuous existence; partly because she thought she liked him (it was hard to be sure because she had so little experience); partly because he was one of the very few people here who seemed to care about what she thought or felt. In addition, she was immediately worried by his appearance of distress. And by his presence outside her door. King Joyse hadn't just ordered the Apt not to answer her questions: he had also said, *You will have no more reason to see or speak with the lady Terisa.* Geraden had already shown himself loyal to his King – and yet he was here in direct disobedience.

And nobody had ever told her that she looked wonderful before.

Flustered, she felt herself blushing. With a gesture at her gown, she said, 'I feel like I'm going to a costume party.'

Glancing back and forth between Terisa and Geraden, Saddith gave a quiet laugh. 'What is a costume party, my lady?' she asked to disguise her amusement.

Terisa tried hard to get her confusion under control. 'It's a party where people dress up in fancy clothes and pretend to be somebody they aren't.'

For some reason, her response brought the strain back to Geraden's eyes.

'La, my lady,' Saddith said at once as if that were the reaction she had been waiting for, 'it must be greatly amusing. But if you will excuse me, I will return your trays to the kitchens. Please call for me at need. If you do not call before then, I will come whenever the lady Elega or the lady Myste asks to see you.

'As for you, Apt Geraden,' she said in a tone of kind mirth as she gathered the dishes together and carried them toward the door, 'a word of friendly advice. Women do not generally admire a man who gapes.'

Laughing, she left the room, hooking the door shut with her foot.

But Geraden ignored Saddith's exit. Gazing at Terisa now with an intensity that matched the color in his cheeks, he asked softly, 'Are you pretending to be somebody you aren't, my lady? What are you pretending?'

She turned her head away. 'I thought I told you to call me Terisa.' This was absurd. Why was she in such a dither? And why was he asking her such silly questions, when he must be risking some kind of serious punishment by defying the King? 'I'm not pretending anything. I'm just wearing this dress because the lady Myste offered it and Saddith said she would be insulted if I turned it down.'

Then she faced him. 'Geraden, what are you doing here? King Joyse told you not to see me. You'll get in trouble.'

At that, a pained smile made his mouth crooked. 'I'm already in trouble. It probably won't get any worse.

'You've met King Joyse. These days, he doesn't punish anyone. I don't think he has the heart for it. Or maybe nothing matters to him that much anymore. The worst thing he might do is turn me over to Castellan Lebbick.' Geraden sighed. 'I guess Lebbick is a good man. Artagel says he is. But he isn't exactly gentle. And he's already started on me. Because I asked Ribuld and Argus to guard you.' That was the source of his distress: Castellan Lebbick must have abused him severely. 'He spent half the night at it. I kept wanting to apologize, even though we both knew I was right.'

Abruptly, he shrugged. 'At least now I'm not afraid of him anymore. After last night, all he can do is lock me up. But he isn't likely to do that to a son of the Domne – not without a better reason.' Slowly, he made the tight lines of his face relax, and his smile improved. 'For a while, anyway, I don't have anything to worry about.'

Her heart twisted for him: she could guess what being scathed by the Castellan might be like. 'But why?' she asked. 'Why did he do that to you? What does he think you did wrong?'

'Well,' mused Geraden, 'I suppose he does have a point. He wants to know why I thought you might be attacked when the idea apparently never occurred to anybody else in Orison. It's his job to know everything that happens here. What do I know that he doesn't?'

'What did you tell him?'

He snorted quietly. 'The truth. Mordant is under siege by Imagery. King Joyse won't let the Congery fight back – but even if he did, the Imagers are so divided they might not be able to accomplish anything. Cadwal and Alend are drooling for a chance to strike at us. And in the meantime the King has taken to acting like a man who left his head in the other room. Who in his right mind would *not* want someone as important as you guarded?'

Again, the Apt mustered a crooked smile. 'Castellan Lebbick didn't like it when I said all that.'

He was putting up a brave front; but the rest of his face still looked as pale as wax around the hot spots of color in his cheeks. Wanting to comfort him, Terisa said, 'I can imagine what that must have been like. He was here for a while last night. After everything was over.'

'I know.' Without transition, his expression became morose, almost grim. 'That was something else he wanted me to explain. How did you manage to save yourself, after both Argus and Ribuld were beaten? And why didn't you answer the question when he asked it?

'He has a point there, too, my lady.' He began to pace in front of her without looking at her. 'Even Artagel couldn't beat both Argus and Ribuld at once. They may not look like much, but they're really pretty good. And you got rid of a man who beat them all by yourself. Do you have any idea what kind of conclusions Lebbick draws from that?'

'No,' she breathed. 'I don't have any idea about any of this.'

'Well, I'll tell you. He thinks you're in league with that man. Or rather, that man is in league with you. He fought his way in here to meet you for some reason – maybe to give you a message, or to let you know what preparations are being made by your allies. But it doesn't have to go that far. Maybe you *aren't* allies. You still got rid of him without being hurt. That took *power*.' The whole notion seemed to offend him to the point of nausea. 'I tried to tell him it was impossible. I wanted to protect you. But when you get right down to it' – he stopped pacing and faced her squarely, his trouble in his eyes – 'I don't have any reason to think it's impossible. Except you keep saying it is.'

'What do you mean?' she protested. 'Of course it's impossible.' She had only wanted to commiserate with him; she hadn't intended to admit anything that might force her to betray Adept Havelock and Master Quillon. 'I don't know anything about Imagery, or Mordant, or' – she saw again in her mind a wild grin, as sharp as hate, and a nose like the blade of a hatchet, and yellow eyes – 'that man who tried to kill me.'

'My lady,' he countered, 'I found you in a room full of mirrors! And it was a room where no known translation could have taken me – unless it was you who did the translating. You were sitting in a chair right in front of the glass, and you were staring at me, concentrating on me. I thought I could feel you calling me.

'My lady,' he repeated in misery and appeal, 'I want to believe you. I want to trust you. But I don't know how.'

Terisa hadn't had much time to adjust to the new rules and emotions of her situation; the sheer seriousness of Geraden's reaction took her by surprise. She was unprepared for the way she was affected, not by his argument, but by his distress.

'I'm sorry. I didn't know you would feel that way about it. Come here.'

Turning, she walked quickly into the bedroom, toward the wardrobe with the hidden door.

She still didn't intend to betray Adept Havelock and Master Quillon. She had no way to evaluate any of the conflicting factions or exigencies that she had already met in Orison, no way to know which side she might actually want to be on. But what Havelock and Quillon had done for her was better than the treatment she had received from either the Congery or the King, and she didn't mean to repay kindness with exposure.

When Geraden joined her, she pulled open the wardrobe and showed him the chair she had wedged there. Then she removed the chair to let him see the secret door.

'Oh,' he said uncomfortably. 'You've got one of those.'

'I didn't know it was here when they gave me these rooms,' she began. 'But in the middle of the night' – she swallowed hard, hoping she would be able to say enough without saying too much – 'Adept Havelock came through that door. I don't think he wanted to scare me, but he talked about hop-board and' – she faltered for an instant – 'and lust until I wanted to scream. So he was here when that man attacked. And he had a piece of glass that let out an intense light. When that man was done with Argus and Ribuld, he came at me. But Adept Havelock shone the light in his eyes. He was blinded. He had to forget me and get away.'

She met Geraden's astonishment as well as she could. 'I probably should have said something to the Castellan. I certainly wasn't trying to get you in trouble. But Adept Havelock saved me. And he seemed to want to keep what he was doing secret. When I found out Argus and Ribuld hadn't seen him, I decided not to tell anybody he was here.'

Then, changing the subject promptly, she went on, 'And I'm not an Imager. Where you found me, mirrors don't do what they do here.' She couldn't have borne the embarrassment of trying to explain why she had decorated her apartment in mirrors, but she had another argument ready. 'When you arrived in my room, you must have noticed the broken glass. It was all over the rug. You even had some in your hair.

'You did that.'

His mouth hung open. 'I?'

'Two objects can't occupy the same space at the same time,' she recited. 'Your translation put you in the same space as my mirror. If I was trying to translate you, it was a failure. The glass was ruined, and I wasn't going to be able to send you back, or go with you. But glass isn't like that where I come from. There's nothing magic about it. When you arrived, it just broke.

'Do you see? I'm telling the truth. The translation was from your side. I've been telling you the truth all along.'

For a long moment, he frowned intently while he absorbed what she had said. Then, slowly, starting at his mouth and rising to his eyes, a grin lit his face. 'Of course,' he breathed, beaming wonder at her. 'I shouldn't have questioned you. Of course I saw the broken glass. Why didn't I think—?' With every sentence, his distress lifted and the weight of worry on him seemed to grow lighter. 'I should have figured it out for myself.'

Exuberant with relief, he put his hands on her shoulders and pulled himself close to her to kiss her cheek. But his enthusiasm tipped him off balance; he missed, knocking his cheekbone against hers instead.

'Oh, I'm sorry, I'm sorry,' he babbled in immediate chagrin. Backing away, he waved both hands as if to assure her that he meant no harm. 'I'm sorry, my lady. Please forgive me.' Then he raised one hand to his mouth. 'Oh, shatter it all to slivers. I bit my tongue.'

Terisa rubbed her cheekbone; the blow had startled more than hurt her. Secretly, she wanted him to try to kiss her again. She was as lost as he was, however. The best she could do was to say with mock severity, 'Apt Geraden, if you don't start calling me Terisa I'm going to tell Castellan Lebbick that you forced your way into my rooms and tried to knock me unconscious.'

At that, he began to laugh. His laugh was strong and clean, and it blew most of the chagrin out of him. 'My lady,' he said finally, 'I've never called a woman like you by her given name in my whole life. I've got at least three brothers who think I'm still young enough to spank – and I'm sure they would try it if they heard me call you anything except "my lady," no matter how badly you threaten me. Be patient. You can probably tell I've still got a lot to learn.'

She, too, had a lot to learn. But she knew enough to say, 'I'll try,' and smile at him as if she knew a great deal more.

She was relieved to see him looking happier – and to have escaped the subject of Havelock so easily.

For a moment, he stood and gazed at her in silence, enjoying what he saw: her smile, the tumble of her hair against the scarlet fabric on her shoulders. Then he shook his head and recollected himself. He ran an unself-conscious hand through his hair, touched his own cheekbone, and said, 'Actually, I do have one official reason for being here. I was just supposed to send you a message, but I can stretch a point by delivering it myself. If anybody asks, that's why I came.

'The Congery wants you to know you won't have to attend their meeting today. That's a polite way of saying you aren't invited. They want to talk about you, and they don't want to be' – he grimaced humorously – 'inhibited by your presence while they do it. In fact, I'm not invited either. They don't want to have to spend the whole meeting arguing with a mere Apt.'

As he spoke, his tone and manner became more serious. When he paused, he did so with an air of hesitation, as if he were unsure of how she would react to what he wanted to say. 'My lady,' he went on slowly, 'I'm already disobeying the King, as you pointed out. And I really don't think I can get into any worse trouble. So I thought' – his gaze dropped to the floor as though he were forcing himself not to stare at her – 'since all the Masters will be in their meeting, and nobody else is likely to stop us' – involuntarily, his eyes rose to hers again, and she saw trepidation and suspense in them – 'I might try to answer some of your questions by showing you the laborium. Where the mirrors of the Congery are kept.'

His audacity made her catch her breath. It was dangerous to flout authority: she knew that intimately. People who disobeyed were punished. In a rush as she forced the air out of her chest, she asked, 'Are you sure that's a good idea?' Then, feeling her apparent ingratitude, she added, 'I mean, it's too much. Too many people are angry at you already. If you do that for me—'

She stopped.

'I'm willing to take the chance.' His open face projected a sober intensity which suggested that he didn't make his offer lightly – that he had thought through the implications of what was involved more clearly than she had. 'I started thinking about it when King Joyse called off the search. If he can't even be bothered to let his guards try to find a man who attacked you—' His voice trailed into an uncomfortable shrug. In the set of his features, she saw how deeply his King had disappointed him. 'Anyway, it's not as dangerous as it sounds. After all, I'm not offering to give you the kind of information you could use – if you were an enemy of Mordant. If you're an Imager, you'll already be familiar with everything I can show you. And if you aren't, you won't be able to do anything with what you learn.'

'Then why—?'

'Because I owe it to you. I'm the one who brought you here. If you're the wrong person – or even if you *are* the right person but you don't want to help us – it's my responsibility to get you back where you came from. I want you to understand enough about Imagery to know what that means.'

He paused, took a grip on his courage, and continued. 'But that's not all. Even if you want to go back – and I want to take you back – the Masters won't permit it. Even if they decide you actually are the wrong person, they won't be able to ignore the importance of what you represent. They won't want to let you go.

'Right now,' he said carefully, 'while they're in their meeting, might be our only chance to get to the right mirror and try to take you home.

'I don't want you to go,' he added at once. 'I believe you're exactly the one we need. I don't know how or why, but you are. If you want to go, I'll beg you to stay. But' – he sighed – 'you have the right to go, if you want to. It would be immoral to keep you here against your will.'

He amazed her. The question of whether it would be possible for her to return to her apartment, her job at the mission, her infrequent dinners with her father hadn't seemed particularly substantial to her. Other matters dominated her attention. But behind the relatively tentative surface of his offer, he was asking her something fundamental.

She glanced down at her gown – at the rich scarlet fabric against her skin, at the snug neckline. Already? she protested. It's too soon. I'm not ready.

Nevertheless the risk he was willing to take in the name of her *right* demanded a different answer.

'I'll go with you,' she said, although her pulse was heavy in her throat and she felt light-headed. 'It might be a good idea if I knew what my choices were.'

Geraden smiled bleakly. 'In that case, we should probably go now. If we delay, we might miss our chance. There's really no telling how long that meeting will last.'

Terisa wished she could take hold of his arm to steady herself. She had a mental image of women in gowns clinging closely to the arms of strong young men and looking happy there, supported and secure. But he gestured politely for her to precede him; she complied by walking toward the door.

He held the door for her, then closed it after her. Outside, he greeted her guards by name, and they replied in a tone of friendly commiseration, as if they knew all about his ordeal with the Castellan. But they didn't move to follow her.

Feeling a resurgence of fright, she hesitated, looking back at them.

'Don't worry,' Geraden answered her concern. 'Nobody is going to attack you in Orison in broad daylight.' On this point, he sounded confident. 'Nobody would dare.'

She wanted to ask him how he could be sure. But this was his world, not hers. She ought to trust what he told her.

Carefully, she moved toward the stairs.

For a while, she and Geraden didn't speak. As he guided her through the halls, she seemed to recognize the route Saddith had used yesterday. Based on what she had seen from her windows, she guessed that Geraden's destination was on the opposite side of the huge open rectangle of Orison: in order to reach it without traversing the mud and snow of the courtyard, he had to take her around through the halls. Once again, they encountered any number of men and women of every rank. But now, instead of staring at Terisa, they deferred to her and bowed their respect, as if her gown marked her as a great lady whom they didn't happen to know.

Every salutation made her more self-conscious. She wasn't accustomed to being noticed so much. To distract herself, she asked Geraden if assassins commonly roamed Orison at night.

'Actually, no.' Sensitive to the tone of her question, he treated it humorously. 'It isn't common at all. If it were, Castellan Lebbick would have piglets. He takes his duties *very* seriously.'

'Then why did King Joyse call off the search?' As she spoke, she remembered the oddness of the orders which had been reported to Lebbick. The King didn't *like all this running around in the middle of the night*. And yet he had known exactly what to expect of his Castellan – and had thought enough of Terisa to protect her from Lebbick's zeal. 'I got the impression attacks were something that happened all the time – not worth the trouble of trying to pursue.'

Geraden shook his head at once, scowling. 'Orison has *always* been safe –

ever since King Joyse conquered the Demesne. I would have expected him to call out the entire guard, instead of letting that man get away.' A moment later, however, he admitted, 'But this is an impossible place to search. It has too many rooms. I don't think anybody knows how they all interconnect. And then there are the secret passages. As long as he had a head start, it would take a miracle to find him.'

Even after Havelock blinded him? she wondered. But she didn't raise the question aloud.

'What *I* want to know,' Geraden went on after he had worried for a while, 'is, how did he know where to find you?'

That wasn't something which would have occurred to Terisa. 'How did Argus and Ribuld find me?'

'That's not the same thing. They knew you would have someone to look after you, so they asked around the maids until they heard Saddith had volunteered. Then all they had to do was locate her. Nobody was trying to keep where you were secret. But how did *he* learn where that was? He's an assassin hiding in Orison. Who did he talk to? He must have talked to someone. He must,' Geraden said more slowly, 'have an ally living here. Someone who could ask questions without making anyone suspicious. Or else—'

'Or else?'

They took a stairway down to a lower level, turned through the base of one of the towers, and continued on around the courtyard. 'Or else,' he rasped, 'he's one of the people of Orison himself. He lives here like anybody else – and presumably serves the King – or acts like he serves the King – and then at night he sneaks around trying to do murder. He might be someone I know.'

'Is that possible?'

He shrugged stiffly. 'Orison is a big place. And it's open all the time, especially to anybody who lives in the Demesne. Nobody keeps track of all the people here. Although Castellan Lebbick tries, of course.' His thoughts were elsewhere. 'My lady, you had better keep your eyes open. If you see anybody who resembles him at all, tell someone right away.'

Frightened by the prospect, she spent a few tense minutes staring hard at every face she saw, searching it for signs of yellow eyes and scarred cheeks and violence. But slowly she talked herself into calming down. The man would be a fool to show himself where she might encounter him. And if he did, she wouldn't have to make a special effort to recognize him. She could see him again anytime she wished, simply by closing her eyes.

Then another stair took them down to the huge, empty hall, the ballroom fallen out of favor, which they had crossed the day before. There were several entrances to the hall; but she recognized the corridor that led down to the meeting room of the Congery.

The air grew colder.

'In the old days,' Geraden commented as he guided her into the corridor, 'before King Joyse unified Mordant – and before Orison was built as big as it is now – these used to be the dungeons. Back then, half of every castle must have been dungeons. But King Joyse gave all the torture chambers, most of the cells, and a hall that used to be a kind of guardroom to the Congery. All that space became the laborium.' There was a note of pride in his voice. 'You've seen the old examination room. That's where the Masters hold their meetings. We'll stay away from there.'

Terisa remembered the downward stair; but she quickly became lost among the doors and turnings that followed. She had no idea where she was when he opened another of the stout, ironbound doors which characterized the dungeon, and a glare of light and heat burst out at her.

This must have been the former guardroom: it looked large enough to sleep a hundred people. Now, however, it contained no beds. Instead, it was crowded with two large furnaces built and roaring like kilns; firewood stacked in cords; piles of finely graded sand; sacks of lime and potash; stone conduits and molds in many shapes polished to a metallic smoothness; worktables supplied with scales, pots, small fires, retorts; iron plates and rollers of arcane function; and shelf after shelf affixed to the walls and laden with any number of stoneware jars in a plethora of sizes and colors.

Working about the room were several young men dressed like Geraden, they tended the furnaces, polished pieces of stone, measured and remeasured tiny quantities of powders from the jars, cleaned up the messes they created, and generally sweated in the heat. One of them saw him and waved. He waved back, then closed the door, sealing the noise and fire of the hall out of the corridor.

'You don't want to go in there,' he said. 'You'll ruin your gown. But that's where we make the glass for our mirrors. The Apts do most of their work there. If a boy wants to be an Imager, but he just doesn't have the power for it in his blood, his inability usually shows up here, before the Masters teach him any of their real secrets. Beginners do the menial chores, like keeping the furnaces at a steady temperature. The more advanced ones learn to mix tinct and prepare molds.'

'Is that what you do when you aren't disobeying the King?'

He grimaced, then fell into a wry grin. 'It was. The one advantage of being older than all the other Apts is that I already know everything they're being taught. I just can't seem to do it right. So now I'm sort of a formal servant for the Masters. I normally attend all the meetings, not because they care what I think, but so I can run errands, take messages, things like that. They don't trust me to carry glass' – Terisa heard a tone of sadness behind his smile – 'so they do that themselves.'

He didn't let himself brood, however, on the consequences of his awkward instinct for mishap. 'Come on,' he said in a brighter voice. 'I want to show you some mirrors.'

He touched her arm; and again she wanted to take hold of his, for encouragement and support. The excitement he seemed to feel at the prospect of mirrors affected her strangely: it made her want to hang back – made her reluctant to face a risk that might be more dangerous than either of them knew.

'What do the Masters do?' she asked wanly.

'Research, mostly.' His eyes watched the way ahead and sparkled. 'They're supposed to be finding proof that Images really do or really don't have an independent reality. But some of them would rather figure out how to predict what Image a particular configuration and color of glass will show. Most research is just done by trial and error. Unfortunately, the Congery hasn't been any better at predicting than at proof. As a more attainable goal, Imagers like Master Barsonage are trying to determine how much one mirror has to vary from another before it shows an entirely unconnected Image.

'But the Congery does practical research, too. That's also King Joyse's idea. He wants Imagery to be useful for something besides war and ruin. Not so long ago, some important progress was made—' Geraden swallowed, frowned to himself, and admitted, 'Actually, Master Eremis did it. He shaped a glass that shows an Image where nothing seems to happen except rain. Nothing at all. The Congery checked the water, and it's fresh. So now we have a good local solution for drought. That mirror can be taken anywhere crops are dying and provide water.' Being fair to a man he didn't like, the Apt pronounced, 'It's quite a discovery.

'More recently, of course,' he added with even less enthusiasm, 'we've spent most of our time worrying about King Joyse's collapse.'

Perhaps to shake off uncomfortable thoughts, he guided Terisa forward with a quickening stride.

Down the corridor, along an intersecting passage, they soon came to a heavy door like the door of a cell. Her step faltered: the door was guarded. But he gave her a reassuring smile, saluted the guards casually; and one of them bowed appreciatively to the lady in the scarlet gown while the other opened the door, ushering her and Geraden into a small, well-lit room like an antechamber, with entryways in the massive walls leading to other rooms.

'These used to be cells,' he explained, 'but the Masters had them rebuilt to make a place where mirrors could be displayed – as well as protected.'

When the guards had closed the door behind him, she whispered, 'Why didn't they stop us?'

He grinned. 'As a matter of protocol, the laborium is under the command of the Congery. Master Barsonage didn't give orders to keep us out because it never occurred to him I might bring you here.

'Come on.'

His excitement was growing. Turning to lead her through the nearest entryway, he caught his toe in the long hem of her gown and fell toward the wall as though he meant to dash his brains out against the stone.

At the last instant, however, he contrived to tuck his dive into a roll. He hit the wall with an audible thud; but the impact wasn't enough to keep him from bouncing back to his feet at once – or from apologizing profusely.

'Don't worry about me,' she said quickly, expressing concern to keep herself from laughing. 'Are you all right?'

He stopped himself with an effort. 'My lady, if I got hurt every time I did something stupid, I would have died by the time I was five. That's the worst part about being such a disaster,' he went on ruefully. 'I do any amount of damage to everybody and everything around me, but I never really hurt myself. It doesn't seem fair.'

For a moment, she did laugh. Then she swallowed it. 'Well, you didn't hurt me. I'm glad you didn't hurt yourself.'

He gazed at her as if the sight made him forget why they were here. 'Thank you, my lady,' he said softly, earnestly.

But he recollected himself almost at once. 'Let's try this again.' With elaborate care, he turned away and walked through the nearest entry into the chamber beyond.

Following him, she found herself in a room which had been enlarged by joining it with three or four other cells. The light came from plentiful oil lamps, which didn't smoke. Aside from the lamps, however, and the slim pedestals that held them, the room contained nothing – no decorations on the walls, no rugs on the floors – except three tall objects hidden under rich satin coverings.

Happily, Geraden pulled off the nearest cover, revealing a glass.

Like the only other mirror she had seen in Orison – the one that had brought her here – this one was nearly as tall as she was; the glass wasn't quite flat or quite clear, and it wasn't perfectly rectangular; it was held in a beautifully polished wooden frame which gave it a secure base on the floor and still allowed it to be tilted from side to side as well as from top to bottom.

In addition, the glass reflected nothing of the stone or the lamps in front of it. It didn't even show Geraden.

What it did show was a fathomless seascape under a bright sun. For an instant, she could have believed that the Image was simply a painting brilliantly contrived to create the illusion of three dimensions. But the waves of the sea were moving. They rolled toward her out of the distance until they came too close to be seen. Small caps of froth broke from their crests and dissolved away before her eyes.

The Image was so real that it made her stomach watery.

'Master Barsonage shaped that one several years ago,' Geraden explained. 'It's the kind of mirror King Joyse wants the Congery to concentrate on. Something useful, practical. Master Barsonage was searching for a world of water – an Image Mordant could use in case of drought. Or fire. The story is that he extrapolated this glass from a small mirror Adept Havelock once had. If that's true, it's an amazing achievement – to reproduce exactly every inflection of curve and color and shape on such a different scale.' With his fingers, he ran a stroke of admiration down the side of the frame. As he re-covered the glass, he added, 'Unfortunately, the water is too bitter for our soil and crops.'

Shaking her head in gingerly astonishment, as if her brain were a bit loose in her skull, she followed him into the next room.

This chamber was roughly the same size as the one they had just left. It was similarly lit with lamps on pedestals. But it contained four satin-covered mirrors.

'I don't mean to lecture you,' he was saying. 'If you really are an Imager, I'll bore you. And if you aren't, I'll just confuse you. Stop me if I get carried away.'

He considered for a moment, then selected a mirror.

When he uncovered it, she gasped involuntarily and stepped back.

From the glass stared a pair of eyes as big as her hands.

They glared at her hungrily, and the teeth under them seemed to drip poison as the mouth gaped in her direction. She had an impression of a body like a gargantuan slug's hulking behind the eyes and the mouth – an impression of a dark, cavernlike space enclosing the body – but she couldn't look away from those eyes to confirm the rest of the Image. They were eyes that wanted, insatiable eyes, consuming—

Geraden stooped to the lower corner of the mirror and nudged the frame. At once, the eyes receded a few dozen feet, and Terisa found herself blinking her horror at them from a safer distance. Now it was plain that she was looking at some kind of huge, sluglike beast in a cave.

'This is how we adjust the focus.' He nudged the frame again: the Image retreated farther. Then he pushed lightly on the side of the frame, and the Image panned in that direction, revealing the mountainside where the cave opened. 'The range is limited, of course. But once a true mirror is made – one that works, instead of just throwing distortion in all directions – we can look at its whole Image – in this case, the whole mountain – by adjusting the focus. If we have that much patience.'

He stood up and tugged the cover back over the glass. She hardly noticed the darkness gathering in his mood. 'The story is that King Joyse captured this mirror during his wars for Mordant's independence. The Imager who made it had already translated that' – he shuddered – 'that abomination, and it was busy eating an entire village, hut by hut.

'But that was in the days before Adept Havelock lost his mind. When King Joyse captured the glass intact, Adept Havelock was able to reverse the translation.

'The Congery was founded to keep Imagery under some kind of control. So that no more mirrors like this one would be made.'

Terisa's arms and legs felt weak, and her head was full of air. 'How—' she asked faintly. 'How could something like that get through?'

'Oh, size is no problem. Imagers discovered long ago that once a mirror reaches a certain size – about the size of the ones you've seen – it can translate anything. Nobody knows quite how that works. But if you had a glass focused at the right place at the right time, you could bring an avalanche through it.

'Come on.'

Without looking at her, he strode into another room.

Viscerally expecting the slug-beast to lift its own cover and come after her, Terisa followed him. Mordant was being threatened by things like *that*? There were people at work here mad or malicious enough to translate things like *that*? Then he was badly mistaken. Mordant didn't need her. It needed the champion in Master Gilbur's mirror. And all the armored men who fought under him. And all the weapons from his ship.

She trailed right on Geraden's heels because this whole situation was crazy and she had to get out of here.

He led her into a chamber larger than the previous ones: apparently, an extra cell or two had been used to make it. Six covered mirrors stood on the smooth stone floor, but four of them had been set back against the walls, leaving room in the center for the remaining two. Those two were the same size. Under their coverings, they seemed to have the same shape.

As he considered the mirrors, his face clenched into an unself-conscious scowl. 'We usually keep the flat mirrors here,' he said toward one of the side walls. 'This is the largest display room, and we have a number of them. But the Masters had some moved out to make room for these two. The Congery does a lot of experimenting with flat glass, trying to find some way to use it – or at least understand it.'

Abruptly, he moved toward one of the mirrors against the wall. 'Here.' He sounded angry; she couldn't tell why. 'I'll show you what happened to Adept Havelock.'

With a rough jerk, he pulled the cover off the glass in front of him.

Involuntarily, she winced.

Nothing terrible happened.

The mirror did in fact appear to be flat. Its color, the sand from which it was made, the slight irregularity of its edges – she guessed that these things determined what Image the mirror showed. But because it was flat its Image existed in this world rather than somewhere else.

Something about the scene looked vaguely familiar.

'It's dangerous,' muttered Geraden. 'I don't know who shaped it, but if it was an accident it was dangerous to make. And even if it wasn't an accident, it's dangerous to keep.'

She was looking at what appeared to be a place where roads came together. The roads were deeply packed in snow, of course, and were only marked by the wheel tracks cut into them by passing wagons. But lines of stark, winter-stripped trees made the roads more obvious than they would otherwise have been against the piled white background. The Image was so vivid that she could see cold aching among the outstretched limbs of the trees.

On the other hand, she had no idea why it was dangerous.

Had she seen those trees or that intersection from her windows this morning?

Apparently so. 'You can see that place from your rooms,' Geraden explained. 'That's where the one road out of Orison branches south toward the Care of Tor, northeast toward Perdon, and northwest toward Armigite. But why would anybody bother to shape a glass that shows a place we can already see from here? If someone is coming it doesn't exactly give us a lot of warning. As I say, it could have been an accident. Or else whoever did it was trying to produce a mirror that would show Orison itself – and only missed by that much.'

'Who would do that?' she asked.

He shrugged. 'Someone who wanted to spy on King Joyse.

'But what makes this dangerous – more dangerous than most flat mirrors – is that we're so close to being able to see ourselves in it. If we took this mirror out to that spot and stood in front of it, we would see ourselves in the Image. And we would be lost forever, erased – caught in a translation that took us away without shifting us an inch from where we stood.'

He dropped the cover to the floor and stepped back to consider the glass. 'I guess we're lucky that didn't happen to Adept Havelock. *He* was lucky, anyway. He's just crazy – he hasn't been erased. But if we tried to use this glass now – if we tried to translate ourselves out to the branching of the roads – we would end up like him. The stress would destroy our minds.

'Nobody knows exactly why.' He began to sound more and more irritated, vexed with himself. 'The people who believe that Images don't exist – that mirrors create what we see – argue that the stress comes from being in a created place that exactly resembles a real place. You expect reality and don't get it, so your mind snaps.'

'And what if Images are real?'

'Then it's the translation itself that does the damage. I guess you could say translation is too powerful to be used so simply. If you want to get from here to there' – he gestured at the scene in the mirror – 'you need a horse, not Imagery. Because you aren't using the true power of translation, it rebounds against you instead of taking you safely where you want to go.

'Anyway, something like that happened to Adept Havelock.' Geraden turned his back on the glass, and now she caught the flash of anger in his eyes. 'That's why the Masters want to understand flat mirrors. They're so dangerous – and fundamental.

'Come on,' he growled. 'I've dragged my feet long enough.'

Brusquely, he moved to the two mirrors in the center of the room.

Now she understood him. He was angry because he was conflicted: he was acting against his own wishes as well as the King's, forcing himself to do what he thought was right despite his belief that Mordant needed her.

And he was risking the accusation that he was a traitor in order to give her a chance to go home.

Despite the warmth of her gown, a chill went through her as he pulled one of the covers off, and she recognized the glass that had stood in the Congery's meeting room the day before – the glass that had brought her here.

Its Image was both different and unchanged. The fighting had stopped. The metallic figures had enlarged their defensive perimeter and were holding it unchallenged. But the alien landscape, red-lit by its old sun, was unaltered, as was the tall ship in the center of the scene.

Like his men, the armored figure who dominated the Image had moved: he now walked the perimeter, pausing briefly at each defensive station as if to check how his forces were placed. Again, his power was almost palpable across the distance between the worlds. He looked like a man who conquered whole continents almost daily, as a matter of course.

Geraden gave her a glance, measuring her reaction. Then he lifted the satin from the second glass.

She saw at once that it was identical to the first. The shape was the same; the tint was the same; the curvature was the same. Even the curved and polished wooden frames were indistinguishable. And yet the Images weren't the same. Under a red-tinged light, against a stark background, a colorless metal helmet with an impenetrable faceplate looked in her direction as if the eyes hidden in it were studying her coldly.

A moment passed before she realized that both mirrors showed the same scene: the first reflected the ship from some distance, while the second depicted the commander of the defense in extreme close-up. Looking at both mirrors, she could see that each portrayed exactly the movements of the commander's helmeted head: only the perspective was different.

Softly, Geraden muttered, 'It's too bad we can't hear thoughts through the glass. It would even help if we could hear language. But of course most of the Masters believe there aren't any thoughts or language in there to be heard.'

He adjusted the focus of the second mirror carefully until it duplicated the first. Then he stepped back to stand beside Terisa. Still he avoided her gaze.

'I made one of those,' he said. 'The one we used yesterday. It's a duplicate. Master Gilbur created the original. I couldn't use his. Imagers learned a long time ago that there's some kind of essential interaction between a mirror and the talent of the man who shapes it. So I made a copy.' He snorted sourly. 'It took me a long time because I kept doing things wrong.

'Can you tell which is which?'

She shook her head. The question didn't matter to her. She cared only about his distress and her opportunity. It might really be possible for her to go back to her world, to her apartment and her job and her father—

—and the man with her wanted her to stay. He wanted it so intensely that the bare thought of letting her go hurt him.

'Actually,' he murmured, 'nobody else can. But Master Gilbur and I don't have any trouble. Any Imager can always feel his own work. The one I shaped makes my nerves tingle.' He pointed to the glass on the left. 'That one.

'My lady.' At last he forced himself to face her. He held his arms clenched over his chest, as if to keep them from reaching out. His scowl had become a knot of worry and pain. 'Are you sure you want to do this?'

'Geraden—' Now that he was finally willing to meet her gaze, she wanted to look away. She had never learned how to refuse other people. If she did what was expected, or asked, or even suggested of her, she could at least fit herself to her circumstances. But she didn't belong here. It made no sense.

As well as she could, she said, 'Please understand. I'm no Imager. None of this could possibly have anything to do with me. You didn't force me to come with you. You just asked me to come, and I came. I don't know why,' she admitted. 'I guess I just wanted to believe my life didn't have to be the way it was. I didn't want to just *sit* there. But now I know I made a mistake. You don't need me. You need that champion. I think the best thing for me to do is just go back where I came from.'

'It's your right.' Behind its dismay, his voice held a note of dignity and even command which she remembered vividly. The importance of what he was saying lit his eyes. 'But you *are* needed here. Mordant's peace will be the first good thing to be lost – and the smallest. In time, the Congery will be perverted, and Orison will be torn down stone from stone, and what remains of the realm will be reduced to nothing but bloodshed and treachery.'

Somewhere in his voice, or his words, she heard a reminder of horns, calling out to her heart in dreams and changing everything.

'You give us hope,' he continued. 'You say you aren't an Imager. Maybe you aren't. And maybe you just don't know yourself yet. Maybe you just don't know yet that you're more powerful than any champion.

'I can't explain it – but I believe you're here because you *must* be here.

'And' – all at once, he relapsed into normalcy, and his gaze clouded – 'you make sense out of my life. As long as I can believe in you, it's all been worthwhile.'

His insistence should have repelled her, frightened her. It was so unreasonable. *She* was necessary? *She* had power? *She* made sense out of his life? No. It was easier to believe that she had already lost herself, faded away into dreams. Or that she had never existed – that the translation had created her.

Nevertheless what he wanted and offered moved her. His appeal and the reminder of horns moved her.

'Aren't we getting a little ahead of ourselves?' she said unsteadily. 'We don't know yet whether this is going to work. We should find that out first, before we worry about anything else.'

He studied her hard, trying to gauge her emotions. Then he nodded. 'You're right, I suppose.' Suddenly decisive, he said, 'Here – hold my hand. I'll go first, just in case something goes wrong.' At the same time, he stepped closer to his mirror. 'You can anchor me.'

She became increasingly conscious that the air in the room was cold. She looked at his hand, the glass, the hard lines of determination on his face. Now that she had gained her point, she found herself hesitating. 'Don't we have to go through some kind of ritual first?' Her ambivalence felt absurd, but she couldn't control it. As soon as she made anything that resembled a choice, she lost confidence. 'There must be magic powders – or spells – or something? Aren't there?'

'Is that how Imagery is done in your world?' he demanded with a glare.

'No, of course not. I mean, we don't have Imagery. I keep telling you. We don't have magic.' Self-consciousness flushed her cheeks. 'I just thought you must need preparation.'

He made a visible effort to unclench himself a bit. 'I'm sorry. I didn't mean to snap at you. Imagery is in the way the glass is made and shaped and colored. That's the preparation. Then it either works or it doesn't, depending on whether the person who tries it has the power. If we wanted to translate something out to us, that would be different. There are words and gestures that help the process. But we aren't going that way. Right now, all we have to do' – he attempted a smile which didn't succeed – 'is do it.'

Again, he extended his hand to her.

This time, she took it.

What she was doing made her feel sick.

He drew her to the mirror and braced his free hand on the frame to keep it – or himself – steady. 'First I'll just stick my head in,' he murmured, thinking aloud, 'and take a look around. Then I'll come back, and you can decide what to do next. Hold on tight,' he added to her. 'As long as we've got a grip on each other, you can pass in and out of the glass as well as I can.'

Abruptly, he dashed his forehead at the surface of the mirror.

And his head vanished, cut off as cleanly as a knife-stroke at the neck. Beyond the glass plane, the Image of the back of his head blocked part of the landscape and the ship.

Instinctively, she braced herself against his weight.

He had pushed himself forward too hard: he was losing his balance, starting to fall. His hand pulled on the frame of the mirror, shifting the focus of the reflection. As he toppled forward, she saw one of the armored defenders aim a hot shaft of light at him.

Somehow, she jerked him back. He pitched out of the glass and stumbled away from it, then caught himself with his feet splayed and his knees locked.

All the color was gone from his cheeks: he was as white as flour paste. Panic and astonishment stared out of his eyes.

'Are you all right?' she asked.

'He shot at me,' whispered the Apt hoarsely. 'He almost hit me.'

'I saw him. I saw the back of your head.'

'Glass and ruination.' He swallowed repeatedly. 'If I had gone there the first time. Instead of finding you. They would have killed me before I could open my mouth.'

Her heart began to hurt as the implications struck her. The mirror that had impossibly taken Geraden to her when it should have put him in front of the champion now did what it was supposed to do. 'I don't believe it.' That mirror was her only doorway home. She was stuck here. 'I want to try.'

'My lady!' His surprise and fear turned instantly to dismay. 'You'll be shot! They might not miss twice.'

'Come on.' Without thinking, she grabbed one of his hands and tugged him toward the mirror. She was stuck here forever. There was no other way she could get back to her own life. 'I've got to try.'

He twisted out of her grip, then clapped his hands to her shoulders and shook her. 'No!' He was shouting at her. 'I'm not going to let you kill yourself!'

'I've got to try!' she yelled back at him. It was quite possible that she had never yelled like that at anybody in her entire life. 'Let me go!'

Wrenching away from him, she swung around toward the mirror – and tripped on the hem of her gown. Helpless to stop herself, she fell as if she were diving straight at the glass.

Apparently, he got one hand on her just in time to make the translation possible. Instead of shattering the glass, she passed into it.

The transition felt shorter this time: it didn't have as much impact on her as the one that had taken her out of her apartment. It was quick and timeless, vast and small, as if eternity had winked at her while she went by; but this time its familiarity made more of an impression on her than its strangeness.

Then she landed hard enough to jar her breath away on a hillside of thick, rich grass dotted with wildflowers.

More precisely, her body from the waist up landed on the grass. She must have been lying with her stomach across the bottom edge of the mirror's frame, because she was cut off at the navel: everything beyond that straight, flat severance was gone. She could feel her legs. They gave her a sensation of movement. Someone was holding them. But she had left them in another world.

This world was warm and tangy with springtime. A low breeze made the bright heads of the wildflowers dance and cooled the touch of the open sunlight on her hair; the sky was so blue it looked whetted. The hillside sloped down to her right toward a fast stream almost big enough to be called a river. The water ran like crystal over the gold background of its rocks and sand and gurgled happily to itself as it rushed past.

She saw now that she was in a valley that closed sharply as the ground rose ahead of her. A few hundred feet away, the valley became a narrow defile, almost a chasm, mounting toward the mountains in the distance; and this cut was given both a marked entryway and a guard by the tall, rugged, ponderous stone pillars like sentinels which the hills had set on either side of the stream. Shaded by the steepness of its walls, the defile looked dark and secretive – and also inviting, like a place where it would be possible to hide and be safe.

Her heart went out to it at once. Because she had grown up in a city, she had seldom seen a place so beautiful before. For a moment, she simply stayed where she was and inhaled the scent of spring grass, the tang of wildflowers.

Soon, however, she thought of Geraden. This wasn't an alien landscape where men in armor shot beams of fire at people. And it certainly wasn't her apartment. She wanted to show it to him.

Too full of wonder to call out, she began to crawl backward.

As she did so, more and more of her body disappeared past the plane of translation. And Geraden was unceremoniously trying to help her. Her chest vanished; then her shoulders.

Shortly, she found herself on her hands and knees in front of the mirror.

The stone under her palms felt cold. The air in the room was cold. Even the lamplight seemed cold.

The scene in the glass had scarcely changed at all. The commander was conferring with the defender who had fired at Geraden. Perhaps they were trying to understand the man's head which had unexpectedly appeared and then vanished before their eyes. Perhaps they thought they were faced with some new trick by the people they were fighting, the natives of the planet.

'My lady,' Geraden panted as if he had been wrestling for her life, 'are you all right? What happened? I couldn't see you. I didn't see them shoot at you. They didn't seem to know you were there. What happened?'

'Geraden—'

She was so shaken and cold that she could hardly lift her weight off her arms, hardly get her legs under her. The change was too abrupt, too complete. It left her gasping, disoriented. Springtime—? A stream dancing in sunlight—? No, not here. Not in this converted stone dungeon. And not in the mirror, where men of violence discussed their work.

Somewhere inside her, the translation was still going on, still happening. Now, however, she knew what it meant. Doubt accumulated in her nerves: she was on the verge of failure. It was the sensation of fading, of losing existence, concentrated to crisis proportions: it was the pure moment in which she lost her hold on herself, on actuality, on life. This was what she had been falling toward ever since she had begun to be unsure of her own being.

It was happening to her now.

Although Geraden hovered beside her, urgent to know what she had seen, she couldn't shift her attention to him. She was staring at the glass he had left uncovered – the flat glass that showed a snow-clogged meeting of roads—

The Image in that mirror had changed.

The way she stared made him turn.

When he saw the mirror, he gasped. 'That's impossible. How did you—?'

He fought to control his amazement. 'I *know* that place. I've been there – I practically grew up there. We used to play there when I was a boy. We called it the Closed Fist. It's in the Care of Domne. It can't be more than five miles from Houseldon.' Through his confusion and surprise, his voice shone with pleasure. 'That valley is a jumble of rocks inside. A great place to climb. And there must be a hundred little caves and secret places to hide. We had the best games—'

She believed him: she had just been there herself. She recognized the contours of the ground, the shape of the valley. The hillside was blanketed in snow, ice choked the stream, the pillars wore frost like thatches of white in their gray hair. But the scene was the same. Only the season had changed; spring had become winter.

Now Geraden was gazing at her as if she had done something wonderful. 'My lady,' he said in awe, 'I don't know how you did that. It isn't possible. Mirrors can't change their Images. But you did it. Somehow.

'You're an Imager. You're certainly an Imager. Nothing like this has ever been done before. It's a good thing for us you're here.'

The color was back in his cheeks.

She had no idea why he had jumped to the conclusion that she was the cause of this impossible change. At the moment, however, that was secondary. She couldn't think about it yet. Other things staggered her.

She had just seen the same scene in two different mirrors. A scene he said was real. But she had seen it in two different seasons. One of the mirrors was wrong. This was winter, not springtime. The mirror that showed the Closed Fist in springtime was wrong.

A sensation of fading drained her heart. It was Geraden's mirror. The mirror that had brought her here. That glass reflected Images that didn't exist.

When she realized that she also was an Image that didn't exist, she nearly collapsed to her knees again.

EIGHT

VARIOUS ENCOUNTERS

Why isn't it possible?' She sounded small and weak, and her head was spinning.

Exaltation had taken hold of Geraden; he didn't seem to be aware of her distress. 'Nobody knows how to change Images. It isn't possible. The Image is part of the glass. But you've just done it. You're the augured champion.'

He didn't know what she had seen in the other mirror. His mirror. He didn't know she had proof that she didn't exist. Her hands made unself-conscious warding gestures, pushing ideas away. The implications were horrifying.

On the other hand, she didn't *feel* horrified. She felt distant, as if she were floating off. The sensation that she was fading grew stronger. Or perhaps she was now more acutely sensitive to it. She had no idea why she was still present in the room with him.

The mirror that had brought her here showed Images that weren't real.

'You said it's a real place. Didn't you? But I've never seen that place before.' Her voice had a brittle edge to it; a tinny pitch of hysteria. She was struggling to recover the sense that she existed. 'I've never been there. I can't change Images if I don't know how.' She hugged her elbows and tried to sound calmer. 'Otherwise it would be easy to get back to my apartment.'

That argument reached him in spite of his elevated state. He thought about it, frowning intently. 'But you *must* have done it. If you didn't – That only leaves me. *I* can't even do simple translations. I've never been able to do anything like that.'

'Have you ever tried?' Whatever she said no longer mattered. Her life was growing farther and farther away.

He stared at her: for a few seconds, he seemed to take her question seriously. Then he shook his head. 'No, of course not. It's nonsense. An Image is a fundamental part of the glass itself. That's why mirrors have such limited range. They can't be focused away from what they are.' Abruptly, he peered more closely at the glass. 'But this one was,' he muttered in bewilderment. 'It changed while we were right here in the room. So it isn't nonsense. One of us must have done it.' He stepped back, his manner abstract and intense with thought. 'Unless there's somebody in Orison who has that much power. And he's here.'

'That is absurd, Apt Geraden,' a crisp voice commented. 'The impossible is the impossible. There must be another explanation.'

Geraden whirled.

Terisa turned also, floating around from far away.

In one of the doorways stood Master Eremis.

He wore the same jet cloak under his chasuble which she had seen the previous day. Again, she was struck by how little conventionally handsome he was: his large nose and narrow, sloping cheeks made his face look like a wedge; the thick, black hair perched on the back of his skull emphasized the baldness of his high forehead. But in his case the conventions lost their usual meaning. He was tall, lean, and strong, his pale eyes shone with intelligence and humor, the smile on his lips promised secrets. And the way he *looked* at her made her hold her breath.

She had been told that he might consider her lovely.

Without warning, her pulse began to beat with excitement in her skin. Inexplicably, the sensation that she was fading lost its urgency.

As grateful as if she had been rescued, she waited to find out what he would do.

For a moment, he looked at the changed mirror, frowning in concentration. 'Yes,' he murmured, 'that is impossible.' Then he turned his attention back to Terisa and Geraden.

'Freshen my memory, Apt. Perhaps I recollect incorrectly. Did or did not Master Barsonage command you to give no knowledge away to the lady?'

Geraden glared at the floor and didn't respond.

Insouciantly, Master Eremis came forward. Before she had moved into her own apartment, Terisa had seen a variety of men who were reputed to be powerful, her father's guests; but none of them had projected the commanding confidence Master Eremis did. Only her father's presence had been comparably effective – and his manner had been considerably less attractive. He had lacked the sparkle of play or passion that would have made her mother's marriage to him comprehensible. As Eremis approached, he spoke to Geraden, but the interest gleaming in his eyes and smiling on his lips was directed at her.

'Well, no matter. I think it a stupid command. The first rule of good courtesy is to deny beautiful women nothing. Nevertheless you are fortunate that the rest of the Masters are too interested in their debate to be vigilant. Master Barsonage might well strip you of your place if he learned what you have done. But he will not learn it from me.'

'Thanks,' Geraden muttered ungraciously. The Master's sudden appearance seemed to reduce him to the stature of a sullen boy.

Eremis glanced at Geraden. 'My forbearance does not please you? I wish I could persuade you that you have no truer friend on the Congery than I am. You know that I opposed the decision to let you attempt an approach to our chosen champion. Do you believe that I did so because I despise either you or your abilities? You are wrong. The champion is dangerous. I was arguing for your safety, Geraden.'

'I might have an easier time being grateful if I understood,' Geraden said through his teeth, still glaring at the floor. 'What good is my safety to you?'

'Shame on you,' laughed the Master. 'Bitterness is not becoming.' He moved behind Geraden and put his hands like a fond parent on the Apt's shoulders. From that position, he gave Terisa a conspiratorial grin. 'Your safety is no "good" to me personally. But I value your intelligence – and your stubbornness. It would not please me to see those qualities wasted.

'Also' – he squeezed and patted Geraden's shoulders – 'the fact that you are safe means that you can now give me formal introduction to this' – his gaze left hers and went down to her neckline, resting there deliberately for a moment before returning to her face – 'delectable lady.'

Stiffly, Geraden said, 'I'm sure you know her name by now.'

'Ah, but I have not heard it from you. You are her translator. As Master Barsonage observed, you are responsible for her.' The particular way he looked at Terisa made the weakness she felt seem more pleasant. 'I want you to introduce me to her properly.'

Geraden flicked a glance at her. His mouth was twisted into a snarl. Nevertheless he complied. 'My lady, may I present Master Eremis. His home is Esmerel, one of the now renowned manors of Tor.' He was as rigid as an iron bar. 'Master Eremis, this is the lady Terisa of Morgan.' Then, in a tone of muffled ferocity, he added, 'She is a guest of King Joyse and under his protection. Castellan Lebbick has her well guarded.'

Once more, Master Eremis laughed. 'Geraden, you are as graceless as a child.' He gave the Apt's shoulders another pat and moved away from his back. 'But I mean to show my friendship in a way that will surprise you.

'Now,' he went on, returning his attention to the mirrors, 'there is the question of how Images can be changed. I doubt that a substitution has been made.' He stroked the flat glass lightly with his fingertips. 'At the same time, a more fundamental change is inconceivable. This requires thought.'

He didn't appear to be interested in thinking about the question at the moment, however, 'In the meantime,' he said unexpectedly, facing Geraden again, 'I naturally wonder what inspired you to bring the lady Terisa here. Your glass and Gilbur's are uncovered. This leads me to suspect that you had some aim of enabling her to leave us – or of proving to her that departure is impossible. I dismiss the first. It is absurd. Even you, Apt, would not risk your life, your future with the Congery, and the survival of Mordant, only to undo everything the next day.'

Geraden met the Master's gaze without flinching, but the muscles of his jaw knotted.

'I conclude, therefore, that her departure is now impossible. Some change has taken place within the glass, closing the door which you opened – somehow! – to bring the lady Terisa here.

'Yet that, too, is impossible.' He smiled as if the idea pleased him. 'We have impossibilities everywhere. Here is a challenge for you, Apt. As I hope I have made plain, I appreciate your intelligence. Your capacity for disaster exerts itself in practice rather than theory. Consider this question: is it theoretically possible to project or transpose the Image of one mirror onto another?' He sounded like a teacher raising issues to which he already knew the answers.

'Would that explain the impossibilities which seem to surround the lady Terisa?

'Study the matter and let me know your conclusions. For my part, I will take up the question with the Congery. You will advance yourself much if you reach an answer more promptly than the Masters do.'

Before Geraden could reply, Master Eremis shifted his concentration to Terisa. 'And now, my lady,' he said, resuming his previous manner, 'perhaps you will do me the kindness to accompany me to my chambers. The space which Orison allows me is not lavish, but I can offer you hospitality and comfort.' At once casual and intent, he moved closer to her. 'There are many matters that I think we can profitably discuss.'

His smile and his nearness seemed to have strong male implications which made the blood rise in her face. She studied his expression until her breathing quickened and she couldn't look away.

'We will not bore you, Apt, by requiring your attendance,' the Master murmured over his shoulder. 'You have more pressing responsibilities to pursue.'

With one hand, he reached out to her. His fingers were long and slim, artist's fingers, their knuckles delicate, their tips made to stroke and probe and know. His index finger touched the skin of her shoulder at the edge of her gown and gently traced the fabric down into the hollow between her breasts.

'My lady, shall we go?'

Involuntarily, her lips parted as if they were waiting for him. She felt too hypnotized and malleable to move, transfixed by his magnetism and the light in his eyes. But if he had put his arm around her, she would have gone with him anywhere.

'Master Eremis' – Geraden's voice was so tight that it cracked – 'what is the Congery debating? If the Masters are trying to make a decision about the lady Terisa, all three of us should be there. I know a lot more about her than I did yesterday.' He sounded at once desperate and angry, yet he kept himself under control. 'And she might want to speak for herself.'

The Master raised an eyebrow; one corner of his smile knotted. 'Apt Geraden,' he said softly, without looking away from Terisa or removing his finger from the V of her gown, 'this is insufferable. I have dismissed you. If you find yourself unable to grow up, return to Houseldon and ask the Domne to put you back among your toys and nursemaids. Orison is no place for children.'

'Master Eremis.' Geraden's tone made Terisa look at him. In his face, she saw an inchoate hardness, a capacity for strength that hadn't come into focus. 'I've been wrong about a lot of things. I make any number of mistakes. But I've never served the Congery wrongly.' A secret ferocity mounted behind his words. 'Something impossible has happened in this room. The Masters need to know what I've learned – what the lady Terisa can tell them. What are they debating?'

'Tinct and silver, boy!' Eremis wheeled away from Terisa sharply. 'Are you blind as well as deaf?' An instant later, however, he restrained himself. 'Oh, very well,' he growled. 'Perhaps if I answer you, you will be content to leave us alone.

'Because they are muddled and ineffectual, those pompous Imagers will today arrive – with much protestation, consideration, expostulation, and inspiration – at the astonishing conclusion that it is not possible to arrive at a conclusion concerning the lady Terisa of Morgan. You cannot explain whether you came upon her by accident or power. Therefore you cannot possibly know whether the power was yours or hers. And nothing she may say for herself can be trusted. *If* she is real in her own existence, and not a creation of Imagery, then she will have her own reasons for any answer she gives. Her motives will most assuredly not be the same as ours. And if she is in fact made by the glass – as seems apparent to me – then all her reasons and answers will be shaped by the Imager who caused you to find her. By someone who chooses to remain secret because he is the obvious enemy of the Congery and Mordant.

'Therefore intelligent decisions concerning her cannot be made as matters stand.

'I anticipate that the Masters will achieve this remarkable insight in another hour or two – well before Master Barsonage is in danger of missing more than one meal.

'Tomorrow they will debate what action should be taken in this dilemma. And by that time I will have spoken to them concerning the lady Terisa's latest impossibilities.

'Apt, are you satisfied?'

Once again, Geraden didn't meet the Master's gaze. His strength appeared to have deserted him. With his head down and his shoulders sagging, he looked like he might begin to kick his boots against the stone in chagrin. But he didn't retreat. Terisa noticed particularly that he didn't accept his dismissal and leave the room.

'You can forget about accidents,' he said, his voice muffled by the way he held his head. 'The mirror that brought her here has been closed. There's power at work. And it has something to do with the lady Terisa.

'She says she's not an Imager. She says there *are* no Imagers in her world. She uses the word *magic* – there is no magic in her world. And when I was there I saw evidence that she didn't draw me to her.

'But that doesn't mean she has no power *here*.'

Terisa winced at this argument. When Master Eremis turned his attention away from her, she began to recover some of her ability to think. As a result, she wished that she could have told Geraden what she saw in his mirror before he tried to argue with anyone. Her proof might have saved him from making a fool of himself.

Unfortunately, it was too late to save him now. 'I believe,' he went on, speaking more slowly and tensely, 'that there's something crucial about her. We need her. *I* know I don't have any kind of undiscovered talent. I would not have found her if she weren't vitally important.'

Then he did look up at the taller man. He appeared to be chewing the inside of his cheek to steady himself. His expression was anxious and abashed, but his gaze didn't falter. 'Master Eremis, I believe she's too important to become just another one of your women.'

'You insolent puppy!' spat the Master. For an instant, he seemed to grow taller, as if he were cocking himself to deliver a blow.

Suddenly, however, he burst out laughing. 'Oh, Geraden, Geraden!' he chortled. 'Is it any wonder that I wish you well? You are beyond price. Tell me, boy.' His voice took on an edge of glee, as if he were playing at outrage. 'Is it actually possible for you to look at this lady' – he indicated Terisa with a broad sweep of his hand – 'and *believe* that she could ever be "just another" woman to any man?' Throwing back his head, he laughed again, loudly and thoroughly.

That was what was wrong with her father, of course. He never laughed. In an odd way, Master Eremis' mirth filled her with sadness. It represented a loss. If she had grown up in a family where people laughed, things might have been entirely different. She might have been entirely—

Almost inevitably, this sorrow brought back the sensation that she was fading.

It had remained with her despite the Master's gaze, his touch. Now it was growing stronger and changing: safety was being transformed into danger. It made her turn her head as if she knew what was happening.

In quick horror, she saw that the flat glass which Geraden had uncovered was shifting.

While she gaped at it, the impossible Image of the Closed Fist modulated as though the mirror were a kaleidoscope of winter. Bleeding out of itself, the stream became roads; the pillars stretched limbs and spread out as trees; the sloping virgin snow slumped into ruts and mud. After only a moment, the scene became unmistakable: it was the intersection outside Orison, where the roads from the Cares came together; it was the mirror's original, real Image.

This time, however, there were riders on the northeast road. At least ten men on horseback flailed their mounts and the snow as if they were frantic to reach Orison.

As if they were being pursued.

'My lady,' breathed Geraden in astonishment.

Then he gasped, 'Glass and splinters!'

Master Eremis also gazed at the mirror, his eyes bright; but he said nothing.

From out of nowhere, a black spot sprang like a predator at one of the riders. It was small, hardly larger than a puppy by comparison, too small to hurt him. Nevertheless it communicated force and fury like a shout across the distance. The rider flung up his arms and plunged from his horse as if he were screaming.

None of his companions turned back to help him. They only goaded their mounts harder, straining toward the castle. His horse veered off the road and fled with a frenzied gait, disappearing past the edge of the glass.

A cold fist clutched at Terisa's stomach and twisted it hard.

She was so frightened she failed to notice that she was no longer fading.

Another black spot appeared out of nowhere.

The whole scene seemed to jump toward her as the spot sprang. Geraden had moved to the edge of the mirror: he was adjusting its focus, bringing the Image closer. Now she could see that the spot was a gnarled, round shape with four limbs outstretched like grappling hooks and terrible jaws that occupied more than half its body. Bounding from whatever invisible perch it had launched itself, it struck a rider in the chest. At once, its limbs took hold; its jaws opened and began ravening.

The mirror showed the man's agony distinctly as he toppled backward in a useless effort to avoid having his heart torn out. It showed the exact shape of the stain his blood made gushing into the snow.

Pointing at one of the riders, Geraden cried, 'The Perdon! He'll be killed!'

'Perhaps not!' countered Master Eremis. 'They have fled this attack for some distance. If they can outrun the range of the mirror which translates those abominations, they will be safe.'

Terisa couldn't tell which one of the riders was the Perdon. All of them looked the same to her, clenched by cold fear and riding for their lives; the eyes of all their horses flashed white panic. She was holding her breath in unconscious alarm, trying to brace herself for the next black spot that would spring out of the empty air, trying to bear the sight of those jaws.

But Master Eremis was right. From that moment until the riders passed out of the Image, out of this flat glass's reach, no more of them were attacked.

Geraden stood with his fists knotted at his sides, panting between his teeth. 'Thank the stars. Thank the stars.'

Pressure in her chest made her draw a shuddering breath. Abruptly, she wanted to throw up. She couldn't find enough words to ease her nausea. 'What *were* those things?'

Master Eremis shrugged. 'Translated things such as that have no names for us. I have a more interesting question.' The fire in his eyes was eager, avid. 'At last report, the Perdon refused to leave Scarping because he believed that matters along the Vertigon required his constant attention – rumors from Cadwal, sneaking spies, hints of armies, forays by bandits. Yet now he is here. What has happened to drive him from his Care?'

Without waiting for an answer, he took hold of Terisa's arm. Brusque with concentration, he drew her away from Geraden and the mirrors. 'Come. I want an explanation.'

Geraden followed with a bleak expression on his face.

Hurrying, Master Eremis' long legs set a rapid pace; she had difficulty keeping up with him. After a moment, however, he seemed to notice that she was struggling. He shortened his strides a bit, smiled at her, and tucked her arm through his so that she could support herself on him.

Even then, she was glad he didn't try to talk to her. Most of her attention was consumed by the necessity to fight down nausea.

He guided her up out of the dungeons, across the unused ballroom, and into the main halls of Orison, along Geraden's route of the previous day toward the tower in which King Joyse had his quarters. In a large chamber like a waiting room in front of the stairs upward, he stopped. Only a few people occupied the chamber, and most of them had the needy and inward look of petitioners – a look which she recognized almost automatically because she had seen so much of it in the mission. But there were more guards here than she remembered. They told Master Eremis readily enough that the Perdon was already with King Joyse. They also made it clear that no one else had been invited to attend that meeting.

Almost at once, Castellan Lebbick strode into the room, heading for the stairs.

Master Eremis detached himself from Terisa and accosted the Castellan. 'Can it be true, Lebbick?' He towered over the shorter man; his intent curiosity couldn't conceal an air of superiority. 'Is the Perdon here? This is strange news. What crisis could possibly inspire that bulwark of Mordant to abandon his domain to the Cadwals?'

'Master Eremis,' Castellan Lebbick replied trenchantly, 'that is the King's business.'

Attacking the stairs, he climbed out of sight.

The Master glared after him. 'Unconscionable lout,' he muttered to no one in particular. 'I require an explanation.'

Terisa glanced at Geraden. He stood a little distance away, his good face marred by a mixture of alarm and bitterness. If he had an answer for Master Eremis, he didn't offer it.

No one else in the waiting room had anything to say. The guards stood motionless, apparently meditating on their duty – or perhaps on their lunch. The petitioners were absorbed in themselves. Terisa steadied her respiration and tried to push gnarled, round shapes with terrible jaws out of her mind.

The Imager's impatience mounted visibly. He seemed to have trouble holding himself still. Abruptly, he announced as if everyone around him were eager for his opinion, 'There is a crisis in the Care of Perdon. That much is obvious. But I doubt that it is the crisis itself which brings the Perdon here. He is not a man who would readily flee trouble – or admit weakness. No, I think it is our illustrious King's response to the crisis which forces the Perdon to Orison. I will wager a dozen gold doubles that he hazarded this journey because he was furious. And he will be more so when he departs.'

As if on cue, a shout echoed downward, a roar of anger:

'No!'

Clattering metal, a man appeared on the stairs. He was big and brawny, and made bigger by the iron palettes on his shoulders above his breastplate, the gorget around his neck, the brassards about his arms. On one hip, he had a longsword that appeared heavy enough to behead cattle; on the other, a fighting dagger. His head above his eyebrows was perfectly bald; but his eyebrows themselves were red and thick, red tufts of hair sprouted from his ears, and his wide mustache was so shaggy that food and drink had stained the fringe over his mouth black. The haste of his arrival showed in the spattered mud on his legs.

His blunt face knotted like a club, he pounded downward as if he were looking for someone to attack.

Behind him hurried a woman. Her sky-blue gown and resplendent jewelry marked her as a high lady; but she moved as though she had no interest in the dignity of a long dress or the good manners of necklaces and earrings. Framed by her pale skin and the short crop of her pale blond hair, her violet eyes flashed vividly.

'My lord Perdon!' she protested, demanded, as she descended. 'You must try again! You must not give up. Surely it is just a failure of understanding. You must explain it to him again. *We* must explain it to him until he grasps its importance.

My *lord*!'

'No!' he repeated, his voice like the shout of a breaking tree. From the stairs, he stamped into the center of the chamber, then whirled to face her. Shaking his fists at the ceiling, he roared, 'He has given his answer! *He will not command it!*'

The force of his anger made her halt. Her skin was so pale that it might have been drained of blood. Yet she didn't flinch. 'But he must!' she replied. 'I say he *must*. *Some* attempt must be made in Mordant's defense. I am certain that Castellan Lebbick tries to reason with him even now. Return with me, my lord. It is vital that you do not fail.'

The Perdon clamped his hands together in front of him, holding down his fury; his brassards gave out a muffled clang against his breastplate. 'No, my lady,' he said thickly. 'I will not endure it. Let him play hop-board until the realm *crumbles!*' His fists made a fierce hammering motion, pounding hope to the floor. 'I fought at his side for ten *years* to make Mordant what it is. I will not grovel asking him for what he should volunteer.

'You tell him *this*, my lady. Every man of mine who falls or dies defending him in his blind inaction, I will send *here*. Let him look to their wounds, or their bereaved families, and explain why he will not' – he couldn't contain himself – '*command it!*'

'My lord Perdon.' Master Eremis sounded suave and easy – and authoritative enough to catch the attention of everyone in the chamber. 'I gather that our admirable lord, King Joyse, has done something foolish. Again. Will you tell me what it was?'

His tone made the blond woman flush, but she bit her lip and didn't retort.

The Perdon turned. 'Master Eremis.' For a moment, his eyes narrowed, gauging the Imager. Then he spat, 'Paugh! It surpasses belief. I would not have believed him capable of it.

'I will not speak of the horrors that befell my men within the hour – horrors hardly a stone's throw from the gates of "our admirable lord." They are Imagery, and I am sick of such things. I fought with King Joyse in part so that the abominations of mirrors would be ended.

'I will not speak of them because there is nothing to be said' – his hard gaze glittered – 'except by the Imager who causes them.

'But you must know that our borders have been raided for some time now. *I* have not kept the matter secret. All along the Vertigon, from end to end of Perdon, North and South, bands of marauders have ridden out of Cadwal despite the season to strike and burn whatever they happen to find. Then they flee. My protests to that fop Festten's regional governor have been met with shrugs. The marauders damage him also – he says. Since its wars with Mordant, Cadwal no longer has the strength to control banditry – he says. And I, Master Eremis' – he hit his breastplate with one fist – '*I* am left to guard every mile of the Vertigon with enough men for no more than a small fraction of the job.

'Lacking support or counsel from Orison,' he went on with massive sarcasm, 'I set out to solve this problem as best I could.

'Among my patrols, I included riders who were trained as scouts and spies, so that when marauders were found – or sign of them was found – they could be followed in secret. I wanted to know where those pieces of rabble went to ground. If I could discover their camps, I would not mind raiding a bit into Cadwal myself, to root some of those bandits from their holes.'

Master Eremis nodded. 'Sound thinking, my lord Perdon. But I gather you were surprised by what you learned.'

'Surprised?' the Perdon growled. 'Death's hatchetmen, Master Eremis! We are speaking of Cadwal. I should not have been surprised.

'Nevertheless,' he went on darkly, 'I was not altogether prepared in my mind for the reports which eventually came to me. Some of my scouts were lost – doubtless because they let what they were doing be discovered. Others were gone so long that I gave them up before they won home. But those that lived all told the same tale.

'It was natural, I trust, that I had believed these marauders to be petty bandits and butchers. Their bands were not over-large. They wore the rags and equipage of men who have grown poor enough to be careless of bloodshed. They struck in motley fashion, as though they meant to overwhelm opposition or be slaughtered without discipline or forethought. They were only a serious trouble to me because they came from Cadwal. And because they were so *many*.

'But I was wrong, Master Eremis.' His fists bunched, and his anger rose again. 'I was wrong. Will you believe it? After forays of two or four or even ten days, all the bands my men followed rode at last to *the same camp*.'

Terisa glanced at Geraden and saw that his face was losing color rapidly.

'And in this camp,' the Perdon continued, 'they mingled freely with Festten's soldiers, men plainly wearing the uniforms of Cadwal. The supply wains bore the High King's sigil. The tents where the officers and supplies and support were housed were of Cadwal design.'

'Indeed,' murmured Master Eremis. 'Perhaps your surprise is understandable, my lord Perdon. *I* am astonished.' He didn't sound astonished. 'How large was this force?'

'Estimates vary. My scouts did not observe it under favorable conditions. And some of them were inclined to panic, where others remained too phlegmatic. But I am convinced that it could not have numbered less than fifteen thousand fighting men.'

One of the guards in the chamber let out a low whistle; Terisa didn't notice who it was.

'All this *in winter*,' snarled the Perdon. 'They mean to throw themselves at our throats as soon as the weather shifts.'

'You see how the matter stands, Master Eremis,' said the blond woman. 'The King *must* be made to admit reason. This threat cannot be ignored.'

'Between North Perdon and South,' the Perdon rasped, 'I have little better than three thousand men. To my certain knowledge, Orison has at least five thousand, all sitting idle in their camps under the command of Castellan Lebbick.'

'More nearly eight thousand, I think,' Master Eremis commented.

'Eight? Yet when I asked for support' – the Perdon ground his teeth to keep himself from shouting – 'the King refused. He has refused repeatedly, but at first I could not believe it. Finally I came in person to demand help. I lost seven men along the road, within sight of his walls. And still he refused.' The brawny lord shook his mustache. 'With an invasion force poised on his eastern border, waiting to take advantage of the chaos of Imagery which assails us from within, and doubtless more peril being plotted in Alend, he refused.'

'It is inconceivable,' the pale woman breathed to herself. Her violet eyes looked distracted and urgent. 'He must command it. How can he not?'

Geraden was frowning hard, deep in thought. What he was thinking made him look sick.

'For ten years, I fought beside him,' finished the Perdon. 'I trusted him. Now I learn that to him it means nothing.'

Master Eremis studied the armored man. 'Then perhaps,' he said quietly, 'it will not amaze you to learn that I have the same problem.'

Both Geraden and the blond lady showed their surprise. The Perdon arched his red eyebrows. 'You, Master Eremis?'

'Indeed.' Glancing around him casually, Eremis moved to the Perdon's side and placed a hand on the pallette protecting the Perdon's shoulder. 'Our plights are remarkably similar, my lord. Will you accompany me to my quarters? The battles of Perdon will not be fought in the next hour or two, and I have some excellent Domne ale. Commiseration will benefit us both.'

For a moment, the Perdon stared at Master Eremis as frankly as Geraden and the lady did. His blunt mouth formed the word, *commiseration*, as though he had never heard it before. Then his expression closed. Carefully, he said, 'I thank you. Your offer is kind. I could drown my anger in a hogshead of good ale, if you have it.'

The Master laughed. 'I have that – and a great deal more, which I think will please you.'

His face blank, the Perdon replied, 'Then I am yours, Master Eremis.'

'Good!' At once, Eremis bowed to the blond woman and Terisa. 'With your permission, my ladies.' His salutation was abrupt: he was clearly eager to leave. As soon as the Perdon also had bowed, Master Eremis steered him out of the chamber.

Slowly, as if involuntarily, Geraden and the lady in blue looked at each other. They both appeared stiff, awkward. She had more self-possession, however. After a few moments, she asked, 'Now why would he do such a thing, Apt?'

Geraden shifted his weight uncomfortably, though he refused to drop her gaze. 'I don't know, my lady. The Perdon has the heart and soul of a soldier. And he has fought Cadwal too long. Master Eremis knows he doesn't trust any Imager.'

She looked away. Cupping her hands about her elbows, she gripped them tightly. 'I *hate* it when he looks at me like that. He smiles and jests, but all I see is scorn.'

'I don't exactly love it myself,' muttered Geraden. 'But that doesn't explain what he thinks he has in common with the Perdon.'

They fell into a discomfitted silence. Now that he didn't have to meet her gaze, he scanned the stone floor. She watched the corridor down which Master Eremis and the Perdon had departed as if she wanted to run after them and demand an answer. Considering Geraden and the lady, Terisa thought suddenly that they had known each other for a long time. The lady was about his age and seemed to Terisa to be a fitting companion for him. The intensity of her violet eyes, especially, seemed appropriate to his awkward intensity of spirit.

Abruptly, the lady gave a start of embarrassment. Turning to Terisa, she said, 'Oh, I *am* sorry. How very rude of me. You have been standing here all this time, and I have not been courteous enough to speak to you. You must be the lady Terisa.' She produced a smile that appeared genuine, if somewhat tentative. 'I know the gown,' she explained. 'If the Apt's manners were any better than mine' – the glance she cast in his direction suggested a scorn of her own – 'he would have introduced us. I am Elega. King Joyse is my father.'

'Oh, yes.' Terisa recognized the name. Because she had never met a king's daughter before and had no idea what kind of salutation was expected, she said what she had so often heard her mother say: 'How nice to meet you.' Then she winced internally because her voice sounded just like her mother's.

Fortunately, the lady Elega hadn't known Terisa's mother. 'Myste and I,' she continued, 'have wished to meet you since we first heard of your – shall I call it your "arrival"? The present circumstances are not of the best. Matters which you have overheard leave me somewhat distracted, I fear.' Despite her words, the way she regarded Terisa implied that she had found something to compensate her for her father's distressing treatment of the Perdon. 'But I would be pleased' – she smiled – 'and Myste would be delighted, I think, if you would visit us in our rooms. You may be unaware of the interest you have aroused in Orison. My sister and I are always eager for new friendships. And I tell you frankly, my lady' – she lowered her voice as if she were imparting a public secret – 'Mordant is a man's world. We women are not often given enough to occupy our talents. So your acquaintance would have a special value to us.

'My lady, will you come?'

Terisa was momentarily frozen. Then she shook herself in disgust. Why did she feel threatened when she was asked for the simplest statements and decisions? It was her mother in her. Her mother would have said, *What a nice idea. When would you like us to come? I'm sure that would be lovely. My husband is so busy these days. Shall I call you next week?* For that reason, Terisa gazed at Elega as straight as she could and said, 'I'm not doing anything right now.'

A second later, she realized how that would sound to Geraden, and a sting of chagrin turned her face crimson. He wasn't looking at her: his expression had gone flat, like nonreflective glass. Only the slight, stretched widening of his eyes betrayed that he had heard her.

Now she remembered why it was natural to fear even simple statements and decisions. They caused trouble.

Apparently, however, the lady Elega considered the assertion a natural one to make in Geraden's company, even though Terisa might be presumed to have come here with him for some reason or another. Her smile seemed as unconstrained as her earlier dismay allowed. 'Thank you, my lady. Have you eaten? We can have a quiet lunch together. I am certain that we have an enormous amount to talk about.'

Yet she stiffened when she turned to Geraden. In a tone of dutiful politeness, she asked, 'Will you join us, Apt?'

The corners of his jaw bunched. He shot a glance at Terisa and murmured, 'No, thanks.' His voice was studiously neutral. 'I think the lady Terisa has had enough of my company for one day. Give the lady Myste my greetings.'

Abruptly, he sketched a bow toward her and headed out of the waiting room.

As he passed through the entryway, he bumped into a doorpost with his shoulder and stumbled until he caught his balance. Several of the guards chuckled at his departing back.

The lady Elega put a hand to her mouth to hide a smile. 'Poor Geraden.' Then she shook her head, dismissing him. 'We must go upward, my lady.' She gestured toward the stairs and started Terisa in that direction. 'My sister and I share rooms a level above the King's. We are told that we must live there so that we will be at least as safe as our father. But I believe,' she said cynically, 'the true reason is so that anything of importance will reach him before it reaches us – and stop.' Trying to blunt the edge of her words, she added more humorously, 'As I said, Mordant is a man's world.'

In a small voice, Terisa said, 'You should call me Terisa.' But the suggestion was abstract; her heart wasn't in it. Part of her remained with Geraden. It pained her that she had hurt him. He was the only one she knew here who made sense to her. And part of her was still nauseated. Had the Perdon told King Joyse about those fatal black spots? Of course he had. He must have. And *still* the King refused to act? If he had only *seen*—

'Terisa. I will,' the lady Elega said with satisfaction. 'And you must call me Elega. I hope we will be great friends.'

'Have you known him long?' asked Terisa. That was better than the memory of jaws and blood.

'Apt Geraden?' Elega laughed, but her mirth sounded brittle. 'You will hardly believe it, but he and I were once betrothed.'

'Betrothed?'

'Yes. Astonishing, is it not? But his father, the Domne, although no fighter – unlike the Perdon – is one of my father's oldest and most trusted friends. Because of' – a hitch in Elega's voice unexpectedly made Terisa think that the King's daughters might also have been warned against revealing too much – 'of his wars, my father wed late. Though I am his eldest, I was born only a year before Geraden, who is the Domne's seventh son. Later, during a difficult period of those wars, my father sent all his family to the Care of Domne for safety. I spent several seasons in the Domne's home in Houseldon, and Geraden and I were natural playmates.' The memory didn't amuse her. 'For that reason, thinking us well suited, our parents arranged a match.'

One flight of stairs took them to the level of the King's suite. Elega passed his high, carved door and took another stairway upward. 'I would have been better pleased with one of his brothers,' she continued. 'All women seem to favor Artagel, and to see Wester is to love him. But both lack ambition. Nyle is more to my taste. Sadly, women are often given little say in these matters.'

'What happened to your betrothal?'

'Oh, I flatly declined to marry him. He is quite impossible, Terisa.' Elega made no effort now to conceal her scorn. 'It is bad enough that he cannot be trusted to walk out of a room safely. But in addition he is *such* a failure. He has already been serving the Imagers for three years longer than any other Apt since the Congery was founded, and he is no nearer a Master's chasuble than he was when he began.

'His determination must be respected – and his desire to better himself. But I am the daughter of Mordant's King, and I do not mean to spend my life cleaning sheds in the Care of Domne, or sweeping broken glass after Geraden's disasters.

'Do you know?' She giggled suddenly. 'The first time he was to be formally presented to my father – we had all ridden out to visit the Domne, some twelve or fourteen years ago now – he was so eager that he had no better sense than to attempt a shortcut across a log which spanned a pig wallow. When he reached us, he was carrying more filth on his person than he left in the wallow.'

Terisa nearly laughed. She could imagine him as clearly as if she had been a witness: mud caked to his hair, his face, his clothes; water and fruit rinds dripping off him. He was exactly the sort of person to whom something like that would happen.

A second later, however, her emotions turned until she was close to tears. Poor guy, she murmured to herself. He deserves better.

'No, Terisa,' Elega concluded. 'Apt Geraden will make an honest husband for some dull woman with her mind in her belly, a strong passion for motherhood, and much tolerance for accidents. But I will not have him.'

In silence, Terisa replied, That's your loss. She never said such things aloud.

From the top of this flight of stairs, they approached another door as high as the King's, which may have been directly below it. But this one wasn't guarded: there was apparently no other way up to this level of the tower, and so whatever protected the King would also ward his family.

Then Terisa remembered the secret passages. Maybe no place in Orison was safe from anyone who knew them well enough.

Smiling, Elega went to the door and swung it open to admit her guest. 'You are welcome here, my lady Terisa of Morgan,' she announced formally. Then she turned and ushered Terisa into the suite of rooms where she and her sister lived.

In a small way, Terisa was surprised to see that these rooms weren't as richly furnished as the ones King Joyse used. The thick, woolen rugs looked more like the work of villagers than the creations of artists – rugs for use rather than display. The divans, chairs, and settees had sturdy frames that emphasized their expanse of cushion rather than their maker's craftsmanship.

Some of the end tables in the first room had the look of having been built for children to stand on; the dining room table which she glimpsed through another doorway had seen better days.

Her own background being what it was, she couldn't help wondering why King Joyse kept his daughters in this less luxurious style. But Elega was already explaining that detail. 'Formerly, these rooms were those used by our family, while the ones below were reserved for the private business of the kingdom – receptions, small audiences, discreet parties, and the like. The Queen, my mother, had no taste for personal ostentation, but she recognized the importance of visible wealth in the craft of governance. For that reason, the public rooms were designed for show rather than comfort.' This arrangement clearly suited her, as far as it went. The way she wore her jewelry revealed that her interest in her father's affairs had nothing to do with wealth or luxury.

Terisa started to ask why the King had moved downstairs – or why, for that matter, the Queen (had Saddith said her name was Madin?) no longer lived in Orison. But asking personal questions wasn't one of her strengths; and before she was ready to take the risk, a woman wearing a flowing gown of yellow silk came out of the back rooms.

'Ah, Myste.' The look Elega gave her sister was at once fond and a bit condescending, as if she loved Myste but didn't hold her in very high esteem. 'I have brought a treat for us. This is Terisa – the lady Terisa of Morgan. She looks well in your gown, does she not? We will have lunch together. Terisa, may I introduce my sister, the lady Myste? She is perhaps the only person in Orison more *avid* – she stressed the word humorously – 'to make your acquaintance than I am.'

This made Myste blush. She was, as both King Joyse and Saddith had observed, very nearly the same size as Terisa, although slimmer in certain dimensions. In much the same way, she very nearly resembled her sister, although she lacked the contrast between Elega's vivid eyes and her pale skin and hair. Standing together, they were outdoor and indoor versions of each other. The deeper blond of Myste's hair might not have looked like fine gold by candlelight, but it would have a burnished richness in sunshine. The tone of her skin promised that it would tan well. At the same time, the less dramatic color of her eyes seemed suited to peering across distances under bright light rather than to penetrating the secrets hidden in corners and conversations.

The faraway quality of Myste's gaze was apparent when she entered the room: her thoughts might have been in another world. But it was strangely emphasized when Elega introduced her to Terisa. All at once, she did look avid, so poised for wonder that she was almost trembling – and yet her eagerness seemed to pass through Terisa in order to fix itself on something behind her, some set of possibilities that she cast like a shadow. This impression was so strong that she instinctively looked around, half expecting to find someone at her back.

'My lady.' Myste bowed to the floor in a pile of yellow silk as if both to honor Terisa and to hide her blush.

Terisa almost panicked. Helpless and alarmed, she cast a mute appeal toward Elega.

In response, Elega put a hand on her sister's shoulder. 'That is well done, Myste,' she said somewhat dryly. 'Nevertheless it appears that so much homage makes Terisa a little uncomfortable. I call her Terisa by her own request. Surely she will want you to do the same.'

'Please,' Terisa begged immediately. This time, she was acutely sincere.

The lady Myste rose. Apparently her blush was a sign of excitement rather than embarrassment: she didn't show any shame or self-consciousness. Her gaze, however, now seemed to be better focused on Terisa. 'You are very welcome here, my lady,' she said in a kind voice. 'I am sure I will be able to call you Terisa in a moment – when I have calmed the beating of my heart.' She laughed in a way that immediately reminded Terisa of King Joyse's smile. 'Forgive me if I have discomfitted you. Perhaps you do not realize the honor you do us. I have so much that I wish to ask you.'

'It *is* an honor,' Elega put in before Terisa could protest. 'By the standards of Mordant, we are merely two women living with our father because he has found us unmarriageable. The lords and personages who pass through Orison do not feel obliged to call upon us or keep us informed. It was only by chance that I happened to be with the King when—'

More urgently, she went on, 'Myste, you will not believe it. Father has outdone himself.' In a few scathing sentences, she told her sister about the Perdon's audience with King Joyse. Then she concluded, 'Fifteen thousand men, Myste. The Perdon has but three thousand. And yet Father will not reinforce him.

'He has gone too far. This must stop.'

'Elega, he is our father,' Myste demurred. 'Of course we do not understand his intent. How can we, when we know so little of what he knows and fears?' Unlike Elega, she didn't complain of her ignorance: she was simply stating a fact. 'But we must not be quick to judge him. High matters are abroad in Mordant. It appears that war is near. A chaos of Imagery threatens us. And the lady—' She glanced at Terisa, blushed again momentarily, and forced herself to say, 'Terisa.' Then she gave Terisa a sweet grin. 'Terisa has come to us out of a mirror. It is rumored that she comes in answer to augury. We must not be quick to judge.'

'Myste, you are incurable.' A small frown pinched Elega's forehead. 'If the High King's Monomach broke in upon us, butchered me before your eyes, and raised your skirts with his sword, you would say that we must not be quick to judge him.'

'I trust,' the lady Myste said gravely, but without irritation, 'that the High King's Monomach has more honor.'

'Oh, you are a fool!' cried Elega softly. Her violet eyes flashed in her pale face. But at once she put her arms around her sister and hugged her until her own vexation faded. When she stepped back, her social graces were restored. 'Yet even a fool and a great lady from another world' – she smiled to show that she was playing – 'must have lunch. I will summon it.'

She went to a nearby bellpull and gave it a tug. Then she retreated to another room.

A short time later, Terisa heard her speaking softly to someone, probably a domestic. And not long after that a maid laden down with trays appeared in the dining room and began to set the table.

In the meantime, however, Terisa was alone with Myste.

The particular quality of Myste's gaze – and attention – made her nervous. She found that she liked Myste readily, but she didn't want the lady to look at her. The way Myste seemed to see things that existed through or behind or beyond Terisa gave her the impression that she was starting to fade again. Involuntarily, she remembered that the mirror which had brought her here was false.

'There's so much about all this I don't understand. Why is the King – your father – why is he being so passive? What reason could there be for not supporting the Perdon?'

'Ah, my la— Terisa. There you touch on a question which has sundered this family to its heart, and still we have no answer.' The lady gestured toward a divan. 'Will you sit?'

They sank deep into the comfortable cushions, and Myste went on, 'You have not been among us long. And it appears to be our policy that we must not reveal too much of ourselves to you.' Her frown expressed her disapproval as effectively as her admission itself did. 'You may be unaware that our father has *three daughters*. Our middle sister, Torrent – accompanying our mother, Queen Madin – no longer lives with us. They make their home in Romish – or in a manor just outside Romish, I believe, for I have not been there – with Mother's family among the Fayle.

'Two years ago, that was not true. We were together then. And I was glad of it, though I cannot say that we were happy.'

Terisa remained still, said nothing. She sensed what kind of story was coming. The mission had taught her how to listen to stories like that.

'I think you would like our mother, my— Terisa. She is a woman who knows her own mind – a fact which upon occasion gave our father no little exasperation.' Myste smiled at the memory. 'If you listen to Elega, she will lead you to believe that there are not five such women in all Mordant. But it is my opinion that she misjudges. It is my opinion that women simply lack the courage to follow their dreams.' As she said this, her gaze seemed to be aimed through the opposite wall, as if the stone were translucent. 'Nevertheless none would deny that Queen Madin is one of the few who know themselves enough – or are brave enough – to insist upon their own wishes.

'This accounts, I think,' she commented as a digression, 'for the fact that she permitted Elega to break her match with Geraden of Domne, though the King himself had made it. Our mother was glad to have a daughter who knew her own mind.

'Now Madin,' the lady resumed, 'loved Joyse from girlhood – long before he became King of Mordant – and he loved her. In fact, it is said only a little in jest that he began the campaigns which led to his kingship in order to rid himself of the obstacles that thwarted his passion for her. Therefore when he had established the Demesne under his rule, and had brought the Care of Fayle to freedom in his service, he threw himself at her feet and begged that she would enter his possession, as her father the Fayle had done.

'To his astonishment' – Myste smiled again – 'she refused him. She did not deny that she loved him utterly, but she would not have him for husband or for lover. He had set his hand to war as a farmer to a plow, and he must not release it until his fields were furrowed and planted. But while his grasp was upon that handle, his time and his life belonged to bloodshed. She was prepared to share him with many things, she said, but not with a mistress as avaricious as warfare, where every spear and arrow and blade of his enemies hungered for the riches of his heart. If his will did not change – and if he were still alive – let him only send word to her when his wars were done, and she would come to him anywhere in all the world.

'Well, he is a man. Of course he was furious. But he is also a good man. When he had been furious for some little while – a time which he describes in days, but which she reports as a *little* while – he laughed loudly and long. He avowed that there was no other woman alive to suit him as well as she did, and he swore on his oath that, whatever happened, her own steadfastness would provide her a minimum estimate of his. Then he rode away, bragging – as young men will – that he meant to conquer both Cadwal and Alend before the next winter.

'Sadly, he did not fulfill that boast. Many years passed before he could call himself King without fear that the title would be ripped from him in the next day's battle. And when that was accomplished, he turned himself to a different kind of warfare, the struggle to unify all Imagery in the Congery. Upon occasion, he visited her so that she could see he had not changed toward her. But his wars were not done.

'At last, she had had enough. Departing Romish on horseback with no other companionship or protection than her maid, she rode the hills and forests of Mordant until at last she found where he fought. He and his men, Adept Havelock among them, had just ended a battle with a malign Imager, and he was covered in ash from head to foot. Yet she rode up to him – as he tells it – as though they were being presented to each other in the audience hall of Orison, and she said, "My lord King, how much longer will this go on?"

'He looked at his men, and he looked at her. For a moment, he says, he was tempted to make some foolish retort. She was a woman riding abroad with no one but a maid beside her, and five of his men had just been slain. But he thought better of it. Instead, he handed her down from her mount and took her into his tent and explained to her all that he was doing and all that he had left to do.

'When he was done, she said, "My lord King, this may occupy another ten years or more."

'He nodded. Her estimate was accurate.

'"That is too much," she said. "I have had enough of waiting. Is there any man in your camp qualified to perform a wedding service?"

'My father says that he gaped at her for fully an hour before he understood, but she insists that he did not appear to have lost his mind for more than a moment or two. Then he let out a yell and embraced her so boisterously that the tentpole broke and the tent collapsed upon them.

'Nevertheless it was he who insisted that they return at once to Orison for a full and elaborate marriage rite. He says that she deserved no less. In her view, however, he wished primarily to take her away from the danger of battles to the safety of his Demesne.

'Their union' – Myste glanced at Terisa as she continued, and Terisa saw both happiness and sorrow in the lady's face – 'was what some have called "gleefully contentious." Certainly both of them knew their own minds with a vengeance. To those who observed them, each compromise they achieved seemed to be twenty years in the making. But we also saw how his eyes shone behind his bluster when she contradicted him. And we heard the warmth and loyalty with which she always spoke of him when he was absent. I call it a good marriage, Terisa.

'Its ending,' she sighed, 'was both slow and sudden.'

'What happened?' Terisa was thinking about her parents, trying to find some point at which their relationship had had anything in common with what she had just heard.

Sadly, Myste said, 'He became passive. The spark faded in him. More and more of the time which should have been occupied with governance, he spent closeted with mad Havelock, playing – so he said – hop-board. Fewer and fewer decisions were made. Perils and signs of peril were ignored. His people were not given justice. Not all at once, but over a period of years, he became what some men call him – an old dodderer. He retains only enough of his rule – and of the loyalty of his followers – to guard that he will not be usurped. The rest he has let go.

'This has been a grief to us all, but for our mother it has been a blow to the heart. As she valued her own mind, so she prized his. Yet now he only argued with her over trifling matters, such as whether his daughters should be taught hop-board in place of needlepoint. This she bore until she had had enough. Then she confronted him.

'"Old man," she said – by her wish all her daughters were present – "this must stop. There is evil Imagery at work. Your enemies gather as thick as jackals at your heels. Unrest grows close to rebellion among the Cares. And while all this transpires, you play hop-board with that fool Havelock. I say it must stop."

'"My dear," he replied, as though she had wounded him unjustly, "you refused to marry me for years because I was at war. Do you wish me to go to war again?"

'"I was young then, and unwed," she retorted. "Now by my own choice I am your wife. As King of Mordant, you are my husband. I have accepted your kingship, and I expect you to do all that your kingship demands. The duty is yours and must be met."

'"As it happens," he answered with a touch of his old hardness, "I *am* King of Mordant. And no one but the King is fit to tell me where my duty lies. I have already consulted myself on the subject, and I follow my own advice exactly."

'At this, our mother rose from her seat. "Then you will follow it without me. I love you as utterly as death, and I cannot bear to watch the ruin which you are making of yourself and everything that you once held precious."

'My father watched her go. When she was gone, he wept fiercely, as though he had been torn out of himself. But he did not say one word to explain himself, or to reassure her, or to call her back.

'Torrent went with her because she believed her to be in the right. Elega remains here—'

By this time, the lady Elega had returned. 'I remain here,' she interrupted, her eyes flashing, 'because something must be done for Mordant – and it will not be done in Romish. Whatever action may be possible to save the realm, it will be taken in Orison. I mean to be a part of it, if I can.

'For her part,' she continued, barely muffling her scorn, 'my sister remains here because she dreams that the King will one day rise up to defend his kingdom – if only we are willing to trust him long enough.'

Myste sighed again. 'Perhaps.'

At once, Elega became apologetic. 'Forgive me, Myste. I should not speak so harshly. His treatment of the Perdon has upset me. Perhaps the true reason you remain here is so that whatever happens he will have the comfort and company of at least one woman who loves him.'

Or perhaps, Terisa thought, she does it because at least one member of his family ought to be willing to witness what happens to him. Her own mother had stayed with her father until her death, but there hadn't been any steadfastness in that. Steadfastness required decision, and her mother had been incapable of it. She had simply been chosen by her husband, and she had accepted his right to do so. That may have been the only way she knew how to believe in herself.

Then Elega turned to Terisa. 'But we did not invite you here to tell you such stories.' She forced herself to sound more good-humored. 'As my sister has said, there is so much that we wish to know of you. And lunch has been set for us. Shall we eat as we talk?'

Almost without thinking, Terisa replied, 'I really don't have much to tell you.' The contrast between her own background and the story she had just heard shamed her somehow, like a demonstration of how insubstantial she had always been. Against the threat of violent death she had no reality at all. 'You're being very kind. But I'm only here by accident. I'm not an Imager. We don't have Imagers – where I come from. Something went wrong when Geraden made his mirror. Or during his translation.' Again, she found herself sounding like her mother. But what else could she say? 'I don't know why I ever let him talk me into coming with him.'

Then, so that it would all be said and done with, she concluded, 'I would have gone back already. But the mirror changed somehow. He can't make it work anymore.'

She stopped. Her heart beat in her throat as if she had just uttered something dangerous, and the strange desire to weep which had touched her when she thought of Geraden in the pig wallow returned.

Gaping through her as though someone a few rooms away were performing a prodigious feat, Myste breathed, 'Is it possible? Oh, is it possible?' She seemed to think that what she had just heard was more marvelous than any other revelation could have been.

In contrast, Elega flung her head back as if a menial had slapped her face, and her eyes flared. Slowly, her voice under rigid control, she asked, 'Do you mean to say, my lady, that you have no reason here? No purpose? That you have not come to play a part in Mordant's need? Do you wish us to believe that you are nothing more than an ordinary woman? That this "accident," as you call it, should not have happened to you?'

Terisa didn't want to answer. The thrust of Elega's demand was hurtful. She had created this situation for herself, however, and she mustered her courage to face it. In that way, at least, she could try not to be like her mother.

'I'm not a lady. I'm a secretary in a mission.' She held her back straight and her head up. 'They need me. Not many people can afford to work for what they pay me. But I'll lose my job if I don't get back soon. Reverend Thatcher can't take care of everything alone.

'That's all. I live in an apartment. I eat and sleep. I go to work. That's all.'

For a moment, she thought that Elega would scorn her. Myste was whispering, 'That's wonderful. It's wonderful.' Her gaze was coming into better focus on Terisa. 'I have always wished that such things were possible.' But Elega's face was made feverish by the intensity of what she felt, and she had drawn herself up as if she meant to spit acid.

'You should have gone after the Perdon,' Terisa said dully. 'He and Master Eremis are the ones you want.'

In response, the lady tried to smile.

It was a sickly expression at first, but Elega mastered her features and forced them to serve her. With an effort of will, she softened her posture. 'My lady, this is unnecessary. We belong to none of the factions of the Congery. We have no secret allies among Mordant's enemies. We will not manipulate or betray you. We are women like yourself, not self-serving men hungry for power. We can be trusted. We are perhaps the only people in Orison whom you may safely trust. This pretense is unnecessary.'

Myste looked at her sister at once. 'Elega, Terisa has no reason to lie to us. I am sure that she has not. It is not a pretense.'

With a savagery that would have done Castellan Lebbick credit, the lady Elega flashed out, '*It must be.*'

An instant later, she recollected herself. Once again, she tried to smile. Now, however, she looked like a woman bravely suppressing an impulse to throw up.

'I'm sorry,' Terisa said. 'I'm sorry.'

NINE

MASTER EREMIS
AT PLAY

The ladies Elega and Myste struggled to engage Terisa in a desultory conversation while they ate lunch together, but they weren't very successful. Myste smiled as if she had a secret behind her faraway gaze; she asked Terisa polite questions about what she had seen and done in Orison. Elega masked a towering impatience by picking at her food and filling the silences with trenchant descriptions of the life Terisa could have expected to lead, had she been born and reared in Mordant – a safe life, insufferably protracted by her essential irrelevance to her own fate. Both of them were obviously not saying what they had in mind.

It was also apparent, however, that both of them were constrained, not by Terisa, but by each other. The quick, stark moment of their disagreement had been intense enough to shock them, make them retreat from her as well as from each other. She felt an active relief when Myste at last suggested that Saddith be summoned to conduct Terisa back to the peacock rooms.

In a state of pronounced awkwardness, the three women awaited an answer to their summons. Fortunately, Saddith's arrival was prompt. A few moments later, Terisa had said a stiff farewell to the ladies Myste and Elega and was on her way back to her rooms.

Saddith had kept her eyes lowered in the presence of the King's daughters. Now, however, she studied Terisa frankly. At first there was uncertainty in her eyes, but it slowly gave way to a look of spice and humor.

When she and Terisa had passed the King's rooms, and were out of earshot of the guards, she said in a cheerful, probing tone, 'Well, my lady. You have met the lady Elega and the lady Myste. They are the two highest ladies in Orison. What do you think of them?'

I think, Terisa mused, they're both miserable. But she didn't want to say anything like that to Saddith.

Terisa's silence seemed to confirm the maid in her opinion. To hide a smirk, she glanced down at her unbuttoned blouse, the cloth stretched open by the pressure of her breasts. 'I think,' she said with satisfaction, 'that they have forgotten who they are.'

'What do you mean?' As she walked, Terisa found herself watching the faces of everyone who passed by, looking for some sign of the man who had attacked her. That was preferable to thinking about what she had seen in the mirrors of the laborium.

'They are the highest ladies in the land,' explained the maid. 'They have position and wealth, rich gowns and rare jewels. All the finest men of Mordant are theirs by right. But what use do they make of their opportunities? The lady Elega scorns suitors. She does not wish a man – she wishes to be one. And the lady Myste will not leave behind her a nursery girl's dreams of romance and adventure.'

Saddith laughed softly. 'They are properly clad and placed to be who they are. But they are too bloodless for it. Neither of them is woman enough to rule the King's court as it should be ruled.

'Some day, my lady,' she added confidently, 'I will stand among them. I will be as high as any of the ladies of Mordant.

'The contrast will not be to their advantage.'

The maid's bluntness was strange to Terisa. She wasn't accustomed to servants who spoke so freely. Curiosity impelled her to ask, 'Don't you like what you're doing now?'

At that, Saddith glanced sharply at Terisa as if to gauge the intent of the question. Whatever she saw, however, reaffirmed her faith in Terisa's innocence; she relaxed at once and replied candidly, 'It is well enough for what it is, my lady. Before I became a maid, I was a scullion in the kitchens of Orison. And before that, I served ale in a tavern near where the army of Mordant is encamped. And before *that* – she grimaced – 'I fed chickens and swept floors in the village where I was born – one of the lesser villages of the Demesne. The place of a lady's maid in Orison is well enough, indeed. For what it is.

'But it is not enough for me.'

Terisa considered this. 'What do you mean?'

Saddith replied with a lubricious grin, and her eyes sparkled. 'My lady, it is in their beds that men put aside their pretenses and become the enslaved children that they are in their hearts. When I learned this, the village of my birth could no longer hold me. A soldier of Mordant could not bear to be parted from me, and so he found me a place in the tavern near his camp. A cook of Orison could not bear that my body should suffer the grimy hands of soldiers, and so he found me a place in his kitchens. The dear son of an overseer could not bear to displease me, and so I was given the work of a maid. The beds of men have lifted me this high, and they will lift me higher.

'Do you remember, my lady, that I spent last night with a Master? Already, my position in Orison rises.'

Her complacency made this information sound to Terisa like an announcement in a foreign language. Under no circumstances would she have revealed to anyone that Master Eremis had touched the curve of her bosom.

'He believes,' Saddith continued, 'that he took me to his bed to reward me because he had asked for a service and I had met it well. But that is only his pretense to himself, by which he preserves the illusion of will and power. He bedded me because he could not do otherwise. He has begun to share his confidence with me. Soon he will find that his pretense disappears in public as it does when we are alone. Then he will find some place for me, to raise me closer to himself. But it will be a place of my choosing, not his – and I assure you, my lady,' she concluded with relish, 'that I will choose a place that will open my way to the strong sons of the lords of Mordant.'

They were nearing the tower where the peacock rooms were. For a moment, Terisa said nothing, though she was conscious of Saddith's gaze on her, half expectant and half amused. She wanted to ask, Does it really *work*? Can you live like that? Can you be happy? But the words stuck in her throat. Without quite intending to speak aloud, she said, 'I've never met anyone like you before.'

'That is plain, my lady.' The maid tried to reply gravely, but she was almost chortling. 'Yet you may rely on me to assist you,' she went on, speaking now more like a kindly sister. 'If you wish it, we will make of you a formidable woman' – she smiled behind her hand – 'eventually.'

Terisa ascended the stairs to her rooms with her head full of haze. She had apologized to the King's daughters. For what? For not being a powerful Imager, come to save the world? Or for simply not being substantial enough to deserve their interest in her, their friendship or alliance?

Did she want Saddith to help her become *formidable*?

'I'll think about it,' she murmured belatedly as she and Saddith approached the guards standing outside her door. 'This is all so new to me. I need time to think.'

'Certainly, my lady.' Saddith spoke as a proper servant, but the looks with which the guards regarded Terisa conveyed the impression that Saddith had winked at them. 'Let me help you undress, and then you will be alone as long as you wish.'

One of the guards made a sound in his throat as though he were choking. Helpless to do otherwise, Terisa blushed again as Saddith ushered her into her rooms. As soon as the door was closed, she turned to see if Castellan Lebbick had kept his word.

He had: the bolt was fixed.

The rooms had also been cleaned and tidied. The strewn peacock feathers of the previous night were gone. A decanter of wine and a few goblets had been set on a table near one wall.

She was relieved when Saddith unfastened the hooks at the back of the gown and the pressure around her chest was released. Her lungs felt tight, as though she hadn't taken a decent breath for hours. Gladly, she dressed herself in her flannel shirt, corduroy pants, and moccasins. Then she waited as patiently as she could until Saddith had built up the fires, replenished the lamps, and made her departure.

At once, Terisa bolted the door. Then she went to the wardrobe with the concealed door and made sure her chair was still propped securely against that entrance. It was impossible that she would ever be *formidable*. She didn't want any man to look at her as Master Eremis did.

Unless Eremis himself did it again. Just once. So that she might have a chance to learn what it meant.

But when she went to one of her windows to gaze out over the winterscape of Orison and try to make some sense of her emotions, the face she remembered most vividly was Geraden's – his expression flat and neutral, held rigidly blank because she had hurt him and he didn't intend to show it.

During the afternoon, as the sun westered toward the cold, white hills, she was watching a squad of guards exercise their mounts in the courtyard when she chanced to see a figure that looked like the Perdon stride out into the wet snow and mud. Men on horseback were waiting for him, their shoulders wrapped in heavy cloaks against the weather. He sprang onto a beast they held ready for him. With as much speed as the horses could manage on that footing, they rode out of Orison.

To her, he looked like a man who had made up his mind.

After breakfast the next morning, she gave herself a bath, put on her own clothes, and tried to decide what she was going to do. For some reason, she hadn't been troubled by the sensation that she was fading – even though she had spent the evening alone with her fears and the strangeness of her situation; even though her existence seemed to be more doubtful than ever; even though there were no mirrors anywhere, no kinds of glass in which she could see herself reflected. Nevertheless her problem remained. The mirror that had brought her here was false. She wasn't an Imager – and Mordant needed help at least as powerful as an Imager's. A man in black had tried to kill her. She had seen men torn apart like raw meat by creatures out of nowhere. People who counted on her were going to get hurt.

She had to do something about it.

Well, *what*, exactly?

She still had no idea.

For that reason, she jumped up and ran to answer it when she heard a knock at her door. It sounded like an offer of rescue.

Unbolting the door, she pulled it open.

Master Eremis stood outside.

He had Geraden with him.

'Good morning, my lady,' the Master said cheerfully. 'I see that you have slept well. Your eyes are altogether brighter this morning – which I had not thought possible. I must confess, however' – he leered at her – 'that I prefer yesterday's apparel. But no matter. I have come to escort you to the meeting of the Congery.'

This was too sudden. Her heart was still pounding in reply to his unexpected presence. 'The Congery?' she asked as if she were deaf or stupid. 'Am I invited?'

Instinctively, she turned to Geraden for an answer.

The Apt's face was deliberately blank. He looked like a man who had taken an oath to stifle his emotions. Apparently, he still felt hurt, but didn't want to show it. Or was he just trying to keep his reactions to Master Eremis under control? She couldn't tell.

Nevertheless he was the one she trusted to tell her what was happening.

He didn't quite meet her gaze. 'Actually, neither of us is invited,' he said neutrally. 'But Master Eremis wants us to go with him anyway.'

'I do, indeed,' said the Master. 'I have told you that I mean to show my friendship toward you. And today the Congery will attempt to decide what action the lady Terisa's presence and Mordant's need require. Surely that discussion will be of some interest to you, my lady?'

Because she had hurt him – and because she had no idea where she stood with Master Eremis or the Congery – she tried to find some way to ask Geraden what she should do. But the words wouldn't come. Eremis' smile seemed to stop them in her throat.

Geraden scanned the room. Still neutrally, he said, 'It may not be pleasant. At least half the Imagers are going to be offended when we show up without being invited. But Master Eremis doesn't seem to care about that. And the opportunity is too important. I don't think we should miss it.'

Listening to him gave Terisa the odd impression that he had aged since the previous day.

In an effort to show him how much she appreciated his reply, she said, 'All right,' without a glance at Eremis. 'I'll go.' Then she stood still under the Master's quick frown of vexation, although it made her heart quake.

Unfortunately, Geraden's gaze didn't rise above her knees; he didn't see that she was trying to apologize.

Master Eremis got even with her by giving her an exaggerated bow in the direction of the door and saying, 'If you will so graciously condescend, my lady?' His mockery was plain, but his quick smile took the sting out of it. The way he looked at her reminded her of his finger's touch on the curve of her breast. Before she was altogether sure of what she was doing, she returned a shy smile of her own. Somehow, she accepted his arm, and he escorted her out of the room.

Geraden followed without expression.

At once, one of the guards stepped forward to call attention to himself. 'Master Eremis.'

Eremis paused, cocked an eyebrow. 'Yes?'

'Castellan Lebbick's orders. We're supposed to know where the lady is at all times. Where are you taking her?'

Terisa was a bit surprised. No mention of those orders had been made the previous day, when she had left her rooms with Geraden. She glanced at him and saw that he, too, was surprised. His blankness lifted, and he concentrated as if he were thinking hard. The exertion improved his appearance considerably.

But this discrepancy in the guards' behavior was something that Master Eremis obviously knew nothing about. 'I have invited her to a meeting of the Congery,' he answered smoothly – acid under a satin surface. 'Doubtless Castellan Lebbick – by which I mean King Joyse – will also wish to know what the Congery means to discuss in her presence.' He wrinkled his nose in distaste. 'And doubtless his spies will tell him shortly after the event. Come, my lady.'

As though she were dressed for a formal ball, he took her grandly down the stairs.

His route toward Orison's former dungeons was the same one Geraden had used yesterday. As they walked, he bent his tall form slightly over her, at once deferential, proprietary, and courtly. They must have looked like they were sharing secrets. She didn't have anything to say, however; all the talk was his. She was looking among the people they passed in the halls for any face that might remind her of the man who had attacked her. So he caught her completely off guard by commenting casually, 'The Perdon and I discussed you at some length yesterday, my lady.'

She was too startled to respond. Surely she wasn't the kind of woman men *discussed at length*?

He chuckled as if she had said something clever. 'He has a – what shall I call it?' – he savored the word in anticipation – 'a *vast* experience of women, but he and I disagreed as to which of your many attractions would prove to be the most delectable. I have promised to give him an answer when he returns to Orison.'

The idea made her shiver. What did he mean? Something intimate and presumptuous – but what? Her mind remained stubbornly blank on the question. How would he touch her? What emotions would he draw out of her? She was too ignorant: ignorant of men, of course, but also of herself.

Unconsciously, she held his arm as though she were cold and needed warmth.

Crossing the disused ballroom with Geraden behind them, they took the corridor which went down to the laborium of the Congery. Again, she lost her bearings immediately among the doors and turns; but at last she recognized the straight passageway leading to the former torture chamber which the Imagers now used for their debates. The guards outside saluted, then opened the massive wooden door for Master Eremis, Terisa, and Geraden to enter the meeting hall.

From its perimeter, beyond the four heavy pillars that supported the ceiling, the large, round chamber seemed to clench around the Masters who had already gathered there. But when Eremis took Terisa toward the curved circle of benches and the better light of the lamps, her perspective changed; the space began to feel a bit less oppressive, a bit less like a crypt buried under a pile of old stone.

There were at least ten Imagers staring at her and Geraden as Master Eremis led them forward. A few of them sat on the benches, leaning toward or away from the carved railing that circled the center of the chamber; the rest stood around the dais. Two days ago, that dais had held the mirror of her translation. No mirrors were present now, however. As a result, the dais looked more like what it had once been: a raised platform to display the interrogation of prisoners.

Terisa had no trouble identifying Master Barsonage: she remembered his bald head, his eyebrows like tufts of gorse, his face the color and texture of cut pine, his wide girth. And two or three of the other Imagers she recollected vaguely: they must have been standing nearby when Geraden had pulled her out of the glass. But most of the Masters had a strange and hostile appearance, as though they were prepared to judge her sight unseen. To put her to the question without mercy.

'What is this, Master Eremis?' Master Barsonage asked darkly. 'Did we not explicitly determine that neither Apt Geraden nor the lady should take part in our discussions?'

Geraden studied the groins of the ceiling.

'You did, Master Barsonage,' replied Master Eremis in good humor. 'But I am prepared to persuade the Congery otherwise.'

The mediator frowned sternly. 'This does not please me. It is frivolous. Our survival – and indeed the fate of all Mordant – hinges on the choices we must make. We have not the time' – he faced Eremis squarely – 'and I have not the patience to reopen finished decisions.'

Several of the Imagers nodded, muttering assent. Eremis didn't appear popular among them.

'Let us not be hasty,' a familiar voice put in, as if the speaker were meek and disliked calling attention to himself. 'For my part, Master Barsonage, I am willing to hear Master Eremis. Perhaps he has too little concern for the dignity of the Congery, but surely he is not frivolous.'

Until she heard his voice, Terisa didn't realize that Master Quillon was sitting on one of the benches halfway around the circle from her. His gray robe and nondescript demeanor blended into the stone background. Involuntarily, her gaze leapt to him, at once glad to see someone she thought of as a friend and fearful that in his presence she wouldn't adequately keep his secret. But he didn't meet her look. His bright eyes watched the other Masters, and his nose twitched alertly.

'In any case,' drawled Master Eremis, 'it is my right to bring whatever I see fit before the Congery. That is one of our rules, Master Barsonage, as you well know.'

An Imager said, 'That's true.' Another agreed.

Master Barsonage made a snorting noise, but he didn't trouble to argue the point. Turning away, he resumed his conversation with the Masters standing near him.

For a moment, Master Eremis grinned at the mediator's back. Then he drew Terisa toward an empty bench and seated her there, with the railing between her and the center of the chamber. With a gesture, half brusque, half cheerful, he commanded Geraden to the bench as well. Eremis himself remained on his feet, however. From her seat, Terisa received an exaggerated impression of how much taller he was than any of the men near him.

The room didn't seem as cold as it had been two days ago.

Alone or in small groups, more Imagers arrived. She noticed now that two or three of them were young enough to be recently elevated Apts – as young as Geraden. Among the others was someone else she recognized: heavyset Master Gilbur, a scowl cut deeply into the thick flesh of his face under his black-flecked white beard, his crooked back counterbalanced by the power of his hands. She remembered his voice, as guttural as the bite of a saw. But young or old, familiar or otherwise, they all stared at her and frowned at Geraden. Apparently, none of the Masters had improved his opinion of the Apt and her. As he passed, Gilbur rasped rhetorically, 'What foolishness is this?'

Shortly, she heard Master Barsonage murmur, 'Well, we are here. Let us begin.' Imagers shuffled themselves to the benches, their yellow chasubles dangling. There was no escape: all the doors were closed. And they were strutted and bolted so that they could only be opened from inside. The Congery valued its privacy. If Master Eremis hadn't brought her here so confidently, she would never have come. She had nothing in her that might enable her to outface twenty-five or thirty antagonistic men.

As soon as all the Masters were seated and the mediator was alone beside the dais, he said abruptly, 'Be brief, Master Eremis. We have more important questions to confront.'

In response, Master Eremis resumed his feet. His smile appeared easy, impervious to insult; but his skin had an underhue of blood, and his pale eyes glittered dangerously. 'Master Barsonage,' he said in a conversational tone, 'with deference to your age, place, and experience, I doubt whether your questions are more important than mine.

'No one here has failed to note that I have brought with me two persons expressly prohibited from this meeting – Apt Geraden and the lady Terisa of Morgan.' He didn't glance at either of them: he was playing to the Masters. 'They *are* the questions we must confront. He is the issue of power, for we still have no understanding of how he contrived to find her in a mirror focused upon our chosen champion.'

Geraden lowered his head and covered his face with his hands.

'She represents action – the action we wish to take for our own preservation and the saving of all Mordant. Who belongs in our discussion, if they do not?

'First let us consider Apt Geraden—'

'Paugh, Eremis!' Master Gilbur interrupted rudely. 'All this has already been said. A child could make the same arguments. Come to the point.'

'The point, Master Gilbur?' Eremis waggled his eyebrows. 'Do you wish me to forgo the fine speech I have prepared for this solemn occasion? Very well. I will trust to your penetrating good sense and make no further defense of my proposal.

'I propose' – suddenly, he raised his voice until it rang around the stone walls – 'that Apt Geraden be granted the chasuble of a Master!'

While his shout died away, the Imagers gaped at him. Geraden's head jerked up, his eyes were wide with emotion. Terisa thought, *I mean to show my friendship toward you.* So this is what he meant. Master Eremis had been planning to gain recognition for the Apt, to see that he was finally rewarded for his years of devotion. She couldn't understand why the expression in Geraden's face was neither pleasure nor gratitude, but rather a kind of fear.

Then through the silence she heard a faint sound like muffled laughter. Scanning the circle, she saw Master Quillon biting the side of his hand to keep himself quiet.

Several other Masters were less successful. One of them let out a guffaw like the burst of a ruptured wineskin, and half the chamber broke into chuckles and hoots of laughter.

Slowly, Geraden's skin turned red until it looked hot enough to catch fire.

Master Eremis' grin was like his gaze – at once sharp, ominous, and vastly amused.

The mediator didn't laugh. He faced Master Eremis, his chin out-thrust. Without effort, he made himself heard through the glee of the Imagers. 'Master Eremis, it is not kind to humiliate the Apt in this way.'

'*Humiliate*, Master Barsonage?' returned Master Eremis instantly in a tone of protest and outrage, though he didn't lose his grin. 'I am entirely serious.' More laughter greeted this assertion. In response, he began to shout at all the Masters together. 'Apt Geraden has accomplished something that no Imager before him has ever achieved! Even the arch-Imager Vagel could not use glass as *he* has! Will you laugh at him? By the pure sand of dreams, you will *not*!' His voice quenched the mirth around. 'Geraden is as worthy of the chasuble as any of you, and I will have my proposal answered!'

Still he didn't lose his grin.

'Oh, forsooth,' said Master Gilbur before anyone else could speak. '"I will have my proposal answered."' His sarcasm was as heavy as a truncheon. 'You dream, Eremis. You have put your head into a flat mirror and brought it out as mad as Havelock. Make Geraden a Master? Must I explain even this to you?'

'You must indeed,' Master Eremis replied like sweet poison, while the rest of the Congery watched him in various states of uncertainty and annoyance. 'I ignore the offense, but I must have the explanation.'

'Have it, then,' Gilbur growled. 'We could not accept him to the Congery, were he the greatest Imager in recorded time. We do not have his loyalty. While his body serves us, his heart and mind belong to King Joyse. It is no secret that when he left with her two days ago he took her straight to that old dodderer. But what did he say to her along the way? Ask him that, Eremis. What did he say of us to the King? Ask him *that*. And how has he served our interests with her since then? Master Barsonage commanded him not to reveal anything to her until the Congery had made its decisions. I will wager that command was broken before Apt Geraden and the lady left this chamber.'

The muscles at the corners of Geraden's eyes flinched at every word. Yet he didn't lower his head or look away. Instead, he grew pale, as though his emotions were being honed out of him, leaving him focused and sharp. Holding her breath for him, Terisa thought that at any moment now someone was going to mention the flat glass which had changed. Then he would be asked to explain what he and she had been doing there.

'Apt Geraden.' Master Barsonage was gazing at Geraden, his eyes level and solemn. 'You must reply to this.'

Geraden's jaws knotted, and he jerked to his feet. His deliberate blankness had failed him like an inadequate mask. 'Master Barsonage,' he said, biting down on his voice so that it wouldn't shake, 'I am loyal to King Joyse – as all of us should be. He created Mordant. He gave us peace. He made the Congery to be what it is. But he' – his voice snapped for a second – 'he has no allegiance to me. I kept your command, Master Barsonage, while I took the lady Terisa of Morgan to the King. But when I reached him, he paid as little attention to me as you have. He gave me your same command. And he dismissed my responsibility for the lady.

'Master Gilbur implies that I'm a spy for my King.' Acid leaked past his control. 'I'm not. What purpose would it serve? If I tried to tell him the secrets of the Congery, he wouldn't listen.'

Stiffly, he sat down.

Terisa heard his hurt and his need. At the same time, she remembered her dream of winter, in which three horsemen rode to kill her, and a young man dressed like Geraden fought to save her. She had remained motionless in that dream, as passive as she had been all her life.

Remembering, she stood up.

'He's telling the truth.' She was trembling, but she didn't let that stop her. 'He obeyed you. And King Joyse dismissed him. He told him not to answer any of my questions.' Then, impelled by a secret flash of anger or adrenaline, she added, 'The King didn't give me any answers either. He feels the same way you do. He doesn't trust me.'

Master Quillon stared vacantly at nothing.

For a second, Geraden's face shone with relief and gladness. The vitality that made him so likable was restored. But the smile Master Eremis turned on her looked as gentle and friendly as the strike of a hawk.

Abruptly, her courage failed. She sat down and bowed her head, trying to hide behind her hair.

'Thank you, my lady,' Master Barsonage said quietly. 'Apt Geraden, it is my opinion that you are owed an apology – by Master Gilbur, if no one else.'

Master Gilbur made a hoarse spitting noise and muttered, 'Do you consider that dogswater the truth?'

'Since it is unlikely' – Master Barsonage whetted his tone – 'that Master Gilbur, or any other Master, will do so, I must apologize for them. Any son of the Domne deserves better treatment than you have received.'

'It's not important,' murmured Geraden. Then he raised his voice. 'I would be satisfied if the Congery simply decided to treat the lady Terisa with more consideration.'

'Very good,' Master Gilbur whispered harshly. 'He is not content with an apology from the mediator of the Congery. Now he must try to teach us our priorities and duties.'

'Have done, Master Gilbur!' snapped Barsonage at once. 'This does not become you. Apt Geraden's manners are not what we must decide here. It is his elevation to the chasuble of a Master.'

Master Gilbur replied with a glare that would have split a wooden plank.

The mediator faced him for a long moment. But what Master Barsonage saw seemed to unsettle or alarm him: he was the one who looked away. The silence in the chamber became strained as he frowned into the distance, looking for self-possession.

'You have made your proposal, Master Eremis. Do you wish to speak further?'

'I will let Apt Geraden's evident merit speak for itself,' replied Master Eremis. Bowing to the Congery, he sat down.

'Very well. Masters!' Barsonage called out formally, 'you have heard the proposal. Shall it be accepted? What is the will of the Congery?'

Terisa was beginning to understand, partly from Master Gilbur's irritation, but mostly from Master Eremis' strange fierceness, that there were more things going on here than she could identify. Ulterior motives were at work. She watched in unexpected suspense as the Imagers voted by show of hands.

For a moment, she thought that Geraden had won. A number of hands were favorably raised, though most of them – with the exception of Eremis' – appeared to be reluctant. Master Quillon's was not among them, however. He was watching Geraden, and his eyes held a look of understanding and empathy, but he only raised his hand to vote against the proposal.

He was in the majority. When Master Barsonage had finished counting, he announced that the proposal was defeated.

Oh, Geraden, Terisa said to him silently. I'm sorry. But she didn't have enough nerve to speak aloud.

'Masters,' Eremis enunciated softly but distinctly, 'you will regret this.'

Master Gilbur replied with a snarl of derision.

'Apt Geraden,' said the mediator in a way that suggested his self-possession was still in doubt, 'the vote has been taken. I must ask you to leave us now.'

To Terisa, Geraden had never looked more like a man with whom the Congery would have to reckon. 'Master Barsonage,' he said as he rose to his feet, 'you must make the lady Terisa a party to your decisions. It is her right to know and understand what is done here.' Perhaps she had hurt his feelings the day before; that didn't appear to affect his sense of justice. 'And it's folly to deny her. If she's simply a woman accidentally translated, then she can't do any harm. And if she's an Imager secretly – if she's the augured champion of Mordant's need – then you're wrong to risk angering her against us.'

His assertion still in the air of the chamber, he turned sharply away from the Imagers and left the meeting hall.

Master Eremis shook his head and sighed. He was smiling at no one in particular.

Geraden's departure twisted Terisa's stomach. She was already in knots when she realized that no mention had been made of the flat glass with the impossibly shifting Image.

'Master Barsonage,' rasped Gilbur, 'may we dismiss this woman also and go about our work? There are reasons for haste. And I do not enjoy spending entire days in debate.'

'You are in haste, Master Gilbur,' put in Master Quillon unexpectedly, 'but you are also hasty. We must not be too quick to set aside the questions Apt Geraden has raised.'

'Masters,' Eremis said, 'I will give you good reason why we must accept the lady Terisa of Morgan among us. It has come to us from her own mouth. King Joyse desires her ignorant. If that is *his* policy, then surely it must be *ours* to inform and enlighten her. Why else do we have these debates, if not to break the mute inaction which our King imposes upon us?'

'Master Eremis' – Quillon's voice had an edge which he usually kept hidden – 'do you propose that we commit treason?'

'If it is treason,' the tall Master responded, 'to fight for our survival – and for the defense of all Mordant – then I will propose it. But for the moment I advocate only that we permit the lady Terisa to remain during our debate.'

'You make all matters complex,' said Master Barsonage stiffly. 'I do not

137

like the direction in which you take us. But with Master Gilbur I wish to reach the meat of the question, so that I will no longer have to guess what is in your mind.

'Masters, you have heard the proposal. Shall it be accepted? What is the will of the Congery?'

This time, Quillon and Gilbur were on opposite sides of the vote. Once again, however, the former was with the majority. By a significant margin, the Congery elected to let Terisa stay.

Suddenly, there were too many eyes on her, too many men looking to see how she would react. She lowered her head to hide her disconcertedness. It was Geraden who should have been allowed to remain.

'Very well.' The mediator sounded tired. 'Now we turn to the matter which must be decided today.'

'At last,' breathed Master Gilbur.

'I will not remind you of the debate which brought us to this point,' Master Barsonage went on. 'It is enough to say that we must choose a policy – or a course of action – to meet the unexpected outcome of Apt Geraden's attempt to translate our chosen champion. We decided on that attempt because it was demanded by our circumstances – and because it appeared to be supported by augury. And we decided to send Geraden into the glass out of respect' – here Master Gilbur snorted again – 'out of *respect*, I say,' the mediator snapped, 'for our King's belief that what is seen in mirrors is not created by Imagery, but rather has its own existence outside our knowledge.

'But that has gone entirely awry. And we have realized that it is impossible for us to know what role the lady Terisa of Morgan will play in the fate of Mordant. Therefore we must now choose where we will stand. Will we accept the consequences of what we have done and await its outcome? Or will we choose some other policy or action to meet our dilemma?

'Masters, you must decide.'

Without rising, Master Eremis said immediately, 'I say that we must accept the consequences of what we have done and await its outcome.' Now he spoke as if he wanted to avoid provoking an adverse reaction. 'As I have observed repeatedly' – he permitted himself no sarcasm – 'the lady Terisa represents an enormous and unprecedented display of power, which we do not understand. We must not take further risks until we have learned more of her.'

'Is this *you*, Master Eremis?' a younger voice interposed. The speaker was an Imager of about Geraden's age; he didn't hesitate to be sarcastic. 'You sound craven. We have already determined that we cannot know *what* the lady represents. So we cannot make our choices on that basis. In our peril, it does not matter that Apt Geraden did something unprecedented. It matters only that he *failed*. The augury itself is sound. It must be, or we have no understanding of Imagery. Only the Apt failed. We must try again.'

A flash of passion showed in Eremis' eyes, but he didn't retort.

Quietly, Master Barsonage asked, 'And did you never fail when you were an Apt?'

'I did not make a lifetime of it,' retorted the young Imager. 'As well you know.'

'In any case,' Master Gilbur cut into the discussion, gathering force as he spoke, 'whether Apts are prone to error is not at issue here. I agree that we must try again. *I* will try again. Using the original glass, of which Apt Geraden's is a copy, I will translate our chosen champion to us' – abruptly, he shook his huge fist at Master Quillon – 'and *blast* the King's scruples, whatever they are! He will sit and play hop-board with that madman Havelock until the ground cracks under him and all Orison is swallowed in ruins. If Mordant is to endure, *we must have power!*'

'Well said, Master Gilbur!' Two or three of the Imagers applauded. But Master Barsonage faced Gilbur with undisguised dismay.

Terisa felt a jolt like a moment of vision as she saw the armored figure again in her mind: though the landscape he faced was alien to him as much as to her, he confronted it as though he were in the habit of victory; and his strange weapons gave him all the strength he needed.

'Then you also,' another Master said, 'advocate what Quillon calls treason? Or do you mean to enter the glass and ask the champion to come to us?' A pause. 'He will shoot you.'

'I do not fear "what Quillon calls treason,"' Master Gilbur returned. 'Do none of you understand the *reason* we are in such peril? It is not Mordant which is truly threatened. It is the Congery. We are in peril because all men who have ever hated King Joyse or loved power covet what we represent – all the resources of Imagery in the world we know. And they dare act on what they covet because King Joyse has abandoned us. He created the Congery, and he shackled it with rules which serve no purpose but his own, and now he has cut it adrift. We must fend for ourselves or die.'

'I agree.' Master Eremis continued to speak carefully. 'But how must we fend for ourselves? That is where we differ.'

'Master Eremis,' Gilbur grated, 'you differ from everyone. You have no sense.'

Tentatively, as though he wished to avert hostility, Master Quillon asked, 'Would it help, perhaps, if we looked again at the augury?'

'Would that help you?' Master Gilbur answered in a nasty tone. 'Have you forgotten what it shows? Or do you believe it may have changed?'

Quillon seemed unwilling to take offense. 'I would like to be sure that it has not.'

'As would I,' said another Imager.

'In addition,' Master Quillon went on, 'there is the question of interpretation. Perhaps the experience of the past few days will teach us to read the augury more clearly.'

A handful of men around the circle promptly indicated their assent.

Master Barsonage sighed. 'It will take a moment to have the glass brought here. Masters, we do not vote on this. Any of you has the right to make such a demand – if the demand is seconded.'

'I wish to see the glass,' one of Master Quillon's supporters said at once.

'And I,' said another.

'Very well.' The mediator nodded toward someone Terisa couldn't see; the sounds of the door as it opened and closed carried distinctly through the chamber.

No one spoke while the Congery waited. Perhaps this was part of the Masters' protocol. Or perhaps none of them wanted to commit himself until Quillon's request had been satisfied. Master Barsonage stared beyond the circle. Master Gilbur ground his big hands together as if he were practicing breaking things. Master Eremis leaned back on the bench and gazed nonchalantly at the ceiling like a man whose good manners kept him from whistling. Master Quillon appeared to be making a conscious effort not to twitch his nose, but he didn't succeed. The other Imagers exhibited varying degrees of impatience, curiosity, assurance, and alarm.

Terisa had the impression that she ought to be more worried. There were undercurrents in this debate which she was able to sense but not define. They might be dangerous. People were plotting – and plots meant harm. What she felt, however, was a small, hesitant eagerness. She wanted to see the augury that had led Geraden to her.

It was brought into the chamber by two Apts, carrying it between them on a beautifully polished wooden tray nearly five feet on a side. As the Apts passed near her on their way toward the dais, she saw that the tray was covered with pieces of broken glass. These pieces had all been laid flat on the wood, and none of them touched each other; but they didn't appear to have been arranged in any other way.

So softly that no one else could hear him, Master Eremis murmured to her, 'Perhaps Apt Geraden neglected to explain how auguring is done, my lady. There are two arts: to create a flat glass of the proper kind, accurately focused; and to interpret the outcome. In simple terms, a flat mirror is made that shows some person, place, or event from which the augury is to be extrapolated. For example, if we wished to determine whether our future contained a war with Cadwal, we might attempt to create a glass focused on Carmag – a glass in which High King Festten could be seen. Mirrors show places, but it is people who cause wars. Then the mirror is dropped. If it has been correctly made, it breaks into fragments that show pieces of what will come from the Image on which it was focused.

'This glass was created by Master Barsonage.' He smiled sardonically. 'For that reason, none of us ask whether it was correctly made.' Then he added, 'The other difficulty, as you will see, is to interpret the results. I have always suspected, my lady, that augury exists primarily in the mind of the interpreter.'

Once the Apts had set their burden down on the dais, most of the Masters left the benches and crowded around it. Only Gilbur and his most outspoken supporters apparently felt no need to look at the broken glass again. Everyone else cast at least a glance at the augury. Taking her arm confidently, Master Eremis guided Terisa among them until she stood at the edge of the dais. The Apts had stepped back: the tray of glass was clearly displayed in front of her.

The mirror had broken into dozens of fragments.

Each of them showed a different Image.

And all the Images were moving. When she first looked at them, they seemed to be groping blindly toward each other, as if they aspired to some kind of wholeness.

Pieces of what will come.

The sight made her momentarily dizzy: it seethed like migraine. She felt that she was going to fall. But she closed her eyes and pushed down her queasiness. When she looked again, she held herself steady by concentrating on one or two Images at a time.

—of what will come.

At first, she was startled by how many of them she recognized – and by how precise they were, despite their small size. In one, King Joyse hunched over a game of hop-board, a game that had collapsed into chaos, the men scattered everywhere. He stared at it as if he were determined to make sense of the confusion, and his hands moved aimlessly over the board. In another, Geraden had begun to step into a mirror; but his body blocked the Image within the Image. In another, he appeared again, this time standing surrounded entirely by mirrors, all of them reflecting scenes of violence and destruction against him. And in yet another, the armored warrior in the alien landscape fired his weapons past the edge of the glass.

But in fact those were only a small handful of the Images. The others reached beyond her experience. One shard showed a castle – she guessed it to be Orison – with a smoking hole torn in one side and a look of death about it. Several pieces of glass held Images of battle: men on horseback hacking at each other so vividly that she could see the blood in the wounds; figures that looked like kings rampaging; soldiers on foot spitted by spears; corpses trampled; carnage. Smoke blotted out the sun. And other Images were of things that could only have come into existence through Imagery: rocks falling from the sky as if off the side of a mountain; creatures so hot that whatever they touched caught fire; devouring worms. Villages were razed. Castles fell. Crops burned. Men, women, children died.

And yet here and there in the squirming mosaic were scenes of peace, perhaps even of victory: a plain purple pennon set on a hillside; a celebration that might have been a wedding, taking place in a high ballroom; farmers planting a field still scarred by battle.

Then another Image caught her eye.

Three riders. Driving their mounts forward, straight out of the glass, driving hard, so that the strain in the shoulders of their horses was as plain as the hate in the keen edges of their upraised swords. Fixed on her across the gulf of augury and translation, and riding hard to hasten the moment when she and her future would come together.

The riders of her dream.

Of course.

At once, a wonderful and ludicrous calm came over her. It lasted for only a moment; but while it endured she lifted her head, half expecting to hear the heart-tug of horns. Of course. Why hadn't she thought of that before?

Not the riders. She didn't know what they meant. She hardly cared. But the *future.* Mirrors didn't simply span distance or dimension: they had the capacity to span *time* as well. *Pieces of what will come.* That was why she had been able to see the same Image in two different seasons, the same scene in spring and winter: time. What she had witnessed wasn't proof that the mirror that had brought her here was false; she had seen only another demonstration of the potential that made augury possible.

And that meant—

From across the dais, Master Quillon asked blandly, 'Does this shed any light for you, my lady?' as though he were inquiring only out of politeness. 'I confess that it baffles me.'

'The secret of interpretation, my lady,' Master Eremis murmured, 'is to read the flow of the Images. Their movement is not random. There is a – perhaps it might be called "current" – which runs from crisis to action to outcome. Unfortunately, this current is not easily discerned. We see Mordant's danger. We see the importance of Geraden. He is in august company – King Joyse, High King Festten, the Alend Monarch. And he is the only individual who appears twice. The champion we thought he would bring to us is here. Also, we see scenes we do not understand.' He pointed at Geraden surrounded by mirrors. 'And we see outcomes – ruin and hope. But how the Images flow is harder to determine. Does Apt Geraden lead to hope, or to ruin? What does King Joyse meditate upon while his enemies ride against him?'

'In brief,' Master Gilbur rasped from his seat, 'nothing has changed. The augury tells us only what we have already seen.'

'When we decided that Apt Geraden should attempt to translate our champion,' explained Master Barsonage, overriding Gilbur, 'the logic of it seemed plain enough. He clearly could not be the cause of ruin. Ruin confronted us already. Therefore he must be a source of hope.

'Now,' he sighed, 'the interpretation is less obvious.'

'Oh, forsooth.' Master Gilbur was growing steadily angrier. '"Less obvious," indeed. Nothing has been more obvious. The Apt's involvement in our plight *is* the path which leads to ruin. Only the champion you see before you offers any hope.'

Through his teeth, the mediator replied, 'That is what we must decide.'

For another moment or two, the Imagers stood around the dais. Some of them whispered among themselves. Others pointed out details of the augury which their companions might have missed. Then, slowly, they returned to their benches. Still holding Terisa's arm, Eremis steered her back to her seat.

But when the Masters were in their places again, a silence fell over the Congery. Everyone except Gilbur seemed lost in thought – perhaps frustrated that the augury didn't provide a clearer answer, perhaps hesitant to consider the drastic solution Master Gilbur had proposed. And he continued glowering about him as if he were determined not to speak first.

At last, an Imager Terisa didn't know asked, 'Is there no middle ground? Must we either do nothing or risk doing too much?'

'No,' another muttered. 'The King has not left us that choice. Our *plight* is extreme. By governing Mordant like a madman, he has made the situation too grave to be met on any middle ground.'

'I have heard a rumor,' said a third Master portentously. 'It is said that the Perdon came yesterday to speak with King Joyse. He reported an army of thirty thousand Cadwals mustering against him beyond the Vertigon, and he demanded reinforcement.

'He was refused.'

The shocked expressions of several of the Imagers showed that this story hadn't reached them. Master Eremis smiled vacantly.

'Nevertheless,' Master Barsonage put in more loudly than necessary, trying to shore up a weak position, 'he is the King. That decision was his to make. We do not know what reasons he may have had for his refusal.'

'True,' retorted Master Gilbur. 'And I, for one, do not care. When an assassin tries to strike a knife into my heart, and the man who is sworn to protect me steps aside, I do not ask for his reasons. First I fight the assassin. And when I have defeated him, and have bound them both in irons, and perhaps broken a few of their limbs for good measure, *then* I ask my sworn protector what his reasons may have been.'

'Master Gilbur.' The mediator swung his bulk to face Gilbur squarely. A combination of anger and fear stained his skin. 'How have you become so savage? Your arguments I understand, but not the tone of hatred in which you utter them. Whatever else we may say of him, we must say that King Joyse created the Congery. He made us who we are.'

'Who we are,' sneered Gilbur. 'Divided and useless.'

Grimly, Master Barsonage continued, 'We cannot make our decisions now on a basis of blind passion. What causes your loathing of him, Master Gilbur?'

Master Gilbur clenched his hands together until the knuckles whitened.

'Personally,' drawled Master Eremis, 'I believe that good Master Gilbur once had the insolence to ask for the hand of one of the King's daughters in marriage. Quite understandably, King Joyse laughed at him.'

A few of the Imagers might have been tempted to laugh, but Master Gilbur silenced them by surging to his feet.

'Am I savage, Master Barsonage? Do you hear hatred in my voice? Do I display loathing? I have cause.

'As you know, I was one of the last Imagers brought into the Congery in the days before the defeat of the arch-Imager Vagel. But the story of how I was brought to the Congery has never been told.

'I have given my life to my researches, and in those days no other question interested me, although of course I knew of the King's invitation to all Imagers to leave their private laboriums and join him in Orison. I did not know, however, that another Imager had moved secretly near to my lone cave in the Armigite hills. This corrupt wretch coveted my research – and he attacked me, seeking to wrest what I knew from me. I defended myself, but he had taken me by surprise, and I could not win. In our struggle, a portion of the ceiling of my cave collapsed, pinning me under a block of stone I was unable to shift. My attacker snatched what he desired most of my possessions and fled.

'As it happened, he fled straight into the arms of King Joyse. The King had learned of my attacker before I had, and he was riding toward us to deal with the man when I fell. Instantly, my attacker turned his power against the King. But he was no match for Adept Havelock in those days, and he was killed.

'Weakened by the damage it had suffered, the ceiling of my cave continued to fall. But King Joyse risked his life to enter and lift the stone and carry me to safety. He could not heal the harm done to my back – the harm which marks me still. But he restored my health, recovered my researches, and gave my life purpose in the Congery.'

'And for this you hate him?' asked Master Barsonage incredulously.

Master Gilbur slashed the air with hooked fingers. 'Yes! Oh, he was wise in the creation of the Congery. He was strong and valiant in the making of Mordant. And he was good to me. But he did not teach me to look upon his subsequent weakness, his folly, his refusal to act, as though such things were anything except *betrayal*.

'I despise what he has *become*, Master Barsonage. If you or I slipped into our dotage, the servants of Orison would tend us in our beds, and our responsibilities would pass elsewhere. Our incontinence or loss of mind would do no hurt. But *he* remains King. And he takes no action except to prevent any action that might offer us hope.

'You should be savage, as I am. The man in all Mordant whom we have most cause to love has *betrayed us!*'

His shout echoed through the chamber. At once, however, he sat down. Into the silence, he growled softly, 'I have been attacked and broken once. We must have power to defend ourselves.'

Then he bowed his head into his hands and sat still.

No one spoke. Master Eremis shifted in his seat as if he wanted to say something, then thought better of it. Master Quillon appeared to be shrinking: he might have been making a conscious effort to disappear into the background. The mediator clenched his arms over his heavy chest like a man who felt like raging and did not intend to let himself go. Some of the Imagers watched the rest of the circle as if they were looking for hints. Others studiously avoided anyone else's gaze.

Terisa listened to the tension and wondered what the implications of being real were. What did it demand of her? What should she do?

Abruptly, Master Gilbur hit the rail in front of him so hard she thought she heard the wood crack. 'Balls of a dog!' he roared. 'Will you sit there forever? If you consider me wrong, say so. Does not one of you possess bowels enough to tell me to my face that I am wrong?'

At once, the young Imager who had jeered at Master Eremis said loudly, 'I second Master Gilbur's proposal. We must call our champion to us.'

His words broke a dam: suddenly, the air was full of voices urging that the matter be put to a vote.

Still gripping himself hard, Master Barsonage waited until quiet was restored. Then he said stiffly, like a breaking board, 'Very well. This is madness, but it must be answered. I know my duty. You have heard the proposal. Shall it be accepted? What is the will of the Congery?'

Terisa counted the show of hands as rapidly as she could. Master Barsonage, Master Eremis, Master Quillon, and several others voted against the proposal.

They were in the minority. Master Gilbur had won.

The mediator snarled his disgust.

As if shocked by what it had just done, the Congery relapsed into silence. Imagers blinked at each other uncertainly. A grin of anticipation bared

Master Gilbur's teeth; but he savored his victory and said nothing. Nobody seemed to know what to do next.

Then Master Eremis rose to his feet. If anything, his manner was more nonchalant than ever; but Terisa saw in his face – especially in his eyes – a new excitement, a taste for the game he was playing.

'I am surprised,' he drawled. 'This *is* madness, as Master Barsonage has said. I will not challenge the vote, however. It is conceivable, I suppose, that my judgment may be in error.' He flashed a smile to which no one responded.

'Be that as it may,' he continued, 'you must next decide *when* to attempt this translation. Let me beg for a delay. Six days should suffice.'

Master Gilbur jerked up his head as though he had been poked in the ribs. Master Quillon watched Eremis like a small animal staring at a snake.

'A delay, Master Eremis?' asked Barsonage. 'Six days?' A quickness had come into his attention; his distress receded. 'If Master Gilbur has his way, we will begin the translation at once. Why should we delay?'

'Why should we not?' Master Gilbur retorted trenchantly. 'The peril thickens around us like quicksand. Thirty thousand Cadwals are poised against Perdon. The Alend Monarch alone knows what treachery he contemplates. We are attacked by Imagery of all kinds – and in all places, as if our enemy has no limitations of time and distance. In six days we may all be dead. But doubtless we will bow to the wisdom of our esteemed Eremis.'

'Master Gilbur' – once again, the insouciant Imager looked hugely and secretly amused – 'I advise you to watch your tongue. If you do not, I will watch it for you. In order to watch it well, I will remove it from your head.'

Gilbur replied with a bark of laughter.

'Master Barsonage,' Eremis went on smoothly, 'I do not make this request lightly. Here is my reason. Yesterday, after his audience with King Joyse, I spoke with the Perdon. We spoke at some length, and we agreed that Mordant's plight is dire, that the King's passivity is insufferable, and that some action must be taken in spite of him.

'Our own dilemma is severe, Masters,' he said to the circle, 'but consider the situation of the Cares. It is Perdon that will die first when Cadwal comes to war, Armigite that has always been the first victim of Alend's aspirations, Termigan and Fayle and Tor that will have their people decimated. Therefore the Perdon promised that he will summon all the lords of the Cares to Orison – with the exception of the Domne, of course, who is too great a friend of the King's – so that they can try to determine an answer to their common need. And so that they can try to forge an alliance with us.'

Terisa saw dismay on Master Quillon's face. On the other hand, the mediator listened with visibly increasing enthusiasm.

'They will meet during the night of the sixth day,' Master Eremis continued. 'I have been asked to confer with them, to speak for the Congery.'

'What? In *six days*? For messengers to ride out and the lords to reply?' an angry Master demanded. 'At this time of year?' A mutter of agreement rose around him. 'If the Armigite is sent for, he may possibly ride the distance in time. Batten is little more than forty miles distant. But the Fayle? The Tor?

That is madness. Under the best conditions, the Termigan has seldom made the journey to Orison in less than *ten* days.'

'Nevertheless,' Master Eremis replied, as suave as poison, 'the Perdon has promised it. Will you call him a liar?' Then he smiled. 'I do believe, however, that he had decided on this gathering – and had sent out his call – well before he spoke to me. I merely persuaded him to include us in his proposed alliance.'

At once, he resumed what he had been saying. 'Masters, I believe that we must not ignore this opportunity to find support for what we do. If we ally ourselves with the lords of the Cares, explaining to them what we propose for Mordant, we will not risk their opposition to our champion. And we will gain friendships across Mordant which may prove of great value in the coming strife.'

Terisa found herself gazing up at him as though her face shone. The boldness and possibilities of what he proposed took her breath away. He was trying to fight for Mordant in a way that made sense to her.

'Also,' Master Barsonage put in promptly, 'it may be that the lords will propose a defense which will make the calling of our champion unnecessary. And we will have six more days in which to be sure of what we do. Master Eremis, I congratulate your foresight and initiative. This is well done.'

'Is it?' demanded one of the younger Imagers. 'By what right does Master Eremis speak for us in front of the lords of the Cares?'

'As Master Barsonage has said,' Master Eremis said with a gleam in his eyes. 'By right of foresight and initiative.'

'But you oppose the calling of our champion,' another man protested. 'How can we be sure that this is not some ploy to undercut our decision? How can we know that you will advocate our knowledge and position fairly to the lords?'

'Masters,' Eremis answered in a tone of good-natured sarcasm, 'the lords will not agree to bare their hearts before the entire Congery. However we may look at the matter, we are the creation of King Joyse, and all men who fear his present *policy* fear us as well.'

'My question remains,' retorted the man who had just spoken. 'How can you be trusted to form an alliance for us, when you oppose what we mean to do?'

For a moment, Master Eremis looked around him – at Master Barsonage, at Master Quillon, whose eyes seemed to bulge with stifled distress, at the Imagers who challenged him. Then he shrugged. 'Very well. I will take one of you with me, to ensure that I deal rightly with your decisions. I will risk the ire of the lords.

'Master Gilbur, will you accompany me in this?'

Surprise echoed around the circle. Gilbur gaped. But he quickly nodded, murmuring, 'I will.'

Master Barsonage permitted himself a sigh of relief. 'Master Gilbur, I take that as a second. Masters, it has been proposed that we delay the translation of our champion for six days, until Master Eremis and Master Gilbur have spoken to the lords of the Cares. Shall it be accepted? What is your will?'

The vote was almost unanimous.

Terisa began breathing more easily, as if a threat had been averted. Six days. Anything could happen in six days.

But Master Eremis wasn't done. Still standing, he said, 'One matter more. The lords of the Cares will come to Orison openly, as befits their station. But they will meet in secret.'

The mediator nodded briskly. 'I understand you.' The postponement appeared to have restored his confidence, his command of the situation. 'Masters,' he said in an incisive voice, his jaw jutting, 'my lady Terisa of Morgan, no one must speak of this. No one. Whatever your private opinion of us, and of what we mean to do, you must not speak.' He addressed the circle generally, but his gaze was fixed on Terisa. 'The lords will not trust us if any word of this meeting precedes them. If King Joyse interferes, all hope of any alliance will be lost. We do what we do, not to aggrandize ourselves, but to save Mordant. We must not be betrayed.' Slowly, he moved until he was standing at the rail in front of her: his eyes held hers. 'My lady,' he said quietly, 'you must not speak of *anything* you have heard today.'

He gave her a wry smile. 'Geraden will question you, I do not doubt. If you become acquainted with her, you will find that the lady Elega is insatiably curious. Castellan Lebbick desires to know everything that takes place in Orison. Even King Joyse may bestir himself to take an interest in you.

'My lady, you must say nothing.'

She tried to meet his eyes, but they were too demanding. He was asking her to make a choice and stand by it – asking her to accept at least a small share of the responsibility for Master Eremis' success. A passive share, perhaps, but a choice nonetheless. Wasn't that what people who believed in themselves did? – made choices and stood by them?

She hesitated because she wasn't ready to promise that she wouldn't talk to Geraden.

Fortunately, Master Eremis came to her rescue. 'Master Barsonage,' he said kindly, 'I am certain that we can trust her.'

The mediator glanced at Eremis, frowning as if he disliked his thoughts – as if something in Eremis' words or tone suddenly raised a host of questions. A moment later, however, he shook his head and turned away.

'Masters,' he said distantly, 'are there other matters we must discuss here?'

No one said anything.

'Then let us have done. I think that we have cast enough votes that will shape Mordant's future for one day.'

Leaving the center of the circle, he passed between the pillars, unbolted a door, and walked out of the chamber.

Terisa looked for Master Quillon. He wasn't present. Apparently, he had already left.

Master Eremis took her arm and raised her to her feet. 'Come, my lady,' he said privately. 'This is only your third day among us, yet already I feel I have been waiting a long time to offer you my hospitality.'

She couldn't resist the way he pulled her arm through his and hugged her to his side. She sensed triumph from him, and anticipation, a secret, whetted enthusiasm. He was moving events too quickly. His confident vitality as he paraded her out of the chamber ahead of most of the Masters made her thoughts swirl.

When she was that close to him, his physical impact on her dominated everything else. He gave off a slight scent of perspiration and cloves, and she could feel muscle working over bone under his jet cloak. Where did his confidence come from, his power? And what did he see in her? Why did he go to such lengths to lay claim to her? She didn't understand him at all.

That made his hold on her stronger. His confidence was like a display of magic, enchanting because it was at once so attractive and so far beyond her experience.

As a result, she walked at his side as if his strength and her uncertainty were a kind of charm, entrancing her in ways she couldn't define.

He made her want something she didn't know how to name.

Still escorting her formally, he took her up out of the laborium and into the public passages of Orison. Once past the ballroom, however, he moved her in the opposite direction from the route to which she was growing accustomed – the route back to her rooms. As they walked, he explained that they were entering a section of the castle devoted to the personal quarters of the Masters – a section that King Joyse had had rebuilt when he first began to form the Congery, so that his Imagers would have fitting, perhaps even sumptuous, places to live, places that would show the respect in which their occupants were held. But she only paid attention to the sound of his voice, not to what he said. At once fascinated and alarmed, she concentrated on him physically as though his voice and his scent and the hard grasp of his arm were a spell that might solve the problem of her existence at last.

Leaving the ballroom behind, they began to pass more and more people. She saw a knowing leer in some of the greetings Master Eremis received from men of rank, a smile of congratulation or envy. Guards rolled their eyes at the ceiling; a few of them were bold enough to wink. Ladies and chambermaids studied her as if they were trying to grasp what made her desirable.

The sensation that she was enchanted and real caused her to feel unexpectedly bold. Undaunted by the way people looked at her, she said, 'That was a nice thing you tried to do for Geraden.'

'Do you think so, my lady?' She heard the grin in his tone. 'You are delightfully naive. A child's spirit in a woman's body.' With his free hand, he stroked her forearm; his touch seemed to leave trails of intensity on her skin. 'I doubt, however, that Quillon takes a similar view. Unless I am quite mistaken, he considers me cruel.'

His mention of Quillon sparked a quick protective reaction in her. There was little in herself or her circumstances of which she was sure; but she was sure that she didn't want to betray either Master Quillon or Adept Havelock. She felt Eremis probing on that point, and she replied immediately – perhaps too immediately – 'Quillon? Which one was he? I haven't been introduced to very many of the Masters.'

He responded with an easy laugh. 'No matter, my lady. I assure you that he is of no significance whatsoever.'

With a wave of his hand, he indicated that they had arrived at his quarters. They had just entered a short hall like a cul-de-sac, with a door or two on either side and one at the end. The stone of the walls was the same almost-smooth gray granite that appeared everywhere in Orison, but the door bore no resemblance to the dungeon doors of the laborium. It was of rosewood, polished to a high sheen so that the bas-relief carved into it was unmistakable: a full-length rendering of Master Eremis himself, complete with a sardonic smile and a look of extraordinary knowledge in his eyes – a look, Terisa realized a moment later, that was achieved by embedding subtle pieces of ivory in the wood.

'I hope you will always be able to find me, my lady,' he remarked. 'The doors of the Masters are marked with their characteristic signs and sigils. But Orison is large, and signs are easily confused. Anyone who knows me will always know which door is mine.'

Deftly, he unlatched the door and steered her into his chambers.

His use of the word *sumptuous* hadn't prepared her for the room she entered. After the relative starkness of the halls and stone outside, the opulence of the furnishings seemed exotic and exquisite. Both light and warmth were provided by perfumed oil fires cunningly hidden in brass shells as large as urns, their sides cut into delicate open filigree. The main piece of furniture was a huge divan swathed in satin and piled with pillows; and before it stood a long, low table, its engraved brass top suspended by chains from rosewood legs at each corner. But there were two or three armchairs in the room as well, each cloaked in satin to match the divan. An ornate washstand and basin, also of brass, filled one niche. Nearby was a wooden cabinet that held what appeared to be wine decanters. The floor was softened by several layers of rugs, the uppermost of which cast a solid sweep of crimson against the predominant blue of the furniture and the canary drapes that covered the windows. The fabric masking the ceiling was also canary; but the tapestries on the walls picked up all three colors, using crimson primarily to focus attention on what they depicted – scenes of women in various stages of seduction.

Grinning his welcome, Master Eremis released Terisa's arm and bolted the door. 'Joyse treats his Imagers well, as you see, my lady,' he commented. 'Mordant, however, is not natively wealthy. For centuries, the Cares produced nothing grander than wheat, grapes, and cattle – and farmers to tend them. Our King's wealth – like his power – is the result of war.' He glanced around him smugly. 'Doubtless some Cadwal noble previously had the use of these riches. That pleases me.'

He moved to the washstand to rinse his hands and sprinkle a few drops of water on his face. When he returned to her side, Terisa smelled a renewed scent of cloves. 'Be comfortable,' he said, gesturing toward the divan. 'Do you like wine?' His smile was fading, and there was an avid smolder in his eyes.

The tang of incense, and the smell of cloves, and the expression on his face shifted the balance of her excitement and alarm, made a sensation like panic rise in her throat. Groping for something to say, some way to gain time so that she could try to think, she blurted out, 'There was something I didn't understand about the mirrors. When Geraden was showing them to me.'

He frowned, perhaps at her mention of Geraden, perhaps at her uncertainty. To cover whatever vexation he felt, he went to the cabinet, took out two goblets, and filled them with a wine as crimson as the rug. Then he came back to her, placed one of the goblets in her hands, and drank from his. He was smiling again, and the urgency in his eyes had receded a bit, become more wary.

'Frankly, my lady,' he said, 'no one understands what you saw. No mirror, flat or otherwise, can change its Image. Since it is impossible, I would not have believed it if I had not seen it myself.

'Doubtless you noticed that we did not discuss that change in our debate today. There is nothing to be said about the impossible, now that it is gone. Most of the Masters did not believe me when I described what had happened. Especially' – he spoke in a musing tone – 'since I did not recognize the new Image and could not identify it.'

'Oh, Geraden recognizes it. It's called the Closed Fist. He says it's somewhere in the Care of Domne.' As soon as she said the words, she felt that she shouldn't have. She had a strange feeling that she had betrayed a secret – that she had betrayed Geraden. But Master Eremis' virile presence compelled her to speak. He bowed slightly over her, listening as though he were waiting for her to finish so that he could take hold of her. She needed time. At once, she explained, 'But that isn't what I meant.'

As if involuntarily, she told Master Eremis what she hadn't told Geraden. She told him what she had found in the glass that showed the champion: not violence, not her apartment, but the Closed Fist in springtime.

Her hasty admission interested him, although it didn't appear to interest him quite as much as she had hoped. His frown now was one of thoughtful consideration. 'That *is* strange,' he admitted. Slowly, he took her to the divan and seated her so that her side was warm against his, with his arm on the cushions behind her and his torso leaning toward her. 'Did Geraden have this experience also?'

She shook her head. 'He tried.' Her senses were full of incense, cloves, and baffled desire. 'He wanted to see if he could take me back where he found me. So that I would at least have the choice of leaving. But when he went into the glass, he was with your champion.'

'Indeed?' He cocked an eyebrow. 'Then it was for you that the translation went astray?'

She didn't want to think like that. 'Or Geraden does it for me. He probably doesn't even know he's doing it. He doesn't know he has the power.' She remembered the way he had left the meeting hall – the way he had spoken out for her; the authority of his first appeal to her. To herself, she murmured, 'They should have accepted him as a Master.'

'Then,' Master Eremis said firmly, 'it is well that this changing of Images was not publicly debated. Unable to believe such power of Geraden, the Masters would have concluded that you are the powerful Imager they both fear and want.

'But you are no Imager, as we both know. I will speak quietly to Masters who may be trusted, and we will attempt to explain the things you do not understand.'

While he spoke, his arm tightened around her; now his lips brushed her hair. 'Are you satisfied? I am ready to begin exploring the territory of your womanhood.'

She felt that she had no choice, that all choices were being swept away. Her body yearned against her clothes. She inhaled his warm breath as his mouth came down and covered hers firmly.

Then somebody knocked at the door.

The knocking was quiet at first, a few gentle taps. Master Eremis ignored it. His tongue stroked her lips, giving her a taste of kisses she had never experienced. But the knock became more insistent. Soon the person outside the door was hammering at the wood.

'Whelp of a dog!' Eremis jerked himself off the divan. Chewing curses under his breath, he strode to the door, unbolted it, and yanked it open.

Terisa saw Geraden standing in the doorway.

She was breathing harder than she should have been, and she could feel her face burning.

He didn't look at her – or at Eremis: he kept his gaze studiously fixed on a vacant spot between them. 'Master Eremis,' he said in a controlled tone, 'how may I serve you?'

'*Serve* me?' snapped the Master. 'Why do you imagine that I have any need of you at all? Go away.'

'I'm in your debt. For no apparent reason, you proposed me for the chasuble of a Master. I'm done with my other duties. I want to repay you somehow.'

'Very good. I accept your indebtedness. Repay me' – with a visible effort, Master Eremis refrained from shouting – 'by leaving me alone.'

At that, Geraden raised his eyes. Steadily, he said, 'The lady Terisa deserves better.'

Then he turned and walked away.

Master Eremis cursed again and started to slam the door. He caught it before it closed, however, shut it gently and restored the bolt. When he turned back to Terisa, there was a distant, peculiar smile on his face – a smile that might almost have been one of admiration. 'That boy is a challenge,' he murmured. He sounded like he was speaking to himself; but the glance he gave Terisa showed that he was aware of her. 'I must think of something truly special for him.'

A moment later, he shrugged the question away and looked at her more directly. The intensity came back into his eyes. He returned to the divan, drained his goblet, then seated himself close beside her again.

Without quite meaning to, she shifted a little away from him. By turning more to face him, she was able to raise her goblet like a barrier between them. Her cheeks still burned: for no clear reason, the sight of Geraden made her feel that she was doing something she should have been ashamed of. *The lady Terisa deserves better.* What did that mean? He knew too little about her to say something like that.

And yet the way he said it – *the lady Terisa deserves better* – touched her. It made her withdraw a bit from the Master leaning expectantly over her.

'That reminds me.' Her voice was soft, even tentative; but inwardly she seemed to be growing bolder all the time – so bold that she could hardly recognize herself. She actually met his avid gaze as she said, 'He told me you don't believe I exist. Remember? And you said you believed I didn't exist until I came out of the mirror. That's something else I don't understand.'

'In what way?' Eremis' tone expressed deliberate patience.

She tried to explain. 'I don't know anything about Imagery. I don't really understand anything about it. But I'm trying. It's easier for me to believe that a mirror is like a window. It lets you see from one place to another. Or from one world to another.' She hoped he couldn't see the way her heart was beating, the way her breath came unsteadily from her chest. She didn't want him to know how important this question was to her. 'It's much harder to believe that a piece of glass *creates* what you see in it.'

Please. Do you *really* think I didn't exist until you saw me for the first time?

'Ah.' He nodded in recognition. 'As you must know by now, my lady, that is the fundamental confusion which divides and weakens the Congery. And Joyse further muddies the issue by insisting upon "ethical" questions, such as, by what right do we translate Images out of their natural existence? But that is extraneous. The matter cannot be resolved until the essential point is known. Is a mirror a "window," as you call it, or are the Images seen in the glass brought into being by Imagery itself, by the act of making and shaping the mirror?'

As he spoke, he moved incrementally closer to her, leaned closer to her. His arm was around her again so that she couldn't retreat, and his spell renewed its power. She had never realized before that the delicate aroma of cloves was sensuous. She could no longer hold his gaze. Instead, she watched his mouth as if in spite of her uncertainty – not to mention her recent embarrassment – she wanted him to kiss her again.

'The true difficulty, however, is not a failure of understanding, but of imagination.' He took the goblet from her and put it aside. His voice became lower, huskier. 'The evidence of the truth is plain, but we do not accept it because, as you have observed, it is harder to credit.'

His mouth dipped to hers, kissed her lightly: once; again. The second time, she responded as if she knew what she was doing.

'My lady,' he breathed, 'it is plain that you did not exist before you were incarnated by translation. Glass is dumb. Mirrors depict Images. They do not transmit sounds. If you come to us from another world' – again, he kissed her – 'complete in its own existence' – and with each kiss her response improved – 'how is it possible that we speak the same language?

'Since Geraden created the glass that conceived you, I must admire his taste in women.'

This time, his mouth took hold of hers and didn't let go. His tongue parted her lips. She was leaning back among the cushions: his arm hugged her there, half reclining. For a moment, all her senses were concentrated on his kiss – and on learning how to kiss him herself. It was true: the mirror had created her. She was free. What she did no longer mattered. At first she didn't realize that he was unbuttoning her shirt. But his kiss was so potent – and his hand, so adept – that she felt no wish to stop him.

'Master Eremis,' a voice said, 'my lady Terisa, would you like something to eat?'

Eremis sprang to his feet, rage flaming in his eyes. Terisa pushed herself out of the cushions and looked up at Geraden.

This time, he had entered through a doorway which led to some of the inner rooms: he must have used a servants' entrance. Once again, his gaze was fixed away from both her and the Master. In his hands, he carried an ornate brass tray on which he had arranged a large wedge of cheese, some bread, and several bunches of grapes.

'While you discuss the fate of Mordant,' he commented in a voice so determinedly nonchalant that it sounded fierce, 'I thought you might like something to eat.' As he spoke, he moved forward into the room. 'It's been a long time since breakfast.'

'Excrement of a pig!' the Master snarled softly. His hands hooked into claws. 'This is insufferable! Must I bolt their doors on my own servants in order to keep you *out?*'

'I've already told you.' Geraden's deference was comparable to his nonchalance. 'I'm in your debt. I'm just trying to find some way to repay you.'

Though she fought to hide it, Terisa could hardly refrain from laughing. The Apt's second interruption wasn't embarrassing: it was absurd. And the butt of the absurdity was Master Eremis, who looked angry enough to tear Geraden's heart out for too small a cause. Standing ridiculously polite and out of place in the middle of Eremis' seduction room, Geraden reminded her why she liked him so much. She was barely able to keep her face straight.

As if sensing that he appeared foolish, Master Eremis pulled himself erect. 'Apt, I believe you,' he rasped, jabbing one finger like the point of a spear at Geraden's face. 'You seek to repay me. But *revenge* would be a better word, would it not? You blame me because the Congery laughed when I proposed you for the chasuble, and now you wish to "repay" me by driving me mad.

'Listen to me, boy.' He managed to look calmer as he spoke, despite the struggle between control and ferocity in his voice. 'I wish you to go away and leave me alone. I have been your friend, whatever you believe. But you will sacrifice my friendship if you continue to torment me. And you will not enjoy my enmity.'

If Geraden felt the force of this threat, he kept his reaction to himself. Without looking at Terisa, he asked – deferentially, nonchalantly – 'My lady, do you want to be left alone?'

As soon as he confronted her with his question, she found that she couldn't answer. She liked him. She wanted to give him a reply that pleased him: it would have made her feel good to please him. But her body had come so close to learning what its womanhood meant – to Master Eremis, at least, and perhaps thereby to herself. She was trembling inside, and her legs felt too weak to lift her off the divan. Her yearning hadn't gone away.

'Are you blind, Apt?' The Master was almost whispering. 'The *only* thing she wants is to be left alone.'

'Then' – for an instant, Geraden's control nearly cracked, and a spasm of pain leaped across his face – 'I must go.' His tone became formal in compensation. 'Please forgive this mad intrusion. I have misjudged.'

Master Eremis made a stiff gesture of dismissal. Geraden turned and left the room the same way he had come.

'Fool.' Eremis glared after the Apt. 'He believes that he is safe to play games with me. I do not play games.' Abruptly, he swung toward Terisa. 'My lady, be warned. I do not play games.'

She met his gaze until it seemed to make her tingle. If what she did no longer mattered, then why did she ache this way? Perhaps her yearning was stronger than she realized, and it was changing her. Or perhaps she felt an inchoate desire to defend Geraden. Whatever the reason, she amazed herself by saying, as if she were accustomed to comment on the behavior of the people around her, 'I can understand why he thinks you do.'

To her surprise, her remark caught his interest. His anger receded, and an inquiring look came into his face. It made him even more attractive than his intent desire. 'Do you, indeed? I am taken aback.' His tone was sardonic, but kindly. 'What have I done to convey such an impression?'

She made an effort to answer him accurately, in part because she enjoyed being free to say what she thought, in part because his question flattered her by conferring substance on her ideas. 'You don't show much respect for people when you talk about them in private, so when you act respectful in public you don't sound sincere. And you aren't consistent. You seem to do things' – her boldness was positively dizzying – 'like propose to make Geraden a Master, not because you believe in them, but because you like surprising people.'

His eyes widened humorously. 'Not consistent, my lady? *I?* You were not present when the Apt's role in the translation that brought you among us was debated. You have not heard how consistently I have always defended and supported him.' He took evident pleasure in questioning her. 'How am I not consistent?'

She considered the matter. This couldn't last: surely he was about to become angry at her. That was what happened whenever she called attention to herself. She didn't want to lose this moment. Trying to minimize the risk, she replied carefully, 'I was surprised when you chose Master Gilbur to go with you to that meeting with the Perdon. He doesn't seem to like you very much.'

That surprise came back in a rush when Eremis burst out laughing.

For a moment, he was too amused to speak. She had apparently touched a point on which he was exceptionally pleased with himself. Chortling loudly, he returned to the divan and sat down beside her again, sprawling back into the cushions and stretching his arms above his head.

When he was able to stop laughing, he drew himself erect, put his hands on her shoulders, and held her for a kiss. 'Ah, that was a fine jest, my lady,' he replied, enjoying her mystification, 'and the richest humor of it lies in its secrecy. I will wager that all the Congery was equally surprised.' Only the hint of calculation in his eyes, the way he seemed to gauge the consequences of what he did, prevented him from looking as unabashedly happy as Geraden sometimes did. 'None of those fools knows that Joyse was not the one who saved Gilbur's life when his cave collapsed. *I* was.'

While she gaped at him – while her thoughts reeled and her conception of everything that had taken place during the meeting of the Congery changed – he pulled her to him and captured her mouth again with his.

He stopped her breath in her chest. But as soon as his kiss eased she panted, 'Wait a minute. Wait. I don't understand.'

Placing kisses on her eyes, her forehead, the corners of her mouth, he eased her back into the cushions. 'What do you not understand?'

'You and Master Gilbur are working together.' Her chest heaved. 'You planned that whole meeting.' You were play-acting all the time. 'Why did you pretend to be enemies?'

'Because, my precious' – his tongue licked at her lips between phrases – 'some of those dunderheaded Imagers truly do not like me. Ideas and hopes are frequently rejected simply because I am the one who presents them.' His warm breath seemed to fill her lungs. 'The truth would have turned them against Gilbur as well.' She felt his hand once more on the buttons of her shirt. 'The lie that he was saved by King Joyse gave him credibility, so that he was able to swing the vote.'

Reclining against the pillows and his arm as though she were helpless, she still asked, 'But why? Why do you want that champion? He's dangerous.'

Master Eremis withdrew enough to let her meet his gaze. His expression was serious, and he spoke candidly. 'Arms and war are dangerous. Power is dangerous. But nothing else can save us.

'You do not know the Perdon. You have seen his rage, however. He loves his people. He is proud of Mordant – and of his place in the realm. And yet his King has refused him aid. Impelled by desperation, he will go to any extreme to defend what he loves.'

She thought she heard a knock at the door. For an instant, Master Eremis stiffened. But the sound was tentative, and it wasn't repeated.

'I will also,' he went on. 'I sneer at my fellow Masters, but that is only because a talent for Imagery is not a guarantee of intelligence or courage. I love the potential the Congery represents. I would gladly do battle in its defense. And I, too, have been refused. My King denies me his aid.

'I will not hesitate at a lie or two in order to gain the strength I need.'

She wasn't sure of what she saw in his eyes or heard in his voice. His manipulation of the Congery was too easy; his explanation for his lies was too tidy. But his nearness and his strong touch took hold of her. His scent of cloves and his kisses were more persuasive than logic.

Her lips answered his as well as they knew how. Slipping under her shirt, his hand cupped her breast. His caress made her nipples ache. Instinctively, she arched her back, pressing her breasts closer to him. He pushed her shirt aside, and they were bared. Then his mouth left hers, and he breathed thickly, 'My lady, I was not wrong. You are made for a man's delight,' and his tongue reached out to her breast until his lips closed over the nipple.

Willing to risk almost anything now, she put her arms around his head and held it where it was so that he wouldn't stop what he was doing.

She was so amazed that she did nothing but stare when Saddith walked into the room.

Like Geraden, the maid studiously didn't look at Master Eremis or Terisa. She held her face slightly averted, and her expression was perfectly bland.

'Master Eremis—' she began.

He bounded off the divan violently, his arm cocked as if he were expecting Geraden and intended to hit first and ask questions later.

'Master Eremis,' she repeated, flinching, speaking quickly to ward off his outrage, 'this intrusion is inexcusable, I know, but you must forgive me. I had no choice. You did not answer the door. My lady, you must forgive me. I have no choice.'

'No *choice*?' As soon as he recognized Saddith, he lowered his arm. Nevertheless he needed a moment to control his anger. 'You are a servant. Why is it a matter of *choice* for you to enter my rooms unbidden?'

'Forgive me. I know that what I have done is inexcusable.' Because Saddith's face was so bland, and her tone was so neutral, she didn't sound particularly contrite. 'But I have been commanded to fetch the lady Terisa. The lady Myste wishes to speak with her. She is the King's daugher, Master Eremis. I could not refuse to obey her. You have the power to insult me – perhaps even to hurt me.' She also didn't sound particularly fearful. 'But if the lady Myste complains of me to Castellan Lebbick—'

Eremis interrupted her. 'You could have told Myste that you were unable to find the lady.' He had already regained his self-possession, however. He sighed. 'But that may have been too much to expect of you.' He turned to Terisa. 'My lady, you must go. Kings' daughters are capricious – and our King lets his do what they will. It is not safe to ignore them.'

Only his eyes betrayed him. They had gone dark and murderous.

Terisa wanted to wail in frustration – and also in unexpected fright. His ferocity was suddenly as vivid as her father's. She felt giddy, almost wild, close to tears – or laughter. Her relief was as acute as her sense of loss, her alarm.

Because she had no idea what else to do, she mutely began buttoning her shirt.

TEN

THE LAST
ALEND AMBASSADOR

Still trembling weakly, full of confusion and trying not to show it, Terisa left with Saddith.

Master Eremis unbolted the door and bowed her out of his rooms. As he did so, his smile displayed a familiar blend of amusement and concupiscence: he might have been proof against his recent vexations. If she hadn't seen his eyes, she wouldn't have been scared.

She breathed an instinctive sigh of relief when the door closed because it had been Saddith, not Geraden, who had interrupted the Master the third time. She didn't like to think of so much anger aimed at the Apt.

For her part, Saddith appeared untroubled by Eremis' ire. Instead of betraying any kind of embarrassment or concern, her expression suggested a barely concealed satisfaction.

Terisa wanted to ask, Why does the lady Myste want to see me? More than that, she wanted to ask, How did you manage to come for me at just that moment? But as soon as she and Saddith left the cul-de-sac of Master Eremis' quarters, Geraden accosted them.

He made no effort to restrain himself. He was gamboling like a puppy.

'Saddith, you're a wonder!' Grabbing her by the arms, he danced her in a circle until he stumbled against the wall and almost knocked her to the floor; then he planted a loud kiss on her cheek and released her. 'I'm in your debt. Forever! How did you *do* it?'

Without waiting for an answer, he turned, practically prancing, toward Terisa.

She kept on walking.

She couldn't tell what he saw in her face, but whatever it was, it sobered him rapidly. For once, however, he didn't apologize. 'I know it was none of my business.' He controlled his glee for her sake. 'I just had the strongest feeling—' He gave her a wry grimace. 'We've talked about my feelings.' I told you they're always wrong. But I have to do what they tell me anyway. I can't ignore them. I just can't. And this time I had the strongest feeling you were in some kind of danger.'

'Danger, indeed,' Saddith replied derisively. 'You mistake those "feelings,"
Apt. You had the strongest "feeling" that you wish to bed the lady yourself,
and you could not bear to think that any man would do so before you.
Perhaps also,' she added with a leer, 'you feared that once she had tasted
Master Eremis' lovemaking she would have no interest in yours.'

At Saddith's words, Geraden's eyes filled up with chagrin, and he began to
blush like a little boy.

Suddenly, Terisa's trembling got worse. She had come so close – so close
to something she couldn't name, some vital awareness of who or what she
was. Master Eremis had told her that she didn't exist. And yet his touch – She
was shaking all over. Her voice shook. 'Do you mean to tell me Myste doesn't
want to see me? You made that up?'

The Apt winced, but it was Saddith who said, 'Certainly *not*,' in a tone of
humorous indignation. 'I am not a liar, my lady.' With evident difficulty, she
suppressed a desire to laugh. 'The lady Myste has most assuredly asked to
speak with you. I spent some considerable time searching for you before I
encountered Apt Geraden and he told me where you were.'

Reassured by this support, Geraden admitted, 'But it *is* true that Myste
isn't the kind of lady who would insist on seeing you right away.'

Saddith nodded. 'I believe she truly does not know what it means to be the
daughter of a king.'

'If she had known where you were,' Geraden continued, with some of his
personal happiness bubbling up past his self-command, 'I'm sure she would
have insisted on waiting until Master Eremis was done with you.'

'Nevertheless,' concluded the maid, 'I made him believe it. In future, he
will be wise to be more careful about his designs.'

Geraden couldn't help himself: he threw back his head and laughed.

Saddith joined him.

In their distinct ways, they both sounded so pleased that the tension which
made Terisa tremble loosened itself involuntarily. She wanted to laugh as
well. 'He got so angry.' At the moment, she felt it would have done her a
world of good to laugh. 'Maybe he isn't used to frustration. He looked pretty
silly.'

The thought of Master Eremis looking *silly* started Geraden and Saddith
again.

Paying no attention to where they were going, they nearly ran into Master
Quillon.

Because of his self-effacing gray robe and unassertive demeanor, he
seemed to appear in front of them out of nowhere. His smile didn't close over
his protruding teeth. 'Ah, there you are, Apt,' he said at once. 'Come with
me. I have need of you.'

Terisa felt that his tone boded ill for Geraden.

'Master Quillon—' Geraden was nonplussed. 'I've finished my duties. I
wanted to spend the afternoon—'

'Precisely,' the Imager cut in. 'You wanted to spend the afternoon helping
me. I am determined to finish my researches before Master Gilbur summons
his champion and we are all required to put aside our personal concerns for
the sake of the war which will ensue. Come.'

158

Abruptly, he turned and started down the hall.

'Master Quillon!' Geraden protested. 'It's customary to let Apts do what they want with their time when they've finished their duties.'

The Master paused. The way he bared his teeth gave him an air of lugubrious savagery. His eyes glittered coldly. 'For shame, Geraden,' he said, speaking more mildly. 'Sloth does not make a Master. Work does. How will you ever learn, if you are unwilling to make an effort?' Then his face tightened. 'This is not a request, Apt. Come with me.'

Walking briskly, he moved away.

Geraden cast a look of appeal and apology at Terisa.

'Go, Geraden,' whispered Saddith. 'Do not be a fool. What will become of your wish to be a Master? You hurt no one but yourself by disobeying.'

The Apt grimaced, nodded, threw up his hands, and trotted after Master Quillon.

Saddith laughed again, this time at Geraden, but her mirth was not unkind. 'He is a good boy, my lady, with many attractive qualities.' She grinned. 'Even his awkwardness might prove piquant. But in your place I would not trouble with him. You can aim higher.

'If you are already able to interest Master Eremis' – now she was serious, perhaps even a trifle vexed – 'making no more effort than you do, you can most certainly aim higher. As an example, consider Castellan Lebbick. You will hardly believe it, having tasted a little of his tongue – and his temper – but he is uxorious to a fault. And now his wife of many years has died, after a protracted illness. *There* is a man in grave need of a woman. If I could attract his notice, I can assure you I would not remain a servant in Orison much longer.'

'Saddith, what should I do?' Terisa asked on impulse. Now that Geraden was gone, she felt an urgent need to talk to him. Despite Master Barsonage's instructions, she wanted to tell Geraden everything. And she wanted to know how he would answer Master Eremis' reasoning. But she couldn't discuss any of those things with the maid. 'I'm not an Imager. I don't know anything about men.' Then, remembering Eremis' hands – and his mouth – she added, 'Master Eremis and Geraden hate each other.'

'My lady,' replied Saddith, trying to speak lightly, 'I would make certain that Master Eremis does not come to hate *me*.'

An open window somewhere let a draft of cold into the corridor. Terisa shivered. Saddith was silent along the way to their destination.

Terisa expected the maid to take her to the suite the lady Myste shared with her sister, in the tower above King Joyse's rooms, but Saddith led Terisa back to her own quarters. Myste was waiting there.

Saddith exchanged her customary badinage with the guards, then opened the door and ushered Terisa inside. They found the lady Myste standing in front of one of the windows. Despite the chill outside, sunshine emphasized the summer tone of her hair and skin, making her more obviously beautiful than she had been in her own rooms, in Elega's company. Nevertheless she gazed out over the castle and the desolate winter as though she longed to be anywhere except where she was.

Her face retained its faraway expression, but she left the window and smiled when Terisa entered the room. 'My lady,' she began, then corrected herself, 'Terisa, it is good of you to come so promptly.' She hadn't lost the strange excitement with which she had greeted the idea that Terisa was far from being an Imager or a woman of power, was in fact nothing more than a mission secretary. 'I hope I have not called you away from anything you would rather do. I fear I have nothing urgent in mind. For Elega everything is urgent, but I want nothing more than a little quiet talk.'

This greeting took Terisa aback. She felt instinctively that Myste was one of the few people here who didn't have some kind of outlandish or even lethal expectations of her – one of the few with whom it might be possible to have a simple friendship. But for that precise reason she wasn't sure how to respond. She knew so little about friendship.

Fortunately, Saddith came to her rescue. Dropping a curtsy, she lied, 'The lady Terisa was already returning here when I found her, my lady. She had attended a meeting of the Congery, but it was ended.

'And it is well past time for a meal,' she went on. 'Shall I bring you something to eat? You will be able to talk at your leisure.'

For a moment, Terisa expected Myste to answer Saddith. Myste was the King's daughter. But then she realized that these were *her* rooms: hospitality was her responsibility.

'Please,' she said quickly. 'I'm hungry.' Hurrying to recover her manners, she asked Myste, 'Are you? I don't know what Saddith can bring us, but I'm sure it won't take long.'

The lady continued to smile. Her gaze was direct – and distant, as if it passed straight through Terisa's eyes and mind to something beyond. 'Thank you. You are kind.'

'Very well, my lady,' said the maid. 'I will return shortly.' On her way to the door, she turned so that her back was to Myste and gave Terisa a sharp look – a look that seemed to say, *Wake up. Pay attention. This woman is the King's daughter.* Then she left, closing the door quietly behind her.

From Terisa's point of view, however, the fact that Myste was the King's daughter really made no difference. What mattered was that she, Terisa, suddenly wanted Myste's friendship so strongly that the desire made her ache. She had never had a *friend—*

Oh, of course, she had had friends: playmates in her early years; girls who spoke to her in the halls and whispered gossip during school. But from the first her parents had never encouraged friendships. In particular, they had never allowed her to visit the homes of her young playmates, had never invited any of those girls to their home. And this separation had carried on into the numerous private institutions to which she had been sent, exclusive schools dedicated more to forming moral character than to nurturing comradeship. Or perhaps the distance that kept everyone away was something she had carried in herself – a gulf of passivity and doubt that no one knew how to cross; an unhealed wound.

She didn't want to lose this opportunity.

Awkwardly, she gestured toward two of the chairs. 'Would you like to sit down?' Then she remembered the decanter on one of the side tables. 'Would you like some wine?' But she sounded so disconcerted to herself that she couldn't endure it. 'I'm sorry,' she said, abandoning the pretense that she knew what she was doing. 'I'm making a mess of everything. I'm so new at all this. I don't think I've ever had a guest in my apartment.'

Myste had no way of knowing that this was the literal truth, but she accepted it anyway. 'Please do not apologize. I think you do amazingly well. Consider what has happened to you in the past three days. You have been taken to a strange and alien world. You have been put down in the middle of a castle full of conflict, machination, and treachery. Half the people around you seem to believe that you can save them from war and chaos. An attempt has been made on your life. If I were in your place' – her tone became wistful – 'I would be proud to manage half as well.'

Without warning, Terisa's eyes filled with tears. Myste's understanding took her completely by surprise. 'Thanks.' Gratefully, she tried to explain. 'Most of the time, I think I must be losing my mind. Everybody wants me to do something, and I barely understand what's going on.'

'Here.' Myste took Terisa's arm and guided her to one of the chairs. Then the lady produced a delicate handkerchief from the sleeve of her gown and handed it to Terisa. 'It is a lonely thing which has happened to you. You must think that everyone you meet plots against you in some way. And now you have been taken to a meeting of the Congery. I doubt they reacted well when you told them you are not an Imager.'

Terisa nodded, wiping her eyes with the handkerchief. 'They're all doing it. The Congery doesn't want me to talk to the King. He doesn't want me to talk to the Congery. None of them want me to talk to anybody else.' She almost said, Except Master Quillon and Adept Havelock. 'And the Masters are all scheming against each other. Master Eremis—' He kissed me. He kissed my breasts. 'Castellan Lebbick yells at me.' She hesitated for a second, then blew her nose on the fine fabric. 'Even Geraden wants to turn me into an Imager.'

'Ah, Geraden.' Myste's voice suggested a smile. 'I cannot speak for the others, but him, at least, you can trust. You may doubt his judgment. His luck is disastrous. Nevertheless you can trust his heart. It is agreed everywhere that the Domne has no bad sons.'

After a pause, she added, 'I would like to be your friend, Terisa.'

Terisa met the lady's eyes. They were focused on her now, not distant at all, and the expression in them was direct and kind.

So that she wouldn't start crying again, Terisa looked away. Myste's offer touched her too deeply to be acknowledged. How was it possible for someone like her to have friends? Evading the important point – and hating herself for doing so – she said, 'You have a better opinion of him than Elega does.'

Myste smiled again; but as she did so her gaze slipped back into the distance, and her face resumed its faraway cast. Quietly, she replied, 'I have a better opinion of many things than she does. She is a king's daughter, and she desires the importance of a high place in the affairs of Mordant. She does not forgive her father – or the society around her – or anything else which she imagines stands between her and her natural right to plot and manipulate and betray as much as any prince. She does not forgive Geraden for the mistaken judgment which once betrothed him to her.' Then she shrugged. 'I think better of being a woman. I think better of those who hold power in Orison.' Her tone was gentle and reassuring, but soft, as if she were speaking in another place, perhaps to someone else; and there was a note of yearning in what she said that didn't entirely agree with her words. 'I think better of myself.'

Terisa nodded as though she understood. 'Was that what you wanted to talk to me about?'

'Oh, no,' Myste replied easily. 'Or perhaps it was. I have nothing special to say. But I would like to know everything about you. You are a pleasure and a wonderment to me. You consider yourself an ordinary woman – and I believe you,' she hastened to add, 'I believe what you say of yourself, though it is difficult for me to call any woman from another world ordinary – and yet you find yourself here, in the great crisis of Mordant's history. If your world has no Imagery, such a translation must seem extraordinary.

'For my part, great things have never happened to me. I have never been to a world other than my own. Indeed, I have hardly been out of Orison in the past few years. What is your world like? How did you live your life there?' She became more animated as she spoke, bright with curiosity. 'How does it feel, to step through a glass and find everything changed? What do mirrors do in your world, since they have no magic?'

'Please. One thing at a time.' In spite of herself, Terisa smiled at Myste's fascination. 'We don't have anything magic. Mirrors just' – she groped for an adequate description – 'just reflect. They show you exactly what you put in front of them. If they're flat. If they aren't flat, they still reflect what you put in front of them, but they distort it.

'In my apartment—' There she faltered. She had never admitted to anyone, I had my walls covered with mirrors so that I would know I existed. Lamely, she finished, 'I had a lot of mirrors.'

'Then you must be very wise,' murmured Myste as if she were clinging to every word.

'Wise? Why?'

'You are able to see yourself exactly as you are. You are able to see everything exactly as it is. I have no such vision. And those who look at me do so with their preconceptions of a king's daughter – perhaps even of a woman – and so their vision is confused. None of us see anything exactly as it is.'

'We do the same thing,' objected Terisa. 'We have the same preconceptions. But we only look at the surface. All we care about is the surface.' She made a deliberate effort to be candid. 'Maybe I've been able to see what I look like. But I don't know what that means. It doesn't help me know who I am.'

Myste seemed to find this notion both humorous and appealing. 'Then you are not wise?'

Slowly, Terisa replied, 'I don't think I've ever known anybody who was wise.' Unless Reverend Thatcher's ineffectual dedication counted as wisdom.

At that, the lady laughed. 'Then you are surely mistaken, Terisa. You yourself are already the wisest woman in Orison, for you have not been misled by those who believe in their own wisdom. You know the difference between what is seen and what is unseen, and you do not attempt to judge the one by the other.'

'Do you call that wisdom?' Terisa wanted to laugh simply because Myste was amused. The lady's mirth betrayed her kinship to her father: her smile was almost as infectious and likable as his. 'Doesn't the fact that I don't understand *anything* count against me?'

Myste went on laughing. 'Of course not. Mere understanding is the business of kings, not of sages – or of ordinary women. And it is always mistaken. It depends upon a knowledge of things which cannot be known – a knowledge of what is unseen.

'I must tell you, Terisa, I wish that Elega had less understanding and more wisdom. You are wiser than she.'

They were silent for a moment while they relapsed to seriousness; then Myste asked, 'Where does such wisdom come from? Tell me about your world. What are its needs and compulsions? How do you spend your days?'

A few minutes earlier, that question would have frozen Terisa. But Myste's friendly manner defused the frank pressure of her curiosity. Almost before she knew what she was going to say, Terisa began talking about her work in the mission.

She had never discussed it before. Words seemed to tumble headlong after each other as she described the mission's work, the human wrecks and relicts it served, the facilities, the surroundings; and her own job, her typing and filing and drudgery, her relationship with Reverend Thatcher; and her reasons for doing the work, because she had believed that in a place like that even she would be able to make a difference, because she could afford to accept the meager pay, because she hadn't considered herself capable of anything more demanding or ambitious. She babbled about it all until the discrepancy between what she was saying and the sparkle of Myste's attention stopped her. The lady absorbed every sentence as if she were hearing a tale of heroism and romance. Abruptly, Terisa said, 'I'm sorry. I didn't mean to go on like that.'

'It is a wonderment,' sighed the lady. A gleam still shone in her faraway gaze. 'Forgive me if I repeat myself. But that such a strange world exists! And you have a part in it.'

'A little part,' Terisa commented, 'and getting less by the minute. Reverend Thatcher must have replaced me by now.' And her father had no reason to want her back.

In her excitement, Myste rose to her feet. 'But that is just the point.' She began to pace the rug, her eyes searching everything except her companion. 'You are an ordinary woman, and you say that your life in your world was utterly ordinary, however brave and self-sacrificing it may appear to me. I, too, am an ordinary woman.

'I am a king's daughter – but what of that? It is an accident of birth. Its effect upon what is seen is merely that I am able to dress well and command servants. Its effect upon what is unseen is – I hardly know whether it has any effect. It seems plain to me that I am an ordinary woman – and that this is good.

'Yet I am surrounded by people who are not content. Her lack of involvement makes Elega savage. Geraden causes himself misery striving for a Mastery he will never attain. Half the Congery wishes to retreat into pure research. The other Masters yearn for power over Mordant. Castellan Lebbick's life has revolved around a woman, and yet in his grief he despises all women. Alend and Cadwal struggle against the peace which has done them more benefit than all their generations of warfare.

'Terisa, I do not consider my father's passivity a good thing. I do not *understand* it. I am his daughter enough to know the importance of striving and risk. Passivity is not content. But surely we must acknowledge that it is not a terrible thing to be who we are.

'You are the proof of this.' Her voice had risen to a pitch of affirmation. 'By your own insistence, you are an ordinary woman, with no experience of power, and no talent for it. Yet your life is not meaningless. Great forces are at work in Mordant, and you are involved in them. There is no life which does not possess its own importance, no life which may not be touched by greatness at any time – yes, be touched by greatness and have a hand in it.'

For a moment, Terisa stared at Myste. With an urgency which surprised her, she wanted to say, *Greatness?* That's ridiculous. How could I have anything to do with *greatness?*

At the same time, she wanted to weep harder than she had ever cried in her life.

Fortunately, Myste realized almost at once what she was doing. Puncturing her own seriousness, she smiled; her manner relapsed to its more usual diffidence. 'In her heart,' she said with a verbal shrug, 'Elega considers me mad. She thinks that such romantic notions render me unfit for my own life.' A note of sadness entered her voice. 'But my father did not despise what I believe. He loved me for it, and it was a bond between us.' Her face hardened. 'Until he changed, and it became impossible for any of us to speak with him.'

Terisa was holding her breath, clamping herself rigid to restrain what she felt. But that wasn't necessary anymore, was it? She was free, wasn't she? The past didn't exist. What she said or did didn't matter. She could tell Myste the truth. By degrees, she released the air from her lungs.

'My father didn't change. He's always been like that.'

'Do you mean passive?' asked Myste. 'Lost and uncaring?'

'No. I mean impossible to talk to.'

Tentatively, like a small animal coming out of a burrow after a storm, she began to smile. She had just spoken critically of her father, as if she had the right to do so – and nothing terrible had happened. Maybe friendship was possible after all.

Myste sat down beside her again. The lady's expression was soft and reassuring. 'Tell me about him.'

By chance, Saddith found that moment to knock on the door and come into the room, carrying trays of food.

Unable to sustain the way she felt in front of the maid, Terisa stood up at once – more abruptly than she intended – to thank Saddith and help her set out the meal.

If Myste was taken aback by the shift in Terisa's manner, she didn't show it. Apparently, she recognized that something important had happened – something that required privacy. She didn't pursue the conversation. When Saddith had served the food and left again, Myste made a polite show of enjoying her meal, and while she ate she kept her curiosity still.

Grateful for Myste's consideration, Terisa spent a few minutes concentrating on her food – a stew baked in a thick pastry shell. Then, to keep the conversation safe for a while, she asked a practical question in which her mission work had taught her to be interested: How did Orison manage to feed so many people so well in the dead of winter?

Myste replied by describing the system that provided Orison with all its food and supplies. After generations, even centuries, of an economic system based on warfare, in which powerful lords fought for the privilege of taking what they needed by violence, Mordant had been reduced almost to destitution, despite its abundance of natural resources. One of King Joyse's most important acts had been to replace war with trade. Essentially, he had established Orison as the principal buyer – and seller – of everything Mordant needed or produced. All the villages of the Demesne, and all the Cares of Mordant, traded with Orison; and Orison used its profits from these transactions to buy what its own people needed, so that its wealth acted as fertilizer to grow more wealth for the kingdom. A similar system applied to trade with Cadwal and Alend – which needed the resources of Mordant too badly to refuse to barter with King Joyse – and those profits were likewise plowed back into the soil and society of Mordant. As a result, all the Cares had come a long way from the fierce poverty that had marked the beginning of King Joyse's reign.

Terisa didn't entirely absorb the details, but she appreciated Myste's explanation nonetheless. She had criticized her father without being punished. When the lady was done, Terisa commented, 'This sounds silly – but I've just realized that I haven't been outside since I got here.' She glanced toward the window, with its thick glass and its tracery of frost. 'I don't have any idea what's out there.'

Myste put down her fork and dabbed at her mouth with her napkin. 'It must be quite a shock for you. As strange as your world seems to me, ours must appear equally strange to you. And we have been so strictly instructed' – she betrayed a moment of embarrassment – 'not to reveal our "secrets" to you. Your ability to accept such things – Well, I have already said that you amaze me.

'How does it feel, Terisa? I have no experience with translation.' There was a rapt undertone in her voice. 'I have never stepped through glass into a different creation. It is another of my romantic notions,' she admitted, 'that such an event in anyone's life must be fundamental in some way, changing them as much as it changes where they are.'

'No,' Terisa said at once, remembering a sensation of impersonal vastness, of temporary eternity, of fading, 'I don't think it changed me at all.' She almost added, I wish it had. 'It didn't last long enough.

'It was like,' she went on, suddenly sure of what she meant, 'dying without any pain. All at once, your whole life is gone, faded, everything you ever knew or understood or cared about, you don't exist anymore, and there's nothing you can do about it except maybe grieve. But it doesn't hurt.

'I'm not talking about physical pain,' she explained, 'or even emotional pain. It just doesn't hurt. Maybe because there's a whole world around you to take the place of the one you've lost. Do you understand? I think that's the only reason I can bear it.'

In response, Myste smiled vaguely – not as if she weren't listening, but rather as if what she heard triggered a wide range of ideas and yearnings. 'I do not really understand. Elega would say that you are talking nonsense. Translation is a physical passage, nothing more. But there is something in what you say' – her hand closed unconsciously into a fist – 'something that is not nonsense to me.

'Perhaps it is only death which gives life meaning.'

But I didn't die, Terisa protested instinctively. That isn't what I meant. I was never there.

The impossibility of explaining herself any better, however, kept her silent.

'Terisa,' Myste went on, quietly, distantly, without looking at her, 'you have given me a great deal to consider. You say that you are not wise' – slowly, she became less abstracted, more present in the room and in Terisa's company – 'but I have met very few fools who challenge me to examine my life so closely.'

'Don't blame *me*.' Terisa didn't know what Myste meant – and at the moment didn't care. She couldn't suppress a grin. 'I didn't do it on purpose.'

At that, Myste started laughing. Happily, Terisa joined her.

They were still chuckling together like old friends when Saddith knocked on the door and reentered the room. She was red-cheeked and panting, as if she had run up several flights of stairs. 'My lady Terisa,' she said breathlessly, 'my lady Myste, the King summons you.

'There is news. Important matters are afoot. Your presence is commanded in the hall of audiences. All the high lords and ladies of Orison must attend.'

'That is news indeed, Saddith,' replied Myste. Her immediate excitement made itself clear in the way her eyes focused on the maid. 'My father has not summoned Orison to the audience hall in more than a year. What occasions this gathering?'

'An ambassador has come, my lady,' Saddith answered through her panting. 'An Alend ambassador – in the dead of winter! He must have paid an awful price in time and men and supplies. And they say it is Prince Kragen himself! What could possibly compel the son of the Alend Monarch here, through such hardship at this time of year, and across so much distance, when all Mordant knows that Alend desires war, not peace?'

Myste dismissed that question. 'And he asks an audience with King Joyse?'

'Asks, my lady? He *demands*. Or so it is said.'

'And the King consents to grant what the Prince demands,' Myste continued. 'That is well. Perhaps it is very well. Perhaps the affairs of the realm begin to interest him again.

'Terisa, we must go.' She was already moving toward the door. 'This must not be missed.'

Because of the background Master Quillon had given her, Terisa caught some of the importance of Saddith's news. She followed without hesitation.

Perhaps this was what being free meant. She could criticize her father and follow her friend and even share in her friend's excitement without having to worry about the consequences.

When they had descended into the body of Orison, Myste turned in a direction new to Terisa. This part of the castle was more open than many of the other halls: the ceiling was higher; the walls, farther apart; the floor, worn smooth by generations of feet. Windows between the arched supports of the ceiling shed winter sunlight on large, colorful pennons fixed so that they jutted out from the stone; under the banners guards stood at attention, their pikes braced by their feet. As a result, the place seemed more formal, less inhabited, than the rest of Orison.

A number of men and women, however, were headed in the same direction as Myste and Terisa. Some were clearly officers of the guard; others wore the rich attire of high rank. Almost everyone saluted or greeted the lady Myste in some respectful or friendly way. She replied with faraway politeness: like her eyes, her attention was aimed ahead. Quite a few people, on the other hand, stared openly at Terisa. What she was wearing made her stand out in the crowd as badly as if she were naked.

Self-conscious now, she looked around and noticed that Saddith was no longer with her. Apparently, the servants of the castle hadn't been commanded to attend the Alend ambassador's audience. She regretted that: she could have used Saddith's worldly advice and support.

The stream of people approached a set of peaked doors, perhaps a dozen feet tall, opening out of the formal corridor. When she and Myste passed between them, Terisa found herself in what was unmistakably the hall of audiences.

It had the look and size of a cathedral. The stone walls were hidden by carved wooden screens, panel after panel around the room, each of them depicting characters and scenes Terisa couldn't identify; and the screens rose into elaborate spikes and finials reaching twenty or thirty feet toward the vaulted ceiling. The deep brown of the wood had the effect of making the hall dark, but it also seemed to distance the ceiling and fill the very air of the chamber with an impression of authority. The light came from two narrow windows up near the ceiling at the end of the hall, from rows of candles set around the walls and in tall holders here and there, and from batteries of cresseted oil lamps in the corners. The spiced oil of the lamps gave the air a sandalwood tang.

Down at the far end, opposite the doors, stood a structure that could only be King Joyse's seat: an ornate mahogany throne on a wooden pediment four or five steps high, dominating the space before it. A large part of the floor before the throne was clear, except for a wide, thick strip of rich carpet which led from the doors to the first step of the throne; but this open space was closed on three sides by benches like pews, in which the people entering the hall seated themselves.

They all stopped talking as soon as they passed through the high doors. The atmosphere of the hall seemed to silence them.

When she looked about her, however, Terisa saw that the hall of audiences hadn't been designed entirely to inspire respect. Above the screens on all four sides of the hall ran a balcony; the guards stationed there were archers rather than pikemen.

Those were the only guards in the hall, except for two at the doors and two more on either side of King Joyse's seat. But they were enough to make Terisa crane her neck as Myste guided her forward and wonder how many assassinations had taken place in Orison before King Joyse or his ancestors had conceived this protective arrangement. It was a convincing defense. As long as the guards remained loyal to their King, he probably had nothing to fear from anyone he met in the audience hall.

Following the lady Myste, Terisa bypassed the benches ranked on three sides of the open space and moved toward the King's seat. On each side of the pediment, a row of chairs reached toward the benches – special places for those who wielded the King's power or had the King's favor.

To the right of the throne, the nearest chair was already occupied by Castellan Lebbick. His perpetual glare and the purple band knotted around his short gray-stained hair made him look like a fanatic.

Fortunately, Terisa wasn't expected to sit near him. The first seats were taken by officers under his command; most of the rest had been filled by Masters, among them Gilbur, Barsonage, and Quillon. (Quillon? Why wasn't he working with Geraden?) Myste led Terisa to the left of the throne, where they joined the lady Elega and several men, most of them old, who resembled counselors more than courtiers. Myste introduced them by such titles as 'Lord of Commerce' and 'Lord of the Privy Purse.' They gaped at Terisa as if she had just arrived from the moon.

Elega showed more enthusiasm. 'I am glad you are here,' she whispered, drawing Terisa into a seat beside her. 'I feared that you would be found too late – or that Myste might not consider a call to audience worth obeying.' She spoke as though she meant no insult, and Myste appeared to take none. 'Kragen himself, Terisa! The son of Margonal, the Alend Monarch, and Prince of the Alend Lieges. Imagine! He has come this entire distance from Scarab in deep winter. His purpose must be both mighty and terrible. Now my father will rise to the stature of his kingship' – her vivid eyes flashed – 'or he will forfeit what little respect he still holds in Mordant.'

'Elega, he is our father,' murmured Myste under her breath. 'Even if he loses his mind completely, he still deserves our respect.'

Elega gave a soft snort of derision. 'Let him abdicate his rule when he loses his mind. Then we will respect him as our father without despising him as a failed King.'

Terisa noticed Lebbick glowering at them as if he heard and hated every word.

His glare struck such a chill into her that several moments passed before she realized that the doors to the hall had been closed.

Around the balcony, each of the guards unlimbered his bow and put an arrow to the string. Instinctively, Terisa clutched at Myste's arm. But the lady shook her head and smiled in reassurance.

Now the Castellan was on his feet. Facing the seated people, he said formally, 'My lords and ladies, attend.' He didn't raise his voice, but his tone cut to the farthest corners of the hall. 'You are commanded to this audience by Joyse, Lord of the Demesne and King of Mordant.'

On cue, King Joyse appeared from behind the tall construct of his seat. He had on what appeared to be the same robe of purple velvet he had been wearing when Terisa last saw him. His white hair was held in place by a circlet of gold; but his beard looked like he had slept on it and forgotten to comb it. Now, however, a brocade strap across his chest over his right shoulder supported a tooled leather sheath which held a long sword with a double-handed hilt and a jeweled pommel. The weight of the sword made him seem even more frail than before, more withered inside his voluminous robe. He was walking very slowly.

He was followed immediately by Adept Havelock.

The people in the hall rose to their feet and bowed while King Joyse ascended the pediment and sat down on his throne; then, responding to some signal Terisa missed, they raised their heads and stood in silence before their King.

At the same time, Adept Havelock walked into the open space before the seat and began to dance.

From one foot to the other he hopped, shaking his head, gesturing with his arms, kicking up his heels behind him.

His dingy surcoat, tattered at the hem, and his stained chasuble, his bare feet and the ratty tufts of hair protruding from his pate made him look like a derelict, a piece of human flotsam that had recently been retrieved from some gutter. His beaklike nose confronted the gathering with a fierceness that his unsteady, sybaritic mouth and confused eyes rendered foolish.

His expression was so lunatic that Terisa nearly laughed aloud. Luckily, she didn't. Everyone else stared at Havelock – or avoided staring at him – in misery, disgust, or horror. Someone she didn't see muttered audibly, bitterly, 'Hail the King's Dastard.' Castellan Lebbick fixed the Adept with a glare that threatened to make his surcoat catch fire. Even Myste's tolerance wasn't equal to the way Havelock capered: she frowned and bit her lower lip, and her eyes were bright with anger or tears.

Nevertheless he reveled in the reaction he caused – or he was proof against it. In one hand, he carried a smoking silver censer shaped like a large baby rattle, and he shook fumes of incense around him while he pranced. Soon his dancing took him close to the people standing in front of their pews. At that point, he began to single out individuals for special attention. He jumped up and down in front of them, flourished his censer until smoke made them cough and their eyes water. And he shouted in a liturgical tone, as if he were intoning specific prayers for each of the people he faced:

'Rut in the halls!'

'Hop-board is the game the stars play with doom!'

'Twelve candles were lit upon the table, twelve for the twelve kinds of madness and mystery.'

'All women are better clothed naked.'

'Dandelions and butterflies. We are nothing more than dandelions and butterflies in the end.'

King Joyse slumped in his seat, propping his elbows on the arms of the throne and supporting his head with both hands.

'Hail King Joyse!' Adept Havelock went on piously, still dancing in front of people, still forcing them to breathe his incense. 'Without him, half of you would be dead. The rest would be slaves in Cadwal.' He had chosen a pretty young woman to receive this utterance. 'If you are dead from the waist up, and the lower half remains alive' – he grinned savagely – 'you will still be of service.'

The woman looked pale enough to faint. Instead of collapsing, however, she tittered nervously behind her hand.

At once, the Adept stopped. He peered at her in astonishment and indignation; with his free hand, he scratched one of the bald patches on his skull. Then he snorted, 'Ballocks!' and tossed the censer away over his shoulder. It cracked open when it hit the floor, and a block of incense fell onto the thick carpet. In a scalding tone, he snapped, 'Do not trouble to say anything more, my lady. I can see that I am wasting my time.'

Abruptly, he turned from her and stalked toward the place where he had made his entrance. 'Do you hear me, Joyse?' he shouted up at the King. His arms flailed fury at his sides. *'I am wasting my time!'*

A moment later, he disappeared behind the pediment.

The hall of audiences was shocked. Apparently, the people of Orison still weren't accustomed to Havelock's quirks. In one or two places among the pews, a different kind of titter began; it was stilled immediately. The mediator of the Congery had a lost expression on his face. Master Quillon covered his eyes with one hand. A scowl of vindication twisted Master Gilbur's face. Elega's eyes flashed anger. Myste looked like she wanted to weep.

Behind the incense of the censer and the perfumed oil of the lamps, Terisa smelled the stink of burning fabric. Spilled incense was making the carpet smolder.

King Joyse seemed to be shrinking inside his robe. The watery blue of his eyes was bleak.

Castellan Lebbick was the first to act. Bristling with anger, he stamped away from his chair, went to the burning patch in the carpet, and ground out the fire with his heel. Then he faced the King, his fists cocked on his hips.

'Perhaps you know the meaning of the Adept's display, my lord King.' He sounded savage. 'I don't. He would be more understandable to me if you had him *chained.'*

At once, however, he regained his self-control. Without any pretense of transition, he said, 'My lord King, Prince Kragen of Alend has requested this audience. He says that he comes as ambassador from his father, Margonal, the Alend Monarch. Shall he be admitted?'

For a while, King Joyse didn't reply. Then he sighed. 'My old friend is wiser than I. All this is a waste of time. But since it must be faced, let us do it and be done.' He made a tired gesture. 'Admit Prince Kragen.' A moment later, he added, 'And sit down, all of you. You exhaust me.'

Lebbick glanced up toward the balcony and nodded. Then he returned to his chair.

Obeying her father promptly, Myste sat down. Terisa followed her example. The Castellan himself took his seat. Shortly the rest of the gathering did the same.

Elega was the last. She remained on her feet for a few seconds, staring up at the King as if she were trying by force of will to make him behave as she wished. He didn't meet her gaze, however, and after a moment she, too, resumed her seat, muttering darkly to herself.

At the same time, the high doors swung open. From somewhere, a cornet sounded a fanfare. Everyone looked toward the doors as three men came striding into the audience hall.

One of them led the way, with the others a step behind him on either side, and Terisa at once took him for the Prince. His bearing was confident, and his stride expressed regal self-assertion. His black hair curled out from under his spiked helmet; his black mustache shone as if it had been waxed; his black eyes gleamed with vigor. In contrast to his swarthy skin, his ceremonial helmet and breastplate were of polished and gleaming brass, and a sword in a fine brass sheath was belted to his hip. The silk flowing around his limbs picked up the same contrast, giving off glimpses of light and dark as he moved.

He looked like a man who wouldn't hesitate to demand an audience of anyone.

Judging by the fact that the two men behind him seemed more wary as well as less assured, Terisa guessed that they were bodyguards. The Prince ignored the archers poised around the balcony above him: his companions didn't.

He strode forward until he was close enough to the throne to show that he considered himself King Joyse's peer, but not so close that the guards would take him for a threat. There he stopped. He gave King Joyse an elaborate bow – which his well-trained companions matched – then announced, 'Hail, Joyse, Lord of the Demesne and King of Mordant. I bring you greetings from Margonal, the Alend Monarch and Lord of the Alend Lieges, whose ambassador I am.' Like his smile, his tone was perfectly courteous. 'Great matters are afoot in the world. The times are perilous, and it well befits rulers to consult with each other as brothers, to meet the danger. My father has sent me to Orison to ask many things – and to propose a few which may be of interest.'

King Joyse didn't stand or in any other way return the Prince's salutation. Gruffly, he muttered, 'Kragen, is it? I know you.' The tremor of age in his voice made him sound petulant.

The Prince's smile shifted a few degrees. 'Have we met, my lord King?'

'Yes, we have, my lord Prince.' King Joyse articulated the title sourly. 'You should remember. It was seventeen years ago. You led several squadrons of Alend horse to protect one of your Imagers from me. When I beat you, I had to have you bound to make you accept defeat – yes, and gagged to make you keep your insults to yourself. You were an overeager puppy, Kragen. I hope that seventeen years have made you wiser.'

Now Prince Kragen wasn't smiling. His men weren't smiling. One of them whispered something Terisa couldn't hear. Nevertheless Kragen's manner remained suave and sure. 'My thanks for the reminder, my lord King. I doubt that I am much wiser, since I have always been too ready to forget my defeats. For that reason, I am not bitter. Howsoever, it is well that I have come as an ambassador instead of as an opponent, is it not? Since I am an ambassador, you will not need to have me bound and gagged in order to save yourself from an overeager puppy.'

At that, Castellan Lebbick made a noise between his teeth that could be heard across the hall. Though he sat back in his chair with his arms folded, he gave the impression that he was ready to spring at Prince Kragen's throat.

King Joyse scowled. 'I have often said,' he answered the Prince slowly, 'that a puppy is more deadly than a dog. A dog learns from experience. A puppy has none, and so his behavior cannot be predicted.'

The Alend ambassador's eyes had a yellowish cast, like a tinge of anger. Yet his manner remained unruffled. His stance suggested that he was incapable of quailing. 'My lord King, do you keep hunting dogs? I do not know if you enjoy the sport. It is one of my passions. Among my people I am not considered a poor master of the hunt. I can assure you that it is never the puppy that brings down the stag.'

The King's hands gripped the arms of his throne. 'That,' he snapped, 'is because dogs hunt in *packs*.'

'Oh, Father,' Elega groaned softly.

The indignation of Prince Kragen's companions was becoming stronger than their training – or their good sense. One of them put a hand on his sword; the other turned his back halfway to the King and whispered hotly in Kragen's ear. But the Prince stilled them both with a sharp cut of his hand. He appeared determined not to take public offense.

'My lord King, it seems that you harbor some enmity toward me – or perhaps toward the Alend Monarch himself. If that is true, it may have a bearing on my mission. I am prepared to discuss it openly, if you desire. But would not a more private audience be better? That was my request, as you will recall.'

'That was your *demand*, as *I* recall,' rasped the Castellan.

'Nevertheless,' King Joyse said as though he were following a different conversation, 'I apologize for calling you a puppy. You have become wiser than you admit. In that, you resemble your father.'

In response, Prince Kragen brought back his smile. 'Oh, I think you misjudge the Alend Monarch, my lord King,' he drawled. 'He has become openly fascinated with wisdom over the years. My mission to you is evidence of that.'

The Castellan continued to glare at Kragen. 'The Alend Monarch,' he said in an acid tone, 'has caused more death in Mordant than any man except the High King of Cadwal. Come to the point, my lord Prince, and we'll judge your father's wisdom for ourselves.'

For the first time, Prince Kragen shifted his attention away from the King. Still smiling, he said, 'You are Castellan Lebbick, are you not? If you do not keep a civil tongue in your head, I will have you garroted.'

Terisa stiffened. Despite his casual manner, the Prince was convincing. She heard stifled gasps around the hall. The guards tightened their grips on their weapons; Lebbick's officers poised themselves. Myste was alarmed; but

Elega watched the Castellan or the Prince – Terisa couldn't tell which – with admiration and envy on her face.

Lebbick's expression didn't flicker, yet he looked more like a threat of violence with every passing moment. Slowly, he rose to his feet. Slowly, he turned toward the King. Then he waited in silence for the King to speak.

King Joyse had slumped back in his seat. He seemed to be shrinking. Wearily, he said, 'I wish you *would* come to the point, Kragen. I'm too old to batter my wits against yours for the rest of the day.' To the Castellan, he added, 'Sit down, Lebbick. If he is puppy enough to attempt harm to anyone or anything in Orison, he'll deserve what happens to him. I'm confident you'll feed his liver to the crows.'

Castellan Lebbick glanced at Kragen, then bowed his acquiescence. 'With pleasure,' he murmured as he sat down.

Terisa heard Elega and several other people sigh. Some of them were relieved; the rest sounded disappointed.

More sternly, King Joyse went on, 'We have little reason to love Alend. I ask you simply, Kragen: Why are you here?'

As if nothing had happened, the Prince replied, 'I will answer you simply, my lord King. The Alend Monarch wishes to know what takes place in Mordant. He wishes to end the chaos of rumor and implication. And' – Kragen paused for an instant of drama – 'he wishes to propose an alliance.'

The reaction in the hall was as strong as he could have desired. Unable to restrain herself, Elega sprang to her feet – as did the Castellan, two of his officers, and Master Barsonage. Master Quillon gaped. Whispers of surprise spattered toward the ceiling. Clapping her hand to her mouth, Myste stared up at her father with excitement and hope.

Terisa had no reason to share Castellan Lebbick's hostility.

As far as she was concerned, the Prince had just spoken the first sensible words she had heard in the hall of audiences.

'An alliance?' snapped Lebbick. 'With Margonal? Sheep-dung!'

One of his officers demanded, 'Does the Alend Monarch think we have lost our minds?'

But another cried, 'But if we are allied against Cadwal? The High King musters his armies beyond the Vertigon. The Perdon should hear this!'

At the same time, Master Barsonage protested, 'An alliance? An alliance against our doom?' He looked almost frantic. 'My lord King, you must accept!' For an instant, Terisa thought he was going to shout, You must accept, so that the Congery will not need to call its champion!

More quietly, but with equal fervor, the lady Elega was saying, 'Bravely said, Prince Kragen! Bravely done.'

But King Joyse said nothing until the hubbub stilled itself. He didn't appear surprised. In fact, he hardly seemed to be interested. His face was tight, as if he were stifling a yawn.

At last the hall became quiet again. Castellan Lebbick and the others seated themselves reluctantly, as though pushed down against their will. Soon, every eye was fixed on King Joyse.

Muttering under his breath, he pulled himself straighter in his seat. His circlet had been nudged askew, and a few strands of hair hung down over his eyes. 'An alliance, Kragen? After several dozen generations of war? Why should I agree to such a thing?'

'My lord King, I have not the least idea,' the Prince replied equably. 'I have no facts. But the rumors coming out of Mordant suggest that you are in need. They suggest that the need is growing dire. Therefore it occurred to the Alend Monarch to offer his assistance.'

'What does the Alend Monarch think our need is?'

The Prince shrugged delicately. 'I must repeat that he hears only rumors. But the import of these tales seems clear.' He nodded past Lebbick toward the Masters. 'It appears that some – perhaps many – of your Imagers have turned against you.'

'Impossible!' Master Barsonage objected at once. 'You are offensive, my lord Prince.'

King Joyse ignored the mediator. 'And what does the Alend Monarch think to gain from this alliance?'

'Your trust, my lord King.'

That made sense to Terisa.

King Joyse had a different reaction, however. He sat forward, his incredulity plain on his face. 'What? *Trust*? He does not wish to rule half of Cadwal? He does not desire Imagers of his own?'

'As I have said,' Prince Kragen explained patiently, 'the Alend Monarch has given himself to wisdom. He understands that things may happen between rulers who trust each other which are impossible otherwise. Of course he desires the resources of Imagery for his people. Of course he desires the wealth of Cadwal, so that he can purchase more of what Mordant has and Alend lacks. But he sees that these wishes will not be fulfilled without trust. And trust must begin somewhere.

'He offers you his assistance and asks nothing in return. If what he wants can be achieved, it will come of its own accord when his cooperation has taught you to know him better.'

'I see.' King Joyse leaned back again. 'Doubtless that explains why Margonal has an army of tremendous size gathering beyond the borders of Fayle and Armigite. I mean, of course, that I have heard rumors of such an army.'

'Then you have also heard,' the Prince answered smoothly, 'that High King Festten musters a massive assault against you. Doubtless' – he allowed himself a hint of sarcasm – 'he means to take advantage of your weakness – I mean your need – to crush your kingship, enslave the Cares, and capture all Imagery for himself. I think you will understand, my lord King, that the Alend Monarch cannot permit Cadwal such a victory. Whether or not you accept his alliance, he must oppose the High King. In forging the Congery, you have created something which must not be surrendered.'

'That is true,' acknowledged the King. 'That is true.'

For a long moment, he stared at the ceiling with his mouth open, stroking his beard as though he were deep in thought. His eyes closed, and Terisa thought suddenly, Oh, no, he's going to sleep! Abruptly, however, he looked back down at Prince Kragen and smiled.

His smile seemed to light his face like a touch of sunshine.

'My lord Prince,' he said as if he were happy for the first time since the audience began, 'do you play hop-board?'

Terisa's throat closed against a mounting sense of panic as Kragen replied, 'Hop-board, my lord King? I am unacquainted with it.'

'A game.' The wobble in the King's voice began to sound like ardor. 'I find it most instructive.'

With a noise like a slap, he clapped his hands together. Instinctively, Terisa flinched. Myste and Elega stared worry and consternation up at their father.

Almost at once, two of the wooden screens across the hall parted, revealing a door in the wall. The door was already open, and through it came two servants carrying a small table between them. Two more followed, each bearing a chair. Heads bowed, they brought their burdens forward to the long run of carpet and set the table and chairs down roughly midway between the Prince and the base of King Joyse's throne. While the lords and ladies of Orison gaped, the chairs were placed at the table as if to accommodate Kragen and the King. Then the servants withdrew, closing the screens and the door after them.

Terisa's alarm tightened another turn. She recognized that table, those chairs: she had last seen them in King Joyse's private apartment.

His checkerboard was set up on the table, ready for play.

'Oh, Father,' Myste whispered, 'have you fallen to this?'

Elega's cheeks were hot with color. 'He is *mad*,' she answered. 'Mad.'

But King Joyse ignored the reactions of his people. Sitting forward eagerly, he said to the Prince, 'On the surface, it is a simple game. A child can master it. Yet it is also subtle. In essence, you force your opponent to win battles against you so that he will lose the war. Will you play?'

'I?' Prince Kragen betrayed some surprise of his own. 'As I have said, I am unacquainted with this game. I will gladly watch it played, if that is your wish. If,' he commented casually, 'you can find no better use for this audience. But I cannot play.'

'Nonsense.' The King's voice held a note that Terisa hadn't heard before – a note of hardness. 'I insist. Hop-board is an excellent gauge of persons.'

'And I must decline.' Kragen spoke firmly, yet he had begun to sweat. 'My lord King, I have spent nearly thirty days in the snow between Scarab and Orison because the mission entrusted to me by the Alend Monarch could not wait another season. I do not like to let it wait another day. If I must, however, I will. Shall we meet again tomorrow, privately?'

King Joyse dismissed this speech with a toss of one hand. Coughing to clear his throat, he said, 'I mean to be as fair as I can. I will not play you myself. Though I am hardly the equal of Adept Havelock, I have had much experience. No, my lord Prince.' His tone became sharper. 'I have not seen you measured for seventeen years. Your strengths and abilities are unknown to me. I will match you against another who is similarly unknown.'

With no forewarning except her own imprecise alarm, Terisa heard the King say formally, 'My lady Terisa of Morgan, will you be so kind as to test Prince Kragen for me?'

Now everyone in the hall was staring at her. Her face grew hot. She looked up at King Joyse. In front of all these people—? Fear made her vision acute, immediate, as if there were no distance between them; every line of him was distinct. She could see the veins pulsing in the thin old skin of his temples. His watery eyes seemed weak, almost lost. The hair straggling across his features caused him to appear faintly ludicrous.

But he was smiling.

And his smile hadn't lost its power. It reassured her, like a promise that he meant her no harm; an assertion that she was too valuable to be mistreated; a belief that she would acquit herself well, whatever he asked of her. It was innocent and clean, and she couldn't resist it.

Without consciously making the decision to move, she rose to her feet and went toward Prince Kragen.

At once, she wished she had remained seated. She understood too much of what was happening to be calm, but not enough to be sure she was doing the right thing. And virtually all of the important people in Orison were going to watch her do it. The daughter of her father wouldn't have done this. She could hardly bring herself to meet the Prince's gaze.

His black brows were knotted over his eyes, and he seemed to be chewing the inside of his cheek. His easy and confident manner had deserted him: he didn't smile at her, bow to her, greet her. The hint of yellow in his eyes darkened as his anger increased. He was strung so tight that she expected him to pull out his sword at any moment.

She went as near to him as she dared – no closer than ten feet. Then she stopped.

'My lady' – King Joyse seemed to be speaking from the far end of a tunnel – 'may I present Kragen, Prince of the Alend Lieges and son of Margonal, the Alend Monarch? My lord Prince, this is the lady Terisa of Morgan.

'My lady, I am sure that Prince Kragen will grant you the first move.' With one hand, the King motioned her toward the chair which faced Kragen and the audience.

The Prince turned back to King Joyse. 'Do not waste your time, my lady,' he said. 'I will not play.'

'I think you will.' King Joyse no longer sounded old – or innocent. He sounded like a sovereign who was nearing the end of his patience. 'Please be seated, my lady.'

As if she were helpless, Terisa went to the chair King Joyse had indicated. She pulled it back, sat down, and focused her eyes on the checkerboard, all without risking a glance at Prince Kragen. If she met his eyes, she felt sure he would scathe her to the ground. The whole hall was focused on her. The air around her was heavy with alarm and doubt.

But surely she wasn't helpless? If the mirror had created her, everything she believed about herself and her past might be an illusion. In that case, she belonged here. She had been created to be where she was, and the things she had to do wouldn't be too much for her.

'You are mistaken, my lord King.' Though he spoke quietly, Kragen's voice was as passionate as a shout. 'I understand you now. When I came to you as my father's ambassador and desired an audience, you determined at once to humiliate me. You chose this public occasion when I wished a private meeting. And you meant from the first to confront me with this' – he swallowed a curse – 'this *game*. You had it ready and waiting for your signal. Doubtless you have chosen the lady Terisa of Morgan because in some way she increases the mockery. Really, my lord King, I am surprised that you troubled to wait until I had explained my mission before beginning this charade.

'It is enough. I will return to the Alend Monarch and inform him that you do not wish an alliance.'

'You will not.' The King's tone made the back of Terisa's neck burn. 'You will sit down and play.'

'No!'

'By my sword, *yes*! I am King in Mordant yet, and my will rules!'

Before the Prince or his bodyguards could react, Castellan Lebbick gave a small signal. Around the balcony, archers raised their bows, pulled back the strings.

All the arrows were aimed at Kragen.

'Treachery!' one of the bodyguards spat. Fortunately, he retained enough sense to leave his sword in its sheath.

'Treachery, is it?' rasped Castellan Lebbick with evident relish. 'Keep a civil tongue in your head, or I'll have you fed to the hogs.'

Slowly, Prince Kragen turned in a complete circle, studying the balcony, the screens, the arrangement of the pews and seats; there was no escape. He faced King Joyse again. His expression was flat, closed. The people in the hall watched him without a sound.

Then the lady Elega cried, 'Go!' as if she were in torment. 'Leave this madness! You are an ambassador. Your mission is one of peace. If he has you killed, the execration of all Mordant will hound him to his grave!'

The Prince didn't glance at her. He didn't speak.

In one swift motion, he seated himself across the table from Terisa and folded his arms over his chest, glaring at her as if his gaze were a spike which he meant to drive through her.

King Joyse said nothing. Castellan Lebbick sneered and said nothing. Master Barsonage fretted in his seat. Master Quillon seemed to have disappeared from her range of vision. Neither of the King's daughters moved. No one came to Terisa's aid.

It was up to her to save the Prince.

She didn't look into his face: she concentrated on the board. It seemed impossible that she had ever played this game before. The servant who had taught her had been fired. Perhaps he had been a friend of hers without quite intending to be. Perhaps that was why he had been fired. Close to panic, she thought, Why? Not, Why is King Joyse doing this? But, Why am I?

She knew the answer. Because the King was behaving like a lunatic, and a humiliation like this would make war with Alend inevitable. Because Mordant couldn't afford a war with Alend. Because Cadwal was already mustering. Master Quillon had given her the answer. He was watching her keenly. And Geraden had shown it to her in a mirror. Because gnarled shapes with terrible jaws had been sent out of nowhere to tear men apart.

If her past didn't exist, what did she have to lose?

After a long moment while sweat gathered on her scalp and fright clogged her chest, she reached out and made her first move.

At once, Prince Kragen unfolded one arm, picked up his matching piece, and slapped it down in a move which mirrored hers. His gesture betrayed the dark stains spreading through the silk under his arm.

She nodded to herself, and a bit of her tension relaxed. What else could he do? He knew nothing about the game. He was in her hands.

Like a distant calling of horns, the realization came to her that there was a way out of this dilemma.

She made another move.

Kragen copied it.

Quickly, so that she wouldn't falter, she moved again. He copied her again.

After a few more moves, she was able to turn in her seat and look up at King Joyse. Her heart pounded as though she had just taken an important risk, done something that would make a difference.

'It's a stalemate.'

The passion on his face resembled apoplexy. He was almost bursting with rage. Or else he was tremendously amused – she couldn't tell which.

The Prince took his cue promptly. Rising to his feet without so much as a glance at Terisa, he gave King Joyse an ironic bow. 'I thank you, my lord King. It is indeed a most instructive game. An excellent gauge of persons. The Alend Monarch will be fascinated to hear of it.

'Now with your permission I will withdraw. I fear that the journey from Scarab has exhausted me. I cannot continue without rest.'

He nodded to his bodyguards; they bowed also. Then he turned and started for the doors.

King Joyse swallowed his emotion with difficulty. 'Go rest, if you have to.' He sounded petulant again, like a disenchanted child. 'You're more of a puppy than I thought.'

Prince Kragen's stride checked for an instant; his shoulders bunched. Shocked by the suddenness with which the ambassador's mission had been refused, the people in the hall stared at him – or at King Joyse.

But the Prince didn't stop. The doors were opened for him, and he stalked out of the hall of audiences.

Before anyone else could react, Elega was on her feet. Lightning flared in her eyes. Her cry rang against the high ceiling of the hall:

'Father, I am *ashamed*!'

As quickly as her long, heavy skirts and petticoats permitted, she ran after the Prince.

No one else said anything. No one else dared.

Softly, King Joyse sighed. With both hands, he pushed the hair out of his face and resettled his circlet. Then he scratched his fingernails through his beard. 'That saddens me,' he murmured as though he didn't know that everyone in the hall could hear him. 'I have always been proud of you.'

Weakly, he climbed to his feet and stepped down the stairs from the throne.

When he started toward the back of the pediment, Myste said in a quiet, aching voice, 'Oh, Father!' and went after him.

Terisa should have been proud of herself. She had achieved a victory of a sort. In spite of that, however, Myste was in pain, and Elega was furious; and King Joyse had become so much less than he was, so much less than he needed to be. Terisa was left with a hollow feeling like a stalemate in her heart.

The memory of horns was gone.

ELEVEN

A FEW DAYS WITH
NOTHING TO DO

Terisa would have had trouble finding her way back to her rooms by herself: she wasn't familiar with this section of Orison. But Castellan Lebbick didn't leave her alone. As soon as the lords and ladies began to depart, muttering and arguing their astonishment among themselves, he assigned one of the guards to escort her.

The walk seemed longer than she remembered; but eventually she was in her suite, with the door bolted behind her, and she had her first chance to think about everything that had happened to her today.

From her windows, she was surprised to see that the sky was clear and the snow-packed roofs and towers of the castle were gilded pink, while dusk shrouded the ground and the distant hills. She hadn't realized that so much of the afternoon was gone. For a moment, she forgot everything else and simply watched the sunset, entranced by the way it made Orison look like a place in a fairy tale – old stone immured in winter and darkness, and yet reaching like hope or dreams toward the light and the sky and the delicate touch of the sun's glory. Now she was able to remember the sound of horns. For a long moment, she ached to leave the castle, not to escape back to the illusion of her old life, but to go out into Mordant's world and find the spot among trees and hills where it was possible to hear hunters or musicians calling joy and passion into the cold.

How had the augury known about the riders in her dream?

She could think of an answer, of course. If she had been created by a mirror, then a mirror had also created her dreams.

For some reason, that didn't help.

She had so much to tell Geraden. Regardless of the way she felt about Master Eremis, Geraden was the only one she trusted to help her decide what to do.

Some decision had to be made – that was obvious. Some action had to be taken. King Joyse was on the path to self-destruction – a path more dangerous than the passivity people ascribed to him. She knew now that he wasn't passive. By refusing to shore up Perdon's defenses, as much as by humiliating Prince Kragen, he was working actively toward Mordant's ruin.

Clearly, Mordant needed a leader strong enough to take command of circumstances – and intelligent enough to be constructive. Not Castellan Lebbick: he was too fiercely loyal to the King. And not the Congery as a body. Despite the power it represented, it was too divided to be effective. Adept Havelock? He was mad. Master Quillon? She didn't know what his motives were, but she couldn't imagine him leading the struggle for Mordant's survival.

That left Master Eremis.

Geraden wouldn't like the idea, of course. But maybe she could convince him. If they agreed to help the Master, she might get the chance to spend more time with him.

The thought brought back the sensation of his mouth on her breasts. She hugged herself with her arms and shivered. Saddith had asserted, *Any Master will tell me whatever I wish – if I conceive a wish for something he knows.* And she had said, *The same is true for you, if you choose to make it so.* Well, why not? She lacked Saddith's experience – and expertise. But Eremis found her desirable.

No one had ever found her desirable before.

While the sun set and darkness swallowed the castle, she turned away from the window, poured a goblet of wine, and made herself comfortable to enjoy what she was thinking.

Later, Saddith brought her supper. The maid wanted to talk: Orison was full of rumors about Prince Kragen's audience, and she had heard them all, but she wanted to know the truth. Terisa found, however, that she was too tired – as well as too self-conscious – to do the subject justice. The day's events had exhausted her emotional resources. And her reveries of Master Eremis had put her in the mood for sleep. After a few halfhearted apologies, she dismissed Saddith. Then she ate her supper, drank one more goblet of wine, hung up her clothes in the wardrobe which didn't have a chair propped in it, and went to bed.

She fell asleep almost at once—

—and was awakened by a dull, wooden pounding. Dreams she couldn't remember fogged her brain: she felt sure, with a certainty like cold, congealed oatmeal, that what she heard was the sound of her clothes knocking on the door of the wardrobe, begging to be let out – frantic to dissociate themselves from the false petticoats and misleading gowns which had been loaned to her to seduce her from herself. Something about that didn't make sense, but she couldn't figure it out: the oatmeal was too thick to stir.

The pounding was repeated. After a long, stupefied moment, she realized that it came from the wrong wardrobe.

It came from the door to the secret passage.

At first, she was so mush-headed with sleep and fatigue that she didn't consider answering the knock. At this rate, she thought as clearly as she could, I'm never going to get any rest. Does everybody here spend all night sneaking around behind everybody else's back?

The problem didn't go away when she ignored it, however. The knock was repeated; a muffled voice croaked, 'My lady!'

As far as she knew, only Master Quillon and Adept Havelock knew about that passage.

If the pounding became any louder, the guards outside would hear it.

'All right,' she muttered as she pushed back the covers and stumbled out of bed, 'I'm coming.'

Fortunately, the fire in the hearth had burned down. As a result, the air was cool – and that reminded her that she was naked. Her head began to clear. She detoured to the safe wardrobe, pulled out her clothes and put them on. The pounding began again. 'I'm *coming*,' she replied as loudly as she dared.

As soon as she had unwedged the chair, the door opened, and lamplight spilled out of the wardrobe.

Though her eyes weren't accustomed to the light, she had no trouble identifying her visitor. Master Quillon shrugged past the hanging clothes and stepped out of the wardrobe. 'My lady,' he whispered with some asperity, 'you are a sound sleeper.'

'I'm sorry.' She made no effort to sound sorry. 'I'm still not used to having people break into my room in the middle of the night.'

'I would rather be asleep myself,' he retorted. 'Some things are more important.' Anger made his nose twitch. In the lamplight, he looked more than ever like a rabbit. But the intensity of his manner didn't suit his face. It gave his eyes a manic gleam, like the gaze of a cute pet gone rabid. 'Have you seen Geraden since Prince Kragen's audience?'

He took her aback. His demeanor was frightening. Intimations of danger suddenly filled the air.

'Is he missing?'

'Missing? Nonsense. Why would he be missing? I only want to know if you have spoken to him at any time today – at any time since I separated you.'

Terisa took a deep breath, tried to steady herself. 'What's going on?'

Half snarling, Quillon demanded, 'My lady, *have you spoken to him?*'

'No,' she retorted defensively. 'I haven't seen him. I haven't spoken to him. What's going on?'

Master Quillon glared at her for a moment. Then he sighed, 'Good,' and his face relaxed a little. 'That is good.' But his gaze didn't release her.

'My lady, you heard a great deal in the meeting of the Congery. And I will venture to guess that you heard a great deal more from Master Eremis. You must not speak of these matters to Geraden. You must tell him *nothing*.'

'What?' A pang went through her; alarm closed around her stomach. She had been looking forward to seeing him again, to spending the day with him, to telling him everything. 'Why?' He's the only one I can talk to!

'Because,' the Master articulated distinctly, 'that is the only way we can keep him alive.'

'*What?*'

'As long as he is ignorant, his enemies may not risk exposure by killing him. If you tell him what you know, he will surely act on it. Then he will become too dangerous, and he will be killed.'

'Killed?' She was reeling inwardly. The floor and the lamplight seemed to tilt. 'Why would anybody want to kill him?'

'My lady,' he returned heavily, 'it must be obvious to you that your presence here cannot be an accident. You were translated through a glass which could not have been used for that purpose. How was that done? No mistake or blunder can explain it. You insist that you are not responsible. Then who is?

'My lady, you are important.' Abruptly, Master Quillon turned and began to push his way back through the wardrobe. His voice was obscured by clothes. 'Geraden is crucial.'

For a moment, she stared after him while he entered the passage and closed the door, cutting off the light. Then she wrenched herself into motion. The thought that Geraden's life depended on her silence was so sharp that it nearly made her cry out. Thrusting garments aside, she reached the door and jerked it open.

Master Quillon was on the stairs below her. He turned at the noise she made, looked up at her. The angle of the lamplight left shadows like pools of darkness in his eyes. 'My lady?'

'Who are his enemies?'

She couldn't see his expression. His voice was flat. 'If we knew that, we would be able to stop them.'

Before she could speak, he turned away again and continued his descent. His silhouette twitched like a marionette.

'Who are his friends?'

The echoes of Master Quillon's feet didn't answer.

When she could no longer hear his sandals on the stair, or be sure of the glow of his lamp, she left the passage. Closing the door, she wedged the chair against it again.

After a while, she went back to bed.

By the next morning, she had made at least one decision.

She wasn't going to talk to Geraden.

Unfortunately, that wouldn't be as easy as it sounded. Her desire to confide in him was strong. And she knew he would be hurt by her silence.

In order to protect him, she would have to avoid him for a while.

So she got up early. Despite her inexperience, she managed to build up the fires in her hearths. Gritting her teeth against the cold, she bathed thoroughly. Then, defying the awkwardness of clothes that hadn't been designed to be put on without help, she struggled into a demure, dove-gray gown which, she hoped, would enable her to blend into the background.

She intended to ask Saddith for a tour of Orison – as complete a tour as possible. If she were occupied doing something Geraden didn't expect and couldn't predict, and if she were camouflaged against accidental discovery, she might win herself a day's respite from choices and crises.

Getting dressed alone took some time, however. When she was done, she didn't have to wait long for breakfast. Saddith soon knocked on her door and entered when it was unbolted, bringing a tray of food with her. Today she appeared a bit more cheerful – or perhaps a bit more highly spiced – than usual: there was more sauce in her smile, more zest in her step. On impulse, Terisa said, 'You look happy. Did you have another night with that Master of yours? Or have you found someone better?'

'Why, my lady,' Saddith protested, fluttering her eyelashes, 'whatever do you mean? I am as chaste as a virgin.' Then she grinned. 'That is to say, I am as chased as most virgins dream of being.'

Giggling at her own humor, she began to set out Terisa's breakfast.

As she ate, Terisa proposed the idea of a tour. The maid agreed at once. 'However,' she said, studying Terisa critically, 'we must first repair your dress. If it was your intention to appear as if you had spent the night in your gown, wrestling for virtue, you have succeeded. Really, my lady, you must let me assist you with such things.'

'I didn't think it was that bad.' Terisa was in a hurry to get going: she didn't want to take the chance that Geraden was on his way to see her. But a closer look at the gown convinced her that Saddith was right. Wryly, she assented to the maid's ministrations.

That was a mistake. Saddith took only a few minutes to adjust and refasten the gown; but as she finished there was another knock at the door.

Terisa's heart sank. She wasn't ready for this. Was she going to have to lie to him? She didn't think she could bear to lie to him.

Saddith, of course, had no idea what was in Terisa's mind. With a sprightly step, she left the bedroom to answer the door. Terisa heard her say in a teasing tone, 'Apt Geraden, what a surprise. Have you come to repay me for my help yesterday? For that we must have privacy. Or do you mean to spurn me, preferring my lady Terisa?'

Geraden's laugh sounded a little uncomfortable. 'Come now, Saddith. You can do better than me. In fact, you *do* do better than me. The best *I* can do is ask the lady Terisa to talk to me. Is she free?'

'Geraden,' Saddith answered with mock severity, 'no woman is *free*.'

Chuckling to herself, she returned to the bedroom, where Terisa waited as though she were cowering. 'My lady, Apt Geraden is here. He will be better company than I for an exploration of Orison. He is male, even if he is awkward, easily embarrassed, and only an Apt. I will leave you to him.'

No, Terisa tried to say. Please. But Saddith was already on her way out of the room. She aimed another riposte at Geraden and closed the door behind her.

For a moment, Terisa remained where she was, wishing stupidly that she knew how to swear. But she couldn't stand there, paralyzed, forever. Eventually, Geraden would come a few steps farther into the sitting room, and then he would see her. Feeling at least as abashed as she ever had in front of the barracuda-like young men whom her father had tried to interest in her – trying to marry her off so that he would no longer be bothered with her – she left the bedroom.

Geraden's grin nearly ruined her good intentions: he looked so happy to see her that she wanted to break down immediately and tell him everything. It was all she could do to glance at him and force her mouth into a smile.

'I'm sorry I didn't get to see you again yesterday,' he began at once; he couldn't swallow the pleasure bubbling up in him. 'I don't know what came over Master Quillon. He isn't usually that unreasonable. He took me down to his private workshop and put me to work grinding sand, of all things. That job is so menial and mindless even new Apts don't usually have to do it. Then the message came that Prince Kragen was here and King Joyse was going to give him an audience. I thought that would save me. Despite whatever came over him, Master Quillon wouldn't expect me to go on grinding sand at a time like that.'

He grimaced. 'I was right, as usual. I didn't have to grind any more sand. Instead, he handed me instructions for the most complex tinct I've ever heard of and told me to prepare it three different ways. "For experimental purposes." Some Masters never let Apts do work that sophisticated. And it's been years since *any* Master gave me a job like that. I didn't know whether to be grateful or cut my throat.

'Anyway, I didn't finish until after midnight. I'm still not sure I got any of them right.

'I guess I missed all the excitement.'

Terisa's throat felt like cotton wadding. She swallowed roughly. 'You must have heard about it.'

He nodded slowly, studying her: the strangeness of her manner cooled his ebullience. 'Did you really play hop-board against Prince Kragen?'

Unable to face him, she went to the window. The clear sky of the previous evening was gone: now low clouds as heavy as stone covered the castle and the surrounding hills, making everything gray. In that light, the gown she had chosen seemed as drab as her spirit.

'Yes.'

Geraden whistled his appreciation. 'Amazing! And he didn't know the game. How did you manage to maneuver him into a stalemate? *That* was impressive. The Alend Monarch ought to give you a title for treating his honor with so much courtesy.' Then his tone darkened. 'Judging by the rumors, that was the most intelligent thing anybody did in that disaster. If King Joyse had half your sense, there would still be hope for us.'

Oh, Geraden. Hating herself for what she had to do, she took advantage of the opening he had unintentionally given her, the chance to deflect – or at least postpone – his inevitable questions. Without turning her head, she said bitterly, 'But that's the point, isn't it? He doesn't have any sense. As far as I can tell, he arranged that whole audience for just one reason – to make fun of the Prince. He *wants* a war with Alend.'

Then she did turn, forcing herself toward him because she was ashamed. 'Geraden, why are you loyal to him? Maybe he was a great king once – I don't know. But there's none of that left.' She spoke as if during the audience she had been capable of refusing the King's smile – as if she could have refused it now. 'Why don't you give him up?'

The quick hurt in his eyes made her want to run into the bedroom and hide her head under the pillows. Lamely, she concluded, 'That's why the Masters don't trust you. Because you're loyal to him, and nobody can understand why.'

'Is that what they told you?' he retorted at once. 'They don't trust me because I still like to serve my King? I thought it was because I haven't done anything right since I was nine years old.'

Stung, she returned to the window, leaning her forehead against the cold glass to cool the pain. Not talk to him? Not tell him the truth? How could she do that, even to save his life?

'I'm sorry,' she heard him say, chagrined by her reaction. 'I didn't mean it that way. This is just a sore point for me. As you can probably tell.

'But I have the strongest feeling—' He stopped.

She waited, but he didn't go on. Finally, she asked, 'What is it this time?'

As if the words were being forced out of him by a deep but involuntary conviction, he replied, 'I have the strongest feeling he knows what he's doing.'

'Oh, Geraden!' She couldn't restrain herself: she faced him again, showing her irritation plainly. 'Do you really think that starting a war with Alend is *wise*? Do you think that's a *good* answer to Mordant's problems?'

'No,' he admitted glumly. 'I've already told you my feelings are always wrong. I just can't ignore them.' After another hesitation, he said, 'I haven't told you about the first time I met him.'

Thinking she knew what was coming, Terisa winced inwardly. 'Would you like to sit down?'

'No, thanks.' His manner was abstracted: his mind was on the story he meant to tell. 'I spent too many hours yesterday hunched over a mortar. My back still hurts.' He began to pace slowly back and forth in front of her.

'I must have been eleven or twelve years old at the time, and I had never been away from home. Oh, there was hardly a mile of Domne where I hadn't ridden or worked, trailing after my brothers, doing the jobs I was given, or' – he smiled – 'trying to avoid my chores. I don't care what anybody else says. Domne is the most beautiful of the Cares – especially in the spring, when the apples trees and dogwood and redbud come out, and some of the hills as far as you can see are wooded in blooms – and I loved exploring it, playing in places like the Closed Fist, riding like wild around the skirts of the mountains.'

He sighed happily. 'But Houseldon was the center of my life. My father, the Domne, is a man who loves his home more than any place in the world. He prefers the company of his family to anyone else – even though people call him one of the King's dearest friends. Every year or two, he had to go somewhere to do something for King Joyse or Mordant, and he always took at least two of my brothers with him. That was how Artagel discovered his talent for fighting, which he would never have done at home. But I was always too young to go. I was my mother's baby, of course. And when she died, Tholden – he's my oldest brother – he and his wife took over as if they thought I was never going to grow up.

'In some ways, it's difficult to describe why I didn't take after my father. Tholden certainly did – when he becomes the Domne, even our father's beloved cherry trees will hardly notice the difference. So did Minick and Wester – he's the handsome one of the family. And the only reason I don't count Stead is that he would rather court every village girl in Domne than do his share of the shearing. Did I tell you that our family raises sheep? We do all kinds of farming, of course. All the Cares do. But wool and cloth are what we're known for.' He sounded proud. 'As soon as my brothers found out how clumsy I was,' he continued wryly, 'they refused to let me near the shears. But one summer I did so much herding that I knew every sheep within five miles by name.

'Looking back on it, I think my father's love should have been irresistible. He can still take off a sheep's wool in one piece so even it can be used as it is. His eyes light up when he sees a new seed sprout or a new crop come up. And he enjoys the company of his sons as if they were the best people in the world. He even manages to appreciate *my* good points – whatever they are. Whenever I go home, I spend the first five days amazed at my good luck and wondering why I ever left.'

Then he shrugged and grinned. 'I spend the *next* five days trying to figure out how to tell the Domne I have to leave again. Maybe it's because I never got to go with him when he traveled. I had to wait until he and my brothers came back and spent the next entire season telling stories about all the exciting things they saw and did. I was like Nyle in that. Except for me, he's the youngest. He had to stay home a lot, too. When Artagel went into training with the armies of Mordant, Nyle and I treated him like visiting royalty. We wanted him to tell us *everything*.

'Or maybe it's because King Joyse sent Queen Madin and their daughters to stay with us for more than a year when I was five or six. What was happening, I think, was that the Alend Monarch and High King Festten were becoming desperate to defend their Imagers, and King Joyse was afraid they might try to stop him by attacking his family. Anyway, the lady Elega and I were about the same age, and we played together most of the time. Even then' – his fondness was evident – 'she was so full of being a king's daughter that I hardly knew what to do with her. But I admired her for it. I loved her stories of wars and power, even though she credited herself with saving the realm more often than most five-year-old girls can manage. Young as I was, she made me ache to explore the whole world the way I did Domne.

'Or maybe it was simply that the most exciting thing I knew about my father was his friendship with the King.

'Whatever the reason, I haven't been content with the idea of being a farmer or sheepherder for as long as I can remember.'

Abruptly, he stopped and looked at Terisa. 'I'm sorry. I didn't mean to go into all that. I just wanted you to understand what kind of boy I was when I first met King Joyse.'

'Don't apologize,' she replied gently. She was grateful for anything that kept him from questioning her. And she liked hearing about his family. His background was as alien to her experience as Mordant and Imagery were; but it was also attractive – as strange and wondrous as a fairy tale. 'If you didn't point it out, I would never know you were digressing.'

He bowed playfully. 'You are too gracious, my lady.' Then he resumed his story.

'As I say, it was probably thirteen years ago. Mordant was approximately at peace because Adept Havelock wasn't ready to expose the arch-Imager and his cabal, and King Joyse was doing a royal circuit, getting ready for the days when his wars would actually be over. After Termigan, he came to Domne.

'The day he arrived, I was weeding corn in one of the fields near Houseldon. It was as far away as I could bear to be, and I only went that far because the field was on a hill that let me watch the road. I was so excited that I kept forgetting to look where I swung the hoe. By the time the King and his party finally rode into view' – he chuckled to himself – 'I had left a swath of ruined corn right through the middle of the field.

'But that didn't bother me. As soon as I saw him coming, I dropped my hoe and ran.

'There's a stockade around Houseldon, mostly to keep the animals out, and unfortunately there was a large pig wallow between me and the nearest gate. However, one of my brothers in an enterprising mood had tossed a long log into the wallow as a shortcut, and I headed for it to save time.

'You can imagine what happened.' He grimaced in mock disgust. 'But I didn't stop. I absolutely *had* to meet King Joyse as fast as possible. It was the most urgent thing in my life. So I managed to arrive in front of our house just as the King and his people – Queen Madin with Elega, Torrent, and Myste, Adept Havelock in his scruffy chasuble, Castellan Lebbick and a handful of guards, two or three of the King's counselors, and a small number of servants – you see, I remember it all – I got there just as they were dismounting.' He snorted. 'I had cherry pits in my hair, orange peels on my clothes, melon rinds sticking to my feet, and I was still dripping mud.

'A lot of people laughed – except Elega, who got angry – but my father and the King didn't. The Domne said, "My lord King, this is my youngest son, Geraden," as if he had never loved me as much as he did right then. Then the King beckoned me to him. In spite of the muck, he put his hands on my shoulders and gripped me hard. "I like you, boy," he said. "Come to Orison in a few years." Just like that. "You already have one fighter in the family, and Artagel does it well. You will be an Imager."'

Again, he stopped pacing to face Terisa firmly. 'He made me happier than I had ever been in my life. And I can't forget that. I'm not as loyal to him as I should be – he doesn't want me to talk to you, remember? – but he is my King, and I won't stop trying to serve him as well as I can.'

Then he laughed self-consciously. 'Anyway, that's the best explanation I can give you. At the rate I'm going, if you ask me any more questions, I'll never give you a chance to tell me what happened to you yesterday.'

A pang went through her. Not quite able to meet his gaze, she said, 'I like hearing about your family. Did you hear Saddith mention a tour? She was going to give me a tour of Orison. I would like to know this place a little better.' Deliberately duplicitous, she added, 'This room is starting to give me cabin fever.'

Forgetting self-consciousness, Geraden became immediately sober and intent. 'I'll gladly give you a tour. After yesterday, I can use the escape myself. But that meeting of the Congery is too important to talk about in public. With my luck, somebody would overhear us. Why don't you tell me what happened after I had to leave? Then we'll go.'

If he secretly wanted to know what she had done with Master Eremis, he concealed the desire well. Nevertheless she needed some way to deflect him again and didn't have any better ideas, so she said, 'Are you sure it isn't

Master Eremis you want to hear about? You were eager enough to interrupt us.'

She tried to make the words teasing – and failed completely. In fact, she sounded just like her mother, feigning playfulness to disguise the intended hurt in what she said.

Involuntarily, Geraden scowled to keep himself from flinching; his face darkened. 'Was I wrong, my lady?' he asked stiffly. 'Does Master Eremis mean you well?'

She couldn't answer that. She was too ashamed of herself. Softly, as if she were apologizing, she said, 'Do you know what he did? He proved I don't exist. Or I didn't exist until you found me in the mirror. You must have created me somehow.'

Suddenly, the Apt was angry. His eyes burned. 'He convinced *you* of that? *You*. That must have been quite a display of logic. What did he actually say? What argument did he use this time?'

Surprised and a bit frightened by Geraden's reaction, she answered, 'Language. Mirrors don't translate sound.' Confusedly, she repeated the gist of what Master Eremis had said to her.

In response, Geraden threw up his hands. Stalking away to the window, he glared out at the winter. 'That son of a mongrel,' he rasped. 'Why does he *do* things like this?' Then, roughly, he swung toward her again.

'That's all pigslop, and he knows it. It's an interesting argument, but it doesn't *prove* anything.'

She stared at him dumbly.

'There is at least one alternative explanation. Translation changes things. That's part of the magic. Language isn't the only issue. When I put my head into that mirror – the one with the champion – I didn't have any trouble breathing the air. But surely a world like that would have different air than we do. Why would a mirror create alien landscapes, alien people, alien power, alien creatures – and not alien air? That doesn't make sense. I must have been changed by the translation so I could breathe. If those people hadn't been so determined to kill me right away, we might have been able to talk to each other.

'I can't prove that either, of course. But proof isn't the point. The point is, the answer Master Eremis gave you isn't inevitable. There is another explanation.

'It isn't love that makes him talk to you like that.' His tone was hard, like a clenched fist. He didn't seem to be aware that she was panicking in front of him.

The past *was* real? She couldn't simply turn her back on it and go ahead, as if she had a role to play and a right to play it? Then she didn't belong here – and everything she did was too important. Her mistakes might do serious damage: the risk she had taken for Prince Kragen against King Joyse might have terrible consequences.

She hardly heard Geraden saying, 'There's some reason why he wants you to believe I created you. He wants something from you.' He grimaced bitterly. 'He wants to bed you – but that isn't what I mean. If it were that simple, he wouldn't take the chance of upsetting you.

'My lady, what happened during the meeting of the Congery after I left? What did they decide?'

She hardly heard him – but all at once the words came into focus, and she grasped what he had said. The color drained from her face. 'Decide?' she breathed, trying not to pant. Even this might be wrong, the decision to protect him. Maybe she shouldn't trust Master Quillon. Or maybe Geraden needed to die – maybe he was a danger to Mordant in some way she could never understand because she didn't belong here. She didn't know enough: the right answer wasn't available to her. A feeling of weakness washed through her, and darkness swirled around the edges of her vision. Her knees started to fold.

Somehow, Geraden crossed the distance between them. He was holding her up, his hands clamped to her arms. 'Terisa!' he hissed like a blaze. 'What did they decide?'

She couldn't stand. If he let her go, she would be lost. A moment later, however, she found that the urgent need in his face brought her strength back. He was more at risk than she would ever be. Master Quillon was right about that: Geraden was too passionate and determined to be safe. She couldn't let him be killed, couldn't give his enemies an excuse to kill him.

But as she straightened her knees, took her own weight, she realized that there was no way out. She couldn't let him be killed. What good was that? She also couldn't lie to him. It would be impossible for her to lie to any man who looked at her like that. Even if she had never existed before in her life, she would have become real at that moment because of the way he stared at her, simultaneously outraged on her behalf and desperate for her help.

One after the other, she shrugged her arms free. Still feeling weak, she said, 'They told me not to tell you. They told me that if you knew what the Congery was going to do your enemies would have you killed.'

As quick as a slap, astonishment stretched his face, and he recoiled a step. 'Killed—?' His eyes flashed from side to side, hunting for comprehension. 'Me? *What* enemies? Why would anyone—?' Questions burst from him in fragments: he couldn't frame them quickly enough to keep up with them. 'And you—? They did *that* to you? Who are—?'

Abruptly, he took hold of himself with an almost visible grip of will, forced down his confusion. In a clenched voice, he murmured, 'You poor woman. You know something I don't, and you know I need to know it, but you think it might cost me my life if you tell me. And if I tell you I don't have any enemies – I can't *imagine* having any enemies – you won't know who to believe.'

She nodded. If he kept going, she was going to weep.

Without warning, he did something that amazed her down to the ground. Nothing in her father's dour unlove or Reverend Thatcher's weakness or Master Eremis' desire had prepared her for the way Geraden unknotted his throat and swallowed his distress and gave her a smile like a gift.

'You know, Terisa, a tour sounds like a grand idea to me.' He met his danger with a sparkle in his eyes. Dimly, she realized that he was using her name at last. 'I would love to show you around Orison. I don't know any of the secret passages everyone keeps talking about, but I think I've explored almost everything else.'

She was so relieved and glad that she went to him without thinking, put her hands on his shoulders, and kissed his cheek.

At once, his pleasure became so bright that she started laughing.

They were still chuckling together when they left her rooms a moment later to begin the tour.

It took considerably longer than she had expected. In fact, it spread out over several days. Geraden was familiar with a bewildering combination of routes which stretched through Orison from end to end and top to bottom. He had never been able to win admittance to the Congery and its secrets; but he could tell the story behind each of the pennons hanging outside the hall of audiences (each one was the standard of some commander who had been beaten by King Joyse in battle). Most of the high-ranking men and women he and Terisa met in passing either didn't know him or recognized him with amusement bordering on disdain; but every guard, maid, scullion, cook, sweeper, wine steward, armorer, apprentice, plumber, stonemason, and merchant from the deepest storerooms to the highest rafters of the castle seemed to be a friend or acquaintance, either of his own or of his family's. And his relationship with all those people was like his knowledge of Orison: he was as clumsy as a puppy, tripping on stairs or his own feet, bumping into walls, dropping things, and falling all over himself with enjoyment whenever someone made a particularly acute jest; yet he held his own among the scullions and armorers and sweepers, in spite of his instinct for mishap, by displaying an unfailing insight and humor that made many of them look at him with affection indistinguishable from respect.

Nearly exhausted after a few hours – and determined not to show it – Terisa asked him how long he could afford to stay away from his duties. 'If they can't catch me,' he replied with a shrug and a laugh, 'they can't tell me what to do. And they can't punish me.' Then he closed the subject by leading her away into one of the huge, hot kitchens where Orison's food was prepared; or perhaps (she couldn't remember after a while) it was into one of the long dining halls crowded with trestle tables where many of the people who worked for the castle ate their meals; or perhaps into one of the warrens of stone rooms and apartments, as crowded and complex as tenements, but scrupulously clean (kept that way by Castellan Lebbick's orders and under his supervision because he was determined that Orison would never fall siege to disease), where the people who served and maintained the castle lived.

Along the way, Geraden chatted amiably with her for a long time. Eventually, however, he became curious enough to wonder aloud why she wasn't asking more questions. 'I've probably made it clear,' he commented, 'that I'm not going to let anybody tell me what to do where you're concerned.' He was trying to sound casual. 'I'll tell you anything you want to know.'

She understood him. He was trying to find out how much she knew already. And where she had learned it.

His offer flustered her. She didn't want to betray what Master Quillon had already done for her. Because she was in a hurry to say something – and because Master Quillon made her think of Adept Havelock, who reminded her of the arch-Imager Vagel and his cabal – she replied, 'Tell me about the High King's Monomach.'

That was such an odd response that Geraden stopped and peered at her. 'Gart? Where did you hear about him?'

She winced at the blundering way she forced herself to prevaricate. In an effort to keep the falsehood to a minimum, she said vaguely, 'One of the Masters mentioned him. They were talking about Vagel and Cadwal.'

For a difficult moment, the Apt continued studying her. Then, fortunately, he shrugged and started walking again, deliberately accepting her explanation at face value.

'Cadwal is a strange country.' His answer was typically rambling. 'With its ships, it has more contact with the rest of the world than Alend does – and we've never had any. That trade brings in wealth like you'll never see here. But wealth isn't good for anything except to buy food, pleasure, or power. Well, food they get from us at reasonable prices – or they did until they started harassing Perdon's borders. Now they rely on brigand commerce. And in other ways power hasn't done them much good since King Joyse established Mordant and the Congery. So the Cadwals buy a *lot* of pleasure.

'On the other hand, the country is bitterly harsh. Most of it is ragged rocks and desert, and the regions with water also have the kind of winds that tear your skin off your bones. Conditions like that teach harshness – they teach anybody who can survive them to be strong and cruel.

'The strange thing is the way the Cadwals combine pleasure and harshness.' Geraden thought for a moment before he explained. 'The High King's Monomach is Festten's traditional champion – a personal defender and assassin. He's supposed to be the greatest fighter in the country – the strongest and cruelest product of the harshest circumstances and training. In fact, the Cadwals like to say the men who fail as the High King's Monomach's Apts are so strong that Carmag is built on their bones. But the reward they give the greatest fighter in the whole country isn't wealth or power – or even freedom. It's just pleasure. That, and the chance to get killed serving – or displeasing – the High King.

'For some reason, power and wealth in Cadwal – and control over pleasure – have always belonged to the sybaritic side of their culture. High King Festten doesn't have an ancestor in the past ten generations who ever lived in a tent in the desert, or survived the wind that cuts the rocks, or measured his life with the edge of his sword. And yet his hold over Cadwal makes the Alend Monarch look like the mediator of the Congery.' He flashed Terisa a grin. 'As far as I can tell, the High King has always wanted to rule Mordant simply to save himself the cost of food, so he'll have more wealth free to spend on pleasure.'

Carried along by what he was saying, Geraden seemed to forget the incongruous fact that she wasn't asking questions. Breathing a sigh of relief, she reflected that both the Congery and King Joyse had good reason to try to protect what they knew from strangers. For instance, if by some wild stretch of the imagination she were in league with Gart, this tour might prove priceless to her. During the second day, Geraden showed her the prodigious reservoir where rainfall, melting snow, and the waters of the small spring that fed Orison were accumulated and stored. That was information any enemy would have known how to use.

This realization increased her appreciation for what the Apt was doing for her. She knew she was perfectly harmless – but he couldn't be equally sure. His trust itself was a risk.

She began to feel that keeping secrets from him wasn't a very satisfying way to thank him. She didn't want him hurt.

The next day, however, he didn't arrive to continue the tour. Instead, he sent a message to let her know that Master Quillon had commandeered him once more. Somewhat to her surprise, she went back to bed and slept through most of the day.

But her dreams were of Master Eremis, and she was restless all night. When morning came she found herself hoping that Geraden would return. If he didn't, she might be tempted to take her questions and decisions in search of the man who had kissed her so intimately.

Where was he? Why had he left her alone? Didn't he want her anymore? Was she so unappealing that he had already lost interest in her?

Fortunately, Geraden knocked on her door soon after breakfast.

He had procured a thick sheepskin coat and boots for her, similar to the ones he was wearing himself. 'Today,' he said sententiously, a grin shining in his eyes, 'the battlements.' When she had wrapped the coat around her gray gown, he bowed her out of the room with a mock-courtly flourish.

As she was able to see from her windows, Orison didn't have a defensive outer perimeter: the same stone served for the rooms and halls inside and their protection outside. But that wall, as Terisa saw when Geraden took her through it, was tremendously thick. Its outward faces were lined with battlements wide enough to carry supply wains, high enough to make archers effective without exposing them to counterattack, and massive enough to resist catapults and battering rams; and it contained (so she was told) storerooms, guardrooms, and passages. Now she was more baffled than ever by the fragment of augury that had shown Orison with a smoking hole torn in its side and a look of death about it. What kind of force was powerful enough to do such damage to a wall like this?

From the battlements, Geraden took her up to the top of the tower that held her rooms.

The air was as sharp as splintered glass, and her nose and ears were chilled. At this elevation, the breeze seemed harsher than it was. The heavy clouds of recent days had lifted slightly, but the increased clarity made the cold worse. The snow packed into the crenellations and corners of the parapet looked old and rotten, gnawed upon but not consumed by the occasional touch of the sun. Her breath steamed in front of her face; she hugged her arms inside the sleeves of her coat and shivered. But she didn't try to persuade Geraden to forgo this exposure. It offered her the best view she had ever had of the countryside surrounding Orison.

The position of the sun enabled her to verify that the long rectangle of the castle ran roughly from northwest to southeast. She and Geraden stood atop the eastmost tower. Churned mud showing through the snow marked the road that left the gates in the northeast-facing wall and branched almost within arrow shot of the castle, one limb turning toward the south, the Broadwine River, and the Care of Tor (as Geraden had explained several days ago), another paralleling the Broadwine northeast into the Care of Perdon, and a third swinging northwest toward the Care of Armigite. The river, he assured her, could be seen in the distance at other times of year, but in winter white snow and ice made it blend among the hills. Nevertheless it was the same river she had seen in one flat mirror, the river that ran out of the narrow defile that he had called the Closed Fist. It came down through the center of Domne, divided Tor from both Termigan and Armigite, separated a portion of the Demesne from Perdon, and finally split Perdon into its North and South regions before joining the Vertigon on the border of Mordant.

It was odd, she thought as she shivered, how much safer this scene looked here than it did in the glass that had let her, Geraden, and Master Eremis witness the attack on the Perdon. Under the open sky, it became almost impossible to believe in savage monsters and fierce death. Surely things like that only existed in mirrors?

She didn't absorb much of what he was telling her. She would need a map to get it all straight. Still her eyes devoured Orison's surroundings. The castle dominated the snow-cloaked hills immediately around it, but those farther away were higher, more rugged, and more interesting. Trees lined the roads after they branched and went their separate ways; yet the hillsides around Orison were so bare that she thought they must have been cleared. Geraden confirmed this: Castellan Lebbick wanted space in which to exercise his men, and Orison's rulers had never wanted cover to hide an approaching enemy. There were woods in the distance, however – trees as thick, black, and secretive as the ones in her dream. And the roads seemed to lead to places so far away that they must be wonderful.

She wanted to say, Take me to Domne. Take me to Termigan and Armigite and Fayle. Take me away from here. But the weather was too cold; the snow, too deep. And she wasn't Prince Kragen or one of his men: she couldn't travel under these conditions. When she saw a group of riders coming up toward Orison from the south, she remembered that she had never been on a horse before.

Squinting into the breeze to keep his vision clear, Geraden stared out at the riders. After a long moment, he breathed softly, 'Sand and tinct! That looks like the Tor. The Tor himself. He hasn't been to Orison since I came here.' To Terisa, he added, 'Some people say he's too fat to travel. But I think he's probably just too old. He's at least ten years older than King Joyse.' Then he murmured distantly, 'If that's him, what's he doing here? At this time of year?'

As he spoke, Terisa felt the cold reach around her heart, and she turned toward the stairs leading back into the tower. The Perdon was keeping the promise he had made to Master Eremis.

But one of the Masters had said – or implied? – that the Tor was incapable of making such a journey. There wasn't enough time? The distance was too great?

194

Without warning, Geraden burst past her, half running for the stairs. 'Come on!' he called over his shoulder. 'That's definitely the Tor! He's got a litter with him!'

For a second, she was frozen. A *litter*? Then Geraden's urgency grabbed hold of her.

He took the descent two steps at a time. The long skirt of her gown made it impossible for her to keep up with him. But he glanced back at her from the first landing, saw her difficulty, and slowed his pace.

Nearly together, they hurried down out of the tower.

A few moments ago, she had been cold. Now she was hot. In spite of his haste, she stopped on the stairway to pull off her coat. He tried to calm himself, but his face betrayed his vexation at the delay. 'I'm sorry,' she murmured as they started moving again.

Before he could reply, he missed a step, let out a yelp, and dove headlong down the length of the stone stairs.

'Geraden!' She rushed after him in panic.

As she reached him, he got to his hands and knees and pushed himself off the floor. His head wobbled from side to side as if he couldn't remember which way was up. She took him by the arm, tried to lift him erect. 'Are you all right?'

Although he looked stunned, he put his weight on her until he propped his feet under him. Then he was able to stand.

'Don't worry. If this didn't happen at least once a day, I wouldn't know who I was.' Awkwardly, he lurched into motion. 'Come on. I've missed everything else recently. I don't want to miss this.'

His strides grew slowly steadier as he led her down more stairways toward the level of the gates.

Abruptly, the air turned cold again. They were approaching a high, wide doorway which gave access to Orison's enormous inner courtyard. Guarded doors made of heavy timbers and bolts stood ready to close the entrance if necessary; but they were open.

Shouts began to echo off the walls of the castle. Guards came running down the hall. More guards splashed out into the mire of the courtyard, running toward the gates. A moment later, Castellan Lebbick appeared. His commands carried more sharpness than the cold as he, too, headed for the gates.

'Put on your coat,' Geraden whispered tensely.

As soon as Terisa had complied, he took her arm and drew her out into the open court.

Her feet sank into the mud up to her ankles. She groaned to think of damaging such nice boots, then had to forget about them in order to concentrate on pulling herself from step to step against the suction of the muck.

She and Geraden were in the southeast end, which was relatively clear. The shops of the bazaar and the wagons of the farmers were crowded to the northwest, and among them were pitched the tents of their attendants, as well as of the guards who were responsible for maintaining order and honesty. But even this half of the courtyard looked large enough to exercise several squadrons of horse.

The castle stood open. The gate itself, a tremendous construct of timbers the size of tree trunks and lashed with iron, had been raised, as it was every day. During the tour, Geraden had showed her the gigantic winches that cranked the gate up into the wall above its architrave. Ahead of her, the Castellan was forming his men into an honor guard to greet the lord of the Care of Tor. A trumpeter blew an announcement. Geraden took her as close as the guards permitted to the place where the Tor's riders would enter Orison and dismount. There they stopped.

The riders were on the road outside the castle. They had almost reached the gate, despite their mourning pace. She saw now that the men were all in black. The breath of the horses steamed silver in the iron cold, but their trappings were black. Black draped the litter that four of the mounts supported from their saddles. The man who led the group hid his face under a black hood, and a black cloak was wrapped around him.

This figure was so fat that Terisa wondered how his horse could bear his weight.

He led his riders toward Castellan Lebbick, then halted within the precise formation of the honor guard. Their horses seemed to sag under the burdens they carried.

'Greetings, my lord Tor,' the Castellan said gruffly. His shoulders were braced as if they had the weight of the whole winter on them; the purple band across his forehead emphasized the anger of his eyebrows. 'You are welcome in Orison. No matter what reason has brought you here at such a time, you are welcome.'

Slowly, the Tor raised his black-gloved hands and lifted his hood, revealing thin white hair that straggled from his pale scalp, features the shape and color of cold potatoes, bleak eyes. His fat cheeks were hurt with cold.

In a husky voice, he rasped, 'I will see the King.'

The sharpness of the air made everything distinct. Terisa saw the shadow of a wince pass across Lebbick's hard face. 'My lord Tor,' he replied, 'King Joyse has been informed of your coming. At present, he is busy with other matters.' He couldn't keep his disdain for those 'other matters' out of his tone. The King was probably playing hop-board. 'I'm sure he'll grant you an audience shortly.'

The clouds sealing the sky were the color of tombstones. Cold seemed to close around the courtyard. For a long moment, the Tor didn't move or speak. His eyes blinked as if he were going blind. Then, with a grunt of effort, he heaved his leg over the back of his horse and dismounted. The guards were silent. The champing of the horses and the squelching sound of his boots in the mud could be heard clearly as he moved like an old man among his people toward the litter.

From the litter, he lifted in his arms the black-draped shape of a man or woman who must have been taller than he was. He didn't look strong enough to bear so much weight; nevertheless he cradled the body against his belly, carrying it forward until he stood directly in front of Castellan Lebbick.

In the same dried-out, hollow voice, he said, 'This is my first son. I will see the King.'

Now the Castellan's distress was unmistakable. 'Your son, my lord Tor? That's a terrible loss.' Terisa remembered that Lebbick was acquainted with loss. 'All Mordant will sorrow with you. How did he die?'

For a moment, a flicker of passion lit the Tor's speech. 'His face was torn away by a wolf such as Mordant and Cadwal and Alend together have never known. Do you care to see the wound?' He extended the shrouded body toward Lebbick.

But almost at once his energy faded. Dully, implacably, he repeated, 'I will see the King.'

'That won't be possible.' Castellan Lebbick sounded thick and hoarse, like a man in pain. 'King Joyse doesn't yet grant you an audience.'

Through the silence, the riders at the Tor's back muttered curses. How far had they ridden in order to present the Tor's slaughtered son to his King?

Abruptly, Geraden left Terisa's side. Striding through the mud as if he couldn't be held back by any slip or accident – as if he had forgotten his talent for mishap – he went toward the Tor. The boyish prance-and-fumble of exuberance and mistake was gone from his manner entirely. The way his chestnut hair crowned the strong lines of his face made him look incontestable, as sure of himself as if he had power and knew how to use it.

Ignoring Castellan Lebbick's fierce glare, he said, 'My lord Tor, I am Geraden, youngest son of the Domne. In the name of my father and all his family, please accept my grief. King Joyse will see you. When he hears why you have come, he will see you.'

'Geraden,' the Castellan snarled in an undertone, 'be warned. You forget yourself, whelp.'

At once, Geraden turned toward Lebbick. 'No, Castellan.' He had become taller almost without transition, certain of his authority. 'Be warned yourself. You may despise me as much as you wish. But the day has not yet come when you may despise the Domne. I speak in his name.

'In his name, I claim the responsibility. Let it crush me if it will. The King will see my lord Tor.'

The Tor said nothing. He stood there with his son in his arms as though he had been stricken mute, unable to articulate his grief except by demanding the King's acknowledgment of it.

A snarl twisted Castellan Lebbick's mouth. His hands knotted at his sides. After a moment, he said softly, 'You can try, whelp. Gestures like that come cheaply to those with no duty – to those who can ignore the consequences of what they do. It's my place to ensure that King Joyse is obeyed, and I will do it' – his fist beat the words against his thigh – 'if I must.'

Then he stepped aside. With a barked command, he ordered the honor guard to do the same.

Geraden put his hand on the Tor's arm to help support the great weight of what the man carried. Together, they moved toward the nearest open door. Perhaps a dozen guards took formal positions behind them and followed.

Terisa started after them.

The Castellan stopped her with a hard gesture. 'No, my lady. There's harm enough here without your contribution.' He spat the words like gusts of steam. 'I won't expose my King's plight to a woman of your dubious allegiance.'

Raising his voice, he instructed two of his guards to return the lady Terisa of Morgan to her rooms.

For a moment, she stood right on the edge of resisting him, though she had never done anything like that before and wouldn't have been able to do it if she had thought about it in advance. She wanted to go with Geraden. If anything could be done for the Tor, she ached to do it. But the quality of Lebbick's glare pushed her back. It was outraged and extreme, and it seemed to say that if she forced him to do her violence she would drive him mad.

She turned to the men he had assigned and let them take charge of her.

As she slogged through the mud, she heard Castellan Lebbick stiffly welcome the Tor's retinue and offer the riders and their mounts Orison's best hospitality. Then he went after the Tor and Geraden himself.

Back in her rooms, with her boots cleaned as well as possible and drying in the bathroom, she reflected that the Tor had obviously *not* come to Orison in response to any summons from the Perdon. On the other hand, what difference did the Tor's reasons for being here make now? His presence was what mattered. It worked in Master Eremis' favor.

Master Eremis wasn't a comfortable subject of contemplation. His absence gave her a secret ache of frustration and fear. Nevertheless thoughts of him were an improvement over the image of the Tor which remained with her – the fat old man standing ankle-deep in mud, his dead son in his arms and his eyes bleak with grief. When her mother had died, and Terisa had dared to cry, her father had hit her, once, to make her stop. Then he had gotten drunk for the first and only time she could remember. Then he had begun bringing other women into the house as though his wife had never existed. Terisa definitely preferred thinking of Master Eremis.

An hour or so passed before she realized how restless she was. She wasn't ordinarily a woman who paced, but now she caught herself tensely measuring the rugs and stone of the floor – waiting for Geraden. He had stood up to the Castellan. She felt that it was a long time since she had seen so much strength in him. Surely he would come tell her what had happened?

He did. Before lunchtime, she heard a knock on her door. When she answered it, she found Geraden outside.

He looked like a little boy. His eyes were still puffy from crying, and the expression in them was so forlorn that she wanted to put her arms around him.

She couldn't go that far. A lifetime of inhibition held her: she had never learned how to reach out to other people. But instinctively, without gauging what she did, she put her hand on his arm and breathed, 'Oh, Geraden. What happened?'

He tried to compose himself, but the effort only made him harsh. 'He got to see the King. Being the Domne's son is good for that, at least. I just didn't let anybody say no to me. But King Joyse didn't—'

Then his throat closed on the words, as if they hurt too much to come out.

For a moment, his features knotted. He glanced rapidly at the guards on either side of the door. 'Please, Terisa. I can't talk about it out here in the hall.'

Her heart was beating double time. 'Come in,' she gulped. 'I'm being stupid. I didn't mean to keep you standing there.'

With her hand still on his arm, she drew him into the sitting room.

If he hadn't been struggling so hard to contain himself – and if she hadn't been so awkward – they might have hugged each other. But he looked untouchable in his distress, and she had to step away to close the door. When she turned back to him, he was standing with his elbows pressed against his sides and his hands in fists over his heart.

'Oh, Geraden,' she murmured again. 'Geraden.'

'I don't know what's going on.' His voice was still harsh, clenched. He was trying to shore up something inside himself. 'I swear I don't understand it.

'It wasn't hard to get in to see him. All I had to do was ignore the guards at the door when they told me the King was busy. Under the circumstances, they weren't likely to stand in the Tor's way.

'King Joyse and Adept Havelock were playing hop-board. You probably guessed that. What else,' he asked acidly, 'would make him too busy to see the man who got him started on the road to becoming King of Mordant? But he didn't seem to resent the interruption. When I barged in, he left his game to welcome us. And he smiled the way he does – the way that makes you want to lie down in front of him so he can walk on you.

'Then he saw what the Tor was carrying. I told him who it was. And for a few moments there I thought I had finally done the right thing. For once in my life, I had *finally* done the right thing.

'He seemed to remember his strength and call it back from somewhere. Suddenly, he was taller, bigger, and his eyes flashed. "How was this done?" he demanded. The Tor couldn't speak, so I said, "Imagery. Some kind of strange wolf." Gambling that I knew what I was doing, I said, "Look at his face."

'King Joyse lifted the cloth.' Geraden shuddered. 'It was terrible. But it would have been worse if the body hadn't been frozen for ten days while the Tor was on the road.

'When King Joyse saw it, he seemed to stand up inside himself. He took the body out of the Tor's arms. He raised his head as if he was going to howl. There was so much outrage and hurt in him that it practically shouted from his face. I thought that finally – *finally* – he was going to get angry enough to do something.

'I was wrong.'

Geraden made no effort to muffle his pain. 'Adept Havelock chose that moment to say, "Joyse, it's your move." As if he didn't know anyone else was in the room.

'And King Joyse just collapsed.

'His face crumpled, and he started crying – softly, almost not making a sound. "Oh, my old friend," he said. "Forgive me. Forgive me." Then he fell to his knees – he couldn't hold up the weight any longer.' Geraden was weeping himself, with his elbows hugged to his ribs and his hands across his chest. 'As carefully as he could, he rested the Tor's son on the floor. For a while, he bowed over the body. Then he got his feet under him again' – Geraden had to grip his determination in both fists in order to say the words – 'and went back to his game.'

For a while, Geraden stood still, fighting to regain control of his emotions while Terisa ached for him and the Tor and King Joyse and said nothing.

'After that,' Geraden resumed with a shuddering sigh, 'he didn't respond to anything. He didn't give any orders for the funeral. He didn't answer any questions. Maybe he forgot we were there. Eventually, he moved one of his pieces. As far as I could see, it improved Havelock's position.

'All this time, the Tor hadn't said a word. He looked too stunned, too hurt, to say anything. I thought he was going to fall on his face. But now he pulled himself together a bit. "My son is dead," he said as if maybe King Joyse had failed to notice that detail. "Is this the best you can do?"

'The King still didn't respond. Adept Havelock said, "Close the door on your way out."'

Geraden shrugged. 'Then Castellan Lebbick made us leave. Two of his men had to move the Tor by main force. But I was actually grateful. He did us a favor by getting us out of there.'

Abruptly, the Apt ground the heels of his palms into his eyes to force down his tears and his pain and his weakness. When he looked at Terisa again, his glare was red-rimmed and lost. Certainty had deserted him. More than anything now, he resembled a young man who was being broken by his involuntary instinct for disaster.

'Castellan Lebbick was right,' he said. 'It would have been better if the Tor had been kept away. All I did was make his misery worse.'

'I'm sorry,' Terisa whispered, hating herself for her inability to help him, heal him. But there was nothing she could do for him except say, 'I'm sorry.'

Later that day, alone in her rooms in the middle of the afternoon, with nothing to do except brood, she was standing at one of her windows and musing out toward the road when more riders appeared.

This group was larger than the Tor's, more military in character. A trumpet announced the approach of the riders to the gate of Orison. Castellan Lebbick greeted them with an honor guard equal to the one which had met the Tor. Then they dispersed into the castle. But she still couldn't make up her mind.

Saddith brought news with her supper. 'Have you heard, my lady? Both the Fayle and the Armigite have come to Orison. Both have demanded audiences with King Joyse. And both have been refused.' The maid was proud of her information, as if it came from some high, secret source. 'It is said that the Fayle carries messages from Queen Madin and the lady Torrent. And yet he has been refused.

'If the reports are true, he bears his disappointment stoically. Not so the Armigite. I have heard him. He wanders the halls, accosting whoever will listen and explaining his indignation.' She tittered. 'I am inclined to question his virility, my lady.'

When Saddith left, Terisa found that she had reached her decision. King Joyse was unwilling to meet with the lords of the Cares: he was unwilling even to receive a message from his wife. He was too far gone. Master Eremis was right. Mordant could only be saved now if someone else took charge of events.

She would have to go to him, talk to him, tell him what she knew.

It was possible that she would have to tell him about her secret conversations with Master Quillon and Adept Havelock. Not to betray them, but to help him; the information might make him more effective.

She made this decision because she wanted to do what was right. She didn't mean to remain passive for the rest of her life. Her presence here made no sense – but as long as she *was* here, she had to make some effort to help. For Geraden's sake, as well as for Mordant's. He was too paralyzed – and too hurt – by his devotion to the King; he wasn't able to see past his dislike of the Master. He was blind to the one fact she saw clearly: Master Eremis was the only man who had any chance of uniting the Congery and the lords against Mordant's enemies.

But she wasn't thinking about Geraden – or about Mordant – when she finally reached her decision. She was thinking about the way Master Eremis had kissed her and touched her.

So the next morning, after a restless night, she got up early. She bathed. She washed and dried her hair. When Saddith brought her breakfast, she found that she couldn't eat it. Instead of risking nausea, she asked the maid to help her put on the gown she had chosen the previous evening – a confection of mauve silk which clung to her thighs and made the hollow between her breasts look deep and desirable. Then she dismissed Saddith for the rest of the day, saying that she meant to spend it with the lady Myste.

Saddith winked at this obvious fabrication, grinned her approval, and left as if she had plans of her own.

When the maid was gone, however, Terisa remained in her rooms for quite a while. She told herself that she wasn't hesitating – precisely. She was waiting for a decent hour. But the truth was that she had lost her confidence. Master Eremis was too much for her – too experienced, too adept, too powerful. Geraden had accused him of trying to manipulate her. He had certainly manipulated the Congery. The explanations he gave for what he did weren't entirely satisfying. And apparently he was no longer interested in her.

Nevertheless in the end her resolve held. Around mid-morning, she went to her door, unbolted it with an unsteady hand, and left her rooms.

One of the guards whistled at her softly through his teeth; she ignored him.

Descending from the tower, she panicked for several moments because she wasn't sure of the route back to Master Eremis' quarters. She hadn't paid close enough attention on the one occasion when she had visited those rooms. And she thought she saw a man following her—

She glimpsed him three or four times, on different levels of the castle. He seemed to disappear as soon as she spotted him. But he was tall; he looked strong. A gray cloak hid his clothes and covered his head, but didn't conceal the end of the long sword jutting down near his boots.

On the other hand, he didn't seem to be the man who had attacked her in her rooms. He wasn't wearing black. And he didn't keep after her. Instead, he seemed to forget her after a while. She didn't see any more sign of him.

After worrying about him probably more than he deserved, she put him out of her mind, concentrating her attention again on the problem of finding Master Eremis' quarters.

What she remembered of Geraden's tour helped. Eventually, she found her way into the section of Orison that had been set aside for the personal use of the Masters. After that, all she had to do was locate the polished rosewood door with the full-length bas-relief carving of Master Eremis.

As soon as she reached it, she raised her hand to knock – and stopped. She was breathing too hard. She needed a moment to become calm. But the carving on the door was really quite extraordinary. The eyes seemed to see everything, and the mouth promised pleasures which she might not like. He was much too much for her. If she had any sense left, she would admit that. She had no business taking a risk like this.

So she didn't knock. Gripped by the demented logic of the obsessed, she put her hand on the latch and eased the door open more quietly than the thudding of her heart.

Exactly as she remembered it, she saw the sumptuous room in which the Master had held her and kissed her. She saw the crimson of the uppermost rug made even more dramatic by the blue of the furniture and the yellow of the drapes. She saw the filigree-cut brass urns from which perfumed lamps provided light and warmth. She saw the tapestries which covered the walls with scenes of seduction. She saw the divan—

Master Eremis was on the divan. Fortunately, he wasn't facing in her direction. He was lying forward, his attention focused on the woman under him. The long, clean muscles of his bare back and buttocks bunched and released to the rhythm of his movements.

The woman's legs were locked around his hips. Her arms clenched his back. She made moaning noises deep in her throat.

Her clothes were scattered across the floor. Terisa recognized them. But she didn't need the confirmation.

The woman was unmistakably Saddith.

She had seen something like this once before. Her parents had had separate rooms. After her mother's death, she had begun using her mother's room as a hiding place, a retreat, as if her mother were a more comforting presence dead than alive. Of course she hadn't told her father; he probably had no way of knowing what he was doing when he took one of his women to her mother's bed. She had watched for a while before she had realized what she was seeing.

Now she closed the door softly. Hugging the cold ache in her heart, she returned to her rooms. Careful not to tear it, she finally worked her way out of the silk gown and put it away. Then she got dressed in her old clothes and went to the window to stare out at the wilderland of winter.

She was still there near sunset when yet another group of riders approached the castle. Like the one she had seen the previous afternoon, it was larger than the Tor's retinue – and less funerary. Again, a trumpet saluted the riders as they approached the gate. Again, Castellan Lebbick met them with a guard of honor. While they were dismounting, she thought she recognized the brawny shape and bald head of the Perdon. But she couldn't be sure.

TWELVE

WHAT MEN DO
WITH WOMEN

She didn't know how she was going to face Saddith again. Fortunately, when the maid brought her supper, old habits came to Terisa's rescue. She responded to Saddith's glow in the same pale, passive, covert way that she had so often dealt with her parents; she put on nonexistence like a cloak, so that nothing about her called attention to itself or disturbed the flow of Saddith's emotions and concerns. As a result, she was able to hear Saddith's hints and elation in safety, as if she felt nothing. And she had no trouble fending off the maid's cheerful, leering attempts to find out how she had spent her day.

It seemed quite possible to her that she did feel nothing. How would she have known if an emotion of any importance had taken hold of her?

Unfortunately, the habits that saved her exacted a price. The sensation that she was fading began to steal over her. A bad night loomed ahead – and she had no mirrors with which to defend herself.

After the maid had cleared away the tray and left for the night, Terisa took another bath, using the cold of the water and the warmth of the fire to create the illusion of physical actuality. Then she spent some time meticulously rearranging the lamps in the room, trying to bring out a reflection from the glass of the window. But the black night outside stubbornly refused to give her image back.

She was tempted to give up, let go of herself and take the consequences. But she had been fighting this battle for years. What did Master Eremis have to do with her, anyway? He hadn't created her problem. Surely she wasn't foolish enough to believe that he could cure it? – that his touch on her body could restore what she lacked? Then why was she wasting her time feeling so miserable about him? Why was she—

—trembling in the middle of the room with her heart in an uproar simply because someone had knocked on her door?

She knew the answer to that one. Tonight was the night when Master Eremis and Master Gilbur were supposed to meet with the lords of the Cares.

For a moment, she wanted to ignore whoever was outside her door. But the knock was repeated, reminding her that she really had no place to hide. Mustering her scant resources of courage, she went to answer the door.

Master Eremis stood there grinning.

The way he looked at her still had too much power: effortlessly, it banished all question of fading, made her real in front of him – real for him. After all, what harm had he done her by making love to Saddith? His eyes promised that his attentions were worth having. Who else did she know who could kiss her with just that combination of ardor, experience, and glee?

And if he lost interest in her, she could bring him back by telling him about Adept Havelock and Master Quillon.

In self-defense, trying to take a stand against him, she said, 'I don't want to go.'

He came easily into the room, as if he knew her better than she did herself. 'My lady,' he said in a teasing tone, 'you must.'

'Why?' The effort not to lose herself in his bright gaze and his smile made her light-headed. 'It doesn't have anything to do with me.'

'Ah,' the Master replied, 'now there you are wrong.' His manner became slightly more sober. 'You must come with me as a demonstration of my good faith. You may be unaware of the ill repute which King Joyse has placed upon all Imagers. Either we are the creatures of his will, honest only as far as he is honest, or we retain allegiances to Cadwal and Alend which make us treacherous, or we are the source of the present peril. We are regarded in this way because the Congery was created by force rather than volition. I must persuade these unruly lords to trust me, and that can only be accomplished if I am honest with them. I must show you to them so that they will grasp what the Congery has attempted in the past – and what we mean to do now.

'My lady, this has a great deal to do with you. If you do not come with me, I will gain nothing from this meeting' – he made an attempt not to look too cheerful – 'and all my efforts to save Mordant will be undone.'

His hands twitched the ends of his chasuble playfully.

She remembered his hands. She had just begun to learn what they could do. Her heart was beating in her throat. She almost said, All right. I'll go with you. If you'll take me back to your rooms afterward. The words came so close to utterance that she felt giddy. She had to swallow more than once before she became able to nod her head.

He reached toward her. 'My lady,' he drawled as he took hold of her arm, 'I was confident that you would understand.'

The guards stopped him as he closed the door after her. They wanted to know where he was taking her. Castellan Lebbick's orders. Even though – she was only vaguely aware of this – Geraden was never questioned when she left with him. Master Eremis replied acerbically that the lady Terisa of Morgan had agreed to join him and several other Masters for a quiet supper in the quarters of the mediator of the Congery. Then he steered her away.

The set of his jaw showed that the guards had made him angry.

Holding her arm, he took her down out of the tower and through several of the main halls. She nearly missed her balance and stopped when she spotted the man in the gray cloak again. But he disappeared almost immediately; she lost sight of him before she could point him out to Master Eremis. Smiling apologetically to excuse her awkwardness, she walked on. The man in the gray cloak didn't reappear.

Master Eremis made no obvious attempt at stealth, but he moved along a route calculated to confuse the few guards they passed. Nevertheless it soon became clear that he wasn't taking Terisa anywhere near the Congery's private section of Orison. Nor was he moving toward the complex rooms and passages of the laborium. Rather, he was descending, circuitously but steadily, into a dank, disused part of the castle which resembled the place where Adept Havelock had his rooms – a place among the foundations of Orison. For a moment, she was struck by the wild thought that Master Eremis had something to do with Master Quillon and the Adept. But though the passages Eremis chose were cold, empty, and untended, they were still public enough to be lighted: lanterns hung from the walls at distant intervals. The side corridors and chambers seemed to indicate that this part of the castle had once been inhabited. Perhaps Orison had settled as it was built higher. Or perhaps the foundations had begun to leak. Whatever the reason, these halls and rooms had clearly been abandoned for drier quarters on some other level. Master Eremis' boots splashed through ice-scummed puddles on the floor, and the sound echoed wetly. Terisa could hear water dripping in the distance.

She hugged her arms against the cold and tried to remember the way back, so that she wouldn't get lost.

Without warning, a dark shape seemed to materialize out of the wall. She flinched involuntarily. The nearest lantern was twenty or thirty feet away, and its dim light made the figure look as bulky and dangerous as a bear.

But Master Eremis chuckled through his teeth; and a moment later she made out a profile with a bald head, thick eyebrows, and a shaggy mustache. The man was wrapped in a fur cloak the same dark, wet color as the shadows. He probably presented such a bestial shape because he was still wearing his pallettes and gorget under the cloak.

Now that she looked harder, she saw the faint outline of a doorway behind him. He must have been waiting concealed there for Master Eremis to come along.

'Master Eremis,' the man breathed. His greeting steamed in the cold. 'They are all foregathered – even that hunchbacked dog you say we must endure to reassure the Congery. You are not what I call prompt.' Terisa could see only half his face in the lantern light, but the one eye on that side glared at her. 'Why do you bring a woman?'

'My lord Perdon,' the Imager replied, 'it is not as easy as you imagine to arrange for a meeting like this to take place in secret.' The softness of his voice muffled his sarcasm. 'Lebbick watches everything – or thinks he does. A number of plausible lies must be placed in a variety of ears. I will explain the woman.'

The Perdon glowered at Terisa a moment longer. 'Explain her well, Master Eremis.' Then he shifted his gaze to the Imager. 'When you persuaded me to this meeting, I promised that I would gather the other lords as quickly as possible. But the task of sending summons and receiving answer across such distances at this season seemed likely to take at least fifteen days.

You assured me, however, that less time would be required. I must confess that I did not entirely believe you. Now I am astonished that you were right to such an impossible degree.'

In surprise, Terisa nearly said aloud, *Fifteen* days? He told us *six*. He told the Congery you promised *six*.

The Master's grip on her arm kept her quiet. 'Imagery has its uses,' he commented enigmatically.

'Doubtless it has,' said the Perdon. 'And doubtless you will explain them, also – when you see fit. But one answer you must give me. I am troubled by the Tor's presence among us.'

'Troubled, my lord Perdon?'

'Yes, Master Eremis.' A clenched fist showed between the edges of the Perdon's cloak. 'I do not trust him here. He has been too steadfastly the King's friend. I agreed to summon him only because I believed him too old – and too fat – to make the journey. His presence now alarms me.'

At that, Master Eremis cocked an eyebrow. 'Now you begin to alarm *me*. I begin to suspect, my lord Perdon, that it is not the Tor you distrust. It is me.'

The Perdon's scowl didn't waver.

'This distresses me.' Eremis let a glint of anger into his voice. 'When you spoke of fifteen days, I knew that the time would be less because the Termigan was already on the road to Orison. I have a flat glass which chances to show his seat in Sternwall, and I saw him depart.

'When the Tor arrived, I did not hesitate to include him. Has no one spoken to you, my lord? Has the Tor himself not told you why he is here? He came to demand a response from our brave King because his eldest son was killed by some instance of vile Imagery. And the King has refused. He refuses even to hear the demand – as he has also refused audiences to the Fayle and the Armigite.

'The Tor loves his sons,' Master Eremis concluded. 'I believe he will be our ally now.'

'Well,' the Perdon murmured. 'Well.' He had turned his head. All his face was in shadow. 'He has been the King's friend for forty years. But perhaps grief will make him bitter. Perhaps it is worth the risk to have him with us.'

'My lord Perdon,' said the Master dryly, 'you have already implied that I am late. If we do not go to them soon, the other lords will become restive, and then we will have no one with us.'

The Perdon's eye came flashing back into the light. He stretched out his fist and touched the Imager's chest lightly. 'Be warned, Master Eremis,' he whispered. 'I am the lord of the Care of Perdon. I do not like manipulation – or abused trust. And I suspect that my fellow lords have similar prejudices.'

Then he turned and strode away down the corridor, his heels loud against the stone.

For a moment, Master Eremis held Terisa where she was. 'Someday,' he said in a musing tone, 'that rash lord really must be taught to be more careful with his threats.'

Almost involuntarily, as if the question were forced out of her, she asked, 'Why did you lie to the Congery? You told them it was the Perdon's idea to meet tonight.'

At once, he raised a finger to his lips. 'My lady,' he whispered, 'I have already explained that some of my fellow Masters do not like or trust me. They only accepted the risk of this meeting because they believed it to be based on the Perdon's honor rather than on my foresight. Now I advise you not to utter a word until you are once again safely in your rooms.'

Still holding her arm tightly, he drew her after the Perdon.

They followed the hard echo of his bootheels until they had passed another turn; then she saw light streaming from an open doorway ahead. The door wasn't guarded: apparently, the lords of the Cares still believed they were safe in Orison. The Perdon strode through the doorway, and Terisa heard low voices greet him. A moment later, Master Eremis took her into the light.

There he released her arm and gave her a small nudge forward. She had the impression that he had stepped back – that he was using her entrance to provide some kind of distraction.

The door opened on a room as plain as a cell and not much larger. The light came from several lanterns set on a long, crude wooden table which filled at least half the space. The heavy chairs around the table made the chamber crowded.

As soon as she entered the room, Terisa noticed Master Gilbur: he sat at the far end of the table, and his features were clenched in an acid scowl, as if he had been trading insults with someone.

The Perdon was still on his feet, but the other lords were seated. She recognized the Tor, of course. He sat near Master Gilbur. Out of direct contact with the winter, his skin had a less abused color; but his face still looked like a handful of mealy potatoes, and his eyes were glazed. There was an enormous flagon on the table in front of him.

Opposite him was a man whom Terisa took at once to be the Armigite, simply because of Saddith's description. The softness of his face made it appear fleshier than it really was, and his expression was petulant; his hair was darkened and pomaded into elaborate curls; his clothes were rich in a way that somehow suggested a lady's bedroom. He was the only man in the room who looked younger than Master Eremis: clearly, he had inherited his place rather than earning it in Mordant's wars.

Like the other lords, he was armed, but the slim blade at his side seemed essentially decorative.

The man next to him was a strong contrast: he appeared to have been chipped from a block of flint. Every line of his face, every glance of his eyes, every gesture of his hands looked like it had been made sharp by blows, hammered to a cutting edge. His skin had a dusty tinge that suited his flat eyes. His eyebrows seemed to have no color.

He must have been the Termigan. Terisa reasoned this because he wasn't old enough to be Queen Madin's father. The lord across from him – beside the Tor – was much more likely to be the Fayle. This man was at least the Tor's age; the sparse white hair on the back of his skull was cut short; he was as lean as a whippet. His face was so long, and had so much jaw, that he might have looked lugubrious if his eyes hadn't been so bright, blue, and precise. The way he sat – upright in his chair, with his arms crisply folded over his thin chest – implied the stoicism Saddith had attributed to him.

With the exception of the Tor – whose attention was fixed on his flagon – everyone was looking at her. The Fayle's keen gaze betrayed nothing; but the Termigan regarded her indignantly, the Armigite's face wore a sneer, and Master Gilbur's customary scowl was black and stormy.

The men and the lanterns made the room considerably wanner than the corridor.

No one offered any introductions. As soon as Master Eremis came into the room, just a moment or two after Terisa, the Perdon announced sourly, 'Master Eremis says that he will explain her.' The red hair of his eyebrows and ears bristled as he took a chair beside the Termigan.

'I would like an explanation,' Master Gilbur growled at once. 'What sort of legerdemain will you use to make us swallow her presence, Eremis?'

Under so much hostile scrutiny, Terisa felt her face growing hot. Anybody who looked at her closely would notice the sweat trickling down her temples. How had she become the linchpin of Master Eremis' plans? Why did everything he wanted in this meeting suddenly hinge on her?

'My lady' – his tone wasn't especially courteous – 'be seated.' He gestured her toward the chair beside the Fayle. Then he sat down himself, at the head of the table opposite Master Gilbur. His leanness, the thatch of black hair behind his high forehead, and the way his cheeks sloped like the sides of a wedge from his ears toward his large nose gave him the appearance of an exotic bird. In some ways, she had never seen him look less serious. The sparkle in his eyes counterbalanced the grim set of his mouth. His hands he folded together on the table in a conspicuously unsuccessful effort to appear grave.

'My lords,' he said briskly, glancing at each of them in turn, 'the problem is time. If we were not in haste, I would not have presumed to make decisions without your knowledge and consent. It is true that this winter may not break for another thirty days, or even fifty. But it may break in ten. In ten days, an army of considerable size may begin to march against us from Cadwal. And only a few days have passed since wise King Joyse saw fit to reject a proposed alliance with Alend, humiliating the ambassador to seal his refusal. The forces of Margonal will not be far behind those of the High King.'

'That is true,' the Armigite said with boyish bitterness. 'If King Joyse had granted me an audience, I would have told him that Margonal's army musters not half a day's march from the Pestil. My commanders say that they cannot stand against it. When Alend decides to attack, I will be swept away. And King Joyse refuses to hear me!'

He would have gone on, but Master Eremis cut in smoothly, 'Worse than armies, however, is Imagery. And Imagery does not wait for spring. All Mordant is already assailed. Strange wolves have slaughtered the Tor's son. Ghouls harry the villages of Fayle. Devouring lizards swarm the storehouses of the Demesne. Pits of fire appear in the ground of Termigan – almost within the fortifications of Sternwall.'

The Termigan nodded bleakly. 'That's why I'm here. I'm a soldier. I'm weaponless against pits of fire in the ground.'

'We have no time, my lords,' Master Eremis concluded. 'For that reason, I have presumed to do what I have done.'

He paused, and Master Gilbur growled, 'Get on with it, Eremis. What have you done?'

Master Eremis' dour expression nearly broke. Suppressing himself stiffly, he said, 'I have invited someone else to our meeting.' Before anyone could react, he called over his shoulder, 'My lord, you may come in now!'

Terisa gaped as Prince Kragen strode into the room, accompanied by his two bodyguards.

His bearing showed that his self-assurance hadn't been dampened. He no longer wore his ceremonial brass helmet, breastplate, and sword sheath. Black silk garments emphasized the darkness of his skin; his mustache gleamed. But once again he had a strong sword belted to his hip. His bodyguards were armed for use rather than show.

Seeing him, the Armigite blanched. The Termigan thrust back his chair and sprang to his feet, hauling at his sword. Master Gilbur's face darkened apoplectically. The Tor took a swig from his flagon and belched.

'This is surprising,' commented the Fayle in a voice like the rustle of dry leaves. 'You are not presumptuous by half measures, Master Eremis.'

'Have you lost your mind?' the Perdon snapped at Eremis. 'I warned you that we will not be manipulated. Will you admit the son of the Alend Monarch to our secret counsels?'

One of the bodyguards braced himself between Prince Kragen and the Termigan. Before the man could draw his sword, however, the Prince stopped him. 'My lords,' he said with a placating gesture, 'hear me. You are surprised – but you are not threatened. Indeed, I am grateful that Master Eremis has provided me this opportunity to meet with you. After my treatment at the hands of your King, I was minded to depart Orison at once. But that would have ensured war between Mordant and Alend. And the Alend Monarch strongly desires peace. It is his greatest wish to form an alliance against the perils of Cadwal and Imagery. Therefore when Master Eremis asked me to remain in Orison, promising me a chance to speak to you, I allowed myself to be persuaded.

'My lords, I have been denied an alliance with Mordant's King. But surely the same end may be achieved by an alliance with Mordant's lords?'

'Alend is my enemy,' the Termigan spat at once, still holding his sword. 'I've had too many brothers and friends killed by Alends who thought it was their right to own our freedom. I didn't realize, Master Eremis, that you called us together to discuss treason.'

'Oh, *treason*, forsooth.' The Armigite fluttered his delicate hands, quickly recovering from his initial fright. 'For myself, I am delighted to see Prince Kragen on grounds of friendship. What is your loyalty, my lord Termigan – to King Joyse, or to Mordant? You know what our King has done – and not done – to meet our need. I call it *treason* to obey him further. Mordant,' he added piously, 'is a higher service.'

'My lord Termigan,' Prince Kragen continued, 'you must understand the Alend Monarch's position. As I have said, his desire for peace is strong. We have known peace since you fought so powerfully for our defeat – and we have learned that peace is better than war. But your King has not been content with peace. He has created the Congery.

'My lords,' he said generally, 'the Congery represents great danger. While your King held it strongly, so that it served the causes of peace, we were able to bear the threat. But now your King has become weak. Mordant is under attack by Imagery – and Imagery is not used in your defense. How are we to explain this? Either your King has gone mad and no longer cares to defend what he fought so long to win. Or he has gone mad and now wields the Congery against his own land, preparing his strength' – Master Gilbur started to protest, but the Prince overrode him – 'so that in time he will be able to destroy us all!'

'*That* is a lie!' Master Gilbur barked, pounding the table. 'Of course King Joyse is mad. But he does *not* use the Congery! By the balls of the arch-Imager's goat, we are *not* the cause of this peril!'

Prince Kragen didn't take offense. 'You speak for yourself, Master Gilbur,' he said mildly, 'and for yourself I believe you. That the Congery desires our meeting augurs well for its honesty. To my mind, Master Eremis has proven himself true by bringing us together – and by gaining the Congery's permission to tell us what the Masters mean to do in Mordant's defense. Sadly, however, that changes nothing. Your King has become weak. Therefore Cadwal aspires to possession of the Congery. And therefore Alend must fight. We cannot permit so many Imagers to become a weapon in the hands of the High King.

'My lord Termigan, you have lost much in war against us. We also have lost much. But Mordant and Alend together will lose a great deal more if Festten becomes the ruler of the Congery.'

'Well said!' cheered the Armigite. 'Well said!'

The Perdon was looking hard at Master Eremis. After a moment, he said softly, 'You are wiser than I realized, Master Eremis. If I had known that you are so farsighted, I would have come to you for counsel sooner.'

Eremis' eyes glittered, but he didn't permit himself to smile.

The Prince's argument was enough to make the Termigan reconsider. He lowered his sword; frowning in thought, he stared at the table.

Unexpectedly, the Tor banged his flagon to the table. 'Oh, sit down, my lord Termigan. So much upright anger makes me tired. Let us learn what more surprises are in store for us.'

'Before we go further,' the Fayle said dryly, 'perhaps Master Eremis will explain why he has brought this young woman to hear what we say and decide.'

Taken by surprise, Terisa's heart started to pound again.

Abruptly, the Termigan slapped his sword back into its sheath and sat down. His flat eyes looked at no one. 'Yes, Master Eremis. Account for the woman. You ask us to accept too much too quickly.'

Master Eremis opened his mouth to answer, but Prince Kragen was faster. 'My lords, she is the lady Terisa of Morgan. I know nothing of her. Yet I am in her debt. During my audience with your King, she did all she could to spare me humiliation. For that, the gratitude of Alend is hers.' He gave Terisa a formal bow. Then, his voice at once velvet and iron, he added, 'My lords, I must ask you to treat her with respect.'

Master Gilbur snorted softly.

The Tor peered past the Fayle at her through a blur of wine. 'You were with that boy of the Domne's,' he said thickly. 'Geraden. When I arrived.' Without warning, his eyes filled with tears. Blinking furiously, he leaned back in his chair, then slapped his hand down on the table. 'Take my gratitude as well. Prince Kragen and I will see that you are treated with respect.'

Gulping from his flagon, he slumped to the side as if he had lost consciousness.

'Very touching,' the Armigite murmured without quite looking at Terisa. 'What will we have next? Offers of marriage?'

The other lords, however, seemed to think better of the Tor than of the Armigite: they didn't acknowledge his sarcasm. Instead, they fixed their attention pointedly on Master Eremis, and the Termigan said, 'I'll respect her well enough when I understand why she's here.'

'My lords' – Eremis spread his hands in an expansive gesture – 'I will tell you. Will you be seated, my lord Prince?'

'Thank you.' Smoothly, Prince Kragen moved to a chair beside Terisa, between her and the Fayle. His eyes gleamed at her. 'May I sit at your side, my lady?' he murmured. He didn't wait for her permission, however. As he sat down, she noticed that his hands were well manicured, but there were ridges of callus on his palms and fingers.

His bodyguards stationed themselves behind him.

'As you have heard,' Master Eremis resumed at once, 'she is the lady Terisa of Morgan. She was brought among us by Imagery.'

No one reacted to this announcement: perhaps it was self-evident.

'Beyond that, you already know as much of her as I do – certain secondary details aside.' He couldn't resist a leering grin that made the Armigite snigger. But he suppressed it quickly. 'She reveals nothing. She has no discernible talent for Imagery. I brought her here so that you will understand what the Congery has done in an effort to answer Mordant's need – and what we now propose to do.

'My lords, our dilemma is yours, and we are not blind to it. Mordant is in great danger. And King Joyse has lost his senses. Therefore we have done what Imagers have always done. We have cast an augury.

'A great amount of time was required to do this. It is not a simple thing to create the glass needed for such specific augury. But when the glass was done, the augury was cast. As best we can, we have acted on what we learned.

'I will not trouble you with lengthy explanations of augury. It is enough to say that the matter of interpretation is difficult. Put simply, our augury shows Mordant's peril. It shows an alien figure of great power. It shows scenes of victory. And it appears to imply a connection between the figure of power and the Domne's youngest boy, Geraden.

'As it happens, this same figure of power is visible in one of Master Gilbur's most celebrated mirrors.'

Master Gilbur gave the room an indiscriminate glare.

'We came to the conclusion,' Eremis continued, 'that this figure was the champion who would save Mordant – if he were translated in the right way. And we agreed – not without some debate – that it must be Geraden's task to perform the translation.'

He leaned back and indicated Terisa with a nod. 'She is the result. In some way that we cannot explain, Geraden's translation went awry.' Then he paused to enjoy the perplexed frowns and muttering of the lords.

The Tor twitched in his seat. 'I know that Geraden,' he rumbled. 'He is a good boy. A true son of his father.' Absentmindedly, he yawned and took another pull from his flagon.

After a moment, the Armigite said in a tone of rising indignation, 'Do you mean us to believe, Master Eremis, that Mordant is to be saved by this' – he waved the back of his hand in Terisa's direction – 'this *woman?*'

'No, my lord Armigite.' The Fayle's voice was as dry and brittle as ever, but it held an unexpected authority. 'Master Eremis would never ask that of a man who has no wife and no daughters. He means us to understand the decisions which the Congery has made because of the lady Terisa's translation.'

'Exactly, my lord Fayle.' Despite his stern expression, the laughter in Master Eremis' eyes implied a comment on the Armigite's embarrassment. 'It is my hope that seeing the lady Terisa will enable you to grasp why we have determined now to turn our backs on the obvious interpretation of our augury.

'Though he figures prominently in the augury, we have decided to forgo , Geraden's assistance. Master Gilbur will perform the translation as soon as you wish him to do so.'

Terisa thought the room was getting colder. But— she protested. But— That wasn't what the Congery had decided. Master Eremis was going too far.

The Tor made a soft snoring noise. The other men were more attentive, however. The Termigan stared at Master Eremis. The Armigite's mouth hung open. Prince Kragen's gaze darted watchfully around the room, gauging what he saw. The Fayle moved his lips as if he were talking to himself. In the surprised silence, Terisa could hear the creak of the bodyguards' leather as they shifted on their feet.

All at once, her sense of the situation changed. Despite his strange manner, Master Eremis had the ability to amaze her. Now she understood what he was doing. He was trying to forge an alliance, trying to place all three of the forces here – the lords, the Congery, and Alend's representative – into positions from which they would find it impossible to refuse him. Lacking the strength of the King, or even the authority of the mediator of the Congery, he was forced to resort to these subtle ploys. But the point of his maneuvering was to save Mordant.

Abruptly, Prince Kragen slapped his hand down on the table and crowed, 'Bravely done, Master Eremis! You are audacious and resourceful, and you have my admiration. This is the union you offer us – Alend and the lords of Mordant and the Congery. I would not have believed there to be a man anywhere bold enough to make such a proposal – and clever enough to make it possible by bringing us together.'

'Master Eremis is indeed audacious and resourceful,' said the Fayle. 'Our reward for forming the union he wishes is the chance to employ the Congery's champion as if he were our own.'

'You say a "figure of power,"' the Termigan put in brusquely. His tone suggested distaste, but his flat eyes revealed nothing. 'What do you mean?'

'A moment, my lord Termigan,' the Fayle insisted mildly. 'I must claim precedence.'

The Termigan closed his mouth.

'Emend me if I am mistaken, Master Eremis.' The Fayle's blue eyes glittered like a bird's. 'Has not King Joyse forbidden any translation that deprives its object of volition?'

'He has,' snapped Master Gilbur. 'The greater our need for Imagery, the more he strives to paralyze us.'

'And is he aware that your champion will be brought among us involuntarily?'

Master Eremis spread his hands like a shrug. 'My lord, that is one of many reasons why we must meet in secret. Our wise King will not lift his hand in Mordant's defense. But he will take Orison stone from stone to prevent a forbidden translation.' Then Eremis indicated Terisa. 'The last time we obeyed his commands, she was the result.'

'I see,' the Fayle replied. 'Forgive my interruption, my lord Termigan.'

'For my part,' said the Perdon fiercely, 'I favor anything that will keep Festten's butchers on their side of the Vertigon. I have sworn to send King Joyse my dead and wounded if I am attacked – and I will do it.'

The Armigite looked like he was going to be sick.

The Termigan hadn't shifted his gaze from Eremis. Softly, he said, 'Tell us about this "figure of power," Master Eremis.'

'What is the need?' Gilbur demanded sourly. 'He is *augured*. We must have him.'

But Master Eremis answered, 'He has weapons that hurl a destructive fire. His armor protects him from all attack. Seeing him in battle, we cannot imagine how even an army would be able to stand against him. Surely he will be proof against wolves and ghouls and devouring lizards. Pits of fire will not harm him. He will be able to fight this vile Imagery to its source.'

'Better and better.' Prince Kragen's smile shone like his mustache. 'What *is* that source, Master Eremis?'

'I believe,' Eremis replied as grimly as his private excitement allowed, 'that he is the arch-Imager Vagel.'

The Tor made a snorting noise. He raised his head, glanced around blearily for a moment, then heaved himself to his feet. 'My lords, I must go to my bed. I have become too old for so much carousal.'

'Do not go, my old friend,' the Fayle remonstrated gently. 'You must help us to a decision.'

The Tor blinked hard. 'What decision? I have none to make. I will not return to Marshalt. I am *old*, I say. These questions are too much for me. If King Joyse means to destroy Mordant, I will be here to assist him. I will stand at his side to the end.' He made a small chuckling noise. 'He deserves me.' Then he began to shuffle his bulk toward the door. 'My son always said I was a fool and a coward for not giving him more than two hundred men when he first set himself to become King. Now my son is dead. I should not have been so cautious.'

Slowly, he lumbered out of the room.

To Terisa's surprise, the Armigite said, 'The Tor is right. We should all go to bed. A decision like this should not be made quickly.' His eyes showed white, and there was sweat on his upper lip. 'What if we are discovered? What if Castellan Lebbick comes upon us? We need time. We must choose with care.' His voice cracked. Struggling for dignity, he concluded, 'I do not like decisions.'

With considerable asperity, the Perdon snapped, 'My lord Armigite, your father is groaning in his grave. Did he fight so many bloody-handed battles against' – he flicked a glance at Prince Kragen – 'against foes of every description, simply to surrender his Care to a half-man who does not like decisions?'

The Armigite flushed, but was too nauseated to retort.

'My lords,' the Perdon went on, 'Armigite is bordered on the east by Perdon, on the west by Fayle and Termigan, on the north by Alend. We are enough. The Armigite cannot oppose us all. He will permit us to make his decisions for him.'

There was a moment of silence while the Armigite squirmed and the Perdon looked hotly around him. Then the Fayle said, 'Be explicit, my lord Perdon.' He sounded like a dry husk. 'What is the decision you propose?'

'I propose the union Master Eremis has offered us,' replied the Perdon at once. 'I propose that we join together to draw up a plan of battle – against Cadwal as well as against these attacks of Imagery. King Joyse we will ignore. When Prince Kragen has had time to ready his forces' – he spoke as though he could hear trumpets, and his bald head seemed to gleam with enthusiasm – 'the lords of the Cares will march with him and the champion of the Congery for the preservation of the realm.'

Master Eremis sat very still, trying not to smile. Down the table from him, Gilbur had covered his face with his heavy hands.

'That's eloquent, my lord Perdon.' The Termigan's tone betrayed neither approval nor sarcasm. 'I'm considered a loveless man. Certainly, I've got little use for any of you, my lords – and none for King Joyse. But Termigan is my *Care*. From the depths of its copper mines to the expanse of its wheat fields and the heights of Sternwall's towers, it is mine.

'Tell me this. When Cadwal is beaten, and the Imagery has been defeated, and Joyse is deprived of kingship, who is going to rule Mordant and Termigan? Who is going to have authority over my Care?'

Prince Kragen replied with surprising promptness, 'The lady Elega.'

Elega? Terisa thought as if she had been kicked.

'She is your King's eldest daughter, his rightful heir. And I have had the pleasure of her acquaintance in recent days. She understands power and rule better than you know.' He paused. 'And she is not Alend.'

'A woman,' groaned the Armigite, apparently seeking to regain lost stature. 'Then you will marry her, and Margonal will become king over us.'

Kragen's eyes glittered dangerously, but he didn't deign to retort. Instead, he asked the Termigan, 'Is she acceptable to you, my lord?'

'My lords,' interposed the Fayle. For the first time, he unfolded his arms and put his long, thin fingers flat on the table. The veins in the backs of his hands bulged crookedly. 'This must stop.'

At once, every eye in the room was on him.

'I have heard enough.' He sounded old and tired; yet there was an undercurrent of firmness in his voice. 'If you mean to accept this alliance, you must be content to do so against my opposition. Fayle will support the King.'

In an apologetic tone, he added, 'You must understand that I am the father of his wife. Queen Madin is a formidable woman. Whatever choice I make here, I must justify to her.'

'Women and women!' The Perdon was on his feet, his features clenched in anger. 'Must Mordant be destroyed because you cannot stand before your own daughter? Or because Prince Kragen is enamored of Elega? Or because' – he brandished his mustache at Terisa – 'Master Eremis desires to bed this product of Imagery? My lords, such questions are not important! Our ruin musters against us while we debate petty considerations. We must—'

'No, my lord Perdon.' Though the Termigan didn't raise his voice, he made himself heard through the Perdon's ire. 'You'll do what you want. But you'll do it without me. My lord Fayle is too polite to say what he thinks. I'm not so courteous. There is some plot here. My lord Prince agrees with all this too easily. I *know* the Alend Monarch. When he closes his hand around Mordant, he won't release it – not unless the lady Elega has already agreed to become his proxy.'

He got to his feet. 'Make all the alliances you can. I trust no Alend or Imager.' Roughly, he strode from the room.

For a moment, no one moved or spoke. The Termigan's unexpected declaration appeared to have shocked everyone. Terisa was reeling at the sudden collapse of Master Eremis' plans. He looked like he wanted to laugh; she interpreted that as fury.

'One thing more,' said the Fayle. He, too, was standing. 'Master Eremis, Master Gilbur – you must not translate this figure of power.'

Master Eremis only cocked an eyebrow. The Armigite looked like he was trying to shrink down in his seat, so that he would be ready to duck under the table. But the Perdon stared accumulated outrage at the Fayle. And Master Gilbur demanded in quick anger, '*Not?*'

'You will violate the King's express commands. And more – you will violate the purpose for which the Congery was conceived. You must not do it.'

'That purpose is Joyse's, not ours!' retorted Gilbur. 'We will not allow some doddering old fool to tell us our duty.' Abruptly, he hit the table so hard that the Tor's abandoned flagon toppled to the floor. '*We mean to survive!*'

'Then,' murmured the Fayle sadly, 'I must tell the King what you intend.'

Terisa felt a sting of panic as she saw everything Master Eremis had tried to achieve backfire.

Prince Kragen was on his feet with his bodyguards.

The Perdon faced the Fayle across the table. 'Do you mean to betray us, my lord Fayle?'

'No, my lord Perdon,' the Fayle answered as though he were grieving. 'I will say nothing of this meeting. I mean only to prevent the Imagers from betraying their King.'

He should have looked foolish as he left the room: he was old and thin, and his erect carriage emphasized his peaked shoulders, his ill-proportioned head. The men he opposed were younger, stronger, handsomer. But he didn't look foolish. To her astonishment, Terisa considered him admirable. His loyalty touched her. She could imagine Geraden greeting the Fayle's exit with applause.

When the old lord was gone, Master Eremis threw back his head and let out a sound like the cry of a loon.

'Oh, control yourself, Eremis!' growled Master Gilbur. The hunchbacked Imager was plainly furious. 'I warned you that this would happen. These *lords* forget every lesson of the past, but they remember that they do not trust Imagery. I have said from the beginning that we must take our own action and let the Cares fend for themselves.'

'Yes, Master Gilbur,' said Eremis. 'You did indeed warn me. You warned me often.' With a sudden push, he left his chair. Speaking rapidly, urgently, he said. 'My lord Prince, my lord Perdon, you must excuse me.' He ignored the Armigite. 'Despite Master Gilbur's warning, I did not anticipate this outcome.' His face was so knotted that Terisa couldn't read it. 'Our fellow Masters are already at work, preparing the champion's translation. We must go to them at once, before the Fayle is able to bring down the King's wrath. If they are caught in the act of a forbidden translation, I fear that our kind King will reinstitute the practice of execution.

'My lord Prince, will you see that the lady Terisa is returned to her rooms?'

Without waiting for an answer, Master Eremis said, 'Come, Master Gilbur,' and hurried away.

Master Gilbur followed as quickly as his bent back allowed.

Terisa sat where she was, too confused to move. Why did she admire the Fayle, when he and the Termigan had ruined Master Eremis' efforts to save Mordant? And why was the translation already started? The Congery had agreed to wait for the outcome of this meeting.

'It is too bad, my lord Prince,' the Armigite was saying, 'that the courage to accept your offer of alliance is so scarce. I would be willing to discuss a private union. I would require protection against reprisals. In exchange, I would—'

His voice trailed away; no one was listening to him.

'My lord Prince,' said the Perdon stiffly, 'please forgive the failure of this meeting – and the insult. I can only assure you that Master Eremis and I meant well. It will not be wise to linger here. Shall I relieve you of the lady Terisa?'

'No apology is needed, my lord Perdon.' Prince Kragen didn't appear as upset as Terisa expected. 'It is true that my mission has met little success. Frankly, I do not see how Mordant and Alend can now be saved from war.' He gave Terisa a sparkling black glance and grinned. 'But perhaps my fortunes will improve. I am in the lady's debt. I will happily escort her.'

'As you wish.' The Perdon bowed brusquely, pulled his cloak around him, and left.

Almost at once, the Armigite scrambled after him, as though the younger lord were afraid to be left behind. When he reached the corridor, Terisa heard him call out to the Perdon, asking for company. She didn't hear the Perdon's answer.

'My lady.' Prince Kragen had his hands on the back of her chair. 'Will you come?' He was bowing slightly over her and smiling. 'As the Perdon has said, it is not wise to linger.'

She didn't know how to interpret his smile. It reminded her to some degree of Master Eremis'. At the same time, it suggested that the Prince was a better diplomat, better able to conceal his feelings. His self-assurance was as good as a mask.

She rose in compliance. She had learned her manners from her father.

He pulled the chair out of her way, then took her arm, holding her closely but without undue intimacy. With one bodyguard ahead of him and one behind, he guided her from the room.

Almost without transition, the temperature of the air dropped. The sound of dripping water seemed to creep around her.

'Are you warm enough, my lady?' the Prince asked softly. 'You are not warmly dressed.'

She should have murmured some noncommittal reply. But she had lost the ability to be as compliant as she appeared. In instinctive self-defense, she answered with a question of her own. 'Do you really know Elega?'

She felt him stiffen. He was silent for a moment. Then he said politely, 'My lady, it is customary to address me by my title.'

'My lord Prince.'

He let an easy laugh into the dank passage. 'Thank you. Yes, it has been my great pleasure to make the acquaintance of the lady Elega. I have had considerable leisure since the debacle of my audience with King Joyse.'

The boots of the bodyguards made crisp crack-and-spatter noises as they strode through puddles of water thinly crusted with ice. When the light of the lanterns was right, she could see her breath steaming. Without conscious boldness, she asked, 'Then why are you interested in me?'

Again, he fell momentarily silent, as though he needed time to digest her question and marshal a reply. 'My lady,' he answered finally, 'if another woman asked that question, I would know better how to respond. Can you be unaware that you have a face and form that would interest any man? Perhaps you can. Yet I suspect that your question had another meaning.

'If you are not a coquette – if your question is not meant to entice me – I will answer frankly. I am much impressed by the lady Elega. King Joyse has done more than he knows in producing such a daughter.'

Terisa breathed an almost audible sigh of relief.

There was a hitch in the leading bodyguard's stride, a flicker of hesitation. Then he resumed his steady pace.

A chill reached both hands through Terisa's shirt.

'Few Mordants clearly understand, I think,' Prince Kragen went on with apparent irrelevance, 'that the rule of Alend is not hereditary. When my father, the present Alend Monarch, dies, I will not automatically assume his

Seat in Scarab. Rather, the new Monarch will be chosen by contest from among all those who wish to vie for rule.

'Incidentally,' he commented, 'it is this method of choosing rulers that has preserved the confederacy of the Alend Lieges. Those unruly barons remain faithful to Scarab because they know that they or their families will always have another opportunity to win the Seat.

'This contest is not formal, of course. It has simply evolved. In former times, it was primarily a test of ruthlessness. Whoever butchered, poisoned, or terrified enough of his opponents into submission became Monarch.

'Peace has its benefits, however,' he continued. His voice formed a murmuring undertone to the damp echo of bootheels. 'And the Alend Monarch is devoted to wisdom, as I have said repeatedly. Now people who desire to rule Alend are not allowed to fester in private, scheming murder. They are publicly acknowledged, and they are tested in the service of the kingdom. Put simply, they are given opportunity to demonstrate that they are fit for the Seat.' He chuckled briefly. 'One mad old baron put his son forward in recent years – and then went privately about the business of trying to slaughter all opposition. His son was given the test of bringing the baron to justice.

'As it happens, he succeeded admirably.

'My lady,' he said ruefully, 'this mission is a test for me. And it does not provide much hope. You could safely wager, I fear, that I will not be the next Alend Monarch.'

At once, however, he assumed a more cheerful tone. 'But we were discussing the lady Elega. I mention all this so that you will understand me when I say that if she were an Alend the Seat of the Monarch would not be closed to her. I believe that she would stand high among the powers of the Kingdom.'

The leading bodyguard hesitated again. This time, he nearly froze in mid-stride. Cold suddenly licked across Terisa's heart. She thought she heard the same thing he did – a quiet leather sound which reminded her of swords and sheaths.

Prince Kragen snatched at his blade. He had time to snap, 'Beware! Guard the lady!' Then the darkness attacked.

Men charged out of a side passage. How many? She couldn't tell – five or six. Cloaks fluttered from their shoulders like wings. Their leather armor was so black it was difficult to see. Lantern light glinted on bare iron.

They struck straight for her through the opposition of the Prince and his bodyguards.

Swords rang, echoing in the passage. Baleful red sparks sprayed from the conflict of blades. Violence streaked her vision. She saw the head of the nearest bodyguard lift from his shoulders and away like a ball negligently tossed aside. Then a handful of hot blood slapped her face, and his corpse fell into her, driving her against the wall.

Slipping on blood and ice, she sprawled beside the body.

Two attackers drove Prince Kragen back. He was quick with his sword, stronger than he appeared; but his opponents were expert. He couldn't dispatch two of them at once. The force of their double-handed blows hammered him down the passage.

One of the attackers stretched out on the stone, coughing his lungs into a puddle of water. The other bodyguard still kept his feet – barely. He held one arm clamped to a gushing wound in his side; with the other, he flailed his sword at his assailant.

With a deft toss, the assailant flipped his cloak over the bodyguard's head.

Then Terisa lost sight of him. A black figure reared over her, sword poised.

The light caught his face. His nose was like the edge of a hatchet. A fierce grin bared his teeth. His eyes gleamed, as yellow as a cat's.

He was trying to kill her again.

This time, he was going to succeed. There was nothing she could do to stop him, and she still didn't know why he wanted her dead, she had no idea, it didn't make any *sense*—

'Stop!'

The shout caught him. It echoed in the corridor, wrenching him away from her to protect his back.

A drawling voice said clearly, 'Five against three are coward's odds. But even a coward wouldn't attack a woman.'

Fighting her eyes into focus, Terisa saw the man with the gray cloak advancing along the passage.

The obscure light left his features unclear: she couldn't tell if she had ever seen his face before. But his sword was in his hands. The smile on his lips didn't soften the glint of battle in his eyes.

An attacker drew his blade out of the cloak-blinded bodyguard and moved to join the man threatening Terisa. Her assailant gestured help away, however, sending his companion toward the struggle to kill Prince Kragen.

Black against gray, Terisa's enemy and the newcomer faced each other.

For a moment, they paused. The man in gray commented pleasantly, 'It might be interesting to know who you are.'

The man in black barked a laugh and exploded at his opponent.

Iron flashed and scraped. Blows resounded. The man in black was knocked to the wall. He recovered and countered as if he were immune to pain. With his cloak, he made an attempt to snare the man in gray. The ploy failed. Their swords clashed, caught and held, clashed again. Attacking, retreating, flinging their bodies from side to side, they wove quick sparks about them like fireworks.

The man in gray kept smiling, but his concentration was savage.

Terisa should have helped. She knew that. She should have gotten to her feet, picked up one of the fallen swords, tried to intervene. For Prince Kragen. Or the man in gray. But she didn't move. Instead, she lay on the cold, wet stone with her hands at her temples, terrified by the enormity of what was happening because of her.

She had no idea *why*. What had she done to deserve such hate? Or to be defended from it?

The man in gray moved with such speed that it was difficult to realize how graceful he was, difficult to follow the way his sword swept and cut as if it were avid in his hands. He and his opponent wove gloom and echoes and hot sparks around each other. In the space between one heartbeat and the next, he blocked his opponent's blade, then dropped one fist from his swordhilt and struck a backhand blow that staggered the man in black.

Smoothly, almost contemptuously, Terisa's attacker brushed aside the onslaught that followed. He gripped her defender's blade with one gloved hand long enough to chop his elbow down on the man in gray's neck.

The man in gray staggered to the floor. He caught himself on one knee, countered a brutal assault, regained his feet. He was still smiling, *still smiling*. But his opponent had single-handedly beaten Argus and Ribuld. Sweat ran from his face. The lanterns showed a glare of desperation in his eyes.

Shouts rang along the corridor. He made the mistake of glancing to see what they meant.

His opponent responded with a belly-thrust so swift it couldn't be parried.

He parried it.

The convulsive effort cost him his balance, however. Although he stopped the next blow with his blade, it was so powerful that it knocked him on his back.

For a fraction of a second, he was as helpless as Terisa.

Then Prince Kragen sprang into the struggle, whirling his bloody blade.

The Perdon was only half a step behind him.

The man in black flung a look of yellow hate at Terisa.

An instant later, he leaped back. His hands and sword made a strange gesture.

Without warning, he disappeared. Before the echoes of combat died, he was gone from the passage as completely as if he had never been there.

The Perdon gaped. Prince Kragen dropped his sword in stunned surprise. The man in gray regained his feet, hunting the air as though he thought he might hear or smell some sign of his opponent.

Shivering, Terisa got her arms under her and pushed her chest off the floor.

The Prince was breathing in harsh gasps, near exhaustion, but he went to look at his men. When he saw that one of them had been beheaded, he clenched his fists over his heart, and his face twisted into a snarl. 'They were my friends,' he rasped. 'I was in your debt, my lady. But now I think I have made repayment.'

The Perdon spat, 'Pigswill!' He wasn't talking to Prince Kragen. 'Who were they? How could they know we would be here?'

Braced on her hands and knees, Terisa watched her rescuer wipe his sword and sheath it, then kneel in front of her to help her to her feet. He had a nice smile – he was trying to reassure her – and his face was strong. It reminded her of someone. Nevertheless his eyes were clouded with trouble.

'My lady, I am Artagel. One of Geraden's numerous brothers. He asked me to watch over you. I haven't done very well.

'Apparently' – he grimaced – 'someone really wants you killed.'

The smell of blood on her clothes was so strong that she simply couldn't help fainting.

THIRTEEN

FOLLY IN
GOOD FAITH

℮

When she came to, she suffered a moment of disorientation. Half of her seemed to be standing up: the other half was upside down. She thought she was going to fall, but something hard held her by the waist.

'We were betrayed,' the Perdon rasped. 'Does this not make you suspicious? Perhaps in Alend the word "alliance" has another meaning. What better way to fill Mordant with dissension than by bringing violence to an unprecedented meeting between the lords of the Cares and the Masters of the Congery? This ensures that we will not be strong enough to defend ourselves.'

'My lord Perdon—' Prince Kragen began in a dangerous tone.

'And if we are not strong enough to defend ourselves,' the Perdon snarled, 'where else shall we turn for help, but to Margonal and you?'

'Two of my friends are *dead*!' the Prince retorted. His diplomatic self-control was badly frayed. 'If I desired dissension in Mordant, I would have one of the *lords* killed, not any of *my men*!'

As her eyes squeezed into focus, she saw that she was indeed upright; but her arms and torso dangled toward the floor. The backs of her hands scraped lightly on the cold stone. A forearm clasped about her waist kept her from falling on her head.

'If you must have traitors,' Prince Kragen went on fiercely, 'I advise you to look for them among your fellow lords. Who gains if the Cares are not united against their King?'

'Precisely, my lord Prince,' demanded the Perdon. 'Who?'

'Any lord who can hope to become King directly, without disloyalty to Joyse. The Tor does not mean to return to Marshalt. Queen Madin has had considerable time to forge a bond between her husband and the Fayle. Is it inconceivable that the road to power may be shorter if it does not pass through a union of the lords with Alend and the Congery?'

'Are you all right, my lady?' Artagel asked. He was the one holding her.

Now she understood: he had put her in that position because she had fainted. He helped her pull herself upright, and she found that she was able to keep her balance. Watching her closely, he withdrew his hands from her waist. A glance down the passage showed her that he had moved her a short distance from the scene of combat. Her clothes still stank, but now she was able to stomach that. She took a deep breath, pushed her hair back from her face, and murmured, 'I think so. Thanks.'

He gave her a fleet smile and at once turned away. 'The alternative, my lords,' he said, striding toward Prince Kragen and the Perdon, 'is that you were betrayed by an Imager.'

'I would like to believe that,' said the Perdon gruffly. He seemed to regard Artagel as an equal. 'But only Master Eremis and Master Gilbur knew the place of our meeting. And it was Master Eremis who brought that meeting about. If he desired disunion among us, he did not need to go to such lengths. All that was required was to leave us alone.' He paused, then said, 'I cannot speak so positively for Master Gilbur.'

'And I,' said Prince Kragen, 'did not know that Imagery could do such things. Is it not true that such a translation would require a flat glass? And is it not true that translation through flat glass produces madness? Who could have performed the feat we have witnessed?'

No one had spoken to Terisa. She wasn't sure they knew she could hear them. But she replied, 'The arch-Imager. Vagel.'

For a moment, the three men stood still. Then the Perdon growled, 'As Master Eremis said. But who in Orison – or in all Mordant – would be foolish or vile enough to ally himself with that fiend?'

'Let us look, my lords.' Artagel moved past the Perdon and Prince Kragen toward the nearest of the fallen attackers.

Terisa followed, walking warily back into the memory of bloodshed. Artagel was kneeling over the body when she drew near him. He turned it onto its back; she flinched at the sight of the gory wound in its chest. Nevertheless she watched as he pushed aside the cloak in order to inspect the dead man's face and armor.

The hardened leather chestplate was so black that she couldn't make out any of the details Artagel appeared to be analyzing. She didn't know what he was talking about when he suddenly tapped the covering over the dead man's heart and said, 'Here.'

'I lack your eyes,' growled the Perdon. 'What is it?'

'A sigil.' Abruptly, Artagel rose to his feet. 'I've seen it before.' His eyes held no expression; his face looked as hard as the stone around him. 'This man is a Cadwal. The sigil indicates that he trains with and serves the High King's Monomach.'

'Gart?' Prince Kragen asked incredulously. '*Here?* Was that Gart you fought?'

'I don't know who I fought.' Artagel's voice was like his face, blank and rigid. 'Whoever he was, he beat me. But this man is one of Gart's Apts. The others must be the same.'

'Entrails and carrion!' spat the Perdon. 'An Apt of the High King's Monomach!'

'But *here?*' the Prince persisted. 'How could such men come here? How could they gain admittance to Orison? They could not simply enter the gates. Castellan Lebbick is not so lax.'

Artagel nodded curtly. 'They must have come the same way their leader vanished.'

'Vagel?' Prince Kragen scowled in frank dismay. 'Why did we ever believe the story that he was dead?'

The Perdon had no answer. At the mention of Lebbick, he had jerked up his head as if he were reminded of something important. Now he glanced rapidly back and forth down the corridor, trying to watch both directions at once. 'I have a better question. Do we wish to be found here when the Castellan comes?'

The Prince became instantly alert. 'Will he come? Are we not beyond earshot of his nearest guard?'

'That spineless fop, the Armigite,' explained the Perdon. His voice dripped venom. 'When we heard the sounds of attack that brought me to your side, he fled in the opposite direction, yowling murder. He must have missed his way, or the Castellan would already be here. In any case, we have little time.'

'He will question me, whatever I do,' mused Kragen. 'My men are dead. But if I am not here, he will not be able to connect me to this bloodshed.' Promptly, he made his decision. 'My lord Perdon, Artagel of Domne – I thank you for my life. But I will not remain with you, to give us all the look of treachery. My lady, farewell.'

Retrieving his sword, he slapped it into its sheath and ran. Swiftly, the sound of his strides receded into the distance.

'I will leave you also,' the Perdon said to Artagel. 'I do not know what role this woman means to play in our doom, but I will not risk an accusation of treason to protect her.'

Muttering angrily, 'Cadwals? Horsepiss,' he rushed away after the Prince.

Terisa looked at Artagel and saw that the gleam was back in his eyes; he was smiling again. In reply to her gaze, he bowed humorously. 'For my part, my lady, I haven't got anything worth hiding. Whatever happens, all Orison will assume I had something to do with this many dead bodies. I'm afraid I have that kind of reputation – I don't know why. In any case, I have a better opinion of Lebbick than most people do. But there's no reason why you should have to spend the rest of the night listening to him sneer at you.' He gestured down the passage. 'Shall we go?'

Again, she said, 'Thanks.' She wished he would take her arm: she needed the support. 'I don't think I can face him. He doesn't like me.'

'Nonsense.' As if guided by inspiration, he slipped his arm through hers and braced her companionably. His tone jollied her along. 'You don't know him as well as I do. Our good Castellan only insults the people he likes. And if he likes you a lot, he becomes positively scathing. His wife – rest her soul – was the only person in Orison who was ever able to get civility as well as affection out of him.'

Together, they moved through the gloom toward the next lantern.

Almost at once, they heard running feet.

He was undismayed. Still grinning, he drew her into a side passage and along a different route back toward the inhabited levels of the castle. With apparent ease, he avoided encountering the guards. In a shorter time than she was expecting, he brought her to the tower where her rooms were.

By then, she had recovered at least some grasp on the situation. Artagel had saved her life. Because Geraden had asked him to keep an eye on her. Now he was taking her away from a session with the grim Castellan, in which she would have had to lie and lie and lie to protect Master Eremis, Prince Kragen, and the lords of the Cares. She should have started thinking about gratitude some time ago.

Off the top of her head, she couldn't imagine many ways to thank Artagel effectively. At least one small one was clear to her, however. So far, they had been fortunate: they hadn't been seen closely enough to expose the mess that blood and dirty water had made of her clothes. But to reach her rooms she would have to pass within arm's reach of the guards outside her door—

At the foot of the stairway, she stopped and disengaged her arm. A bit awkwardly – she wasn't accustomed to making decisions in this way, with a tall, strong man smiling at her quizzically – she explained, 'I can go alone from here. We've been lucky so far. I don't think you want to be seen with me.'

He cocked an amused eyebrow. 'I don't, my lady?' The events of the evening hadn't seriously ruffled his self-confidence. 'Well, I admit you aren't as clean as you should be. But I don't choose my friends on the basis of accidents like that.' He chuckled. 'If I did, poor Geraden would be at the bottom of my list.'

His smile was disarming, but she persisted. 'That's not what I meant. The guards are going to notice' – she twisted her mouth in disgust – 'the way I look. And someone is going to realize that a woman covered with blood must have something to do with all those dead men. If you're seen with me, you'll be implicated.'

'I know you aren't worried about that. But you should be. How are you going to explain it to the Castellan?'

He was unpersuaded. Lebbick didn't worry him. And she couldn't ask him to lie, either for herself or for Master Eremis. So she shifted to a different argument. 'Do you know what he did to Geraden the last time he caught him trying to give me independent protection?'

At that, Artagel frowned thoughtfully. 'You have a point, my lady. He tried to explain why he doesn't trust the guards, but I didn't understand all of it. It had something to do with the orders King Joyse gave the Castellan? Or the way he interprets those orders?' He shrugged. 'Geraden has always had a subtler mind than I do. Is it true that the guards don't even ask where you're going when you leave your rooms?'

Terisa felt a new touch of panic. So she wasn't imagining it: the guards *did* treat Geraden differently than the other people who came for her. She nodded mutely.

'That doesn't make sense,' Artagel commented. Then he shook his frown away. 'But I'm sure it will eventually. That's Geraden's only fault. I mean, aside from clumsiness. He's too impatient. Things always make sense eventually, if you don't think about them too hard.'

Smiling again, he added, 'But you're right. I don't want to get him in any more trouble. I'll leave you here.' For a moment, his expression grew sober. 'I'm still going to keep an eye on you. I take him seriously when he's that worried. And this time he has good reason. The High King's Monomach is training his Apts better than he used to. If you need me, I'll usually be somewhere nearby.'

He put on a jaunty grin. With a graceful and humorous bow, he saluted her. 'Rest well, my lady.' Then he strode away.

She smiled at his departing back. As soon as he was gone, however, she began to shiver again, as if she had brought the chill of the lower levels up with her. Shock and reaction were setting in.

She was alone. She would have no defense if more men in black appeared suddenly out of nowhere to attack her.

She was going to have to face Castellan Lebbick by herself.

She wanted to sit down. Her knees felt too weak to hold her. But she put her feet on the stairs and forced her legs to take her upward.

When the guards at her door caught sight of her, they became immediately tense with concern. One of them said, 'My lady, are you all right? Do you need any help?'

She couldn't meet their eyes. As firmly as possible, she said, 'No, thanks. I'm fine.'

Trying not to hurry, she went into her rooms. At once, she bolted the door. Then she checked to be sure that the entrance to the secret passage was still blocked.

After that, she kicked her moccasins away and flung off her clothes in a rush of revulsion, alarm, and determination, unable to bear the touch of drying blood against her skin any longer. First she took a bath, splashing icy water over herself as though she thought she could sting or shock herself into being brave enough for what she had to do. Next she scrubbed her clothes thoroughly, almost brutally, and set them out to dry in front of the fire.

She intended to be ready for Castellan Lebbick when he came.

But she couldn't stop trembling.

He came early the next morning, a barely polite interval after she had finished breakfast. She was wearing her dove-gray gown because a cowardly instinct told her it would make her look more vulnerable, less deserving of abuse. But she met him in her sitting room as bravely as she could.

As always, he wore the symbols of his office – the purple band around his cropped gray hair, the purple sash over one shoulder across his mail. But his real authority was expressed in the glare of his eyes, the stiff swagger of his movements, the thrust of his jaw. If he had held no position in Orison at all, he would still have commanded the room when he entered it.

'My lady.' His tone was as subtle as an iron bar. 'I trust you slept well after your adventures last night.'

She was determined to lie to him. It would have been better to face him squarely, but that great a display of courage was beyond her. After all, she had never lied to an angry man in her life. 'What adventures?' She cursed herself for sounding so small and weak, but perhaps that would work to her advantage in the end.

226

Castellan Lebbick, however, appeared to be unsympathetic toward small, weak women. 'Don't be coy with me, my lady. I do my duty under a number of disadvantages, but stupidity isn't among them.'

'I'm not being coy.' That was true, at any rate. She was doing everything in her power to refrain from running into the next room and hiding under the bed. Or from blurting out the truth. 'I went out with Master Eremis. I came back alone. We didn't have any adventures. You can ask him. He'll tell you the same thing.'

'My lady' – he feigned a tiredness which didn't show in his eyes – 'I have no taste for manure this morning. Whatever you were doing, my night was longer than yours, and when I went to my bed it was cold. Do me the courtesy of being honest.'

Her resolve was crumbling: she could feel it. The promises she had made to herself were all very well – but what did any of this have to do with her? Her father hadn't raised her to be strong. 'I *am* being honest,' she said without conviction, already flinching in anticipation of his retort.

It came quickly. 'Dogshit! You haven't spoken a true word since you arrived. By the stars, woman, you will answer me! The Armigite came squalling out of the abandoned foundations of Orison – where he never should have been in the first place – and insisted there was a battle going on. Naturally, he had no idea who was involved. He has rotten fruit for brains. But an investigation was required, so it was done. We found two men dead – Prince Kragen's bodyguards, by some towering coincidence – and enough blood for a small war. But we found no explanation.'

For two or three heartbeats, her mind went completely blank. *Two* men dead? There should have been six. Four Cadwals. She was on the verge of crying out, I'm sorry I didn't mean it it wasn't my fault *what happened to the four Cadwals?*

Fortunately, Lebbick didn't pause. 'I questioned Prince Kragen. He put on righteous indignation and accused *someone* of having his men murdered. *Someone*, he said, wants to provoke a war. *Someone*' – the Castellan's reference to King Joyse was unmistakable – 'wants to be sure he returns to Alend with every conceivable provocation. On top of that, those bodyguards were *friends* of his.'

He clenched his fists. 'My lady, I know how to get the truth from men like him. Some of the old engines of torture have been preserved. Unfortunately, he's an ambassador. I can't touch him.

'You are another matter.'

Abruptly, her head cleared. She didn't become less afraid, but a sense of urgency made what she was thinking sharp and precise. Four bodies were missing. Someone had taken them. Probably in the same way her attacker had vanished. So Castellan Lebbick didn't know there were Cadwals in Orison. He had no inkling of the truth. Master Eremis was safe. Artagel was safe. If she didn't lose her nerve.

Her voice was almost steady as she asked, 'You mean you're going to torture me?'

Instead of answering directly, he snarled, 'After my discussion with Prince Kragen, imagine my surprise when I learned that you had returned *alone*' –

his tone was pure vitriol – 'from your supper with Master Eremis and the mediator of the Congery – and that you were covered with blood.'

He cocked his fists on his hips. 'Do you want me to believe that Prince Kragen's bodyguards killed each other in a contest for your affections? Will you ask me to credit that you *happened* to wander down to that part of Orison, and you *happened* to find those two bodies in all the miles of corridors down there, and you *happened* to slip and fall while their blood was still warm – all by the most monumental coincidence? No, my lady. I won't have it. You returned here alone and covered with blood. But you told no one what had happened, when the common sense of a small dog would have led you to report it to the guards. Therefore you want to keep what happened secret. You have something to hide. I'll have *that*, my lady.'

The lash of his outrage brought up an unexpected anger from among the secrets of her heart. How much sarcasm was she expected to swallow in one lifetime? 'Your guards must have been mistaken,' she retorted. 'Maybe the shadows fooled them. Or maybe they were half asleep. I wasn't covered with blood. I've never been down there. I don't know what you're talking about.'

When she was done, she wanted to give out a crow of joy which would announce to the world what she had achieved.

But the Castellan behaved as if she hadn't spoken – or as if he hadn't heard her. Lowering his voice until it sounded like the thongs of a flail being stroked between eager fingers, he said, 'I am the Castellan of Orison and commander of the King's forces in Mordant. Do you wonder how I came to this high position? It's simple. Midway through his wars for Mordant's freedom, King Joyse found me prisoner in the stockade of an Alend garrison near the borders of the Care of Termigan. I was hardly more than a boy, but I had been wed' – his throat knotted – 'for nearly ten days. Our families were farmers and peasants of Termigan, and those folk wed early. So I had been a married man for ten days – and of those ten I had spent six in the stockade. As it happened, the garrison commander had ridden across my little farm, noticed my wife, and taken a fancy to her. Because I was foolish enough to resist, I was imprisoned.

'But I wasn't mistreated. No harm was done to me.' He bared his teeth. 'I was merely held spectator, so that I had to watch the great variety of things that were done to my wife, by the commander as well as most of the garrison.

'Then King Joyse surprised the garrison. We were released.'

The Castellan's voice sank as he spoke. 'When he observed the zeal with which I took revenge upon the commander, he gave me work which put that zeal to good use. And when I displayed a talent for that work, I rose in his service.

'Now he has lost his mind' – Lebbick was barely whispering – 'and it's my duty to preserve his life and power for the day when he may recover himself and need everything he entrusted to me. Don't tell me any lies, my lady. If you don't give me the truth, I'll tear it out of you.'

Terisa's throat had gone dry. She had trouble finding her voice. 'The King told you to leave me alone.'

'My lady' – a touch of the whip – 'I'm rapidly losing patience for the instructions of a madman. My King was in full possession of his wits when he made me his Castellan and commander. That's the responsibility I intend to fulfill.'

In a strange way, he frightened and moved her at the same time. But she couldn't afford to feel either fear or sympathy. She had to find some way to defend herself.

'I'm sure you will,' she said as if her small fund of anger were equal to his. 'But I think you learned your moral sense from that garrison commander. I've told you what I did. Before you call me a liar, you ought to find out if I'm telling the truth. Look at my clothes. They're clean. Ask Master Eremis. Ask him. Or have you already decided he's a liar too, without bothering to check what he says? You want to do your job the easy way, by bullying the weakest person you can find. If you did a little work, you might learn something different.'

Then she stopped and held her breath while her heart shook.

A look of pain clouded his glare. 'That's enough, woman,' he said thickly. 'When you've suffered the way my wife did, I'll permit that imputation. Until then, you don't have the right. You are an enemy of Mordant and King Joyse, and you don't have the *right*.'

She wanted to babble, I know I don't I didn't mean it that way. The pressure to give up everything and tell him what he wanted to know was maddening. Somehow, however, she kept it under control. Instead, she replied, 'No, I'm not. I'm nobody's enemy. Not even yours. We have one thing in common. I'm just a spectator. I don't have anything to *do* with any of this.'

For a moment, his jaws clenched, and his eyes darkened, and she thought he was going to let out a blast which would rip her to the bone. Yet he didn't. He was more dangerous than that: he knew what to do with his anger.

'Have it your way, my lady. I'll talk to Master Eremis – I'll check your story. I'll *persuade*' – the word was a snarl – 'that pig-brained Armigite to go over every step of his tale with me. I'll talk to every guard in Orison who may have encountered Prince Kragen's bodyguards – or seen where you were going with Master Eremis. I've already studied the place where those men died. They could not have shed so much blood. And at least four people walked through the blood while it was wet. One of them had feet the size of a lady's.' Though the threat was unmistakable, he emphasized it by raising one hand and cupping it lightly over her cheek. 'I'll have the truth. I don't care how.'

Turning sharply, he strode out of the room. The door slammed behind him hard. He was capable of hitting her like that. If Master Eremis didn't somehow convince him that she was telling the truth, she would be at his mercy.

But she had kept her promises to herself. She had done it, *done* it: she had fended Lebbick away from the truth. There was still hope for Mordant. Because of what she had done. She, Terisa Morgan – a woman who had never learned how to believe in herself. She had made a *difference*. The idea made her want to start singing. She imagined herself going to the window, flinging open the casement, and shouting out to the world below her – the muddy courtyard, the roofs clogged with snow, the smoking chimneys, the guards patrolling the battlements – 'I did it! I lied to the Castellan!' The vision struck her as so ludicrous that she laughed.

She was having such fun that the quick knock at her door didn't interrupt her. 'Come in!' she called without so much as pausing to wonder who might be there.

It was Master Eremis.

He had Geraden with him again.

The Apt wore a baffled expression: he didn't know why he was there. Nevertheless Terisa was instantly glad to see him. Although she couldn't tell him what she had just accomplished, she was free to smile at him, and she did that with unfamiliar pleasure.

He grinned back through his confusion, then shrugged in the direction of Master Eremis.

The Imager was scowling as though he wanted no one to realize that he had never been happier in his life.

Closing the door quickly, he strode toward her in a hurry. He seemed to give off an electricity of excitement and urgency, so that simply being in the same room with him made her nerves tingle and jump, ready to go off in any direction. 'The Castellan,' he demanded in a rapid half whisper as he crossed the peacock rugs. 'He was just here. Why?'

The question closed her throat like a hand clamped around her windpipe.

She knew immediately what he was after: he wanted to know how much of his night's activities had been betrayed to Lebbick. But she didn't know how to answer. Geraden was staring at her, perplexed and alarmed by her consternation. She had been warned to keep everything secret from him. How could she reply without putting his life in danger – and without exposing what the Master was trying to do?

Eremis reached her and caught hold of her shoulders, gripped them so hard that he nearly lifted her from the floor. 'Tell me!' he hissed furiously, his eyes sparkling. 'Why was Lebbick here?'

She felt his power so strongly that for just a moment, perhaps no more than one or two heartbeats, she was nearly overwhelmed by an irrational desire to say, Why did you leave me last night? I wanted to go back to your rooms. But he needed more than that from her. And Geraden was watching. He needed better – and didn't deserve to be hurt.

Meeting the Master's strange gaze, she said as clearly as she could, 'He doesn't know anything.'

'Nothing?' He cocked an eyebrow, eased his grip on her shoulders. 'Then why was he here?'

At that, her tension increased to the level of fright. Suddenly, a new dimension of uncertainty was added to the situation. Perhaps Master Eremis didn't know what had happened after he left the meeting. If he didn't, she should tell him, make him aware that Apts of the High King's Monomach had the power to appear and disappear in Orison. But again she couldn't talk about such things in front of Geraden.

Geraden was watching her with frank worry. If he felt any personal pain over the fact that she and Master Eremis were sharing secrets, it was secondary to his direct concern for her.

She had to say less than she meant. Striving for nonchalance, she replied, 'The guards told him I went out with you' – she darted a glance at Geraden – 'and came back alone. That made him curious.'

For a second longer, the Master studied her, searching for the truth behind her words. Then he let her go, turned away, and started laughing as if he were having the best time of his life. 'Curious?' he chortled. 'That old lecher. I will wager gold doubles to coppers that he was more than curious. He must have been *avid*.'

Geraden looked away. A dull flush spread over his face.

All at once, Terisa was ashamed of herself.

Fortunately, Master Eremis' mirth was quick to subside. 'Well, the stars have smiled on us,' he said, resuming his haste. 'I am certain that the Fayle spoke to King Joyse. So it follows that the King said nothing to Lebbick. Either our illustrious sovereign has lost the capacity to understand what he hears, or he does not believe it, or he is unable to achieve a decision. We must act while he leaves us time.'

Immediately, he started for the door. Over his shoulder, he said, 'The Masters are gathering. Come.'

Terisa remained where she was. This was too fast. She still felt obscurely ashamed. And she hadn't told Master Eremis all the things he needed to know.

For that matter, why was the Congery in such a rush to meet? Hadn't Master Eremis stopped it from summoning the champion last night? What had changed since then?

But Eremis wasn't prepared to wait. From the doorway, he snapped, 'Geraden, bring her!' and stalked out of the room.

That brought the Apt's gaze back to hers. In a hurry himself, he whispered, 'Terisa,' as if the words were being wrung from him, '*what* is going on?'

'I can't tell you,' she replied. She was trying to make sense. 'I want to. It's too much for me.' But what she really wanted was to reassure him. 'I don't know what he was laughing about. I didn't spend the night with him.'

He looked away. At first, she thought he was still in pain. Then she realized that he was just trying to hide his relief. When he turned to her again, his expression was clear.

'We ought to go.' He tried not to smile. 'He told me to bring you. I won't be an Apt much longer if I start disobeying commands this simple.'

He made her feel better. 'All right,' she said. 'I really don't know what the Congery is going to do. But we might as well not get ourselves in trouble.'

Enjoying his helpless, idiotic grin, she took his arm. Together, they went after Master Eremis.

On her way down the stone stairs, she missed her moccasins. They were warmer and protected her feet better than the delicate buskins Saddith had recommended. But her discomfort wasn't enough to make her go back.

When she and Geraden left the tower and entered the main halls, they caught up with Master Eremis: he had stopped to talk to someone. His stance briefly obscured who that someone was; as her angle of vision changed, however, she recognized Artagel.

'That's Artagel,' Geraden whispered quickly. 'I've mentioned him. He's one of my brothers. I asked him to keep an eye on you – give you some extra protection. I would introduce you if we weren't supposed to be in a hurry.'

His words left a trail of electricity across her mind. So Artagel hadn't told Geraden about last night. And if he hadn't told Geraden, he probably hadn't told anybody. There was a real chance that Master Eremis didn't know she had been attacked.

Artagel was leaning casually against the wall, a smile on his lips, his sword prominent on his hip. He seemed to be sneering politely at something the Imager had said.

Master Eremis shook his head. 'Artagel, Artagel,' he murmured sadly, 'I thought we were friends.'

'So did I.' Artagel's smile might have been an insult. 'But Geraden assures me you're no friend of his – so I'm no friend of yours.'

The Master turned a gaze Terisa couldn't interpret on Geraden. Then he looked back to Artagel. 'Do you always let him choose your friends for you?'

Artagel laughed easily. 'Always. He's my brother.'

For a moment, Master Eremis stood motionless. His back was to Terisa; the only face she could see was Artagel's. Somehow, the confident mischief in his eyes increased his resemblance to his brother. Abruptly, Eremis strode away. As he left, he said, 'Geraden is mistaken. I am a better friend than he knows.'

Artagel glanced past Geraden and Terisa and shrugged eloquently. As if he were speaking to the air, he commented, 'He wants to hire me. He thinks he needs protection. In Orison, of all places. I wonder what he's afraid of.'

Geraden snorted. 'Probably his friends.'

Artagel went on smiling. 'Speaking of friends, did you know Nyle is here?'

'No.' Geraden sounded surprised.

'I met him by accident. He didn't seem especially pleased to see me. But I got him to admit he's been here for eight or ten days now. I have no idea why he made a journey like that in the dead of winter. He said he just wanted to get away from Houseldon for a while.'

'Sounds like one of your expeditions,' Geraden muttered. Then he added, 'He must be hiding. Otherwise I would have run into him. Do you suppose he's in some kind of trouble?'

'That's what I thought.' Artagel pushed himself away from the wall. 'You should go. I don't think Master Eremis is feeling patient today.

'My lady.' He gave Terisa a bow and sauntered off down the hall, heading away from the laborium.

At once, Geraden tugged her into motion. 'He's right. We'd better hurry.'

She went with him as quickly as her skirts permitted, but her brain was spinning. After a moment, she asked, 'Isn't Nyle one of your brothers? Why would he come here in the middle of winter and then not try to see you?'

He shrugged without looking at her, as if the question were painful.

She let it go. Instead, she asked, 'What kind of "expeditions" does Artagel go on?'

This proved to be a safe topic. 'Didn't I tell you about him? He says he's too lazy to be a regular soldier, but the truth is that he hates to take orders. So he does what you might call piecework for Castellan Lebbick. Whenever he's in the mood, he volunteers for something. The Castellan sends him all over Mordant – and probably into Cadwal and Alend, too, but nobody says that out loud. He just came back a few days ago from stopping a smuggler who was selling our crops to High King Festten's army suppliers.

'When I heard he was here, I couldn't resist asking for some help. Did I tell you he's the best swordsman in Mordant?'

She shot a glance of concern and sympathy at him which – fortunately – he didn't notice. His brother may have been the best swordsman in Mordant, but the man in black was better.

The idea that Artagel could be beaten by a man who appeared and disappeared in Orison at will gave her a shiver of trepidation.

Shortly, she and Geraden crossed the vacant ballroom to the corridor that gave entrance to the laborium and descended the stairs into the former dungeon. Soon they were walking along the passageway that led to the Congery's meeting hall. Ahead of them, Eremis and another Master entered the chamber. The guards saluted correctly – they certainly betrayed no sign that King Joyse or Castellan Lebbick knew what the Imagers had in mind. Nevertheless Terisa felt a tightening in her chest as she and Geraden followed Master Eremis.

Two or three more Masters arrived after she and Geraden did; then all the doors were closed and bolted, and the Imagers gathered around the curved circle of benches within the pillars. She was starting to recognize more of them by sight. All the familiar faces were there. Except Master Quillon. That surprised her. She expected— no, there he was, already seated partway around the circle from her. He nodded at the floor as though he were half asleep.

He was the only man in the hall who wasn't staring at Geraden, Terisa, and Master Eremis with some degree of confusion, curiosity, or indignation.

The light of the oil lamps and torches flickered, making the Masters appear hot-eyed and hollow-cheeked, spectral.

Then Terisa's attention was drawn to the open center of the chamber. Some of the Masters in her way sat down; others stepped aside to make room for Eremis. She saw the tall mirror which had been set ready on the low stone dais.

The mirror of the champion.

The scene in the glass had changed: the spaceship was gone. But hadn't Geraden told her that mirrors focused on *places*, not on *people*? Had the ship taken off? Or was it simply out of sight? The alien landscape certainly seemed unaltered, despite the shift of details: it was stark, red, and dim, composed of jagged old rocks and sand under the light of a dying sun.

The metallic figures were clustered in the center of the Image – and they were fighting for their lives.

Black flame as liquid as water and as flexible as whips licked at them from all directions. Three or four bodies sprawled around the scene, their machinery and flesh still smoking from great, ragged gashes. The remaining men used the rocks for protection as much as possible and struck back at the black flame with the incessant fire of their guns.

The champion was distinct among them. His gestures directed the fire of his companions, and his huge rifle gave out blasts that chopped the edges of the landscape into new configurations.

He conveyed an impression of desperation that Terisa hadn't seen in him before. For the first time, she realized that he, too, was someone who could be beaten.

But Master Eremis took a different view of the matter. Rubbing his hands together vigorously, he said, 'Excellent! Whether he exists in his own right or is a creation of the glass, he will have no cause to complain of our translation.'

'Master Eremis, you presume too much!' The mediator of the Congery stood beside the mirror, his fists braced on his large girth and his pine-colored face mottled with anger. Apparently, his fear of what Master Gilbur and the others proposed had concentrated into ire. 'Your arrogance is offensive. You call us together in urgent haste, you have this glass brought before us, and once again you bring Geraden with you without permission – as if our course were already decided. Our course is *not* decided. You were deputized to speak for us before the lords of the Cares. You have not told us the outcome of that meeting. You have not told us what was said – what position the lords take. Our course cannot be decided until we have heard a full report, both from you and from Master Gilbur.

'Also the lady has no place in this,' he added grimly. 'Correct your presumption by sending her and the Apt away.'

'Oh, presumption!' the guttural voice of Master Gilbur growled before Eremis could reply. 'It is not presumption. It is survival. We must act or die. Stop trying to shirk the situation, Barsonage. The woman does not matter. But look at Geraden!' He made a hacking gesture with one powerful hand. Every eye in the chamber turned to the Apt. 'He is fumble-footed and disastrous. But he has never been stupid. *Look* at him.'

Geraden appeared unaware of the way he was regarded. He was chewing his lower lip and thinking so hard that the effort made his eyes look wild.

'Where else would you have him? You have already blurted out all the information he needs. In a moment, he will guess the import of what we propose – and then he will be on his way to inform the King. Here, at least, he will have no one to tell.'

As if to prove Gilbur right, Geraden abruptly faced Terisa. At that moment, no one else in the room seemed to exist for him. What he was thinking filled him with dismay.

'Is that what you couldn't tell me?' he whispered. 'They've decided to call the champion? And Master Eremis had some kind of meeting with the lords of the Cares?' An instant later, he went further. 'But they waited until after the meeting. Master Eremis went to suggest some kind of alliance. The Congery and the lords against King Joyse?'

She couldn't help him. Her heart pounded in her throat as she felt the danger suddenly thicken around him, but there was nothing she could do.

'I've got to warn him.'

So quickly that she had no chance to try to stop him, Geraden headed for the nearest door.

With unexpected speed, Master Gilbur pounced after the Apt. In an effort to reach him, Gilbur struck him from behind. The blow made Geraden trip, so that he slammed against one of the pillars and sprawled to the floor.

At once, Master Gilbur knotted one great fist in the back of Geraden's leather jerkin, and wrenched him to his feet. 'No, whelp,' he grated. 'You have heard too much. Now you will hear it all.'

Blood trickled from Geraden's temple. The impact of his head left a small red stain on the pillar. For a moment, he struggled as though his heart were breaking. But he couldn't twist away from Gilbur's powerful grip – and his jerkin refused to tear. The fight went out of him, and he sagged into submission.

Terisa wanted to rage at Master Gilbur. The fact that she thought Geraden was wrong made no difference. In misery, she met his dumb pain. 'I'm sorry.'

'It's not your fault,' he replied dully. 'Somebody told you I would be killed if I knew what was going on. Whoever that was, it's his fault.'

Terisa looked around quickly. Master Quillon hadn't raised his head. But Master Eremis' face showed an instant of honest surprise.

He recovered rapidly, however. Frowning, he said, 'She was told the truth, Geraden. You will not believe it – but I brought you here to save your life. Now that you cannot leave, you will live.'

Immediately, he turned to face the rest of the Imagers.

'Masters, if you will sit down and compose yourselves long enough to hear me, I will tell you what happened at my meeting with the lords of the Cares – and why we must act without delay on our decision to translate our champion.'

His manner was commanding; he emanated urgency. After a moment, Master Barsonage said between his teeth, 'Very well, Master Eremis. So far I will go with you. But there is much that I expect you to explain.'

Scowling dourly, he left the center of the circle to Eremis.

The other Masters followed his example. Before she could be separated from him, Terisa caught Geraden's arm. Master Gilbur's controlling grip forced the two of them to a seat on the bench. At the same time, Master Eremis strode toward the dais.

Almost at once, he began.

'Masters, I can make this quite simple.' His tone was soft, but it seemed to carry an echo to the farthest reaches of the room. 'Our meeting with the lords of the Cares was broken up without useful issue because they do not trust us. They believe that we serve King Joyse and wish only to entrap them. Or they believe that we serve ourselves and wish only to make them serve us also.'

'And Master Eremis is accused of arrogance,' one of the younger Imagers put in. 'Are the lords not arrogant?'

As softly as possible, Terisa whispered in Geraden's ear, 'Don't worry. King Joyse already knows.'

He gaped at her in surprise.

'Of course,' Master Eremis went on with deceptive sarcasm, 'the discussion itself was not so simple. First I must inform you that I have been more "presumptuous" than you know. When I learned of the outcome of his embassy among us, I invited Prince Kragen of Alend to the meeting.'

At that announcement, several of the Masters stiffened. Eremis had their complete attention now. The mediator glared at him furiously but didn't interrupt.

'I cannot honestly say that I trust any representative of the Alend Monarch. But he protests that he desires peace. And I am certain that he desires to preserve us from Cadwal. For that reason, I considered that his presence would cost nothing at worst, and at best would open the possibility of a much stronger alliance than one uniting only the Congery with the lords.'

'The Fayle told him,' Terisa explained to Geraden. 'About the champion, anyway. Not about the meeting.'

'Then why—?' For a second, he forgot to whisper. But the sharp glares of the Masters – and Master Gilbur's grasp on his jerkin – reminded him. 'Why doesn't he do something?'

Visibly mollified, Master Barsonage murmured, 'You surpass yourself, Master Eremis. You are entirely presumptuous – but you are not thick-witted. I feared that this gamble would make the lords unwilling to heed you. Was I wrong?'

Eremis sighed. 'That is the second matter I must explain. The lords were indeed unwilling to heed me, but not because of Prince Kragen's presence. In truth, I think they would have listened to him well if I had not been there. Their hatred of Alends is less than their distrust of Imagers.'

Several Masters expressed surprise. Others muttered angry curses. But Master Eremis raised his hands to ward off their reactions. 'I do not mean to be unjust. Prince Kragen himself was much interested in our proposal. The Perdon was interested, even eager. But as for the others—' He shrugged. 'The Armigite has too little sense to know his own mind. And the Tor was too steeped in wine to have a mind.'

'Don't you understand?' Terisa returned, trying to make herself clear to Geraden. 'That's why Master Eremis doesn't have any choice.'

His gaze was dark with pain. Apparently, he didn't want to understand her as well as he did.

'I believe the Termigan could have been persuaded, under other circumstances,' Master Eremis continued. 'With the Perdon, he might have been enough. We would have had a base on which to build. But it is all made hopeless by the intensity of the Fayle's prejudice against Imagery.'

'The Fayle?' asked Master Barsonage. 'He has the reputation of a reasonable man.'

Master Quillon was paying close attention now. His eyes glittered at everything he saw.

'Oh, he is *reasonable*,' Gilbur put in, 'if you call it reasonable that he rejected everything we proposed simply because we mean to call our champion without King Joyse's approval.'

Another Master protested, 'Are you serious? Why did he think you were meeting in secret? Why did he accept your invitation, if the King's approval is so important to him?'

'To spy on us,' Master Gilbur growled. 'Why else?'

The mediator was staggered. 'Is this true?'

'It is,' Master Eremis said crisply. 'He admitted his intention to inform

King Joyse, so that we would be prevented from any exercise of our own judgment or will.'

Startled out of concentrating on Geraden, Terisa thought, That's not really the way it happened. Is it? But it was. The more she tried to remember, the more she had to agree with Master Eremis and Master Gilbur. It was only her personal reaction to the Fayle's dignity that misled her.

'Then why,' Master Quillon inquired unexpectedly, 'has the King done nothing to prevent us?'

Suddenly angry, Master Eremis whirled to face Quillon. 'You ask me to explain *his* decisions? If I had *that* power, I could save Mordant single-handedly.'

'We can't explain them,' an Imager who hadn't spoken before said urgently. 'We've got to act – before Lebbick and his men get here to stop us.'

Geraden's face wore an intent frown, as if he were listening hard.

'Very well.' Master Barsonage rose heavily to his feet. 'I have conceded everything else.' He had an air of defeat; even his eyebrows looked wilted. 'I concede the need for haste also. Be plain, Master Eremis. What do you propose?'

Eremis turned to the mediator. The way he pivoted, balanced himself, and faced Master Barsonage conveyed so much sharp energy that he seemed to give off sparks. His expression was too intense for Terisa to interpret.

'Translate our champion,' he said. 'Now.'

Master Barsonage nodded. For a moment, he said nothing. Then he asked, 'Why?'

Master Eremis was ready. 'To prove our good faith. We are not heeded because it is believed that we have no commitment to anything except ourselves. Or because as the King's tools we have, in effect, lost our minds as badly as he has.'

Now he raised his voice so that it throbbed and thrilled in the chamber, as clarion and moving as a trumpet. 'We have no way to convince anyone otherwise except by taking single and unselfish action in Mordant's defense. Only by opposing the evil ourselves can we show that we are worthy of trust and alliance.'

That might have been enough to gain what he wanted. It was enough for Terisa: his electricity and passion swept her with him. But Master Gilbur didn't leave it alone.

'In addition,' he rasped, 'we must consider the possibility that Prince Kragen and the lords came to our meeting for an entirely different reason. We were created by Joyse. He set an example for Cadwal and Alend to follow. They think we are to be used as they see fit, and they maneuver against each other in order to *possess* us.' His hands made fierce fists on the railing in front of him. 'They want to own us as if we were things instead of men.

'We have no swords or soldiers.' His voice lacked resonance, but it had the force to be terrifying. 'We can never protect ourselves *unless we show our power!*'

Through the silence which followed his shout, everyone heard the hammering at the door. It sounded like the shaft of a sword or the butt of a pike belaboring the wood.

Everyone heard the command:

'In the King's name, open this door!'

For a fraction of a second, Terisa had time to wonder why King Joyse had changed his mind.

Then Geraden jerked up his head. '*The Castellan.*' At once, he tried to gain his feet, yelling, 'Castellan Lebbick! Break down the door! Stop them!'

Gilbur jerked him back. With one stone fist, the Master struck him so hard across the side of his head that his whole body flopped soddenly. His eyes glazed.

Terisa froze. Everything was happening at once. King Joyse had finally made a decision. Master Eremis' plans were in danger. *Geraden was hurt.*

Most of the Imagers were on their feet, shouting at each other frantically; but Master Barsonage sank to the bench. His face had no strength left: he looked lost. 'Then it must be done,' he murmured to no one in particular. 'Or else we will cease to exist.'

'Gilbur!' Master Eremis barked. A grin bared his teeth. 'Do it now!'

Master Gilbur dropped Geraden and hurried into the center of the chamber, toward the dais and his mirror.

Several of the Imagers cheered. Others dithered in alarm. They all got out of Gilbur's way, however. They crowded past the pillars toward the walls, as far as possible from Castellan Lebbick's hammering and the mirror.

Eremis took Master Gilbur's place, lifting Geraden from the stone and holding both him and Terisa with a grip they couldn't break.

The mirror faced them directly. Geraden plainly had no idea what was going on – he couldn't even hold up his head – but Terisa had a perfect view.

Master Gilbur put his hand on the frame and deftly began to adjust the focus of the glass. After one heartbeat, the champion was centered in the Image. After another, he seemed to sweep forward until he filled the mirror.

The pounding on the door had become a heavy, rhythmic thud. Terisa could hear wood cracking. But the ironbound timbers were too stout to yield easily. Between blows, Castellan Lebbick shouted, 'Master Barsonage! Imagers! By the stars, I will have this door open!'

Master Gilbur shot a glance toward Master Eremis.

'*Translate him!*' Eremis hissed.

Geraden stirred, shook his head. Blinking rapidly, he tried to clear his vision.

Master Gilbur braced his hands against the edge of the mirror as though he were preparing to pull the champion through by main force. His guttural voice rasped words Terisa couldn't understand.

'Got to stop him.' Geraden sounded like he was choking. Somehow, he fell forward over the rail. Climbing unsteadily to his feet, he stumbled toward Master Gilbur.

Master Eremis was no longer holding Terisa. Had he tried to grab Geraden and missed? Lost his grip on her at the same time? She had no idea: she didn't see him. Her attention was concentrated on Geraden.

Swinging her legs over the rail, she went after him.

He was too late. If he hadn't been stupefied by Master Gilbur's blow, he would have seen that he couldn't reach the glass in time.

In front of him, the surface of the mirror went dark as the champion surged through it.

His armor made him at least seven feet tall. His head showed no face, but only a thick plate that must have been a visor. The metallic skin that protected him was scored black in several places: it had been breached at least twice. Acrid smoke curled from the wounds. He moved as if he were hurt.

But his huge rifle was ready. As he caught his balance on the dais, he aimed the muzzle straight at Geraden's chest.

Terisa got her arms onto Geraden's shoulders. He was so weak and woozy that her weight pulled him to the floor.

The first shot went over them. The Masters shouted. At least one of them screamed.

Trying to pull her legs under her, fighting to stand, she suddenly found herself staring down the barrel of the rifle.

For a period of time as quick and intense as a crisis of the heart, she watched the champion's metal-clad hand tighten on the firing mechanism.

Then he jerked up the barrel, and the blast hit the ceiling.

Broken stone began falling into the chamber.

The champion unclosed one hand from his rifle, gripped her neck, and forced her down on top of Geraden. 'Stay there.' His voice blared like a megaphone, but it was barely audible through the thunder of collasping rock. 'I don't shoot women.'

The next instant, he started firing again.

In a rush, the entire ceiling came down.

Book Two

FOURTEEN

OUT OF THE
RUBBLE

Castellan Lebbick suspected that he was foundering inside. Of course, life in Orison had been going from bad to worse for some time now; but suddenly the purpose of his life had sprung leaks in all directions.

Because of the Congery's gamble, he had several crises to deal with at once. But they were only symptoms; they weren't fundamental. As he strode to face them, he was smiling like a hawk; and only his wife – and perhaps King Joyse – had ever known him well enough to realize that this smile was a bad sign. To other people, he probably looked like he was in his element, eager for the conflicts or disasters that would provide an outlet and a justification for his rage. Only his wife and his oldest friend could have understood the particular ferocity of his grin.

Unfortunately, his wife was dead – miserably dead, killed by a long, hacking illness that cut her life out as effectively as a knife in her lungs. Nearly a year had passed, and he still missed her so acutely that it seemed to make his guts tremble.

And King Joyse had cast him adrift.

He had refused to hear the Fayle. One way or another, he blocked every vital act, interfered with every hope.

The Castellan clenched his teeth tighter, stretched his smile thinner, and refused to think about it. King Joyse was his reason for living. The passions that had led to the founding of Mordant, the ideals that had inspired the creation of the Congery – these things were the blood in his veins, the air in his chest. He was the King's hands. The King had rescued him—

Now the King *had refused to hear the Fayle.* He had abandoned it all to die, Mordant and passion and purpose, abandoned it to die miserably, hacking its life out while Castellan Lebbick cradled it in his arms and couldn't let go.

No, he was definitely not going to think about that. He had too many other problems in front of him.

That woman.

To himself, he chewed out a long, scathing curse. She was in everything somehow. The connections were there, if he could find them: she was doing this to Orison and Mordant somehow.

And she made the back of his throat ache with a desire he hadn't felt since the days of his wife's best beauty.

He wasn't going to think about that, either. He was going to do his job, *cling* to it until he recovered what it meant.

For a start, he was going to sort out the consequences of the latest catastrophe perpetrated by those pig-brained Imagers.

His task had the advantage of being both dramatic and subtle. All the crises were linked together in some way.

First in point of time, if not in degree of urgency, there was the matter of Prince Kragen's dead bodyguards.

Clearly, they had been killed for *some* reason. And they couldn't have shed all that blood by themselves. Furthermore, it seemed unlikely that they were responsible for tracking their own blood away from the places where they lay dead.

And that woman had returned to her rooms liberally besmirched with blood.

There was a band of renegade soldiers – or worse – loose in Orison. They were skilled and numerous enough – or worse – to kill trained bodyguards and carry away their own dead or wounded. They had friends to conceal them. They had something to do with that woman. And their purpose was to instigate a war between Mordant and Alend. Or worse.

That brought up other matters. What had happened to the man in black who had tried to kill her during the night after her arrival? He had escaped easily enough. Why hadn't he made another attempt?

What came next? An attack on the King himself?

And King Joyse *had refused to hear the Fayle*. The old lord had tried to warn the King of the Congery's intentions, and the King had refused to hear him. The Fayle had spoken directly to the Castellan because he had no other recourse.

Which raised the question of how the Fayle had come to know what those Imagers meant to do. He had flatly declined to answer when Lebbick had demanded an answer.

As for the Congery's crazy defiance of King Joyse's prohibition against forced translations, Castellan Lebbick knew who was responsible – or, more accurately, he knew whom he could blame. He had compelled the Fayle to mention a name or two. But they would have to wait. The results of that translation posed more immediate problems.

Apparently to defend them against Alend or Cadwal, the Imagers had chosen some alien man of war whom they had discovered in their mirrors – a soldier of commanding power, weaponry, and fierceness. So what did they expect after snatching a fighter like that out of his own life? A docile bow? A humble offer of service? They were lucky he had simply brought down the ceiling of their meeting hall, instead of murdering them individually as they deserved.

Judging by the way he had blasted an escape up out of the laborium and through the thick northwest wall of Orison to open air, he was certainly powerful enough to have murdered any number of people. In fact, Lebbick had at first feared he would turn and attempt to raze the castle itself. If that had happened, the Castellan would have had no choice but to hale whatever Imagers he could find to the defense. Completely unforewarned, his own forces and siege engines weren't in position for war.

Fortunately, the champion kept on going – away from Orison, lumbering madly through the snow like a rogue animal. Something about the way he moved suggested to Castellan Lebbick's experienced observation that he was hurt.

That left two exigent dilemmas, neither of which was the gaping breach in the wall. Of course, the breach was an enormous problem, and it was going to become urgent – but not yet. First the champion had to be pursued. That was obvious. His location had to be known, so that some effort could be made to control him, stop him. His present rampage would take him through the most densely populated region of the Demesne straight toward Batten and the heart of the Care of Armigite.

On the other hand, Master Quillon kept harrying the Castellan's heels like a ferret, thrusting his dust-caked face forward whenever Lebbick paused and shouting that the woman and Geraden had been buried under the collapse of the ceiling.

Castellan Lebbick bared his teeth. 'Do you mean you think they're still alive?'

'I don't know!' returned Quillon. 'But they won't be if you don't get them out!'

Lebbick debated the question with himself. He didn't have enough men available to both pursue the champion and dig effectively in the rubble. Some time would be needed to call up reinforcements from the encampments among the hills around Orison.

One of those encampments, however, lay reasonably close to the path the champion appeared to be taking.

Without hesitation, the Castellan did his job. He sent one aide to summon all the guards of the castle to the ruined meeting hall. Another ran for the courtyard to get a horse, bearing explicit instructions for several detachments of the King's forces. Then Lebbick turned back to Master Quillon.

'This will be slow. We can't shift all that stone in just a few hours.' Gauging the relative positions of the chamber and the breach, he commented, 'It'll have to be shifted uphill. If that woman and Geraden aren't dead yet, they'll suffocate soon.' Almost without malice, he added, 'Unless you and the rest of the Congery can think of some way to be helpful for a change.'

Unaware that he was smiling, he strode away.

Quillon went to find Master Barsonage.

He located the mediator on the floor outside one of the doors of the chamber. Those doors had saved the Congery. Not knowing what to expect from the champion, the Masters had retreated to the walls, and so they had been able to reach the doors almost instantly. As a result, only two of them were dead: one hit by the champion's first blast; another fallen under a block of stone. The rest were safe – including Master Gilbur and Master Eremis, although no one knew how they had contrived to get away in time.

245

But Master Barsonage didn't look particularly safe. He was covered with dust, chips of stone, and flakes of ancient mortar – as Quillon was himself – which gave him the appearance of a derelict. The rims of his eyes showed red through the caking dust; his mouth hung open; he sat with his hands dangling between his knees. He might have been in shock from a wound that didn't show because it was hidden by dirt.

'Barsonage!' snapped Master Quillon. 'Get up! We must hurry.'

For a moment, Master Barsonage didn't respond. He stared sightlessly past Quillon as though the ruin of the chamber had made him deaf. But when Master Quillon began to fume, the mediator raised his head and blinked.

'Quillon,' he croaked in recognition, his voice husky with dust and dismay. 'I knew it was a mistake. From the first. We should never have tampered with someone that powerful. But there was no alternative. Was there? The augury— And everyone was against us. The lords, Cadwal and Alend, King Joyse—'

He lowered his head again. 'It was a mistake.'

'Never mind,' Master Quillon cut in impatiently. 'We all make mistakes. Come *on*.'

Master Barsonage gave Master Quillon a look of blank incomprehension.

'Geraden and the lady Terisa!' Quillon was practically hopping from foot to foot. 'They are buried under all that stone!'

The mediator's expression didn't change. 'So is Gilbur's glass. It is powder. We have no way to undo what we have done. Geraden's mirror has shown that it does not translate properly. And any other glass will be a sentence of death, either for our "champion" or for the Image that receives him.'

'Mirrors preserve us! Wake *up*, Master Barsonage! Forget the champion. We must rescue Geraden and the lady! Castellan Lebbick's men will make the attempt, but it will be too slow. All that stone must be moved up and out. *It will be too slow.*'

Slowly, Master Barsonage began to understand. 'They cannot be alive,' he muttered. 'Under all that? It is impossible.'

'They must be!' shouted Master Quillon so hard that his voice squeaked. 'We have no other hope! *Come on!*'

Urgently, he reached down and tried to pull the much larger Imager upright.

For a moment longer, the mediator seemed unable to achieve enough resolution to get his legs under him. But then he muttered, 'I suppose we must. Even if it is hopeless. After this disaster, how else can we show our good will?'

Puffing dust, he heaved himself to his feet.

As quickly as possible, Quillon took Master Barsonage toward the warren of converted cells where the mirrors of the Congery were displayed and protected. After a certain amount of dithering, the mediator chose the glass Master Quillon had had in mind all along – the tall mirror reflecting a fathomless seascape, nothing but water in all directions. Strong under his girth, Master Barsonage picked up the glass without assistance and carried it back to the meeting hall.

He was starting to move faster. His carriage became steadier. When he and Master Quillon encountered other Imagers – retreating from the debacle, milling around in the halls – he issued commands with increasing authority, summoning the rest of the Congery to his support.

The two Masters soon reached the chamber.

The nearest door stood open, letting winter blow dust and cold and snow into the corridor.

Inside, the pile of rubble was substantial: it reached halfway to where the ceiling had once been. To the stone of that ceiling had been added a wide portion of the level above it, as well as all the damage the champion had left behind him on his way up to and through the outer wall. Much of the mound was composed of cut granite – ponderous foundation slabs, huge monoliths from the interior of the walls and pillars, smaller pieces which the builders of Orison had used like bricks – but the champion's rifle had reduced enormous quantities of rock to powder and pebbles.

Now Master Quillon understood the Castellan's point better. The only way the guards could clear the space was by somehow transporting the rubble up and out of the hole. Even with the help of every appropriate mirror in Orison, the job might take all day.

The whole place was in gloom, blocked from light by Orison's bulk and the thickening snowfall. Nevertheless he could see the cloud-clogged morning sky, the pall of dust in the air, the guards and other servants of the castle who had already arrived and begun fighting the pile with shovels, picks, and crowbars.

He could see Artagel on top of the mound, wrestling like a madman to shift blocks and shards nearly as large as himself. His curses sounded like cries.

At once, Master Quillon clambered up the side of the pile toward Geraden's brother. Encumbered by the mirror, the mediator followed more slowly.

When he reached Artagel, Quillon caught at his arm. Artagel brushed the Master aside without a glance. The fixed wildness in his eyes made him look dangerous.

'Make room, Artagel!' barked Master Quillon. 'We can do this better. It will be of no help to Geraden if you rupture yourself. We can reach him, but we need cooperation, not stupid single-mindedness.'

'He is my brother,' Artagel panted between exertions.

The Master spat an obscenity that sounded silly, coming from him. 'I do not care if he is your mother, your father, and the bastard offspring of every act of fornication in all the history of Mordant. Help us or get away.'

Artagel's fists clenched murderously; he forced them to relax. 'Show me, Imager,' he breathed through his teeth. 'Show me you can do better.'

By this time, Master Barsonage had gained the top of the mound. Master Quillon rasped at Artagel, 'Then make room,' as the mediator positioned his mirror beside the block Artagel had been trying to move.

Quillon helped hold the glass. While the mediator murmured the invocations that had gone into the shaping of this mirror, the two Imagers lowered the glass toward the block—

—and the block was translated away into the rolling sea.

Artagel gaped for a second. Then he started to grin.

More Imagers and many more guards were arriving. Several of the Masters had mirrors with them, Eremis among them. Master Quillon noticed Gilbur's absence; but he had no time to worry about that. While he and Master Barsonage shifted their glass, he shouted instructions to the guards. Rapidly, they organized themselves into teams around each mirror. Someone threw a shovel up to Artagel. At a nod from Master Barsonage, he began heaving rubble at the mirror, working to clear an approach to the next large piece of granite.

Powder and pebbles and hunks of rock large enough to shatter any glass passed into the Image and were swallowed by the sea. If Master Quillon had cared to do so, he could have watched the splash as each shovelful of rubble hit the water.

Glancing around the pile, he recognized the other mirrors as they were put to work. Only two of them were as large as the one he and Master Barsonage held, but they had all been intelligently chosen: none were flat; none showed scenes where the sudden appearance of huge heaps of rock would do any damage. The only possible exception was the glass Master Eremis employed with the flustered assistance of a young Apt. It reflected a gigantic and ravenous sluglike beast, with fangs that looked poisonous and malign eyes. The guards around Eremis shoveled rubble straight into the creature's face.

The creature appeared to be roaring in fury.

'Quillon!' Master Barsonage demanded. 'Pay attention!'

Hurriedly, Master Quillon helped the mediator adjust his mirror to translate another large chunk of stone.

'Is there a chance?' Artagel asked. 'Can they really be alive down there?'

'They must be,' Quillon averred again. That conviction was becoming harder and harder to sustain, however.

Terisa knew she was alive.

The scant air she was able to draw into her lungs was thick with dust: they were full of it, and whenever that dry suffocation forced her to cough, the pressure against the edges and corners of rock gouging her chest threatened to crack her ribs. Every breath raised grit into her face, scouring her eyeballs, blinding her to the darkness. And she could feel the weight of the rubble pressing down on her, slowly compressing her until her weak flesh and bones would burst and break. In addition, the rocks were hot, charred by the champion's rifle. The air was so warm it ached.

She knew she was alive. But she had no idea why.

The champion had pressed her face-down on top of Geraden: she had been in no position to observe the way his metal-clad form and his destructive fire shielded her from the worst of the stone-fall. Blocks of stone came down on him and bounced aside, forming a pocket around her; slabs of rock were cut into pieces and powder which made a cushion over her body and Geraden's. In consequence, when he turned away to burn a path for himself out of Orison, the rubble that fell immediately onto her and Geraden came, not from the ceiling and the upper level, but from the sides of the protective pocket. And smaller pieces wedged the fall securely enough to hold it in place as more and more debris from the champion's rampage was added to the pile.

She was still breathing. Against all likelihood, there was still air trapped in the stone heap.

It wasn't going to last.

With a palpable shift, a hard ridge clamping the middle of her back pressed down another fraction of an inch. She struggled frantically, but couldn't move anything more than her fingers. The heat and the dust made her want to gag on each shallow breath she sucked through the rocks. Pain like the caress of flame increased in her lungs, her eyes, her outstretched limbs. To die like this, slowly, feeling it happen moment by moment, feeling the hurt grow worse with each feather-width change in the poise of the rubble—

Something like this had happened to her before. Sometimes, when her mother and father had been angry at her, they had locked her in the closet. No one had answered her cries, her timid or hysterical appeals, until she had been quiet long enough to appease her parents. And once – for an offense which might have been heinous or trivial – she had been thrust into the back of the closet and armfuls of clothes had been tossed in on top of her before the door was locked, so that the house would be insulated from any protest she might make.

There in the dark, she had had her first experience with fading.

The clothes had choked her, and the dark was locked and absolute on all sides; and suddenly she had understood that her distress and panic meant nothing, that sensations like fear and asphyxiation meant nothing – that the locked door and the piled clothes and the dark made her unreal. For the first time, she had felt herself losing reality, felt her existence leaching out into the enshrouding blackness.

She hadn't realized it at the time – perhaps she had never realized it – but this response to the crisis had protected her. It had prevented the dark and her parents' unlove from creeping *in*.

This time, unfortunately, there was no protection. Her mind was going to snap. She could feel a crazy desire to scream rising from the bottom of her stomach. Then she would inhale so much dust that the effort to breathe would tear her heart.

'Geraden.' Her voice was a whisper, as desperate as the powder burning in her lungs. 'Geraden. Can you hear me?'

But of course he couldn't hear her. She had been lying on top of him, but not in a position that afforded him any protection. And he had been on his back, facing the stone-fall. His head must have been crushed immediately. He must still be under her somewhere, but nothing there felt soft enough to be a body.

'Geraden.' Her mind was definitely going to snap. 'Geraden.'

There was a way out, however. It came to her without drama, almost without surprise. She could fade now. She could let go of herself, of her long struggle against unreality, and allow the darkness to bear her away. Then she would be safe. Whether she lived or died, she would be safe because she would be gone.

As soon as the idea occurred to her, she knew it would be easy. That kind of failure would be easy. It had been calling out to her all her life, offering to protect her – offering her peace.

'Terisa?'

The word was a rustle of dry pain, so far away that she couldn't believe it.

'Terisa!' Impossibly weak, hurt, crushed – and stubborn, determined to reach her. 'Are you all right?'

Sudden weeping closed her throat. Now she couldn't escape. Safety was impossible. He was here with her. She was too relieved to hear his voice. She had to stay.

'Terisa?' He fought to control his alarm. 'Are you all right?' He coughed. 'Can you hear me?'

'Geraden.' Raw strain knotted her chest. 'I can't breathe. I can't stand it.'

'Don't try so hard.' His whisper came to her from some place entirely out of reach. 'Take shallow breaths. Make yourself relax. I'm getting air from somewhere.'

Despite the awful distance between them, she could hear his distress. He, too, was being crushed.

'We're going to be rescued. They'll dig us out. All we have to do is wait.'

'I can't. Can't.' The pressure of rejecting her one chance for escape drove her toward hysteria. 'Can't move. It's breaking my back. Geraden!'

'Don't think about it.' His voice sifted like dust between the stones. 'Put it out of your mind.'

'I can't.' She locked her teeth to keep from screaming.

'You can.' Somehow, he managed to speak more strongly. 'Nothing to it. Think about something else. Tell me what happened. I don't remember anything – after Master Gilbur hit me. Did he translate the champion? Did the Castellan stop him?'

Just for a moment, he startled her out of her panic. He didn't remember—? He had come back to consciousness without any notion of where he was or why—

'Terisa.'

Until she heard the edge of need in his appeal, she didn't realize how much he was depending on her. If he lost her now, he, too, might start screaming.

Deep inside, she wailed, I can't I'm being crushed *I can't stand it!* Let me *go!* But she struggled to do what he was doing, struggled to think about him instead of herself. He didn't even know how he had come to be buried alive. 'I'll try.'

In quick, broken phrases, pieces of explanation like her breathing, she described the outcome of Master Gilbur's translation.

When she finished, he groaned, then fell silent. Before she could panic again, however, he said, 'That proves one thing. You're definitely the one. The one who's going to save Mordant. The champion.'

'What?' she panted. 'What're you talking about?'

'It was always possible' – the words came out as if he were retching them – 'you were just an accident. I went wrong somehow. But that means Master Gilbur was right. Now we know he wasn't. His champion isn't going to rescue us.

'You must be the real champion.'

'That's crazy.' She could feel the bones of her spine being squeezed to chips and splinters. The air was getting worse. *You can. Think about something else.* 'Nothing's changed. I'm not an Imager. I don't understand anything. Master Eremis is the only one who can save Mordant.'

The words trailed away. If he were still alive— He was right behind her when the champion emerged. Wasn't he? What if the collapse of the ceiling caught him? What if he were dead? A pang made her twitch against the press of stone. The ridge across her back settled closer to her.

'Master Eremis.' Somehow, Geraden managed a snort. 'You think he can save Mordant? If you can make me believe that, you don't need Imagery. You're powerful enough already.'

She bit her lips to keep from crying out, I can't stand it!

When she didn't respond, he changed his approach. 'Maybe you should tell me the stuff that was supposed to get me killed. I want to understand' – he seemed to be gritting his teeth – 'why you trust Master Eremis.'

'All right.' I can't! *You can.* His voice was the only thing that kept the rock from breaking her apart.

With a clench of will, she fought to push the pain and the dust out of her mind, the close heat, the immuring weight of the stone. To take their place, she fixed her attention on images of Geraden – the line of his cheek, the way his hair curled above his forehead (*the blood trickling from his temple, the way Master Gilbur hit him, that good face smashed under the rubble*— No! not that, don't think about things like that), the quick potential for happiness and misery in his eyes. He was the reason she couldn't fail, couldn't fade. Picturing him helped her remember the things he wanted to know.

Her account was erratic, filtered and altered by the press of rock. Nevertheless she told him everything as well as she could. She related what he had already surmised about the decision of the Congery to translate its champion, as well as to send Master Eremis and Master Gilbur to a meeting with the lords of the Cares. Master Eremis had arranged that meeting, but had opposed the translation of the champion. Master Quillon was the one who had warned her not to talk to Geraden. *You can.* The meeting and its outcome. What she could remember about Prince Kragen. The attack of the man in black.

When she was done, she held her breath for a moment, hoping that would ease the pressure in her chest. But it didn't.

Geraden's reaction surprised her. Sounding even more distant and forlorn, he murmured, 'So Quillon's a traitor.'

'What do you mean?'

'He warned you not to talk to me because he knew I would tell King Joyse about that meeting. And about the champion.'

'No.' The dust was turning to stone in her lungs. She couldn't maintain her equilibrium, could not— 'If you put it that way, all the Masters are traitors. They voted for the champion *and* the meeting. Master Quillon is just more loyal to them than to King Joyse. And he's been trying to keep you alive.'

Geraden, help me.

He considered for a while. 'There has to be a traitor on the Congery.' The pain in his voice was growing stronger. 'The man who attacked you had to know where you were going to be. That leaves out the lords and Prince Kragen.

'Ah!' he groaned sharply.

A moment later, however, he continued at a higher pitch, 'Even if Eremis told them he was going to bring you, none of them knew you existed when you were attacked the first time. Only the Congery. And for that man to just disappear— It takes Imagery. Some Master wants you dead. He knows you're the only one who can save Mordant.

'If it isn't Quillon, it must be Eremis.'

'No,' she said again. That isn't what I meant. You don't understand. I need him. The rubble shifted again. She thought she could feel her ribs starting to give. I need him to teach me who I am.

On the other hand, the air seemed to be cooling. That was one small blessing, at any rate.

'He's trying to *save* Mordant. Can't you see that? He's trying to make alliances. Find ways to fight. Because King Joyse won't.'

'No, I don't see that,' Geraden replied distantly. 'Don't you think it was odd for him to take you to that meeting? You didn't know he was going to do that. How could the man who attacked you know? And why did he rush off and leave you? Maybe he went to use the mirrors so that man could appear and disappear.'

'No. No.' You don't understand. Pressure. Dust. I put on the sexiest gown I could find and went to his rooms by myself. Come on – *think* about it. 'You aren't being fair. You were with him this morning. When he came to get me. You saw the way he behaved. He didn't know I was attacked.

'It had to be set up in advance. How could he know how the meeting was going to turn out? He wanted it to succeed. He certainly didn't sabotage it.'

'The Fayle was there,' Geraden muttered. 'He wouldn't have anything to do with illicit Imagery. Everybody knows that.'

She wasn't listening. Her concentration was focused on what she was trying to say. It was important – she knew it was important. *You can.* If she survived this – and Master Eremis survived it – she had to talk to him right away. He needed to know there was a traitor on the Congery. 'And how could he know where King Joyse would put me? The first attack had to be set up in advance too. But none of the Masters knew you were going to find me instead of the champion.'

Geraden coughed thinly. Then she heard him gagging.

Instantly, everything else rushed out of her head. He was being crushed. 'Geraden! Are you all right? What's wrong?'

For a time, he didn't answer. She saw him in her mind, dangling from Master Gilbur's grasp, falling, always falling, his head a smear of blood and splinters of bone. Again she struggled crazily, helplessly, to move.

'*Geraden.*'

'I'm sorry.' To her amazed relief, he sounded better. 'I didn't mean to scare you. The rock keeps shifting. It came down harder on my throat for a while. Are you having an easier time breathing?'

At first, she had no idea what he meant. If anything, the dust was thicker than ever. But then she realized that the air had become cooler – noticeably cooler than the rubble piled around her. It was almost cold.

'They're coming,' he said. 'They're going to rescue us. We're going to be rescued.'

Unable to control herself, Terisa burst into tears.

It seemed to take forever. Then it happened all at once. The air grew colder and colder, cooling the rocks, cooling the desperate pressure in her lungs; but there was no other change except an increase in the shifting. That nearly pushed her into panic: every subtle movement threatened to break the bones of her back. She couldn't keep from sobbing. Nevertheless Geraden's nearness helped her. And she knew how to hang on when every part of her seemed to be fading.

And suddenly the weight on her simply vanished as though it were no longer real. She heard voices; more stone vanished. Hands came scrabbling through the debris to grab her arms with alarmed roughness and haul her upright.

She was still crying, but the tears washed the grit out of her eyes. She got her vision back in time to see Artagel pull Geraden out from under the place where she had been lying.

Master Quillon held her. 'Are you all right, my lady?' He seemed to be weeping himself. 'Are you all right?' His concern sounded as wonderful as the grip of his arms, and the cold, open air full of snow, and the freedom to move.

Geraden clung to his brother and coughed as if his lungs were torn. Yet he was breathing. Nothing about him looked crushed. Dust hid the traces of blood on his temple.

Falling snow made the air as dim as twilight, but she could discern what was left of the Congery's meeting hall. Beyond the shattered stumps of the pillars, the doors were open. Enormous quantities of broken stone still covered the floor. At least a dozen Masters – and many guards with shovels, picks, and crowbars – stood holding mirrors among the debris.

She caught a glimpse of Master Eremis; then he strode away as if he were in a hurry.

Abruptly, Artagel shouted, 'We did it!' and the guards dropped their tools and started cheering.

'It was a terrible mistake,' muttered Master Barsonage. Behind the dust caking his face, his eyes were red with weariness. He gripped a tall mirror that she recognized – the glass with the reflected seascape. The mediator's shoulders shook in exhaustion. 'We should never have risked that champion. We were all mad. Castellan Lebbick has fifty men chasing him, but I doubt they will be enough. Still, we have been luckier than we deserve. We have lost only two Masters.' He named men she didn't know. 'And you are alive.

'Please forgive us, my lady,' he finished unsteadily. 'We were stupid – but we did not mean you harm.'

Geraden rubbed a cloud of dust from his hair. 'Tell that to Master Gilbur.' He was smiling. 'If he hit me any harder, he would have broken my neck.'

But he seemed unable to keep his eyes in focus. 'With your permission, my lady,' he said to Terisa, 'I think I'll lie down for a while.'

Smoothly, as though it were the most graceful thing he had ever done, he fainted in Artagel's grasp.

There was a gaping breach in the ceiling of the chamber, and that section of the level above it had been gutted; but the worst damage was off to the side, where the champion had burned his way up and out through the wall. Snow swirled inward on an eddying wind. It was falling heavily enough to gather in Master Quillon's hair and form clumps on the mediator's wide shoulders.

Geraden believed that she was going to save Mordant.

When she looked up into the snow, she thought she heard the distant thrill of horns.

FIFTEEN

ROMANTIC NOTIONS

She was shivering. The temperature of the air seemed to drop rapidly –
although that was just reaction, she knew, just her body and mind suffering
the consequences of what she had been through. Her gray gown, so warm
and self-effacing earlier, now gave her no protection at all. Granite dust
coated every fiber of the material, covered every inch of her skin, made her
hair feel like ruined wool.

On the other hand, she was able to understand why Geraden had fainted.

But someone thrust a rude, soldier's goblet in front of her face. She took it
and swallowed deeply because she thought it contained wine.

The liquid turned out to be harsh brandy. A spasm knotted her chest.
When she was done coughing and gasping, however, she felt better. More
dirt had been washed from her eyes, and her lungs were clearing. She felt
warmer.

Geraden remained unconscious. Artagel had stretched him out on the
rubble, and a man in a gray doublet and baggy cotton breeches was
examining him. After listening to his chest and feeling his pulse, the man
sponged the dirt from his face, noticed and cleaned the wound on his temple,
then took a vial from a leather satchel and poured some liquid between his
lips.

Rising to his feet, the man announced quietly, 'He sleeps.' Apparently, he
was a physician. 'He does not appear seriously hurt. Take him to his bed. Let
him rest for an hour or two. Then awaken him for a bath and food. If he has
any complaint – or if he is difficult to awaken – I will come at once.'

Artagel nodded, and the man turned to Terisa. 'Are you hurt, my lady?'

She tested her arms and legs. They felt unnaturally stiff, and she couldn't
stop shivering, but nothing was damaged.

The physician watched her analytically. 'Bruises and headaches must be
expected. But if you discover any deep pains or swelling – or if you suffer
dizziness or prolonged faintness – you must send for me.'

Taking his satchel, he left the chamber.

Artagel scooped Geraden into his arms. 'Take care of him,' Terisa
murmured. He gave her a smile and moved away, carrying his brother easily.

'Come, my lady.' Master Quillon was still supporting her. 'We will return to your rooms. You, too, will profit from rest, a bath, and food.'

'Yes,' sighed Master Barsonage. 'We must all rest. And think. We must find some way to combat this champion. Now that his proper glass is broken, we have no good weapon against him.'

Leaning on Master Quillon because her legs seemed to have developed ideas of their own, Terisa let him help her out of the meeting hall.

As soon as they gained the relative privacy – and the warmer air – of the corridors leading out of the laborium, she asked the question that was uppermost in her mind. 'Is Geraden safe now? Do his enemies have any reason to kill him now?'

He hesitated momentarily. 'My lady, let me first explain that I do not know what the enemies of Mordant hope to gain by the presence of this champion. For that matter,' he added, 'I do not know what *we* hoped to gain. I abide by the decisions of the Congery because I am an Imager – but that decision I do not understand. He appears to be a danger without aim, allegiance, or purpose. As such, his actions will be random in effect. Perhaps they will aid our enemies, perhaps us.

'Nevertheless,' he continued, 'it is clear that Geraden's immediate peril is now less. If you were to tell him everything you have heard, what action could he take that would threaten those who do not wish him well?

'And yet, my lady,' he said pointedly, 'the *reason* for his peril – I have never been able to say what that is. I do not know what it is that makes him a threat to his enemies, and so I cannot claim that their malice against him has been made less. The reason for his peril remains.'

Master Quillon's words drew a shudder from her; but she accepted them. She needed to keep her mind moving. Since he seemed willing to talk, she asked, 'Why didn't King Joyse stop them? Why did he wait so long before sending Castellan Lebbick?'

The Master cleared his throat uncomfortably. 'My lady, the Fayle tried to warn King Joyse, but he was not heard. The King refused. Castellan Lebbick had no orders to intervene. He acted upon his own initiative, after the Fayle spoke to him.'

'But why?' she pursued. 'I thought King Joyse opposed that kind of translation. I thought that was one reason he created the Congery in the first place – so he could have all the Imagers in one place and make sure they didn't do any more involuntary translations.'

Master Quillon gave a snort of exasperation. 'If I were in a position to explain our King's actions and inactions, Mordant's need would be very different than it is now.'

That was the best answer she was able to get out of him.

He took her through frightened, tense, and curious crowds in the direction of her tower. When they reached her suite, they found the doors unguarded.

'Wonderful!' he muttered angrily. 'By the stars, this is perfect.'

Confusion had begun to creep like fog through the cracks and crevices of her brain. Her reaction to what had happened was growing stronger. Like a woman with a head full of cotton, she asked, 'What's perfect?'

'The guards.' He stopped and cocked his fists on his hips; his head made twitching movements as his gaze darted in all directions. 'They were all called to dig in the rubble. You are unprotected. If that butcher who desires your life should choose this moment to attack again, you are lost.'

Obviously, what he was saying was important to him. Yet somehow she had missed the point. Carefully, she inquired, 'How do you know about that?'

He looked at her sharply, his nose wrinkling. 'My lady, you need rest. And I suggest a quantity of wine. But you are unprotected.'

'I mean it.' It was difficult to speak aloud. I didn't tell anybody. Artagel didn't. I'm sure Prince Kragen and the Perdon didn't. 'How do you know I was attacked last night?'

'Last night?' Surprise made his voice squeak. 'You were attacked last night? By the same man?'

She nodded dumbly.

'Ruination! By the pure sand of dreams, why does Lebbick bother to train the dead meat he uses for guards?' With an effort, Quillon controlled himself. Facing her squarely, he asked, 'My lady, how did you survive?'

'Artagel saved me. Geraden asked him to keep an eye on me.'

'Thank the stars,' Master Quillon breathed fervently, 'for that impetuous puppy's interminable interference!' Almost at once, he demanded, 'Why did you tell no one?'

She blinked at him, unable to fathom his distress. This was going on too long. She wanted to lie down. To make him stop, she asked, 'Who do you expect me to trust?'

For just a moment, he looked as miserable and desperate as a soaked rabbit. Then he shook his head and scowled. 'I take your point, my lady. You are not in an easy position. Someday it will improve – if you live that long.

'Go to your rooms,' he continued brusquely. 'Bolt the door. I will guard you until Lebbick's men return to duty.

'As soon as I can, I will have your maid bring food and wine.'

The fog was growing thicker. She stared at him blankly.

His expression softened. 'Go, my lady.' He took her arm to urge her toward the door. 'You need rest. And if you remain standing here your mistrust will become unbearable to me.'

Somehow, his strange mixture of concern and sorrow was enough to move her. She entered her rooms, and he closed the door behind her.

After that, however, the capacity to act abandoned her. She forgot to bolt the door. Standing in the center of the room, she looked at her windows. They were blinded by the storm. Snow mounted on the ledge outside the glass; snow caught the light from the room and reflected it back. Flakes swirled and swirled forward like bits of light, but behind them everything was dark, as impenetrable as stone.

After a while, she realized that she was lying on the rug.

She felt weak and light-headed, but clearer, less fog-bound.

Cautiously, she got to her feet and located the decanter of wine. It had been refilled, a fact that gave her a sensation of detached surprise until she realized that her bed had also been made, her fires rebuilt, her stores of firewood replenished – until she remembered that a long time had passed since she had left her rooms this morning. Plenty of time for Saddith to do that part of her job.

Because Master Quillon had told her to do so, she poured a goblet of wine, drank it, and poured another.

The wine seemed to increase her detachment as well as make her feel steadier. Now she wasn't surprised when she heard voices outside her door.

'How is she?' a woman asked.

'Quiet, my lady,' replied Master Quillon.

'I do not like it that she is alone.' The woman seemed to be hesitating. 'But if she is resting a knock may disturb her.'

'Try the door,' the Master suggested. Terisa couldn't gauge his tone through the wood. 'I think she did not bolt it.'

'Thank you, Master Quillon.'

The latch lifted, and the lady Myste let herself into the room.

She bolted the door before she turned and saw Terisa.

She had on a bulky cloak the color of old snow, too heavy and warm to be worn around Orison. Held closed by her arms, it covered everything from her neck to the floor and made her look like she was trying to conceal the embarrassment of having suddenly gained forty or fifty pounds. The flush of her cheeks and the perspiration on her forehead showed that she was in fact too warmly dressed. But she smiled, and her eyes seemed to sparkle with accuracy, as if she were seeing things in good focus for the first time in years.

'Terisa,' she said, studying her quickly, 'you are well. You need a bath' – she grimaced humorously – 'but you are well. I am pleased.' Her pleasure was unmistakable. 'All Orison knows what you have suffered today. Taking that into consideration, you are impossibly well. Have I not tried to tell you that you are more special than you realize?'

This reaction left Terisa nonplussed. She was sure that she wasn't special. On the other hand, she was glad to see Myste. Although several days had passed since their last conversation, she remembered that the King's daughter wanted to be her friend.

Awkwardly, she asked, 'Would you like some wine?'

The lady's smile became laughter, then faded to seriousness. 'I would love some wine. But first' – she faltered as if a touch of fear made her stumble – 'you must agree to hide me.'

Terisa's detachment wasn't equal to the challenge. '*Hide* you?'

'Just until tonight,' said Myste quickly. 'Until after dark. Then I will be gone, and no one will know that you have aided me.

'If you will not,' she went on, 'I have no time for wine. I must go at once, hoping that I will be able to hide myself.'

'Wait a minute.' Terisa began to feel faint again. 'Wait a minute.' She made a warding gesture with both hands. 'What do you mean, no one will know? Master Quillon already knows. He knows you're here.'

'Yes, but who will he tell? The guards? Your maid? The Masters of the Congery are not inclined to tell such people anything. And if we manage matters properly, he will not realize the significance of what he knows until I am safely gone.

'Then' – the lady's expression was pained, but she held Terisa's gaze – 'I will ask you to lie for me. When Master Quillon tells what he knows – and you are asked what became of me – say that I left again shortly after I arrived, and the guards failed to notice me. Or say only that you do not know where I have gone.

'Terisa, I would not ask this if I had any choice.'

'No, wait a minute,' Terisa said again. 'I don't understand. Where are you going?'

Myste started to reply, then suddenly gestured for silence.

Terisa heard Saddith's voice. 'Is my lady all right? I came as soon as I heard that she has been rescued.'

'She will be all right,' replied Master Quillon. 'Before you see her, go call the guards who are supposed to be here. I have better things to do than stand outside her door for the rest of the afternoon. And bring food and wine.'

'Yes, Master.'

As Saddith moved away, Myste lifted her shoulders in an I-told-you-so shrug.

'She'll be back,' Terisa hissed urgently. '*Where are you going?*'

The King's daughter looked uncomfortable, a little sad – and yet excited, burning inside with a personal fever. 'If I tell you, you will be able to stop me. You must promise that you will keep my secret and not interfere.'

Terisa stopped. Her mind had cleared enough to grasp that she was being asked to do something she couldn't evaluate, something that would have consequences she couldn't predict. She hesitated because she didn't know what to say.

Her silence deepened the pain in Myste's face. 'Forgive me,' the lady said softly. 'I should not demand so much of you. Your own burdens are already severe. I will go at once.'

'No!' Startled out of her uncertainty, Terisa answered, 'Don't do that. I won't tell anybody where you're going. I'll hide you. I just want an explanation.

'The Masters translated their champion, and he went berserk. Geraden and I were buried alive. People are being killed. They appear and disappear. Everybody is betraying everybody else.' Geraden thinks I'm going to save Mordant. 'I feel like I'm falling apart. I would like to understand *something*.'

To her relief, Myste at once gave her a smile and a nod. 'I will gladly explain as well as I can. It would ease my heart. If you were Elega' – her smile became a wry grimace – 'you would believe that I have lost my mind. Doubtless this is another of what she calls my "romantic notions" – the worst of a bad lot. But I hope you will understand it.

'May I have some wine?'

'Of course.'

Half flustered and half pleased, Terisa filled a second goblet and handed it to the lady. At the same time, Myste opened her cloak, shrugged it off her shoulders, and set it aside.

Under the cloak, she wore a heavy leather jacket with a masculine cut, pants stitched of the same material, and boots clearly made for traveling. The bulk that the cloak covered was caused by a number of sacks – apparently full of supplies – slung over her shoulders on a strap like a bandolier. Knives hung at her belt – a long fencing dagger and a short poniard.

She asked permission to sit. Terisa nodded at once and gladly took a chair herself: her knees seemed to be growing weaker rather than stronger.

'Terisa,' Myste began after a long draught of wine, 'I believed from the first that you would be willing to help me. I believe you will understand. But I do not willingly impose what I mean to do on anyone. I truly have no choice.

'Are you aware,' she asked slowly, 'that Orison is riddled with secret passages?'

Taken aback, Terisa said before she had a chance to think, 'Yes. There's one in the bedroom.'

Myste smiled inwardly, and the focus of her eyes drifted into the distance. 'You have been among us for hardly ten days, and already you have learned so much. I would not have done as well. I have always been a woman who could live for years without learning such things. But Elega has a different spirit. By the time she was twelve, exploring secret passages had become her favorite pastime.

'She could not interest Torrent in this, so she often urged me to go with her.

'If you were to characterize us when we were girls,' she commented, 'you would say that Elega was bold; Torrent, timid; Myste, dreamy. In a sense, I found secret passages more exciting than Elega did. She would say that I found them "romantic." But in another sense I did not need them. I explored them with her enough to please my imagination. Then I was satisfied. Eventually, I began to ignore her urging.

'But I had learned enough for what I mean to do now.

'Terisa, you may not know that all the passages do not connect. They were built at different times, for different purposes. Most provide admittance to only a few locations in Orison.

'My knowledge of the passages is not extensive. The only entrance I am aware of to the one I need – the passage that goes where I need to go – is from the wardrobe in your bedroom. That is why I had no choice but to come to you.'

Terisa was about to ask, You mean you want to go where Adept Havelock lives? But she remembered that the passage had several branchings and kept her mouth shut.

'If I have not forgotten what Elega and I learned together,' Myste said carefully, 'if I am not confusing imagination and memory, a branch of this passage leads down into the laborium, near the meeting hall of the Masters.'

Terisa couldn't help herself. 'Why do you want to go *there*?'

Firmly, the lady answered, 'From there I may be able to leave Orison unseen through the breach in the wall. I know of no private exits, and Castellan Lebbick watches the public ones better than most people realize. If I do not get out unseen, I will be brought back involuntarily, and what I must do will come to nothing.

'Of course, the breach will be watched. But that duty will be new to the guards. They will be watching for enemies who desire to enter, not friends who wish to leave. And if this snowfall continues, it will cover me. Perhaps it can be done.'

The sensation of fog began to fill Terisa's head again. She needed sleep – a bath, a meal, and sleep, in that order. Slowly, as if she were becoming stupid, she asked, 'What do you want to do? What's so important that you have to sneak out in this kind of weather?'

Articulating each word precisely, like a woman controlling an impulse to rush, Myste said, 'I mean to find that poor, lost man the Masters call their champion. He needs help desperately.'

'*Help?*' Terisa nearly choked. 'He needs *help?*'

Myste made a warning gesture, urging Terisa to lower her voice.

'He could have burned this whole place to the ground,' she whispered intensely, He almost killed me, 'and you think he needs *help?*'

He almost killed me. Even though he said, *I don't shoot women.*

'He could have,' the lady returned promptly. 'He could have killed us all. But he did not. Does that not say something important about him – something crucial to an understanding of him and his plight?'

'Yes!' Terisa hissed back. 'It says he doesn't want to waste his power until he knows what kind of mess he's in – how many people he's going to have to slaughter to stay alive.'

Suddenly, Myste was angry. She rose to her feet. 'Perhaps you are right,' she retorted. 'Perhaps he seeks only to ration his capacity for slaughter. Do you think that Castellan Lebbick's soldiers will teach him restraint? No. They will harry him from murder to murder, searching for their opportunity to kill him in turn. If he is to be stopped, it will only be by someone who cannot harm him.'

The lady would have gone on: she plainly had more to say. But she paused at the sound of voices.

'The Castellan sends his apologies, Master.' Saddith's tone was pert and insincere: apparently, she didn't aspire to Master Quillon's bed. 'He regrets that you have been held so long on guard duty. You will be relieved shortly.'

She gave the door a saucy rap.

'Will you hide me?' Myste breathed.

'I said I would,' Terisa retorted softly. Then she admitted, 'I don't know how.'

The lady picked up her cloak. 'Let her in. I will conceal myself in one of the wardrobes.' She didn't forget her goblet. 'Try to keep her here for a while – long enough so that the guards will relieve Master Quillon. They will not know that I am here, so they will not expect to see me leave.' Her excitement had returned. 'But do not let her bring you clean clothes from the wardrobe. If she finds me there, she will surely talk about it.'

Without a sound, Myste left the room.

Saddith knocked again.

For a moment that felt like an icicle in her stomach, Terisa was unable to move. This was worse than merely telling lies: this was active subterfuge. She had to trick Saddith. And she felt too weak and befuddled to so much as stand up, never mind trick anyone. The cold paralyzed her.

But the next instant a leap of imagination told her what was about to happen. Saddith would knock again. If there was no answer, she would turn to Master Quillon and ask him what to do. And Master Quillon would be concerned. He would say something like, 'The lady Terisa may be asleep. But the lady Myste is with her. She should answer.' Then Myste would be lost.

Stung by panic, Terisa got her legs under her and hurried to the door.

When it opened, Saddith sailed grandly into the room like a yacht on show, the lower buttons of her blouse straining to contain her breasts. Her demeanor made it clear that she didn't think very highly of Master Quillon.

She carried a well-laden tray to a table while Terisa closed the door. 'That man,' she said as if she intended to be overheard, 'ought to be more civil. I can perform my duties very nicely without the benefit of his instructions.'

Putting down her tray, she surveyed Terisa.

Her immediate reaction was a gleam of mirth and a quick giggle. 'My lady, you look awful!' At once, however, she made an effort to swallow her amusement. 'My poor lady, how terrible! To be buried like that. And to be recovered in such a state, with all those men around—!' She frowned. 'What a shame that this dull gown was not damaged more. A few strategic tears would have done much to make your appearance more appealing.'

The maid continued to babble, apparently controlling her desire to laugh by saying whatever came into her head. Until that moment, Terisa had had no idea what to do. But the sense of weakness which made her want to simply fold at the knees and forget everything came to her rescue like a flash of inspiration.

'I need help,' she murmured. 'I'm so weak.' Her voice sounded wan and distant in her ears. 'I want a bath, but I keep passing out when I try to get undressed.' She had left enough dust on the rug to make that statement credible. 'I can't seem to get warm.'

Through the fog in her head, she felt remarkably clever. No one could say she was really lying. And she would gain precious time while Saddith arranged to have hot water brought to her rooms.

But her imitation of frailty was perhaps a little too convincing. With increased sympathy, Saddith came to her and took her arm. 'My poor lady, lean on me. You should sit down.' Gently, she moved Terisa toward a chair. 'It will take me only a moment to begin heating water. Then we will remove that foul gown, and I will bathe you.'

Unable to raise a reasonable objection, Terisa allowed herself to be seated.

Saddith went into the bathroom. Terisa heard running water; then the maid emerged carrying the tin bucket, which she set in the fireplace as close to the grate as possible. As she added wood to the fire, she announced, 'It is too cold in the bathroom. I will bathe you here.'

Pushing back the rug, she made room in front of the fire. Then she brought the tub from the bathroom and positioned it next to the hearth. After that, she began unfastening Terisa's gown.

For the first time since chidhood, Terisa had the experience of being undressed and washed like an invalid. It made her acutely self-conscious.

The result was undeniably pleasant, however – sitting in the tub before a hot fire while Saddith poured warm water through her freshly scrubbed hair.

The relief of being clean and warm compensated for the embarrassment of Saddith's comments on her body. When she heard the unmistakable sounds indicating that guards were now on duty outside – unmistakable because Master Quillon complained peevishly about the delay as he left – she felt almost equal to her next trick, which was to get rid of Saddith without allowing the maid to bring her any clothes.

'This feels wonderful,' she murmured. 'I think I'll just soak here for a while,' it'll be all right for you to leave, 'and then go to bed.'

Saddith nodded approval. 'I will bring you a robe.'

'No, thanks.' Terisa barely escaped betraying her fright. 'I don't need one. The fire's warm, and I have plenty of towels.' Hoping it would help, she added shamefacedly, 'I don't wear anything in bed.'

'Nonsense, my lady,' replied the maid. 'What if you change your mind and decide to eat something before going to bed? You must not risk a chill.'

Before Terisa could stop her, Saddith walked into the bedroom.

Terisa nearly fell out of the tub. Water splashed and steamed on the hearth as she scrambled to her feet.

But Saddith returned almost immediately with the burgundy velvet robe in her arms and a puzzled expression on her face.

'What's the matter?' asked Terisa, her heart hammering.

'Nothing, my lady.' Saddith shook her perplexity away. 'I cannot remember leaving your robe on the chair when I cleaned the room this morning.'

Terisa felt so light-headed with relief that she almost collapsed. Myste was more quick-witted than she would have believed possible. 'I got it out' – she seemed to hear herself from far away – 'when I thought I was going to be able to undress myself.'

'My lady,' Saddith said reprovingly, 'you must not stand there wet.'

As calmly as if she were levitating, Terisa reached for a towel.

Saddith wound a second towel around her hair while Terisa dried herself. When she was done, she stepped out of the tub and let Saddith lift the robe onto her shoulders. 'Thanks,' she said again. 'You can go now.' She had lost the capacity to be subtle. 'I'll be all right.'

The maid studied her for a moment. Then she winked. 'I believe,' she said mock-seriously, 'that I recognized the voice of one of your guards. He has a good reputation in these matters. You may find it restful – and rewarding – if you ask him to warm your bed. If I had come so close to death, I would be eager to remind myself' – she moved her hands suggestively down her thighs – 'that life is worth living.

'He is the tall one with the green eyes,' Saddith added, laughing happily as she let herself out of the room.

Immediately, Terisa rushed to the door and bolted it.

When she turned around, she found Myste standing in the doorway of the bedroom. The lady's face wore a distracted and thoughtful expression.

'That was close,' breathed Terisa. 'I don't know how you can think so fast.'

'Hmm?' Myste murmured. Her mind was obviously elsewhere. 'Oh, the robe.' With a shrug, she dismissed the subject. 'Terisa, I think it is not a good idea to leave that chair in your wardrobe.'

'Why not?' Surprise and reaction gave Terisa's tone a note of asperity. '*I* don't know where those passages go. I've got to do something to keep people out of here.'

A smile quirked Myste's lips. 'I see your point. The precaution is tempting. The difficulty is that the position of the chair announces to anyone who sees it that you are aware of the passage. I want to ask how you chanced to notice it—'

Terisa held her breath.

'—but you owe me no explanations. We must simply hope that your maid will not volunteer what she knows to the wrong ears. I assure you, however, that your life will become much more burdensome if Castellan Lebbick sees a chair in your wardrobe.'

'Oh.' Terisa let the air out of her lungs in a sigh of self-disgust. 'You're right.' Why wasn't she able to think of things like that for herself?

At once, Myste became reassuring. 'I doubt that you have any cause for worry. Your maid has already told everyone she is likely to tell. And Castellan Lebbick has had no reason to search your rooms.'

'I hope so.' Terisa made an effort to relax. Of course the Castellan had no reason to search her rooms. She was probably safe. And Myste's kind refusal to pursue the question of how she had become aware of the passage was another relief.

By degrees, she began to feel that her bath had done her a lot of good. And a tray of food was waiting for her. When she sniffed it, she discovered that she was hungry. Inviting Myste to join her, she sat down to a meal.

Myste had left her cloak in the bedroom. Taking off her bandolier, she accepted Terisa's invitation.

While they ate, Terisa returned to the subject of Myste's intentions. 'You were telling me why you think the champion needs your help. That's the point, isn't it? At least that's what I don't understand. You don't even know him. What difference does he make to you?'

The lady cleared her throat with a swallow of wine. 'You ask several questions at once. The truth is probably nothing more profound than that when I heard of his plight it wrung my heart – and when I thought that I might help him the pain turned to gladness. But I will try to give you reasons.

'That he needs help is obvious. Consider.' Her gaze was fixed on something beyond the wall of the room. 'He is a man of war, accustomed to hostility on all sides. Subjugation and destruction are his life. And now – suddenly, without explanation – he is alone in a world surely as unfamiliar to him as any he has ever conquered.

'You are aware of the great debate of Imagery. Do the people, places, and creatures seen in mirrors have independent existence, or are they merely like reflections in a pool of water, unreal apart from the glass in which they have been cast? Is the champion a man, deserving the rights and respect of a man? Or is he, in effect, nothing more than an animal – a being like a horse that can be decently, even honorably, deprived of its own will?

'Terisa, by either standard he must have help.'

Myste's excitement impelled her to her feet. She began to pace the rug. 'If he is a man – as my father would surely insist he is – then what the Masters have done is abominable. We cannot judge whether he is a good man. Perhaps he is a foul enslaver – that lies outside our knowledge. But any man deserves better than to be wrenched out of life, away from world, home, family, purpose, and explanation, to serve what are, essentially, the whims of Imagers. Think of him! He knows no one here, understands nothing. He was not invited to cast his lot among us. To him we must appear simply as enemies. He will fight us until weapons, food, and hope fail him. Then he will die.

'If he is a man, his death will be murder—

'If he is less than a man,' she continued after a long pause, 'a being comparable to a horse or a hunting dog, then it is his right to have help. There is a responsibility which accompanies the service we impose on animals. In exchange for what we take away, we give food, shelter, healing, perhaps even kindness. If we do not, few will call us admirable. Does not a champion with the mind and needs and desires of a man deserve at least as much consideration as a beast? Even if he did not truly exist until the moment of his translation, he is real now and should not be harried to death simply because, like an animal, he does not understand what we require of him.'

Perhaps reaction to the day's events left Terisa punchy; perhaps her emotions were bouncing out of control. Whatever the cause, her heart lifted as she listened to the lady. She was glad that she had decided to help Myste, very glad. This was worth doing. Simply because she wanted confirmation, she said, 'Maybe all that is true. But what does it have to do with you? Why do you think you have to sneak out of Orison and chase after him on foot in this weather?'

Myste frowned for a moment. Then she smiled self-deprecatingly. 'There you touch me on my weakest point. I am a bundle of romantic ideas which defy common sense.' As she spoke, however, she became stronger. 'Yet I have always believed that problems should be solved by those who see them – that when a difficulty presents itself the person who becomes aware of it should answer it instead of trying to pass it to someone else.' Her voice cast hints of passion like glints of gold in the firelight. 'This is more true rather than less for a king's daughter. What is a king if not a man who accepts responsibility for problems when he sees them? And should his daughter not do the same?'

Her eyes flashing like Elega's, she faced Terisa. 'But the truth,' she said as intensely as a cry, 'is that I *want* to go. I am tired of waiting for my life to have some kind of purpose.'

At once, however, she made an effort to tone down her manner. '"Romantic," as I say.' She laughed awkwardly. 'But I cannot claim that I have been happy since the hall of audiences, since my father' – she was uncomfortable mentioning him – 'forced you to play hop-board against Prince Kragen. When my mother and Torrent left, I remained in Orison because I thought I had a purpose. I wanted there to be at least one person at the King's side who would believe him if he chose to explain himself. Perhaps I could not help him solve Mordant's problems, but I could offer him the company and support of my willingness.

'But when for a whim he insulted an ambassador of Alend to the point of war – for a *whim*, Terisa! – and I went after him, he refused to hear me.' She couldn't keep her emotion down. '"My daughter and that Kragen mean to betray me," he snapped. "They have already begun. Do not hover. I am tired of daughters." Then he slammed his door.'

Again, Myste was silent for a while. But then she shrugged, and that small gesture seemed to restore her balance, her excitement. 'I am still enough his daughter to want to take action when I see a need. And I do *not* want to watch him continue as he is going.'

Terisa did the best she could to help. Slowly, she said, 'When the champion first appeared, he nearly killed me. But he stopped himself. He said, "I don't shoot women."'

Myste smiled like a beam of sunshine through the storm piling snow over Orison.

The snowfall began to lessen shortly after sunset. Because she didn't want to risk departing Orison under an open sky and a clear moon, across an expanse of new snow in which she would leave obvious tracks, Myste left Terisa's room promptly. Her supplies over her shoulder under her cloak, a small oil lamp in one hand, she opened the hidden door and clambered through the wardrobe into the passage.

'Be careful,' Terisa whispered after her. 'If you get lost, and Castellan Lebbick has to send a search party down there to find you, we're both going to look pretty silly.'

'Do not let him bully you,' replied the lady almost gaily. 'He only does it because he loves my father. I thank you with all my heart. I think I have not been this happy for years.'

As an afterthought, Terisa asked, 'What shall I tell Elega?'

With the lamp in front of her, Myste seemed to be standing on the lip of a well of darkness. 'Tell her nothing.' Her voice carried a hollow sound like an echo. 'Watch her. If she truly means to betray the King, stop her.'

How do you expect me to do that? Terisa demanded. But she didn't speak aloud. Myste was already gone.

Oh, well. Terisa closed the passage and got out of the wardrobe. Tomorrow she would have to go looking for Master Eremis. He needed to know how he had been betrayed. For some reason, the prospect of talking to him didn't appeal to her. She preferred to think about Myste.

She wanted to believe that someday she would have as much courage as the King's daughter.

As soon as she went to bed, she slept like a dead woman all night.

She was awakened early the next morning by the sound of horns.

It snatched her out of bed as if it were the call from her dreams, the distant appeal and ache of music or hunting. In too much of a hurry to notice that her fires had almost died out and the air was chilly, she strode naked out of the bedroom, looking for the source of what she had heard.

It came again.

It wasn't the call she remembered. It was the blare of a trumpet, the same solitary fanfare that had greeted the arrival of the lords of the Cares to Orison.

Now she recollected herself enough to feel the cold. Nevertheless she went to the window and looked out over the muddy courtyard.

The trumpet winded again. Apparently, each of the departing lords was being given a personal salutation. She saw the Fayle and his entourage emerge from the gate with the Perdon behind him, while the Termigan turned his horse away from the guards ranked formally behind Castellan Lebbick. Then came the Armigite, accompanied by his guards and courtiers – and by two or three women. Perhaps they were his mistresses or courtesans.

Last was Prince Kragen.

So he was leaving also. Apparently he – like the lords – had decided to remain only long enough to assess the consequences of what the Congery had done. Were they all abandoning Orison now because it was no longer safe, no longer proof against siege – or even against weather? Did Prince Kragen intend to bring down the war that the lords of the Cares fled?

How much was the translation of the champion going to cost Mordant in the end?

The cold of the stone against her arms and breasts made her shiver. The tempo of events was accelerating. She thought she heard a wild note of warning in the way the trumpeter blew his salute as Prince Kragen received his abrupt farewell from Lebbick and turned toward the gate, surrounded by his coterie of bodyguards.

Shivering violently, she left the window.

First she retrieved her robe and sashed it tightly; then she worked on her fires, stoking them with fresh kindling, blowing on the coals until the kindling caught flame, feeding the flames with generous quantities of wood. After a while, she began to feel warmer.

She had become surprisingly hungry during the night. But Saddith didn't usually bring her breakfast quite this early. When she had completely stopped shivering, she decided that she would get dressed, then ask one of her guards to call for the maid and a tray.

She wanted to wear her own clothes: she had had enough of gowns for the time being. To her bafflement, however, she couldn't find her moccasins. That was strange. When had she last worn them? The night before last, to the meeting of the lords. Where were they?

Had Saddith taken them for some reason?

Frowning, she finished dressing, put on the delicate buskins again, then went to the door and unbolted it.

The guards outside looked vaguely familiar: they must have had this duty sometime recently. They saluted her, and one of them asked if she needed anything.

'Can you call my maid?' she asked. 'I want breakfast.'

'Of course, my lady.' A moment later, the man added, 'Apt Geraden was here earlier, asking if you're all right. I won't be surprised if I see him again soon.' He grinned. 'Should I tell him you're ready for visitors?'

'Yes, thank you.'

Smiling because Geraden must be well if his brother and the physician were willing to let him worry about others, she closed the door and returned to her windows to watch people – guards on duty, servants carrying supplies, men and women who had business with the few shops already open in the northwest end – watch them slogging through the cold and mud of the courtyard while she waited for Saddith or the Apt.

Soon there was a knock at her door. Before she could answer it, Castellan Lebbick stalked into the room and slammed the door behind him.

In the center of the rug, he stopped to face her. He had one arm clamped at his back, the other cocked on his hip. His jaws chewed anger; his shoulders were stiff with it.

Nevertheless he was smiling.

'My lady' – his tone was practically cheerful – 'you are done lying to me.'

To her surprise and relief, she didn't cringe. She had already outfaced him once. She could do it again.

'I would have come sooner,' he commented in a conversational way, 'but I've been busy. I'm sure you don't want to hear about it, but I'll tell you anyway.

'I was on my way to confront you again yesterday when the Fayle found me and told me what those pigshit Imagers were doing. After that, of course, I had to organize my men to help dig you and Geraden out of the rubble. I had to provide protection for the lords of the Cares and' – his mouth sneered – 'Prince Kragen as well as King Joyse, in case that *champion* turned to attack us. I had to arrange to follow and trap him, so that he wouldn't do any more damage. Since I knew where Eremis was, I didn't have to worry about him. But I had to spend hours and good men searching for Gilbur.

'I suspect you already know the outcome. I'm going to tell you anyway.

'Gilbur is gone. Vanished as completely as if he's mad and can use any flat glass he wants. The lords are gone. Since they think the Masters are insane, they aren't willing to stay and stand by their King. I had to let Prince Kragen go. He's an *ambassador*.' He grinned as though considering the prospect of tearing into her with his teeth. 'In addition, the champion is free.'

'Free?' The Castellan had made no mention of Myste. He wasn't saying the things Terisa expected. It was happening too fast. Why did he want to 'confront' her? How could Master Gilbur have vanished? 'What do you mean?'

'I mean, my lady,' he replied like the edge of an axe, 'that my men failed. Of course, I only sent fifty – but two hundred might have done no better.

'Oh, they found him easily enough. That strange armor of his doesn't include wings. In any case, I think he's wounded. So they should have been able to keep him. I didn't tell them to fight. I didn't want him provoked. I just wanted him to stay in one place until we had a chance to decide what to do with him.

'But his translation was planned well. Gilbur and Eremis must have been working on this for a long time.' Now the fury in his grin couldn't be mistaken. 'My men succeeded. They made him stop. But before they could do anything more than send a rider back to me, they were attacked. The air in front of them opened, and a cat the size of a small *horse* jumped out.'

In some strange way, the Castellan's ire sustained him, as if it were the food on which he lived.

'A beast that large would have been formidable under any circumstances. But this one, my lady – *this* one set fire to everything it touched. Flesh and iron were tinder for it, and it butchered my men like cattle. Only two escaped. They left it feeding on charred carcasses. I'm lucky I didn't send two hundred men. I can't afford to lose two hundred men.

'Since then,' he went on more quietly, 'I've been out there. The snow makes it easy to see that the champion and that firecat left in different directions. Clearly, they didn't do us the courtesy of destroying each other. Now we have two abominations on our hands, instead of just one.'

Terisa shuddered involuntarily. Fifty men! And that was where Myste had gone— She nearly groaned aloud, *That's where Myste went!*

But all this had happened yesterday, and Myste hadn't left Orison until last night. The odds were great that both the champion and the firecat were so long gone that she would never catch up with them.

Taking a deep breath to steady herself, Terisa said, 'That's terrible. I just don't understand what it has to do with me.'

'My lady,' he replied like a blade, 'in some way you are responsible.'

She started to protest, but he cut her off. 'Yesterday morning, right after you left here with Eremis and Geraden, I took your advice. I did "a little work." I searched your room.'

For some reason, she found that she had to brace herself against the wall to keep her knees from folding.

'I discovered a chair in your wardrobe.' His satisfaction was as keen as his anger. 'And I found these.'

From behind his back, he produced her moccasins.

While she stared at them, he said, 'You were able to wash the blood out of your clothes. But these are leather. You couldn't do anything about the bloodstains on the soles.'

At that moment, a knock on the door interrupted him.

'Come in!' he snapped harshly.

The door opened, and Geraden entered the room.

Her attention jumped to him like a leap of the heart. For an instant, she saw his ready smile and the light of pleasure in his eyes, and she felt that she was already rescued, that his mere presence would be enough to save her. He was loyal to King Joyse – therefore logically on the Castellan's side against her. But she was confident that he would stand by her, whatever happened.

The next instant, however, his pleasure vanished in alarm as he grasped what was going on. Warily, he inquired, 'Castellan Lebbick? My lady?'

Lebbick nodded in recognition. 'Geraden. Is this an accident, or are you intruding on purpose? Are you in this with her?'

'In what?' asked Geraden.

For a moment, the Castellan studied him. Then Lebbick said sourly, almost bitterly, as though he were disappointed, 'No, I don't believe it. You're capable of almost anything misguided or blind. But you know better than to betray your King. The Domne would birchwhip you to ribbons if you tried it.'

'Are you accusing the lady Terisa of treason?' Geraden sounded a little frightened by his own temerity, but determined nonetheless. 'Isn't that awkward? I mean, she isn't one of his subjects. He has no claim on her. How can she commit treason?'

Castellan Lebbick returned his gaze to Terisa. She met it so that she wouldn't look at Geraden, wouldn't let her need for him show in her face.

Softly, her accuser growled, 'Why are you here, boy?'

'This morning,' replied Geraden promptly, 'the Congery will hold a funerary commemoration for the two Masters who died yesterday. The lady Terisa is asked to attend.'

'In other words' – Lebbick's tone sharpened into a lash – 'the Masters need to decide what to do about Eremis and Gilbur, and they don't want anybody else to know it.' He didn't allow Geraden a chance to respond, however. 'You can tell them the lady Terisa won't be coming. She's under arrest. You can visit her in the dungeon when I'm done questioning her.'

Unable to restrain herself, she flung a mute appeal toward Geraden. She saw him mouth the words 'under arrest' as if he were appalled. During the space between one heartbeat and the next, she believed that he would protest on her behalf, do something – that he might even jump at Lebbick and try to defend her physically.

But he didn't. He said, 'I'll tell them.' Turning away, he walked out of the room and closed the door behind him.

Geraden! He had abandoned her to Castellan Lebbick's anger. *Geraden!* When she needed him, he turned and walked away.

Her knees threatened to fail her. She could feel the courage running out of her like water from a broken jug. She had been so *sure* that he was her friend—

'I see I finally have your attention,' the Castellan commented maliciously. 'Yes, you're under arrest. For lack of anything better, you're accused of participating in the murder of Prince Kragen's bodyguards.'

Really, it would have been better if she had never come here, if she hadn't let Geraden's smile and his earnestness (and his brief, unaccountable authority) persuade her to ignore her common sense. She had no business pretending that she had anything to do in this place, that she could make a difference.

'I'm going to lock you in the deepest, darkest cell I've got – the one with the biggest rats – and let you rot there until you tell me the truth.'

Everybody was betraying everybody else; she was just a minor item on everybody's list. She couldn't defend herself because she couldn't figure it all out. And she didn't have anybody to betray because there was nobody on her side.

'If you get lonely, you'll be able to talk to your lover. Eremis will be in the cell beside you. If I have my way, you'll get to hear him scream.'

That halted the downward spiral of her dismay. Eremis? Eremis was arrested? That was bad – worse than what was happening to her. He needed his freedom. Mordant needed him to be free. Especially now, with the hope of the champion turned to disaster and the lords gone back to their Cares.

'I wish you knew how silly that sounds,' she said as if a total stranger were speaking for her. 'I haven't done anything. I never do anything.'

'Is that a fact?' Lebbick's sarcasm was as thick as blood.

'You're really doing a good job,' she continued so that she wouldn't stop, wouldn't realize how dangerously she was behaving. 'I'm probably the only person in Orison who is innocent of everything. And Master Eremis is probably the only one who doesn't deserve to be locked up.'

'Sheepguts!' snarled the Castellan. 'You're trying my patience, my lady.'

'Which was never your best feature anyway,' she retorted.

For a moment, he gazed at her in silence, perhaps in surprise; and for that moment she failed to realize she was giving him exactly what he wanted. Then his smile warned her. But of course the warning came too late. Her unpremeditated goading had already provided his anger the object it desired.

'No,' he said almost mildly, 'it was never my best feature.' He was grinning like a barracuda.

Her audacity turned to fright. Instinctively, she tried to retreat; but the wall held her where she was.

'Of course, as you pointed out earlier, I don't have much proof. Yesterday I was too busy to question either the Fayle or that whelp the Armigite. And today they insisted on leaving. I couldn't refuse them.

'But I'm not stupid.

'The night before last – the same night my guards found Prince Kragen's men, after the Armigite warned them – the Fayle somehow came by the knowledge that Eremis and Gilbur intended to translate their champion. The same night, you left here with Eremis – and came back alone, covered with *blood*.' He flung the word at her. 'Of course, you're innocent. You innocently washed the blood out of your clothes, trying to get rid of anything that might connect you to those dead bodyguards. You innocently lied to me. But you innocently *forgot*' – he brandished her moccasins – 'that your footwear would give you away.

'By some staggering coincidence, all of the lords except the Domne were here at the same time. Prince Kragen was here, the Alend ambassador. The next day the Congery rushed to its translation, hurrying to get done before I could interfere. When my men tried to stop that champion, he was rescued by another exercise of Imagery.

'What do you expect me to make of all this, my lady? Do you expect me to be impressed by the purity of your innocence, my lady, or by the sincerity of your lover's motives, my lady?'

He swore at her with intense relish. 'I'll tell you what I make of it.' His oaths were unfamiliar to her, but their passion made her quail. 'First, it's obvious that this translation has been planned for a long time. Mirrors don't come into existence overnight. Although I don't know how they did it,' he muttered half to himself. 'Where's the glass that worked the translation?' Then he resumed his attack. 'Since Eremis and Gilbur were the ones who spoke to the Fayle – and since Gilbur has disappeared now – it's obvious they're responsible.

'But what happened to produce two men dead and enough blood for five or six more?

271

'One of two things, my lady, both of them treason. Either Eremis and Gilbur met with the lords to plan the betrayal of Mordant by means of their champion, and Prince Kragen was caught spying on them, and his men died saving his life. Or Eremis and Gilbur met with Prince Kragen, and the lords caught them planning the betrayal of Mordant, and his men died saving his life. Either way, the Fayle spoke to me because what Eremis and Gilbur intended to do appalled him.

'How do I account for the quantity of blood – or the insufficiency of bodies? The chair in your closet answers that. The men who fought for you and *died* were removed into one of the secret passages.

'In fact, that chair explains a lot. It tells me how you contrived to survive being attacked the first night you were here. Your allies – I mean Eremis' allies – came out of the passage long enough to save you. Then they went back into hiding.'

A sensation of horror rose in her throat, choking her. He was so close!

'In addition,' he went on, 'ordinarily, I would have said you haven't been here long enough to become so deeply involved in treachery. Eremis may be the greatest fornicator in all Mordant, but even women usually need time to be so degraded. But you've had more time than I realized – you've had all the time I thought you were safely locked in your room.

'What do you think, my lady? Which evil did you share? Or is there a third explanation, a worse crime?'

He stepped closer to her, aimed his rage straight into her face. She flinched, but couldn't look away. His passion held her.

'What do you gain here? Is the way Eremis abuses his lovers reward enough for you? Or do you have some other purpose? Did the arch-Imager send you here to destroy us?'

Tossing aside her moccasins, he gripped her arms and ground his fingers into her triceps.

'Who fought for the King, my lady? Is *everyone* a traitor?'

No leave me alone it's not my fault I don't know what you're talking about!

He shook her as if he meant to fasten his teeth in her throat. '*Why didn't you use your secret passage to come back to your rooms?* That way, you would have been safe. No one would have known you had anything to do with those dead bodyguards.'

'Because that isn't where it goes!' she cried.

Then she stopped and stared at him while the blood froze around her heart and a look of triumph filled his face.

'That's a start, my lady,' he whispered between clenched jaws. 'Where *does* it go?'

She couldn't tell him that. If she did, she would expose Master Quillon and Adept Havelock, as well as Myste. She had already said too much.

This time she defied the Castellan deliberately. It was Terisa herself, not some audacious stranger, who said, 'I don't deserve to be treated like this. If your wife were here, she would be ashamed of you.'

After that, panic made her giddy. She saw the widening like a flare of madness in his eyes, but she didn't understand it. She heard him say, as if he were speaking in a foreign language, 'Thank you, my lady. I haven't had this

much fun since King Joyse let me punish that garrison commander.'
Through a veil of dread, she watched him let go of her arms, cock himself
back, and swing the back of his hand at her head.

Instinctively, she jerked her head down, jerked her arms up.

Deflected, his blow was still hard enough to knock her to the floor. Pain
began to roar in her ears. She had the impression that she was going blind:
the only thing she could see was the Castellan staring at his hand as though it
belonged to someone else.

The pain had a voice. It said distinctly, 'What am I doing?'

Then she heard someone pounding at the door.

'Go away!' Lebbick roared.

'Your pardon, Castellan.' A guard's voice. 'The King's orders.'

'The King?' Castellan Lebbick verged on apoplexy.

'He wants to speak with the lady Terisa. I'm instructed to take her to him.'
The man's tone conveyed a squirm in the face of Lebbick's rage. 'He wants
to speak with her now.'

'She's under arrest. She should be in the dungeon.'

'Castellan, I was specifically told to assure the lady she isn't under arrest.'

The Castellan made a hoarse, strangled noise.

Abruptly, hands took hold of her and stood her on her feet. After a
moment, she saw that they were his. 'Someday, my lady,' he said softly, 'my
chance will come. When that happens, you aren't going to escape me.'

He left her to the support of the guard.

SIXTEEN

WHO YOUR FRIENDS ARE

On the whole, she reflected with a loopy clarity while pain clanged back and forth in her head and the guard held her upright, she liked being rescued. It was better than not being rescued. Definitely.

But what had inspired King Joyse to send for her now? How did he know she needed rescuing?

How did he know she was under arrest?

Considering how little information she herself possessed, it was truly astonishing how much everybody else seemed to know.

'Are you all right, my lady?' asked the guard.

She heard relief and concern in his tone. On the other hand, no one had mentioned Myste. Hadn't they missed her yet? She speculated on that until she forgot the guard's question.

He shook her gently and repeated, 'Are you all right?'

Her vision appeared normal. Nevertheless she had the odd impression that everything was distorted. The angles where the walls met the floor looked false. The doorway was insidiously straight, not to be trusted. She was out of her mind, of course. She didn't object, however. This kind of craziness helped her bear the way her head hurt.

'My lady?' The guard's concern was becoming stronger than his relief.

Do you know—? she began, but no sound came out. She made an effort to clear her throat, hold her head more upright. 'Do you know why he hit me?'

'No, my lady.' The guard was standing beside her with one arm around her back and the other hand on her shoulder. She still had no idea what he looked like. 'I wasn't here.'

'He hit me,' she said precisely, 'because I insulted him.' Suddenly, she wanted to laugh. Or cry: it was hard to tell the difference. She had insulted him, *she*, Terisa Morgan. It was worth getting hit for. Maybe. 'Oh, my head hurts.'

'Here, my lady.'

Carefully, the guard maneuvered her into a chair, then pressed a goblet of wine into her hands. She drank deeply; for a moment she felt spikes hammering through her skull. After that, however, she began to feel better.

With an effort, she said, 'Thanks.' Now what she wanted was a nap. But there was some reason why she couldn't take one. What was it? Oh, yes. 'Did you say the King wants to see me?'

'Yes, my lady. When you're well enough to walk.'

She turned her head to look at him and smile. She didn't remember ever having seen him before. He was a relatively young man with a thin face and earnest eyes – perhaps not the most promising candidate to convey a message that would infuriate Castellan Lebbick. But he had carried out his orders. And she was grateful for his courtesy.

'We might as well try,' she said. 'Maybe the walk will do me good.'

Nodding encouragement, he assisted her to her feet. Then he gave her his arm to lean on. She took a few experimental steps and found that the condition of her head continued to improve. Incredible. Judging by appearances, it was actually possible to survive having a man like the Castellan furious at her. A man like her father. She could hardly believe it.

Moving cautiously, she let her escort guide her to the tower where King Joyse and his daughters had their suites. By the time she arrived at the high, carved door of the King's apartment, she felt reasonably stable – balanced between light-headedness and the aftereffects of Lebbick's vehemence.

The King's guards opened his door without question: clearly they were expecting her. One of them announced her while the other bowed her inward. In a moment, she found herself standing for the second time in the richly furnished chamber where King Joyse played his games of hop-board.

The room was lit by candles in candelabra and brass wall-holders, and the thick blue-and-red rug contrasted warmly with the decorated blond wood paneling of the walls, bringing out the carving and the delicate black inlay-work. An ornamental mantel framed the fireplace. On the hop-board table, a game was in progress. No one was playing, however.

'My lord King,' the guard pronounced firmly, 'here is the lady Terisa of Morgan.' Then he withdrew, taking his companion and Terisa's escort with him and closing the door. But King Joyse didn't react. He sprawled in a gilt-edged armchair with his legs extended on a fat hassock and his head propped against the chair back. His purple velvet robe covered him like a shroud: it was starting to look as old and ratty as Adept Havelock's surcoat. A long sheet of parchment – an open scroll – was draped over his face; his arms dangled beside him, his swollen knuckles nearly scraping the rug. The floor around his chair was littered with more scrolls, some of them open, others haphazardly tied with string.

He was snoring decorously. The stiff parchment rustled whenever he breathed.

The King's Dastard wasn't present. Instead, King Joyse was being kept company by Geraden and the Tor.

Involuntarily, she gaped at them.

'My lady,' rumbled the Tor. 'It is a pleasure to renew your acquaintance.' His fat overflowed his chair, and his plump hands gripped a flagon of wine as if he couldn't function without it. His thin white hair straggled disconsolately from his pale scalp. But his voluminous black robe was clean; his jowls were decently shaved. Although his small eyes were bleary, they seemed marginally less blurred than she remembered them.

275

Geraden met her surprise with a grin. Almost at once, however, his expression changed to distress. He jumped out of his chair and approached her. Lightly, he stroked the hot skin of her cheek. 'That unscrupulous bastard,' he whispered. 'He hit you.' Then chagrin overcame him. 'I'm so sorry. It's my fault. I didn't think he would go that far. I thought I would be fast enough. I ran all the way – all the way—'

'Enough, young Geraden,' the Tor interposed, peering morosely into his flagon. 'You are a son of the Domne. Have more dignity.'

'I don't understand.' Terisa felt that she had abruptly become stupid. 'What are you doing here?'

'As little as I can,' the Tor replied as though she had spoken to him. 'King Joyse keeps good wine and an excellent fire. I have no other needs.

'It was awkward, I admit,' he mused, frowning to himself. 'He refused to see me. After that cell, I felt as cold as my son. I wanted to be warm again. And I thought I would share a last flagon with my old friend the King of Mordant. Did I say that I would not leave him? I meant to say so. But he refused to see me. Very awkward.'

Unexpectedly, he smiled. Under other circumstances, it would have been a happy smile; but it didn't touch the sadness in his eyes. 'He underestimated me. I sat down outside his door and commenced howling. Not polite, deferential howling, I assure you, but howling to alarm the dead.'

'You did that?' Geraden grinned in spite of himself, surprised out of his contrition.

The Tor nodded. 'It is well that my family did not see me. They would not have thought better of me for it. But I succeeded.' He glanced toward King Joyse and commented, 'Since admitting me, he has found it impossible to make me depart.'

This didn't make much sense to Terisa. She shook her head to clear it, but the movement had the opposite effect. She needed to sit down. Or lie down.

'But why?' She couldn't forget how the Tor had looked standing in the mud of the courtyard with his dead son in his arms, or what Geraden had told her about King Joyse's reaction to the Tor's son's death. 'All the other lords left. Why do you want to stay?'

The Tor grimaced.

'Revenge.'

Geraden was startled. 'Revenge?'

'For most of my life,' explained the lord in a husky voice, 'I have been haunted by the knowledge that I did not give King Joyse my full support when he needed it. This would have been wise policy – if he had failed. But he succeeded, thereby making me a conniving ingrate in the eyes of all Mordant. I mean to be revenged for that.'

'I don't understand,' Terisa repeated weakly. Maybe the Tor was joking. But what kind of joke was it?

'The King needs a chancellor.' The lord didn't raise his head. 'Someone who can put two coherent commands together better than that mad Imager. As long as I sit here' – he flopped one hand on the arm of his chair – 'and speak as though I have authority, I will be obeyed. Whether he wishes it or not, Joyse will no longer be a passive ruler. Either I will take action in his name, or he must take action to stop me.'

Geraden's eyes gleamed appreciatively; but Terisa said, 'Wait a minute.' She was too slow: she had to catch up. She had believed that the Apt was abandoning her when he left her to Lebbick. 'You're giving orders in the King's name.' She turned to Geraden. 'You came here – you ran here – to get King Joyse to stop Castellan Lebbick.' Geraden nodded. She glanced over at the King. 'Does he really want to see me?'

With the exaggerated care of too much wine, the Tor scanned the room as if searching for eavesdroppers. Then he said, 'No.' At once, one plump finger jumped to his lips to hush himself. In a thick whisper, he added, 'But he would if he had any sense. He was asleep, so I took the liberty of speaking for him.

'Young Geraden is right,' he continued sententiously. 'The good Castellan should not be allowed to make decisions where women are concerned.'

She felt that she hadn't stopped gaping at him. She wanted to say several things at once. What do you hope to accomplish? Oh, Geraden, I'm sorry! Do you really think he'll let you get away with this? But that wasn't the point, of course. The point was to make King Joyse declare himself – to make Mordant's sovereign take a stand that would reveal his true intentions. So she didn't ask any of her questions. Instead, she said sincerely, 'I'm glad you did it. I needed rescuing.'

The Tor gave her a lugubrious wink. To Geraden, he commented, 'You see? Already my revenge begins to bear fruit.'

'My father tells a lot of stories about you, my lord,' said Geraden. 'I don't think they do you justice.'

But Terisa wasn't done. She turned to Geraden. Because she had become brave enough to tell lies – and even to speak insults – she was brave enough to say, 'I'm sorry. When you left, I thought you were running out on me. I should have known better.'

He met her gaze sharply, and his shoulders straightened. 'That's right.' His tone was earnest. 'You should have known better. I would rather cut off my hands than run out on you.'

Almost at once, however, he relapsed to self-consciousness. 'I'm glad I did something right.' His smile was embarrassed and happy. 'Please don't count on it. It doesn't happen that often.'

'Tush, young Geraden,' the Tor interposed. 'You malign yourself.' He drained his flagon and waved it until the Apt found a decanter and poured more wine for him. 'Your difficulty is quite simple. You have not found your true abilities. As the King's chancellor, I dispense advice freely to all. Born swordsmen make very clumsy farmers, as I am sure your brother Artagel would agree. Give up Imagery. A son of the Domne should not spend his life providing jokes for Imagers.'

Geraden's face darkened, not with anger, but with pain. 'I would if I could.' The quick distress in his voice went straight to Terisa's heart. 'I'm a disappointment to my whole family. I know that. But I can't – I can not give it up.'

The Tor studied his wine with the air of a man who didn't want to meet

Geraden's eyes. 'At least you are your father's son. Take comfort in that. He, too, is stubborn. I have heard King Joyse say that he would rather break his head on a stone wall than argue with the Domne.'

Privately, Terisa thought that if Artagel had been present he would have denied being disappointed in his brother at all.

Abruptly, the King made a snorting noise. A twitch of his head dislodged the scroll, and the parchment slipped aside, curling around itself among the others on the rug. Blinking, he raised his hands to his chest and flexed them as if they had gone numb. 'The Domne,' he muttered at the ceiling. 'Stubborn man. Rather break my head on a stone wall.'

In an effort to push himself upright, he fumbled at the arms of his chair, but he seemed too stunned with dreams – or too weak – to succeed.

'My lord King.' Geraden went to him and helped him.

With awkward hands, King Joyse tried to rub the sleep off his face. Seen in this way, his old skin and watery eyes had a vulnerability which pained Terisa. He didn't look like a perverse or half-mad ruler who refused to defend his kingdom: he looked like a frail semi-invalid, nearly crippled by arthritis and age, who had lost most of the people he loved and now could barely keep his grip on reason.

But when he saw her – when he got his eyes into focus and saw who she was – he answered her unspoken concern with a smile of clean, uncluttered joy.

That was where the lady Myste had come by her look of sunshine: she had inherited it from her father. Terisa tried to distance herself from his transparent pleasure, but she couldn't. If he had simply smiled at her like that and done nothing to change the way she felt about him, she would have done anything for him.

Unfortunately, he spoke.

'My lady, have you come to offer me a game? How kind of you. I have a problem here' – he gestured toward his hop-board table – 'that defies my poor brain.'

Her disappointment was so acute that she had to turn her head away.

He levered himself upright in a way that suggested his legs weren't as weak as his arms. 'Havelock set it up for me. If I understand him – which isn't always easy – he once found a solution. These are his notes.' King Joyse nudged a nearby scroll with one foot. 'Since I haven't been able to design a solution for myself, I've been reading his notes, hunting—' His voice trailed away as he lost the thread of what he was saying. His gaze shifted toward the Tor and Geraden as if he couldn't quite remember who they were. Then he looked back to Terisa and resumed, '—hunting for his answer.' He shrugged. 'Without success. Maybe you can give me some fresh ideas.'

Memories of her game with Prince Kragen made her stomach twist. King Joyse had lured her into that situation with his smile. She didn't want to find herself in a similar mess again. Carefully, she said, 'I'm sorry. I didn't come for that. The Tor' – she hoped the lord would forgive her for putting him on the spot – 'had your guards bring me here.'

'Ah, my old friend the Tor.' King Joyse grimaced as though his mouth were full of bile. 'He is one of the few mummers in this masque who defies prediction.' He seemed to drift between colloquial and more formal diction according to his mood. 'Who could have foreseen that he would feel compelled to force his service upon me, after all the indignities I have required him to suffer?' He didn't glance in the direction of the old lord. 'This is not in the rules. It is enough to drive me mad, my lady.'

'My lord King' – the Tor's voice was quiet and harsh – 'I am sure you understand that I am not motivated by benevolence.'

The King ignored him. 'Nevertheless,' he said to Terisa, working visibly to recover his equanimity, 'we must all bear our burdens as we can. Mine is hop-board.' Again, he gestured toward the table. 'This problem beats me. Are you sure you won't take a look at it for me? It's really quite demonic.' Slowly, the skin around his eyes crinkled with humor and enjoyment. 'And I think you know something about it.'

'Please?'

Without quite intending to do so, she faced the table. After all, it wasn't entirely fair to say that his smile alone had seduced her into her game with Prince Kragen. She had had her own odd reasons for what she did. It wasn't fair to place all the blame on King Joyse.

When she saw the arrangement of the men on the board, she understood his idea that she knew something about it. The position was virtually a stalement: it was the same position she had played for against Prince Kragen. Whose move was it? If white's, the game could go on; if red's, the only available play would complete the stalemate.

'It's red's turn,' answered the King, although she hadn't spoken.

'I see what you mean,' she murmured. 'There's no way out of that. Adept Havelock must be joking.'

'Oh, I don't think so. He doesn't have that kind of humor' King Joyse frowned at the board. 'There is a way out. I'm sure of it. I simply can't imagine what it is.'

Terisa shook her head. The subject of hop-board held no interest for her. To dismiss it, she said, 'I haven't played for years. The only thing I can see is to back up and start over again. Try to avoid arriving in this position.'

He gave her another of his radiant smiles. 'My lady, I wish life were that simple.'

Under the influence of his joy, she thought suddenly that she caught Havelock's joke. 'In that case,' she said, 'try this.' Without pausing to reflect, she took hold of the edge of the table and tilted it back and forth just enough to slide most of the men off their squares. In an instant, the impending stalement became chaos.

Grinning, she turned back to the King.

He obviously didn't think what she had done was funny. A look of nausea on his face, he stared at the board. His frailty came back over him; his eyes filled as if he were on the verge of tears.

Hastily, she tried to explain. 'I still think Adept Havelock was joking.' She indicated the board. 'Does he have *that* kind of humor?'

King Joyse gave no sign that he heard her.

'I'm sorry. I didn't mean to upset you. It's just a game.'

Without warning, his eyes flashed like steel glimpsed through water. 'To you, it's just a game. To me, it's the difference between life and ruin.'

Moving so feebly that he nearly tottered, he went back to his chair. The difficulty with which he lowered himself into his seat made her ache as if in some way it were her fault.

'My lord King,' Geraden asked, 'are you all right? Can I get anything for you?'

Slowly, King Joyse shifted his damp blue gaze toward the Apt. 'I notice you haven't been paying much attention to my orders,' he rasped aciduously. 'I distinctly told you not to see or speak with the lady Terisa. I told you not to answer her questions. Do you call what you've been doing obedience? I expected better loyalty from a son of the Domne.'

His accusation surprised Geraden. The Apt's head jerked up; his concern changed to a scowl. 'My lord King,' he replied slowly, holding his emotions like a bit clamped between his teeth, 'I would obey your orders if I understood them. But they don't make any sense.

'You've lost interest in Mordant. You insulted Prince Kragen badly enough to start a war with Alend. You let the Congery summon that champion, when the Fayle did everything he could to warn you. We need all the friends we can get. I'm not willing to treat the lady Terisa like an enemy.'

King Joyse looked too tired and old to keep his head up, but his gaze didn't waver. 'Are you through?'

Geraden took a sharp breath. 'No.' Stiffly, he said like a formal confession, 'My lord King, the day after you commanded me not to see or speak with the lady Terisa, I took her to the mirror which brought her here and attempted to return her to her own world.' Then he stopped, held himself still.

Like Geraden, Terisa expected anger from King Joyse. She wouldn't have been surprised if he had sent for the Castellan. Apparently anticipating the same reaction, the Tor shifted forward in his chair, braced himself to speak.

But the King only sighed. He leaned back and rested his chin on his chest. Staring vaguely into the rug, he murmured, 'One grows old so quickly. This should have happened when I was younger. I was strong enough when I was younger.'

Terisa wanted to ask – gently, gently – What should have happened? But Geraden had been too shaken by the King's accusation to let it drop.

'I tried to translate her back to her own world because I believe all the things you used to say about the reality and integrity of what we see in mirrors. I think she deserves the freedom to leave whenever she wants. If I had known you were going to let the Masters translate their champion – if I had known you were going to turn your back on the ideals you talked about when you created the Congery in the first place – I would have tried a lot harder to get her out of here.' What he was saying wasn't recrimination: it was an appeal. Terisa could hear his heart in it. 'Why did you do it? Their champion nearly killed us. He left a hole the size of a small mansion in the northwest wall. We might as well invite Cadwal and Alend to besiege us. And he's still out there, ready to tear down anybody who gets in his way.'

And Myste is out there, Terisa thought. Your daughter. She's trying to catch up with him.

'My lord King, the Fayle tried to warn you. Why didn't you let him warn you?'

King Joyse didn't bother to glance at the Apt. When Geraden finally fell silent, the King remained still for a moment. Then he said, 'Because I didn't see fit to do so.' A tremor of bitterness and pain ran through his voice. 'Do you think you're qualified to make my decisions for me? I was fighting to make Mordant and the Congery whole long before you were old enough to fall on your face in pig wallows.'

Geraden flushed at this gibe, but couldn't retort to it.

'I let the Masters have their champion because I didn't choose to stop them.

'Besides,' King Joyse added sourly, 'Eremis is under arrest. That should make you happy. Lebbick will arrest Gilbur when he finds him. The perpetrators are going to be punished. What more do you want?'

'I want to *understand*,' cried Geraden.

'Tush, young Geraden,' the Tor rumbled unexpectedly. 'I doubt that the Domne has any thick-skulled sons. Surely you are not stupid. It must be obvious by now that my lord King does not *wish* you to understand.'

Geraden whirled to face the Tor. 'But *why*? I'm just an Apt. I'll never become a Master. What harm would it do if I understood? Who would it hurt?'

The Tor lifted his shoulders fatly. Speaking half into his flagon, he asked, 'How did I gain an audience with the King?'

Hauled up short, Geraden blinked at the old lord. Slowly, he said, 'You howled outside the door until he let you in.'

King Joyse snorted quietly.

In disgust, the Tor grimaced. 'You cannot convince me that you are stupid. I insist that you are not. How did I gain an audience with the King when I first arrived in Orison?'

Geraden opened his mouth. 'I—' Then he closed it again.

'Young Geraden' – the Tor emphasized each word – 'the King does not wish you to understand. I suggest that you return to your quarters and beat your head against the wall until your skull cracks enough to let a little light shine in.'

'Yes, go,' King Joyse muttered at once. 'I'm tired of being reminded how little my own people respect their King.'

Sharply, Geraden turned back to the King. Now Terisa saw something wild in his eyes, something extreme enough to be dangerous. Nevertheless his balance had become steady, as if urgency improved his poise. 'Actually,' he said, 'I should be used to this.' His tone was almost calm. 'I was always the youngest. My brothers didn't have the patience to explain things to me very often.' Almost calm – and almost threatening. 'I probably do better when I figure it out for myself.'

Without glancing away from King Joyse, he asked Terisa, 'My lady, will you come with me?'

'She will stay here,' King Joyse answered for her. 'I want to talk to her.'

So he did want to talk to her. Terisa didn't know whether to be relieved or concerned. To Geraden, she said, 'I'll see you later,' trying to reassure him.

'We'll think of something.' Then she waited while he made up his mind to leave.

Before he left, he gave her a look like an iron promise – a look that hinted at passion and authority. Then he was gone.

As the door closed, the Tor sighed thickly. He emptied his flagon and settled his bulk more comfortably in the chair as though he intended to take a nap.

Terisa faced King Joyse.

Instinctively, she felt sure she knew why King Joyse wanted to talk to her. And she meant to take advantage of the opportunity. She was angry. Castellan Lebbick had hit her. King Joyse insisted on causing Geraden pain. Master Eremis had been arrested. She was angrier than she had realized.

Her voice shook slightly as she said, 'You knew Master Eremis was arrested. Castellan Lebbick has been reporting everything to you.' That seemed a safe deduction. 'You knew he was going to arrest me. You *let* him attack me like that. If the Tor hadn't stopped him, I would be in a cell by now.

'I seem to recall hearing you argue I might be a powerful Imager – I was like an ambassador – I had to be treated with respect. Do you call this respect?'

As if he intended to answer her, he raised his head. He shifted in his chair to face her squarely. Now there was no petulance or bitterness in his expression. He looked grave with all the seriousness of his years, as intent on her as his watery gaze permitted – and so sorrowful that she was taken aback.

'My lady,' he asked softly, 'where is my daughter?'

So she was right. Her pulse beat faster. At last she had something somebody else wanted, something she could use. As long as she didn't betray Myste, this was her chance.

This prospect frightened her, but she clung to it with both hands. 'Which daughter?' she returned despite the tremor in her voice. 'You have several.'

She expected indignation and anger – that was what she always expected – but King Joyse remained quiet. His expression didn't change. For a long moment, he studied her through the moisture in his eyes. Then he indicated the chair across the table from him. 'My lady, will you be seated?'

At first she hesitated. Perhaps she would be stronger if she stayed on her feet. But his sadness was as persuasive as his smile. She went to the chair, pulled it away from the table to dissociate herself from hop-board, and sat down.

When she was seated, he said in the same soft, grieving tone, 'My lady, my daughter Myste is gone. Where is she?'

Suddenly, her tongue was so dry that she could hardly swallow. Like a frightened but stubborn child, she asked, 'My lord King, why did you let Castellan Lebbick arrest me?'

The room seemed uncomfortably warm. Again, the King's eyes gave a hint of steel. He held her gaze until she faltered and looked down. Then he breathed almost inaudibly, 'My lady, do not play this game with me. It is more dangerous than you imagine.'

For a few seconds while her heart hammered and her stomach knotted, she nearly backed down. She didn't have the strength to face him. Anybody was stronger than she was. As she had with Saddith, she felt that vulnerability and weakness were her only defense, her only weapon.

But backing down now wouldn't accomplish anything. The King would still want to know about his daughter. He would still demand answers. If she gave up what she wanted, she wouldn't make herself safer. And it would be more difficult for her to avoid betraying Myste.

And she was too angry to give up. Deliberately, she raised her eyes to the King's again. 'I don't have any choice. Geraden tried to take me back where I belong, but that mirror doesn't seem to work anymore. I have to play.

'Why did you let Castellan Lebbick arrest me?'

Something shifted in the background of King Joyse's expression, like clouds moving their shadows across a distant landscape. Without any definable change, his attention became sharper and more cautious.

'My lady' – his tone was caustic in an oddly impersonal way, as if he didn't mean it – 'do you know who your friends are?'

She stared at him in surprise and bit her lip and didn't try to answer.

'Well, I don't either. Having you arrested would have been a good way to find out. It would have been very interesting to see who tried to help you, or communicate with you, or persuade me to let you go. But of course Geraden interfered. With his usual instinct for disaster. I already knew *he* was a friend of yours.'

This reply startled her. It drew a different sketch of him – of the way his mind worked – than she was expecting: it seemed to imply that he was paying attention to what happened in Orison. 'Wait a minute,' she protested weakly. 'Wait a minute. You mean you *planned* to have me arrested? It was just a ploy?'

'No, my lady.' He waved one sore-knuckled finger at her. 'You aren't playing the game. It's my turn now. Where is my daughter?'

Terisa drew a sharp breath. For a moment, she considered trying to extort information from him without revealing anything herself. In spite of his age, however, he looked too strong for that tactic. And it wouldn't be fair. He was Myste's father.

Carefully, she responded, 'She came to see me yesterday afternoon. In my rooms. We talked for a long time.'

He nodded. 'I guessed that. But I don't understand it. What do you have that she wanted? What did she tell you?'

'No, my lord King. It's my turn now.'

She had so *many* questions. Too many to remember them all at once. And she didn't want to waste an opportunity like this on the one she had blurted out a moment earlier. So she concentrated on the issue that had brought her to the King's suite – on Castellan Lebbick and his behavior.

'When I leave my rooms with someone – with Master Eremis, for example – my guards always want to know where I'm going. But when I leave with Geraden, nobody seems to care. Why is that?'

King Joyse snorted as if she had just made a particularly bad move. In the same caustic, impersonal way, he said, 'You should have figured that out for yourself. I already know Geraden is your friend.'

Right. Of course. She really *should* have figured that out for herself. A sense of panic rose in her. She wasn't thinking quickly enough.

Impatiently, the King continued, 'You were speaking of my daughter, my lady.'

'Yes.' She needed to be smarter. Sharper. She was tempted to turn to the Tor for help. But she could hear him breathing deeply, heavily, as though he were about to snore. Groping for inspiration, she asked, 'Can you be more specific?'

'Certainly,' he snapped. 'Where is she?'

Fortunately, his tone brought back her anger. All right. If that was the way he wanted to play. 'I don't actually know where she is.' She made an effort to sound sweet. 'But you asked what I have that she wanted. There's an entrance to a secret passage in my wardrobe. She wanted to use it.'

Again, he nodded. Apparently, Terisa was only confirming his own suspicions. 'Why?'

Anger was a great help. She was being cruel to him – but only because she had been so badly treated herself. 'My lord King,' she said stiffly, 'the first night I was here a man tried to kill me. When he was chased away, Castellan Lebbick started a search for him. But you called it off.' Despite her inexperience, she worked to match his tone. 'Why?'

For an instant, King Joyse hesitated. The shadows shifted behind his eyes. Then he said trenchantly, 'Because I didn't want him caught.'

'What? Why not?'

'I didn't think he was stupid, so I didn't think he would lead Lebbick to his allies. And I didn't think he was a coward, so I didn't think he would tell me anything if Lebbick caught him. The only way to learn anything about him was to leave him alone and wait for what he did next.' His voice grew harsher, but it still sounded impersonal, as if his ire were calculated rather than real. 'Are you satisfied, my lady?'

'Why did my daughter want to use a secret passage?'

'Because' – Terisa's anger made her stronger than she would have believed possible – 'she wanted to leave Orison.'

That struck him, hurt him. 'Leave Orison?'

'She knew you would stop her if you could, so she used that passage to get down into the laborium. Then she sneaked out through the hole in the wall.'

'Leave Orison?' he repeated. 'Why?'

'No.' She clenched her fists to make herself ignore his distress. 'Why did you make me play hop-board against Prince Kragen? You did everything you could to force a war. I didn't enjoy being used like that.'

So suddenly that she had no chance to defend herself, King Joyse surged out of his chair. As if he had never been weak or old in his life, he knotted his hands in the front of her shirt and jerked her to her feet. 'This is intolerable! She is my *daughter*!' His eyes ran as if he were weeping. 'Her mother and one of her sisters left me. Her other sister holds me in contempt. *Where did she go?*'

Terisa should have broken then: she knew that about herself. She should have given up everything and betrayed Myste in simple fear. Her own anger should have evaporated.

But it didn't.

'Back to her mother,' she retorted. Myste was her friend. 'She wanted to be loyal. She wanted to help you. But when you insulted Prince Kragen like that, you broke her heart. She was raised to be the daughter of a *king*, not some petty tyrant who likes war and can't be bothered to defend his own people. She—'

Terisa stopped. His anguish stopped her. His sudden strength collapsed. He let go of her shirt. His hands dropped. His eyes squeezed shut, but tears went on spilling past his old eyelids. 'If you lie to me—' he rasped far back in his throat. 'If you dare lie to me—' It wasn't a threat: it was a plea. Fumbling behind him, he found the arm of his chair and braced himself on it while he sat down. His robe covered him as if he were lost inside it. 'My daughter, what have I done to you?'

'Why did you do it?' Terisa asked so that his pain wouldn't tear the truth out of her. 'Why did you make me play hop-board against Prince Kragen?'

'To test him,' he replied like a man who had no idea what he was saying. 'No other reason. How could I trust him? Alend has been Mordant's enemy for generations. He has a personal grudge against me. If his mission were honorable, he would refuse to play. He would have no reason to brook that insult to the Alend Monarch. But if he intended treachery he would acquiesce because he could not risk my displeasure – risk expulsion from Orison before his work was done.' He covered his face with his hands. 'Oh, my daughter.'

So it was true. He knew what he was doing, what was happening around him. The thought seemed to chill her blood. Where had she gotten the idea that it was too warm in this room? She wanted to shiver violently. Ignorance or senility had nothing to do with it.

He was intentionally destroying Mordant.

And yet his distress swept her anger away. She could fear him, but she couldn't be angry at him. 'I'm sorry,' she said, trying to be kind. 'I guess this game is a stalemate too.'

Roughly, he pulled down his hands. They shook as he clasped them together in his lap. He didn't look at her. Quietly and distinctly, he said, 'My lady, I suggest that you give the matter more consideration before you once again attempt to end a stalemate by tilting the board.' Then he indicated the door with a twitch of his head, dismissing her.

She turned to leave as if she were fleeing.

The Tor was awake. He watched the King with a look that resembled hunger. As she passed his chair, he gave her a firm nod of approval.

She had already closed the door behind her before it occurred to her to wonder how King Joyse had been able to guess that Myste had come to her for help.

SEVENTEEN

TERISA TAKES ACTION

She had the impression that she was hurrying inside, racing to keep ahead of her emotions, ahead of the consequences and implications of what she was doing. She needed to outrun the lie she had told King Joyse. She had caused him too much pain. Liars surrounded her. Even Master Eremis didn't trust her with the truth to any remarkable extent. It was possible that the King himself had been lying to her. Falsehood was her only weapon, the only way she could defend herself. She wanted to flee from it.

She had descended two flights of stairs and was about to enter one of the main halls before she realized that she had no idea how to get where she wanted to go.

She tried to swear at herself, but the unaccustomed words lacked conviction. Geraden's tour hadn't included the information she needed. She was off to a great start.

She scanned the hall in both directions. It was full of people; she might conceivably ask one of them for directions. But she had no idea how to approach them. What were they all doing here? Floor- and chimney-sweeps, stonemasons, supply porters, chambermaids, scullery maids, seamstresses, even blacksmiths: she understood the servants of the castle. But who were the rest of these men and women, these lords and ladies? Myste had made a point of explaining how much Mordant and Orison depended upon trade. Were these people all involved in commerce and finance? – warehouse managers? goods inspectors? tax collectors? shipment foremen? bookkeepers? supply allocaters? black marketeers? If so, her father would have felt right at home.

Her father, she firmly believed, wouldn't have hesitated to tell King Joyse any number of lies. She believed this despite the fact that she had never heard him utter an untruth.

Still running inside, she spotted Artagel.

Some distance away, he sauntered across the hall. Judging by his manner, he might have been unaware of her. But a moment after she noticed him – before she had time to raise her hand and wave – he changed course and came toward her.

'My lady.' He gave her an amiable bow. 'Have you recovered from your adventures already? If I had a similar experience, I would get into bed and not get out again for several days.'

'Call me Terisa,' she said to dismiss the subject of her recovery. She was in a hurry. What she had in mind was even more uncharacteristic of her than her conversation with King Joyse. If she paused or faltered, it would fall apart; she might never be able to pick up the pieces again. 'Where are the dungeons?'

He cocked an eyebrow. 'I can't call you Terisa, my lady. If I do, I'll be in danger of forgetting that Geraden is my brother. I'm not like Stead – Has Geraden mentioned that we have one brother who is absolutely insatiable for women? But I'm also not immune to beauty. Why in the world do you want to know where the dungeons are?'

Remembering the conversation she had overheard between him and Master Eremis, she hesitated. But she couldn't afford the luxury of hesitation. 'Castellan Lebbick has arrested Master Eremis,' she said, trying to sound like she knew what she was doing. 'I need to talk to him.'

That announcement widened his eyes. She saw him consider and reject a variety of responses in rapid succession – surprise, disapproval, curiosity. When he spoke, he had decided on unruffled amusement. 'If Eremis is safely locked up, I don't think Lebbick will want him to receive social visits.'

He had a good point. Grasping at possibilities that hadn't crossed her mind until that moment, she said, 'But you can get me in. If we don't ask the Castellan's permission. If we just go to his cell. The guards will let you in,' she concluded awkwardly, 'because of who you are.'

His expression became wary. 'Maybe. But you'll be taking a chance. Even if Lebbick doesn't catch you, he'll still be told you were there. I assume there must be some *reason* why Eremis was arrested. You'll make yourself look like his accomplice. You'll make *me* look like an accomplice. What good is that going to do?'

For a moment, she froze. The matter was too urgent to be explained. King Joyse knew what he was doing. He was doing it on purpose. *My daughter, what have I done to you?* Master Eremis needed to know that. He couldn't act or plan accurately unless he knew what he was up against. And he was Mordant's only hope.

Unfortunately, that also couldn't be explained – to Artagel even less than to Geraden. The sons of the Domne were too loyal.

Impelled by her sense of haste, she tried another prevarication. 'Maybe I'm being naive, but I think what's really wrong here is that none of the people who want to defend Mordant are willing to talk to each other. The Congery doesn't trust Geraden. The King doesn't trust the Congery. Nobody trusts Master Eremis. Castellan Lebbick doesn't trust anybody. And meanwhile the whole kingdom is going to hell.' She was pleased to hear that she sounded like she knew what she was talking about. 'I want to see if I can make people start talking to each other.

'I've just had a talk with King Joyse. Now I want to talk to Master Eremis. I think he's the key to the whole thing.'

Artagel watched her while she spoke, a bemused smile on his lips. When she finished, he shook his head, not in refusal, but in wonder. 'You amaze me, my lady. You make it so simple. There must be some reason why it's never been attempted.' Then his smile broadened into a grin. 'It might be fun. It might even work.' Bowing extravagantly, he offered her his arm. 'Shall we give it a try?'

At once grateful for his acquiescence and alarmed by her own behavior, she accepted his arm and let him guide her down to the dungeons of Orison.

The cells were physically close to the laborium. After the conversion of the original dungeons, the place where the Castellan kept his prisoners was separated from the workrooms of the Masters only by a masonry wall. Artagel took Terisa to the disused ballroom which was becoming so familiar to her – its emptiness a symbol of Orison's loss of heart. Beyond it, a passage paralleling the entrance to the laborium led to a corresponding stairwell. There, however, the similarities ended. The atmosphere of the dungeon was a world away from the laborium.

Ill-lit by torches guttering at intervals along the old walls, the place was dank and oppressive; she could feel the huge pile of Orison's stone impending over her. Straw that smelled of rot – and perhaps, faintly, of blood – covered the floor. It had originally been scattered to sop up whatever the prisoners of the castle spilled, but now it served primarily to control moisture. The corridor was narrow but direct: after a second downward stair, it brought Terisa and Artagel to the guardroom.

Here the men who were about to go on duty, or had just been released, or were taking a break could warm or refresh or relieve themselves; but the guardroom also served as part of the dungeon's defenses. Although the chamber was appointed like a crude tavern, with trestle tables and rough benches for the guards, a few beds against the walls, a large hearth in which a fire struggled against the wet chill of the stone, and a short bar from which a servingman provided ale and meat, it also gave the only admittance to the cells: no one could get in or out of the dungeon without passing through the guardroom. Racks of swords and pikes along the walls above the beds suggested that the men in the guardroom were expected to be ready to fight at a moment's notice.

Discipline was slack, however – perhaps because most of Orison's guards were exhausted by the previous day's exertions; perhaps because the dungeon wasn't the most vital or interesting part of the castle. One man sat honing his sword with the studious attention of diminished intelligence; the rest were less involved in their duties. Three guards at one table had obviously consumed more ale than was good for them; two more occupied beds, snoring in a perfect third; the rest threw dice in a corner of the room with more vehemence than pleasure.

Artagel frowned at what he saw, then changed his expression to an insouciant smile. His eyes glittering, he said to no one in particular, 'What a collection of slovens and aleheads. I could walk every prisoner you have through this room singing, and you wouldn't notice until the Castellan locked you in irons.'

Glaring with surprise, irritation, and stupidity, everyone who was awake turned toward him.

When the guards recognized him, however, their hostility vanished. Expressions of gruff humor stretched their faces. Several of them guffawed hoarsely, and one riposted, 'That's true. Who cares about prisoners? But just try getting that woman past us.'

'Anyway,' another said, 'the Castellan never comes here. Except when he wants to question Master Eremis. We always have plenty of warning.'

'The fact is,' explained a third, 'Master Eremis is the only prisoner we've got. That's bad enough – but you don't know what misery is until you've spent an entire night turning away women who want to see him.' Staring straight at Terisa, he clutched his groin. 'I would give my left hand to know how he does it.'

Terisa noticed that all the guards were now staring at her.

Suddenly, she wanted to forget the whole thing and go back to her rooms.

Then one of the dicers rose to his feet. A purple band knotted around his right bicep marked him as a captain of some kind. 'Take it easy, you louts,' he drawled. 'Unless I'm confused in my old age, Artagel's companion is the lady Terisa of Morgan. She isn't one of Master Eremis's toys – or yours either.

'My lady' – he gave Terisa a decent bow – 'don't look so worried. You aren't in as much danger as you think. Artagel can unman half the rubbish here before they get their hands on their swords. And Castellan Lebbick would feed the other half to the pigs just for touching an unwilling woman.'

Artagel's answering smile made the captain straighten his shoulders. In a more rigid manner, he asked, 'What can I do for you?'

She had no idea how to respond, but her companion replied easily, 'The lady Terisa is taking a tour of Orison. She wants to see the dungeon.'

The guard with the armband hesitated; his eyes narrowed. 'The Castellan isn't going to like that.'

Artagel's smile stretched wider. 'The Castellan isn't going to hear about it.'

Terisa was holding her breath. She felt rather than saw the men around her stiffen.

'If he does,' the captain observed slowly, 'you won't be the one who gets eaten alive. *I* will.'

'That's probably true.' Artagel seemed to enjoy himself more and more by the minute. 'But there's one consolation. You'll be safe from me. Whoever tells Lebbick we were here won't be that lucky.'

For a moment, Artagel and the guard captain measured each other. By degrees, the guard's expression changed until it resembled Artagel's threatening grin. He unhooked a ring of keys from his belt and tossed it to Terisa's companion. 'I don't have any idea why you want to talk to Master Eremis. I don't want to know. Just don't let him out.'

'"Talk to Master Eremis"?' Artagel was gleaming. 'You aren't serious. I would rather lie down in a nest of snakes.'

'That's a mistake,' someone chortled. 'There aren't any women in a nest of snakes.'

All the men laughed – with the exception of the guard honing his blade, who frowned as though the people around him spoke a foreign language.

Artagel jingled the keys. 'We'll be back soon.' Then he said to Terisa, 'Come, my lady,' as though she weren't clinging tightly to his arm. Together, they crossed to the doorway which led to the corridors and cells of the dungeon.

Beyond the guardroom, she asked softly, 'Would you really kill somebody who betrayed us?'

'Of course not,' he replied negligently. 'That's why we're safe. If they were really afraid of me, someone would talk.'

For some reason, his tone didn't carry conviction.

Breathing deeply to ease the pressure in her chest, she inhaled the rotten air and tried to remember why she was here.

To talk to Master Eremis. To tell him what she had learned from the King. So that he would know better where he stood, what Mordant's true danger was. So that he could decide what to do, now that his attempts to unite the Congery with the lords of the Cares and Prince Kragen had failed.

To see him again, so that she could try to understand what he meant to her, why the mere thought of him was enough to make her nerves tingle.

Her heart laboring, she went with Artagel past a first turn in the passage, past a second, and into the area of the cells.

Perhaps because the dungeon itself was so obviously closed, the cells were relatively open. They didn't have solid doors to shut their occupants in. Instead, each of them was essentially a deep niche cut into the foundation stone of the castle, eight or ten feet deep and just wide enough to accommodate a low cot and a washstand against the back wall. A heavy iron grid bolted to the stone served as the near wall for each cell; a barred door in the grid provided entrance and egress.

All the nearby cells were empty: apparently, King Joyse's recent rule hadn't supplied the Castellan with a significant number of prisoners. Nevertheless the glow of a lamp some distance ahead implied that one cell, at least, was occupied. Terisa and Artagel walked toward it, their feet rustling through the straw on the floor. As they passed, the one lantern that provided dim illumination for this corridor made ghoulish shadows leap in and out of the cells on either side.

Before they reached his cell, Master Eremis said in a voice pitched to carry, 'Astonishing. I thought that I would be left alone longer. The time is not right for a meal. Have more innocents been arrested? Has the Castellan already obtained King Joyse's permission to torture me?' He sounded almost jovial. 'Can it be that I have been granted a visitor?'

'You're in good spirits, Master Eremis,' commented Artagel dryly as he and Terisa reached the cell. 'I hope you have reason. As I remember, the last time Lebbick locked somebody up down here, she was executed two days later. A Cadwal spy, I think she was. Before that, it was a brigand who lost both hands for his trouble.'

At first glance, this cell seemed as empty as the others. A small oil lamp balanced on the washstand revealed that a rumpled blanket covered the dirty mattress on the cot; but the light didn't show Master Eremis. Instead, it reflected delicately in the fine trails of moisture dripping down the granite.

Then, however, a darker place – a place without reflections – took shape against the wall.

He was sitting on the end of the cot as far from the lamp as possible, and his jet cloak blended him into the shadows. Until Terisa's eyes adjusted, she saw the pale skin of his face and hands as nothing more than stains on the old stone of the wall.

He wasn't wearing his chasuble. He had given it up – or it had been taken from him.

'My lady,' he murmured. Now his voice didn't carry: it was soft, almost intimate. 'I wanted you to come.'

That statement went straight into her heart. It was pitched to a key which made her whole being resonate. Nobody else except Geraden had ever said anything like that to her. And nobody else in the world had ever spoken to her with that specific magnetic vibration, that knowing and personal passion. In an instant, all her reasons for being here changed to suit the tone in which he said, *I wanted you to come.*

Without thinking, she said to Artagel, 'Let me in. I need to talk to him.'

Artagel glanced at her strangely. But the expression on her face must have convinced him not to argue with her. With a shrug, he stepped to the door, tried a few keys until he found the right one, then unlocked the Imager's cell.

Before either common sense or timidity could inspire her to question what she was doing, she entered the cell.

At once, Artagel closed the door. In a distant, noncommittal manner, he said, 'I'll be nearby. Just raise your voice. If he tries to do anything, I'll kill him so fast he won't know he's dead until afterward.'

Quietly, he moved a few paces away down the corridor.

Terisa paid no attention to him. She was focused on Master Eremis.

He hadn't left his seat on the end of the cot. He didn't speak. He was still hard to see in the dim light. Involuntarily, she slowed down as she moved toward him.

The cot was low: despite his height, his head only reached her shoulders. When she was near enough, however, he sat forward, drew her between his spread knees, and pulled her head down to take her mouth in an urgent kiss. She tasted wine and desire on his breath.

The strength of his embrace and the insistence of his tongue seemed to complete the change in her. She responded with everything he had taught her, trying to make her kiss as intimate as his. A long moment passed before she remembered that she had other reasons for being here: that without having planned to do so she had joined the ranks of King Joyse's opponents; that Mordant's fate might hinge on what she could tell Master Eremis. And they weren't really alone.

Deliberately, she pushed herself back a little way. Trying to recover her breath, she murmured, 'That's not why I came.'

'Is it not?' Still holding her with both knees and one arm, he raised his free hand to the buttons of her shirt. 'It would be enough for me.'

Again, he kissed her.

When he let her pull back once more, his deft fingers began to open her shirt.

'Artagel will see us.' In spite of her anxiety, she kept her protest low. She wanted the Master to touch her.

'He will not if you do not raise your voice. Artagel is scrupulous.'

His hand slipped inside her shirt. His fingers were cold, bringing her nipples erect at once, making her breasts ache for him.

His behavior and her own unexpected emotions confused her; she could hardly think. Nevertheless she made one more attempt to draw away. 'I've just talked to the King. I came straight to you from him.'

Somewhat to her chagrin – as well as to her relief – Master Eremis loosened his grip. 'A talk with the King,' he murmured, tilting his head back to peer into her face. 'That is an honor which all Orison and half of Mordant would envy you. What did the old dodderer desire?' He caressed one of her breasts. 'Does he have enough life left in him to covet my place?'

'Castellan Lebbick came to arrest me.' She wanted to explain everything clearly, make the importance of what she had learned plain; but she felt that she was babbling. 'The Tor and Geraden stopped him. But King Joyse wanted to talk to me anyway.' Quickly furious at her incoherence, she halted, took a deep breath, then said distinctly, 'He's not an old dodderer. He knows what he's doing. He's doing it on purpose.'

The Master's sharp face betrayed no reaction; yet his sudden stillness suggested that she had touched on something important. Slowly, he lowered his hand. 'My lady, you must tell me everything. Begin at the beginning. Why did Lebbick decide to arrest you?'

His attitude was like magic: it made her firmer, stronger. At once, her confusion receded. 'I think it's the same reason he arrested you. You broke one of the King's rules, I know that – but I don't think it's the real reason. I think the real reason is that he figured out we went to a meeting with the lords and Prince Kragen. He believes we're all traitors.'

It was his embrace that confirmed her, his expressionless face, the steady pressure of his knees. She might have been willing to tell him anything. Yet she made no mention of Myste or secret passages; she said nothing about Master Quillon. Instinctively, she focused on the attack after Eremis' clandestine meeting two nights ago; on the bloodshed that had led Castellan Lebbick to her; on the Castellan's conclusions. Then she explained how the Tor and Geraden had rescued her from arrest.

After that, she had to be more careful. Acutely conscious that she wasn't a good liar, she said, 'He wanted to talk to me about his daughter Myste. She's vanished. He thought I might know where she's gone. I pretended I did to make him talk to me.' Hurrying once more to get past her falsehood, she described the answers King Joyse had given to her questions.

Now Master Eremis did react. By the weak lamplight, she thought she saw surprise, anger, excitement emerge in glimpses from the darkness surrounding him. At one point, he breathed as if involuntarily, 'That old butcher.' At another, he whispered, 'Cunning. Cunning. I was warned, but I did not believe—' Calculations as quick as his emotions ran behind his eyes.

When she was done, he thought soberly for several moments. Without releasing her, he gave the impression that they had become distant from each other. As though she weren't still clasped in his arms, he said, 'This will be a better contest than I anticipated.'

Almost immediately, however, his notice returned to her. Tightening his embrace, he studied her face and said in a detached tone, 'You have done me a considerable kindness, my lady. I wonder why. I have claimed you' – he squeezed her with his knees – 'and you are mine. No woman refuses me. But I can hardly fail to observe that you are enamored of that puppy Geraden. And you risk more than Lebbick's rage by coming here. Why have you done it?'

So she had done the right thing. She had helped him. The knowledge made her feel so weak, so ready for him, that she could hardly answer his question. If she had been braver, she would have bent to kiss him again. A kiss might be a better explanation than any rationale. But he needed this answer as much as anything else she had told him.

Awkward with conflicting priorities, she said, 'King Joyse is doing everything on purpose. I don't know why – it's insane. But he's refusing to defend Mordant on purpose. Somebody has to resist him. You're the only one who seems to have enough initiative – or intelligence – or determination – to *do* something. Everyone else is just waiting around for King Joyse to finally wake up and explain himself.'

The Master remained silent, untouched by her account of herself.

For an instant, she faltered. Then she blurted out, 'You have enemies. There's a traitor on the Congery. You were betrayed.'

In response, the lines of his face became stone. His eyes searched her face; his whole body was still. 'My lady' – softly, sardonically – 'you did not come to that conclusion alone. Who told you?'

Please. You can make me sure of myself. You can do anything with me. She hardly heard herself say, 'Geraden.'

That was the wrong answer. She could feel the Master's quick anger through her skin. 'Now I understand you,' he snapped. 'You are worse enamored than I realized. Of course *Geraden* believes there is a traitor on the Congery. There *is* a traitor on the Congery.' He glared up at her. 'But why did he reveal that fact to you?'

Before she could reply – before she could imagine what she had done to infuriate him – his anger changed to surprise. 'That cunning son of a mongrel,' he murmured. 'Naturally he spoke to you. For that reason alone, if for no other, you will never credit that he himself serves the traitor.'

Now she was too shocked to speak. *He himself serves*—? It was cold in the cell, too cold. She ought to button her shirt. No warmth seemed to come to her from the Master. Could Artagel overhear what was being said? Probably not: otherwise he would already have a blade at Eremis' throat.

Geraden?

'My lady, you must learn to think more clearly.' The Imager sounded almost sympathetic. 'I know that the young son of the Domne is attractive to you. That is understandable, considering that he created you. If you had not come to me of your own volition, I would not say such things. I would simply give your fine body the love it craves – the love for which it was made – and keep my thoughts to myself. But if you wish to help me, you must use your mind to better effect.

'Take into account whatever reasons Geraden may have given for his belief that the Congery conceals a traitor, and add to them what we have learned since. Along with his initial questions, Lebbick did not fail to mention that

Master Gilbur has disappeared. Does it not seem likely, my lady, that he himself is the traitor?'

Yes, she thought, held by his arms and knees and his intent gaze. No. How could he foresee that I would go to your meeting? How could he know where I would be after the meeting, so he could translate those men to attack me? (Don't translations with flat mirrors drive people crazy?) But those arguments no longer seemed to make sense. Gilbur was the one who had vanished.

'I confess,' Master Eremis went on softly, 'I did not foresee his treachery. Foolishly, I trusted him simply because he has cause to feel gratitude toward me. But when Geraden went into his glass, purportedly seeking our champion, and brought you to us instead, my eyes were opened.

'My lady, do you never try to understand why I do what I do? Did you never ask yourself why I involved Master Gilbur in my meeting with the lords of the Cares, when it was plain to all the Congery that he and I stood on opposite sides of every issue? I was trying to expose him, to give him means and opportunity to betray himself. And I succeeded—

'At a greater cost than I had anticipated,' he commented. 'Orison's wall breached. The champion gone. Myself arrested. And stripped of my chasuble by that officious lout Barsonage to prove the Congery's good faith to the Castellan.'

He snarled in disgust, then resumed his reasoning. 'Did you never wonder why I have placed so much value on Geraden's life? I wanted him alive so that I might try to gain his friendship, insinuate myself into his counsels, study his strange abilities.

'Did you never ask yourself why I attempted to have him admitted to the Congery as a Master? Surely that must have seemed gratuitous, even to someone who knew so little of Orison and its conflicts. In that I did not succeed. Oh, I gained a part of what I wanted – I learned how our good King had reacted to his first encounter with you. That information might have aided me, if I had possessed the key to understand it.' His voice grew sharper as he spoke, more urgent and demanding. 'But I did not accomplish my chief end, which was to tighten a snare around Geraden – to place him where he would be watched, even by fools who did not fear him, where his secrets might be forced into the open, and where the achievement of his lifelong dream might help blind him to his true talents.'

'No.' Terisa's protest was too strong to be kept still. 'That doesn't make sense.' The Master's assertion hurt everything in her chest. 'What talents?' As though she were rising up inside herself, she demanded, 'What makes you think that he and Master Gilbur have anything to do with each other?'

'Use your mind!' Eremis replied between his teeth. 'It was Gilbur who shaped the mirror that first showed the champion. It was he who taught Geraden to copy that glass, he who watched and verified every step of the process, from the refining of the finest tinct to the sifting of the precise sand to the polishing of the exact mold. He must have seen what went wrong, what was changed, to produce the mirror which translated you here.

'Think. While he shaped his glass, Geraden showed abilities which have never been seen before, abilities which allowed him to twist all the laws of

Imagery to his own purposes – abilities as great in their way as the arch-Imager's ability to pass through flat glass and remain sane.

'Gilbur must have known this. He must have witnessed it. Yet *he said nothing*. Something fundamental occurred under his nose, and he made no mention of it.

'What conclusion do *you* draw, my lady? What conclusion *can* you draw? Are you able to insist that I am wrong?'

No. She shook her head leadenly, and her heart reeled. This time she couldn't contradict him. In his logic, as in his physical magnetism, he was too much for her. If she accepted the proposition of Master Gilbur's treachery, then all the rest followed impeccably. *It was he who taught Geraden* – Why hadn't she thought of that for herself?

It was still possible, she argued dimly, like a woman who was about to faint, it was still possible that Geraden was her friend. That he meant her well. If he was as ignorant and accident-prone as everyone believed—

Clutching at straws, she breathed, 'Maybe. Maybe you are. You saw what happened when he tried to stop Master Gilbur from translating the champion. Maybe he's being used and doesn't know it.' Her temples were beginning to ache. 'Maybe he was misled while he was making his mirror – maybe he thought it *was* an exact copy. How would he know if Master Gilbur lied to him? Maybe these "abilities" are Master Gilbur's, not Geraden's.'

Master Eremis shook his head. 'That is conceivable.' His face seemed to be growing darker. 'Why do you imagine that I have relied on subterfuge rather than direct action? I have not wanted to risk harm to anyone who might be innocent. But remember two things, my lady.

'The first is a fact. It is Geraden who figures so prominently in the augury, not Gilbur. That cannot be meaningless.

'The second is a possibility. As it is conceivable that Geraden is being manipulated, so it is also conceivable that he and Gilbur feigned their conflict in order to disguise their relationship, thereby freeing Geraden to continue his work when Gilbur was forced to flee.'

At once, Terisa retorted, 'That's crazy!' so strongly that she surprised herself. She and Geraden had been buried alive together. 'Master Gilbur almost got him killed!'

'Paugh!' Abruptly, the Master was angry again. 'Gilbur could not have foreseen that – or caused it. He was busy with his translation.' The pressure of his knees increased. 'Do not insult my intelligence.'

As quickly as it had come, her resistance evaporated. 'I'm sorry,' she said like a wince. Don't hurt me. His face had gone completely dark: she could see nothing but the outlines of his form against the wall. 'I'm not used to thinking like this.'

Unfortunately, that wasn't what he wished to hear. His grip felt like rock, bruising her flesh. In rising panic, she asked, 'What do you want me to do?'

He didn't ease the clench of his knees or release his embrace, yet the vehemence of his posture softened. 'Under other circumstances,' he murmured harshly, 'I would not ask such flesh to serve any purpose but its own. But I must have your help.

'This is what I want you to do.' He undid the last buttons and jerked her shirt open. 'I want you to pretend friendship for young Geraden.' Her breasts were exposed to the cold air and his moist breath. 'I want you to watch him for me, study him for any sign of betrayal or talent, scrutinize him for any word or deed or implication which may reveal his secrets to me.

'And tell him nothing. Do not tell him that you have spoken to me. Swear Artagel to silence if you must. Give no hint to anyone that we are allies.'

Moving his head from side to side, he stroked his wet tongue across her nipples, bringing them to hardness, making them demand him. Then he put his mouth to work, sucking and kissing her breasts.

She couldn't resist him. She felt herself giving up balance, leaning into him, so that his hand and his lips would caress her more strongly. He made it imaginable that she could clinch her arms around his neck and hug herself to him.

And yet he asked her to pretend – to watch. The bare conception knotted her stomach. He was asking her to betray Geraden, *Geraden!* She had already doubted him once today, and he had proved his faithfulness almost immediately. He had kept her sane and actual under the rubble of the meeting hall. Simply to admit the intellectual possibility that he might be dishonest felt like an essential injustice. He was more loyal than this. Didn't he deserve more loyalty?

How could she betray him?

How could she ignore Master Eremis' reasons for what he did, his commitment to Mordant's survival, his ardor?

Both he and Geraden were trying to tell her who she was.

Without raising his head – without ceasing his kisses and caresses, which seemed to draw her heart to the surface of her skin and inspire it with every touch – he whispered surely, 'You are mine. I have claimed you. Whenever you think of another man – whenever you are tempted to doubt me – you will remember my lips upon your breasts, and you will cleave to me. You will do what I ask with Geraden.'

'Yes.' She was helpless to say anything else. What stubbornness she had left was already committed, holding her arms back from his neck, holding herself passive in his embrace. It would have been easier to give him her inexperienced passion and let him do what he desired with it. But she was too deeply sickened for that submission.

'You will do what I ask,' he repeated as if in litany.

'I will do what you ask.'

'When I am freed from this cell – for I will be freed. Do not ever doubt that I will be freed. If Lebbick does not recognize my innocence, I will free myself in spite of him. And when I am free, I will come to you. Then we will consummate these kisses, and I will take possession of your fine beauty utterly. There will be no part of your womanhood which I have not claimed – and no portion of my manhood which you have not accepted.'

'Yes,' she said again. For a moment, she wanted what he wanted, despite her nausea. 'Yes.' As if she knew what her acquiescence meant.

'In that case' – he leaned back without warning, dropped his arms, released his knees – 'you must leave me. You will be of no help at all if Lebbick finds you here. If he does not stretch his authority so far as to imprison you, he will certainly do his best to make sure that we cannot meet and talk again. Button your shirt and call Artagel.'

His change of mood and manner was so abrupt that she flushed with shame. 'Yes.' Why did she keep repeating herself, offering him her assent over and over again like an idiot child? 'Yes.' Her father's moods had been sharply and inexplicably changeable, flashing from tolerance to anger for reasons she could never understand. Because of the ache in her stomach and the heat in her face, she didn't look at Master Eremis again. She turned away; her hands shook as she hurried to do up her shirt and tuck it back into her pants.

For a moment, her throat refused to work. The she whispered, 'Artagel.'

'Speak louder, my lady,' Master Eremis suggested with cold mirth. 'I doubt that he can hear you.'

Louder.

'Artagel. I'm done.' A croak in the back of her throat.

He wants me to betray Geraden.

Like a flowing shadow, Artagel appeared past the edge of the cell and reached the door. Then the door was open. 'My lady,' he murmured, offering her his hand, his arm.

With the Master's silence behind her like a wall, she moved to accept Artagel's support.

He drew her out of the cell, paused almost negligibly to relock the door, then took her down the passage, out of sight of Master Eremis' imprisonment.

'My lady,' he growled as soon as they were beyond hearing, 'are you all right? What did he say to you?'

The concern in his voice was so quick and true – so much like his brother – that her knees grew weak, and she stumbled.

Sickness and shame. Desire and dismay. Master Eremis was right: she could never forget the touch of his lips and tongue; she was his; he could do anything he wanted with her. But what he wanted—! To spy on the person she most needed to trust, the man whose smile lifted her heart. To betray—

Artagel held her. '*Terisa.*' His eyes were bright and extreme. '*What did that bastard say to you?*'

It hurt. She should have cried out in simple protest. But that would ruin everything. He was Geraden's brother. Despite his concern, the light in his eyes and the murderous half-smile on his lips, she couldn't tell him what was wrong. If she did, he would tell Geraden. She understood that clearly. He might be willing to keep one or two things secret from Castellan Lebbick for her sake, but he wouldn't keep secrets from Geraden.

To speak to him now would be the coward's way to betray Master Eremis, to withdraw her allegiance and aid, her new passion, without having the courage to face Geraden and admit that she had chosen his side by default, that she preferred his friendship to Eremis' love for no better reason than because she wasn't brave enough to do otherwise.

With an effort, she found her balance and took her weight on her legs, easing the urgency of Artagel's grasp. 'I'm sorry.' When he let go of her arms, she pushed her hands through her hair. 'I guess I really haven't recovered from yesterday.'

'Are you sure that's it?' Artagel's concern made his voice rough. 'You were better before you went in there. You look like Eremis just tried to rape you.'

He was so far from the truth that she let out a giggle.

That didn't reassure him, however. Her giggle sounded ominously hysterical. And she had trouble making it stop.

She would have to give him a more cogent explanation if she wanted to deflect his alarm. 'I'm sorry,' she repeated. Still giggling – and fighting it. 'I don't know what's come over me. I've just had a lesson in humility.

'I told you I wanted to see if I could make people start talking to each other.' Abruptly, the artificial mirth ran out of her, and she found herself close to tears. 'That's going to be a lot harder than I thought.'

For a moment, he studied her sharply. Then he took her hand, drew it through his arm to comfort her, and moved her again in the direction of the guardroom. 'Don't worry about it, my lady. It was worth trying. It's still worth trying. Master Eremis just' – his smile was perhaps a shade too fierce to offer much consolation – 'isn't very promising material to work with.'

In an effort to distract him, she asked, 'Is it true that you and he used to be friends? Before Geraden turned you against him?'

He shrugged. 'Sort of. Not really. I was never actually able to like him, but I didn't have any reason for the way I felt, so I kept it to myself.' He glanced at her. 'Geraden understands these things better than I do. And he knows Eremis a lot better. You ought to talk to him about it.'

She didn't meet his gaze. 'You trust Geraden completely, don't you.'

Without hesitation, he replied, 'He's my brother.'

'Is that the only reason?'

Her question made him chuckle. 'No, my lady, that's not the only reason. It's at least two reasons – experience and blood. We have five other brothers, you know. I've watched him with all of them.' Then his face darkened, and he turned her so that she had to look at him. 'My lady, does Eremis think you shouldn't trust Geraden?'

Kicking herself, she countered, 'That isn't what I meant. I don't know if you realize what a strange position you're in. As far as I can tell, you're the only person in Orison everybody trusts. Even Master Eremis wants you on his side.' Her unexpected facility for lies – for using parts of the truth to disguise other parts – amazed and frightened her. 'I want to know why you trust Geraden because I'm trying to understand *you*.'

Apparently, he believed her explanation; but he still didn't know how to respond. After an awkward moment, he said in a tone of deliberate foolishness, as if her question embarrassed him, 'It's clean living, my lady. Nobody trusts anybody who overindulges in clean living. I'm more dissolute than practically everybody else, so I'm easier to trust.'

His reply was clearly intended as a joke, but she accepted it simply because she was relieved to get away from his seriousness. 'I never thought about it that way,' she murmured as she let him guide her down the corridor to the guardroom.

From the guardroom, they returned to the ballroom and the main halls of Orison. Now she wanted him to leave her; she couldn't go on talking to him and still keep her emotions hidden. With frustrating gallantry, however, he insisted on escorting her most of the way toward her rooms. She was unable to detach herself from his attendance until they reached the tower that held her rooms. After thanking him abruptly, she hurried up the stairs as if she were fleeing from him.

But of course what she really fled from was the danger he represented – the danger that she would betray the choice she had to make before she was sure of it. She had said *yes* to Master Eremis, and *yes* again; but the illness in her stomach was getting worse. Artagel bore just enough resemblance to Geraden – and she had been just dishonest enough with him – to make what the Imager wanted of her vivid and appalling.

Pretend friendship.

Watch him.

Tell him nothing.

She feared she would throw up before she reached safety.

When she approached her door, however, one of the guards stepped forward, gave her a stiff bow, and said with gruff courtesy, 'My lady, you have a visitor.'

For a second, she thought her knees were going to fail again. A visitor. Now? Oh, please. But she was tired of being so weak. Her emotional nausea itself acted like a kind of strength, enabling her to keep her legs under her, her head up, her voice quiet. 'Who is it?'

The guard seemed discomfited. 'We couldn't refuse to let her in, my lady. You've never asked us to keep visitors out of your rooms.'

His self-defense made no sense, but Terisa didn't try to understand it. 'Who is it?' she repeated.

'The lady Elega.' At once, the guard added, 'We couldn't refuse her, could we? She's the King's daughter.'

From a distance, Terisa heard herself say, 'Of course not. You did the right thing.' But she wasn't paying much attention. The lady Elega – Myste's impatient and discontented sister. Terisa hadn't spoken to her since their awkward, disappointing lunch. On that occasion, Elega had protested, *We are women like yourself, not self-serving men hungry for power. We can be trusted. This pretense is not needed with us.* When Terisa had refused to give up her pretense of ordinariness, the lady Elega had looked the way Terisa herself felt now.

What does she want this time? Terisa wondered dimly.

Then it came to her, and a sting of adrenaline ran down her veins.

Myste.

With a pang of embarrassment, she realized that she was standing slack-faced in the hall while one of the guards held her door open and both men made obvious efforts to appear unaware of her distraction. Pushing herself into motion, she entered her sitting room as if she were still in a hurry.

Elega stood before one of the windows, much as Myste had once stood. And, like Myste, she was beautiful. But her beauty seemed to be a reflection of the lamp- and firelight in the room, a contrast to the lowering gray winter outside the glass. In its own way, her skin was as pale as her short blond hair; and both emphasized the striking violet flash of her eyes. Although she was clad and jeweled like a queen, her manner was too forthright, too assertive for ornaments. Nevertheless she had a queen's spirit, a queen's instincts.

She left the window at once. As the door closed, she moved a few steps toward Terisa; there she stopped. Her gaze reminded Terisa of another contrast between the King's daughters. Unlike Myste's, Elega's glances were so immediate and fiery that they threw what she saw into stark relief. Both, however, were able to convey an impression of excitement, a sense of possibilities. 'My lady,' she said in a low voice. 'Terisa. I hope you will forgive this intrusion. I did not know when you would return – and I did not want to wait in the hall.'

Terisa didn't feel equal to the situation. All she wanted to do was huddle near the fire to drive the cold out of her bones and drink wine until her stomach either calmed down or got rid of its distress. But she had to face Elega for Myste's sake. Responding almost automatically, she waved a hand toward the wine goblets and decanter, which Saddith had mercifully replenished. 'Would you like to join me? I'm going to have some wine.'

'Thank you.' Elega obviously had no interest in wine. Nevertheless she accepted the goblet Terisa handed her as if she appreciated the gesture.

Terisa took a longer draught than good manners or wisdom suggested and refilled her goblet. Without thinking to offer Elega a seat, she sat down in the chair nearest the fire. The flames were oddly entrancing. She hadn't realized how cold she was. How long had she stood in Master Eremis' cell with her shirt open—?

'Terisa?' She heard Elega as clearly as a voice in a fever. 'Are you well?'

With an effort, she pulled her attention away from the fire. 'Too much is happening.' Unlike Elega's, her own voice sounded muffled. 'I don't understand it all.' In an effort to be polite, she added, 'Why don't you sit down and tell me what's on your mind?'

For a moment, Elega hesitated. Her doubts were plain in her face. I must look awful, Terisa thought vaguely. Abruptly, however, the lady became resolute. First she accepted a chair. Then she asked softly, firmly, 'Terisa, where is Myste?'

It was symptomatic of Terisa's condition that she leaped from this question to the conclusion that King Joyse had somehow seen through her lie. With an inward wince, she replied suspiciously, 'Did your father send you to talk to me?'

Elega raised her eyebrows in surprise. 'No. Why would he?' Gradually her tone took on a tinge of contempt. 'I doubt he knows that she is gone. And if he does know – and if he thought to have me ask for him the questions a father should ask – I would refuse. I am his daughter, but he has broken that duty for me by breaking all other duties for himself.

'No,' she repeated, pushing the subject of her father aside, 'I ask because I am afraid. My sister is not the wisest or the most practical woman in Orison. Her dreams often do not contain enough plain sense for ballast. I fear she has done something very foolish.

'Terisa, where is she?'

Terisa turned back to the fire to avoid Elega's vivid gaze. So her lie to the King hadn't been caught. That was a relief. Unfortunately, Elega's question still had to be answered.

Staring into the flames as though they might hypnotize her and thereby make her strong, Terisa murmured, 'What are you afraid she's done?'

'I hardly know.' The lady's uncertainty sounded sincere. 'I freely admit I do not understand her, Terisa. She prefers dreams to realities. I know that she is hurt – as I am – by what our father has done, and especially by his humiliation of Prince Kragen. That the King of Mordant' – she forgot her concern for a moment in anger – 'should actively seek war with Alend is abominable.' Then she steadied herself. 'But what Myste might do because of her pain, I cannot guess. Perhaps she has left Orison for some mad reason.' Her tone tightened. 'Perhaps she has gone after Prince Kragen, thinking to persuade him to ignore the extent of his insults.'

Elega had come just close enough to the truth to frighten Terisa. Dimly, she asked, 'What makes you think I know where she is?'

Again, Elega hesitated. When she spoke, her tone was carefully neutral, distinct but unaccusing. 'First, because I doubt that anyone else in Orison would assist her in anything greatly foolish. She is the King's daughter. Orison's people value her too highly to help her into trouble.

'But primarily,' she went on, 'because I have seen how she responds to your insistence that you are only an ordinary woman.'

Terisa gazed vacantly into the fire and waited.

'It was an astonishment to me,' admitted Elega frankly. 'I consider that people are as ordinary or as exceptional as they choose to be. Oh, I am assured that no one can conceive a talent for Imagery or statecraft by effort of will' – she didn't sound entirely convinced – 'and it is true past argument that anyone who has the misfortune to be born a woman must oppose the prejudices of all the world in order to prove herself. Yet I believe that in the end I am limited only by the limits of my determination, not by accidents of talent or preconceptions of sex.

'Myste,' she sighed, 'thinks otherwise. She does not want to open doors. She dreams that doors will be opened for her. And she sees you, Terisa, as proof that into *any* life – be it drab and dreary enough to numb the mind forever – a door of magic and mystery may open, offering the least drudge an opportunity for grandeur.' Her tone suggested frustration rather than disdain. 'In the meantime, it behooves us to be contented while we wait.

'I have no reason to believe that you know where she is. Yet I think you do, if anyone does. You are a flame which she is too mothlike to resist.'

This view of Myste struck Terisa as so poignant – and so mistaken – that she didn't know how to reply to it. If anything, Elega's ideas seemed less realistic than Myste's, rather than more. And Terisa had questions of her own about the King's eldest daughter. But that wasn't the point, of course. What she thought didn't matter. In this situation, only her promise to Myste mattered.

As if she were reading her answer in the flames and coals, she murmured, 'She came here yesterday because she wanted to get into the passage behind my wardrobe.' She felt rather than saw Elega stiffen. 'She used it to sneak out of Orison without being stopped.' Behind the soft snap of the fire and the distant soughing of wind past the edges of the tower, the silence in the room was intense. 'She went back to her mother.'

For a moment, Elega remained still – so still that Terisa couldn't imagine what she was doing. Then, in a tone soft with surprise, as if she had just received a revelation, the lady breathed, 'That cannot be true.'

Anxiety twisted through Terisa. Half involuntarily, she turned to look at Elega.

The lady had risen to her feet. Her eyes flashed as though their violet depths were lit by lightning. Yet her demeanor remained quiet, almost perfectly self-possessed.

'I believe that Myste has left Orison. Thank you for telling me how it was done. But she has no intention of going to the Care of Fayle, to Romish – to Queen Madin, our mother.'

Because she was lying, Terisa wanted to protest that she wasn't: she wanted to use all her distress and fear to feign as much anger as possible. But she was restrained by Elega's eagerness. It bore so little resemblance to the reaction she had expected.

With slow caution, she said, 'She was disgusted by what the King did to Prince Kragen. She couldn't stand to watch him destroy himself and Mordant anymore, so she decided to go back to the rest of her family.'

'Terisa—' The lady's arms made a gesture of appeal, which she controlled abruptly. 'Do not continue. That is unimportant now. A lie is an exercise of power, and I rejoice to see it. You are not passive – you are no longer content to hide behind a mask of ordinariness. You have decided to take your part in Mordant's need. That is a great step – a step which I can only hope Myste has taken also – and I honor you for it.'

Nonplussed to the point of chagrin, Terisa stared at her visitor. Simply because she had to say something, she muttered, 'I'm not lying.'

Elega shook her head decisively. 'I will attempt to persuade you this charade is not necessary with me.' But then she paused. Her eyes scanned the room as if searching for the best line of argument. In an abstract way, like a woman digressing momentarily while she prepared her thoughts, she asked, 'Terisa, what do you consider Orison's greatest internal weakness?'

Taken completely by surprise, Terisa said without thinking, 'The water supply.'

The lady didn't appear to be paying attention. 'In what way?'

'If you poisoned the reservoir, the whole castle would be helpless.' Not permanently, of course. The small spring under the walls supplied some water. The open roof and the collecting pipes could bring in large quantities during any heavy snow- or rainfall. But for a few days, at least—

Why were she and Elega having this conversation?

Smiling, the lady Elega returned to her chair, seated herself, smoothed out her skirt. The electricity of her gaze made Terisa shiver. Without transition, she said in a relaxed, conversational tone, 'You have been in Orison for some time now. I fear that you have seen few of us at our best. Nevertheless you have had time to form impressions, perhaps even to draw conclusions.

302

'What do you think of us? Is there hope for Orison and Mordant? What is your opinion of King Joyse?'

Baffled and vexed, Terisa was tempted to retort, No, I don't think there's any hope. Not as long as you insist on behaving like this. But she could feel danger around her. Whatever she said would have consequences. Carefully, she replied, 'I think he knows what he's doing.'

Elega's smile seemed to grow a degree brighter. 'And the Congery? What do you think of the Imagers? They have put us in grave peril. Are they honest? Or perhaps I should ask, Are they honorable?'

Terisa shrugged. She wasn't about to begin discussing either Master Eremis' or Geraden's ideas with the King's strange daughter. 'Some of them seem to be. Others don't.' Then she added, 'I don't think very many of them expected the champion to go wild like that.'

This answer gave Elega less satisfaction, but she didn't dwell on it. 'And the lords of the Cares? What are your opinions of them?'

In reaction, alarm flushed through Terisa. How did—? Trying to cover her fright, she jerked to her feet, went to the wine decanter, and refilled her goblet. How did Elega know she had met the lords of the Cares? Suddenly, the whole room felt threatening, as though the walls were transparent and the floor might yawn open. Elega knew because someone had told her. That was simple enough. Or because she had had a hand in the attack on Terisa. That wasn't so simple. But still somebody must have told her about the meeting. Who would have any reason in the world to do that?

Unexpectedly, Terisa found that she had reached her limit. She was already in distress – and Elega was making no sense at all. Apparently, she was trying to probe Terisa, test her somehow. But for what?

She drained her goblet, faced the King's daughter squarely, and said, 'Prince Kragen and I were talking about you. You've made a conquest. He's really quite impressed. What did he say about you?' she asked rhetorically. 'He said if you were an Alend you would "stand high among the powers of the Kingdom."' Then she stopped to let Elega draw as many inferences as possible.

The lady rose to her feet immediately to meet Terisa's stare. Her smile was like the lights in the dining room of Terisa's mirror-walled apartment: it was on a rheostat which made it brighter at every turn. 'Terisa,' she said softly, 'you take my breath away. Is this what being ordinary means in your world? That place must be brave beyond conception. You have begun working to shape events with a vengeance.

'I understand you,' she affirmed. 'Do you understand me?'

Terisa didn't answer. She was afraid to open her mouth.

'Terisa,' Elega urged in a whisper, 'I have said that this charade is not necessary with me. You can no longer pretend passivity – and you need not pretend ignorance.'

Still Terisa didn't answer.

Slowly, Elega's brightness dimmed. She didn't give up, however. 'Since you have mentioned Prince Kragen, perhaps you will tell me your impression of him.'

With an effort, Terisa recovered her voice. 'Did you know the Alend monarchy isn't hereditary? It has to be earned. That's what he's doing here. He's trying to earn the right to become the next Alend Monarch.' She studied Elega closely, but the lady's expression betrayed nothing except its underlying intensity. 'I think that's more important to him than peace.'

This riposte was rewarded with a slight widening of Elega's eyes, a slow congealing of her smile. The way her pleasure curdled reminded Terisa that she had no real idea what was going on. Elega clearly understood what Terisa was saying better than Terisa did herself.

In a voice scarcely louder than a whisper, the lady asked, 'Do you not believe that you can trust me? We are women, you and I – despised in a world of men. There is no one here whom you *can* trust but me. No one else intends as much good to both Mordant and yourself. What may I do to convince you?'

That, at least, was a question Terisa could meet. Without hesitation, she said, 'Tell me what's going on. Before you ask me to trust you, start trusting me.'

Slowly, Elega nodded in acknowledgment. She was no longer looking at Terisa, and her smile was gone. 'You are better at this than I suspected. I cannot trust you until you have first trusted me. I have more to lose.'

Sadly, she turned to go.

In her confusion and frustration, Terisa wanted to demand, What is *that,* exactly? What have you got to lose that's more than everybody else in this mess? But she let it go. Instead, she said before Elega reached the door, 'Just tell me one thing. What makes you think I'm lying about Myste?'

The lady paused with her hand on the latch. A different smile touched her mouth, a smile like the affectionate and faintly condescending one she had occasionally given her sister. 'You do well, as I have said, Terisa. But you do not know Mordant well enough to exert power without risk. Plainly, you do not know that what you have said of Myste is impossible. Romish is too far. In this winter, it would be easier for a lone woman to rebuild our breached wall than to cross the Demesne and Armigite on foot.' A suggestion of triumph. 'I doubt that you intend me to believe my sister has decided to kill herself.'

Still smiling, she left the room.

Terisa hardly noticed her departure. She was remembering the way King Joyse had stood in front of her with his eyes squeezed shut and tears spilling down his cheeks, in anguish at the idea that Myste had gone back to her mother. *If you lie to me,* he had said like a appeal. *If you dare lie to me* – But he must have guessed even then that she wasn't telling the truth.

Her stomach heaved. Unfortunately, all the lies and plots and pain she had swallowed refused to be ejected. After a moment, she went to the door and opened it long enough to tell the guards that she didn't want any more visitors today. Then she bolted the door, sat down again in front of the fire, and had more to drink than she had ever had in her life.

EIGHTEEN

A LITTLE CONVERSATION

The next morning, she had the kind of headache that made strong men swear off drink. Internal pressure seemed to be prying the bones of her skull apart, and her brain felt bruised. In addition, her throat had apparently been treated with sandpaper, and her stomach gave the impression that it was sloshing wetly from side to side in her abdomen.

Nevertheless she was no longer so badly baffled by her talk with Elega.

The lady and Prince Kragen must have formed some kind of alliance. Elega knew about Terisa's meeting with the lords of the Cares because the Prince had told her. What they hoped to accomplish, Terisa wasn't sure; but she was sure that whatever it was wouldn't make King Joyse either comfortable or happy.

And they hoped to include her for some reason.

Sometime during her fourth or fifth goblet of wine, she had found – rather to her surprise – that she didn't like what Elega was doing. King Joyse persistently refused to remind her of her own father. He had perhaps sacrificed most ordinary claims on the loyalty of his people, but he didn't deserve to be betrayed by his daughter.

So the question she was left with – the question on which neither too much wine nor a night thick with bad dreams had shed any particular light – was the one that had made her sick in the first place. What was she going to do about Geraden? Or about Master Eremis?

Since she was hung over, the Master's caresses no longer seemed entirely inevitable or convincing. Yet his arguments were still important. In fact, his reasons for distrusting Geraden made more sense than Geraden's for believing the worst of him. On the other hand, the idea that Geraden was a traitor felt absurd.

Groaning more to persuade herself she was alive than because it relieved the pain, she climbed weakly out of the knotted chaos that her dreams had made of the bed. The rooms were cold: by bolting the door, she had locked Saddith out; and she couldn't remember having put wood on the fires herself more than once or twice. But the cold forced her to take better command of the situation. Struggling into her robe, she went deliberately into the bathroom to drink as much water as her stomach could bear. Then she returned to the hearth in her sitting room and began trying to coax a little flame out of the warm coals.

In her condition, blowing on the coals was as painful as batting her head against the wall. Nevertheless she persevered because she was determined not to let anyone into the suite to help her. She didn't want an audience while she suffered the consequences of her folly. So she got the fire going despite the sharp pressure in her brain. She took a bath, even washed her hair out of sheer stubbornness. And she dressed herself alone, working her way into one of Myste's relatively demure gowns, a warm sheath of yellow velvet. Only then did she permit herself to unbolt the door to see if Saddith had left a tray for her.

In fact, the maid had done so. And, as a mercy, there was no one waiting to talk to her. In peace, she was able to eat a little porridge and drink a great deal of a hot beverage which she thought of as tea – although it tasted more like cinnamon and rose petals – before a knock at the door announced that she had a visitor.

She didn't trust her voice, so she moved carefully to the door and opened it.

Geraden stood outside.

Oh, terrific. That was just what she needed.

'I hope I'm not disturbing you,' he began at once. 'We didn't get a chance to talk yesterday. I wanted to tell you—' Then his smile faded. 'Are you all right? You look a little sick.'

Thanks to Master Eremis, the sight of the Apt made anxiety throb in her veins – which in turn threatened to split her head. 'It's the gown.' Her voice came out like a croak. 'Yellow isn't my color.' Doggedly, she gave him a smile that felt like a crack across a porcelain vase, and invited him in.

Studying her, he said as soon as the door was closed, 'I tried to see you yesterday, but the guards told me to leave you alone. I couldn't help worrying.' Behind his concern, he looked self-conscious. 'How did your talk with Master Eremis go?'

She concentrated on keeping herself from groaning or shutting her eyes. 'Artagel told you.'

He nodded. 'He might have anyway. But you looked so bad when you came out of the cell, he felt he didn't have any choice.'

'Then he must have told you what happened.' Her sudden bitterness surprised her. When had she begun to believe that she had the right to resent the way she was treated? 'I thought I was going to be able to accomplish something – I thought I was going to make a difference. I was going to persuade you to start cooperating with each other.' Instead, I'm supposed to spy on you, even though you're the only friend I've got left, now that Myste is gone. Even though you're the only one who cares about me enough to *do* anything. 'Instead, all I did was make a fool of myself.'

No, she wouldn't do it. She couldn't. The promise of a few intimate kisses didn't suffice. Geraden was too important to her. She would watch him, yes. But she wouldn't tell anyone what she learned. Not unless he did something that forced her to believe Master Eremis was right about him. And she would make the decision for herself. No matter what the Master offered her.

Unexpectedly, she felt better. In spite of her resolution, she found herself saying, 'I had too much to drink yesterday,' so that his feelings wouldn't be hurt. 'I suppose I was trying to drown my sorrows. My head feels like a football.'

This time there was a quirk of relief in his smile. 'I've done that a few times,' he admitted, pretending rue. 'I still don't know what made me think it was a good idea. I guess I'd just had more of my own fumble-footedness than I could stand.

'Anyway, I'm sorry that happened to you,' he added in a way that suggested it wasn't his biggest regret. 'For your sake, I wish he had listened to you.

'Terisa, I—'

He stopped abruptly, and his eyes began to fill with tears.

Suddenly, she thought he had come to tell her something terrible. Instinctively defensive, she went back to the door and bolted it. Then she faced his troubled brown gaze.

'What's the matter, Geraden?'

'Nothing,' he said quickly. 'Nothing.' Too quickly. 'I mean, you survived, didn't you? It turned out all right.'

He couldn't sustain his pretense, however. 'I'm sorry.' His voice rasped, but he didn't turn away to hide what he was feeling. 'I'm really sorry. After we were rescued – after they got us out from underneath all that rock – Artagel took me back to my room. I drank quite a bit of wine myself. But when I went to sleep I kept having the same dream over and over again, exactly the same.' His expression twisted. 'For a long time, I thought it was a nightmare. It was the *worst*—'

He took a breath to steady himself. 'But I finally realized it wasn't a nightmare. I wasn't dreaming at all. I was just remembering.' He had to grit his teeth to make himself say, 'I was remembering that you almost got killed.'

Oh, is that all? She tried not to show her relief. What he was saying wasn't terrible after all.

'That only happened because of me.'

Now she stared at him.

'I brought you here,' he explained miserably. 'I don't know how to take you back where you belong. People want you dead. They want to manipulate you. And the champion—

'You went through that whole ordeal – you were buried alive and came within inches of being crushed to death – because of me.

'When I saw Castellan Lebbick harassing you, I wanted to club him with a chair. I'm sorry. That's what I should have done. Just to make him *stop*. It's my fault you got hit.

'If anything happens to you, it'll break my heart.'

If she had felt healthier, she might have laughed. Instead, she put her hand on his arm, touched the muscles knotted along his bones. 'Geraden,' she protested, 'he would have snapped you in half. He wants somebody to defy him, so he can crush them.'

In response, he looked at her in pain; and she recognized that he needed a better answer than that. No one else had ever declared so much concern for her. It was strange, really – and endearing. He had nightmares because of her?

She did the best she could. 'You kept me *sane*. You were in as much trouble as I was. Worse. Master Gilbur nearly knocked your head off. But you were still able to hold me together. If you hadn't helped me, I would have lost my mind hours before we were rescued.'

She should have gone on – should have said, You and Myste are the only friends I've ever had. No one has ever been as good to me as you have. I'm glad I'm here. But that was too much for her self-consciousness, her fragile sense of herself. Awkwardly, she dropped her hand.

And yet she had to do something for him that would mean as much as a touch. Rather than attempting to match his declaration, she tried to joke with him. 'This has got to stop. I'm going to start rationing you. If you apologize to me more than once a day, I'll kick you.'

He peered at her dubiously, uncertain how to take her. 'Do you mean that? I know I apologize a lot. If you caused as much trouble as I do, you would too. So far, you're the only thing I haven't been wrong about. You shouldn't have to bear the brunt of my disasters.'

There was no question about it: he deserved better from her. Trying to provide it, she looked straight into his eyes and said, 'You don't get me in trouble. You save me. Orison is full of disasters, but as far as I'm concerned you haven't caused any of them. You're one of the few people who wants to do something about them.

'You don't have anything to apologize for.'

He continued to study her warily. When she didn't drop her gaze, however, he began to relax. His shoulders lifted; the chagrin let go of his face; his eyes brightened as if they had been wiped clean. After a moment, he said softly, 'Thank you.'

Now her heart was eased. She was willing to fight the pain in her head if that enabled her to make him happier. Smiling more successfully, she sat down in one of the chairs near the fire, then gestured toward her tray. 'Have you had breakfast? I've got more than I can eat.'

He shook his head. He seemed to be suppressing a burst of exuberance, a desire to shout or sing or hug her. Moving with comic care, so that he wouldn't trip or lose his balance, he turned a chair to face hers and seated himself. Then he gleamed in humorous triumph, as if to say, And you thought I couldn't do it.

What he actually said, however, was, 'What did King Joyse want to talk to you about?'

She hoped without much optimism that her sudden surge of anxiety didn't show. In the press of more recent events, she had forgotten the question of what to tell him about her discussion with the King. He might be appalled by what she had discovered, deeply grieved to learn that his father's old friend and his own childhood hero was deliberately embarked on the destruction of Mordant. And Master Quillon had made a point of explaining that Geraden was still in danger from his nameless enemies, still liable to pay a high price for knowing too much. Or had Master Quillon come to Master Eremis' conclusion that Geraden himself was dangerous, not to be trusted? Were Eremis' reasons for his distrust that good?

When she didn't reply at once, Geraden went on, 'Being thrown out of his rooms like that wasn't exactly the highlight of my life.' He sounded incongruously cheerful, as if he wanted to encourage her. 'I didn't think the Tor would take his side.' He shrugged. 'On the other hand, I don't have any reason to believe I ever know what the Tor is going to do. I just want to understand. I want King Joyse to say something that makes sense.'

Terisa wasn't listening. The question in front of her was too complex to be answered casually. She needed more time to think. More time to watch. Unconscious of her own abruptness, she said, 'He wanted to talk about checkers some more.' Her headache was getting ahead of her. On impulse, she added, 'Elega was here.'

Geraden waited expectantly. When she didn't continue, he asked, 'The lady Elega? My former betrothed? When was that?'

She tried to clear her thoughts. Actually, she had a number of things she wanted to talk to Geraden about. Elega might be a safe place to start. If she could get her hangover under control.

'She was waiting here for me. When I got back from seeing Master Eremis.'

'What did she want?'

Terisa hesitated momentarily. Was she sure she wanted to say this to Geraden?

Yes. She was already carrying too many questions alone.

With unexpected ire, she articulated distinctly, 'The lady Elega wanted to enlist me in a plot against her father.'

Geraden froze. 'What kind of plot?'

'I don't have any idea.' As fully as she could, she told him what had been said – and what she surmised. His eyes narrowed at Prince Kragen's name, but he listened without interrupting. Sourly, she concluded, 'That was why I didn't want any more visitors yesterday. I didn't want to take the chance I might hear anything else like that for a while.'

He frowned without speaking for a moment – long enough to make her wonder whether he believed her. She wanted him to believe her. The more secrets she kept, the more lies she told, the greater her need to be believed became, especially when she was being honest. Fortunately, he began to nod.

'That's always worried me about her,' he murmured, brooding. 'I've always had the feeling she was more interested in what kings are than in what they do. More interested in the power than in what the power is for. She might be capable of some pretty unscrupulous decisions.'

'So you don't think I'm jumping to conclusions?'

'No.' His face was tense with thought. 'Not after your conversation with Prince Kragen. By that time, they had probably already agreed to approach you.'

'I wish I knew what they think I can do,' she complained, simply because she felt like complaining. 'It's the same problem I have with everybody. Even you. You all think I can *do* something.' But her parents had never permitted

309

her to whine, and she found she didn't care for the sound of it herself. 'I haven't shown much sign of it yet,' she finished.

Geraden went on musing morosely. 'What should *we* do?' he wondered. 'Should we tell King Joyse?'

Careful not to reveal too much, she countered, 'If we could get him to listen, do you think he would pay any attention?'

He let out a dejected sigh. 'Probably not.' Then he asked, 'What about Castellan Lebbick?'

She shrugged. 'I don't like telling him anything. I don't like the way he treats me.

'He'll certainly *do* something. He may or may not be able to stop her – but whatever he does will give away the fact that we told him. She'll know she can't trust me. That'll be the end of our chances to find out what she's doing.'

The Apt shot her a glance and a quick grin. 'For someone who can't do anything, you seem determined to try. What's your suggestion?'

She was about to say, I don't have any idea, when she had what felt like an inspiration. 'You could ask Argus and Ribuld to keep an eye on her.'

He blinked at the unexpected notion. 'They didn't exactly enjoy what happened the last time they did me a favor,' he muttered, thinking aloud. 'But this time Artagel is here to back me up. They might be willing – especially if they can think of a way to do it without making Castellan Lebbick suspicious.' He met Terisa's gaze as he added, 'It might be worth it. If we can just learn how she intends to communicate with Prince Kragen, that'll be an improvement.

'I'll ask them.' The decision brought back his sense of humor. With a mischievous glint, he commented, 'If you do it, they may try to talk you into making it worth their while. You can guess what that means. The worst they can do to me is say no.'

Smiling at him was becoming easier. Her headache had begun to recede. And her anxiety had turned to relief again. The sensation that here, at least, was one subject on which she wasn't alone – and on which Geraden agreed with her – was a positive pleasure. When he smiled back, she felt good enough to broach another of her many areas of incomprehension.

'That conversation I had with Prince Kragen reminds me. What's an arch-Imager?'

Her question made Geraden sit up straighter. 'It reminds you—? What connection—?' Almost at once, however, he pushed down his confusion, unwilling to give his questions precedence over hers. 'An arch-Imager is someone who has mastered what we consider the apex of translation – the ability to pass safely through flat glass. As far as we know, only one man has ever done it – the arch-Imager Vagel.

'In theory, the difficulty is that translation changes whatever it touches. When the translation involves a passage between separate worlds – or, if Master Eremis is right' – he grimaced – 'between our world and Images which are known not to exist in our world – the changes are appropriate. For instance, they solve the problems of language and breathing. But when you pass through a flat glass, you don't actually go anywhere. I mean, you move from place to place, but you stay in the same world. So you don't need to be changed. But you are anyway.' He looked down at his hands. 'It made Adept Havelock mad.

'Theoretically, if you looked into a flat mirror that showed you to yourself – in other words, a mirror that was focused on the exact spot where you were standing, so that you were also in the Image looking out at yourself – you would go into a kind of translation cycle, passing simultaneously back and forth between yourself and your Image, changing literally without going anywhere. Probably nobody who looked at you would be able to see the difference. But your mind would be gone. Not just mad. Taken away.

'I still don't know how I survived seeing myself in that room where I found you. I have to believe mirrors *are* different in your world. Or you're the most powerful Imager we've ever heard of.

'Anyway, the other important point is that the capacity to be an arch-Imager seems to be just that – a capacity. It isn't a skill you can learn, it's a talent you're born with. If it were a skill, Havelock would have mastered it somehow. "The Adept" isn't an honorary title. He earned it by being better at translations than anybody else. In particular, he was better at working translations with mirrors he didn't make. *I* can't even work them with mirrors I *did* make.

'Does that answer your question?'

Terisa nodded. She was trying to make what he told her fit her experience.

'Then answer mine. What does all this have to do with your conversation with Prince Kragen?'

'Oh, that. I'm sorry. I wasn't trying to be cryptic. It just seems like this is crucial somehow. I was talking to him right before we were attacked. That's why it reminded me.'

Then she got to the point of her question. 'When Artagel examined the dead men – the ones who vanished later – he said he found an insignia – a "sigil" – that meant they were Cadwals. They were Apts of the High King's Monomach. But when they attacked, they seemed to come out of nowhere. And when the rest of them were dead, their leader didn't have to run away. He just disappeared.

'He and his men must have come and gone through a flat mirror. But isn't that impossible? The Perdon and Prince Kragen decided Vagel must be involved, but that doesn't explain it. If passing through a flat glass safely is a matter of talent rather than training, then all of those men must have been arch-Imagers.'

And, now that she thought about it, how had Master Gilbur contrived to elude the Castellan? If it was conceivable that the man in black and Master Gilbur were allies, surely it was also conceivable that the Master had disappeared in the same way?

For a long moment, Geraden regarded her thoughtfully. 'You know,' he said with a wry chuckle, 'a lifetime ago, when I was still a new Apt, and I believed I was going to accomplish glorious things, I used to lie awake at night stewing about questions like that. And I came up with an idea that might work.

'First you shape a flat glass which just happens to be focused exactly where you want it.' He shrugged humorously. 'A trivial problem for the Imager I intended to be. Then you make another mirror – a normal one this time – that just happens to show a world which is essentially inert. No people or animals – and preferably no weather – to interfere with what you're doing. Then you translate the first mirror into the second and position it so that it fills as much of the Image as possible. And then, if the first mirror hasn't changed – and if it's actually possible to work two translations almost simultaneously – you might be able to pass through and keep your mind in one piece.'

He grinned. 'Ingenious, don't you think?'

'Yes.' Actually, she thought it was more than ingenious: she thought it was brilliant. But some of the implications – 'It would take two people, wouldn't it? One to translate the other?'

'Not to go. But it would to come back. That's true of any translation.'

Therefore if Master Gilbur had escaped by the same device that had saved the man in black, then Geraden was proven innocent. Everyone in Orison was innocent (especially Geraden, but also Master Eremis, who was locked up in the dungeon and had no access to mirrors) because they were *here* rather than wherever the mirrors were located. They could not have pulled Master Gilbur away.

Almost shivering, she said, 'I wish there was some way we could find out what really happened. If your idea is right, Master Gilbur probably left Orison the same way the men who attacked me came in.'

'But who did the translation?'

'Could it have been Vagel? That makes sense now – or it does as long as there actually is some way to move people around Mordant by Imagery without making them lose their minds.'

The Apt threw up his hands. '*I* don't know. For years, everybody thought the arch-Imager was dead. Now they all think he's alive.

'But you know,' he went on, looking at her appraisingly, a hint of eagerness rising in his voice, 'there might be a way to verify that Imagery was involved when you were attacked. There might even' – he sat forward – 'be a way to check out my idea.'

She watched him closely as he explained. Excitement animated his face, making it more and more attractive to her.

'Obviously, there's a lot we don't know about Imagery. Some things seem like they might be theoretically possible, but we've never had any way to test them. For instance, it's theoretically possible that an Imager with a certain kind of talent might be sensitive to mirrors from the other side. I mean, if he were to walk into a place that you could see in some mirror somewhere else, he would be able to feel it. He would know he was in an Image.

'Of course, you have to assume the Image actually exists. Otherwise what you see in a flat glass is just a copy of something real, and there would be nothing to feel.

'But if he *could* feel it' – Geraden jumped to his feet, no longer able to sit still – 'then it's *also* theoretically possible that he might be able to work the translation from the other side. Do you see what that means? He could just step out of the Image into wherever the mirror happened to be.'

As he spoke, her heart began to beat faster. His excitement took her with

312

him. 'If you're right,' she said slowly, 'then it wouldn't have to take two people. Master Gilbur could do it alone. He could come and go from Orison whenever he pleased.'

'Yes!' returned Geraden impatiently. 'But that's not the point. The point is that it might be *possible*.' In his enthusiasm, he gripped the arms of her chair so that he could look into her face closely. 'It might be possible for *you*.'

Unfortunately, he misjudged the distance. Their foreheads cracked together with a sound like breaking bone.

'Oh, Terisa, I'm sorry!' he sputtered. 'I'm sorry, I'm sorry.' One hand clapped to his head, he reached out to her with the other. 'Are you all right? I'm so sorry.'

Just for an instant, the whole room looked like it was on fire. Then the hot red and orange flames resolved themselves into flares of pain across her vision, and her skull began to clang as if he had used it for a gong.

But she hadn't been hit as hard as all that: her hangover accentuated the blow. When she was sure that her forehead was neither crushed nor bleeding, she pushed Geraden's apologetic hand away. Rising purposefully to her feet even though she now had an entire carillon ringing between her ears, she did her best to kick one of his shins.

First he gaped at her as though she had lost her mind. Then he let out a shout of laughter.

'I warned you,' she muttered through the pain. It was starting to decline. She was almost able to hear herself. 'One apology a day. That's all you get.' Helpless to spare herself, she was laughing as well. 'I'm not some lord or Master you can trifle with.'

Gales of glee rose from him.

'Please don't make me laugh.' Weakly, she lowered herself back into her chair. 'My head is going to split open.'

He took a deep breath to control his mirth. When he was able to stop laughing, he came over to her. Cupping his palm to her cheek, he kissed her bruised forehead tenderly.

For a moment, she thought he would lower his mouth to hers. If she could have stifled the throbbing in her skull, she would have tilted her head back to meet him halfway. But the pain wasn't fading quickly enough. She didn't know whether to be relieved or vexed when he withdrew to his chair.

'Terisa,' he repeated quietly, 'it might be possible for you.'

She sighed and closed her eyes. With both hands, she massaged the back of her neck. 'You must have broken something in your head. That's the craziest idea you've had yet.'

'Not really,' he replied good-naturedly. 'It's only an idea, of course. But you want to know why you're here – what you can do. Well, we can't teach you enough about making mirrors to find out if you can be an ordinary Imager. The Masters made it clear that they won't stand for it, and they control the laborium. But maybe you have a different kind of talent. Maybe that's why I was drawn to you when all the rules of Imagery should have taken me to the champion.

'We could try to find out, anyway. What have we got to lose?'

Opening her eyes, she stared at him hard. 'You're serious, aren't you?' He didn't look like a man who had just become dangerously insane. 'You think there might be some way to test what you're saying? To verify—?'

He nodded brightly.

Maybe you have a different kind of talent. Unexpectedly, her headache became less important. 'I'm almost afraid to ask how.'

Excitement gathered in him again, and his gaze shone. Making an effort to be reasonable, he said, 'I hope you understand that I don't really know any more about this than you do. It's only theory. And most of the Masters wouldn't even be interested. Shaping mirrors takes too much practical research and effort.' Then his enthusiasm broke out, pulling him once more to his feet. 'But all we have to do is go back to where you were attacked. Once we're in the right vicinity, all you have to do is move around slowly and concentrate on what you feel.'

The responses he aroused in her were so unfamiliar that she didn't know what to call them. Was this fear or eagerness? Her question was more complex than it sounded as she asked, 'What am I expected to feel?'

'Who knows?' he replied, unaware of the extent of her confusion. 'But it'll probably be subtle. A slight tugging sensation? An impression that something in front of you looks blurred? That sick feeling some people get when they look down from a cliff?

'If you don't feel anything, it won't prove anything. You might or might not have talent. Imagery might or might not be involved.' He chuckled. 'We might or might not be in the right place. But if you *do* feel something—' He made a visible effort to appear calm. '*That* would be interesting.

'Do you want to try it? Shall we go?'

For a moment, she couldn't answer. Peering into the fire, she almost heard a voice saying, That's the stupidest thing you've said today. Stop wasting my time. It sounded like her father's voice. And she knew what her mother would have said. Little girls don't do things like that.

Things like that.

What if Geraden were right?

If he were wrong, there would be no problem. Nothing in her life would change. But if he were right – she would never be the same again.

'It isn't that simple,' she murmured. 'I don't think I can find the place again. I was only there once. And – and my mind was on other things.'

His brief hesitation before he spoke suggested that he was paying strict attention to her now, that he had realized the importance of the issue he raised. 'We can solve that problem,' he said carefully. 'We can ask Artagel to help us. He'll remember the exact spot.' Then softly he repeated his earlier question. 'Terisa, what have you got to lose?'

She wanted to say, My self. Who I am. But that seemed impossibly melodramatic. Why was she taking all this so seriously? As a treatment for headache, it worked admirably: her head still hurt, but now she was able to forget about it. On the other hand, the danger she apparently feared was so improbable that she should have considered it silly. Really, she ought to have more common sense.

Intending a flippant retort, she faced Geraden.

His intent demeanor stopped her: he was looking at her as he might have looked at someone who was about to risk her life. He had made a leap of empathy that carried him into the center of her fear. In a husky voice, as if he were full of pity, he said, 'I would take you back to your world if I knew how. You know that.'

For an instant, something like grief rose in her throat. His eyes held a sharp awareness of what she had lost. He had already cost her her former life. Now he asked her to risk her sense of herself, the little she understood about who she was.

Mustering a smile, she said, 'Yes, I know. Don't you dare apologize.' Then she stood up. Whatever happened, she had no intention of wasting his friendship. 'Maybe the exercise will do me good.'

The pleasure in his face was so brilliant that she nearly started laughing again.

They found Artagel in one of the halls near her tower. By then, she had discovered that exercise made her head hurt worse at first; but by degrees circulating blood seemed to cleanse her brain, and she began to feel better. Thinking about Geraden's brother, she wondered if he had any system for keeping an eye on her. The hall where they found him didn't look like an especially logical station for a bodyguard. On the other hand, they had no trouble locating him.

He greeted her with a humorous bow and a comradely comment on her questionable appearance. Geraden defended her with mock indignation and received for his pains a cuff on the shoulder which did him no appreciable damage. Then he explained what he had in mind – leaving out, she thought, most of the salient details – and asked for Artagel's help.

Artagel took this more grimly than Terisa had expected. 'Thank your good fortune,' he snapped, 'the lady Terisa *doesn't* remember how to find that place. Did you leave your brains under that pile of rubble? Or maybe you just *forgot* she was attacked down there by Apts of the High King's Monomach. It's even possible Gart himself was among them.' He digressed momentarily. 'I would hate to think anyone less could give me that much trouble.' Then he resumed, 'What were you planning to do if she was attacked again? Ask them nicely to go away?'

'Not exactly.' His brother's anger clearly didn't trouble Geraden. 'I thought I would just ask them to wait until you caught up with us.

'Actually,' he explained, 'they probably can't attack us. They won't be ready for us. They don't have any way of knowing what we're doing – and I'm sure they don't spend *all* their time crouched in front of the mirror waiting for a likely victim to appear by coincidence. We should be safe.'

In spite of himself, Artagel was mollified. 'You're too clever for your own good. But it does happen that I don't have anything better to do this morning.' Without apparent difficulty, he forgot his anger and grinned at Terisa. 'My lady,' he said formally, offering her his arm, 'shall we go?'

When she accepted, he gave Geraden a smile of good-humored malice and swept her away, leaving his brother to tag along behind.

As he followed, Geraden's face wore an expression of lopsided fondness. After all, she reflected, he had six older brothers – and all of them probably delighted in teasing him. The way he looked now gave another lift to her spirits. He and Artagel made it easy for her to think she was doing the right thing.

As she returned to the damp, disused passages among the foundations of Orison, however, she began to reconsider. She didn't have fond memories of this place. The endless dripping of water promised peril. Although there were enough lanterns to enable Artagel to find his way, their scattered and distant reflections in the puddles and smears of water on the floor gave the stone an evil aspect, as though dark secrets were hidden behind the gleams. The echo of bootheels chased the silence down side passages and around corners until she felt irrationally sure that she was being stalked. The warmth of day never reached down this far, and the air felt colder than she remembered it: certainly, more of the moisture had become ice. Whenever she or her companions broke the surface of a frozen puddle, the ice crackled like fire.

And if Geraden were right – if by some strange chance she had the kind of talent he described—

She clung to Artagel's arm harder than she realized. Apparently thinking she was cold, he draped the edge of his gray cloak over her shoulders.

'Whoever made that mirror,' Geraden commented like whistling in the dark, 'was either very lucky or very good. It's hard to imagine anyone *accidentally* shaping a mirror that shows this part of Orison. On the other hand, it isn't exactly easy to figure out how he could have made it deliberately. Even the best Masters have to do decades of research to get what they want.'

'I hope you know what you're doing,' muttered Terisa nervously. 'I don't like this at all.'

Artagel gave her a little hug. 'He probably does. The only time you really have to worry about him is when he looks like he has everything under control.'

She wanted Geraden to reply, but he didn't. After a moment, she asked, 'Who keeps these lanterns lit?'

Her escort shrugged. 'Servants.'

'But why?' she pursued. 'Hasn't this whole area been abandoned?'

'Well, not quite *abandoned*. I've heard that many of the damp, cold rooms down here are used to store wine. If we just knew which ones, we could die happy. And I know for a fact that the Castellan uses sections of this place to train his guards, especially in winter.

'Besides,' he added wryly, 'I think he hates the dark. He might put lanterns here even if no one but the people who took care of them came here from one year to the next.'

The thought of Castellan Lebbick wasn't much comfort. 'How much farther?' she asked.

'We're almost there.' Artagel sounded nonchalant, but when she glanced at him she saw wariness in the flick of his eyes, the movement of his head. 'Lebbick must have had the floor cleaned. Otherwise you could see the blood by now.'

He was right. After another dozen paces, the look of the corridor began to match her memory of it, despite the absence of blood.

'Here,' she said softly. Even though she understood that sound didn't pass through mirrors, she was viscerally afraid of being overheard by unfriendly ears. This was the place. She could almost detect the residual tremor of her own fear, vibrations left over from the man in black's assault. 'It was here.'

'Yes.' Artagel stopped, turned. Then he moved her until her back touched one wall. 'You were there.' With a gesture, he indicated the passage. 'We fought there.' The obscure illumination made his face as grim as his voice. 'The Perdon and Prince Kragen came from the other side. They rescued us.' Abruptly, he confronted his brother. 'I'm not sure you realize,' he grated through his teeth, 'that the bastard beat me – whoever he was. The last time that happened, I was a lot younger than you are now.'

Light gleamed dimly across Geraden's forehead as though he were sweating in spite of the cold. 'Somehow,' he muttered, 'I'm sure you'll get a chance to try him again. I just hope it doesn't come today. *I* won't be very good at rescuing you.

'But this isn't what we're looking for.' He moved past his brother and peered at Terisa through the gloom. 'We need to find the exact point of translation. If there is one.

'Where did they come from?'

She closed her eyes. She had been walking with Prince Kragen. He had been talking about Elega. One bodyguard was ahead of them; the other, behind. She heard a quiet leather sound – a sword leaving a sheath? Then the men charged forward. The black leather of their armor made them difficult to see. Their naked swords were more distinct, glinting lanternlight—

'There,' she breathed and opened her eyes. She was pointing at what appeared to be a dark side passage diagonally across the corridor from her. 'They came out of there.'

'Good.' Geraden was whispering as though he, too, feared being overheard. 'Let's take a look.'

His breath left a wreath of steam in the air as he moved away.

Artagel had his sword out. It seemed to flex with the movement of his wrist. He touched her arm with his free hand, and she went with him after Geraden.

The way ahead remained black. If it was a side passage, it was too short to merit a lantern of its own. Illumination reflecting from the main corridor faded rapidly. After a moment, Artagel asked, 'Do you want to wait while I get us a light?'

'No,' hissed Geraden. 'If there is a mirror focused here, light will just make it easier for us to be seen.'

Artagel nodded. He was keeping Terisa positioned between him and the wall, to reduce the number of directions from which she could be threatened.

'Concentrate,' Geraden said to her over his shoulder. 'The point of translation could be anywhere. Try to feel it. Forget everything else and just try to feel it.'

'Concentrate yourself,' she retorted. Her whisper came out hoarsely. 'I'm not the only one who doesn't know what his talents are.'

Geraden paused for a second. 'Good point.'

Artagel flashed her a grin she could barely see in the thickening dark.

This is silly, she enunciated to herself. All three of them were supposed to be adults – yet here they were, groping their way down a blind hall looking for some place where the air or the stone or who knew what would give one of them twinges. We must be out of our minds. If somebody had jumped at her and said, Boo! she would have screamed.

That idea made her want to giggle.

It distracted her. She didn't realize what was happening until a touch of cold as thin as a feather and as sharp as steel slid straight through the center of her abdomen.

Before she could react – before she could try to shout a warning – a man stepped out of the wall. His body felt like a block of stone as he collided with her heavily, knocking her against Artagel.

Artagel clinched her arm. 'Back!' he snapped. 'Back to the light!' and flung her away from him.

At once, the cold sensation vanished.

She didn't notice the difference.

She stumbled, caught her balance. Where was Geraden? Every muscle in her body wanted to run, but she turned in time to see Artagel thrust Geraden after her while threatening a shadowy figure with his blade.

Urgently, she raced for the main passage and the lanterns.

Geraden was faster. He was beside her when he reached the corridor. He steered her to the right, toward the nearer lantern. Their momentum took them to the opposite wall, to the place where she had fallen and waited for the man in black to kill her. There they both whirled to see what was happening to Artagel.

He came into the light with his sword still poised between him and the obscure figure. No, it wasn't one figure: she saw two. Three. Four. They moved slowly, massively; the menace of Artagel's blade didn't hinder them.

Four. That was bad. But at least there weren't any more. As they reached the light, she saw that they did in fact look like men. They had the heads and faces and limbs of men. Their nakedness showed that they had the bodies of men. Their arms were extended for embraces.

But their eyes were dead. And under their skin lumps the size of hands moved visibly – lumps that couldn't be muscle.

They carried no weapons, however. And their movements were so leaden that Artagel would surely be able to handle them.

He retreated in the other direction, trying to lead them away. His fighting grin was absent. Behind his perplexity, his eyes hinted at horror.

The four men ignored him. As they emerged from the side passage, they headed for Terisa and Geraden.

Artagel shouted to distract them. They ignored that as well. They might have been deaf. Lumbering woodenly, they went after their chosen object.

In an effort to turn them, he struck. His sword whirled and flashed and came down on the wrist of the leading figure with such force that Terisa winced, expecting to see the hand flop to the stone.

But the hand didn't fall. There wasn't any blood. Instead, the skin of the wrist peeled back from the point of the blow, revealing an insect like a monstrous cockroach where the bones of the hand should have been.

The skin withered away; the insect dropped from the wrist-stump to the floor.

It tasted the air with its feelers for a second, worked its mandibles, then scurried toward Terisa and Geraden.

At the same time, a second insect started to squirm out of the lumbering figure's wrist. The skin of the wrist withered, as if the cockroach inside it were all that had preserved it as living tissue.

Terisa would have screamed if she could have found her voice. But the insect was faster than the heavy body or host that had carried it; and Geraden had shouted at her, grabbed her arm, trying to tug her away; and some residue of the incisive cold that had presaged this assault seemed to knot up her chest, so that she was hardly able to breathe.

While the second insect dropped to the floor from the tattered flesh of the figure's wrist, a third fought into view out of his forearm.

She couldn't tear her eyes away from what was happening. Geraden had to drag her backward. She saw wild revulsion in Artagel's eyes as he sprang to the attack.

One high hard blow of his sword bit into the nearest figure's shoulder at the base of the neck, cutting deeply through the man's chest. Another swing – so quick that it seemed to be part of the first – came around from the other side, licking murderously far between his ribs.

But there was no blood. He didn't fall.

Like a rotten husk, his torso split open. His head continued staring straight ahead; his legs continued walking stiffly, heavily, down the corridor after his fellows – and dozens and dozens of cockroaches came tumbling out of his ruptured chest and abdomen.

For an instant, they seethed around each other, searching for a scent. Then they ran like a rush of blood after Terisa and Geraden.

Abruptly, the man's head burst, scattering a knot of insects among the rest. After that, his legs seemed to lose their way. They tottered to the side, hit the wall, and fell over, while more and more huge cockroaches swarmed out of the crumbling remains of his waist and hips and thighs.

Soon there was nothing left of him except hurrying insects.

Terisa heard Artagel swearing in vicious desperation, as if he were about to vomit.

'Terisa!' Geraden hauled on her arm. 'Run!'

Transfixed by Artagel's attack and its result, she hadn't realized how much she was hindering Geraden – how swiftly the insects were moving. The nearest one had nearly reached the skirt of her gown.

Gasping, she whirled away.

For a few strides, she ran, ran with all her heart. But then she had to stop and turn, to see—

Artagel had put away his sword. With his face clenched and bleak, his lower lip bitten between his teeth, he came up behind one of the remaining figures, stooped rapidly, hooked his hands around the squirming ankles, and pulled as hard as he could.

The man toppled forward with the slow, unreactive violence of felled timber.

When he hit the floor, the impact broke his whole body open. All the insects that had packed themselves into his flesh were released at once.

They flooded the passage from wall to wall. Lanternlight gleamed and glinted on their dark backs; they formed a flowing current as they sped forward, champing their mandibles for the flesh of their victims.

Terisa fled again.

Geraden ran with her. 'We can keep ahead of them,' he panted. His chest heaved, urgent for air. 'Don't stop. We can outrun them.'

'How far?' Her heart was on fire, as if she had already run for miles. She seemed to be suffocating on fear and cold. 'How far can you run?'

'Far enough,' he promised grimly. Yet he sounded like each breath he took hurt his lungs.

She stopped near a lantern and looked back. She and Geraden were twenty or thirty feet ahead of the leading cockroaches. From this angle, the whole floor of the passage seemed to boil with menace as the insects rushed forward. Behind them, the figure Artagel had struck first was just finishing his collapse, releasing the last of his occupants among the swarm. The remaining man increased his pace to keep up with the hunting torrent.

Artagel followed in a frenzy. 'Geraden!' His call echoed down the corridor like a wail. 'What can I do? Tell me what to do!'

'No,' Terisa rasped. She fought for air, but was too frightened to get it. 'I can't run far enough. We don't know where we're going. If we get out of here, we'll just lead those things into Orison.'

In response, Geraden gave her a look of pure anguish.

'We've got to fight somehow,' she said as if a total stranger were talking, someone who had no acquaintance with the panic which hammered in her heart, the dread and revulsion that twisted her stomach. 'We've got to fight.'

For one more moment while the cockroaches rushed closer, he stared at her as though he were about to start sobbing. Then he gave an inarticulate shout like a cry of battle and leaped for the lantern.

Wrenching it from its hooks regardless of the way the heated iron scorched his hands, he flung it at the insects.

It hit in a splash of burning oil, and a dozen or more of the creatures caught fire.

They burned almost instantly, spouting flames as bright as torches: they were incendiary in some way. After two or three heartbeats, nothing remained of them except bits of charred carapace—

—nothing except a black vapor which rose into the air and spread quickly.

It smelled like a strong combination of formaldehyde and partially digested meat, and it clawed at Terisa's throat and lungs like acid. Gagging, she doubled over: the spasm that gripped her chest was too fierce to let her cough.

The passage had gone dim without the lantern, but she was close enough to the floor to see the nearest cockroaches scuttling rapidly forward, unconcerned by a few deaths. She had to run, *had* to—

She couldn't. It was impossible. She could not break the hold of that black vapor on the inside of her chest.

Retching hard enough to crack his ribs, Geraden got his arms around her and somehow found the strength to lift her off her feet. With her convulsed weight awkward in his embrace, he stumbled away, struggling to outrun the insects again.

In a few strides, he set her down to see if she could carry herself now. She snatched a whooping breath, and the spasm began to unclench. Still clinging to him for support, she fled farther before turning to look back.

She was in time to see Artagel run up with a lantern that he must have retrieved from the opposite direction and throw it like a madman at the head of the last erect attacker.

He didn't know his danger: he was too far away to have seen accurately what had happened to Geraden and her. But she couldn't shout a warning. Her raw throat could barely whisper his name as the lantern hit and broke – and the lumbering figure went up in flames, burning with such sudden fury that he seemed incandescent – and the spouting black exhalations of that many insects engulfed Artagel, causing him to collapse as effectively as a sword-thrust in the belly.

'Artagel,' croaked Geraden. '*Artagel.*'

Terisa watched Artagel and the insects while her fear turned to a cold, dark anger. This time, she was the one who grabbed at Geraden's arm and pulled. 'Come on.' Her voice was only a scrape of pain in her throat, but now the chill seemed to be doing her some good, slowly numbing the hurt of the black vapor. 'Come *on.*'

Ahead, she saw that the corridor came to a T, branching left and right. More light seemed to emanate from the right than from the left.

When she reached the T, she scanned both passages to ascertain that there was in fact a lantern nearby off to the right. Then she released Geraden. The cockroaches were after her. They had come through the same mirror that the man in black had used to attack her. She was the only person she knew who had active enemies.

'Get the lantern,' she choked out. 'I'll lead them away.'

He gaped at her as though his brother's fall had cost him his wits.

Urgently, she pushed him into motion. '*Go!* I'll lead them away. You follow. Every lantern we pass, you can kill a few more. Just don't breathe that vapor.'

At last, he appeared to understand. He moved into the right-hand corridor a few steps ahead of the cockroaches.

Retreating backward so that she could see what he did, she went to the left.

Unfortunately, her assumption was mistaken. The entire swarm swept after Geraden, ignoring her completely.

Geraden!

Her anger crumbled into horror and incomprehension. The strength ran out of her: she nearly sank to her knees. Slowly, she raised her hands to her mouth, and fear filled her eyes.

He didn't realize his danger until he reached the lantern, unhooked it, and turned back. Then he saw the oncoming rush. For a second, he was paralyzed. Dismay wiped the combative stubbornness off his face. His hands lowered the lantern: it looked like it was about to fall.

One of her knees failed. She lost her balance and stumbled to the floor, breaking the ice that scummed a wide puddle. Water soaked into her gown. She wasn't even on her feet when she heard him howl, 'Terisa! Get help!'

But she was watching him, watching with all she had left, yearning for him in voiceless desperation, as Adept Havelock arrived at his side and leveled a beam of light against the onslaught.

Apparently, the mad old Imager had been waiting in the hall for just this purpose. The reflections from his eyes danced insanely, but his movements betrayed none of the erratic frenzy, the hysteria of intent, which she had seen in the past: they were deft and sure, almost calm.

One hand took hold of Geraden's collar and pulled him back; the other directed his beam at the seething cockroaches.

Terisa was past surprise, so she noticed as if it were a matter of course that the Adept's weapon was the same small piece of glass he had used before to light her way and save her life. Now, however, that mirror shone much more hotly: its light was as fierce as fire. More powerfully than burning oil, it ignited the insects. They took flame and were incinerated almost instantly, popping like firecrackers as they died.

Then billowing black vapor filled the corridor so thickly that the illumination of Geraden's lantern was obscured. Only Adept Havelock's fire was bright enough to show through the sudden midnight as the beam swept the floor and cockroaches by the hundreds burned.

At the last moment, Terisa remembered to hold her breath.

For what felt like a long time – a dozen heartbeats, two dozen – the Adept's light moved swiftly and methodically over the stone, boiling the damp to steam in order to achieve the death of each insect. Of course, the creatures simplified this process by marching with mindless determination in Geraden's direction. Adept Havelock didn't need to be concerned that any of them would sneak past him along the walls, or would turn and flee. Nevertheless he was careful, and so the cleansing of the passage took time. She felt her mind going giddy as she wondered whether the Adept had enough sense – or Geraden enough self-awareness – to stop breathing.

Then the vapor became thick enough to block even Adept Havelock's beam. The air began to sting her eyes. She lowered her forehead to the floor. The ache of her bruise against the cold stone gave her a focal point for her concentration, and she clung to it so that she wouldn't breathe.

Unexpectedly, something nudged her shoulder.

Believing in panic that she had been found by one of the cockroaches, she flipped to the side and gasped for air so that she could scream.

Adept Havelock stood over her, dressed as usual in his worn surcoat and tattered chasuble. His light played on the ceiling, filling the corridor.

He looked like a dangerous lunatic. His disfocused eyes bulged; the few remaining tufts of his hair protruded wildly. His fleshy grin was gleeful and lecherous. Behind the dirty stubble on his cheeks, his skin seemed to be turning purple.

As she began to cough, however, he let his own breath out with a burst and started breathing again. The air made him cough as well, and a few tears trickled from his eyes; but his eyes stopped bulging almost at once, and his skin lost its purple intensity.

'I see,' he rasped hoarsely, 'that the air is now tolerable. It was kind of you to sample it for me.'

Geraden stumbled into her range of vision. His eyes were raw, and the difficulty of breathing showed in his face. Nevertheless he was on his feet. As soon as he saw that she, too, would survive, he groaned, 'Artagel,' and pushed himself into a coughing run toward his brother.

'Artagel?' Although one of Havelock's eyes leered, the other was sane and serious. His nose, as fierce and ascetic as a hawk's beak, made every word he uttered count. 'Was he caught in this trap as well?'

'Back there.' A spasm of retching wracked Terisa. After that, however, the pain in her lungs eased, and she was able to breathe more normally. With an effort, she climbed to her hands and knees, then to her feet. 'He tried to save us. That vapor got him.'

'Balls of a goat!' the Adept snapped. At once, he strode away.

Struggling not to be left behind, she reeled after him.

Slowly her balance improved as the effects of the vapor faded. She was nearly steady as she and Adept Havelock reached Geraden.

He didn't notice them. He sat on the floor, cradling Artagel's head in his arms.

Artagel's face was mottled with exertion and pain, and his eyes gaped at the ceiling as though he had gone blind. But he was breathing.

Her relief was so acute that her eyes spilled tears.

Stooping to Geraden, Adept Havelock tapped him crisply on the shoulder. 'Come along, Geraden. Carry him if you have to. I don't like staying this close to that translation point. Who knows how many more surprises Vagel has for us? I'll take you somewhere safe.'

Geraden hugged his brother harder and didn't move. Terisa couldn't tell whether he had heard the Adept.

As if he were making a concession, the old Imager said, 'I have some wine. I think it'll help him.' Then he lost patience. 'Horror and ballocks, boy! If you're attacked again, I might not be able to save you!'

Still Geraden didn't move. But Artagel jerked his head in a nod as if he understood. When Terisa took hold of his arm and tried to pull him upright, he made a feeble effort to assist her.

Roughly, Geraden rubbed his eyes with the back of his hand. Then he helped Terisa lift his brother off the stone.

'Come along,' repeated Havelock. With a brisk stride, he moved away.

Supporting Artagel between them, Terisa and Geraden followed. Artagel was unable to keep his feet under him, but she heard an improvement in his breathing. He was beginning to sound like he would live.

She found that she was completely disoriented: she had no idea where Adept Havelock was taking them. After a short distance, he entered a side passage which led at once to a sturdy wooden door that looked like the entrance to a storeroom. In fact, it was the entrance to a storeroom. The storeroom, however, appeared to be full of nothing but empty crates in various stages of disrepair. Adept Havelock ignored them as he picked his way to another door hidden in a niche at the back of the room.

This door looked ordinary enough from the outside, but inside it held enough bars and bolts to seal a dungeon. Havelock shut it behind Terisa, Geraden, and Artagel, then led them down a passage that opened almost immediately into a room crowded with a disarray of mirrors.

'King Joyse confiscated most of these during his wars,' the Adept explained offhandedly as he crossed the room to another corridor. 'After he created the Congery, he restored quite a few mirrors to the Masters. But he kept more than he gave up.

'I wish they did me some good.'

The sight astonished Geraden out of his distress, at least for a moment. Adept Havelock had the only light, however, and he left the room promptly. Terisa and Geraden followed with Artagel.

After two or three turns, as many short hallways, and another door, they suddenly found themselves in the large, square room where Terisa had listened to Master Quillon explain the history of Mordant's need.

The place appeared unchanged: it was still furnished and cluttered like the study of a man whose mind had gone. Lamps set into the walls and the central pillar shed plenty of light toward the doors that lined the walls, giving admittance to Orison's secret passages.

Perhaps because she was suffering from reaction, Terisa was struck by the odd thought that Adept Havelock resembled a spider. This room was the center of his web; the secret passages were the strands. Now she and Geraden and Artagel had been caught.

She wondered what the Adept was plotting.

He bustled away behind the pillar. While he was out of sight, Terisa and Geraden helped Artagel to one of the chairs at the checker table. Artagel's breathing still had a thick tubercular wheeze that was painful to hear, but he was strong enough to take notice of his surroundings. With an effort, he choked out, 'Does he *live* here?'

'Looks like it,' replied Terisa vaguely. She still wasn't ready to tell anyone that she had been here before.

'I wish I knew what he was doing with all those mirrors,' Geraden muttered. Fear and strain and bafflement gave him a feverish look.

Carrying a large flagon, Adept Havelock returned.

At last she had an opportunity to observe him more closely. He conveyed an impression of suppressed haste, as though he were trying to resist the acceleration of some internal process. His movements were deliberate, tightly controlled; but his eyes flicked from side to side with a discernible rhythm, like a heartbeat being gradually goaded faster by adrenaline.

He handed the flagon directly to Artagel. 'Drink it all. It's going to taste terrible. I put some balm in it to heal your throat.' Brusquely, he addressed Geraden. 'Make sure he drinks it all. If he recovers, make him play hop-board with you.' He indicated his empty checkerboard table. 'You need the practice. I want to talk to the lady.'

Without waiting for a reaction, he took Terisa's arm and drew her away, around the pillar until she could no longer see Geraden and Artagel.

When he stopped, however, he didn't speak. His eyes took turns flicking toward her and off again, flicking – Their rhythm and the aftertaste of black vapor made her stomach queasy. A grimace clenched his sybaritic mouth, as if he had taken a vow not to let himself grin at her. Slowly, he raised his scrawny old arms and folded them across his chest.

From beyond the pillar came harsh gagging noises. The wine must have been worse than terrible. Fortunately, the noises soon ceased.

Facing the Adept alone, Terisa felt a strong desire to become hysterical. That would solve a number of problems. It would give her an escape from his loony gaze. It would provide a much-needed rest. It would free her from the responsibility of trying to figure out what was going on. But he had saved her life. He had saved Geraden. And he clearly had some kind of purpose for bringing her here. In return, she had to make some kind of effort to rise to the occasion.

Swallowing hard to clear her throat, she said, 'You're not really as crazy as people think.'

In response, he let out a bark of laughter. 'Oh, yes I am. This is just one of my lucid moments. Quillon told you I have lucid moments. This is one of them.'

Abruptly, he unfolded one age-spotted hand from his chest to stab his index finger in her direction. 'The important thing,' he whispered intensely, 'is, don't ask me any questions. *Don't.* I'm having a hard enough time as it is.'

At once, he resumed his stance and went on flicking his eyes at her, back and forth in turn, their rhythm eloquent of mounting pressure, perhaps even of violence.

She felt her mouth hanging open, so she closed it. Apparently, he needed her to help him in some way. But without asking any questions. Did he want her to guess at something? Or did it matter what she said?

Maybe it didn't matter. Cautiously, she ventured, 'I haven't thanked you for saving us. I don't know how the arch-Imager or whoever it was managed to spring that trap on us. I can't think of any way for him to know what we were going to do. But if you hadn't come along, we—' She shuddered, unable to complete the thought.

Without warning, he snapped, 'Vagel!' He sounded grimly angry, yet his expression conveyed gratitude. 'If I could get just one hand on him, I would tear his heart out. But it isn't good for me to lose my temper.' Whatever emotions appeared on his face or in his voice had no effect on his posture or the movement of his eyes. 'That was just coincidence. The first piece of good luck we've had in a long time. I've seen those creatures before – just once, when I was in a cabal of Imagers High King Festten built around Vagel in Carmag. I saw what they do. But I've never actually seen the glass.

'We were told they're like hunting dogs. If you translate something with the scent of the man you want hunted on it into their world, those insects go wild. But apparently they can't be translated directly. They forget the scent and just attack the first thing they find. So you have to give them living bodies to serve as hosts.'

As he spoke, the edges of her vision went dim as if she were about to faint.

'They eat their way into those bodies and breed, and then they can be translated without losing the scent.'

'That's what they would have done to Geraden,' she murmured weakly. Then she raised a hand to her mouth, fighting to keep her nausea at bay.

'And anybody else who got in their way,' added the Adept. He seemed to be growing calmer. 'That's why I say we were lucky. If he hadn't happened to be near the translation point when those creatures came through, they would have had to go looking for him. We would have had to fight them in the public halls of Orison. Who knows how many people would have been killed.'

Struggling to get her mind off the idea of Geraden as a host for the monstrous insects, Terisa started to ask a question. Fortunately, she caught it in time to rephrase it.

'It's a good thing you were there to rescue us.'

She felt an unexpected, poignant desire to say, I saw the riders of my dream in the augury. Geraden thinks I'm an Imager.

'I said I'm crazy,' the Adept replied with some asperity. 'I didn't say I'm stupid.' Then, to her surprise, he smiled, baring his crooked yellow teeth. 'It's obvious that Vagel has plans for that translation point. After going to all the trouble to create it, he isn't likely to leave it unused. I've been watching it, more or less ever since you told Quillon about it – the day after Gart came through and almost killed you.'

She couldn't help herself: she blurted out, 'Gart? The High King's Mono—?'

At once, a spasm of fury twisted his face. He squeezed his eyes shut. As if they weren't under his control, his hands rose into fists and began punching at his temples. She saw that he was holding his breath.

'I'm sorry,' she whispered fervently, frightened without knowing why. 'I'm sorry. I didn't mean it. I just didn't know it was Gart—' She faltered and fell silent.

Fiercely, he sucked a deep breath in through his nose and opened his eyes. 'Of course it was Gart.' One muscle at a time, as if by a supreme act of will, he resumed his stance. His mouth grimaced again. He appeared to be in command of himself. 'The alliance between Vagel and Festten still holds. Cadwal wants you dead even more than Alend and that treacherous Prince do.' The rhythm of his eyes was faster, however, flicking to her and away like the stalking beat of his madness.

He tried to smile again – this time unsuccessfully. Without transition, he said, 'You're probably wondering why I brought you here. Well, I can't tell you that. If I knew the answer myself, it probably wouldn't make sense. But I want to tell you a little bit about King Joyse.'

Terisa swallowed the change of subject as well as she could and waited for him to go on.

'You know, the relationship between Imagery, augury, and fate is an interesting philosophical question.' His tone was peaceful now, but his eyes contradicted it. His manner brought back the idea of a lurking spider. 'Before Joyse was born, I was what some people called the "pet Imager" of the Cadwal prince who ruled Orison and the Demesne. He was a petty tyrant, but imaginative in his cruelties, and I was growing desperate for hope. So I tried to arrange an augury for the coming birth.

'Unfortunately, I was unable to shape a flat glass to show the room where he would be born. The best I could create was an Image of a hill just outside Orison – a hill,' he added by the way, 'which is now *in* the castle. In fact, it forms the foundation for the tower where he has his rooms.

'But at the time,' he resumed, 'the focus of my mirror refused to be adjusted any farther than the stables where our prince allowed us to keep our mangy horses.

'Of course, I could have waited until the child was born and grew up enough to go to the stables on his own. But as I say I was growing desperate. So one black night soon after he was born, I stole little Joyse from his cradle and took him down to the stables and risked leaving him there alone in a pile of straw while I raced back to my small laborium to work the augury.

'He took cold and nearly died – but I got what I wanted.'

From where he stood, he couldn't see Geraden and Artagel as they crept past the edge of the pillar. Terisa glanced at them to reassure herself about Artagel's condition – and to try to warn them not to interfere. Then she returned her attention to the Adept.

'It was a remarkable augury, unusually distinct in some ways, maddeningly vague in others. On the one hand, it clearly showed Joyse making himself a king. On the other, it proved to have almost nothing to do with the process by which he actually did become King. It didn't show the battles he actually fought, the victories he actually won, the decisions he actually made. So it was no help at all to us along the way. The best it gave us was an occasional bit of confirmation, when the results of something he did – like the creation of the Congery – unexpectedly matched the Images in the augury.

'Let me give you an example,' he said blandly while the pace of his gaze increased. 'According to my augury, he became King as an old man. Sometime *after* a large, unexplained hole was torn in the side of Orison.'

While Terisa stared – and Geraden and Artagel fought to muffle their surprise – Havelock permitted himself a stiff shrug. She felt sure he was trying to tell her something urgent, something she couldn't possibly understand. 'At the time, the idea that I would have to wait until he was old was so depressing – I almost didn't bother to go rescue him from the stables. But since then I've had a lot of time to ask myself what went wrong. Did I falsify my augury by not allowing the conditions for it to happen naturally? Does the very act of casting an augury change events? Or are there other possibilities? Has King Joyse changed his own fate by being stronger – or weaker – than he would have been if he hadn't taken cold that night and nearly died?

'We would be better off if we could answer questions like these.'

As if he were pausing to briefly become a completely different person, he relaxed his rigid posture and scratched himself unceremoniously. Whatever dignity and command he possessed vanished at once. His surcoat looked old and grimy enough to carry lice: perhaps the itching was unbearable. Then he drew back into his clenched stance.

'I'll tell you something else that was in my augury. If you promise never to

327

tell anybody. Never never never.' He spoke to the rhythm of his eyes. 'Never never never.' The strain of holding on to his lucidity brought sweat to his forehead, despite the cool of the room, 'His daughters were in it.

'Of course, I didn't know they were his daughters then. But now it's obvious.'

A crafty look broke over his features. 'You'll never guess what I saw Myste doing.'

Terisa had to gouge her nails into her palms to keep herself quiet. At the edge of her attention, she was aware of Geraden's agitation, but she had no time to spare for him.

With a visible effort, Adept Havelock wrestled his expression back to sternness. 'Of course you'll never guess,' he snapped as if she had just said something insulting. 'How could you? That's why I'm going to tell you.

'I saw her,' he said sarcastically, 'with a figure who bore an astonishing resemblance to Gilbur's champion. She looked like she was begging him not to kill her.'

Terisa must have been stronger, more resilient, than she realized. How else was it possible for her to feel such panic, after everything she had already been through? Havelock knew where Myste had gone. Perhaps King Joyse also knew. Perhaps he had known all along. *Begging him not to kill her.* Myste!

Numb with fright, she asked, 'Did he kill her? Did she go through all that just to get herself killed?'

But it was likely that Adept Havelock didn't hear her. While she breathed her question, Geraden surged forward, demanding, 'Myste is with that champion? Is that why no one's seen her recently? Does King Joyse know about this?'

Rage on his face, Havelock whirled as if he intended to strike Geraden down. Instantly, however, his turn changed into a pirouette, and he spun circles, flapping his arms like an old crow. When he stopped, he looked like he wanted to storm at Geraden, yet he was giggling, and his voice was thick with mirth.

'Do you know what the difference is between an Apt and an Adept?'

Frozen with chagrin, Geraden gaped at the mad Imager.

Lugubriously solemn, Adept Havelock raised his fingers to his fat lips and flapped them, making a *de-de-de-de* sound. Then he cackled appreciation for his own humor and turned to Terisa. 'Do you get it? De-de-de-de. *D-e.* A-*d-e*-p-t.' But he quit laughing as soon as he saw the dismay on her face. 'Women!' he snorted. 'Whoever invented women gave them teats instead of brains. By the hoary goat of the arch-Imager! No wonder Mordant is in such a mess.'

Suddenly, her throat filled with pain. He was so valuable – and so lost. 'I'm sorry,' she whispered. 'You poor man. I'm so sorry.'

But no amount of regret could bring his mind back. He leered at her, smacked his lips, and pronounced in a tone of finality:

'Sheepdung.'

When Artagel had recovered sufficiently, he and his companions found their way back up to the public halls of Orison. 'You'd better tell Castellan Lebbick about the attack,' said Geraden glumly as they walked. 'He needs to guard that translation point.'

Artagel nodded and left. He still carried himself stiffly, as if his lungs were tender, but all he needed now was rest.

The prospect of being alone made Terisa's skin crawl, so she asked Geraden to keep her company in her rooms. Inborn consideration seemed to warn him off sensitive topics: deliberately casual, he whiled away part of the afternoon for her by chatting about his family, giving her brief sketches of his brothers and their life in the Care of Domne. Soothed by his gentle talk and affectionate memories, she began to feel restored enough to consider the implications of the day's events.

Unfortunately, he was called away at that point: one of the younger Apts found him and summoned him to his neglected chores.

The remainder of the afternoon was bad. And the evening threatened to be worse, until she discovered – to her surprise and relief – that she was too exhausted to keep her eyes open. Grateful for small blessings, she went to bed.

The next morning, after a night full of dreams from which Terisa awakened as though she had been screaming, Saddith bustled into her rooms and announced gleefully that Master Eremis had been released.

'Really? Are you sure?' Terisa tried to conceal her emotions, but her heart was pounding. The Master had said, *When I am free, I will come to you*. As if by magic, the events of the previous day became less important. *There will be no part of your womanhood which I have not claimed*. 'Why would Castellan Lebbick let him out?'

Saddith looked positively exultant. 'I do not know the entire story, my lady. Apparently, the Castellan is teaching his men to keep their mouths closed. But it is rumored' – she lowered her voice dramatically – 'that Orison was attacked by Imagery yesterday. Master Eremis had been imprisoned because he was believed to be responsible for such things.' The recollection made her indignant. 'But of course he could not have attacked Orison by Imagery while locked in the Castellan's dungeon. No proof can be found that he is guilty.' She chortled. 'Even our dour Castellan cannot justify imprisoning an innocent man.'

Terisa made a conscious effort not to speculate about the meaning of Saddith's pleasure. Her own expectations were already too confused: she didn't want to have them complicated further by memories of the way Saddith had moaned and clung while Master Eremis thrust into her. Instead, she remembered the touch of his lips and tongue on her breasts – the way he had instructed her to betray Geraden – and waited impatiently for the maid to leave.

She wanted the Master – and was afraid to face him with her refusal to take his part against Geraden. Opposing desires made her forehead ache. As soon as Saddith closed the door, she rushed to give herself a quick, intense bath, trying to get ready. But then she forced herself to put on the dingiest gown she had, as if she wished to be unattractive. Master Eremis. Geraden. She yearned for both in different ways and had no idea what to do about the contradiction.

But Master Eremis didn't come.

She had thought she was going to find out who she was. But neither of the men who tried to claim her had given her an answer. She had risked accompanying Geraden to Vagel's translation point for nothing more than the sensation of thin, sharp cold – a sensation that made no difference. And she had known all along that Master Eremis could have any woman he wanted.

Apparently, he didn't want her.

Perhaps for that reason – perhaps simply because she couldn't have him – she found that she wanted him badly.

NINETEEN

THE ADVANTAGES OF
AN EARLY THAW

ౌ

Four days later, the weather broke.

By that time, Terisa had forced down the pain of Master Eremis' implicit rejection. She continued to function, which meant that she spent as much time as possible with Geraden – talking, trying to understand. Nevertheless the knowledge that she didn't have anything better to do, anything more constructive to offer, wore on her constantly. She couldn't shake free of a gray depression that took the edge off everything she thought and felt; her behavior resembled her former existence more than anything she had done since she had come to Orison. As a result, her conversations with Geraden were like many of the sessions she had had with Reverend Thatcher. But now the underlying futility was on her side rather than on anyone else's.

She had lost her fragile sense of purpose, of direction. The conclusions she was occasionally tempted to draw from the appearance in the Congery's augury of the riders of her dream had never seemed so foolish. She had no reason for being where she was. And she didn't seem able to invent one. The real point of her long conversations with Geraden was not to shed any light into the dark corners of her situation, but rather to keep him with her, so that he wouldn't fade from her life like Master Eremis.

So while snow as sharp and brittle as ice rattled against her windows and lorn wind keened past the edges of the tower and all Orison seemed to fall into a kind of static calm, frozen not by peace but by waiting, she did essentially nothing except eat, sleep, and sit in her rooms, talking with the Apt whenever he got free of his duties.

He brought her news from around Orison. The Masters were involved in a fierce and apparently endless debate, trying to decide what to do about their champion – and about their own vulnerability. Castellan Lebbick's guards and every stonemason available were busy using the rubble of the champion's departure to build a wall across the breach in Orison's side. And Argus and Ribuld were doing what they could to keep an eye on the lady Elega.

The rest of the time, Terisa and Geraden talked about their circumstances. On his side, this meant fighting a steady but subdued, almost covert struggle to raise her spirits. As if he knew that any despondency in him could hurt her, he practiced good cheer. As if he knew that the sore places in her weren't ready to be touched, he preserved a tactful emotional distance. As if he knew that she wasn't strong enough to be pushed, he urged nothing. With a delicate gentleness that made his physical mishaps look like they belonged to a completely separate person, he cared for her.

Even though he needed care himself and wasn't getting it. His enemies were as savage as hers, wanted him dead as badly – and for as little reason. But if he was afraid, he kept his fear to himself.

At one point, he asked rather wistfully, 'Did you feel anything at the translation point? Could you tell it was there?'

A touch of cold as thin as a feather and as sharp as steel. That was something she didn't want to talk about; it frightened her too badly. 'It was so cold down there, and I was so scared. Just before those' – she shivered involuntarily – 'those men appeared, I seemed to get even colder and more scared.' She already knew that she was never going to mention it to Master Eremis. 'That's probably all it was.'

He looked at her hard before glancing away.

'What about you?' she countered. 'That would explain a lot. If you have that kind of talent, and Master Gilbur got a hint of it while he was teaching you, we would at least have an explanation for why you were attacked.'

He rolled his eyes at the ceiling. 'Wouldn't that be fun? I would love an explanation. But all I can remember is thinking that it was a silly idea. I was dragging you and Artagel around in the cold and damp for an empty theory. I didn't even see the translation start.'

She sighed morosely.

Several times, they both returned to the matter of their strange session with Adept Havelock. 'What was all that about, do you suppose?' he wondered. 'Why did he want to tell you all that? Why those specific details?'

She had no idea. 'He's crazy. Maybe what he calls "lucidity" just means he's able to put a few sentences together in order.'

But that explanation didn't satisfy either of them. Eventually, an old resolve crumbled, and she found herself telling him about her first night in Orison. She described how Adept Havelock had fetched her to his chamber, what Master Quillon had told her of Mordant's history, and how the Adept had saved her from the man in black.

He listened in mingled astonishment and incomprehension. When she was done, he breathed, 'They already knew. The first night you were here, they already knew you were in danger. Master Quillon has been busy.' He scowled wryly. 'If you told the rest of the Congery about this, they wouldn't believe it. Master *Quillon*? Trying to change what happens to anyone?' Then he said more seriously, 'At least now we know who my enemies are. Master Gilbur and arch-Imager Vagel.'

She nodded. She could feel herself sinking deeper into gloom.

He didn't let the idea of his enemies dismay him, however. Smiling, he said, 'There's one advantage to all this, anyway. Now I know how you feel. You don't understand what everybody thinks you can do. I don't understand why men like that think highly enough of me to consider me worth killing.'

She was too despondent to be amused. 'I want to know whose side Master Quillon and Adept Havelock are on. Not the King's. Not the Congery's. Not Master Gilbur's.' She could have also said, Not Master Eremis'.

How many sides *were* there?

But that brought them back to their encounter with the Adept – and to the presumed hints hidden in what he had said. Finally, she decided to give up another of her few remaining secrets. She was committed to him – not because she knew what she was doing, but because he was her friend. And Master Eremis didn't want her. There would be no harm in telling Geraden about Myste.

He listened in close silence. As she explained Myste's reasons for going after the champion, he held his head up like a salute, and tears stood in his eyes. When she was finished, he remained silent for a long moment before murmuring gruffly, 'I always liked her.

'Of course,' he added, 'I know Elega better. And Torrent is so sweet she makes you want to lie down on the floor for her to stand on so her feet won't get cold. King Joyse doesn't have any unattractive daughters. But Myste—' His voice trailed away.

Begging him not to kill her. Terisa felt like crying herself.

Early in the morning of the fifth day, however, she was awakened from a thin, unrestful sleep by the sound of rain.

Groggy with sleep and surprise, she climbed out of bed and went to the nearest window.

For a moment, she was baffled because she couldn't see any rain. In fact, the sky was completely free of clouds. The early sun cast a genial light over the walls and battlements, and the heavens were a vital blue, shaded closer to purple than azure. The distant hills seemed softer under their thick robes of snow, and the crooked bulk of Orison looked considerably more picturesque than it had the previous day, more like a grand castle in a fairy tale.

Then she realized that the sound came from the melting of the snow.

Water ran thickly from the roofs and towers, streamed off the eaves like a downpour. Already, the courtyard resembled a quagmire: its churned mud lay hidden beneath brown puddles as vast as ponds. Guards and people bustling in and out of the courtyard, to and from the huddled maze of shops and shanties and tents, had to wear cloaks against the runoff and high boots against the standing water; but under the open sky they pushed back their cloaks or doffed them altogether to revel in the new warmth.

The winter had turned to thaw.

A little thrill ran through her as she thought she might get a chance to go outside for a while. It might be possible to stop feeling depressed for a while.

Hurrying, she went to wash her face and put on her clothes.

She wasn't surprised when Geraden arrived before Saddith had brought her breakfast. His cheeks were flushed with exertion, and he was breathing hard. He must have run up the stairs. At first glance, she thought he was simply eager, caught up in a stronger version of her own reaction. But the way his eyes shone was more complex than that.

'Have you seen it?' he panted as soon as she shut the door.

'Yes.'

They went to the windows together, drawn by the prospect of sun and warmth and springtime after the long, tense winter.

'Glass and splinters,' he muttered while he regained his breath, 'this is awful.'

She blinked at him like a startled owl. 'Awful?'

At once, he started laughing. 'Isn't that silly? I feel this eager every spring. Like the whole world is coming back to life. The first thaw always makes me want to go out and play like a boy.

'But it's still awful. Even though I love it.' He tried to sound somber. 'Terisa, this is *very* bad news.'

His laughter drew a smile from her. 'It's a good thing I've known you so long. If you were a stranger, I would have to assume you've lost your mind. *Why* is this bad news?'

'You mean, since you know me, you don't have to *assume* I've lost my mind? You can take it for granted?' He dismissed her protest with a chortle. 'Because it's early. Too early. Right now, winter is about the only thing protecting us. If too much of the snow melts, there won't be anything to prevent Cadwal and even Alend from marching against us *today*.

'You heard what the Perdon said. High King Festten has already mustered an army. He can do that because Cadwal gets so much less snow than we do. And you can be sure the Alend Monarch didn't send his son on a mission as dangerous as a visit to Orison without having an army prepared to support or rescue him. Or avenge him.

'We're the only ones who aren't ready,' he continued. 'Oh, I'm sure Castellan Lebbick has done everything he can. But we didn't get ready for war last autumn because King Joyse refused to command it' – now Geraden managed to sound grim – 'and we aren't ready now because he hasn't been paying attention all winter. Our only hope has been that the snow would last until he came back to his senses.'

Terisa frowned in an effort to concentrate. 'If they start marching today, who's going to get here first?'

Unable to preserve an appropriately dire expression, he flashed a grin. 'That's complicated. Cadwal is closer, especially if they march up through Perdon from the southeast. Alend's best route comes almost due south through the Care of Armigite. That's nearly twice as far.

'But South Perdon is mostly hills, some of them rugged. Armigite is almost all lowland. To reach us, the High King's army has to cross two rivers, the Vertigon and the Broadwine. The Alends only have to ford the Pestil. And the Perdon will fight Cadwal every step of the way. The Armigite, on the other hand—' Geraden sighed. 'We would be lucky, I guess, if he fired a few catapults at Margonal's army while it went by.'

Although the air outside was obviously much warmer than it had been, it wasn't balmy: when he leaned close to the window, his words left small, brief ovals of condensation on the glass. 'But it's even more complicated than that. How long has Prince Kragen been gone? Six days? I presume he's riding hard, but he won't be able to go very fast. Not even today. This much snow will take days to melt off. So he's still a long way from home. Will the Alend Monarch do anything without him? I don't know.

'Giving you my utmost wisdom' – he grimaced – 'I would say at this point anything can happen. With our luck, it probably will.'

'Well, that's all right,' she murmured. '"Anything" is what's been happening ever since I got here.'

He responded with a chuckle and a bow. 'My lady, you have an enviable gift for understatement.' Then he added, 'We're probably lucky. If it stopped happening, we might get confused.'

'Speak for yourself,' she replied. 'Confusion is my natural state.' She feigned puzzlement. 'Or I *think* so, anyway.'

He laughed. 'A kindred spirit. No wonder I like you.'

Gazing out at the thaw, he sighed happily, 'This really is terrible.'

Sometime later, there was a knock on the door.

'I am sorry to be late, my lady,' Saddith said as she entered the room carrying a large breakfast tray. 'The guards told me that Apt Geraden was with you – already.' She winked. 'So I went back for more food.'

Feeling light-headed and impervious to discomfort because of the thaw, Terisa asked foolishly, 'How is Master Eremis this morning?'

Saddith glanced down at her tight bosom. 'He has been very busy. Or so it is rumored. But he is well.' When she looked up, her face wore a deliberate veil of blandness, but the corner of her mouth quirked. 'Or so it is rumored.'

Terisa realized that she didn't feel quite as cheerful as she thought.

Geraden watched her with a quizzical expression; however, he made no comment. He had apparently decided that he didn't want to know what her present relationship with the Master was.

When the maid had left, Terisa tried to recover her good humor by eating a big breakfast. Nevertheless her mood had turned restless. She wanted to *do* something, wanted to go as far away from this room – and from herself – as she could. Abruptly, she demanded, 'Let's get out of here. Today. This morning.'

He stared at her with his mouth full. 'Get out? You already know I can't—'

'I didn't mean that. I meant, out of this room. Out of Orison. Outside.' Trying to make sense, she urged, 'Maybe we could rent some horses. I don't know how to ride, but you could teach me. Anything. I just want to *get out* for a while.'

He struggled to understand. 'I'll do anything you want. What is "rent"?'

For no very admirable reason, she thought it might be fun to scream at him. Or maybe not *fun*, exactly. Maybe *satisfying*?

Fortuitously, someone chose that moment to knock at her door.

Swallowing her baser impulses, she called, 'Come in.'

On command, a guard opened the door formally and announced, 'The lady Elega.' Then he stepped aside and bowed the King's eldest daughter into the room.

She was dressed as if for an excursion in a warm, high-collared fur robe and ornately tooled leather boots.

Geraden jumped to his feet. Instinctively, Terisa did the same.

Elega studied both of them. 'I am sorry,' she said with an ironic smile. 'I did not mean to frighten you.'

'Guilty secrets,' Geraden replied promptly. 'You know me, my lady.' His smile was no more innocent than hers. 'I'm always plotting something.'

The lady measured him with a glance. Then she turned to Terisa. 'Whatever he plots, Terisa,' she said, 'I hope you will not let him entangle you in it. I do not know what he has in mind, of course. But surely he plots in the same way he does everything else.' She grinned around the word: 'Notoriously.'

In response, Geraden bowed. 'You're too kind, my lady.'

Instead of shouting, Cut it out! Terisa asked Elega, 'Would you like some breakfast?'

'Thank you, no.' The King's daughter accepted the change of subject smoothly. She comported herself as though she were ready for anything. 'I have breakfasted. What I would like – if it would please you – is to take you shopping.'

Shopping? Terisa gaped helplessly, struck as much by the familiarity of the word as by the strangeness of hearing it from Elega.

'I fear it will not be a very elegant experience. Because of the mud,' explained the lady. 'But this thaw is wonderful. If it lasts as much as a day or two, it will open the roads around Orison enough to permit the merchants to replenish their stores. This late in the winter, the shops have become too depleted to be worth visiting. Now they may be resupplied.

'Terisa, I would like to take you to buy cloth and engage a seamster, so that you can have clothes made' – she hesitated almost imperceptibly – 'to your own fit and fashion.'

'Clothes?'

'Whatever clothes you like. Of course,' said Elega firmly, 'I will offer you advice as to weather and custom. But what I wish is to help you please yourself.'

'But' – it was the first thought that came to her – 'I don't have any money.'

The lady raised a delicate eyebrow in surprise. 'You are a friend of the King's daughter. Why do you need money?'

Terisa couldn't find the words to protest. Fortunately, Geraden was sensitive to the particular character of her ignorance. 'The lady Elega is right,' he said, supplying more reassurance than the situation superficially required. 'As long as you're with her, any merchant or artisan in Mordant will give you anything you want. That's one of the privileges of the ruling family.

'It isn't actually fair.' His tone reminded her that most of his friendships were among the workers of Orison, rather than among the lords and ladies. 'But the way King Joyse runs the country puts more wealth back than it takes out, so his privileges don't do any harm.' He seemed to be urging her to accept Elega's offer.

She made an effort to collect her scattered wits. Really, she ought to be accustomed to surprises by now. They were becoming the story of her life. And when she thought about it, she found that she was excited.

'Thanks,' she said to the lady. 'That sounds like fun. I was just telling Geraden I wanted to get out of this room. I'm about to start screaming.'

Elega smiled. 'I know just what you mean. I have felt that way for years at a time. When would you like to go?'

Terisa glanced at Geraden, but his features were composed into a neutral mask. 'How about right now?'

'That suits me admirably.' Elega looked pleased.

'If you will take my advice from the start, however,' she continued, 'you will change your garments before we go. The seamsters who serve the ladies of Orison are accustomed to gowns. I suspect that they have scant acquaintance with' – she searched for a graceful description – 'the styles of your world. If you wear a gown and carry your own clothing with you, you will be able to leave it for the seamster to use as a pattern. Then they should be able to match it.'

Although Terisa wasn't at all sure that she wanted shirts and pants instead of gowns, Elega's advice seemed too reasonable to ignore. 'Just give me a minute.' From the wardrobe in the bedroom, she quickly fetched her demure gray gown. Then she retreated to the bathroom to change.

'Dress warmly,' Elega called. 'And be prepared for mud.'

As soon as she had worked her way into the gown, Terisa located the thick sheepskin coat and boots that Geraden had supplied for her tour of Orison's battlements. In a few moments, she was ready to go. She carried her old clothes under her coat. Her heart was beating like a schoolgirl's.

'Will you accompany us, Geraden?' inquired Elega. 'I doubt that choosing fabrics and studying styles will be of much interest to you. But it is unwise for ladies to go unescorted to the shops.' To Terisa, she explained, 'Despite Castellan Lebbick's best efforts, the bazaar attracts any number of rude fellows – pickthieves, gypsies, clowns, and ruffians. The guards maintain good order, but they cannot prevent all small crimes.' Then she addressed Geraden again. 'If you would like an escape from your routine duties, I will be happy to pretend that I have commanded your attendance.'

'Again you are too kind, my lady.' Behind his deference, he was laughing. 'But the King's daughter's pretense is probably as good as a command. I'll go with you, of course.'

Elega smiled at him as though he were an amiable child. 'Then perhaps you should get a coat.'

He was taken aback: he seemed almost suspicious, as if he thought the lady might have some ulterior motive. He swallowed his concern, however. 'That's a good idea. Which door are you going to use? I'll catch up with you.'

She told him.

Bowing to Terisa, he left.

Brightly, Elega asked, 'Shall we go?'

Terisa wasn't sure what she was doing as she followed the King's daughter out of the room.

Chatting easily about trivial subjects, Elega led her around through Orison to the northwest end of the castle. Along the way, she spotted Ribuld and Argus. The two guards were loitering in the hall as if they were off watch and had no better use for their time.

Her eagerness began to change color. What had started as a simple case of spring fever was becoming yet another gambit in the plots and schemes that surrounded Mordant's need.

She accepted this. At the moment, all she really wanted was to *get out* of her recent depression.

Then she and Elega reached a door that gave access to the courtyard. With its massive timbers and thick iron bolts, it was made to be sealed; but it was open, and its guards stood outside, watching the crowd that spilled out of Orison to swirl and mill around the shops and tents.

Geraden was already there: he had been running again. Now, however, he had a coat to keep him warm.

Just for a second, his face showed a relief he couldn't conceal. Apparently, one of his fears had been proved groundless. Then he greeted the two women with a smile.

Terisa inhaled the springlike air deeply and plunged with her companions through the downpour from the eaves out into the mud.

Once again, she was struck by the size of the courtyard. Hidden in its own shadow, the eastern edifice of the castle was dark against the fathomless blue sky; but to the west Orison's whole inward face held the sun and reflected the browns and grays of its stones, making the atmosphere around her warmer than the weather. In this light, the erratic pile of the castle seemed protective, rising high on all sides to keep what it enclosed safe. Windows caught the sunlight and flashed; from oriels and poles and projections among the balconies and walkways, clotheslines had been strung, and drying laundry decorated the walls in particolor; up on the towers, pennons made tiny by distance fluttered and gleamed.

The mud wasn't as bad as she had expected. In this end of the courtyard, away from the area where the guards exercised their horses, gravel had been strewn over the dirt. That didn't solve the problem, but it did make the inevitable muck less deep and cloying. The hem of her gown became soaked and stained immediately, but she was able to walk with unanticipated ease.

Doubtless inspired by their own species of spring fever, the people of the courtyard had flung wide the wooden fronts of their shops, decked their tents with ribbons, brought out carts loaded with refreshments which no one would have braved the cold to enjoy yesterday. They had put on their gay clothes and declared the day a spontaneous festival. Terisa heard the music of pipes and lutes punctuated by tambourines. Somewhere, there was probably dancing. Cooking smells and spices followed the tang of wood-smoke which drifted along the slight breeze from tin chimneys in the roofs of wooden structures, from smoke holes at the tops of tents, and from open fires crackling frequently in the gaps between the buildings.

For no reason except that she suddenly felt wonderful, she began laughing.

Geraden shared her mood. And Elega smiled, although the assessing quality of her gaze suggested that her pleasure was more complex. Terisa grinned at both of them and made an effort not to hurry.

'Here!' Passing among the shops and the crowds, Geraden presumed on his apparent stature as a *friend of the King's daughter* to dash over to a cart and capture some of its wares, which were charred chunks of meat on long cane sticks. 'This is my favorite food in the whole world.' The vendor bowed again and again like a bobbing cork as Geraden carried his booty triumphantly back to Terisa and Elega. 'It's called "treasure of Domne." The meat is just lamb, but it's basted with a sauce that will melt your heart.' With a flourish, he offered a stick to each of his companions. 'Eat! And grieve that you weren't born in the Care of Domne.'

'I think,' Elega murmured without malice, 'we would be more likely to grieve if we *were* born in the Care of Domne.'

Juice ran down Terisa's chin as she bit into the tender meat. It was spiced like nothing she had ever tasted before. Stale coriander? Cumin that hadn't been stored properly? For Geraden's sake, she finished the piece she had in her mouth, then tried to think of an excuse not to eat the rest. Luckily, he savored the treat so much himself that he was temporarily deaf and blind to his companions. Elega deftly handed her stick to the nearest passerby. After a momentary hesitation, Terisa did the same. A bit self-consciously, she wiped her chin.

She and Elega walked on. The crowd made too much noise for quiet conversation. People were laughing gaily, shouting rowdy encouragements and insults at each other, greeting friends and hawking merchandise. But she didn't want to talk – she wanted to see everything and absorb it all. The loud bustle seemed entirely unlike the frenetic activity of the city streets with which she was familiar. These people weren't thinking about making fortunes or losing their jobs or fighting off muggers or being evicted from their homes. And they also weren't thinking about war with Cadwal and Alend, the ethics of Imagery, or their King's inexplicable decline. Their minds were on more important things.

Geraden rejoined her, grinning a little foolishly. With Elega, they took the path of least resistance through the throng.

Everything here had been set down or built up unsystematically, without a thought to such questions as ease of access or advantageous display – and with very little concern for sanitation. Apparently Castellan Lebbick's authority didn't entirely rule this little village which had sprung up to serve the demands of Orison. Rickety wooden buildings that looked too tall for their underpinnings, and too hastily hammered together to be more than semi-permanent, leaned against each other, often making it difficult for prospective buyers to find the entrances to the shops. Some of the tents assertively overfilled the available space, with the result that they couldn't be passed except by squatting under or straddling over the ropes. Cooking fires sent up sparks dangerously close to weathered planks and dry canvas. Terisa was jostled so frequently that she began to be glad she wasn't carrying any money.

Around one corner, she and her companions came upon a mountebank selling nostrums from a brightly painted wagon. His shirt was several sizes too small for him; his trousers, far too large. And both had been worn to tatters. But he had made a virtue of necessity by tying himself up from neck to ankles in ribbons of all colors, so that his tatters looked like a deliberate part of his costume. His mustache was as tangled as his hair, which had the added attraction of being streaked with ash. More ash stained his swarthy skin; his eyes rolled feverishly.

His nostrums were contained in crooked little glass bottles, large and uneven clay pots, and baskets woven of reeds. He advertised them with a high-pitched cry like the whine of a halfwit. If he had worn a red sign around his neck that said CHARLATAN, he would have appeared no less reliable than he did now. Large numbers of people showed interest in his wares, but he didn't seem to have many buyers.

'Where does somebody like that *come* from?' Terisa asked Elega. 'I can't believe he sells enough to keep himself alive.'

'You have never been beyond the walls of Orison.' The lady's tone and expression were cool: she obviously didn't share Terisa's curiosity. 'Do not let your experiences among us paint a false picture. Away from the Demesne – and, to a lesser extent, from the principal cities of the Cares – Mordant's people include a predictable number of simpletons and gulls. Fellows such as this often live better than you might guess.'

Nevertheless Terisa thought the man was fascinating. In fact, she found him more fascinating than she could explain. Something about the way he rolled his eyes and leered made her suspect that he knew what he was doing – that there was cunning in his performance. Was it all an act? Did he disarm suspicion by making himself so plainly untrustworthy?

Her companions wanted to go on, however. After a moment, she let them draw her away.

Shortly, Elega raised her voice and pointed. 'All the fabric and tailor shops are there. They have been set almost one on top of the other. It is not usually a quiet place. I think they are often more interested in stealing custom from each other than in attracting buyers. But they will restrain themselves as long as I am with you.'

Terisa was tempted to reply, You seem to have that effect on everybody. She bit her tongue, however, and said nothing.

They passed a cart selling what looked like fried bread. Another offered the sort of trinkets that a guard might buy for a serving girl. In an open area where no one had yet built a shop or pitched a tent, a juggler in a voluminous black robe handled sharp, silver pieces of metal shaped like stars as if they were plates or ninepins. His robe whipped and spun around him like a whirl of midnight. Then Terisa and her escorts were near enough to the tailors and cloth merchants to see swaths of material draped invitingly out windows and over doors, and to hear men with measuring tapes around their necks and pins stuck in their clothing haggling over the passersby.

Suddenly, Geraden let out a yelp of surprise and pleasure and took off at a run, splashing mud.

Terisa and Elega stared after him. 'I swear to you, Terisa,' the lady said, 'that man becomes more like a boy every year.' Despite her tone, she looked perplexed – perhaps even a little worried. 'Surely he knows that it is neither courteous nor wise to abandon us?'

Terisa watched him dodging recklessly through the crowd and held her breath, afraid that he would fall. But he didn't. Instead, he came to a stop as suddenly as he had started.

'Let's go see what he's doing.' Without waiting for agreement, she headed in that direction.

Elega sighed audibly and joined her.

Geraden hadn't gone far. They found him with another man, who appeared to be considerably less than delighted by the fact that Geraden had spotted him.

'Terisa,' the Apt announced as she and Elega reached him, 'this is my brother Nyle.'

Then he began babbling.

'Artagel told me you were here, but I almost didn't believe him. I haven't been able to find you. Where have you been hiding? It's great to see you. Why are you here? The last I heard, you were in Houseldon for the winter. You were trying to talk yourself out of – well, never mind that. Is everyone all right? How is Father? And Tholden? How about—'

'Let him answer, Geraden,' chided Elega firmly. 'I am sure he did not come out of "hiding," as you call it, specifically so that you could drive him to distraction.'

With an effort, Geraden cut off his rush of words.

Unabashedly curious, Terisa studied Nyle. She would have known him as Geraden's brother anywhere. He had Geraden's hair and coloring, Geraden's build, only an inch less than Geraden's height. And he would have had Geraden's face, if his features hadn't been set for brooding instead of openheartedness. He looked like a discontented version of his younger brother, a man whose basically serious nature had curdled.

It was clear that he took no joy in meeting Geraden.

Stiffly, he bowed to the two women. 'My lady Elega.' He and Elega didn't look at each other. 'My lady Terisa. I'm glad to meet you' – Terisa heard no pleasure in his voice – 'even though my brother hasn't bothered to introduce us.'

Geraden started to apologize, but Nyle cut him off. 'You haven't been able to find me because I've been busy with my private affairs.' He glared at Geraden, and his tone was acid. 'They don't have anything to do with you, so there's no reason why you should be involved in them.'

'What do you mean, "private affairs"?' snorted Geraden. 'I'm your *brother*. You don't *have* private affairs. Even Stead' – he laughed shortly – 'doesn't have private affairs, and he needs them more than you do. Half the husbands in Domne flinch every time he walks into the room. What can you possibly be doing that doesn't involve your own family?'

A muscle in Nyle's cheek twitched; however, he kept the rest of his face still. Turning from Geraden, he bowed again to Terisa and Elega. 'My ladies, I hope you enjoy your outing. We're lucky to have this weather.'

With his shoulders squared and his back rigid, he strode away between the shops.

Terisa shot a look at Geraden. His face was knotted: for an instant, he seemed on the verge of chasing after his brother, shouting something. Then he swung toward Elega. 'My lady' – he bit down to keep his voice steady – 'is this your doing?'

She wasn't taken aback by the accusation. Watching Nyle's departing figure vividly, she murmured, 'It may have something to do with me. I should speak to him. Excuse me.'

Pulling up her skirts, she hurried after him.

Geraden moved to follow. Instinctively, Terisa put a hand on his arm.

Hadn't she heard Elega mention Nyle once? When was that? Oh, yes. When Elega first took her to meet Myste. *Nyle is more to my taste.* Geraden looked at her to see why she had restrained him; she asked, 'How could it be her doing?'

Elega caught up with Nyle and stopped him. Their faces couldn't be seen clearly: too many people intervened, moving in both directions. And of course what they said was inaudible.

Distantly, Geraden replied, 'He's been nursing a passion for her for years, but he thinks it's hopeless. He thinks—' He frowned in vexation. 'I don't understand it. He thinks he isn't grand or special enough for her. He hasn't done anything dramatic in the world. He knows she's ambitious, and he's sure she won't have him. I think it galls him that *I* was the one who was betrothed to her – and I let her get away.

'He told us he was going to stay in Houseldon all winter to talk himself out of asking for her hand.'

'So you think he came to Orison to see if she'll have him?'

Geraden nodded. His face was tight with empathy. 'But I guess he hasn't asked her yet. If he did, and she turned him down, he wouldn't stick around. So she must have done something to hurt him before he got his courage nailed down tightly enough to actually propose. He can't leave because he hasn't done what he came for. But he's in too much pain to do it.

'Blast her.' He glanced at Terisa. 'I'm guessing, of course. But look at them. Whatever it is, she knows what's eating at him.'

The glimpses Terisa caught through the crowd seemed to confirm Geraden's opinion. Elega was talking to Nyle – pleading with him? – as though she knew what to say. And his answers – brusque as they were – suggested understanding, even approval.

Because she didn't know how to comfort Geraden, Terisa changed the subject. 'What did you think of that mountebank? The man in the ribbons and tatters.'

At first, Nyle and Elega held Geraden's attention. With an effort, however, he dragged his gaze back to Terisa. 'What did you say? I didn't hear you.'

'The mountebank we passed a little while ago. What did you think of him?'

'Think of him? Nothing special. Why?'

She could see the difference when he actually *looked* at her. 'Just curious,' she said casually. 'Something about him—'

Another characteristic of Geraden's that she liked was his willingness to accept her whims. He wracked his memory, then said, 'I haven't seen him before. I wonder why. He doesn't look young enough to be new at this.'

'Well, he isn't exactly old,' she began. 'He—'

A moment later, the truth struck her.

'He looks familiar.' That was why she found him so interesting. 'I *have* seen him before.'

Geraden stared at her. 'You what?'

'I've *seen* him somewhere,' she insisted. 'I'm sure of it. But not like this. He's in disguise.'

'Where was that?' Geraden was instantly ready to believe her. 'Was it the man who attacked you?'

Gart? 'No.' She closed her eyes and tried to calm her excitement. 'It's not him.' But the hints and pieces didn't come together. 'I don't know. Somewhere.' The more she pictured the mountebank, the less familiar he looked. 'I can't remember.'

'Don't try to force it. The quicker you forget about it, the quicker it'll come to you.' Then he added, 'And thanks.'

She shook her head. 'Thanks for what?'

He nodded toward Elega and Nyle. 'I needed the distraction.'

As Terisa looked in that direction, Nyle moved off into the throng and Elega returned to her companions.

Her determined smile and veiled gaze made it clear at once that she had no intention of revealing what had passed between her and Nyle. 'I am sorry I kept you waiting,' she said before either Terisa or Geraden could speak. 'The best of the cloth shops is just over there. Shall we go?'

Taking their acquiescence for granted, she started toward the shop.

Geraden met Terisa's eyes behind Elega's back and shrugged. The twist of his mouth suggested regret rather than anger. After all, this wasn't his first experience with the King's eldest daughter. He seemed to know the trick of not being offended by what she did.

He and Terisa followed her together.

As they approached the fabric and tailor shops, the noise rose to a din. The merchants there fought over possible customers so aggressively that Terisa would never have considered approaching them if she had been alone. The lady Elega wasn't in the least disconcerted, however. Smiling good-naturedly, she walked into the midst of the shopkeepers and said without raising her voice, 'Good sirs, you do not need this raucous display. You know that I am not persuaded by it.' Her tone was mild but sure. 'Perhaps you will indulge me with a bit more moderation.'

Almost immediately, quiet spread out around her as people saw who she was and nudged their neighbors.

In response, Elega inclined her head graciously – a gesture that made Geraden roll his eyes. Nevertheless Terisa saw that the deference of the shopkeepers was perfectly serious. The King's daughter's patronage must have been well worth what it cost.

Selecting a shop, Elega sailed toward it as if she were leading a fleet. Like many of the wooden structures, this one was built up a bit so that its flooring didn't rest in the mud. A few apparently reliable steps led to a narrow porch that inspired less confidence; then an open door gave admittance to the small room where the merchant showed his wares.

Most of the room's light came from unglassed windows with their shutters pushed aside, but a brazier in the center of the floor provided some warmth. Scurrying ahead of Elega, the shopkeeper stationed himself behind a counter and began to murmur obsequious enthusiasm for her presence.

Aside from the brazier and the counter, the room was empty. Bare planking without shelves formed the walls. In fact, there was no cloth to be seen in the shop, apart from the swaths hanging out the windows and over the porch.

Elega greeted this fact with equanimity. 'I see that I have come to the right place.'

The shopkeeper was bold enough to say, 'You have, my lady. All my winter stock is sold. I have nothing left except my samples.'

'I take that as testimony to the quality of your goods.'

He bowed in humble pride. 'But I will have everything you wish as soon as the roads are open,' he added quickly.

'Very good. Let us see your samples.' Elega indicated her companions. 'The lady Terisa of Morgan needs to improve her wardrobe.'

'At once, my lady.'

From beneath the counter, the man started producing long, thin strips of cloth which he spread out for inspection.

Geraden cleared his throat. 'With your permission, my lady,' he said to Elega, 'I'll leave you for a while. My opinions aren't likely to be much help. And if anybody troubles you while you're choosing cloth or talking to tailors, every merchant in the area will leap to your defense.'

'Leave Nyle alone,' Elega replied by way of assent. 'I think he is in no mood to be pestered by his family today.' Then she chose two or three of the strips and showed them to Terisa.

'What do you think of these?'

Only Terisa noticed the Apt's bow as he left the shop.

Trying to sound casual, she took this opportunity to ask Elega, 'Did you know Nyle was in Orison? Geraden was surprised to hear it.'

'No. Why?' Elega's disinterest was nearly flawless. 'I should have been more surprised than he was. I did not know Nyle was here until we saw him. But I fear I am losing the ability to be surprised by anything the sons of the Domne do.'

Terisa shrugged. 'I just thought you might have seen him around. You mentioned him to me once. I got the impression you liked him.'

'I do.' Elega was better at nonchalance than Terisa was. 'I consider him a friend. And I respect him. He has a – a seriousness of mind? – no, a seriousness of *desire* which his brothers apparently lack. It is inconceivable, for instance, that he would spend Geraden's years trying and failing to become an Imager. And it is also inconceivable that he would learn Artagel's skills and then refuse to use them – as Artagel has refused – to rise in command of the King's guards.

'There was a time,' she admitted, 'when if he had expressed an interest in my hand I would have taken him as seriously as he took me.' She spoke without any noticeable concern for the shopkeeper's presence. 'Still, I did not know that he had come to Orison. His "private affairs" – whatever they may be have nothing to do with me.'

'I was just curious.' Lamely, Terisa turned her attention to the question of fabrics.

Elega proved to have a good eye. The materials she selected for consideration were excellent – some warm twills and light poplins for everyday wear, some fine silks and velvets for formal occasions – and the colors she advised were right for Terisa's hair and eyes and skin. Soon Terisa had the ten samples she liked best arranged in front of her. She was trying to pick one or two (or three?) when Elega said to the shopkeeper, 'These will be enough at present. As soon as the material arrives, deliver it to Mindlin the seamster. He will tell you how much he needs.'

'Certainly, my lady. With pleasure.' The prospect of supplying enough free cloth to make ten outfits didn't appear to distress him.

Terisa herself was too astonished to protest. *Ten* new outfits? What was she going to do with *ten* new outfits?

Elega seemed to enjoy the look on Terisa's face. 'Come,' she said with a smile. 'Mindlin has always made my clothes. I am sure he will be glad to do the same for you.'

'Without question, my lady,' the shopkeeper put in, 'without question. An outstanding choice, if I may say so. Mindlin's work is superb. Superb. I'll provide him these fabrics the instant they arrive.'

Bestowing a nod, the lady drew Terisa out of the shop.

Mindlin's establishment was nearby. If anything, it was even less elaborate or pretentious than the fabric shop. Mindlin himself was a tall man with sunken gray cheeks and an austere manner, and he spoke in a haughty tone which seemed to come out of a different mouth than the subservient words he actually uttered. In fact, the content of his speech was so fawning that even Elega was embarrassed. 'Unfortunately,' she explained to Terisa, 'he has become wealthy on the strength of his reputation as my seamster.'

Terisa was unable to suppress a grin.

Embarrassment, however, didn't cost Elega her command of the situation. Briskly, she told Mindlin what materials would be supplied to him, and by whom. Then she asked Terisa, 'What would you like?'

For a moment, Terisa's imagination was paralyzed. 'I've never had clothes made for me before.'

'Then the experience will be good for you,' Elega replied with satisfaction. She thought briefly, then informed Mindlin that the lady Terisa needed two formal gowns, two warm winter gowns, two lighter ones for spring, and – she gave him the bundle of Terisa's old clothes – four outfits made on that unfamiliar pattern, again two for winter and two for spring. She also specified which fabric should be used in each case – a test of memory that would have defeated Terisa.

'But you must choose the details,' she told Terisa, 'unless you wish to abandon yourself to Mindlin's taste. There is no hurry, however, if you are unsure. He will bring you his work well before it is complete, so that it can be fitted properly. You will have that opportunity to discuss the way your skirts hang, or the amount of lace and finery you wish to display, or even' – she indicated ironic tolerance for the foibles of woman – 'the degree of décolletage that interests you.'

'That would be nice,' Terisa said, feeling shy as well as excited.

'Then I will leave you in his hands,' Elega announced smoothly. There seemed to be a hint of anticipation in the way she started toward the door.

At the idea of having to face this situation by herself, Terisa went into a schoolgirl's panic. 'Where are you going? Aren't you going to stay with me?'

The lady beamed reassurance. 'I must do a few trifling errands of my own.

And I have already tried to make too many of your decisions. I will return – almost at once. If I do not, wait for me here. I will be with you soon.'

Before Terisa could protest further, Elega was gone.

Terisa wanted to run after the lady. She felt suddenly alone in a hostile world. She had so many questions. How was Mindlin going to measure her? Was she expected to disrobe right here in his shop? How could she?

To make matters worse, the seamster's demeanor changed immediately. His manner became less austere: he even went so far as to attempt a ghastly smile. At the same time, the subservience dropped out of his speech. Holding up her clothes disdainfully, he asked, 'Does my lady seriously intend to wear such garments?'

Reduced by alarm – and by echoes of her father's sarcasm – to feeling like a child, she was on the verge of blurting out, No, of course not, not if you don't think it's a good idea, what do you recommend? Fortunately, she caught herself in time. Really, she ought to be ashamed of herself. Hadn't she already stood up to Castellan Lebbick more than once? And now she was going to let herself be driven to drivel by a *seamster*?

With a conscious effort, she raised her eyes to meet his, and as she did so her spirits also rose. Smiling, she asked, 'What's wrong with them?'

His expression looked suspiciously like a sneer. 'They are not flattering, my lady. Not womanly.'

'Do you think so? Where I come from, they're considered' – she rolled the word around in her mouth and realized that she could have fun doing this – 'delectable.'

Mindlin seemed shocked. She suspected he was afraid of having misjudged her meekness. The haughtiness in his face came up as the self-assertion in his voice went down. 'As my lady wishes. I will certainly work to the best of my humble abilities to please her.'

There was no question about it: she could have fun doing this. She didn't want to overdo it, however. 'But you're probably right,' she said as though he had persuaded her. 'I don't need four outfits like that. Two should be enough.' In a flash of inspiration, she added, 'Why don't you use the rest of the material to make me two riding habits?'

'Riding habits?' Suppressed apoplexy constricted his tone. 'Does my lady intend to go riding? On horseback?'

'Of course,' she answered sweetly. 'Where I come from, all the ladies do it. Don't you know how to make clothes like that?'

He dropped his gaze. 'I am not accustomed to make such garments for women of rank. But I will do as my lady wishes.'

'Good.' She was starting to feel inordinately proud of herself.

Still studying the floor instead of her face, he said, 'If it pleases my lady, I will take a measure from these' – his fingers twitched her shirt and pants – 'and return them to her no later than this evening. Then, sadly, I must await the arrival of the fabrics in order to serve her. As the lady Elega, my illustrious patroness, has said, the details can be discussed when the work is ready for fitting.'

'That's fine,' Terisa pronounced. Then, because she knew she would never be able to stand where she was and keep her composure, she turned to leave.

Trying to emulate Elega's regal bearing, she walked out of the shop into the crowds and the sunlight.

If Geraden had been there, she would have burst out laughing: all she needed was someone to share her humor with. But he was nowhere in sight. And Elega, too, didn't appear. The clamor of the merchants had risen to its former pitch. If anyone had called her name, she might not have heard it. The flow of the throng made it easier to move than to stand still, so she let herself be nudged and jostled slowly away from Mindlin's shop.

Before she had gone far enough to consider turning back, she caught a glimpse of Nyle.

He shifted purposefully through the crowd – not hurrying, but also not wasting any time. His path took him out of view again almost immediately; but a moment later he became briefly visible between shops, still heading in the same direction.

On impulse, Terisa started after him.

She would have been hard pressed to account for what she was doing. He was a familiar face, of course, and she didn't like being alone among all these people. Her curiosity about him as Geraden's brother was probably a more fundamental explanation, however. And more fundamental still was her instinctive interest in his purpose. Whatever it was, it was enough to make him snub Geraden. But not Elega.

Was he unaware that Elega plotted to betray his father's best friend?

Quickly, she walked to the shops between which she had just seen him. Taking that narrow lane, she reached the place where he had passed. Almost at once, she spotted him.

He seemed very far away.

She didn't want to call attention to herself by running. At the same time, she didn't want to lose him. After an instant of hesitation, she decided to run.

It was a fortunate decision, despite the fact that it caused her to bump into people and made total strangers mutter curses at her: it enabled her to gain enough ground so that he didn't vanish when he turned along a row of food stalls and turned again. She reached the row of stalls barely in time to see him clamber over the ropes and disappear behind a tent which had been pitched much too close to the neighboring buildings.

She went as far as the tent; then she had to stop. Could she follow him? Her gown and coat would make her awkward over the tent ropes. And there appeared to be no exit from where Nyle had gone except around one side of the tent or the other. If he knew of another, she had already lost him. And if he came back while she tried to go after him, he would catch her.

Finally she moved to the opening of the tent and made an effort to wait there inconspicuously, watching both sides.

The tent seemed to be about the size of a comfortable cottage. In a ring around the tent pole, rough tables had been set up in the mud (there was no ground cover), and from these tables a number of men and women sold beads and sequins, shawls and trinkets. None of the people behind the tables were particularly busy; one man called out to Terisa, inviting her in. She ignored him and remained at her post.

Several minutes after she began to feel foolish, but still a minute or two before her stubbornness would have given out, a slight quiver ran through the tent as Nyle returned, pushing himself over the ropes.

With her heart pounding, she ducked partway into the tent to avoid being seen, then turned to watch him, holding herself steady with one hand on the canvas.

His face was focused, intent. Whatever he was doing didn't appear to give him any pleasure: his frown was so deep that it seemed to describe the underlying set of his bones. Nevertheless he was obviously not a man who hesitated simply because he wasn't enjoying himself. Perhaps he didn't expect enjoyment from life.

Without noticing her, he strode off the way he had come.

She was about to go after him when another quiver warned her that someone else was climbing over the tent ropes.

She froze in time to get a clear, close look at the man who emerged from the place where Nyle had just been.

It was the mountebank, his ribbons and tatters fluttering extravagantly.

The *mountebank*? That was surprising enough. By itself, it would have astounded her. But the fact that stunned her into openmouthed immobility was that she knew him. He passed so near to her that she was able to recognize him.

Behind the distracting way he dressed, under the ash that marked his face and hair, he was Prince Kragen. The Alend Contender.

Around her, the whole day shifted. Meanings changed everywhere. It *can't* be, she protested. I saw him *leave*. I saw him ride out of Orison with all his men.

But if he wanted to come back secretly, how else could he do it? Pressure filled her throat, rising there until she thought she would choke. How else could he and Elega communicate? How else could they make plans together?

And Nyle was involved with them. Elega had lied. Of course she had lied. His 'private affairs' had everything to do with her. No wonder he didn't want to encounter his brother.

He was plotting with Elega and Prince Kragen against the King of Mordant.

And Elega's invitation to Terisa to come here with her wasn't innocent at all. It had nothing to do with any desire for a mere friendly outing. Shopping was just an excuse. Elega was still trying to snare her somehow.

Terisa was so staggered that she didn't notice the black-clad juggler with the sharp silver stars until he began performing directly in front of her, hardly more than twenty feet away.

The midnight whirl of his cloak caught her attention. His stars began to dance in his hands. They cast a glitter of sunshine, lovely and bewitching, as they arced through the air, passing between his fingers like flakes of light. Soon he was surrounded with spangles.

He didn't watch what he was doing. He had no need to watch: his hands knew their skill. Instead, he regarded Terisa narrowly.

The stars cast a trance. For a moment like the touch of a dream, she saw everything.

Here in the middle of the bazaar, a good distance from the torrents of water pouring off the eaves and roofs of Orison, the mud was beginning to dry under the warmth of the sun and the passage of so many feet. The boots of the men were stained, of course, and the skirts of the women were filthy; but they were no longer clogged in mire.

Nyle had disappeared into the throng in one direction; Prince Kragen would soon be out of sight in the other. As if to balance the scene, however, Geraden and Elega were approaching from opposite ends of the row of food stalls.

The sunlight seemed to make the smells from the stalls stronger. Sweets, oils, nuts, pungent meats – they were all part of the arcing dance of the stars.

Elega was apparently looking for someone – maybe for Terisa herself. The way Elega squinted reminded Terisa that sunshine wasn't the lady's natural element, not the kind of illumination that brought out her beauty.

Geraden, on the other hand, had already spotted Terisa. He waved his arm and moved toward her, smiling.

The sky overhead looked as blue as a dream, blue and perfect, the ideal background for the whirl of silver.

But the juggler *had a nose like the blade of a hatchet; his teeth were bared in a feral grin. She had the indistinct impression that there were scars on his cheeks.* His burning yellow eyes were fixed on her—

Then the moment ended, and she didn't see how things happened.

Without forewarning, the stars changed their dance. From the juggler's hands, they began to float straight at her head like bright, metal leaves on a long breeze.

Hardly aware of what she did, she twitched her face away from the first star. The second licked along her cheek.

The rest of them should have hit her. But they were pulled off target when Geraden crashed into the juggler, grappling for his arm.

The juggler delivered a blow with his elbow that crumpled Geraden into the mud. Then his robe swirled aside, and a longsword appeared like a slash of steel fire in his hands.

He sprang at Terisa.

She was already falling backward, stumbling into the tent.

Everything seemed to go dark. People screamed, cursed. She collided with one of the display tables and overturned it. Someone shrieked, bitten by the juggler's blade. In a flurry of trinkets, she fell past the table and hit the tent pole.

Then she was able to see again.

As black and irresistible as midnight, the juggler came after her, wielding his sword like a flail to clear terrified merchants and shoppers out of his way.

Somehow, she got her legs under her, put the tent pole between her and her attacker. Then she lost her footing and went down again.

'Gart!' a man barked.

The shout turned the juggler away from her.

'Don't tell me,' drawled Artagel as he sauntered forward, grinning sharply, 'that the High King's Monomach can't find a worthier opponent than an unarmed woman. I've already warned you about that.'

'Do you think yourself worthy?' the man in black hissed like silk. 'I already know you are not.'

Artagel kicked a table aside. Almost in the same motion, he jumped to the attack.

Gart wheeled and leveled a blow like the cut of an axe at Terisa.

His swing was hard enough to split her in half. Fortunately, Artagel anticipated Gart's move. He came around the other side of the tent pole in time to parry the blow and save her.

Then he was between her and the High King's Monomach.

The tent was deserted now except for Terisa and the two combatants. Their boots ground beads and lace into the mud as they probed and riposted. Their blades struck sparks from each other, a darkened and baleful version of the sunlit dance of stars. She could hear Artagel's harsh breathing: he sounded as though he hadn't fully recovered from the damage to his lungs. Gart's respiration was so firm and even that it made no noise.

Attack. Parry. The clangor of iron.

Artagel had trouble with the tables. They hampered his strokes, interfered with his parries: they caught his feet so that he nearly fell. His movements were tight with strain. Gart, on the other hand, seemed to float among the obstacles as if he had placed them where they were to suit his training and experience.

Bracing herself on the tent pole, Terisa climbed upright. Her hands were slippery with blood. Where had it come from? Probably from her cheek. Artagel was going to get killed because of her. Because of her. She wanted to run away. That was the only thing she could do. If she distracted Gart by running away, Artagel might have a chance. But the High King's Monomach stayed so close to the opening of the tent that she couldn't escape.

She would have cried out; but the ringing clash of iron and the hoarse rasp of Artagel's breath made every other sound impossible.

As it happened, she didn't need to cry out. Roaring like maddened bulls, Argus and Ribuld charged out of sunlight into the gloom of the tent.

Even if she had known what to watch for, she might not have seen how Gart saved himself. It was too fast. Perhaps he took advantage of the moment their eyes needed to adjust. All she knew was that she heard him snarl as he whirled and met Argus and Ribuld with a blow which somehow forced them to recoil separately, away from each other.

Artagel sprang after him.

Too wild, too desperate. Off balance.

Gart met that onslaught also, caught and held Artagel's blade on his, then slipped it aside and swept his own steel in a slicing cut that laid open Artagel's side and brought blood spurting between his ribs.

Gasping, he staggered to one knee.

That was all the time Ribuld and Argus needed to recover and attack again. Still Gart was too quick for them. Before they could hit him, he leaped for the tent pole – vaulting over the blow Artagel aimed at his legs – and dealt a high cut to the rope that pulled the canvas up the pole.

Then he dove and rolled for the opening, passing as slick as oil between Argus and Ribuld while the tent came down on their heads.

The wet, heavy canvas pushed Terisa into the mud again. She groveled there, smothering slowly. In her mind Gart's blade bit into Artagel's side and the dark blood flowed. She hardly heard the clamor of the onlookers as the High King's Monomach made his escape.

Roused by the tumult, a number of guards arrived almost immediately. They cut Terisa and Artagel, Argus and Ribuld free. They improvised a litter and raced Artagel toward the nearest physician. They picked up Geraden, chaffed and slapped him back to consciousness. They started a search. Soon Castellan Lebbick came on the scene with reinforcements, organization, and tongue-lashings. The whole bazaar was searched.

But no one found Gart.

TWENTY

FAMILY MATTERS

Terisa wanted to go after Artagel with Geraden. She was the one who had seen Artagel hit, seen him fall. Fighting to save her. But even if she hadn't been a witness, as well as the cause – in fact, even if she hadn't known Artagel at all – she would have felt the same. Befuddled by Gart's blow, Geraden let his anguish show nakedly on his face. His concentration on his brother was so urgent that he was blind to everything else. Awkwardly, he struggled to free himself from guards and questions and astonished onlookers so that he could go after Artagel. Seeing him like that made her believe that he needed her. In spite of her own shock and fear, she wanted to go with him.

Elega didn't release her.

The lady came to Terisa's side as soon as the guards had fanned out to search for the High King's Monomach. As she held Terisa's arm and dabbed at the blood on Terisa's cheek, she made soft comforting noises which sounded a little artificial, coming from her. Terisa would have had to repulse her vehemently in order to get away from her.

Terisa didn't have it in her to do that. Not now: not while every muscle in her arms and legs trembled, and her stomach twisted around itself, trying to decide what to do about the sight of Artagel's blood. So she was caught where she was as Geraden stumbled away through the crowd, pursuing the litter that carried his brother.

Touched by something that might have been pity, the Castellan let him go.

On the other hand, Lebbick didn't appear to feel anything as soft as pity when he turned to question Terisa.

Elega shielded her, however. 'Castellan,' she interposed firmly, 'you are not surprised to learn that the lady Terisa has an enemy who wishes her dead. You are only surprised that her enemy is a man as important and dangerous as the High King's Monomach. And you are surprised that he has such freedom of movement in Orison, despite the fact that you are responsible for such matters.'

A muscle in the Castellan's jaw twitched.

'You will agree, I am sure,' she continued, 'that the lady Terisa is the last person likely to relieve your surprise. What does she know of Cadwal's secrets – or of Orison's defenses? If you must question her, do so in her own rooms, when she is stronger.'

In response, Lebbick gave Terisa a look that made her heart turn over. Then he bowed stiffly, ordered an escort for the two women, and turned away.

Elega took Terisa back toward the peacock rooms.

At first, she felt no pain in her cheek. With the odd detachment of shock, she wondered if she were cold enough to be numb. Then she wondered whether Gart put poison on the edges of his weapons.

After a while, however, the relative warmth in Orison and the exertion of walking brought back the sensation of bright metal as it licked the side of her face. The cut was too thin to hurt. What she felt now wasn't pain. It was a trail of moisture, a long wet touch like the stroke of a tongue.

Once, trying to explain the way coming here had disrupted her life, she had said to Myste, *It was like dying without any pain. It doesn't hurt.* That idea recurred now in a kind of panic. If her cheek had hurt, she would have known what to do about it. Suddenly, she ached for a mirror, for any looking glass which would have told her whether she had been disfigured.

She didn't realize that Elega was talking until the lady stopped her, took her by the shoulders, and insisted, 'Terisa, I know that you are afraid. Nevertheless you must listen to me. It may appear that your reasons for fear become less if you do not think about them, but I assure you they do not. The reverse is true. You can only make your danger less by understanding it and acting against it.'

At the moment, Elega didn't appear to be a woman who had much sympathy for fear.

They were standing on the stairs that led up to Terisa's rooms. Elega seemed unconscious of the escorting guards; perhaps she thought that the urgency of her questions outweighed caution. But Terisa didn't want to talk at all: she certainly didn't want to talk in front of two men she didn't know. Somewhere in Orison, a physician was trying to save Artagel's life. And Geraden was there – She was surprised to hear the anger in her voice as she demanded, 'What do you think I can do?'

'Put your fear aside and try to grasp the truth,' Elega replied at once. 'There must be a reason why the High King's Monomach risks his own life in order to threaten yours.'

Terisa stared at the lady and thought, She still believes I'm some kind of Imager. That's why she wants me on her side. With Prince Kragen. And Nyle. A moment later, however, she realized that Elega's thoughts were more complex than that. The lady was also considering the idea that Terisa had already involved herself in someone else's machinations – a plot so far-ranging and insidious that High King Festten took it as a personal threat. A plot about which Elega knew nothing; a plot which might undo everything she herself wanted to achieve.

With unfeigned fatigue, Terisa asked, 'Do you really want to discuss it here?'

Elega lifted an eyebrow and glanced around her. A flush stained her cheeks. Was she embarrassed by her own carelessness? Abruptly, she moved on up the stairs.

Stifling the temptation to turn and flee in the opposite direction, Terisa followed her.

When they had reached the safety of the peacock rooms and closed the door behind them, Elega poured out a goblet of wine for each of them. By then, she had regained her composure. Watching Terisa over the rim of her goblet, she drank a few swallows. Then, with an air of decision, she put the goblet aside.

'You must forgive me for speaking of such things at such a time. I understand that you have been badly frightened. And I am sure that you are concerned for Artagel. But you must understand that it is madness to ignore my question. Terisa' – her eyes were vivid in her pale face – 'you surely have some idea why Gart is here to kill you. It is inconceivable that you could pose such a threat to the High King without being aware of it.'

Terisa sighed. She didn't want to deal with Elega. She wanted to lie down and sleep for a few years. At the same time, she wanted to go find Artagel. The sharp wet sensation of her cut was starting to resemble pain. When she drank, the wine seemed to make the cut worse. Carefully, she raised her hand to her cheek. Her fingers came down marked with dried blood. Her face must be a mess. Afraid of the damage, she asked unsteadily, 'How bad is it?'

Elega frowned in vexation, but she quickly smoothed her expression. With a gesture that asked Terisa to wait, she went into the bathroom and returned with a damp towel. Then she motioned Terisa to sit on the couch. When Terisa was settled, Elega began stroking her cut gently with the towel, washing away blood and dirt from the wound.

After studying the cut for a moment, the lady pronounced, 'It is clean. It still bleeds a little' – she dabbed the towel at Terisa's cheek – 'but that only serves to keep it clean. We can summon a physician if you wish, but I doubt that you need so much care. It is only as long as my finger' – at the moment, her fingers looked exceptionally long – 'and rather delicate. When it heals, you will have a fine, straight scar that no one will see except in certain lights.' She drew back to consider the matter from farther away. 'And no one will see it at all if they do not stand near you.'

In a neutral tone, she concluded, 'When it heals, I expect that most men will feel that your beauty has been enhanced rather than diminished.'

'I wish I could see it,' Terisa admitted lamely. 'Where I come from, that's all we use mirrors for. To see ourselves.'

Still neutrally, Elega replied, 'For that reason we have maids, so that women who care for the decoration of their appearance will not make fools of themselves.' She couldn't hold down her real interests, however. More quickly, she asked,

'Then all the mirrors in your world are flat?'

Terisa tried to swallow another sigh. 'Yes.'

'And you are not translated by them?'

'No.'

The lady rose to her feet. Facing the hearth, she cupped her hands under her elbows, holding her forearms across her midriff as if to restrain herself

354

from an outbreak of emotion. 'You insist that you are an ordinary woman. Perhaps that is true in your world. But is it possible that you are translated and do not know it – or take it for granted? Here, we are told that any man who faces a flat glass in which he sees himself facing himself will be lost in a translation which never ends. But what if you – if all the people of your world – possess a power which we lack? A power to master the most dangerous manifestation of Imagery? You might be unaware of it – and yet it would be fundamental enough to alter all our preconceptions.'

'No.' Terisa denied that idea as she had denied everything like it from the beginning. 'Where I come from, mirrors are just *things*. They aren't magic.' In an effort to shorten the discussion, she faced what she took to be Elega's point. 'I really *do not* know why the High King's Monomach wants to kill me.'

Her eyes flaming, Elega turned from the fire. 'That is not possible.'

Terisa raised the towel to her cheek to hide her anger. 'It's still true.'

For an instant, Elega was on the verge of a shout. 'Then—' But at once she caught herself; calculations ran behind her eyes so clearly that they were almost legible. 'Then you must be protected.'

'Protected?'

'The King will not do it. He will not understand the need. And because the King will not understand the need, the Castellan *cannot* do it. He is too hampered. He has shown that he cannot even limit Gart's access to Orison.

'The lords of the Cares are useless to you. The Tor has become an old drunkard. The Armigite's foppishness shames the memory of his father. The Fayle does not know where his loyalties should lie. And neither the Perdon nor the Termigan is *here*.

'As for the Congery' – she made a dismissive gesture – 'the Masters are too divided among themselves to protect anyone. They all resemble Master Quillon, who is too timid to take risks – or Master Barsonage, who is too concerned for the reputation of the Congery to take action – or Master Eremis, who is too self-absorbed to take interest.

'Terisa—' Elega seemed to hesitate, as if doubting whether she should finish what she had started to say. But hesitation wasn't a prominent part of her nature. Distinctly, like an avowal of faith, she said, 'You must let me protect you.'

Terisa was so startled that she stared.

'For the present, I admit,' Elega hurried on, 'I can do little more than hide you. But that I can do very well. My knowledge of Orison's secrets is extensive. Soon, however, I will be able to protect anyone I choose.

'I can provide you safety, if you will entrust yourself to me.'

Though she wanted to think clearly – it was important to think clearly – Terisa's head whirled. She believed that she understood Elega. On the other hand, she would gain more information if she pretended ignorance. At the same time, however, her cheek hurt, and she was worried about Artagel and Geraden, and she feared that Elega was too cunning for her. And she was still angry.

With difficulty, she managed to ask, 'How?' instead of losing her temper. 'I've heard you complain about how left out you are. How little you have to do with what's going on. How are you going to protect me?'

355

Elega met Terisa's gaze steadily. 'I can provide you safety,' she repeated, 'if you will *entrust* yourself to me.' Then she added, 'Terisa, I have shown you nothing but friendship. I desire only your well-being, and the preservation of Mordant – and an end to evil in the realm. But if you will not trust me I can do nothing.'

You surely have some idea why Gart is here to kill you.

It was too much. 'You're going to have power,' retorted Terisa harshly. 'Where are you going to get it? I can only think of one place. From your father. But he won't just give it to you. That isn't the way he does things. You're going to betray him. You're going to cut his throne out from under him somehow. You and Prince Kragen.' She barely stopped herself from saying, And Nyle. You've even turned Geraden's brother against him. But the shock on Elega's face warned her that she had already gone too far. 'I don't want to have anything to do with that.'

'And why not?' Ire mounted through the lady's surprise. 'Do you have any alternative? Are you so pure that you can conceive some answer to Mordant's need that does not require betrayal?'

'He's your father. That ought to make a difference.'

Elega drew back her shoulders, straightened her spine. The violet flash of her eyes made her look regal and certain, like a woman who was within her rights. 'I assure you, my lady,' she said austerely, 'that it does make a difference. You understand me so well that I am sorry to find you understand me so little.'

Giving Terisa a bow as correct and defiant as an offer of combat, the lady Elega left the room.

Terisa watched the door long after it closed. She had made a serious mistake: she had just ruined her only chance to learn how Elega and Prince Kragen intended to take Mordant away from King Joyse. In disgust, she tried to swear at herself. Her heart wasn't in it, however. After all, what Elega had offered her made no sense.

To keep her hidden. For how long? Until the end of winter? Until the Alend army arrived? Until Orison fell to siege? Twenty or thirty or forty days?

It made no sense.

She didn't want to think about such things. They were either irrelevant or impossible. She wanted to know what was happening to Artagel and Geraden.

And she wanted to know what made her so valuable that people were willing to risk their lives over her. What was there about her that made her worth Gart's hate and Artagel's blood?

Outside, the sun shone warmly, as if it were immensely pleased with itself.

If she had been required to wait long alone, she might have done something foolish. That is to say, she might have done *something*; and she felt sure that anything she decided to do would be foolish. Fortunately, while she was still unable to make up her mind, Geraden arrived at her door.

He had a high spot of color in each cheek and a slightly glazed look in his eyes; he was frowning deeply, as if he were in pain; his fingers made small twitching movements, though his hands were held pressed to his sides. Nevertheless he had come to her.

Because she had grown up in a household where she was seldom offered comfort – and was never asked for it – she didn't put her arms around him, either for his sake or for her own. She invited him in quickly, however, and closed the door and swallowed the congestion in her throat to ask, 'How is he?'

He made an effort to look at her, to pull himself out of his distress and *look* at her. Gently, he reached out a hand and touched her cut cheek with his fingertips. Somehow, he managed to twist his mouth into a smile. 'Does it hurt? It doesn't look too bad. I'm glad you're all right.'

'*Geraden.* How *is* he?'

A spasm cracked his control. His smile broke, and his eyes brimmed with tears. 'The physician is doing everything he can. He doesn't know what's going to happen. Artagel's lost a lot of blood. He might die.'

Slowly, he hunched forward, and his arms rose to his chest as if he were crumpling inwardly, collapsing in on himself.

For just an instant, Terisa remained still. Then, as if she were turning her back on everything she had ever been taught about people and pain, she went to him and caught him in a hug as hard as she could.

They stood that way together for a long time.

When she finally let him go, he didn't look at her at first. Rubbing his face, he murmured, 'I don't think I ever told you. My mother died when I was just a kid. A fever of some kind – we never knew what it was, but it dragged on for a long time. *I* thought it was a long time, anyway. I was only five – and I was her baby, so she wanted me with her – and watching her die I thought I was being torn apart. I *swore*—' Slowly, he raised his head, letting Terisa see his grief. 'I was only five, but I swore I was never going to let anybody I loved die ever again.'

Then he sighed, and by degrees his expression cleared. 'I hope Artagel doesn't hold me to it, because there's nothing I can do to save him.'

'I'm sorry.' She didn't know what else to say. 'This is all my fault somehow. I'm the one Gart wants to kill. I just don't understand why.'

He sniffed to clear his nose. 'Don't be silly. It's Gart's fault, not yours.' His frown came back as he tried to reassure her. 'Or you could say it's my fault, since I failed to stop him. Or, if you want to look at it that way, it's High King Festten's fault. After all, Gart is the High King's Monomach. He's just following orders.' His features clenched. 'You could even say it's King Joyse's fault. If he weren't being so detached, the High King wouldn't dare send Gart here.

'In fact' – he tried unsuccessfully to smile for her – 'if you look at it right, you're the only one whose fault it *isn't.*'

He misunderstood her. What she felt about Artagel's wound wasn't blame, but rather a regret as piercing as iron. The distinction was unimportant at the moment, however. Instead of trying to explain it, she said as if she were still on the same subject, 'I'm not so sure. I think I've done something pretty stupid.'

His incomprehension seemed to warn him to listen to her closely. 'Wait a minute. You mean you think Gart attacked you because you've done something stupid?'

She shook her head. 'Elega brought me back here. She offered to protect me.'

He scowled at her; his jaws knotted. Unexpectedly, she became aware that it might be possible to be afraid of him: the intensity he focused on her was daunting. As if he were holding back an eruption, he said, 'Maybe you'd better tell me the whole story.'

As simply as she could, she described her conversation with Elega and watched his anger mount. Then she concluded, 'As soon as I mentioned Prince Kragen, I ruined the chance that she would ever tell me what she's doing. She's never going to trust me.'

Geraden turned away to hide his face. 'Glass and splinters!' he muttered fiercely. 'Now she's been warned. She'll be more careful. Before long, she's bound to notice Argus and Ribuld. As soon as that happens, they won't be able to follow her anymore. We've lost before we even got started.'

This time, Terisa could have said, I'm sorry, without being misinterpreted. But the apology she owed him now was nothing compared to the one he would deserve soon. For a moment, she quailed. Why not keep *this* a secret as well? At least until his unfamiliar rage declined. Who would be hurt?

Nevertheless she knew the answer. She had learned it in this place of secrets. Whenever he discovered the truth, he would be hurt. And the fact that she had kept the truth from him would cripple their friendship.

Taking a deep breath for courage, she said, 'Maybe we haven't lost yet.'

He swung around to confront her.

He looked so extreme and vulnerable that she could hardly speak. 'She left me alone with her seamster. I was finished before she got back, so I left his shop.' Remembering what had happened, a momentary faintness passed over her. 'I saw Nyle.'

Without transition, Geraden's anger disappeared.

'I followed him – I don't know why. I guess I wanted to know why he snubbed you.' A feeling of despair rose in her. Geraden would hate her for this. 'He met someone behind that tent. He didn't see me, but I saw him. I saw who it was.'

She faltered. Geraden looked nauseous with anticipation.

'It was that mountebank. The one we talked about. This time I recognized him. I know who he is. I'm sure of it.' Rapidly, so that she wouldn't break down, she said, 'He's Prince Kragen. He met Nyle behind that tent.'

For a second, Geraden looked as surprised and wounded as she had feared. His love for his family was one of his sovereign passions – and she had just accused his brother of plotting treason. The stark and intimate dismay on his face was more than she could bear.

After that first second, however, his entire posture shifted. The bones in his spine and shoulders straightened themselves, making him taller. His expression became at once bleaker and stronger, as if all the weaker or more awkward lines of his cheeks and jaw were being honed away. His eyes gave hints of authority.

'That explains it,' he said flatly. 'No wonder he wants to stay away from Artagel and me.'

Then he added, 'Elega got him into this.'

She knew on some level that his crisis wasn't over – that perhaps it was just beginning – but his immediate reaction relieved her so much that she almost kissed him. 'So we haven't necessarily lost,' she breathed. 'You can tell Argus and Ribuld to forget Elega. They can follow Nyle.'

Geraden didn't appear to be listening: he looked like he was concentrating hotly on his own thoughts. But he replied in a murmur, '*If* they can find him. That's going to be the hard part. If they can find him, maybe we can stop him before he does something even King Joyse will have to punish.'

Abruptly, he swung into motion. 'Come on. We've got to tell somebody about this.'

He was already at the door. Starting after him, Terisa blurted, 'Tell who? Why?'

'Not King Joyse,' he answered as if she were thinking fast enough to keep up with him. 'He probably wouldn't listen anyway. And Castellan Lebbick would probably overreact. He might have Nyle cut down on sight. The Tor would be better.' The way he held the door for her was like a command for haste. 'It's the only thing we can do right now to protect Nyle. If we aren't able to stop him – and he gets caught – he'll be less likely to be executed if what he's doing doesn't come as a surprise.'

He said this with such conviction that she believed him. In spite of her mud-streaked clothes and blood-marked skin, she kept pace with him.

He hurried all the way to the King's apartment without tripping once.

They were admitted to the suite readily because King Joyse wasn't there. 'Off somewhere with his Imager, I suppose,' the Tor muttered in explanation. 'His courtesy never fails, but he tells me as little as he can to keep me from howling.'

His voice was a subterranean gurgle, as though it emerged from somewhere deep in his great fat, and the passages that let it out were filling up with wine. Days of use were marked on his green robe by wine and food stains. His unshaven jowls and oily hair showed that he had been neglecting his toilet.

'I am a patient man, young Geraden,' he confided past his flagon. 'I have spent no small number of years in the world, and I have learned that fat is more enduring than stone. But the truth is that my presence here has not accomplished quite what I intended.' He flapped one hand in a gesture that made Terisa notice the absence of the King's hop-board table. 'He has simply moved his games elsewhere.'

He sighed lugubriously, and his eyes misted. 'It is a sad thing to be neglected at my age.'

Listening to the Tor, Terisa began to lose confidence. Nevertheless Geraden was wound too tightly to be deflected.

'You appointed yourself chancellor, my lord,' he reminded the Tor. 'You said you would take action in the King's name. That ought to be easy, if he isn't here to contradict you.'

The Tor gave Geraden a sour look. 'You are too young to understand. If I wish mutton rather than duckling for my next meal, I have only to speak. If I decide to appoint a holiday and make every lady in Orison do without her maid, I can do so without raising my voice. Who here has any desire to oppose the will of the King's old friend?' One fist beat out the words as his anger rose. 'If I take it upon myself to declare war tomorrow, I have no doubt that I will be obeyed.

'But the *King*, young Geraden!' He raised his bulk to emphasize his point. 'Where is the *King*? Where is the man who ought to be shamed by every command I issue in his name? Off playing *hop-board* with Adept Havelock while his realm *crumbles*.'

Slowly, the Tor subsided. 'As for Castellan Lebbick,' he sighed, 'he now holds what little effective power is left in Orison. But even he finds it difficult to ignore me. And he does not want to submit his decisions for my opinion, so he avoids me. I suspect he secretly passes judgment on all my orders before they are carried out.

'It appears I have chosen a foolish way to grieve for my son.'

Terisa tried to catch Geraden's eye; she wanted to send him a mental message, urging him not to tell the Tor about Nyle and Elega. The old lord was starting to remind her of Reverend Thatcher.

Geraden refused to receive her signal, however. He was fixed on the Tor, and his expression had softened, although his manner remained grim. 'I'm sorry, my lord,' he said roughly. 'I don't have time for your grief.'

Under his fat, the muscles of the Tor's face tightened dangerously, but Geraden went ahead without pausing. 'I need to talk to King Joyse. Since he isn't here, I'll have to talk to you. I can't take this to the Castellan. I'm not going to tell it to anybody who isn't a friend of my father's.'

He had caught the Tor's attention. 'I consider the Domne a friend,' the lord rumbled slowly. 'And your past courtesy outweighs your present rudeness.' He had blinked the blur of wine from his eyes: his gaze was hard. 'I am interested in what you need to tell the King.'

Terisa was suddenly ashamed of herself. Rather than distrusting the Tor's despondency, Geraden was trying to help.

The perception made her squirm. She had never done anything to help Reverend Thatcher. She had listened to him for hours, but she had never tried to help.

'You've probably heard the rumor that King Joyse thinks the lady Elega has turned against him.' Geraden didn't need to feign harshness; the bleak strength that had brought him here rasped in his voice. 'Well, he's right.'

As gently as the bite of a crosscut saw, Geraden told the Tor what he knew about Elega and Prince Kragen and Nyle. When he had recited the basic facts, he added, 'Two of my friends – two guards – are following her around. But she knows we're suspicious of her now. She'll be more careful. I'm going to tell my friends to forget her and concentrate on Nyle.' He said his brother's name in a tone of forced impersonality. 'Maybe he'll lead us to the answers.'

The Tor's gaze held: his eyes looked like bits of glass embedded in pastry dough. 'I hear quite a number of rumors,' he commented when Geraden was done. 'Duty outside this door is dull, and many of the guards liven it with conversation. I have heard a rumor that your brother Artagel, who is reputed to be the best swordsman in Mordant, faced the High King's Monomach and fell.' His tone didn't become clear until he asked, 'Is he seriously injured?'

Geraden swallowed convulsively. 'Yes.'

Unblinking, the Tor studied Geraden for a moment. Then he said, 'I have lost a son. I will not have it said to the Domne that I sat drunk on my hams while one of his sons was killed by the High King's Monomach and another sold himself to the Alend Monarch. What do you wish me to do?'

At once, Geraden replied, 'Don't let Castellan Lebbick interfere. Make him leave Nyle alone.' He was plainly relieved to get away from the subject of Artagel. 'And tell him to assign Argus and Ribuld to me. Tell him I'm doing you some kind of favor and I need their help.' He sounded clear, almost authoritative, as if he had been involved in situations like this all his life. 'The last time they tried to help me, he roasted them for it. They'll do a better job if they don't have to dodge him the whole time.'

He sounded so sure of what he was doing that Terisa wanted to give him a round of applause.

Nevertheless he was sweating by the time he was done.

The Tor regarded him gravely for a little while longer. Then he turned his head and let out a cheerful yell that made Terisa jump and brought the guards promptly into the room.

'Yes, my lord Tor?' one of them inquired. He was on good terms with the self-appointed chancellor. 'You bellowed?'

'Mongrel!' snorted the Tor. 'That was not a bellow. That was a polite request for attention.' His chuckle sounded like belching. 'If you ever have the misfortune to hear me bellow, you will not speak of it so calmly.

'But now that you are here—' He rolled his eyes at the ceiling as though he were contemplating an entire litany of desires. 'I want cranberry sauce with that duckling which the cook is already so late in providing. I want more wine. I want peace or war with our enemies, whichever will cause them the most consternation.' He rubbed a fat hand over his jowls. 'I believe I want a barber. But most of all' – suddenly, his voice seemed to have a knife hidden in it somewhere – 'I want the Castellan.'

Briskly now, he said, 'Be so kind as to inform him that I require a few moments of his time – almost immediately.'

'As you wish, my lord Tor.' Grinning, the guards withdrew.

The Tor looked at Geraden and shrugged. 'He may not come at once, but I will nag until he does.'

'Thank you, my lord Tor,' the Apt breathed sincerely. 'That should make things easier.'

With a flutter of his free hand, the Tor waved gratitude aside. After a moment's consideration, he said severely, 'Young Geraden, your reputation for mishap is entirely misleading. You have shown me that my King has a need for his chancellor which I did not suspect. I believe I will begin to assert myself.'

Pointing a pudgy finger at the Apt, he added in an ominous rumble, 'In the meantime, I advise you to stop Nyle before he goes too far. The union of the Cares already grows fragile. An open rupture now between King Joyse and the Care of Domne may bring us all to grief.'

361

Quickly, he emptied his flagon. Then he drawled happily, 'While you are otherwise occupied, I will take it upon myself to teach my lady Elega the fear of discovery.'

For an odd moment, Terisa felt like laughing. The idea of a confrontation between the huge old lord and the regal princess tweaked her fancy. But her amusement was primarily a reaction to strain: as soon as she glanced at Geraden, it evaporated. His grin was a rather feverish imitation of the smile Artagel wore into combat.

Fortunately, the Tor also noticed his expression. 'You may go now, young Geraden,' he said firmly, 'unless you have more treachery to reveal? I do not mean to share my duckling with anyone. Send me word as soon as you have news of Artagel.'

'Thank you, my lord.' At once, Geraden headed for the door.

Terisa wanted to thank the Tor more thoroughly, let him know how much he did for Geraden. But she couldn't do that and still follow the Apt.

The old lord seemed to understand, however. 'Take care of him, my lady,' he muttered, dismissing her. 'He has need of you.'

Flashing him her best smile, she left the apartment and pursued Geraden down the stairs.

He slowed his pace after a flight or two so that she could catch up with him. 'I've been away from Artagel too long,' he said. 'Will you excuse me? I would take you with me, but the physician won't let you in. I practically had to threaten his life to see Artagel myself. You can find your way back to your rooms, can't you? Will you be all right?'

'Geraden—' She put her hand on his arm to make him hear her. 'You did the right thing with the Tor. You gave him what he needed.' Unaccustomed to saying such things, she sounded terribly stilted to herself – and she hated it. But she didn't back down. 'I'm proud of you.'

That reached him. The muscles around his eyes unclenched, and something that looked like a smile caught at the corners of his mouth. 'I like him,' he explained simply.

'I'll be all right,' she promised. 'Go see Artagel. Send me a message right away.'

He nodded and immediately took off at a run.

She went back to her rooms alone and spent the rest of the day trying not to think.

The next morning, Artagel's physician ventured the opinion that his patient might live.

At once haggard with exhaustion and giddy with relief, Geraden brought the news to Terisa before going to his own rooms for some rest. 'Now it's just a question of infection,' he reported. 'If he can get through that, he's going to make it.'

As an afterthought, he added, 'The Tor did it. Argus and Ribuld are working for me now. Castellan Lebbick doesn't like it, but I guess the Tor told him I had some ideas about how to protect you from Gart. So far, they haven't been able to locate Nyle.'

Terisa wanted him to stay with her. She was losing whatever ability she once had to support being alone. When she was by herself, the High King's Monomach and Castellan Lebbick and Master Eremis seemed to crouch in hiding all around her, waiting for her most vulnerable moment. And she wasn't much comforted when she succeeded in concentrating on Elega, Nyle, and the Alend Contender, or worrying about Myste and the champion, or trying to analyze the relationships between Master Quillon, Adept Havelock, and King Joyse, or wondering what obscure talent for Imagery either she or Geraden might have. Every question was dangerous.

But Geraden looked so tired – emotionally drained as well as physically weary – that she took pity on him. As firmly as she could, she sent him on his way, ordering him not to return until he had caught up on his sleep.

Alone, she turned to meet the day in the same spirit in which she had too often faced her evenings in her old apartment: as if the only thing she could hope to do with her time was cling to a tenuous and necessary sense of her own existence.

The view from her windows interested her for a while. The early thaw was settling in as if for a long stay. Sunlight poured over the piled bulk of Orison, melting more snow, raising more mud. Crowds milled through the bazaar, as eager as they had been the previous day. Carts and wains lumbered down the road to the gate of the castle, their iron-rimmed wooden wheels cutting the snow and mud together. Again, she wanted to go outside. But she couldn't – not alone.

She felt lost in her own company.

Before long, Mindlin the seamster arrived to return her old clothes and announce that he expected to receive the material he needed for her tomorrow, or the day after tomorrow at the very latest, unless something dramatic happened to the weather. As a friend of the lady Elega, she would command his first and best attention, so he believed he could promise with confidence that her new garments would be ready for their first fitting no later than six days from now.

Unfortunately, the question of what her new clothes should look like had no power to divert her. She had other things on her mind.

Where was Master Eremis?

What was she doing here?

How could she know anything about herself without a mirror?

Why was it that the only times she was able to reach out to Geraden were when he was hurt? Why was she still keeping secrets from him as if she didn't trust him?

If she kept this up, she might drive herself crazy. These impossible questions only reminded her of what she lacked. They ignored what she had: Geraden's friendship, and Artagel's; the Tor's respect; perhaps even Myste's gratitude, if Myste were still alive. So she was glad for the distraction when a knock at the door announced that she had a visitor. It could be Master Eremis. And even Castellan Lebbick might be an improvement over her own company.

It was Master Barsonage.

The mediator of the Congery was such an unexpected arrival that at first

363

she didn't notice the change in his appearance. But the vague way he failed to meet her gaze as he greeted her made her look past her surprise and see his distress.

'Master Barsonage. Come in.'

'Thank you, my lady.' With an aimless air, as if he didn't quite know where he was going, he shuffled into the sitting room.

He appeared *deflated* – that was the only description she could think of to fit him. When she had first met him, his girth had appeared almost equal to his height. His eyebrows had sprouted thickly, like bracken. His skin had had the color and texture of cut pine. Now, however, that yellow hue had turned sickly, and his flesh seemed slack across his bald skull. His eyebrows sagged; lines ran down his cheeks. His movements and his bulk resembled each other: they were flaccid, like bladders without enough substance in them.

'This is an honor.' She spoke without sarcasm because he looked so woebegone – and so unconscious of it. 'What can I do for you?'

His eyes persisted in missing hers. 'I hardly know, my lady.'

Well, she couldn't leave him standing in the middle of the peacock rug. 'Why don't you sit down?' She gestured toward one of the chairs. 'Would you like some wine?'

He accepted the chair. A weak push of his hands rejected the wine. When he spoke, his tone was as aimless as his appearance. 'You were attacked, my lady.'

At that, she groaned to herself. She had already had this conversation more than she wanted. But then she reflected that it wasn't her fault he was unhappy. With more asperity than she intended, she replied, 'Again. That was actually the third time.'

He blinked in her general direction. 'The third?'

'Didn't Master Eremis tell you about the second? It was right after his meeting with the lords. Prince Kragen and the Perdon almost got killed.'

'No,' he breathed. His voice also was deflated. 'Master Eremis made no mention – He has left Orison. To return to Esmerel, he said. Yesterday – when the thaw began. I had to restore his chasuble, of course. There is no evidence against him. He could not bear our debates, he said.' Unconscious of her reactions, he asked simply, as if they were both children, 'Why were you attacked, my lady?'

He made her heart flutter against her ribs. So there was a reason why Master Eremis hadn't come to see her since Gart's attack. He had probably left Orison before it happened. On the other hand, he hadn't said goodbye—

Painfully confused, she tried to concentrate on the mediator. 'Everybody wants to know why I was attacked.' Her mother would have sent her to her room for speaking in that tone. 'You, Castellan Lebbick, Geraden and Artagel, Prince Kragen' – with an effort, she prevented herself from mentioning Elega – 'even King Joyse. Even *I* want to know why I was attacked. What difference does it make to you, Master Barsonage?'

Still his gaze wouldn't shift to hers. All the anger seemed to have gone out of him. In that same simple voice, he answered, 'I have given my life to it. The Congery is ruined, my lady.'

'Ruined?' What he said was more unexpected than his appearance. 'How? What do you mean?'

'We are disbanded.'

She stared at him. 'Wait a minute. Say that again. You've *disbanded* the Congery?'

'The name still exists, of course. King Joyse does not will that we should come to an end. Therefore we continue. But it has no meaning now. We are done with it – done with our King's impossible ideals and his abandonment of us. Each of us will go his own way.

'Unless you will tell me why you were attacked.'

Her blood felt like cold tallow around her heart, congealed and sickly.

'My lady, we have debated and debated until we have lost our voices – and our hearts. I will not trouble you with the arguments. Without purpose, we are nothing. Either Master Gilbur is a traitor or he is not. In either case, there is nothing we can do. He is beyond our reach. Either the translation of the champion was a mistake or it was not. In either case, there is nothing we can do. We have no glass to return him to his own life. And we cannot reach him for any other translation.

'Either the translation that brought you among us was a mistake or it was not. In either case, there is nothing we can do. Unless we know.'

'Know?'

His limp hands gestured nowhere. 'We could serve you, my lady. If you had a reason for being here. The High King's Monomach risks his life to end yours. Are you not a threat? Are you not an Imager? Then turn to us, my lady. Give us your purpose. Let us serve you.'

No. That was too much. No. She backed away from it. 'Aren't you afraid I might be an enemy?'

He shrugged his empty shoulders. 'The High King's Monomach risks his life to end yours,' he repeated. 'You are not a friend of Cadwal. That is more certain than anything else we have. We will trust it – if you will give us purpose.'

He couldn't *do* that. She couldn't let him make her responsible for the Congery – for all those Masters who despised her, despised Geraden. This was the same man who had forbidden her information when she had first arrived. Bitterly, she retorted, 'You haven't got any easy answers, so you're just going to give up. Have you told Geraden about this yet?'

Quietly, Master Barsonage admitted, 'I have not had the courage.' Then he added, 'None of the Apts have been informed. They continue to tend the fires and the laborium, so that we will be able to do our work – if we are able to find any purpose for it.'

For just a moment, she considered telling him what she had never told Geraden, or anyone else: that she had seen the three riders of her dream in the Congery's augury. But the thought of what he might to with the knowledge stopped her.

He might put the responsibility for the Congery on her shoulders in earnest, making demands that she wouldn't know how to either meet or refuse.

'Master Barsonage,' she said while the pressure increased in her veins, 'don't you think you're asking a little too much? You've barely been *civil* to me since I got here. You certainly haven't been *decent*. You've ignored my ignorance – and what it cost me. And you're still ignoring it. You're ignoring me. I don't know why Gart wants to kill me. Where I come from, mirrors just reflect. They don't *do* anything. *I am not an Imager.'*

In spite of her vehemence, he still didn't meet her eyes. Instead, he took several deep breaths, as though he were pumping himself up, and his hands closed into fists.

'My lady, this is wrong. The Congery is precious, whatever King Joyse now thinks of it. It stands between us and bloody chaos – between Mordant and horror. War is only war. Men are killed. Women are mistreated. Then the struggle shifts elsewhere, and there is peace for a while. But without the Congery to control it Imagery will wreak such evil upon the innocent—

'It will, my lady. It must. Even if every Imager living is a man of good heart, intending what is beneficial, his Imagery must come to abomination in the end. Because he will fall to High King Festten, or to the Alend Monarch, or to whoever takes power in Orison – and these rulers will require his Imagery for destruction. They must, because they are at war. Yet it is not they who suffer. Their soldiers pay a price – and the rest is borne by the innocent of the world.

'Because King Joyse has turned his back on us, there is no other hope. Only the Congery can prevent this. If it is safe and strong – if it has a purpose to unite it.

'You are the answer, my lady. You must not leave us to ruin.'

He moved her. In spite of her anger, her instinctive rejection, he moved her. Perhaps his belief that she could help him was an illusion. Nevertheless the fear that drove him to it was real.

'Master Barsonage,' she said softly, 'the honest fact is that I don't know what's going on. I don't understand any of this. But I'm like you. I don't think Imagery should be used for destruction.

'I'll tell you the truth about me – as soon as I find out what it is. If it turns out to be an answer, it'll help both of us.'

She couldn't tell whether he grasped what she was saying. In fact, she couldn't tell whether he so much as heard her. His eyes stayed away from hers, and his face sagged on his skull as if she had refused his appeal completely.

After a while, he rose from his chair and slumped away.

She was left with one more terrible thing that she would have to tell Geraden.

The advantage was that she no longer had to worry about her grasp on substantiality. She was too worried about him to be in any danger of fading.

Around noon the following day, he came to her rooms to take her to see Artagel.

She had spent the night groping for courage. But there was no kind way to say what needed to be said, so she simply described her conversation with the mediator. Then she bit her lip and held her breath, waiting to see how he would take the news.

To her dismay, he took it laughing.

He laughed so hard that he had to lean against the wall – a strange, silent laughter which shook his whole body but didn't make a noise. He huddled into himself as if he were weeping; tears smeared his face like grief. Yet he was obviously laughing, so astonished with amusement that he was almost hysterical. His hands pounded against each other like applause.

'Well, you have to admit,' he cried through his mirth, 'it's logical.'

She had no idea what to do. Was he really hysterical? He had a right to be: he was under enough strain. Did that mean she was supposed to slap him?

She was supposed to tell him about the riders of her dream. She knew that. Yet she couldn't do it. She was afraid.

'It all comes back to you.' Trying to stop himself, he set his teeth into one knuckle hard enough to draw blood. The pain helped him regain a measure of steadiness. 'Even if you didn't have anything to do with it. Even if you're just here because I have some amazing new talent no one has ever heard of before. There still has to be a reason. A reason why I translated you instead of somebody else. Otherwise it was only an accident. Doesn't mean anything. One way or another, it's the fundamental question of Imagery.

'You *are* the answer.'

Like Master Barsonage, he couldn't meet her gaze.

'Disbanded. My whole life – ever since I came to Orison—

'Oh, Terisa.'

But he didn't let her touch him. 'It's probably just as well,' he said, making a gallant and miserable attempt to sound gay. 'I spent most of my time trying to get out of doing my work anyway. Now I can concentrate on more important things.'

Roughly, he insisted on escorting her to visit Artagel.

Along the way, he walked like a man who had something broken in his chest and didn't know what it was. Nevertheless he kept moving. His self-control gave the impression that he had no conception of how much he had been hurt.

Artagel's quarters were in a part of Orison she had only visited once, during Geraden's tour – a vast warren of rooms built every which way around and on top of each other. She wouldn't have taken it for the castle's equivalent of a barracks if she and Geraden hadn't encountered so many guards, and if she hadn't seen interspersed among the rooms the obviously military halls where the guards mustered. From the look of the place, she guessed that each man had at best one room to himself; the larger rooms were probably shared. Artagel, however, had a modest suite – a bedroom, sitting room, pantry, and lavatory which together took up less space than her bedroom.

Most of the suite was unadorned, almost unfurnished: its occupant apparently didn't spend enough time in Orison to care about his rooms. Or perhaps his sense of home was focused exclusively on Houseldon. Whatever the reason, his quarters contained only one piece of decoration – a long rack, stretching across two walls of the sitting room, from which hung a clutter of variously snapped and shattered swords.

'They're all blades that failed him,' Geraden whispered in explanation as he led her toward the bedroom.

There Artagel lay on an austere bed, a simple wooden frame with strips of cloth woven across it to support a pallet. He had no fireplace, and the air was cool. In addition, he was naked to the waist, except for the bindings wrapped around his middle. Nevertheless sweat streaked his skin, and his eyes smoldered darkly, like secret fires.

Geraden had warned her that he was feverish; but she was still taken aback to see him grinning as though he were about to go down under Gart's next attack.

She had rehearsed a speech for him, wanting to thank him, but it failed her. There was no fat on him: all his muscles were outlined clearly under his skin. And the sweat emphasized his scars, making them catch the light differently so that she couldn't ignore them. He had been cut and cut – part of his chest looked like someone had once stuck a pole through it, and he hadn't been able to grow enough tissue to refill the wound. And under his bandages was another wound.

Her eyes spilled tears, making him a blur of reflected lamplight. 'I'm sorry. I don't know why he wants to kill me. I swear I don't know why he wants to kill me.'

'My lady.' His eyes glittered through the blur, and his voice sounded like his eyes. 'Your cheek is almost healed. That's good. When he hit you, I couldn't see how bad it was. I thought I was too late. Then this idiot' – he was referring to Geraden – 'jumped him and nearly got his neck broken. I thought you were both lost. I'm glad you've got quick reflexes.'

While Terisa blinked her vision clear, he added, 'I've been practicing that counter he used on me. I think I know what to do about it now.'

'If you ever get the chance to find out,' Geraden put in gruffly, 'I'm going to tie you down until it's all over. That way, we won't have to find out whether he can beat you three times in a row. I can't stand the suspense.'

Artagel's smile looked like the fire in his gaze. 'That's the trouble with you. You don't have any confidence in me.'

Geraden wasn't having a good day. For a moment, Terisa feared he might lose his grip on himself. But somehow he managed to smile back at his brother. 'Oh, shut up,' he muttered in a thick growl. 'You're breaking my heart.'

'You heard him, my lady.' Unexpectedly, Artagel began falling asleep. 'If you wake up one morning and find yourself dead, with me tied up on the floor beside you, you'll know what happened. No confidence.' He closed his eyes, and a subtle tension faded out of him.

She and Geraden left him to rest.

For two more days, nothing happened. The thaw weakened, but didn't break. Mindlin sent word that her material had arrived. Argus and Ribuld found no trace of Nyle. To pass the time, Terisa took long, aimless walks through Orison; she even revisited the bazaar because she wanted some fresh air. Now whenever she left her rooms alone at least one guard accompanied her:

Castellan Lebbick had made his orders for her protection stricter. But she saw no sign of Prince Kragen or the High King's Monomach anywhere.

Not long after breakfast on the third day, however, Geraden came to her rooms. 'I've just had a talk with the Tor,' he announced, trying to sound cheerful. He was feeling too much stress to carry it off, unfortunately.

She asked the natural question. 'What did he want?'

'He wanted to tell me about his conversation with Elega.'

'And how did it go?'

'Not very well. I think he underestimated her.' Geraden shook his head. He didn't like what he was thinking. 'You remember he said he wanted to teach her "the fear of discovery." Unfortunately, she doesn't seem to fear discovery. "She declines to be taught," he said. In fact, she defied him to produce one scrap of proof that she was in communication with Prince Kragen.

'That was bad enough,' he commented. 'Whatever her plan is, it's already at work. And she's sure we can't stop her. But—' He grimaced and met Terisa's gaze glumly. 'She was so convincing the Tor isn't sure he believes us anymore.'

Terisa winced.

'He made quite a speech about it. He told me that before I aimed any more accusations at my own brother and the King's eldest daughter I should make an effort to produce a witness or two, instead of relying on empty-headed suspicions.'

'But I *saw* Prince Kragen and Nyle meet each other,' she protested.

He shook his head again. 'They both emerged from behind the same tent. Maybe they just happened to go back there at the same time to relieve themselves.'

'Do you think I'm wrong?'

'No,' he answered at once. 'He's behaving too strangely. There has to be an explanation.' A moment later, however, he added in a pained tone, 'But I wouldn't want Castellan Lebbick to throw him in the dungeon for reasons as thin as what we have.'

That expression of certainty did little to make her feel better.

Geraden returned to spend the evening with her. They were together when a guard brought a message from Argus and Ribuld.

It was cryptic:

'Got Nyle. See Artagel.'

So Terisa and Geraden went to see Artagel.

He was half sitting up in bed, with several pillows propped behind his back, and he looked clearer and cooler of eye, less feverish. His smile was distant and a little sad, rather than fierce. 'He came to visit me,' he explained. 'They picked him up when he left.'

'I don't understand,' muttered Geraden. 'He's been hiding out for days. Why did he suddenly decide to visit you?'

Artagel tried to shrug; the movement hurt his torso. 'If *you* don't understand, don't expect *me* to figure it out.' He wasn't being sarcastic. 'I don't understand him any better than I understand you.'

Geraden ignored that remark. 'What did he want to talk about? What did he say?'

The memory emphasized Artagel's unaccustomed sadness. In a thin voice, he said, 'He didn't look glad to see me. I suppose that's because I'm hurt. But he's seen me hurt before. At least I'm not dead. If he was worried about me, wouldn't he be glad to see I'm getting better?

'Anyway, he asked me if there was any news from Houseldon. But he's been there more recently than I have. He asked me' – Artagel's eyes avoided Geraden's – 'when you were going to stop embarrassing the family here and go back home where you belong. I didn't try to answer that.'

Geraden held himself still.

'Then he asked me what would happen to Orison in a siege, now that we've got that breach. The last time I saw it, the wall Lebbick is building wasn't very impressive. He asked me if we had any defense left. He asked me how long I thought it would be before King Joyse got us into a war with *some*body. But he wasn't listening to the answers.

'Then—' Artagel stared at the ceiling while the lines in his face got deeper, cut by what he remembered. 'Then he told me how much he admired me. I was his hero – I was *always* his hero. The first thing he could remember about his own life was wanting to be like me. But he just didn't have the balance, or the reflexes. And his muscles refused to develop the right kind of strength for a longsword.

'And everybody in the family seemed to be content with him the way he was, when the way he was wasn't what *he* wanted. Having his parents and his brothers content with him did nothing except make his heart ache. Nobody expected him to be *good* at anything. They were proud of me. And they were ambitious for you. They wanted you to marry Elega and become a great Imager. But nobody wanted anything from him. Or for him.'

Swallowing hard, Artagel stopped.

'Is that it?' asked Geraden quietly. 'He didn't say anything else?'

'I told you,' Artagel snarled. 'Don't expect me to explain it.' But his anger wasn't aimed at Geraden. 'The best I could think of was to ask him how he managed to admire me, when I didn't even have a home of my own or a woman who could put up with me, not to mention children, and I was lying here with a stupid *hole* in my ribs after the High King's Monomach had already beaten me twice.'

Geraden put a hand on his brother's shoulder. 'Don't worry about it. There was nothing you could have said that would have made a difference. He's already committed.' His tone was more reassuring than his expression. 'He was just trying to apologize.'

'Apologize? For what?'

'For choosing the other side.' Geraden sounded like he understood perfectly. 'If everything he and Elega and Prince Kragen are planning works out – and you and I don't turn our backs on King Joyse – he might end up being responsible for our deaths.' A note of grimness came into his voice. 'That's why we have to stop him. He'll hardly be able to stand the rest of his life if he has both of us on his conscience. On top of everything else.'

Terisa watched the two brothers study each other. Finally, Artagel managed a crooked smile. 'Well, I'm not going to be much help. That physician swore he'll have me clubbed if I try to get out of bed too soon. But there probably isn't a guard in Orison who doesn't know Ribuld and Argus are trying to do you a favor for me. You should be able to get all the support you need.'

Somehow, Geraden chuckled. 'I would rather have you. But I suppose I ought to be satisfied with one or two thousand of Castellan Lebbick's best men.' Then he sighed. 'I hope he doesn't keep us waiting much longer. I want to know what's going on.'

Terisa felt the same way.

As it happened, Nyle didn't keep them waiting much longer. In fact, if Argus and Ribuld hadn't found him when they did, they probably would have missed him altogether. Before dawn the next morning, while Terisa was still in bed, tangled in sweaty sheets and dreaming that she could see Gart's blade as it came for her like the edge of a star, she was awakened by a wooden pounding and Geraden's voice.

'Terisa. *Terisa.*'

Naturally, she decided the noise must be coming from the door to the secret passage. She peeled the sheet off her naked back and climbed, instantly shivering, out of bed to let Master Quillon or Adept Havelock in. But that didn't make any sense. Why were they knocking so loudly, when she had forgotten to put a chair in the wardrobe to block the door?

With a wrench, her perceptions corrected their orientation. Was it really this *cold*, or was she just chilled by the effect of her dreams? Her robe was on the chair that should have been in the wardrobe. She snatched it up, got her arms into the sleeves, knotted the sash around the deep velvet. Geraden? Shivering so hard she nearly lost her balance, she went into the sitting room and unbolted the door.

Light from the lamps outside washed inward, sweeping Geraden with it.

'Come on,' he whispered at once. 'We've got to hurry. He's leaving.'

'Leaving?' Her voice shook wildly. 'What are you talking about? What time is it?'

'Almost dawn.' He was breathing hard: he had been running. 'It's Nyle. This is our chance to find out what he's doing. Maybe it's our chance to stop him.'

'Leaving?' she repeated. Her robe seemed to hold no warmth at all. 'How can he be leaving? Where can he go?'

'That's what we'll find out,' Geraden hissed. 'Just *get ready*. He was in the stables when Argus and Ribuld finally figured out what he was doing. He's probably in the courtyard by now. He'll be out the gate by the time you get your clothes on. We've got to *hurry*.'

Some of his tension reached her. She turned to look for some clothes. Which clothes? Her old shirt and pants. And the sheepskin coat. The warm boots. There was still a small fire in the hearth. Why was she so *cold*? 'How can we follow him?' she asked, trying to get herself under control. 'He's practically gone already.'

Geraden permitted himself a growl of exasperation. 'Argus is waiting for us. Ribuld will follow Nyle. He'll leave us a trail. *Come on.*'

She got herself moving and tried to hurry.

Violent tremors made her hands fumble. As familiar as these clothes were, she had trouble putting them on. From the privacy of the bathroom, she asked, 'What's happened to the weather? I'm freezing.'

'Bitter, isn't it,' he muttered. 'The thaw is over – at least for a while. But there's no new snow. We would be better off if there was. It would slow down anybody who might be marching in this direction. And it might make it easier for us to follow Nyle.'

A part of her was glad that she was too cold and rushed to think about what she was doing. If she thought about it, it might turn out to be crazy. Her rooms were still full of nightmares. It would be good to escape them.

A moment later, she pulled on her coat and left the bathroom. 'I'm ready,' she said, although that was probably nonsense. 'Let's go.'

He took her hand, and they left.

They went down the stairs almost at a run. Holding his hand gave her the illusion that she could keep him from falling, but he didn't stumble. All she remembered about the stables was that they were somewhere near the warren of rooms where the guards were quartered. And she had never ridden a horse. The route he chose appeared convoluted because it bypassed a number of long, straight halls and passages that ran in the wrong direction. The exercise was just starting to generate a little human warmth inside her coat when he brought her to the place where Orison wintered its horses.

The guard at the side entrance nodded sleepily and said. 'Argus is waiting. Keep it quiet. Nobody's supposed to be here this early. Upsets the horses.' Then he let them in.

The low ceiling was supported by a great number of stone pillars, as well as by bulky wooden posts which also anchored the sides and rails and gates of the individual stalls. In addition, many of the stalls had been constructed haphazardly, with the result that the aisles between them were crooked. Consequently, the true dimensions of the place were hard to see. Its size was only apparent from one of the main aisles, which met like roads in the center of the stables.

During his tour, Geraden had taken Terisa to the center and showed her that the stalls stretched cavernously for a hundred yards in each direction.

The ceiling multiplied noise; but the place was much quieter now than she remembered it. Still, a constant rustling murmur punctuated with staccato thuds and coughs filled the air as hundreds of horses snuffled in their sleep, broke wind, shifted positions, and knocked their hooves against the slats of the stalls. So many animals put out enough heat to make the cavern warm, one of the most noticeable effects of which was to perfect the sweet, thick stench of horse droppings and urine fermenting in sodden straw. Together, the noise and the warmth and the smell were comforting in an odd way, like a return to a primitive womb. And the womblike atmosphere was increased by the fact that at night the stables were lit only by a few small lanterns placed at considerable intervals along the aisles. Nevertheless the air made Terisa feel that she had fungus growing in her lungs.

Geraden put his finger to his lips unnecessarily and led her forward.

She spared as much attention as she could to keep her feet out of the brown piles that dotted the aisles, but she had a number of other things to think about. Now that she was more awake, she was both excited and fearful. She was going to go out. For the first time since this whole experience began, she was going to see the outside of Orison. On the other hand, she believed instinctively that something was about to go wrong.

Geraden spotted Argus. The guard stood near a lantern with three horses, already saddled. They nickered and snorted softly, complaining about being put to work so early in the morning. Geraden waved and hurried toward the grizzled veteran.

Bracing herself to endure Argus' crude sense of humor, Terisa followed.

Over leather clothes, Argus wore a mail shirt and leggings; over his mail, a cloak that looked like a bearskin. His iron cap was on his head. A dagger hung at his belt opposite his longsword, but he had left his pike behind. As Geraden and Terisa reached him, he grinned, showing the gaps where several of his teeth had been knocked out. 'Good,' he leered. 'I have horses. I even have brandy.' He indicated a small pouch tied to the back of one saddle. 'You have a woman. This is going to be more fun than guard duty.'

Geraden brushed that remark aside. 'How far ahead do you think he is?'

'She's in my debt, don't you think?' Argus persisted. 'I don't care how fine a lady she is. The finer the better. I've risked my life for her twice now. She owes me a little gratitude.' He reached a grubby hand toward Terisa's cheek.

'Argus.' Suddenly, Geraden clamped a hold on the guard's wrist. Though Argus was much larger, Geraden wrenched his hand down. 'Do not trifle with me.' Strength echoed in his voice – strength that Terisa hadn't heard for a long time. 'Nyle is my brother. How far ahead is he?'

Involuntarily, Argus winced. 'He has his own horse,' he replied as if he were surprised to find himself backing down.

'He didn't have to get permission to take it and go. And he didn't have to stand around here waiting for you. But Ribuld has him. We should be able to catch up.'

'Then let's go,' said Geraden impatiently. The echo was gone. 'Who gets which horse?'

'This one's mine.' With a slap to its rump, Argus shifted a rawboned roan stallion out of his way. 'You get the mare.' He indicated a smaller horse the color of fresh axle grease. 'She likes to kick, but you can handle her. At least she's tough.

'The lady can have the gelding.'

Terisa found herself staring at a horse with rancid eyes, a mottled coat, and an expression of sublime stupidity.

With an effort, she cleared her throat. Her voice sounded small and lost. 'I don't actually know how to ride.'

Argus flashed her a look that might have been anger or glee. 'Geraden mentioned that. He didn't explain why you have to come with us. I mean, if you can't ride, and you think you're too good to spread your legs for a man who saved your life, why bother?' He gave a massive shrug. 'But at least he warned me.

'The only way this gelding can hurt you is if he steps on you. He hasn't got the brains to do anything except follow the nearest thing he recognizes – and the only thing he ever recognizes is another horse. Just hold on to the saddle horn and let him do the rest.'

Still she hesitated. Geraden and Argus stared at her. Abruptly, Geraden came and took her to the side of the mount. Holding the stirrup, he said, 'Put your left foot here, grab the saddle horn, and swing your right leg over. Leave the reins where they are. We'll adjust the stirrups when you're in the saddle.'

She looked at him hard and saw that his eyes were dark with suppressed urgency. Swallowing a lump of alarm, she nodded her head. Then, before she had time to panic, she put her foot into the stirrup and lunged for the saddle.

Argus caught her on the other side and squared her in her seat. The ceiling seemed perilously close. Argus and Geraden made her stirrups longer or shorter without consulting her. The gelding shifted its weight. She gripped the saddle horn until her knuckles ached. To no one in particular, she said, 'Why am I doing this?'

'Because' – Argus flashed his remaining teeth – 'you've heard it said that a few hours on a horse make a woman desperate for a man.'

Geraden was already on the mare. 'If you don't stop harassing her,' he muttered, 'I'm going to wait until we're several miles from here, and then I'm going to break all your legs and leave you to walk back.'

Argus let out a guffaw which made several of the nearby horses whinny in protest and brought an angry insult from a watching stablehand whom Terisa hadn't noticed before. Argus wasn't daunted, however. Chuckling to himself, he took hold of the gelding's reins and tugged the beast into motion behind him.

Terisa clung to the saddle while Argus led her and Geraden out to one of the main aisles and along it toward the closed passage that went in the direction of the courtyard.

The guards at the main entrance lifted the gate without a word: apparently, Argus had already spoken to them. But when he and his companion reached the gate to the courtyard – with Terisa shivering again at the sudden drop in temperature – he had to stop and speak to the sentries for several minutes. She saw him point at Geraden, heard him mention Artagel. Finally, the gate opened, and the horses crunched out into the frozen mud of the courtyard.

'One more gate,' Geraden told her softly. 'Then we can start hurrying.'

The sky was clear above the high, dark walls of Orison, but most of the stars were gone, washed out by the oncoming gray flood of dawn. The air was so sharp it cut her throat: she could feel it in the bottom of her lungs, pricking like needles. From horseback, the ground looked faraway and dangerous. The cold seemed to make the leather of her saddle slick; because she couldn't stick to it, she had trouble keeping her balance over the stiff-legged lurch of the gelding's stride. Geraden looked like a shadow beside her. Argus was nearly invisible against the darkness of the wall ahead.

Other people moved in the courtyard, waking up, getting ready for another day. Small lights flickered on the inner balconies. A few more showed in the bazaar. One or two cooking fires had been started. Terisa barely noticed them.

The predawn gloom and the shadow of the walls hid the gate, but she remembered it – a massive shutter raised or lowered by winches. Because Mordant was said to be at peace, the gate stood open during the day. At night it was down.

When the horses reached it, Argus dismounted and went to talk to its guards. For some reason – perhaps because his back was turned – his voice was an indeterminate murmur, but the sentry could be heard clearly.

'You're out of your mind, Argus.'

Argus made some response.

'We *had* to let him out. He's a son of the Domne. We don't have any orders to keep him in.'

Again.

'Try explaining *that* to the Castellan.'

Geraden shifted in his saddle, fretting. Terisa could feel her face freezing stiff.

Then: 'All right. He's a son of the Domne too. And you're assigned to him. And we thought it was just some strumpet with you. If you don't back us up, I'll personally see to it you never have children.'

A faint call rose. Geraden let a breath of relief through his teeth as Argus came back to his horse. His boots on the mud sounded like he was striding through broken glass. After a moment, Terisa heard a long creaking noise as rope began to stretch between the winches and the gate.

She saw the gate go up, a deep darkness lifting off the lighter background of the road.

'Come on,' Argus muttered. Taking Terisa's reins again, he put his heels to the stallion and started forward so sharply that she let out a yelp and nearly lost her seat.

When they were outside, Geraden caught up with Argus. 'Well done,' he rasped sarcastically. 'Do you *want* her to fall?'

'Don't be so prickly,' replied the guard. '*I* didn't know she's a squealer.' Terisa had the impression he was grinning.

She unknotted her muscles, flexed her grip on the saddlehorn, and began making a conscious effort to find the point of balance on the gelding's back.

Overhead, the paling sky seemed impossibly open. The gradual hills immediately around the castle were naked of trees, kept that way so that Castellan Lebbick could watch his enemies approach him; in the dawn twilight the bareness of the slopes made them feel as expansive as the heavens, wide and unmeasured to the extreme horizons after the relative constriction of Orison. In spite of her precarious perch, she felt her excitement rise.

If anything, the air was even colder here. Most of the road had been chewed to mud and iron ruts by days of wagon wheels, but whenever the hooves of the horses hit a patch of snow, the distinct clatter of horseshoes against hard dirt changed to an oddly resonant crumpling sound, a break-and-echo as the hooves stamped to the ground through the iced surface, the snow melted by the thaw and then refrozen. The graying of the sky grew stronger, enabling her to see the black trees that lined the road after it branched. One branch, she remembered, went south; another, northwest; the third continued northeast toward the Care of Perdon: roads running toward secrets and surprises in every direction. The world was something she had hardly begun to discover.

Although spring was drawing closer, the sun was still so far to the south that she couldn't glimpse the source of the dawn past Orison's bulk until she had ridden almost to the road's branching. By then, the trees were tipped with light as if they were catching fire. Sunshine glowed coldly on the towers and battlements behind her, making Orison look less dire – but larger somehow, as though a sense of its true size were impossible from inside. Its gray stone appeared stronger and more enduring than she had expected.

From the branching, she watched the sun come up and wished she were a little less cold so that she could feel its touch on her face.

'Now what?' Geraden demanded of Argus. His mind was clenched to what he was doing. 'How do we know which way to go?'

'That's Ribuld's job.' Argus scanned the area. 'He's supposed to leave signs. Probably in the snow beside the road.' Tossing her reins to Terisa, he moved toward the left edge of the road. 'Start looking.'

Geraden took the other side. The two men began to work around the branching. Experimentally, Terisa picked up her reins, gripped them as her companions did, and gave the gelding a tentative kick, trying to make it follow Geraden. But it went after Argus instead.

When Argus burst out laughing, she looked where he pointed and saw a mark shaped like an arrow in the snow. It had been drawn rather unsteadily with a warm, yellow liquid.

Northwest.

Geraden came to look at the sign and grinned in spite of himself. 'That's got to be him.'

'Right. Now we can start moving faster.' The guard glanced at Terisa as if he anticipated entertainment. 'But we've got to be careful. They might turn off.'

Geraden nodded and cantered his mare to the northern side of the road. Although he didn't appear especially smooth or self-contained in the saddle – his elbows flapped, and his weight bounced with the horse's gait – his experience was evident. He knew how to ride well enough to do so without thinking about it.

Argus hadn't resumed his hold on Terisa's reins. 'Come on. You've got to learn sometime.' Watching her over his shoulder, he started away, matching Geraden's pace along the western margin of the road.

She was still trying to decide how hard to kick her mount when it lumbered ahead, following the stallion.

For one moment that seemed to last a long time because it was frozen by panic and cold, she dropped the reins and clutched for the saddle horn, but the gelding's gait hit her so hard that she missed her grip and started to fall.

When she failed to fall, she didn't immediately understand why. By degrees, however, the strain in her legs made her aware that she was clenching the beast with her knees.

This development amazed her so thoroughly that she only put one hand back on the saddle horn. With the other, she retrieved the reins. Then, borne

376

along by a burst of exhilaration, she kicked the gelding to make it catch up with Argus.

The guard gave her a nod of disappointed approval and turned his attention to the road.

Her mount's spine pounded her up and down. Its tack jangled so loudly – and her legs and rear slapped the leather so hard – that she wanted to shout, Do we have to go this fast? But a residue of common sense told her that for her sake Argus and Geraden were already going more slowly than they wished. She closed her mouth so that she wouldn't bite her tongue and held on.

Orison looked surprisingly far away. She had to glance back over her left shoulder to see the castle. A purple flag flew from the King's tower now, raised to meet the day. Then the road crested a hill, dipped into a hollow, and Orison was gone.

A short distance later, a spur of the road ran north to a village nestled picturesquely in a little glen. Most of the twenty or thirty houses had wooden frames, but a few had obviously been constructed of stone. The snow had melted off their slate roofs; smoke curled from their chimneys as fires were built up for cooking and warmth. The angle of the sunlight enabled her to make out cattle pens in the shelter of the hills. These people raised meat for the castle.

In a war, a siege, they would have to evacuate their homes and live in Orison.

Geraden found no indication that Ribuld had taken the spur. The three riders went on.

Terisa's hands were red and freezing, despite the exertion of holding herself on her mount's back. Her face was so stiff it felt like it might break. Whenever a scrap of breeze caught her eyes, tears ran to ice on her cheeks. Gradually, she understood that it would actually be easier to keep her seat if the horse moved a bit faster. But Argus and Geraden now seemed to be going as fast as they dared. They had to watch for Ribuld's signs.

Over the rise of another hill, they came suddenly upon a wain loaded – Terisa would have said overloaded – with barrels of all sizes. Although it faced toward Orison, it was stopped by the side of the road for no apparent reason. At a glance, Terisa couldn't tell which looked more miserable, the shaggy, club-headed workhorse in the traces, or the driver huddling on the wagonbench, clutching his reins with hands that barely protruded from the mound of wool blankets wrapped around him. A moment later, however, the driver explained himself by croaking, 'Argus? One of you Argus?'

The stallion skittered to a halt beside the wain. 'I'm Argus,' the guard said, studying the driver.

'Guard like you gave me a silver double to wait here.' The driver sounded like he was being strangled by the weight of his blankets. 'Too cold for that. About to give you up.'

'Now why would Ribuld do that?' drawled Argus.

The man's eyes glittered shrewdly. 'Too cold. One silver double—' His horse snorted vapor. 'Not enough.'

At that, Argus guffawed. 'Pigshit! Taking this load into Orison won't earn

377

you more than half a dozen coppers. You've already tripled your take. Don't push your luck.'

The mound of blankets moved in a shrug. The driver made a clucking noise, and his horse pricked up its ears. When he twitched the reins, the horse leaned into its harness, and the wagon started to move.

Geraden swore under his breath. Argus was unperturbed, however. Over the groaning of the wain's axletrees, he commented amiably, 'I'm thirsty. Before you leave, I think I'll knock a few holes in some of these casks.' He drew his longs-word. 'Most of it's probably swill, but you may have something drinkable back there.'

The driver tugged his horse to a halt. He considered for a moment, then said, 'Glad to help the King's guards. Guard like you left the road here. Asked me to mark the place.'

'Which direction?' demanded Geraden.

'North.'

The Apt fisted his mare to the north side of the road. Almost at once, he called, 'I've got his tracks. It looks like at least two riders went this way.'

Argus sheathed his sword and gave the driver an elaborate bow. In a tone of gratitude, he said, 'I'm sure it's *all* swill,' and went to join Geraden.

Terisa's gelding followed with an air of lugubrious endurance.

As soon as she and her companions left the road, she was surprised by the noise they made. Crunching through the frozen white crust and thudding to the ground beneath, the horses' hooves were loud enough to be heard half a mile away – a sound like a cross between shattering glass and a distant cannonade. Nevertheless Argus set a somewhat faster pace and pulled ahead. After a moment, she realized that he was trying to match the stallion's gait to Ribuld's trail, riding as much as possible on already broken snow. When Geraden swung in behind him, and the gelding transferred its affections from the stallion to the mare, their progress became noticeably less noisy.

Ribuld's trail ran along a shallow valley between small hills, then crossed a ridge and began to descend a series of slopes marked with brittle thickets and black copses. Woods filled a fold in the terrain ahead, and the fold deepened as the ground around it rose into sharper hills. Argus followed the trail straight into the woods.

There he had to slow down. The ground between the trunks wasn't particularly cluttered; the wood itself wasn't thick. But many of the branches grew low enough to swipe at riders.

Barely cantering now, listening to the way the metallic sound of tack seemed to echo delicately back from every tree because of the steeper hills on either side, and wondering why she felt so much like holding her breath, Terisa followed Geraden into a gully which became a rocky streambed with its bottom less than half full of ice and crusted water. The trees on the slopes grew more thickly together, pointing their dark twigs like fingers at each other; but the bed remained clear. Now when the horses broke fresh crust their hooves clicked and clattered on stone.

Her legs ached. Her hands hurt like raw ice. She had the impression that the cold had begun to peel her face back from the bone. How else could she explain the sensation of numb pain in her cheek and chin and nose? She should have been as miserable as the driver and his workhorse.

But she wasn't.

For some reason, she expected to hear horns.

Then the streambed debouched into a valley where its waters joined a larger stream which had cut a ravine for itself among the hills. The ravine went roughly from east to west, and its northward wall especially was steep but climbable. As soon as Argus hissed a warning and pointed, she saw the horse tethered in the low flat made by the joining of the streams.

Ribuld crouched at the crest of the northward wall, peering over the rim: his cloak made him look like a shaggy rock. He turned his head, gazed downward, and waved.

'This is it,' muttered Geraden. 'That ridge probably blocks the sound. But we still need to be quiet.'

'Right.' Argus dismounted, and Terisa did the same. While he tethered his stallion as Ribuld had done to an old piece of deadwood sticking up out of the snow, she nearly collapsed because her legs were suddenly knotted with cramps. She had forgotten how cold her feet were. And her feet had forgotten the ground: she expected it to wobble like the gelding.

Her companions were already laboring up the side of the ravine.

Determined not to be left behind, she struggled after them.

The climb was easier than she expected. There was enough rock under the snow and dirt and the autumn's layer of fallen leaves to give her secure footing; and her legs were glad to do almost anything that didn't involve clutching at a horse. She reached Ribuld only a moment or two behind Geraden and Argus.

'Good timing,' Ribuld whispered, grimacing around the old scar that ran from his hairline between his eyes almost to his mouth. 'He's been here awhile. The others just arrived.'

Kneeling in the snow at Geraden's side, she looked past the edge of the ridge into another ravine like the one behind her. Directly below her, a horse champed at the cold. Near it, a man with his back to her stood beside a small fire that burned almost without smoke. She took him to be Nyle. His fire seemed so wonderful to her that she could practically taste its warmth.

On the other side of the bottom, four men were busy securing more horses. Three of them looked like bodyguards.

The fourth was Prince Kragen.

TWENTY-ONE

AT LEAST ONE
PLOT DISCOVERED

'Nyle,' the Prince said.

Geraden's brother returned the greeting. 'My lord Prince.'

Terisa could hear them perfectly. It was astonishing how well the cold and the ravine wall brought the sound up to her.

'I hope you were not kept waiting long.'

'Just long enough to build a fire.'

Like his men, Prince Kragen was wrapped in a white robe, with boots of white fur on his feet and a white fur cap on his head, using the winter itself for concealment. At first glance, Nyle's black-brown garb, his half-cloak and leggings, looked like a bad choice by comparison. But his clothes were indistinguishable from the colors of the driftwood in the ravine, the dark trunks of the trees. If he stood still, no one would see him.

'What news do you have of Orison?'

'What's the news of Alend, my lord Prince?'

A fringe of black hair showed around the rim of Prince Kragen's cap, hair as black as his eyes. He studied Nyle for a moment, then turned to his men and gave them a gesture that set them in motion. Two of them went in opposite directions to keep watch up and down the ravine. The third began to unpack bundles tied to the back of his saddle.

A bit sadly, Prince Kragen commented, 'You still do not really trust me, do you, Nyle?'

'Yes and no, my lord Prince.' Nyle's voice emerged from a clenched throat. 'I'm committed to you. But we're traditional enemies. That's hard to forget.'

At Terisa's side, Geraden picked up a handful of snow and rubbed it across his face to cool a reckless inner fire.

'I understand,' replied the Prince evenly. 'But I am more at risk here. You can ride back to Orison and resume your life. As soon as we separate, you are innocent. If *I* am caught, Castellan Lebbick might have me executed before anybody can explain to him that killing foreign princes is rarely wise.'

'What news do you have of Orison?'

Argus turned away. Ribuld hissed at him for silence; he ignored the warning and began to pick his way back down the slope. Fortunately, the wall cut off the noise he made.

Grudgingly, Nyle answered, 'Elega is in trouble.'

Prince Kragen flashed a glance. 'What trouble?'

'For some reason – I don't know how – that woman Terisa of Morgan decided you and Elega are plotting against the King. She convinced my brother Geraden. And he convinced the Tor.

'I told you the Tor has set himself up as some kind of chancellor. He issues orders as if he has the King's authority behind him, and no one questions him. It might be true. After all, he *is* the Tor – the lord who gave King Joyse his start.'

'He is also,' the Prince put in, 'a drunken fool.'

'He is. That's probably why he believed Geraden. There aren't many people left who can muster that much optimism.'

Geraden heard this with a grimace that reminded Terisa of Artagel's fighting grin.

'And what trouble has this drunken fool caused for the lady Elega?' pursued Prince Kragen.

'He told her he knows what she's doing. Then he went off on a long lecture about the loyalty children owe their parents.' Nyle shrugged. 'She says it wasn't much. She gave him a piece of her mind and left him looking – she says he looked cowed. And she *says* he won't be able to interfere with her part of your plan. I'm not so sure. All he has to do is drop a few hints to Lebbick, and she won't be able to take a step without half the guards in Orison watching her.'

'I see.' Prince Kragen thought for a moment. 'I regret that she is at hazard. But she has assured me many times that her role is secure – and she is a woman who conveys conviction.'

In a decisive tone, he concluded, 'We must trust that she will do what she has said.'

Nyle's voice sounded like he had both fists knotted around it. 'I'm still waiting to hear exactly what that is.'

The Prince stiffened. With misleading casualness, he said, 'My lord Prince.'

'My lord Prince.'

Prince Kragen's nod advised, Remember it. His mouth commented, 'The lady Elega's safety and success depend upon secrecy.'

'Then maybe you'll tell me the news of Alend. My lord Prince.' Nyle's anger was controlled, but unmistakable. 'Maybe you'll tell me why we had to meet today. Not sooner. Not later. All I've had so far are assurances and rhetoric. Maybe you'll tell me what's going on.'

Geraden bobbed his head in approval. 'Good,' he breathed. 'Make him tell you what's going on.'

Ribuld glowered at the Apt for speaking.

'In a moment.' Prince Kragen's composure was equal to the occasion. 'I will answer a number of your questions in a moment. First, however, I prefer to tell you what I want you to do.'

Nyle still had his back to the eavesdroppers: Terisa couldn't see his face. But his shoulders hunched as though he were strangling things inside himself.

'I asked you to meet me here on this particular day,' the Prince said steadily, 'and I asked you to be prepared to leave Orison, because I want you to ride to Perdon. I want you to find the Perdon and offer him the kingship of Mordant.'

Breathing too loudly, Argus came back up the hill carrying his pouch of brandy. His companions paid no attention to him. At Prince Kragen's announcement, Geraden's whole body twitched. Terisa stared. At least temporarily, even Ribuld was too interested in what he heard to be interrupted by liquor.

Nyle's surprise showed in the way he stood. 'Why?'

'Why the Perdon?' Prince Kragen hid a trace of amusement under his black mustache. 'Why the kingship? Or why you?'

Nyle seemed unable to do anything except nod.

'The Perdon is my only reasonable choice. You see, I profited from my meeting with the lords, although it did not have the outcome I desired. The Fayle is too old – and too loyal. The Tor has become a drunken fool. The Domne would refuse. The Armigite—' Prince Kragen snorted. 'As for the Termigan, he is too far away. Also he is concerned only for the fate of his own Care.

'The Perdon must be offered the kingship to prove our good faith.'

Furiously, Geraden whispered, 'Not to mention the fact that the Perdon is the only lord with an army close enough to threaten you, my lord Prince.'

'Despite what King Joyse and Castellan Lebbick believe,' Prince Kragen continued reasonably, 'it has never been the Alend Monarch's intention to conquer Mordant for himself. His first priority – his only overriding commitment – is to fill the vacuum of power in Mordant so that the Congery of Imagers will not fall into the hands of Cadwal. To accomplish that, we will conquer Mordant because we have no alternative. What else can we do? The King insulted my mission. The lords refused the union Master Eremis and I offered them.

'But we will not take Mordant for ourselves if the Perdon can be persuaded to be King. That will be your job. He might not listen to such a proposal from me. We are traditional enemies, as you have said. But a son of the Domne – a lifelong friend of the lady Elega – may perhaps persuade him. For the good of all who oppose Festten and Cadwal.

'Will you do it, Nyle?'

Nyle was silent for a long time. When he spoke, he sounded both astonished and relieved.

'Yes.' In spite of its softness, the word came out with too much steam, as if it were exploding from inside him. 'Yes, my lord Prince. I'll do it.'

Geraden covered his head with his hands, inadvertently smearing snow into his hair.

'Good.' Prince Kragen stepped closer to the fire to warm his hands. 'Then you will need to know "what's going on," in order to convey that information to the Perdon.'

Argus put his brandy pouch down in front of Terisa. Noticing it, she realized that she was miserably cold. With a shiver, she loosened the neck of the pouch and raised it to her mouth. Like her cheeks, her lips were too numb to know what they were doing, but her tongue verified that the brandy was going into her mouth rather than down her chin. It tasted like badly perfumed tarnish remover, but it did what it was supposed to do: it raised the temperature of her blood several degrees.

She passed the pouch to Geraden.

Down in the ravine, Prince Kragen crooked a finger at the bodyguard who had unpacked the bundles. The man came to him and handed him a stylus and a small writing tablet. Standing by the fire, Prince Kragen began to write. His fingers held the stylus as though they knew nothing about swords and had never helped save Terisa's life.

'Is that a message to the Perdon, my lord Prince?' Nyle's tone suggested impatience.

The Prince shook his head. 'To my father. The Alend Monarch needs to know that you have agreed to approach the Perdon for us.'

'What will he do?'

'What he is already doing.' Prince Kragen's mind was on his message. 'In the bazaar of Orison during the first morning of the thaw, you brought me the lady Elega's word that she had learned a way to fulfill her part of our plans. You noticed, I think, that I was pleased by this news.

'I was pleased because much hinges on her role. While you and I spoke together – while we chose the day and place for this meeting – my father and his armies were already crossing the Pestil into Armigite.'

Argus, Ribuld, and Geraden became still: all movement was sucked out of them. They didn't blink or glance around; they didn't appear to breathe. Every part of them – their arms and legs, the angles of their backs, the set of their shoulders – concentrated on what they were hearing.

So it was all a lie, thought Terisa. His *peaceful* mission. His meeting with the lords. A lie. The Alend Monarch had begun marching before he even had time to learn the outcome of his son's mission. He had never intended to do anything except invade Mordant.

Like an echo of her shocked thoughts, Nyle articulated softly, 'You never wanted peace. You never meant King Joyse to take your mission seriously. You just came here looking for people to help you betray him.' Both arms leaped outward in a gesture full of violence, fiercely truncated. 'This is what you call good faith.'

Distinct and sibilant in the cold, a sword came out of its sheath. Prince Kragen's bodyguard moved forward, aiming the tip of his blade at Nyle's throat.

Ribuld clutched at his own sword.

But a quick wave of the Prince's hand stopped the bodyguard. The man shrugged stiffly and resheathed his longsword.

'I understand your anger, Nyle.' Prince Kragen spoke calmly, almost casually, but his tone warned Nyle not to push him too far. 'You misunderstand me, however. The problem is one of communication, is it not? Knowing that I spent nearly thirty days in the worst of this winter making my way from the Alend Monarch's seat in Scarab to Orison, you believe that we have had no time to exchange messages since my arrival here. Therefore you conclude that I have come merely to serve plans which he made before I left him.'

Nyle didn't move.

With a faint smile, the Prince continued, 'Those unruly barons, the Alend Lieges, are always striving to gain the advantage over each other. At last their petty wrestling has produced something useful.' Another gesture to his bodyguard brought the man forward carrying a bundle that appeared to be a swath of cloth wrapped around a rigid frame.

Prince Kragen rolled his message tightly and tied it into a tiny packet with a piece of thread. When he was done, his bodyguard unveiled the bundle, revealing a bird in a square cage.

'A carrier pigeon,' Terisa breathed in astonishment. 'They're using *carrier pigeons*.'

Argus, Ribuld, and Geraden all stared at her for an instant, then snapped their attention back down into the ravine.

The bird was unmistakably a pigeon. It cooed comfortably as the bodyguard removed it from the cage and held it so that Prince Kragen could bind his message to its leg. 'One of the Lieges,' the Prince explained, 'discovered that these birds have the ability to find their way over any distance back to the place they have been trained to recognize as home. This one has learned to identify a combination of tents, standards, and wagonlines that invariably occurs in my father's encampments. It will fly to him when it is released.

'Now do you understand?' Prince Kragen's tone was hard, a threat behind his amicable manner. 'I brought a number of these birds from Alend. They bear messages to my father in a day – perhaps less. In this way, I make decisions for him.

'I came to Orison charged with the responsibility of resolving the dilemma of the Congery, Cadwal, and war – the dilemma of your King's strange weakness. I am the Alend Contender. I wish strongly to earn the throne. For that reason, my mission of peace was sincere, I assure you. But when King Joyse rejected it, I began to think of war. I sent messages accordingly. Then, however, both Master Eremis and the lady Elega offered me hopes that were much preferable to war. Again I sent messages. When the lords of the Cares refused the pact Master Eremis suggested to them – and most especially when I experienced how vulnerable Orison, and therefore the Congery, was to attack from Cadwal – I determined to act on the possibilities the lady Elega and I had discussed.

'The Alend Monarch is doing what I ask of him. And I ask it because I believe it to be the least bloody and most effective answer to an intolerable danger. *High King Festten must not gain control of the Congery.* The breach of Orison's wall is an opportunity I *can not* ignore.'

Firmly, the Prince concluded, 'What is your answer now?'

Nyle looked like he was swallowing hard, trying to adjust his preconceptions to fit new information. At the moment, Geraden appeared to have no opinion about what his brother should do. He seemed to be scrambling to catch up with the implications of what he had just heard. Both Argus and Ribuld watched the encounter below with trouble in their eyes.

'My lord Prince,' Nyle began thickly, 'I should probably apologize. I didn't know this was possible.' His hands moved helplessly at his sides. 'Of course I'll go to Perdon. I'll persuade the Perdon somehow.'

Prince Kragen studied Nyle for a moment. Then he nodded.

His bodyguard released the pigeon.

It took to the air in a flash of gray, a hint of blue and green. Terisa watched it go, an easy labor of wings against the chill sky – watched it as if it were on its way to bring bloodshed down on Orison. After circling briefly, it turned north.

Ribuld glared at her. 'You knew about that bird,' he murmured.

'We have them where I come from.' Defensively, she added, 'We have horses, too, but I've never ridden one before.'

Geraden nudged the guard silent.

Nyle was still struggling to improve his grasp on the situation. 'But is there time?' he asked after some thought. 'When do you think the Alend Monarch will get to Orison? I don't know where the Perdon is. He might not be in Scarping. He might be anywhere along the Vertigon, fighting Cadwals.'

'I have chosen the time with some care,' replied Prince Kragen as if this would reassure Nyle. 'It is important that you not reach the Perdon too soon. If you do, and he is not persuaded, and so he brings his forces against us, he might be able to block us from Orison. For that reason, we did not meet until today. I calculate that if you find him immediately – and he rejects you and comes against us in furious haste – he will not reach Orison until after we have mastered it.'

Geraden shook his head. 'It's not that easy,' he whispered.

'You think it's going to be that easy?' The idea seemed to incense Nyle. 'A siege might take all spring. Even with that breach in the wall. You can't just—'

'Nyle,' the Prince cut in. 'I am not a child. Do not harangue me about sieges. I have studied them deeply. And I assure you that we will be able to master Orison.'

Nyle received this assertion like a man struggling not to let what he heard stun him. 'Still, my lord Prince,' he said slowly, 'it seems to me you're trying to control events too delicately. What if the weather turns against you? We're almost sure to get another storm.'

Prince Kragen shrugged. His patience was wearing thin. 'Then you and the Perdon will be hindered as much as we are.'

'And what about the Armigite?' Nyle seemed unable to keep his anger down. 'Is he going to let you march your army – and *supply* it – straight through his Care without making at least an effort to slow you down?'

At that, Prince Kragen laughed shortly. 'I doubt that I need to concern myself with the Armigite.' His laugh held a note of scorn that made Terisa feel suddenly colder. 'Nevertheless I have done so. He and I have negotiated a pact.

'Sweating fear all the while, he offered me an unhindered passage through his Care for as many armies as I chose to name. And what did he ask in exchange? That we do no violence to his people in their towns and villages? That we leave untouched the cattle pens and storehouses that feed his Care? No. He asked only that he be allowed to remain safe and ignorant – *ignorant,* Nyle – while the fate of Mordant was decided.'

Argus swore under his breath. But Terisa had met the Armigite: she wasn't surprised.

'Personally,' the Prince went on with more nonchalance, 'I would enjoy damaging his ignorance a little. His Care deserves better of him. But we will respect the pact. And we will do no harm to his people or his cattle or his stores. Our aim is to find an answer to your King's weakness – and to oppose Cadwal – not to worsen the old enmity between Mordant and Alend.

'Have I satisfied you, Nyle?'

From the back, Nyle didn't look satisfied: there was too much tension in his stance. Terisa would have expected him to be grateful to Prince Kragen for giving him so few causes for mistrust, so many reasons to believe he was doing the right thing. Why was he still angry? Why did he sound almost livid with fury as he replied, 'Yes, my lord Prince.'

For a moment, Prince Kragen regarded his ally as though he, too, didn't understand Nyle's mood. But apparently what he saw in Nyle's face assured him. 'Good,' he said, suddenly brisk. 'The Perdon will listen to you. Let us begin.'

At once, he signaled to his bodyguards.

The men watching either end of the ravine returned to their horses. Moving stiffly, Nyle readied his own mount. At last, Terisa saw his face. His features were set and implacable, as if nothing – not even his own passion – could dissuade him from the course he had chosen.

Argus rose into a crouch and loosened his sword. 'We'll jump them before they get out of the ravine. Maybe we'll be able to stop them.' The grimace that exposed his missing teeth didn't show much fear. Fighting was his job; he and Ribuld seemed to take it for granted.

But Geraden stopped them. 'Don't be stupid. There are four of them. And if the Prince has any sense, he has more men nearby.

'You.' Speaking quickly so that the guards had no chance to argue with him, he stabbed an index finger at Argus. 'Follow the Prince. Find where he's camped. Keep an eye on him. And leave a trail.

'Ribuld, you get back to Orison.' The lines of Geraden's face were as sharp as the cold. Frost in his eyebrows and snow in his hair made him look strangely feral. 'Tell Castellan Lebbick what you heard. Lead him here. Tell him if he captures the Prince we can use him as hostage. We still have a chance to get out of this mess.

'*Go.*' He gave the guard an urgent push.

Ribuld looked once at Argus and back at Geraden, puckering his scar in concentration. Then he launched himself down the steep slope almost at a run.

Prince Kragen and his bodyguards swung up into their saddles. Nyle began dousing his fire with handfuls of crusted snow.

'Thanks a lot,' Argus whispered sarcastically to Geraden. 'You gave *me* the hard job. If they go west, these two ravines join. I can pick up their trail there. But if they go east—' He jerked a thumb behind him. 'That one ends. The other opens out of these hills. I won't be able to get my horse over the ridge. I'll have to follow them on foot.'

'Then you're in luck.' Geraden pointed downward.

Below him, Nyle mounted his horse. The son of the Domne and the son of the Alend Monarch faced each other, and Prince Kragen raised a salute. Together, the Alends turned to the left and started along the frozen stream.

Argus punched Geraden lightly on the arm and left, bounding down the side of the ridge toward his mount.

Terisa continued watching Nyle. Over her shoulder, she heard Ribuld ride away.

Nyle remained where he was for a moment, perhaps considering the best route to Perdon, perhaps wondering what he could say to persuade Perdon's lord – perhaps simply hesitating. Then he urged his mount forward with his heels and went east.

Geraden caught hold of Terisa's hand. 'Come on. We've got to stop him.' He almost pulled her off balance as he followed Argus toward the horses.

At once, he fell. Fortunately, some instinct inspired him to let go of her hand as he went down. And he caught himself before he had a chance to break any bones on the rocks. He reached the bottom of the ravine several strides ahead of her.

Awkward with haste, he leaped into the saddle of his mare. From the low valley where the streams met, Ribuld had disappeared along the streambed in the direction of Orison. At a more cautious pace, Argus was going west, toward the joining of the ravines. Flapping his boots against the mare's sides, Geraden goaded her into a gallop eastward.

Terisa reached out a hand to him, called as loudly as she dared, 'Wait!'

He didn't see or hear her.

By the time she had descended to her gelding, she had decided to forget everything else and just follow Ribuld home. She was chilled to the heart; she didn't know how much more of this cold she could endure. She was afraid of everything she had heard.

Ignoring her own decision, she continued to hurry as fast as she could. Somehow, she untethered the gelding; somehow, she got her left foot into the stirrup, her right leg over its back. With the reins, she hauled its head toward the east.

Gritting her teeth, she kicked it.

She nearly panicked when the gelding went from a trot into a canter and then a run, trying for reasons of its own to catch up with Geraden's mare.

This speed felt tremendous. And the bottom of the ravine was treacherous. She ought to control her mount somehow – slow it; steer it to safer footing. Of course. And while she was at it, she ought to defeat the Alend Monarch's army, take care of Master Gilbur and the arch-Imager Vagel, and produce peace on earth. While composing great music with her free hand. Instead of doing all that, however, she concentrated with a pure white intensity that resembled terror on simply staying in the saddle.

The northern wall of the ravine became sheer gray stone, then relaxed its slope a little. Along the top, it was thick with brush. The south side was much more gradual, held down by heavy black trees with their roots gripped in the soil. But soon the trees drew back, and the side became steeper.

While the gelding hurtled along, she promised and promised herself that if she ever got off it alive she would never ride again, never as long as she lived, never.

All at once, as if the terrain itself had taken pity on her, the walls of the ravine jumped up and came together, ending the watercourse. At one time, it must have continued on to the east, but apparently its sides had fallen inward, forcing the water to find another channel. The horses had nowhere to go.

Roughly, Geraden wrenched his mare to a halt and sprang from her back. He hit the ground too fast: he fell again, slamming his whole body into the snow. He looked like a wild man as he regained his feet and charged the north slope.

She had no breath to shout at him, call him back, so she had to figure out how to make the gelding stop by herself.

Unintentionally kind, it took care of that detail for her. Having rejoined the mare, it seemed suddenly content with its lot in life. At the mare's side, it nuzzled her once, then lowered its head and lapsed into a state of impenetrable stupidity.

Terisa was still in one piece. Amazing.

It would have been nice to sit there and enjoy her survival for a moment. But Geraden was scrambling frantically up the slope. At first, the climb looked too steep for him. Then she saw that he was going to make it. Soon he would be out of sight.

She struggled off her horse, took a few tentative steps to test the solidity of the world, then pushed herself into a tight run.

The ridge side was certainly steep. It was well supplied with embedded rocks and protruding roots, however. And Geraden's upward scramble had cleared away a remarkable amount of snow. She found that if she didn't hurry – and didn't look down – she could make the ascent quite easily.

On the way, she tried not to think about how far ahead he was. Or what he intended to do.

Gasping at the icy air, she reached the crest.

The spine separating the two ravines was much the same here as it had been back where she and Geraden had eavesdropped on Nyle and Prince Kragen: a bit gentler down its northward face; marked with brush, jutting piles of rock, a few trees; but still steep. The stream that had cut the ravine clung to the base of the spine, wandering slowly out of sight to the east. The ravine itself was gone, however. Its own north side had slumped down and opened up into a wood which filled the lower ground between this spine and another ridge of hills. The ridge was plainly visible through the bare treetops, although it appeared to be some distance away.

Geraden, on the other hand, was nowhere to be seen.

She would have panicked, but she had no time. Almost at once, she spotted Nyle.

He rode at a trot along the streambed. He was still off to her left, coming eastward; but in a moment he would be directly below her. If she were the kind of person who did such things, she could have hit him with a rock.

More because Nyle's movement drew her gaze in that direction than because she had recovered her common sense, she looked at the slope in front of her and saw the marks of Geraden's descent. They went straight into a thick clump of brush poised above the streambed.

She figured out what was happening just in time to control her surprise as Geraden sprang out of the brush at his brother.

His elevation and proximity gave him an advantage: he could hardly have missed. And he jumped hard. His momentum carried Nyle out of the saddle and plunged both of them into the snow on the far side of the horse with a sound that made Terisa think of snapped arms and broken backs.

She started down the slope, a shout locked in her throat.

Geraden's experience with falls stood him in good stead. He was on his feet again almost instantly. Scattering flurries of snow, he dashed after the startled horse and struck the beast on its rump, sending it away at a gallop, out of reach. Then he turned back to his brother.

Nyle lifted his head. For a moment, he didn't appear to realize that he was blind because his face was caked with snow. When he scraped his features clear, however, he was able to see.

'Are you all right?' asked Geraden. 'I didn't mean to hurt you. I just wanted to stop you.'

Blinking fiercely, Nyle shook his head. In a series of jerks, he moved each of his arms, then his legs. He slapped snow off his half-cloak. All at once, he yanked himself to his feet like a knife blade opening.

'If you think this is a joke,' he said between his teeth, 'it isn't funny.'

Terisa's exhausted legs nearly failed her; she stumbled and had to catch herself on a tree. But she was almost there.

'It isn't a joke.' Geraden was so caked and white that he looked like he had been rolled together by children. Nevertheless there was nothing childlike in his manner. 'I'm not going to let you do it.'

Terisa reached the streambed and skittered across the frozen surface toward the two brothers.

'Do *what*?' snapped Nyle. 'You've lost your mind. I was just *riding*. On a *horse*. Remember horses? You act like that's a crime against humanity.'

'Nyle.' Geraden held himself still. Even his voice became still. 'I heard you. I was there.' He included Terisa. 'We were there. We heard everything you said. And Prince Kragen.'

For just a second, Nyle gaped at his brother. He gaped at Terisa.

Mutely, she nodded in confirmation.

He straightened his shoulders, and anger closed his face like a shutter.

'So you've decided to stop me. Full of moral superiority, you've decided to stop me because you cling to the astonishing belief that King Joyse and chaos and terrible Imagery and a fresh start to the wars that crippled Mordant for generations are somehow *preferable* to putting the Perdon on the throne and saving the entire kingdom. You—'

'No.' Geraden shook his head, suppressing violence. 'It won't work. The Perdon will never accept Prince Kragen's offer – he knows that. He's sending you to do this to confuse the issue, so the Perdon won't have a chance to fight for Orison when Alend attacks.'

'You're wrong, Geraden.' Terisa was surprised to hear herself speak. Her voice was like a small animal huddling against the cold and barely alive. 'I'm sorry. I've met the Perdon. I've seen him and Prince Kragen together. He's desperate. He won't turn the Prince down.'

Geraden gave her a quick look of dismay; but Nyle didn't glance away from his brother. 'Even if that's not true,' he resumed, 'you're acting like a child. Prince Kragen is right. The Alend Monarch is right. The *worst* thing that can happen to us is for High King Festten to get his hands on the Congery.

'We're already being torn apart by an Imager no one can find or stop. Cadwal will be able to decimate everything west of the Vertigon if the Congery falls. On our mother's grave, Geraden, we ought to *beg* Margonal to invade us.

'Instead of interfering, why don't you figure out what you're going to say to all the families who are going to be butchered – all the children who are going to be bereaved – all the men and women who are going to be maimed and massacred when King Joyse finally collapses and no power strong enough to hold the realm together takes his place?

'In the meantime, get out of my way.'

Thrusting between Geraden and Terisa, he stamped off after his horse.

The dismay on Geraden's face got worse. For a moment, he seemed unable to move. Confused and alarmed, Terisa reached out a hand to him. 'Geraden?'

Abruptly, his features knotted, and he swung into motion.

Chasing Nyle, he yelled, 'That's great! Wonderful! You're right, of course. You're being perfectly reasonable. Our father is going to be very proud of you.'

Nyle flinched, but kept on walking.

'There's just one thing. What about loyalty? King Joyse is our father's *friend*. What about self-respect? You're betraying your *King*, the man who made Mordant and peace out of nothing but bloodshed. How are you planning to live the rest of your life without loyalty or self-respect?'

'Loyalty to *whom*?' Though Nyle's stride didn't falter, his shout was like a cry. 'King Joyse? When was he ever loyal to *me*?

'He met all of us. He must have seen me dying for his notice, his approval. But *you're* the one he invited to Orison. When he decided to betroth Elega, he chose *you*. And a brilliant choice it was, too. You've certainly vindicated his good judgment, haven't you? Forgive me, but I find it a little difficult to feel warm and sentimental about that man.

'And he's going to get us all *killed*!' Small pieces of his distress echoed back from the tree trunks. 'Don't you understand that? How much *self-respect* are you going to get out of giving your life for a man who sacrificed you simply because he *couldn't be bothered* to hold his realm together? If you want to talk about self-respect, ask yourself why you place so little value on your own blood. I won't even mention the blood of all the people you claim to care about.'

'Then why—'

Geraden caught up with Nyle and grabbed his arm. Nyle flung off

Geraden's grip. The two brothers faced each other, their breath steaming furiously.

'Then why,' Geraden repeated, 'are you so angry about it?' He was no longer shouting. His voice sank to a whisper. 'You're doing what you know is right. Doesn't that make you feel good? And you're doing what Elega wants. She'll love you for it. She won't be able to help herself. Doesn't that make you feel good?'

'No.' Like Geraden, Nyle lowered his voice as if he didn't want the trees or the snow to hear him. 'No, it doesn't.' Each word hurt. 'That's how I got into this, but it doesn't help. She doesn't love me. She'll never love me. She loves Prince Kragen.'

All around him, the wood was silent. The only noise came from Terisa's boots as she neared the brothers. The sunlight out of the leaden sky seemed to have no weight, no effect against the cold.

Geraden spread his hands in a gesture of appeal. 'Then give it up. Please. This is all craziness anyway. There's no way the Alend Monarch can take Orison without a terrible siege – without killing any number of people. I don't care what Prince Kragen says. The Tor and Castellan Lebbick won't give up. The only lives you're going to save are Alend's, not ours. Don't throw yourself away for a woman who wants to betray her own father.'

Terisa saw at once that Geraden had made a mistake. He should have left Nyle's grief to gnaw at him unaided – shouldn't have mentioned Elega again. But it was too late now: the damage was done. As if the bones of his skull were shifting, Nyle's face took on the implacable set that had persuaded Prince Kragen to trust him. His eyes were as dull as weathered stone.

'If you want my advice' – he had a white-knuckled grip on himself – 'go home while you can. And take Artagel with you. He isn't going to enjoy losing his famous independence.'

'Nyle,' Geraden protested.

Nyle glanced over his shoulder. 'I see my horse. He'll let me catch him – if you haven't spooked him too badly.' He returned his gaze to Geraden's. 'You're going to stay here while I go get him. Then I'm going to ride away. If your mind is as weak as your talent for Imagery, you'll go back to Orison and tell Lebbick the whole story. It won't do him any good, but at least he'll have something to fret about for a few days. But if you have any sense, you'll keep your mouth shut.'

Softly, Geraden replied, 'No.' Clogged with snow, he looked white and foolish beside his dark-clad brother. Pain came from him in gouts of vapor, but his voice and his eyes and his hands were steady. 'No, Nyle. I won't let you go.'

Briefly, Nyle's features twisted as though he were trying to smile. Then his shoulders and arms relaxed. 'I guess I knew you were going to say that.' He made an unsuccessful effort to sound casual. 'You always were pretty stubborn.'

Terisa struggled to give warning, but her voice failed her. As if she were helpless, she watched Nyle start into a full-circle spin which seemed to lift him off the ground, out of the snow, bringing one of his boots to Geraden's head.

His kick slammed his brother down.

For a moment, Geraden arched his back and clawed at the crust. Then he lay still as if his neck were broken.

Quickly, Nyle bent to examine his brother.

When he was satisfied, he swung to face Terisa. Now he couldn't contain his fury. His hands clenched and unclenched spasmodically at his sides. The muscles of his jaw worked.

'Take care of him. If you let him die out here, I'll come back and throttle you with my bare hands.'

He headed for his horse at a run, as though there were hounds at his heels.

She never saw him go. Her hands were too cold; she couldn't find any sensation in her fingers. She was weeping with fear and frustration when she finally located the pulse in Geraden's throat and understood that he wasn't dead already.

A long time seemed to pass before she noticed that her surroundings looked familiar.

Through the black-trunked trees, she saw a ridge of hills. She had seen it earlier without paying any attention to it, but now its crisp line against the wintery sky tugged at her memory. Where—? It had been slightly different. What was different? The snow. The snow was different. She remembered dry, light flakes frothing like steam, churned to boiling by the haste of horses. She remembered the creaking of leather, the jangle of tack. And she remembered—

She remembered horns.

Her dream. This place was in her dream, the dream that had come to her the night before her life changed – come as if to prepare her for Geraden's arrival. The trees and the cold were the same. The ridge was the same. And Geraden was here, the young man in her dream who had appeared, coatless and unarmed, to save her life. All she lacked were three riders who hated her and drove their mounts through the snow for a chance to strike her dead. And the sound of horns, reaching her through the chill and the wood like the call for which her heart waited.

She didn't hear any horns. Though she yearned and strained for it, she couldn't conjure that hunting music out of her mind and into the air.

Nevertheless she heard the labor of horses in the distance, crashing through the snow crust. The cold brought every sound off the ridge into the wood, as edged as a shard of glass.

The sensation that she had wandered into her dream made everything distinct and slow: she had time to see clearly, time to hear every sound except the horns she desired. There they were, where she knew they would be: three men on horseback charging along the skirt of the ridge. She saw them through the wide gaps between the trees. She saw steam trailing furiously from the nostrils of the mounts. Each plunge of their hooves, each crunch-and-thud through ice and snow reached her ears.

Unheralded by the high, winging call that would have made the dream complete, the three riders swung abruptly away from the hills and aimed their mounts in her direction.

She was watching them so hard that she didn't realize Geraden was conscious until he gained his feet beside her, rubbing his head.

Caught up in the double experience of what was happening and what she had dreamed, she was unable to speak, unable to shift her concentration from the riders. Like hers, however, his attention was on them. 'You recognize them?' His voice was dull with the aftereffects of his brother's blow.

The riders were still too far away to be recognized, although she already knew the look of their hate. She shook her head.

'They're probably after you.' He didn't need to speak quickly; there was no hurry, he had plenty of time. 'It wouldn't be impossible for somebody to find us. If they asked the right questions at the stables and the gates. And they met that wagon driver.' He turned away, then back again. 'There's no point in trying to run. Our horses are too far away.'

Swords appeared in the hands of the riders – blades as long as sabers, but viciously curved, like scimitars. They were going to hack her into the snow where she stood. She ought to move. She and Geraden ought to do something. At the moment, however, she was more interested in the odd recollection that the swords raised against her in her dream had been straight, not curved.

Geraden seemed equally out of touch with reality. He was too calm. For some reason he chose this moment to kick at lumps in the snow. Then his behavior began to make sense. From the snow, he uncovered fallen branches. They were crooked and dead; but two of them were stout, as thick as her arm, long enough to be useful.

This wasn't right. This wasn't the way it happened in her dream.

But there was still plenty of time. He gave one branch to her, kept one for himself.

'When they reach that tree' – he pointed – 'we'll separate. If they split up, we might have a better chance against them. If they don't, I'll be able to hit them from the side when they attack you.'

She had the impression that if she really *looked* at him, she would see that he was terrified. Yet her ears insisted on hearing him as if he were calm.

'Don't worry about the riders. Go for the horses. Try to hit one of them in the face. If we get lucky, the rider will fall and hurt himself.'

She didn't respond. Her attention was on the riders while she waited to hear horns.

Then their faces came into focus for her, and she saw that she was wrong about them. They weren't the riders in her dream.

They weren't men at all.

They had eyes in the wrong places. Long whiskers sprouted around the orbs. Snouts hid their mouths, but not their tusks. She was able to see their heads because the hoods of their riding capes had been swept back. Their heads were covered with mottled red fur.

They seemed to have more limbs than they needed. Each of them seemed to be waving two swords.

No. It wasn't like this.

Nevertheless the sensation that she was acting out a dream grew stronger.

She remained motionless, waiting. The air was whetted with cold, as hard as a slap and as penetrating as splinters. She could hear the separate sound made by each pounding hoof.

When the riders reached the tree Geraden had indicated, he hissed, 'Now!' and dashed away as if he had decided at the last moment to flee. He ran kicking his feet high to break them free of the icy surface. But she didn't move.

Without hesitation, all three of the riders turned their mounts and plunged after him. None of their strange eyes so much as glanced at her.

Out of nowhere, a pang of fear nailed her.

Geraden? *Geraden?*

So suddenly that he nearly fell, he turned and saw his danger. He flung a look like a cry in her direction, then raised his club. The riders were almost on top of him.

Gripping his branch in both hands, he broke it across the forehead of the first horse.

The mount squealed in pain, tried too late to leap aside. Wrenched off balance, the rider spilled into the snow in front of the second attacker.

Frantically trying to avoid a collision, the second horse and rider went down.

Geraden hit the downed rider with the remains of his club, then dodged around the struggling horse to evade his third attacker – and tripped. He landed on his face in an untrampled patch of snow.

As he fell, the first rider hacked at him from the ground. But the crusted snow hampered movement: the blow missed. Geraden and his attacker struggled to their feet at the same time, while the third rider turned to come in for another charge.

Awkwardly, Geraden stumbled out of reach long enough to snatch up a sword from the rider he had stunned. He obviously didn't know how to use it, however. Clenching it like a bludgeon, he turned to face his attacker.

The creature let out a snort of scorn and started swinging.

Geraden blocked the first cut.

He was helpless to parry the second.

In her dream, Terisa had watched a man hazard his life to save her. Despite his evident lack of experience with weapons, he had downed one assailant for her sake. Then another. And she had watched. Nothing more. She had seen the third rider come up behind him. Sword held high, the rider had positioned himself to cut her rescuer down. And she had made no effort to help him. She had startled herself out of the dream altogether by shouting a warning.

But it was Geraden who was being attacked, Geraden who needed rescuing. And she still had the branch he had given her. She felt that she had been running for a long time, that the distance was too great, she would never reach him in time; but she ran harder than she had ever run in her life, and before his attacker could kill him she swung her club against the side of that furred head.

Several things seemed to be happening simultaneously. Nevertheless she saw them all.

She saw a flat patch appear in the mottled red fur. While the attacker

394

stumbled to his knees, the patch began to bleed, first slowly, then in a sickening gush. He hit the snow, and his life splashed a red-black stain across the crust. He was never going to move again.

Geraden gaped at her, momentarily astonished.

At the same time, she saw the third rider come up behind him. Swords held high, the rider positioned himself to cut Geraden down.

Geraden was looking at her. He had forgotten the third rider entirely.

There was no time for warning, no time for her to move, no time for him to duck or dodge.

Yet there was time for her to see another horseman reach the creature and drive a long poniard like a spike into the center of his back. She saw him cough blood onto Geraden's shoulders and pitch from his horse, almost knocking Geraden down as he dropped.

Nyle hauled his mount to a stop and sprang out of the saddle. 'Are you all right?' Without waiting for an answer, he began to check the fallen riders. 'Where did you get enemies like *this*?' When he found that the first attacker was still alive, he produced a length of rope from one of his saddlebags and lashed the creature's wrists and ankles together. 'I saw them heading this way. Since they were in such a hurry to get to the place where I just left you, I decided I ought to follow them.'

Geraden and Terisa stared at him as if he had arrived from the moon.

'Are you all right?' he repeated. There was concern in his eyes; but there was also a glint of humor, a suggestion of pride; for a moment he looked so much like Artagel and Geraden that the resemblance closed Terisa's throat. 'I get the impression you aren't used to fighting enemies like this.'

'Thank you,' said Geraden as if he felt the same way she did. A nauseated expression distorted his features. With a shudder of disgust, he dropped the sword he was holding. 'Thanks for coming back.'

In the same motion, he picked up another sturdy branch and knocked his brother unconscious in front of him.

Then he stood hunched over Nyle with his chin thrust out and his face like the winter, breathing in great gasps that seemed to hurt his chest.

Terisa strained her ears for the distant calling of horns. But it was all in her mind.

TWENTY-TWO

QUESTIONS ABOUT BEING BESIEGED

Eventually, Terisa and Geraden were found by a squad of Castellan Lebbick's guards.

By that time, both Nyle and the attacker were conscious. Nyle wasn't particularly amused to discover that he was trussed with his own rope; but after a few minutes of bitter cursing – which did nothing to warm the bleak cold of Geraden's expression – he lapsed into silence.

The attacker snarled periodically and twisted his strange features. He didn't waste his strength on futile efforts to break his bonds, however.

The guards brought Geraden's mare and Terisa's gelding along with enough of their rough brandy to push the worst of the chill back from her vitals – and enough questions to make her ache for sleep. Fortunately, Geraden took charge before anyone – perhaps including the Apt himself – realized what he was doing; he quickly established that the guards' questions were less important than the need to join the men on Argus' trail, pursuing Prince Kragen.

All Terisa wanted was to get out of this weather and lie down somewhere warm, where it might be possible to forget the way that flat patch in the mottled red fur had begun to gush blood – or the way Geraden had struck Nyle down. Chasing after Argus and the Prince would only prolong her misery.

But at least no one had time to insist on questions.

Although she had promised she would never ride again, she soon found herself mounted on the gelding. Ignoring the reins, she clung to the saddle horn and went wherever her horse took her.

Once Nyle and Geraden's attacker had been secured on their own beasts, and the guards were mounted again, her horse took her with everyone else back the way they had come.

Eager for more speed, Geraden surged ahead.

'Relax,' one of the guards advised him. 'There are already at least a dozen men on that trail. They'll catch him. It won't happen any sooner just because you're in a hurry.'

Terisa caught the look Geraden flashed at the guard. It was wild and sick; and she understood almost automatically why he wanted to go faster. He didn't want to help capture Prince Kragen. He wanted to get away from what he had done to his brother.

Instinctively, she straightened her back and tried to improve her balance, as if that would enable the gelding and all the horses to go faster.

The guards swung east and didn't cross the stream until a fold in the south wall provided them access to those hills. Their route back to the southern ravine was circuitous, but quicker than walking – and much quicker than getting lost, as Terisa would have done if she had tried to find her own way. Still, it took long enough to make her numb. She was blind to herself, and the passing of the dark tree trunks on either side, and the tight mood of the riders around her as they reached the joining of the streambeds where Ribuld had ridden south to rouse Orison and Argus had gone west after Prince Kragen – blind enough to be surprised by the fact that the valley was full of guards.

Although they were mounted, they didn't appear to be doing anything except waiting.

All their eyes were on Geraden and her. None of them spoke.

Ribuld sat erect on his horse with his head high, brandishing his scar as though he were about to let out a yell.

Involuntarily, Geraden jerked his mare to a halt. The men with him stopped. Terisa's gelding blundered against the mare's rump and stopped also.

'What is it? Why aren't—?' Geraden's voice caught.

Near Ribuld stood a horse without a rider. But not without a burden: the man on its back hung from his stomach; his wrists and ankles had been tied to the girth so that he wouldn't fall. His back was wet. Blinking stupidly, Terisa recognized Argus' stallion before she recognized Argus himself.

'I'm sorry,' a guard with a captain's purple band knotted around his bicep rasped. 'I know he was a friend of yours.'

'What—?' Geraden tried again, but couldn't make the words come out. 'What—?'

The captain was a stocky, middle-aged man with a face that suggested more decency than imagination. 'We found him about a mile down the ravine. I guess he wasn't careful enough. There wasn't even a struggle. He was just there on the ground with a hole in his back. Probably made by an arrow.'

The captain spat a curse into the snow, then continued, 'After that, the trail gets confused. When that Alend butcher found out he was being followed, he knew what to do. He and his men did a good job of it, I'll give them that. I've got my best trackers working on it, but I think it's hopeless. By the time we locate his trail, he'll hit a road or a stream and disappear.'

Geraden wasn't listening. He stared at the body hanging from the stallion. Terisa could see the contours of his face aging. 'Argus,' he said thickly. 'I got you killed.'

'Very good,' Nyle snarled at him. 'This is wonderful. Now you've got the worst of both sides. Without Prince Kragen, you can't stop Margonal's army.

397

But you insisted on stopping me. This way, the Alend Monarch won't have any choice. After he breaks Orison, he'll have to keep it for himself.'

Geraden flinched; but he didn't answer his brother. Kicking his horse into motion, he went to face Ribuld.

'I'm sorry,' he said. 'It's my fault. I should have sent you with him.'

Ribuld lowered his head. For a moment, Terisa feared he was going to strike Geraden; he looked savage enough for that. Without thinking, she urged her mount after Geraden so she would be near him.

'Nyle is right,' Geraden went on. 'I should have let him go. We should have concentrated on catching the Prince.'

Ribuld clenched his fists. 'Do I look like the kind of man who takes orders from an inexperienced puppy?' he growled. 'I thought he was smart enough to watch his back.'

Geraden bowed his head and couldn't speak.

The only sounds in the valley were the stamping of the horses, the jangle of tack. Then one of the guards pointed at the bound creature and asked in dismay, 'What kind of thing is *that?*'

The Apt turned. Terisa could hardly recognize him: he appeared more dangerous than Artagel had ever been.

'I intend to find out.'

'Come on, men,' the captain ordered. 'The Castellan is going to shit brass when he hears about this. The longer we make him wait, the worse it's going to get. Form up.'

He spent a moment arranging more support for the trackers, assigning men to carry messages. Around the streambed, the guards pulled into formation. Terisa found herself beside Geraden between two files of riders who, among other things, clearly wanted to know what she was doing there.

She glanced back at Nyle; his face was closed and locked. Any resemblance between him and his brother had been struck away by Geraden's blow.

Her attacker had eyes in the wrong places, surrounded by long whiskers; he had a snout and tusks. But she didn't notice those things. Instead, she saw blood seeping to a rush out of mottled red fur, blood and death spilling to the white snow.

She was hardly aware of the way her seat and legs hurt as the gelding lumbered into a trot to keep up with the rest of the horses.

The ride back to Orison was cold and gloomy; it might as well have been interminable. Terisa lost track of herself and didn't regain her bearings until she realized that the host of red-furred riders waving scimitars that swept toward her every time she turned her head was just a hallucination, the product of too much gray sunlight glaring deceptively off too much snow. Orison wasn't as far away as her physical condition seemed to indicate, however. Eventually, the riders entered the courtyard of the castle and stopped.

Sliding off her mount's back, she planted her feet in the churned mud and stood on her own, trembling.

The guards dismounted. For a moment, she was surrounded by confusion – men moving here and there, muttering to each other. For reasons of their own, more men came out of Orison, hurrying in groups. The whole courtyard appeared full of guards who ran in one direction or another. Peasants or merchants pushed wagons about. She didn't know what to do with her horse. There was warmth nearby now: it was somewhere in the high walls looming around her. She couldn't imagine how to get to it.

Then the captain barked an order. His squad sorted out its disarray, came to attention.

Castellan Lebbick strode toward them.

Disdaining winter gear, he wore only his characteristic mail and leather, with his purple sash draped diagonally down his chest and his purple band knotted above his eyebrows. Cold steamed off his skin, but he didn't appear to notice it: he had enough fire inside to keep him warm. Though he was shorter than Terisa, he dominated her and the men and even the horses as if he were much taller. Ire glinted in his eyes.

Brusquely, he returned the captain's salute, but didn't speak. Instead, he surveyed the men before him. When he spotted Ribuld with Argus' body, he went abruptly in that direction.

Geraden put a hand on Terisa's arm as if to steady or comfort her. But his expression was too harsh to be convincing.

Rigid with silence, the guards waited as Castellan Lebbick thrust among them to Argus' side. Roughly, he clenched a fist in Argus' hair and lifted the dead man's head as if to check his face, verify his identity. The look the Castellan gave Ribuld was enough to make the veteran turn away.

Lebbick aimed a glare at Nyle's sealed belligerence. Then he considered the inhuman attacker. For a moment, the two measured each other across the gulf of their antagonism and strangeness. Without turning his head, he demanded unexpectedly, 'Is this his horse?'

'Yes,' answered Geraden between his teeth. 'There were three of them. One was killed. Terisa and I would have died, but Nyle killed the other.'

The Castellan, however, wasn't interested in how many red-furred creatures had been killed. '*This* horse?' he insisted. '*This* tack?'

'Yes.'

Castellan Lebbick moved toward Geraden. In a soft voice, hardly louder than a whisper, which nevertheless sounded like it could be heard on the highest ramparts, he said, 'I don't like losing men. Do you understand me, boy? I don't like it.'

Geraden didn't try to respond. In any case, the Castellan turned away without waiting for a reply. To the captain he snapped, 'Put Nyle and that monster of Imagery in the dungeon. I'll see you, Geraden, and' – he sneered her name – 'the lady Terisa of Morgan in the south guardroom.'

Trailing wisps of vapor from his shoulders, he stalked away.

'The dungeon,' Geraden groaned to himself. He put his hands over his face. 'Oh, Nyle. What am I doing to you?'

Nyle raised his voice sharply. 'Don't worry about it, little brother. This isn't any different than what you've done with the rest of your life. And Lebbick probably hasn't had anybody to torture for a long time. For him, this will be more fun than a carouse.'

Geraden's shoulders tightened. Terisa stared at Nyle numbly. But it was Ribuld who spoke.

'I advise you to keep your mouth shut.' He tried to sound casual in spite of the way his voice shook. 'Nobody cares what happens to you. If you weren't a son of the Domne – and if your brothers weren't so much better men than you are – we would have let you ride off and make a shitass of yourself in front of the Perdon. You talk about *fun*.'

'Ribuld,' warned the captain, 'that's enough.'

But Ribuld couldn't stop. 'I'm sure the Perdon would have thought it was fun to be offered the kingship of Mordant' – he was ventilating a vicious grief – 'if we captured that fornicating Prince, and the whole Alend army was helpless against us. Geraden did you a *favor*.'

Nyle avoided the guard's gaze.

'*Argus* did you a favor, you rotten—'

'*Ribuld!*' The captain's voice cut like a whip. 'I said, that's enough.'

Ribuld rolled the whites of his eyes, glaring like a wounded predator. His scar flamed with blood. Nevertheless the captain's command caught and held him. He turned his back on Nyle, began untying Argus' wrists.

'He doesn't have any family. Somebody has to bury him.'

Lifting the body in his arms, he carried his friend away, out of the courtyard.

Terisa feared that if she didn't get inside soon she would begin to cry.

Dourly, the captain issued instructions to his men. Nyle and Geraden's attacker were escorted rather ungently in the direction of the dungeon. The remaining guards took charge of the horses while the captain himself guided Geraden and Terisa toward the south guardroom.

She seemed to have no sensation left in her. What was going on made no sense, and she was afraid of the Castellan. How had she survived being so cold? It was probably a lie that there was warmth in Orison. She was afraid of Castellan Lebbick because of his relentless anger. Or was it because she had lied to him?

When had she lied to him? How many times? She had killed one of Geraden's attackers, and all these falsehoods were going to destroy her.

In spite of lies and cold, however, a door opened and closed, and suddenly something blissful touched her face. She was inside the castle; she was still cold, frozen almost to the marrow, carrying her misery with her like a cocoon of ice; but the air was warm, warm. She could breathe it. She could stretch out her fingers to it. She tried to clear her throat, and a snuffling noise like a sob emerged.

'Here.' Geraden stopped her and undid the front of her coat to let more warmth reach her. 'You aren't used to this.' He took her hands and slapped them, firmly but not too hard, then rubbed her wrists. 'I'm sorry. I didn't realize you were feeling it so much.'

She began to shiver again.

He put his arm around her and helped her toward the guardroom.

It proved to be a low hall with a bare stone floor and all its walls unadorned except one, which supported a large slate chalkboard. Most of the space was taken up by rows of wooden benches facing the chalkboard: apparently, this was where Castellan Lebbick explained their orders to his captains and men. The warmth was stronger here; it made her shivering worse.

The Castellan arrived a moment after she entered the guardroom. Slamming the door behind him, he confronted her and Geraden. For some reason, she noticed his hands were curled. At first, she thought that was because he was angry. Then she realized he had spent so much of his life with a heavy sword in his grasp that he could no longer completely straighten his fingers.

He was looking at her closely, and something strange happened in his face. His expression softened; his constant, simmering rage let go of his features.

As abruptly as he had entered the guardroom, he left again.

Mystified, she and Geraden turned to the captain. He shrugged and tried to keep his own surprise from showing.

They waited. Geraden glowered at the ceiling. Terisa shivered.

When Castellan Lebbick returned, he was followed by a maid carrying a tray. There were three brass goblets on the tray. Whatever was in them gave off a sweet, heavy steam.

'Mulled wine,' he announced without quite meeting anyone's stare. His manner suggested that he was ashamed of himself. 'You look like you could use it.'

The maid delivered the goblets to Terisa, Geraden, and the captain, then withdrew.

Straining to conceal his surprise, the captain emptied his goblet with unceremonious haste. Then he gaped into it as though he were fervid for more wine to occupy his attention until someone else spoke.

Geraden looked at his drink suspiciously, as if he were wondering if it was drugged.

Terisa couldn't wait for him to make up his mind. Wrapping her hands around the heat of the metal, she sipped at the dark liquid as though she were sampling nectar.

Mulled wine. She sipped some more. She had never had mulled wine. In fact, she had never had hot wine before. It was lovely. She drank a large swallow. It ran down into her, as delicate as the guards' brandy was rough; and it tightened her shivering into a knot and then released it, so that all the strain seemed to flow suddenly out of her muscles. She was warm again, warm in places that had given up hope. Mulled wine. Her goblet didn't hold enough, but she drank what there was down to the last drop.

In sudden resolution, Geraden tossed down several swallows too quickly, with the result that he inhaled some of the spiced liquid and went into a spasm of gagging and coughing. Trying to help, the captain pounded him discreetly between the shoulderblades.

'Thank you,' Terisa said to Castellan Lebbick as she lowered the goblet. 'Thanks.'

'Don't thank me.' The Castellan sounded bitter, but his expression was still soft and ashamed. 'You should be more like Geraden. He thinks I put something in it to make you talk.'

She sighed – and was relieved to hear no quaver or catch in her breathing.

'That's all right. You didn't bring it for him. You brought it for me. I'm grateful.'

Scowling, Castellan Lebbick turned to the captain.

'Your report?'

Back on familiar ground, the captain regained his poise. Without wasting time, he conveyed what he knew, described what he had done, and pointed out – rather unnecessarily – that he himself still had no idea what had happened to Geraden and the lady Terisa after Ribuld had left them.

The Castellan absorbed the details, nodded once. 'All right. Muster a squad. Send them back where your men found Geraden and her. I want them to backtrack those three creatures. As far as possible. I want to know where they came from. I want to know how creatures of Imagery happened to be mounted on horses and saddles like that.

'While you're at it, set up supplies and relays for your trackers. Prince Kragen isn't going to make any mistakes – but if he does, I want him to pay for them.

'And,' he concluded, 'find me a falconer. I want to know more about these' – he snarled the words, glancing at Terisa – 'carrier pigeons.'

The captain saluted. With an unmistakable air of relief, he left the guardroom.

For a long time, Castellan Lebbick didn't say anything. Initially, he didn't look at Terisa and Geraden: he acted like a man lost in thought. Then he began to study them carefully, scrutinizing each of them in turn while his choler mounted. He seemed to be waiting for one of them to speak first, to blurt out something he could use. Or he might have been giving himself a chance to recover from his unaccustomed charity.

The expression with which Geraden met the Castellan's scrutiny wasn't belligerent, but it was tight and wary, and he didn't open his mouth.

For her part, Terisa had nothing to say. The hate in the strange faces of her attackers held her.

Finally, the Castellan pulled up a chair for himself and sat down, folding his arms on his chest. His manner didn't invite Terisa and Geraden to do the same. 'So,' he said. His gaze was aimed somewhere between them, ready to strike in either direction. 'Again something strange happens, and again the lady Terisa of Morgan is involved.' He articulated each word with hard-edged consonants and blunt vowels, so that it had an almost tangible impact. 'This time, at least one mystery is solved. I don't know who she's plotting with. I don't know why. But finally I know how.'

'Plotting?' Geraden was immediately incensed. 'Terisa? What are you talking about?'

Castellan Lebbick looked at the Apt. A baleful light was growing in his eyes. 'I'm talking about carrier pigeons.'

'But that's crazy! She doesn't have any pigeons. Where would she keep them?'

'Perhaps they bring messages to her first and carry her answers back. Then all she has to do is open her window to hatch treachery with anyone in the world.'

'No,' Geraden insisted. 'No, that's still crazy. They would still have to be trained. When has she had a chance to do that?'

'We don't know how much training they need.' Lebbick's face had been forged out of iron and extremity. He seemed deaf to the impossibility of what he was saying. 'But that's really unimportant. Didn't she come here out of a mirror? A mirror that couldn't possibly have anything to do with her? She's an Imager of some kind.' His tone slapped down contradiction. 'How do you know how much chance she's had? For all you know, she's already spent years here secretly, getting ready to betray King Joyse.'

Terisa shook her head. 'You don't understand.' She couldn't take Lebbick's charge personally. It was too loony. And she was too tired. 'Carrier pigeons only work one way. You take them away from home, and they fly back. That's all. Prince Kragen can send messages to his father. He can't receive them.' Then she stopped because the effort of explaining to him that he ought to concentrate on Elega was beyond her.

'You see?' demanded Geraden. 'It's crazy. The Alend Monarch is marching an army through Armigite *right now*, and you're wasting your time on impossible accusations. We're going to be *besieged*. Don't you understand *that*?'

For just a moment, the muscles in Castellan Lebbick's neck corded, and his arms clamped hard across his chest. He was at the edge of his self-control. Nevertheless he shifted his glare deliberately to Terisa, as if Geraden hadn't spoken.

'A falconer may be able to tell me whether you're telling the truth. If you are, I'll have to assume that your pigeons are being kept for you by an ally here in Orison.'

Geraden threw up his hands, but the Castellan ignored him. 'How do you communicate with an ally, when you're reasonably well watched by my men? Through the secret passage in your wardrobe. A child could do it.

'But let that pass for now. In the meantime, my lady, why don't you tell me how you happened to know Nyle was going to meet with Prince Kragen this morning?'

Terisa blinked at him, her heart suddenly quailing.

'For someone as innocent as you are, I call it remarkable that you managed to be in just the right place to spy on that meeting. May I take it as proven that the people you're plotting with aren't Alend? Or are you exposing your own allies to conceal your real plans?'

Worn down by exposure and lulled by wine, she couldn't meet his eyes. Maybe she was as guilty as he thought. That seemed possible. She understood the secret of recrimination: it was deserved because it was received; accusations instilled the sense of guilt that justified them. Because the Castellan looked at her so harshly, spoke to her so bitterly, she deserved it. She had no defense.

But Geraden was already speaking for her.

'Listen to me.' His voice lacked Lebbick's clenched and whetted capacity for violence. 'I'm going to explain a few things to you.' Yet he made the Castellan heed him.

'The first day of the thaw, Terisa and I went out to the bazaar with the lady

403

Elega. You know that.' And the more he spoke the more he seemed to push back the pall that Castellan Lebbick had cast over her. 'While we were there, we saw a mountebank. Terisa recognized him. He was Prince Kragen.'

Terisa felt rather than saw the Castellan's gaze shift to Geraden.

'Purely by chance,' the Apt went on, 'she happened to see the mountebank and Nyle' – he said the name as if it didn't hurt him – 'come out from behind a tent as if they'd just had a private conversation. That was before Gart attacked her.

'I decided the best way to find out what was going on was to have Nyle followed. So I asked the Tor to get Argus and Ribuld released from their duties, and I put them to work on Nyle's trail.'

Lebbick's jaw jutted ominously.

'It's that simple.' Geraden stood his ground as though he were the Castellan's equal in courage and determination. 'She isn't plotting with anyone. If she were using carrier pigeons herself, it would be incredibly stupid of her to let us know she knew anything about them.'

Terisa hung her head and kept quiet.

'Very interesting, boy.' Lebbick's tone was like the thrust of a dagger. 'She told you what she saw, and you decided what to do about it. But I'm the Castellan of Orison. Defending the King from all enemies is my job. If there's any danger in the Demesne or Orison, I need to know it.' He was a coiled spring, tightened to the point of outbreak. 'Why didn't you tell *me*?'

'Because, good Castellan,' a familiar voice rumbled, 'you are prone to excess.'

Terisa looked up in surprise as the Tor entered the guardroom.

He seemed to be in an affable mood – a bit unsteady on his feet, perhaps, but full of good will. He came into the room wearing a fleshy smile that appeared to have nothing behind it except more fat. The way he walked suggested that he had filled every cavern and crevice of his bulk with wine before venturing out of the King's suite.

'My lord Tor,' said Castellan Lebbick between his teeth. He didn't get up. 'I'm surprised you trouble to join us. Today would be a good day for men with nothing better to do to stay in bed.'

'Ah, true,' replied the lord amiably. 'Very true. It is my extreme misfortune that there is a voice which brings me the news of this stone pile – brings me the news implacably. Its custom is to whisper, but the closer I drowse toward sleep, the louder it shouts. This morning I thought it imaginable that King Joyse himself would awaken.

'Alas,' he went on, 'the King seems unlikely to take an interest in the great events of the day. Therefore the burden falls to his chancellor.'

Lumbering forward to the nearest bench, he seated himself with a sigh. The stout plank groaned under him.

'That's very diligent of you, my lord Tor,' grated Lebbick. 'It also happens to be unnecessary. I'm perfectly capable of handling "the great events of the day" myself.'

'Certainly you are.' The Tor was like a lump of pastry dough, impervious to sarcasm – and immune to argument. 'Doubtless you understand sieges as well as most men understand their wives. I am sure you will do everything that must be done to prepare for the coming of the Alend Monarch. Nevertheless, good Castellan, I must point out' – he sounded kindly, almost avuncular – 'that if the matter had been left to you, you would still be unaware of Margonal's approach. As I say, you are prone to excess.'

Castellan Lebbick's eyes bulged slightly in their sockets. 'In what way, my lord?'

The Tor spread his plump hands. 'Suppose young Geraden had come to you with his suspicions of his brother? What would you have done? Why, you would have arrested Nyle, of course. Instead of following him to his assignation and overhearing his plans, you would have tried to take those plans from him by persuasion or force. And if he had resisted both persuasion and force—' The lord rolled his thick shoulders.

'Or suppose again that young Geraden had given you his *reasons* for suspecting his brother? Suppose he had mentioned that hints dropped by the King's daughter Elega led the lady Terisa to suspect that she was involved with Prince Kragen?' Now the lord was no longer pastry dough talking. His voice became like the grinding of heavy stones against each other. 'Suppose he had revealed that the guards Argus and Ribuld were following Elega – that in fact they had no other reason for being near enough to save Artagel's life when the High King's Monomach assailed the lady Terisa?' His hands lay limp on his fat thighs, but his eyes grew harder. 'Suppose he had informed you that the lady Terisa had rejected Elega's effort to win her support for the Prince – and that, forewarned by this rejection, Elega had made herself fruitless for Argus and Ribuld to trail? What would you have done then, good Castellan?

'Would you have raised a cry against her?' At last he was not an obese old drunk: he was the lord of the Care of Tor, King Joyse's first ally in the campaign that had created Mordant. 'Would you have sent men to arrest her so that she could be hailed before her father and publicly accused of treason?'

The Castellan's face was dark with blood, but he didn't unclose his teeth. 'It's already done.'

For a moment, the Tor looked like he might rise to his feet and shout something. Instead, however, he smiled sadly and slumped back into softness. 'Just so. And what is the result?'

'We can't find her.'

'Certainly you cannot. She has gone into hiding. And she has bragged, good Castellan, that she knows the secrets of Orison well enough to remain hidden for a long time. And so the opportunity has been lost to learn her intent – the intent on which Prince Kragen's plans hinge, the intent which will deliver Orison to the Alend Monarch without a protracted siege.

'Good Castellan, you have a greater need of me than you realize.'

Geraden looked like he wanted to applaud.

The muscles at the corners of Castellan Lebbick's jaws bunched. His eyes scanned the guardroom as though he were looking for the perfect stretch of bare wall against which to spill the Tor's blood. But he didn't rise from his chair.

Slowly, he said, 'Geraden, my lady Terisa – you haven't told us where you got those creatures of Imagery. In fact, you haven't told us how you managed to catch Nyle. He's your brother. He knows you. Surely he didn't let you just trip and fall on him. You've been telling the Tor so many stories. Why don't you tell him that one?'

'"Creatures of Imagery"?' The lord smiled pleasantly at Geraden. 'Yes, young Geraden. Do tell us.'

Geraden glanced back and forth between the two men, gauging where he stood with each of them, before he shrugged and said, 'All right.'

Just a few minutes ago, Terisa would have sworn it as impossible, but now she found that she was too warm. She loosened her coat a bit, shifted it back from her neck.

'I wasn't thinking straight,' admitted Geraden stiffly. 'Nyle wasn't the real danger. I should have let him go so we could concentrate on trying to catch Prince Kragen. But that never crossed my mind. Stopping him was too important—' In an awkward way, he seemed to be asking for understanding. 'He's my brother. I couldn't let him make a traitor of himself.'

The Tor nodded in an absentminded fashion; his attention appeared to be elsewhere. Sourly, Castellan Lebbick muttered, 'It was a little late for that, don't you think?'

Geraden flushed. He didn't permit himself to react, however.

'But I made a mess out of that, too. He got away, and we were stuck out there without our horses.

'That was when those "creatures of Imagery" attacked. They came from the east, but that could have just been because of the terrain. I thought they were after the lady Terisa, so I wasn't ready for it when they came for me.'

'You?' demanded the Castellan. 'They came for you, boy?'

'That's what it looked like.' With a visible effort, Geraden held himself steady. 'We separated. They ignored her. All three of them chased me.'

Although he still didn't seem to be paying attention, the Tor's expression was beatific, as if he had just received a piece of good news. 'Young Geraden, you are a wonderment. I have mentioned – have I not? – that you underestimate yourself. Even the lady Terisa of Morgan does not have such enemies.'

'Oh, yes,' snarled Lebbick. 'That seems especially plausible because you're still alive. You were alone against the three of them. What did you do? Accident them to death?'

Somehow, Geraden retained his self-command. Carefully, he said, 'I used a club on their horses. Two of them went down. One was killed. The other is your prisoner.'

'No,' Terisa breathed.

Castellan Lebbick ignored her. 'And the third?'

'Nyle got him. He saw them heading toward us, so he came back. Terisa and I might both be dead if it weren't for him. While he was still thinking about that, I knocked him out. I hit him with a tree branch. That was how I caught him.'

'No,' Terisa repeated. She couldn't help herself: it all came back to her. It was as vivid as dreaming in front of her.

'He was fighting for his life,' she whispered. 'I had to help him. Didn't I? I can't spend my whole life just sitting on my hands and wondering when I'm going to fade. I can't. That's worse than doing something wrong. Isn't it?

'He got two of them off their horses. He stunned one of them. The other went after him with those swords.' She shivered as though she had become cold again, but the truth was that she could hardly bear the weight of her coat. 'I had to help him. I killed— With a club. I hit him from behind and broke his skull.' A small patch of red fur on the back of the skull had turned wet and begun to gush blood. 'Then Nyle came.

'Geraden didn't kill anybody.'

She ran out of words and fell silent.

The men stared at her. Geraden's throat worked as if he were choking on her name. After a moment, the Tor rumbled gently, 'My dear lady, of course you had to help him. You would not forgive yourself if you had not helped him. And perhaps you would both be dead.'

Castellan Lebbick turned away. 'Women.' Every line of his posture was knotted and bitter. 'Always women. It's indecent. If I'm ever saved by a woman, I'll do away with myself.'

Then he rasped, 'But the horses. That's the point. The saddles and *tack*, my lord Tor. Tell him about the horses and saddles and *tack*, Geraden.'

In his uncertainty, Geraden faced the Castellan while he spoke to the Tor. 'Our attackers were obviously creatures of Imagery. But their horses looked normal to me. I didn't notice anything else.'

Abruptly, Lebbick jerked to his feet. '*Normal* horses, my lord Tor. *Normal* saddles and tack. What do you make of that?'

The lord pursed his lips. 'These creatures were mounted after their translation. Either they stole mounts and gear for themselves, or they were equipped by their translators. Equipped and instructed.'

'Exactly.' Castellan Lebbick faced the lord like a fuse burning dangerously close to powder. 'The horses were normal. The saddles definitely didn't come from Cadwal – in Cadwal they use barbed stirrups – but they could have come from anywhere in Mordant or Alend.'

'And the tack?' asked the Tor obligingly.

'The tack—' Lebbick stifled a furious gesture by clenching his fists on his hips. 'The tack includes a hackamore you won't find anywhere in Cadwal or Alend or Mordant – anywhere except the Care of Tor.' His glare was hard enough to strike sparks from flint. 'Only your people use it, my lord Tor.'

The Tor gazed back at the Castellan as though Lebbick were a curious specimen pinned to a mounting board.

'Perhaps,' the Castellan gritted, 'you think this is just another of my *excesses*.'

He took Terisa so completely aback that a moment passed before she grasped how serious he was. The *Tor*? In league with Vagel against Geraden and King Joyse and Mordant? Her legs were weaker than she realized: she had to sit down. Riding a horse wasn't easy. Without quite noticing what she was doing, she went to the nearest bench and seated herself beside the lord.

Geraden was aghast. 'You can't mean that,' he protested. 'Do you know what you're saying?'

Without warning, Castellan Lebbick grinned. His teeth flashed fiercely.

'Oh, I am sure that our good Castellan knows entirely what he is saying.' The Tor had resumed his pastry dough aspect, impervious to affront. 'One of Mordant's greatest problems has always been that the vile attacks of Imagery which harass us come from no known source. My son was killed by an enemy who might be hidden anywhere in Alend or Cadwal – or Mordant.'

'If indeed your son was killed,' the Castellan interrupted. 'I only have your word for that – and the word of your men. The corpse you showed us could have been anybody.'

Geraden went white at this insult to the lord. The Tor, however, shrugged it aside. 'But now,' he persisted, 'we have taken a great step forward. Now we know where to look.'

'In the Care of Tor.' Lebbick was remorseless. 'In your domain, my lord.'

The Tor permitted himself a subtle flare of anger. 'Astonishing, is it not?'

'Unquestionably,' the Castellan grated with pleasure.

'Unfortunately' – the Tor's ire was instantly gone – 'a search is impossible at present. We are otherwise occupied. Please tell me what you are doing to prepare Orison for siege. It is reported that Prince Kragen places great faith in the Alend Monarch's ability to master us almost without difficulty. That seems absurd on its face – and yet I doubt that Prince Kragen is given to trusting the absurd. It is a pity that we cannot question – or observe – the lady Elega. That is beyond help, however. We must be very ready, good Castellan.'

'I'll be ready,' retorted Castellan Lebbick. 'By my estimation, we still have a few days left, but I've sent out scouts to make sure. The fact that the Armigite is a traitor probably has one advantage for us.' As he spoke, he seemed to fall unconsciously into the manner of an old soldier delivering a report. 'We can assume Margonal will use the main roads through Armigite. They're the easiest, quickest route. So his army shouldn't be hard to find.

'Also, I've sent messengers to the Cares that ought to help us. Fayle. Perdon.' Glowering at Geraden, he commented, 'What the Perdon hears isn't going to be what your dear brother had in mind.' Then he resumed his report. 'I've sent men to the Termigan, but he's too far away to do us much good.

'I haven't had time to talk to the Congery yet, but I'll do that soon. Maybe I'll finally be able to scare some sense into those Imagers.'

Apparently, none of the Masters had seen fit to announce their intention to disband the Congery.

'In the meantime, I'm calling my garrisoned troops into Orison. Most of the men hunting for the Congery's *champion*' – he was snarling— 'have come back, and I won't send them out again. The only men I'm going to risk outside are the ones who still have a chance to locate Prince Kragen before he joins his father, and the ones who're trying to backtrack those creatures. I'll have all my strength here and organized by dawn tomorrow.'

The Tor nodded, but didn't interrupt.

'Because we're near the end of winter, our stores are low. That's a problem. But there are quite a few merchants and villages we can call on for supplies. That won't cause them any unfair hardship – with a war about to start, most of them are going to want sanctuary in Orison anyway, so they might as well pay for their safety with food. If Margonal gives us three days, we should be as well stocked as possible.

'But our biggest problem is that breach in the wall.'

Again, the Tor nodded. This time, however, his eyes were closed. He looked like he was going to sleep.

'Without that,' Castellan Lebbick rasped, 'I could hold Orison against anybody. Long before our stores were gone, at least one of the lords of the Cares would take it into his head to come to our rescue. But that breach changes things. I've had all the stonemasons I could find working to build a rough curtain wall across the gap. It's serviceable, but it won't take the kind of pounding Margonal is going to give it.

'Am I boring you, my lord Tor?'

The lord opened one eye. 'Not at all, good Castellan. I am merely resting my mind from the chore of trying to imagine the source of Prince Kragen's confidence.'

The Castellan's mention of the champion reminded Terisa that she wanted to ask a question. She felt that she was coming back to herself now, recovering some presence of mind and attention. But this wasn't her chance to speak.

'Young Geraden,' the Tor went on, 'can you remember exactly what Nyle and the Prince said to each other?'

'Pretty much,' Geraden answered. 'Prince Kragen was worried about Elega. Nyle told him about your talk with her. That shows she knew you were suspicious of her. And it proves she and Nyle were in communication before he left this morning. Then he said that she said that you won't be able to interfere with her part of the plan.'

Castellan Lebbick grunted. The Tor raised an eyebrow.

'Nyle had trouble believing that. But – let me try to get it right.' Geraden looked at the ceiling while he searched his memory. 'Prince Kragen said, "I regret that she is at hazard. But she has assured me many times that her role is secure. We must trust that she will do what she has said." '

'Is that all?' demanded the Castellan.

Geraden shrugged. 'Nyle still wasn't convinced. But Prince Kragen said, "The lady Elega's safety and success depend upon secrecy." He was pretty careful. I'm not sure Nyle realized how many of his questions weren't being answered.'

'Poor Nyle,' the Castellan sneered.

'Unfortunate,' contributed the Tor thoughtfully. 'What can one woman hidden in Orison do to ensure the success – the *instant* success – of the Alend Monarch's siege? I confess that I am baffled. I need wine.'

With an effort, he heaved himself to his feet. The bench under Terisa flexed in relief.

'Good Castellan,' he murmured, 'I suggest that you question your prisoners. But try not to harm them. You really must curb your instinct for excess. I suspect that Nyle will be more amenable to persuasion than force. Perhaps he will speak frankly if he can be made to believe that Elega has been caught – that the only way to spare her distress is by revealing what he knows. And the creature of Imagery may let slip something helpful.'

'Thanks for the advice, my lord Tor,' Castellan Lebbick replied. 'Question the prisoners. I would never have thought of that.

'While you're waiting for me to tell you what I've found out, what will you be doing?' His question was an obvious reference to the lord's drinking.

The Tor sighed. For a moment, his thick flesh dropped into lines of sorrow. 'Good Castellan, I trust you more than you know. I am sure that you have done everything in your power. Nevertheless I am not content with matters as they stand. I will make one more attempt to interest King Joyse in the fate of his kingdom.'

With that, he waddled out of the guardroom.

At once, Lebbick turned a glare like the cut of a hatchet at Terisa and Geraden. 'I *like* that. I've been wrestling with this problem for years, and one fat old man thinks he can solve it by howling outside the King's door.'

Here it comes, Terisa thought glumly. Now he's really going to tear into us.

She was wrong: the Castellan had more imagination than that. There was malice and anticipation in his tone as he said, 'You two still haven't told me what I want to know. But I don't want to be accused of *excess*. And you won't be leaving Orison anytime soon. You'll have plenty of time to talk yourselves into telling me the truth.

'In the meantime, I want you to help me question the prisoners. You should enjoy that.'

She and Geraden looked at each other. The room wasn't so warm after all; she no longer wanted to take off her coat. His face held an expression of alarm that worried her. She was so full of her own problems that she tended to forget how much he was suffering. *Help me question* – Did the Castellan really intend to use him against his brother? After what he had already done?

Because she believed Geraden needed her, she rose to her feet and met Castellan Lebbick's scowl.

'You're searching for Elega.' She was still afraid of him. Nevertheless she had stood up to him in the past; she could do it again. 'Do you think there's any chance you'll find her?'

His jaws chewed iron. Yet in spite of his ire he answered her. He looked oddly helpless, as if he didn't have any choice. 'That depends on how many secret passages she knows. I can't spare enough men to search them all at the same time.'

'I understand.' She had expected that. It was unimportant, however. Her next question was the one that mattered. As if she weren't going off in a completely different direction, she asked, 'Is it true that your men never found the champion?'

Is it true that your men never found Myste?

'Those pigshit Imagers,' he rasped. 'No, my men never found the *champion*. And that doesn't make sense. He must have left a trail. He needs to eat, doesn't he? He must have raided villages for food. That's not the kind of thing a farmer or cattleherd forgets. Even if he went straight for Cadwal, we should have been able to follow him at least that far. But my men couldn't even find *rumors* about him.

'Either he's dead under a snowdrift somewhere, or Gilbur and Vagel translated him to safety. Or he sprouted wings and flew away. *You tell me.*

'As for the firecat' – Lebbick gave a bleak shrug – 'it just disappeared. They must have sent it back where it came from.'

But what about Myste? What happened to Myste?

If the man she risked her life to find had disappeared, what did she do?

'Castellan,' Geraden interposed. Terisa had given him enough time to recover his self-possession. 'If you're planning to tell Nyle lies about Elega, you don't want me with you. He knows me too well. He'll see the truth in my face. I won't be able to hide it.'

Lebbick looked at the Apt. For the second time, his face went through a strange transformation. Terisa expected him to be livid, but he wasn't. Taken by surprise, he was open, accessible to pain: Geraden had hurt his feelings. 'I have no intention of lying to anyone.' He spoke sternly, but his sternness wasn't anger. 'I don't tell lies.'

'I'm sorry,' Geraden said at once, abashed by the change in the Castellan. 'I knew that. I'm just not thinking straight.'

'It wouldn't make any difference if you were.' Castellan Lebbick's tone was rude, yet his intent may have been kind. 'No matter how important the Tor thinks you are, you didn't cause this mess. Prince Kragen told your brother a lot of hogslop. I know Margonal. He hasn't suddenly been converted to benevolence and peace. He's been planning to invade Mordant ever since he heard about King Joyse.

'Come on.'

Dismissing Geraden's apology along with his own odd vulnerability, the Castellan strode toward the door.

The guardroom that gave access to Orison's dungeon was unaltered from the time when Terisa had passed through it with Artagel, going to talk to Master Eremis. Despite its resemblance to a crude tavern – its trestle tables and rough benches, its beds and hearth, its refreshment bar – its defensive function was unmistakable. The racks fixed along all the walls held enough pikes and swords to equip forty or fifty fighting men. And the room itself was the only way into or out of the passages that led to the cells.

Remembering Master Eremis made her heart feel weak. He had left Orison without coming to her, without fulfilling his promise. An ache of desire passed over her.

If the room hadn't changed, however, the men in it had. They weren't ill-disciplined and resting: they were on their feet, at attention to meet the Castellan's arrival.

He saluted their captain and stalked on through the guardroom without speaking.

Geraden shrugged and grimaced companionably at the guards as he and Terisa followed the Castellan. One or two of them nodded to him slightly, little signs that they understood his circumstances.

The air beyond the guardroom remained dank, foul with rotting straw and recollections of torture, fretted with hints of old blood. The infrequent lanterns seemed to create more gloom than illumination; the passage wandered as if it led down into the dark places of Orison's soul. Castellan Lebbick took one turn, then another, and reached the region of the cells.

Past his shoulders, Terisa saw two guards coming along the corridor. They walked in single file, apparently lugging something heavy between them.

An instant later, she realized that they were carrying a litter.

Panic leaped in Geraden's face.

She thought dumbly, Nyle?

When Castellan Lebbick shifted to one side of the passage, however, and the guards took the other, she saw that the man lying in the litter wasn't Nyle.

'Artagel!' Geraden cried in relief and consternation. 'You're supposed to be in bed.'

The guards stopped, and Artagel hitched himself up on one elbow.

'What're you doing here?' snapped the Castellan. 'This is none of your business. I've already lost one man today, along with my best chance to catch Margonal's pigslime son. I don't need you bleeding to death on top of my other problems.'

'Are you all right?' Geraden put in. Suddenly, he had so much to say that it all tried to tumble out at once. 'There was no other way I could stop him. I couldn't talk him out of it. He saved us. He could have let us be killed, but he didn't. It makes me sick. I hit—' His voice caught; he couldn't go on. His whole face burned for Artagel's forgiveness.

But Artagel didn't glance at Geraden. 'He's my brother,' he replied to the Castellan in a voice like a dry husk. He looked like he had suffered a relapse of fever; his mouth had lost its humor, and his eyes glittered like polished stones. 'I had to see him.'

One of the guards shrugged against the weight of the litter. 'We couldn't talk him out of it, Castellan. He was going to walk if we didn't carry him.'

Castellan Lebbick ignored the guards. Facing Artagel, he demanded, 'What did he say?'

With surprising strength, Artagel reached out, caught at Lebbick's sash, pulled the Castellan closer to him. 'He told me the truth. He got into this because he loves that crazy woman. And because he thinks it's right. Somebody has got to save Mordant. He thinks Margonal is our only chance.' Staring at him, Terisa understood that he wasn't angry. He grinned when he was angry. No, what he felt now was closer to despair. 'She talked to him about everything in the world except her part in Kragen's plans. He doesn't know where she is, or what she's going to do.'

On the other hand, Castellan Lebbick was angry enough for both of them. 'Do you expect me to believe that?'

'Artagel?' Geraden insisted. 'Artagel?'

Artagel met the Castellan's glare. Slowly, he let go of the sash and eased himself onto his back in the litter. 'I don't care whether you believe me or not. I don't even care if you torture him. He's a son of the Domne. No matter what you do, this is going to kill my father.'

Geraden raised a hand and clamped it around his mouth to keep himself still.

The Castellan drew himself up. His face showed no softening. Nevertheless he said, 'All right. I'll try believing him for a while and see what happens.'

For the first time, Artagel turned his eyes to Geraden. The angle of the light from the one lantern filled his face with shadows.

Geraden flinched. Terisa had never seen him look more like a puppy cringing because he had offended someone he loved and didn't know what to do about it. He needed understanding if not forgiveness, needed some kind of consolation from his brother.

He didn't get it.

'You're the smart one of the family.' Artagel's voice was still as dry as fever. 'You find that woman and stop her. If you don't – and she betrays us – I swear to you I'm not going to let Margonal's men in here, no matter who tells me to surrender. I'll fight them all if I have to.'

In response, Geraden's face twisted as if he were about to throw up.

'Oh, get him out of here,' Castellan Lebbick rasped to the guards. 'Put him back in bed. Tie him down if you have to. Then call his physician. This air is making him crazy. Right now, he couldn't fight a pregnant cripple.'

'Yes, Castellan.' The guards settled their shoulders into the load and took Artagel in the direction of the guardroom.

'Geraden?' Terisa put her hand on his arm and felt the pressure that knotted his muscles. 'He didn't mean it. He still has a fever. He shouldn't have gotten out of bed.' He was so hurt that she wanted to embrace him, but Castellan Lebbick's presence prevented that. 'Listen to me. He didn't mean to blame you.'

The Apt turned to her. Gloom hid his eyes. He had his back to the lantern; the lines of his face were dark. He didn't respond to what she said. But he continued to face her as he addressed the Castellan.

'That just leaves the creature who attacked us.' His tone was as empty as one of the cells. 'What do you think you can learn from him?'

'That depends,' replied Lebbick. 'You're the student of Imagery. You tell me. Is there any chance he speaks a language we can understand?'

Geraden had once discussed that subject with Terisa; he didn't go into it now. 'Let's find out.'

He and Lebbick started down the passage – and a shadowy figure brushed past them, hurrying toward the creature's cell. 'Nobody tells me anything,' the man muttered into the air as he passed.

Terisa caught a glimpse of his face and recognized Adept Havelock.

Adept Havelock?

Automatically, the Castellan grabbed at his sword; then he slapped it back into its scabbard. With Geraden, he pursued the mad old man.

Jumping to sudden conclusions, Terisa ran after them.

They were moving too quickly: she couldn't catch up with them in time. In the grip of a sudden alarm, she called, 'Don't ask him any questions.'

Castellan Lebbick whirled toward her so unexpectedly that Geraden ran into him. Their collision sent the Apt staggering against the bars of a cell. Swearing viciously, Lebbick took hold of Terisa's coat and snatched her to him.

'*Don't ask him any questions?*'

'That's right. Questions just make him worse.' The Castellan's breath was dry and sour. She wanted to explain herself clearly, but everything was happening too fast. 'He might tell us something. But not if we ask him any questions.'

'My lady,' Castellan Lebbick whispered through his teeth, 'how do you know that?'

'He told me.'

'He *told* you?'

Fortunately, she had no chance to think about what she would say. A chance to think would also have been a chance to make a mistake, to reveal something accidentally. Almost without hesitation, she repeated, 'He told me. I guess he wanted to talk to me. But I didn't understand. When I didn't obey, he nearly had a fit.'

The Castellan tightened his grip on her. His grin made him look mad, nearly out of control. A second later, however, he dropped his hands and went after Adept Havelock again.

Geraden had caught up with the Adept. They stood together in front of a cell. Lamplight glowed from inside the grid wall.

A snarl throbbed down the corridor. Four furred arms with claws on their fingers sprang between the bars, reaching for Geraden. He jerked backward just in time.

Vehemently, Adept Havelock shoved the last digits of both hands up his nostrils and waggled the rest of his fingers at the creature like a child trying to make his face as horrible as possible.

Castellan Lebbick grabbed Havelock by the scruff of his surcoat and pulled him a safe distance away from the bars. When Terisa joined the three men, the creature was clinging to the grid with all four hands. His chest heaved, and the whiskers around his eyes bristled like weapons. Maybe they're poisoned, she thought, staring at him. Though his features were completely alien, they plainly promised violence.

Swept away from rationality by the creature's strangeness, the Adept's unexpected appearance, the pressure of too many unanswered questions, she observed in a tone of lunatic calm, 'The weather sure got cold today.'

Trying to lure Havelock into talking with her.

He didn't look in her direction. First he pinched his lips with his fingers and pulled them apart, making a wild grimace. Then he commented, 'I've heard of these, but I've never seen one before.'

The Castellan started to explode. Geraden slapped a hand against his chest to stop him.

All at once, Terisa's throat went dry. She had to swallow several times before she was able to say, 'We went riding today. I nearly froze to death.'

Havelock experimented with another monstrous face, but it had no discernible impact on the creature. 'A couple of Vagel's Imagers talked about them,' he muttered. 'Not Vagel himself. But he was eager. In the mirror, all they did was hunt for things to kill. And they seemed to be able to find what they were after without seeing it. They went past the mirror in swarms. But obviously intelligent. They had domesticated animals they used for mounts. He wanted a whole army of them.'

In an effort to keep the Adept going, she said the first words that popped into her head. 'We were following Geraden's brother Nyle. He went to meet Prince Kragen.'

Geraden winced.

'That's right,' replied Havelock as though he were in complete agreement. 'Festten kept interfering.' He bared his teeth in a humorless grin, then put his thumbs in his ears and stretched his eyes to slits with his fingers. 'If Vagel had his own army, he wouldn't need the High King. Festten found ways to interrupt the research before those two Imagers could finish it. One of them finally disappeared. I think he was killed.'

Terisa did her best to pull her thoughts together. Her concentration was in tatters. She had killed—

What were the Imagers researching? What kept them from translating the army the arch-Imager wanted?

Was it language?

Aiming a mute apology at the Apt, she said, 'We tried to stop Nyle. That was when they attacked us. They were after Geraden. Not me.'

The Adept gave her a smile as high-pitched and unexpected as a giggle. 'I know exactly what you mean.' The lamplight made his eyes look milky, as if he were going blind.

From one of his sleeves, he produced the palm-sized bit of mirror that Terisa had twice seen him use as a weapon.

For a piece of time that seemed to have no measurable duration, she gaped at him while he murmured to the glass and passed his hand over it. Then a sting of intuition warned her, and she wrenched herself forward, grabbed at his wrist.

She missed. He had already turned away.

Blissfully unaware of her, he focused his glass and shot out a beam so hot that the creature went up in flames like a bundle of kindling.

With a howl of inarticulate frustration and rage, the Castellan flung Havelock aside. Instantly, the beam stopped as Adept Havelock stumbled against the wall and fell to the floor.

But the creature burned like a torch. No sound came from him; he didn't recoil or wave his arms or loose his grip on the bars. Slowly, slowly, he slumped down the grid.

As if in slow motion, Terisa felt a blast of heat. The stench of scorched fur and sizzling flesh filled the air.

Unable to control her reactions, she staggered to her knees. Down near the floor, the air was still cool. The rotten stink of the straw was too much for her, however. Adept Havelock had risen to his hands and knees to watch the creature. When he saw that she was looking at him, he gave her a huge, conspiratorial wink.

Then darkness welled up in her, and she fainted as though she were fading inward.

TWENTY-THREE

ANTICIPATING DISASTER

She had the distinct impression that she was gone for a long time.

A man bending over her: she remembered that.

But who was he? Master Eremis? The idea gave her a liquid feeling in the pit of her stomach. She didn't want to be unconscious. If he were to touch her in any way, she didn't want to miss it.

Now, however, the figure with her was more like a woman. Gradually, she became aware that she wasn't lying on the floor in the dungeon. For one thing, she was warm, really warm – warm all the way down to her toes. There must be a bed under her; no stone was this soft. And blankets—

With an effort, she got her eyes open.

Over her hung the familiar peacock-feather canopy of her bed.

Saddith met her bleary gaze and called softly, 'Geraden, I think she is waking up.'

At once, Geraden came to her side. His face was stretched with fatigue and worry, and his expression was harried; but when he looked into her eyes he smiled as though she made everything in the world all right. 'Thank the stars,' he murmured in a husky voice. 'I'm glad to see you conscious again.'

She coughed at a throat full of gluey cotton. 'How long have I been out?'

'Long enough.'

Saddith gave a light laugh. 'My lady, the Apt is sotted with you. Every moment that your eyes are not open for him is "long enough" to fill him with alarm. You have had a much-needed rest. When you have had food and' – she wrinkled her nose – 'a bath, you will feel well enough to be amused by his concern.'

Terisa smelled the faint rotten scent. It seemed to be in her hair. And in—

Her coat was draped over the back of another chair, but she was still wearing her clothes under the blankets. The smell was in her shirt and pants as well. When she lifted the covers, it wafted delicately into her face.

She pushed the blankets away and let Saddith and Geraden steady her in a sitting position on the edge of the bed. A bright fire crackled in her hearth, and the creature had burned—

'What happened?' she asked.

Geraden's smile twisted. 'Not much. You passed out. Adept Havelock left.

416

The Castellan swore at everybody. One of the physicians and I brought you here. He said you were going to be all right, but I didn't believe him.' He looked away. 'Saddith has been telling me her life story to keep me from screaming while you slept.'

'Why did—?' Terisa ran her fingers into her hair, then grimaced at the odor which clung to them. She had to breathe deeply to make her head stop spinning. 'Why did Adept Havelock kill that poor—?'

At that, Geraden's expression turned harsh. 'He's crazy. Even if we knew why he does anything, it wouldn't make sense.'

'I can explain it,' said Saddith in a teasing tone. 'If the rumors are true, the Adept has not had a woman since he returned from Cadwal.' With her elbow, she nudged Geraden's ribs. 'All men become madmen if they do not bed women often enough.'

For no very clear reason, Geraden appeared to be blushing.

Terisa had to get the creature's immolation out of her mind. She had to get the stink out of her clothes and hair. Ignoring Saddith, she said to Geraden, 'I don't understand. Why didn't those Imagers who worked with Vagel translate the army he wanted? What research did they have to do?'

Promptly, as if he were relieved by her question, he answered, 'I don't have any way of knowing, of course – but I'm pretty sure I can guess. We've talked about language.' He watched Terisa's face intently. 'When the arch-Imager's cabal came up with an Image of what looked to them like the ideal warrior, they had no way of knowing whether they would be able to talk to him. They didn't believe the question of language would be resolved by the translation itself. That's what they needed to research.'

He snorted a sour laugh. 'It's funny, in a way. Either High King Festten or the arch-Imager could have had an entire army of those creatures, if they just believed the same thing King Joyse believes. They might have been able to beat him.

'Now we'll never know the answer,' he concluded bitterly.

Terisa nodded, letting Geraden push back the memories she wanted to escape from. For her part, however, Saddith didn't appear particularly pleased by this turn of the conversation. As soon as Geraden stopped, she said, 'My lady, I have no food or bathwater ready for you. I did not know when you would awaken. But both can be provided almost immediately. With your permission, I will go to bring what you need.'

'Thanks.' As usual, Terisa's eyes were drawn to Saddith's open blouse and bursting breasts. She made an effort to raise her head so that she felt less like she was talking to Saddith's chest. 'I would like that.'

In response, Saddith swung a saucy gaze at Geraden. 'Be warned,' she said slyly. 'I will be back too soon for what you desire. Even the hottest youth must have a certain amount of time.'

Laughing, she left the rooms.

Terisa eased herself experimentally to her feet.

In a hurry to steady her, Geraden jerked forward. Unfortunately, he missed his balance and nearly fell onto the bed. Terisa found herself holding him up rather than being supported.

Swearing at himself, he pulled away. Apparently, he had lost his balance in more ways than one. Now he looked like he was on the verge of tears.

Geraden? What's the matter? She wasn't sure of what she was seeing. Or she wasn't sure of herself. She wasn't in particularly good shape. In fact, she felt lousy. Where was the Geraden who always took care of her as if she were the most important person in his life?

Inanely, she said the first words she could think of that had nothing to do with what she felt. 'I thought I saw you blush. What were you and she really doing while I was asleep?'

He stiffened. Retreating to his chair allowed him to turn his face away from her for a moment. When he sat down, his features were set into hard lines, as if he were angry. Nevertheless she knew he wasn't angry. His eyes were hot with grief.

'I don't understand that woman,' he muttered without meeting her gaze. 'I mean, I understand. I'm not as ignorant as she thinks. It just doesn't make sense to me.' He scowled at the vista of his confusion. 'While you were asleep, she wasn't telling me her life story. She was trying to persuade me to bed her right here on the floor.'

For some reason, Terisa didn't find this amusing. All at once, the muscles around her heart felt tight.

'She said she hadn't had a man for a while. She talked about it like it was just scratching a complicated kind of itch. Of course, there are probably two hundred men within a stone's throw of us right now who would be glad to oblige her. But she didn't want to do anything that might get back to the man she's really interested in. I got the impression he's been away. Whoever he is.' He sighed, but still couldn't bring himself to look at Terisa. 'She said I was safe because my heart was set on you, not her. And she would be doing me a favor by teaching me what to do with your body when I finally got my hands on it.

'I couldn't get it through her head that if she kept talking like that she was going to make me throw up.'

'Why?' Terisa tried to sound casual, but didn't succeed. 'Don't you think she's attractive?'

His gaze turned cold as he faced her. 'Sure, she's attractive. A stone wall would be attractive if it looked like that. It's her attitude I don't like. There's more to love than just getting your itches scratched.

'Tell me something.' Now he was angry. 'Some time ago – I think it was the first morning of the thaw – I was here with you, and Saddith came in. You asked her how Master Eremis was.'

The knot around Terisa's heart pulled tighter.

'At the time, I thought that was a strange question. I just didn't want to pry. But the more I think about it, the stranger it gets. Why ask *her*? What would she know about Master Eremis?'

Saddith had tried to seduce Geraden. Terisa sat back down on the bed to conceal the fact that she was trembling – and to control it. In a small voice – putting her emotions at a distance because she was afraid of them – she said, 'She's having an affair with him. She tells me about it.' She would never be able to admit that she had seen Master Eremis and Saddith together. 'I think she believes if she sleeps with enough men she'll end up queen of Mordant.'

After a moment, he murmured, 'That explains it.' He no longer sounded angry. He sounded frayed and alone.

Abruptly, he rose to his feet. 'I got a message earlier. Artagel has had a relapse. His physician says it's temporary. He'll be all right. But I ought to go see him. Saddith will be back soon. That may not cheer you up, but at least you'll get some food and a hot bath.'

Unable to keep his distress from showing, he turned to leave.

'Geraden, wait.' The sight of his departing back seemed to pull everything inside her in a different direction. She jumped upright, reached a hand he couldn't see toward him. 'Don't go.'

He paused in the doorway. His voice was cramped in his throat. His shoulders hunched as if he were huddling over a pain in his chest. 'I have to.'

'Please,' she said. 'I've been very selfish. You're always so good to me that I let myself forget you have problems of your own. Please tell me what's the matter.'

He didn't move. Slowly, he put out one hand to brace himself on the doorframe. 'Terisa,' he said, aching, 'this mess really is my fault.'

'No, it isn't.' She was ready to defend him at once. 'You aren't Prince Kragen. You aren't Elega.'

He raised his free hand to his face. 'Nyle was right. I've been a fool about everything. He was doing what he thought was right. But he was also doing something that wouldn't do any serious damage if he turned out to be wrong. That's important. We didn't need to worry about him. He didn't pose any threat. You and I should have gone back to Orison so that Ribuld could stay with Argus. We should have told Castellan Lebbick about Elega right away.'

Slowly, his voice became edged with iron, like the hit of a chisel. He cut off words like chips of stone. 'You wouldn't be here if I hadn't gone wrong with that translation. The champion would be here instead. Or else he would have refused, in which case he wouldn't have been translated against his will. Orison's walls would be intact. And Myste would still be here. If anybody could stop Elega, she could.'

'Geraden.' Terisa went to him; tentatively, she rested her hands on his back. It felt like it had been bound with cords to keep him from exploding. The boyish side of him was dying. He was being taken apart piece by piece, deprived of the things he loved, the things that sustained him. 'Please, Geraden.'

She would have to tell him.

He had gone too far to stop. 'The Alend Monarch is going to take Orison. It's impossible – it *ought* to be impossible – but he's going to do it. And it's my fault. I was *betrothed* to that woman. Maybe we don't have much in common, but I thought I knew her better than this. First Nyle. Now her. Everything I love—'

His throat closed. She felt him struggle to open it. Then he said, 'Artagel is right. This is going to kill my father.'

She should have told him long ago. 'Geraden, don't do this to yourself.'

Without warning, he turned to face her. His cheeks were wet with tears, but he didn't look like he was weeping: he looked flagrantly unhappy, almost demented with contempt for himself and his mistakes.

'Artagel thinks it's my fault.' He spoke quietly – so quietly that he sounded unreachable. 'I expected that from Nyle. But Artagel thinks it's my fault too.'

'*Geraden.*' She had passed the limit of what she could stand. To steady herself – because she was afraid – she took hold of the front of his shirt with both hands. 'You aren't wrong. I don't know why – or how. But you aren't wrong.

'Do you remember the augury? Do you remember seeing riders?' *Three riders. Driving their mounts forward, straight out of the glass, driving hard, so that the strain in the shoulders of their horses was as plain as the hate in the keen edges of their upraised swords.* 'I saw them – I dreamed them before I ever saw the augury. Before I ever met you. I had a dream that was exactly the same as one Image in the augury.'

Searching his face, she saw surprise and bafflement dawn into joy. 'So there *is* a reason,' he breathed in wonder. 'I didn't go wrong. You *are* the champion.'

'I don't know why,' she repeated, insisted. It was the only gift she had to give him, the only consolation. 'I don't know how. But there is a reason. You didn't go wrong.'

In response, he became brighter and brighter, as if he were burning. His arms closed around her; his mouth came down to hers.

Ardently, she put her arms around his neck and kissed him.

They hugged and held each other until Saddith returned with a tray of food and a porter carrying bathwater.

After a meal, they did what they could to get ready for the coming siege.

By noon the next day, Castellan Lebbick had deployed virtually all the King's guards in Orison, sorting them according to their responsibilities for the defense and maintenance of the castle, and billeting them wherever he could find room. When the barracks became overcrowded, some of the abandoned passages and quarters under the main habitation were brought back into use. Cooks complained about the extra work. Servingmen and -women whose jobs included sanitation complained vehemently. Nevertheless Orison swallowed the additional troops.

Work on the curtain wall across the breach continued.

At the same time, scouts crossed from the Demesne into the Care of Armigite. Although they would have been appalled to encounter the Alend Monarch's army so soon, they began to travel with more caution.

During the night, the men tracking Prince Kragen had returned. The Alend Contender had lost his pursuers in the simplest way possible – by riding onto a road, where his trail couldn't be distinguished from anyone else's. This report inspired the Castellan to curse extensively, but there was nothing he could do to change it.

Nothing was heard from the guards who were trying to find out where Geraden's alien attackers had come from.

Most of the farmers and merchants in the nearer environs of the castle had started to empty their sheds and warehouses and pens and barns toward

Orison. Plenty of people still alive in the villages remembered what life had been like before King Joyse had taken power over Mordant and created peace by the strength of his good right hand. They goaded the folk around them into motion.

Grandmothers and flocks of goats didn't move quickly – but they were on their way.

As a result, the courtyard was crowded with activity, and an atmosphere of bustle pervaded the halls. The situation could easily have degenerated into chaos and choler. Castellan Lebbick knew his job, however – and his men knew their orders. Most of the incoming populace found places and got settled without noticing how closely they were supervised. And those who did notice probably didn't guess that the highest priority of the guards wasn't to preserve order, but rather to make sure that Alends or spies didn't sneak into Orison.

Satisfied with the progress of his preparations, Castellan Lebbick paid a visit to Master Barsonage.

The outcome of that visit was less satisfactory. Since the Masters had seen fit to interfere in Mordant's affairs by translating their champion, the Castellan argued that they couldn't now claim to be detached from what was happening. It was their responsibility, therefore, to assist in the defense of Orison and their King. That seemed clear enough.

But Master Barsonage replied with the almost treasonous information that the Congery had disbanded itself. Paralyzed by the very ideals that had brought them together, the Masters couldn't agree on anything. They had no credible purpose. Castellan Lebbick was free to approach individual Imagers as he saw fit – unlike Master Eremis, most of them had remained in Orison – but he couldn't look for concerted decision or action. King Joyse's abandonment of the Congery had finally arrived at its logical conclusion.

Fuming, Castellan Lebbick left.

For his part, the Tor spoke to King Joyse. Or, more precisely, he spoke *at* King Joyse. He wheedled and demanded; he whispered and shouted. He made himself lugubrious, and he tried sincerely to make himself noble. Unfortunately, he received nothing for his pains except a rather strained smile and the absentminded assertion that the King was sure his old friend the Tor would do whatever he, the Tor, thought best. King Joyse himself was really too busy trying to solve the latest hop-board puzzle Adept Havelock had set for him to be distracted by a mere siege. Nevertheless he became irrationally angry when the Tor risked mentioning the lady Elega. The Tor eventually gave up and retreated to the solace of his chancellor's flagon.

As for Elega, two squadrons of guards had searched what they called twenty-five miles of hidden passages in Orison without finding her. The Castellan sent them back to the beginning to start over again.

Pacing the peacock rug in Terisa's sitting room, Geraden demanded, 'But what can she *do*?' Terisa had forgotten how many times he had asked the same question, but at least he had the decency not to expect an answer. 'I mean, stop and think about it. She has essentially promised that she'll deliver Orison to Prince Kragen single-handed. And she made him believe it. But he knows what a siege is. And he's seen Orison. What could she possibly have said to him that he would believe?'

Terisa sighed and gazed glumly out the window.

As he had promised, Mindlin brought her new clothes for a preliminary fitting. She made a few arbitrary decisions, accepted a few adjustments; he went away.

She returned to the window. Although she loved the spring-like sunshine which made the hillsides sparkle and the roads treacherous, she was hoping for snow.

In fact, most of Orison's burgeoning population was hoping for snow. But the next morning brought, not clouds and cold, but a warming trend. Apparently, the weather was on Alend's side.

Castellan Lebbick wasted no time cursing the weather, however. He had other things to swear about.

The influx of people and livestock and supplies was actually going quite well. Of course, life in the courtyard was little better than thinly structured chaos; and people who found themselves quartered in the once unused depths of the castle had to contend with a damp that only grew worse as the walls were warmed by fires and bodies. But there was room for everybody somewhere. And the added livestock and supplies compensated for the increased number of people who had to be fed.

The causes of Castellan Lebbick's compressed fury lay elsewhere.

He had heard nothing from his scouts – but that was good news, not bad. On the other hand, he had also heard nothing from the men who were backtracking Geraden's attackers. As news, that was uncontestably bad. It left open the ominous possibility that an entire horde of creatures was gathering somewhere to sweep down on Orison at the worst possible moment.

Unfortunately, the Castellan also had other provocations. One was that the Tor refused to leave him alone. Having failed to dent King Joyse's detachment, the fat old lord now insisted on knowing everything about Orison's defenses. He wasn't content with generalities: he wanted specifics – the names of officers who had been given certain orders; the quantity and disposition of certain stores; the important routes for moving men and weapons (and water – was the Castellan ready in case of fire?) through the castle. The lord's interference was enough to make a kind man savage.

As another provocation, King Joyse refused to take seriously Lebbick's report from Master Barsonage. 'Disbanded?' he snorted. 'Nonsense. Barsonage has just lost his nerve. Find Master Quillon.' The King hopped a piece on his board and studied the resulting position. 'Tell him he's the new mediator. I need those Imagers.'

Although Castellan Lebbick gnawed at an outrage that was starting to taste like despair, King Joyse refused to say anything further.

And the lady Elega appeared to have vanished without a trace. The guards not only failed to find her, they also failed to find any sign of her – any little stores of food and water; any clothes; any lamps or candles; any (the guards were thorough) carrier pigeons. All they found was Adept Havelock, who appeared at awkward intervals and treated them to displays of wisdom and decorum that would have embarrassed the ruffians at a carnival. The Adept seemed to be having the time of his life. Nevertheless Castellan Lebbick wasn't diverted.

Behind his anger, and his concentration on his duty, and his determined belief that no one woman could deliver him and Orison to the King's enemies, he was beginning to sweat.

'Do you think,' Geraden asked Terisa, 'it's something stupid and obvious, like suborning the guards? That might work if nobody suspected her. It's at least imaginable that she could arrange to have the gates opened in the middle of the night.'

He was calmer today, which relieved her sense of responsibility for him and freed her to feel worse herself. Perhaps his obsession was starting to soak into her, making her tense and irritable for no good reason. Or perhaps there was something – She ground her teeth at the idea. Something she knew and couldn't remember? Something she ought to understand?

Damn it.

Scowling at the Apt as if he were to blame, she tried to make sense out of the little she knew.

'Tell me something. Why haven't Alend or Cadwal – or both – attacked Mordant long before this?'

'They were afraid of King Joyse. They were afraid of what he would do with the Congery.'

She nodded. 'And why is Margonal attacking now? Why isn't he still afraid?'

'Because he's heard' – this was painful for Geraden to say – 'from Prince Kragen and probably a few dozen other sources that King Joyse doesn't care anymore.'

'No.' She felt that she was pouncing. 'That's not good enough. So what if the King doesn't care? Why isn't Margonal still afraid of the Congery? Why isn't he afraid the Masters will defend themselves no matter what King Joyse does?'

'Because they've disbanded.'

'He doesn't know that. *She* probably doesn't know it.'

At that, Geraden faced her with an awakening light in his eyes, as if she had suddenly become more beautiful or brilliant. 'In that case, she's promised to do something that will keep the Masters from fighting back.'

'Yes.' That made sense to her. For a moment, she felt vindicated, sharply triumphant.

But she was misleading herself, of course. After scrutinizing what she had suggested, he asked, 'What, exactly? What *can* she do? What power does she have over the Congery?'

Terisa had no idea.

This time, it was Geraden who stared morosely out the window. 'I told you an early thaw was dangerous,' he muttered for no particular reason.

The next day was overcast and gloomy, full of cold wind: it seemed to promise a return of winter. Castellan Lebbick kept an eye cocked at the sky while he fretted at the Tor's persistent attention and stewed over the fact that his scouts hadn't come back. Without realizing it, he fell into the pattern of announcing, when he had nothing more direct or withering to say, that he intended to have the Armigite charbroiled at his earliest convenience.

From a superficial point of view, Orison demanded a great deal of him. The castle was overcrowded – and overcrowding bred quarrels as well as vermin. People were angry because they had been forced to leave their homes. Some merchants were angry because everything they owned had been commandeered; others were angry because almost no one could afford to pay the exorbitant prices dictated by scarcity. Guards were angry because they were being cooped up, or drilled too hard, or assigned to duties they didn't like. Lords and ladies were angry because anger was in the air. Everybody was angry because everybody was afraid. And fear made anger seem more urgent, righteous, and justified.

The truth was, however, that Castellan Lebbick now had the castle organized to function almost entirely without him. His men knew what to do; their officers knew what to do. Everybody was angry, but virtually no one got hurt. The Castellan really had nothing to do but fret and stew – and keep an eye on the weather.

That night, what was left of the squadron backtracking Geraden's attackers rode into Orison: two battered veterans with wounds that still bled, kept open by hard riding. The squadron had been ambushed by a number of the same creatures. And the ambush had taken place not far south of the Broadwine – not far into the Care of Tor.

To commemorate the occasion, the Tor broached a new hogshead of wine. But Castellan Lebbick concentrated on snow. If the weather turned to snow, the men he had sent to the Perdon, the Fayle, even the Termigan might have time to get through.

In the morning, the weather turned to spring.

Sunlight poured through the windows, leaving a gold largesse on the stone floors and the thick rugs. A breeze like a harbinger of flowers wafted through the courtyard. A few patches of bare ground appeared on the hillsides, and some of the distant trees looked distinctly like they intended to bud. Unexpected flocks of birds swirled over the roofs of the castle, lit in loud clusters on the tiles and gutters, and sang.

Shortly after noon, the Castellan's scouts returned to report that the Alend army was already in the Demesne. Barring a cataclysmic disaster or a miraculous reprieve, Orison would be under siege no later than noon the next day.

The scouts gauged that Margonal had ten thousand men – two thousand mounted, eight thousand on foot – and enough engines of war to take the castle apart stone from stone. As it happened, many of the engines were of Armigite design. Apparently, Prince Kragen's dealings with the Armigite hadn't been as simple as the story he had told Nyle.

Unfortunately, that wasn't the only bad news.

Shortly before sunset, a trumpet announced the arrival of riders. Nearly a hundred soldiers came down the road from the Care of Perdon. They looked old and weary, as if they had been traveling for an indecent length of time. They carried the Perdon's banner and wore the Perdon's insignia, and they moved slowly. All of them were injured: limbs were missing; heads and chests, bandaged; faces, haggard. Many of their horses supported litters bearing dead men.

When he realized who the riders were, the trumpeter changed his note to the wail of a dirge.

'Oh, no,' Terisa groaned, watching from her window as the procession approached. 'He said he was going to do this.'

'Cadwal is marching,' muttered Geraden grimly. 'The Perdon isn't going to come to our rescue. He's already at war.'

Then he bit his lip. 'We have got to stop her. If she betrays us now, we don't have any hope.'

Castellan Lebbick and the Tor met the riders at the gate. The Tor made a short speech. The Castellan didn't know how to express grief or compassion, so he remained silent.

To Orison's welcome and the Tor's speech, the captain of the riders replied only, 'We are dying. The Perdon commanded us to come.'

The sunset that evening was especially glorious.

Terisa pushed her supper away untasted. Geraden picked at a piece of bread, rolling bits of dough into pellets and tossing them at the hearth. The mood in the room was as dark as the night outside the window. Neither of them had spoken for a long time.

At last, he murmured, 'It isn't enough.'

'Hmm?' she asked vaguely.

For no special reason, they had both neglected to light the lamps. The only illumination came from the hearth. Flickering firelight cast streaks of orange and shadow across the Apt's face; bits of flame echoed in and out of his eyes.

'It isn't enough,' he repeated. 'Suppose Elega knows some way to neutralize the Masters. For example, suppose – just for the sake of supposing – that she has some kind of acid that eats glass. And she knows a way to sneak into the laborium where the mirrors are kept. *And* she knows where all the Masters keep all their private mirrors. Suppose she has time to ruin every mirror in Orison. That's a lot – but it isn't enough.'

As he spoke, she was gradually struck by the impression that his face had changed. The firelight seemed to emphasize an alteration in the line of his jaw, the planes of his cheeks, the shape of his frown. The pressure of the past few days had ground the puppy out of him. He no longer looked like a man who tripped over his own feet and smiled lopsidedly at the results.

'It wouldn't defeat Orison,' he mused into the fire, talking mostly to himself. 'Castellan Lebbick wouldn't surrender for a reason like that. There has to be some other answer.'

Yes, she said inside herself. There has to be some other answer. But she wasn't agreeing with him. She was consciously and explicitly angry. She was angry at Artagel and Castellan Lebbick and Nyle. She was angry at King Joyse, who knew what he was doing to people who had spent their lives trusting him. She was angry at the Masters for their derision, their unwillingness to understand. She had *liked* Geraden's puppyish look. She

425

had *liked* his ability to tumble all over himself without feeling that he was to blame for the destruction of everything he loved.

Why are *we* responsible for Elega? Why is it *our* fault she's probably going to betray everybody?

A moment later, however, her memory brought another image back to her, as vivid as Geraden's face – an image of the lady Myste. Sitting in this same room, Myste had explained to Terisa why she wanted to go after the champion. *I have always believed*, she had said, *that problems should be solved by those who see them. This is more true rather than less for a king's daughter.*

Myste! Terisa murmured with a silent ache. What happened to you? Where are you?

What is Elega doing?

Without thinking, she said aloud, 'Water.'

Geraden's face shifted through patches of light and darkness until he was looking at her. 'Water?'

'Where do we get water?'

His brows knotted in perplexity. 'I told you about that during our tour. Orison was built over a spring. But of course it's grown a lot. And we use a lot of water. I think I mentioned Castellan Lebbick has strong ideas about sanitation. The spring has been inadequate for a long time. So we store rainwater and melted snow. Gutters and pipes from all the roofs take water to the reservoir – I showed you the reservoir.'

'And now,' she said slowly while a keen pulse began to beat in her temple and a hand of tension closed around her heart, 'we have all these extra people. And we haven't had any more snow.'

'That's one of the dangers of an early thaw.' He was watching her closely. 'Until the rains start, we won't have anything except the spring to keep us going.'

She took a deep breath and held it to prevent her head from spinning. When she was ready to speak steadily, she asked, 'What if something happens to the reservoir?'

He still didn't understand. 'Happens? What could happen?'

'Is it guarded?'

'No. Why should it be guarded?'

Unable to suppress the excitement or fear charging through her, she jumped to her feet. With both hands, she took him by one arm and pulled him upright.

'What if she *poisons* it?'

The idea hit him as if she had thrown open a window and shown him a completely alien world. His lips shaped the words *poisons it* while he scrambled to catch up with her. In a strangled tone, he argued, 'There's always the spring.'

'What difference does that make? Fresh water won't help. We'll all be *poisoned*. As long as nobody knows we're in danger, we'll all be *poisoned*. There won't be anybody left to fight. Even if we aren't killed – even if we're just sick for a few hours – Margonal will be able to take Orison almost without a struggle.'

'That's right.' His face twisted as his thoughts raced. 'We've got to warn Castellan Lebbick.'

'*Geraden.*' For just a second, she wanted to yell at him. He was being so obtuse.

Almost at once, however, her mood changed, and she wanted to laugh. She wasn't used to being ahead of him. Carefully, she said, 'Don't you think it would be better if we *stopped* her?'

He stared at her momentarily with his mouth wide open. Then he let out a whoop that sounded like glee. The firelight was as bright as laughter in his eyes. 'Excuse me, my lady.' He hugged himself and chortled. 'I've got wax in my ears. I'm not sure I heard you right.' But joy and relief weren't the only emotions reflecting from his gaze. The flames were warm and glad – and they were also fierce, burning sharply. 'Did you say, Don't you think it would be better if we saved Orison all by ourselves? Just you and me?'

She nodded.

'Why should we tell Lebbick? We're just guessing. He might not believe us. If he believes us, we might be wrong. But if we're right this is our chance to prove that you're innocent – that you aren't secretly plotting Orison's destruction.'

She nodded again, more because she liked the life in his face than because she thought the Castellan would believe any demonstration of her innocence.

'Blast all glass to splinters!' He hissed the words between his teeth, grinning like Artagel. 'Get your coat. It's going to be cold up there.'

Terisa got her coat.

It was cold up there.

The reservoir had been built in the highest part of Orison's main body – a labor of construction that was justified by the amount of work saved by being able to distribute water around the castle with gravity instead of pumps. The towers, of course, required pumps; and the waters of the spring had to be pumped up to the reservoir. But those were relatively simple jobs compared to the chore of supplying water for all of Orison.

Terisa had to fill in many of the details from memory. The place was dark: the only light came from the screened openings that let rain and snow and the night air into the reservoir while keeping birds out; and the bright moon outside did little more than glint vague silver across the surface of the water. But she remembered that the reservoir had been built like a pool, deep and rectangular, with a smooth stone walk on all four sides.

Around the walk rose heavy timbers, crisscrossing toward the roof to hold up the network of pipes that carried rainfall and melted snow and even dew from the roofs of Orison – and to support also the scaffolding that made possible the cleaning and repair of the screens. Because of these timbers, the reservoir resembled a cathedral. Against the faint, wet, lapping susurrus, the overarching silence felt like awe. In the darkness, the water looked vast.

It seemed to absorb whatever warmth endured after the onset of night. The reservoir was cold enough to make her chill despite her coat.

'We need a light,' she whispered unsteadily.

'She'll see us,' answered Geraden, putting his mouth close to her ear so that he wouldn't be overheard.

Terisa nodded. She had hoped she would never have to be cold again in her life.

'Where can we hide?'

For a moment, he didn't move. 'How long do you think we'll have to wait?'

'How should I know? I'm just guessing about all of this.'

'Well, guess some more.'

She made an effort to control her shivers. 'All right. Whatever she puts in the water will need time to dissolve – or spread out – or whatever it does. But if she does it too soon, people will start getting sick' – or dying – 'too soon. The Castellan or somebody might have time to figure out what's going on. Before Margonal is ready.

'If I were her, I might wait until the siege starts.' No later than noon the next day. 'We might be stuck here all night.'

'No.' Geraden was thinking too hard to be polite. 'If she does that, practically all our forces will already be on duty. She'll get the farmers and servingwomen and cooks, but that will just warn Lebbick. She needs to strike tonight, so the water will be bad when the guards get out of bed tomorrow morning. Tomorrow morning early.'

That made sense. 'Where can we hide?' she repeated.

He took her by the arm and pulled her softly into motion. 'There may be any number of ways in here. The floor is riddled with pipes. Maybe it's riddled with passages, too. But we can't do anything about that. And there really isn't anyplace to hide. We'll just put ourselves where we can watch the entrances – the way we came in, and the other one' – he pointed across the reservoir – 'and hope we get lucky.'

'That should be fun,' she retorted simply because she needed to say something. 'We're famous for our good luck.'

He let out a breath of stifled laughter. 'Very true.'

Muffled though it was, his laugh made her feel better.

She wanted to test her way with her feet to be sure she didn't fall into the pool, but he urged her forward as if he were afraid of nothing. He didn't lead her into the water, however. Instead, he guided her to a place where a pair of timbers met the floor close together. They were located roughly midway between the entrances to the reservoir, and the gap between them was just wide enough for two people. In this dark, she and Geraden would be effectively invisible as long as they stood near the timbers.

Side by side in the gap, they were pressed against each other a bit at the shoulder and hip. Initially, she tried to squeeze away from him, so that he wouldn't feel her shivering. But she would be warmer if they were closer together. She would be warmer still if he put his arm around her. After a moment, she found that she didn't mind letting him know how cold she was.

Turning his head, he breathed her name into her hair and gave her a companionable hug. Almost at once, the pressure that made her shiver seemed to grow less.

She quickly got tired of straining her eyes into the deep dark of the pool, of trying to tell the difference between the light lap-and-slap of water and the possible sound of footsteps. Shifting more toward Geraden so that she fit better against his side, she whispered, 'What're we going to do when she comes?'

'Stop her.'

She poked at his ribs through his coat. 'I know that, idiot. *How* are we going to stop her?'

'Not so loud,' he cautioned. 'Water carries sound.'

She wished she could see his face. He sounded tense and far away, caught up in his responsibility for what happened to Orison. Stopping Elega was like stopping Nyle for him: she was his King's daughter, a childhood friend, and his former betrothed. Precisely because the situation was so painful for him, he couldn't afford to fail.

Almost in spite of herself, Terisa understood his allegiance to King Joyse and Mordant.

'She'll have a light,' he went on softly. 'She doesn't expect to be caught. And she needs to see what she's doing.' Like his attention, his voice seemed to be aimed out into the dark. 'When we see her light we'll try to sneak up on her.'

Terisa nodded, but her mind was elsewhere. Her head nestled against his shoulder; his coat warmed her cheek. Was it really better for him to remain loyal to the people and ideas he loved? Was that preferable to facing the truth when those people and ideas failed him? preferable to doing what Nyle and Elega were doing – what Master Eremis had been trying to do all along? *How are you planning to live the rest of your life without loyalty or self-respect?* Of course it was always better to face the truth. Wasn't it? Nyle and Elega and Master Eremis had all faced the truth. But she couldn't shake the odd feeling that what Geraden was trying to do was harder.

For that reason, it was a good thing he hadn't been able to return her to her old life. Maybe the sense of unreality that had dogged her for so long was the result of living in the wrong world: maybe she truly had never been a solid being until she came here. Or maybe her evanescence was the result of striving for the wrong things – despite what Reverend Thatcher might have taught her – of not understanding what Geraden understood so well. It was even possible—

Across the water, she saw a wink of light.

Geraden stiffened.

It was no larger or brighter than a candle flame – it flickered like a candle flame. But it flickered because it was moving, passing behind the timbers on the opposite side of the pool. When it stopped, she saw that it was a small lantern.

The hand that carried it set it down on the flat stone near the lip of the pool. The light shone on a woman's features. She seemed to be cloaked in midnight: nothing of her was visible except her hands and face.

Elega.

She scanned the reservoir for a moment, and Terisa cowered; but the lady's lamp was too weak to reach so far. Almost at once, Elega withdrew into the darkness.

Geraden drew a hissing breath. 'Now.' He shrugged himself out from the timbers. With his mouth at Terisa's ear, he whispered, 'You go that way.' He gave her a slight nudge in the direction he meant. 'When you get close enough, distract her. I'll come up behind her.

'Go.'

She felt rather than saw him fade into the dark.

Go. Yes. Good idea. But how? One misstep would take her into the pool. Dragged down by her coat, she would drown. She would never learn whether she was right about Elega.

Cautiously, she turned and put one hand on the nearest timber.

The timbers were all the same distance from the edge of the pool. If she felt her way along them, she would be safe. And she had another sign to navigate with: the reflection of the lamp in the water. That gleam was tiny, but it helped her keep her bearings.

Hoping that the pool's wet noises would cover the sound of her steps, she concentrated all her attention on the timbers and the reflection and started moving.

Elega was still nowhere to be seen.

Geraden had disappeared completely.

More quickly than she would have believed possible, Terisa reached the corner of the pool. This side; another corner; a straight walk to the lamp. She was cold, but she had no time for that. She wasn't conscious of shivering.

Elega returned to the light.

Instinctively, Terisa froze.

The lady brought with her a sack about the size of a large purse. She supported it with both hands as though it were heavy. In contrast, however, her walk and posture didn't betray much strain. Apparently, she feared that the material of the sack might tear, spilling its contents. Her care was obvious as she put the sack down beside the lamp.

I'm going to be too late. With an effort of will, Terisa forced herself into motion again.

But she wasn't too late. Instead of opening the sack, Elega retreated once again into the dark.

This side; another corner. How long would Elega be gone? How far did the light reach?

Where was Geraden?

The lamp made everything behind it blank, impenetrable.

She felt that she was breathing louder than the sound of the water; the effort of muffling her respiration made her want to gasp. Now she didn't need to guide herself by the timbers: the lamp showed her the rim of the pool. But she had to be quiet, *quiet*. No sound from her boots on the stone; none from her heart; none from the tense fear that constricted her chest.

How long would Elega be gone?

Not long enough. While Terisa was still too far away, the lady reentered the reach of her light.

She was carrying a second sack. It was just like the first one. She cradled it with both hands.

Terisa wanted to freeze again.

Instead, she began to run.

At the noise of Terisa's boots, Elega whirled. The cowl of a cape flipped back from her head, and her eyes seemed to gather up all the light, flaring like violet gems. Her face was whetted and intense.

'Terisa, *stop!*'

Terisa jerked to a halt.

'Come no closer!' the lady warned. 'You cannot prevent me from flinging my sack into the water. That is not the best way to distribute the powder – but it will suffice.' In this light, with such extremity in her eyes, her beauty was astonishing. She looked as certain as a queen. 'And one sack will suffice, though I have brought two for safety. Do not interfere with me.'

'Elega—' Terisa had to gasp hard to clear her throat, unlock her chest. 'Don't do this. It's crazy. You're—'

'Who is with you?' demanded Elega.

'You're going to kill thousands of people. Some of them are your friends. A lot of them know and respect you.'

'*Terisa!* Who is with you? Answer me!'

'*You're going to kill your father.*'

Deliberately, Elega adjusted her grip on her sack and started to swing it toward the water. The sack appeared to be made of some unusually supple leather.

Geraden hadn't come. There was nothing beyond the lamp except the dimly silvered night of the reservoir. 'I'm alone!' Terisa cried urgently.

The lady checked her swing.

'There's nobody with me. I'm alone.'

Elega's eyes burned. 'How can I believe that?'

Helpless to do anything else, Terisa replied bitterly, 'No one trusts me. Who would believe me if I told them you were going to do this?'

'Geraden trusts you. Together, you persuaded the Tor to be suspicious of me.'

'I know,' Terisa shot back in desperation. 'But you made him back down.' Where was Geraden? 'And Geraden *can't* believe anything like this about you. You're the King's daughter.'

For a moment, Elega studied Terisa. Slowly, she straightened her back; she faced Terisa regally. She didn't put down her sack, however.

'If no one else would believe this, why do you? How do you come to be here?'

Terisa met the lady's scrutiny as well as she could and struggled to hold down her panic. 'I guessed. We talked about the water supply. I think I suggested it.' Her self-control was fraying. In another minute, she would begin to babble. 'Elega, *why?* This is your home. You're the King's daughter. You're going to kill—'

'I am going to kill,' cut in Elega impatiently, 'a few of Orison's oldest and most infirm inhabitants. That is regrettable. Perhaps my father will be one of them.' She grimaced. 'Even that is regrettable. But no one else who drinks this tainted water will die. They will simply be too sick to fight.

'Orison will fall with little loss of life.' Her voice rose. 'At small cost to the realm, my father will be deposed, and a new power will take his place. Then Mordant will be *defended*' – she had to shout in order to hold back an uprush of passion – 'defended against Cadwal and Imagery, and the dreams with which King Joyse reared his daughters will be restored!' Her cry was strong – yet it echoed like mourning in the high silence of the reservoir. 'To accomplish that, I am willing to cause a few deaths.'

She might have continued: the force of what she felt might have impelled her to say more. But she didn't get the chance. All the illumination behind her condensed at once, transforming Geraden instantly out of the dark; and he charged wildly.

In fact, he charged so wildly that he caught his foot on the butt of one of the timbers.

The sound alerted Elega. As quick as a bird, she leaped aside while he crashed to the stone on the spot where she had been standing.

'Geraden!'

The impact seemed to stun him: he looked hurt. Although he bounded up almost instantly to his hands and knees, into a poised crouch, his balance shifted as if the flat stone under him were moving, and his head wobbled on his neck.

Nevertheless he was between Elega and the water.

Terisa hurried to his side. She wanted to help him up, find out how badly he was hurt. But she couldn't take her eyes off the lady.

The two women studied each other across a space of no more than ten feet. Elega's face was dark around the violet smolder of her eyes; she clutched her sack with both hands. Despite the fear pounding in her head, Terisa braced herself to block Elega's approach to the pool.

The corners of the lady's mouth hinted at a smile. In a formal tone, as if she wanted the reservoir to hear her, she said, 'My lady Terisa, I am sorry that I did not persuade you to join me. I believed you when you said you were alone. Clearly, you are a better player of this game than I realized.'

Nothing about her gave the impression that she was caught or beaten.

Geraden, get up!

Abruptly, he wrenched himself to his feet, stumbled sideways, then recovered. His gaze appeared oddly out of focus, as if his eyes were aimed in slightly different directions. Breathing heavily, he bent over and braced his hands on his knees to support the weight of his sore head.

'Blast you, Elega,' he panted, 'don't you know we caught Nyle? Castellan Lebbick has him. I don't expect you to care what happens to anybody as minor as a son of the Domne, but you ought to care about the fact that he didn't get through to the Perdon.

'You made a nice speech about defending the realm and restoring dreams. But you can't pretend that anymore. You aren't doing this for Mordant. You're doing it for Alend.'

The lady's eyes flared.

'Or you're doing it for Prince Kragen, which comes to the same thing. When you're done, we'll all be ruled by the Alend Monarch. Then it won't be you who decides what happens to your dreams. It won't even be your personal Prince. It'll be Margonal. Once Orison falls, you won't be anybody except the oldest daughter of the Alend Monarch's worst enemy.

'Give it up before you get hurt.'

As if she were in pain, Elega lowered her gaze. 'Perhaps you are right,' she murmured. 'You have caught me. I was a fool to believe the word of an Alend.' Her grip on the sack shifted.

Terisa shouted a warning – too late, as usual – as the lady flung her sack over Geraden's head.

At the edge of the light, it arched toward the still, dark water.

Geraden leaped for it.

So did Terisa.

Before they collided with each other, his reaching fingers hooked the soft leather and deflected it.

They fell tangled together. His arms and legs were all around her: she couldn't sort her way out of them.

After an interminable instant, she found herself on the floor while he scrambled to regain his feet. She was gazing straight along the smooth stone at the sack. It had landed right at the rim of the pool – so close that she could have put her hand on it.

But it had split open when it hit. A strange green powder was already pouring into the water. As she watched, the sack slumped empty.

Then the light went out.

A heavy splash cast sibilant applause around the reservoir as the other sack sank into the pool.

Across the dark, Elega said, 'Prince Kragen is a truer man than you are, Geraden fumble-foot. He will not be false to me.'

Small waves continued to slap and echo against the sides of the pool long after the King's daughter was gone.

TWENTY-FOUR

THE BEGINNING
OF THE END

Later that night, a small band of men on horseback launched an attack that no one understood at the time against the heavy gates of Orison. With a great whooping and hallooing, the men charged forward, shot burning arrows into the wood or up at the parapets, then brandished their swords and challenged the defenders to come out and fight instead of cowering inside the walls like girls.

Their arrows had no effect on the gates: some of Castellan Lebbick's guards had spent the past four days soaking the wood with water. And the attackers themselves seemed more drunk than dangerous. Nevertheless they made enough noise to be heard by every man on duty around the walls.

While the captain in command of the watch readied a sortie, the riders escaped. They could be heard laughing derisively for a few moments after the night had swallowed their retreat.

When this was reported to the Castellan, he had less to say about it than might have been expected. By that time, he had passed from his usual fulminating outrage into a tightly coiled fury that resembled equanimity. He looked almost cheerful as he went about his work, preparing Orison to meet an Alend siege with a totally inadequate supply of clean water.

Sometime earlier, Terisa and Geraden had had the disconcerting experience of appearing to improve his mood by telling him about their encounter with the lady Elega.

When they first approached him, he acted like a man who was savage with lack of sleep. His eyes had a harried cast, and some of his gestures seemed aimless, as if he weren't aware of making them. His personality changed stress and fatigue into ire, however. His problem was that he had nothing to do: Orison was as ready as possible for a struggle he had no expectation of winning. Because he couldn't rest, he was in danger of driving his own forces ragged before the real test of their strength began.

He had never been very good at resting. The strict urgency inside him kept him on his feet. Now, however, he couldn't rest because rest meant sleep – and sleep meant dreams.

His dreams were haunted.

As a younger man, he had occasionally had nightmares about his revenge on the Alend garrison commander who had raped and tortured his wife of four days with such relish and variety. But over the years the stable mildness of her companionship – and the clear worth of the work he did for his King – had taken the sting out of those dreams.

But now she was dead. He was alone – effectively abandoned even by King Joyse. And when he dreamed, he didn't dream of revenge.

He dreamed that he was an Alend garrison commander with a young Termigan sod's nubile bride tied helpless in front of him. He dreamed of all the things that could be done to her to make her scream and her husband mad.

He dreamed of relish.

And he awoke trembling – *he*, Castellan Lebbick, *trembling*, a man who hadn't quailed in the face of any dread or danger since the day when King Joyse had cut him free and let him take his revenge.

At the sight of Geraden's stiff-faced determination and the woman Terisa's stubbornly controlled alarm – alarm which he instinctively wanted to justify – something leaped through him like fire in a mound of dry brush.

By the time Geraden finished describing what Elega had done, Castellan Lebbick was smiling.

'Congratulations,' he said almost genially, 'Here's another triumph for you. The lady Terisa' – he spoke as if she weren't present – 'gave you the perfect chance to do something right for a change – and what did you do? You decided to be a hero by saving Orison alone. You must be particularly proud of yourself.'

'That's not fair,' the woman put in unexpectedly. Despite her alarm and her downcast gaze, she had courage. 'You make it impossible for anybody to tell you anything. If I turned out to be wrong – if Elega did something else while you were guarding the reservoir – you would accuse us of conspiring to distract you.'

Yes, the Castellan mused, she was an interesting woman. And her turn was coming. Someday soon he would have her in his power. Then she would learn what it really meant to be accused. He would teach her thoroughly.

He still found it difficult to distrust the Apt: as the Domne's son and Artagel's brother, Geraden had an automatic claim on Castellan Lebbick's good opinion. And he had stopped Nyle. That may have been stupid, but it was certainly honorable.

The woman, on the other hand—

Curious, wasn't it, how she just happened to be the one who became suspicious of Elega – how she just happened to be the one who figured out what Elega was doing. All Lebbick knew of her was that she was an Imager. And that she acted like an enemy of Alend. And that High King Festten wanted her dead. And that she lied to him when the truth would have helped him serve his King. The rest was inference, speculation, dream.

The smile with which he regarded her would have curdled milk. Still addressing Geraden, he asked, 'Do you know what I'm going to have to do now?'

'Yes, Castellan.' The Apt sighed as though he anticipated more abuse. 'You're going to have to face this whole siege with only the spring for water.'

'That's right. We've doubled our population. That spring doesn't give a tenth of what we need. We're going to have to ration water severely. I'm going to have to put pregnant women and tired old men and children on rations that will make them ache with thirst. Because you thought it would be fun to be a hero for a change. And that's not all.'

'No, it's not.'

Regardless of what Geraden felt, he faced Lebbick without flinching. The Castellan liked that. Not so long ago, the Apt would have flinched.

'You're also going to have to flush out the reservoir and all the pipes. If you don't do it – and do it soon – people who get thirstier than they can stand are going to start sneaking drinks. If they're weak enough, they'll die.'

'Flushing everything will use water, too. You won't have much left to ration.'

The Castellan nodded. No matter how stupidly he behaved, the Apt wasn't stupid. In fact, considering his obvious intelligence, it was amazing how consistently he managed to go wrong.

'Are you sure she poisoned the water?'

Geraden frowned. 'Do you mean, am I sure she knew what she was doing? No. And I haven't tested it. But whatever was in those sacks was a powder, and it was green. I only know one kind of green powder. It's a tinct the Masters use. They call it "ortical" – it was first mixed by an Imager named Ortic. There must be a hundredweight of it stored in the laborium.' He didn't look away. 'That stuff will make you sick if you just get too much of it on your hands.'

'Is there a counteragent?'

'Who knows? Imagers don't *eat* tinct. And they don't spend their time trying to cure people who do.'

'If I ask your Master Barsonage, will he be able to tell me if any ortical is missing?'

'No. Nobody supervises the Masters when they're working. Quite a few of them still like to keep the ingredients they use secret. But one of the younger Apts might have noticed a sudden drop in the amount of ortical on the shelves.'

Again, the Castellan nodded. Without warning, he addressed Terisa for the first time. 'How did you know what the lady Elega was going to do?'

In a small voice, she replied, 'I guessed.'

'You *guessed*?'

'I put together some things she said.' She became stronger as she spoke. 'They weren't even enough to be called hints. I put them together and just guessed.'

'My lady,' Castellan Lebbick announced in a contented tone, 'I don't believe that.' Then he dismissed her and Geraden.

He didn't need to plan what had to be done. It was already clear to him, step by step. He was the Castellan of Orison; he knew how to serve his King. In the end, it made no difference what the odds were against him. How badly Orison was damaged. How much he was outmanned. How far King Joyse

failed. Castellan Lebbick had made himself more like a sword than a man –
and a sword knew nothing about surrender.

In the meantime, he had something to look forward to. That woman's turn
was coming.

Geraden took her back to the peacock suite, then went to his own rooms to
try to get some sleep. But neither of them slept much.

No one in Orison slept much.

Of course, many of the castle's inhabitants were awake because they were
too tense to sleep. A large number of people didn't have that problem,
however. They were guards who were either too experienced or too tired to
stay awake; parents whose overexcited children had worn them out;
merchants who knew that their own survival – and even their profits – would
probably be more rather than less valuable after the siege, regardless of who
won. They were servants who were so badly overworked that they couldn't
afford sleeplessness; Masters who lacked imagination; lords who didn't
understand and ladies who were philosophical.

These people didn't get much sleep because Castellan Lebbick and his
men woke them up.

Despite his quickness, the Castellan was too late to save two old men who
were accustomed to make several trips to the lavatory during the night, a
handful of guards who came off watch and refreshed themselves before they
were warned, and several children who roused their parents crying for water.
But these unfortunate incidents at least served to confirm that Elega *had*
poisoned the reservoir – that the harsh measures which Lebbick imposed on
the castle were necessary. The children were desperately sick, but no one
died except one of the old men.

And in the morning nearly everybody tried to crowd out onto the
battlements or around a window to watch for the Alend army.

In that respect, Terisa and Geraden were fortunate. They had no trouble
gaining access to the top of the tower that held her rooms.

During the night, the weather had turned cold again. A featureless gray
cloud wrack had closed down over Mordant, turning the castle and the
landscape the color of gloom; a chill wind blew like a scythe, reaping away
every sign of an early spring. The nearby hills lost depth; the ones farther
away looked higher, more dangerous. The black trees tossed their limbs as if
they were writhing. Corrupt snow still clung to most of the slopes, making the
bare ground appear unwell. At first, she could hardly see: the cold felt like a
slap, and the wind in her face made her eyes tear. Gradually, however, her
vision improved until she was able to scrutinize the horizons in the direction
of Armigite and Alend just as the crowds on the lower battlements and the
people on the other towers did.

There was nothing to see.

For a long time, there was nothing to see. By degrees, the crowds thinned.
Twice, Terisa and Geraden broke their vigil and returned to her rooms to get
warm.

'When are they coming?' she asked.

'How should I know?' he replied with uncharacteristic asperity. He was taking his failure to stop Elega hard.

She knew how he felt and didn't blame him.

'Which direction are they going to come from?'

He repented his testiness. 'Along the road. That's longer, but it should be quicker. And it's the only way they can bring their supplies. Or the "engines of war" we keep hearing about.'

When they went back outside, she learned that he was right. Warned by an indefinable stiffening of attention around her, she peered harder into the harsh wind and saw the vanguard of the Alend army coming.

It was on the northwest road from the Care of Armigite.

The Alend Monarch's flags flew in the hands of his standard-bearers. The gray light and the distance made them look black.

Slowly, the army marched toward Orison – a body of men that seemed huge beyond counting. Soldiers on horses. Soldiers on foot. Dozens of drivers goading the mules that dragged the supply wains. Swarms of transformed servants and impressed peasants who steered and tended the lumbering siege engines. And a second army of porters and camp followers.

All come to take Orison away from Mordant's King.

Held by a kind of awe, she stared out from the tower and tried to imagine the amount of bloodshed King Joyse's actions threatened to bring down on his people.

Perhaps he was imagining the same thing. Geraden nudged her and pointed toward the north tower. Squinting in that direction, she saw King Joyse standing before the parapets with Castellan Lebbick.

He looked small across the length of Orison, despite his heavy fur cloak. Both he and his Castellan studied the Alend advance without moving. Perhaps there was nothing they could do. The flags of Mordant had been raised over the battlements, but the King's personal banner snapped painfully from the end of a pole on the tower where he stood. It was a plain purple swath that might have appeared jaunty and brave under bright sunlight. Now it looked as if it was about to be torn away by the wind.

After a while, he and Castellan Lebbick left the tower.

For no reason that Terisa could see, Orison's trumpeter winded his horn. He may have been blowing a call to arms; it sounded more like a wail.

With ponderous precision, like a display of inevitability, Alend's army invested the castle.

Ten thousand soldiers surrounded the walls and presented their weapons. The siege engines were rolled into position. Then the Alends bugled a signal of their own, and a party of riders formed around the Alend Monarch's standard-bearer. The standard-bearer added a flag of truce to Margonal's assertive green-and-red pennon. Together, the flags and the riders approached the gates of Orison.

Orison's trumpeter responded. The gates rose.

With six men behind him, Castellan Lebbick rode out to meet the Alend party.

He wasn't surprised to see that the Alends were led by Prince Kragen. Nor, after his conversation with King Joyse, was he surprised by the fact that one of the riders was the lady Elega.

The two groups stopped and eyed each other across a short distance. The Prince was steady, but Elega didn't meet Castellan Lebbick's glare.

After a long silence, Prince Kragen said, 'Greetings, Castellan. Your King's folly has brought us to this.'

The Castellan was holding his horse with too tight a rein: the beast couldn't stand still. As it shied from side to side, he rasped, 'Say what you came to say and be done with it, my lord Prince. I have better things to do with my time.'

Prince Kragen's gaze darkened. 'Very well,' he snapped. 'Listen carefully, Castellan.'

In a formal tone, he announced, 'Margonal, the Alend Monarch and Lord of the Alend Lieges, sends greetings to Joyse, Lord of the Demesne and King of Mordant. The Alend Monarch asks King Joyse to meet with him under a flag of truce, so that together they may find some way to avert this conflict. King Joyse has refused to hear requests for peace from the Alend Monarch's ambassador. Nevertheless it is peace the Alend Monarch desires, and he will pursue that desire openly and fairly with King Joyse, if the King will consent to meet him.'

'A pretty speech,' Castellan Lebbick retorted without hesitation. 'Why should we believe you?'

'Because,' the Prince shot back, 'I do not need to make pretty speeches. Your wall is broken – and not well repaired, I observe. You have no stores of clean water. Your men are too few. You cannot endure a siege, Castellan. The Alend Monarch has no reason to offer you peace – no reason except the sincerity of his desire.'

'"The sincerity of his desire."' Lebbick jerked at his mount. 'I like that – from an Alend.

'All right. Here's your answer.

'King Joyse asks me to point out to you – and to your illustrious father – that neither of you understands hop-board. You wouldn't have gotten as far as a stalemate without help. Instead of waving your swords at us, you ought to remember what happened the last time you went to war with Mordant.'

The wind cut between the horses. 'By the stars, Lebbick,' cried out the lady Elega, 'is he *still* playing hop-board? Tell him to *surrender!*'

The Castellan didn't shift his gaze from Prince Kragen's face. 'The King's daughter,' he remarked. 'That attack last night was a diversion, so she could get out of Orison.' As soon as King Joyse had said this, Lebbick had cursed himself for not realizing the truth immediately. 'What do you plan to do with her now? Is she a hostage?'

Prince Kragen spat an oath. With an effort, he resumed his formal tone. 'The Alend Monarch welcomes the lady Elega as a friend. He has no intention of offering any harm, either to her, or to her father in her person. This courtesy, also, he provides as a demonstration of his desire for peace.'

'I have an answer for that, too.' For the first time, Castellan Lebbick used the exact words he had been given. 'King Joyse replies, "I am sure that my daughter Elega has acted for the best reasons. She carries my pride with her wherever she goes. For her sake, as well as for my own, I hope that the best reasons will also produce the best results."'

The lady Elega stared at Castellan Lebbick as if he had said something horrible.

'*That* is an *answer?*' demanded the Prince.

'Take it and be satisfied,' the Castellan replied. 'You ought to like it better than the denunciation she deserves. Ask her' – King Joyse had specifically forbidden him to say this – 'if she wants to know how many people died this morning.'

Prince Kragen ignored that jibe. 'You misunderstand me deliberately, Castellan. Have you given me your King's answer to the Alend Monarch's desire for truce? Is he that far out of his senses?'

Riding the strength of the fact that King Joyse had actually talked to him – however strangely – Castellan Lebbick had no trouble finding a retort. 'I don't advise you to put it to the test.'

'Then hear me. Hear me well, Castellan.' Prince Kragen's anger was fierce. 'This is my last word.

'Your King leaves us no choice. We *cannot* "be satisfied." Cadwal is marching. You know that Cadwal is marching. Where we stand, we are more vulnerable than you to the High King's great force. We cannot defend you, or your people, or the Congery—'

'Or yourselves.'

'—or *ourselves* if we do not take Orison. King Joyse compels us all to a war he cannot win, regardless of the cost to us. He *must* offer peace. By peace or by blood, we *must* have Orison.'

The Castellan fought his horse still. '*That* is your *last word?*' He was grinning.

'Yes!'

'Then here's mine.' Lebbick knew what to say, although he didn't understand it. 'King Joyse assures the Alend Monarch that he has more choices than he realizes. King Joyse suggests you withdraw to the west of the Demesne and await developments. If you do that, he'll be glad to meet the Alend Monarch under a flag of truce and offer more suggestions.

'If you don't' – the Castellan could barely conceal his own surprise at the threat he had been instructed to deliver – 'King Joyse intends to unleash the full force of the Congery against you and rout you from the earth!'

At the moment, he didn't care whether or not the King's gambit would succeed. He was simply glad that he had been allowed to say those words.

Silence seemed to shock the gathering. For a time, no one could respond. In spite of himself, Prince Kragen gaped in anger and dismay.

Then the lady Elega whispered intensely, 'Castellan Lebbick, you lie.' Her face was pale in the harsh wind. 'My father would never do such a thing.'

As if she had commanded it, the Prince snatched the flag of truce from the standard-bearer, broke its shaft across his knee, and threw the pieces into the road. Wheeling his mount, he led his party back to the Alend lines.

Castellan Lebbick and his men returned to Orison. The gates thudded shut behind them.

The Alend bugler sounded another call. All around the castle, camp followers and servants began to unpack wagons and pitch tents. The siege of Orison had commenced.

'I've got to go see Artagel,' Geraden said as if he were proposing to have his legs broken. 'He'll want to hear what's happened.' The cold made his nose run; he sounded congested and miserable. 'If he can't forgive me for letting Prince Kragen get away, at least there isn't anything worse he can do to me for letting Elega poison the water.'

Terisa offered to go with him, but he declined her company. He wanted to face his distress alone.

When he left, she went back to her rooms.

She had a great deal to think about. She needed to decide where she stood in relation to what was happening around her. She needed to define her own loyalties. She needed to decide how far she was willing – or able – to pursue the commitment she had apparently given Geraden by telling him about the connection between her dream and the augury.

Instead, she found herself thinking about Reverend Thatcher.

She had worked for him for almost a year – long enough to forget why she had originally accepted the job as his mission secretary. Since then, what she tended to remember about him was his dogged ineffectuality. But she hadn't seen him that way at first. No, at first she had gone looking for a mission job to make up for the emptiness and wealth of her background, the uselessness which eroded her sense of herself. And she had taken the job Reverend Thatcher offered because of his dedication against impossible poverty and callous disregard.

At the time, of course, she hadn't realized that he was ineffectual. Now, however, she began to wonder whether that perception was accurate. In his place, wouldn't Geraden have done just what he did? Wouldn't Geraden have held true in the face of any failure? Wasn't the real failure of her mission work in her? A failure of heart?

Wasn't it possible to live as if she could hear horns?

What she was thinking didn't solve anything. But it was necessary, and she stayed with it. At least it taught her to understand that she owed Reverend Thatcher an apology.

Later, she became aware that she was tired enough to sleep.

The idea of a nap was unexpectedly appealing. She hadn't slept well the night before. And no amount of fatigue or wakefulness was going to do Orison any good. Humming to herself, she added wood to both fires to keep her rooms warm. Then she took off all her clothes, tossed them onto a chair, and slipped herself into bed.

For a while, she listened to the hungry wind scraping its claws on her window, on the corners of the tower. But as soon as the cool sheets gained heat from her skin, she fell asleep.

Deep in dreams, she received the delicious impression that she was being kissed.

A strong mouth covered hers. A tongue stroked her lips, probing delicately between them. She tasted cloves.

Under the blankets, a hand caressed her belly, then moved up to her breasts. Its touch was just cool enough to make her nipples harden.

When she realized that she wasn't dreaming, she opened her eyes.

Master Eremis was bending over her; his pale gaze met hers. Her father had eyes like that. But the crinkles around them suggested that he was grinning.

He startled her so much that she clutched at the blankets and jerked her head away from him.

Pulling back a little, he withdrew his hand from her body. The ends of his chasuble swung carelessly against the front of his accustomed jet cloak. He was definitely grinning. In fact, he seemed to be in excellent spirits.

'My lady,' he said, 'I fear I have frightened you. Do forgive me.'

Staring up at him through the gray light from the windows, she thought that he was uglier than she remembered: his face was too much like a wedge; his hair sprouted too far back on his skull. Yet that only made the lively intelligence of his expression more magnetic.

She pulled the covers tightly over her shoulders and blinked at him in confusion. 'How—?'

'The wardrobe.' His smile stretched wider. 'I was exploring hidden passages and had the good fortune to find your room.'

'Where—?' She sat up a bit. Her mind refused to function. She had been more deeply asleep than she realized. How had she gotten out of the habit of putting a chair in that wardrobe? 'Where were you? I thought I would see you.'

He seated himself on the edge of the bed, then reached out a hand and ran his fingertips down the line of her neck from her ear to her shoulder. 'I was required at home. I think I have mentioned Esmerel?' His touch felt like a signature on her skin. 'My grandfather called it our "ancestral seat," though Esmerel is not really as grand as that. My father is still less grand, however, and does not use such language.'

Master Eremis plucked lightly at the sheet she held in front of her. 'In his blunt way, he demanded my presence. I seems that one of my brothers killed the other – although with that pair the truth has often been difficult to determine. My father wanted me in front of him while he decided whether to disinherit the survivor in my favor.

'Esmerel is in the Care of Tor – fortunately a ride of only two days beyond the Broadwine. I have just returned.'

She could hardly swallow. If he went on looking at her like that, she was going to forget everything that had happened while he was away. His fingers were curled gently over the edge of the sheet covering her. Soon he would begin to pull it down, and she wouldn't be able to resist. She didn't know that she wanted to resist. Her head seemed to be full of forgotten dreams. It was impossible to think.

With an effort, she asked, 'What did he decide?'

The Imager shrugged to show his disinterest. 'My father hates me. As do – or did – both my brothers. So it is remarkable that they have always done what I wished. I have no use for Esmerel at present. Therefore my brother will inherit it. If my father has the good sense to die soon.'

He leaned toward her, and his mouth took hers again. The scent of cloves seemed to fill her senses. His hand urged the sheet downward, and his tongue had to be answered. No, she couldn't resist. His palm rubbed her nipple until she shivered at his touch; then he cupped her breast possessively. She was his—

Somehow, she pushed him back. A flush on her cheeks, and breathing raggedly, she faced him as well as she could. 'Why does your family hate you?'

His smile was gone: his eyes burned with an intensity that made her melt. 'My lady, I did not come here to discuss my family. I came to claim you at last.'

Without thinking, she rolled away from him and got out of bed. Momentarily defying her nakedness, she went to the chair where she had left her robe. Her hands shook as she pulled the velvet onto her shoulders and knotted the sash; her voice shook as she spoke.

'You were gone for a long time. I waited for you. I wanted to help you. I was ready—' Ready to do almost anything. 'But you didn't come. I didn't hear from you.'

Despite her resistance, she was close to panic at the thought that he might take offense and leave, that by retreating from him she had sacrificed her chance to be touched and kissed. He didn't look offended, however. His smile was too acute to be affectionate; yet he gazed at her with a new eagerness, as if she had become a challenge.

'My lady,' he said thoughtfully, 'I regret that you did not hear from me. That was not my intention. I sent word to you several times. But perhaps my messages were intercepted.'

She started to ask, Who would intercept—? before she understood what he was saying. He hadn't meant to leave her without saying goodbye. That changed everything. Didn't it? Almost babbling, she said, 'You sent messages with Saddith. But she's your lover. She wants you for herself, so she didn't give me any of your messages.'

For an instant, the Master's eyes widened as if she had surprised him. A grin quickly altered his expression, however. Now his excitement was unmistakable. His tone was both careful and jocose as he said, 'My lady, you cannot possibly be jealous of a maid like Saddith. Nearly all the men she has ever known have been between her legs. I can believe that she did not deliver my messages. But I cannot believe it matters that I have taken advantage of her crass charms.'

Terisa's emotions were in an alarming muddle. Her relief that he had tried to send word to her lasted only a moment. It was replaced almost at once by the sense that the information came too late. It didn't change anything after all. She had made her commitment without him – had put herself on Geraden's side. And not just by default: not just because the Apt was present and Master Eremis was absent. She had chosen Geraden because to distrust him – to spy on him, to betray him, as the Master had demanded – was intolerable. If only Eremis had come to her sooner. She bit her lip to try to keep her distress from showing on her face.

Still smiling, he studied her narrowly. After a moment, he said, 'Saddith is of no importance, however. I will dispense with her to please you. You asked about my family.'

She nodded dumbly, hanging on every word he said while her heart hurt.

'It is a small family. Esmerel is a small estate, though beautiful. My grandfather was a man of high intelligence – and even higher refinement. He had an exceptional understanding of both knowledge and pleasure. And he dabbled in Imagery. In truth, one of our family legends is that he was acquainted with the arch-Imager Vagel. Of course, that was before the wars for Mordant, during which the arch-Imager went into High King Festten's service.

'Unhappily, my grandfather had but one son, and that one son was a lout. Beauty and refinement were as blank as stone walls to him. He understood nothing except violence – and the pleasures of violence. When he came into possession of Esmerel, he spent years debauching its beauties as well as himself. Then he became a petty brigand to preserve some semblance of wealth in his "ancestral seat."

'The accidental result of his debauchery was that he had three sons. The first was an exact duplicate of himself – therefore much loved. The second was a bit smaller, a bit less muscular, and a bit more cunning – therefore tolerable.

'I was the third.'

The Master's voice was part of his spell. Terisa expected him to move toward her. The way he studied her made her feel that he was moving toward her. Her pain seemed to hypnotize her. But he remained motionless beside the bed.

'Fortunately,' he observed, 'I was a good deal stronger than I looked. To all appearances, I was the runt of the litter, and my father despised me accordingly. For that reason, my brothers sought to earn his approval by tormenting me.' He spoke calmly, but the glint in his eyes was as calm as a hatchet. 'On one occasion, I recall, they locked me in a wooden shed and set it afire to see what I would do.'

Breathing through parted lips as if she were rapt – or appalled – she asked, 'What did you do?'

He chuckled. 'I tricked them. I was no heir to Esmerel, but I was my grandfather's heir in intelligence. Before I was old enough to be afraid, I was clever enough to protect myself. And soon I learned that the surest protection was to turn them all against each other. So I set out to teach each of them that he needed my help against the others. With a little judicious prodding, I was able to make them do whatever I wished.'

Drawn by what he described – things that must have been acutely painful, things that reminded her of closets and fading – she took a step toward him. 'What did you make them do?'

He betrayed a glint of anticipation. 'I made them all good citizens of the Care of Tor. I tamed my brothers. I deprived my father of his debaucheries. And I made them restore the resources of knowledge which Esmerel had once boasted, so that I could claim my grandfather's true inheritance. It was his interest and researches that led me into Imagery.

'Since leaving Esmerel, I have done what I can to keep my family from

444

bestiality. But a distance of two days' ride seems like the world to men like them. I regret that there was nothing I could do to prevent the altercation that left my father's firstborn dead.' His manner suggested that his regret wasn't especially profound.

She took another step. His pale gaze seemed to be devouring her. 'You came to claim me. What do you want me to do?'

He opened his hands as if to show her their strength. 'Take off your robe.'

She touched her sash as a giddy acquiescence swept through her. But she shook it away. 'I mean after that. What do you want me to do for Mordant?'

'Why must there be an "after that"?' he countered. 'I will content your womanhood in ways you have not dreamed.'

In a small voice, she insisted, 'I want to help you. I want to help Mordant.'

'Very well.' As though he were confident that she already knew and had accepted the answer, he replied, 'Together, we will persuade Castellan Lebbick and the Congery that Geraden has betrayed us.'

When he said that, her heart gave a lurch – and then her courage was gone, as if he had kicked out the bottom of her spirit. Geraden? Was he back to Geraden? Still arguing that Geraden was in league with Gilbur and Vagel? Or did he have some new accusation to level against her only friend? She barely had the fortitude to ask, 'What has he done?'

'Done? What has he not done? Has he not convinced you that *I* am a traitor?'

She shook her head.

'Then he is wiser than I thought. You would have become suspicious of him if he had tried to turn you against me.'

The Master considered her for a moment, then said, 'Because he has been wise, you will probably not believe that he arranged to leave you alone in the bazaar so that Gart could attack you. You will probably not believe that his failure to stop Elega was no accident.'

She stared at him in frank horror.

'Those are subtle points,' he went on. 'I grant it is difficult to credit him with such subtlety. But I will tell you something you must believe. Cadwal is marching. Have you never asked yourself *why* Cadwal is marching? Have you never wondered why High King Festten feels he must attack *now*?'

Terisa didn't reply. Her mind was blank with dismay. A new accusation. New reasons to believe that the only man who cared about her and encouraged her and stayed with her was a traitor.

'In the ordinary course of events,' Eremis explained, 'the High King's spies must have told him that Alend was coming to Orison. What would he do?' His voice was like the wind, growing harsher as it filled the room. Light from the hearth made his face unnaturally ruddy. 'On one side is the risk that Orison might fall, giving the Congery into the Alend Monarch's hands. But with Castellan Lebbick – if not our good King – defending the castle, that is unlikely. On the other side is the certainty that the forces of Perdon would be drawn to Orison's support. Alend and Mordant might easily cripple each other in that battle – and then everything the High King wants could be taken almost without cost. *Why* did he not wait for his enemies to destroy each other?

'I will tell you why, my lady.' The Master made a short, brutal gesture with both hands. 'He did not wait because he knew of Elega's intentions. He knew our danger was greatly increased by the fact that Orison would be betrayed from within by Prince Kragen's allies.

'Think, woman. How could High King Festten have known that Orison would be betrayed to Alend? By Imagery, his Monomach can enter or leave the castle – although how this is done remains a mystery. But access to our halls does not give him access to our secrets. Who but a traitor would tell Gart that Elega meant to poison the reservoir, depriving us of water and exposing us to summary defeat?'

'No,' Terisa murmured. She wanted to collapse into a chair. 'No.'

Master Eremis ignored her protest. 'And who but Geraden knew the danger?'

'But he was attacked,' she objected. 'By Imagery. Twice. They tried to kill him – Gilbur, Vagel—'

'Whelp of a bitch!' Eremis sounded furious. 'Those were *ploys*, woman. Tricks. They show only that Gilbur and Vagel are desperate that you do not turn against their ally. By attacking Geraden, they make him appear innocent. The truth is that they feint his death for the same reason that they actively desire yours – so that you will not expose him.

'If he had not been rescued as he was, I assure you that they would have recalled their insects before he was slain.'

She was no longer looking at the Imager. She wasn't looking at anything. Tears streamed down her cheeks. 'How could I expose him?'

'You have been with him for many days. You have watched him, spoken to him, studied him. And you met in private in your own world, before he translated you here. You alone possess the knowledge – the experience – that will persuade the Congery of his treachery.'

'No,' she repeated softly. She wasn't speaking to him, however. She was speaking to herself. She hardly heard what he said: she heard only his voice, his anger, the threat of losing him. Geraden was no traitor. Of course not. She knew that precisely because she had spent so much time with him. But she was being forced to a choice. No, more than that. She was being forced to do something about what she believed. She couldn't defend Geraden without turning her back on Master Eremis and everything he represented.

'You said you wished to help Mordant.' He spoke in a hectoring tone that reminded her of her father. 'While you protect the man who betrays us, we are doomed.'

What could she do? She couldn't argue with him. She had never been able to argue with her father. She could only take his side or refuse. That was clear enough.

Quietly, she asked, 'What are you going to do to me?'

'Take off your robe,' he snapped. 'Your body, at least, will not disappoint me.'

Now at last she understood the anger and secret triumph she had so often heard in her father's voice, the desire to inflict pain. For that reason, what she had to do was clear to her in the end – clear and simple – and so difficult that it was nearly impossible.

446

Her hands were on the sash of her robe. Deliberately, she pulled it tighter. 'No,' she said to the Master.

She thought that he would shout at her or strike her. He started toward her, and his expression sharpened into a grin of violence. Instead of shouting, however, he whispered intensely, 'My lady, I have claimed you. I have placed my hands and my kisses where you will never forget them.' He was close enough to grasp her shoulders. Echoing firelight, his hot gaze held her. 'Every curve of your flesh and pulsebeat of your womanhood desires me, and I will not be refused.'

He pulled her to him and kissed her forcefully. Somehow, her robe was gone from between them. He felt as hard as iron against her inexperienced belly.

She didn't struggle: she was too weak to struggle. But her body had gone cold; her nerves and her sore heart no longer responded to him. His kiss was only pressure against her face, nothing more. His hardness had lost its fascination.

No, she protested. I said *no*.

Someone knocked at her door so hard that it thudded against the latch.

Swearing viciously, Master Eremis pushed her away. For an instant, he measured the distance to the wardrobe. 'Do not answer!' he hissed.

She was about to faint. 'I forgot to lock it.'

Without waiting for admission, Geraden burst into the room and slammed the door behind him.

But when he saw Terisa standing near the entryway to the bedroom with her robe open and Master Eremis near her, he stopped as if he were turned to stone.

Convulsively, she jerked the robe closed and sashed it. Surprise and mortification made her feel like a lunatic. She sounded like a lunatic as she asked, 'How is Artagel?'

The Master's eyes were savage.

Geraden stared at Terisa as though she were appalling. 'I didn't go see him.'

'Then what *did* you do, boy?' inquired the Imager. 'It must have been quite interesting, if it drives you to enter a lady's bedchamber so discourteously.'

'Terisa.' With the light of the hearth behind him, Geraden's features were dark. His gaze glittered at her out of the shadows. 'Tell him to leave.'

Master Eremis made a snickering noise in the back of his throat. She was facing Geraden: she didn't know that the Master had moved until she felt him beside her. He put one arm around her waist. With the other, he slid his hand into her robe and began to fondle her breast. 'The lady Terisa,' he said, 'does not wish me to leave.'

Shame flushed down the length of her body. 'Please,' she breathed to Eremis, to Geraden, on the verge of weeping. Don't do this to me. It doesn't mean what you think. 'Please.'

'In fact, it *was* interesting,' Geraden replied in a voice thick with blood. 'I had a talk with Saddith.'

Terisa felt Master Eremis stiffen. Slowly, he took back his hand, although he didn't release her. 'What an odd thing to do. Almost as odd as the urgency you attach to it. Are you quite sure you are well, boy?'

With an effort, she swallowed the distress that clogged her throat. She felt that she was fighting for her life. 'What did Saddith say?'

Without a glance at the Imager, Geraden retorted, 'Your guards told me you were alone. How did he get in here?'

She knew immediately that Master Eremis didn't want her to answer. She could feel his will in the harsh strength of his grasp.

'The wardrobe,' she said thinly. 'The secret passage.'

Geraden nodded once, abruptly. 'And how did he know it was there?'

In an even tone, as though he were in danger of becoming bored, Eremis drawled, 'He had no idea it was there. He was exploring a passage new to him and found the lady Terisa's rooms by chance.'

The Apt turned a gaze like stone on the Master. Shadows shifted along his jaw. 'Actually, that's not true.' Then he addressed Terisa again. 'How did Saddith become your maid?'

She was having difficulty breathing: the pressure growing in her chest seemed to cramp her lungs. 'King Joyse told her to take care of me.'

'Did he choose her himself?'

It was astonishing how vividly the memory came back to her. The King had said, *Saddith will attend upon you as your maid.* He had even greeted her by saying, *Just the one I wanted.* But he hadn't looked pleased.

'I don't think so. He didn't ask for her by name. He just told the guard I needed a maid.'

'I begin to see why you found this so interesting,' commented Master Eremis. He seemed to be laughing to himself. 'Trivial matters always interest men who fail at everything else.'

'Terisa' – now Geraden's tone cast hints of authority, as if he stood taller under the weight of the Master's derision – 'do you remember what we talked about after the first time Gart tried to kill you?'

Dumbly, she shook her head. She couldn't think. That memory was gone, as blank as the previous one was distinct. The dim gray light from the windows appeared to be failing.

'We talked about how he found you.'

How he found me.

'It was obvious that he had an ally in Orison. Somebody must have told him where you were.'

'That is very good, Geraden,' Master Eremis sneered, 'A prodigious display of reasoning. Somebody must indeed have told him. Perhaps it was you. You knew where she was. I have heard that her room was guarded at your request.'

Terisa didn't look away from Geraden.

He met her gaze to the exclusion of everything else. 'Saddith didn't tell me as much as I wanted. But she told me enough so I can guess the rest. She volunteered to be your maid.'

Volunteered?

'I wondered about that. Why would she volunteer, when the only people who knew you were here – and knew you were important – were King Joyse and the Masters? With a little prodding, she told me. She did it to please one of her lovers. Or rather someone she wanted for a lover. One of the Masters. He asked her to take care of you for his sake, and she did it to make him grateful.'

A log fell in the hearth; flames spurted higher. Gently, Master Eremis wrapped his long fingers around the back of Terisa's neck.

'That's also how he found out about the secret passage to your room,' Geraden went on. 'From her. She could hardly help noticing you kept a chair in your wardrobe.'

'This is outrageous, boy.' The Master's grip on the back of Terisa's neck tightened. 'Have you lost your mind? Do you seriously mean to accuse me – *me*! – of being in league with the High King's Monomach?' Beneath his scorn ran an undercurrent of mirth.

Still Geraden kept his hard gaze on Terisa, away from Master Eremis. 'He's one of the few people who knew where you were that first night. He's one of the few who know about that secret passage. And he's the only one who could have set up that ambush for you after the lords met Prince Kragen. He's the only one who knew you would be there. He *took* you.

'He put you right in front of the champion so you might get shot. You were together – but *he* escaped. He could have taken you with him. He could have stopped me. Why didn't he?'

The fires seemed to be dying. The suite was filling up with gloom.

Geraden, help me. He's going to break my neck.

'Geraden,' said the Master casually, 'this is inexcusable. You have gone beyond insult.' The pressure of his fingers began to make Terisa light-headed. 'You cannot place the blame for your own crimes on my shoulders. I will not carry it.'

Geraden shifted his glare to Eremis.

'All of this is silly supposition except the question of Gart's attempt on her life after the meeting of the Lords. And *that* you could have arranged as well as I. Your brother Artagel was following her. You knew at all times where she was. It is only good fortune that Gart did not come upon all the lords together. Some of them would surely have died.'

'Let her go,' the Apt said in a voice like a piece of granite. 'If you have to have a hostage, take me. I'm a lot more dangerous than she is.'

At that, Master Eremis laughed like a splash of acid. 'Oh, you flatter yourself, boy. You flatter yourself.'

Before she could try to twist free, she heard the sound of someone thrashing his way through clothes. In a sudden flurry, her wardrobe disgorged most of its contents, and a man burst out from the hidden passage.

His cloak and leather armor were so black that he seemed like an incarnation of the darkness behind him; he moved like a shadow. But the long steel of his sword caught reflections of fire and scattered them in front of him. His nose jutted between his yellow eyes like the blade of a hatchet.

He sprang into the room, coiled for bloodshed.

Nevertheless he was unmistakably surprised to find Master Eremis, Terisa, and Geraden all in front of him. Despite himself, he checked his attack. The aim of his sword wavered.

'Gart!' Master Eremis shouted. 'Whelp of a dog! Your timing is miraculous!'

So quickly that his movement staggered her, he released Terisa and bounded to the bed. While Gart swung into motion, Master Eremis snatched down the peacock-feather canopy and flung it over Gart's head.

At the same moment, Geraden grabbed Terisa and jerked her away, thrust her into the sitting room behind him. She stumbled toward the fire, barely caught her balance.

With a wet sound like water on hot iron, Gart's sword swept the canopy to shreds. Feathers settled to the floor on all sides: their eyes watched everything.

Master Eremis jumped up onto the bed.

As he faced the Monomach, firelight glared across his features. The red flash gave him a look of almost ghoulish glee as he pitched a pillow at Gart.

Snarling, Gart separated the pillowcase from its stuffing with the tip of his sword so fiercely that the pillow appeared to explode. Feathers billowed toward the ceiling and came snowing down on him.

Instantly, a second pillow followed the first.

This one, however, he caught on the flat of his blade. Swinging his longsword like a bat, he sent the pillow back at Master Eremis.

It hit him in the chest hard enough to knock him against the wall.

Gart turned on Geraden and Terisa.

'Guards!' roared Master Eremis before the High King's Monomach could strike. '*Guards!*'

For the second time, Gart was startled enough to hesitate. He stopped the driving swing which had carried him into the sitting room – the swing which would have carried Geraden's head from his body. Swiftly, the Monomach gauged the distance past Geraden to Terisa; he looked at the door as the latch lifted; he glanced over his shoulder at Eremis.

With his left hand, he reached to his belt and produced a keen iron dirk.

As the door pounded open and the first guard started into the room, Gart cocked his arm.

A third pillow thumped against his shoulder and spoiled his aim. He missed Terisa.

Master Eremis let out a cackle of laughter.

Now the Monomach had no time for hesitation. Cursing vehemently, he met the first guard's blow with his sword, then kicked the man's legs out from under him. While the second struggled to avoid trampling his comrade, Gart retreated into the bedroom.

Without a glance at Master Eremis, he dove into the wardrobe.

'After him!' Eremis yelled at the guards. 'That passage leads to Havelock's chambers! *Go!* I will summon reinforcements!'

Terisa saw the guards falter distinctly before they plunged into the wardrobe. Perhaps they didn't want to face the High King's Monomach in a narrow place. Or perhaps they were reluctant to intrude on Adept Havelock's private domain – especially if, as Master Eremis seemed to suggest, the Adept were in league with Gart.

With a bouncing stride, Master Eremis left the bed and came into the sitting room. The glow of the fire and his own mirth lit his face, but Terisa thought he had never looked more dangerous. Briskly, he approached Geraden and stabbed a finger at the Apt's chest.

'I intend to call a meeting of the Congery.' Despite his humorous expression, his tone was savage. 'You will answer me for this in front of the Masters, boy.'

'No, I won't,' Geraden replied unsteadily. 'They've disbanded themselves.'

Master Eremis snorted. 'Again you are mistaken. Quillon holds them together with the King's authority.'

Flourishing his chasuble like a threat under Geraden's nose, he left the room.

Geraden's features twisted as if he had just been kicked in the stomach.

Terisa sat straight down on the floor. The noise of the guards' boots echoed dimly out of the wardrobe, but she heard nothing that sounded like the clash of swords.

TWENTY-FIVE

MASTER EREMIS
IN EARNEST

'Are you all right?' Geraden asked. His tone wasn't sympathetic.

Sitting cross-legged on the rug, Terisa clamped her hands to the sides of her head to keep her mind from flying apart. She didn't understand: none of it made any sense. Master Eremis. Gart. What were they doing to her?

'Terisa?'

And why was Geraden so angry at her? He was her friend. Why was he suddenly blind to her pain?

'Did he hurt you?'

He was her friend. He must have a good reason for snarling at her as if she had broken his heart. She struggled to concentrate. The room was full of disaster. She had to *think*.

Heavy boots hammered the stone. Three guards burst into the room with their swords out. Master Eremis had certainly gotten their attention. Once in the room, however, they hesitated, waving their blades warily, until Geraden snapped, 'There's a wardrobe in the bedroom with a passage behind it.' Then they charged away. The boards of the wardrobe resounded as they went through it.

How many different kinds of pain were there? There was the dull ache where Master Eremis had gripped the back of her neck. There was the grief that seemed to throb in the secret places of her heart. There was the sharp strain around her chest which grew tighter every time Geraden spoke to her in that clenched and bitter tone. There was the belabored sensation inside her skull, as if her mind had been beaten with clubs.

And somewhere else – somewhere indefinable – there was a new certainty as pure as a knife. It needed a name. Perhaps that was why it hurt so much: because she had no name for it.

Dully, she said, 'At least now we know he and Gart aren't working together.'

'*Terisa*.' That word would have sounded like a cry if Geraden hadn't whispered it so softly.

Before she could reply, another voice intervened. 'Don't torture yourself,

Geraden,' Castellan Lebbick said from the doorway. Four more guards clattered past him on their way to the wardrobe. 'She isn't worth it.'

She scrambled to her feet so that she wouldn't appear so defeated in front of the Castellan.

Geraden stood with his back to the wall, his arms folded like fetters across his chest. His face looked like a stone mask from which all the joy had been chipped away. Firelight reflected out of his eyes, as dry as fever.

'Save your insults, Castellan,' he rasped quietly. 'We don't need them.'

Castellan Lebbick cocked an eyebrow. 'All right. I'll be civil. You be cooperative. For a change. What happened?'

Geraden seemed to shrink slightly, as if he were being compacted by the pressure of his grip on himself – as if he were squeezing himself down to his essence. 'We were attacked. The High King's Monomach tried to kill her again.'

A grin pulled the Castellan's lips back from his teeth. 'And you're still alive? How did you manage that?'

'Master Eremis saved us. He fought Gart off until the guards could get in.'

'Master Eremis? What was *he* doing here?'

Bitterly, Geraden didn't look at Terisa.

With an effort, she met Lebbick's gaze. 'He came to see me.'

'And do you always receive him dressed like that?'

In shame, she bit her lip. Shame was yet another kind of pain. Somehow, she murmured, 'He came when I was asleep.'

The Castellan turned back to Geraden. 'Apparently, Master Eremis was welcome. In that case, what were *you* doing here? I doubt that either one of them invited you.'

'When I arrived,' Geraden said like a piece of the wall where he stood, 'her guards said she was alone. Don't you want to know how he got in? Don't you want to know how Gart got in?'

'Go on. Tell me.'

'Both of them used the secret passage behind her wardrobe.'

At that, Castellan Lebbick drew a hissing breath through his teeth. 'Ballocks! How did they know about it?'

'Saddith and Master Eremis are lovers. In fact, she volunteered to be Terisa's maid to please him. She noticed the chair in the wardrobe and told him about it. I presume he told Gart.'

'Wait a moment. You said Master Eremis saved you. Now you say he is in league with Gart?'

'Where else could Gart find out about the passage?' retorted the Apt. 'Who else knew enough to tell him? There's just me and Terisa. Saddith and Master Eremis. And you, Castellan. Even Artagel doesn't know about it.'

Involuntarily, Terisa remembered that Myste knew.

Clenching his fists on his hips, the Castellan rasped, 'All right. If Gart knew, why didn't he use it to kill her long ago?'

'At first,' Geraden said, 'he didn't know. Saddith told Master Eremis where Terisa was, but she didn't know any more than that. I don't know when she found the passage. And I don't know when he got her to tell him about it. I certainly don't know how busy Gart is. But I think Master Eremis decided he

453

wanted to let her live because he wanted her for himself. He didn't tell Gart about the passage until the Alend army arrived and they both ran out of time.'

Abruptly, Castellan Lebbick turned on Terisa. 'Is this true? Have you been making it worthwhile for Master Eremis to keep you alive when he really wants you dead?'

His tone made her wince. She was starting to understand Geraden's hurt, and his reasons dismayed her. Nevertheless she met the Castellan squarely.

'He did save us.' And her certainty was precise, if only she could put a name to it. 'He said he's going to make Geraden answer for this in front of the Congery.'

She wasn't prepared for the virulence with which Lebbick snarled under his breath, 'Bitch!' Fortunately, he swung back to Geraden too soon to see her flinch.

'I have a few questions myself. I want to know how you suddenly became an expert on what Saddith does or doesn't tell her lovers. And I want to know some of the things you haven't told me yet.

'But as it happens, you're not my only problem right now. I have the rest of Orison to worry about. I'll wait until the Congery meets.

'When my men come back from not finding Gart, tell them to report to me.'

Brusquely, Castellan Lebbick strode to the door and left.

Without thinking about what she was doing, Terisa turned toward the fire so that she wouldn't have to look at Geraden. She was afraid to look at him. He was so hurt – And almost everything he believed about her was true. He had saved her from her own weakness. Master Eremis had claimed her – and she had resisted him so little. Even choosing against him, she had been unable to struggle. Shame seemed to demoralize her; she couldn't face the accusation of his pain.

Yet her cowardice disgusted her. He had never let fear prevent him from doing anything for her. At last, she forced herself to turn again and meet his distress.

'Geraden, I—'

He hadn't shifted his stance an inch. Dim gray from the windows and dull red from the hearth lay along the stone lines of his cheeks and jaw, his straight nose, his strong forehead. Not a muscle moved. His hair curled into darkness.

But his eyes were closed.

This was her fault: he was in so much pain because of her. Because he had found her nearly naked with Master Eremis. Because he had seen the Master touch her so intimately. Helplessly, she asked, 'What're we going to do?'

He didn't open his eyes. Perhaps the sight of her was intolerable. When he spoke, he couldn't restrain his voice. It shook as if he were freezing.

'I need to know whose side you're on. You don't have to tell me anything else. You have to make your own choices. I can't tell you who to love. But I'm going to have to stand up in front of the Masters and tell them everything I can think of. They aren't going to want to believe me. I've spent too many years making too many mistakes.

454

'You're my only witness. You're the only one who can tell them I'm telling the truth. If you're planning to call me a liar—' He couldn't go on.

She wanted to reply at once, but his distress closed her throat. What could she say? Nothing was adequate. He had touched her near the point of her certainty, but she still didn't know what to call it.

Yet she was unable to bear his rigid silence. Somehow, she mustered an answer.

'I didn't invite Master Eremis here. He came while I was asleep. That's why I'm dressed like this.

'He wanted me to choose between you.'

A muscle twitched in Geraden's cheek, a knot of pain.

'I think he's probably the only man in Orison who has a chance to save Mordant. He has the ability to make things happen.' That was the limit of her honesty. 'But I chose you.'

His eyes popped open. A subtle alteration of the planes and lines of his expression made him appear both astonished and suspicious. His voice continued to shake.

'Your robe was open.'

'He did that. I didn't.'

For a long moment, he remained motionless – and yet, in spite of the fact that he wasn't moving, she seemed to see the entire structure of his face being transfigured, the whole landscape behind his eyes and emotions reforming. He didn't smile: he wasn't ready for that. But the potential for a smile was restored.

Slowly, he unbent his arms from his chest. Slowly, he reached out his hand and stroked her cheek as if to wipe away tears she hadn't shed.

Unable to hold back, she flung her arms around him and hugged him desperately, as if he could cure her shame.

The embrace with which he answered her was as tight and needy as hers, as hungry for solace. And somehow, because he wanted so much from her, he gave her what she needed.

A short time later, nine guards came trooping up out of the passage behind her wardrobe. They had nothing of any use to report.

The gray afternoon wore down toward evening. All around Orison, campfires glimmered against the wind. Tents everywhere formed a ripple of hillocks over the bare ground. Even the siege engines looked small in this light, at this distance. Wind thudded without remorse at the windowpanes of Terisa's rooms, until the atmosphere felt crowded and bitter, full of threats.

Late afternoon brought her an incongruous visitor: the seamster, Mindlin, come to deliver her new clothes. He wanted to give them a second fitting, to be sure that she was satisfied – perhaps he thought her approval would have some value when the siege was over – but she accepted them and sent him away.

For the fourth or fifth time, she said, 'We've got to *do* something.'

Geraden sighed. 'I know the feeling. But I'm not exactly brimming with ideas.'

She needed to put her certainty into words, so that it would be good for

455

something. It would come to her, she told herself, if she stopped pushing it. Or if she pushed it in the right way. Abruptly, she shook off her irresolution.

'You wanted to talk to Artagel, but you didn't get the chance. Why don't you do that now?'

The suggestion surprised him. 'What's that going to accomplish?'

'It might make you feel better.'

'And you think I might not get another chance? You think I might have a little trouble getting my brother to forgive me after I've been tossed in the dungeon for treachery?'

She couldn't suppress a grin. 'I didn't say that.'

'You didn't have to.' In spite of himself, he caught her mood. 'I said it for you.'

'So you did. If you think it's such a terrible idea' – now she was grinning broadly – 'I'm afraid I'll have to apologize for bringing it up.'

At once, he waved his hands defensively. 'No, no. Anything but that. I'll do it.' His playfulness faded almost immediately, however. 'Do you want to come with me?'

She shook her head.

'What *are* you going to do?'

Firmly, as if she were sure of herself, she said, 'I'm going to make sense out of this. Somehow.'

He spent a moment studying her. Then, in a purposely sententious tone, he said, 'My lady, I've got the strongest feeling you'll succeed.'

'Oh, get out of here,' she returned.

Nevertheless she hoped he was right. As soon as he was gone, she got dressed, putting on her warm new riding clothes and her winter boots because she didn't want to be hampered by her more ladylike gowns. Then she went to see the King.

She had no clear plan in mind. She simply wanted him to intervene on Geraden's behalf.

As she climbed the stairs toward the royal suite, however, she remembered more and more vividly that she had lied to the King the last time she had talked to him. And she still had no idea how he had guessed that she had helped his daughter Myste sneak out of Orison. Before she reached his door, she was tempted to turn back.

The ordeal Geraden had ahead of him determined her to keep going. He needed answers. She needed answers in order to help him. If King Joyse would do nothing else for her, or for the Domne's son, or for Mordant, he might at least supply a few answers. The chance was worth what it might cost her.

And if the King refused to see her, she could always talk to the Tor.

The guards outside the suite saluted her. Practicing steadiness, she asked them if she could be admitted. One of them stayed at the door while the other entered the suite. A moment later, she was given permission to go in.

Her pulse was laboring enough to make her regret her temerity. Blind to the room's luxurious appointments, she had eyes only for the three old men sitting like bosom companions before the ornate fireplace.

456

King Joyse lay as much as sat in an armchair with his legs stretched over a hassock toward the fire. His purple velvet robe showed the benefits of a recent cleaning, and his cheeks were freshly shaved: his appearance, if not his posture, suggested readiness.

In contrast, the Tor slumped as if his skeleton no longer had enough willpower to support his fat. Like his flesh, his robe spilled over the arms of his chair; the green fabric was stained with splotches of wine. Too plump to look haggard, his face sagged like wet laundry. He gave the impression that he had become so involved in Orison's preparations for defense that he had stopped taking care of himself.

Between the two old friends sat the King's Dastard, Adept Havelock, looking grimier and loonier than ever in his ancient surcoat, with his unruly tufts of hair and his disfocused gaze.

All three men held large, elegant goblets.

All three turned their heads toward Terisa as she was announced. The Tor peered at her through a haze of exhaustion and wine. Adept Havelock licked his lips salaciously. King Joyse nodded but didn't smile.

She had been hoping that he would smile. It would have done her good to see his luminous smile again.

He greeted her casually; his tone implied that he was a bit the worse for drink. 'My lady, come join us.' His cheeks were red, scraped raw with shaving, but behind their color his skin looked pale. 'Pour yourself some wine.' He nodded toward a decanter and extra goblets on a table against the paneled wall. 'It's quite good – a fine wine from—' A look of perplexity crossed his face. 'Where did you say this wine is from?' he asked the Tor.

The Tor shook himself as if he were in danger of falling asleep. 'Rostrum. A small village near the border of Termigan and Domne, where the babes drink wine instead of milk from their mothers' breasts, and even the children can do exquisite things with grapes. Rostrum wine.'

King Joyse nodded again. 'Rostrum wine,' he said to Terisa. 'Have some. We're celebrating.'

She stood in the center of the thick blue-and-red rug and tried to watch all three men simultaneously. 'What're you celebrating?'

Adept Havelock giggled.

'Are we celebrating?' The Tor's voice sounded damp. 'I thought we were grieving.'

'Grieving? My old friend.' King Joyse glanced at the Tor kindly. 'What for? This is a celebration, I tell you.'

'Oh, of course, my lord King.' The Tor waggled a hand. 'A celebration. I misspoke.' His fatigue was plain. 'Orison has been invested by the Alend Monarch. Your daughter has poisoned our water. While we sit here, the men of Perdon die, spending themselves without hope against Cadwal. And the royal Imager, Adept Havelock' – he inclined his head courteously in Havelock's direction – 'has burned to death our only clue as to where – and who – our chief enemy is. We do well to celebrate, since we can accomplish nothing with sorrow.'

'Nonsense,' replied the King at once. Although his expression was grave, he appeared to be in good spirits. 'Things aren't as bad as you think. Lebbick knows a trick or two about sieges. We still have plenty of Rostrum wine, so we don't need much water. As soon as he realizes we can't reinforce him, the Perdon is going to back off and let Festten through. That will stop the killing.'

He seemed unaware that what he was saying didn't convey much reassurance.

'And the death of the prisoner?' inquired the Tor glumly.

King Joyse dismissed that question. 'Also, we have another reason to celebrate. The lady Terisa is here. Aren't you, my lady?' he asked Terisa, then went on speaking to the Tor. 'Unless I've gotten it all wrong, she's here to tell us that she has found a new cure for stalemate.'

Again Adept Havelock giggled.

For a second, Terisa nearly lost her head. A *cure*? A cure for *stalemate*? She wanted to laugh feverishly. Did King Joyse really think this was all just one big game of hop-board? Then they were all doomed.

Fortunately, she caught hold of her reason for being here before all her thoughts veered off into panic. Geraden. That was the important thing. Geraden.

'I don't know anything about stalements. Or cures.' Her tone was too curt. She made an effort to moderate it. 'My lord King. I came because I'm worried about Geraden. Master Eremis is going to try to ruin him in front of the Congery.'

The King gave her his attention politely. 'Ruin him, my lady?'

'He and Master Eremis are going to accuse each other of betraying Mordant.'

'I see. And don't you call that a stalemate?'

'No.' She wasn't getting through. She had to do better. 'No, my lord King. The Congery will believe Master Eremis.' And yet she was certain – 'But he's lying.'

The Tor twisted in his seat to study her more closely. With a show of effort, Adept Havelock picked up his chair, turned it, and plumped it down again so that he could sit facing her.

King Joyse, however, gazed toward the fire. 'Master Eremis?' he asked as if he were losing interest. 'Lying? That would be risky. He might get caught. Only innocent men can afford to tell lies.'

'My lady,' said the Tor quietly, 'such accusations are serious. Master Eremis is a man of proven stature. The Congery might have some justification to take the word of one of their own number over the charges of a mere failed Apt. How do you know that Master Eremis is lying?'

She opened her mouth, then closed it again. What could she say? The piece of information lodged in her brain refused to come clear. Something Master Eremis had said, or revealed – Or was it Geraden? After a moment, she admitted, 'I haven't figured that out yet.'

'I see, my lady.' The old lord returned his attention to the fire. 'You simply trust Geraden. That is understandable. I trust him myself. There is no help that I can give you, however. I am no longer my lord King's chancellor.'

What?

Adept Havelock grinned at her.

King Joyse sighed and leaned his head against the back of his chair. 'My old friend was wearing himself toward his grave with the business of Orison. He doesn't want to admit he's no longer young. Sadly, it's true.'

'My lord King,' the Tor explained, 'has given instructions that I am not to be obeyed, except in matters of my personal comfort. With the arrival of Alend's army, my power ended.' He snorted to himself. 'You may imagine Castellan Lebbick's delight. Remember, he thinks it possible that I am a traitor myself. He did not like my interest in our defenses. Though my lord King does not say so, I believe he has taken away my position to protect himself in case the good Castellan's suspicions prove correct.'

At that, King Joyse jerked up his head. His watery eyes were suddenly acute, and his mouth twisted. He didn't reply to the Tor, however. Glaring at Terisa, he demanded, 'Just what is it you want, my lady?'

She was startled: for a moment, she had lost herself in empathy for the old lord. Almost stammering, she said, 'Geraden doesn't stand a chance in front of the Masters. Master Eremis will chew him to pieces. You've got to stop them. Don't let them do this to him.'

'But if Master Eremis is telling the truth,' returned the King in a voice like a rasp, 'Geraden deserves to be caught and punished.'

'No.' She couldn't think. It was maddening. 'You don't believe that.'

King Joyse aimed his gaze at her like a nail and spoke as if he were tapping his words into wood. 'That is not the point, my lady. At the moment, it isn't him I doubt. It's you.'

She blinked. Her heart began to labor again, pounding alarm in all directions. 'Why?'

'Are you surprised? You underestimate me. I warned you this game is dangerous.

'After we talked, I had Myste's rooms searched. She took nothing personal with her – none of her little mementos of childhood, none of her favorite gifts. Does that seem likely to you? If she had gone back to her mother, she would have taken everything she could carry.

'You lied to me, my lady. You lied to me about my daughter.'

Inside her chest, a cold hand knotted into a fist. Both the Tor and Adept Havelock squinted at her as if she were being transformed to ugliness in front of them.

'Where did she really go?'

This was what Terisa had feared: King Joyse had found her out. She learned the danger of lies when she was still a child. Falsehood had been exquisitely tempting to her; her dread of being punished had made her ache to deflect every manifestation of parental irritation, discontent, or disapproval. She had learned, however, that the punishment was worse when she got caught.

In simple defensiveness, she tried to counter as if she had cause to complain. 'How did you know she came to see me? Were you having your own daughter spied on?'

Adept Havelock swung his chair back to face the fire, sat down again, and began to twiddle his fingers.

The King continued to glare at her for a moment. She met his gaze because she was afraid to do anything else. Then, abruptly, he too turned away. 'You were warned,' he muttered. 'Remember that. You were warned.

'My lord Tor, be so good as to summon the guards. I want this woman locked in the dungeon until she condescends to tell me the truth about my daughter.'

'No!' The cry burst from her before she could stop it. 'I'll tell you. I'll tell you anything. Geraden needs me. If I'm not there, he'll have to face the Congery alone.'

None of the men were looking at her. The Tor emptied his goblet, but didn't trouble to refill it.

Terisa took a deep breath, squeezed her eyes shut for a second. 'She went after the champion. She thought he needed help.' She swallowed hard. 'I'm sorry.'

To Terisa's astonishment, King Joyse's profile quirked toward a smile. But almost at once his expression turned sorrowful, and he leaned his head morosely to rest against his chair again. 'More wine would be nice, don't you think?' he commented in the direction of the ceiling.

The Tor seemed to slump farther down in his seat.

With a strangled chortle, Adept Havelock tossed his wine into the fire. While the wine hissed and burned, he threw his goblet behind him, narrowly missing Terisa.

'Fornication,' he pronounced, 'is hard to do well alone.'

'My lady,' the King breathed as if he were going to sleep, 'I didn't *know* Myste went to see you. I *reasoned* it. If you were more honest, I would have less trouble trusting you. You ought to try using a little reason yourself.'

Terisa had expected him to be appalled and angry. Obviously he wasn't. Preconceptions were being jerked out from under her. This new surprise seemed to knock the last bit of sense out of the situation. Myste was doing something that had been foreseen in Havelock's augury of King Joyse. Was that why a lie made the King furious and the truth had nearly made him smile?

'I don't understand,' she murmured weakly. 'Don't you care?'

King Joyse reached out a swollen, unsteady hand and nudged Adept Havelock, who in turn nudged the Tor. 'My lord, I said, "More wine would be nice."'

Sighing, the Tor pried his bulk out of his chair and moved to fetch the decanter.

'You want me to use a little *reason*.' Terisa had difficulty holding her voice down. 'How about giving me some information to reason *with*? Myste is probably dead. If the cold didn't kill her – and the champion didn't kill her – then that firecat probably did. You act like the only thing you care about is that she didn't go see her mother!'

'No.' The King sounded sad, but he answered without rancor. 'What I care about is that she did something I can be proud of.'

Like an echo, Terisa seemed to hear Castellan Lebbick quoting King Joyse to Prince Kragen: *She carries my pride with her wherever she goes. For her sake, as well as for my own, I hope that the best reasons will also produce the best results.*

She wanted to yell, But that doesn't make any *sense*! Elega betrayed you!

Myste is probably dead! The words died in her throat, however: they were hopeless. The thought that she would have to go support Geraden with nothing except more confusion made her feel sick.

The Tor refilled the King's goblet and his own, then eased himself into his chair. 'The lady Terisa is distressed,' he remarked distantly. 'It would be a kindness, my lord King, if you gave her what she desires.'

King Joyse lifted his head once more, scowling sourly as if he meant to say something acid to the Tor.

But he didn't. Instead, he growled, 'Oh, very well.'

Over his shoulder, he addressed Terisa. 'The reason I told Geraden not to talk to you when you were first brought here is the same reason I didn't intervene when the Masters decided to translate their champion. It's the same reason I'm not going to intervene now. I'm trying to protect you. Both of you.'

'Protect us!' She was too upset to restrain herself. 'How does it protect me to keep me ignorant? How does it protect us to let that champion be translated? We were buried alive.' I almost lost my mind. 'How does it protect him to let Master Eremis destroy him? All you're doing is making us look foolish.'

The King turned his head away and sketched a frail gesture with both hands. 'You see?' he observed to the Tor. 'She doesn't reason.' Then his tone grew bitter.

'You're still alive, aren't you? Do you have any conception how unlikely that was when you first arrived? Better minds than yours were sure neither of you would last for three days. A little foolishness is a small price to pay for your lives.'

Terisa stared at the back of his head with her mouth open as if he had taken all the air out of the room.

'"Better minds"!' crowed Adept Havelock like a man addressing a crowd of admirers. 'He means me. *He means me.*'

'If I had welcomed you with open arms,' King Joyse went on, 'my enemies would have formed a higher estimate of how dangerous you are. They would have put more effort into killing you.' He sounded querulous and old, peevishly incapable of the things he ascribed to himself. 'As long as they thought I had no interest in you – that I was too stupid or senile to have an interest in you – they could afford patience. Wait and see. Gart attacked you that first night because my enemies hadn't had time to find out I hadn't welcomed you. But as soon as people heard that I wasn't treating you like an ally, Gart held back for a while.

'Are you satisfied?'

His demand took her by surprise. She scrambled to ask, 'Do you mean the reason you can't help Geraden now is that if you do your enemies will know you're his friend and they'll start trying even harder to have him killed?'

'I mean much more than that,' he snapped. 'I mean that if I had given him permission to tell you whatever you wanted to know I would have doomed you both. My enemies would have taken anything like that as a sign that you were on my side.

'*Now* are you satisfied?'

461

'But what—?' It was too much: his explanation increased her confusion. It had all been an elaborate charade. 'Who *are* your enemies? Why can't you protect anybody you want in your own castle?' Images of Geraden and Myste and Elega and Queen Madin and Master Barsonage and even Castellan Lebbick rose in her, all of them lost and aggrieved. *'Why do you have to make everybody who's loyal to you think you don't care what happens?'*

'My lady.' His tone was no longer petulant. Now it was as keen and cutting as ice. 'If I had any desire to answer such questions, I would have done so earlier. As a courtesy to your distress, I have already told you more than I consider wise.' Like Geraden's, his speech became more formal as it gathered authority. Despite his years, his voice still had the potential to lash at her. 'I advise reason and *silence*, my lady. You will not prolong your life by speaking of what you have heard.'

He dismissed her without a glance. 'You may go.'

But—? But—? She knew she should have been stronger. She should have demanded a better explanation. But what she wanted to ask couldn't get past her mental stutter into words. She had no sure ideas left to stand on. King Joyse knew what he was doing – he knew with a vengeance. He was being passive and obtuse on purpose – hurting the people who loved him on purpose. But what purpose was that? It was inconceivable. He—

'My lady,' he said again, 'you may go.'

In a tone of faraway sadness, the Tor murmured, 'My lady, it is generally unwise to disregard the will of a king.' He spoke as if from personal experience.

With a fierce effort, Terisa quelled her insistent incomprehension. The exertion left her angry and panting, but in control of herself.

'Thank you, my lord Tor,' she said stiffly. 'My lord King, I'm sorry. I lied to you about Myste because she trusted me. She was afraid somebody would try to stop her. She asked me to protect her. I lied to you because I didn't know you would have let her go.'

None of the three men looked at her. They stared vacantly into the fire, as if they had used up their allotment of words for the day and had nothing left to think with. King Joyse let her get as far as the door before he breathed softly, 'Thank you, my lady.'

She left as if she were escaping.

Geraden joined her in her rooms for supper.

His expression was a strange mixture of relief and dread. His conversation with Artagel made his spirits soar; the upcoming meeting of the Congery hung on him like lead. The good news, he reported, was that Artagel was healing well after his earlier setbacks. And Artagel was still his friend. The bad news was that the swordsman was still in no condition to stand up in front of the Masters and defend his brother.

'When will the meeting be?' she asked.

'I don't know what kind of mediator Master Quillon is. I used to think he wasn't assertive enough to pull a meeting together. But now—' He shrugged.

Fervently, he listened while she described her session with King Joyse, the Tor, and Adept Havelock. Unfortunately, it changed nothing. 'You know,' he commented after a while, 'all this would do us a lot more good if we had any idea why we're so important.'

'I don't think so.' She felt sour and imperfectly resigned. 'It doesn't cheer me up to believe King Joyse is really our friend only he can't risk doing anything about it. What good are friends who treat you just like your enemies do?'

He nodded slowly without agreeing with her. 'The important thing is, it's hope. He certainly sounds like he has reasons for what he's doing.' Geraden's mood seemed to improve as hers deteriorated. 'And if he has reasons, we can at least *hope* they're good ones.'

'On the other hand,' she countered, 'look at the way he's treating the Tor.'

That made Geraden scowl. 'You heard King Joyse say he "defies prediction." There's probably a danger he'll do something to mess up one of the King's plans. So King Joyse is trying to keep him under control.'

A moment later, he added in a black tone, 'I don't like plans that hurt the Tor.'

'Neither do I,' said Terisa.

After a while, he remarked with more humor, 'It's too bad nobody much cares what we think of their plans.'

Damn you, Geraden, she thought, you're starting to cheer up again. I don't understand it.

In spite of his improved humor, however, he didn't smile when one of the younger Apts knocked on the door and announced that the Congery wanted him. When the Apt used the words 'at once,' Geraden's eyes widened slightly.

'That was fast,' he muttered to Terisa. 'Master Eremis knows how to get action.'

The young Apt avoided looking at Geraden. 'The lady Terisa isn't invited.'

'The lady Terisa,' she snapped, 'is coming anyway.'

The Apt didn't look at her, either.

Geraden tried to give her one of Artagel's combative grins; but its failure only made him appear sick. 'Let's go get it over with.'

Together, they followed the young Apt through Orison down to the laborium.

Until her knuckles began to ache, she didn't realize that she was clenching her fists.

Although she was warmly dressed, she felt the chill as soon as she crossed the disused ballroom and descended into the domain of the Masters. Castellan Lebbick's new curtain wall defended the breach the champion had made, but didn't seal it. Because of the strong wind outside, there was a noticeable breeze in the passages. As a result, the atmosphere was cold enough to make her wish she had brought a coat.

If Geraden noticed the cold, he didn't show it. His manner was distracted. As he entered the laborium, he grew tense. He had spent all his adult life – and a good part of his adolescence – trying to earn a place for himself in these halls and passages, and now his failure threatened to become so dramatic that it would be considered treason.

For his sake as well as her own, Terisa was getting angrier.

The young Apt led her and Geraden to a part of the laborium where she had never been before – to the room the Masters had used for their gatherings ever since the champion had destroyed their meeting chamber.

This room was small by comparison, but still more than large enough. It was a long rectangle; and something in the color or cut of its cold, gray stone, in the worn but uneven floor, in the number of black iron brackets set into the walls created the impression that it had originally served as a storeroom for the instruments of torture. It was the kind of place where ways of inflicting pain might wait while they weren't needed: racks and iron maidens being taken to and from the interrogation chamber might have rubbed those hollows in the floor; thumb-screws and flails might have hung in the brackets. A few of the brackets had been adapted to hold lamps, but the rest were empty. The empty ones seemed especially grim.

The Masters were already gathered.

They sat in heavy iron-pegged chairs which lined the two long walls, roughly half of them on either side facing each other as if they had deliberately set out to form a gauntlet. Because of the length of the room, however, a sizable space at each end was unused. The doors were there, several strides from the nearest seats.

Two guards on strict duty held the door through which Terisa and Geraden entered the chamber. Neither man acknowledged the Apt's glum nod.

As the door closed behind her, she scanned the room. At first, the only face she recognized was that of Master Barsonage. Since she had last seen him, the former mediator seemed to have developed a nervous tick: one of his thick, stiff eyebrows twitched involuntarily. Under the pressure of the Congery's mistakes and indecision, his face had taken on a jaundiced hue. She saw no hope there.

Looking for Master Quillon, her eye was caught by Castellan Lebbick.

When she saw him, her throat suddenly went dry.

He had Nyle with him.

Geraden's brother sat beside the Castellan at the far end of one row of chairs. He wore a brown worsted cloak over his clothes. Inside it, his arms bunched across his chest, holding the cloak shut. His head hung at a dejected angle. He didn't look up at Terisa and Geraden.

Geraden was frozen with shock. All expression had been wiped from his face. The spark that animated his features most of the time was gone – hidden or extinguished – and he seemed smaller, as if he were shrinking in on himself. He stared blankly at Nyle while two bright spots of color slowly spread in his cheeks. She had never seen him look so lost. The glazing of his eyes made her irrationally afraid that he was having a heart attack.

'The lady Terisa was *not* invited,' said one of the Masters loudly.

'But she *is* welcome,' rasped Castellan Lebbick. 'Isn't she, Master Quillon.'

The rabbity mediator rose to his feet, gazing brightly at everything and nobody. Wrinkling his nose, he answered, 'As welcome as you are, Castellan.'

Castellan Lebbick grinned like a snarl.

Master Eremis was sitting on the other side of the Castellan.

'Oh, I insist,' he said at once. 'If Castellan Lebbick and Nyle are permitted, it is only fair to permit the lady Terisa also.' His expression was difficult to read. For no clear reason, he looked pleased.

'Why is he here?' Geraden asked. He sounded like a sleepwalker.

Everyone understood to whom Geraden was referring. Master Quillon started to reply, but Castellan Lebbick spoke first. Still grinning, he said, 'Master Eremis claims he's going to support the accusations against you.'

'Nyle!' Terisa cried softly.

All the Masters were staring at her, but none of them seemed to have faces. She didn't know who they were.

Geraden moved to the nearest chair and sat down as if he were crumbling. Nyle tightened his grip on his cloak. He didn't raise his head.

'Castellan Lebbick,' Master Quillon said as if he were thinking about something else, 'this is the meeting of the Congery, not a congregation of your guards. You have no authority here. You are permitted only because you refuse to let Nyle among us without you. Please be quiet.'

The Castellan accepted this admonition without retort, but also without acquiescence.

'My lady,' the mediator continued in the same tone, 'will you sit down so that we may begin?'

Terisa wrestled with an impulse to start shouting. Abruptly, she turned and took a seat beside Geraden.

He looked so stunned that she whispered, 'What is Nyle going to say about you?'

He didn't answer.

Master Eremis watched Geraden curiously, as though he were genuinely interested in what the Apt was thinking.

'Very well,' said Master Quillon. He took one or two quick steps out into the middle of the floor between the rows of chairs. 'Let us begin.'

The chairs were old; perhaps they were left over from the days when the lords and ladies of Orison liked to watch the way prisoners were questioned. The wood was dry and porous enough to hold bloodstains.

'We hold this meeting to consider a question which I will not attempt to soften.' His manner suggested that he might be looking for a place to hide, yet his voice was firm. 'As you all know, Master Eremis claims that Apt Geraden is a traitor – a traitor to the Congery and to Orison, to King Joyse and to Mordant. He also says that Apt Geraden will make the same claim of him. We will hear both speak. They will give their reasons. They will provide what corroboration they can. And we will try to determine the truth.'

'And when the truth has been determined,' Castellan Lebbick put in casually, 'I'll act on it.'

Master Quillon ignored the interruption. 'This matter must be dealt with speedily. There is a blot on the honor of the Congery, and it must be removed at once. Orison is under siege because of us – because we are desirable to the King's enemies. And we are not much trusted at the best of times. Therefore it is urgent that we determine the truth – and that any traitor is delivered to the Castellan.'

'Apt Geraden' – the mediator's eyes sparkled – 'will you speak first?'

Everybody turned to look at Geraden – everybody except Nyle, who slumped in his chair as if he were contemplating suicide.

Terisa wanted to say, demand, No. Make Master Eremis go first. But the words didn't come. She watched like one of the Imagers as Geraden got slowly to his feet.

The spots of color in his cheeks had darkened until they resembled a flush of exertion. His movements were tight, constrained. His chest rose and fell as if he were trying to take a deep breath and couldn't. He didn't look at Nyle: in fact, he didn't look at anybody. He had been given a shock he didn't know how to face.

Terisa found herself thinking, Nyle is doing this because Geraden stopped him.

'Masters—' The Apt had to swallow hard to clear his throat. His voice seemed to be choking him. His life's ambition had been to belong to the Congery. He had spent years obeying and honoring these men. 'We've all been betrayed. I can't prove any of it.'

Oh, Geraden.

Master Eremis appeared to be suppressing a desire to laugh.

'You must make the effort, Geraden.' The mediator's words were sterner than his tone. 'Master Eremis will prove everything he can. Are you speaking of Master Gilbur, or of someone else?'

Geraden nodded aimlessly. His gaze stumbled to the floor. Yet he said nothing.

At the sight of his pain, something turned over in Terisa. He had suffered too much, borne too much. And now his brother hurt him like this – personally, deliberately. He was finally breaking under the strain.

'It's simple, really,' she said in a voice she hardly recognized. 'There *has* to be a traitor. Someone else – not just Master Gilbur.'

Master Quillon swung toward her. His nose seemed to twitch with eagerness, but the rest of his face was still.

'It's simple, really,' Geraden echoed like a ghost. 'There *has* to be a traitor. Someone else.'

Then he raised his head.

'It has to be somebody here.'

Terisa held her breath, praying that he would go on.

'She's been attacked by Gart four times.' His tone was a little slurred, but the glaze in his eyes seemed to be fading. 'The third time was out in the bazaar. That doesn't prove anything. But the fourth time Gart came through a secret passage in her room. Somebody must have told him about that passage.'

He stopped.

'That is true,' Master Eremis observed as if he were agreeing with Geraden. 'Someone must have told him. I was there to feel his attack. It is possible, I suppose, that I was his intended victim.'

'Master Eremis,' said the mediator with unexpected force, 'you will be given all the time you need to speak. Defend yourself then. The Apt must be left to say what he will.'

466

A Master with a heavy paunch and no eyebrows interposed, 'You were there, Master Eremis? How did you survive? How did any of you survive?'

Smiling, Eremis made a deferential gesture for silence.

Without hesitation, Master Quillon prompted Geraden, 'Continue, Apt. Who knew of the secret passage?'

At once, Geraden said, 'The Castellan, of course. King Joyse. His daughters. Terisa. Her maid. And Master Eremis.'

Terisa released an inward sigh of relief because he hadn't mentioned Master Quillon or Adept Havelock. He still had enough sense to keep that secret.

The mediator, however, gave no sign that he had noticed Geraden's restraint. 'And what does this prove?'

'Everybody knew about the passage all along. Except Master Eremis. He only found out about it recently. Soon after he found out about it, Gart used it.'

'That means nothing!' protested Master Eremis at once. 'What opportunity have I had to confer with the High King's Monomach? I have been away, as you all know. I have been visiting Esmerel.'

Geraden straightened his back. 'But that's not the crucial one.' At last he began to sound stronger. He was breathing more easily, and his gaze had come into focus. 'It's the second attack that's crucial. It was right after Master Eremis and Master Gilbur met with Prince Kragen and the lords of the Cares.'

A look of outrage jerked across Castellan Lebbick's face as old suspicions were confirmed. 'They *met*—?'

Geraden overrode the Castellan. 'That lets out everybody else. Everybody who didn't know about the meeting. But Master Eremis took her to it. When it broke up, he left her with Prince Kragen. Gart came out of a mirror with four of his men to attack them. The Perdon and Artagel saved them. Only Master Eremis could have arranged that. He's the only one who knew she would be there. He's the only one who had any control over where she would be after the meeting.'

An expression of mock horror widened Master Eremis' eyes and stretched his mouth.

'And,' Geraden insisted, 'he may be the only Master who knew where she was that first night, when Gart broke into her rooms to kill her. He's Saddith's lover. She volunteered to be her maid because he asked her to.

'Master Eremis is the only man in Orison who could have told Gart where and when to attack Terisa.'

As if he were having trouble keeping his balance, Geraden sat down and braced his hands on his knees.

Castellan Lebbick was on his feet, dangerously calm. 'I suspected something like this. Tell me about that meeting.'

'Is that *all*, Apt?' demanded an Imager with a red complexion and bad teeth. 'Do you expect us to *believe* that?'

'Be seated, Castellan,' advised Master Quillon. 'This does not concern you.'

'What does Artagel say?' someone else asked.

'I still do not understand why the High King's Monomach wants to kill the lady Terisa. What threat is she to Cadwal?'

'Why weren't we told about the second attack?'

'He hasn't done anything right since I've known him. I think we can take it for granted that if he says something it must be wrong.'

'Ballocks and pigsoil!' Castellan Lebbick roared over the babble. '*Tell me about that meeting!*'

Silence echoed after his shout.

'You have reached a hasty conclusion, Castellan,' Master Eremis volunteered without rising from his seat. 'The Perdon suggested a meeting between the lords of the Cares and the Congery so that we could discuss our mutual problem – the inaction of our good King. He arranged the coming of the lords to Orison. Master Gilbur and I were chosen to represent the Congery – I because I favored the meeting, he because he opposed it. I took it upon myself to invite Prince Kragen, believing his mission of peace to be sincere.'

He shrugged eloquently. 'Nothing came of it. The Fayle and the Termigan were too stiff-necked, the Tor too drunk, the Armigite too cowardly. Only the Perdon and Prince Kragen displayed any understanding of each other.

'Incidentally, if I am trusted by Alend, I am unlikely to be a servant of Cadwal. Don't you agree?

'I believe,' he concluded, 'that the blood you found belonged to Gart's men. Their bodies left as they came – by Imagery. We can only assume that Master Gilbur escaped in the same way, as the arch-Imager Vagel's ally.'

His explanation was so close to the truth that it made Terisa squirm. The air in the room seemed to be getting colder. She wondered if she would ever be warm again.

'It was treason,' Castellan Lebbick breathed through his teeth. 'You were plotting treason.'

'It was nothing of the kind,' sighed Master Barsonage, speaking for the first time. His weariness cut deep. 'The truth is that we were hoping the lords would give us cogent reasons not to risk the translation of our champion. We only took the risk of that translation because the lords convinced us they had no answer to Mordant's plight.'

'In any case,' Master Eremis said more sharply, 'it came to nothing. There is no cause for your outrage, Castellan, because no harm was done. In retrospect, it is clear that the gravest danger arose simply from the presence of so many lords – and Prince Kragen – here at the same time. If the champion had chosen to blast his way in some other direction' – Master Eremis rolled his eyes humorously, but his tone didn't lose its edge – 'he might have brought Orison down on the head of every important man in the kingdom.'

Castellan Lebbick muttered a few dark oaths.

'Can we get on with it?' Terisa asked, still speaking in the voice she hardly knew. 'I want to hear why Nyle thinks Geraden is a traitor.'

The Master with the paunch snapped, 'My lady, what you want is not of great consequence to us at present.'

With a gesture, Master Quillon demanded silence. Facing Lebbick, he inquired acerbically, 'Castellan, may we continue? Or do you wish to go on abusing us because we see our circumstances and Mordant's need differently than you do?'

Castellan Lebbick spat another curse, then clamped his mouth shut. Like a coiled spring, he returned to his seat.

The mediator rubbed his nose, trying to stop its twitch. 'Apt Geraden, have you finished what you wish to say?'

Geraden gave an abrupt nod.

'Do you have any corroboration? Is there anything you can show us or tell us to support your assertions?'

Geraden shook his head.

An odd thought crossed Terisa's mind. Geraden, she realized, had done what King Joyse wanted her to do: he had used his reason. His accusation against Master Eremis was based on reason rather than on proof.

Unfortunately, it was proof the Masters wanted. 'Master Eremis was the only one who knew I would be at the meeting,' she said. 'I was there. Everyone else was surprised to see me.'

'No, my lady,' Master Eremis put in immediately. 'That is incorrect. You cannot be sure that I did not mention my intent to Master Gilbur – or even to Prince Kragen. You cannot be sure that the surprise you saw did not have another cause.

'But even if your assertion is true, what does it mean? Master Gilbur and I left the meeting together, going – as you know – to report what had happened to our fellow Masters. But he parted from me almost at once, saying that he had an urgent need to visit his rooms. Knowing now that *he*, at least, is a traitor, how can you believe that he did not take that opportunity – unforeseen though it may have been – to translate Gart against you?'

'Because,' someone Terisa didn't know remarked incisively, 'such an attack could not have been done without preparation. The necessary mirror could not have been made on a whim. Indeed, the location of the meeting must have been chosen to match the proximity of the mirror. Was it not you who chose the location of the meeting, Master Eremis?'

Almost instantly, everyone in the room fell still. Attention concentrated the atmosphere. Geraden took a deep breath, and some of the unnatural color left his face.

Master Eremis, however, wasn't daunted. 'Of course it was,' he snapped. 'I had that responsibility because neither the Perdon nor Prince Kragen knew Orison well enough to make the choice themselves. But you assume that the mirror was created for the sake of Gart's attack on the lady. There were only six days between the planning of the meeting and the meeting itself. Do you think such a mirror could be conceived and researched and shaped in six days? Is it not more probable that the mirror was created for an entirely different purpose – perhaps to give Gart access to Orison whenever he wanted it – and that the opportunity to attack the lady was merely fortuitous, an accident of circumstance which Master Gilbur hurried to turn to his advantage?'

Several of the Imagers shuffled their feet; few of them met Eremis' gaze.

The ease with which he had turned the accusation made Terisa's thoughts spin.

'Very well, Master Eremis,' the mediator murmured after a long pause. 'I presume that Geraden has no more to say. Since you have already begun to defend yourself, please continue.'

'Thank you, Master Quillon,' Eremis said as if he were deliberately suppressing contempt. He didn't trouble to rise. 'I will give you my reasons. Only if they do not persuade you will I call on Nyle to prove what I say. He is understandably reluctant to condemn his brother.'

That statement may have been true. Nyle did look reluctant: he looked reluctant to go on living.

'I have been curious about Apt Geraden since the moment when he brought the lady Terisa to us from a mirror which could not have performed that translation.' The Master sat nonchalantly, half sprawled in his chair with his legs outstretched. While he spoke, his long fingers played with the ends of his chasuble. His manner was so negligent that Terisa had to study him closely to notice that he was watching the entire room. 'The link between him and Master Gilbur turned my curiosity to suspicion. When Master Gilbur finally proved himself false, my worst doubts were confirmed.'

No one interrupted him as he recited the arguments he had already presented to Terisa. She had to admit that they sounded plausible, almost inevitable. It was Master Gilbur who shaped the glass which first showed the champion, Master Gilbur who guided every step of Geraden's attempt to match that mirror. Therefore if Geraden's abilities had made a mirror which could do things no mirror had ever done before, Master Gilbur must have been a witness to them. Or else Master Gilbur must have been responsible for the mysteries of that mirror himself, guiding Geraden to accomplishments which the Apt couldn't have achieved for himself. In either case, the two men were confederates. Geraden's difficulties had always been ones of talent rather than of knowledge: Master Gilbur couldn't have employed him to do something unprecedented without the Apt's awareness of it.

'No,' Geraden murmured. 'I had no idea.' But no one paid any attention to him.

Master Eremis also explained his theory about why Cadwal was marching. On that basis, he claimed, the rest was obvious. Who was the only man who always knew exactly where the lady Terisa was? Apt Geraden, of course, who first arranged to have her rooms guarded, then persuaded his brother Artagel to follow her. Who was the man most likely to have aided Master Gilbur in translating Gart after the meeting of the lords? Apt Geraden, of course, Master Gilbur's confederate. Why was it that all Geraden's apparent loyalty to King Joyse came to nothing? Because it was only a clever disguise to help him hurt those who most trusted him. He was in league with Gart and High King Festten.

Listening to this made Terisa feel sick.

The pain in Geraden's eyes was acute, but he said nothing.

When Master Eremis was done, the rest of the Imagers were slow to speak. A few of them looked shocked. More were relieved, however, as if they had been rescued from believing that a member of the Congery had betrayed them. And some were plainly delighted by the prospect of finally being rid of Geraden.

After a moment, however, a slightly cross-eyed young Master countered, 'But this is inconsistent, Master Eremis. If I understand rightly, it is Geraden who has kept the lady alive by providing her with defenders.'

'Nonsense,' retorted Master Eremis shortly. 'The guards he first arranged for her could not be a match for the High King's Monomach. And since then his duplicity has been more profound than you realize. He has put Artagel at the lady's side so that Mordant's best swordsman might also be killed, thus freeing Cadwal of two important enemies with one betrayal.'

'You can't believe that!' Geraden's protest was like a groan. At once, however, he closed his mouth again.

'No, Geraden.' Master Barsonage heaved his bulk upright. His gaze lingered momentarily, sadly, on Terisa. 'I do not believe that.' His face had the color and texture of prolonged strain. 'The truth is that I do not believe anything I have heard here. You and Master Eremis denounce each other as though what you say cannot be doubted, but you do not answer the most important question, the question on which all else stands or falls. You do not explain *why*.

'*Why* does the High King's Monomach go to such lengths to attack the lady Terisa? *Why* does Master Eremis wish her killed?' Over his shoulder, he demanded, 'Master Eremis, *why* does Geraden wish her killed?' Then he addressed the Congery. 'Nothing that these men have said has any meaning unless they can tell us *why*.'

Before either accuser could answer, Terisa stood up. 'I'll tell you why.' A shiver ran through her voice – a shiver of anger rather than of cold. She wasn't cold: she was sure. The frustrating certainty that she hadn't been able to name was suddenly clear. 'I'll tell you exactly why.' *If he had not been rescued—* She wasn't talking about Master Barsonage's question; she had no answer to that. But it gave her a way to say what she meant.

'Geraden doesn't have any reason to want me dead. He's spent enough time with me since I got here to know I'm no threat to anybody. If he were in league with Gart, I would never be attacked. He wouldn't risk the High King's Monomach on someone like me.

'But Master Eremis has a reason.'

The Master sat up straighter. He appeared to be taken aback. 'My lady,' he said wonderingly, 'I have saved your life. I have done everything a man can do to gain your love. How can you think that I wish you harm?'

She wanted to throw up. 'Because I know you're lying.'

At that, his expression darkened. She heard a hiss of indrawn breath from the Imagers behind her as he rose ominously to his feet. 'Be sure of what you say, my lady,' he murmured in warning.

'I'm sure,' she flung back at him. Pressure mounted in her voice. She didn't want to yell, but she needed passion to control her fear, to keep her going despite the fact that she had never defied anyone like this before and didn't believe she could do it, certainly not Master Eremis, he was too much for her, he was like her father, he had been too much for her from the start. 'You know all about the attack after the meeting. I told you that. I've made a lot of mistakes. But you left without coming to see me again.' *If he had not been rescued*— 'I never had a chance to tell you about the attacks on Geraden. Who told you about them?

'You could know about those riders in the woods. That's common knowledge now. Anybody could have told you.' – *rescued as he was, I assure you* – 'But you knew about the first time, too.'

Master Eremis stared at her as if she had caught him completely by surprise.

'Nobody knew about that except Artagel, Geraden, and me. And Adept Havelock. *He* didn't tell you.' Master Eremis had made a mistake. Under the pressure of Geraden's accusations, he had made a mistake. 'Artagel told the Castellan.' Lebbick nodded shortly. 'None of us told you. You weren't *here*. But you still said that attack was just a ploy. You knew all about it. You said, "If he had not been rescued as he was, I assure you that they would have recalled their insects before he was slain."

'You said "their insects." How did you know he was attacked by insects?'

A light of amazement and vindication broke across Geraden's face.

Struggling for self-control, she concluded, 'You're trying to accuse Geraden for the same reason you want me dead. Because we're dangerous to you. We know you're the traitor.'

For just a moment, Master Eremis continued to gape. Then he began chuckling.

His mirth didn't sound particularly cheerful.

'My lady,' he said, 'you are outrageous. You told me about the attack youself.'

'That's another lie,' she shot back in fury.

'No, my lady. The lie is yours. I had the story from your lips between kisses.'

'I don't think so, Master Eremis.' Geraden stood at Terisa's side. Her audacity had galvanized him: he was poised for battle, and his eyes burned. 'She doesn't have any reason to lie. She doesn't have anything to gain here.'

'Does she not?' Master Eremis' mouth twisted scornfully.

'You are naive, boy – or a fool. You are her reason. She has you to gain.'

That argument stopped Terisa: it set her back on her heels, like a dash of cold water in her face. It was true—

It was true enough to make her look foolish.

Nevertheless it was a miscalculation. Before Eremis could go on, several of the Masters burst out laughing.

'With *your* reputation for women?' said the Imager with the bad teeth. 'Do you ask us to credit that she prefers Geraden fumble-foot?'

'I would not have believed any other proof,' another Master put in, 'but I believe this. If Master Eremis is reduced to claiming that he could not win a woman away from the Apt, then there is no truth in him.'

'On the contrary,' someone else returned uproariously. 'If Master Eremis is reduced to admitting that he could not win a woman away from the Apt, then he must be speaking the truth.'

'*Enough!*' barked Master Eremis. He slashed the air with his hands, demanding silence. 'I have endured *enough!*'

His shout made the walls ring fiercely. The fury in his voice and the relish in his eyes stilled the room, commanding everyone's attention.

'It is intolerable that all my service to Mordant and the Congery is met with distrust. It is *intolerable* that any of you will believe this weak boy when I am accused. Now I will prove what I say. I will ask Nyle to speak.'

The Masters stared. Geraden opened his mouth, closed it again; the color seeped out of his skin. Down inside her, Terisa's shivering suddenly got worse.

Master Quillon cocked his head reflectively. After a moment, he commented in a tone that almost sounded threatening, 'For the sake of everyone here, Master Eremis, I hope that you are sure of what he will say.'

'I am sure.' Eremis' certainty was absolute, as unshakable as his grin.

Everyone looked at Nyle.

Geraden's brother seemed unaware of what was going on. His dejected posture didn't shift: his head didn't rise. The grimace that distorted his features was as deep as despair.

Abruptly, he turned and whispered in Castellan Lebbick's ear.

Nyle returned his gaze to the floor.

No one moved. Terisa's heart pounded against the base of her throat. Geraden knotted his fists and kept his head high; his jaw jutted. Master Eremis turned a measuring gaze on Nyle, but didn't say what he was thinking. The Imagers glanced uncertainly at each other, at the Castellan, at Master Quillon.

At last, the mediator asked curiously, 'Why?'

Castellan Lebbick shrugged. 'Maybe he thinks he can persuade Geraden to confess.'

'Do you object?'

Lebbick shook his head. 'The room is guarded.' Then he added sarcastically, 'Anything Geraden has to confess is bound to be fascinating.'

Once again, Master Quillon looked as though he wanted to run and hide. Nevertheless he said, 'Then let us be seated. Nyle and Geraden may go to the end of the room.'

Master Eremis shrugged and complied. The other Masters resumed their seats.

Terisa turned to Geraden. What is Nyle going to say about you? Oh, Geraden, what's wrong?

But Geraden didn't meet her gaze. Everything in him was focused on his brother – the brother he had tried to save from committing treachery; the brother he had humiliated to the bone.

'Be careful,' Terisa breathed. She could feel disaster gathering around him. There was no way to forestall it. 'Please.'

Aching with suspense, she sat down.

Stiffly, Geraden moved to stand in front of Nyle.

When he saw Geraden's boots near his own, Nyle wrenched himself to his feet. Without releasing his grip on his cloak, he strode away to the far end of the room – as far as he could get from the Masters; the farthest point from Terisa.

There he waited for Geraden to join him.

The Masters watched without moving. Castellan Lebbick's jaws chewed indigestible thoughts; his gaze didn't shift an inch from the brothers.

They stood with Geraden's back to the room. Terisa could see Nyle's face: it was set and savage, more implacable – and more desperate – than it had been when he had ridden away to betray Orison. He looked at once homicidal and appalled, as if he were involved in a crime which made every inch of him cringe.

Whispering, he said something to Geraden.

It must have been something hurtful: Geraden reacted as though he had been struck. He flinched; he surged forward. From the back, he appeared to have taken hold of Nyle's cloak.

Between the brothers, an iron dagger dropped to the floor, clattering metallically on the stone.

It was covered with blood.

Nyle slumped against the wall. His eyes rolled shut. Then his knees bent. Geraden tried to catch him, but he collapsed on his back. His cloak fell open, exposing the red mess the knife had made of his abdomen.

Like the dagger, Geraden's hands were covered with blood.

TWENTY-SIX

FRATRICIDE

𝓮

In the stunned silence of her mind, Terisa started screaming. Fortunately, she didn't scream aloud. For a moment, no one said anything aloud. No one did anything at all. Everyone simply gaped at Geraden and Nyle.

Then Geraden made a constricted noise like a sob, and the Congery erupted.

Masters jumped out of their chairs and headed in all directions. Castellan Lebbick burst into motion, hurtling like a destructive projectile toward Geraden. Geraden cowered against the wall as if he were cornered.

Over the chaos, Terisa cried out, 'Geraden! *Run!*'

As if she had set him on fire, he flung himself at the door.

He was too late, too slow: he was in a state of shock and couldn't match the Castellan's instinct for action. But a few of the Masters were also rushing at him, perhaps wanting to capture him, perhaps hoping to help Nyle. One of them was Master Quillon.

As fast as a rabbit, he dove after Geraden – and stumbled.

He fell directly in front of Castellan Lebbick, accidentally cutting the Castellan's legs out from under him. Lebbick plunged to the stone.

Geraden reached the door and jerked it open.

'*Stop him!*' Castellan Lebbick roared at the guards outside. '*Stop Geraden!*'

The door slammed shut in time to cut off his shout.

Master Barsonage stood alone in the middle of the confusion. While Imagers shouted at each other and tried to decide which way to run, he clasped his hands together and gaped at nothing. Even his involuntary tic was paralyzed.

Still roaring, the Castellan sprang upright, heaved Masters away from him on both sides, charged the door.

Master Eremis wasn't the first to reach Nyle. Nevertheless he shoved everyone else aside, swept the bloody form up in his arms, and began dodging toward the far exit. 'A physician!' he barked although no one was listening to him. 'He must have a physician!'

Automatically, Terisa followed Master Eremis and Nyle.

Without warning, someone caught her by the arm. Forced to turn, she found herself facing Master Quillon.

His bright eyes shone; his nose twitched extravagantly. 'Come!' he demanded in a voice that seemed to pierce straight through the confusion into her heart. 'We must help him!'

At once, he started forward, hauling her into motion toward the door Master Eremis had just taken.

The two guards assigned to that door were in the room, shouting for order and answers. Master Quillon ducked past them. They made an effort to stop Terisa, then let her go: the turmoil of the Congery demanded their attention.

With his gray robe flapping against his knees, Master Quillon broke into a run.

She had no idea where he was going: she followed him simply because he had used the word *help*. But suddenly she began to recognize this part of the laborium. Down a corridor, then along an intersecting passage, Master Quillon brought her to a door small and heavy enough to be the door of a cell.

This door also was guarded.

'Quickly!' Master Quillon shouted at the men. 'Someone has been killed!' He pointed back the way he and Terisa had come. 'The Castellan needs you!'

His urgency was so convincing that both guards left their post at full speed, drawing their swords as they ran.

Immediately, Master Quillon swung the door open, ushered Terisa through it, and closed it again.

They had entered the antechamber of the network of cells that had been rebuilt for the storage and display of the Congery's mirrors.

'Will he come here?' she asked. She was panting hard.

With unintended brutality, Master Quillon replied, 'He has nowhere else to go.' Taking her arm again, he impelled her through the nearest entryway into the warren of showrooms.

But he didn't accompany her.

When he stopped, she turned back to question him.

'Go!' he snapped. 'Help him! I will gain as much time as I can. I will be believed when I say he did not come here – at least for a minute or two.'

She stared. *Help* him?

'*Go*, I say!' He gave her a push.

She stumbled, caught her balance, and fled the antechamber.

Help him? Geraden?

Nyle was dead. His belly had been cut open with a knife.

Why?

So he wouldn't speak to the Congery. So he wouldn't support Master Eremis' accusations.

Geraden!

As soon as she found the room where the mirror that had brought her to Orison was on display, she spotted him. He was trying to dodge past an entryway, trying to hide, but he wasn't quick enough to avoid her.

Master Gilbur's original glass had been destroyed by the champion, of course: this mirror was Geraden's copy. Because it was covered, she couldn't see what scene it showed.

'Geraden!' she whispered. She was afraid to shout. 'It's me. Terisa.'

After a moment, he came out of hiding to confront her.

He had become a different person. His face was iron; his eyes were steel. He spoke as if he could call up authority against her at any time.

'Have you come to persuade me to surrender?'

'No.' She could hardly force out words. Something inside her was breaking. 'He told me to help you.'

'He?'

'Master Quillon.'

'He should have come himself.'

The sound of a door echoed faintly through the rooms. Terisa heard a distant murmur of voices.

'If you are an Imager, my lady,' Geraden went on, 'you may be able to help me. Otherwise, I have no escape.'

'You know I'm not an Imager.' Oh, my love! 'What was Nyle going to say about you?'

He looked unreachable – too hard and inhuman to be touched. Yet something in her voice or her face or the way she stood must have penetrated him. His defenses cracked.

'Nothing,' he said as if he had arrived without transition on the verge of tears. 'Nothing at all. It's a trick. Something Master Eremis cooked up against me.

'Terisa, I did not kill my brother.'

She heard Castellan Lebbick clearly. 'Spread out! He's got to be in here. I want him alive.'

'I'm not an Imager!' she cried. 'I can't help you!'

In misery, she flung her arms around Geraden's neck.

He clung to her until they both heard the sound of hard boots approaching them from one of the other rooms. At once, they sprang apart.

He had become iron again.

Without hesitation, he turned to the mirror and swept off its cover.

The glass showed the bitter alien landscape where the champion and his men had failed.

'No, Geraden!' she gasped. 'You'll be lost! You'll never get back.'

He didn't heed her. 'As soon as I am translated, my lady,' he said as if she were a stranger, 'please shift the focus of the mirror. If I am visible in the Image, I will be pursued.'

He said something she didn't understand. His fingers stroked the wooden frame in parting; his hands made a gesture of farewell.

Then he stepped into the mirror and left her alone.

But he didn't appear in the Image.

She searched the scene feverishly: there was no sign of him. Once again, his glass had performed an impossible translation. It had taken him to a place it didn't show.

This time, however, no one was holding on to his foot. He had no way to come back. He was gone completely.

Castellan Lebbick came upon her so suddenly that she would have wailed if she hadn't been in such dismay.

He looked around the room, peered into the glass. Then he put his hands on her arms and ground his fingers into her weak flesh. A ferocious triumph burned in his face.

'Now you've done it, woman,' he said almost cheerfully. 'You've done something so vile that nobody is going to protect you. You've helped a murderer escape.'

She should have said something to defend herself. A denial would have cost Geraden nothing. He was beyond harm. But she only held her head up and met the Castellan's flagrant gaze as well as she could with her own distress and didn't speak.

'Now,' he said through his teeth, 'you are *mine.*'

A MAN RIDES THROUGH

'Steeped in the vacuum of her dreams,
A mirror's empty till
A man rides through it.'

– John Myers Myers, Silverlock

Book Three

TWENTY-SEVEN

THE PRINCE'S SIEGE

Early the next morning, the siege of Orison began. The huge, rectangular pile of the castle stood on slightly lower ground, surrounded by bare dirt and straggling grass – and surrounded, too, by the Alend army, with its supporting horde of servants and camp followers. From Prince Kragen's perspective, Orison looked too massive – and the ring of attackers around it too thin – for the siege to succeed. He understood sieges, however. He knew his force was strong enough to take the castle.

Nevertheless the Prince didn't risk any men. He felt the pressure of time, of course: he could almost taste High King Festten's army marching out of Cadwal against him, a sensation as disturbing as a stench borne along on the edges of the raw wind. And that army was large – the Prince knew this because he had captured a number of the Perdon's wounded men on their way to Orison and had taken the information from them. Composed half of mercenaries, half of his own troops, the High King's troops numbered at least twenty thousand. And of the Alend Monarch's men there were barely ten thousand.

So Kragen had to hurry. He needed to take Orison and fortify it before those twenty thousand Cadwals crossed the Broadwine into the Demesne. Otherwise when the High King came he would have no choice but to retreat ignominiously. Unless he was willing to lose his entire force in an effort to help Joyse keep the Congery out of Cadwal's hands. The lady Elega's plan to paralyze Orison from within had failed, and now time was not on the Alend Contender's side.

Still he didn't risk any men. He was going to need them soon enough.

Instead, he ordered his catapults into position to heave rocks at the scant curtain-wall which protected the hole in the side of the castle.

He had seen that wound from a similar vantage point the day after the Congery's mad champion had blasted his way to freedom, the day when as the Alend Monarch's ambassador he had formally departed Orison: a smoking breach with a look of death about it torn in one face of the blunt stone. The damage had been impressive then, seen against a background of cold and snow, like a fatal hurt that steamed because the corpse was still warm. The sight of it had simultaneously lifted and chilled Prince Kragen's heart, promising as it did that Orison could be taken – that a power which had once ruled Mordant and controlled the ancient conflict between Alend and Cadwal was doomed.

In some ways, however, King Joyse's seat looked more vulnerable now. The inadequacies of the curtain-wall were so simple that a child could measure them. Considering his circumstances, Castellan Lebbick had done well – quite well, in fact. But circumstantial excuses wouldn't help the wall stand against siege engines. The Prince's captain of catapults was privately taking bets as to whether the curtain-wall could survive more than one good hit.

No, the obvious question facing Prince Kragen was not whether he could break into Orison, but rather how hard the castle would defend itself. The lady Elega had failed to poison Lebbick's guards – but she *had* poisoned the reservoir, putting the badly overcrowded castle into a state of severe rationing. And as for King Joyse – He wasn't just the leader of his people: he was their hero, the man who had given them identity as well as ideals. Now he had lost his mind. Leaderless and desperate, how fiercely would the Mordants fight?

They might find it in themselves to fight very fiercely, if Joyse kept his word. He had certainly lost his mind, there was no doubt about that. Yet he had met Alend's demand for surrender with the one threat which might give heart to his followers: *King Joyse intends to unleash the full force of the Congery against you and rout you from the Earth!*

Elega didn't believe that, but the Prince lacked her confidence. If Joyse did indeed *unleash the Congery*, then what happened to Alend's army might be worse than a rout. It might be complete ruin.

So Prince Kragen held his troops back from the walls of Orison. Wearing his spiked helmet over his curly black hair, with his moustache waxed to a bold gloss that matched his eyes, and his longsword and breastplate exposed by the negligent way he wore his white fur robe, he was the image of assurance and vitality as he readied his forces, warned back the army's camp followers, discussed weights and trajectories with his captain of catapults. Nevertheless every thought in his head was hedged with doubts. He didn't intend to risk any men until he had to. He was afraid that he might soon need them all.

The terrain suited catapults. For one thing, it was clear. Except for the trees edging the roads, the ground was uncluttered: virtually all the natural brush had been cut away, and even the grass struggling to come out for the spring was having a hard time because of the chill and the lack of rain. And the roads weren't in Kragen's way: they met some distance outside Orison's gates to the northeast of the castle, and the wound in the wall faced more toward the northwest. For another, Orison's immediate setting was either level with or slightly lower than the positions of Alend's army. As Prince Kragen's military teachers and advisors had drummed into him for years, it was exceptionally difficult to aim catapults uphill. Here, however, the shot which actually presented itself to his siege engines was an easy one.

The lady Elega came to his side while the most powerful of the catapults was being loaded. His mind was preoccupied; but she had the capacity to get his attention at any time, and he greeted her with a smile that was warmer than his distracted words.

'My lady, we are about to begin.'

Clutching her robe about her, she looked hard at her home. 'What will happen, my lord Prince?' she murmured as if she didn't expect an answer. 'Will the curtain-wall hold? The Castellan is a cunning old veteran. Surely he had done his best for Orison.'

Prince Kragen studied her face while she studied the castle. Because he loved her, even admired her – and because he was reluctant to acknowledge that he didn't entirely trust a woman who had tried so hard to betray her own father – it was difficult for him to admit that she wasn't at her best under these conditions. Cold and wind took the spark out of her vivid eyes, turning them sore and puffy; stark sunlight made her look wan, bloodless, like a woman with no heart. She was only lovely when she was within doors, seen by the light of candles and intrigue. Yet her present lack of beauty only caused the Prince to love her more. He knew that she did indeed have a heart. The fingers that held her robe closed were pale and urgent. Every word she said, and every line of her stance, told him that she was mourning.

'Oh, the wall will fall,' he replied in the same distracted tone. 'We will have it down before sunset – perhaps before noon. It was raised in winter. Let Lebbick be as cunning and experienced as you wish.' Kragen didn't much like the dour Castellan. 'He has had nothing to use for mortar. If he took all the sand of the Congery – and then butchered every Imager for blood – he would still be unable to seal those stones against us.'

The lady winced slightly. 'And when it comes down?' she asked, pursuing an unspoken worry. 'What then?'

'When this blow is struck,' he said, suddenly harsh, 'there will be no turning back. Alend will be at war with Mordant. And we cannot wait for thirst and fear to do our work for us. The Perdon is all that stands between us and High King Festten. We will make the breach as large as we can. Then we will fight our way in.' A moment later, however, he took pity on her and added, 'Orison will be given every conceivable opportunity to surrender. I want no slaughter. Every man, woman, and child there will be needed against Cadwal.'

Elega looked at him, mute gratitude on her chafed and swollen face. She thought for a while, then nodded. 'Castellan Lebbick will never surrender. My father has never surrendered in his life.'

'Then they must begin here,' snapped the Prince.

He believed that. He believed that the curtain-wall couldn't hold – that apart from Imagery, Orison didn't have the resources to withstand his assault. Yet doubts he could hardly name tightened their grip on his stomach as he ordered the captain to throw the first stone.

In unison, two brawny men swung mallets against the hooks on either side of the catapult; the great arm leaped forward and slammed against its stops; a boulder as heavy as a man arced out of the cup. The throw raised a shout of anticipation from the army, but Prince Kragen watched it go grimly. The flat smack of the mallets, the groan of stress in the timbers, the thud of the stops and the protest of the wheels: he seemed to feel them in his chest, as if they were blows struck against him – as if he could tell simply by the sound that the stone was going to miss.

It did.

Not entirely, of course: Orison was too big a target for that. But the boulder hit high and to the left, away from the curtain-wall.

The impact left a scar on the face of the castle. That was trivial, however: the projectile itself shattered. The plain purple swath of the King's personal banner continued to snap and flutter, untouched, unconcerned.

Under his breath, Kragen cursed the wind, although he knew it had nothing to do with the miss. In fact, a miss was normal: a hit would have been uncommon. The captain of catapults needed a few throws to adjust his engine, get the range. Yet Prince Kragen felt an irrational pang, as if the miss were an omen.

Perhaps it was. Before the captain's men could start hauling on the tackle which pulled back the arm of the catapult, the entire besieging force heard the cry of a trumpet.

It wasn't one of the familiar fanfares, announcing messengers or defiance. It was a high, shrill wail on one note, as if the trumpeter himself didn't know what he was doing, but had simply been instructed to attract attention.

Kragen glanced at the lady Elega, implicitly asking for an explanation. She shrugged and nodded toward Orison.

From his present position, the Prince couldn't see the castle gates. They must have been opened, however, because a man on a horse came around the corner of the wall, riding in the direction of the catapult.

He was a small man – too small for his mount, Prince Kragen gauged automatically. And not accustomed to horses, judging by the precarious way he kept his seat. If he carried any weapons or armor, they were hidden under his thick mantle.

But over his shoulders, outside his mantle, he wore the yellow chasuble of a Master. The wind made the ends of the chasuble flap so that they couldn't be missed.

The Prince cocked a black eyebrow, but didn't let anything else show. Conscious that everything he said would be heard and reported throughout the army, he murmured calmly, 'Interesting. An Imager. A Master of the Congery. Do you know him, my lady?'

She waited until there was no possibility of mistake. Then she responded softly, 'Quillon, my lord Prince.' She was frowning hard. 'Why him? He has never been important, either to the Congery or to my father.'

Prince Kragen smiled toward the approaching Master. So that only Elega could hear him, he commented, 'I suspect we will learn the answer shortly.'

Master Quillon came forward, red-faced and laughable on his oversized mount. His eyes watered as if he were weeping, though there was no sorrow in his expression. His nose twitched like a rabbit's; his lips exposed his protruding teeth. But as the Master brought his horse to a halt in front of Prince Kragen and the lady Elega – as Quillon dismounted almost as if he were falling, blown out of his seat by the wind – the Alend Contender had no difficulty suppressing his mirth. Regardless of what Quillon looked like, he was an Imager. If he had a mirror with him, he might be able to do considerable damage before he was taken prisoner or killed.

'My lord Prince,' he said without preamble – without a glance at King Joyse's daughter or a bow for the Alend Monarch's son – 'I have come to warn you.'

The men around the Prince stiffened; the captain of catapults put his hand on his sword. But Prince Kragen's demeanor gave no hint of offense.

'To warn us, Master Quillon?' His tone was smooth, despite the piercing glitter of his gaze. 'That is an unexpected courtesy. I distinctly heard Castellan Lebbick threaten to "unleash the Congery" against us. Have I misunderstood your King's intent? Have I not already been warned? Or' – he held Quillon's eyes sharply – 'is your warning different in some way? Does your presence here imply that the Congery is no longer under Joyse's rule?'

'No, my lord Prince.' The Imager had such an appearance of being frightened that the assertion in his voice sounded unnatural, unexpectedly ominous. 'You rush to conclusions. That is a dangerous weakness in a leader of men. If you wish to survive this war, you must show greater care.'

'Must I?' replied the Prince, still smoothly. 'I beg your pardon. You have misled me. Your own incaution in coming to speak to me inspired my incautious speculations. If you mean merely to repeat the Castellan's threats, you could have spared yourself an uncomfortable ride.'

'I mean nothing of the kind. I came to warn you that we will destroy this catapult. If you remain near it, you may be injured – perhaps killed. King Joyse does not wish you killed. This war is not of his doing, and he has no interest in your death.'

A cold, unfamiliar tingle ran across Kragen's scalp and down the back of his neck. *We will destroy*— Like everyone else he had ever known, he was afraid of Imagers, afraid of the strange power to produce atrocities out of nothing more than glass and talent. One consequence of this was that he had distorted the shape of his siege to avoid the crossroads because he knew from Elega that the Perdon had once been attacked by Imagery there. And Quillon's manner made his words seem mad – unpredictable and therefore perilous. *King Joyse does not wish you killed.*

At the same time, Margonal's son was the Alend Contender: he occupied a position, and carried a responsibility, which no one had forced on him. In other lands, other princes might become kings whether they deserved the place or not; but the Alend Monarch's Seat in Scarab could only be earned, never inherited. And Kragen wanted that Seat, both because he trusted his father and because he trusted himself. More than anyone else who desired to rule Alend, he believed in what his father was doing. And he felt sure that none of his competitors was better qualified than himself.

So there was no fear in the way he looked at Quillon, or in the way he stood, or in the way he spoke. There was only watchfulness – and a superficial amusement which wasn't intended to fool anybody.

'What, no interest at all?' he asked easily. 'Even though I have taken his daughter from him and brought the full strength of the Alend Monarch to the gates of Orison? Forgive me if I seem skeptical, Master Quillon. Your King's concern for my life appears to be – I mean no offense – a little eccentric.' As if he were bowing, he nodded his head; but his men understood him and closed around Quillon, blocking the Imager's retreat. 'And you risk much to make me aware of his regard for me.'

Master Quillon's gaze flicked from side to side, trying to watch everything at once. 'Not so much,' he commented as if he hadn't noticed his own anxiety. 'Only my life. I prefer to live, but nothing of importance will be lost if I am killed. This catapult will still be destroyed. Every catapult which you presume to aim against us will be destroyed. As I say, King Joyse has no interest in your death. If you insist on dying, however, he will not prohibit you.

'The risk to my life is your assurance that I speak the truth.'

'Fascinating,' drawled the Prince. 'From this distance, you will destroy my siege engines? What new horror has the Congery devised, that you are now able to project destruction so far from your glass?'

The Master didn't answer that question. 'Withdraw or not, as you choose,' he said. 'Kill me or not.' The twitching of his nose was unmistakably rabbitlike. 'But do not make the error of believing that you will be permitted to enter or occupy Orison. Rather than surrender his Seat and his strength, King Joyse will allow you to be crushed between the hammer of Cadwal and the anvil of the Congery.'

The lady Elega couldn't restrain herself. 'Quillon, this is madness.' Her protest sounded at once angry and forlorn. 'You are a minor Imager, a lesser member of the Congery. You admit that your life has no importance. Yet you dare threaten the Alend Monarch and his son. How have you gained such stature, that you claim to speak with my father's voice?'

For the first time, Master Quillon looked at her. Suddenly, his face knotted, and an incongruous note of ferocity sharpened his tone. 'My lady, I have been given my stature by the King's command. I am the mediator of the Congery.' Without moving, he confronted her as if he had abruptly become taller. 'Unlike his daughter, I have not betrayed him.'

Loyal to their Prince, the Alend soldiers tensed; a number of them put their hands on their swords.

But Elega met the Master's reply squarely. She had a King's daughter's pride, as well as a King's daughter's commitment to what she was doing. 'That is unjust,' she snapped. 'He has betrayed all Mordant. You cannot be blind to the truth. You cannot—'

Deliberately, Master Quillon turned away as if she had ceased to exist for him.

Unheeded, her protest trailed into silence. In the chill spring wind she looked like she might weep.

With difficulty, Prince Kragen checked his anger. The Master's attitude infuriated him because he understood it too well. Nevertheless he resisted the impulse to have Quillon struck down. Instead, he murmured through his teeth, 'You risk more than you realize, Master Quillon. Perhaps you do not consider death to be of great importance, but I assure you that you will attach more significance to pain.'

At that, Elega's head jerked, and her gaze widened, as if she were shocked. The Prince and the Imager faced each other, however, ignoring her reaction.

Master Quillon's eyes flicked; his nose twitched. He might have been on the verge of panic. But his tone contradicted that impression. It cut fearlessly.

'Is that your answer to what you do not understand, my lord Prince? Torture? Or do you inflict pain for the simple pleasure of it? Be warned again, son of the Alend Monarch, you are being tested here, as surely as you were tested in Orison, at the hop-board table – and elsewhere. I do not advise you to prove unworthy.'

Without Prince Kragen's permission, Quillon left. He mounted his horse awkwardly, gathered up the reins. He was surrounded by Alends; yet when he pulled his mount's head toward Orison the soldiers seemed to open a path for him involuntarily, without instructions from their captain or their Prince, as if they were ruled by the Imager's peculiar dignity.

Looking slightly ridiculous – or perhaps valiant – on his big horse, he rode back the way he had come. In a short time, he rounded the corner of Orison and disappeared from sight.

Kragen chewed his lips under his moustache as he turned to the lady. *You are being tested here—* He would have asked, What was the meaning of *that?* but the darkness in her eyes stopped him.

'Elega?' he inquired softly.

Her jaw tightened as she met his gaze. '"Pain," my lord Prince?'

Her indignation made him want to shout at her. We are at *war* here, my lady. Do you believe that we can fight a *war* without hurting anyone? He restrained himself, however, because he was also a little ashamed of having threatened Master Quillon.

It was certainly true that in the old days of the constant struggle between Alend and Cadwal, no supporter or adherent of the Alend Monarch would have hesitated to twist a few screams out of any Mordant or Cadwal. And the barons of the Lieges still tended to be a bloodthirsty lot. But since his defeat at King Joyse's hands, Margonal hadn't failed to notice that his opponent was able to rule Mordant with considerable ease by winning loyalty rather than extorting it. Never a stupid man, the Alend Monarch had experimented with techniques of kingship other than those which hinged upon fear, violence, and pain, and had been pleased with the results. Even the barons were becoming easier to command.

That was one of the things Margonal had done which Prince Kragen believed in. He wanted to make more such experiments himself.

So despite the fact that he was angry and alarmed and full of doubt, he lowered his guard enough to offer Elega a piece of difficult honesty.

'I said more than I meant. The Imager affronted you, my lady. I do not like it when you are affronted.'

His explanation seemed to give her what she needed. Slowly, her expression cleared; moisture softened her gaze until it looked like a promise. 'I should not be so easily offended,' she replied. 'Surely it is obvious that anyone who still trusts my father will be unable to trust me.' Then, as if she were trying to match his candor, she added, 'Yet I thank you for your anger, my lord Prince. It is a comfort that you consider me worth defending.'

For a moment, Prince Kragen studied her, measuring his hunger for her against the exigencies of the situation. Then he bowed and turned away.

The wind seemed to be getting colder. Spring had come early – therefore it was possible that winter would return. That, the Prince thought bitterly, would be just what he and his army needed: to be encamped and paralyzed by winter outside Orison like curs outside a village, cold and hungry, and helpless to do anything except hope for table scraps. Yes, that would be perfect.

But he kept his bile to himself. To his captain of catapults, he said briskly, as if he were sure of what he was doing, 'We will heed the Imager's warning, I think. Withdraw all who are unnecessary, and prepare the rest to retreat. Then resume the attack.'

The captain saluted, began to issue orders. Men obeyed with nervous alacrity, artificially quick to demonstrate that they weren't concerned. Taking Elega with him, Prince Kragen walked in the direction of his father's tents until he had put nearly a hundred yards between himself and the catapult. There he turned to watch.

He didn't have to wait long for Master Quillon's threat to be carried out. The mediator of the Congery must have given the signal almost as soon as he entered the courtyard of the castle. Moments after the Prince began to study Orison's heavy gray profile for some hint of what was coming, he saw a brown shape as imprecise as a puff of smoke lift off the ramparts of the northwest wall.

It looked like it would dissipate like smoke; yet it held together. It looked like it was no bigger than a large dog, no more than twice the size of a buzzard; yet the way it rose seething and shifting into the sky made it seem as dangerous as a thunderbolt. A bit of brown smoke – Like nearly ten thousand other men and virtually all his army's adherents, Prince Kragen craned his neck and squinted his eyes to trace the shape's movement against the dull background of the clouds.

So high that it was almost certainly beyond arrow range, even for the iron-trussed crossbows some of the Alends carried, the brown shape sailed out toward the catapult and over it and away again, back in the direction of the castle. The Prince thought he heard a faint, thin cry, like the wail of a seabird.

And from out of the smoke as it passed overhead came plummeting a rock as big as the one which the catapult had pitched at Orison.

Powerful with the force of its fall, the rock struck the catapult and shattered the wood as easily as if the engine had been built of kindling. Splinters and bolts burst loose on all sides; chunks of timber arced away from the impact and hit the ground like rubble. Two of the men fleeing from the catapult went down, one with a ragged stave driven through his leg, the other with his skull crushed by a bit of the engine's iron. The rest were luckier.

The vague brown shape had already dropped out of sight beyond the parapets of the castle.

A shout went up from the army – anger and fear demanding an outlet, calling for blood. But Prince Kragen stood still, his face impassive, as if he had never been surprised in his life. Only the white lines of his mouth hidden under his moustache betrayed what he felt.

'My lady,' he said to Elega in a tone of grim nonchalance, 'you have lived for years in the proximity of Imagers. Surely Orison has always been full of rumors concerning the Congery. Have you ever heard of or seen such a thing before?'

She shook her head dumbly and studied the wreckage of the catapult as if she couldn't believe her eyes.

'It is possible,' he muttered for her ears alone, 'that during King Joyse's peace we have forgotten too much of the abomination of Imagery. Clearly the Masters have not been inactive under his rule.

'My lady'– he closed his eyes just for a moment and allowed himself to be appalled – 'the Congery *must not* fall into the hands of High King Festten.'

Then the Prince took command of himself again and left her. First he ordered the captain of catapults to bring forward another siege engine and try again, taking whatever precautions were necessary to protect the men. After that, he went to talk to his father.

The Alend Monarch's tents were sumptuous by his standards. Margonal liked to travel in comfort. Also he knew that upon occasion a grand public display was good for morale. Nevertheless High King Festten would have considered the Monarch's quarters a hovel. Alend lacked the seaports and hence the trade of Cadwal. Compared to Festten, Margonal was no wealthier than one of his Lieges. If Mordant hadn't lain between Cadwal and Alend – and if the Cares of Mordant hadn't been so contentious, so difficult to rule – a quality which made them an effective buffer – the High King and the forces which his wealth could procure would long since have swallowed up his ancient enemy.

Prince Kragen was conscious of this, not because he was jealous of the High King's riches, but because he felt acutely vulnerable to Cadwal, as he pushed the canvas door-flap aside and was admitted to his father's presence. He could feel Alend's peril in the cold wind that curled about his neck like a garotte.

The Alend Monarch sat in the fore-tent where he held councils and consultations. The Prince could see him well enough: braziers intended for warmth gave off a flickering illumination that danced among the tentpoles and around the meeting chairs. But there was no other light. The seams of the tent were sealed with flaps, and Margonal didn't permit lamps or torches or even candles in his presence. Privately, Prince Kragen considered this arbitrary prohibition a vestige of the tyranny to which his father had formerly been accustomed. Nevertheless he accepted it without question. As anyone who looked on the Alend Monarch's face in good light could see, Margonal was stone blind.

It was unimaginable that any vision could penetrate the white film which covered his eyes like curtains.

Obviously, his battles with King Joyse hadn't been his only losses in life. And it had been when he had begun to lose his sight that he had first started to search for surer ways to rule, safer means of preserving the kingship for himself and his successor. As he had repeated until everyone near him was sick of it, 'Loss teaches many things.' Again privately, however – and without any disrespect – Prince Kragen dropped *loss* and substituted *fear*. A man who couldn't see his enemies couldn't strike at them. For that reason, he had to find new ways to protect himself. Kragen understood his father's fear and honored it. A lesser man than Margonal would have retreated into terror and violence.

Old and no longer strong, the Alend Monarch sprawled in the most comfortable of the meeting chairs and turned his head toward the sound of his son's entrance. Because he was punctilious, he didn't speak until the Alend Contender had been announced, and had greeted him in the formal manner prescribed by custom. Then he sighed as if he were especially tired. 'Well, my son. My guards have already been here, whispering lurid reports which they were unable to explain. Perhaps you will tell me something comprehensible.'

'My lord,' Prince Kragen replied, 'I fear I can only increase the range of your incomprehension.' Succinctly, he described Master Quillon's visit and the destruction of the catapult. When he was done, he told his father what he was thinking.

'The Imager's actions were strange, unquestionably. But to my mind the great mystery is that King Joyse behaves as if he had not made himself weak – as if we were nothing more than an annoyance to a sovereign in an invulnerable position. And he is able to command men such as Castellan Lebbick and Master Quillon to preserve that illusion.

'Yet we know it *is* an illusion. Cadwal marches against him. He has a hole in his wall, few men to defend it, and no water for them to drink. Despite his control over the Congery, the Imagers who serve his enemies are more powerful. They are able to strike him at will anywhere in Mordant or Orison, passing through flat glass as if they were immune to madness. In addition, there are Masters on the Congery who would abandon his cause if they could. Men such as Eremis may be loyal to Mordant, but they are no longer committed to their King.

'His lords will not help him. The Armigite is a coward. The Termigan values nothing but his own affairs. And the Perdon resists Cadwal, not for King Joyse, but for his own survival. Of the Cares, only Domne, Tor, and Fayle are truly loyal. Yet the Domne does not fight. The Tor is old, sodden with wine – and *here*, where he is unable to muster his people. And the Fayle cannot come to Orison's aid because we stand in his way.

'And *still* King Joyse treats us as if we lack the means to harm him.'

The more he thought about it, the more unsure the Prince became. For a moment, he chewed on his moustache while his doubts chewed on him. Then he concluded, 'In truth, my lord, I cannot decide in my own mind whether his audacity constitutes raving or deep policy.'

Again, the Alend Monarch sighed. With apparent irrelevance, he murmured, 'I suffered an uncomfortable night. The loss of sight has sharpened my powers of recollection. Instead of sleeping, I saw every trick and subterfuge he has ever practiced against me. I felt every blow of our battles. Such memories would curdle the blood of a young sovereign with his eyes clear in his head. For me, they are fatal.'

Facing his son as if he could see, Margonal asked in a husky voice, 'Can you think of anything – anything at all – that a king such as Joyse might gain by feigning weakness – by allowing Imagers to bring atrocities down on the heads of his people – by permitting us to invest him when his defenses are so poor?'

'No.' Prince Kragen shook his head for his own benefit. 'It is madness. It must be madness.'

'And the lady Elega? She is his daughter. Her knowledge of him is greater than yours – greater even than mine. Can she think of anything that he might gain?'

Again, the Prince said, 'No.' He trusted her, didn't he? He believed what she believed about her father, didn't he?

Abruptly, the Alend Monarch raised his voice. 'Then he is a madman, a *madman*. He must be rooted out of his stronghold and made to pay for this. Do you hear me? It is unsufferable!'

As if he didn't know what they were doing, his fists began to beat on the arms of his chair.

'I understand his desire to take Mordant from us and rule it as his own. He was able to do it – therefore he did it. Who would not? And I understand his desire to gather all the resources of Imagery for himself. Again he was able to do it – therefore he did it. Who would not? And perhaps I understand also his restraint when he had created the Congery, his refusal to use his power for conquest. That is not what Festten would have done. It is not what *I* would have done. But perhaps in that he was saner than we.

'But *this*—! To create all he has created, and then abandon it to destruction!' Now the Alend Monarch was shouting. 'To forge such a weapon as the Congery, and then make himself vulnerable to attack, neglect responsibility, turn his back on those who serve and trust him, so that his enemies have no choice but to attempt to wrest his weapon from him for their own survival!' Margonal half rose from his seat, as if he intended to go to demand sense from King Joyse in person. 'I say it is *unsufferable*! It must not *continue!*'

As quickly as it had come up, however, his passion subsided. Sinking back, he wiped his hands across his face.

'My son,' he whispered hoarsely, 'when I received your message asking us to march, a chill went into my heart. I cannot warm it away. I *know* that man. He has beaten me too often. I fear that he has lured us here to destroy us – that his weakness is a pose to bring us and Cadwal within reach, so we can be crushed at his ease, instead of met in honest battle. You say this cannot be true. The lady Elega says it cannot be true. My own reason says it cannot be true – if only because in fifty years he has never shown any desire to crush us. And yet I fear it.

'He has witched me. We have come here to our doom.'

Prince Kragen stared at what his father was saying and tried not to shudder. Fear teaches many things, he thought. Have all the rest of us been blind? Why have we never believed that Joyse is malign? Softly, he answered, 'My lord, say the word, and we will retreat. You are the Alend Monarch. And I trust your wisdom. We will—'

'No!' Margonal's refusal sounded more like pain than anger or protest. 'No,' he repeated almost at once, in a steadier tone. 'He has witched me, I

493

say. I am certain of only one thing – I cannot make decisions where he is concerned.

'No, my son, this siege is yours. You are the Alend Contender. I have given our doom into your hands.' A moment later, he added in warning, 'If you choose retreat, be very certain that you can answer for your decision to the others who seek my Seat.'

Mutely, the Prince nodded. He had caught Margonal's chill much earlier: long before this conversation, the cold of the wind had crept into his vitals. But the Alend Monarch had named his doubt for him – and the name seemed to make the doubt more palpable, more potent. *We have come here to our doom.* When his father asked, 'What will you do?' he chewed his lip and replied, 'I do not know.'

'Choose soon.' Now Margonal spoke to him harshly, as he himself had spoken harshly to the lady Elega. 'Festten will not be patient with your uncertainty.'

In response, Kragen stiffened his spine. 'Perhaps not, my lord. Nevertheless our doom will be Cadwal's as well. Until the issue is proven, I will do my best to teach the High King better uses for his impatience.'

Slowly, the Alend Monarch relaxed until he was sprawling in his chair once again. Unexpectedly, he smiled. 'Festten, I have heard, has many sons. I have only one. I am inclined to think, however, that I have already bested him in the matter.'

Because he didn't know what else to do, Prince Kragen bowed deeply. Then he withdrew from his father's presence and went to watch a vague brown shape rise above the walls of Orison and wreck another of his best catapults.

Fortunately, his men escaped without injury this time.

His face showed nothing but confidence as he went to consult with all his captains.

TWENTY-EIGHT

A DAY OF
TROUBLE

Castellan Lebbick stood with the three Imagers on the ramparts of the northwest wall and watched as the brown shape which Adept Havelock had translated reduced the second Alend catapult to firewood and splinters. At this elevation, behind the defensive parapet built into Orison's outward face, he had a good view despite the distance.

Judging by the old scowl cut into the lines of his face, the knot of his jaw muscles, the bleak glare in his eyes, he wasn't impressed.

He ought to have been impressed. He had had no idea that this mirror existed – or that a creature with no more definition than dense smoke could be translated *and controlled*, could be made to carry rocks as heavy as a man anywhere the Adept commanded. And that wasn't all. In plain fact, he had had no idea that Havelock was still sane enough to cooperate in Orison's defense – that plans could be designed on the assumption that the Adept would carry out his part in them. In some way, the Castellan's warrior spirit probably was impressed. Unquestionably he ought to have been.

He wasn't conscious of it, however. He certainly didn't show it. The truth was that only a harsh act of will enabled him to keep his mind on what he was doing, pay any attention to the situation at all.

'Well done,' Master Quillon breathed as the airborne shape returned to Havelock's glass, gusting easily across the wind. 'You surpass yourself, indeed you do.' And he actually patted the Adept's shoulder like an old friend – which would have surprised Lebbick under other circumstances, since Havelock's lunacy had made friendship with him impossible for everyone except King Joyse. Who was himself, the Castellan thought sourly, no longer particularly sane.

'Fornication,' Adept Havelock replied negligently, as if he normally performed such feats of Imagery standing on his head. 'Piss on the slut.' In spite of his tone, however, he was concentrating so hard that his misaimed eyes bulged slightly.

'Of course,' murmured Master Eremis. 'My thought exactly.' He was the only other man near the mirror, although a number of guards and several

Apts were clustered a short distance away, watching raptly. 'Yet it occurs to me that you have been a bit too coy with your talents, Adept Havelock.'

Nominally, Eremis was here only because the Castellan wasn't done with him. Too many questions remained to be answered. Nevertheless his interest in what happened was intense: his wedge-shaped head followed everything, studied every movement; his eyes gleamed as if he were having a wonderful time. 'If the Congery had known of your resources, we might have made different decisions entirely.'

Master Quillon glanced rapidly at the taller Imager. 'Is that so? Such as?'

In response, Master Eremis smiled distinctly at the Castellan. 'We might have decided to defend Mordant ourselves, rather than waiting politely for our beloved King to fall off the precarious perch of his reason.'

Lebbick really should have replied to that jibe. Eremis intended to provoke him – and provocation was his bread and meat. It fed the fires of dedication and outrage which kept him going, sustained him so that he could continue to serve his King past the point where his own common sense rebelled and his instinct for fidelity turned against him. In addition, he had work to do where Master Eremis was concerned – issues to resolve, explanations to obtain. But this time the Master's sarcasm didn't touch him. His heart was elsewhere, and without it he wasn't able to think clearly.

His heart was in the dungeon, where he had left that woman.

Curse her, anyway, *curse* her. She was the source of all the trouble, all the harm. He was even starting to think that she was the reason for King Joyse's weakness, even though the King had been walking that path for years before her first appearance. But now Lebbick would get the truth out of her. He would tear her limbs off if necessary to get the truth out of her. He would take the soft flesh of her body in his hands—

He would do anything he wanted to her. He had permission.

Now you've done it, woman. You've done something so heinous that nobody is going to protect you. That was true. The Tor had tried – and failed. *You've helped a murderer escape.*

Now you are mine.

Even though he had been warned.

Mine.

If only he could control the way he trembled whenever he thought of her.

He answered Master Eremis for no reason at all except to mask what was happening to him, disguise the tremors in his muscles.

But he wasn't thinking about what he said. He couldn't. He was too busy remembering the way her arms felt when he ground his fingers into them.

'No,' he heard her whisper. Her protest was like the horror in her soft brown eyes, like the quivering of her delicately cleft chin. She was afraid of him, deeply afraid. His anger touched a sore place in her – he could see that vividly, even though she had stood up to him in the past, had lied to him, forced him to swallow his passion against her time and again. She feared him as if she deserved to be terrified, as if she already knew that anything he might do to her was justified. 'No,' she whispered, but it wasn't his accusations she denied; it was *him*, the Castellan himself, his violence and authority.

'Yes,' he replied through his teeth, smiling at her fiercely as if she made him happy for the last time in his life.

Holding her as hard as he wished, without regard for her pain – or for the way the Masters and guards looked at him despite the chaos of Nyle's murder and Geraden's disappearance – he escorted her to the dungeon himself.

Along the way, she babbled.

'No, you don't understand, it's a trick, Geraden didn't kill Nyle, please listen to me, *listen* to me, Eremis did this somehow, it's a *trick.*'

He liked that. He liked her fear. He wanted her prostrate in front of him. At the same time, however, her reaction disturbed him. For some reason, it reminded him of his wife.

For no good reason, obviously, since his wife hadn't been a babbler. In fact, she hadn't been afraid of anything, not since King Joyse had rescued them from the Alend garrison commander who was having her raped so imaginatively. Not since he, Lebbick, had ripped that dogshit Alend apart with his teeth.

But before that she had been afraid. Yes, he remembered her fear as well. She babbled. Yes. He heard her – watched her – was forced to watch her – and couldn't do anything about it, anything at all. He heard and saw her do every desperate and terrible thing she could think of to try to make those men stop.

Castellan Lebbick wasn't going to stop. Never. Let her babble to her heart's content, cry out, scream if she wanted to. She was *his*.

Yet it disturbed him.

When he thrust her into her cell so that she nearly sprawled on the cot against the far wall, he had no intention of stopping. But he didn't start right away. Instead, he closed the iron door behind him without bothering to lock it, folded his arms across his chest to keep them from shaking, and faced her past the light of the single lamp. Its wick needed trimming; the flame guttered wildly, making shadows dance fright over her pale features.

Still smiling through his teeth, he demanded, 'How?'

'I don't know.' Babbling. 'Somehow. To get rid of Geraden. Geraden is the only one who doesn't trust him.' Terrified. 'Eremis and Gilbur are working together. And Vagel. He lied to the Congery.' Trying to distract him. 'Eremis brought Nyle to the meeting of the Congery. He said Nyle would prove Geraden is a traitor, but that was a lie. They set this up together. They planned it.' Trying to create the illusion that she made sense. 'It's a fake. They staged it. They must have.'

Deaf to the illogic of her own defense, she insisted, 'Nyle is still alive.'

Watching her, the Castellan wanted to crow for joy. 'No, woman.' His jaws throbbed with the effort of not sinking his teeth into her. 'Tell me *how*. How did he escape? How did you help him escape?'

Finally she caught hold of herself, closed her mouth on her panic. Shadows flickered in and out of her eyes; she looked as desirable as an immolation.

'*He's* no Imager,' Lebbick went on. 'And there isn't any way he could have left those rooms except by Imagery. So *you* did it. You translated him somewhere.

'Where is he, woman? I want him.'

She stared at him. Her dismay seemed to become a kind of calm; she was less frantic simply because she was so afraid. 'You've gone crazy,' she whispered. 'You've snapped. It's been too much for you.'

'I won't hurt him.' The Castellan's face felt like it was being split apart by the stress of restraint. 'It isn't really his fault. I know that. You seduced him into it. Until you arrived, he was just another son of the Domne – too clumsy for his own good, but a decent boy. Everybody liked him, even though he couldn't do anything right. You changed that. You involved him in treachery. When I get my hands on him, I won't even punish him. I just want him to tell me the truth.'

Suddenly, like dry brush on a smoldering blaze, Lebbick yelled at her, '*Where* IS *he?*'

She flinched, cowered. Just for a second, he believed that she was going to answer. But then something inside her stiffened. She raised her head and faced him squarely.

'Go to hell.'

At that, he laughed. He couldn't help himself: he laughed as if his heart were breaking. 'You little whore,' he chortled, 'don't try to defy *me*. You aren't strong enough.'

At once, he began to speak more precisely, more formally, tapping words into her fear like coffin nails. 'I'm going to start by taking off your clothes. I might do it gently, just for fun. Women are especially vulnerable when they don't have any clothes on.

'Then I'll begin to hurt you.' He took a step toward her, but didn't release his arms from his chest. 'Just a little at first. One breast or the other. Or perhaps a few barbs across your belly. A rough piece of wood between your legs. Just to get your attention.' He wished she could see what he saw: his wife being stretched out in the dirt by those Alends, her limbs spread-eagled and staked so that she couldn't move, the delicate things the garrison commander had done to her with small knives. 'Then I'll begin to hurt you in earnest.

'You'll beg me to stop. You'll tell me everything I desire, and you'll beg me to stop. But it will be too late. Your chance will be lost. Once I begin to hurt you, I will never stop. I will never stop.'

She was so vividly appalled – the fright on her face was so stark – that the sight of it cost him his grip on himself. His arms burst out of his control; his hands caught her shoulders. Snatching her to him, he covered her mouth with his and kissed her as hard as a blow, aching to consume her with his passion before it tore him to pieces. Then he hugged her, hugged her so urgently that the muscles in his shoulders stood out like iron.

'Tell me the truth.' His voice shook, feverish with distress. 'Don't make me hurt you.'

She had her arms between them, her hands against his chest. But she didn't struggle: she surrendered to his embrace as if the resistance had been squeezed out of her. If he had released her without warning, she would have fallen.

Nevertheless when she spoke all she said was, 'Please don't do this. Please.' The way he held her muffled her words in his shoulder, but he could still hear them. 'I'll beg now, if that's what you want. Please don't do this to me.'

For a moment, the gloom in the cell grew unexpectedly darker. It rose up around the Castellan, swept over his head; it made a roaring noise like a black torrent in his ears. Then it cleared, and the back of his hand hurt. The woman was slumped on the floor; the wall barely braced her up in a sitting position. Blood oozed like midnight from the corner of her mouth. Her eyes seemed glazed, as if she were scarcely conscious.

'The lady Terisa is too polite,' someone else said. 'I will not speak so courteously. The next blow will be your last. If you strike her again, I will not rest until you are sent to the gallows.'

Staggering, Castellan Lebbick turned and saw the Tor at the entrance of the cell.

'My lord Tor—' The Castellan croaked as if he were choking. 'This isn't your concern. Crimes committed in Orison are *my* responsibility.'

The old lord was as fat as a holiday goose and as pasty-faced as poorly kneaded dough. Yet his small eyes glinted in the lamplight as if he were capable of murder. Under his fat, there was strength which enabled him to support his immense weight. 'Then,' he shot back, 'you will be especially responsible for crimes you commit yourself. What if she is innocent?'

'"*Innocent*"?'

Lebbick was ashamed to hear himself cry out the word like a man who was about to start weeping. With a savage effort, he regained control of himself.

'"Innocent"?' he repeated more steadily. 'You weren't there, my lord. You didn't see Geraden kill his brother. I caught her helping him escape – helping a *murderer* escape, my lord Tor. You have strange ideas of innocence.'

'And your ideas of guilt have cost you your *reason*, Castellan.' The Tor's outrage sounded as acute as Lebbick's own. 'You accuse her of helping a murderer *escape*, not of shedding blood herself. When I heard that you had brought her here, I could hardly believe my ears. You have no right and no *reason* to punish her until King Joyse has judged her guilt for himself and given you his consent.'

'Do you think he'll refuse me?' countered Castellan Lebbick, fighting to shore up his self-command. '*Now*, when Orison is besieged, and all his enemies are conspiring against him? My lord, you misjudge him. *This*' – he made a slapping gesture in that woman's direction – 'is one problem he'll leave to me.'

Without hesitation, the Tor snapped, 'Shall we ask him?'

The Castellan had no choice; he couldn't refuse. In spite of the way his bones ached and his guts shook, so that he seemed to be dying on his feet, he turned his back on that woman and went with the Tor to talk to King Joyse.

When Lebbick demanded an audience, the King answered in his nightshirt.

Instead of admitting the Castellan and the Tor to his presence, he opened the door of his formal rooms and stood there between the guards, blinking his watery old eyes at the lamplight as if he had become timid – as if he feared he might not be safe in his own castle in the middle of the night. He hadn't been asleep: he had come to the door too promptly for that. And he neglected or forgot to close it behind him. The Castellan saw that King Joyse already had company.

Two men sat in front of his hearth, looking over their shoulders toward the door.

Adept Havelock. Of course. And Master Quillon, the recently designated mediator of the Congery.

Master Quillon, who had *accidentally* contrived to help Geraden escape by tripping Lebbick. Master Quillon, who had *mistakenly* given that woman time to help Geraden by sending the guards away from the rooms where the mirrors were kept.

The Castellan ground curses between his teeth.

King Joyse gaped at Castellan Lebbick and then the Tor with a foolish expression on his face. His beard was tangled in all directions; his white hair jutted wildly around the rim of his tattered and lumpy nightcap – a cap, Lebbick happened to know, which Queen Madin had given him nearly twenty years ago. His hands were swollen with arthritis, and his back stooped for the same reason. The result was that he looked small and a little silly, too much reduced in physical and mental stature to be a credible ruler for his people.

And yet the Castellan loved him. Looking at him now, Lebbick found that what he missed most wasn't Joyse's former leadership – or his former trust. It was the Queen: blunt, beautiful, pragmatic Madin. She had done everything in her power to keep King Joyse from becoming so much less than he was. She wouldn't have let anybody see him in this condition.

That recognition surprised Castellan Lebbick out of the fierce speech he was primed to make. Instead of spitting his bitter demands in Joyse's face, he muttered almost gently, 'Forgive the intrusion, my lord King. Couldn't you sleep?'

'No,' King Joyse assented in a vague tone. 'I meant what I told you to tell Kragen. I want to use the Congery. But I didn't know how. It was keeping me awake. So I sent for Quillon.' As if he believed this to be the reason Castellan Lebbick had come to him, he asked distractedly, 'If you were them, what would you do tomorrow?'

Involuntarily, Lebbick exchanged a glance of incomprehension with the Tor. '"Them," my lord King? The Masters?'

'The Alends,' King Joyse explained without impatience. 'Prince Kragen. What's he going to do tomorrow?'

That question didn't require thought. 'Catapults. He'll try to break down the curtain-wall.'

King Joyse nodded. 'That's what I thought.' He seemed too sleepy to concentrate well. 'Quillon and Havelock are going to do something about it.' As an afterthought, he added, 'They'll need advice. And you need to know what they're doing. Meet Quillon at dawn.'

'Good night.' He turned back toward his rooms.

'My lord King.' It was the Tor who spoke.

The King raised his eyebrows tiredly. 'Was there something else?'

'Yes,' the Tor said sharply before Castellan Lebbick could break in. 'Yes, my lord King. Lebbick has put the lady Terisa of Morgan in the dungeon. He struck her. He means to question her with pain. And he may' – the Tor looked at Lebbick and fought to contain his anger – 'may have other intentions as well.

'He must be stopped.'

The Castellan started to protest, then caught himself. To his astonishment, King Joyse was glaring at the Tor as if the old lord had begun to stink in some way.

'What difference does it make to you, my lord Tor?' retorted the King. 'Nyle was *killed*. Maybe you didn't realize that. The son of the *Domne*, my lord Tor – the son of a *friend*.' He spoke as if he had forgotten why the old lord had come to Orison in the first place. 'Lebbick is just doing his job.'

In response, the Tor's expression turned to nausea; his mouth opened and closed stupidly. He was so appalled that a moment passed before he was able to breathe; then he said as if he were suppressing an attack of apoplexy, 'Do I understand you, my lord King?' His lips stretched tight, baring his wine-stained teeth. 'Does Castellan Lebbick have your permission to torture and rape the lady Terisa of Morgan?'

A muscle in King Joyse's cheek twitched. Suddenly, his eyes were no longer watery: they flashed blue fire. 'That's enough!' Echoes of the man he used to be rang off the walls as he articulated distinctly, 'You fat, old, useless sot, you've interfered with me enough. I'm sick of your self-righteousness. I'm sick of being judged. Castellan Lebbick has my permission to *do his job*.'

Behind his constant scowl, inside his clenched heart, Lebbick felt like cheering.

The Tor's face swelled purple; his eyes bulged. His fists came up trembling, as if he were in the throes of a seizure – as if he had finally been provoked to strike his King. When he lowered them again, the act cost him a supreme effort. As the blood left his face, his skin became waxen.

'I do not believe you. You are my King. My friend.' His voice rattled in his throat; his gaze was no longer focused on anything. 'I, too, have lost a son. I will not believe you.

'Be warned, Castellan. You will suffer for it if you believe him.'

His flesh seemed to slump on his bones as he moved away and went slowly down the stairs, carrying himself as if his years had caught up with him without warning and made him frail.

Softly, so that he wouldn't betray his jubilation, Castellan Lebbick murmured, 'My lord King.'

At once, King Joyse turned on him. The King's blue eyes continued to burn, but now they were unexpectedly rimmed with red. 'That woman must be pushed,' he rasped under his breath. 'She must be made to declare herself – or to discover herself.' Then he thrust a crooked finger into Lebbick's face and snarled, 'Be ready to answer for everything you do.'

Without allowing Lebbick time to reply, he reentered his rooms and slammed the door.

Since the guards were studiously not looking at him, Castellan Lebbick glowered at them to conceal his satisfaction. He hadn't forgotten the rest of his job: Master Quillon, Master Eremis, Nyle; the organization and defense of Orison. But those things carried no emotional weight with him now; he would deal with them simply to get them out of his way. King Joyse had given him permission. His King trusted him to discover that woman's secrets.

His King's trust was the only answer he needed. The answer for everything.

Deliberately postponing the pleasure he desired most, he didn't return to the dungeon. Instead, he went looking for Master Eremis – and Nyle's body. *Nyle is still alive.* He had time before dawn to give himself the luxury of confirming that that woman had lied.

He found the Imager in the corridor leading away from the section of Orison where all the Masters had their quarters. Eremis was striding purposefully in Lebbick's direction, and he greeted the Castellan by saying without preamble, 'Nyle is still alive.'

Castellan Lebbick halted, braced his fists on his hips, faced the Imager fiercely. Now that Eremis had his attention, he remembered why he hated the tall, lean Master so much. He hated the lively and sardonic superiority in Eremis' gaze, the combination of intelligence and ridicule in Eremis' manner. Most of all, however, he hated Eremis' success with women. Women whose faces wore an implicit sneer for the Castellan spread their legs for Eremis whenever the Master simply lifted an eyebrow at them. It probably wasn't surprising that the sluttish maid Saddith was eager for the prestige she could get from a Master. But it knotted the Castellan's guts to recollect the mute yearning he had occasionally seen in his prisoner's expression at the mere mention of Master Eremis.

Lebbick himself would have been tempted to kill any woman who acquiesced to him without being his wife.

Unfortunately, he didn't have time to hate Eremis at the moment. Too much was happening; the Master's words seemed to open an abyss under his feet. 'Alive?' he snapped. 'What're you talking about?'

'I hoped this was possible,' replied Master Eremis as if the Castellan had asked his question politely. 'That is why I rushed him to my rooms. I have never seen Geraden do anything well, so I hoped that he might find it impossible to murder his brother successfully. Apparently, his knife missed Nyle's heart.'

At once, relief reeled through Lebbick's head. That woman *was* lying. She still belonged to him. For a moment, he was so giddy that he couldn't pull his thoughts together enough to speak.

'Underwell is with him,' continued Eremis. Underwell was one of the best physicians in Orison. In fact, he was the physician Castellan Lebbick himself would have chosen to take care of Nyle. 'If he can be saved, Underwell will do it.

'In addition, I took the liberty of making a few demands on your guards.' The Master's eyes glittered with mirth or malice, as if he could read Lebbick's confusion plainly. 'If Geraden wants his brother dead badly enough, he may try again. It seems clear that he is in league with Gilbur as well as Gart – and almost certainly with the arch-Imager also. You may recall that they are apparently able to come and go in Orison as they wish. So I insisted on being obeyed by four of your men. Two of them are with Underwell and Nyle. The other two guard my door.

'Do you approve of my arrangements' – Master Eremis smiled amiably – 'good Castellan?'

With some difficulty, the Castellan imposed a bit of order on his inner riot. He *did* approve of Eremis' arrangements. They were right. No, more than that: they were so right that they made that woman's accusations against Master Eremis look ludicrous. Just for a second, he found himself wondering whether Eremis had jilted her, whether her behavior could be explained by jealousy. But speculations like that only led him back into turmoil. What he needed at the moment was to forget about her for a while.

'They'll do for now,' he replied, speaking roughly because he resented the necessity of giving Eremis even that much satisfaction. 'In the meantime, I want you to come with me. I want some answers, but I haven't got time to stand here talking.'

Master Eremis frowned, although his eyes continued smiling. With a hint of acid, he said, 'My time is valuable also, Castellan. Our brave King threatened the Alend army with the strength of the Congery, did he not? And yet we have made no plans to back up his threat. It seems likely that our new mediator will call a second meeting of the Congery before this night ends.' The Imager's tone gave nothing away. 'If he does, I must attend.'

Lebbick consulted his mental hourglass and retorted, 'I don't think so. There isn't time.' His anger matched Eremis'. 'I've been commanded to meet Quillon at dawn. You can talk to him then.

'Come on.'

He almost hoped that Eremis would refuse. The Castellan would have enjoyed having the insolent Imager tied up and dragged along behind him. On the other hand, he had too much else on his mind and wouldn't be able to give an experience like that the attention it deserved. So he waited until Master Eremis acceded; then he strode away.

His questions were the same ones which had come up during that ill-fated meeting of the Congery earlier in the evening. How did Eremis account for the fact that he was the only man in Orison who had been consistently able to know where that woman was when the High King's Monomach attacked her? And why was Gart trying to kill her anyway, if he and Geraden were plotting together and Geraden loved her? And what had the lords of the Cares and Prince Kragen said to each other when they had treacherously met at Eremis' instigation? And what was that story about an attack of Imagery on Geraden – translated insects trying to kill him? With or without Eremis' knowledge?

Of course, Master Eremis had replied to all those questions during the meeting. But Castellan Lebbick hadn't liked the answers. Taken together, they all contained one fatal flaw: they all presupposed that Geraden was a smooth and expert traitor; that he not only possessed but concealed unprecedented talents; that he had allied himself with Gart and Cadwal long before that woman's translation into Orison; that all his clumsiness, his appearance of being a confused puppy, was a sham.

Lebbick found the whole idea incredible.

He believed that Geraden had tried to kill Nyle: he had seen it with his own eyes. But Geraden secretly plotting Mordant's downfall? Artagel's brother in league with Gart? The son of the Domne seducing that woman to crimes she wouldn't otherwise have committed? Those things Castellan Lebbick didn't believe. No, the crimes and the plotting and the seduction were hers, not Geraden's.

And Eremis was a fool for blaming him. Or else the Master hadn't started to tell the truth yet.

So while he went about readying Orison to meet the dawn, Castellan Lebbick made Master Eremis go through all his explanations again, with more care, in greater detail. After a day without water, the castle was already experiencing considerable distress. Strict rationing created hundreds of hardships; dozens of people cheated – or tried to cheat – and had to be dealt with. On the other hand, the difficulties were much less now than they would be soon. Severity was Orison's only hope. Therefore Lebbick dispensed severity everywhere he went. And Eremis watched him. Answered his questions. Betrayed nothing.

Perhaps that was why Castellan Lebbick couldn't think of a good retort when Eremis goaded him about his loyalty to the King, on the ramparts of Orison after Adept Havelock had demonstrated the effectiveness of his defense against catapults. The Master had betrayed nothing. *We might have decided to defend Mordant ourselves, rather than waiting politely for our beloved King to fall off the precarious perch of his reason.* Some reply was essential: Lebbick knew that. But he couldn't seem to pull his yearning spirit this far away from the dungeon. Without paying much attention to what he said, he muttered, 'Prove it. Get me water.'

Then he didn't want to look at Eremis anymore. The tall Master's smile had become abruptly intolerable: it was too bemused, too secretly triumphant. Instead, he did his best to concentrate on what Havelock and Quillon were doing.

At first glance, the Adept seemed to be in a state of unnatural self-possession, even though the obscenities he muttered as he worked were so extravagant that they would have earned him a round of applause from any squad of the Castellan's guard. Lebbick wasn't used to seeing him do what was asked of him. The mad walleyed old goat who capered and jeered in the hall of audiences – or who incinerated important prisoners before they could be questioned – was the Havelock Lebbick knew: the man working with Master Quillon was a relative stranger. A throwback to the potent and cunning Imager who had helped King Joyse found and secure Mordant. Only the Adept's appearance seemed unchanged. He wore nothing but an ancient, unclean surcoat; what was left of his hair stuck out from his skull in wild tufts. Between the craziness of his imperfectly focused eyes and the trembling, sybaritic flesh of his lips, his nose jutted fiercely.

But a closer look showed the cost of Adept Havelock's self-possession.

He was sweating, despite the chill of the breeze. His whole body shook as if he were in the grip of a fever – as if he stood where he was and worked his Imagery by an act of will so harsh that his entire frame rebelled against it. With an unexpected pang, Lebbick noticed that there was blood running down Havelock's chin. The Adept had chewed on his lower lip until he had torn it to shreds.

For all practical purposes, he was Orison's only defense against catapults. Master Quillon had made it clear that the Congery possessed no other mirrors which could meet this particular need. Everything the Castellan had ever served or cared about depended on Havelock – and Havelock obviously wasn't going to last much longer.

'Dogswater!' Roughly, Castellan Lebbick took hold of Quillon's arm, demanded the Master's attention. 'How much longer can he keep going?'

Before Quillon could answer, the Adept swung away from his glass, cackling like a demented crone.

'Long enough! Hee-hee! Long *enough!*' Havelock brandished a mouth full of bloody teeth toward Lebbick, but neither of his eyes succeeded at aiming itself at the Castellan. His voice scaled higher, tittering on the verge of hysteria. 'They're throwing *rocks* at him, rocks rocks rocks rocks rocks! And *we're* the only friends he has left! *We're the only friends he has left!*'

Moving too quickly to be stopped, he wiped blood from his chin onto his hands and slapped them across Lebbick's cheeks, smearing red into the grizzled stubble of the Castellan's whiskers. 'And *you've* lost your *mind!*'

Suddenly wild, Castellan Lebbick knocked Havelock's arms away. He snatched at his sword, barely stopped himself from sweeping it out and gutting the Adept where he stood. Trembling as badly as Havelock, he jammed his blade back into its scabbard, then clamped his arms across his chest. 'Whelp of a slut,' he muttered through his teeth. 'You should have been locked up years ago.'

For a moment, Adept Havelock grinned blood at the Castellan. Then he turned to Master Quillon. Jerking a thumb at Lebbick, he whispered as if no one but Quillon could hear him, 'Did you ever know his wife?' Havelock stressed the word *know* suggestively. 'I did.' Without warning, he started to cackle again. 'She was a better man than he'll ever be.'

Still laughing, he returned to his mirror.

Master Eremis also was laughing; his eyes sparkled with mirth. 'Master Quillon,' he chuckled to the pained consternation in Quillon's face, 'we are well and truly fortunate that only one of the King's last friends has lost his mind.'

The Alend forces wheeled a third catapult into position. Adept Havelock, the King's Dastard, caused it to be destroyed also. After that, no more catapults were advanced against the castle for a while. Prince Kragen had apparently decided to reconsider his options.

But Castellan Lebbick didn't stay to watch. The mention of his wife made him so angry that he could barely endure it – and in any case his guards were perfectly capable of reporting whatever happened to him. While the blood dried on his cheeks, he stormed back into Orison and headed toward the dungeon, taking Master Eremis with him.

After a moment, of course, he realized that the last thing he wanted was to have the leering Imager with him when he confronted that woman again. Luckily, he was able to deflect his course before Eremis could guess where he was going. Instead of exposing his obsession, he led Eremis toward the Masters' quarters to check on Nyle.

'A good thought,' Master Eremis commented when it became clear where Lebbick was headed. 'I wish for news of Nyle's condition myself.'

'Sure you do,' rasped the Castellan. 'He's the one who was going to prove your innocence. He was going to prove his own brother is the real traitor. Isn't that what you said?'

'Indeed.' Obviously, Eremis wasn't afraid of Lebbick at all. 'You find it impossible to believe that I am concerned about him for his own sake. I understand perfectly. Considering your attitude toward me, I am gratified that you believe I wish him well for my own reasons.' The Master's sarcasm seemed to contain an undercurrent of hilarity; he sounded like he was trying to conceal his enjoyment of a good joke. 'As I said, he is my proof that I am innocent of Geraden's accusations.'

Lebbick kept on walking. When he replied, he hardly cared whether Eremis heard him or not. Primarily for his own benefit, he muttered under his breath, 'Laugh now, you goat-rutting bastard. Someday I'm going to learn the truth about you. When I do, I'll have an excuse to feed you your balls.'

He was so clenched inside himself, so obsessed with his own thoughts, that he didn't expect a retort. After Master Eremis spoke, the Castellan wasn't sure that he had heard his companion correctly.

'Try it.'

Behind his bland smile, Eremis looked as eager as an axe.

Grinding his teeth, Castellan Lebbick strode down the corridor toward the Imager's quarters.

They were reached by a short hall like a cul-de-sac, with servants' doors on either side and the main entrance at the end. Master Eremis' ostentatious rosewood door made Lebbick sneer: it was carved in a bas-relief of the Imager himself, representing clearly his sense of his own superiority. But the door itself wasn't important; it changed nothing. No, what mattered – Castellan Lebbick clung to what mattered with both fists – was that the door was properly closed, and that two reliable guards were on duty in the hall, controlling access to Master Eremis' chambers.

The guards saluted, and Lebbick demanded a report.

'Underwell and two of our men have been in there all night, Castellan,' the senior guard said. 'Nyle must still be alive, or Underwell would have come out. But we haven't heard anything.'

Master Eremis said, 'Good,' but the Castellan ignored him. Brushing past the guards, Lebbick jerked the door open.

Then for a long moment he just stood there and stared dumbly into the room, trying as if all his common sense and reason had evaporated to figure out why the guards hadn't heard anything. That much carnage should have made some noise.

Behind him, his men stifled curses. Master Eremis murmured, 'Excrement of a pig!' and began whistling thinly between his teeth.

There were three men in Eremis' sitting room, the two guards and Nyle. All three of them had been slaughtered.

Well, not *slaughtered*, exactly. Lebbick's brain struggled to function. The dead men hadn't actually been cut to pieces. The damage didn't look like it had been done with any kind of blade. No, instead of being victims of slaughter, human butchery, the men resembled carcases on which predators had gorged. Huge predators, with jaws that took hunks the size of helmets out of the chest and guts and limbs of his guards, *his guards*. The bodies lay in a slop of blood and entrails and splintered bones.

As for Nyle—

In some ways, he was in better condition; in some ways, worse. He hadn't been as thoroughly chewed on as the guards. But both his arms were gone, one at the elbow, the other at the shoulder. And his head had been bitten open to the brain: his whole face was gone. He was recognizable only by his general size and shape, and by his position on Eremis' sumptuous divan.

The Castellan started grinning. He wanted to laugh. He couldn't help himself: despair was the only joke he understood. Almost cheerfully, he said, 'You aren't going to be seducing any women here for a while, Imager. You won't be able to get all this blood out. You'll have to replace everything.'

Eremis didn't seem to hear. He was asking softly, 'Underwell? Underwell?'

Of course, there should have been *four* men here: Lebbick knew that. His two guards. Nyle. And Underwell. With a feral smile, he sent a guard to search the other rooms. He still had that much self-possession. But he was sure the physician was gone. Why would Underwell want to stay and get caught after committing treachery like this?

For some reason, the fact that what had happened should have been impossible didn't bother Lebbick.

'Castellan,' the senior guard said in a constricted voice, as if the air were being squeezed from his chest, 'nobody went in or out. I swear it.'

'Imagery.' Castellan Lebbick relished the word: it hurt so much that he seemed to enjoy it. 'They must have been hit too hard, too fast. Maybe it was that firecat. Or those round things with teeth the Perdon talked about.' The desire to at least chuckle was almost unsupportable. 'They didn't even have a chance to shout. Imagery.'

'I fear so.' Master Eremis' manner was unusually subdued, but his eyes shone like bits of glass. 'Our enemies have been able to do such things ever since the lady Terisa of Morgan was brought here.'

'And in your quarters, Imager.' Lebbick kept on grinning. 'In your care. Protected by arrangements you made.'

At that, Eremis' eyes widened; he blinked at the Castellan. 'Are you serious? Do you blame me for this?'

'It was done by Imagery. You're an Imager. They're your rooms.'

'He was alive when I left him,' Master Eremis protested. 'Ask your guards.' For the first time, Lebbick saw him look worried. 'And I have spent all the rest of my time with you.'

The Master's point was reasonable, but Castellan Lebbick ignored it. 'You're an Imager,' he repeated. As he spoke, his voice took on a slight singsong tone, as if deep inside himself he were trying to rock his hurt like a sick child. 'You think you're a good one. Do you expect me to believe "our enemies" have a flat glass that shows your rooms and you don't know about it? They made it and then never used it, never gave you any kind of hint, never did anything that might possibly have made a good Imager like you aware of what they had? Are *you* serious?'

To his astonishment, Lebbick discovered that he was almost in tears. His men had never had a chance to defend themselves, and there was nothing he could do to help them now, no way he could ever bring them back. Grinning as hard as he could, he twisted his voice down into a snarl. 'I don't like it when my men are slaughtered.'

'An admirable sentiment.' Master Eremis' face was tight; the concern in his eyes had become anger. 'It does you credit. But it has no relevance. *Our* enemies appear to have flat glass which admits them everywhere. If I knew how that trick is done, I would do it myself. But that also has no relevance. Nyle was alive when I left him. A blind man could see that I was with you when he was killed. I am not to blame for this.'

'Prove it,' retorted the Castellan as if he were recovering his good humor. 'I know you didn't do this yourself. The traitors you're in league with did it. But *you* set it up. All *you* did' – with difficulty, he resisted a tremendous impulse to hit Eremis a few times – '*all* you did was bring Nyle here so that Gart and Gilbur and the rest of your *friends* could get at him.'

He wanted to roar, *All you did was have my men slaughtered!* But the words caught in his throat, choking him.

'Castellan Lebbick, listen to me. Listen to me.' Master Eremis spoke as if he had been trying to get Lebbick's attention for some time – as if Lebbick were in the grip of delirium. 'That makes no sense.

'If you believe I am responsible for Nyle's death, then you must believe he would not have defended me from Geraden's accusations. Therefore you must believe I had no reason to take him to the meeting of the Congery. What, so that he could speak against me? I say that makes no sense.

'And if you believe I am responsible for his death, you must also believe I have the means to leave Orison whenever I wish – by the same glass which enabled Gilbur to escape. Then why do I remain? Why did I go to face Geraden before the Congery, when I could have fled his charges so easily? Why have I submitted myself to this siege? Castellan, that makes *no sense*.

'I am not a traitor. I serve Mordant and Orison. I am not to blame for Nyle's death.'

Unable to think coherently, Lebbick rasped again, 'Prove it.' He wanted to howl. Eremis' argument was too persuasive: he didn't know what was wrong with it. 'Talk doesn't mean anything. You can say whatever you want.' And yet there had to be something wrong with it. There *had* to be, because he needed that so badly. He needed to do something with his despair. 'Just prove it.'

Unfortunately, Master Eremis had recovered his confidence. The Imager's expression was again full of secrets – hidden facts or intentions which made Eremis want to laugh, restored his look of untarnished superiority.

Smiling amiably, hatefully, he remarked, 'You said that once before. Out on the battlements. Do you remember?'

The gentle suggestion that Lebbick might not remember – that he might not have that much grasp on what he was doing – infuriated him enough to restore some of his self-command. 'I remember,' he shot back, relieved to hear himself sound trenchant and familiar. 'You didn't do anything about it then, either.'

'No,' the Master agreed. 'But a possibility occurred to me. I was about to discuss it when the Adept treated us to another of his fits. That distracted me, and I forgot my thought until now.

'You mentioned water.'

Involuntarily, Castellan Lebbick froze. Water! Complex pressures seized his heart: he could hardly breathe.

'I can provide it.'

Orison was desperate for water. The lack of water hurt a lot of people. And it was Lebbick's job to supervise that hurt. Because of his duties, he was responsible, culpable, as if he caused the hurt himself.

But he would have preferred to be gutted by whores than to accept any vital help from Master Eremis.

'I have a glass,' Eremis explained, 'which shows a scene in which the rain is incessant. The Image is always in a state of torrential downpour. I can take that mirror to the reservoir and translate rain to replenish our supply of water.' He shrugged slightly. 'The process may take some time. The volume of rain that I can bring out at any given instant will be limited. But surely I can ease the need for rationing. Perhaps in a few days I can refill the reservoir.'

Deliberately, he smiled as if he knew precisely how much distress he was causing Lebbick. 'Will that prove my loyalty, good Castellan? Will that demonstrate the sincerity of my desire to serve Orison and Mordant?'

Castellan Lebbick made a rattling noise far back in his throat. Eremis' offer was so bitter to him that he was in danger of strangling on it. He couldn't refuse it, he knew that. It was just what King Joyse had always wanted from the Congery, from Imagery: the ability to heal wounds, solve problems, rectify losses without doing any injustice – real or theoretical – to the Images themselves. And it was just what Orison needed.

With enough water to keep them going, the castle's defenders might prove strong enough to repulse Alend, even if that bastard Kragen's catapults succeeded at tearing down the curtain-wall.

The offer had to be accepted. There was no way around it. The Castellan had to swallow it somehow, had to sacrifice that much more of himself for the sake of his duty. But he could not, *could* not choke down such a mortification directly. Instead of replying to Master Eremis, he turned on the senior guard so savagely that the veteran flinched.

'Pay attention,' he snapped unnecessarily. 'You were supposed to protect these people, and you did a great job of it. This is your chance to redeem yourself.

'Take this Imager to the King. Make him tell the King what happened here. Make sure he tells the King everything he just told me. Beat it out of him if you have to. Then take him to get that mirror of his. Take him up to the reservoir. Make him do what he promised.

'Use as many men as you need. He's your problem until that reservoir is full.

'Do it now.'

'Yes, Castellan.' Shock, fear, and anger made the guard zealous. Glad for something specific and physical to do, he clamped a fist around Master Eremis' arm. 'Are you coming, or do I have to drag you?'

In response, the expression on Master Eremis' face became positively blissful.

He had more strength than Lebbick suspected – and better leverage. A twist freed his arm: a nudge knocked the guard off balance: a strategically placed knee doubled the man over. With sarcastic elegance, Eremis adjusted his jet cloak, straightened his chasuble. Then, in an excessively polite tone, he commented, 'Good Castellan, I fear that your men are not trained well enough for this siege.'

Before Lebbick could find words for his fury, the Master turned to the guard. 'Shall we go? I believe the Castellan wishes me to speak to King Joyse.'

Flourishing his arms, he left the hallway.

Paralyzed by pain and consternation, the guard stayed where he was. After a moment, however, the murder in Castellan Lebbick's glare sent him hobbling after Master Eremis with his comrade.

Lebbick remained alone. He didn't look at Nyle's mutilated corpse again, or at the bodies of his men. Slowly and steadily, unconscious of what he was doing, he beat his forehead against the wall until he had regained enough self-possession to call for more guards without howling. Then he had the dead carried out and gave orders for the sealing of the rooms, in case Geraden or his allies wanted to use this way into Orison again.

Geraden wasn't just a murderer. He was a butcher, crazy with hate for his own brother, and nothing made sense anymore.

For the rest of the day, Castellan Lebbick concentrated on keeping himself busy, so that he wouldn't go down to the dungeon. Eremis' innocence seemed to weaken him in ways he couldn't explain, cut the ground out from under his rage. He was afraid that if he saw that woman now he would end up begging her to forgive him.

Keeping himself busy was easy: he had plenty of duties. While he heard reports about the state of the siege, however, while he settled disputes among Orison's overcrowded population, or discussed tactical alternatives in case Adept Havelock became ineffective against the Alend catapults, he didn't say anything about water to anyone. He didn't want to raise any hopes until Master Eremis proved himself. Nevertheless he sent men to adjust all the valves of the water system and incurred the outrage of hundreds of thirsty people by using the little water which the castle's spring had accumulated to flush any possible residue of the lady Elega's poison out of the pipes.

And when one of his men finally brought him word that Master Eremis was at work in the reservoir, he went to watch.

The Imager was doing what he had said he could do. In the high, cathedral-like vault of the reservoir, he stood on the stone lip of the empty pool and held his mirror leaning out over the edge. The glass was nearly as tall as he was, and set in an ornate frame; therefore it was heavy: even a man with his unexpected strength wouldn't be able to support its weight in that position for any length of time. He had solved the problem, however, by bringing two Apts to help him. One braced the bottom of the mirror to keep it steady; the other held the top of the mirror by means of a rope looped over one of the timbers which propped up the network of pipes and screens above the pool. The assistance of the Apts enabled Master Eremis to concentrate exclusively on his translation.

As he stroked the frame and murmured whatever invocations triggered the relationship between his talent and the glass, rain came gushing from the uneven surface of the mirror.

He was right: the process was going to take time. However torrential the rain was, the amount which could be translated through the mirror was small compared to the size of the pool and Orison's need. Nevertheless Castellan Lebbick could see that the glass gave significantly more water than the spring. If Master Eremis was able to keep going – and if the water was good.

Lebbick tested one worry by requiring the Imager to drink two cups of the rainwater himself – which Master Eremis did with no discernible hesitation. But a close look at him only increased the Castellan's other concern.

Master Eremis was sweating in the cool air of the reservoir. His breathing was deep and hard, and his features had the tight pallor of clenched knuckles. His expression was uncharacteristically simple: for once, what he was doing required him to concentrate so acutely, exert himself so fully, that he had no energy to spare for secrets.

He had been at work for only a short time, and already the strain had begun to tell on him. To keep his translation going, he would need more than unexpected strength. He would need the stamina of an iron bar.

Castellan Lebbick didn't bother to curse. He could feel something inside him failing: the Imager was beating him. This was just perfect. Eremis was going to save Orison – but that wasn't enough for him, oh, no, not enough at all. He was going to save Orison *heroically*, exhausting himself with a translation which would leave no doubt in anyone's mind about where his loyalties lay.

A curious weakness dragged at Lebbick's muscles. He had trouble keeping his back straight. His cheeks felt unnaturally stiff; when he rubbed them, dried blood came off on his fingers. Maybe Havelock was right about him. Maybe he had lost his mind. Two of his men and Nyle had been *slaughtered*, and it was his fault, not because he had trusted Eremis, whom he hated, but because he had refused to believe that bright, clumsy, likable Geraden was sick with evil. Geraden had translated atrocities to butcher his own brother. Or he had made someone else do it for him.

The Castellan wanted his wife. He wanted to hide his face against her shoulder and feel her arms around him. But she was dead, and he was never going to be comforted again.

Master Eremis wasn't cold now, but he would be chilled as soon as he stopped for rest. Mortifying himself further, Castellan Lebbick ordered a cot and food, warmer clothes, a fire on the edge of the pool, brandy. Then, when he had done everything he could think of for Orison's savior, he went back to his duties.

During the afternoon, the Alends brought up a catapult against Orison's gates – the only other part of the castle which might prove vulnerable without a prolonged assault. Master Quillon roused Havelock from a loud snooze, and the two Imagers took the Adept's mirror around to Orison's long northeast face to protect the gates. Castellan Lebbick, however, remained out of sight above the curtain-wall. When several hundred Alends rushed forward suddenly, carrying scaling ladders, the Castellan was ready for them. His archers forced them to retreat.

That success relieved some of his weakness. But it wasn't enough. Nothing was enough anymore. To keep himself from foundering, he fell back on the one distinct, comprehensible instruction he had received from his King.

To do his job.

That woman must be pushed.

After dark, when the loss of light alleviated the threat of catapults, allowing the guards to concentrate on defending Orison from simpler forms of attack, Castellan Lebbick went back to the dungeon to do what King Joyse had told him.

TWENTY-NINE

TERISA HAS VISITORS

After the Castellan hit her and left, Terisa Morgan remained against the wall for a long time, held up in a sitting position more by the blank stone than by any desire to keep herself from crumpling.

It's a trick. She told him that, didn't she? *Eremis did this somehow.* Yes, she told him. *To get rid of Geraden.* She told him all that. She even tried to beg – tried to call on the part of herself which had babbled and pleaded with her parents, her father, No, I didn't do it, it isn't my fault, I'll never do it again, *please don't do this.* Don't lock me in the closet. That's where I fade. It's dark, and it sucks me away, and I stop existing. *Nyle is still alive.*

But the Castellan didn't listen to her. He took hold of her shoulders and kissed her like a blow. Then he did hit her; she staggered against the wall and fell. It was the second time he had hit her. The first time, she had been full of audacity. She had told him that his wife would have been ashamed of him. She could almost have foreseen that he would hit her. But this time she was begging. *Please don't do this to me.* And he hit her anyway. Like her father, he didn't stop.

The third time was going to be the end of her. She felt sure of that. He had promised to hurt her, and he was going to keep his promise. *Just a little at first. One breast or the other. Or perhaps a few barbs across your belly. A rough piece of wood between your legs.* He was going to hit and hurt her until she broke.

She didn't understand why he kissed her. She didn't want to understand. *Go to hell.* All she wanted was to fade. The cell was cold, and the lamp was afflicted with a ghoulish flicker like a promise that it might go out at any moment, plunging her into blackness. When she was a child, the prospect of fading had always terrified her. It still did. But soon being locked in the closet had reminded her of the safety of the dark, had taught her again that she could fade to escape from being alone and unloved, scarcely able to breathe. If she didn't exist, she couldn't be hurt.

If she didn't exist, she couldn't be hurt.

Go to hell.

But now, when she needed it most, it was taken away from her. She couldn't fade: she had lost the trick of letting go. The Castellan was going to hurt her in a way she had never experienced before. That wasn't like the relatively passive violence of being locked in a closet. It wasn't like being left alone to save herself or go mad. It was a new kind of pain—

And Geraden—

Oh, Geraden!

She needed to fade, *had* to escape, in order to protect him, just in case he was still alive, just in case he had somehow succeeded at working another impossible translation. Fading was her only defense against the pressure to betray him. If she were gone, she wouldn't be able to tell the Castellan where he was.

And yet he was the other reason she couldn't let go. She was too afraid for him. She couldn't forget the way she had last seen him, the poignant mixture of anguish and iron in his face, the fatal authority in his voice and movements. The sweet and openhearted young man she loved wasn't gone. No. That would have been bad enough, but what had happened to him was worse. He had been melted and beaten to iron without losing any of his vulnerabilities, so that the strength or desperation which led him to cast himself into a mirror wasn't a measure of how hard he had become, but rather of how much pain he was in.

She had cried, *I'm not an Imager! I can't help you!* And he had turned away from her because he didn't have any other choice. She wasn't the answer to his need. He had flung himself into the glass and was gone, unreachable, so far beyond hope or help that he didn't even appear in the Image of the mirror. Even an Adept couldn't have brought him back.

That was how she knew where he was.

If he were still alive at all. And if the translation hadn't cost him his sanity.

She should have gone with him.

Yes. She should have gone with him. That was another reason she couldn't fade: she couldn't forget that she had already failed him. And failed herself at the same time. She loved him, didn't she? Wasn't that what she had learned in their last day together? – that he was more important to her even than Master Eremis' strange power to draw a response from her body? that she believed in him and trusted him no matter what the evidence against him was? that she cared about him too much to take any side but his in the machinations and betrayals which embroiled Mordant? Then what was she doing *here*? Why had she stood still and simply watched him risk his life and his mind, without making the slightest effort to go with him?

She should have gone.

She was blocked from escaping inside herself by her fear of the Castellan. By her fear for Geraden. And by shame.

After a while, the wall began to pain her back. Imperfectly fitted pieces of granite pressed against her spine, her shoulder blades. Cold seemed to soak into her from the floor, despite the warm riding clothes Mindlin had made for her, despite her boots. Perhaps it would be wiser if she got up and went to the cot. But she didn't have the heart to move, or the strength.

Now you are mine.

Geraden, forgive me.

'My lady.'

She couldn't see who spoke. Nevertheless his voice didn't frighten her, so after a while she was able to raise her head.

The Tor stood at the door of her cell. His voice shook as he murmured again, 'My lady.' His fat fists gripped the bars of the door as if he were the one who had been locked up – as if he were imprisoned and she were free. Dully, she noticed the lamplit tears spreading across his cheeks.

'My lady, help me.'

His appeal reached her. He was her friend, one of the few people in Orison who seemed to wish her well. He had saved her from the Castellan. More than once. Biting back a groan, she shifted onto her hands and knees. Then she got her feet under her and tottered upright.

Swaying and afraid that she might faint, she moved closer to the door. For the moment, that was the best she could do.

'My lady, you must help me.' The old lord's voice shook, not because he was urgent, but because he was fighting grief. 'King Joyse has given Lebbick permission to do anything he wants to you.'

She didn't understand. Like the Castellan's kiss, this was incomprehensible. Somehow, she found herself sitting on the floor again, hunched forward so that her graceless and untended hair hid her face. *Permission to do anything.* King Joyse had smiled at her, and his smile was wonderful, a sunrise that could have lit the dark of her life. She could have loved that smile, as she loved Geraden. But it was all a lie. *Anything he wants to you.* It was all a lie, and there was no hope left.

'Please,' the Tor breathed in supplication. 'My lady. Terisa.' He was barely able to contain his distress. 'In the name of everything you respect – everything you would find good and worthy about him, if he had not fallen so far below himself. Tell us where Geraden has gone.'

Involuntarily, her head jerked up. Her eyes were full of shadows. You, too? Nausea closed around her stomach. You've turned against him, too? She couldn't reply: there weren't any words. If she tried to say anything, she would start to cry herself. Or throw up. Not you, *too*.

'You will not hurt him, my lady.' The Tor was pleading. He was an old man and carried every pound of his weight as if it were burdensome. 'I care nothing for his guilt. If he lives, he is far from here, safe from Lebbick's outrage. We are besieged. Lebbick cannot pursue him. And no one else can use his glass. It will cost him nothing if you speak.

'But King Joyse—' The lord's throat closed convulsively. When he was able to speak again, his voice rattled in his chest like a hint of mortality. 'King Joyse has trusted the Castellan too long. And he is no longer himself. He does not understand the permission he has given. He does not know that Lebbick is mad.

'My lady, he is my friend. I have served him with my life, and with the lives of all my Care, for decades. Now he is not what he was. I acknowledge that. At one time, he was the hero of all Mordant. Now it is the best he can do to defend Orison intelligently.

'But he has only become smaller, my lady, not less good. He means well. I swear to you on my heart that he means well.

'If you defy Lebbick, the Castellan will do his worst. And when *King Joyse* understands what his permission has done to you, he will lose the little of himself that remains.

'Help me, my lady. Save him. Tell us where Geraden has gone, so that Lebbick will have no excuse to hurt you.'

Terisa couldn't focus her eyes. All she seemed to see was the light reflecting on his cheeks. He was asking her to rescue herself. After all, he was right: if she revealed where Geraden was, the Castellan would have no more excuse to harm her. And in the process King Joyse would be saved from doing something cruel. And the Tor himself – the only one of the three she cared about – might be able to stop crying.

With more strength than she knew she had, she got to her feet. 'King Joyse is your friend.' To herself, she sounded dry and unmoved, vaguely heartless. 'Geraden is mine.' Then, trying to ease the old man's distress, she murmured, 'I'm sorry.'

'"Sorry"?' His voice broke momentarily. 'Why are you sorry? You will suffer – and perhaps you will die – out of loyalty to a man who has killed his own brother, and it will do him no good. Perhaps he will never know that you have done it. You will endure the worst Lebbick can do to you and accomplish nothing.' His hands struggled with the bars. 'You have no cause to be sorry. In all Orison, you alone will pay a higher price for your loyalty than King Joyse will.

'No, my lady. The sorrow is mine.' The rattle in the Tor's chest made every word he said painful to hear. 'It is *mine*. You will meet your agony heroically, and you will either speak or hold still, as you are able. But I am left to watch my friend bring to ruin everything he loves.

'I did not come to you with this at once. Do not think that. Since King Joyse gave his orders, I have been in torment, wracking my heart for the means to persuade him, move him – to understand him. I have begged at his door. I have bullied servants and guards. Do not think that I bring my pain to you lightly.

'But I have nowhere else to turn.

'My lady, your loyalty is too expensive.

'Whatever I have done, I have done in my King's name. He is all that remains to me. I beg of you – do not let him destroy himself.'

'No.' Terisa couldn't bear the sight any longer, so she turned her back on the Tor's dismay. 'Geraden is innocent. Eremis set this all up.' She spoke as if she were reciting a litany, fitting pieces of faith together in an effort to build conviction. 'He faked Nyle's death to make Geraden look bad, because he knew Nyle was never going to support his accusations against Geraden. If the King lets me be hurt' – a moment of dizziness swirled through her, and she nearly fell – 'he's going to have to live with the consequences. Geraden is innocent.'

'No, my lady,' the Tor repeated; but now she heard something new in his voice – a different kind of distress, almost a note of horror. 'In this you are wrong. I care nothing for Geraden's guilt. I have said that. Only the King matters to me. But you have placed your trust in someone evil.'

She stood still, her pulse loud in her ears and doubt gathering in her gut.

'Nyle is unquestionably dead.' The lord sounded as sick as she felt. 'I have seen his body myself.'

Unquestionably dead. That made her move. Groping, she found her way to the cot. It smelled of stale straw and old damp, but she sat down on it gratefully. Then she closed her eyes. She had to have a little rest. In a minute or two, when her heart had stopped quaking, she would answer the Tor. Surely she would be able to think of an answer? Surely Geraden *was* innocent?

But a moment later the thought that Nyle really had been murdered cut through her, and everything inside her seemed to spill away. Unconscious of what she was doing, she stretched out on the cot and covered her face with her hands.

Eventually, the Tor gave up and left, but she didn't hear him go.

At noon, the guards brought her a meal – hard bread and some watery stew. She panicked at their approach because she thought they might be the Castellan; her relief when she saw who they were left her too weak to get off the cot.

In fact, she felt too weak to eat at all, to take care of herself in any way. As soon as Castellan Lebbick spoke to her, she would tell him anything he wanted. But that wouldn't stop him. She could see his face in her mind, and she knew the truth. He didn't want to stop. Now that he had King Joyse's permission, nothing would stop him.

Where were the people who had shown her courtesy or kindness, the people who might be supposed to have some interest in her? Elega had gone with Prince Kragen. Myste had left Orison on a crazy quest to help the Congery's lost and rampaging champion. Adept Havelock was mad. Master Quillon had become mediator of the Congery because that was what King Joyse wanted – and King Joyse had given the Castellan permission to do whatever he wished to her. Saddith? She was only a maid, in spite of her ambitions. Maybe she *had* inadvertently betrayed Terisa to Eremis. That didn't mean there was anything she could do to correct the situation. Ribuld, the coarse veteran who had fought for Terisa more than once? He was only a guard – not even a captain.

She couldn't lift the whole weight of Mordant's need by herself. She was hardly able to lift her head off the lumpy pallet which served as her mattress. The Tor had seen Nyle's body. Geraden's brother was *unquestionably dead.*

Why should she bother to eat? What was the point?

Maybe if she got hungry enough, she would regain the ability to let go of her own existence.

She tried to sleep – tried to relax so that the tension and reality would flow out of her muscles – but another set of boots stumbled toward her down the corridor. Just one: someone was coming in her direction alone. A slow, limping stride, hesitant or frail. Deliberately, she closed her eyes again. She didn't want to know who it was. She didn't want to be distracted.

For the first time, he called her by her name.

'Terisa.'

It wasn't a good omen.

Startled, she raised her head and saw Geraden's brother at the door of her cell.

'Artagel?'

He wore a nightshirt and breeches – clothes which seemed to increase his family resemblance to Geraden and Nyle because they weren't right for a swordsman. His dress and his way of standing as if someone had just stuck a knife in his side made it clear that he was still supposed to be in bed. He had been too weak yesterday – was it really only yesterday? – to support Geraden in front of the Congery. Obviously, he was too weak to walk around in the dungeon alone today.

Yet he was here.

It was definitely not a good omen that he had called her *Terisa*.

Forgetting her own lack of strength, she swung her legs off the cot and went toward him. 'Oh, Artagel, I'm so glad to see you, I'm in so much trouble, I need you, I need a friend, Artagel, they think Geraden killed Nyle, they—'

His pallor stopped her. The sweat of strain on his forehead and the tremor of pain in his mouth stopped her. His eyes were glazed, as if he were about to lose consciousness. Gart, the High King's Monomach, had wounded him severely, and he drove himself into relapses by struggling out of bed when he should have been resting. The fact that Gart had beaten him; Nyle's treasonous alliance with Prince Kragen and the lady Elega; the accusations against Geraden: things like that tormented the Domne's most famous son, goading him to fight his weakness – and his recovery.

'Artagel,' she groaned, 'you shouldn't be here. You should be in bed. You're making yourself sick again.'

'*No.*' The word came out like a gurgle. With one arm, he clamped his other hand against his side. 'No.' Because he was too sick to remain standing without help, he leaned on the door, pressing his forehead against the bars. The dullness in his eyes made him look like he was going blind. 'This is your doing.'

She halted: pain went through her like a burn. 'Artagel?' There were, after all, more kinds of pain in the world than she would ever have guessed. Except for Geraden, Artagel was the best friend she had. She would have trusted him without question. 'You don't mean that.' He thought *she* was responsible? 'You can't.'

'I didn't mean to say it.' He was having trouble with his respiration. His breath seemed to struggle past an obstruction in his chest. 'That isn't why I'm here. Lebbick is going to take care of you. I just want to know where Geraden is.

'I'm going to hunt him down and cut his heart out.'

Suddenly, she was filled with a desire to wail or weep. It would have done her good to cry out. But this was too important. Somehow, she kept her cry down. Panting because the cell was too small and if she didn't get more air soon she was going to fail, she protested, 'No. Eremis did this. It's a trick. I tell you, it's a *trick*. The Tor says he's seen the body and Nyle is really dead, but I don't believe it. Geraden didn't have anything to do with this.'

'Ah!' Artagel gasped as if he were hurt and furious. 'Don't lie to me. Don't lie to me anymore.' Now his eyes were clear and hot, bright with passion or fever. 'I've seen the body myself.'

And while she reeled inside herself he continued, 'After Geraden stabbed him, he was still alive. That much is true. Eremis rushed him to his own rooms and got a physician for him. That was his only chance to stay alive. Eremis got him that chance. Then Eremis put guards on him – inside the room and outside the door. In case Geraden tried again.

'It didn't work.' Artagel's forehead seemed to bulge between the bars; he might have been trying to break his skull. 'Lebbick found them. The guards were killed. Some kind of beast fed off them. Geraden must have translated something into the room – something they couldn't fight.

'Nyle was killed. It chewed his face off.'

Just for a second, that image struck her so horribly that she quailed. Oh, Nyle! Oh, my God. Visceral revulsion churned inside her, and her hands leaped to cover her mouth. Geraden, no!

She should have gone with him. To prevent all this.

But then she saw iron and anguish, and Geraden came back to her. She knew him. And she loved him. *Terisa, I did not kill my brother.* Without warning, she was angry. Years of outrage which she had stored away in the secret places of her heart abruptly sprang out, touching her with fire.

'Say that again,' she breathed, panted. 'Go on. Say it.'

Artagel was beyond the reach of surprise. Baring his teeth in a snarl, he repeated, 'Nyle was killed. The beast chewed his face off.'

'And you believe *Geraden* did that?' She lashed her protest at him. 'Are you out of your mind? Has everybody in this whole place gone crazy?'

He blinked dumbly; for one brief moment, he seemed to regard her in a different light. Almost at once, however, his own horror returned. His legs were failing. Slowly, he began to slip down the bars.

'I saw his body. I held it. I've still got his blood on my clothes.'

That was true. Her lamp was bright enough to reveal the dried stains on his nightshirt.

'I don't care.' She was too angry to imagine what the experience had been like for him – to hold his own brother's outraged corpse in his arms and have no way to bring the body back to life. 'Geraden is your brother. You've known him all his life. You know him better than that.'

Artagel continued slipping. His side hurt too much: apparently, he couldn't use his hands. She reached through the bars and grabbed his nightshirt to support him somehow; but he was too heavy for her. Finally he bent his legs and caught his weight on his knees. 'I tell you I've seen his body.'

He pulled her down with him until she was on her knees as well. Raging into his face, she gasped, 'I don't care. *Geraden* didn't do it.'

'And I tell you I've seen his body.' In spite of weakness and fever, Artagel met her with the unflinching passion which had twice led him to hurl himself against the High King's Monomach. 'You deny it, but it isn't going to go away. An Imager did it. Translation is the only way a beast could get into that room and out again. But it wasn't Eremis. He was with Lebbick the whole time.

'Right now, he's up in the reservoir translating a new water supply. He's the only reason we've got any hope at all. I took Geraden's side against him' – Artagel's voice seemed to be thick with blood – 'and I was wrong. He's *saving* us.

'Geraden killed Nyle. I'm going to track him down whether you tell me where he is or not. The only difference it's going to make is time.'

'And then you're going to cut his heart out.' Terisa couldn't bear any more. He made her want to shriek. With an effort of will, she let go of his shirt, drew back from him. 'Get out of here,' she muttered. 'I don't want to hear this.' The image of what had happened to Nyle sucked at her concentration. She thrust it away with both hands. 'Just get out of here.'

Then the sight of him – fierce and in pain on his knees against her bars – touched her, and she relented a little. 'You really ought to be in bed. You aren't going to be hunting anybody for a while. If the Castellan doesn't tear it out of me – and if he lets me live – I promise I'll tell you everything I can when you're well enough to do something about it.'

He didn't raise his head for a long time. When he finally looked up, the light had gone out of his gaze.

Tortuously, like an old man whose joints had begun to betray him, he pulled himself up the bars, regained his feet. 'I always trusted him,' he murmured as if he were alone, deaf and blind to her presence. 'More than Nyle or any of the others. He was so clumsy and decent. And smarter than I am. I can't figure it out.

'You came along, and I thought that was good because it gave him something to fight for. It gave him a reason to stop letting those Masters humiliate him. So then he kills Nyle, kills' – Artagel shuddered, his eyes focused on nothing – 'and you're the only explanation I can think of, you must be evil in some terrible way I don't understand, but you want me to go on trusting him. I can't figure it out.

'I saw his body.' Like an old man, he turned from the door and began shuffling down the corridor. 'I picked it up and held it.' Brushing at the dried stains on his nightshirt, he passed beyond Terisa's range of vision. His boots scuffed along the floor until she couldn't hear them anymore.

She stood rigidly and watched the empty passage for a while, as erect as a witness testifying to what she believed. Like the Tor, he said that Nyle was dead. And he could hardly be wrong. He ought to be able to identify his own brother's body. And yet she didn't recant. Unexpectedly, she found that she was supported by a lifetime's anger. A childhood of punishment and neglect had taught her many things – and she was only now starting to realize what some of those things were.

Her hands shook. She steadied them as well as she could and began to eat the bread and stew she had been brought, pacing back and forth across the cell as she ate. She needed strength, needed to pull all her resources together. King Joyse had told her to think, to *reason*. Now more than at any other time in her life, she needed the stamina and determination to think clearly.

To the extent that it was possible for anyone to do so, she intended to defy the Castellan.

When he came at last – several hours and another meal later – she was almost glad to see him. Waiting was no doubt much easier to bear than rape or torture, but it was harder than defiance. Solitude eroded courage. Half a dozen times during those hours, she quailed, and her resolution ran out of her. Once she panicked so badly that afterward she found herself on the floor in the corner with her knees hugged against her chest and no idea how she got there.

But she was brought back from failure of nerve by the fact that she knew how to survive waiting alone in a cold, ill-lit cell. She had recovered her ability to blank out the dark and the fear. Paradoxically, the decision to meet her danger head-on restored her capacity for escape. And when she surrendered to fading, she rediscovered the safety hidden in it and felt better.

For this she didn't need a mirror. Mirrors helped her fight the erosion of her existence; they weren't necessary if she wanted to let go. And it was letting go, not desperate clinging, which had kept her sane when her parents had locked her in the closet.

Nevertheless the time and the waiting, the cold and the inadequate food exacted their toll. There were limits to how far she could stretch her determination. She was almost glad to see him when the stamp of boots announced his coming and Castellan Lebbick appeared past the stone edge of her cell.

Now he would hurt her as much as he could. And she would find out what she was good for.

But the sight of him shocked her: it wasn't what she had expected. She was braced for rage and violence, for the intensity like hate in his glare and his knotted jaws, for the potential murder tightly coiled in all his muscles. She wasn't ready for the distracted man, noticeably shorter than she was, who entered her cell with no swagger in his shoulders and no authority on his face.

The Castellan looked like someone who had suffered an essential defeat.

Dully, he let himself into the cell. Again, he didn't bother to lock the door behind him. He was enough of a bar to her escape. And if she got past him and out of her cell, where could she go? She could run the corridors like a trapped rat, but she couldn't get out of the dungeon without passing through the guardroom. Castellan Lebbick didn't need to lock the door.

For a moment, he didn't meet her gaze; he glanced around the cell, glanced up and down her body without quite looking at her face. Then he murmured as if he were speaking primarily to himself, 'You're better. The last time I saw you, you were about to fall apart. Now you look like you want to fight.' Without sarcasm, he commented, 'I had no idea being thrown in the dungeon was going to be good for you.'

Terisa shrugged, studying him hard. 'I've had time to think.'

At last, he raised his eyes to hers. The smolder she was accustomed to seeing in them had been extinguished – or tamped down, at any rate. He seemed almost calm, almost stable – almost lost. 'Does that mean,' he asked quietly, 'you're going to tell me where he is?'

She shook her head.

In the same tone, the Castellan continued, 'Are you going to tell me what you've been plotting? Are you going to tell me why he did it?'

Once more, she shook her head. For some reason, her throat had gone dry. Lebbick's uncharacteristic demeanor began to frighten her.

'That doesn't surprise me.' He seemed to have no sarcasm left. Turning away, he started to walk back and forth in front of the bars. His manner was almost casual; he might have been out for a stroll. 'King Joyse told me to push you. He wants you to declare yourself. Does that surprise you?' The question was rhetorical. 'It should. It isn't like him. He was always able to get what he wanted without beating up women.

'I've been looking forward to it all day.

'But now—' He spread his hands in a way that almost gave the impression he was asking her for help. 'Everything is inside out. Clumsy, decent, *loyal* Geraden has turned rotten. Crazy Adept Havelock spent most of the day protecting us from catapults. Master Eremis is busy refilling the reservoir.' Apparently, he didn't know that she had been visited by both the Tor and Artagel, that she was already aware of the things he told her. 'And King Joyse wants me to hurt you. He wants me to find out who you are – what you are.'

A suggestion of yearning came into Lebbick's voice, a hint of wistfulness. 'Sometimes – a long time ago – he used to let me get even with his enemies. Sometimes, Men like that garrison commander— But he's never given me permission to hurt someone like you.'

Then the Castellan faced her – and still he seemed almost casual, almost lost. 'He must be afraid of you. He must be more afraid of you than he's ever been of Margonal or Festten or Gart or even Vagel.

'Why is that? What are you?'

Meeting his extinguished, unreadable gaze, Terisa swallowed roughly. She didn't understand what had happened to him, what had taken the fire out of him or stifled his hate; but this was the best chance she would ever get to distract him, deflect his intentions against her.

'I don't know,' she said as steadily as she could. 'You're asking the wrong questions.'

'The wrong questions?'

'I can't tell you why King Joyse is afraid of me. *If* he's afraid of me. And I won't tell you where Geraden is. Because he didn't do it. I'm not going to give him away.

'But I'll tell you anything else.'

'Anything else?' Castellan Lebbick sounded no more than mildly interested in the idea. 'Like what?'

His manner gave her a moment of panic. She was afraid that he had become unreachable – that whatever was happening to him had taken him beyond the point where anybody could talk to him, argue with him, guess what he would do next. Breathing deeply to shore up her courage, she replied, 'Like how did I survive when Gart tried to kill me the first night I was here. Like what was I using that secret passage in my rooms for. Like what really happened the night Eremis had his meeting with the lords and Prince Kragen. Like what happened the first time Geraden was attacked.' Her own passion mounted against the Castellan's blankness. 'Like how I can be sure Eremis is lying.'

At that, something like a spark showed in Lebbick's eyes. His posture didn't shift, but his whole body seemed to become unnaturally still. 'Tell me.'

'It all fits together,' she answered. King Joyse had told her to *reason*, and *reason* was the only weapon she had. 'I can even tell you why they're afraid of Geraden – Vagel and Eremis and Gilbur – why they're trying so hard to get him out of their way.'

Lebbick didn't blink. 'Tell me,' he repeated.

So she told him. As clearly as she could, she told him how Adept Havelock had saved her from the High King's Monomach. She described how Havelock and Master Quillon had used the passage hidden behind her wardrobe. She related every detail she could remember about Eremis' clandestine meeting with the lords of the Cares, including Artagel's role in saving her. And then she told the Castellan what conclusions she drew.

'The first time Gart tried to kill me, he obviously didn't know about that secret passage. The last time, he did. How did he find out? You knew it was there. Myste and Elega knew.' Lebbick didn't react to this revelation. 'Quillon and Havelock, of course. Geraden knew. And Saddith, my maid. But Myste and Elega and Havelock and Quillon all knew about it long before I came here. They could have told Gart that first night. Forget them. What about Geraden? He didn't know when I first moved into those rooms. You think he's in with Gart. Well, I told him about it the next morning. After I talked to you. Why did he wait all that time before letting Gart know the best way to kill me?

'On the other hand' – she was determined to hold back nothing that might help her – 'Saddith and Eremis are lovers. She could have told him about the passage – and she could have taken a long time to do it.

'She could have told him where I was that first night.'

'I know all that,' the Castellan murmured without inflection. 'Tell me something I don't know. Tell me why Eremis rescued you. Gart came through the passage, and Eremis could have gotten rid of you both at the same time. How do you explain that?'

Because she was only guessing, Terisa did her best to sound plausible. 'There were witnesses. If Gart just killed me, Geraden would see that Eremis let it happen. And if Gart tried to get both of us, the guards outside might catch him at it. All they had to do was open the door. Either way, everyone would know Eremis is a traitor.

'What he thought he was going to do' – she forced herself to say this also – 'was make love to me. And then while I was asleep or distracted Gart would sneak in and kill me. And no one would ever know Eremis had been there.

'He wasn't expecting Geraden to interrupt.'

Still the Castellan didn't show what he was thinking. All he said was, 'Go on.'

Grimly, Terisa continued.

'Eremis controlled every detail of that meeting with the lords. He arranged the location, the time, who was going to be there. He arranged where I would be afterward. Geraden couldn't have known any of his plans. The only thing Eremis didn't arrange was Artagel. He didn't arrange for me to be saved.

'When Gart attacked, he obviously came and went through a mirror. I don't know how he did that without losing his mind – but Artagel and I figured out where the point of translation was, the place in the Image. He and Geraden and I went to look at the place again, and the same mirror translated those insects. Artagel told you about that. They almost killed all three of us.

'Eremis says it was a feint, a trick to make Geraden look innocent, but that's nonsense. If Havelock hadn't rescued him, he would have died. And no one could have predicted that the Adept would show up there to help us. And Eremis knows all about it, even though he wasn't there and no one told him. He says I did, but I didn't. He must have been on the other side of the glass, watching.'

Lebbick had begun to scowl. His eyes gave out glints of dark fire. For better or worse, Terisa was bringing the banked heat in him to flame. If that was a mistake, she was sealing her own doom. Nevertheless she kept going.

'They want Geraden dead or ruined because he really is an Imager – a kind of Imager no one has ever seen before.'

Obliquely, it occurred to her that she should have grasped this before. But she hadn't forced herself to think until now. And because of that Geraden was paying a fearful price. At the moment, however, she had no time for regret. She was too busy defending herself from the Castellan.

'That's why he isn't able to recognize what he is for himself. He can do translations that don't have anything to do with the Image in his mirror. He got me out of a glass that showed the champion the Congery wanted. And Eremis knew that was going to happen. Or Gilbur did, anyway. He taught Geraden how to make that mirror. He must have seen Geraden wasn't making it right. When the mirror was made wrong and it still showed the Image with the champion, Gilbur must have realized what Geraden can do.

'If he ever figures out what his power is or how to use it, he'll be the strongest Master there ever was. And he's loyal to King Joyse. Even though it's breaking his heart. Gilbur and Vagel and Eremis have to get rid of him before he learns how to fight them.

'That's why they attacked him with insects, tried to kill him. And that's why they set him up to look like he killed Nyle. They're afraid of him. And he's trying to expose them. They need to get rid of him in a way that makes them look innocent.

'Nyle isn't really dead. He can't be. Eremis couldn't have used him like that without his cooperation – and he wouldn't have cooperated if he thought he was going to be killed.'

Distinctly, the Castellan said, 'Pigshit.' The muscles bunched along his jaw; his eyes glared balefully. 'My men are dead, and I saw his body. His entire face was eaten through to the brain.' She had succeeded at restoring his outrage. 'Eremis is at the reservoir right now *saving us*. He's the hero of Orison. No one will believe a word you say.' His raised his fists in front of her face, hammered them at the unresisting air. 'That whoreson physician betrayed us, and *two of my men are dead!*'

Now it was her turn to stare at him, stunned with surprise. 'Physician?' Artagel hadn't mentioned a physician.

'*Underwell*, you bitch! The best physician in Orison. Eremis did everything perfectly. He got Nyle to his rooms fast. He got Underwell. He set guards.

While you were out helping Geraden escape and that pisspot Quillon was getting in my way, Eremis was actually trying to *save Nyle*.'

She should have been afraid of his new rage, but she wasn't. 'Physician?' Instead, she was astonished by the sudden clarity of her thoughts. 'What happened to him? Didn't he see what attacked your men and Nyle?'

'*Escaped!*' snarled Lebbick. 'What do you think? Did you expect him to wait around and let us catch him?' Rage swelled the cords of his neck. 'He was translated away the same way Geraden's bloody creature was translated in.'

'But why?'

'How should *I* know? I've never looked inside his head. Maybe he just hated Nyle. Maybe Festten offered to make him rich. Maybe Gart took his relatives hostage. I don't know and I don't care. As far as I'm concerned, he just *did* it.'

'No,' Terisa said as if now she had nothing to fear. 'That isn't what I meant. Why did he do it that way? Why have the guards killed? Why—?' Why do that horrible thing to Nyle? 'They might have been interrupted. They might have been caught. What about the noise? Wouldn't being attacked by some kind of beast make noise – warn the guards outside? Why take the chance?'

Fuming, the Castellan started to spit an explanation at her. But she didn't want to hear him say anything more against Geraden. She ignored him.

'He's a physician,' she said. '"The best physician in Orison." He didn't need any help getting rid of Nyle. And he didn't need to make himself look like a traitor. Don't you understand?' Lebbick's slowness to grasp the implications surprised her almost as much as her own certainty. 'All he had to do was *fail*. Let Nyle die. Put something toxic in the wound and cover it with bandages. No one would ever know. No one would even suspect.

'Why take the stupid, *stupid* risk of all that bloodshed?'

Castellan Lebbick stared at her as if she were growing noxious in front of him. 'So maybe he didn't do it.'

'Then where is he?' shot back Terisa.

'He wouldn't let them kill Nyle without trying to stop them – without trying to get help.' Lebbick was making a visible effort to understand her. 'Maybe they killed him, too, and took the body with them.'

'Why?' she repeated. 'Why bother? To create the illusion they had a confederate they didn't need? To make you think Underwell is guilty when he really isn't? What does that accomplish? What would be the point?'

'*Right!*' The Castellan clenched his fury in both fists. '*What would be the point?*'

And still she wasn't afraid. *His entire face was eaten* – Calmly, she asked, 'What did Underwell look like?'

Lebbick made a strangling noise. '"Look like"?'

'Compared to Nyle,' she explained. 'Were they about the same height? The same weight? About the same coloring?'

'NO!' the Castellan yelled as if she had gone too far, as if this time she had finally pushed him past the point where he could hold back his hands. And then, an instant later, what she was getting at hit him, and he stopped.

525

In a thin voice, he said, 'Yes. About the same.'

Quietly, as if she didn't mean anything personal, she pursued her argument. 'If you put Underwell in Nyle's clothes, would you still be able to recognize him? If you gave him wounds to match the ones Nyle was supposed to have – and if you disfigured him – and if you covered the rest of him with blood – would you still be able to recognize him?'

Castellan Lebbick stared at her with apoplexy on his face.

'I think Nyle is alive,' she finished, not because she thought the Castellan still didn't understand her, but simply because she had to say something to control the silence, keep him from exploding. 'I think the poor man who got butchered was Underwell.'

With an effort, Lebbick pulled a breath between his teeth. 'All that,' he chewed out distinctly, 'you think all that, and you haven't set foot outside this cell. Sheep-rut! How do you do it? What do you use for reasons? What do you use for proof?'

Now that she had arrived at her conclusion, she lost her invulnerability. He was beginning to scare her again. 'I've already explained it.' She was determined not to let her voice shake. 'Eremis wants to shift the blame onto Geraden. Partly to get him out of the way, so he can't understand his talent and start using it. And partly because Eremis isn't ready to betray you yet. Maybe his plans aren't finished. If he sprang his trap now, Prince Kragen would get Orison. Alend would get the Congery. Isn't that right? But Eremis is in with Gart – with High King Festten and Cadwal. He wants to keep us all safe until Cadwal gets here – until Alend is out of the way.

'If Geraden is working with Gart – if he really does serve Cadwal – he wouldn't have done any of this. He wouldn't have risked accusing Eremis, he wouldn't have done anything to undermine Orison. Until Cadwal got here. He wouldn't have ruined his own position by killing his brother.'

She would have gone on, trying to build a wall of words between herself and the Castellan, but he cut her off. 'That's enough!' he snapped fiercely. 'It's just talk. It isn't a reason. It isn't *proof.* You've been in this cell all day. What makes you think you know what's going on? You say he's doing everything because he's guilty – but he would do exactly the same things if he was innocent. I want *proof.* If you expect me to go arrest the "hero of Orison," you'll have to give me *proof.'*

Just for a second, Terisa nearly failed. Proof. Her mind went dark; a lid closed over her courage. What kind of proof *was* there, in a world like this? If Underwell had been stretched out naked in front of her, she wouldn't have been able to tell the difference between him and Nyle. She didn't know men. Only the crudest physical characteristics would have enabled her to distinguish between him and, say, Eremis. Or Barsonage.

Then, abruptly, the answer came to her. In sudden, giddy relief, she said, 'Ask Artagel.'

'Artagel?' demanded the Castellan suspiciously. '*Geraden's* brother?'

'And Nyle's,' she countered. 'Make him look at the body. Take the clothes off and make him look. He ought to be able to recognize his own brother's body.'

Lebbick glared at that idea as if he found it offensive. Under one eye, a muscle twitched, giving his gaze a manic cast. She had gone too far, said something wrong, accidentally convinced him her arguments were false. He was going to do what he had come for in the first place. He was going to hurt her.

He didn't. He said, 'All right. I'll try that.

'It's too bad Underwell doesn't have any family here. It would be better to look at this from both sides. But I'll try Artagel.'

Terisa felt faint. She wanted to sit down. The Castellan's scowl was still fixed on her, however. He made no move to leave. After a moment, he said, 'While I'm gone, remember something. Even if that *is* Underwell's corpse, it doesn't prove Nyle is alive. It doesn't prove anything about Geraden or Eremis. All it proves is that some shit-lover is still plotting something. If you want me to arrest the whore-bait "hero of Orison," don't show me Underwell is dead. Show me Nyle is alive.'

Then he left. The cell door banged; the key scraped in the lock; hard bootheels echoed away on the stone of the passage.

Terisa sat down on the cot, leaned her back against the wall, and let herself evaporate for a while.

THIRTY

ODD CHOICES

The bars of the cell were of old, rough iron, crudely forged and cast. Little marks of rust pitted the metal like smallpox; it looked ancient and corrupt. Nevertheless the bars were still intact, despite their age. Against the gnawing of rust, which the rude workmanship and the damp atmosphere aggravated, the iron was defended by generations of human oil and fear. Since the dungeons were first constructed, dozens or hundreds of men and women and perhaps children had stood in this cell, holding the bars because they didn't have anything else to do with their need. And now the ooze of sweat and dirt left behind by their knotted, aching, condemned hands protected the metal from its accumulated years. Sections of iron could be brought to a dull shine, if Terisa rubbed them with the sleeve of her new shirt.

So. He was right. It didn't prove Nyle was alive. She couldn't argue with that.

So the Castellan would be coming back.

She wondered whether the places where people suffered were always made stronger by the residue of pain. And – not for the first time – she wondered how many different kinds of pain it was possible to feel.

When he came back, whatever he did would be out of her control. She had used up all her weapons. She wasn't Saddith: she couldn't use her body to protect her spirit, even though he apparently desired her. Even if she had been willing to make the attempt – a purely theoretical question – she lacked the knowledge, the experience. And somewhere between the poles of love and violence Castellan Lebbick had lost his way. He might no longer be able to distinguish between them.

She should have gone with Geraden.

She should have come to her own conclusions about him earlier, much earlier.

She should have stuck a knife in Master Eremis when she had the chance. If, in fact, she had ever had the chance.

The Castellan would be coming back.

What hope was there for her now? Only one: that Artagel might look at the body and be sure it wasn't Nyle's. If that happened – if she were proved right on that point – the Castellan might doubt his own rage enough to treat her more carefully. He might. She had to hope for *something*, now that she couldn't hope to be left alone.

She had to hope that Geraden's talent was strong enough to save him. Somehow, he had bent his mirror away from its Image in order to appear in her apartment and translate her to Orison. That was one thing. But to bend the same mirror so that it functioned as if it were flat – that was something else. A more hazardous attempt altogether. And yet she had reason to think it was within his abilities. With that same glass, he had put her partway into a scene which bore no resemblance to the Image, a scene which he called 'the Closed Fist' in the Care of Domne, and she hadn't gone mad. If he could do that for her, surely he could do it for himself?

Surely?

Oh, Geraden.

The truth was that she wasn't sure of anything anymore. She wasn't accustomed to the confidence she had projected in front of Castellan Lebbick: it was easier to forget than to sustain. Unfortunately, there wasn't anything inevitable about the explanation of events she had urged on him. Like her capacity for love, it was purely theoretical. She knew how Master Eremis would laugh, if anyone told him what she had said. At bottom, her defense of herself rested entirely and exclusively on the conviction that Geraden was innocent. If she was wrong about that—

The implications were intolerable, so she tried to close her mind to them. Because she didn't know whether the Castellan would come back soon or late – and either way it could mean anything, good or bad – she made an effort to distract herself by counting the granite blocks which formed the walls of the cell.

Both of the end walls had been built in the same way. At a glance, the construction looked careless: ill-fitting blocks had simply been piled on top of each other. So it might be possible to work some of them loose, especially up near the ceiling. But time and use had worn off the rough edges, leaving a surface that couldn't be hurt. In contrast, the back of the cell was flat, seamless stone – cut, not built. No doubt the work had been done by the Mordant-born slaves of Alend or Cadwal, during the long years of conflict between those powers.

And now she was a prisoner of the same conflict. In a sense, dungeons never gave up their victims. The faces and the bodies changed – died and were dragged away – but the old stone clung to its purpose, and the anguish of the men and women locked within it never changed. King Joyse hadn't gone far enough when he had altered Orison to make it a place of peace. Much of the extensive dungeons had been given over to the Congery for a laborium: that was good – but not good enough. The whole place should have been put to some other use. Then perhaps the Castellan wouldn't have spent so many years thinking about the things he could do to people who offended him.

She didn't know what to say to him.

She had never known what to say to her father, either. So far, however, she had had better luck with the Castellan. But that was finished. She had done everything she could think of. Now she was at the mercy of events and attitudes she couldn't control, men who were losing their minds, men who hated, men who—

'Deep in thought, I see, my lady,' said Master Eremis. 'It makes you especially lovely.'

She turned, her heart thudding in her throat, and saw him at the door of her cell. With one hand, he twirled the ends of his chasuble negligently. His relaxed stance suggested that he had been watching her for several minutes.

'You are quite remarkable,' he continued. 'Ordinarily, cogitation in a woman produces only ugliness. Were you thinking of me?'

She opened her mouth to say his name, but she couldn't swallow her heart; it was beating too hard. Staring at him as if she had been stricken dumb, she took an involuntary step backward.

'That would explain this increased beauty – if you were thinking of me. My lady' – he smiled as if she were naked in front of him – 'I have certainly been thinking of you.'

'How—?' She fought to regain her voice. 'How did you get in here?'

At that, he laughed. 'On my legs, my lady. I walked.'

'No.' She shook her head. Slowly, her immediate panic receded. 'You're supposed to be up at the reservoir. Saving Orison. Castellan Lebbick wouldn't let you just walk in here.'

'Unfortunately, no,' the Master agreed. His tone became marginally more sober. 'I was forced to resort to a little chicanery. Some cayenne in my wine to produce a sweat, so that he would be impressed by the strain of my exertions. A gentle potion in the brandy I offered to the men he set to guard me, so that they would sleep. A passage which has been secretly built from my workrooms in the laborium into an unused part of the dungeons – tremendous forethought on my part, do you not agree? considering that it was never possible for me to be certain Lebbick would arrest you.'

Terisa ignored the cayenne and the potion; they meant nothing to her. But a secret passage out of the dungeon – A way of escape – She had to take hold of herself with both hands to keep her sudden, irrational hope under command.

Struggling to muffle the tremor in her voice, she said, 'You went to a lot of trouble. What do you want? Do you expect me to tell you where Geraden is?'

Again, Master Eremis laughed. 'Oh, no, my lady.' She was beginning to loathe his laugh. 'You told me that a long time ago.'

When he said that, a sting of panic went through her – a fear different than all her other frights and alarms. She forgot about the secret passage; it was secondary. She wanted to shout, No, I didn't, I never did that! But as soon as he said it she knew it was true.

She had refused the Tor and Artagel and Castellan Lebbick – but Eremis already knew.

'Then why?' she demanded as though she were genuinely capable of belligerence. 'Have you come to kill me? Do you want to keep me from talking to the Castellan? You're too late. I've already told him everything.'

'"Everything"?' The Imager's dark gaze glinted as if he were no longer as amused as he sounded. 'Which "everything" is that, my lady? Did you tell him that I have held your sweet breasts in my hands? Did you tell him that I have tasted your nipples with my tongue?'

The recollection twisted her stomach. More angrily, she retorted, 'I told him you faked Nyle's death. You and Nyle set it up as an attack on Geraden. So no one would believe the things he said about you.

'I told him Nyle is still alive. You ambushed Underwell and those guards so everyone would think Geraden came back and killed him, but he's still alive. You've got him hidden somewhere. You talked him into being on your side somehow – maybe he hates Geraden for stopping him when he tried to help Elega and Prince Kragen – and now you've got him safe somewhere.

'That's what I told the Castellan.'

In the uncertain lamplight, Master Eremis' smile seemed to grow harder, sharper. 'Then I am glad it was never my intention to harm you. If I were to hurt you now, everyone would assume that there is some justice in your accusations.

'But I do not hold a grievance against you. I will demonstrate,' he said smoothly, 'the injustice of those accusations.'

'How?' she shot back, trying to shore up her courage – trying not to think about the fact that she had betrayed Geraden to the Imager. 'What new lies have you got in mind?'

His smile flashed like a blade. 'No lies at all, my lady. I will not lie to you again. Behold!' Flourishing one hand, he produced a long iron key from the sleeve of his cloak. 'I have come to let you out.'

She stared at him; shock made her want to lie down and close her eyes. He had a key to the cell. He wanted to let her out, help her escape – he wanted to get her away from the Castellan. She was too confused, she couldn't think. Start over again. He had a key to the cell. He wanted— It didn't make any sense.

'Why?' she murmured, asking herself the question, not expecting him to answer.

'Because,' he said distinctly, 'your body is mine. I have claimed it, and I mean to have it. I do not allow my desires to be frustrated or refused. Other women have such skin and loins as yours, such breasts – but they do not prefer a gangling, stupid, inept Apt after I have offered myself to them. When I conceive a desire, my lady, I satisfy it.'

'No,' she said again, 'no,' not because she meant to argue with him, but because he had given her a way to think. 'You wouldn't risk it. You wouldn't take the chance you might get caught here. You want to use me for something.'

Then it came to her.

'Does Geraden really scare you that badly?'

Master Eremis' smile turned crooked and faded from his face; his eyes burned at her. 'Have you lost your senses, my lady? *Scare me? Geraden?* Forgive my bluntness – but if you believe that Geraden Fumblefoot frightens me in any way, you are out of your wits. Lebbick and his dungeon have cost you your mind.'

'I don't think so.' In a manner that strangely resembled the Castellan's, she clenched her fists and tapped them on the sides of her legs as if to emphasize the rhythm of her thoughts, the inevitability. 'I don't think so.

'You know what he can do. You pretend you don't, but you know what he can do better than anybody – better than he does. Gilbur watched him make that mirror. You knew something unexpected was going to happen when the Congery decided to let him go ahead and try to translate the champion. That's why you argued against him. You weren't trying to protect him. You wanted to keep him from discovering who he is.

'The reason you tried to get him accepted into the Congery was just to distract him, confuse him – make it harder for him to understand.

'When Gilbur translated the champion' – she swung her fists harder, harder – 'you left Geraden and me in front of the mirror, *directly* in front of the mirror. You probably pushed him. You wanted the champion to kill him.' To kill both of us. The Master had been trying to take her life as well for a long time. But that was the only flaw in her convictions, the only thing which didn't make any sense: why anybody would want to have her killed. 'There isn't any doubt about it. You're definitely afraid of him.'

This time, the bark of Master Eremis' laugh held no humor, no mirth at all. 'You misjudge me, my lady. You misjudge me badly.'

She didn't stop; it was too late to draw back. 'That's why you're here,' she said, beating out the words against her thighs. 'Why you want to let me out. You want me to be your prisoner. You know he cares about me,' *cares* about me, oh, Geraden! 'and you want to use me against him. You think if you threaten to hurt me he'll do whatever you want.'

'You misjudge me, I say. It is not fear. Fear *that* puppy? I would rather lose my manhood.'

She heard him, but she didn't slow down. 'The only thing' – which was already a lie, but she had no intention of telling him the truth – 'the only thing I don't understand is why you didn't just send Gart to kill the lords of the Cares and Prince Kragen. Why else did you get them all together? You didn't want any alliance – you knew that meeting would fail. You were just trying to undermine all of Cadwal's enemies at the same time.

'Why didn't you finish the job? With the lords and Prince Kragen dead, Alend and Mordant and even Orison would be in chaos. What were you afraid of?'

Abruptly, Master Eremis swung his own fists and hit the bars so hard that the door clanged against its latch. '*It was not fear.* Are you *deaf*? Do you have the arrogance to ignore me? It was not *fear*!

'It was *policy*.'

Terisa stared at him past the bars, past the stark conflict of lamplight and shadows on his face, and murmured softly, in recognition, 'Oh.'

'I did not send Gart against the lords and Kragen,' he said harshly, 'because it was impossible to be sure that he would succeed. The Termigan and the Perdon and Kragen are all fierce fighters. Kragen had bodyguards. And any man who killed the Tor might drown in all his blood. Also it was much too soon to risk revealing my intentions. The gamble I chose to take was safer.

'When Gilbur performed his translation, the champion came to us facing the direction we wanted him to go – in toward the most crowded parts of Orison, the rooms and towers where his havoc would be most likely to bring the lords and Kragen to ruin. That was why I wanted him, the only reason I permitted his translation to take place.

'Of course,' the Master said in digression, 'once he had been translated, it was necessary to preserve him from Lebbick. I could not allow some bizarre happenstance to bring him into alliance with Orison and Mordant. Let him rampage now and do harm as he wishes, without friends or understanding. That also serves me. But my chief intent was more immediate.

'I wanted him to gut Orison, destroying all my principal enemies at once. If he had gone that way – if you had not turned him, my lady – my gamble would have brought a rich return.

'*Policy*, my lady. If it succeeds, I succeed with it. If it fails, I remain to pursue my ends by other means.

'And what I have done where Geraden is concerned is also *policy*, not *fear*. He is my enemy – and he appears to possess a strange talent. Therefore I will destroy him. But I will destroy him in a way that serves my ends rather than risks them. I do not' – vehemence bared his teeth – '*fear* that ignorant and impossible son of a coward.'

So he admitted it. She was right about him – she had reasoned her way to the truth. That discovery simultaneously relieved and terrified her. She was right about him, *right* about him. Geraden was innocent, and she had reached the truth alone, without anyone to help or rescue her. It was an intense relief just to recollect that he had never been able to finish anything he started with her: that he hadn't gotten her killed – or into his bed; hadn't gotten her confused enough to turn her back on Geraden.

On the other hand, there were no witnesses; no one else had heard him. She was alone with her knowledge – alone with him.

And he had a key to her cell.

Without meaning to do it, she had stripped herself of her only protection – the appearance of incomprehension that let him think she wasn't a threat to him, led him to believe he could do anything he wanted with her.

In quick panic, she tried to fake a defense. 'Prove it,' she replied, groaning inwardly at the way her voice shook. 'Leave me here. Go back to the reservoir and save Orison from Alend. If you aren't afraid of him, you don't need me.'

Her own alarm was too obvious: it seemed to restore his humor, his equanimity. He began to smile again, voraciously.

'Tush, my lady,' he said in deprecation, 'you do not truly wish that. I have touched you in places you will never forget. No man will ever treasure the ardor of your loins or the supplication of your breasts as I do – most assuredly not that lout Geraden, whose clumsiness will make his every caress a misery to you. If you consult your heart, you will accompany me willingly.

'If you should prove useful to me, how does that harm you? You will still be my lady. And you will be rewarded. I am going to *win* this contest. King Joyse considers it a mere game, an exercise in hop-board, and that is one of many reasons why Mordant will be defeated. Alend will be defeated, and Cadwal will be consumed. When I am done, there will be no power left in all this world which is not *mine*. Then the woman who stands with me will have riches and indulgence beyond her wildest imaginings.

'You would look well in that place, my lady. If you accompany me willingly, it will be yours.'

Terisa studied him hard. She didn't listen to what he was saying; his offer meant nothing to her. But the fact that he made it meant something. It *meant* something. When he stopped, she muttered, 'Take Saddith. She wants the job,' speaking aloud for her own benefit, so that the sound of the words would help her think. 'I'm still trying to figure out why you bother pretending to seduce me. You've got a key. You're bigger than I am. Why don't you just come in here, rape me, club me over the head, and let Gilbur or Vagel translate me to some other dungeon where you can use me without having to be nice about it?'

'Because' – he had recovered from the unpleasant surprise she had given him; now he was very sure of himself – 'that is not what you truly wish, my lady. Your deepest desire is not to defy me, but to open yourself so that I may teach you the joy of your body – and mine.'

She shook her head, hardly hearing him. Any explanation he gave was automatically false. Still for her own benefit, she went on, 'You're not just afraid of Geraden. You're afraid of *me*.' She felt a growing sense of wonder and dismay. 'You're trying to trick me for the same reason you've been trying to have me killed. You're *afraid* of me.'

This time when Master Eremis laughed his amusement was unforced and unmistakable. 'Oh, my lady,' he chortled, 'you are a wonderment. You flatter yourself beyond recognition. If you were not so earnest, I would believe you drunk with pride.

'Nevertheless I will respect what you say. Perhaps you desire a little force. Perhaps that will add spice to your eventual surrender. Since you suggest it—'

With a final chuckle, he pushed the key into the lock and turned it.

Without a second's hesitation, Terisa reared back and yelled at the top of her lungs, 'Guards!'

Master Eremis froze. His gaze flicked away down the passage, then sprang back to her in instant fury.

She put her whole heart into it:

'*Guards!*'

A door clanged in the distance. A rumor of boots ran along the corridor.

The Imager snarled a curse. 'Very well, my lady,' he hissed savagely. 'That was your last chance, and you have lost it.' In a swirl of darkness, he turned to leave. 'Now you will face the consequences of your foolishness. When Lebbick is done with you' – he spoke sharply enough to raise echoes after him, so that she could hear him as he left – 'expect worse from me.'

Then he was gone.

His departure was so abrupt – and the approach of the guards sounded so ominous – that just for an instant she thought she had made a mistake.

That concern evaporated almost immediately, however: it was burned away by the swift, hot awareness that she preferred being left to the Castellan's mercy. He was unpredictable and violent, capable of almost any atrocity when his loyalties were outraged. Yet he was *faithful* – far more trustworthy than the people in whom he had placed his faith. In fact, that discrepancy was what drove him wild. She would rather fight a man like him, who was at least true to his King, than be seduced by a man like Master Eremis, who was false to everybody.

The guards arrived at her cell, demanded an explanation threateningly because Castellan Lebbick might take them to task for anything they did in regard to her. For a moment, she was right on the edge of telling them what had happened. Master Eremis was here. He's got a secret entrance to the dungeons. He's a traitor. But her instinct for subterfuge made her swallow the words. No. She might need them. The Castellan would be back: she might need everything she could possibly tell him.

Facing the guards as if she had become bold, she replied, 'I want to see him.'

The two men gaped at her. One of them asked stupidly, 'Who? The Castellan?'

She nodded.

The other leered, 'Waste of effort. Last time a woman wanted to *see* him, he had her stripped and flogged and thrown out of Orison.' He grinned at the memory. 'Had nice tits, too. Would have done better to come to me.'

Terisa closed her eyes to control an upswelling of disgust. 'Tell him,' she demanded. 'Just tell him.'

The guards looked at each other. The first one said, 'He isn't going to like it.' But the other shrugged.

Walking loudly, they went away.

She sat down on her cot and tried to believe that she knew what she was doing.

She didn't have much time to prepare herself. Scant moments after the guards left, she heard Castellan Lebbick's rage echoing along the corridor.

'I don't give a trough of horseshit who she wants to see! You irresponsible sons-of-sheep are going to be cleaning latrines before morning! You're going to clean latrines until everything you eat tastes like piss and your wives and even your children stink as bad as you do! Who gave you the fornicating permission to let her have *visitors?*'

Then the door between the guardroom and the dungeons rang viciously against its frame; and boots came, as hard as hate, along the damp stone corridor.

Shocked, she found herself murmuring helplessly, Oh, no, oh, no, oh, no, on the verge of panic.

The Castellan stamped to the front of her cell like a man with murder on his mind. The glare in his eyes was fierce enough to wither what little courage she had left; his jaws were knotted with violence. Like a blow, he rammed the key into the lock, turned it, and slammed the door open. The door hit the bars so hard that they belled like a carillon.

'You heartless *slut!*' He came into the cell, came straight at her. 'I've been tearing my guts out over you all day, and you've been having *visitors!*'

Involuntarily, she flinched back onto the cot, cowered against the wall.

'The Tor!' she cried out, trying to keep him from hitting her. 'Artagel! They came here. I didn't ask to see them.'

'You didn't *have* to!' His fists caught her shirt, wrenched her off the cot so fiercely that the seam at one shoulder parted and the fabric ripped like a wail. 'Artagel is still too sick to get out of bed, and King Joyse personally told the Tor to let me do my job with you. So instead they both came to see *you*.

'What are you plotting? Did they tell you what to say to me? They must have. I half believed that dogpiss story about Eremis and Gart. You couldn't make that up yourself – you don't know enough. No, you're all doing this together. Those riders with the red fur came from the Care of Tor. Artagel is Geraden's brother.' Convulsive with anger, he twisted her shirt so that it tore down one seam to the hem. *'What are you plotting?'*

'Nothing.' She ought to be able to resist him, but her strength had deserted her. 'Nothing.' His fury was thrust so closely into her face that she could hardly focus her eyes on it, hardly see him at all; he was a darkness roaring in front of her, clawing at her – too much hate to be endured. She couldn't do anything more than whimper in protest. 'Nothing.'

'You're *lying*!' His intensity seemed to strangle him. 'You're *lying* to me!' His voice was like a howl stuck in his throat, too congested for utterance. 'You've got friends, allies. Even when you're locked in the dungeon, I can't stop you from plotting. You're going to *destroy* us! You're going to destroy *me*!'

She felt him gathering force as if he rose up to consume her; he blotted out her vision. A spasm of his grip nearly dislocated her shoulders. Then he caught his arms around her and began to kiss her as if he had been starving for her so long that the pressure of his need had snapped his self-command.

She sank into his embrace, into the dark. She let herself fall limp, so that she scarcely felt the violence of his kisses, scarcely felt the iron of his breastplate against her chest. The darkness sucked her away, out of herself, out of existence – out of danger. It took her to a place where he couldn't touch her and she was safe—

No. Fading wasn't the answer. She had to do better than this. It accomplished nothing. Oh, it kept her safe, kept her spirit hidden among the secrets of her heart – but her body would still be harmed. And no one would be left to help Geraden. No one would be left to stop Master Eremis. No one would be left to champion Orison against the real enemy, against Master Eremis and his dire alliance with Master Gilbur and the arch-Imager Vagel, with Gart and Cadwal. It came down to her in the end. Myste had said, *Problems should be solved by those who see them.* There wasn't anybody else.

She was terrified – but the fact that she was capable of escape gave her courage. She remained limp, lifeless, until the Castellan eased his embrace and shifted his hands to the waistband of her pants, bending her backward over the cot. Then she opened her eyes and looked at him.

She could see him clearly now, the distress bulging along the line of his jaw, the pale intensity on either side of his nose, the darkness like mania in his eyes. He scared her down to the bottom of her soul, where her fear of her father still lived and burned, distorting her. Nevertheless she caught at his wrists and held them as hard as she could, trying to stop him.

As if his kisses had made her lucid and crazy, immune to fright, she said, 'You didn't ask them why they came to see me. You didn't bother. You didn't ask Artagel to look at Nyle's body. You didn't even *try* to find out the truth. You just want to hurt me more than anything else in the world, and they finally gave you an excuse.'

Roaring almost silently behind the constriction in his chest, he let go of her and drew back his arm. He was going to hit her hard enough to crush her skull against the wall.

'They came to see me,' she said – lucid and completely out of touch with the reality of her plight – 'because they want me to tell you where Geraden is.'

While his arm rose and his teeth flashed, he stopped. Surprise or doubt or self-disgust seemed to seize hold of him, cramp all his muscles. Hoarsely, he panted, 'You're lying. You're still lying.'

'No.' She shook her head calmly. It was madness to be so calm. 'Is it true that you didn't ask Artagel to look at Nyle's body?'

The Castellan was going to hit her. Or else he was going to break down right there in front of her. Precariously balanced between the extremes, he choked, 'I asked. He's had another relapse. Too sick to understand the question.'

Steady and unafraid, she shrugged away her disappointment as if it were trivial. 'Never mind,' she murmured. She might have been trying to console Castellan Lebbick. 'I had another visitor. One you don't know about.

'Master Eremis was here.

'Now I can prove he's a traitor.'

Lamplight flickered in the Castellan's gaze. He straightened his back and stood over her as though his body had become stone; he held himself back from bloodshed with an effort of will so savage that it made him gasp for air.

'How?'

Unnatural quiet and clenched wildness, Terisa and the Castellan spoke to each other.

'He put cayenne in his wine to make himself sweat, so you would think he was exhausted.'

'You'll never prove that.'

'He gave your guards a potion to make them sleep, so he could get away.'

'If they're awake when I check on them, you'll never prove *that*, either.'

'He has a secret way into the dungeon. It comes from his workroom in the laborium. You ought to be able to find it without too much trouble.'

When she said that, Castellan Lebbick flinched backward. He didn't loosen his grip on himself, but his eyes betrayed a vast accumulation of pain.

'If he came here,' he asked, still breathing hard, 'why didn't you go with him? Why didn't you escape?'

For some reason, that question cracked her mad calm. She seemed to feel herself shattering, like an eggshell. Without transition, she went from lucidity to the edge of hysteria.

'Because—' Her voice broke, and her heart hammered as if it couldn't bear the strain any longer. 'Because he wanted to use me against Geraden. The same way he used Nyle.'

A muscle began to twitch in the Castellan's right cheek. The twitch spread until the whole side of his face felt the spasm. He was losing control.

'So if you're telling the truth' – for the first time since she had met him, he sounded like a man who might weep – 'Geraden has always been true to King Joyse. *True*, when almost nobody else is. And you're true to Geraden. And I've been hurting my King by distrusting you – by trying to protect him from you.'

Dumbly, Terisa nodded.

Without warning, the Castellan whirled away. 'I've got to see this "secret way" for myself.' Slamming the cell door so hard that flakes of rust scattered to the stone, he started down the corridor.

Almost at once, he broke into a run. His voice echoed across the sound of his boots as he shouted as if he were calling farewell to her – or to himself – 'I am loyal to my King!'

Stricken numb and hardly able to care what happened to her at the moment, Terisa pulled the torn seam of her shirt closed as well as she could. Grief threatened to overwhelm her: her own; the Castellan's; the hurt and sorrow of anyone who had to bear the consequences of King Joyse's decline. No, *decline* wasn't the right word. He still knew what he was doing. He had brought Mordant and Orison to this dilemma deliberately. Dully, she thought about that to keep herself from considering how close she and Castellan Lebbick had come to destroying each other.

When she finally looked up from her futile attempt to make her shirt decent – or at least warm – she saw Master Quillon inexplicably standing outside the bars of her cell.

'That was bravely done, my lady,' he said in a distant tone. 'Unfortunately, it was a mistake.'

She looked at him, gaped at him; her mouth hung open, and there was nothing she could do about it.

'Master Eremis lied to you. He has no passage from his workroom into the dungeon. He came to you by translation.

'When the Castellan learns that no passage exists, he will not believe another word you say. His rage will be so great that I fear he will be unable to hold himself back from killing you.'

It was too much. Fear and loneliness filled Terisa's chest, and she started crying.

THIRTY-ONE

HOP-BOARD

After a while, she felt a hand on her shoulder.

She was crying hard; but the touch was unexpected, and it startled her. She looked up to find Master Quillon beside her. His nose was twitching, and his eyes were gentle; clearly, he intended to comfort her.

'My lady,' he murmured, 'it has been painful for you, I know. And it must seem unjustified. You asked for none of this. And though we did not choose you, we have not hesitated to use you. I will give you all the help I can.'

Help, she thought through her tears. All the help I can. It was too late. The Castellan was too strong. He had too much power. She couldn't prove anything against Master Eremis. Nobody was going to be able to help her.

But Master Quillon was standing beside her. With his hand on her shoulder. Inside her cell. When she blinked her eyes clear, she saw that the door was open.

The Imager glanced where she was looking and commented like a shrug, 'Fortunately, the Castellan was in such dudgeon that he forgot to lock it. I doubt that any of the guards would be willing to open it for us when he is at this level of outrage.'

By degrees, the open door and Master Quillon's unexplained presence fixed her attention. The pressure of sobs receded in her chest; her breathing grew steadier. Without meeting the Master's gaze, she muttered, 'Did Havelock send you this time?'

'Indirectly,' Quillon replied. 'I am here for his benefit – and for the King's. To save all Mordant. But primarily' – his grip on her shoulder tightened a bit – 'I have come to let you out of this prison.'

Let me out—? Her eyes jerked to his: she stared at him, unable to control the way her face suddenly burned with yearning and hope. Her mouth shaped words she couldn't find her voice to say out loud: You're going to set me *free*?

Abruptly, Master Quillon took his hand from her shoulder and sat down next to her on the cot. Now his gaze studied the floor instead of meeting hers. 'My lady,' he said to the stones, 'it pains me to see you so surprised. And it pains me even more to know that we deserve your surprise. I do not like some of the things we have done to you. And I lack King Joyse's talent for risks. We deserve any recrimination you might make against us.'

Then his tone became more sardonic. 'The truth is that we deserve to be betrayed – by you as well as by Geraden, if by no one else. But a blind man could see now that you are faithful to him, and so you will not betray us. In that we are exceptionally fortunate. Perhaps our good fortune is as great as our need.'

Because she was too confused to follow what he was saying, she asked, 'Is this going to be another lecture?'

He winced; perhaps he thought she was being sarcastic. But he didn't back down. 'Not if you do not wish it, my lady. If you wish me to keep my mouth shut, I will simply take you away from here and let you do whatever you choose without argument – or explanation. But I tell you plainly' – then he did look at her, letting her see the pain on his face – 'that you will wound me if you do not permit me to explain. And I think you will increase the difficulty of your own decisions.'

She could hardly believe what she heard. To be helped, to be offered explanations, to be offered *freedom*—! Far from resenting him, as he apparently expected, she was hard pressed to restrain herself from weeping again in gratitude.

But she had to have more self-command than *this*. Otherwise it would all be wasted on her. She would go wrong. So she didn't jump to accept his offer. Instead, she did her best to *think* again, to make her brain resume functioning. Tentatively, groping for what she wanted to understand first, she asked, 'How do you know Master Eremis doesn't have a secret way in here? How do you know what he said to me?'

'I *heard* him,' Master Quillon retorted with sudden sharpness. He didn't seem to like what he had heard. 'I have been secreted down here since noon, when Prince Kragen stopped bringing up catapults against us. I heard your conversations with both the Castellan and Eremis – and with the Castellan again.' He made an effort to speak more softly. 'That is how I became certain of your loyalty to Geraden.'

As if he thought she wasn't asking the right questions – not being hard enough on him – he said almost at once, 'You will ask why I did not intervene when the Castellan threatened you. My lady, please believe that I would have done so. You found your own answer to his violence, however. Because he must not know my part in all this, if that can be avoided, I left you to deal with him alone.'

'No,' she said reflexively, abstract with concentration. He was right: that was something she wanted to ask him, a subject she wanted to pursue. But not yet. 'Tell me about that later.' First things first. She had to pull her mind into some kind of order. 'He said he built a secret way from his workroom into the dungeon. How can you be sure that isn't true?'

The Master rubbed his nose to make it stop twitching. 'It would be impossible to do such work secretly, with so many Apts everywhere in the laborium. Regardless of that, however, I know Eremis did not use a passage to come here. I saw him arrive and depart. He was translated.'

'You mean—' *He* can pass through flat glass, too, and not lose his mind? Can *everybody* do it? 'You mean he has a mirror with this dungeon in its Image?'

How is it possible to fight people who can pass through flat glass without going mad?

'I fear so, my lady. I suspect it is the same mirror which translated those hunting insects against Geraden. The passages of Orison are confusing, I know, but actually we are not far from the translation point they used – and Gart used when he attacked you and the Prince. There is considerable stone between this cell and that corridor, but of course stone would be no obstacle to an Image, if the focus of its glass could be shifted that far.

'Incidentally, you may wonder why your enemies do not send more of those insects against you while you are here and helpless.' Actually, she hadn't wondered anything of the kind, but Master Quillon went on anyway, 'It is the Adept's opinion that they must be given the scent of their victim before they will hunt. For anyone associated with the Congery, it would be easy to obtain something belonging to Geraden – a small possession, a piece of clothing. But opportunities to loot your rooms or wardrobes have been kept as near to nonexistent as possible. Without your scent, the insects cannot be sent against you.'

Involuntarily, Terisa shuddered. She didn't want to think about those hideous—

Master Quillon saved her. He continued talking.

'Considering that Eremis wants you – perhaps as a hostage, perhaps as a lover – wants you enough to risk coming here, it is an interesting question why he has not used his mirror to translate you away. You would be entirely in his power then. But I suspect that the focus of his mirror has already been shifted as far as it will go.

'He must find it quite exasperating that the perfect solution to his dilemma is denied him by the small fact that you are *here* rather than eight cells farther down the corridor. As I say, we have been more fortunate than we deserve.'

The Master had done it again, gone off at a tangent, distracted her. Sudden frustration welled up in her. 'Then why don't you *stop* him?' She turned toward Quillon, demanding an answer with her whole body. 'Get the Castellan to arrest him. Lock him up somewhere safe. He's going to betray *everybody*. You've got to *stop* him.'

'My lady' – Master Quillon's voice was soft, and his eyes studied her as if he wondered how much of the truth she would be able to bear – 'it is too soon.'

Too *soon*? Too *soon*? She gaped at him, unable to speak.

'We do not know where his strength is located. We do not know how this trick of translation is done. We do not know how far his alliances extend, or how many powers he is prepared to bring out of his mirrors against us. We do not know what his plans are – how he means to destroy us. Until his trap is sprung, we have no effective way to strike back at him.'

Still she gaped at him. Her head was spinning. With an effort, she asked thinly, '"We"?'

The Master smiled slightly, sourly. 'Yes, my lady. King Joyse, for the most part. And Adept Havelock, when he is able. I follow their instructions.' He paused while she went pale with shock; then he admitted, 'Not a very impressive cabal, I fear. There is no one else.'

A moment later – perhaps because she couldn't stop staring at him – he seemed to take pity on her. 'We cannot afford allies,' he explained. 'It is the essence of the King's policy to appear weak. Confused in his priorities. Unable to achieve decisions. Careless of his kingdom. And it would be impossible to create that appearance if his intentions were not kept secret. If Queen Madin knew the truth, would she turn her back on her husband in his time of gravest peril? If the Tor knew the truth, how well would he play the part of the forlorn and hectoring friend? If Castellan Lebbick knew the truth – No, it would be disastrous. He has no subterfuge in him. And no one would believe that King Joyse had lost his will or his wits, while Lebbick remained confident.'

We, she murmured to herself, *King Joyse*, as if the words made no sense, *We cannot afford allies*. It was all deliberate.

'The fact is,' said Quillon, 'that everyone who loves the King would behave differently if they understood him. And so it would all come to nothing. I am trusted only because throughout Orison I am so easily taken for granted – and because King Joyse must have *one* friend and Imager who is more reliable than the Adept.'

'But *why?*' The words burst from Terisa. '*Why?* Mordant is falling! Orison is under siege! Everybody who loves him or is loyal to him has been hurt!' All deliberate. Of course. She knew that. But the *reason*—! 'He's destroying his whole world, the world *he* created. Why would he do such a terrible thing?'

Abruptly, the Imager jerked to his feet. He was suddenly angry: he bristled with indignation. Quietly, but with such intensity that he shocked her to silence, he replied, 'So that he would attack here.'

What—?

'We did not know who he was, my lady. Remember that. We did not know who he was until last night, when he erred by trying to make us believe that Geraden had killed Nyle. Before that, we had few suspicions – and less proof. *We did not know who he was.*' Red spots flamed on the Master's cheeks. 'We knew only that he was powerful – that he had the ability, unprecedented in the history of Imagery, to inflict his translations wherever he chose. We had no way to find him, no way to combat him. No way to protect Mordant from him.

'But worse than the danger to Mordant was the threat to Alend and Cadwal, that had no Imagers to defend them. *That* King Joyse had accomplished with his ideal of the Congery and peace, that Cadwal and Alend were more helpless than Mordant against the enemy. *That* he was responsible for. His past victories have left Alend and Cadwal at the mercy of his new foes.

'Therefore' – Master Quillon gritted his teeth to keep from shouting – 'King Joyse set himself to save the world.

'His weakness is an ambush. He lures the enemy to strike *here* rather than elsewhere – to inflict their peril and harm *here* rather than on the people he has made vulnerable – to attack Mordant and Orison rather than first swallowing Cadwal and Alend and thereby growing too strong to be defeated. We did not know who he was.'

Roughly, Quillon shrugged, trying to restrain his anger. 'That is the reason for everything King Joyse has done. That – and the Congery's augury – and Geraden's strange translation, which brought you here. When you came among us, your importance was obvious at once. Clearly, it was vital to make you aware of the world you had entered, so that you could choose your own role in Mordant's need. Even a good person may do ill out of ignorance, but only a destructive one would do ill out of knowledge. The augury made it clear that we had to trust you or die.

'But Geraden was also at risk – and his importance was also plain in the augury. His only protection lay in King Joyse's weakness. If Geraden were granted the ability to elicit intelligent, decisive action from his King, the enemy would surely kill him. In addition, the belief that you were ignorant was a form of protection for you. So it was vital also to spurn Geraden's loyalty – and then to make you aware of Mordant's history in secret.

'My lady, I argued against that decision. From the beginning, I found it difficult to trust you – a woman of such passivity. What hope did you represent to us? But King Joyse insisted. That is why Adept Havelock and I approached you and spoke to you, giving you in secret the knowledge which both the Congery and the King had denied to you publicly.'

Oh, of course, now I understand. Terisa felt herself smiling into the quagmire of her own stupidity. Had she really spent her entire life like this – helpless, passive, unable to think?

'The translation of the Congery's champion,' rasped Quillon, 'presented a similar problem in a different guise. Again, the champion's importance in the augury is plain. Therefore King Joyse must oppose that translation, in order to appear determined on his own defeat. And yet he must be too weak to oppose the translation successfully. And I was at risk there, in addition to Geraden and yourself. My loyalties had to be concealed. So King Joyse had no choice but to refuse to hear the Fayle's warnings – and to ensure that Castellan Lebbick did not learn what transpired until the translation could no longer be stopped.

'My lady' – now Master Quillon faced her squarely, and Terisa saw that some of his anger was directed at her – 'it will be easy for you to be outraged at what we have done. You have already said that everybody who loves King Joyse or is loyal to him has been hurt – and you are right. His policy is dangerous. Therefore the only way he can save those who love him is to drive them away – to make them distance themselves from the seat of peril he has chosen for himself. He succeeded with Queen Madin. But his failure with such men as the Tor and Geraden haunts him. If harm comes to them, he will carry the fault on his own head, even though they have chosen to do what they do.

'Nevertheless you should understand what he does before you protest against it. He hazards himself so that thousands of men and women from the mountains of Alend to the coast of Cadwal will be spared. He tears his own heart so that the people he loves may be spared. He places the kingdom that he built with his own hands in danger so that his traditional enemies can be spared.

'If you cannot trust him or serve him, my lady, you must at least respect him. He created his own dilemma, and he accepts its consequences. He does what he is *able* to do, so that the harm his enemies do will be suffered by a few instead of by many.'

Because the Imager was angry at her – and because she was angry herself and didn't know how to conceal it – she turned away. The light seemed to be failing; maybe the lamp was running out of oil. Darkness gathered in all the corners: fatal implications spilled past the bars from the corridor into the cell. *You must at least respect him.* A man whose idea of wise policy was to twist a knife in his friends' hearts and leave his enemies unscathed. Of course she had to respect that. Sure.

She could hear Castellan Lebbick crying like a farewell, *I am loyal to my King!*

With more bitterness than she had realized she contained, more indignation than she had ever been aware of possessing, she asked softly, 'What about the Castellan?'

'What about him?' returned Master Quillon. Perhaps he was too irate to guess what she meant.

'Maybe the Tor and Geraden have made their own choices. They're more stable than he is. What choice did you ever give *him*? If he tried to quit serving, King Joyse would have to stop him. This whole *policy*' – she sneered the word – 'depends on the Castellan. If he doesn't stay faithful – if he doesn't do his utter best to keep Orison strong while King Joyse is busy being weak – then the whole thing collapses. When King Joyse finally decides to fight, he won't have anything to fight *with*. Unless the Castellan stays faithful.'

Master Quillon nodded. 'That is true. What is your point?'

'He doesn't have any choice, and it's *killing him*.' Sudden pity surged up through her bitterness. The man Lebbick had once been would probably have treated her with nothing more terrible than detached sarcasm or kindness. But the entire weight of King Joyse's *policy* had come down on his shoulders, and now he could hardly refrain from raping or murdering her. 'Don't you *see* that? What you're doing is expensive, and you're making him pay for all of it.' Without warning, she began to weep again. Her distress and the Castellan's were too intimately interconnected. 'You and your precious King are destroying him.'

She expected Master Quillon to yell at her. She was ready for that: she didn't care how angry he got, what he said. Somehow she had gone past the point where mere outrage could threaten her. She had anger of her own, and it was no longer hidden away. If her father had appeared before her there and lost his temper, she would have known how to respond.

The Imager didn't yell at her, however. He didn't raise his voice. Slowly, he moved to the door of the cell. Perhaps he intended to leave, give up on her: she didn't know – and didn't care. But he didn't do that, either. He waited until she looked up at him, lifted her head defiantly and glared at him through her tears. Then he said quietly, 'We didn't know this was going to happen. We thought he was stronger.'

Just for a second, she almost stopped crying in order to laugh. Imagine it. An aging King and a madman and a minor Imager got together to save the world – and the best plan they could come up with required them to drive the only man in Orison who knew how to fight for them out of his mind. It was funny, really. The only thing she didn't understand was, what made them think it would work? How could they possibly believe—?

The sound of a door rang down the passage: iron hit stone with such savagery that the echo seemed to carry a hint of snapped hinges.

'*Lying slut!*' howled the Castellan. 'I'll have you *gutted* for this!'

His boots started toward her from the guardroom.

Terisa froze in shock. Castellan Lebbick was coming to get her. He was coming to get her, and there was nothing she could do. Master Quillon said something, but she didn't hear what it was. In her mind, she saw the corridor from the guardroom: one turn; another; then the long line of the cells. The Castellan was coming hard, but he wasn't running; he might run as he drew closer, but he wasn't running yet; he was at the first turn – on his way to the next. He would reach her cell in half a minute. Her life had that many seconds left. No more.

'Are you deaf?' Quillon grabbed her wrist and hauled her off the cot. 'I said, *Come on.*'

She didn't have a chance to think, to choose. He wrenched her through the open door out into the passage. But he was pulling on her too hard, away from the guardroom: she staggered against the far wall and fell; her weight twisted her wrist from his grasp.

As she scrambled to her feet again, she saw Castellan Lebbick come into view past the second turn.

He saw her as well. For an instant, their eyes met across the distance, as if they had become astonishing to each other.

Then he let out a roar of fury – and she skittered in the opposite direction, her boots slipping on the rotten straw.

She could hear him coming after her. That was impossible; her feet and breathing and Master Quillon's shouts made too much noise. Nevertheless her sense of his overwhelming rage, his ache for destruction, made his pursuit loud in her mind. She could feel his hate reaching out—

And ahead of her the Imager was losing ground. He slowed his flight; took the time to turn and beckon frantically.

A second later, he whipped open the door to another cell, dashed inside.

She followed without thinking. She had no time to think. Deflecting her momentum against the bars, she flung herself into the cell faster than Master Quillon was moving and nearly ran him down when he stopped.

Quickly, he opened a door in the side wall.

It was well hidden: the spring that released it was so cunningly concealed that she would never have found it for herself; and until he hit the spring she couldn't see the door itself. Then it swung wide, moving smoothly, as if it were counterbalanced on its hinges and controlled by weights. It must have been built in when this cell was first constructed.

That was how Master Quillon had gained access to the dungeon. How he had been able to listen to her conversations with Eremis and Lebbick. Another secret passage. But she didn't have time to be surprised. As soon as the door opened, Quillon caught at her arm again and thrust her forward, into the unlit passage.

He followed on her heels. Trying to make room for him without advancing into the dark, she found a wall and put her back to it. He was only a silhouette against the dim reflection from the dungeon lamps. At once, he tripped the mechanism that moved the weights to close and seal the door—

—and Castellan Lebbick burst into the cell.

He was too late: he wasn't going to be able to prevent the door from shutting. And once it was shut he would have to find the spring to open it again.

Nevertheless he was fast, and his sword was already in his hands. Driving wildly to spit Terisa through the closing of the door, he plunged forward, hurled himself headlong toward her.

The door's weight swept his thrust aside. His swordtip missed her by several inches.

Then his sword was caught in the crack of the door. The iron held, jamming the stone so that it couldn't seal.

His body thudded against the door; he recoiled, staggering.

A moment later, his voice came, muffled, into the dark. 'Guards! *Guards!*'

'Come on!' hissed Master Quillon. He took Terisa by the wrist once more and tugged her away from the thin slit of illumination. 'Curse him! As soon as his men arrive, he will be able to open that door. We must escape *now*.'

Struggling for balance, she hurried after her rescuer into a blind passage.

Stone seemed to whirl about her head like a swarm of bats, probing for some way to strike at her. There was no light – no light of any kind. Except for his grip, Master Quillon had ceased to exist. Her shoulders kept hitting the walls as if she were reeling. She couldn't keep up this pace; she had no idea where the passage went, or how it got there. 'Slow down!' she panted. 'I can't see.'

'You do not need to see,' Quillon snapped. 'You need to hurry.'

Still trying to make him slacken speed, she protested, 'How long?'

Without warning, he halted. At the same time, he let go of her. She collided with him, stumbled against the wall again, flung up her arms to protect her head.

'Not long,' he muttered acerbically. 'This passage was put in when the dungeons were rebuilt to provide room for the laborium. In other words, it is relatively recent. So it does not connect to the more extensive passage systems.'

Unseen beside her, he tripped another release, and the wall she had just hit opened, letting cold air wash over her. Her torn shirt couldn't keep the chill out.

The space into which the door gave admittance was dim, almost black; but after a moment her eyes adjusted, and she saw ahead of her a truncated bit of hall leading to a wider corridor. Lanterns out of sight along the corridor in one direction or the other supplied just enough reflected glow to soften the gloom.

When she caught her breath to listen, the sound which came to her was the delicate spatter of dripping water.

Cold and wet. And a side passage too short to be worth lighting with a lantern of its own. A passage that seemed to go nowhere, as long as this door was closed and hidden.

Despite the distractions of fear, exertion, and surprise, her nerves turned to ice as if she had been here before.

'Now, my lady,' whispered Master Quillon, 'we must be both quick and quiet. These are the disused passages beneath the foundations of Orison, where twice you were attacked. They are back in use now, housing our increased population, but that is not our chief worry. Those people will be asleep – or too confused to hinder us. No, the difficulty is that these halls are now guarded to keep the peace – regularly patrolled. Somehow, we must avoid the Castellan's men.'

No, she thought dumbly. That isn't right. Her brain felt like rock, impermeable to understanding. She had never seen the hall from this side, but it looked the same; the hairs on her forearms lifted as if the hall were the same. When Master Quillon started forward, she managed to reach out and stop him.

'No,' she whispered, almost croaking. 'This is the place. I'm sure of it.'

He stood motionless and studied her narrowly. 'What place?' The air grew colder on her skin while he stared at her.

'The translation point.' The cold made her shiver. Long tremors seemed to start in her bones and build outward until her voice shook. 'Where those insects came through to get Geraden. And Gart—'

Closing her arms across her chest, she hugged herself to silence.

'What, here?' the Imager asked in surprise. 'Exactly here?'

She nodded as well as she could.

'We did not know that,' he muttered; he appeared to be thinking rapidly. 'We knew the general area, of course.' His quick eyes studied the passage. 'But the Adept did not observe the actual translations. And we could hardly afford to betray our interest by asking you or Artagel to show us specifically where the attacks took place.'

Terisa ignored what he was saying; it didn't matter. What mattered was the mirror which brought people who wanted to kill her into Orison. 'We can't go there,' she breathed through her shivers. 'I can't go there. They'll see us.'

They'll come after us.

'A good point, my lady.' Master Quillon's nose twitched as though he were trying to sniff out a way of escape. 'If they saw us in the Image – and if they were ready for us—'

A grunting noise, a sound of strain or protest, carried along the passage from the entrance to the dungeons behind them.

The Master and Terisa froze.

'Put your backs into it, shit-lickers.' Castellan Lebbick's voice was obscured by stone and distance, but unmistakable. 'Get that door open before we lose them completely.'

Terisa wanted to groan, but she couldn't stop shivering.

'Glass and splinters!' Quillon swore under his breath. 'This is a tidy predicament.'

An instant later, however, he grabbed her by the shoulders and shook her to get her attention. 'My lady, listen.

'The focus of that glass was shifted. I saw Eremis translated into the dungeon. I saw him depart. He must have used the same mirror which

brought your attackers here. Why else was I permitted to eavesdrop on him –
to hear him reveal his intentions? Had his allies seen me enter the passage this
way, they would have had no difficulty in disposing of me. Therefore they
did not see me. Therefore the translation point of that mirror has been
shifted.'

'They could shift it back,' she objected.

'They could be watching us right now,' he retorted. 'But if that is true, why
are we still unharmed?'

The groan of stressed ropes and counterbalances came quietly out of the
dark. A man gasped, and Castellan Lebbick barked, 'That does it!'

'We must take the risk!' Master Quillon hissed.

Again, Terisa nodded. But she remained still, caught between fears. Gart
was there somewhere, the High King's Monomach. And from that translation
point had come four lumbering assailants who had themselves been eaten
alive from the inside by the most terrible—

'You must go first!' Urgency made Quillon's rabbity face slightly ludicrous.
'First is safest. Any man will need a moment to react when he sees us.

'*Go.*'

He shoved her, and she went.

Two stumbling steps toward the main corridor; three; four. For some
reason, the strength had gone out of her legs. She felt like a woman in a
nightmare, frantic to run, but powerless to do anything except ache with
fright while her enemies rushed toward her.

Master Quillon caught up with her and shoved her again to keep her going.

For the second time, she felt *a touch of cold as thin as a feather and as sharp
as steel slide straight through the center of her abdomen.*

Running now, but hardly aware of it, hardly conscious of what she was
doing at all, she reached the main passage and the light and turned, whirled
around in time to see Master Quillon following her and a black shape with a
face full of hate and glee rising behind him, clutching a long dagger to strike
him down.

No, Quillon! *Quillon!*

The shape rose and swept after him while she tried to cry out a warning
and couldn't do it fast enough: black arms rose and then plunged down
viciously, driving the dagger into the joining of his shoulders with such fury
that blood burst from his mouth and the blade came through his chest and he
was crushed to the floor as if he had been hit with a sledgehammer.

'*Got* you, you insipid rodent!' Master Gilbur barked in guttural triumph.
'That is the *last* time you will interfere with anything we wish to do!'

When he wrenched his blade out of Quillon's back, blood ran from his
hands like water.

Oh, Quillon!

Terisa remembered Master Gilbur's hands. They looked strong enough to
bend iron bars; strong enough to grind bones. Their backs were covered with
black hair – hair that contrasted starkly with his white beard. The hunch in his
spine only seemed to increase his physical power; the flesh of his face was
knotted with murder.

Gloating, he looked up from Quillon's corpse. 'My lady,' he coughed like a curse, 'this is fortuitous. I had not expected the pleasure of killing you. That was intended to be Gart's task, after Eremis had finished with you. But my vigilance has been rewarded. Neither Festten's dog nor cocksure Eremis were with me when I found you in the Image.'

She watched him as if he were a snake, waited for him to strike.

'It is a delight to rid the world of Quillon at last' – Gilbur licked spittle from his thick lips as he stepped over the body at his feet – 'but to twist my knife in your soft flesh will be plain ecstasy.'

Reaching out with his blade and his bloody hands, he started toward her. She turned and fled.

She ran with all her heart this time, pushed all her strength through her legs. In spite of his crooked back, Master Gilbur was fast. His first blow nearly caught her. The gap she opened between them as she sped was less than a stride; then two; then three and a bit more. Instinctively, she had run to the left; she was taking the same direction she and Geraden had taken when they had fled from the insects.

Black arms rose and then plunged down—

Now she would have been glad – delirious with relief – to encounter a guard. An old codger hunting for the public lavatories. A servant. Anyone to witness what was happening, distract Gilbur. But the corridor was deserted. Master Gilbur spat curses as he pursued her. She was young, and running for her life; slowly, she widened the gap. But the air had already become fire in her lungs, and he didn't seem to be tiring.

Plunged down—

In one way, she had no idea where she was going. She didn't know these passages, had never been down here without a guide. The only thought in her mind was to find help. Before she faltered. She could feel her strength ebbing now. In another way, however, her instinctive sense of direction was sure, and she followed it unhesitatingly. To escape the fierce Imager, she tapped resources in herself that she didn't know she possessed.

She took the route to Adept Havelock's quarters.

There: the side passage. A thick wooden door, apparently the entrance to a storeroom. Yes, the entrance to a storeroom. A storeroom which hadn't been appropriated to help house Orison's increased population. She heaved the door open, pulled it shut behind her. It had a bolt. Didn't it have a bolt? It had to have a bolt – *had* to have – but she couldn't find it, couldn't see, there was no light in the storeroom, no illumination except thin yellow slivers from the cracks around the door.

Master Gilbur's bulk blocked even that light—

—and her fingers found the bolt, slapped it home just as he crashed against the door, trying to crush her with the weight of the wood and his own momentum.

The bolt twisted against its staples. But it held.

It wasn't going to hold for long. Gilbur hit the door again, raging at it and her. She couldn't see the bolt – but she could hear the metallic screaming noise as iron rusted into wood was forced out. The staples were going to give. It was only a matter of time.

Ignoring her frantic need for air and rest, she groped across the storeroom toward the door hidden at the back – the entrance to Adept Havelock's secret rooms.

Because she was moving by instinct rather than conscious thought, she didn't remember the possibility that the hidden door might be bolted until she found it open. Master Quillon had probably left it that way. He had probably intended to bring her here himself. Weak with relief and need, she opened the door and hurried into the lighted passage which led to Havelock's domain.

The first room she came to was cluttered with mirrors.

Nothing had changed since her last visit here. The disarray was composed of full-length mirrors so uneven in shape and color that they showed Images she couldn't begin to interpret; bits of flat glass that would have fit in her pocket; mirrors the right size for a dressing table, but piled on top of each other and scattered as if to keep anyone from seeing what they showed. All of them had been gleaned by King Joyse during his wars and never restored to the Congery; all of them were set in rich or loving frames which belied the neglect of their present circumstances. And all of them were useless. The Imagers who had made them were dead.

They didn't have anything to do with her. She rushed past them.

The passage took two or three turns, but she didn't lose her way. In a moment, she reached another door. She thought she could hear Master Gilbur still pounding to get into the storeroom – or perhaps the sound was simply caused by panic beating in her ears – so she pulled the door open and stumbled into the large, square chamber which Adept Havelock used as a study, and which gave him access to Orison's networks of secret passages.

The air was musty, disused – something had gone wrong with the ventilation. There were too many people in the castle. Smoke from lamps with wicks that needed trimming curled lazily around the pillar which held up the center of the ceiling.

The Adept was there, lurking in his madness like a spider.

Master Quillon had asked Terisa to believe that Havelock had helped King Joyse plan the destruction of Mordant. Quillon had expected her to believe it – expected her to believe that the old Adept's insanity didn't prevent him from wisdom or cunning. And perhaps her dead rescuer was right. Perhaps only a madman like Havelock could have conceived a strategy which relied for its sole chance of success on Castellan Lebbick's stability.

Nevertheless Terisa had nowhere else to turn now. Surely Quillon would have brought her here, if he had lived. The Adept had to help her. He had helped her in the past. He had tried to answer her questions. And Master Gilbur might catch up with her at any moment. He might kill the Adept as well, if he got the opportunity. And the Castellan was still after her.

'Havelock!' she gasped, wracking her lungs to force out words, 'Gilbur killed Master Quillon. He's after me. I need help. You've got to help me.'

Got to. As soon as she stopped running, she knew that she wouldn't be able to stay on her feet much longer.

The Adept stood beside his hop-board table, hunching over it as if he had a game in progress, studying the board intently even though there were no men on it. He didn't look up until she spoke; then, however, he raised his head and smiled amiably. Smoke eddied around him. One eye considered her casually; the other began a scrutiny of the wall behind her.

'My lady Terisa of Morgan,' he said in a tone of loopy mildness. 'What a pleasant surprise. Fornicate you between the eyes. I trust you are well?'

'*Havelock*,' she insisted. 'Listen to me. I need help. Gilbur killed Master Quillon. He's right behind me.'

The Adept's smile showed his teeth. 'I'm glad to hear it,' he replied as if she had just indulged in a pleasantry. 'You certainly *look* well. Rest and peace do wonders for the female complexion.

'Now, tell me what you would like to know. I'm completely at your service today.'

Horror welled up in her; she could hardly control it. The strain of defending Orison had finished him. He was gone, entirely out of touch with sanity. The air was too thick to give her lungs any relief. Quillon had been killed, and she was going to be killed, and the Adept himself was probably going to be killed. She didn't know how to get through to him. Nearly weeping, she cried, 'Don't you understand? Can't you hear me? *Gilbur just killed Master Quillon. He's coming here.*'

Abruptly, he switched eyes, regarded her with the orb which had been staring at the wall. His nose cut the air like the beak of a hawk. On the other hand, his fleshy smile didn't waver.

'My lady Terisa of Morgan,' he said again, 'it would be my very great pleasure to rip the rest of your clothes off and throw you in a pigsty. Today I can answer questions. Ask me anything you want.

'But,' he commented as if this particular detail were trivial, 'I can't help you. Not today.'

She stopped and stared at him, almost retching for air and aid. I can't help you. Not today.

Oh, Quillon!

'Almost everybody,' he went on in the same tone of relaxed good cheer, 'wants to know why I burned up that creature of Imagery who tried to get Geraden. Timing, that's the answer. Good timing. It doesn't matter what you look like. It doesn't even matter what you smell like. Anybody will lick your ass if you've got good timing. We weren't ready. If Lebbick found out who our enemies are from that creature, it would all collapse. We wouldn't be weak enough to defend ourselves.'

'*Havelock!*' Terisa wanted to hit him, curse at him, tear her hair. 'Master Quillon was your *friend*! Gilbur just killed him! Don't you even *care*?'

Without transition, Adept Havelock passed from amiable lunacy to wild fury. 'Cunt!' With a roar, he brandished his right hand, pinching the fingers together as if he held a checker. 'This is you!' Wheeling to the table, he banged his hand down on the board several times, jumping imaginary pieces; then he mimed flinging his checker savagely into the corner of the room. 'Gone! Do you understand me? *Gone!*

'Don't you think I *want* to be sane? Don't you think I *want* to help? He was the only one who knew how to help *me*. But I used it all up! This morning – against those catapults! *I used it all up!*'

Dumb with shock, Terisa gaped at him. He was too far gone. She didn't know how to reach him.

An instant later, however, his rage disappeared as suddenly as it had come. Both his eyes seemed to grow glassy with sorrow, and he turned his back on her slowly. 'Today I can't help you,' he murmured to the blank checkerboard. 'Go deal with Gilbur yourself.'

He lowered himself into a chair near the table. His shoulders began to shake, and a high, small whine came from his clenched throat. After a moment, Terisa realized that he was sobbing.

Lost and numb, she left him alone there and went to deal with Gilbur herself.

She was so sick with dread and dismay and grief that she didn't even wince when she heard the Adept bolting his door after her, locking her away from any possibility of escape.

Like a sleepwalker – like a woman trying to locate herself, discover who she was, in a glass made from the pure sand of dreams – she returned to the room where Havelock kept his mirrors.

Master Gilbur was already there.

He didn't notice her. He was too full of wonder at what he had found: mirrors he had never known existed, dozens of them; a priceless treasure for any Imager with the talent to use them, any Adept. She could have tried to hide. The look on his face made her think that it might even be possible to sneak past him. He was so caught up in what he was seeing—

With a forlorn shrug, she took one of the small mirrors stacked on a trestle table near her and tossed it to the floor so that it shattered in all directions.

A cloud of dust billowed from the impact, softening the sound. The whole room was thick in dust; the mirrors apparently hadn't been cleaned in decades.

Nevertheless the sound of breakage got his attention. He jerked around to face her, raised his massive fists. His eyes burned; fury seemed to fume from his beard. 'You dare!' he coughed. 'You dare to destroy such wealth, such power! For that, I will not simply kill you. I will hack you apart.'

'No, you won't.' To her astonishment, her voice was steady. Perhaps she was too numb to be afraid any longer. As if she did this kind of thing all the time, she put the trestle table between them so that it blocked his approach. 'If you take one step toward me, I'll break another mirror. Every time you do anything to threaten me, I'll break another mirror. Maybe I'll break everything here before you get your hands on me.'

Numbness was a good start. It led to fading. She could stand here and confront Master Gilbur with all his hate like a woman full of courage – and at the same time she could go away, evaporate from in front of him. Give up her existence and follow mist and smoke to safety. By the time he got his hands on her – she knew he was going to get his hands on her somehow – she would be gone.

And in the meantime she might delay him long enough—

'You would not!' protested Gilbur, momentarily surprised out of his rage.

Terisa picked up another mirror and measured the distance to the Master's head. 'Try me.'

Numbness. Fading.

Time.

'No, my lady.' His features gathered into their familiar scowl. He was breathing heavily, as if his back pained him. '*You* try *me*. All this glass is beyond price – in the abstract. In practice, it is useless. A mirror can only be used by the man who made it. There are new talents in the world, and mine is one of them. I can make mirrors with a speed and accuracy which would astound the Congery, if those pompous fools only knew of it. But only an Adept has the talent to work translations with a glass he did not make.'

'If you believe I will not kill you, you are stupid as well as foolish.'

He took a step toward her.

She threw the glass at him and snatched up another.

The delicate tinkling noise of broken glass shrouded by dust filled the room.

He halted.

'Maybe nobody except Havelock actually has that talent,' she said, nobody except Havelock, for all the good that did her, 'but you think you might be able to learn it. It might be a skill, not a talent. You've never had a chance to find out the truth because other Imagers won't let you experiment with their mirrors. With these, you could do all the experimenting you want. You could learn anything there is to learn.'

Fading. Time. With her peripheral vision, she picked out the mirror she wanted – a flat glass in a rosewood frame, nearly as tall as she was. Through a layer of dust, its Image showed a bare sand dune, nothing else. Somewhere in Cadwal, she guessed. One of the less hospitable portions of High King Festten's land. In the Image, the wind was blowing hard enough to raise sand from the dune like steam.

Carefully, she edged toward it.

'But I'm not going to let you have them,' she continued without pausing. 'Not if you try to get me.'

Master Gilbur faced her as if he ached to leap for her throat. One hand clutched his dagger; the other curled in anticipation. He restrained himself, however. 'A clever point,' he snarled. 'You are cleverer than I thought. But it is futile. You cannot leave this room without coming within my reach. Or without moving out of reach of the mirrors. In either case, I will cut you down instantly. What do you hope to gain?'

Time. It was amazing how little fear she felt. Her substance was leaching away before his eyes, and he was blind to it. Now she could ease herself into the dark whenever she wished, and then there would be nothing he could do to hurt her. Nothing that would make any difference. All she wanted was time.

She took another small step toward the glass she had chosen.

Then she went still because she thought she heard boots.

'I'm not greedy.' Now her voice tried to shake, but she didn't let it. Instead, she began to speak louder, doing what she could to hold the Master's attention. 'I don't want much. I just want to frustrate you.

'You and Eremis are so arrogant – you manipulate, you kill. You don't have the slightest interest in what happens to the people you hurt. You're *sick* with arrogance. It's worth breaking a few mirrors just to upset you.'

Suddenly, she saw movement in the passage behind him.

Trying to gain all the time she could – trying to strike some kind of blow in Master Quillon's name, and Geraden's, and her own – she flung the mirror she held at Gilbur's head.

He dodged her throw effortlessly.

And even that went wrong for her. Her life had become such a disaster that she couldn't even throw something at a man who hated her without saving him. Dodging, he pivoted and leaped toward the table to close on her. As a result, the first guard charging into the room missed his swing.

Before the man could recover, Master Gilbur hammered him to the floor with a fist like a bludgeon.

The second guard had the opposite problem: he had to check the sweep of his sword in order to avoid his companion. That took only an instant – but an instant was all the time Gilbur needed to plant his dagger in the guard's throat.

Castellan Lebbick entered the room behind his men alone.

He held his longsword poised; the tip of the blade moved warily. He glanced at Terisa, then returned his gaze to the Master. He was coiled to fight, ready and dangerous. She thought that she had never seen him look so calm. This was what he needed: a chance to do battle for Orison and King Joyse.

'So here it is,' he commented distinctly. 'The truth at last. Geraden's seducer and a renegade Imager, together. And poor Quillon dead in the corridor. Did he try to stop you? I thought it was him helping her escape, but I must have been wrong. The light isn't very good.

'You're lucky you're alive. If she hadn't thrown that glass, my men would have cut you down.'

Master Gilbur's face twisted with laughter.

Terisa was past caring what the Castellan thought of her. She took another small step toward the mirror she wanted. Despite the intervening layer of dust, the sand in the Image seemed real to her, more solid than she was herself.

'Drop that pigsticker,' Lebbick growled at Master Gilbur. 'It isn't going to help you. Lie down. Put your face on the floor. I'm going to tie you up. I'd rather kill you, but King Joyse will want you alive. Maybe he'll let me question you.

'Do it *now*. Before I change my mind.'

As if the provocation had become too great to be endured, Gilbur let out a harsh guffaw. 'My lady,' he said, scowling thunderously, 'tell Lebbick why we are not going to let him take us prisoner.'

She started to retort. The suggestion that she really was an ally of his nearly broke her careful hold on fading. Her anger had come out of hiding, and she wanted to scathe the Master's skin from his bones.

Unfortunately, his ploy had already accomplished its purpose: it had tricked Castellan Lebbick into glancing at her again.

During that brief glance, Master Gilbur pitched a handful of dust into the Castellan's face.

Cursing, the Castellan recoiled; he swung his blade defensively. His balance and reflexes were so good that he almost saved himself. Without sight, however, he couldn't counter Gilbur's quickness; he couldn't prevent Gilbur from picking up one of the guard's swords and clubbing him senseless.

Terisa paused in front of the mirror she had chosen. Her only rational hope was gone. Now nothing stood between her and whatever the Master might do. She should have been terrified. Yet she wasn't. Her capacity for surrender protected her. The hope she had placed in the Castellan hadn't been hope for herself, but only hope against Gilbur. She hadn't lost anything crucial. Inside herself, she was on the verge of extinction, and Master Gilbur had no way to stop her. When he looked up from Lebbick's body, she asked, 'Why don't you kill him?'

'I have a better idea,' he snarled, feral with glee. 'I will take you with me. When he comes back to consciousness, he will report that we are allies. Joyse and his fools will have no conception of their real danger until we destroy them.'

He was right, of course. The Castellan would be believed. Master Quillon was dead – her sole witness to Master Eremis' admission of guilt. And Quillon certainly hadn't had time to tell anyone what he had learned. Gilbur would come after her in a moment. She might be able to slow him down by breaking a few more mirrors, but that would only postpone the inevitable. He had won. If he called this winning.

Deliberately, she began to let go.

Nevertheless on the outside she continued to challenge him. 'Someone will stop you,' she said as if she were accustomed to defiance. Defiance was what led to being locked in the closet. 'If Geraden doesn't do it, I will. You're going to be stopped.'

'Geraden?' spat Gilbur. '*You*?' He really was remarkably quick. In the space between one heartbeat and the next, he ducked under the trestle table and came upright again, bringing his knife toward her. Every knot and fold of his expression promised butchery. 'How are *you* going to stop me?'

How?

Like this.

She didn't need to say it aloud. He was still bearing down on her with his bloody hands when he seemed to run into a wall. Surprise wiped the violence from his face: his eyes sprang wide as he saw what was happening to the mirror behind her.

'Vagel's balls,' he muttered. 'How did you do *that*?'

She didn't look. The last time she had done this, she had done it entirely by accident, without knowing what she was doing; she didn't try to coerce it now. In any case, at the moment she didn't care whether she lived or died. She only cared about escape.

Still astonished, but recovering his wits, Master Gilbur reached for her.

Gently, Terisa closed her eyes and drifted backward into the dark.

THIRTY-TWO

THE BENEFIT
OF SONS

She lay still for a long time. The fact was that she went to sleep. Two nights ago, the lady Elega had poisoned the reservoir of Orison. Last night, Geraden had faced Master Eremis in front of the Congery, and she, Terisa, had become the Castellan's prisoner. And tonight— She was exhausted. Master Gilbur reached for her, but he must have missed. Even though her eyes were closed, she knew the light was gone. And as the light vanished, she felt herself enter the zone of transition, where time and distance contradicted each other. It was working: she was being translated. Somewhere.

That was enough. The sensation that she had taken a vast, eternal plunge in no time at all sucked the last bit of her out of herself, completed her self-erasure; and she slept.

The cold wasn't what awakened her. The dungeon had been as cold as this. No, it was the faint, damp smell of grass, and the breeze curling kindly through the tear in her shirt, and the high calling of birds, and the impression of space. When she opened her eyes, she saw that she was covered from horizon to horizon by the wide sky. It was still purple with dawn, but already the birds had begun to flit through it everywhere, looking as swift and keen as their own songs against the heavens.

Then she heard the rich chuckle of running water.

She raised her head and looked down the hillside toward a fast stream. The melted snow of spring filled its banks and made it hurry, eager to go on its downland journey. In that direction, the water ran toward a valley still shrouded by the receding night; upstream, it came from a high, dark silhouette piled against the purple sky, a sense of mountains.

The air was as cold as the dungeon, but not as dank, as oppressive; the life hadn't been squeezed out of it by Orison's great weight and overloaded ventilation. She took a deep breath, put her hands into the new grass to push herself onto her feet, and stood up.

Almost at once, the mountains in the distance took light. The sun was rising. For no reason except that it was morning and the air was clear and she was alive, her heart started to sing like the birds, and she knew what she was going to see before the sun reached the massed shadow from which the stream emerged.

The Closed Fist.

There.

Starting from the west, sunshine caught the heavy stone pillar which guarded the stream's egress from the hills on that side. Then it touched the eastside pillar, and the defile between them came clear, the narrow, secret cut from which the Broadwine River ran toward the heart of the Care of Domne.

The Closed Fist. Geraden had played here as a boy. The jumble of rocks inside the defile must have been wonderful for children, a source of endless climbing games and cunning hideaways.

And she had brought herself here. Against all the odds. Despite her utter ignorance of Imagery – and despite Master Eremis' best efforts to confuse her. She had translated herself to safety using a flat glass. And she hadn't lost her mind.

Abruptly, her eyes filled with tears, and she wanted to cry out in relief and joy.

'Terisa.'

She heard feet running over the grass. Through her tears, she glimpsed a shape, a man blurred by weeping. She turned to face him – to face the sun – and as its clean, new light shone through her, she found herself in Geraden's arms.

'*Terisa.*'

Oh, Geraden. Oh, love.

'Thank the stars! I thought I was never going to see you again.'

You're here. You made it. You made it.

Then he pulled back. 'Let me look at you.'

She blinked her sight clear and saw him gazing at her hungrily through his own tears.

'I've been watching for you, waiting, almost ever since I got here. It was the only hope I had. I just went in to Houseldon to tell my family what's going on. They didn't want me to come back alone, but I couldn't bear it any other way. I couldn't bear having somebody watch me wait. I left you there – with Eremis and Lebbick – and I thought I was never going to see you again.'

She wanted to say, Did you think they could keep me away? The delight of him shone like the sun in front of her. He was the same Geraden he had always been – openhearted, vulnerable, dear. His tears made him look hardly older than a boy. His chestnut hair curled in all directions, full of possibilities above his strong forehead; his bright gaze and his good face were like birdsong in the spring air. I fought Eremis and the Castellan and Master Gilbur for you. Did you think they could keep me away?

But then he took in her rent shirt, her battered appearance, the strain impacted around her eyes; and his face changed.

The bones underlying his features seemed to become iron; his eyes seemed to catch and reflect light like tempered and polished iron. As completely as if he had been translated, the boy was gone, and in his place stood a man she hardly knew, a man who resembled Nyle more than Artagel – Nyle when he had set himself to do something which would both humiliate him and hurt the people he cared about. The metal of Geraden's character had been tempered by bitterness, polished by dismay. When he spoke again, his voice was thick with muffled strength – and veiled threats.

'Why didn't Eremis kill you? It looks like he tried.'

Terisa put out her arms to him; she wanted to hug him again, embrace him, bring back the Geraden she had first learned to love. The Geraden who had willingly taken on so many different kinds of pain for her. But he only gripped her hands and held them still, requiring her to stand before him with all her sufferings exposed.

So she had to try to match him, to meet him where he was. She shook her head – not contradicting him, but denying her desire for comfort – and said, 'Oh, he tried. Or Master Gilbur tried for him. But the Castellan did this.'

Distinctly, like the sound of a breaking twig, he said, 'Lebbick.' The skin of his face was tight over his iron bones. His threats weren't directed at her. 'Tell me.'

Involuntarily, she faltered. She wanted to be equal to him – to be worthy of him – but she couldn't do it. Tears filled her eyes again. 'There's so much—'

'Terisa.'

At least he could still be reached. He put his arms around her again and let her cling to him as hard as she was able. Then he murmured, 'You're cold. And you look like you could use some food.' He hadn't become softer: he was simply holding himself back. Turning her with his arm on her waist, he started her moving up the hillside in the direction of the pillars. 'My camp is over there.'

She nodded, unable to speak – unable to separate the joy and the grief of seeing him.

'When I first came through the mirror,' he explained distantly, 'when I discovered I was still alive, I planned to hide up here. It's the best place I could think of. And I didn't want to put Houseldon in danger, if Eremis tried to get me again. And I'd already lost you. I thought I would go crazy if anybody else got hurt trying to protect me.

'But we finally figured out what Nyle is doing. There's no way I can keep my family out of danger. So there's no point in hiding. I just came back here because somebody had to do it – in case you managed to get through somehow and then couldn't find Houseldon – and it might as well be me because I was going to spend all my time waiting for you anyway.'

The sun had risen farther. The valley below the Closed Fist would remain in shadow for some time; but now there was enough light to reveal two horses tethered near the rocks ahead. One of them looked up at Terisa and Geraden. The other went on cropping grass unconcernedly. With an effort, she cleared her throat. 'It sounds like you've figured out a lot of things.'

He snorted sardonically. 'After that last day we spent together, I knew Eremis was a traitor. When I finally realized I do have a talent for Imagery – an unprecedented talent – it wasn't too hard to start drawing conclusions. Then all I had to do was hope you really have a talent, too – and you would find it – and you would be able to get at a mirror.

'On the whole, it seemed more plausible that Eremis would just fall down dead and save us that way, but I didn't have anything else left.'

There were a couple of packs on the ground near the horses, and a small jumble of blankets – Geraden's bed. As he and Terisa entered the shadow of the rocks, he dropped his arm and hurried ahead to pick up one of the blankets. At once, he draped it over her shoulders. 'I don't have a fire,' he muttered. 'I didn't want to be exposed, in case the wrong people came after me.'

She shrugged: the blanket was enough. Grateful for its warmth, she asked, 'What did you figure out about Nyle?' She dreaded everything she would have to say to him about Nyle.

Without meeting her gaze, he squatted to his packs and began pulling out foodskins, a jug, some fruit. His tone was harsh as he replied, 'Falling in love with Elega and letting her talk him into betraying Mordant for Prince Kragen – that was bad enough, but it sort of makes sense. Quiss – that's Tholden's wife – she says Nyle has been unhappy enough to do something like that for years. Not everybody agrees with her' – he grimaced – 'but I do. The Domne does.

'But faking his own murder to ruin me and help Master Eremis, right after he heard us prove Eremis was the only man in Orison who could have been working with the High King's Monomach— *That* doesn't make sense. It doesn't sound like him. He came back and saved my life, remember? Right after he rode away to betray Mordant. Helping a known traitor isn't something he would do of his own free will.

'He must have been pushed.'

Geraden put cheese, dried apples, and a hunk of mutton on a plate of flat bread. Terisa accepted it and sank to the grass to start eating. Nevertheless her attention was fixed on him.

'Pushed how?' he went on. 'What kind of threat or bribe would make him do something like that? What does he value that Eremis could give him – or take away?' Again, Geraden grimaced. He got out food for himself, but didn't eat it. 'His family. What else? Eremis must have a mirror that gives him access to the Care of Domne – to Houseldon. He can send those insects here – or creatures with red fur and too many arms – or even Gart. He must have threatened Nyle with something like that.'

A pang seized Terisa's heart, and she nearly dropped her food; she stared at him through the shadow. 'Then they're still in danger. Your home – your whole family – He might attack any time. Especially now – now that I got away from him.

'He knows where you are.' She had told Eremis that, she had told him that herself.

Geraden jerked up his head.

'He can guess I'm here,' she rushed on. 'He saw that mirror change – the day you tried to find a way for me to go home. Master Gilbur saw what I was doing. How can they protect themselves? What are they doing to protect themselves?'

He met her alarm squarely. Gloom veiled his eyes, but his voice was iron. 'Everything they can.'

His tone halted her panic. She was still afraid, however, and there were so many things she had to say which might hurt him. Trying to swallow her shame, she said, 'He really does know where you are. I'm sorry – that's my fault. I never told you—' His gaze made it hard for her to speak, but she forced herself. 'That day you tried to get me back to my apartment. When you translated me into your mirror. You never asked where I went. I didn't go to the champion – but I didn't go to my apartment, either. I came here.' She felt like she was confessing to an essential infidelity. 'I never told you, but I told him.'

Keeping himself clenched and neutral, he asked, 'Why?'

Despite his restraint, he put his finger on the sore place. She could have made excuses. He hypnotized me. He was the first man I knew who ever wanted me. But Geraden deserved better than that. And she was responsible for what had happened. No one else.

'I was wrong,' she said. 'I thought I wanted him.'

Geraden was silent until she looked up at him again. She still wasn't able to read his expression, but he didn't seem angry. His voice only sounded sad as he murmured, 'I wish you'd told me the mirror didn't take you to the champion. I would have had an easier time doing what I did. I would have felt less like I was throwing myself away.'

She felt the pain he didn't express more acutely than the regret he did. In an effort to make amends somehow, she offered, 'But Nyle is still alive. I'm sure of that. Eremis admitted it.'

As coherently as she could, she described what had happened to the physician and guards who had been left with Nyle's supposed corpse. The thought of their devoured bodies twisted in her belly; she forced herself to concentrate on her reasoning.

Geraden listened without showing any reaction. He was too tight to react. When she was finished, he said absently, 'Poor Nyle. Right now he probably wishes he actually were dead. Being used like that must be horrible for him. As long as Eremis has him, he can be hurt again. He can be used against us again.

'It's my fault, of course. If I hadn't stopped him from going to the Perdon – if I hadn't tried to make his decisions for him, he never would have been vulnerable to this. He wouldn't have been in the dungeon, where Eremis could get at him.' Geraden sighed as if blame were a part of what made him strong. 'I don't know how much of it he can stand.'

Must be horrible. That was true. She knew the feeling. She had come this far herself so that she wouldn't be used against the people she cared for.

Softly, she asked, 'What're you going to do, when you try to fight him, and he tells you to surrender or he'll kill Nyle?'

Unexpectedly, Geraden snorted again. If he hadn't been so angry, he might have laughed. 'I'm not going to fight him.'

You're what? She stared at him through the shadow as if he had struck her. Not going to fight him? The world was full of different kinds of pain, ways of being hurt – more than she had ever suspected. The wrenching sensation she felt now was new to her. I'm not going to fight him. Just for a second, her own anger began to blaze, and she wanted to rage at him.

He hadn't looked away, however. He was facing her like a hard wall; anything she hurled might simply hit him and fall to the ground. He had been that badly hurt himself: she seemed to see the sources of his pain as if the gloom were full of them. He had been hurt by the desperation which had made him translate himself away from Orison with no clear hope of ever being able to return – or to control where he was going. And by all the implications of what he had discovered about Master Eremis. By the fact that no one in Orison trusted or valued him enough to believe him – not one of the Masters, not Castellan Lebbick, not even King Joyse.

By the threat to his home.

And everything else he had ever tried to do with his life had failed. He was even responsible for Nyle's plight. How could she be angry at him now? What gave her the right?

She had to swallow the thick sensation of grief in her throat before she was able to ask, 'What *are* you going to do?'

Her quietness seemed to ease him in some way. His posture became marginally less rigid; his features relaxed a bit. With a faint echo of his former humor, he said, 'First I'm going to get you to tell me what happened to you. Then I'm going to take you back to Houseldon for a decent shirt.'

Involuntarily, she winced. 'You know that isn't what I meant.'

'All right.' The iron came back into his voice. 'I'm going to make a mirror. Any mirror, it doesn't matter – as long as it's big enough – as long as it isn't flat. I'm an Imager now. I know how to do it. I always went wrong before because I was trying to do the wrong thing, trying to use my talent wrong. Now I know better.

'I'm going to make a mirror. And I'm going to kill any son of a whore who comes here and tries to hurt my family.'

Terisa held her breath to keep herself still.

He shrugged stiffly. 'Is that what you wanted to hear?'

Oh, Geraden.

She didn't know what to do for him – but she had to do *something*. She couldn't bear to see him like this. He needed a better way to deal with what had been done to him.

That realization gave her the strength to start talking herself.

'You asked what happened to me. I think I better tell you.'

It was easier than she had expected: she was able to leave so much out. On a practical level, she discreetly excised the information that both the Tor and Artagel had asked her to betray him. He didn't need any more of that kind of hurt. And emotionally she could talk as if the Castellan's fury and her own terror hadn't touched her. In any case, she had no language for such things – or for the way they had changed her. Instead, she concentrated on Master Eremis.

'He has them fooled, Geraden,' she said after she had described her time in the dungeon, her visits from the Castellan and Eremis and Master Quillon, her escape with Quillon – after she had told him about Gilbur and Havelock, and about Quillon's murder. 'What he did with Nyle is just an example. That physician, Underwell, is dead, and everybody thinks you're a butcher, and the only person in Orison who looks innocent is Master Eremis. He's making himself a hero by refilling the reservoir – but that's only an excuse, he's just doing that so he can sneak around while everyone thinks he's busy. He's in league with Gart and Cadwal, and he's just waiting until his plans are ready.'

Policy, my lady. If it succeeds, I succeed with it. If it fails, I remain to pursue my ends by other means. In spite of her determination to be detached, the memory made her shudder.

'He's going to spring some kind of terrible trap, and no one knows he's the one behind it all. Master Quillon is my only witness, and he's dead. Since the Castellan saw me with Master Gilbur, he thinks *I* killed Quillon.'

Her own anger gathered as she spoke; she was full of accumulated outrage. She didn't want to put pressure on Geraden, she wanted to persuade him. But she simply couldn't think about Eremis without trembling.

'Geraden, he's going to destroy *them all*, and they don't even know it's him. What King Joyse is trying to do is crazy anyway, but it's hopeless if nobody knows who his enemy is. Everything he ever fought for, everything he ever made, Mordant and the Congery, all his ideals,' everything that made you love him, 'Eremis is going to destroy them all.'

Out of the mountains' dusk, Geraden made a cutting gesture, silencing her. His face might have been stone. '"Eremis is going to destroy them all." Of course. And you want me to stop him. You think there's something I can do to stop him.'

She tightened her grip on herself, forced herself to speak softly. 'Somebody has to warn them. Otherwise they don't stand a chance.'

What about the augury? What about Mordant's need?

Abruptly, he surged to his feet. For a moment, he stalked away as if he never intended to come back; then he swung around harshly and returned to confront her over the new grass and the neglected food.

'You want me to warn them,' he rasped. '*Do you think I haven't already considered that?* Talk is easy. Do you know how *far* Orison is from here? Do you know how long it would take me to get there? The siege has already started. Cadwal is already marching. Everything he wants to destroy will be in ruins before I get halfway there. I'll arrive like a good boy, panting and desperate, wanting something to save, and he'll just laugh at me.

'He'll just *laugh* at me.

'Terisa' – he was controlling himself with a visible effort, holding down a desire to yell at her – 'I am very, very tired of being laughed at.'

All her insides ached as she watched him; he made her so sad that her anger faded, at least temporarily. She didn't know what to say. What could she have said? She understood: of course she understood. He was beaten, and he was trying to accept it. But what she did or didn't understand changed nothing. It didn't help him – or Mordant. Yet she had to give him something. If she didn't, she was going to start crying again.

Quietly, stifling her unhappiness, she asked, 'What do you want me to do?'

He had considered that as well. 'You're an arch-Imager,' he said promptly. 'Like Vagel. You've just proved that. You can pass through a mirror without changing worlds. And without losing your mind. But you're more than that, too. You can change the Images themselves. You can do the same thing with flat glass that I do with a normal mirror. Together, we're two of the most powerful people in Mordant. All we need is practice. And mirrors. I want you to stay here and help me defend the only thing left that's worth fighting for.'

In the same tone, she asked, 'Do you have any glass at all?'

'No, not yet. We've got a bit of equipment and tinct my father confiscated from some sort of hedgerow Imager back in the early days of Mordant's peace, but we've never used it.

'I was worried while you were back in Orison, where Eremis could attack you – or put pressure on you by attacking me. But after what you've just told me, I don't think we need to hurry. We aren't much of a threat to him right now. He's got us out of Orison, and he still looks innocent. We can't hurt him where we are. And he's got a lot of other things on his mind. He's got to spring this trap of his – whatever it is. I think he'll leave us alone until he's done with Orison. He won't worry about cleaning up minor problems like us until afterward.'

Terisa sighed softly. 'We're "two of the most powerful people in Mordant," but we're only a "minor problem."'

'All we need is practice,' he repeated as if that would reassure her. 'By the time he gets around to us, we'll be ready for him. If he tries to touch Domne, we're going to tear his hand off at the wrist.'

After a pause, he concluded like a man affirming an article of faith, 'There isn't anything else.'

Maybe that was true – she didn't know. She had gone as far as she could at the moment. He assumed she would do what he wanted: that was enough. It would give her time to think. Time to *rest*. She needed rest badly. With everything still unresolved, she looked up at him and said, 'Speaking of Domne, I think you ought to take me to Houseldon. I want to meet your family.'

She couldn't be sure in the dim light, but she thought she saw him almost smile.

For some reason, however, her acquiescence – and the idea of returning home – didn't improve his mood. If he did smile, he did so in a way which denied laughter. His bitterness may have lifted a bit, but the dour humor which replaced it was equally iron and ungiving.

With a crisp accuracy entirely unlike the eager, accident-prone manner she remembered, he repacked his supplies, then watered the horses and saddled them. 'Take the bay,' he said, indicating one of the mounts. 'Quiss had her trained to carry pregnant women. Quiss has been pregnant a lot. I think Tholden wants to have seven sons, too.' His tone seemed gentler when he talked about such things, but that impression may have been created by what he was saying rather than by the way he said it. 'But so far he only has five children, and two of them are daughters.'

The air was warmer now; nevertheless Terisa kept the blanket over her shoulders as she climbed onto the bay. This was only her second experience with a horse, and the saddle seemed dangerously high. The blanket was awkward to hold closed – but not as awkward as her torn shirt. The last thing she wanted at a time like this was to ride into Houseldon with her chest exposed.

When she was seated, he adjusted her stirrups. Then he swung up onto his own mount, an appaloosa with a look of harmless lunacy in its eyes, and led her away.

The hillside sloped downward from the Closed Fist for some distance, then became rumpled, like a rucked-up skirt. Even in the shadow of the mountains, the light was strong enough now so that she could see wildflowers scattered across the grass; but she didn't realize how bright they were – how much brighter they were than she remembered them – until she and Geraden reached the direct sunshine. Then color seemed to burst from the grass wherever she looked: blue and lavender; mauve; yellow shot with orange; the rich, rich red of poppies. There were trees on the hillsides, too, but most of them grew down in the folds of the terrain, along the river. Mountains with snow still on them ranged north and east as well as south of her, so that she and Geraden seemed to be riding out from between their arms. As far as she could see toward the northeast, however, toward the Care of Domne, the hills were primarily covered with open grass and wildflowers.

Geraden was right: the bay was easy to ride; her gait instilled confidence. He and Terisa were soon down among the low hills, and she began to feel secure enough to attempt a trot. The whole sensation – the horse, the morning sunshine, his presence beside her – was so much more pleasant than the time she had gone riding with him and Argus that she couldn't hold in a smile.

'Yes,' she heard him murmur as if he were answering a question. 'The Care of Domne is beautiful. It's always beautiful, no matter what happens to it – or to Mordant. No matter who lives or dies, no matter what changes. Some things—' He looked around in an effort to see everything at once. 'Some things remain.'

He thought for a moment, then said, 'Maybe that's why the Domne was never willing to fight. And why King Joyse loved him anyway.'

'I don't understand.'

Geraden shrugged. 'In a way, my father *is* the Care of Domne. The things he values most don't need to be fought for because they can't be hurt.'

Terisa concentrated on her seat while the horses worked their way up a steeper hillside. After that, the ground seemed to have been smoothed out by the hand of the sun. It wasn't level, but the slopes were long and comfortable, and the grass appeared to flow all the way to the horizon.

She probably should have been thinking about her strange talent for Imagery. After any number of denials, she had discovered that her talent was real. Surely that changed her situation, her responsibilities? But she didn't feel that anything had changed. She had already chosen her loyalties in the struggle for Mordant, committed herself. And without glass there was nothing she could do to explore or define her abilities – whatever they actually were.

At the moment, she wasn't interested in herself. She was interested in Geraden.

'Tell me about your family,' she suggested. 'You've talked about them before, but it feels like a long time ago. I'd like to know who I'm going to meet.'

'Well, you won't meet Wester,' Geraden answered absently, as if his family had nothing to do with what he was thinking. 'He's away rallying the farmsteads. That's probably just as well. He's the handsome one. Women fall in love with him all the time. But he'll break your heart. The only thing he cares about is wool. If wool were glass, he'd be the greatest Imager in the world. We aren't sure he knows women even exist.

'Tholden is the oldest, of course. He's the heir – he'll be the Domne when our father dies – and he takes that very seriously. He wants to *be* the Care the same way our father is. And he's good at it. But he'd be better if he trusted himself enough to relax.

'He and the Domne can be pretty funny sometimes. He's a compulsive fertilizer – he wants everything to grow like crazy. So he goes around shoveling manure onto anything that has a root system. And my father follows him with a pruning saw, muttering about waste and cutting back everything Tholden just encouraged to grow.'

In the distance, Terisa saw a flock of sheep, moving gently like foam rolling on the green sea of the grass. Two small dogs and a shepherd kept the flock together without much difficulty: the day was untroubled, and the animals were placid. Geraden and the shepherd waved at each other, but neither of them risked disturbing the flock with a shout.

'The sheep are still out,' Geraden commented. 'We could drive them into Houseldon, but what good would that do? They're probably safer as far away as they can get.'

He rode for a while in silence before returning to her question. 'Anyway, you'll meet Tholden's wife, Quiss. And their children. She'll make you comfortable in Houseldon, or die trying.

'Minick is the second son. He's married, too, but you probably won't see his wife. She hardly ever leaves the house. That's too bad – I like her. But she's so shy she gets in a flutter when you just smile at her. Once she ruined her best gown by curtseying to the Domne in a mud puddle.

'I like Minick, too, but he's a little dim. He's the only man I know who thinks shearing sheep is fun. He and his wife are perfect for each other.

'That leaves Stead, the family scapegrace. He's in bed right now with a broken collarbone and several cracked ribs. He just couldn't keep his hands off the wife of a traveling tinker, and the tinker expressed his disapproval with the handle of a pitchfork.

'The strange thing is that Stead means well. He works hard. He's generous. Every day is a new joy. He simply adores women – and he can't imagine why any man doesn't make love to every woman there is. They're too precious to belong to anyone. *He* isn't jealous of the husbands he cuckolds. Why should *they* be jealous of him?

'Other than that, only about three hundred people live in Houseldon. It's the seat of the Domne. What serves as government in this Care is there. Anywhere else, Houseldon would be just another village, but in Domne it's the marketplace as well as the counting-house and the court of justice.

'Also the military camp. The Domne maintains six trained bowmen, mainly in case a bear or two or a pack of wolves comes out of the mountains and starts raiding sheep. But it's also their job to do things like rescue Stead from that tinker, or sit on people who get belligerent when they've had too much ale. On the rare occasions when the Domne decides he has to fine somebody for something, they collect it.

'That's what we have to defend ourselves with,' Geraden concluded as if this were the question Terisa had asked. 'Six bowmen, plus farmers with hoes and shepherds with crooks – as many as Wester can talk into it.

'That's why Houseldon needs us.'

The way he drifted from his subject disturbed her. She had always liked hearing him talk about his relatives. Sometimes, the contrast to her own family had saddened her; today it was a pleasure. She was looking forward to meeting his father and brothers. She wasn't ready to start thinking again about the trouble which had driven her here.

And what he suggested didn't sound right, coming from him. To give up everything to which he had ever aspired in order to do nothing more than fight for his home: that didn't sound like him. Like Artagel and Nyle in their different ways, he had never been able to stay at home. He had too much itch for the rest of the world, too much sense of possibility: he couldn't contain himself in Domne. She didn't question his love for Houseldon and the Care, for his father and brothers. But she felt strongly that he was the wrong man for the job he had chosen. He had chosen it as much out of bitterness as out of love: it didn't fit him.

She saw another flock of sheep. Then the ground became more level; fields appeared, watered by ditches from the river and streaked with the delicate green shoots of new corn; the horses reached a road. She and Geraden were the only people on it, but that came as no surprise to her. Everyone except the shepherds was probably busy preparing for the defense of Houseldon.

Then she saw Houseldon itself ahead.

She had forgotten that Geraden had called it a stockade.

The whole village was walled by timbers taller than she was; from horseback, she was barely able to see the thatched roofs of the houses past the top of the stockade. The timbers had been set into the ground and then lashed together with vines of some kind. To her, the idea of a stockade didn't sound especially impressive; she had grown up with concrete and steel. But when she actually saw that timber wall, she thought it looked remarkably sturdy. Mere men on horses wouldn't be able to break it down. Red-furred creatures armed with scimitars and hate wouldn't be able to break it down. They would need a catapult or a battering ram.

Or fire.

Thinking about fire, she clutched the blanket around her shoulders and shivered.

The gate, a massive shutter of timbers trussed with strips of iron, stood open. The men guarding it hailed Geraden in a way that suggested they knew where he had gone, and why. Houseldon wasn't a place for people who liked secrets.

As he and Terisa rode through the gate, Geraden asked the guards, 'Where's the Domne?'

One of them shrugged. 'At home? With that leg, he doesn't get around as easily as he used to.'

Geraden nodded and led Terisa down the main street of the village.

She wanted to ask what was wrong with the Domne's leg, but she was too busy looking around. The dirt street was little more than a lane; yet it served as a thoroughfare for wagons and cattle as well as people. If the street had been busy, she and Geraden would have had trouble getting through. This morning, however, they caused most of the traffic themselves: it was composed almost entirely of people who came out to see Geraden – and her.

In contrast to the lane, the square-fronted buildings on either side were substantial: solidly erected as well as large. They had stone foundations, deep porches, windows covered with oiled sheepskins. Working with rough planks and mud plaster, the inhabitants of Houseldon had constructed homes and shops meant to endure; and the characteristic thatch of the roofs was apparently used because it was practical – cool in summer, warm in winter, easy to replace – rather than because it was cheap. In that way, the houses were like the people, who were dressed primarily in tough fabrics and simple styles, intended to last.

The spectators looked at Geraden and studied Terisa with unabashed curiosity. One rowdy spirit – she didn't see who it was – shouted unexpectedly, 'Looks like you made a good choice, Geraden!' but Geraden didn't react.

He certainly didn't need to defend himself. Several voices muttered imprecations at the rowdy spirit on his behalf, and one old man said clearly, 'Hold your tongue, puppy. If you had his problems, you would drown yourself in the Broadwine.'

Just for a second, the gloom in the background of Geraden's expression lifted, and his eyes sparkled a little.

Terisa was abashed by the realization that she was blushing.

For several minutes, he steered her horse past a number of intersecting lanes and paths – past public watering troughs, a granary or two, a shop that sold foodstuffs and utensils, at least six merchantries which dealt in wool and sheepskins, and one tavern rendered unmistakable by a huge sign over the door that announced succinctly: TAVERN. Then, without warning, he stopped in front of a house and swung off his mount.

This building was somewhat larger than its neighbors. Apart from its size, however, its only distinguishing feature was the plain, brown-and-russet pennon that fluttered from a pole jutting out of its thatch. Geraden tossed his reins over the porch rail, then turned to offer Terisa a lift down, muttering, 'This is it.'

There was a woman on the porch. A line of rope ran from one end of the porch to the other, and over it hung a large rug, rag-woven from scraps of wool. The woman held a short flail in one hand, and the air around her was dim with dust: apparently, she had been beating the rug. Terisa was immediately struck by her corn silk hair and sky blue eyes, by the flush of exertion on her cheeks and the strength in her hands. She had the bosom of an Earth Mother and the shoulders of a stonemason, and she propped her fists on her hips to greet Geraden as if she weren't entirely ready to let him enter her house.

A child only a little bigger than a toddler peered from behind her skirts, then ducked into hiding.

'You took long enough,' she said in a voice that directly contradicted the severity of her manner. 'Da's been fretting.'

'Quiss,' he replied like a man who had forgotten how to laugh and didn't want to get angry, 'this is Terisa. The lady Terisa of Morgan. She's an arch-Imager.' He seemed to fear that Quiss wouldn't take his companion seriously enough. 'After Vagel, she's the most powerful Imager in the country.'

Quiss raised her blue eyes to Terisa's face. She didn't smile, but her gaze felt as friendly as sunshine. All at once, Terisa forgot to be self-conscious.

'She's also cold and tired, and probably hungry,' Quiss pronounced, 'and she isn't used to horses. What are you waiting for? Bring her in.'

Terisa smiled helplessly.

Geraden reached up for her hand. His eyes gave away nothing: he was too iron to be dented by Quiss' manner. Terisa included him with her smile, then lost it because she suddenly began to ache for the Geraden who would have chuckled happily at Tholden's wife. When he didn't respond, either to her smile or to her sadness, she took a deep breath for courage and let him help her off the bay.

Her legs began to shake as soon as her feet hit the ground – a consequence of her unfamiliarity with horseback riding – but after she took a step or two the trembling eased. Geraden might have wanted to withdraw his hand, but she didn't give him the chance; she clung to him as she went up the steps onto the porch.

Still without smiling, Quiss unexpectedly took hold of Terisa's shoulders and gave her a quick hug, a kiss on the cheek. 'Welcome, Terisa of Morgan,' she said. 'I don't know anything about Imagery – but I know Geraden. You are very welcome here.'

Terisa had no reply. An awkward moment passed while she groped for a way to explain how glad she was to be here. Then the child hiding behind Quiss' skirts broke the silence.

'Ma, the lady don't smell good.'

Quiss started to turn. '"Doesn't," Ruesha. Not "don't." And that's no way to talk to a lady.'

Geraden was faster, however. 'Imp!' he barked. 'Come here. I'm going to paddle your behind until you can't walk for a week.'

Squealing with an obvious lack of fright, the child sprinted into the house. Geraden followed, thundering his boots on the floorboards as he pretended to run.

This time, Quiss did smile, half in apology, half in pleasure. 'Ruesha says what she thinks,' she said, 'like too many of her uncles.' Then she wrinkled her nose humorously. 'But it's true, you know. You don't smell good. They must have treated you pretty badly after Geraden got away.'

Terisa was smiling herself; a small trill of music ran around her heart. There was hope for Geraden yet. Perhaps just for a second, he had been surprised out of his defeat. She sounded incongruously happy as she replied, 'They put me in the dungeon.'

Quiss' eyes resumed their sky blue sobriety. 'A dungeon they haven't cleaned for decades, apparently.' The bare idea affronted her. 'Come. I'll introduce you to the Domne. Then we can go get you a bath. And some clean clothes. That will give his father a chance to try to make sense out of Geraden.'

With one strong arm wrapped companionably around Terisa's shoulders, Quiss steered her into the house.

The room they entered was so dark that she could hardly see. The only light came from the coals in the hearth, the barely translucent window covers, and the reflection of daylight through the doorway. As her eyes adjusted, however, shapes began to emerge from the dimness: a bulky cast-iron stove beside the fireplace, several doors into other rooms, a rectangular wooden table long enough to seat ten or twelve people.

At the head of the table sat a man with one leg propped on a stool.

'Did you see Geraden, Da?' Quiss asked.

'He went through here,' a warm voice rumbled. 'He was too busy trying to beat the spit out of your youngest to talk to his mere father. But he's back in one piece – and he's got a woman with him. I gather something good has happened.'

'I think so,' said Quiss briskly. 'Da, this is Terisa – the lady Terisa of Morgan. As soon as you tell her how welcome she is, I'm going to take her and get her a bath and clothes and food. In the meantime—' She paused significantly before saying. 'Now that she's here, maybe he'll unbend enough to tell you what's going on.

'My lady Terisa of Morgan, this is the Domne.'

Through the gloom, Terisa saw that the Domne was a tall man, as lean and curved as an axe handle. He had Geraden's face, and Artagel's, and Nyle's, but more so in some way, as if they were attractive yet inaccurate copies of him. The hair on his head was thick, but he had no beard. The silver streaks at his temples were the only obvious signs of his age. Perhaps because the light was weak, he didn't appear to be more than half as old as King Joyse.

The leg propped on the stool was plump with bandages. He had a pair of canes nearby, but he made no attempt to rise when Quiss introduced him. Instead, he said, 'My lady,' in a voice as warm as a hug, 'you're welcome in Houseldon – and in my house. If we could do it, we would put on a feast for you, a celebration. But I'm afraid we're a little too busy. Geraden seems to think we might be attacked. That doesn't happen every day, and we have to brace ourselves.

'But don't worry about that right now. I've wanted him to bring a woman home with him for a long time. That's the benefit of sons. When they marry – or only fall in love – or merely feel like flirting a bit – they bring their women home with them. Quiss is a good example. If she were my daughter, and Tholden was someone else's son, she would have left to go with him, and we would have been lost without her.'

At that, Quiss snorted affectionately. 'Sons, is it? Is that why you treat Ruesha like she's worth the weight of her three brothers in fine brandy?'

The Domne didn't deign to acknowledge this jibe. Noticing the direction of Terisa's gaze, he explained, 'A hunting accident. I'm afraid I finally have to admit that I'm not a young man. Occasionally, packs of wild pigs wander into

Domne from the Care of Termigan. I'd be willing to let them wander, but unfortunately they can trample an entire cornfield overnight, so we're forced to hunt them. This time, one of my sons had the bad sense to suggest that I was getting too old to hunt wild pig. The truth must be told, Quiss, it was Tholden. Naturally, I insisted on leading the hunt myself.

'When the boar charged, my thrice-cursed horse panicked and threw me. Then at last I had to admit that indeed I have put on a few years since my youth. I simply wasn't spry enough to prevent the pig from sticking his tusk in my leg.

'It heals slowly, alas,' he sighed. 'Another sign of age.'

Almost at once, Terisa found that she liked the Domne. The relaxed way he talked put her at ease, made her feel more welcome than any elaborate speech or feast; made her feel at home. 'My lord,' she said impulsively because she didn't have any other words for her gratitude, 'I'm very glad to be here.'

'"My lord"?' the Domne returned humorously. 'I hope not. The last time a woman insisted on calling me "my lord," I had to marry her to make her stop.'

Smiling, Terisa asked, 'What should I call you?'

'"Da,"' he answered without hesitation. 'It's probably presumptuous of me, but I like it. My sons refuse, of course. Another benefit of sons – they keep me humble. In the name of my dignity. If I have any – which I doubt, sitting here half crippled because I wasn't able to get out of the way of a pig. But the rest of my family won't call me anything else.'

'Da,' she murmured experimentally. It had a nice sound. She had never called her own father anything except *Father*.

'Thank you,' said the Domne as if she had done him a favor.

'Come, Terisa.' Quiss put an arm on Terisa's shoulders again. 'If I let you stay, he'll keep you talking until lunchtime. That's a "benefit of sons" he doesn't mention. When they were small, he always had someone to listen to him. They taught him bad habits. Any daughter with sense in her head would have known better.'

The Domne nodded gravely. 'We can talk later, Terisa, when you've had a chance to rest and refresh yourself.

'If you find Geraden,' he added to Quiss, 'tell him I want to see him. I refuse to be ignored all morning merely because Ruesha wants to play.'

'Yes, Da,' Quiss replied in a tone of gently mocking subservience. With her arm, she took Terisa out of the room.

Almost immediately, they encountered a serving girl in the hall. Quiss instructed her to bring hot water for a bath, then to fetch Geraden for the Domne. The girl bobbed an acknowledgment, and Quiss and Terisa walked on.

The house was big – bigger than Terisa had realized. Behind its wide front, it seemed to sprawl for a considerable distance. Beyond the room where the Domne sat, the windows were open, letting light and spring air into the hall, and she found that she could see the grain in the polished hardwood of the floor, the fitted planks of the walls. Here she realized for herself how strong the odor of the dungeon was on her – realized it because everything around her smelled of soap, beeswax, and old resin. Years of wear and polish had brought out a glow from the floorboards down the center of the hall, and that warmer hue seemed to mark the way ahead like a path, a way of making sure that no one got lost.

Quiss took her past a door that stood slightly ajar. As they crossed the opening, a plaintive voice called out, 'Quiss! In the name of decency!' The tone of the appeal was both lugubrious and funny. 'I'm dying.'

'And about time, too,' muttered Quiss without stopping – or letting Terisa pause.

'Who was that?' Terisa asked in surprise.

Then she was surprised even further to see Quiss' entire face turn red.

'Stead. One of the sons Da seems to value so highly. He hasn't had a woman since a tinker broke his collarbone, and he wants me to bed him. As soon as he learns you're here, he'll get the same idea about you.

'Take my advice,' Quiss continued primly. 'Have nothing to do with him. He's the only one of the Domne's sons who has no sense at all. Personally, I won't even let the serving girls go in his room. A groom and one of the shearers are taking care of him.'

Terisa made an effort to keep from laughing. 'What does he think he can do – with a broken collarbone?'

Quiss stopped in the hall and gave Terisa the full force of her bright blue eyes. Softly, she said, 'You must not have much experience with men. It isn't what he thinks he can do. It's what he thinks you can do.'

Her expression, however, suggested that she wasn't listening to herself – that her own thoughts had gone in a different direction. She had become grave, almost somber; perplexity knotted her brows. 'Before yesterday,' she murmured, 'none of us knew you existed. Then Geraden arrived out of nowhere, breathing fire about a possible attack and at the same time acting like all the heart and hope had been beaten out of him. He said he left a woman behind who was probably being tortured because she was his friend. Now that I see you, it seems astonishing how little he actually told us about you.

'He never mentioned that you could have any man you wanted.'

Terisa bit back an impulse to ask, Is that really what you think? She wanted to believe that she was pretty; and Quiss' opinion seemed to have tremendous value. But Tholden's wife obviously wanted to get reassurance, not give it. She wanted to believe that Geraden wouldn't be hurt anymore. Deliberately, Terisa put her questions aside.

'They put me in the dungeon,' she said, 'because I wouldn't tell them where he was. He rescued me when my old life was going nowhere. He's risked himself for me any number of times. He even tried to fight the High King's Monomach for me once.' Quiss was impressed; but Terisa didn't stop. 'He's the only reason I'm alive – the only reason I'm here. Even if I didn't like him so much, I wouldn't be interested in anybody else.'

Certainly not Stead, who sounded suspiciously like Master Eremis.

That was what Quiss wanted to hear. She didn't smile – apparently, she rarely smiled when she was happy – but warmth shone from her. 'Then I'll stop worrying about him and leave him to you. If anybody can get him out of the pig wallow he's in, you can.'

Briskly, she moved Terisa again in the direction of a bath.

Three turns, two doorways, and another long hall brought them to a bedroom with a low, flat cot that contrasted strangely with the rest of the furnishings: the heavy armchairs and the sturdy washstand. 'This is Artagel's room,' Quiss explained. 'It's relatively private, but I can get you a softer bed if his cot is too hard. I don't know how he sleeps on it. Sometimes I think he may actually be as tough as he thinks he is.'

'I'll try it and let you know,' said Terisa. The bed in her former apartment had had the firmest mattress she could find.

'The advantage,' Quiss went on, 'is that you get your own bathroom.' She pointed at the other door to the room. 'Why don't you get started? There's water – and the hot water should be here in a minute. I'll go find you some clothes.'

Terisa agreed gratefully. As soon as Tholden's wife left, she closed the bedroom door, pulled off her boots, and went into the bathroom.

It had no running water – apparently the Care of Domne didn't know as much about plumbing as Orison did – but clay pipes had been set in the floor to carry bathwater and waste away. Which explained, now that she thought about it, why she hadn't seen water, not to mention sewage, standing in the ditches alongside Houseldon's streets: underground drains. And that perception, in turn, made her laugh softly at herself. Her time in Orison, and Elega's attempt on the reservoir, had taught her some strange lessons. The woman she used to be would never have noticed plumbing or drains unless they didn't work.

As Quiss had said, however, there was water, plenty of it in a vat beside the wooden bathtub.

Instead of filling the tub right away, however, Terisa went back into the bedroom, sat down on Artagel's hard cot, closed her eyes, and tried to absorb the fact that she was here and safe; that she had finally made her way to a place where she could feel the sun's warmth in the wood of the wall beside the bed, and where the people around her were moved by simple things like family and friendship and wool, rather than by treachery, ambition, and revenge.

She sat there, soaking up the peace of the house, until two serving girls arrived with four buckets of hot water between them. Then she gave herself what felt like the most luxurious bath she had ever had in her life.

Some time later, she dried her scrubbed body and her now-lustrous hair, drained the tub, and tried on the clothes Quiss had left for her.

The undergarments were of fine linen; the shirt and skirt, of unlined sheepskin, supple and delicate against her skin, yet remarkably tough. The long skirt was wide around the hem, and had been slit to the knees both in front and in back, so that it could be worn on horseback; the shirt was decorated only by its buttons, which appeared to be polished pieces of obsidian. Both the shirt and the skirt went well with her winter boots.

Now all she needed was earrings to match the buttons. And a mirror, so that she could do something with her hair.

Of course, she didn't really want a mirror – not for something as simple as vanity. What she actually desired was a chance to see what she looked like, so that she might begin to believe in herself – to believe that Geraden would notice her enough, and care enough about what he saw, to let her reach him.

Get him out of the pig wallow—

She didn't trust any of the conclusions he had reached. And she couldn't bear to see him like that.

When Quiss came to take her back to the Domne, she went both hesitantly and eagerly, unsure of herself, and yet sure that what she wished to do was worth doing.

'Da likes an early lunch,' Quiss explained, 'and he doesn't like to admit that he's too impatient to wait while you eat, so he asks you to eat with him. Also Tholden is here, and I'm sure he wants to question you. If you don't mind.'

Terisa couldn't think of a quick way to describe how important the Domne and his concerns were to her, so she replied simply, 'I don't mind.'

In the front room, the light had been improved by the raising of the window covers and the altered angle of the sun. Two men sat at the table, and as Terisa entered the room she had no difficulty seeing that one of them was the Domne – or that his companion was huge.

'Ah, Terisa,' said the Domne in his warm, comfortable voice, 'I'm glad you could join us. I want someone to share my lunch. And Tholden thinks he can't wait to talk to you.' Gesturing toward the huge man, he went on, 'Terisa, this is Tholden, my eldest. Another of the benefits of sons is that one of them is bound to be the right man to inherit their father's place. Tholden is the right man for mine.

'That's fortunate, since he's also' – the Domne laughed softly – 'the only one of my sons who wants the responsibility.'

Tholden stood beside his father like a bear; his stiff hair nearly brushed the beams of the ceiling; his beard was so long and wild that it made his chest seem even thicker – and his chest was already thick enough to create the illusion that his shoulders were round and stooped. When he sketched a bow toward her, Terisa saw that his hands were ridged with calluses: they looked more like gardening implements than normal hands.

She also noticed that he had straw and a few twigs caught in his beard. Involuntarily, she smiled. Then, trying to recover her manners, she said, 'I'm glad to meet you. Geraden talks about you a lot.'

Tholden grinned – a smile which lifted his beard, but didn't soften his expression. 'I'm sure he does.' His voice was unexpectedly high and gentle; he sounded like a man who wasn't able to shout. 'Quiss and I had the doubtful pleasure of raising him after our mother passed away. He probably remembers every beating he deserved in agonizing detail.'

Quiss went to the stove and began pulling a meal together. Politely, Terisa replied, 'No, nothing like that. He has a higher opinion of you than you think.' Then she asked, 'Where is he, by the way?'

'He was here,' said the Domne. 'We talked for a while—'

'Then I sent him to help Minick.' Tholden let his smile drop. 'Minick is trying to explain to an assortment of farmers, shepherds, merchants, and servants how we want them to defend the walls. He's the most meticulous man in Houseldon, and he's certainly thorough, but he can be a bit slow, and his explanations have a tendency to confuse people. Geraden will get more done in less time, even if he has lost his sense of humor.'

Terisa glanced at the Domne, then looked up at Tholden again. 'In other words, you want to talk to me alone.'

The Domne began chuckling to himself.

From the stove, Quiss said, 'I warned you subtlety would be wasted on her.' Her tone made it clear that she wasn't laughing at Terisa.

'Silence, upstart woman.' Without so much as glancing in his wife's direction, Tholden swung his arm and managed to slap her across the bottom. 'Don't be pert. Women should be seen and not heard. As much as possible.'

Rather than retorting, Quiss looked at Terisa and rolled her eyes in mock-despair.

Terisa herself wasn't amused, however. Holding herself still, she asked in a neutral tone, 'What's the matter? Don't you trust him?'

Tholden opened his mouth as if he had been stung; the Domne waved him silent. 'Terisa,' the older man said quietly, and this time she could hear his years in his voice, 'I would sell my soul at the word of any of my sons. Even Nyle, who seems to have forgotten who he is. But this Geraden who came storming into Houseldon only yesterday, warning of imminent destruction – who is he? He isn't the Geraden who left us for Orison with more hope in his heart than most simple flesh and blood can hold. It's not just that he has become hard. I know him better than that, Terisa. He has become closed. He talks about defending his home as if the mere idea was terrible.

'A change like that' – the Domne spread his hands – 'it could mean anything.'

'And you want me to explain it,' said Terisa stiffly.

The lord and Tholden nodded together. Quiss watched mutely from the stove. 'I will sell my soul for him now, if I must,' murmured the Domne, 'without another word from you – or from him. But I would prefer to understand what I'm trusting.'

Without warning, Terisa found that she wanted to say, It isn't your fault. It isn't anything you did. He's just been so badly beaten— He's failed you, he's failed Artagel and Nyle, he's failed Orison and King Joyse – and now, when it's too late to do any good, he finds out he really is an Imager. He could have made a difference. He went through all those years of humiliation, and now it's too late.

But the words refused to be spoken. They weren't hers to say: they were his. She could feel it in the room that she couldn't try to explain him without erecting a wall between him and his family – a wall with pity on one side and loneliness on the other. The more they knew about his pain, the more difficulty they would have confronting it, challenging it. She herself was almost paralyzed by knowing too much. If he didn't speak for himself, he would never be whole again.

So she said, 'I'm sorry. That's between you and him. He'll have to tell you himself.'

Then she said, 'But *I* trust him.'

Tholden was scowling. Quiss concentrated on her pots and pans as if she were leery of what she might say if she spoke. But the Domne smiled at Terisa with sunlight in his eyes.

Distinctly, Tholden asked, 'Do you consider yourself a friend of his?'

Almost without interrupting her preparations, Quiss swung an elbow into her husband's ribs. Then, ignoring his muffled grunt, his sharp glare, she lifted two platters heaped with food and carried them to the table. 'Sit down, Terisa,' she said, 'eat,' placing one platter in front of the Domne, the other before the chair nearest Terisa. 'If I've given you too much, don't worry about it. I'm used to cooking for this great ox and the farmers he consorts with.'

A bland expression on her face, Quiss pulled out the chair and held it for Terisa.

On the platter, Terisa saw fried yams, panbread, greens, some kind of meat covered with gravy, and what looked like apple fritters. If she ate all that, she wouldn't be able to move for two days.

'I'm sorry,' said Tholden. With a hand like a shovel, he gestured toward the chair. 'Please sit down. Eat.'

When Terisa still didn't move, he added, 'I don't mean to question your integrity. I'm just scared. I don't like the way Geraden has changed. I don't like the news from Orison. I don't like what he says it means. Houseldon has never been very good at defending itself.'

'Good enough,' put in the Domne gently.

'So far,' countered Tholden. 'But I don't want to watch people I've known and worked with all my life get killed because something horrendous has happened to Geraden.'

The Domne pointed at the chair Quiss held. 'Terisa, *sit down*. I haven't heard him apologize that much in twenty years. In another minute, you're going to hurt his feelings.'

Terisa sat down and let Quiss adjust the chair.

Now it was her turn. 'I'm sorry,' she said again. 'I'm scared, too. And I'm groping. Quiss says Geraden didn't tell you much about me. He didn't tell you I'm new at all this. I've never been in a place like this. I've never met people like you.' I've never been *important* before. 'And I'm not used to having enemies.

'I want to help. I'll do anything I can. I just don't want to talk about things that Geraden ought to tell you himself.'

Tholden studied her hard for a moment. Then he grinned – a new smile that brightened his whole face. Abruptly, he swept a chair out of his way and sat down opposite her. 'When you're done eating, push that plate over here. I could use a snack.'

From the stove, Quiss gave Terisa a look of grave, sky blue gladness. Then, wiping her hands on her apron, she turned to the Domne. 'Da, I've heard a rumor that some of the women are panicking. They don't know where to hide their daughters – or themselves. With your permission, I'll go try to talk some sense into them.'

The Domne nodded. 'Of course.'

'Tell them to come here if we're attacked,' said Tholden. 'This house will be our last bastion, if everything else goes down. We'll put the women and children down in the beer cellar, and the rest of us will protect them as long as we can.'

With one hand, Quiss placed a brief touch of affection on her husband's shoulder. Nodding to Terisa, she left the room and the house.

Calmly, as if everything were normal, the Domne picked up his knife and fork, and began to eat.

Terisa was moderately hungry, but she couldn't force herself to tackle all that food. These people were seriously considering the necessity of hiding their women and children in a beer cellar while Houseldon was destroyed. Facing Tholden, she said, 'Ask me something. Let me help.'

Tholden met her gaze squarely. 'When Geraden got here yesterday, he thought we were going to be attacked almost immediately. Now he says we've got time to plan our defense. As long as you're here, he thinks Master Eremis doesn't have any reason to attack us right away. What do you think?'

Without hesitation, she said, 'I think he's wrong.'

The Domne cocked an eyebrow. His mouth full of yams, he asked, 'Why?'

'I don't think he realizes how dangerous he is. Or how dangerous Eremis thinks he is. Eremis has been working hard for a long time now to keep him from understanding his own talent. And he's tried to have him killed. I don't think Eremis will believe he's safe until Geraden is dead.'

'That's speculation,' murmured Tholden.

'This isn't.' Terisa spoke with the confidence of a woman who had been able to out-think Castellan Lebbick. 'Eremis can't possibly know how Geraden's feeling. And he can't possibly know there aren't any mirrors here. Now that Geraden knows what his talent is, Eremis has to be afraid of being attacked himself.

'And that's not all. Geraden thinks Eremis will postpone attacking Houseldon until after he's done with Orison. But the last thing he was doing in Orison was refilling the reservoir. That doesn't sound like a man with a trap ready to spring. It sounds like a man who wants to help Orison fight off Prince Kragen until Cadwal is in position.

'If I'm right, Eremis has time to strike at you right now.

'And he knows I'm here.' This had to be said, although it was difficult for her. The Domne and his son needed to know the extent of their danger. 'Master Gilbur saw the mirror change. He knows I've discovered my talent, too. He knows I can go anywhere in Mordant – or Cadwal or Alend, for that matter – if I just know what it looks like. If I just know how to visualize it. I could show up in his rooms some night when he's asleep and nail him to the bed.

'He's not just afraid of Geraden. He's afraid of me.'

He needs to be afraid of me. I'm going to make him afraid of me. Somehow.

The Domne continued to eat without any obvious concern; but Tholden watched Terisa with growing chagrin on his face. When she was done, he muttered as if no one were listening to him, 'Sheep-dung. I'm not used to this myself. I'm not Artagel – I never wanted to be a soldier. What am I supposed to do?'

The Domne put down his knife and fork. 'What *are* you doing?'

Tholden made a dismissive gesture. 'You know what. Wester is sending farmers and their families here as fast as he can talk them into it. Every empty hogshead and barrel we've got is being filled with water and positioned around the stockade, in case of fire. Every pitchfork and scythe and axe in Houseldon is being sharpened.' Slowly, a frantic look came into his eyes, and his hands knotted on the table in front of him; but he kept his voice steady. 'Banquettes are being knocked together inside the wall, so that anyone with a bow will have a place to stand. Minick – and Geraden, I hope – are laying out lines of retreat. They're trying to explain to the men with bows how to retreat – how to use the houses for cover, how to set ambushes.

'What good is that going to do against Imagery?'

Listening to him, Terisa understood how he felt.

The Domne was undismayed, however. 'Who knows?' he said calmly. 'I don't. I can't see the future.

'But I can see you're the right man for the job. You've already thought of things that wouldn't have occurred to me. You'll think of more. If Artagel were here, he wouldn't be able to defend Houseldon any better.'

Tholden wasn't convinced. With a sour snort, he asked, 'Is this what you call selling your soul at the word of one of your sons?'

At that, the Domne sat up straighter in his chair; his eyes flashed. 'Tholden, I know you think you're a grown man, but you still aren't too old to be punished for disrespect. Maybe I'm only your father, and half crippled as well, but I'm still man enough to prune your apricots within an inch of their lives. Consider *that* before you risk being pert with me.'

Involuntarily, Tholden smiled. His beard rustled on his chest. Nevertheless his eyes remained full of trouble, and his smile didn't last long. Too worried to sit where he was, he pushed himself up from the table. 'Excuse me, Terisa,' he murmured. 'I'm afraid you'll have to eat lunch without my help. I've lost my appetite.'

With the hunched gait of a man who was accustomed to ducking under doorways and low ceilings, he left the house.

The Domne watched him go and sighed. 'You don't know it, Terisa,' he commented after Tholden was gone, 'but those are the saddest words anyone has said in my house for a long time. "I've lost my appetite." I hope you aren't planning to tell me the same thing.'

Terisa meant to say Yes. The pile of food on the platter daunted her. The size and consequences of the danger she and Geraden had brought to Houseldon daunted her. Yet the way the Domne looked at her seemed so warm and companionable, so willing to accept whatever she represented, that when she opened her mouth the word which came out was, 'No.'

He smiled approvingly as she lifted her fork to sample Quiss' panbread and gravy.

For several minutes while she ate a little of everything on the platter, he sat in silence, gazing out into the sunshine through the nearest window. She had the impression that he was waiting for her to finish; but he didn't seem impatient. In fact, he appeared quite content to look out on the street and nod amiably at anyone who caught his eye. If war was coming to Houseldon, it didn't show on the face of the Domne. Geraden had said of him, *The things he values most don't need to be fought for because they can't be hurt.* Yet Terisa wasn't sure that was accurate. Despite his look of contentment, she thought he cared deeply about a number of things which could be hurt very easily.

When she put down her utensils to indicate that she was done, he glanced over at her, then returned his gaze to the window. In a relaxed way, as if he were continuing an earlier conversation, he asked, 'What was your impression of Nyle?'

Her stomach knotted around the food she had just eaten. Cautiously, she countered, 'What did Geraden tell you?'

The Domne's manner disarmed anxiety. 'That you think Nyle is still alive. That this Master Eremis still wants to use him against us. That's not what I want to know. What did you think of him? How is he?'

Because the answer was painful, she said shortly, 'He's miserable.'

'Ah,' sighed the Domne as if he had both expected and feared her reply.

This time, she let herself say, 'I don't blame him. Everything he believed that got him into trouble – everything about King Joyse and Orison and Elega and Prince Kragen – it was all plausible. King Joyse has been working for years, setting himself up to be betrayed. Nyle was just unlucky enough to fall into the trap – the same trap Elega fell into herself. He believed what his King wanted him to believe.'

Ignoring the Domne's reputation as one of the King's dearest friends, she went on, 'He's really just a victim. Eremis probably would never have been able to get his hands on Nyle if Nyle hadn't been stuck in the dungeon with nowhere to turn for hope.'

If anything she said offended the Domne, however, he didn't show it. 'Families,' he murmured mildly. 'They are endlessly interesting. Elega and her father. Geraden and Nyle. Sometimes I think the fate of the world depends on how people feel about their families.

'What sort of family do you come from, Terisa? Did you have sisters? Not *six* sisters, by any chance?'

The idea was so absurd that she almost laughed aloud. 'No, Da. I was an only child.'

He looked at her again, more sharply this time. 'Do you mean to say that after you your parents were able to restrain their enthusiasm for children? Were you that bad? Or were you so good that any other child would be a disappointment?'

'No,' she answered as candidly as she could. 'I was an accident. My father sure didn't have time for children. And he didn't want my mother to have time either.'

'"Didn't have time"?' Abruptly, the Domne pushed his sore leg off the stool. Grimacing, he shifted the position of the stool so that he could face her more directly, then heaved his leg back onto it. Propped straight with his elbows on the table, he asked, 'What vital and consuming work did your father do, that he "didn't have time for children"?'

Unsure of where the discussion was headed – and uncomfortable because she was always uncomfortable when she talked about her parents – Terisa replied briefly, 'He made money.'

Odd how both she and the Domne were speaking of her father in the past tense. But she thought about him in the past, as part of something which wasn't true anymore.

'For what purpose?' inquired the Domne.

She shrugged. 'To make more money. I don't think he had any other reason for doing it. He did it because that was what he was good at.' She thought about conversations she had overheard from the dining room while she sat out of sight on the stairs, listening when her parents thought she had gone to bed. 'Money was the best way to get things that weren't his. Social standing. Political influence.' Then she remembered some of the valets her father had hired. Muscle.

'He made money because he believed if you can do that you can buy everything else.'

'Very strange,' pronounced the Domne. 'He would have flourished in Cadwal.

'And what did your mother do while your father made money?'

With an understated vehemence which unsettled her, Terisa said, 'I think she practiced.'

'"Practiced"?'

'Being ornamental. So my father could show her off whenever he was in the mood.'

'"Women should be seen and not heard"?' The Domne couldn't restrain a burst of laughter. 'That explains where you got your beauty. Terisa, I don't know how to tell you this – but I think you've already met High King Festten. Even though you wouldn't recognize him if you saw him.'

Terisa tried to smile, but she didn't succeed.

The Domne studied her; sunlight from the windows reflected in his eyes. 'However, that raises a fascinating question. How did you get here from there? How did the daughter of parents like that become the kind of woman my youngest son – perhaps my best son – would kill for?'

She wanted to answer him. At the same time, she wanted to stop talking about her parents. Roughly, she told him something that she hadn't revealed to anyone else in Mordant, not even to Geraden.

'When I did something my father didn't like, he used to lock me in a closet until I got scared enough to stop crying.'

For a long moment, the Domne stared at her without expression, as if the energy of life had been wiped off his face. Then, slowly, carefully, he turned away. He took his leg from the stool in order to put it back in its former position, toward the window. He settled himself again with his leg up and his spine stretched against the back of the chair; he might have been getting comfortable for a nap.

After that, one at a time, he picked up his canes and flung them out the window. The first sailed clear; the second clattered against the frame and fell just outside.

So fiercely that she winced, he whispered, 'What are you doing to me, Joyse? Everybody who is worth anything in your entire kingdom is being hurt, and I'm sitting here crippled. What are you *doing*?'

There was nothing she could say. Geraden had surely told his father what she knew about the King's intentions. There was nothing else.

Briefly, the Domne put his hands over his face, and his shoulders clenched. Almost at once, however, he rubbed his cheeks briskly, as if he were scrubbing passion off his features; with a long, slow exhalation, he let his anger go.

'It's remarkable, don't you think,' he murmured, 'that we're such good friends, King Joyse and I?

'Of course, that isn't the reason our friendship is famous. It's famous because I refused to fight in any of his wars. I refused to let him make me into one of his soldiers. People consider that strange. Don't I think Mordant is worth fighting for? Of course I do. Don't I think his ideal of a Congery that turns Imagery into something benign is worth fighting for? Of course I do. Then why don't I fight? What's the matter with me?

'But I think our friendship is more remarkable than anything I have or haven't refused to do in my life.'

'What do you mean?' Terisa asked, wanting him to go on.

'Well—' The Domne spread his hands. 'We have next to nothing in common. For one thing, he has little sense of humor. He's not incapable of seeing the funny side. He just thinks on such an heroic scale. Everything is serious – everything is a matter of life and death. You don't have much time for jokes when you're busy saving the world.

'Terisa, it would never occur to *me* to save the world. I don't object to the world being saved. In fact, I want it to be saved. I just can't imagine that it has anything to do with me.

'There's a cottonwood tree down by the river. It lost a branch in a heavy snowfall this winter, and now sap is starting to leak from the wound. If someone doesn't go down there soon, trim the stump, and cover it with pitch, that tree is going to die. Blights or parasites will get in through the wound.

'*That* has something to do with me.

'One of our shepherds has a ewe that keeps dropping stillborn lambs. *That* has something to do with me. There's a woman in a farmstead a few miles away who suffers from a strange fever, and the only thing that helps her is a brew made from the bark of a tree that doesn't grow in Domne. It grows in the Care of Armigite. *That* has something to do with me.

'If you asked me to save the world, I wouldn't know how.

'King Joyse knows how. Or he thinks he does, anyway.'

Terisa thought that perhaps King Joyse and his old friend had more in common than the Domne appeared to realize. *Problems should be solved by those who see them.* But she preferred the Domne's way of doing it. Controlling her tendency to get angry whenever she thought about the King, she inquired, 'Then why *are* you friends?'

'I'm not sure I can explain it,' he said musingly. 'We need each other.

'When I first met him – when he chased away the minor Cadwal prince who had been using the Care of Domne as his private vassalage for the better part of a decade and set us free – I hadn't thought to refuse anything. I had as much fire in my blood as any young man who had just been released from a servitude he hated, and I seem to recall that I was perfectly willing to start learning how to use a sword.

'But when I actually met him—

'Terisa, that smile of his went right through my heart. As if it came down to me from the sky, I knew that I loved him. And I knew that the Care of Domne was never going to be what I wanted it to be if he didn't protect it. And I knew that he needed something from me – something he wasn't going to be able to get from anybody else.'

'Like what?'

'*Balance*,' replied the Domne distinctly. 'He needed *balance*. He wanted to save the world. Do you have any idea how dangerous that is? Men who want to save the world – and who make a few mistakes – become tyrants. The things they really want and love slip out of their fingers, and they end up clinging to the power because it's all they have left. The possibility was written all over him. He was the brightest and keenest man I had ever met – the kind of man who just naturally makes you want to lie down in the dirt for him – and I simply couldn't bear the idea that he might go too far and turn all the good in him rotten.

'It all came to me in a burst, like a sunrise. And it terrified me, because if I refused him he might just ride away and leave the Care of Domne to fend for itself. But it was necessary. We needed each other.

'He rode into Houseldon, as bright as a new day, but I stood my ground as if I had the right to it. "Well, my lord Domne," he said with that smile, wringing my heart because until he came I'd never believed that I would be lord of my own land, "you're free. At least for a while. How many men can you give me?"

'"None, my lord King," I said.

'"What, none?" He stopped smiling. I seem to remember he put his hand on his sword.

'I was terrified, but I said, "This is the foaling season. I need every man I have."

'He was angry, furious. But he was also perplexed. "Let me understand you," he said. "Domne has been butchered back and forth between Alend and Cadwal for generations. You've been a vassal yourself your entire life until today. And all you care about is your *sheep*?"

'I swear to you, Terisa, his anger nearly blinded me. And I was getting a crick in my neck from staring up at him. "I didn't say that, my lord King," I replied. "You asked how many men I can send away to be killed in your wars. The answer is, none. I need help with my foals."

'He really has very little sense of humor. But he has a wonderful sense of joy. Or had. Instead of splitting my head open, he started to laugh.

'That night, we had one of the best feasts I've ever attended. I thought he was going to laugh for days. He kept saying, "Sheep. *Sheep*," and falling out of his chair.

581

'We've been friends ever since.'

Terisa was surprised to find that she felt like crying. She knew what King Joyse's smile was like. From the first, she had wanted to like him, please him; she had wanted to serve him. The Domne reminded her of that – and of the fact that it was impossible. King Joyse himself had made it impossible.

In a soft voice, she asked, 'And now? Are you still friends now?' After what he did to Nyle and Geraden and his own daughters? After what he's doing to the Congery and Mordant?

Slowly, the Domne turned his head, shifted his gaze from the window to look at her. His eyes seemed partially blind – adjusted to the brightness outside and unable to make her out clearly.

'He isn't responsible for Nyle's choices. He isn't even responsible for Castellan Lebbick's sanity. Both of them could have trusted him. At the same time, he went to a lot of trouble to keep you and Geraden as safe as he could.

'He's still my friend, Terisa. We need each other. Do you really want me to turn my back on him?'

After a while, she found that she was able to say, 'No.' In spite of her anger, she had no intention of turning her own back on the King.

THIRTY-THREE

PEACE IN HOUSELDON

She was determined to do something for Geraden.

Unfortunately, she didn't know what.

In an odd way, her conversation with the Domne had crystallized her resolve. At the same time, the things he had revealed about his family and King Joyse hadn't shed any useful light. So she wanted to help Geraden. Good: so what? When she got right down to it, what could she actually say to him? Don't be so hurt, it isn't worth it? Nonsense. Snap out of it, you're just feeling sorry for yourself? Ridiculous. I'm sure you can beat Master Eremis if you put your mind to it? Perfect.

Thinking about him wrung her heart, but she didn't know what to do.

Soon the Domne became even less helpful. Gazing out the window with his arms folded over his lean chest, he slipped abruptly into a nap. He was older than he looked, after all. Terisa studied his posture for a moment to make sure that he wasn't about to fall out of his chair. Then she got to her feet; she wanted to go outside and see more of Houseldon.

Before she reached the door, it opened, and a man came in off the porch.

He was brown: that was her first impression. Years of outdoor labor had left his skin the same deep color as his leather jerkin and breeches. His hair was the color of the new mud on his old boots. And his eyes were nearly the same hue as his skin and clothes; they seemed to get lost in his general brownness. In fact, most of the details of his face and expression were blurred. Behind the brown, he looked like a cross between a turnip and a fence post.

But then he smiled – shyly, almost deferentially – and his smile pulled his features into definition. Immediately, it became obvious that he was one of Geraden's brothers.

He glanced at the Domne, saw that his father was asleep. Gesturing for silence, he put a hand on Terisa's arm and drew her outside. As soon as they reached the porch, however, he let go of her as if he felt his touch was presumptuous and had only risked it to avoid disturbing the Domne. He even backed a step or two away from her.

'Hello, Terisa,' he said earnestly, without quite meeting her eyes. 'I'm Minick. Geraden sent me to get you.'

'Hello, Minick,' she replied. 'I'm glad to meet you.'

As if she had surprised him, he asked, 'You are?'

She nodded. 'I'm glad to meet Geraden's family. I'm glad to be in Houseldon – in the Care of Domne.' This was so true that she didn't know how to explain it. 'I've wanted to meet all of you for a long time.'

Minick seemed to recognize the inadequacy behind her words. 'Well, I'm glad to meet you, too. I wasn't sure before. I don't like it when Geraden's unhappy. But now I am.'

He baffled her a bit. 'What makes you sure?'

He indicated the house with a lift of one shoulder. 'You were in the room with the Domne,' he explained, 'and now he's taking a nap. He trusts you. So you must be all right. You aren't the reason Geraden's unhappy.'

Minick's confidence was so unjustified that Terisa felt compelled to say, 'It's probably more complicated than that. Sometimes I think I *am* the reason he's unhappy – sort of. I have a lot to do with a lot of things that hurt him.'

'No.' Minick shook his head mildly. 'It isn't complicated. You're like him. He always thinks things are complicated. But they aren't. Important things are simple. He needs somebody to love him. That's simple. The Domne trusts you. That's simple. So now I can be glad to meet you, when I wasn't sure before.'

Unexpectedly, she found herself relaxing. 'I guess you're right.' A world of difficulties apparently evaporated when Minick touched them. 'I hadn't thought of it that way.'

'Let's go see Geraden.'

'Oh, no.' Minick became suddenly serious. 'That isn't what he wants. He's too busy.' For a second, the brown man almost shuddered. 'When he gets like this, he yells at people a lot. He thinks they're fast. He's fast, and he thinks they are, too. But they aren't fast. They're just farmers and shepherds. They're like me. They like having things explained to them.'

The thought of Geraden ranting with impatience was so incongruous that Terisa nearly laughed aloud. At the same time, it gave her a pang. Poor man, he must be almost out of his mind. Deliberately, she controlled herself. 'I don't understand. I thought you said he sent you to get me.'

Minick nodded. 'He did. I thought he was just making an excuse to send me away. But since you're glad to be here I guess I was wrong.

'He sent me to show you around. The Domne can't walk very far, and Tholden is too busy, and Quiss prefers to stay at home with Ruesha. Geraden said, "She likes tours. She might like a tour of Houseldon." So I came to get you.'

Terisa accepted the suggestion, despite the vexed spirit in which Geraden had probably made it. She understood how he felt. And she wanted to see more of Houseldon. She suspected – in an entirely uncritical way – that there wasn't a great deal to see. On the other hand, if Master Eremis launched an attack soon, she might need to know everything she could learn about the Domne's seat.

Giving Minick a smile which would have astonished Reverend Thatcher – or her father – she went with him to explore Houseldon.

In fact, there was more to see in Houseldon than she had expected.

At any rate, Minick thought there was a great deal to see. And he liked to see it all thoroughly, with an attention to detail which was both loving and analytical. For instance, Houseldon contained no less than three livery stables, to accommodate the numbers of people who came here from all over the Care, as well as from other regions of Mordant. Each of these was exactly what it claimed to be: a place where horses were left and cared for while their masters transacted business, visited relatives, appealed for justice, pursued crafts or apprenticeships. Yet to Minick each was worth looking at closely; each had virtues and drawbacks which required evaluation; each prospered or declined according to factors which he took pains to understand.

And he was a motherlode of information. He knew exactly where all the drainage pipes had been laid, and when, and how many square yards of leachfield they required. He knew who had first conceived the idea of trussing the eavesthatch of the roofs with *that* particular kind of binding, and why it was superior to the way eavesthatch used to be trussed. He knew where Houseldon's supplies of tallow came from, and how long they would last in an emergency. And he knew every child he saw by name, parentage, and predilection for mischief.

In a short time, Terisa realized that she had only two choices. She could cut off the tour now, before he drove her to distraction. Or she could relax and let him do whatever he wanted. With him there wasn't any middle ground.

Well, that fit, she mused. In their separate ways, Geraden, Artagel, and Nyle were all intolerant of middle ground. Wester was said to be a fanatic about wool. Stead couldn't keep his hands off women. Geraden had called Tholden *a compulsive fertilizer*. The Domne himself had given up on middle ground when he first met King Joyse. Why should Minick be any different?

Just for a minute, she considered stopping him – telling him that she had had enough, going her own way. But then she noticed that in his company she did very little except smile; he filled her alternately with amusement and affection. He was perfectly capable of distinguishing precisely between good workmanship and bad, sensible husbandry and careless, forethought and its absence; but he liked everybody around him; he loved the details he expounded for her. The more he talked, the more gentle and companionable he seemed. And the more she listened, the more she could feel her tensions and fears going to sleep.

Instead of stopping, she relaxed and let him give her the whole tour.

As a result, the day seemed to evaporate the way complexities did when he analyzed them. He began showing her around a little before noon – and then the shadows were slanting toward late afternoon, and her legs hurt gently with so much walking and standing, and her boots had rubbed a sore place onto one of her toes, and her heart was full of rest for the first time since she could remember. Minick wasn't just amusing, likable, and meticulous: he was a healer. Somewhere in Houseldon, she knew, preparations were being made for battle – but they didn't come near him; he seemed to carry peace with him wherever he went. Now, she thought, all she needed was one really good night's sleep, and then she would be ready to start thinking again.

So when he brought her back to the Domne's house and started to say good-bye, she didn't want him to leave. 'Where are you going?' she asked to forestall him.

This time his grin was shy in a new way, self-conscious about things which hadn't come up before. 'I like to go home before supper,' he murmured, 'and play with the children for a while. It gives their mother a chance to cook. And it uses up some of their energy so they go to bed more easily.'

The thought of this earnest brown man playing with his children delighted her – and reminded her that during the whole afternoon he hadn't said anything personal about himself or his life. Maybe he would have considered it presumptuous to talk about himself. Impulsively, because he had done her so much good and hadn't asked her for anything, she leaned forward and thanked him with a quick kiss.

His eyes widened; he stared at her for a moment. Then he ducked his head as if he were blushing.

'I think I'm not going to tell my wife you did that,' he said softly. 'She might not be pleased.' It was obvious that he was enormously pleased. 'I like her to be pleased. She's the only other woman who's ever been so patient with me.

'Good-bye, Terisa.'

After he left, she went up the steps, across the porch, and into the bustle of Quiss' cooking. Her cheeks ached from smiling so much. Clearly, those muscles needed the exercise.

The scene in the front room stopped her as soon as she came through the doorway.

Quiss was stirring what looked like enough stew to feed half of Houseldon. Her cheeks were red from heat and exertion; sweat made her hair stick to the sides of her face in streaks. Behind her, servants clattered around the room, setting platters, utensils, and pitchers on the table, bringing pots and tureens and trays from a back kitchen Terisa hadn't seen – and talking to each other loudly through the din. The Domne and Tholden sat together at the end of the table, discussing something intently, raising their voices to make themselves heard. In one corner of the room, a boy perhaps fifteen years old and a girl somewhat younger were arguing hotly; but the only part of their discussion Terisa could make out was the part that went: Did so. Did not. Did so! Did not! Another boy, this one no older than eight or nine, sat near Tholden trying to sharpen a wooden sword with a piece of tile for a whetstone. A third, still-younger boy used a stick the size of a club to experiment with the resonant qualities of a tin washbasin.

For a second, the clamor seemed so intimidating – so at odds with the peace inside her – that Terisa almost turned away. Nothing in her life with her parents, or in her life alone, had prepared her for a home where people acted like this.

But then Quiss raised her head, saw Terisa, and smiled.

Quiss' pleasure changed the meaning of the din altogether. Or changed the way Terisa saw it. All this noise and activity wasn't angry, distressed, or alarmed, didn't represent pain: it was just loud. As soon as Quiss smiled, Terisa knew that Tholden's wife was in her element, flourishing precisely because her family and her household were so busy, so noisy; so full of themselves and each other. And then Terisa understood that the tumult was just another form of peace – hot and hectic, of course; not particularly restful to a novice like herself; but completely without fear.

Smiling back at Quiss, she came forward to meet the noise.

'I understand you spent the afternoon with Minick.' Quiss was nearly shouting, but Terisa could hardly hear her. 'The whole afternoon? Letting him show you around?'

Terisa nodded.

'Good for you. I knew I liked you as soon as I saw you. He's your friend for life. Most people aren't willing to listen to him that long.'

'They ought to give it a try.' Terisa tried to speak loudly enough to be audible. 'He's nice.'

It was Quiss' turn to nod. 'Fortunately, his nieces and nephews dote on him.' She indicated the children at the other end of the room. 'I mean, fortunately for them.

'If his wife weren't so shy, he'd be here tonight. I know it saddens him sometimes that he can't spend more time with us. But I think the poor woman panics every time she sets foot outside her house.' Quiss started to laugh, but Terisa couldn't hear what her laughter sounded like through the noise. 'They must have had a rousing courtship.'

Terisa grinned again, then raised her hands to rub the muscles in her cheeks.

A serving woman appeared in front of her, carrying a foaming tankard on a tray. 'Do you like ale? My husband brews for the Domne. You won't find a better ale in the Care.'

'Thanks.' Terisa didn't know anything about ale, but she knew she was thirsty; she accepted the tankard and sampled it. The serving woman watched her while she discovered that the ale had a bite which wasn't quite sour, wasn't quite bitter, but which seemed to be both. After a second taste, however, the flavor had improved dramatically. Soon it became wonderful. She beamed her approval, and the serving woman went away delighted.

'Terisa!' Tholden gestured to her. She went over to him, and he pulled out a chair for her. 'Sit down. I want to tell you what we're doing to get ready. Maybe you can think of something I've forgotten.'

The Domne looked a little skeptical; he may have been sensitive to her general bewilderment. Nevertheless he nodded as if he also wanted to hear what she might say. At once, Tholden began to describe his specific arrangements for the possibility of battle.

She couldn't absorb them. In fact, she only heard every third word; the rest of his explanation was lost in a chorus directed at the Domne: Da, it's her fault, No, it's his fault, she did it first, *he* did it first! And she couldn't help noticing that even the Domne appeared more interested in the bickering of the children than in Tholden's preparations. Feeling vaguely irresponsible – but not enough to worry about it – she said once, 'Maybe it'll be quieter after supper,' then drank her ale and stopped trying to listen.

The chaos of getting supper ready seemed to approach a climax as an inner door burst open and a squall of children blew into the room. They were all about Ruesha's size and age – too many of them too close together in age to belong to any one family. Or any three families. They were all buck naked, full of glee, and glistening with water. And they were followed by Geraden, dripping copiously. He had a couple of towels in his hands, but they were too wet to be much use.

'Come back here, you little monsters!' he roared. 'I'm going to towel you until your heads fall off!'

Squealing with delight, small, naked bodies scattered in all directions.

Terisa hadn't seen Geraden for most of the day. She looked at him eagerly, and saw at once that he was still clenched and dour, knotted inside himself. Perhaps for the sake of the children, however, he had pushed his hardness into the background. Or perhaps they elicited that response from him involuntarily: perhaps it was something they did for him, rather than he for them.

It was enough. She could wait for more until they had a better opportunity together. Giving him her best smile, whether he noticed it or not, she relaxed and let the clamor continue to grow on her, like a milling and vociferous form of contentment.

Quiss, Tholden, and the servants snatched up wet children indiscriminately; soon all of Geraden's victims were caught in adult arms. Stifling a laugh, Quiss said to one of the serving women, 'Your boys are responsible for this.'

'I beg your pardon,' the woman protested in tart amusement. 'I'm sure Ruesha is the cause. She's the most notorious truant in Houseldon. Ask anyone.'

'They're all monsters!' growled Geraden. 'They're all going to suffer horribly when I get my hands on them!' Doing his best wild gorilla imitation, he began stalking children.

With the help of three or four servants, he succeeded in herding his fugitives from torture and cleanliness out of the room.

If he hadn't been so busy – and if she hadn't been so comfortably settled with her tankard of ale – Terisa would have gone after him. She felt an unaccountable desire to kiss him far more seriously than she had kissed Minick.

He came back after a while to join his family – and half a dozen men who arrived in the meantime – for supper. These men were the leaders of teams which had been organized to perform various functions during the defense of Houseldon. As soon as the meal was over, and the table had been cleared, the talk turned to the subject that seemed to be uppermost in everyone's mind, except Terisa's: what kind of attack was coming, and when, and how to meet it.

Geraden described a few of the uses of Imagery which Master Eremis had already made against Mordant; and the men quickly lost whatever self-confidence they had brought with them to the Domne's house. Finally, one of them asked almost timidly, 'Is there anything you can do?'

He shook his head. 'Not until I get a chance to make a mirror.'

'But how can such things be fought?' another man inquired. 'What can we do?'

'We're already doing it,' the Domne said flatly, as if he were sure. 'Everything that can be done. We're doing it.'

Without looking at her, Geraden added, 'Just hope the lady Terisa is wrong. Just hope he gives us a little time. Today we got ready. Tomorrow I'll fire up a furnace and start mixing sand.'

To her own surprise as much as anyone else's, Terisa got up and left the room.

She didn't want to hear it, that was all: she just didn't want to hear it. She was too recently come from Orison – from the Castellan's distrust and Eremis' cunning and Gilbur's violence. She hadn't had any sleep except for the short rest which had come over her unexpectedly in the grass below the Closed Fist. And the sense of peace inside her was fragile; it would collapse if she let herself get caught up in the anxiety of Houseldon's defenders, if she let herself get caught up in her own concern for Geraden. Sleep, that was what she needed, not all this talk. In the morning, she would be readier – maybe braver.

Nodding to the servants she encountered along the way, she retreated to Artagel's room.

It was dark. For a moment, she thought about asking someone for help; then she remembered where one of the room's lamps was. On a small table at the head of the bed. She went to it by the light from the open door, picked it up and brought it back to the doorway. Another lamp hung on the wall outside; she used it to light the lamp in her hands. When it was burning brightly, she entered the room again and closed the door.

A second lamp lit from the first helped fill the room with a comforting yellow glow. Amazing how nice Artagel's cot looked in that light. She visited the bathroom, then took off her clothes and doused the lamp she had set across the room. The early spring chill in the air encouraged her to get into bed immediately, cover herself with clean sheets and sweet blankets.

At once, she knew she was right: this was what she needed. As soon as her head reached the pillow, the peace inside her seemed to rise up and swell outward. It reached through the house growing quiet around her; it reached out to Geraden and the men trying to plan Houseldon's survival; it reached up into the deep heavens and across the Care toward Domne's mountains.

Silence and rest spread so far in all directions that they carried her away.

She went to sleep in such sudden contentment that she forgot to extinguish the lamp on the small table at the head of the bed.

That was what saved her from rousing the household and embarrassing herself unnecessarily, that forgotten lamp. In the dark, she might have lost her head; might have screamed.

For the second time in her life, after she had been asleep for a while she felt herself being kissed.

A strong mouth began to nibble on her lips; a tongue slipped between them, searching for hers. A hand just cool enough to call attention to itself found her hip under the blankets, then rose in a long caress across her belly to her breasts. While the tongue probed her mouth more deeply, the hand began to play with her nipples.

Her eyes flew open. In one quick glimpse, she saw the curly hair and intent brown eyes of the man kneeling beside the cot to embrace her; she saw that he wasn't Master Eremis or Castellan Lebbick, wasn't Gilbur or anyone else who terrified her. So she didn't scream. Instead, she swung her arms with all her strength in an effort to fling him away.

One of her elbows caught him squarely on the collarbone.

With a muffled yelp, he fell off her, sprawled to the floor. His arms tried to protect the bandages over his ribs and around his shoulders, but the fall sent a jolt through his fractured bones. For a moment, his back arched in real pain. Then he went limp on the floorboards.

Looking up at her and panting carefully as the pain receded, he murmured, 'Terisa,' in a wounded tone, 'what're you doing? I just want to make love to you. You don't need to hurt me.'

Now that she could see his whole face, she couldn't mistake his resemblance to the rest of the Domne's sons. Judging by his bandages, his cracked or broken ribs and collarbone, his crooked features, he must be Stead.

Glaring down at him angrily, she said the first thing that came into her head. 'I thought you had too many broken bones to get out of bed.'

He gave up sounding wounded and experimented with a smile instead. 'So did I. But that was before I saw you in the hall – outside my door. So I waited until everyone was asleep. Then I gave it a try. I guess a man can stand almost anything if he wants to badly enough.'

When she didn't reply, he asked, 'Will you help me up? I really am hurt, and the floor is hard.'

Fortunately, he was wearing a pair of light cotton sleeping trousers below his bandages. If he had been naked, she might have had trouble keeping her composure. Under the circumstances, however, she was able to look at him squarely and say, 'If you try to get up, I'm going to kick you until you wish you hadn't.'

But as soon as she said that she nearly started laughing. She had once threatened to kick Geraden. In fact, she *had* kicked him. To make him stop apologizing.

'That isn't kind,' Stead protested. His expression was lugubrious for a moment. But then another thought occurred to him, and he grinned. 'On the other hand, it might be worth it. You won't be able to get out of that bed to kick me without letting me see what you look like. The way you walk makes me think you must look glorious.' His grin sharpened. 'I've never been turned down by a woman who let me catch even a glimpse of her breasts.'

'In that case' – her desire to laugh was getting stronger – 'I won't kick you. I won't get out of bed at all.' Stead looked astonishingly like Geraden trying to do an imitation of Master Eremis – with limited success. Keeping herself carefully covered with her blankets, she sat up and indicated the lamp. 'I'll just throw burning oil at you.'

Stead didn't appear to take this threat very seriously. 'No, you won't.'

In an effort to stifle her mirth, she glowered back at him. 'What makes you think that?'

'You don't really want to hurt me.' With no arrogance at all, he explained, 'What you really want is a man.'

She stared at him. 'I do?'

He nodded. 'Every woman does. That's what men and women are for. First they want each other. Then they get into bed and enjoy each other.'

That sounded dangerously plausible. She countered by asking, 'What about Geraden? He's your brother, after all. And I came here with him. Don't you consider him a man?'

'Ah, Geraden.' Stead's smile seemed genuinely affectionate. 'Of course I consider him a man. If you want my opinion, he's the best one of us all. Oh, he isn't half the farmer Tholden is. He isn't half the shepherd Wester is. He isn't half the swordsman Artagel is. And he sure doesn't know anything about women. But he's still the best.

'But that's not the point, is it?' he continued rhetorically. It was remarkable how little arrogance he had in him, how little assumption of superiority. He didn't belittle anyone. 'The point is, *you* don't consider him a man.'

Terisa's mouth fell open. She closed it with an effort. Suddenly, the situation wasn't funny anymore. '*I* don't?'

'You came here with him. He worships every inch of you. If you thought of him as a man, you'd be in his room right now.' Nothing in Stead's tone suggested the slightest criticism of Geraden – or of her. His view of the situation was essentially impersonal.

'There must be someone else you want.'

Holding her gaze, he began to ease himself up from the floor. Every moment was obviously painful to him, but the pain only accentuated the appeal in his eyes.

'I think you want me,' he murmured. '*I* certainly want *you*.'

There was something of Master Eremis in the way he looked at her, an intensity of interest which hypnotized. And he had distinct advantages over the Master. He wouldn't demean her. He wouldn't do anything cruel.

'I started wanting you as soon as I saw you,' he said as he got his feet under him. 'Your lips cry out for kisses. Breasts like yours should be fondled until they give you bliss. The place of passion between your legs aches to be pierced. Terisa, I want you. I want to revel in you until your joy is as great as mine.'

Upright despite the way his ribs and collarbone hurt, he moved gently toward her.

He had some of Master Eremis' magnetism. And his desire was less threatening than the Master's.

At the same time, he forced her to think of Geraden.

If you thought of him as a man—

She dropped the blankets. Stead's eyes grew bright, and he reached toward her, but she ignored him. Fending his arms away, she left the bed and crossed the room to her clothes.

'Terisa?'

The shirt and skirt Quiss had given her weren't warm enough to hold out the chill. They were warm enough for the time being, however; she didn't want to spend time looking for an alternative. And the boots helped.

Stead came up behind her, put his hands on her shoulders. 'Terisa?'

She turned to face him. 'Take me to Geraden's room.'

He frowned in puzzlement. 'Geraden's room? Why do you want to go there? He doesn't want you. He thinks he does, but he doesn't really. If he did, he would be here already.'

Terisa shook her head; she knew Geraden better than that. 'Stead,' she said quietly, 'I'm not going to threaten you. I'm not going to kick you – or set you on fire. I just don't want you.

'Take me to Geraden's room.'

Stead blinked at her. 'You don't mean that.'

Taking care not to hurt him, she moved around him toward the door. Outside, the lamps had been extinguished. She returned to the table at the head of the bed and took the lamp. 'Make yourself comfortable,' she said. 'You might as well sleep here. I won't be back.'

She was out the door and had started to close it before she heard him pant, 'Terisa, wait,' and come shuffling after her.

His injuries prevented him from walking quickly; he took a moment to catch up with her. Then he braced himself against the door and paused to rest. His expression didn't make sense to her. Behind the strain of movement, he seemed sadder than she'd expected – and happier.

'Quiss always refuses me,' he said, breathing carefully. 'I don't understand that. I've tried to tell her how much I want her. That's all that matters. But she always refuses.

'I have to admit, though' – by degrees, his happiness took over his face – 'she certainly makes me think well of Tholden.

'Geraden's room is that way.' Grinning, he pointed down the hall.

Now she found it easy to smile back at him. To help him walk, she slipped her arm through his. That appeared to confuse him – but of course he had no way of knowing how much he was improved by the comparison to Master Eremis. In any case, he let her assist him, and they went down the hall like old friends.

Past two corners and down a long passage, Stead stopped in front of another door. 'Here,' he murmured softly. Then he put his arm around her waist and hugged her. Touching his mouth to her ear, he whispered, 'Are you sure you wouldn't rather come with me? No matter how much he worships you, he can't want you more than I do.'

Gently, she disentangled herself. 'Go away,' she replied as kindly as she could. 'This is too important.'

He sighed; nodded; shook his head in bafflement. But he didn't argue. A bit morosely, he turned and began to shamble down the hall, holding his arms protectively across his ribs.

She waited until he was out of sight around the corner. Then, before she had a chance to lose her nerve, she lifted the doorlatch and let herself into the room.

By the light of her lamp, she saw that Stead had brought her to the right place. In the wide bed against the far wall, Geraden sprawled among his blankets. Judging by appearances, he had lost a fierce struggle with his covers; now he lay outstretched in defeat, snoring slightly on the battlefield.

Asleep, his face gave up its bitter hardness, the iron of despair. He looked young and vulnerable, and inexpressibly dear. She wanted to go to him immediately and put her arms around him, hold him close to her heart, comfort away everything that hurt him. At the same time, she wanted to let him sleep – let him rest and dream until all his distress was healed. She shut the door behind her gently, so that he wouldn't be disturbed.

But the lamp woke him. He didn't flinch, or jerk himself out of bed; he simply opened his eyes, and yellow light reflected back at her. Without transition, he no longer looked young or vulnerable. He looked poised and deadly, like a wounded predator.

Master Eremis had understood from the beginning how dangerous Geraden was. All at once, the Master's *policy* toward him made sense to her.

'Geraden,' she murmured in sudden confusion, 'I'm sorry, I didn't mean to wake you. Or I guess I did. I don't know why I came. I couldn't stay away.'

Then, mercifully, he sat up, and the change in his position changed the way the light caught his eyes. He relapsed to the Geraden she knew: hard and hurt, closed like a fist around the sources of his pain; but nonetheless human, precious to her.

She took a deep breath to steady herself. 'There's so much we need to talk about.'

Like Stead, he was dressed only in a pair of sleeping trousers; apparently, he didn't feel the cold as much as she did. He didn't get up from the bed or reach out to her. Yet when he spoke his voice sounded like the voice she remembered: capable of kindness; accessible to pain or hope.

'After supper – after you left – I went to see Minick. I wanted to apologize for yelling at him. People shouldn't yell at him, even though he never gets angry about it.

'Do you know what he said? He said, "I spent the afternoon with your Terisa. She's nice. If you make her unhappy, you won't be welcome in my house anymore." Minick said that, my mild brother who never gets angry.'

Geraden shrugged. 'I didn't tell him that I've already made you unhappy.'

'No,' she replied at once, 'that's not true,' reacting too quickly for thought. 'How can you say that?'

He watched her impassively. 'I look at you, Terisa. I see the way you look at me.'

'And what do you see?'

He held her eyes, but he didn't answer.

'I like your family,' she protested. 'I feel comfortable in Houseldon. Ever since you talked me into leaving my old life, you've done more to make me happy than anyone else I've ever known. How can you—?'

She stopped. It would have been nice if he'd had a fire in his room: she needed an external source of warmth. The darkness beyond the lamplight seemed full of sorrow. Making a special effort to speak calmly, she continued, 'Geraden, I think I probably could have made that mirror translate me anywhere. Anywhere I could visualize – anywhere vivid enough in my mind.' *And I just came from Stead. He touched my breasts. He wanted to make love to me.* 'Why do you think I'm here?'

His eyes didn't waver. 'You're here because you think I'm wrong. You

593

think I should have stayed in Orison to fight. You think there are still things I can do against Eremis.'

As he said that, she suddenly knew she had to be very careful with him. Maybe it was true that he had become iron. But iron was brittle; he might break. He was blaming himself – She wanted to cry out, Oh, Geraden, are you *blaming* yourself? For Eremis and Gilbur? For the Castellan? For Nyle and Quillon? Are you *blaming* yourself because some of the best minds around you worked so hard to keep you from understanding your talent? But she couldn't say that to him. He would just turn away. More than ever, she couldn't bear the idea that he would turn away.

Softly, she asked, 'Why do you believe I think you're wrong?'

'I told you.' The kindness was gone from his voice. 'I can see it in your eyes.'

'*What* do you see?' she insisted. '*What* do you see in my eyes?'

For a long moment, he hesitated. Then he said roughly, 'Pain.'

She thought she might feel better if she hit him. She might feel even better if she put her arms around him. Yet she stayed where she was, with her back to the door, holding the only light in the room.

'That's how I know I'm real. Master Eremis says I was created by your mirror, but that can't be true. If I didn't exist, I couldn't be hurt.'

'Terisa.' He swallowed hard. She had touched him: she thought she could see grief shifting behind the rigid lines of his face. 'Nobody says you don't exist. Not even Master Eremis. You're here. You're real. Everything you do has consequences. The question is, were you real before I translated you?'

Automatically, she wanted to ask, Have you changed your mind? Do you still think I was real – back where you found me? But she pushed that question down.

'I must have been,' she said. King Joyse had told her to *reason*. 'If the place I came from was only created by the mirror you saw me in, then that must be true of every mirror, every Image. So when you look in a flat glass, you don't actually see a real place. You see a created copy of a real place. So when I translated myself into the Image of the Closed Fist, I shouldn't have arrived in a real place. I should have arrived in the copy – a different copy than the one you went to. I should have stopped being real myself until somebody translated me back out again.

'Isn't that right?'

The light of the lamp was imprecise, but she seemed to see a hint of a smile at the corners of his mouth. The shadows there deepened as he listened to her. The sight caused her heart to accelerate a bit.

'That's good,' he said. 'I wish I'd come up with that argument myself. But I don't think it's enough. Eremis will just say, That's why translations through flat glass produce madness. The only translation that can be done safely is one between the real world and a created Image. Reality is too powerful to tolerate the manipulations of Imagery.' In spite of his clenched condition, he began to sound more like his old self as he talked – more like he was interested in the discussion for its own sake. 'So the closer a created Image gets to reality, the more dangerous it becomes. And when the Image actually copies reality, reality takes precedence. It rips the translation away from the Image, and the force of that distortion is what causes madness.'

She hung on the change in his tone, hoped for it to continue. Almost at once, however, he closed himself again. 'Terisa, you didn't come here in the middle of the night to debate the ethics of Imagery.'

'Is that right?' Pained to feel the side of him she wanted to nurture slipping away, she made a mistake. 'To you it's just a debate. To me it's my life. I can't make sense out of who I am unless I know the truth.'

Right away, she knew she'd gone wrong: his gaze dropped from hers; his eyes filled up with shadows. He didn't need to be reminded that other people were suffering: he was already too sensitive to that; he already believed he had made her unhappy. But she refused to back down. She had come too far to retreat. Instead, she changed tactics.

'If I wasn't real until you brought me out of that mirror of yours, how did I become an arch-Imager?'

He didn't lift his head. In a muffled voice, he said, 'You know I don't believe that. That's Eremis, not me.'

Unexpectedly angry, she retorted, 'Wake up. What do you think we're talking about here?' She put the lamp down on a nearby table to free her hands, as if she were getting ready to wrestle with him. 'Why do you think who I am and where I come from matters? What he believes is going to affect everything he does to both of us.'

'Tell me how I became an arch-Imager.'

Now Geraden raised his eyes. Studying her closely – and holding himself completely still, as though he feared what she might do if he moved – he replied, 'I created you. When I shaped my glass, I made you.' Almost silently, he caught his breath in surprise and recognition; the implications took him aback. 'I have the capacity to create arch-Imagers.'

'Not just arch-Imagers,' she amended for him. 'Arch-Imagers who can shift glass the way you do, arch-Imagers who can work translations that are irrelevant to what you see in the Image.'

'I could create a whole army of them. A whole army of Imagers as powerful as Vagel. He wouldn't stand a chance.' Staring at her – at the ideas she proposed – Geraden murmured, 'No wonder he wants me dead.'

'And that's not all.' Gripping her courage, Terisa took the risk. 'How does he know you don't have glass here?'

Geraden jerked his head back, glowered at her in astonishment or dismay. 'What—?'

'How does he know' – she forced herself to complete the thought, even though Geraden's expression made her feel that she was accomplishing the opposite of what she wanted – 'you aren't busy creating an army of arch-Imagers right now?'

She horrified him. What a pleasure. All she wanted was to help him – to comfort or encourage the Geraden who had gotten lost and become iron – and what did she achieve? Horror. For a moment, he was so shocked that the lamplight made him look as pale as bone. Then he sprang off the bed, rushed to her and caught her by the shoulders, groaned through his teeth as if he were stifling a wail, 'I've got to get out of here.'

She stared at him dumbly.

'He'll send everything he's got after me. If he catches me here, he'll reduce Houseldon to rubble to get at me.'

It had to be said. She had gone too far to turn back. And this was the point, wasn't it? The reason she had brought the subject up in the first place? Distinctly, she remarked, 'He has to try that no matter what you do.'

He stared at her in dismay.

'He knows you're here,' she said. 'But he won't know it when you leave. Unless he has a mirror that lets him see you here. If you run, he won't know it until he's destroyed Houseldon looking for you.

'*I* did that.' For a moment, her eyes filled with tears. She blinked them back fiercely. 'It's *my* doing. When I told him about seeing the Closed Fist in your mirror, I set you up.

'You didn't know you were coming here. I told him, but I didn't tell you. You were just trying to escape – and hoping you wouldn't end up somewhere you couldn't get back from. He has to destroy Houseldon so that he can stop you, and I set you up for it.'

Geraden, it's not your *fault*. None of this is your *fault*.

His face was thrust close to hers, his fingers ground into her arms; but she couldn't seem to read his face. His passion was part of his skull, definitive under his features; yet the flesh over it was so tight and strict that she couldn't distinguish between them.

When he spoke, however, his voice shook her as hard as if he had shoved her against the wall. It was strong, compulsory; it had the power to command her.

'Terisa, people I have known and loved all my life are going to die because I came here.'

I swore I was never going to let anybody I loved die ever again.

But there was nothing he could do. Houseldon was already as well prepared to defend itself as possible. He was helpless to save anything or anybody. Because he needed so much from her, she didn't cry or apologize or defend herself or get angry. She faced him squarely and said, 'I think I would probably feel better if you hit me.'

He looked like he might hit her: he was angry or desperate enough to hit something.

'Why didn't you *tell* me?'

Slowly, she shook her head. At least he wasn't closed anymore. She had achieved that much. And even fury was preferable to his rigid isolation, his mute hurt. 'That's not the point,' she countered. 'It doesn't matter. I just made a mistake, that's all. I didn't know how important all this is.' And later on she had been so embarrassed by her submission to Master Eremis that she found it impossible to speak.

'The point is, *I* had a choice.' It seemed loony to speak so calmly when he was in such distress. It seemed loony to prefer anyone's anger. 'I could have gone anywhere.' At the same time, her own misery inexplicably began to become something else, something that bore a crazy and astounding resemblance to joy. She could reach him – she could make him furious. Because of that, everything else was possible. 'I *chose* to come here.

'Geraden, listen to me. Why do you suppose I *chose* to come here?'

He was so angry, so frightened for his home and family and friends, that he could hardly refrain from raging. Involuntarily, he bared his teeth. Yet he was still Geraden, still the man who had always done everything he could imagine for her. Panting at the effort he made to restrain himself, he said, 'You tell me. Why?'

'No.' Again she shook her head. 'Come on, think about it. Why did I come here?'

Through his passion, he rasped, 'You didn't know where else to go. To escape.'

'*No*. Come on, *think*. I could have gone anywhere. Prince Kragen would have been glad to have me. All I had to do was translate myself out of Orison. Anywhere outside the gates.'

Now she had him. It was strange how much power she had with him. Her mistakes might result in the complete destruction of his home and family: his reasons for outrage were that good. And yet he felt compelled to try to understand her.

He didn't let go of her, but his fingers stopped grinding into her arms. With less fury, he said, 'You wanted to warn me.'

'*Yes*.' She didn't smile; yet the inexplicable joy in her started to sing. 'I wanted to warn you.

'Why do you suppose I bothered? Why do you suppose I care what happens here? I didn't know your family. I'd never been here before. Why do you suppose I was willing to come here and face you when I knew it was my fault you were in danger – when I knew you had every reason in the world to be angry at me or even hate me and there was nothing I could do to change any of it?'

Oh, she had him. She wanted to shout it out: she *had* him. He wasn't iron now, closed and bitter. His fury had receded. He was scrutinizing her intently: perplexed, almost dumbfounded; fundamentally baffled by her; touched by hope.

'*Think* about it,' she murmured to keep herself from crowing aloud.

He opened his mouth, but no words came.

'You idiot. I did it because I love you.'

Then she reached her arms around his neck and pulled herself up to kiss him.

He took a moment to recover from the shock. Fortunately, he didn't take too long. Before she could lose the elation singing through her, he clasped her to him and returned her kiss as if his answer came all the way up from the bottom of his soul.

The fabric of his sleeping trousers was so thin that she couldn't mistake the way he felt about her, in spite of her inexperience. She kissed him for a long time while his arms strained around her. Then she eased back from his embrace and began to unbutton her shirt.

His eyes darkened, as if they were on fire with shadows. A bit awkwardly, she kicked off her boots. When she slipped the shirt from her shoulders and dropped her skirt, he caught his breath. Even the hair on his head seemed to burn with desire.

Abruptly, he jerked down his pants and took her to his bed.

He was almost devout in the way he kissed and touched her; torn between wonder and alarm, as if he wanted her so much that he didn't trust himself. As a result, he was tentative when she most wished him to be sure. Master Eremis was right. During the Master's brief stay in the dungeon after the summoning of the Congery's champion, he had said to her, *Whenever you think of another man, you will remember my lips upon your breasts.* That was true: Geraden's touch reminded her of the Imager – of his assurance, his willingness to take possession of her completely.

And yet Geraden conveyed an intensity that moved her deeply. She felt that she had spent most of her life waiting for this time in bed with him. She could do without assurance. They would learn what they needed to know together.

But it went wrong, the way everything went wrong for him. He had discovered his talent for Imagery too late, when he was no longer able to do anything with it. Now he discovered her love for him too late, he held her in his arms too late: he had lost the ability to do anything with her. Maybe his own inexperience made him too anxious. Maybe he couldn't stop worrying about Houseldon and his family. She wasn't sure what the reason was – and in a sense she didn't care. She cared only that he swore under his breath and rolled away from her, lay on his back with his fists clenched at his sides and his muscles knotted, trying to withdraw into iron.

She watched him lock himself away from her, and her joy began to crumble. For a moment, she thought about weeping.

Then she got an idea.

With the tip of one finger, she stroked the hard line of his jaw. 'Guess what,' she said as if they were engaged in a casual and even bantering conversation. 'I've just thought of a reason to believe I'm really real.'

'I already believe it,' he muttered from the opposite side of the world. 'You know that.'

'But you don't know why,' she returned playfully. 'That's the trouble with you. You don't have enough reasons. You just have your "strongest feelings" – you do everything on faith.

'I'll give you a reason.

'People like Eremis say I was created by Imagery. I came out of you and your talent when you made that mirror. But if that's true, don't you think you would have created a woman you could have an easier time making love with?'

She took him so entirely by surprise that he couldn't stop himself. As unexpectedly as a shout, he burst out laughing.

And once he started to laugh he lost control.

'That's perfect,' he gasped between gales of mirth. 'I'm so confused I can't figure out my own talent. I can't help my family. Or my King. Or the woman I love. But that's not enough for me. I'm not satisfied with just that.'

Briefly, she heard a note of hysteria in his laughter, and she nearly panicked. But the simple act of laughing seemed to clean the sorrow and self-pity out of him; the more he laughed, the more he relaxed.

'No, I'm so confused that when I create a woman to love I make her so perverse she accidentally betrays my whole life. Then she wants to bed me when I'm so scared I can hardly think.

'I don't need enemies. As soon as I stop laughing, I'm going to kill myself.

'Oh, Terisa.'

He said her name as if it made him ache. Rolling back to her, he put his hands on the sides of her face to hold her and began kissing her again.

Unquestionably, his kisses lacked Master Eremis' assured passion. But they were sweet and compelling, like the remembered call of horns. And when she remembered horns, the music came back into her.

This time, it went right.

It went right nearly until dawn. When she finally slept, she still clung to him like a promise that she was never going to let him go.

At dawn, the house stirred around them; but she and Geraden continued sleeping.

Fortunately, Houseldon wasn't relying on Terisa and Geraden for vigilance. When the attack came, the men on watch spotted it immediately and raised the alarm.

Shouts echoed like wails among the houses and taverns, the livery stables and granaries. As fast as they could get out of bed, men spilled from their homes, clutching pitchforks and scythes, axes, shepherd's crooks sharpened to resemble pikes, sledgehammers, knives and bucksaws, ordinary clubs, an occasional sword, and more than a few hunting bows. The Domne's six trained bowmen took their command positions around the stockade almost instantly. Shouting for his canes, the Domne himself thrashed out of his twisted bedclothes.

Tholden was ahead of his father. The truth was that he had been too worried for sleep. After trying uselessly to rest until after midnight, he had gotten up, put on his clothes. If Quiss hadn't restrained him, he would have gone to wear himself out pacing around the stockade to no purpose. But she had compelled him – almost by force – to sit down and drink a flagon of wine; she had kneaded the knots in his neck and shoulders and back until her hands ached; she had made love to him. After that, he pretended to sleep until she let down her guard. Then he got out of bed again.

He was in the front room stirring up the fire when he heard the alarm. Roaring in a voice that wasn't made to convey anger or violence, he left the house. For a second, he wheeled, trying to find which direction the alarm came from. Then he set off at a run, his beard lifting in the dawn breeze.

Terisa groped awake, roused more by the way Geraden exploded out of bed than by the shouts. He seemed to jump unerringly into his clothes while she fumbled to follow him, catch up with him; he flung the door open before she had begun to button her shirt.

Nevertheless she did catch up with him. Out in the hall, he collided with Stead and had to stop to lift his injured brother off the floor. Stead clung to him for a moment. 'Get me a knife,' he panted. 'I can't run anywhere. But I can fight here if I have to.'

'I'll tell Quiss,' Geraden replied as he pulled away.

With Terisa beside him now, he reached the front room, shouted Stead's message to Quiss, then dashed out of the house.

'Where?' he demanded of the first man he met.

The man looked too frightened to have any idea what he was doing 'West.'

'West,' Geraden muttered, thinking hard. 'So it isn't soldiers. Soldiers would come from the north. The northeast.'

Terisa saw what he was getting at; but her heart was pounding in her throat, and she couldn't speak.

'Eremis is sending Imagery against us.'

She nodded. They ran west among the buildings.

Everyone was running west. Tholden's instructions to Houseldon had been explicit: women and children, stay at home; anyone who was too young or too frail or too sick to fight, stay at home. Unfortunately, the people of Domne had lost the habit of taking orders. The streets were crowded with people who shouldn't have been there. Some of the men who were prepared or equipped or at least determined to fight had difficulty working their way through the throng.

But Tholden had replied to the alarm so quickly that he was ahead of the crowds; he didn't know he was being imperfectly obeyed. He reached the guardpost and climbed onto the platform where the man who had raised the alarm was on watch in time to see the whole attack clearly.

They came in without a sound except for the rush of their paws and the harsh murmur of their breathing: strange wolves with spines bristling down their curved backs, a double row of fangs in each slavering jaw, and something like intelligence in their wild eyes. Only a few dozen of them, Tholden thought when he first spotted them. Enough to ravage a herd of sheep. Or terrorize a farmstead. Not enough to threaten Houseldon. They won't be able to get past the stockade.

Then the leader of the pack sprang at the wall.

The wolf seemed to come straight up at him. Leaping at least eight feet in the air, it got its forelegs over the wall. While its hind legs scrambled for a purchase on the wood, its jaws stretched toward his face.

For an instant more horrible than anything he had imagined, Tholden couldn't move. He was a farmer, not a soldier: he didn't know anything about fighting. Deep down in his heart, he had always believed there was something secretly crazy about people like Artagel, who went into battle with such fierce joy. The men standing on the platform with him had already flinched away. One of the bowmen rushed to bring up his bow. But Tholden just couldn't move.

Then hot slaver splashed into his face as the fangs drew near, and something inside him shifted. Although he never thought about it, he was prodigiously strong, and his strength came to his rescue. He reached out, caught the wolf by the throat, and heaved it backward.

It fell among the pack, breaking the charge, preventing the wolves behind it from gathering themselves to spring. The pack burst into snarls – a raw, red sound, avid for blood. Jaws snapped. Then the wolves swirled around to regain their momentum so that they could leap.

'Bowmen!' the Domne's son cried desperately, 'get some arrows into those things! If they get over the wall—!'

Not fast enough. Already three wolves were leaping, four, six. And instead of attacking the guardpost directly, they hurled themselves at a part of the wall where there were no immediate defenders.

He was appalled by the realization that these beasts knew what they were doing. They were at their most vulnerable while they tried to cross the top of the wall – so they moved out of reach.

But an arrow thudded into the chest of the nearest wolf. It fell away, coughing blood. While the bowman snatched up another shaft, someone below the platform threw a hatchet that buried itself between a pair of glaring, wild eyes. Someone else tried to use a pitchfork as if it were a javelin; the tines missed, but the wolf was forced to drop back.

Three down.

The other three got over the wall.

Tholden saw a farmer swing an axe and miss – saw him go down with his throat torn out by an effortless toss of the wolf's head. Luckily, the next man struck a solid blow with a club, and the wolf wobbled. While the beast was still unsteady on its legs, one long sweep of a scythe disemboweled it.

Defenders arrived as quickly as the narrow streets and the crowds permitted. The second wolf over the wall ducked between two hostlers – who nearly brained each other trying to hit it – ripped open the best baker in Houseldon before he could raise his hands, then flung itself at a knot of young boys who had escaped from their mothers. But it went down when an ancient sword in the hands of an old man who remembered the wars struck between the spines protecting its back.

The third wolf took an arrow in its hindquarters from a terrified young apprentice bowman. As if it thrived on pain, it killed the young man, bit off another man's hand at the wrist when the man tried to stab the creature with a knife, then raced down an alley toward the heart of Houseldon.

At the same time, more wolves sprang to the attack.

Only a few dozen of them, Tholden thought. He wanted to tear his hair.

A second bowman ran up from the guardpost where he had been stationed. Like his comrade, he began picking wolves off the top of the wall as fast as he could nock arrows to the string. But they were only two. Every time one of them reached for a new shaft, three or four beasts got into Houseldon.

Calling frantically for help, Tholden leaped off the platform.

The other bowmen were on their way, but hampered by the crowds. And the defenders at the scene of attack didn't know how to fight an enemy like this; they got in each other's way. In a sense, the wolves were losing. They would all be killed eventually. But if enough of them ran loose in the streets, they would do terrible carnage before they were hunted down.

And if they killed the bowmen—

Maybe the wolves wouldn't lose.

Tholden snatched an axe from a man who obviously didn't know how to use it effectively. Planting himself in the path of the wolves, he hewed at them as if they were nothing more than a stand of timber. He had no idea what else to do.

So he didn't see what happened to the beasts that got past him. He didn't see the arrival of the remaining bowmen, or the efforts they made to thin out the attack; he didn't see the wall of defenders behind him crumble and fail as people panicked and fled and even men who knew how to wield their weapons went down.

On the other hand, he was one of the few people in a position to see that the wolves were only the vanguard of the attack.

No one else guessed that. No one else thought about it. The wolves were trouble enough. Cursing the folly which had taken them outside, women rushed back to their homes, hauling their children along behind them. Men dove into hiding. Flocks of chickens fled in a squall of feathers and fright, running crazily in all directions or battering their way heavily up to the rooftops. The whole west side of Houseldon was in disarray, instructions and defenses forgotten.

Suddenly, the street in front of Terisa and Geraden cleared, and they found themselves facing a beast with blood on its jaws and an arrow sticking out of its hindquarters.

The spines along its back made it look like a hedgehog of monstrous size. The double row of its fangs made it look like a great shark.

Terisa was reminded of riders with red fur and too many arms.

The wolf stopped, scented the air. Its eyes seemed to burn with the possibility of intelligence.

'It's hunting us,' she said. At any rate, she thought she said that; she couldn't tell whether she spoke aloud.

'When I push you,' Geraden whispered, 'go for that house.' He nudged her slightly toward the nearest building. 'Get inside. Close the door. Try to bolt it.'

The wolf began to snarl deep in his chest – a sound like a distant rumble of thunder.

'What're you going to do?'

She must have spoken aloud. Otherwise he wouldn't have answered.

'Same thing in the opposite direction.'

Automatically, she nodded, too frightened to do anything else.

As if her nod were a signal, the wolf sprang at them, slavering murderously. Geraden hit her shoulder so hard that she stumbled and fell.

At least she fell out of the way of the beast's charge. Trying frantically to bounce up from the ground, she jammed her legs under her, pounded up onto the porch of the house—

—whirled to see what was happening to Geraden.

He hadn't made any attempt to do what she was doing. After pushing her aside, he had simply ducked. By the time the wolf checked its spring, landed, and came back at him, he was on his feet facing the creature, poised as if he intended to kick its brains out.

'Geraden!'

'*Get in the house!*'

So fast that she hardly saw it happen, he jumped sideways. The wolf flashed past him. She heard the savage click as jaws strong enough to crush bone tried to close on him. The sleeve of his jerkin burst into tatters.

But there was no blood. Yet.

Faster this time because its second charge had been less headlong, the wolf turned and went for him again.

If he had tripped, if he had missed his footing or misjudged the assault, he would have died. No one could do what he was doing, not for long. The arrow in the wolf's hindquarters wasn't enough of a handicap. Nevertheless he dodged a third time – ripped himself out of the way, ducked and rolled, came to his feet to face the wolf again just before it sprang.

Blindly, stupidly, Terisa started back into the street to help him.

At that instant, a woman came out of the house in mortal terror. So scared that she could hardly control her limbs, she thrust a pitchfork into Terisa's hands. Then she slammed the door behind her, slammed a bar into place against the door.

Terisa took the pitchfork without thinking. Wailing like a madwoman to distract the wolf, she leaped off the porch and did her utter best to spear the beast on the tines.

She missed. The wolf was too fast, too smart for her inexpert onslaught. When it came around at her, however, she was able to fend it off, almost by accident; it shied away from impaling itself on the pitchfork.

As if out of nowhere, the head of a cane whizzed through the air and cracked the wolf across the base of its skull.

Coughing a howl, the beast spun and hurled itself on the Domne.

Geraden yelped a helpless warning. Terisa froze, holding her weapon as if she had forgotten its existence.

The Domne couldn't run or dodge. With his bad leg, he could scarcely hobble. But he had a cane in his other hand as well, and when the beast leaped at him he rammed the end of that stick down its throat.

At the same time, Geraden went past Terisa, tearing the pitchfork from her hands in one motion and hammering it into the wolfs back with all his strength.

Spiked to the ground, the beast writhed for a moment, snarling horribly and spitting blood on the Domne's boots. Then it lay still.

'Thank you, Father,' panted Geraden. 'Glass and splinters! that was close. You shouldn't take chances like that.'

The Domne balanced unsteadily on his feet. His face was white. Yet he contrived to speak calmly. 'Someday,' he remarked, 'you're going to call me "Da." I think you'll like it.'

Geraden shook his head as if he had lost his voice.

With one cane, the Domne prodded the body at his feet. 'How many of them are there?'

'Enough to get past Tholden,' croaked Geraden.

Terisa had the vivid impression that she was about to faint. Fortunately, Geraden turned and caught her before her knees folded.

As the last wolf came over the stockade with an arrow in its heart, the bowman on the guardpost platform yelled, almost shrieked, '*Tholden!*' and

Tholden gasped a curse because there was nothing else he could say while he retched for breath.

Half the pack had been slaughtered in front of him. Carcasses lay along the bottom of the wall, in piles on both sides of him, among the dead bodies of his people at his back. His axe was covered with blood; his hands and arms ran red; blood dripped from his beard and soaked his shirt. His eyes held a wildness of their own which bore no resemblance to the feral intelligence of the wolves. How many of them had gotten past him? He didn't know. He didn't know what the people of Houseldon were doing to defend themselves. He only knew that the bowman on the platform sounded frantic.

There was more. The wolves were only the vanguard.

Forcing himself into motion, he staggered to the guardpost, heaved his bulk up the ladder to the platform.

When he looked over the top of the stockade and saw what the bowman was pointing at, his first reaction was one of deflation, almost of disappointment.

Oh, is *that* all?

He was gazing across a hundred yards of open ground at a cat.

Just a cat. One cat. Nothing more.

The realization came to him slowly, however, that this cat was bigger than he was. It was at least as big as a horse. At least—

Then he noticed that wherever the cat put its paws the new grass and old leaves caught fire. It had already left a smoldering trail away into the distance, where the wolfpack had come from. And it was approaching – not rapidly, but without any hesitation – advancing as steadily and inevitably as a stormfront.

'Tholden,' the bowman murmured like a prayer, 'what *is* it?'

This was foolishness, really. Who was he to pretend that he could fill his father's boots, that he could succeed as the next Domne? He didn't understand anything about Imagery. The only real accomplishment of his life, from his point of view, was to figure out the best time of year and the best conditions to fertilize apricot trees. Unless he counted marrying Quiss, or having five children: his family was also an accomplishment that gave him pride.

'How many arrows do you have left?' he asked the bowman.

'None.' It was a question the man understood. 'I'll have to get them from the wolves.'

'Don't bother. Go.' Tholden pushed him gently. 'Get men for the watertubs. If that thing doesn't just break the stockade, it'll burn it down.'

The bowman clattered off the ladder, sped away. Tholden turned to the other bowmen, actually turned his back on the advancing firecat. 'If you're out of arrows,' he said as if he were speaking to a small circle of friends on an occasion of no great importance, 'go rally Houseldon. We need help.

'If you've still got some left, come up here.'

No more than fifty yards away, the firecat brushed past a discarded corn shock. At once, the shock sprang into flame and withered to crisp ash.

The platform wobbled as two bowmen clambered up to join Tholden. Nodding toward the firecat, he said, 'Aim for the eyes.'

'Will that kill it?' asked one of the men huskily.

'Who knows? You got any better ideas?'

The man shook his head. His face was taut with fear, but he didn't back away.

The bowmen nocked their shafts, strained their bows. Almost simultaneously, they let fly.

The firecat flicked its head aside negligently. The arrows caught fire and became charcoal before their heads could pierce the cat's hide.

'I think we need a better idea,' the second bowman muttered as he and his comrade readied more shafts.

As if he were losing his mind, Tholden turned again and shouted, 'Geraden? Where's *Geraden?*'

The first of his reinforcements had begun to arrive: men who hadn't encountered the wolves; others who grasped that a greater danger was coming; some who were so frightened that the bowmen had to goad them along. No one had seen Geraden. A few of the defenders stared at Tholden as if he were speaking an alien tongue.

'All right,' he rasped. 'We'll do it ourselves.' The wildness in his eyes was getting worse. Suddenly furious, he roared, 'Don't just stand there! Get those watertubs up onto the banquette!'

Galvanized by the incongruous desperation in his high, kind voice, the men below him started hurrying.

The bowmen exhausted their shafts – to no purpose – and jumped out of the way of the watertubs. The firecat was so close now that Tholden thought he could feel its heat. Or maybe that was just the sun. The sky was clear and gorgeous to the horizons, and the air was growing warm. With blood running from his face like sweat, he helped several men boost a watertub into position.

Just in time – barely in time. The cat reached the stockade, paused, tested the wood with its nose. Instant flames swept upward, building swiftly from a small flicker to a savage blaze. The hands and arms supporting the watertubs were scorched. Tholden lost his beard and eyebrows; he nearly lost his eyes.

Then two half hogsheads went over the wall almost simultaneously, and water hit the flames and the heat with a roar like an explosion.

The fire in the timbers went out. But the concussion as that much water erupted into steam blasted the men off the platform, off the banquette.

Tholden landed on his shoulder and spent a stunned and useless moment staring paralyzed at the sky while all his muscles locked up around the jolt. It was possible that his shoulder was broken. It seemed possible to him that he would never breathe again. The hard, hot steam disappeared into the air almost immediately, leaving the heavens blue and perfect, untouched.

After a momentary delay, the wet wood of the stockade began to smolder.

Wrenching air into his lungs, Tholden rolled sideways, got his legs under him.

His shoulder was numb. He couldn't move that arm.

Flames licked between the timbers. The lashings that held the timbers began to snap.

With a howl of heat, the wall caught fire again and blazed up like the blast of a furnace.

Tholden and his men staggered backward, stared as the timbers flamed –
and the firecat thrust its way between the beams as if they were nothing more
than charcoal twigs.

'*Tholden!*' people screamed.

'Help!'

'Tell us what to do!'

'We don't know what to do!'

'Run,' he coughed weakly. He had never felt such intense fire in his life,
never seen anything that terrified him as much as this firecat did. 'Run.' The
heat drew tears from his eyes as if he were weeping. Houseldon was built of
wood. The whole place would burn. 'Get out of the way.'

Automatically, without thought, he retreated to keep the heat at a distance.
The firecat ambled after him with an indirect, even nonchalant gait, as if he
were an especially tasty and helpless mouse.

Moving like a madman, he led the firecat in among the buildings.

The cat moved to the side of the lane while it followed him. Fire swept up
the wall of a granary; then, with a detonation like a thunderclap, the grain
itself took flame. Fire and smoke and blazing grain swirled a hundred feet
into the air.

The merchant who owned the granary lived in a house beside it. He was an
old man with a vast quantity of fat and no reputation whatsoever for valor;
yet he ran raging out onto his porch and flung a washbasin full of water at the
cat.

The cat didn't notice his attack.

Almost instantly, the fire consumed him.

Tholden retreated as slowly as he could bear, bringing Houseldon's
destruction with him.

He nearly missed what had happened when the firecat abruptly let out a
roar of vexation – perhaps even of pain – and flinched to the side. A bit of
flame clung to the pads of one forepaw. The beast hunched over and licked
its paw clean; its tail switched malevolently. When it started moving again, it
appeared angrier, more determined; it looked like it intended to pounce on
him without further delay.

Tholden gaped dumbly, transfixed by the incomprehensible fact that the
creature had hurt itself by stepping in a small pile of sheepdung.

As if this information were too much for him, his eyes rolled in his head;
his scorched and naked face stretched into a wail; his numb arm flapped
against his side.

Awkwardly, he turned and dashed out of the firecat's path, fled between
the nearest houses as if he had vultures beating around his head. The people
who saw him go believed that his mind had snapped.

The cat didn't pursue him. It was after other prey.

Setting homes and shops ablaze almost casually as it went, it continued its
malign stroll into the heart of Houseldon.

Toward Terisa and Geraden.

Terisa and Geraden and the Domne heard the screams; they saw fire and smoke blasting into the sky. 'Glass and splinters!' Geraden hissed between his teeth. 'What's *that*?'

'Not wolves, I'm afraid,' muttered the Domne. He nudged the carcass at his feet. 'Even wolves like that don't set fires.'

Alarm cleared the giddiness out of Terisa's head. She took her weight on her legs and tried to think.

'Where's Tholden?'

Geraden glanced at her. He and the Domne didn't look at each other.

One of the bowmen led the rout down the street. Waving people past him, he stopped in front of the Domne. 'My lord,' he gasped, urgent for breath, 'the wall is breached. Houses are burning.'

'I can see that,' replied the Domne with uncharacteristic asperity. 'How did it happen?'

'A creature of Imagery. A cat as big as a steer. It sets fire to everything. 'It's coming this way.'

Terisa felt a cold hand close around her heart. Sets fire to everything. 'Castellan Lebbick told me about a cat like that. It killed his guards.' He sent out fifty men, and it killed them. 'When they were trying to capture the Congery's champion.'

Geraden nodded grimly. 'Eremis hasn't got enough men. Or enough men to spare. Or he can't translate enough of them here if without making them mad. So he's using Imagery to attack us. Trying to slaughter us wholesale instead of murdering us individually.'

The fires came closer. A warehouse tossed flames in all directions as kegs of oil exploded. The destruction of Houseldon already seemed to be raging out of control.

The Domne watched his people flee past him as if the sight made him want to throw up. He kept his voice quiet, however. 'You're the only Imager in the family, Geraden. How do we defend ourselves?'

'With mirrors,' Geraden snarled. Terisa thought he looked exactly like his father at that moment – so hard and horrified that he wanted to throw up. 'Which we haven't got.'

Then she caught her first glimpse of the firecat. Involuntarily, she took a step backward.

'Where's Tholden?' she asked again. She was suddenly afraid that he was already dead.

Tholden was running for his life.

His shoulder wasn't broken. If it were broken, it would have started to hurt before this. Nevertheless it remained numb; he still couldn't use it. It hampered his balance, his gait. Because of it, he ran like a hunchback.

Ran between the houses and along the lanes of Houseldon as if he were terrified.

He had forgotten the wolves – forgotten them completely. His desperation didn't hold room for any other danger. One of the houses he passed had had its door torn off the hinges, but he didn't notice that. He didn't hear the dying whimpers from inside, didn't see the beast munching flesh in the doorway.

He had no idea what was happening when the wolf left the infant it was eating and leaped at his head.

Because of his lurching gait, it missed his head. Yet its claws raked his back as it went by him.

That pain got his attention. He and the wolf wheeled to meet each other; as fierce as the beast, he faced its charge.

Slobbering blood, it sprang again.

He had no time for fear or forethought. In fact, he had no time for the wolf. Striding forward as the beast leaped, he kicked it in the ribcage so hard that he ruptured its heart.

Then he ran on.

His back bled as if it were on fire. Coughing for help, he ran toward the nearest wastepit where Houseldon accumulated fertilizer for the orchards and fields.

He didn't have much time. The people fleeing along the street had scattered; Terisa, Geraden, and the Domne could see the firecat clearly now.

And it could see them: that was obvious. Its eyes were fixed on them as if at last it had recognized its true prey.

Well, of course. Stunned with fright and helplessness, Terisa had been reduced to talking to herself. Eremis wouldn't trust random violence to kill them. And he must be able to talk to that thing. Otherwise how could he get it to do what he wanted? It might have attacked the champion instead of the Castellan's guards. He probably gave it a description of the people it was supposed to kill.

Uselessly, she wondered what kind of description the firecat would understand. Could Eremis really talk to it?

'Terisa.' Geraden had a hand on her arm; he shook her. 'Terisa, listen to me. If that creature is after me, you can get away. You've got to get away. Get out of here – get out of Houseldon. Go north. To the Termigan. Maybe he's got some glass you can use. At least you can warn him. He'll protect you.

'I'll try to give you as much time as I can.'

'Thanks.' What was she talking about? She had no idea. 'I appreciate that.' Words seem to come out of her mouth without passing through her consciousness first. 'What if it's after me? How are *you* going to get away?'

'An interesting question,' the Domne put in dryly. 'Let's discuss it later, shall we? Start running, both of you. If it's engrossed in destroying Houseldon, you might both get away.' Abruptly, he started to shout, cracking his command at them like a whip. 'I said *start running!*'

Both Terisa and Geraden nodded.

Neither of them moved.

She began to feel the heat of the fire on her face. The firecat was so close now that she could have hit it with a rock. It wasn't in any hurry – but it was definitely coming straight for them. Its eyes stared malice; its tail lashed the dust.

She and Geraden and the Domne stood their ground as if they had lost their minds.

And the firecat stopped. It regarded them warily. They acted like they weren't afraid of it. Why was that? Terisa had the odd impression that she knew exactly what the cat was thinking. Why were they standing there as if fire and fangs couldn't hurt them? What kind of danger did they represent?

Beyond question, she had lost her mind, even if the men with her were still sane. While the firecat studied them all, she waved her hand at it and said, 'Scat. Go away.' She could feel her hair growing crisp in the heat. 'We won't hurt you. If you go away.'

Good. Brilliant. Instead of retreating, the creature crouched to spring.

Unexpectedly, Minick arrived at the Domne's side. In spite of his apparent haste, he didn't seem to be breathing hard – didn't seem to be breathing at all.

Each of his strong, brown hands carried a large wooden bucket.

Water, Terisa thought. Good idea. Too bad it won't work. The firecat certainly hadn't been hindered by the snow when it had attacked Castellan Lebbick's men.

Precisely, as if he were following an elaborate set of instructions, Minick set the buckets down beside him.

Gasping and blowing as though his chest were about to burst, Tholden came into the street. He nearly ran up against the firecat's flank; the heat must have been tremendous.

He held one of the watertubs hugged in his arms.

Full of water, it must have been far too heavy for any one man to lift. Nevertheless he supported it alone, staggered out into the open without help; there he let the tub thud into the dirt.

That dull, hard sound distracted the creature. Dancing aside as daintily as a kitten, it turned to see what he was doing.

'Now!' Tholden croaked hoarsely.

Reaching into his watertub with both hands, he scooped a load of sheepdung into the firecat's face.

The hard pellets hit the cat's whiskers, cheeks, jaws, eyes.

Hit and stuck.

They were fuel: they burned hotly. But they didn't fall away, as water and wood and even iron fell away. They clung to the creature's fur and flesh.

With a scream, the firecat did a complete backflip. Immediately, it began to scrub at its face, trying to dislodge the fiery pellets.

In an instant, its forepaws were covered with fire.

Minick was a little slow; even in an emergency, he couldn't act without his usual care. On this occasion, however, he was quick enough. Before the cat could turn, he stepped forward and splashed its back with the contents of his first bucket.

More sheepdung.

This time, the creature's scream seemed to come from the marrow of its bones. It wrenched itself around in a circle and rammed its burning side into the dirt to extinguish the fire of the pellets.

Abruptly, five or six more men rushed into the street, carrying buckets and baskets and pots of sheepdung; they hurled more fuel into the cat's flames. Stooping to his tub, Tholden shoveled up great handfuls of pellets. Minick emptied his second bucket at the mounting conflagration.

Then all the men had to stop, had to draw back. The creature had begun to burn so hotly that they couldn't get near it. Terisa put up her hands to protect her face.

With a sizzling noise like the shriek of meat on a griddle, of hot iron in oil, the firecat died horribly, consumed by its own blaze.

Tholden staggered, stumbled to his knees; his scorched and beardless face gaped at the charred carcass.

Slowly, the Domne limped around the circle of heat to his eldest son. Minick, Geraden, and Terisa followed; they were there when the Domne put his arms around Tholden's bloody back.

'As I said,' the Domne murmured in a voice congested with pride and pain. 'The right man for the job.'

Before Terisa could think of it, Geraden left to go get Quiss.

Quiss took care of her husband grimly. Like the Domne's, her emotions were too strong – and too mixed – to let her be calm about Tholden's condition.

Standing in the street with his canes propped under his hands, the Domne rallied his bowmen and put them in charge of the hunt for the remaining wolves.

Gently, Minick helped Stead out of the Domne's house. Together, the brothers set about organizing the evacuation of Houseldon.

The firecat's blaze was too well established to be fought. Even without the distraction and damage of the wolves, with nothing on their minds except the safety of their homes, the Domne's people might not have been able to beat this fire. But the truth was that they were seriously distracted, badly hurt. And there might be more attacks – When Minick suggested fighting the flames, the Domne forbade him flatly.

Instead of trying uselessly to save Houseldon, every man, woman, and child who could move himself, lift weight, or accept responsibility was put to work getting supplies and possessions, horses and livestock, infants and invalids out of the stockade.

Geraden ignored all this activity. Taking Terisa with him, he put together a breakfast for the two of them, then found a quiet corner in his father's house where they could eat in peace.

Baffled, she asked him what he thought he was doing.

'Saving time,' he muttered through a cold chicken sandwich. 'We've got to eat sometime. Better now than later.'

That didn't shed any light. She tried again. 'What's going to happen?'

'They'll go up to the Closed Fist and dig in. With all the stuff they have to carry, they won't get there for two or three days. But I don't think that matters. If Eremis had anything else ready to attack with, he would have used it by now. I think the first danger is over. And once they're entrenched in those caves and rocks, he'll need an army to root them out.'

Terisa didn't understand him at all. Dimly, it occurred to her that the Closed Fist would be an impossible place in which to work glass. 'You keep saying "they." Aren't you going with them?'

He shook his head and tried to hide the gleam in his eyes.

She studied him as if she had become stupid. His home was in flames around him. Soon Houseldon would be reduced to ashes and cinders. The survivors were being forced into hiding. One of his brothers had been seriously hurt. People he had known all his life were dead. Really, it was astonishing how much his mood had improved.

He was hard and strong, she could see that; but the grim iron was gone, the bitterness. Last night, he had remembered how to laugh. The shine in his gaze promised that he would be able to laugh again.

Looking at him, the numbness which too much fear and destruction had imposed on her heart began to fade. Almost smiling, as if she already knew the answer, she asked, 'Why not?'

He shrugged cheerfully. 'I've been looking at everything backward. My usual instinct for mishap. In a sense, what happened today is good news. What Eremis did today is good news. It means he's afraid of us – too afraid to wait until he can strike intelligently and be sure of killing us. He thinks there's something we can do to hurt him.

'If he thinks that, he's probably right. He's too smart to scare himself over nothing. All we have to do is find it.'

Incongruously, while Houseldon burned, Terisa felt some of the past night's joy come back. 'Maybe his plans aren't ready,' she said. 'Maybe we still have time to warn Orison.'

'Right. And along the way we can try to warn some of the lords. When they know what's going on, maybe the Fayle or even the Termigan can be persuaded to do something against him.'

She couldn't help herself; she jumped up and kissed him, hugged him so hard she thought her arms would break.

'Come on, mooncalves,' Stead snorted from the doorway. 'The fire's already on the other side of the lane. This house is going next.'

In response, both Terisa and Geraden started to laugh.

They left Houseldon holding hands.

By midmorning, the Domne's seat was little more than a smoldering husk.

From his stretcher, Tholden watched the ruin and wept as if he had failed; but his father would have none of it. 'Don't be silly, boy. You saved all our lives. Houses can be built again. You saved your *people*. I call it a great victory. Nobody else could have done it.'

'That's right, Da,' Quiss said because her husband was too emotional to reply. 'He'll agree with you when he's had a little rest. If he knows what's good for him.'

Ignoring embarrassment, Geraden kissed all three of them. Quiss and the Domne kissed Terisa. Then Terisa and Geraden went to their horses, the bay and the appaloosa which had brought them down from the Closed Fist.

'Now it's your turn, Geraden,' the Domne announced in front of all the inhabitants of Houseldon. 'Make us proud of you. Make what we're doing worthwhile.' Then he added, 'And, in the name of sanity, remember to call me "Da."'

Helplessly, Geraden colored.

Terisa wanted to laugh again. 'Don't worry, Da. I won't let him forget.'

When the Domne's people began cheering, she and Geraden rode away to meet Mordant's need.

THIRTY-FOUR

FRUSTRATED STATES

Toward the end of the first day of the siege – the day which eventually led to Master Quillon's murder and Terisa's escape – Prince Kragen indicated his ruined catapults and asked the lady Elega what she thought he should do.

'Attack,' she replied at once. 'Attack and attack.'

Raising one eyebrow, he waited for an explanation.

'I am no Imager – but everyone knows that Imagery requires strength and concentration. Translations are exhausting. And in this' – she gestured at the catapults – 'you have only one opponent. Only one Master can use the glass which frustrates you. He must be weary by now. Perhaps he has already worn out his endurance.

'If you apply enough pressure, he must fail. Then you will be able to bring down that curtain-wall. Orison will be opened to you.'

Despite his confident demeanor, his air of assurance, Prince Kragen couldn't restrain a scowl. 'My lady,' he asked softly, harshly, 'how many siege engines do you think I have? They are difficult to move. If we had brought them from Alend, we would be on the road yet – and Cadwal's victory would be unchallenged. We were forced to rely on what we could appropriate from the Armigite.' Thinking about the Armigite always made Kragen want to spit. 'It seems likely to me that we will run out of catapults before that cursed Imager is exhausted.

'Then, my lady' – almost involuntarily, he wrapped his fingers around her arm and squeezed to get her attention, make her hear the things he didn't say – 'our first, quickest, and best hope will be lost.'

'Then what do you mean to do, my lord Prince?' demanded Elega. Apparently, she didn't hear him. Perhaps she couldn't. 'Are you prepared to simply *wait* here until the High King arrives to crush you?'

Prince Kragen lifted his head. Too many of his people were watching. By an act of will, he smoothed his scowl, put on a sharp smile.

'I am prepared to do what I must.'

Bowing to conceal the grimness in his eyes, he walked away.

That night, covered by the dark, he sent a squadron of sappers to try to dig the keystones out of the curtain-wall.

Another failure. Scant moments after his men set to work, Orison's defenders poured oil down the face of the wall and fired it. The flames forced the sappers back – and gave enough light for Lebbick's archers. Less than half the squadron escaped.

The next morning, when he had had time to absorb the latest news, Prince Kragen announced that he would take no more risks.

He didn't withdraw from his position. He spent all his time projecting confidence to his forces, or designing contingency plans with his captains, or consulting with the Alend Monarch. But he took no chances, incurred no losses. He might have been waiting for High King Festten to join him in some elaborate and harmless wargame.

Elega understood why he did this. He told her why, publicly and privately. And his explanations made sense. Nevertheless his passivity drove her to distraction. At times, she couldn't face him under the eyes of his troops; at times, she could hardly bring herself to be civil to him in bed. She wanted *action* – wanted the wall down, the battle joined; she wanted King Joyse deposed, and Prince Kragen in his place.

She wanted the fact that she had betrayed her own father to mean something. While the Alend forces spent their time in training or leisure – enjoying the suddenly beautiful spring – instead of in bringing Orison to its knees, everything she had done was pointless.

She kept track of the days; nearly kept track of the hours, gnawing them like a dry bone. It was late in the evening of the fifth day of Kragen's inactivity, the sixth day of the siege, while she waited in her tent for the Prince to finish discussing his day and his plans with Margonal, that a soldier from one of the sentry posts brought her a visitor.

'Forgive the intrusion, my lady.' The soldier was a wary old veteran, and he appeared unsure that he was doing the right thing. 'Wouldn't trouble you with her, but she wasn't trying to sneak into camp. Walked right up to the sentry and asked to see you. Isn't carrying any weapons – not even a knife. I said I would take her to the Prince. Or at least the sentry captain. She said she didn't think that was a good idea. Said if I brought her here you could decide what to do with her.'

Elega made an effort to be patient with all this explanation. 'Who is she?'

The soldier shifted his weight uncomfortably. 'Says she's your sister.'

Elega blinked at him while the blood seemed to drain out of her heart.

Carefully, so that her voice wouldn't betray her, she replied, 'You did well. You can leave her with me. I'll decide what to do with her when I hear what she has to say.'

The soldier lifted his shoulders in a small shrug. Pushing the tentflap aside, he ushered Myste into Elega's presence.

The two sisters stood as if they were stunned and stared at each other. The soldier left them alone, closed the tentflap behind him; they stood and stared at each other.

Physically, Elega was in her element. She was wrapped in a gauzy robe the Prince liked. Lamps and candlelight brought out the lustre of her short, blond hair, the beauty of her pale skin, the vividness of her violet eyes. In contrast, Myste needed sunshine to look her best. Indoors, by the light of fires, she tended to appear sullen or dreamy, and her gaze had a faraway quality that gave the impression she was immersed in her own thoughts – less interested in events around her than Elega was; therefore less important. Her thick cloak had seen hard use.

Yet Myste had changed – Elega saw that at once. Her carriage had become straighter; the set of her shoulders and the lift of her chin made her look like a woman who had lost her doubts. A scar that looked like a healed burn ran from her cheekbone to her ear on the right side; instead of marring her beauty, however, it had the effect of increasing her air of conviction. She had earned whatever certainty she felt. For the first time in their lives, Myste's simple presence caused Elega to feel smaller in some way, less sure of herself.

A quick intuition told her that Myste had done something that would make her own efforts to shape Mordant's fate appear trivial by comparison.

Myste met Elega's regard for a long moment. Then, slowly, she began to smile.

It was too much, that smile; it was the way their father used to smile, back in the days when he was still himself; a smile like a sunrise. She couldn't bear it: her eyes filled with tears.

'Oh, Myste,' she breathed. 'You scared me to death, disappearing like that. I thought you were dead long ago.'

Helplessly, she opened her arms and caught her sister in a tight hug.

'I am sorry,' Myste whispered while they clung to each other. 'I know you were scared. I had no wish to do it that way. I had no other choice.'

Awkwardly, Elega stepped back, wiped her eyes, found a handkerchief and blew her nose. 'You rotten child,' she said, smiling gamely.

Myste smiled back and borrowed the handkerchief when Elega was done with it.

'Do you remember?' Elega murmured. 'I used to call you that. When we were little. When I did something forbidden and got into trouble, I used to try to blame it on you. Even when you were so small you could hardly walk, I used to try to convince Mother you tricked me into – whatever it was. I told her you were a rotten child.'

Lightly, Myste laughed. 'No, I do not remember. I was too young. Anyway, I can hardly believe you ever tried to pass responsibility off on anyone else.' She sighed as if the sight of her sister gave her great pleasure. 'And now after all these years I have proved that you were right.'

'Yes, you have.' Elega wanted to joke, and laugh, and yell at Myste, all at the same time. 'Completely despicable.' She tried to pull some organization into her head, keep her thoughts from spinning out of control. 'Sit down. Have some wine.' She pointed toward a pair of canvas camp chairs beside a small, brass table. 'I really am delighted to see you. I have been so alone—' But she couldn't do it; Myste's unexpected appearance made her brain reel. 'Oh, Myste, *where have you been?*'

A hint of self-consciousness touched Myste's gaze. No, Elega realized almost at once, it was more than self-consciousness. It was caution. Slowly, Myste's smile faded.

'That is a long story,' she replied quietly. 'I have come to you because I must make a number of decisions. Among them is whether I should tell you where I have been and what I have been doing.'

More than self-consciousness. More than caution.

Distrust.

Elega felt like crying again.

At the same time, however, her own instinct for caution sprang awake. The Alend camp was a dangerous place in more ways than one; it was especially dangerous for a daughter of King Joyse who hadn't demonstrated her loyalty to Prince Kragen.

'What is the difficulty?' she asked carefully. 'I am your sister. Why should you not tell me?'

Whose side are you on?

'Thank you.' Myste's manner was firm, unflawed. 'I will have wine. As you see' – she dropped her cloak, revealing a battered leather jacket and pants which apparently had nothing in the world to do with lovers and bedchambers – 'amenities have been few in my life for some time.'

But Elega couldn't respond. She was too busy fighting down an impulse to demand, *Whose side are you on?*

'Elega,' sighed Myste, 'I cannot tell you my story because I do not know why you are here. I do not know how an Alend army came to besiege Orison. I do not know' – for an instant, she blinked back tears of her own – 'if our father still lives, or still holds his throne. Or still seems mad.

'I can decide nothing wisely without the answers to such questions.

'I knew that you were here,' she explained. 'I saw you ride with Prince Kragen to meet Castellan Lebbick on the day Orison was invested. The distance was considerable,' she admitted, 'but I was sure I saw you. It has taken me this long, however, to persuade' – she faltered oddly – 'persuade myself to approach you.'

Obviously trying to defuse Elega's tension, she asked pleadingly, '*May* I have some wine?'

'Of course. Surely.' Jerking herself out of her paralysis, Elega went to the brass table. It held a jug and two goblets. Despite the possibility that she might eventually have to explain to the Prince how his goblet came to be used in his absence, she poured wine for herself and Myste, then sat down and urged Myste to do the same.

Myste accepted the chair and the wine. Over the goblet's rim as she drank, another sun dawned in her eyes. When she lowered the goblet, she grinned longingly past Elega's shoulder. 'That is good. I wish I could take a hogshead of it with me.'

A few swallows of wine helped restore Elega's composure. With a better grasp on herself, she asked, 'Why do you speak of going? You have only just arrived. And' – she attempted her best smile – 'you have not yet said anything I can understand about why you came in the first place.'

Myste drank again, then held the goblet in both palms and gazed into its depths. 'I came to ask the answers to questions, so that I can make my decisions with some hope that they will lead to good rather than ill.'

'In other words' – Elega kept her voice steady – 'you wish me to trust you enough to help you decide whether you can trust me.' Her question refused to be stifled. 'Myste, who has your allegiance now? Whom do you serve?'

Myste's eyes darkened. All at once, the distance in them seemed poignant to Elega. Myste was the youngest of the King's daughters, and in some ways the least respected; alone in her romantic dreams, her strange notion that there were no real limits to the lives of ordinary men and women. Only her father had ever listened to her with anything except kind contempt or outright mockery – and now his kingdom was in ruins, and the fault for it was his alone.

Yet here she was, clad more completely in her own courage than in the worn leather on her body. It was quite possible that she was out of her mind. How else to explain the fact that she was here, that she considered it reasonable to simply walk into the Alend camp and ask for answers? Even if she were sane, she had become something Elega didn't know how to evaluate or touch.

On the other hand, what harm could she do, one brave, foolish daughter of a failed King? Was it conceivable that she had somehow gone over to Cadwal? No. The High King's army was too far away – and the Perdon's forces still intervened. Then what harm could she do?

Why, none.

She made no attempt to answer Elega's question. After a long moment, Elega let it drop. Feeling an unexpected sympathy – and a hint of nameless admiration – toward her lonely sister, she decided suddenly, irrationally, to gamble. 'Very well,' she said. After all, risks came to her more naturally than caution. Prince Kragen's inaction had her at her wit's end. 'Ask me something specific.'

Her words lit a spark in Myste's gaze.

Myste raised an unself-conscious hand to her cheek. 'Again, thank you,' she murmured. 'It will be a great service to me.'

Almost at once, she inquired, 'Is Father well? Is he' – she swallowed quickly – 'still alive?'

'To the best of my knowledge.' As soon as she heard the question, Elega's throat went dry. 'It has been some days since I spoke to him.' Now that she had decided to gamble, she realized that her own story would be hard to tell. Myste's fundamental assumptions were so different. 'Nevertheless emissaries and messengers such as the Castellan and Master Quillon make reference to him without hesitation. He remains King in his own castle, even though his rule over Mordant has collapsed.'

Myste let a breath of relief between her lips. 'I am glad,' she said, nodding to herself.

'And Terisa? How is she?'

Elega muffled her discomfort with asperity. 'I fear that the lady Terisa has fallen victim to Geraden's instinct for mishap.'

'How so?' Myste's tone conveyed a suggestion of alarm.

Remembering the reservoir, Elega drawled, 'She has learned to make the same mistakes he does.'

Again, Myste nodded; she clearly didn't understand what Elega meant – and didn't want to pursue it. She thought for a moment, then asked slowly, as if she wanted better words, 'Elega, *why* are you here? If our father still rules in Orison, how have you come to take the part of his enemies?'

There it was: the place where all their common ground fell away, the point on which they would never comprehend each other. If the truth hit Myste too hard, Elega might be forced to summon guards and have her sister delivered to Prince Kragen.

Nevertheless she was faithful to the risk she'd chosen. Dryly, she replied, 'That is the wrong question, Myste. You should ask why the Prince and his forces are here. My reasons hinge on theirs.'

Myste studied her intently. 'I suspected as much. That is why I feared for Father. I thought the Alends might have come because he was dead. But I had no wish to offend you by leaping to erroneous conclusions.

'When I left Orison, Prince Kragen had been insulted in the hall of audiences. Yet the fact that he remained made me think that he had not given up hope for peace.

'Why *is* he here, attempting to pull the King from his Seat?'

'Because,' Elega answered, bracing herself for Myste's reaction, 'I persuaded him to do it.'

In a sense, Myste didn't react at all; she simply went still, like an animal in hiding. The change was so unlike her, however, that it seemed as vehement as a shout. Where had she learned so much self-possession – and so much caution?

'I made his acquaintance after his audience with the King.' Elega struggled to keep a defensive tone out of her voice. 'He taught me to believe him when he said that Margonal's desire for peace was sincere. Yet Alend faced a dilemma he must resolve. Cadwal has no desire for peace – and the King's strength had become plainly inadequate to keep the Congery out of Festten's hands. Alend must take some action, so that the High King would not gain all Imagery for himself.

'First I required of the Prince some indication of his good faith. He replied with the promise that if Orison fell to him he would make the Perdon King of Mordant – that Alend would keep nothing for itself if the Congery was made safe from Cadwal.

'Then I persuaded him that a siege was his best hope.'

'But, Elega,' Myste protested, 'that is untrue. Father is the only man who has ever taken Orison by storm. A siege may well last for seasons. And High King Festten surely will not allow seasons to pass before he comes to prevent the Alend Monarch from claiming the Congery.'

'It *is* true,' insisted Elega. Honesty, however, forced her to admit, 'Or it *was*. Two things made it so. First, the curtain-wall is fragile at best – and no one could have foreseen that one of the Masters would conceive a way to defend it.

'And second—'

Involuntarily, she wavered. This lay at the heart of her ache for action, her desire to see the siege succeed. It was her doing: she had convinced Kragen to attempt it.

If he held her to blame for her failure, he gave no sign of it. Perhaps he had accepted the hazards of what he did, and felt no recrimination. Or perhaps he found a new hope in the reasons for his present inaction. In either case, she blamed herself enough for both of them. Sure of herself, determined to save her world, she had taken Mordant's fate in her own hands.

And she had dropped it.

'Second?' Myste prompted.

'Second,' said Elega, more harshly than she intended, 'I promised to deliver Orison to him with little or no bloodshed.'

Myste sat completely still; not a muscle in her face shifted. Yet her eyes seemed to burn with outrage.

'How?'

Elega's knuckles tightened on her goblet. 'By poisoning the reservoir. Not fatally. But enough to indispose the defense until the castle could be taken.'

Without a flicker of expression, almost without moving her mouth, Myste said, 'That should have sufficed. What went wrong?'

Deliberately, Elega permitted herself an obscenity which she knew Myste particularly disliked. Then she said, 'Geraden and Terisa caught me. They were unable to stop me – or indeed capture me. But they warned the Castellan. No one was indisposed because no one drank the water. The defense holds – and I was forced to flee.'

Unable to contain her self-disgust, she concluded, 'Does that answer your questions? Can you make your decisions wisely now?'

Gradually, Myste let herself move. Her gaze left Elega's face; she lifted her goblet and drained it. Automatically, far away in her thoughts, she poured more wine and drank again.

'Ah, Elega. How terrible that must be for you – to attempt the betrayal of your own home and family, and to fail.'

'It is worse,' retorted Elega fiercely, 'to do *nothing* – to let every good thing in the world go to ruin because the man who created it cannot be bothered to defend it.'

Still slowly, still peering into the distance, Myste nodded. 'Perhaps. That is one of the decisions I must make.

'Please tell me. Why does the Prince "do nothing"? Since the first day of the siege, he has taken no action I can see. To all appearances, he is simply waiting for High King Festten to come and destroy him.'

Abruptly, as if a stunned part of her mind had just been kicked, Elega realized that Prince Kragen was overdue. Usually, he finished discussing the day with his father and came to her tent before this.

If he caught Myste here, he would have no real choice but to make her a prisoner. Her potential value as King Joyse's daughter was too great to be ignored. But Myste was also Elega's sister – and Elega wasn't sure yet what her own decision would be. The only thing she was sure of was that Myste wouldn't reveal any of her secrets as Prince Kragen's prisoner.

Muttering, 'Wait here,' Elega jumped up and hurried past the curtains into the back of the tent.

There she roused the Alend girl who served as her maid. 'Hurry, child,' she hissed. 'Find the Prince. He may still be with his father, or on his way here. Beg him to forgive me. Tell him I feel unwell. Tell him I am half blind with headache – but it will pass if I am allowed to sleep.

'Go quickly.'

She hustled the girl out into the night, paused to quiet the hammering of her heart, then returned to Myste.

Myste looked at her inquiringly. Elega explained what she had done – and was more relieved than she considered reasonable when she saw that Myste believed her. So Myste's new caution, her distrust, had its limits. Despite the things Elega had already done, Myste didn't expect her sister to betray her.

In the back of her mind, Elega began to wonder whose side she herself was on.

She sat down again, poured more wine. Myste was still waiting for an explanation of Prince Kragen's inaction. Elega took a deep breath because for the first time what she was about to say might be interpreted as evidence of disloyalty. Then she asked, 'Do you remember the day we first met Terisa? The day the Perdon came storming into Orison, demanding help, and King Joyse refused him?'

'Yes.' Once again, Myste's sober gaze was fixed on Elega's face.

'I think I told you about it.' Elega remembered the Perdon's rage vividly. *You tell him* this, *my lady*, he had roared at her. *Every man of mine who falls or dies defending him in his blind inaction, I will send* here. 'Well, he is doing what he said he would. In small groups and squadrons, injured or dead men and their families arrive almost daily from the Care of Perdon, sent to the purported safety of Orison – and as a reproach to King Joyse.

'They are Alend prisoners now – although it would be more just to say that they are under the care of the army's physicians, and not permitted to leave. Being hurt, exhausted, or bereaved, few of them have the will to refuse when they are questioned.'

Myste watched Elega's face and said nothing.

'From them,' Elega sighed, 'we have learned that the High King's army is not coming here.'

At that, Myste's eyes widened. 'Not?' she whispered as if she couldn't believe what she was hearing. 'Not?'

Elega nodded. 'Not directly, in any case. That much is certain. Festten's forces move with what speed they can manage through the hills of Perdon – through the Perdon's resistance. But all recent reports agree that the High King's movement brings him no nearer Orison.

'That is why Prince Kragen believes he can afford to wait.'

At last, Myste sounded like her self-control might slip. 'Then where is High King Festten going?'

'South and west,' Elega answered. 'Into the Care of Tor.

'The Perdon's survivors say that the Cadwal army moves along the best route it can find toward Marshalt, the Tor's seat.'

'But *why?*' demanded Myste. 'Why go *there?* The Congery is *here.*'

Elega had no idea. 'I have heard it rumored,' she said for the sake of hearing how Myste would reply, 'that the Castellan considers the Tor a traitor.'

Myste's head twitched. 'The Tor? Nonsense.' She thought for a moment, then continued, 'And if he *is* a traitor, that would be even less reason for High King Festten to invade Tor. It makes no sense.

'What is the Perdon doing?'

To preserve her composure, Elega put on a hard front. 'Apparently, he is more dedicated to Mordant's service than his King deserves.' The truth was that every thought of the Perdon made her chest ache – made her want to scream because there was nothing she could do. 'Festten appears uninterested in Orison. But rather than taking this opportunity to flee – perhaps here, perhaps toward a dubious alliance with the Armigite, or a stronger one with the Fayle – the Perdon shifts his forces so that they are always in Cadwal's way. He began with scarcely three thousand men against at least twenty thousand. If the reports are true, he has less than two thousand now, and every day he is whittled down. And yet he continues fighting. He spends every life in his command merely to hinder Festten's approach to whatever it is the High King wants.

'Clearly, he is engaged in a personal struggle against Cadwal. If King Joyse had not abandoned him long ago, he would have saved himself – and aided Orison – by coming here.

'Does *that* answer your questions?'

While Elega spoke, Myste's expression changed. Her gaze turned toward Orison; her eyes filled with tears. 'Oh, Father,' she murmured thickly. 'How have you been brought to this? How do you bear it?'

Elega's urge to scream intensified. 'If it does,' she snapped, 'perhaps you will consent to answer mine. I have told you enough to get myself beheaded if I were not in the Prince's favor. I would like some return for my risk.'

'Yes.' Suddenly, Myste rose to her feet, facing through the wall of the tent toward Orison as though Elega weren't present. 'I can make my decisions now. Thank you.

'I must go.'

Without a glance at her sister, she started toward the tentflap.

For an instant, Elega was stuck, caught between contradictory reactions. She was full of outrage; she wanted to make scathing demands which would rip Myste's reticence aside. At the same time, the thought that her sister was about to leave her – without trusting her, without *trusting* her – went into her heart like a spike.

She was about to shout for a soldier when a new thought flashed through her like a bolt of illumination.

Before her sister reached the tentflap, she said, 'Father sent me a message, Myste.'

Myste stopped immediately; she turned, came back toward Elega. As if involuntarily, she asked, 'What was it?'

Too absorbed in Myste's importance to be self-conscious, Elega answered, 'Castellan Lebbick brought it. According to him, father said, "I am sure that my daughter Elega has acted for the best reasons. She carries my pride with her wherever she goes. For her sake, as well as for my own, I hope that the best reasons will also produce the best results."'

Unexpectedly, Myste closed her eyes. Tears spread under her lashes and down her cheeks, but for a long moment she didn't move or speak. Then she looked radiantly at her sister, smiling like a new day.

'Of course,' she breathed. 'Why did I not see it for myself?'

At once, she returned to her chair. Smiling so beautifully that she wrung Elega's heart, she said, 'Very well. Ask me something specific.'

Elega gaped at her – gaped like a fish until Myste started laughing.

Elega couldn't help herself; she was suddenly so full of joy and relief and confusion that she laughed herself.

After a while, Myste subsided. 'Ah, Elega, we have not done that together since we were girls.'

Mocking her own dignity, Elega replied primly, 'Do not be arrogant, child. You are hardly old enough yet to be called a woman.'

Myste chuckled happily. For a moment, the only thing that prevented her from looking like the Myste Elega remembered – romantic and dear, vaguely foolish, not to be taken seriously – was the scar on her cheek.

But that scar changed everything. It made the new Myste impossible to ignore or forget. She inspired a rush of confusion in Elega.

'Myste, where *were* you? Where did you go? *Why* did you go? And those *clothes*. What have you been doing all this time?'

'Elega,' Myste protested humorously, 'I said, "Ask me something *specific*." ' But then she sighed, and slowly the laughter faded from her face. 'Well, I will tell you.' Her expression became one Elega didn't know how to interpret: sober and contemplative; a little sad; a little excited. 'If you do not take it well, however, there will be trouble for us all.

'I left Orison to search for the Congery's champion.'

Elega was so surprised that she cried, 'You did *what*?' before she could catch herself.

The Myste Elega used to know would have flinched or blushed; she might have hung her head or sounded defensive. The new Myste did none of these things. She only raised her head slightly, squared her jaw a bit, and repeated, 'I left Orison to search for the Congery's champion.'

A moment later, she added, 'Terisa helped me.'

Take it well. Elega didn't want to make a fool of herself, so she stared at her sister and said nothing.

'I went from her rooms through the secret passages down to the breach he made in the wall. It was not very well guarded then, so I was able to escape without being seen. From there, I followed his trail in the snow.'

Elega stared, waiting for Myste to say or do something that made sense.

'Eventually,' Myste continued, 'I caught up with him. He was hurt, not able to move quickly. In fact, he was down in the snow, bleeding his life into his armor.

'I startled him – he thought he was being attacked again.' Myste's tone remained mild and firm. 'He fired at me.' She touched her cheek. 'Fortunately, he did little harm. Then he saw that I was a woman, and dropped his weapon. I was able to approach him.'

Elega forced herself to blink her eyes, clear her throat, shake some of the astonishment out of her head. Carefully, she said, 'Go back to the beginning. Tell me why.'

'Why?' Myste's gaze drifted into the distance. 'Why not? There were so many reasons. There was Father's strange decline, his impulse of destruction – and our helplessness, which I enjoyed no more than you did. There was Terisa, who faced a world she did not know or understand with more courage and resourcefulness than I could find in myself. And there was the dishonesty of the Congery's action.'

'"Dishonesty"?' objected Elega. 'The Masters were trying to defend Mordant. The translation of their champion was the only action they could have taken that might have aided us.'

'No.' Myste was certain. 'I will not speak of the ethical question – whether it is ever permissible to impose an involuntary translation on any living thing. But the Masters were not honest with themselves. They claim that they translated their champion in response to Mordant's need, trying to find the hope of their auguries – but how did they expect him to react to what they did? He was injured – he and all his men were embattled for their lives – and suddenly he found himself in another world.' Her voice took on a hint of passion. 'What could he think? Surely he could think nothing except that this change was yet another attack by his enemies.

'If the Masters had been honest, they would have admitted that the only way such a champion could ever become an ally of theirs was if they approached him peacefully, unthreateningly, rather than playing upon his instinct for violence.'

In some ways, Elega found Myste's argument as surprising as her previous revelations. What she said seemed perfectly clear, eminently logical. Elega wasn't accustomed to hearing her sister reason in such terms.

'I never thought of it that way,' she admitted. Then she added almost accusingly, 'But you did. And you decided to do something about it.'

Myste shrugged as if to dismiss the suggestion that she had shown bravery or initiative. 'The Fayle attempted to warn Father of the Masters' intention. When Father permitted that translation to take place, I realized that if I remained where I was and did nothing I would begin to hate him. And when I conceived the idea of trying to help the champion, my heart lifted.'

Speaking dryly to control herself, Elega said, 'So you put on your warm clothes and went out into a hard winter for the sake of a warrior who might kill you as soon as he saw you. For no reason, really, except that you felt sorry for him.'

A small smile touched Myste's lips.

'And you found him and helped him. How was that possible? Was he a man inside his armor?'

'Oh, yes. Different in little ways – but very much like us. Like us in everything that matters.'

To Elega's renewed amazement, Myste blushed. Myste hurried on promptly, however.

'Like Terisa, he speaks our language – perhaps because of the translation. His name is Darsint,' she commented by the way. 'His instructions enabled me to get him from his armor and tend his wound. His weapon made a fire for us easily, and I had food.

'Since then, we have been together, hiding when we can, fleeing when we must. Shelter and even food have been simple to find in abandoned villages and farms—'

'And since the army's arrival,' Elega interrupted, speaking in a rush to catch up with the implications of what her sister revealed, 'you have been watching us. *Together* – you and the Congery's champion. You said it took you several days to persuade yourself to come to me. It was not *you* you had to persuade, it was *him*. You are his knowledge, his guide.'

Inspired by the fire of ideas in her head, she paused to say, 'His lover.' The mind which aims the weapon. Then she sped on.

'*That* is the decision you have had to make. You are companion to the mightiest man in any of the kingdoms. He loves you – he is dependent on you. And you must decide how to use his power.'

Now it was Myste's turn to stare. Unable to contain her sudden, urgent hope, Elega swept out of her chair to confront her sister. 'Myste, you must help us.

'All that force, all that strength, only waiting to be used. Oh, my sister, why have you delayed? You can bring this siege to an end almost without effort. Do you not understand what must be done? We must take Orison. We must put an end to the King's foolish resistance, so that the battle against Mordant's true enemies can begin while the realm and the Congery remain intact.'

'No, Elega.' Myste came to her own feet swiftly, met Elega's passion face to face. 'It is you who do not understand.' Her scar made her look fiery and unanswerable. 'The question I have sought to resolve is not whether I should help you, but whether I should help Orison against you.

'The Alend forces are too large for even a man with Darsint's weapons to combat alone. Also his strength goes from him with every use. The word he uses is "recharged." His weapons cannot be "recharged" in this world. For that reason, we must be cautious. Nevertheless I have been thinking long and hard about the damage he could do to the Alend Monarch's army. The truth is that I have only held back because of your presence – and because of Prince Kragen's inaction.'

Elega started to protest, but Myste cut her off.

'I must warn you, Elega. I am more certain now than ever that I must fight for Father and Mordant. If you require Darsint's guns to be used, they will be used against you.'

'Myste,' Elega gasped in dismay, 'are you *mad*?'

'Only if it is madness to trust our father.'

'Yes, that *is* madness! You said so yourself – you spoke of his "strange decline, his impulse to destruction." Were you not listening to yourself? You would not have left Orison and gone to help this Darsint if you *trusted* our father.'

'Yes.' Without warning, Myste's intensity broke into a grin. She seemed at once sheepish and secure. 'And no. I have spent days laboring through high snow. I have tended the wounds of an alien warrior and held him in my arms. And I have heard Father's message to you. Fear and exhaustion teach many things. So does love. I have learned to think differently.

'It is hard to say that I trust his decline. But I have come to trust the fact that he allowed the Congery to work this translation. I have even come to think that he did it for me – in the same way that he insulted Prince Kragen for you. Do you not see how he has made us powerful? I can guide Darsint's choices. I can ask his help. And you are in a place to affect the actions of Alend's entire army.'

I am sure that my daughter Elega has acted for the best reasons. For her sake, as well as for my own, I hope that the best reasons will also produce the best results.

'Elega, we are doing what he intended us to do. He has plans for us. Perhaps his decline itself is only a goad to make us do what we can.'

Elega floundered in her sister's smile. This optimistic interpretation of the King's behavior was insane. 'Myste, you are a fool,' she muttered as if she were speaking to herself. 'A fool.' King Joyse had driven his own wife away rather than make the effort to defend his kingdom. Or to explain himself. Piece by piece, he had chipped the hope and trust out of Elega's heart. 'Are you not hurt? Do the things he has done not cause you any pain?'

'Of course they do.' Myste's smile became fond and sad at the same time. 'I only say that there is another way to look at what he has done. We ask ourselves whether he deserves our faith. But we do not have his burdens. *He* is the King. We should ask, I think, whether we deserve *his* faith.

'It appears to me that he has tried to let us know that he trusts us.

'Elega, do you never ask yourself what kind of man he must be, to place his trust in the people he has most hurt? Between us, we have the might to destroy him. Darsint's weapons and the Prince's army could accomplish that. And our father has pushed us into this position.

'Either his lunacy is complete, or his need for us is so desperate that he cannot explain what he wants without making what he wants impossible.'

Groping, Elega asked, 'What do you mean? What can you possibly mean?'

Myste shrugged. 'Oh, I mean nothing. I only speculate. But suppose' – her gaze came into focus on her sister – 'it is in some way vital to Father's defense of Mordant that you are trusted by the Prince. How can a trust like that be achieved between two such old and mortal enemies? Any attempt to trick or mislead the Prince would almost surely fail. You are – pardon me for saying this – not much of a liar. You could not persuade the Prince to believe anything you did not believe yourself.'

'No.' Elega shook her head, not in denial, but in exasperation. 'You suppose too much too quickly. How can it possibly be "vital" to Father that Prince Kragen trusts me?'

'Elega, *think*. You have already come so close to your own answer. What did Father accomplish by refusing to reinforce the Perdon, when the Perdon came to Orison and demanded help?'

'What did he *accomplish*?'

'Or put it another way. What would have happened when Cadwal marched if the Perdon had been supported by several thousand guards? As you have observed, the Perdon would have retreated *here*, to preserve his forces and defend his King. And High King Festten could not have permitted an enemy that strong to disengage, to maneuver freely. He would have been forced to follow.

'By refusing to reinforce the Perdon, Father made it possible that the Cadwals would not come here directly.

'Do you still not understand, Elega?'

'Time,' Elega breathed. At last, she seemed to be catching up. 'Since Cadwal is not here, Alend can afford to wait. By refusing to support the Perdon, he gained time.'

'Yes!' Myste whispered.

'And by pushing us where we are, he also gained time. He made it possible that I might use my influence with the Prince to encourage inaction. But primarily' – Elega was amazed by how convincing she found this – 'he pushed us to be where we are so that if the Prince attacked fiercely you would defend Orison – and so the Alend attack would be frustrated – and because you and I are sisters we might find a way to keep the violence between our forces to a minimum.'

'Yes,' repeated Myste. Her manner began to relax.

'But *why*?' Elega didn't know whether to laugh or shriek. '*Why* does he need time? What is he *doing*? What is his plan? How can he believe that Mordant will be saved by the things he has done to destroy it?'

Apparently, Myste felt no need to shriek. Chuckling softly, she said, 'If I knew *that* – if I could so much as make an intelligent guess – I would tell it to Prince Kragen myself.'

Unexpectedly, Elega also began chuckling. 'So this is all talk? You can think of no reason why Father might need time – therefore no reason to believe he actually does need time – therefore no reason to trust any of your speculations?'

Myste shook her head cheerfully. 'None.'

'Except,' Elega murmured after a moment, 'for the fact that it all seems too tidy to be accidental.'

Myste's smile was so complete that it made even the burn on her cheek look like a mark of beauty.

Elega sighed. Slowly, her inexplicable humor faded. 'I must say, Myste,' she commented, 'that I have a powerful wish to make you tell all this to Prince Kragen anyway. Unfortunately, he would make you a prisoner. He would want to use you as a lever against Father – or against your champion.'

'In that case,' Myste replied, 'Darsint would come for me. I doubt that he would be inclined to let me be used as a lever.'

'And Alends would be killed,' added Elega. 'And the force in his weapons might be exhausted. And nothing would be gained.'

'That' – Myste grinned sharply, like a woman who had learned to enjoy risks – 'is the reasoning I used to persuade him to let me come to you.'

As a final surprise in an evening full of surprises, Elega found that she had never liked her sister as much as she did at this moment. 'In that case,' she drawled, 'it behooves me, I think, to help you leave the camp before any word of your visit reaches Prince Kragen. Come, get your cloak. We will take a few skins of this wine with us and go out the back.'

Before they left, she and Myste shared a hug as if they had recognized each other for the first time.

The next morning, after he had received the night's reports from his captains, Prince Kragen called Elega out of her tent.

She had never seen him so angry. Even his moustache seemed to have been waxed with outrage.

'My lady,' he said, 'last night a woman entered the camp. She claimed to be your sister. She was taken to your tent.'

Elega faced him boldly, hiding the fright in her heart. 'Yes, my lord Prince. My sister Myste.'

'The one who disappeared after the Imagers translated their champion.' That may have been all he knew about her. 'Where is she now?'

Remembering that she was a bad liar, Elega held his gaze and replied, 'We talked for a long time. Then I helped her to depart without bothering the sentries.'

'King Joyse's daughter. One of the most valuable women in Mordant. You "helped her to depart."' The Prince's tone made every soldier within earshot avert his head. 'Why?'

Elega did her best to smile the way Myste had smiled, as if she enjoyed risks. 'Come into my tent, my lord Prince. I have a story to tell you that will make you doubt your reason.'

That was why she loved him. Despite the fact that she was the daughter of his enemy – that she had betrayed her own father and might therefore be capable of betraying anyone – that she had helped another of the King's daughters escape – Prince Kragen went into her tent and heard her story.

At roughly the same hour, Artagel was given permission to leave his bed for the first time. His side was healing well, and he had been free of fever long enough to reassure his physician. In addition, ever since his delirious visit to the dungeons he had been a model patient. So he was advised to get out of bed for a little mild, repeat, *mild* exercise.

He smiled at his physician's severe manner. He smiled at the gap-toothed kitchen maid who brought his meals. He smiled at the sweep who cleaned his rooms. But he didn't actually try to stand and dress himself and walk until he was sure he wouldn't be interrupted.

He didn't want any witnesses while he tested himself to see how weak he was.

The effort of putting on a loose shirt and trousers made him sweat. Bending over to shove his feet into his boots made him light-headed. Simply lifting the weight of his longsword made him tremble. With every movement, his injury pulled as if it were about to tear open.

Grinning unsteady defiance, he left his rooms – mild exercise, *mild* – and went to see Castellan Lebbick.

He had a number of reasons for wanting to talk to the Castellan. One was that Lebbick had tried to see *him* a few days ago, and had been turned away because of his fever. Another was that – if he could be persuaded to talk – the Castellan was the best available source of information about several subjects which interested Artagel keenly: the siege; King Joyse's plans; the Congery's preparations; the search for Geraden.

Thanks to the fact that most of his friends were guards, a number of whom had come to see him while he was ill, he knew that the siege had been passive since the first day. But that could mean almost anything; he wanted to know what it *did* mean. Of course, Master Eremis' solution to the water problem was common knowledge. In addition, Artagel had heard that Master Quillon was dead, that Master Barsonage had resumed his place as mediator of the Congery. He had heard that Terisa was gone. He had even heard that there was a connection between Quillon's death and Terisa's disappearance. And just once someone – probably Artagel's physician himself – had mentioned that questions were still being asked about Underwell.

Curiosity about such things might have been enough to make Artagel visit the Castellan. He and Lebbick were old friends, after all – to the extent that the Castellan could be said to have friends. In fact, he had been Artagel's teacher and commander until Artagel had reached the point where it was no longer reasonable for anyone to tell him what to do. Because of this, he was widely believed – at least among the castle's active defenders – to be the only man in Orison who could go to the Castellan and ask him questions and actually get answers.

As it happened, however, Artagel had two additional reasons for wanting a conversation with the Castellan, reasons more compelling than any of the others.

First, he had thought long and searchingly – not his favorite form of exertion – about his last conversation with the lady Terisa, and he didn't like any of the conclusions he reached.

Second, he had heard from no less than six reliable friends that early in the morning after Terisa's disappearance Castellan Lebbick had returned to his quarters and found a woman in his bed.

Terisa's former maid, Saddith.

He had beaten her nearly to death.

Even now – what was it, five days later? – her physician wasn't sure she would ever use her hands again. And as for her face— Well, no one wanted to describe her disfigurement.

Since then, the Castellan hadn't been out of his rooms. He directed the defense of Orison entirely through an intermediary – through the one man he had chosen to bring him information and carry his instructions.

By a coincidence so odd that it made Artagel's guts knot, the man Castellan Lebbick had chosen was Ribuld, the scarred veteran who had occasionally helped protect Terisa as a favor to Geraden, and who had lost his best friend, Argus, in a failed attempt to trap Prince Kragen.

Why *Ribuld*, of all people? Lebbick had never put him in a position of responsibility before. In fact, Ribuld would have said that the Castellan never noticed him except when he did something wrong.

Even though the effort of walking made his heart labor and his bones ache, Artagel was determined to confront Castellan Lebbick and get some answers.

He didn't like remembering the way Terisa had cried at him, *Are you out of your mind? Geraden is your brother.* At the time, he hadn't understood her. Well, he had been delirious, emotionally and morally sick at what had been done to Nyle. But now her words stuck in him like an accusation.

When he arrived at Lebbick's quarters, he was a little surprised to find the door guarded. The Castellan had never felt the need for protection in his own rooms before. Nevertheless Artagel didn't hesitate. He went up to the guard on duty, a man he had known for years, and asked, 'He still refusing to see anybody?'

The man nodded. Despite his evident pleasure that Artagel was out of bed at last, he commented, 'And he isn't going to make an exception in your case, either.'

Artagel smiled. It was probably a good thing he hadn't tried to bring his sword. He would have looked like a fool pulling it out – and then letting its weight stretch him flat on the floor. As if he'd never been ill, however, he said, 'I want to go in there. You aren't really going to stand in my way.'

'You're going to get past me?' the guard snorted. 'In *your* condition?' But then he put up his hands. 'Well, since you force me – Somebody's got to get sense out of him. Might as well be you. After what he did to that woman— If he doesn't answer for it soon, we're going to have trouble on our hands. Too many people who don't have anything better to do are getting ugly about it.

'If he hits you, give a croak, and I'll carry you back to your rooms.'

Artagel faked a bow with one arm. 'Thanks ever so much. It always feels good to have a man like you behind me.'

'I know,' the guard replied. 'As far behind you as possible.'

Chuckling, he opened the door.

Convinced that he really wasn't going to be able to stay on his feet much longer, Artagel entered the Castellan's quarters.

The front room was ill-lit, unswept, and undecorated – which hadn't been the case when Artagel was last here, some time before Lebbick's wife died. Although he wasn't given to luxury, the Castellan had claimed an extensive suite for himself and his wife; he had insisted for decades that they meant to have children, regardless of the damage she had suffered as an Alend prisoner. And she had humored him by keeping up their quarters like a home where children would be welcome. But since her death he had stripped the walls and floor to the bare stone; he had moved a hard cot into the front room and sealed the rest of the doors – even in Orison's overcrowded state, those rooms stood empty. And since Terisa's disappearance he had obviously given up all pretense of housekeeping. The one lamp on the table beside his cot gave just enough light to show that the room was filthy.

So was he: he hadn't shaved, or washed, or changed his clothes for days. His eyes were red with exhaustion and malice – or grief – and his hands curled in front of him as if he badly needed a sword.

Facing Artagel from the edge of his cot, he rasped distinctly, 'I'm going to disembowel the man who let *you* in here.'

The air was foul with dirt, rancid sweat, food gone to maggots. Artagel stifled an impulse to gag. Pretending that his nauseated expression was a smile, he replied, 'No, you won't.' Deliberately, he found a chair and sat down. 'If you want to get him, you'll have to get me first. And you won't do that. You won't dare. I'm the most popular man in Orison.'

'Hog-puke.' The Castellan blinked malevolently. 'Eremis is the most popular man in Orison.' In spite of his tone, however, he didn't leave the bed. 'You're just an invalid who's still alive because he got lucky the last time he met Gart.

'That's probably why they sent you. They think I won't hurt a man who's so weak a woman could knock him over.'

Feigning nonchalance, Artagel inquired, '"They"?'

'*They*. The Tor. King Joyse. Half the rutting dogs in this stink-hole. The

628

bastard who let you in. The ones who think Eremis is the best thing since King Joyse invented sunshine. The ones who think I ought to be castrated because I slapped that rank whore a couple of times. *They*.

'They want me to come out so they can jump me. They want you to make me come out.'

'Sorry.' Artagel loathed dealing with Lebbick like this; he would have preferred to meet the High King's Monomach without a sword. As a result, he sounded incongruously happy, as if he were having a wonderful time. 'I hate to contradict you when you're in such a good mood. But the truth is, I don't have any idea what you're talking about. I just came to tell you Geraden didn't kill Nyle.'

'*I* know *that*,' snapped Lebbick. 'Don't tell *me*. Tell *them*.'

'Wait a minute.' Artagel would have been less startled if the Castellan had started foaming at the mouth. 'Wait. What do you mean, you know that? *How* do you know?'

'I know' – Castellan Lebbick glared at his visitor as if Artagel were hideous – 'because that piss-drinking slut was in my bed. *In my bed*.'

Now it was Artagel's turn to blink. 'Wait a minute,' he repeated. 'Wait.'

Lebbick didn't wait. 'I came right through that door' – he pointed fiercely at the door – 'and she was in my *bed*.' He pounded the cot. 'Naked as shit. *Smiling* at me. Wagging her tits. Of *course* Geraden didn't kill Nyle.'

Then his ferocity dimmed. 'I would have believed anybody except that woman.'

Artagel held his breath and said nothing.

'She made me think about it over and over again. She kept making me go back to the beginning. But when she was wrong about that secret passage – I was *sure*. And I saw her escaping, I *saw* her. With Quillon. King Joyse's friend. Then I found his body. I caught up with her. She was with Gilbur. I was *sure*. Gilbur *told* me they were allies. Of course I was sure. Of course Geraden killed Nyle. She must have escaped with Gilbur, not Quillon. She was a traitor, a murderer. That proved Geraden was guilty.

'Isn't that what *they* told you?'

'No,' Artagel murmured. 'They haven't told me a thing.'

'Well, they will,' Lebbick snarled. 'Give them a chance. They're all talking about me. They whisper behind my back.' A wild grin stretched his mouth. 'Eremis is a hero. Everything that woman said about him is a lie. Geraden killed Nyle. She put him up to it. She helped him escape. Then Gilbur helped her escape. They killed Quillon. I'm a monster. Nobody understands why King Joyse hasn't had me gutted.

'Eremis is a hero.'

Groping for some measure of sanity in the conversation, Artagel drawled, 'I doubt it. Terisa must have told you Nyle is still alive. She certainly tried to tell me.

'I didn't believe her,' he admitted, 'but I've been kicking myself for that ever since.' Generally, he wasn't much inclined to regret; nevertheless he regretted intensely the things he had said to Terisa. He should have looked at that body more closely. 'I finally figured out what must have happened.' *Geraden is your brother. You've known him all his life.* 'They must have

629

switched the bodies. Underwell and Nyle. That's why they used Imagery – why they let creatures feed on the bodies. To disfigure them. So we would think Underwell was Nyle.

'Geraden wouldn't do a thing like that. It's impossible. I know him better than that.'

As if he were discussing the weather, Artagel added, 'If *he* didn't do it, that just leaves Eremis. We don't have anybody else to blame it on.'

'I *know* that.' Grief twisted Castellan Lebbick's features. Softly, he repeated, 'I *know* that. Why do you think I hit her so hard? Why do you think I kept hitting her? I was trying to get her to tell me the truth.

'It *was* Quillon who helped that woman escape. That's the truth. He did it because King Joyse told him to. To get her away from me. He ordered me to do my job, and then he tried to sneak her away from me. That's why he leaves me alone now. He hasn't sent for me in days. He knows I was just following orders.

'He wants to break me. He wants me to hide down here until I rot. Because he doesn't trust me.'

Artagel felt frantically that he was getting nowhere. He was tempted to back out of the room, put some distance between himself and the Castellan's lunacy. But his regret was stronger than his alarm. He had already let both Terisa and Geraden down.

Instead of retreating, he tried a different approach.

'Well, he must trust you some.' Artagel made an effort to sound hearty, without much success. 'You're still in command, aren't you? You're still the Castellan.'

Lebbick nodded as if he hadn't heard the question.

'Speaking of things you're in command of, how's the defense going?' continued Artagel. 'I heard a rumor that Kragen hasn't so much as thrown a rock at us since the first day. Is that true?'

The Castellan nodded again. 'Margonal's whoreson,' he growled, 'is just sitting out there staring at us.'

'Why? What makes him think he can get away with that? Isn't he afraid of Cadwal?'

'I can only think of two explanations.' As if by accident, some of the tension in Lebbick's face loosened. On some level, Artagel had distracted him. 'He knows Festten isn't coming – for some reason – and we don't because he doesn't let the news get to us. Or Alend and Cadwal have made an alliance.'

There: that was an improvement. Castellan Lebbick still had some lucidity left in him. Carefully, Artagel said, 'Then I guess Cadwal isn't coming. If Festten and Margonal had an alliance, Kragen wouldn't have tried to attack us alone.'

'That's probably true,' agreed the Castellan morosely. 'Festten wouldn't have made an alliance unless he could be sure Margonal wouldn't get to the Congery ahead of him.'

Artagel nodded. After a moment, he went on, 'Speaking of the Congery—'

Lebbick interrupted him balefully. 'Were we?'

Artagel frowned. 'Were we what?'

'Speaking of the Congery. Or were you just prying?'

'I was prying.' Artagel grinned. 'And I'm going to keep prying until you say three sentences in a row that make sense. If you don't pull yourself together, you *will* rot.'

'Speaking of the Congery, what're they doing about poor Master Quillon?'

Castellan Lebbick studied his visitor as if at last he had begun to wonder why Artagel was here. 'Nothing,' he articulated. 'As far as I can tell, the only thing they do all day is sit around wiping each other's bums. By which I mean to say, of course' – he began to sound like he was quoting scornfully – 'that they are dedicating all their efforts night and day toward discovering how Gilbur and Geraden and that woman are able to use flat glass without going mad.

'That blind lump Barsonage has suddenly' – Lebbick's tone was savage – 'figured out King Joyse is right. He's gone all virtuous and noble about it. Mirrors don't create their own Images. The places they show are real. So we don't have the right to take anything that can tell the difference out of them. Which is a dogshit way of saying they aren't going to help defend us. They refuse to touch the only things that might do us some good.'

The Castellan barked humorlessly. 'It's actually funny. They discovered purity just when King Joyse gave it up. The only real reason we haven't been overrun already is, Kragen can't use his catapults. Whenever he tries, Havelock destroys them with some kind of smoke-bird from one of his mirrors.'

Artagel began to hope that he was on the right track. Castellan Lebbick seemed to be recovering his self-command. Maybe it was time to risk—

Because he was the sort of man who took chances, Artagel said conversationally, 'That's better. You're doing much better. Any minute now, you're going to be your old self again. There's just one thing I still want to know.

'Castellan' – he took a deep breath – 'what in the name of sanity is the connection between Saddith and Nyle? Why does the fact that she showed up in your bed prove Geraden didn't kill him?'

For a long moment, the Castellan glowered as if he meant to explode. A muscle in his cheek twitched. His gaze burned red, drawing the darkness of the room around him; his expression was full of doom.

Like a man chewing iron pellets, he said, 'Not Saddith and Nyle. Saddith and Eremis. She's his whore.'

Artagel waited.

'He sent her. That's what I was trying to get her to admit. That's why I kept hitting her. Why I didn't stop.'

Still Artagel waited.

'He did that to me.' Without warning, Lebbick's eyes began to spill tears. They ran down into his dirty beard, leaving streaks through the grime on his cheeks. 'I was already so close to the edge. That woman was trying to tell me the truth, and I didn't know how to believe her. And he did that to me. He sent his whore to give me the last push. Because I'm the only one King Joyse has left. Even though he doesn't trust me.

'Master fornicating Eremis,' the Castellan said through his loss, 'wouldn't

631

have sent his whore to my bed if everything that woman said about him wasn't true. He was trying to distract me.'

With difficulty, Artagel resisted the temptation to whistle through his teeth. This time, he found the Castellan's reasoning comprehensible. He had always appreciated Saddith's frank lust; but at the moment he wasn't thinking about her. He was thinking that her appearance in Lebbick's bed was the worst thing Eremis could have done to the Castellan.

It was almost as if Eremis and King Joyse were conspiring together to destroy him.

Gruffly, Artagel said, 'That makes sense.' Words seemed to stick in his throat; he had to force them out. 'What did Terisa actually tell you about our hero, Eremis?'

The Castellan scrubbed his face with his hands, grinding his tears into the dirt. 'The same thing you did.' On the cot beside him, he found a rank piece of rag and used it to blow his nose. 'They must have switched the bodies. If Underwell really wanted Nyle dead, he could have made it happen without the stupid risk of all that bloodshed. But if Geraden was innocent, Underwell must have discovered right away that Nyle wasn't hurt. So Underwell had to be killed. To protect Eremis.

'Nyle is probably still alive. Unless Eremis doesn't need him anymore.

'Eremis is busy acting like the hero of Orison because his plans aren't ready. Cadwal isn't ready to attack. That's obvious – Cadwal isn't even *here*. Or he's waiting for something else to happen. He doesn't want Kragen to get the Congery.'

Artagel was right on the edge of asking, So why don't you stop him? Go cut his heart out. Instead of holing up here like a beaten dog? Fortunately, he stopped himself in time. As soon as the question occurred to him, he caught a glimpse of how Castellan Lebbick would react to it. *They want me to come out so they can jump me. He wants to break me. He doesn't trust me.*

Artagel liked to live dangerously, but he wasn't willing to risk pushing Lebbick back into turmoil.

He couldn't grasp what King Joyse was doing. But that wasn't his problem: someone else would have to figure it out. Eremis was another matter, however. Artagel was very sure that he wanted to oppose or hinder the Master in any way possible.

Gazing around the room in search of inspiration, he grabbed the first idea that came to him.

'You know, Castellan, if your wife saw this pigsty she'd spit granite.'

Artagel was probably the only man in Orison who would have dared mention Lebbick's wife to his face.

By luck or intuition, however, Artagel had found the right approach. Instead of erupting, the Castellan looked chagrined. 'I know,' he muttered. 'I'm going to clean it up. I'll get around to it soon.'

The sorrow in his face wrung Artagel's heart. Without premeditation or forethought, he said quietly, 'Don't bother. Leave it. I've got an extra room. I've even got an extra bed. Come stay with me.'

Castellan Lebbick stared dumbly. His mouth worked as if Artagel had asked him to give up his link to the only thing that held him in one piece.

'She's dead,' Artagel said as gently as he could. 'It can't be helped. She doesn't need you anymore.

'*We're* the ones who need you.'

Roughly, fighting collapse, the Castellan rasped, '"We"? Who is "we"?'

'Me.' Artagel didn't hesitate. 'Geraden. Terisa. Anybody who thinks King Joyse is still worth trying to save, even though he does act like he's got his head stuck up his ass.'

Lebbick thought for a long time, gazing away into the gloom around him. He looked like a man lost in memories – lost in love, in old instances of violence; a man who might never find his way back. But then his shoulders sagged, and he sighed.

'All right.'

'Good.' Artagel sighed as well, let the suspense exhale from him so hard that the release made him shudder. 'It's time.'

Without suspense and sorrow to keep him tight, however, his muscles went slack, and his limbs turned to rubber. Ruefully, he added, 'You can start by helping me get back there. I'm afraid I overdid it coming here.'

'Idiot,' Lebbick growled. Slowly, he got to his feet. 'You're supposed to be resting. I've seen shrubbery with better sense than you've got.'

'That's easy.' Artagel made a determined effort not to fall out of his chair. 'I've seen shrubbery with better sense than any of us.

'Just tell me one more thing.' He paused to collect his fraying thoughts. 'Why Ribuld? I didn't know you had such a good opinion of him.'

Almost gently, Castellan Lebbick helped Artagel to his feet. Supporting Artagel with his shoulder, he started toward the door.

'I need somebody I can trust. He likes Geraden. That's all I've got to work with.'

Artagel couldn't help himself: he had to ask, 'Are you really in that much trouble? Just because of Eremis and Saddith?'

The muscles along Lebbick's jaw knotted. His eyes were full of gloom. 'Wait and see.'

On the way back to his rooms, Artagel found himself positively aching with the intensity of his desire to see Geraden again. He wanted somebody to tell him what was going on.

THIRTY-FIVE

AN OLD ALLY
OF THE KING

That same day, Terisa and Geraden rode out of the southwestern hills of the Care of Termigan and began to approach Sternwall, the Termigan's seat and his Care's principal city.

The relatively direct road from Houseldon – and the lack of rain, atypical at this time of year – had made the journey an easy one, at least for Geraden. He was accustomed to horses, acquainted with roadside comfort, experienced at camping. And he seemed to have become sure of himself. For the first time in his life, he knew exactly what he was doing. The only thing that reduced his eagerness to get where he was going was the pleasure he had with Terisa along the way.

Terisa's eagerness to reach Sternwall was completely different. In a visceral sense, she had lost interest in Orison – in Master Eremis and King Joyse. Her concerns were more immediate. She was aching in every joint, bone-weary, sick of horses. She wanted a hot bath and clean sheets. Thanks to the otherwise-much-desired way Geraden used his weight at night, the hard ground had given her bruises from her shoulder blades to her tailbone. At times, she felt she would have killed for a pillow under her hips. After a day or two in the saddle, every jolt of the bay's gait seemed to grind her bones together. After another day or two, she could hardly keep from groaning whenever Geraden embraced her.

Nevertheless she hugged him back as hard and as often as possible; she locked her legs over his and held him on top of her despite the pain. She was so full of love that she could hardly take her eyes off him, hardly bear to let her skin be out of contact with his. If necessary, she could endure a few bruises.

She had to admit, however, that she had learned to hate horses. Any culture which couldn't devise a better way to travel than *this* really ought to let itself die out. When Geraden announced that they were within reach of Sternwall, she said, 'Thank God!' with such sincerity that he burst out laughing.

'You think it's funny,' she groused. 'I've never been so miserable in my entire life, and you think it's hilarious. I swear I don't know what I see in you.

'Of course,' she added considerately, 'if I *did* know I'd probably want to put my eyes out.'

'Be careful, my lady,' he replied in an aggrieved tone. 'I have a sensitive nature. If you give me any excuse – *any excuse at all* – I'll have to start apologizing.'

'Oh, great,' she growled, trying to sound bitter even though she was grinning with her whole body. 'The last time you did that, we didn't get to sleep until after midnight.'

She made him laugh again. Then he leaned out of his saddle and kissed her dramatically. 'Ah, Terisa,' he sighed when he had subsided, 'you do me good. I wouldn't have believed it was possible. After all those years serving the Congery and failing – after making the wrong choice and stopping Nyle instead of concentrating on Prince Kragen – after botching our chance to stop Elega – after being made to look like my own brother's murderer, and then having to just hurl myself into a mirror without any idea what would happen—' His list of disasters was really quite impressive when he toted it up like that. 'I wouldn't have believed it was actually possible to feel this good.'

'How much farther do we have to go?' she asked because she didn't have anything better to say. 'I want a bed.'

Geraden grinned and gave her the best answer he had.

This was their fourth day on the road, and since they had left behind the smoking ruins of Houseldon they hadn't seen the slightest indication that Mordant was at war. Heading almost directly north-east, they had crossed the Broadwine on its way east-northeast toward the Demesne, and had followed the road in the direction of the Care of Termigan. 'The Termigan will help us,' Geraden had said confidently. 'He's an old ally of the King's. There's a story that he saved King Joyse's life in the last of the big battles against Alend – roughly thirty years ago.'

Terisa had nodded without taking her eyes off the surrounding landscape. She had met the Termigan: she had the impression that he was a man who could be trusted absolutely – but only on his own terms.

North and east of Houseldon, the Care of Domne seemed to be composed almost entirely of the kind of fertile hills which made cultivation difficult, but which provided abundant rich grass for sheep. Toward the south and the west, mountains remained visible, but they became steadily harder to descry as the road wound out of the Care. Geraden explained that the border of Domne stretched from the eastmost point of the spur of mountains on the north – a point called Pestil's Mouth because there the Pestil River came out of the spur – along a relatively straight line toward a distinctive peak in the southern range, a mighty and unmistakable head of rock named, for no known reason, Kelendumble. That line divided Domne from both the Care of Termigan to the north of the Broadwine and the Care of Tor to the south.

Although the border was purely theoretical, the countryside did appear to change after Terisa and Geraden entered Termigan. The edges of the landscape became flintier; the grasses and shrubs, the wildflowers and stands of trees all had an air of toughness, as if they endured in ungiving dirt against unkind weather. 'The soil is good for grapes,' Geraden explained, 'and not bad for hops. But it isn't much use for corn, or wheat, or worren.' Worren was one of the few grains – in fact, one of the few foods – that she found strange in this world. 'In Domne, they joke that everybody who lives here develops a permanent case of dyspepsia from eating the food – and then from trying to feel better by drinking too much.

'On the other hand, I've heard it said that High King Festten won't drink anything except Termigan wine.'

As the soil changed, so did the hills: they began to look less rumbled, more ragged, as if they had been cut by erosion rather than raised by the ground's underlying bones. The road twisted through ravines and gullies rather than along shallow vales and hollows. In contrast, however, the weather turned increasingly springlike – warm in the sun despite the cool nights and shadows; full of green and flowering scents; hinting at moisture.

Terisa wanted a bath so badly that the mere idea made her scalp itch.

Forcing herself to think about other things, she occasionally reflected that ravines and gullies were ideal places for ambushes. Such things seemed entirely unreal, however. After all, Alend had sent its strength to the siege of Orison. And the forces of Cadwal were on the far side of Mordant to the east. So the only real danger came from Imagery. And any attack that struck by Imagery wouldn't need to rely on ravines and gullies for success.

She reasoned that Master Eremis probably didn't know where they were. He couldn't know, unless they happened to pass through a place that showed in one of his mirrors – and he happened to look during the brief time they were visible.

She couldn't bring herself to worry about the possibility.

In fact, she didn't even remember what the Termigan had said about trouble in his Care until Geraden brought her in sight of Sternwall itself, late in the afternoon of their fourth day on the road.

The sight made her wonder how she could have forgotten.

Pits of fire in the ground, the Termigan had said.

Sternwall was a fortified stone city. It had a buttressed wall built of quarried granite; and within the wall all the houses and other edifices were of stone. From this distance, the basic style of construction seemed to be mud-plaster pointed with cement. The Termigan's people could have laughed at the attack which had destroyed Houseldon.

Nevertheless Terisa was sure they weren't laughing.

Even from several hundred yards away, she could sense the heat of the glowing liquid rock which seethed and bubbled in long pools outside the walls. There were half a dozen of them, all set in higher ground which sloped down toward the city, all shaped as if they were flowing slowly, inexorably toward the walls. Eremis had said, *Pits of fire appear in the ground of Termigan – almost within the fortifications of Sternwall.* He must have had a hard time restraining his mirth. Fed by translation, the pits melted the earth between them and the city. She didn't know how long this had been going on, but she guessed that it wouldn't continue much longer. Already, the granite wall had begun to slump like heated wax at four different points; wide sections of the city's outward face reflected the magma redly, as if they were slick with sweat.

The people of Sternwall were eventually going to be burned out of their homes. Orange-red glared into the sky like a presage of sunset.

Geraden scowled at the sight bitterly. 'Glass and splinters!' he murmured. 'Oh, Eremis. No wonder the Termigan doesn't trust Imagers.'

'I don't understand.' Terisa had to swallow hard to make her throat work. 'Why? I mean, why do it this way? Why not put this – this lava – why not translate this lava right into the city and be done with it?'

'It's more fun this way,' grated Geraden. Then he shook his head. 'No, that's not it. Sternwall itself probably isn't in the Image. The mirror they're using probably shows a place up the hill somewhere. This is as far as they can adjust the focus.'

Guards paced the wall without getting too close to the heat. Terisa saw two men stop, point toward her and Geraden; one of them left the wall. She supposed that under the circumstances Sternwall didn't get many visitors. Trying to force down the taste of bile, she nudged her horse into motion.

Grimly, she and Geraden rode past the pits toward the gate on the far side of the city.

Near the lava, she could hear it seething, a deep, almost inaudible rumble that seemed to echo in the marrow of her bones; the sound of the earth being eaten away.

As quiet as that noise was, however, it seemed to deafen her. She hardly heard the lonely cry of a bugle rising from the walls of the city. She hardly heard Geraden say, 'Looks like the Termigan is sending men out to meet us. Maybe he doesn't want to risk letting us in until he knows who we are.'

She should have been ready. She was near an Image: she should have understood that she and Geraden were in danger of being spotted. Unfortunately, she wasn't thinking that clearly. She was too full of Sternwall's plight to think clearly.

She was taken completely by surprise when *a touch of cold as thin as a feather and as sharp as steel slid straight through the center of her abdomen.*

Yet the surprise itself may have been what saved her. She had no time to be frightened, paralyzed. Instead, she yelped a warning and flung herself to the side, out of the saddle, out of the way.

The fangs missed her. They came so close, however, that they snagged her shirt at the shoulder, nearly tore it off her body.

She hit the ground awkwardly, wrenched her knee, fell flat on her face. Desperately, she scrabbled her legs under her and pitched to her feet—

—just in time to see a gnarled black spot the size of a puppy get up on its limbs and come scrambling toward her. Its savage jaws took up more than half its body: they stretched for her, ravening.

At her yell, Geraden had wheeled his mount. Bounding from an invisible perch on the other side of a translation, a black, round shape flipped past him. With all four limbs, it caught the appaloosa by the head.

Its jaws ripped the horse's skull apart. Fountaining blood, the appaloosa went down as if it had crashed into a wall. Geraden landed hard: he was momentarily stunned. Before he could recover, his mount's convulsions rolled the horse over onto his legs.

Munching brains and bone, the black creature began to eat its way through the horse toward him.

Another fierce shape appeared out of nowhere – and another – struck the ground – rolled to a stop—

One of them went for Geraden. The other rushed at Terisa.

She had no choice, no time: when the nearest creature sprang at her, she ducked, flinched aside. Geraden had given her a knife – for cooking, he had said, teasing her because he did all the cooking – and she groped for it while she dodged; she jerked it from its sheath, hacked blindly at her assailant.

Her blow caught nothing but air. Off balance, barely able to support her weight with her twisted knee, she stumbled directly into the path of the second attacking shape.

Its fangs were curved and jagged, made for rending. In a mirror, she had seen a creature like this tear a man's heart out. It was going to rip her to tatters. And there was another one turning to jump her from behind.

Geraden had a few more seconds to live than she did. The red meat of his horse had distracted both of his attackers: they were feeding voraciously. He was safe until they reached his trapped legs.

Wildly, he struggled to open his mount's saddlebags.

The blade he had given Terisa was little more than a filleting knife; a hunter might have used it to skin a rabbit. It was the only thing she had to fight with, however; she didn't question it. Since she was off balance anyway, she thrust her weight in the direction she was falling, so that her arm and the knife came around in a wide, sweeping slash.

Somehow, this blow found the creature before the creature reached her face. The black shape tumbled to the side, spattering green blood everywhere.

She tried to catch herself, but her knee gave out. She toppled with a cry just as the second attacker leaped at her back.

Geraden's assailants were working on the appaloosa's shoulders.

From the nearest saddlebag, he pulled out a sackful of corn meal and flung it.

The sack burst open on the first creature's teeth.

With a sound like thick fabric being shredded, the shape sneezed.

Like its jaws and its appetite, its sneeze was too big for its body. The blast knocked it backward, off the dead horse; tucking its legs around itself, it rolled away.

Another sneeze: another roll.

Geraden searched frantically for something else to throw.

Terisa was down. She couldn't get back up. Her legs shoved at the ground as if her back were broken, but she couldn't bring them under her.

One of the black shapes moved toward her.

As if sensing her helplessness, it stopped hurrying: its steps were almost dainty as it approached. Its huge jaws opened delicately. Each one of its teeth was sharp for her flesh.

Then the quarrel from a crossbow struck the creature so hard that it skipped off the ground and sailed through the air as though it had been kicked by a giant. A few drops of its green blood splashed into her hair as it flew past.

Like a spike driven by a sledgehammer, another quarrel nailed the feeding beast to the appaloosa's carcass. Without a sound, the creature gaped and died, gushing rank fluids around its fangs.

One of the Termigan's men pounded the last black shape into a pulp under the shod hooves of his mount.

A moment later, the three men halted in front of Terisa and Geraden. They peered down from their high seats. Snarling, one of them demanded, 'What in the name of goatshit and fornication *are* those things?'

Geraden didn't seem to notice that he had been rescued. He continued thrashing through the saddlebag, hunting uselessly for a weapon. 'That bastard,' he panted between his teeth. 'That bastard. If I had a mirror—' His whole face was wet with sweat or tears. 'If I just had a mirror—'

Terisa still couldn't get her legs under her. Her knee felt numb, dead. She wanted to say, insist, Help me, is he all right, did you kill them all? The only thing her throat and stomach agreed to do, however, was retch. She had green blood in her hair, and it *stank* – it smelled like corpses rotting in sewage. The head and most of the shoulders of Geraden's horse had been chewed away, devoured— Like the Castellan's two guards and Underwell. She kept gagging, but nothing came up.

Maybe Mordant wasn't at war. But she and Geraden were.

Oh, yes.

The Termigan's men dismounted. Two of them heaved the appaloosa's carcass off Geraden; the third lifted Terisa to her feet. They were hard men with grim mouths and red eyes: they had spent too much time staring into the destruction of Sternwall, watching it boil closer. 'All right,' one of them said harshly, 'you're safe. We've saved you. Who are you? What're those things?'

'Imagery,' Geraden gasped. He still seemed unaware of the men. His attention was on Terisa. 'There could be more. He could translate them right now. We've got to get out of range.'

The men wanted answers – but they also understood Geraden. Just for a second, they glanced at each other, hesitating. Then the man who had helped Terisa off the ground picked her up and leaped for his horse.

The other two mounted instantly; one of them pulled Geraden up behind him. The horses stretched into a gallop back toward the city's gates, putting as much distance as possible between the riders and the point of translation.

Terisa still had her knife clenched in her fist. Her hand and the knife were covered with foul, green blood.

'Relax!' the man holding her gritted into her ear. 'We can keep your balance better if you relax.'

She couldn't relax. She couldn't stop trying to retch.

'How far?' one of the other men asked Geraden. 'How far do we have to go to be safe?'

At last, Geraden began to respond to his rescuers. 'Can't be sure.' The pounding of hooves muffled his voice. 'Depends on the size of the mirror. And how far the focus was adjusted to reach us.' A moment later, he added, 'A hundred yards should be enough.'

'Right!'

The Termigans drove their mounts up to the gates of Sternwall. There they risked stopping.

Terisa didn't feel anything sharp or cold in her stomach. She didn't feel anything except nausea. No more of the gnarled, black shapes jumped out of the air.

Now instead of wanting to throw up she began to think it would be nice to faint.

She didn't get the chance. The man carrying her dropped her to the ground, then slid down beside her. The pressure of his grip made it clear he had no intention of letting her go. One of the other men held onto Geraden as he dismounted.

There was sunset in the air now, as well as the glare of lava. The heavy timbers of the gate were tinged crimson; red ran in streaks along the edges of the buildings. The faces of the men hinted at bloodshed.

'All right,' one of them repeated. 'Now tell us who you are. Before we decide to close the gate and leave you outside.'

Terisa could still hear the deep, visceral boiling of the lava. That noise seemed to undermine everything around her; it made the Termigans sound malign, full of coiled malice.

But Geraden nodded to them. 'We've just come from Domne,' he panted. 'I'm Geraden, the Domne's son. One of his sons, anyway. Houseldon has been burned to the ground.'

The men stood motionless, caught between who he was and what he said. A crowd began to gather in the gate: more of the Termigan's men, hostlers to take care of the horses, merchants, passersby. They all had the same red light in their eyes.

After a moment, one of the men said noncommittally, 'You better tell us who the woman is. And why you were attacked.'

Instinctively, Terisa put a hand on Geraden's arm, reaching out for protection against a threat she couldn't identify.

He also seemed to feel the menace. His arm was tight; he held himself poised. His gaze searched the faces around him. Carefully, he said, 'My father has been a good and loyal neighbor to the Termigan all his life. The last time I was here, I slept in the Termigan's house as a welcome guest.'

No one wavered; no eyes dropped. The man who appeared to be the leader of the guards rested a hand deliberately on his sword. 'I'm sure that's true,' he growled. 'You'll probably be a guest there tonight again. But not until you tell me who she is and why you were attacked.'

The man's tone nettled Geraden. He straightened his shoulders; his voice gave off hints of authority, as if he were accustomed to command respect. 'She is the lady Terisa of Morgan, arch-Imager and augured champion. For that reason, the foes of Mordant wish to destroy—'

He didn't get any further. Or if he did she didn't hear him. Somebody hit her on the back of the neck so hard that the ground seemed to flip over and rush away into the sky.

As she lost consciousness, she grasped that the Termigan was also at war.

★

Later, the war seemed to be taking place somewhere between the back of her neck and the front of her skull. There was a contest of pain going on. Her forehead hurt as if someone on the inside belabored it with a cudgel; the back of her neck ached stiffly. But which was winning? She didn't want to think about it.

Then she remembered Geraden.

Groaning, she tried to roll out of bed.

At once, both sides of the war joined forces against her. Every movement anywhere in her body took on a dimension of agony.

She sat up anyway and pushed her feet over the edge of the bed.

Her knee commemorated the occasion with a throb as sharp as a howl. She gave an inarticulate gasp. For a moment, she had to sit without moving, hold herself stationary while she tried to regain some measure of control.

She still had the smell of green blood in her hair. It was still nauseating.

Geraden, she thought.

Who hit me?

Despite the pain, she forced her eyes into focus.

She was sitting on the edge of the bed in a large but rather austere bedchamber. A number of candles lit the stone walls and wooden ceiling, the mats of woven reeds on the floor; the massive chairs, so heavy that they might have been designed to accommodate the Tor; the dark planks of the door. Compared to the places she had slept recently, the bed was luxurious.

She wasn't alone.

A man sat across the room from her, in a chair beside the door. He wore a plain brown shirt and breeches, simple boots; he had no weapons that she could see. His eyes were flat; his hair seemed to have no color. The lines of his face and the edges of his features were rough, crudely shaped. His arms were folded across his chest as if he were prepared to wait for her indefinitely.

She recognized him.

The Termigan. The lord of the Care.

'So,' he said after scrutinizing her for a while. 'You turn up unexpectedly, my lady.'

She stared back, trying to fight down the pain so that she could think.

'The last time I saw you,' he went on, 'you were there for no good reason except to demonstrate that things went wrong when the Congery tried to obey King Joyse. We were supposed to believe you were just an accident, a nothing – only a woman. Now you're here, and Geraden says you're an arch-Imager.

'I want an explanation.'

His posture suggested that he would never let her leave this room until she satisfied him.

Terisa made an effort to clear her throat. 'Where's Geraden?'

The Termigan shrugged slightly. 'Next door. My men didn't have the nerve to hit a son of the Domne, so he's been struggling and shouting ever since I had you taken away from him. But he's bolted in, and he won't get out until I decide to let him see you.'

'When is that going to happen?'

The lord shrugged again. His flat gaze didn't shift from Terisa's face. 'I'll make up my mind when I hear what you're going to tell me.'

She couldn't keep her voice from shaking. 'Your men didn't hit Geraden. Why did they hit *me*? Do you beat up women as a matter of general policy, or have I done something personally to offend you?'

Sarcasm had no effect on the Termigan. 'My men,' he explained evenly, 'didn't know I knew you. They just heard Geraden say you're an Imager. I don't like Imagers, my lady. When my father was killed in the wars, and I became the Termigan, I fought beside King Joyse for years because I don't like Imagers. All my life, most of the people I value have been killed by Imagers. Or Alends. I've never let Havelock inside these walls. Even when he wasn't crazy.

'Now we're under attack by Imagery. Sternwall is going to fall soon, and there's nothing we can do to defend ourselves. My men have standing orders to make any Imager who comes here helpless first and ask questions later.

'My lady, how did you become an Imager? Or how did you convince Eremis and Gilbur you weren't an Imager? Or' – his tone sharpened – 'why did they lie to us about you?'

The Termigan was definitely at war.

She looked away. Searching for the means to control her anger and pain – and her nausea at the stink in her hair – she scanned the room. I don't like Imagers. Almost immediately, she spotted a decanter of wine and a pair of goblets on a table near the bed, beside a tray that held what appeared to be a cold collation. Carefully, moving her head and neck as little as possible, she stood up, limped to the table, poured some wine. Helpless first and ask questions later. On the other hand, he didn't mean to starve her. Tremors ran down her arms from her shoulders, but she was able to keep most of the wine in the goblet. Lifting it with both hands, she drained it.

Just for a second, her stomach heaved and her head pounded; she thought she'd made an idiotic mistake. Then, however, she began to feel a little better.

Deliberately, she faced the Termigan. In effect, he had taken Geraden prisoner. Geraden was probably worried sick about her. And he, too, was an Imager. What would the Termigan do if he knew that the son of the Domne was also an Imager? He might keep them locked up for the rest of the war – until Sternwall fell, and Mordant was destroyed, and Master Eremis had slaughtered everybody who stood in his way. Anger gave her the strength she needed.

'My lord, they were lying to both of us. Practically everything they said to us was a lie.'

The Termigan didn't move; he hardly blinked. 'Why would they lie to *you*? You're one of *them*.'

She gaped at him. Her brain was sluggish; a moment passed before she was able to say, 'No, I'm not.

'I didn't even find out I've got a talent until' – she counted backward quickly – 'five days ago. How could I be "one of *them*"? They didn't want me to know I had any talent. That's why they were lying to me. That's why they've been trying to kill me. That's why Houseldon got burned. They were trying to kill us. They think I'm some kind of threat to them.'

'What kind of threat?'

'I don't know,' she admitted bitterly. She wanted Geraden with her. She didn't like the risk of talking to the Termigan by herself. 'But we're trying to find out. In the meantime, we want to make as much trouble for Eremis and Gilbur as we can. That's why we're here.'

Abruptly, the lord nodded. 'Now I'm beginning to believe you. They want to kill you. You want to cause trouble for them. All this' – his manner referred to more than just the pits of fire outside Sternwall – 'is just another contest between Imagers. We're the victims' – now he meant the people of his Care – 'but we aren't really the point.

'The point is *power*.'

He had misunderstood her. She made an effort to explain. 'That isn't what I meant. We're trying to defend Mordant. It's King Joyse that Eremis and Gilbur want to destroy. We're secondary – Geraden and I are in the way, that's all. It's King Joyse who needs your help.'

Without a flicker of expression or inflection, the Termigan replied, 'Pigslime.'

Terisa stopped and studied him, trying to see past his face into his mind. But he was as closed as a piece of flint. In an effort to pull herself together, she poured more wine for herself, then returned to the bed and sat down again.

Slowly, she said, 'You don't like Imagers. Is that it?'

'Joyse needs my help, I'm sure of that,' he retorted, 'but not because you ask it. You don't care about him. You want me to do something that will help you against Eremis and Gilbur. If that helps the King today, it will help destroy him tomorrow.'

'Is it because I'm an Imager?' Terisa asked, speaking mostly to herself. 'It must be. Everybody who knows the Domne trusts his sons.'

'The one thing you all want is to get rid of *him*. That's the one thing you're all united on. He's the only man who's ever succeeded at *controlling* you.'

'I see.' Terisa had learned a lot from Castellan Lebbick: she had learned how to speak harshly to angry men. 'You think an Imager can't be honest. You think that talent – an accident of birth – precludes loyalty. Or compassion. Or even ethics.'

Still the Termigan didn't shift in his seat; he didn't raise his head or his voice. 'In the end,' he articulated flatly, 'no Imager is loyal to anyone but himself. That's the nature of power. It seduces – it requires. An Imager can appear loyal only as long as his power and his loyalty don't come into conflict. The only thing' – now just for a moment he did raise his voice – 'my lady, the *only* thing which has saved us for the past ten years is Havelock's madness. If Vagel hadn't cost him his mind, he would have gotten rid of Joyse as soon as the Congery was complete. He would have established a tyranny in Mordant to make the atrocities of Margonal and Festten look like boys pulling wings off butterflies.'

The virulence, not of his tone, but of his belief, shocked her. 'You think that? Even though Havelock was the King's friend and counselor for – what was it? – more than forty years? Even though he gave up his *sanity* for his King?' Pain and the aftereffects of nearly being killed made her savage. 'What would he have to do to make you trust him? Slaughter every Imager ever born? Exterminate talent from the world?'

With a small flick of his hand, the lord dismissed her protest. 'Even that wouldn't be enough. The Imager I trust is the one who kills himself.

'If you're telling me the truth – which is always possible, I suppose – you haven't known about your talent very long. You've only had a few days to discover what it does to you. My lady, I'll tell you what it does.

'It teaches you – no, it *forces* you to believe you're more important than other people. Because you can *do* more. If you're smart enough, and strong enough, and nobody gets in your way, you can change the outcome of the world. You can remake Mordant in your own image. So how can you let anybody stand in your way? How can you let anybody tell you what to do? How can you submit to any kind of control?

'You can't, my lady. You'll find out that you can't.

'And when you find that out, you'll learn Joyse is your enemy. *I'm* your enemy. Even if you think you're honest now, and loyal, and trustworthy, you'll learn you want us all dead. You'll learn it's better to translate pits of fire to roast us out of our homes than to take the risk that we might get in your way.'

Terisa was more than shocked: she was appalled. *How can you let anybody stand in your way?* The Termigan was right: she knew Imagers who met his description. And more than that: she knew people who would meet his description if they became Imagers. Her father was one of them.

If she was her father's daughter, she might be one of them herself.

'Now, my lady,' the Termigan said like a sharp stone, 'tell me what you think I can do to help my King.'

Fortunately, she didn't get a chance to answer. A knock at the door saved her from babbling incoherently. The Termigan turned his head, rasped, 'Enter,' and one of his soldiers came into the room.

'My lord,' the man said in a pale voice. His face was ashen, but his eyes still held the red glow of lava. 'It's getting worse.'

'"Worse"?' the lord demanded without moving.

The soldier jerked a nod. 'They're translating more lava. We can see it pouring out of the air. It's building up against us faster. Two of the pits ran together.' He hesitated, then said, 'Part of the wall just gave way.'

A sting of alarm went through Terisa. Half involuntarily, she said, 'That's because we're here. We're too dangerous.'

And because they were approaching the crisis – the point where Master Quillon said Eremis would be vulnerable. *So that he would attack here.* The point at which King Joyse intended to strike back. If in fact he had ever had the *policy* Quillon ascribed to him – or if he were still King enough to carry it out. Eremis needed to kill or paralyze the King's allies before that moment, so that King Joyse wouldn't have any force with which to strike.

It was probably true – although the thought made her sick – that Eremis wouldn't try so hard to kill her and Geraden if she hadn't convinced the Master that King Joyse knew what he was doing, that the King's choices were deliberate, purposive, rather than passive or accidental.

'"We"?' asked the Termigan. He sounded fatal – too calm for the extremity of his outrage and dismay. 'One new Imager and a failed Apt? I don't believe it.'

'You should.' Terisa couldn't bear it. Sternwall was going to be destroyed. Like Houseldon. Because of her and Geraden. 'He's an Imager, too. He's even more powerful than I am. Let him make a mirror, and he'll get rid of that lava for you.

'Eremis wants us dead. He can't take the chance we'll talk you into helping us.'

Then she closed her eyes, trying to rest her head from this prolonged struggle against pain; trying to believe that she hadn't condemned Geraden and herself to spend the rest of their short lives in the Termigan's dungeons.

She expected the lord to do something vehement: spring to his feet, storm around the room, perhaps have her locked in irons. He did none of those things, however. He murmured to his soldier, and the man left the room. Then he sat still, studying Terisa flatly; his gaze was so unreadable that when she finally met it it made her want to scream.

A few moments later, the soldier returned, ushering Geraden into the Termigan's presence.

After that, the man left.

Geraden looked at her, at the lord. He said, 'My lord Termigan,' roughly, his only concession to politeness. He was already hurrying toward Terisa.

'Are you all right?' he asked in a low voice. 'You were hit so hard, I thought they broke your neck.'

She managed a crooked smile, a stiff nod. Putting her hand in his, she pulled herself to her feet. 'The lava's getting worse,' she said, speaking carefully so that she wouldn't start to yell. 'I think it's another way of attacking us.' She faced the Termigan although she spoke to Geraden, held Geraden's hand; with all her strength, she willed the lord not to harm Geraden. 'And I think Eremis is afraid of the Termigan. There must be something he can do to fight back.' Because she wanted the lord to understand that she was threatening him, she concluded to Geraden, 'I told him you're an Imager.'

And Geraden – without hesitation, almost without trepidation – supported her even though he probably had no idea what he was getting into. 'That's right,' he said. 'If you've got any sand here, any kind of furnace or kiln, I might be able to make a mirror. I could translate that fire away.'

Terisa squeezed his hand hard and held her breath.

For the first time, she saw the Termigan react plainly. A muscle twitched in his cheek; his brows knotted into a hurt scowl. The emotion she felt wash from him wasn't anger or even disgust; it was grief.

In a ragged voice, he said, 'No. Even if you're telling the truth. I won't have it. I won't have Imagery here.'

His own severity cost him this hope.

Geraden blew a sigh; but he still didn't hesitate. 'Then, my lord,' he said clearly, 'there's only one thing you can do for your people.' Terisa marveled at him – at the strength in his voice, at the certainty with which he met a dilemma that confounded her. 'Evacuate Sternwall. Get your men together. Go fight for King Joyse. Before it's too late.'

It didn't work. '"Evacuate Sternwall"?' the Termigan spat as if he had discovered a piece of glass in his food. 'Leave my people? Abandon my Care?' Softly, but so intensely that it sounded like a cry from his heart, he demanded, *'For what?'*

'For Mordant,' answered Geraden. 'For peace.'

The Termigan didn't respond, so Geraden went on, 'Orison is under siege. Prince Kragen brought the Alend army against us – at least ten thousand men. And Cadwal is marching. The High King's army is even bigger – I don't know how long the Perdon can hold out against it. Right now, the Alend Monarch may be in the strange position of defending Orison from Cadwal.'

'I don't think you can do anything about that. I don't think you've got enough men.'

'But you could attack Eremis directly.' He released Terisa's hand so that he could move closer to the Termigan, face the lord more squarely. 'He's in league with High King Festten. But Cadwal has to fight Alend and Orison. So the place where Eremis keeps his mirrors is vulnerable – the place where he does translations like this one, the one destroying Sternwall. The place where he and Gilbur and Vagel hid to do their plotting and shape their mirrors.

'You could attack him there. In the Care of Tor. In his home. Esmerel.'

Esmerel? Terisa was surprised. That didn't make sense. 'What about his father – his brothers?' she asked stupidly. They would have betrayed him long ago. 'He couldn't use Esmerel.'

Geraden turned to her. Frowning at the distraction, he said, 'Eremis doesn't have any family. They all died in a fire years ago. Some of his servants in Orison are people who used to serve his father. I've heard them talk about it.'

So that also was a lie, just another of Eremis' attempts to manipulate her. She ground her teeth. Suddenly, she felt a fierce desire to do what Geraden was proposing: ride into the Care of Tor, ride to Esmerel, attack— Get even with that bastard.

But the Termigan wasn't moved. 'Will that save Sternwall?' he asked Geraden in a voice like a winter wind.

'Probably not,' Geraden admitted. 'It'll take too long. Sternwall is probably doomed – unless something good happens for a change. Unless something happens to distract Eremis or Gilbur so they can't keep translating that lava.'

'Then I repeat,' gritted the lord. *'For what?'*

This time, Geraden said simply, 'You might be able to save King Joyse.'

The Termigan chewed on that for a while. Then he said harshly, 'So you think there's something worth saving? You think Joyse hasn't just gone passive or anile?' He'd been pushed too far: he was losing his calm, his inhuman self-restraint. 'You think there's some *reason* why he let those shit-eating Imagers do this to my Care?'

'Yes,' Terisa said at once, before the lord's sorrow and distress became too much for her. 'I don't like it very well. I don't think it's good enough. But there *is* a reason.'

In a few stiff sentences, while the Termigan stared at her as if she were lice-

646

ridden, she told him what Master Quillon had told her about King Joyse's reasons.

The lord surged to his feet; almost before she was done, he snapped, 'Is that *all*? He turned his back on us, left his realm to rot, let Imagers do whatever they wanted to his people – just so Mordant would be attacked, instead of Alend or Cadwal?'

His passion stopped Terisa's voice. She nodded dumbly.

Without warning, the Termigan let out a snarl of laughter. Candlelight reflected in his eyes like an echo of lava. 'Brilliant. Destroy your friends to save your enemies. Completely brilliant.'

'He needs the help anyway, my lord,' murmured Geraden. 'No matter how slim it is, the possibility that he knows what he's doing is the only hope we have left. You might be able to do him some good by striking against Esmerel.'

For a moment, the lord remained motionless, holding himself as though a gale were gathering inside him. Then, abruptly, he lifted his fists and roared, '*No!*

'He decided to sacrifice Sternwall without consulting me! Let him pay for the rest of his reasons himself!'

When he left the room, he slammed the door so hard that splinters jumped from the latch and one of the crossmembers cracked.

Geraden looked at Terisa with trouble in his eyes. 'Well,' he said finally, 'at least I haven't lost my talent for mishap.'

She went to him and hugged him. 'Wait and see,' she muttered dryly. 'If he doesn't tie us up and throw us in the lava, you got more out of him than I did.'

That enabled him to chuckle a little. 'Do you mean,' he asked, 'that if we simply survive this experience I'm supposed to consider it a success?'

'Wait and see,' she repeated. She didn't know what else to offer him.

They waited.

Eventually, a servant brought them hot water, so Geraden braced a chair against the door, and they bathed each other. They drank the wine and ate the food; they took advantage of the bed. They even got some sleep.

The next morning, they answered a knock at their door, and another servant came into the room carrying their breakfast.

A soldier visited them as well. Brusquely, as if he had no time for this, he asked Terisa and Geraden what they needed for their journey.

They were surprised – but not so surprised that Geraden couldn't think of a list. After all, the Termigan had a reputation for fidelity. He may have hated Imagers and lost confidence in his King, but apparently he couldn't forget his lifelong loyalties. To the Domne, for instance. And Geraden and Terisa had lost their horses and supplies outside Sternwall; they needed anything the lord was willing to give them. So Geraden talked to the soldier for several minutes; and by the time he and Terisa had finished their breakfast the man returned to report that their new horses and fresh supplies were ready to go.

In fact, the Termigan sent them on their way better equipped than they had been when they entered his Care. In addition to the horses, he gave them plenty of food, full wineskins, cooking utensils, a short sword for each of them, and bedding that seemed luxurious compared to the thin blankets with which they had left Houseldon. He even provided a rough map which showed a direct route across country toward the Care of Fayle and Romish.

But he didn't do anything to help King Joyse.

THIRTY-SIX

GATHERING SUPPORT

According to the map, Romish was situated near the southeast point of the Care of Fayle, where the border between Fayle and Armigite met the border between Termigan and Fayle.

Terisa and Geraden wanted to hurry. From one perspective, the attack on Sternwall was a good sign: it implied that Master Eremis was still waiting for his plans to mature, still vulnerable. In every other way, however, the Termigan's plight was cause for alarm. So far, Houseldon had been burned down; Sternwall was falling into a pit of fire. The Armigite had made an agreement with Prince Kragen. The Perdon was alone against all of High King Festten's power. What came next? If this process continued much longer, Mordant would soon have nothing left to save.

Terisa and Geraden had reason to hurry.

Unfortunately, the terrain didn't let them.

They made good progress for a day after they left Sternwall, but that was only because they were able to remain on the road which led eventually to the Demesne and Orison. The second day, their route required them to angle away from the road, heading more to the north as the road shifted east. And this part of Termigan was the roughest land she had yet seen in Mordant.

'Now if this were Armigite—' Geraden panted as he tugged his horse, a rangy gray with a head like a mallet, up an interminable hillside that was too flinty and steep for safe riding. 'Armigite in spring is worth seeing. The soil is so sweet they say you only have to wave a few squash seeds at the ground and you'll be up to your hips in vines. The early hay should be just coming up – it smells so fresh you want to take up dancing. And the women—' He glanced at Terisa and grinned. 'All that rich soil and relaxed countryside makes their work so easy they really don't have anything better to do than sit around and become gorgeous.'

Terisa snorted softly. At the moment, she would have been delighted to be in Armigite. Let the women there become as gorgeous as they pleased. As far as she was concerned, the only thing worse than riding a horse was trying to haul it by main force up a hill it didn't want to climb, when her knee still pained her. Generally, she was willing to put up with the mount the Termigan had provided for her – a roan gelding with a decent gait and no malice. In the present circumstances, however, she would cheerfully have dropped the beast into one of Eremis' fiery pits.

Nevertheless she didn't suggest that she and Geraden forget about the Fayle; that they return to the road and head straight for Orison. The Fayle was the only lord left whom they might bring to the King's support.

And Queen Madin lived in Fayle, in Romish. Myste had mentioned a manor just outside Romish.

Terisa felt a strong, if rather irrational, conviction that Queen Madin had a right to know what her husband was doing. Otherwise the Queen might go to her grave believing that King Joyse had lost his interest in life, his commitment to Mordant; his love for her.

It was typical of Terisa's mood – her soul shocked by Sternwall's danger, her thoughts troubled by the ramifications of what Master Eremis was doing, and yet her heart full of Geraden – that she considered Queen Madin's feelings at least as important as King Joyse's need for help.

So she wrestled her roan up the hillsides, rode it gingerly down the gullies, and trotted it inexpertly across the flats, not precisely without complaint, but without significant self-pity.

The Care of Termigan, as Geraden explained, wasn't heavily populated. And most of the towns and villages were spread out along the Broadwine River, away from the Pestil and Alend. After the second day, the two riders seemed alone in the stringent landscape. Terisa began to think that Termigan had already lost everything it had ever contained worth fighting for.

For three days, dark clouds locked the sky, threatening rain. Water and mud would have perfected the pleasure of her journey; nevertheless she wished for rain. Orison could always use water. And mud would make the movements of armies more difficult.

Despite the fierce way they glowered down at the earth, however, the clouds were only able to spit a few brief sprinkles before they blew away. The weather itself seemed to have Master Eremis' best interests at heart.

On the other hand, as the clouds drifted off, the terrain improved, as if sunlight had an ameliorating effect on the slopes and soil. Trees became more common: soon the errant and bedraggled copses of the rest of Termigan began to accumulate into long stands of elder and sycamore, ash and wattle. 'We're getting closer,' commented Geraden. 'Fayle is known for its wood.

'Actually, that's one reason Alend traditionally attacks through Termigan or Armigite rather than Fayle. And it's why the Fayle was King Joyse's second ally, after the Tor. You could make yourself old trying to run a military campaign through the forests of Fayle. The Care has more history of resistance – or maybe I should say of successful resistance – than most of the rest of Mordant.

'That probably explains,' he concluded humorously, 'where the Fayle got his loyalty – and Queen Madin got her stubbornness.'

Terisa felt that if she never saw another hillside covered with gorse and nettles again she could die happy. 'How much farther?'

He consulted the map. 'Two days, if we're lucky. It's easy to get lost in woods and forests. And I've never been in Fayle before. Actually, Batten in Armigite is the closest I've ever been to Romish.

'But the good news' – he looked around – 'is that we ought to start seeing people again soon. According to the map, we'll go right through several villages. Technically, some of them will still be Termigan. But for all practical purposes we're coming into the Care of Fayle right now.'

Simply because he said those words, she took a harder look ahead – and spotted what appeared to be a smudge against the horizon.

Frowning, she tried to squint her vision into better focus.

Geraden noticed the direction of her gaze. 'What do you see?'

'I don't know. Smoke?'

He squinted as well, then shook his head. 'I can't tell.' Terisa didn't need to say anything; he had the same memories she did. After scanning the map again, he added, 'That might actually be the first village. A place called Aperyte. Unless I'm wrong about where we are. If it has a smithy, the forge will smoke.'

'Let's find out,' she said under her breath.

Self-consciously, he loosened his sword in its scabbard. Then he tightened his grip on the reins and urged his gray into a canter.

Her gelding followed. She was getting better at telling it what to do.

Between the trees, the ground was covered with clumps of dull grass and bracken. The first hint of evening was in the air, but she didn't notice it; she was concentrating ahead, trying to see past a number of intervening wattle thickets. The wattle had bright yellow flowers that grew in sprays like mimosa blooms. The ground was rising: if she had turned in her saddle, she could have seen a panorama unrolled behind her. But she had watched Houseldon burn; she didn't have any attention to spare for flowers and vistas.

The distance was greater than she expected. She began to think that the smudge she had seen was a trick of the light.

Then, abruptly, a knot of copses stood back from a clearing.

A corral with a split-rail fence filled most of the clearing. It wasn't as big as it first appeared; but it was plainly big enough for ten or fifteen horses. Terisa – who felt that she was becoming an expert on horse manure – was sure that the corral had been full of horses.

Recently.

But not now.

Geraden stopped. He studied the clearing. 'That's odd.'

'What's odd?'

'The gate's closed.'

He was right: the gate wasn't just closed; it was tied shut.

'Why?' he muttered softly. 'Why take all your horses out and then tie the gate?'

She lowered her voice. 'Why not?'

'Why bother?' he returned.

Terisa had no idea.

After a moment, he breathed, 'Come on,' and slipped out of his saddle. 'Let's go see what we're getting into.'

When she had dismounted, he led the gray and her gelding away until they were hidden among the copses, out of sight of the clearing. There he tied the reins to a tree; but he didn't uncinch the girths or drop the saddlebags.

Taking Terisa's hand, he moved quietly toward the village.

Because she was trying so hard to look ahead, peer between the trees, she had trouble with her footing. Geraden, on the other hand, didn't trip or stumble. For a moment, she couldn't figure out how he knew where he was going. Then she realized that he was following worn lines in the dirt – marks made by people and animals that had reason to go in every conceivable direction from their homes.

He brought her to the back of a daub-and-wattle shed. Actually, it was little more than a shelter intended to protect straw for the horses from the weather.

Beyond it lay the village.

At a glance, Terisa could see perhaps a dozen huts, all built of daub-and-wattle, all with roofs made from what appeared to be bundles of banana leaves. Among them stood an open-sided structure that might have served as a meeting hall. The size of the cleared space gave the impression that there were more houses and buildings out of sight behind the ones nearby.

From somewhere among them rose a stream of thin, dirty smoke.

The village was disturbingly quiet. No people shouting to each other. No people at all. No dogs. No chickens scratching the dirt. No children whimpering or playing in the distance. The breeze raised a little furl of dust along the hard ground between the huts, but it didn't make any noise.

'Oh, shit,' Geraden growled softly.

'Maybe they're all at work,' she murmured. 'In the fields or something.'

He shook his head. 'A village like this is never empty. Not like this.'

'Evacuation? Maybe the Fayle got them all away?'

He thought for a moment. 'I like that idea better.' Then he said, 'As long as we're whispering, let's go see if they really are gone.'

Together, they crept into the village.

Its inhabitants really were gone.

So were all its animals and fowl; beasts of burden; pets. Terisa had the impression that even the vermin had disappeared.

Shadows lengthened across the bare ground. Dusk seemed to gather in the huts and peek out from their gaping doorways, their eyeless windows. The breeze brought the taste of something cold, a hint of something rotten.

She was afraid to ask Geraden if he recognized it.

The village did in fact contain a smithy, but the forge was cold. The smoke came from somewhere else.

Shortly, she and Geraden discovered its source. At the northern edge of the village, three huts in a cluster were on fire.

They had been burning for some time – had nearly burned themselves out. Only their blackened frames still stood. Small flames licked in and out of the fallen remains of the roofs; the smoke drifting upward had a bitter smell.

All three were full of corpses.

Terisa gagged when she saw the stumps of charred arms and legs, the lumps of heads protruding from the ash. 'Is that all of them?' she choked thickly. '*All* of them?'

'No.' Geraden was having trouble breathing. 'Probably just a few families. The whole village wouldn't fit. These are the ones who didn't get away.'

Inspired by nausea – and by the strange scent on the breeze, which didn't have anything to do with burned wattle and charred bodies – Terisa muttered, 'Or they're the ones who did.'

He gave her a look like a whiplash.

She heard a faint, rustling noise – bare feet scuttling across the dirt. She looked around; her peripheral vision seemed to catch a glimpse of something as it slipped into the evening shadows. Then it was gone. She couldn't be sure that she had actually seen anything.

Yet a chill went down her back as she remembered what Master Eremis had told the lords of the Cares. *All Mordant is already assailed. Strange wolves have slaughtered the Tor's son. Devouring lizards swarm the storehouses of the Demesne. Pits of fire appear in the ground of Termigan.*

But that wasn't all. Now she remembered it precisely.

Ghouls harry the villages of Fayle.

'Geraden—' She was barely able to clear her throat. 'Let's get out of here.'

He was still staring at the huts; he hadn't heard what she heard. But he nodded roughly.

For no apparent reason, he pulled out his sword as he started back toward the horses.

She hoped he didn't have a reason. Nevertheless she was glad that he was armed – and that he was determined, if not skilled. She stayed close to his shoulder all the way through the village and past the corral.

Their boots made too much noise on the hard ground: she wouldn't have been able to hear any soft rustling sounds. But twice she thought she saw movement in the heart of a shadow, the depths of a hut, as if the dark were coming to life.

She was irrationally relieved to find the horses where she and Geraden had left them – and to find them alive. They were both uneasy: the gray bobbed its head fretfully; the roan kept rolling its eyes. Maybe they smelled the same scent that made her so nervous. They were difficult to manage at first, until they realized that they were no longer tied to the tree.

Respecting the uneasiness of the horses – and his own distress – Geraden led Terisa in a wide circuit beyond the empty village before returning to the route marked on the Termigan's map.

Until nightfall forced them to stop, they put as much distance as they could between themselves and Aperyte. She didn't want to stop at all; but of course they couldn't find their way safely in the dark. A flashlight would have come in handy. A *big* flashlight. Sure, she muttered to herself sourly. And while she was at it, why not an armored car to ride in? Or even an airplane to drop a few strategic bombs on Esmerel? On High King Festten's army?

All Geraden needed was a mirror.

He could do it, if he could get to his glass – the one which had brought her here.

Sure.

When they made camp, she helped him build the biggest fire they could. She hunted as far as she dared, collecting firewood. Then, while they ate supper, she commented morosely, 'I don't know what made me say that.'

Geraden looked at her across the stewpot out of which he was eating.

'You said they were the ones who didn't get away. I said they were the ones who did. I don't know why I said that.'

He tried without much success to smile. 'Let's hope you just have a morbid imagination.' The firelight on his face reminded her of the Termigan.

She couldn't smile, either. 'Why is it,' she went on, trying to exorcise images which haunted her, 'everything that comes here by translation is so destructive? Why is it so easy to find terrible things in mirrors? Is the universe really so malign?'

'I certainly hope not.' In a transparent effort to reassure her, Geraden grimaced lugubriously. Then he set himself to give her an answer.

'It's probably true that every world has predators. But even if a world didn't contain any violence at all, its creatures or powers might still be destructive if they were translated – if they were taken out of their natural place. There's nothing immoral about a pit of fire – as long as you leave it where it belongs. What's really destructive is the man who translates it somewhere else.

'Would you call a fox destructive? After all, it hunts chickens. And people need those chickens. Even so, there's nothing wrong with the fox.

'For all we know, the firecat that burned Houseldon might be the same thing as a fox in its own world. It might be anything. It might even be an administer of charity.'

An administer of charity. Just for a moment, she took the idea seriously. Someone who ran a mission, for example. Then, however, she was struck by the thought of Reverend Thatcher going around setting towns on fire. On his own terms, that would please him. But *literally* setting towns on fire—

Involuntarily, she grinned. When Geraden rolled his eyes at her, she started laughing.

She felt like a fool – like she was losing her mind. But she went on laughing, and after a while she felt better.

Nevertheless she didn't sleep very well that night. She kept expecting the horses to snort and shy – kept expecting to smell something cold and slightly rotten in the dark. And for some reason Geraden spent most of the night snoring like a bandsaw. When she nudged him awake in the early gray of dawn, so that they could be on their way, she felt cold herself and vaguely stupid, as if the matter inside her skull had begun to turn rancid.

The day began well. The air was clear and crisp, and the horses moved easily along the increasingly traveled paths. And before noon she and Geraden came upon a village that had nothing wrong with it.

Nothing, that is, except anxiety. When the people of the village heard what Terisa and Geraden had found in Aperyte, they muttered nervously and scanned the woods around their homes and began to talk about leaving.

'Ghouls,' a woman pronounced, confirming Terisa's guess. 'Don't know what else to call them. Never seen one – but the lord sent men to warn us. Attack at dusk or dawn. Little critters, almost like children. Green and smelly.

'Eat every kind of flesh. Don't even leave the grease and bones. That's what the lord's men said.'

Geraden scowled as if he were in pain. 'That's why the gate was closed,' he muttered. 'The horses never got out. They were eaten right there in the corral.'

Terisa was thinking, *They're the ones who did.* They escaped into their huts and somehow sealed the doors. And then they were incinerated in their own homes.

Eremis.

She was beginning to understand why King Joyse had fought for twenty years to strip Alend and Cadwal of Imagers and create the Congery. He wanted to prevent creatures like ghouls from being translated into the world.

Through a haze of nausea and anger, she asked one of the villagers, 'What're you going to do?'

'What the lord's men told us,' came the reply. 'If we heard any rumor of ghouls around here, saw any sign. Get to Romish as fast as we can.'

'*Good,*' said Geraden fiercely.

He and Terisa rode on.

She still felt like the meat of her brain was going bad. Even though those villagers were safe, she couldn't rid herself of the impression that the day was getting worse. How many ghouls had Eremis already translated into the Care of Fayle? How much of the Fayle's strength had already been eaten away?

How could he help King Joyse and defend his own people at the same time?

She practiced saying *oh, shit* to herself until it began to feel more natural.

'Here's some more good news,' Geraden remarked the next time he studied the map. 'At the rate we're going, we're due to reach another village just about sunset. A place called Naybel.'

Oh, shit.

Grimly, she made an effort to think. 'Maybe we should stay away from it. Maybe those things are following us.'

He glared at her. 'You *do* have a morbid imagination.' After a moment, he added, 'If we're being followed, we've got to warn the village. We can't lead ghouls past Naybel and expect them to leave it alone.'

The day was definitely going downhill.

The afternoon wore on, as miserable and prolonged as a toothache. Eventually, Terisa concluded that there were after all worse things than spending so much of the day on horseback. She couldn't get that *smell* out of her mind—

Without making an explicit decision to hurry, she and Geraden began to urge their horses faster. They wanted to reach Naybel before dusk.

Mishap continued to dog them. Because they were hurrying, they rode into the village precisely as the sun began to dip into the horizon. At a slower pace, they wouldn't have arrived until full dark.

The decision to ride straight into the village was also one which they hadn't made explicitly: they did it simply because the need to warn Naybel's people blanketed other considerations. As a result, they were already among the huts, on their way in toward the center of the village, when they realized that Naybel was as empty as Aperyte.

Geraden slowed the gray's canter. The beast's head went up and down like a hammer, fighting the reins. Terisa's gelding had its ears back. Where the sunlight came through the trees, the shadows of the huts were as sharp as blades.

'Geraden,' she whispered, 'we're too late. Let's get *out* of here.' Geraden hesitated, turned his head to fling a look around him – and lost control of his mount. The gray caught its bit between its teeth and bolted.

Terisa couldn't stop her roan from following.

Almost at once, she heard the squeal of a pig. Geraden nearly lost his seat as the gray wrenched itself aside to avoid collision with a fat porker. Immediately, his horse blundered into a squall of chickens. Terisa followed him through feathers and shadows.

Into the center of the village.

Like Aperyte, Naybel had an open-sided meeting hall among its houses.

In the hall stood a group of men – six or eight of them. They wore heavy boots and battle-leathers; they were armed with swords, pikes, longbows.

As soon as they saw Geraden and Terisa, they began to yell, waving their arms wildly.

'Fools!'

'Fornication!'

'Get away!'

'Stop!'

Several of them apparently wanted to chase the horses off. Fortunately, one man had a different idea. Or he realized that the gray was a runaway. With the practiced ease of someone who had worked with horses all his life, he jumped at the gray's head and caught the reins. The gray wheeled to a halt so hard that Geraden was nearly snapped out of the saddle.

More to avoid hitting the gray than because of anything Terisa did, the gelding also blundered to a stop.

'Fools!' a man shouted. 'You're going to be killed!'

Terisa tried to hold herself still, but the whole village seemed to be spinning. A shadow as distinct as a cut lay across the roan's head. The men from the meeting hall shifted in and out of shadows; their weapons disappeared, caught the sun, disappeared again. Geraden had nearly run into a pig. And chickens. Naybel wasn't empty, not like Aperyte.

Then what—?

It was true: she could smell something cold, something that had begun to rot; something like the exhalation from a neglected tomb.

Out of a hut beyond the meeting hall came a little boy. She *thought* he was a little boy, oddly naked. A grin split his face, leaving a wide, empty place. He didn't leave the shadows; because of the dim illumination, a moment passed before she noticed that he had a chicken in his hands.

The chicken was melting. It slumped over his fingers like heated wax. But none of it dripped to the ground. Instead, as it oozed it was absorbed into his flesh.

Now she realized that his whole body was covered with slime. Maybe the shadows were playing tricks on her eyes. The boy looked *green*—

A hoarse cry broke from the men. Two of them already had their longbows up, arrows nocked. Bows like that could have flung their yards straight through the walls of one of these huts. The two arrows that hit the little boy spiked him to the dirt.

Terisa distinctly heard a popping noise, a sound of rupture; she heard a brief wail claw the air.

Instantly, three more green children appeared in the shadow beside the little boy. They grinned as they began to feed.

Somewhere out of sight, the pig squealed – a shriek of porcine agony. The gelding took this occasion to pitch Terisa off its back. With a whinny like a scream, it rushed out of the village.

Terisa landed heavily, knocking the air out of her chest. In the distance, Geraden yelled her name, but she couldn't react to it. The jolt of impact stunned her. A streak of sunlight fell over her face: she looked up and saw one of the ghouls standing in shadow no more than four or five feet away. She could *smell* the child—

In fact, the odor wasn't particularly strong. It was insidious, however, and its subtlety seemed to make it more nauseating, more corrosive, than a stronger stench would have been. Smelling it, staring at the small girl who grinned at her as if she were an especially tasty snack, Terisa decided that the slime on the ghoul's skin was acid. It rendered flesh down to a tallow the creature could take in through its pores. And when someone tried to escape by barring the door of a hut, the acid probably set the wood on fire.

The ghoul was so hungry that she started out of the shadow into the light that covered Terisa's face.

Geraden leaped over her and swept the girl's head off with a long swing of his sword.

The popping noise, the sound of rupture; a high, thin cry.

Two, three, no, at least six more ghouls came at once to feed on their fallen sister.

Around the meeting hall, a weird battle raged. Superficially, it was an uneven struggle: the men slaughtered the ghouls with relative ease. Swords, pikes, arrows, even stones thrown hard – everything worked. Panting, raging, the men hacked down, sliced up, or spitted the ghouls as fast as possible. They were only children, as simple to kill as children.

But they were so many—

No, they weren't as many as all that. The truth was more complex. As soon as one of them got enough to eat, the creature split apart, became two. And whenever one of them died, the body provided enough food for three or four other ghouls to multiply.

And with every death wail, more creatures swarmed out of the shadows.

In addition, the weapons of the men didn't last long. Every arrow that struck home caught fire; every blade that cut came back pitted and weakened, streaked with ruin; every pike that pierced a ghoul lost its head.

Geraden tried to wrestle Terisa toward the meeting hall, into the relative center of the battle, where the men watched each other's backs. She thought she ought to help him, but she couldn't get her legs under her; the fall from her horse seemed to have broken the connection between what her brain suggested and what her muscles did. She wanted to say, Water. Try water.

Maybe the acid could be washed away. Or diluted. Unfortunately, all that came between her lips was a hoarse gasp for air.

And the air was full of wails and death; the stench of rot; men cursing for their lives; sunset.

Then, so suddenly that the sound of it almost relaxed her chest enough to let her breathe, she heard a trumpet.

That high penetrating call seemed to change everything.

At its signal, twenty or thirty men charged through the village on horseback.

They knew what they were doing: they didn't risk any of their mounts in an attempt to trample the ghouls. Instead, they carried lights of every description – torches, lanterns, blazing fagots, even oil lamps. Shining like a host of glory, the riders swept into Naybel at dusk.

Obliquely, Terisa noticed that one of them was the Fayle himself. She recognized him by his age, his leanness, his long, heavy jaw.

She didn't have the strength to wonder what he was doing here. She was too busy watching.

The light seemed to hurt the ghouls worse than death did: it paralyzed them. They lost their grins, their hunger, the power of movement. And when they couldn't move, they couldn't feed on each other; they couldn't multiply.

Clearly, the Fayle's men knew this would happen. At once, they took advantage of it.

In grim concentration, as if they had never been able to reconcile themselves to killing creatures that looked like children, they began hacking the ghouls apart and setting the pieces to the torch.

They used cast-iron tongs and shovels to pile the dismembered corpses together so that the flames fed on each other. Before long, the bonfire beside the meeting hall of Naybel grew so large that its flames seemed to reach the darkening heavens. After the last of the sun went down, there was no other light in the village except fire.

Hot fire and acrid smoke slowly took the cold, rotting odor out of the air. A gust of wind carried smoke into Terisa's eyes; tears ran down her cheeks as if she were weeping. But she was able to breathe again, able to get air all the way down into the bottom of her lungs, able to move her shoulder. So that was why, she thought deliberately, distracting herself from the slaughter she had just witnessed so it wouldn't overwhelm her, that was why the bodies in those burned huts in Aperyte hadn't been consumed, when every other form of flesh in the village was gone. Once the acid had set fire to the wood, the flames had cast enough light to keep the ghouls away.

After a minute or two, she became aware that Geraden still had his arms around her. Like her, he had taken a faceful of smoke; like her, he appeared to be weeping. The light of burning children reflected in his eyes.

She hugged him, held him; clung to him. She didn't know how much more she could bear.

Trying to recover his composure, he muttered, 'I'm never going to tell Quiss about this. Never as long as I live.'

Terisa coughed at the smoke, cleared her throat. Remembering the way he had kept her sane when the Congery's champion had brought the ceiling of the hall down on her, she made an effort to return the favor. 'That's probably a good idea. If I hadn't seen it myself, I wouldn't want you to tell me about it.'

In the same tone, as if he were talking about the same thing, he said, 'If I ever get my hands on Master Eremis, I swear I'm going to kill him.'

Distinctly, so that there would be no mistake about it, she replied, 'You'll have to get to him before I do.'

Geraden studied her through the dusk and firelight. Then, just for a moment, he grinned. 'If he knew we're this angry at him, he would break into a sweat.'

He made it possible for her to smile as well. 'You know,' she murmured close to his ear, 'until I met you, it never once occurred to me that someday I would be able to make my enemies sweat.'

'Your enemies, my lady?' Geraden gave her an extra hug. 'You make *me* sweat.'

When she saw the Fayle riding toward her, she realized that she felt able to face him now.

He dismounted carefully and gave her an old man's brittle bow. 'My lady Terisa,' he said in a voice like dry leaves, 'you astonish me. When last we met, I believed that Master Eremis was the source of my surprise, but now I can see that I was mistaken. The surprise is in you.

'This trap was set for ghouls, my lady. It was never my intention to ensnare you – to endanger you.'

'Of course not, my lord Fayle.' She didn't know what kind of bow to give him. Fortunately, he didn't seem to expect one. 'We were just—' She caught herself, made an effort to take one thing at a time. 'My lord, this is Geraden.'

The Fayle looked at Geraden. 'Son of the Domne,' he murmured. 'Translator of the lady Terisa of Morgan. A prominent figure in the Congery's augury of Mordant's need.' Again, he bowed. 'You are welcome in the Care of Fayle.'

Geraden returned the bow. Terisa wondered whether he – whether she herself – would still be welcome if the lord knew of their talents; but she wasn't given a chance to explore the issue. Without pausing, the Fayle went on, 'I must get out of this smoke. Our camp is a mile from here. There we can offer you hot food and a safe bed. If you will consent to accompany me, we will hear your story in better comfort.

'In the morning, the villagers will return to cleanse their homes, and we will ride to attempt this tactic again elsewhere. You will be welcome to accompany us then, also, if you wish.'

'Thanks, my lord,' Geraden answered promptly. 'We'll be glad to go with you – at least for tonight. We've got a lot to tell you.'

'I am sure you do,' said the Fayle. 'Perhaps you will be able tell me whether Master Eremis is honest – whether I was wrong to betray his intentions to Castellan Lebbick.

'Come.'

As if all his joints ached, he climbed back onto his horse.

All his joints probably did ache. Terisa would have thought that he was too old for ambushes and battles. Privately, she wondered what drove him to it.

She also wondered how much it would be safe to tell him. She and Geraden had come close to disaster by telling the Termigan too much.

Before she had time to wonder what had become of the roan gelding, one of the Fayle's men returned it to her; he had found it in the woods. Soon she and Geraden were riding among the Fayle's companions toward his camp.

After the turmoil and fright of the battle, the ride seemed reassuring and peaceful, too brief. In a short time, she found herself dismounted before a bright fire near the center of a clearing. Around her were servants and supply wains, bedrolls set out on the ground, more men, extra horses; a few of Naybel's people had come to hear what had happened to their village. A steward brought a flagon of heated wine for the Fayle, then hurried away to get more for the lord's unexpected guests. The way the men looked at her reminded Terisa that she hadn't had a decent bath for days. Her hair probably looked like a rat's nest, and her clothes were filthy. Unfortunately, there was nothing she could do about those things at the moment. Instead, she attempted to ignore the stares of the Fayle's men.

A campstool was brought for the lord, and he seated himself near the fire as if he were chilled. Almost at once, more stools appeared for Terisa and Geraden. They sat down, accepted warm flagons of wine. Terisa took a sip, then forgot her self-consciousness – forgot that at least thirty people were watching her – long enough to give a grateful sigh. The wine was full of cinnamon and oranges, a blissful antidote for the smell of ghouls. If she had enough to drink, she might be able to get that reek completely out of her mind.

She wanted to spend a while savoring the sensation that she was safe.

But Geraden was already eager to talk. 'My lord Fayle,' he said before she was ready, 'we've come a long way to tell you Master Eremis isn't honest. He's the one who translates these ghouls into your Care – he and Master Gilbur, and probably the arch-Imager Vagel.

'We came to tell you King Joyse needs help. If he doesn't get it, Master Eremis may destroy him.'

By force of habit, the Fayle sat upright on his stool. His eyes were keenly blue; his gaze was precise. Looking at him, Terisa was struck by the odd thought that he would never have been able to do what King Joyse had done – make himself appear weak and foolish for years. No one who met the Fayle's gaze would doubt that he knew what he was doing.

'It is comforting to know,' he muttered dryly, 'that Master Eremis deserved to be thwarted. We will discuss that further. Nevertheless his dishonesty does little to explain how you came to fall into a trap which I had set for ghouls.'

'Actually, it explains a lot, my lord,' countered Geraden. 'The rest is just details.' For reasons Terisa understood perfectly, he was being cautious. 'We rode here from Sternwall. The Termigan wasn't especially glad to see us.

'Like yours, his Care is being badly hurt by one of Eremis' translations. We told him the same thing I just told you. King Joyse needs help. He didn't seem to care about that. I think we were lucky he let us leave.

'My lord, I don't want that to happen again. The lady Terisa and I are going to fight for the King. Even if we have to do it alone, we're going to do it. If you stand in our way, we'll have to fight you, too.

'I'd rather cut off my hands.'

All the men around the camp were listening. Some of them pretended to be busy with their weapons or their bedding, but they were listening. A focused hush covered everything except the snorts and rustling of the horses.

The Fayle gazed at Geraden steadily. 'You must have told the Termigan something he especially did not wish to hear.'

Geraden nodded.

'What was it?' asked the Fayle. 'What could you have said to him that would make a loyal and trustworthy ally of the King suspicious of you?'

Geraden referred the question to Terisa.

Simply because the lord's eyes were so blue, so exact, she assented to the risk.

'We told him the truth,' Geraden answered the Fayle. 'We've both become Imagers. Terisa is an arch-Imager. The ghouls have started getting worse, haven't they? Just recently?'

It was the lord's turn to nod.

'That's because of us. Eremis knew we were coming here. Or he figured it out. We were at Houseldon first. Then we were in Sternwall. Where else would we be going?

'He wants to kill us before we find a way to hurt him.'

'And have you found a way?' the Fayle inquired dryly.

'We've been trying. That's why we went to Sternwall – why we came here. We've been trying to gather support for the King.' Geraden took a deep breath. 'And if we can't do that, we want to find somebody who can help me make a mirror.'

'You have no glass?' The Fayle's gaze was sharp.

Geraden straightened his shoulders, and Terisa thought she heard a distant echo of strength in his voice, a strange menace. 'My lord,' he said, 'a number of things would be different if we had as much as one small mirror between us. For one, we would have helped you fight those ghouls.' He was speaking through his teeth. 'That's what our talents are good for.'

After a moment, however, the menace faded from his tone. 'Unfortunately, we're helpless. So far.'

The Fayle considered Geraden and Terisa for a while. He turned away to request food and more wine. Then he commented, 'Perhaps you should tell me your story now. While we eat.'

Geraden glanced at Terisa again. She nodded without hesitation. She was remembering the way the old lord had left the meeting Master Eremis had arranged between the lords and Prince Kragen. *Queen Madin is a formidable woman,* he had explained in an apologetic and even vaguely foolish tone. *Whatever choice I make here, I must justify to her.* His peaked shoulders and elongated head should have made him look silly as he walked out on Eremis' plotting. And yet he hadn't looked silly at all. His clear loyalty had made him admirable.

Under the circumstances, she didn't know what to expect from the Fayle. She was willing to trust him anyway.

Apparently, Geraden felt the same. As soon as the decision to speak freely had been taken, he began to relax.

661

He didn't try to include everything, however. He still wanted an answer from the Fayle. So he only described the broad outlines of what he and Terisa had learned, what they had done. The Fayle flinched at the news of what had happened to Houseldon, what was happening to Sternwall; but Geraden kept on talking. Whenever the lord stopped him with a question, however, he replied in more detail.

Most of the men were listening openly now. A few of them fingered their weapons in anger or fear. But because their attention wasn't on Terisa she was able to ignore them.

While Geraden and the lord spoke, she drank her wine, ate the food placed in front of her, and did a little calculating backward. That brought her to the unexpected realization that thirteen days had passed, *thirteen*, since her translation from Orison. In thirteen days, anything could have happened, anything at all. Prince Kragen could have taken the castle – and the Congery. High King Festten could have taken the castle and the Congery *and* Prince Kragen. On the other hand, Castellan Lebbick could have stuck a quiet knife in Master Eremis' back.

'The problem is,' she put in when Geraden paused, 'we've been away from Orison too long.' Abruptly, she became the focus of attention. Swallowing a rush of self-consciousness, she forced herself to say, 'Thirteen days for me. Fourteen for him.

'We don't have any way of knowing what's happened in the meantime.'

'So perhaps,' the Fayle murmured slowly, 'this strange *policy* of the King's has already come to its crisis. Perhaps he is already victorious. Or perhaps he has already been defeated and killed.'

'We can't know,' she agreed. 'All we have to go on is that when we left Orison Eremis was still working hard to look innocent. And since then he's been working hard to get us killed. He's still afraid we can hurt him somehow.' She shrugged. 'It isn't much. But as long as he's afraid of us, we have something to hope for.'

'That's something else we might be able to do if we had a mirror,' Geraden added. 'Get an Image of Orison. See what's going on.'

The Fayle faced Geraden acutely. He looked at Terisa, searched her. After a moment, he spread his hands. The gesture was small, but it seemed full of resignation.

'I have no glass, and no way to make it. I have no Imagers – what use do I have for mirrors? Every product or tool of Imagery which has ever been found in the Care of Fayle, I have given to King Joyse and Adept Havelock.'

By degrees, his gaze drifted away toward the fire. 'Without Imagers, my Care is helpless against these ghouls. You have been away from Orison for thirteen or fourteen days. I have not seen Romish since the day I returned from Master Eremis' meeting. I have been in the saddle, in the villages of my Care – fighting—'

Terisa had never heard him sound so old.

'I cannot win this struggle. In the end, I must fail.' He wasn't looking at his men. His men didn't look at him. None of them contradicted him. 'You saw that I have failed Aperyte. It is only one among many villages dead, gutted—

'These ghouls are too many. I have hardly enough trained horsemen for four bands such as this one. I must fail.'

'Then, my lord,' Geraden said softly, formally, hinting at authority, 'fight another way. Gather your men. Strike at Eremis in Esmerel. While any hope at all remains.'

The old lord studied the heart of the fire. His erect posture didn't shift, didn't sag, but his hands hung between his knees as if they were useless. After a while, he whispered, 'No.'

'My lord—' Geraden began.

'No,' breathed the Fayle. 'Joyse is my King – and the husband of my daughter. I love him. I do not understand this *policy*. I do not like it. Yet I love him.

'But he has *never*' – one hand came up into a fist, fell again – 'in all his years of warfare against Cadwal and Alend and Imagery, he has *never* asked a lord for aid when that lord's Care was under attack. He came to *me*, freed *my* people. He did not ask me for any help until my Care was safe.

'He will not ask me now. He has no wish to break my heart.'

Geraden tried again. 'My lord—'

'No.' The Fayle didn't sound angry: he sounded sad. 'Today we saved Naybel. You were witness. Tomorrow – or in five days – or in *fifty* days' – now both hands were fists, beating the rhythm of his words against each other – 'we will spring another trap, and it will succeed. People will live who would die if I left them to the mercy of these ghouls.

'Do you hear me, Geraden? Did your father ride away from his Care? Did the Termigan?

'I will not leave my people to die undefended.'

'I understand, my lord.' Geraden's voice was as soft and sad as the lord's, but there was no bitterness in it. 'It doesn't matter how desperate King Joyse is. He wouldn't want you to abandon your own Care. He didn't create Mordant or the Congery because he was desperate. He created them because he believes the same things you do.'

The Fayle stared into the fire, nodded several times. In a voice like a winter breeze, he sighed, 'Thank you.'

Geraden hesitated momentarily, then ventured to say, 'Unfortunately, that doesn't change our problem. Is there anything you can do to help Terisa and me?'

With a shift of his head, the lord brought his blue gaze to Geraden's face. For an instant, Terisa thought he was angry. Then, however, she saw a suggestion of a smile touch his old mouth. 'That is true, Geraden,' he said. 'My stubbornness does nothing to change your problem. You and the lady Terisa are Imagers, and the evil of Imagery must be met and answered by Imagers. That is your "Care," in a manner of speaking.

'I will give you supplies. If you need it, I will give you a map. And I will give you two men to ride with you as far as you choose – to Orison, even to Esmerel. They will be useless against Imagers, but they will know how to use their swords to guard your backs and clear your road.'

Before Geraden could reply, Terisa asked, 'Can they take us to the Queen?'

Geraden was surprised: apparently, he hadn't given much thought to

Queen Madin. The Fayle raised an eyebrow; but this time his smile was plain. 'A good thought, my lady,' he murmured. 'It would have come to me in a moment. My men can certainly take you to the Queen. She has a clear right to know what her husband has been doing.' His smile faded at the memory. 'After all, she has been deeply hurt by his *policy*. And it is possible that she may want to do something about it.'

In response, Terisa swallowed hard and said, 'Thanks. I appreciate that.' The force of her relief took her aback. She had known that she wanted to meet the Queen, but she hadn't realized before just how terrible she would feel if she and Geraden came all this way and then left without taking the time to share what they knew with King Joyse's wife.

Geraden stared at her, but he didn't argue; he didn't say, That's a delay we don't need, a day we could spend better on the way to Orison. Luckily, his instinct to trust her was still intact. After a moment, he let the matter drop and concentrated on eating his supper.

Later that night, however, when she and Geraden were in their bedding together, a short distance away from the Fayle's men, he said under his breath, 'I didn't know you wanted to meet Queen Madin. Or is it Torrent you're so interested in?'

Terisa didn't answer directly. After musing for a while, she murmured, 'Do you remember what the Castellan said to Elega – the message he said King Joyse sent to her?' In case he didn't remember, she reminded him: ' "I am sure that my daughter Elega has acted for the best reasons. She carries my pride with her wherever she goes. For her sake, as well as for my own, I hope that the best reasons will also produce the best results." '

'Yes,' returned Geraden. 'It still doesn't make sense. It still doesn't fit with what Master Quillon told you.'

'Wait a minute,' she said to keep him quiet. 'Do you remember that talk I had with Adept Havelock, while you and Artagel were on the other side of the pillar – after he rescued us from those insects?'

Obediently, Geraden nodded.

'He talked about Myste,' she whispered, 'and the Congery's champion. He said he had cast an augury about King Joyse, and one of the Images showed Myste and the champion together.'

Obediently, Geraden didn't interrupt.

'I've always wondered why he told us that. If it wasn't just because he's crazy. And I've always wondered why King Joyse got so upset when I lied to him about Myste – when I said she went back to her mother. Why he was relieved when I told him I helped her go after the champion.'

In silence, Geraden waited patiently. At last, he suggested, 'Why don't you tell me what you think?'

'I think—' Terisa held her breath, then forged ahead. 'I think there's more to King Joyse's plans than Master Quillon told us. I think his daughters are important – I think his whole family is important somehow. I think he wanted to throw Elega and Prince Kragen together. I think he wanted Myste to go after the champion.'

'You think he wanted us to go talk to Queen Madin and Torrent? Isn't that a little farfetched? After all, he didn't know either one of us had any talent. There was no way he could have predicted we would ever be here.'

That was true. And it made everything more dangerous. Nevertheless Terisa persisted. 'I think,' she said, '*I* want to go talk to Queen Madin and Torrent. Just in case.' After a moment, she added, 'He had reason to think we *might* have talent.'

She could feel Geraden grinning in the dark. 'My lady, you've got a remarkably subtle mind. Or indigestion – I can't figure out which.'

She got a hand under his jerkin and poked him in the ribs until he apologized.

Then she poked him for apologizing.

With so many potential spectators nearby, she and Geraden actually got more sleep than usual. And the next day two of the Fayle's men guided them to Romish.

The lord's seat was situated on a fertile plain uncharacteristically – for this Care – devoid of trees. The land for a mile or two in each direction had been cleared to make room for the fields which fed the city. But Terisa saw no more of Romish itself than the earthwork wall around it. As Myste had said, Queen Madin and Torrent lived in a manor outside the city.

The manor, Vale House, which a former Cadwal prince had raised to shelter his poor relations while he ruled Fayle, was tucked into a fold among small hills perhaps half a mile upstream along the small Kolted River which provided most of the water for Romish and the fields. As a defensive position – Terisa surprised herself by thinking about such things – the location of Vale House left a lot to be desired: in full daylight, a rider could probably get within twenty yards of the building unnoticed. On the other hand, the House was so easily reached from Romish, and so stoutly constructed, that it was probably in no danger most of the time. Its walls were of stone – strong against ghouls – and the timbers of its doors were banded with iron.

Through the long dusk of the plain, the Fayle's men guided Terisa and Geraden among the hills to Vale House. They dismounted before the high doors. The Fayle's men told the emerging servants to fetch torches for light, grooms for the horses; also the lady Queen Madin. The windows of the House filled up with brightness as lamps and lanterns were lit inside. In a short time, a woman came across the porch to the steps with a blaze of illumination behind her, as regal as if she ruled the world.

The Fayle's men bowed and stepped back.

'My lady Queen.' Geraden bowed as well, bending so low that he nearly fell over. There was a suggestion of tears in his voice. Madin was a sovereign to him, after all – and the wife of the King he loved. 'It does my heart good to see you again.'

'Geraden.' Queen Madin's tone conveyed the immediate impression that she knew how to make up her mind. 'This is quite a surprise. But a good one – so far.' She didn't sound harsh, and certainly not cold; she only sounded quick to choose. Decisiveness was a power she wielded without noticing it. 'I am glad to see a friendly face from home. And I will be glad to hear your news, whatever it is.' A moment later, she added, 'But if that old fool Joyse sent you here to plead his case, you can forget about it and go back. I will not have it.'

'My lady Queen,' repeated Geraden. He bowed again, this time to cover a smile. 'This is the lady Terisa of Morgan.'

'Ah.' Queen Madin turned toward Terisa, but Terisa still couldn't see her face; dark against the glow from the house, her features were undecipherable. 'The lady Terisa. My father mentioned you, after his return from Orison.

'My lady – Geraden – you are welcome in Vale House. Please enter.'

She turned and walked back into the light.

Geraden touched Terisa's shoulder, nudged her toward the steps and the porch. The light shone on his face, and she was filled for a moment with the unexpected conviction that they had done the right thing by coming here. He had never looked taller; his gaze had never seemed keener. This was the way he might have appeared when he stood in front of King Joyse – if his King hadn't been so studiously dedicated to breaking his loyalty.

She slipped her arm through his and hugged it so that they went up to the porch and entered the high doorway of Vale House together.

They followed the Queen's back and a bowing servant along an entryway hall with tapestries and portraits on the walls, several doors on each side, and a wide stair at the end. Queen Madin chose a door on the left; the servant held it open for Terisa and Geraden, and they found themselves in what looked like a large sitting room. A blazing fireplace dominated the outer wall, and two deep couches and four or five plush armchairs were semicircled before the hearth with their backs to the paneling in the rest of the room. Queen Madin sent the servant for some wine, then gestured her guests toward the chairs; but she remained standing beside the fireplace.

Neither Terisa nor Geraden sat. He may have stayed upright out of courtesy, but her thoughts were elsewhere. At last, she could see Queen Madin clearly, and what she saw kept her on her feet.

Until that moment, she hadn't realized how much she was expecting the Queen to resemble Elega. From Terisa's point of view, Myste favored her father: Myste's laugh was so much like King Joyse's smile that the resemblance seemed more important than any differences. Simply on that basis, because the contrast between Myste and Elega was so pronounced, Terisa had assumed that Queen Madin would prove to be the parent Elega favored.

It was clear now, however, in the light of the fire and the bright chandelier and the surrounding lamps, that Terisa's assumptions were mistaken. One good look at the Queen made it plain that both Elega and Myste in fact resembled their father. Madin was still a luminous woman, despite her years; her gaze was strong, and the years hadn't cost her manner any discernible loss of firmness. But her features were at once too blunt and too forthright to be the model for Myste's and Elega's faces.

What kept Terisa on her feet, however, wasn't the Queen's appearance, but rather her bearing: she stood the way a queen should stand, as if not just her authority but her wise use of it as well came to her so naturally that both were beyond question. She was the Fayle's daughter in more ways than one;

she even conveyed a suggestion of the same sorrow which harried the old lord. Nevertheless, perhaps because her frame was more solidly constructed than his, she projected more force of personality, more of both the ability and the willingness to make other people do what she wanted.

Her failure to make King Joyse put down his passivity and become a decent ruler for Mordant again must have been more galling to her than any other wound she had suffered in her life.

But she was obviously not a woman who felt much self-pity, and she wasn't feeling sorry for herself at the moment. She was studying both Terisa and Geraden with keen interest. And she seemed to find him especially intriguing, even though Terisa was the one who had come to Mordant from an alien world. After a moment, she explained her attention by saying, 'Geraden, you have changed.'

Terisa's immediate reaction was, No, he hasn't. From her perspective, he had come back to his essential self from iron and despair. Queen Madin's observation made her think again, however. In fact, he *had* changed. He hadn't simply lost his clumsiness: he had lost his puppyish look, his appearance of being a boy hidden inside a man. His back was straight and strong, and she had a hard time imagining him making a mistake.

As if to demonstrate the change, he smiled almost without embarrassment. 'It's Terisa's influence, my lady Queen. She made me stop apologizing.'

'No,' Queen Madin replied firmly. 'The difference is that you are more at peace within yourself.' She was sure of her own judgment. 'You have become an Imager.'

In response, he shrugged self-deprecatingly; but he held her gaze. 'I didn't know it shows.'

'Oh, it shows, Geraden,' the Queen affirmed, 'it shows. No one would mistake you now for the oldest failed Apt ever to serve the Congery.

'As for you, my lady,' she went on, turning to Terisa, 'you are less clear to me. Your surprises are better concealed, I think. You both have a great deal to tell me.'

'That's true, my lady Queen,' Geraden said at once. His awareness of how hard that job would be showed in the way he asked, 'But what of yourself? Won't you first tell us how you are? And Torrent?'

The Queen shook her head. 'What I tell you of myself will depend entirely on whether you were sent here by that old dodderer the King. I have asked you that once, but you did not answer clearly.'

For a moment, Geraden measured his reply. Then he said flatly, 'King Joyse didn't send us. I think he would be *astonished* if he knew we were here.'

Queen Madin appeared to receive this information as if it inflicted a deep hurt which she had no intention of showing. As she spoke, however, she couldn't muffle the roughness in her voice. 'In that case, Geraden – Torrent and I are well. But not as well as we would be if our family were whole again. The King's aberrations exact a price from us all.

'Will you not be seated?' she continued, shaking herself out of her thoughts. 'Here is wine.' The servant had reentered the room carrying a silver tray. 'And Torrent will be with us soon, I am sure.

'Ah,' the Queen concluded as the door opened again, 'here she is now.'

Terisa turned in time to see King Joyse and Queen Madin's second daughter close the door behind her and approach the fire.

Torrent's carriage and downcast eyes and demure gown conveyed two impressions almost simultaneously: first, she was so shy that she made Myste and Elega seem as extroverted as mountebanks; and second, despite her shyness, she was nearly the image of her mother. She could have been Queen Madin's shadow: they were as alike as reflections of each other. Only her mother's decisiveness was missing, her mother's assurance.

'Torrent,' the Queen said, 'here are Geraden and the lady Terisa of Morgan. They have a great deal to tell us. She has done something all the Masters of the Congery together could not do. She has made him an Imager.'

Torrent paused among the chairs. The gaze which she raised beneath her lashes was at once so hesitant and so full of wonder that Terisa blushed involuntarily.

'Under the circumstances,' Geraden muttered humorously – perhaps for Torrent's benefit, perhaps for Terisa's – 'I don't think that's much of a compliment. The only benefit I've gotten from the change is that now people want to kill me.

'My lady Torrent,' he went on, 'I'm glad to see you. When you and the Queen left Orison, I didn't think I'd ever have that privilege again.'

'Oh, "privilege," Geraden.' Torrent spoke as if she, too, were blushing; yet her cheeks remained pale, untouched. 'You're making fun of me.'

Before he could reply – perhaps so that he wouldn't have a chance to reply – she came abruptly toward Terisa. Facing Terisa as if holding her chin up were an act of courage, she said, 'I'm sure Mother has made you welcome, my lady, but let me welcome you also. Grandfather – the Fayle – told us everything he knew about you, but it only made us more curious. I'm afraid we'll exhaust you with questions.'

'Please.' Terisa had no idea why she was blushing. She made a special effort to speak calmly, comfortably, to put Torrent at ease. 'Call me Terisa. Both Myste and Elega do.'

That brought a smile to Torrent's face, a lift of self-confidence. 'Do you know Myste and Elega? I suppose you must, since you've been in Orison. Are you friends? How are they?' After an instant of hesitation, a quick glance at Queen Madin, she asked, 'And Father? How is he?'

'Torrent,' the Queen said both kindly and firmly, 'we must sit down. If we do not, Geraden and the lady Terisa will remain standing all night.'

In a convincing imitation of a woman with no will of her own, Torrent immediately sat down in the nearest chair.

Queen Madin took an armchair near the fire. Geraden and Terisa seated themselves on a couch between the Queen and her daughter. Promptly, the servant brought around goblets of wine on a tray, then set the wine down near Torrent and withdrew.

'You are tired from your journey,' Queen Madin said after she had tasted her wine. 'We will bathe and feed you shortly. You will be given all the rest you can allow yourselves. But you must understand that we are hungry for news. In Vale House, we do not hear even rumors from Romish, not to mention truth from Orison. How *are* Elega and Myste?' Just for an instant, her throat closed. 'How is the King?'

Now Geraden hesitated; the change Queen Madin had observed seemed to desert him momentarily. Which made perfect sense to Terisa. Her heart was suddenly thick, and she felt an ache gathering around her. It was possible that the Queen and Torrent would take the news of King Joyse gladly: possible, but very unlikely.

'This is difficult,' Geraden murmured awkwardly. 'I can't really tell you anything without telling you everything – and I don't know where to start. I can't think of any way to say this that won't be hurtful.'

Torrent studied her hands, but Terisa could see that she was breathing deeply to steady herself. Queen Madin, on the other hand, faced Geraden's uncertainty without blinking.

'Tell us the truth,' she said bluntly. 'Speculation will be more hurtful to us than any news.'

Still Geraden faltered.

Grimly, because the only thing worse than knowledge was ignorance, Terisa said, 'The King knows what he's doing. He's doing it on purpose.'

Torrent didn't raise her eyes; she seemed to freeze in her seat.

'"On purpose,"' Queen Madin echoed slowly. 'My lady, you must explain that observation.'

'Unfortunately, it's true,' Geraden rushed in. 'Terisa knows more about King Joyse's reasons and intentions than anybody else. She's had several talks with him – he answered questions for her. He's gone out of his way to give her explanations. I think it's because of the way she came to Orison. An impossible translation – or we all thought it was impossible until I realized I can do it anytime I want. She was so obviously important. She's involved in the Congery's augury. We didn't know what her talent is, but it was obvious she had to have some kind of unprecedented power.'

Abruptly, he made himself stop. Speaking distinctly, he said, 'The last we heard, Elega is fine. We don't know about Myste.'

'It's a trap, my lady Queen,' Terisa tried to explain. 'He's setting a trap for his enemies, for Mordant's enemies. They were too powerful – and he didn't know who they were. And he was afraid that they would keep getting stronger – that they might swallow Alend or Cadwal or both – and leave him alone while they got stronger and stronger, until they were too strong for him, too strong for anyone. He was afraid that if he didn't find out who his enemies were and stop them he would lose everything.'

'That was true,' the Queen put in crisply. 'Any fool could see it.'

'So,' Terisa went on with an inward groan, 'he made himself weak.'

Queen Madin stared at her. 'I do not believe you. What nonsense! What good is weakness? How is it used against Imagers and armies?'

She might have said more, but Geraden intervened. The unexpected authority in the way he raised his hand stopped her. 'Listen to us, my lady Queen,' he breathed gently. 'Please listen.'

'I'm sorry,' Terisa murmured. 'It's the truth. It's all we have.

'He paralyzed his own strength. He made it impossible for the Congery to do anything effectively. He undercut the Castellan. He abandoned the

Perdon without reinforcements. He insulted Prince Kragen – the Fayle probably told you that. He made himself look like a fool. He' – her voice caught briefly – 'he did his best to drive his family away.' She thought she ought to mention the Tor's son, but she didn't have the heart for it. 'He practically punished people like Geraden for being loyal.'

Queen Madin sat without moving a muscle, listened without any reaction except a slow reddening of her cheeks. Torrent was breathing so hard she was almost panting.

'My lady Queen, he made himself a *target*. So that his enemies would attack *him*, instead of chewing Alend and Cadwal and Mordant up slowly until they were too strong to be beaten. It was all a ruse, a trick to make his enemies try to destroy him before they became strong enough to be safe.'

The Domne had put his finger on it. King Joyse wanted to save the world. He hurt all the people he loved best because saving the world was more important to him than anything else.

That was a terrible burden for him to bear.

On the other hand, it wasn't exactly easy for the people he loved.

Without warning – and almost without transition, as if she had been secretly standing all along – Queen Madin swept to her feet. 'Why?' she demanded in a voice that made Terisa want to hide under the couch. 'If this is true, why did he not tell me?' She didn't shout, but her tone had the impact of a yell. 'Did he not trust me? Did he believe that I would not understand? – that I would not *approve*?'

Geraden stood to face her. 'My lady Queen,' he asked softly, intently, 'what would you have done if he told you?'

'I would not have *come here*.' The Queen might as well have been shouting. 'I would have stood by him, instead of allowing all the world to think that I have lost my love for him and his ideals and the realm.'

Geraden gave Terisa a look full of pain and sorrow, a look that brought her to her feet at his side, but he didn't back down. 'That's the problem, my lady Queen. You would have stood by him. And as long as you were there, no one would believe he was collapsing. Not really. Or if they did believe it, they would know you were there to make decisions for him, Queen Madin, daughter of the Fayle, the most formidable woman in Orison. His trap would have failed. No one would fall into it.

'And if he had asked you to leave?' Geraden went on. 'If he had explained his trap and asked you to cooperate by abandoning him? Could you have borne it? Could you have sat on your hands here for – what is it, two years now? – while he risked his life and everything you both believe in?'

He was right: this was hurtful with a vengeance. Nevertheless Terisa was certain these things had to be said. She was just grateful that she wasn't the one saying them.

And Queen Madin was hurt: that was unmistakable. She had been dealt a blow which shook her to the bone.

'My lady Queen,' Geraden concluded in a voice thick with regret, 'if this policy is to succeed – if there's any chance to save Mordant – what else could he have done?'

'Oh, Father.' Torrent was so distressed that she watched Geraden's face openly, without shyness, without self-consciousness. 'What have I done? I should have stayed with you. Like Myste and Elega.'

'No, Torrent.' Queen Madin tried to speak as if she had no tears spilling down her cheeks, no grief in her chest. 'We would have broken his heart. It was a hard thing for him to drive us away. It would have been terrible to try to drive us away and fail – and so lose the chance to save his kingdom.'

'But he's caused all this pain' – sitting, Torrent looked small and helpless, too little to understand or be consoled – 'and we left him to endure it alone. I left him. He has no wish to cause pain. His heart is broken already, or he wouldn't have done something so desperate—'

Despite her own hurt, the Queen gave her daughter a comforting response. 'Hush, child. Do not be in a hurry to call him desperate. Your father has always been given to risks. We must not believe the worst until it is proven.'

Then she wiped her eyes and faced Geraden and Terisa squarely. 'Now,' she said in a tone of barely concealed ferocity, 'you must tell us what the outcome of the King's weakness has been.'

Geraden nodded. Terisa murmured, 'Yes.'

In pieces back and forth as details and developments occurred to them, they told their story as coherently as they could.

And while they told it, Queen Madin became another woman before their eyes. She seemed to find sustenance in the events they described, the implications they discussed. She knew, of course, about the disaster of the Congery's champion, and about Master Eremis' strange attempt to make an alliance of the lords of the Cares, Prince Kragen, and the Congery: reminders of that information had no effect on her now. But the presence – and the freedom – of the High King's Monomach in Orison made her straighten her shoulders. King Joyse's treatment of the Perdon and Prince Kragen seemed to strengthen her bones. Myste's foolish and gallant pursuit of the champion caused her eyes to glow. And Elega's plot with Nyle and Prince Kragen to betray Orison – which Geraden explained with considerable difficulty because it, too, must be hurtful – seemed to bring a flush of youth to the Queen's cheeks. 'Brave Elega,' she murmured as if she would have done the same thing in her daughter's place. But when she heard that Orison was besieged, she snapped like a soldier, 'Then why are you *here*? Why are you not *there*, fighting for King Joyse and Mordant?'

'My lady Queen,' replied Geraden, 'we still have a lot to tell you.'

Just for a second, the Queen paused – not hesitating, but simply allowing the forces inside her time to come together. Then, surprisingly, she said, 'Let it wait. Until dinner, perhaps. I have no time for it now.'

At once, she clapped her hands twice, summoning a servant.

Almost immediately, the servant who had brought the wine came into the room. Without a glance at her guests, she commanded, 'Please conduct Geraden and the lady Terisa to their rooms. Supply them with bathwater and clean clothes. Announce dinner for them in an hour. Then bring the Fayle's men to me.

'Come, Torrent. We must prepare.'

As the servant bowed, Queen Madin swept toward the door as regally as if she had an entire procession behind her.

671

With a flustered look, Torrent jumped up and hurried after her mother.

Geraden met Terisa's gaze in quick apprehension; then he mustered his temerity to ask, demand, 'My lady Queen, what're you going to do?'

Queen Madin paused in the doorway. '"Do," Geraden? My husband and my home are besieged. One of my daughters has allied herself with Alends. Another – if she still lives – is embarked on a mad quest after a champion from another world. I will not be left out of such events. I am going to Orison.

'I intend to be there in three days.'

She left the room with Torrent nearly gasping in her wake.

For a long moment, Terisa and Geraden stood where they were as if they expected the ceiling to collapse on them. Then she took hold of herself, made an effort to shake the surprise out of her head. To break the shock, she murmured, 'Well, at least she's going to let us have time for a bath and some food.'

He snorted. 'I should have guessed something like this would happen. I've known her long enough.

'The truth is' – he shrugged rather helplessly – 'I've always liked her.'

Terisa was quietly disturbed to find herself thinking of her own mother, who hadn't resembled Queen Madin in any meaningful way. And she, Terisa, could so easily have become her mother's image: passive and wan, all her passion kept secret. If Geraden hadn't come for her—

Slipping her arm like a promise through his, she accompanied him out of the sitting room.

Dinner at the long table in the formal dining room of Vale House was an odd experience.

An abundance of candles made the ornaments and paneling glitter. There was a deep rug underfoot, thick cushions on the chairs. The food was good, better than anything Terisa and Geraden had eaten for quite a while; the wine was almost equal to the food. And the sensation of being clean again from head to toe, of being wrapped in clean clothes, of having a clean bed to look forward to, was so luxurious that it seemed practically indecent.

In addition, Torrent was fascinated by the personal side of Terisa and Geraden's story. Before she finished her soup, she was so caught up in what she heard that she forgot to be shy. She was indignant at Master Eremis' manipulations, horrified by Master Quillon's murder. Terisa's repeated rescues from Gart thrilled her. She grieved for Castellan Lebbick, and yet couldn't refrain from shuddering at the things the Castellan had done to Terisa. Artagel's injuries and Nyle's unhappiness touched her heart. The discovery of talent in her guests filled her with wonder. She heard about the destruction of Houseldon and the danger to Sternwall with parted lips and flushed cheeks.

Unwittingly, unself-consciously, she helped make the meal as pleasant as possible for her guests.

It was Queen Madin who provided the occasion with its oddness. She didn't appear to hear a word either Terisa or Geraden said.

She wasn't vague or befuddled: she was simply absent. Her attention was so sharply focused elsewhere that she had none to spare for such comparative details as Master Eremis' mendacity or Castellan Lebbick's accumulated distress.

As a result, neither Geraden nor Terisa was able to relax. Unexpectedly, she found herself thinking that the Queen was rather an old woman to attempt something as arduous as a wild ride to Orison. So she resolved to speak to Torrent privately after supper, to ask whether there was anything Torrent could do to dissuade the Queen.

Unfortunately, when Queen Madin announced the end of dinner she took Torrent with her at once. Instead of saying good night, she informed her guests that the men who had brought them here would procure a team of horses from Romish, 'So that we need not stop too often on the road. We will depart as soon as the mounts are able to see their footing.' Then she led Torrent away.

Terisa returned with Geraden to her room, troubled by the sense that this visit to the Queen wasn't producing the results she had intended. Whatever those were.

When they were alone, she asked him, 'Is this a good idea?'

'What?' he replied disingenuously, 'this rush to reach Orison in only three days?'

She poked his shoulder to get his attention. 'Of course, you idiot. What else did you think I was talking about? Isn't she a little old to try something like that?'

He snickered. '*You* tell her she's too old – if you've got the nerve.' Before Terisa could poke him again, however, he tried to give her a serious answer. 'It isn't the ride I'm worried about. Either she can do it or she can't. Either way, it's out of our hands. What I'm worried about is the siege. Prince Kragen and his ten thousand Alends. Or, worse yet, High King Festten and twice that many Cadwals.

'How does she propose to get past them into Orison? Assuming it hasn't already been taken. When they find out who she is, they aren't exactly going to step aside for her. She's the perfect hostage. King Joyse may have been able to turn his back on the Perdon. He may have been able to swallow what happened to the Tor's son. He may even have been able to let Myste and Elega go. But he is not' – Geraden said the words distinctly, like drum beats – 'going to be able to sit still when someone like the High King threatens his wife.

'She's the only weapon Alend or Cadwal needs to beat him.'

At the thought, Terisa's stomach turned over. 'Oh, good,' she muttered. 'I'm so glad you told me that.'

'Sleep well,' he replied with a malicious grin and rolled away from her.

She had to poke him several times to get him back where he belonged.

For a variety of reasons, neither of them slept much. Long before dawn, they got up, got dressed, and went to help with the preparations for the road.

Outside the protective stone of the manor, the air seemed colder than it had for several days. Even in the gray light before the sun came up, the day had an almost prescient clarity, a dimension of visual precision which made

Terisa shiver. She hugged the half cloak the Termigan had given her around her shoulders and tried not to think about how tired she was.

The boards of the porch creaked under her feet.

From the porch of Vale House, the hills which enfolded the Kolted River appeared to bulk larger than they had the previous evening. They were dark in the dim forecasting of dawn, deep with potential; the whole world lay beyond them, completely hidden. They reminded her that Vale House would be easy to ambush.

On the other hand, an ambush didn't seem very likely at the moment. Even self-respecting villains and traitors were still in bed at this hour. And the Fayle's two men were already there, along with a groom they had brought from Romish to care for the horses and a servant to look after the needs of the ladies Queen Madin and Torrent. As for the horses—

There must have been sixteen or seventeen of them, filling the hollow between the manor and the river. Terisa's and Geraden's mounts. Horses for the four men and the two ladies. A pack animal to carry supplies. And a second mount for everyone, so that the horses could be rested while the Queen kept moving.

They shuffled their hooves, shook their manes; two or three of them snorted disconsolately. Their tack jangled softly, muffled by leather. The groom moved among them, settling the saddles of the ones that would be ridden first, cinching up their girths. Queen Madin's servant was busy checking the contents of his packs again.

Because she was cold and had to do something, Terisa asked Geraden, 'Do you think we should try to stop her?'

He shrugged; the dimness hid his expression. 'I'll try. But don't get your hopes up.'

The sky spanning the hills grew to the color of mother-of-pearl, but without that nacreous flatness: it was at once deep and impenetrable. If anything, the approach of dawn made the hills darker; they clenched themselves around the river and Vale House, brooding. Nevertheless a stretch of water near the bend of the hills caught the air's reflection and gleamed silver.

Terisa wished that she could stop shivering.

After a moment, Queen Madin came out onto the porch with Torrent beside her. The light was improving: Terisa saw that both ladies were wrapped in warm cloaks; riding boots protected their feet and calves; they had scarves bound around their heads to keep their hair out of their faces.

'Are we ready?' the Queen asked anyone who could answer her. 'Can we go?'

'In a moment, my lady Queen,' replied the groom. He was busy inspecting the hooves of the horses.

Geraden cleared his throat. 'My lady Queen, are you sure this is wise? I have qualms about it.'

'Geraden' – Queen Madin wasn't looking at him; her gaze was fixed on the sharp outline of the hills – 'you underestimate me if you think that any "qualms" of yours will stand between me and my husband.'

674

He let a little sharpness into his voice. 'Maybe *you* underestimate *me*, my lady Queen. You don't know what my qualms are.'

'Do I not?' She still didn't look at him. 'You are concerned that I may fall hostage to the forces besieging Orison.'

'Yes,' he admitted. His tone told Terisa that he felt rather foolish.

'That is an important concern. I have no intention of allowing any Alend or Cadwal to use me against the King.' She paused, then said, 'It will be your duty to help me insure that the difficulty does not arise.'

'Yes, my lady Queen,' Geraden murmured glumly.

Terisa put her hand on his arm and gave him a small squeeze of consolation.

'Now, my lady Queen,' the groom announced over the champing and rustling of the horses. 'You can mount whenever you wish.'

Torrent gave a stifled gasp. 'A moment,' she said quickly. 'I have forgotten something.' Before anyone could react, she hurried back into the manor.

Softly, so that no one except Terisa and Geraden heard her, the Queen breathed, 'Probably one of her dolls. She does not like to sleep without her dolls.' Her tone was affectionate, but it suggested that she didn't know how she had managed to produce a daughter like Torrent.

It was astonishing how distinct everything was to Terisa. Every one of the hills across the river had a particular shape, an individual character. Each of the mounts was facing in a different direction, stubbornly determined to see life from its own angle. Geraden held his head up as if he had caught some of the Queen's mood. Queen Madin herself was a knot of controlled impatience. The groom and the servant waited. The Fayle's men had begun to move toward the porch in order to help the ladies mount.

And *a touch of cold as thin as a feather and as sharp as steel slid straight through the center of her abdomen.*

'*Geraden!*' she shouted, almost wailed because her desperation was so sudden. 'There's a translation coming!'

As if she and Geraden had the same mind, the same will, they grabbed Queen Madin by her arms, one on each side, and practically flung her off the porch, down the steps, out among the abruptly milling horses.

Terisa had time to hear one of the men curse as if a horse had kicked him. She registered the Queen's quick gasp of surprise, her swift self-command. She felt rather than saw the tethered mounts twist their heavy bodies around her, blunder against each other, stumble, start to panic.

Then she turned in time to see a fall of rock appear out of the empty sky and crash down on the roof of Vale House.

A fall of rock as massive as an avalanche. A few heavy, bounding stones hit, followed instantly by rushing thunder, the side of a mountain coming down.

The slates and beams of the roof couldn't hold, couldn't begin to think of holding. Almost without transition, the whole attic storey of the manor buckled and collapsed, plunging down into the level where the bedrooms were.

'Torrent!' cried Queen Madin. Without thinking, she twisted against Terisa and Geraden's grasp, tried to run back into the house. '*Torrent!*'

Terisa helped Geraden drag the Queen backward.

675

A frightened horse hit them with its hindquarters and knocked them all off balance.

The rockfall went on with a sound as if the hills themselves had begun to rumble and break. The bedroom level of the manor held until too many tons of rubble piled into it; then, one room at a time, it crumbled toward the ground floor.

Bouncing like balls, huge rocks came off the pile into the hollow. A horse screamed horribly; others squealed, wheeling in wild circles. They were tethered, had no way to escape. Behind Terisa, the groom was trampled to death. She didn't know how any of the stones missed her. The rockfall and the horses made so much noise that she couldn't hear any of the stones splash into the river; couldn't hear any cries, commands, any warnings.

Slowly, almost one stone at a time, the avalanche thinned. The rush of rock turned to scree and gravel, loose dirt.

Terisa stared in shock as the thunder subsided and huge clouds of dust swelled into the dawn.

The fact that she wasn't moving nearly got her killed.

There were men on horseback in the middle of the chaos, at least half a dozen of them. They lashed their beasts among the tethered mounts.

One of them clubbed Geraden to the ground; he never knew they were coming. Another knocked Terisa into a swirl of panic-stricken hooves.

And yet somehow, before she covered her head and curled into a ball to protect herself from being stamped on and broken, she had time to see three men leap from their mounts and snatch up the Queen.

She had time to see that they were armed and armored just like the men of Prince Kragen's army.

They were Alends.

Then hooves danced on all sides of her, thudded the dirt, hammered at her life, and she couldn't do anything except cling to herself and clench her eyes shut until the horses either killed her or backed away.

They backed away. Geraden was on his feet: he yelled at the horses, slapped at them until they retreated. At once, he reached down and pulled her to her feet.

'The Queen!' he panted as if he had broken something in his chest. 'What happened to the Queen?'

At the same time, another woman cried from the bottom of her heart, 'Mother? Mother!'

Staggering, Terisa turned; she dragged Geraden with her.

Torrent stood amid the ruins of the porch as if she had never been touched. Her arms were locked and rigid at her sides; one of her hands clutched a knife. She didn't look down into the hollow, at the horses, down at Terisa and Geraden; her face was lifted to the sky.

'*Mother!*'

Terisa stumbled in that direction, out of the confusion of horses, trying to reach the Queen's daughter before Torrent went mad. With Geraden behind her, she clambered among the splintered and canting remains of the porch.

'She wasn't killed!' she answered Torrent's wail, shouting to make herself heard over the memory of thunder. 'They took her! She's been kidnapped!'

Master Eremis had sprung another of his imponderable traps. But this one changed everything. Alends—! He was in league with Alends? As well as Gart and the High King? What in the name of heaven was going *on*?

Terisa's shout snapped Torrent's head down, brought her frantic gaze out of the sky to Terisa's face.

'What?'

And Geraden demanded fiercely, 'What? Kidnapped?'

'Soldiers came.' Terisa could hardly distinguish between her own voice and the long, deep rumble echoing inside her. 'Alend soldiers. They took her. That's why this happened. So they would have a chance to take her.'

'*Alend* soldiers?' Geraden began to snarl uncharacteristic obscenities, ones Terisa had never heard him use before.

'Why?' Torrent asked softly, as if she were being split apart.

'Because she's so important!' Geraden rasped at once. 'King Joyse will do anything to save her. He'll surrender Orison and the Congery and every one of us to save her.'

Slowly, Torrent raised her knife, stared at it. 'It's my fault.' Terisa was amazed that Torrent wasn't weeping. The Queen's daughter sounded like she was weeping. 'I wanted to take a knife. So I could help defend us. Elega would have been ready for that. Myste would have been ready. But I forgot. I ran to the kitchen.' She turned the blade from side to side as if she had the idea of stabbing herself. 'If I'd been with her – if I hadn't forgotten – I could have saved her. I could have tried to save her.'

There was no doubt about it in Terisa's mind: Torrent was going mad.

If she had gone to her bedroom, as her mother had expected, instead of to the kitchen, she would have been killed almost instantly.

'No!' Terisa replied as loudly as she could, trying to convey conviction through her mounting sense of horror. 'None of us could have saved her. They took us by surprise. The horses caused too much confusion. The men—'

Abruptly, she pivoted away to see what had happened to the groom, the servant, the Fayle's men.

The dawn was brighter now: it didn't raise much color, but it showed everything clearly.

A hoof had crushed the groom's head: he lay in the dirt as if he were abasing himself. One of the Fayle's men clutched at an incapacitating wound in his left shoulder; the other had been hacked to death. Dead and dying horses sprawled everywhere, some of them still quivering. Perhaps ten of the beasts remained alive, but of those at least half showed injuries of one kind or another.

In the middle of the carnage, Queen Madin's servant knelt beside his mount, whimpering for his life.

Swallowing nausea, Terisa whipped herself back to face Torrent. 'None of us could have saved her,' she repeated hoarsely.

'Then' – Torrent's voice shook wildly, but she drew herself up as if she had become a different woman – 'we must rescue her.'

Terisa stared at her, shocked by the strange sensation that she could see King Joyse in Torrent's eyes.

'How?' With a visible effort, Geraden forced himself to speak gently, reasonably. 'We don't have any weapons – and there aren't enough of us. By the time we get help from Romish, they'll be long gone. They'll have plenty of time to hide their trail.'

Torrent shook her head. 'Not Romish.' She took several deep breaths as if she were hyperventilating, with the result that she was then able to control the wobble in her voice. 'You must get help from Orison.'

Both Geraden and Terisa gaped at her.

'They will not hide their trail from me. I will follow and make a new one behind them. I am helpless for everything else, but that I can do. He' – she indicated the man with the badly cut shoulder – 'will get support for me from Romish. But you must ride to Orison. You must warn Father.'

She had lost her mind. There was no question about it.

Torrent couldn't entirely stifle her rising hysteria. 'Do you not understand? It is his only hope!'

Terisa and Geraden stared at her, gaped, held their breath – and suddenly he gasped, 'She's right!' He grabbed at Terisa's arm, wheeling toward the horses. 'Come on! We've got to get out of here!'

Terisa froze: she couldn't move at all. Get out of here. Of course. Why didn't I think of that? Ride like crazy people halfway across Mordant to Orison, while she goes after those Alends and her mother *alone*. You've done this once before. Don't you remember? You sent Argus after Prince Kragen, and he got killed. And stopping Nyle didn't do us any good.

'*Terisa*,' he demanded. 'I tell you, she's *right*. It's his only hope.'

'What—?' She couldn't make her throat work. An avalanche had come *this close* to falling on her. Like the collapse of the Congery's meeting hall. 'What're you talking about?'

In response, Geraden made one of his supreme and unselfish efforts to control himself for her sake. Intensely, he said, 'His only hope is if he finds out what happened to her before the people who took her know he knows. Before they can tell him. Before they start trying to use her against him. During that gap – if we can give him a gap – between when he knows and when they know he knows – he can still act. He can do something to save her. Or himself.'

'Yes,' Torrent breathed. 'It is the only thing I can do.'

Abruptly, she climbed out of the ruin of the porch, heading toward the horses. Her knife was still gripped in her fist.

As if she were her mother, she commanded the injured man, 'Take a horse, ride to Romish. You'll be tended there. Tell them what happened. Tell them I require help. I'll leave a trail for them.' Then her tone softened. 'You're badly hurt, I know. There's nothing I can do for you. I must attempt to save the Queen – and my father's realm.'

As if she were accustomed to extreme decisions – not to mention horses – she chose a horse, untethered it, and swung up into the saddle.

Terisa would have tried to stop her, but Geraden's acquiescence held her. 'Geraden—' she murmured, pleading with him. 'Geraden—'

'Terisa,' he replied, so full of certainty that she couldn't argue with him, 'she's right. I've got the strongest feeling she's right.'

'Farewell, Geraden,' Torrent broke in. 'Farewell, my lady Terisa. Save the King.

'Do that, and together we will rescue Queen Madin.'

Geraden turned to give the King's daughter a formal bow. 'Farewell also, my lady Torrent. This story will fill King Joyse with pride, whatever comes of it.' A moment later, he added, 'And both Myste and Elega are going to be *impressed*.'

That almost made Torrent smile.

Alone, she rode out of the hollow on the trail of Queen Madin's abductors.

Terisa put the best tourniquet she could manage on the wounded man's shoulder. Gritting his teeth, Geraden slapped a measure of sense into the Queen's whimpering servant, then instructed him to make sure the Fayle's man reached Romish.

After that, they selected the two best horses, packed a third to carry their supplies, and started toward the Demesne and Orison.

THIRTY-SEVEN

POISED FOR
VICTORY

The Alend army didn't move.

It hadn't moved for days.

Oh, Prince Kragen kept his men busy enough: he was determined to be ready for anything. But he didn't waste another catapult; didn't risk any kind of sortie, much less a massed assault; didn't make anything more than covert efforts to spy on the castle. In fact, the only thing he apparently did to advance his siege was to completely prevent anyone from getting into or out of Orison: he cut King Joyse off from any conceivable source of news. Other than that, he and his forces might as well have been engaged in training exercises.

He was busy in other ways, of course. For instance, he had quite a number of men out at all times, furtively searching for some sign of the Congery's champion. Knowing what the champion had done to Orison, Prince Kragen felt a positive dislike for the prospect of being attacked from behind by that lone fighter. In addition, he spent quite a bit of time, both alone and with his father, trying to fathom King Joyse's daughters.

But King Joyse's warnings haunted him – and Master Quillon's. He took no direct action to hasten the fall of Orison.

That changed during the night which Terisa and Geraden had spent with Queen Madin.

Naturally, Prince Kragen had no way of knowing where Terisa and Geraden were. He couldn't know that they had ever left Orison – or that Mordant's need was coming to a crisis around him.

On the other hand, he was alert to every outward sign of what was happening in the castle.

When the men who had the duty of watching the ramparts more closely after dark reported to him that they heard shouts and turmoil, saw lights in the vicinity of the curtain-wall, he didn't hesitate: he sent half a dozen hand-picked scouts to creep as near to the wall as possible, climb it if necessary, and find out what was going on.

The news they brought back tightened excitement or dread around his heart.

There was a riot taking place on the other side of the curtain-wall.

Apparently, the overcrowded and raw-nerved populace of Orison was breaking into active rebellion against Castellan Lebbick.

After a while, the noise receded, as if the riot were moving into the main body of the castle. But light continued to show at the rim of the wall, blazing up in gusts like a fire out of control. And when dawn came the Prince saw dirty plumes of smoke curling upward from the wound in Orison's side, giving the castle a look of death it hadn't had since the day the champion had first injured it.

Again, Prince Kragen didn't hesitate: he had spent the night preparing his response. At his signal, fifty men carrying a battering ram in a protective frame ran forward to try the gates. The walls and roof which received the arrows of the defenders made the ram look as unwieldy as a shed; but the use of the frame could be an effective tactic, as long as the gate failed before the defenders had time to ready a counterattack – or as long as they were distracted by trouble elsewhere.

As a distraction, Prince Kragen sent several hundred soldiers with storming ladders and grappling hooks to assail the curtain-wall.

Unfortunately, Orison's guards proved equal to the occasion. A tub of lamp oil and a burning fagot turned the ram's protective frame into a charnal. And the Castellan – or whoever had taken command after the riot – had obviously expected the attack on the curtain-wall; so the defense there had been reinforced.

When Prince Kragen saw that his men were taking more than their share of losses and getting nowhere, he chewed his moustache, swore, and shook his fists at the sky – all inwardly, in the privacy of his thoughts, so that no one witnessed his frustration. Then he ordered a withdrawal.

Rather tentatively, as if sensing the Prince's state, one of his captains commented, 'Well, they have to run out of oil *some*time.'

Prince Kragen swore again – out loud, this time. Then he instructed the captain to begin raiding the surrounding villages and trees for wood: he wanted more battering rams, more protective frames. And while that raid was underway, he set about using up the rams and frames he already had.

If the defenders had left any of the battering rams he now sent against them alone, they would have soon learned that none of the rams had enough men with it to actually threaten the gates. This time, however – for once! – his tactics succeeded. The defenders faithfully burned every ram and frame to charcoal.

The Prince grinned grimly under his moustache. Apparently, Castellan Lebbick – or whoever had replaced him after the riot – was still human enough to be outwitted once in a while.

The riot which had taken place in Orison that night was an ugly one.

It had a number of excuses. The castle was indeed overcrowded, badly so – detail which became increasingly onerous for everyone as the siege wore on. And of course the siege had come at the end of a hard winter, before spring could do anybody any good; so supplies were relatively short, and everything from food and water to blankets and space was strictly – a swelling number of people said *harshly* – rationed. By Castellan Lebbick, naturally. Despite Master Eremis' heroic replenishment of the reservoir.

And Orison's surplus population had nothing to do. Nobody really had anything to do. As long as the Alend army just sat there with all their heads crammed up the Prince's ass – as one tired old guard put it – nobody had any outlet for long days of pent-up fear.

Why didn't Prince Kragen *do* something?

Where was High King Festten?

For that matter, where was the Perdon?

How much longer was this going to go on?

Tempers grew ragged; hostility fed on frustration and uselessness; grievances multiplied in all directions. Orison's sewers kept backing up because the drainfields weren't adequate to the population. And the leaders of Orison, the men in command – King Joyse, Castellan Lebbick, Master Barsonage – did nothing to ease the pressure. They all went about their lives in isolation, as if the burgeoning misery sealed within these walls were immaterial to them. Even the castle's most comfortable inhabitants – men of position, women of privilege – were in an ugly mood; and the ugliness was spreading.

But even ugliness couldn't function in a vacuum: it needed a focus, a target.

It needed the Castellan.

He would have been a likely candidate in any case. After all, the responsibility for deciding and implementing Orison's distress was on his shoulders. Merchants and farmers had time to become bitter about the confiscation of their goods. Mothers with sick children had cause to complain about the rationing of medicines. People with a normal need for activity – and privacy – didn't have anyone else to blame for the lack of those necessities.

The guards, however, were loyal to their commander. Most of them had had years to become familiar with his loyalties – to them as well as to King Joyse. And they were accustomed to taking his orders. One way or another, they worked to control the pressure building against the Castellan.

As a result, there was no riot – no outbreak of resentment – until someone threw a spark into the tinder of Orison's mood.

That someone was Saddith.

She was on her feet now, able to get around. Despite the loss of a few teeth, and the rather dramatic damage done to the rest of her face, she was able to talk. And that was what she had been doing ever since she had healed enough to climb out of her sickbed: getting around; talking.

She had started with every man in Orison who had ever visited between her legs – or had let her know he'd like to visit. She had told those men what the Castellan had done to her, and why: she had gone to his bed out of simple pity for his loneliness, out of compassion for the pressure he was under; and he had hurt her *here*, and *here*, and *here*. But as her strength returned she broadened her range. She carried her injuries everywhere in public: her left hand broken and useless, the right nearly so; her face so badly battered that it would never regain its shape, one cheek crushed, one eye unable to close properly, scars in all directions. If anything, she wore her blouses unbuttoned farther than before, enabling the world to see what Lebbick had done to her there.

And everywhere she went, her message was the same.

You sods were quick enough for fornication when I had my beauty. If you were men now, you'd hoist Castellan Lebbick's balls on a stick.

His violence had no reason and no justification: it was as senseless as it was brutal. As senseless as all the other little brutalities he committed throughout the castle.

How long would it be before some other helpless woman received the same treatment? How long would it be before brutality became the governing principle in Orison?

How much longer will you sods and sheepfuckers permit this to go on?

Of course, when she spoke to women – which she did often, more every day – her words were different. Her message, however, remained the same.

Her disfigurement, as well as her intensity, made her impossible to look away from. She compelled stares and pity; nausea and indignation. It was impossible to look at her and not feel fear.

Because of the way she talked, and the way the men who had once reveled in her talked, and the way the women who were terrified of the same fate talked, this fear took the form of a call for justice, a thinly concealed demand for retribution. With Alend just outside, rape and murder were on everybody's mind.

At the time, few people had any notion of how this demand came to be translated into action. One day, people were growling to each other, muttering vague threats which they had no actual intention of acting on: the next, rumors seemed to filter everywhere that voices would be raised, justice insisted upon; action taken. Come to the disused ballroom this evening, the great hall where King Joyse and Queen Madin were married, and where the peace of Mordant had been celebrated.

Oh, yes? Whose idea was this?

No one knew.

We're besieged. Is it really a good idea to challenge the Castellan at a time like this?

Perhaps not. But it's gone too far to be stopped. Better to support it, make sure it succeeds, than take the chance he'll be able to crush it – the chance he'll be left alone to do something worse the next time.

Yes. All right.

So that evening the crowd began to gather in the high, vast, dusty ballroom. At first, it was plainly a crowd rather than a mob, despite the fact that its numbers quickly swelled to several hundred: the fear threatening to become violence was counterbalanced by uncertainty; by habits of mind learned during many years of King Joyse's peaceful rule; by the perfectly reasonable idea that it was dangerous to weaken Orison during a siege; by the manifest presence of Castellan Lebbick's guards all around the hall. Nevertheless, as darkness deepened outside the windows, the only light came from torches which someone had thought to provide, and the erratic illumination of the flames had a disturbing effect on faces and rationality. People began to look garish to each other, wild and strange; the air was full of grotesque shadows; the atmosphere seemed to flicker. And through the shadows and the orange-yellow light Saddith appeared, around and around in the ballroom, displaying her wounds, speaking of outrage. The seething murmur of several hundred voices took shape in fits and bursts as more and more people found occasion to say the name *Lebbick*.

Lebbick.

And the guard captain who had been detailed to preserve order made a mistake.

He was a tough old fighter with bottomless determination and not much intelligence; and during one of King Joyse's battles the Castellan had saved his entire family from being cut down when they were caught in the path of an Alend raid. He heard all these whimpering shitholes – they were practically puking with self-pity – start to mutter *Lebbick*, *Lebbick*, as if they had the right, and he decided that the crowd had to be dispersed.

Even though the odds were against him, he might have succeeded if he had been able to drive people out of the ballroom back into the public halls and passages. Unfortunately, he failed to do that. Someone with more presence of mind – or maybe just a nastier sense of humor – than the rest of the mob went to the entryway which led to the laborium and called everyone else to follow.

Fear of the Castellan and fear of Imagers formed a powerful combination. Several hundred people surged in that direction as if they had lost the capacity to think.

Somehow, they forced the guards back. Somehow, they were swept into the laborium, where the great majority of them had never set foot in their lives. Somehow, they found themselves packed into the ruined hall where the Congery had held meetings until the champion had blasted one wall open to the world.

Men closed the doors against the guards, shot the bolts. Torches ringed the stumps of pillars which used to hold up the ceiling. Because the curtain-wall didn't completely seal the hole in Orison's side, the hall was theoretically exposed to the guards defending the wall. The wall, however, had been built to protect against siege rather than against riot: its defensive positions faced outward rather than back down into the hall below. Only the archers could have taken any action. And even Lebbick's staunchest supporters knew better than to begin slaughtering Orison's inhabitants.

Lebbick. Men and women shouted back and forth, made threats. *Lebbick.* Their mood grew uglier by the moment. They started demanding blood.

Lebbick. Lebbick!

Back against the wall near one of the doors stood a tall man who wasn't shouting, didn't make any demands. Wrapped in his jet cloak, he was nearly invisible among the shadows. But the hood of his cloak couldn't hide the way his eyes caught the reflection of the torches, or the way his teeth gleamed when he grinned.

'Very good so far,' he said in a conversational tone because absolutely no one could hear him. 'Now the time has come. Do what I told you.'

Around him, the confusion began to change. Something caught the attention of the mob, focused it.

Amid the torches, Saddith stood on the dais of the Masters.

She was just tall enough to be seen over the heads of the people nearest her.

'Listen to me!' There was nothing left of her beauty: it had all become disfigurement and rage. Her voice rang off the stones, rang through the mob. 'Look at me!'

She raised her hands into the light.

'Look at me!'

The mob snarled.

She shook her hair away from her face.

'Look at me!'

The mob hissed.

She stripped open her blouse, exposing her maimed breasts.

'Look at me!'

The mob shouted.

'Lebbick did this! He did this to me!'

The mob roared.

'Yes, my sweet little slut,' the man in the jet cloak commented. 'And you deserved it. Perhaps that will teach you the folly of betraying my secrets.'

'Now he has threatened you,' Saddith went on, as fierce as her nakedness, 'for no reason except that you think this should not have been done to me!'

Lebbick! Lebbick!

'I went to him because I pitied him!' she shouted. 'I went to offer him my love when I was beautiful and all men desired me! This is the result!'

'No,' said the man in the jet cloak, entirely unheard. 'You went to him because you were ambitious. And you went when I told you to go. I understood his need far better than you did.'

Her voice seemed to turn the torchlight the color of blood. '*He must pay!*'

Lebbick! Pay! Lebbick!

'Think about this gambit, Joyse.' The man in the jet cloak was no longer grinning. 'Save him if you can. Stop me if you can. You thought to play this game against me, but you are outmatched.'

Then he cocked an eyebrow in mild surprise and peered over the heads of the crowd as a figure wrapped in a brown robe stepped unexpectedly up onto the dais beside Saddith.

Lit by torches and looking like an image out of a dream, the figure turned sharply; the robe seemed to swirl through the air and float away, thrown off as the man revealed himself.

Castellan Lebbick.

He wore the purple sash of his authority over his mail, the purple band of his position knotted around his short, gray hair. He had a longsword in a scabbard on his hip, but he didn't touch it; he didn't appear to need it. His familiar scowl answered the torches blackly. The lift of his head, the thrust of his jaw, the movements of his arms and shoulders were tight with passion and command. He wasn't tall, yet he made himself felt everywhere in the hall.

He had never looked more like a man who beat up women.

'All right.' His voice carried; it promised violence, like a hammer knocking chips from stone. 'This has gone on long enough. Get out of here. Go back to your rooms. The Masters don't like having their precious laborium invaded. If they decide to defend it themselves, they might translate the whole lice-ridden lot of you out of existence.'

An interesting threat, thought the man in the jet cloak – plainly hollow, but interesting. Nevertheless everyone stared at the Castellan. He had clapped a hush over the mob. Surprise and old respect and inbred alarm did more for him than fifty guards.

Saddith ignored his threats. She ignored his appearance, his proven capacity for harm. After what he had cost her, she had nothing left to lose, no more reason to be afraid. And she hated him – oh, she hated him. Her face was a scabbed and deformed clench of hate as she spat his name:

'*Lebbick.*'

Despite his authority and fury, he turned to look at her as though she had the power to compel him.

'What do you wish here?' she asked thickly. 'Have you come to gloat? Have you come to lay claim to your handiwork? Are you proud of it?'

'No.' His voice was quiet, yet it could be heard throughout the hall. 'I was wrong.'

'"Wrong"?' she cried.

'It wasn't your fault. It probably wasn't even your idea. I shouldn't have taken it out on you.'

At a calmer moment, the crowd might have been utterly astounded to hear Castellan Lebbick say something that sounded so much like an apology, almost a self-abasement. But the people weren't thinking as individuals: they were feeling like a mob, ugly and extreme. *Lebbick*, someone murmured – and another, *Lebbick* – a chant began, far back in the throat, through the teeth, a hunting growl, *Lebbick, Lebbick.*

'"Wrong"?' repeated Saddith. She was breathing hard, trying to get enough air for her vituperation. 'You admit that you were *wrong*?' Her damaged breasts shone with sweat. 'Do you think that *heals* me? Do you think that one small piece of my pain is made less, or one small scar is removed?' Her arms beat time to her respiration, *Lebbick, Lebbick*, the snarl of the mob. 'I tell you, you will pay with *blood*!

'Blood!' she howled, matching the rhythm in the hall: '*Blood!*'

And the mob responded, 'Lebbick! *Lebbick!*'

The man in the jet cloak grinned with undisguised relish.

Nevertheless Castellan Lebbick wasn't daunted. Maybe he wasn't even afraid. 'Oh, stop it!' he snapped over the heavy shout as if the people surrounding him were nothing more than bad children and he had no time for their misbehavior. 'Do you think all this surprises me? I knew it was going to happen. I've been ready for *days*.'

His voice wielded enough of the whip to slash through the beat of his name, the outrage. Men and women faltered, began to listen.

'I had you driven in here so I could do what I wanted with you. You didn't know I was here. You don't know how many of my men are here. Well, I'll tell you. Ninety-four. All disguised. All pretending to be one of you. The person standing next to you shouting *Lebbick, Lebbick* like a dog with the mange is probably one of my men. If anyone raises a hand at me, he'll be cut down where he stands. And the rest of you will be *remembered!*'

It was a remarkable ploy. The man in the jet cloak was virtually certain that it was in fact a ploy, that the Castellan was in fact undefended, as vulnerable as he would ever be; but that changed nothing. It worked. Like water on hot coals, it transformed the fury of the mob back into fear.

All the shouting stopped. Men and women glanced at each other, tried to edge away from each other. When the Castellan barked, 'Now get out of here. Open the doors and get out of here. You've all been stupid enough for one night,' the people near the doors undid the bolts, and the crowd began to move.

This was too much for Saddith – as the man in the jet cloak knew it would be. Of course, he was as surprised as anyone by Castellan Lebbick's appearance in the hall; and more vexed than most, although he didn't show it. From the beginning, however, he had been prepared for the possibility that she might fail – that the crowd might refuse to gather, that it might not become a mob, that the mob might not rise to bloodshed. And then she would break. The hate inside her would refuse to be contained.

That was why he had given her a knife.

She had it in her hand now, and she wailed in a high, shrill voice as she flung herself at Lebbick.

Maybe he wasn't as ready as he pretended to be. Or maybe something had distracted him. Or maybe this was what he had had in mind all along. Whatever the reason, he was slow turning, slow with his hands; too slow to prevent Saddith from driving her blade through his throat.

Nevertheless she didn't so much as scratch him.

While she swung, Ribuld came up onto the dais in a headlong charge and spitted her on his longsword, ran her through so hard that they both crashed into the throng on the far side and fell to the floor.

Just for a second, the Castellan's features seemed to crumple as if he were disappointed. Almost immediately, however, he swept out his own sword and went to stand over Ribuld so that no one would try to strike at the guard who had saved his life.

The man in the jet cloak was mildly entertained to hear Castellan Lebbick rasp at Ribuld, 'Next time don't be in such a hurry.'

The time had come to go with the crowd. If the man in the jet cloak lingered, he might get pulled along when the crowd's departure became flight, people hurrying and then running to get away from the Castellan and trouble. With a shrug, he eased out of the hall.

The next morning, however, he was gratified to hear that some of Saddith's supporters had been sincere enough in their outrage to burn everything flammable they could find before guards arrived to drive them out of the laborium. She deserved at least that much recognition. She had become too ugly to go on living, of course; but while she lasted she had been worth the risk of knowing her. Although he wasn't exactly grieved by her loss, he admired the aesthetic judgment of the man or men who had tried to commemorate her death by doing a little trivial damage to the laborium.

687

On the other hand, he was both surprised and rather amused that the better part of the day passed before anyone discovered that during the riot someone had broken into the warren of rooms where the Congery's mirrors were kept and had shattered several of them.

Treachery was everywhere, it seemed. What a shame.

Chew on that, Joyse, you old goat. I hope it chokes you.

The next morning, with Orison full of news which he might be presumed to have come by honestly, Master Eremis went to visit the mediator of the Congery.

He had a number of matters that he wanted to pursue with Master Barsonage. He had been putting them off for days, partly because he hadn't wished to call attention to himself, partly because he'd been busy elsewhere. But the time was ripe for a little probing. Perhaps he would be able to learn something useful – and sow a hint or two of uncertainty in the process.

Twirling the ends of his chasuble, he walked through the tower which held King Joyse's private quarters. In fact, he made a point of passing that way often, whatever his destination might be. If anyone had asked him why he occasionally walked a considerable unnecessary distance in order to cross the waiting room in front of the stairs up to the King's rooms, he would have replied that he always hoped to overhear something – any gossip or rumor which might reveal where he stood with his sovereign.

After all, King Joyse had said exactly nothing to him, either in person or by message, after his solution to the problem of Orison's water supply. Since what he had done was so obviously the kind of thing which King Joyse had always demanded from his Imagers, he, Master Eremis, might be forgiven for drawing worrisome inferences from the King's silence. Was Eremis not trusted? Were his enemies speaking against him? Had he offended against King Joyse's apparent desire to bring about the collapse of the realm? Or was it true that the King's insistence upon an ethical use of Imagery had never been sincere?

Surely Master Eremis' interest in any news which might somehow emanate from the King was understandable? Under the circumstances, how could he be confident that his life wasn't in danger, even though he had saved Orison from terrible suffering and inevitable defeat?

This explanation – although Master Eremis would have supplied it with perfect assurance – was no more than a by-blow of the truth.

The truth was that he had come this way by accident several days ago, and had chanced to find the Tor in the waiting room.

The old lord was alone, of course. The waiting room was almost always empty, now that King Joyse had made plain his disinclination to respond intelligently – if at all – to the petitions of his subjects. It was possible that the Tor had been alone there for hours – and would be alone for hours more.

He was asleep on the floor, with his face pressed into the corner between the floor and wall; his fat made a quivering mountain, and he snored like a sawmill; he was so drunk that Master Eremis might have been unable to awaken him with a trumpet. The stink exhaling from him was so strong that simply breathing it made Master Eremis feel tipsy and arrogant.

While the old lord's thick flesh shook from his raucous snoring, Master Eremis paused to think. He considered taking this opportunity to slip an unobtrusive knife between the Tor's ribs. That might be helpful – not at the moment, naturally, but later on. Vagel would do it without hesitation; Gilbur, with glee. On the other hand, it would be almost no fun at all. Eremis wanted to humiliate the Tor before killing him.

In addition, there was only one lord whom Master Eremis feared less, and that was the Armigite, who had already sold his Care to Prince Kragen to purchase a temporary safety for himself and his women and his fresh boys. Upon reflection, Eremis let the chance for murder pass.

But he didn't forget it.

If the Tor was occasionally to be found in the waiting room alone and drunk and asleep, then it was possible that he might also occasionally be found there alone and drunk and awake. Awake enough to talk – and too drunk to be cautious.

Master Eremis believed that opportunities were like women: they came to men who knew how to court them.

As a rule, he was given more to flashes of inspiration than to steady labor. That was why he – and Vagel as well – needed Master Gilbur. Nevertheless he began courting this opportunity assiduously. He made sure that he passed through the waiting room more often than any other man in Orison.

Today, on his way to talk with Master Barsonage, his diligence reaped its just reward. The Tor was sitting on one of the deserted benches, so drunk that he could hardly find his head with both hands. His eyes were red and miserable, self-abused, and he exuded a sour smell of old sweat and acid vomit. What was left of his hair straggled into his face.

Clearly, the long, strange wait while Prince Kragen sat outside Orison and did nothing had begun to bear fruit. A riot against Castellan Lebbick, what a shame. Mirrors broken in the laborium. And the King's oldest friend reduced to this, drinking himself to death in full view of anyone who bothered to notice.

It was odd and wonderful that the man who bothered to notice wasn't the King at all, wasn't the one at whom this display was directed. Instead he was Master Eremis.

'My lord Tor,' the Master said amiably, 'this is fortuitous.'

Slowly, as if he were bringing long forgotten muscles into service, the Tor raised his head; he peered at Eremis through a haze of drink. With no discernible self-awareness, he belched.

Then he said in a surprisingly clear voice, 'Got any wine?'

Master Eremis smiled across his teeth. 'I have wished to speak with you, my lord. Great events transpire in Orison.'

The old lord considered this assertion soddenly. After a moment, he dropped his head; it lolled on his neck. Nevertheless when he spoke every word was as distinct as a piece of glass: broken and precise, like augury.

'Too far to get. Too many stairs.'

He belched again, aimlessly.

'We have had a riot against the good Castellan,' explained Master Eremis.

'And it may have been premeditated. While the guards were distracted by the riot, several of the Congery's mirrors were destroyed.'

The Tor's head continued rolling back and forth, back and forth, as if he were rocking himself to sleep.

'And now, like a man who knows what happens within our walls, Prince Kragen attacks at last – although I must confess that I am less impressed by the audacity of his assault than by its circumspection.'

And may the attacks continue, the Master wished, daring fate to deny him. They are an admirable distraction.

Simply because he was so willing to pursue his aims even if everything went against him, he felt confident that fate would in fact heed his desires.

The Tor met Master Eremis' remarks with a snort; he might have been starting into a snore. A quiver ran through him then, however, and he blinked his bloodshot eyes. 'Wine,' he pronounced, as if he expected a cask to appear magically before him.

Master Eremis had difficulty restraining a laugh. True, some of King Joyse's supporters were proving to be more resourceful than Eremis could have predicted. Others, however, only saved themselves from appearing pathetic by being ridiculous.

'What do you make of it all, my lord Tor?' he asked in kind good humor. 'Where are the forces of Cadwal? Where is the Perdon? How has Prince Kragen dared to let us endure against him so long?'

Without looking up, the Tor countered absentmindedly, 'Did I tell you my son was killed?'

'It seems clear, does it not' – at the moment, Eremis was delighted that he hadn't knifed the old lord – 'that the Prince and his illustrious father know something we do not.' This conversation was too much fun to be missed. 'They would not have wasted so much as a day in hesitation, unless they had reason to believe that High King Festten would not arrive against them. What conclusions do you draw, my lord?'

The Tor appeared to suffer from the delusion that he was actually participating in the discussion. 'Did I tell you,' he replied, 'that he gave Lebbick permission to torture her?'

That was an interesting revelation; but Master Eremis could guess its import too easily to pursue it. Instead, he inquired, 'What conclusions can you draw? There are only two. The first is that Festten and Margonal are in alliance – and Festten trusts Margonal enough to give him time to capture the Congery for himself. And if you are able to believe that, I fear we have nothing more to say to each other.'

'*Torture* her,' repeated the Tor, 'despite her obvious decency – and her proven desire to help him.'

'The second,' continued Master Eremis, grinning, 'is that the Prince has cut us off from information which he himself possesses – from the knowledge that we are not indeed threatened by Cadwal at all. High King Festten has other intentions. He has mustered his army, not against us and Alend, but to wage another war entirely. And if you are able to believe *that*, I fear you have nothing left to say to anyone.'

'I begged her.' Fat tears rolled down the old lord's aggrieved cheeks. 'I should have begged him, of course, but he was past hearing me. I begged her. Betray Geraden. So that he would not be responsible for what Lebbick would do. So that he would not have her on his conscience.' He seemed unaware that he was weeping. His ability to speak so exactly when he was barely sober enough to keep his eyes from crossing was delightful, even entertaining, like a trick done by a mountebank. 'But she has the only loyal heart left in Mordant. She would not betray Geraden, even to save herself from Lebbick.'

Master Eremis was so pleased that he could hardly contain his relish. Because his exuberance absolutely had to have some outlet, he spun the ends of his chasuble like pinwheels.

'My lord Tor,' he asked nonchalantly, coming at last to the point, 'what has he been doing all this time, while his people riot, and mirrors are shattered, and women are maimed and murdered? What has good King Joyse been doing?'

As if the word had been surprised out of him, the Tor replied, 'Practicing.'

'Practicing?' A brief giggle burst from the Master: he couldn't hold it down. 'What, hop-board? Still? Has he not given up that folly yet?'

The old lord shook his head, as morose as cold potatoes and congealed gravy.

'Swordsmanship.'

That stopped Master Eremis' mirth: it made him stare involuntarily, as if the Tor had somehow, miraculously, opened a pit of vipers at his feet – or had told him a joke so funny that he couldn't believe it, couldn't laugh at it until he had thought about it for a while. *Swordsmanship?* At *his* age? Was he strong enough to do as much as *lift* a longsword?

'My lord Tor,' Eremis said casually to conceal the intensity of his attention, 'you jest with me. Our brave King cannot swing a sword. He can barely *stand* without assistance.'

Abruptly, with an effort that seemed to make his whole body gurgle, the Tor heaved himself to his feet. He hadn't looked at Master Eremis since the start of the conversation. Dully, as if he were losing his gift for enunciation, he announced, 'Got to have wine.'

With his hams rolling unsteadily under him, he lurched away.

Master Eremis was about to spring after him, pull him back, wrench an explanation out of him, when the true point of the joke struck home. King Joyse intended to fight – and he was years or even decades past the time when he was strong enough to do so. That shed a new light on everything – on every sign that the King knew what he was doing, that he did what he did out of deliberate policy rather than petulant foolishness. He intended to fight because he didn't know or couldn't admit he no longer had the strength. He wasn't self-destructive or apathetic: he was just blind to age and time. He risked his kingdom in an effort to prove himself still capable of saving it.

That was a rich jest, too rich for any coarse display of mirth. Instead of laughing aloud, Eremis whistled cheerfully through his teeth as he continued on his way to see Master Barsonage.

The mediator answered his door wearing only a towel knotted around his middle – a style of dress which emphasized his girth at the expense of his dignity. Water glistened on his pine-colored skin, his bald pate: apparently, Master Eremis had caught him bathing, and his servants were out. His flesh didn't sag on him as the Tor's did, however; his bulk was solid, tightly packed over muscle and bone. He didn't seem especially embarrassed to receive Master Eremis in this damp, disrobed condition.

In fact, he sounded almost friendly as he said, 'Master Eremis, good day to you. Come in, come in.' He stood back from the door, waved a dripping arm. 'It is an honor to be visited by the man who saved Orison. Let us hope that you have saved us permanently. Have you recovered from your ordeal? You look well.'

Master Eremis laughed lightly at Barsonage's uncharacteristic gush. 'And a good day to you, Master Barsonage. I have clearly come at an inopportune moment. I can return later.'

'Nonsense.' The mediator touched the sleeve of Eremis' cloak, urged him into the room. 'Orison is under siege. In one sense, all times are inopportune. In another, the present moment is always better than any other. Some wine?'

Thinking of the Tor, Master Eremis said deliberately, 'With pleasure.'

He accepted a goblet of a very mediocre Armigite vintage, then seated himself in the chair Master Barsonage indicated. He had visited the mediator's rooms on any number of occasions – disputes privately arbitrated at one extreme, formal feasts welcoming new Masters at the other – but whenever he came here he always took a moment to admire the furniture.

It had all been made by Master Barsonage himself.

Eremis did him the justice of admitting that the mediator was a competent Imager. In particular, the preparation for and execution of the Congery's most important augury had been deftly done. On the other hand, he was much more than competent with wood: he was an artist. It was universally acknowledged around the Congery that his frames were better than anyone else's: better made, better fitted; altogether finer. And his furniture could have graced the finest salon in Orison – or in Carmag, for that matter. The expanse of his table had been so well shaped and polished that it seemed to glow from within; the arms of his chairs flowed so naturally with the grain of the wood that it was surprising to find them comfortable.

Secretly, Eremis laughed at Master Barsonage for dedicating himself to his lesser talents – for wasting his time with Imagery when he could have contributed some real beauty to the world in another way.

And he wanted to laugh more now. Instead of leaving the room to put on at least a robe, Barsonage sat down as he was, drank off his wine in a gulp, wiped the water out of his stiff eyebrows, and began to prattle.

'You are much admired now, Master Eremis. Of course, you have always been admired. But it will not surprise you to hear that you have not always been liked. You are too able, too quick. And you mock people. You have not made yourself easy to like.

'Ah, but now— The refilling of the reservoir was a clever action as well as a courageous one. No, do not deny it,' he said although Eremis hadn't moved a muscle. 'The exhaustion of so much prolonged translation. If I had made that attempt, my heart would have failed me. Yet you did not hesitate to risk complete prostration. And, as I say, it was clever. Your reputation has not been the only beneficiary of your action. Your heroism and Master Quillon's foul murder have combined to raise the esteem in which all the Congery is held.

'Shall I give you an example? My servants no longer sneer at me when I put them to work.'

Grinning, Master Eremis raised his hands to ward off the babble. 'Master Barsonage, please. I did not come to you for flattery. I am precisely aware of my own virtues, and they do not merit this praise.'

'Really?' the mediator returned. 'I think you are too modest.' His eyes were as bland as bits of glass. 'But if praise is offensive I will cease. Of course you did not come for flattery. How may I serve you?'

'I am well rested now, as you see,' Eremis answered. 'And another matter which required my attention has come to an end. It is no secret that the maid Saddith was my lover.' He spoke with admirable sincerity. 'After I recovered my strength, I spent much of my time with her. She needed friends—'

He grimaced. 'Sadly, she would not give up her hatred of our good Castellan. There was nothing I could do with her.' Grief wasn't his best pose, but he projected as much of it as possible. As if he were putting Saddith and her death behind him by an act of will, he said, 'Master Barsonage, I am ready.'

The mediator raised an eyebrow. As his skin dried, it looked more and more like cut pine. '"Ready"?'

'I have heard that the Masters are busy – that since Quillon's death you have rediscovered your sense of purpose. I am ready to rejoin the work of the Congery.'

'Our work?' Master Barsonage's features reflected nothing. 'What work do you mean?'

Master Eremis had difficulty suppressing a smile. The mediator was almost ludicrously transparent. Fixing him with a glittering gaze which was intended to express indignation as well as penetration, Eremis replied slowly, 'So it is true. I am still not trusted. That is the reason I have not been summoned to any of your meetings – to any of your labors. I have saved Orison from a quick fall to Alend. I did everything any man could do to keep Nyle alive – and I was the only man here who so much as made the attempt. I have been striving with unmatched diligence to find some means to avert Mordant's fate. It was not *I* who disbanded the Congery. And I am *still* not trusted. That murderous puppy, Geraden, casts a few groundless aspersions on my good name, and suddenly nothing I can do is enough to redeem it.'

'Oh, no, Master Eremis.' Barsonage put up a thick hand in protest. 'You misunderstand me. You misunderstand us all.' In a tone as bland as his expression, he explained, 'You fail to grasp, I think, how high your standing has become. The man who refilled the reservoir – the man who did so much to save Nyle – is not someone who can be "summoned" to meetings like an Apt. He cannot be put to labor like a packhorse. You have been much involved in your own concerns – and you have earned the right to be. The Congery does not distrust you. We only respect your high standing – and your privacy.'

Firmly, Eremis resisted a giddy temptation to snort, During a *siege*? With

Orison's fall tied like a noose around your neck, and no hope anywhere? Can you truly believe me silly enough to swallow that lie? The mediator, however, didn't look like a man who had an opinion about Master Eremis' silliness, one way or the other. He looked – his blandness itself betrayed him – like a man who had spent some time preparing for this encounter.

Master Eremis sat forward in his chair; his relish for the conversation sharpened.

'Perhaps,' he said in a skeptical drawl. 'You will forgive me if I reserve judgment on that point.

'It remains true, does it not, that there have been meetings to which I have not been invited? That there is work in progress which I have not been asked to share? That the Congery has rediscovered its purpose?'

Master Barsonage nodded. 'Indeed.' Something about him – perhaps it was the way his eyebrow bristled – suggested an intensification which his mild gaze contradicted. 'I am glad to say that is the case.'

'Am I permitted to ask how it came about?'

'Certainly. At last we are able to see clearly that the lady Terisa is an Imager.'

Eremis scowled to conceal the fact that he didn't like what he heard. 'Master Barsonage, that is an answer which explains nothing.'

'Well, perhaps not.' Apparently, the mediator had prepared himself quite well for this encounter. 'A man of your assurance and ability may have difficulty understanding men whose chief talent lies in their capacity for doubt.

'Nevertheless in practice – as distinct from theory – the great stumbling block for the Congery has been the question of the lady Terisa. What does she signify? What does her presence among us indicate? Is there a *reason* for her unexpected appearance, or was Geraden merely the agent of a monumental accident?

'If she is an accident, then all Imagery is accidental in the end, and our research, like our morality, is only foolishness. Geraden's role in the augury has no meaning.'

Master Eremis nodded as if the truth were obvious to him.

'But if,' the mediator continued, 'there is a *reason*, then two conclusions are inescapable. So inescapable,' he commented without discernible sarcasm or humor, 'that even our most contentious members have accepted them. First, the responsibility she represents falls upon us. Imagery is our demesne. Second, since the problem she represents exists it must have a solution. What one Imager can do, another can understand and counter.

'It has been demonstrated,' he concluded, 'that there *is* a reason. She is an Imager. We can regret that she has chosen to ally herself with Master Gilbur and arch-Imager Vagel, but we cannot shirk either the responsibility or the hope which that knowledge implies.'

'Yes, very well.' Master Eremis made an impatient gesture. 'That is all reasonable as far as it goes, but you have not yet explained it. How do you know she is an Imager? What evidence has she given? Lebbick reports that Gilbur freed her from her cell. He killed Quillon. He took her to the room where Havelock's mirrors are kept. Lebbick found them there. After Gilbur felled Lebbick, he and she disappeared from Orison. What does that demonstrate? Gilbur's ability to come and go is as well established as Gart's – and as unexplained. There is no reason to attribute Imagery to her.'

Master Barsonage shrugged, scratched his chest. As if to compensate for his baldness, his chest was matted with yellow hair. Water clung to it like beads of sap. 'That is true,' he replied without hurry or hesitation. 'On the other side, it could be argued that Master Gilbur and the arch-Imager would have no reason to free her – just as the High King's Monomach would have no reason to kill her – if she were *not* an Imager. Speaking only for myself, I have examined that argument and found it persuasive. In fact, it persuaded me to accept the position of the Congery's mediator once again.

'Since then, however, we have been given evidence instead of argument, the kind of evidence you and several of the other Masters require.'

Maddeningly, he halted and gazed at Eremis as if he had said enough.

Master Eremis forced himself to take a deep breath, relax, stop grinding his teeth. When he had recovered his nonchalance, he said, 'You say that you do not distrust me. Do you trust me enough to tell me what that evidence is?'

Once again, Master Barsonage replied, 'Of course.

'The Castellan is a hard man, hard to defeat. He was already coming back to consciousness when the lady Terisa and Master Gilbur left the storeroom of Adept Havelock's mirrors. He saw that they did not depart together.

'The lady Terisa vanished into a glass. Master Gilbur was too far from her to have translated her. He left the room the same way he entered it, along the corridor.'

The mediator favored Master Eremis with a smile as bland as milk.

Eremis prided himself on his restraint. Nevertheless he betrayed some surprise as he protested, 'That is not the story Lebbick tells.'

He was surprised because he hadn't expected Barsonage to know so much. And a man who knew more than he was expected to might also *do* more than he was expected to.

And if he really didn't trust Eremis, as his manner made clear, why was he revealing what he knew?

'No' – the mediator corrected his visitor amicably – 'it is not the story Castellan Lebbick has told in public. I gather from what I have heard that at first he was too full of fury and desperation to grasp the significance of what he had seen. And since then he has chosen to keep his thoughts to himself. But he did speak to Artagel. And Artagel brought the story to me. He believed – quite rightly – that his information was vital to the Congery.'

In a tone that made him sound like a simpleton, Master Barsonage said, 'It has enabled me to unite the Masters for the first time since the Congery was created.'

Master Eremis drank more wine to conceal the fact that all these surprises were beginning to affect him. Lebbick told Artagel. Artagel told Barsonage. But Gilbur had sworn that Lebbick was still out cold when he left. Was he just trying to cover up a mistake? Or was Barsonage lying – *Barsonage*, of all people? Was he playing some kind of game?

Eremis grinned around the rim of his goblet. This was better than he had anticipated, more fun. He liked opponents who were capable of surprises. He

695

had grown almost fond of King Joyse. Even Lebbick had his good side. Geraden was almost likable. And as for Terisa—

That made their destruction especially exciting.

Unite the Masters, was that it? Then they would have to be un-united.

He twirled his goblet in his long fingers. 'Thank you, Master Barsonage,' he said happily. 'I understand you now.

'What work is the Congery doing with its rediscovered purpose?'

Again the mediator shrugged. A trickle of water ran out of his chest hair across his belly. 'It will not surprise you. We labor to learn how it is that men such as the High King's Monomach, who is no Imager, and Master Gilbur, whose talents are known to us, can be translated in and out of Orison at no cost to their sanity. Translation through flat glass drives men mad. That has been true since the dawn of Imagery. Why, then, are our enemies not destroyed by the very weapons they use against us?'

Ah. That was a subject which Master Eremis had come prepared to discuss. With a small, inward sigh – relief, perhaps, or disappointment – he said, 'There I may be able to help you. I have an idea that may shed some light.'

For the first time since the conversation began, Master Barsonage looked interested. 'Please explain it,' he said at once. 'You know that the matter is urgent.'

'Certainly.' Matching the blandness of Master Barsonage's tone, Eremis explained. 'To the best of our understanding, as you know, the peril of flat glass arises from the translation itself, not from the simple movement from place to place within our world. Put crudely, translation is too strong for simple movement. The power which makes passage possible between entirely separate Images turns against the man translated because it is not needed.'

Barsonage nodded.

'On the assumption that our understanding is accurate,' Master Eremis went on, 'my idea is this. Suppose that two mirrors were made – one flat, showing, say, an unused chamber in Orison, the other normal, showing a barren, deserted plain. Suppose then that the flat glass is now translated into the other, so that it stands upon the plain in the Image, and the focus of the Image is adjusted so that the flat mirror fills the glass. Is it not conceivable that the Imager who shaped those mirrors could now step straight through them, performing in effect two safe translations rather than one which would make him mad?'

The mediator was listening intently; he seemed to soak up Eremis' words through his pores. Softly, as if he were astonished, he breathed, 'It is conceivable.'

'Of course,' Master Eremis continued, simply marking time while he watched the mediator's reaction, 'the difficulty is that if the Imager stepped through himself he would not be able to step back. And to send and then retrieve someone else by such a method, he would need to be able to perform both translations simultaneously. We have no way of knowing whether such a thing is possible.' Like most of his lies, this one bore an insidious resemblance to the truth. 'There Vagel is ahead of us. He may have spent fifteen years perfecting simultaneous translations.

'But surely we can attempt it? We can learn for ourselves whether this idea is indeed possible as well as conceivable?'

'Yes.' Master Barsonage had lost his air of studied mildness, of deliberate simplicity. His eyes shone. 'We can.'

Abruptly, he surged to his feet like a breaker off the sea. 'We can and we will. Today. Give me an hour to gather the Masters. Come to the laborium. We will begin experimenting.' Almost in the same breath, he added, 'It is a brilliant idea. Two mirrors – simultaneous translations. Even if it fails, it remains brilliant. Brilliant.'

Having hooked his fish, Master Eremis proceeded to act as if he were letting the mediator go. He agreed to everything, stood up, started to leave, then paused at the door. As if he were innocent of all malice, he said, 'Oh, Master Barsonage, one other matter – in case I forget it later. There is a rumor that some of our mirrors have been broken. Can that be true?'

Master Barsonage turned immediately grim: apparently, he was shocked by what had happened. 'During the riot against Castellan Lebbick,' he admitted. 'Five mirrors.' He shook his head. 'It is plain that someone hates us. But why only five? Why those five? If you were insane enough to deprive us of the means to defend Orison and ourselves, would you not break every glass you found?'

'Certainly.' Master Eremis made a sincere effort to look shocked himself. 'Unfortunately, insane actions are by their very nature insane. Which mirrors were broken?'

The mediator replied promptly: once again, he was prepared. 'The glass with which you refilled the reservoir. That was an attack on Orison. And Geraden's mirror, the one that brought the lady Terisa here. Either he or she is stranded now, wherever they are – as is our lost champion. That was an attack on one of the three of them. But the third was a flat mirror of Quillon's, showing a field of Termigan grapes. The fourth was the one with the Image of the starless sky. The fifth, the one where that gigantic slug-beast can be seen – one of the mirrors King Joyse captured in his wars. An attack on wine? On the heavens? An attack on monsters? It makes no sense.

'Geraden and the lady Terisa and our champion – if he still lives – may have been stranded entirely at random, by someone who had no idea what he did.'

Trying to sound disturbed, perhaps even grim, Eremis said, 'My glass. Then we must depend on the weather for water. I cannot save us again.'

'That is true,' replied Barsonage. 'Prince Kragen's position is now much stronger. We must hope he does not know it.'

Master Eremis swallowed a final smile and made his way out of the mediator's quarters. He wanted to reach his own rooms quickly, where he could afford to laugh out loud.

He realized, of course, that he was in a tricky situation. But it was a situation of his own devising. Thanks to the seeds he had just planted, Barsonage and the other Masters might spend the rest of their time until they died trying to work a simultaneous translation because they didn't know it was impossible. Or, rather, it was trivial. The trick was not in the translation, but in the glass.

697

For all practical purposes, he had neutralized the Congery – the only force in Orison still capable of fighting him.

On the other hand, he would have to be very careful. Lebbick had said something to Artagel, who had told it to Barsonage. Not something about Terisa: something about Eremis himself. The mediator had lied to him.

For him, the trick would be to determine exactly what that lie was.

Thinking about things like this made him look like he was about to burst with good humor.

THIRTY-EIGHT

CONFLICT AT
THE GATES

ℰ

'The trick,' Geraden said the first time they rested the horses, 'is not to get stopped.'

They had ridden hard for most of the morning: the road from Romish was easy going, and he was in a hurry. But the horses couldn't sustain a pace like that indefinitely.

'Oh, really?' Terisa didn't realize how sourly she spoke. She was still thinking about Torrent: the idea of the King's shy daughter riding away alone in a foolish and dangerous effort to rescue Queen Madin clung to her mind like a splash of acid. 'We're going back to Orison. Where Master Eremis wants us. Why would anybody try to stop us?'

Geraden looked at her sharply; for a moment, he seemed unsure how to respond. As if he had missed the point, he said, 'We've been riding so long – and it feels so good to be with you – I keep thinking you know Mordant better than you do. Would you like to look at the map again?'

She shook her head. She didn't care about the map. She didn't care about being stopped. At the moment, she didn't even care about having to face Eremis again.

Geraden, that's how Argus got killed.

'Well,' he explained, still missing the point, 'there's really only one fast way to get from Romish to Orison, and that's along this road – the main road through Armigite. Which just happens to be the route Prince Kragen used. It's his link to Alend – his supply line, his line of retreat. It'll be crawling with his men.

'On top of that, even the Armigite can't be as stupid as people think. He's got to have scouts and spies everywhere, especially along the road. He needs to know what's happening. And right now he probably wants an Imager or two more than anything in the world. If his men get their hands on us, they aren't going to let us go just because we smile and say please.'

Terisa stared into the trees without saying anything.

'And on top of *that*' – Geraden's tone became slowly harsher – 'I assume Orison is still under siege. I *assume* it hasn't already fallen, or there wouldn't be any reason to kidnap Queen Madin. If we're going to get in to see King Joyse, we'll have to get past the whole Alend army.

'The men who took the Queen were Alends. It looks like this is some plot of Prince Kragen's. So he's the one we have to worry about. And he won't let us in to Orison until he's ready – until his trap is ready.'

He surprised her, and she winced. 'Do you really think that's true? Do you really think Prince Kragen is responsible for kidnapping the Queen?'

'Don't you? You said those men were Alends. They took her toward Alend.'

The acid in her mind was turning to nausea. 'But if he's responsible—' Until now, she hadn't considered the question closely. 'That means he's working with Master Eremis. Where else would he get an Imager who could translate an avalanche?'

Geraden watched her and waited.

'But if that's true, why did Eremis refill the reservoir? Why didn't he just let Prince Kragen into Orison?'

'An interesting question,' Geraden murmured past his teeth.

She tried to imagine an explanation; but almost at once another aspect of the situation struck her. 'If the Prince did it, he must have done it behind Elega's back. She'd never approve of something like that.'

Geraden nodded once, roughly.

The implications brought Terisa to a halt. 'Elega's being betrayed herself.' She faced Geraden squarely, showed him her distress. 'What're we going to do?'

The way he met her gaze gave the impression that he had accomplished his goal: he had shifted the direction of her thoughts. 'We'll stay on the road until we get close to Batten,' he replied. 'That's where the Alends will pick it up. And it turns south there to meet the road from Sternwall. We can go straight southeast toward Orison. We'll save some miles – and maybe we won't lose much time.

'When we reach the siege, we'll try to get to Elega before the Prince realizes what we're doing.' Abruptly, he grinned – a sharp smile with no humor in it. 'If she knows what happened to her mother – if she allowed it to happen, if she approves of it – I'm going to be *very* disappointed in her.'

'And if she doesn't know,' Terisa completed for him, trying to reassure herself, 'she might be willing to help us.'

He nodded again.

After a while, they mounted their horses and went on.

They rode out of the last hills of Fayle onto one of Armigite's many fertile flatlands at what felt like a breakneck pace. Leaving the woods behind increased Terisa's anxiety: Armigite appeared to be almost unnaturally open, as if everything that moved through it were somehow exposed. Perhaps that was why the Armigite had become what he was: perhaps his personality had been distorted by the pressure of being so exposed. But actually there were quite a few trees around, even in lowlands which had obviously been under cultivation before Prince Kragen and his army crossed the Pestil. Concealment was scarce, but shade was available. Partly for that reason, and partly because of the soil's richness, the flats of Armigite bore no resemblance to the arid spaces of Termigan.

Terisa and Geraden made good progress, despite the lack of fresh mounts. He studied the map repeatedly – they were still crossing a part of Mordant where he had never been before – and assured her that their progress was good. He may have been trying to shore up her spirits. For some reason, his own didn't appear to need support: his keenness suggested that he liked this rush across the landscape, this clear and urgent sense of purpose; that he was eager to return to Orison. By the time nightfall forced them to halt and make camp, they were well on their way toward making the journey to Orison as Queen Madin had intended it, in three days.

The more he looked ahead, however, the more her attention turned backward. Torrent had touched her unexpectedly, made her aware of her own inadequacies. In their separate ways, each of the King's daughters had daunted her. They had inherited more courage than she seemed to possess. Her determination to oppose Master Eremis was little more than a pretense, after all – a pretense that she could somehow transcend her past.

As she gazed across the campfire into the open dark of Armigite, she murmured, 'Geraden, there's something I don't understand.'

'Just "something"?' he returned, making a transparent effort to jolly her out of her mood. 'Then you are marvelous to me, my lady. *My* lack of understanding doesn't stop at "something." It's as vast as the world.'

She looked over at him. His face was as dear as ever. And if anything he had become more handsome; the excitement he had felt since Torrent left brought out the best in his eyes, in the lines of his features. He didn't deserve her gloom. For his sake, she made an effort to smile.

'That's probably true. But I'll bet you know the answer to this one.'

He met her eyes and smiled back. 'Try me.' The dancing light of the campfire created the impression that his smile went all the way to the bone.

Almost at once, she found that the weight pushing down on her spirit wasn't quite as heavy as she had thought.

'I think I will,' she said. 'But first I want you to explain something.'

The gleam in his eyes grew brighter as he waited for her to continue.

'That avalanche,' she said. 'They must have used two mirrors. Isn't that right? One to translate it away from wherever they found it. One to translate it *to* Vale House.'

'Yes,' Geraden replied at once. 'But that's been true of everything we've seen. Those pits of fire outside Sternwall. The ghouls in Fayle. Even the creatures that attacked Houseldon.' A shadow which might have been grief or rage darkened his gaze briefly. 'They all needed two mirrors. That must be Eremis' secret. It must be how he's able to attack so many different places in Mordant without actually going to them. And it must be how he's able to move people in and out of Orison without costing them their minds.'

'We've talked about that before,' he added.

'I remember. It's the only explanation I've heard that seems to make sense. Two mirrors. One shows a scene with a lot of landslides. The other is a flat glass with Vale House in the Image. That means' – her heart tightened as she came to the point – 'Eremis could have seen us in the Image. He *must* have

701

seen us. I know I was in the Image. Otherwise I wouldn't have felt the translation.

'That means he knows where we are.

'And it means we're responsible for what happened to Queen Madin. She was taken because of us.'

'No.' Geraden rejected the idea without hesitation. 'That can't be true. It wasn't because of us.'

'Why not?'

'It's too complicated. He had men ready for that attack. They must have been on their way before we ever got near Fayle. If we had anything to do with it, he must have known we were going there – and not to Romish – long before we did. And his men wouldn't have ignored us. He would have been glad for a chance to capture us.

'That attack was aimed at the Queen herself. Even the timing was just a coincidence. Eremis couldn't control the avalanches in his mirror. He had to be ready to act whenever the opportunity came along.'

Involuntarily, Terisa shook her head. She didn't like what she was thinking. 'No. He probably *can* control the avalanches. I mean he can cause one whenever he wants. All he has to do is focus his mirror on the right kind of mountainside. Then, when he wants a landslide, all he has to do is translate away the rock supporting the mountainside.'

Geraden stared at her, his eyes glittering flames. 'You're right. I never thought of that.'

'The attack wasn't aimed at us,' she assented. 'But he knows we *were* there. He could have seen that we survived. He could have seen us ride away. He could guess where we're going.

'That means we can't warn King Joyse. It won't do any good. There won't be any gap between when he knows what happened to the Queen and when Eremis knows he knows. He won't have a chance to act. What we're trying to do doesn't make any sense.'

She stopped and watched Geraden's face, holding her breath as if she feared his reaction.

She was relieved to see that he wasn't discouraged. His expression became intently thoughtful, but he didn't look especially alarmed; he certainly didn't look horrified. Softly, he commented, 'I've said it before. You have a morbid imagination. No wonder you've been so depressed all day.

'This time,' he said after a moment, 'I think you're wrong.'

Quietly, she let the air sigh out of her lungs.

'If Eremis saw us,' he asked by way of explanation, 'where's Gart?'

Terisa's mouth fell open. She wasn't the only one with a morbid imagination.

'While we were talking with Torrent,' Geraden continued, 'while we were trying to help the Fayle's man, while we were packing our horses – that was the best chance Gart's ever had to kill us both. We were defenseless. Why didn't Eremis get rid of us while he had the chance?

'I don't think he saw us.

'He *could* have seen us, of course. We found that out outside Sternwall. But this time I don't think he did.

'I'm sure he didn't before the avalanche. We were on the porch, under the roof, and his mirror was focused in the air over the house. After all, he didn't want to kill Queen Madin. She wouldn't have done him any good dead. But that's not really the point. The point is, if you're translating several hundred tons of rock out of one glass into another, what do you do with it while it's between translations? If you make even the tiniest mistake, all that rock will shatter the second mirror, and you'll have the entire avalanche in your lap.'

In spite of herself, Terisa let out a slightly hysterical giggle. That would have been perfect justice, if the landslide Eremis had planned for Vale House had come down on his own head.

Geraden flashed her a grin. 'The solution,' he said, 'is the one we talked about – a hundred years ago or so in Orison, when we didn't know we were two of the most powerful people alive. Translate the second glass into the first. In effect, the rock goes straight into the flat mirror.

'But.' He held up a hand to forestall interruption. 'This is what saved us. When you do a translation like that – when you put the second mirror into the first before you start – what can you see? You can see the mountainside. You can see the rock. But you can't see the Image in the second mirror. The *back* of the flat mirror faces you, so the front can translate the rock.

'And once you start a process like that you have to keep it going until the dust clears and you're sure you're safe. If you stop while there's *any* chance one or two boulders are still hopping down the mountainside, the flat glass could be crushed, and the boulders could end up in your face. So you can't be in a hurry to translate the second mirror back out of the first and turn it around and refocus it.

'That's why we had time to get away.'

Listening to him, Terisa felt a knot inside her loosen at last. He was right. It was possible that Eremis hadn't seen them. If he had, surely he would have sent an attack after them – wolves or a firecat, if not Gart himself. There was still hope for the wild scheme Torrent and Geraden had conceived.

That night, she experienced some of the benefits of Geraden's keenness. She began to feel a bit keener herself.

At about the same time, when the embers had died down, and clouds covered the moon, Prince Kragen sent men to clear the charred remains of his battering rams and their protective shells away from Orison's gates. He wanted the new rams and shells being hammered together to have an unimpeded approach.

And the next morning, he pressed his attack.

Well, they have to run out of oil sometime.

It seemed a rather thin tactic on which to hinge Alend's hopes for survival, never mind victory. Nevertheless he persisted. He simply didn't have any better ideas. With enough time, he could have sat where he was in perfect safety, discussing governance with his father, or with the lady Elega, training his forces – and waiting for Orison to starve itself into submission. That was the way sieges were supposed to go. But nothing that had anything to do with King Joyse ever went the way it was supposed to go. And as for High King Festten—

If the Prince could use up Orison's supplies of lamp oil, cooking oil, flammable grease, he might be able to bring his battering rams to bear on the gates more effectively. All he needed was to get the gates open.

He knew he had enough men to overwhelm the castle, if he could just get the gates open.

Around midafternoon that day, while the fifth of Prince Kragen's makeshift rams burned like a bonfire, Terisa and Geraden sighted Batten and left the road to work eastward around the city.

This was one of the tricky parts, Geraden explained. Here they had to cross Alend's supply route. The danger of encountering Alend soldiers was now severe. And the Armigite's scouts or spies would almost certainly be concentrated along the lines where Alend forces were expected. Geraden and Terisa slowed their pace almost to a walk; and he spent long moments on the crest of every rise, straining his eyes toward the horizons. From time to time, he found a tree and climbed it to study the terrain from that vantage.

For no good reason except that she saw nothing – not even the walls of the city, once she and Geraden had left the road – she began to think these pauses for caution were unnecessary. They crossed the unmistakable swath of ground which had brought the Alend army to the road – unmistakable because the soil still held the cut of wheels, the gouge of hooves, the pressure of boots – but they didn't see any sign of Alend supply wains or Armigite spotters. She would have preferred the risk of speed to the frustration of delay.

She changed her mind, however, when he came down out of a tree so fast that he nearly fell like the fumblefoot he had once been. Hissing instructions rapidly, he dragged the mounts into a nearby thicket; with her help, he forced the beasts to lie down, then did his best to muffle their noses, prevent them from whickering as the other horses came near.

A small band of riders with grime-caked clothes and eyes made evil by fear passed so close that Terisa could have hit them with a stone.

'Mercenaries,' Geraden grated under his breath after the riders were gone. 'Men like that – if they were in a hurry, they might cut your throat *before* they raped you.

'I thought every mercenary in the world worked for Cadwal.'

Terisa was having trouble with her pulse. 'Then what're they doing here?'

He shrugged stiffly, as if all his muscles were in knots. 'Working for somebody else. Or spying for the High King. If the Lieges send Prince Kragen reinforcements, Festten will want to know about it. He may have men all over this part of Mordant by now.'

Oh, good, Terisa muttered to herself. Just what we need.

She and Geraden had to hide twice more before the end of the day, but both times they were able to avoid discovery with relative ease. The scouts or mercenaries expected many things, but they clearly didn't expect to encounter a man and a woman with three horses cutting across open ground around Batten.

In a fireless camp that night in a small gully, she remarked, 'I can't live this way.'

'What, sneaking around like this? Surrounded by people who would gut us unless they had the good sense to take us prisoner if they only knew we were here? You aren't having fun?' Geraden snorted softly. 'Terisa, I'm surprised at you.'

Actually, she was surprised at herself. Without warning, she was filled with a sense of how strange her circumstances were. Wasn't she Terisa Morgan, the passive girl who had typed sad letters for Reverend Thatcher until she had lost faith in him and his mission? Wasn't she the lonely woman who had decorated her apartment in mirrors because she didn't know any other way to prove she existed? So what was she doing *here*? – surrounded, as Geraden observed, by enemies; struggling across country on horseback in a nearly crazy effort to warn King Joyse that his wife had been abducted; so angry at Master Eremis that she couldn't think about it without trembling. What was she *doing*?

'So am I,' she murmured; but Geraden had been teasing her, and she was serious. The night on all sides felt at once vast and subtle, too big to be faced, too cunning to be escaped. And the stars— She knew in her bones that the city where her apartment was had nowhere near this many stars watching it. 'Right now, it seems like there isn't another place in the universe farther away from where I used to live than this.'

'Are you afraid?' he asked gently. 'We still have a long way to go.'

He wasn't talking about the distance to Orison.

'That's the funny part,' she mused. 'When I stop and take my pulse, I get the impression I've never been so scared in all my life. But when I think about where I came from' – my apartment, my job, my parents – 'I think I've never been so brave.'

After a while, he said, 'It makes an amazing difference when you have good, clear reasons for what you're doing. I think I used to have so many accidents because I was confused. In conflict with myself.'

She agreed, but she didn't say so. Instead, she said, 'Don't get cocky. I saw you almost fall out of that tree.'

That made him laugh. And his laughter always made her feel better.

Prince Kragen also had reasons for his actions.

What he was doing was unprecedented. Despite the darkness – despite the fact that his men couldn't see Orison's counterattacks in time to defend themselves very well – he was belaboring the gates with the heaviest battering ram he had.

He had two reasons for risking the blood of his army so lavishly, one immediate, the other alarming.

His immediate reason was that just before sunset the defenders had stopped pouring oil on the shells of his rams. The particular ram spared by this forbearance wasn't especially impressive: its shell protected only enough men to move it, not enough to seriously threaten the gates. Nevertheless the forbearance itself was significant. Without hesitation, the Prince called back that ram and sent out a bigger one, fully manned.

This one, also, was allowed to do its work without being set afire.

Two interpretations immediately suggested themselves. Orison was out of oil. Or Orison was trying to conserve oil – was trusting the dark for protection.

Under other circumstances, this chance to hit the gates wouldn't have been worth the risk. At night, protected by darkness from archers, the castle's defenders would be able to swing down from the walls on ropes and strike at the ram in a matter of minutes. But the Prince was too worried to miss any opportunity, however costly it might prove.

He was alarmed because during the afternoon his scouts had intercepted two hacked and dying men who were apparently the last survivors the Perdon would ever send to Orison.

They weren't actually sure of their lord's fate. When he sent them away, he still had several hundred men around him, was still fighting. But he knew he was finished. He sent these two soldiers to warn King Joyse.

They were too badly hurt to last the night; but Prince Kragen pieced their story together from their confused and feverish babblings. What had apparently happened was that High King Festten had suddenly changed his tactics. He had halted his unexplained march into the Care of Tor: for a while, he had even stopped striking at the Perdon. Instead, he had camped his huge army as if he had gained his goal, as if his only real purpose had been to capture the ground where he now stood – a relatively uninhabited region of complex hills and thin rivers no closer to Marshalt than to Orison.

And then, while the Perdon was still trying to figure out what Festten was doing, the High King had sent out nearly five thousand soldiers to encircle and trap the lord. In the end, only the terrain had enabled these two wounded men to escape. They had hidden in a tree-clogged ravine until darkness allowed them to creep away northward.

How many days ago? Prince Kragen wanted to know. How far exactly? In fact, he wanted to know so badly that out of raw frustration he was tempted to resort to some of the harsher forms of questioning. But it was obvious that the Perdon's men, in effect, had already been tortured past the point where they were able to think or speak coherently. Prince Kragen was left with very little idea when they had left their lord, or where Festten was.

So he attacked Orison's gates at night, despite the losses he knew he was going to incur. He was afraid: he could feel a kind of doom stalking him through the dark. An enemy who would march at least twenty thousand men that far into the middle of nowhere – in this case, the middle of the Care of Tor – for no discernible purpose except to *make camp* was capable of anything.

Through the hours of darkness, Kragen listened to the flat, dull booming of the ram against the gates, to the shouts of the defenders and the cries of his own forces – listened, and ground his teeth to restrain his rage at a war he couldn't either avoid or understand.

Castellan Lebbick appeared to be in a completely different mood. If he felt any desire to rage, he didn't show it. From the battlements above the gate, he watched the massive Alend ram at work with a twisted expression on his face, as if something inside him were being torn; yet he didn't so much as raise his voice or curse. He didn't even grin. For no very clear reason, he muttered in disgust words that sounded to the guards around him like, 'fool woman.' Then he called for ropes and began mustering men to fight for the gates.

He didn't stay to watch the struggle, however. A number of his captains knew what to do in a situation like this. Wandering away like a shadow of the man he used to be, he went to spend as much of the night as possible drinking with Artagel.

Unfortunately, ale – even in that quantity – did nothing to quench the hot, dry sensation in his mind. He was full of foreboding; his brain chewed anticipations of disaster. So he was grimly amazed when he woke up the next morning and learned that something good was happening.

It was raining.

A hard rain, so thick that it blinded the castle and turned the dirt of the courtyard into immediate soup; what the people where Lebbick had grown up called a real gully-washer. And long overdue: Mordant expected rain like this in the spring.

Of course, it made Orison impossible to defend. The guards above the gates wouldn't have known if the entire Alend army had come within a stone's throw of their noses.

On the other hand, the rain also made attack impossible.

The Alends had no footing. They could bring up battering rams until they broke their hearts; but they couldn't swing them effectively. The gates would stand forever against any pounding they might receive in this rain. And other siege engines were equally useless.

The rain didn't cheer Castellan Lebbick up. He was past the point where anything could have cheered him. But it did give him a breathing space, a bit of time in which to get a better grip on himself.

It also helped Terisa and Geraden.

That surprised her. She got so wet and so cold so quickly that she felt defeated before the day had well begun. She soon realized, however, that she and Geraden were in next to no danger of being spotted or captured through this downpour. If she had let him get more than ten feet away, she wouldn't have been able to spot him herself.

Now the trick had nothing to do with being stopped. The trick was to know where they were going.

'How do you know we're not lost?' she shouted into the deluge.

'The rain!' Despite the water streaming down his face, he grinned. 'At this time of year, it always comes from the west! We're going south, so all we have to do is cut across the wind!'

She would have been impressed if her whole body hadn't felt so miserable.

Nevertheless she kept going; she and Geraden kept each other going. While their enemies were blinded was the best time for them to go forward. The rain might make it impossible for Torrent to follow her mother; but Terisa was too cold and soaked to worry about something that far out of her control. She concentrated solely on Geraden and motion until the storm finally blew away an hour or two before sunset, and he had an opportunity to find his bearings.

'Tomorrow.' There was relief in his voice; yet she had never heard him sound so tired. 'We'll be in the Demesne tomorrow morning. Tomorrow afternoon or evening we'll reach Orison.'

Just for something to say, she muttered, 'If Prince Kragen doesn't give me some dry clothes, I'm going to spit right in his face.'

Geraden nodded his approval. 'Just don't kick him. I've heard princes tend to get cranky when they're kicked.'

'I don't care,' she retorted. 'I've been on a horse for as long as I can remember, and my whole body hurts. I'm going to kick anybody I want.'

Again, he nodded. 'You may have to.' It was obvious that his thoughts were elsewhere. 'We've been carrying a lot of questions around for a long time. Tomorrow we'll start getting answers. You may have to kick everybody we meet.'

Terisa refused to worry about that. All she wanted at the moment was to be warm and dry.

The inhabitants of Orison had the opposite reaction: they prayed for more rain.

Unluckily, they didn't get it. By the next morning, the ground was dry enough for Prince Kragen to resume his attack.

The mud was still thick: a sea of it surrounded Orison. But decades or centuries of use had packed the roadbed hard; it gave the Alends enough footing to put some heft into the swing of their ram.

Protected by shields and shells, nearly a thousand men edged close to the walls to ward the ram as it hammered the gates. Every blow seemed to carry through the stone to the tops of the towers, the bottoms of the dungeons.

In response, Castellan Lebbick's guards cranked up mangonels powerful enough to dent iron and splinter wood. The mangonels shattered Alend shields almost effortlessly, reduced the flesh under the shields to pulp and crushed bone. Lebbick didn't have many of the ponderous crossbows, however. And his men had to fire scores of lead bolts in order to damage the shell protecting the ram.

Slowly, inevitably, one blow at a time, the gates began to fail.

The wood started to compress and crack; stress showed along the iron strutwork; mortar sifted from between the stones which held the gates in the wall; bolts began to work loose.

At the moment, Prince Kragen was paying for this success with dozens and then hundreds of his men. Inside the castle, Orison's defenders suffered no losses. But that imbalance would shift as soon as the gates broke.

'Tomorrow,' Lebbick muttered, inspecting their timbers with an expert eye. 'Those shitlickers'll be in here tomorrow. We've got that long to live.'

He didn't sound upset. He didn't even sound angry.

He sounded satisfied.

Dutifully, he sent a report to King Joyse. Then he reduced Orison's defenders to a minimum. Every guard who could be spared he ordered away to spend as much time as possible with whatever friends or family the man had left.

His wife would have approved of that.

Amiably, Artagel asked him, 'What do you suppose King Joyse will do to save us?'

Entirely without warning, Castellan Lebbick recovered his rage. 'The way our luck's going' – he was clenching his teeth so hard his forehead felt like it might crack – 'he'll challenge Prince fornicating Kragen to a *duel*.'

With fury crackling in every muscle, he left the gates and the courtyard. While he was angry, at least, he couldn't bear to watch what was happening.

Like the Prince, he had no way of knowing that Terisa and Geraden were already in the Demesne.

Late that afternoon, they rode as if they were fearless straight up to the first Alend patrol they met and demanded to be taken to the lady Elega.

Swords and distrust surrounded them promptly. Terisa's mount showed a distressing inclination to shy in all directions; she had to fight to keep the beast under control. She was conscious that the weather had turned chilly since the previous day's rain. Alends? she wondered. Not Cadwals? Does that mean Orison is still standing? But she had no intention of asking those questions aloud. After all, these soldiers were dressed and armored just like the men who had taken Queen Madin.

The leader of the patrol snapped, 'What makes pigslop like you two think you've got a reason to see the Prince's lady?'

Geraden's mouth smiled, but his eyes were hard. 'We're servants,' he answered with a hint of danger in his voice. 'Our parents have served her family since before we were born. We grew up with her.

'We've come from Romish. The Queen sent us to see her.'

The Alend leader snarled a curse. 'The Queen? Madin, that shithole Joyse's wife?'

The effort of controlling her horse disguised Terisa's face as effectively as a mask. Geraden's expression was positively serene: only his eyes threatened to betray him. 'So you've heard of her,' he said blandly. 'Good. Then you'll understand that the lady Elega won't take it kindly if you prevent us from delivering our messages.'

'Queen Madin?' the Alend repeated in a voice congested with hostility. 'You've got messages from Queen Madin?'

Geraden's mouth smiled again. 'My, you *are* quick.' Then, softly, he said, 'Take us to see the lady Elega.'

A little thrill touched Terisa's heart as she heard the authority in his tone.

The leader of the patrol hesitated; he was taken aback – a fact which seemed to surprise him. To compensate, he growled an obscenity. Then he said, 'I think the Prince is going to want to hear your messages.'

'As long as we get to talk to her,' replied Geraden, 'I don't care who else hears us. Take us to see them both.

'Just do it.'

To his own obvious astonishment, the Alend leader turned and organized his men to escort Geraden and Terisa toward the encampment. A pair of the Alends galloped ahead; the rest formed a knot around the travelers.

Suddenly giddy with relief – perhaps because her horse had stopped shying – she took the risk of giving Geraden a wink. He pretended not to notice it.

They were closer to the siege than she had realized. In only a short time, they came in sight of the Alend army and Orison.

She was surprised by how small the castle looked under these circumstances, invested by ten thousand soldiers, half a hundred siege engines, and an uncounted number of servants and camp followers. Orison's bluff gray stone, which should have appeared impregnable, bore an unexpected resemblance to cardboard; tiny flags fluttering from the towers gave the place the air of a child's plaything.

At the same time, the breach partially covered by the curtain-wall seemed to gape unnaturally wide, as if it were bigger than it used to be, darker; a fatal wound.

The men who had ridden ahead had already caused a commotion: Terisa could see the army and its adherents shifting to receive her and Geraden. People ran forward to stare; questions were called which the Alend leader either ignored or shouted down. The attack on the gates used only a fraction of Prince Kragen's forces; the rest had nothing to do at the moment except wait and worry. Some of the soldiers only wanted news. But others offered jokes and insults that turned Geraden's eyes as sharp as bits of glass. He preserved his expression of serenity, however, and followed the patrol in through the camp.

They passed an area of tattered and scruffy tents where the poorest of the camp followers lived, ankle-deep in the overflow of their own squalor. Then the order and cleanliness of the encampment began to improve, according to the increasing status of its occupants. In minutes, the patrol brought Terisa and Geraden to an open area like an imitation of a courtyard, around which were pitched several tents so large and luxurious that she felt sure she and Geraden had reached their goal.

Their immediate goal, at any rate. In order to enter Orison, they first had to get past Prince Kragen.

He came out of one of the tents into the evening shadows before anyone had a chance to dismount. He moved as if he intended to approach the riders directly; but as soon as he saw them he stopped. He planted his fists on his hips when Terisa met his gaze; his black eyes flashed as if she had given him a slap. For a moment, forcing himself to be thorough, he turned his head and considered Geraden; then he faced Terisa again.

'"Servants of the Queen"?' he demanded of his men in a tone that might have been jesting or bitter. 'They said that, and you believed them? Did not one of you louts think to ask them their *names*?'

He didn't give the leader of the patrol a chance to respond, however. 'Oh, let it pass. They would have lied about their names as well, and then you would have been worse fooled than before.

'At least have the common sense to disarm them. Then go.'

Stung, the leader of the patrol snatched away Terisa's and Geraden's weapons, the swords the Termigan had given them. Then the men withdrew.

Prince Kragen gave the impression that the patrol had already ceased to exist as far as he was concerned. He was concentrating exclusively on Terisa.

'My lady Terisa of Morgan.' He spoke slowly, drawling in a way which suggested humor or scorn. 'You astonish me entirely. And your companion must be the infamous Apt Geraden, the butt alike of mirth and augury. I can think of no other possibility.

'However, you may amaze me there as well. Since you are *out here*' – he released one fist from his hip to gesture at the ground between the tents – 'when it is obvious that you ought to be *in there*' – he indicated Orison – 'I conclude that you have a remarkable story to tell me.

'You will tell it' – gradually, his tone convinced Terisa that he wasn't in a happy mood – 'now.'

'My lord Prince,' Geraden put in steadily, as if he weren't interrupting the Alend Contender, 'where is the lady Elega?'

'I am here, Geraden.'

Terisa turned in her saddle and saw the King's daughter.

Elega stood between the flaps of one of the tents. A streak of sunset caught her face, so that her usual paleness was covered with an orange-gold blush, and light muffled the vividness of her eyes. In that way, she looked like she had become an entirely different woman since Terisa had last seen her.

'So it is true, my lady Terisa,' she said clearly, lifting up her voice as though this were a formal occasion. 'It was always true. You are an Imager.'

Prince Kragen's mouth moved under his moustache, swearing. When he spoke, however, he kept his tone neutral. 'How do you reach that conclusion, my lady Elega?'

Elega's gaze didn't shift from Terisa; she studied Terisa through the failing beams of the sun. 'As you said, my lord Prince, they are not in Orison. It is doubtful that they were able to creep out through your siege. Therefore they must have removed themselves by Imagery.'

'Or someone else removed us,' Geraden put in acerbically. 'Don't forget that possibility. You don't think Gart does his own translations, do you?'

An unexpected silence fell over the tents. Elega half raised a hand to her mouth, then dropped it. A glint of white teeth showed between Prince Kragen's lips. From somewhere in the distance, Terisa heard a methodical booming, a deep thud at once so hard and so far away that it seemed to come through the ground rather than the air. Men shouted faintly. Her presence there, and Geraden's, must have come as a complete surprise to Elega and the Prince. Now the idea Geraden suggested appeared to shock them further, as if it made the whole situation incomprehensible.

Well, Terisa thought, this was better than being tied up – or cut down. She felt an off-center, almost loony desire to give Geraden a round of applause. The men who had taken Queen Madin were Alends. And Terisa and Geraden had so many questions— And they wanted to get into Orison. If Kragen really had ordered the Queen's abduction, their only hope was to keep him off balance and pray for something unexpected to happen.

Trying to make a contribution, she asked, 'My lord Prince, may we get down? I've been on this horse ever since I can remember.'

A small shudder seemed to pass through Prince Kragen, a brief convulsion of will. At once, he became calmer, as if his self-possession had been tightened a notch.

'Of course, my lady Terisa.' He moved toward her. 'Where other matters are concerned, I have said that the debts between us are settled. Yet you are a friend of the lady Elega's, and so you are welcome among us. Permit me to offer you the Alend Monarch's hospitality.'

He reached up his hands to help her dismount.

That was a courtesy to which she wasn't accustomed, but she did her best to let him assist her. Geraden swung down and came to her side; at once, he bowed formally to Prince Kragen.

'My lord Prince, I haven't been properly presented, but you've named me. I'm Geraden, the seventh son of the Domne, an Apt of the Congery of Imagers.

'As you say, we have a remarkable story to tell.' Somehow, he contrived to sound like he couldn't think of a single reason to distrust the Prince. 'And there must be a lot you could tell us, if we can persuade you to do it.'

'Geraden.' Elega had come forward while Terisa was focused on Prince Kragen. Her face and form were in shadow now, with the paradoxical result that she looked brighter, keener; more capable. 'What does this mean?' she demanded. 'Why are you here? And *how*? Surely you will not ask us to believe that this is nothing more than another of your colossal mishaps?'

'No,' Geraden replied. 'On the other hand, I do expect you to believe that it's hard for me to trust you enough to tell you anything.'

There: he had given the first hint of his loyalties; therefore of his intentions. Terisa held her breath, afraid that he might be risking too much too soon.

Fortunately, Kragen wasn't surprised enough to react badly. He knew what had happened to Nyle's attempt to reach the Perdon: he was probably able to take Geraden's loyalties for granted. Before Elega could respond to Geraden's gibe, Prince Kragen stepped between them and took Terisa's arm.

'We will discuss such things thoroughly, I assure you,' he remarked, 'but I can see no reason why we should not discuss them in comfort – and in private.' With his hand on her arm, he urged Terisa into motion, steering her toward the largest of the surrounding tents. 'In addition, I have offered you the Alend Monarch's hospitality, and he does not like to be refused.' As if she weren't already moving – as if she had a choice – he asked, 'Will you come with me?'

Terisa nodded. But she didn't let out her breath until she saw that both Geraden and Elega were following.

The Prince took her into what she realized after a moment was a fore-tent. It was lit only by the braziers which warmed it, with the result that its furnishings were obscure, vaguely ominous; the chairs seemed to crouch in the dimness, as unpredictable as beasts. Prince Kragen clapped his hands, however, and called for lamps as well as wine. The servants responded almost instantly; soon warm yellow light filled the fore-tent, and the danger crept away, hiding in the darkness at the tops of the tentpoles, or in the shadows behind the chairs.

'The Alend Monarch has gone to his bed,' Prince Kragen said casually. 'Otherwise he would welcome you himself. This tent serves as his council chamber, and I doubt' – he smiled – 'that there is a man in all the camp who would dare eavesdrop on what is said here. We will speak freely.'

Briskly, he got Terisa, Geraden, and Elega seated. When the wine had been served, he took a chair himself. Terisa drank a gulp of the fine vintage, trying to control her nervousness; but Elega watched her and Geraden, while Geraden faced the Prince.

Prince Kragen toyed with his goblet. 'My lady Terisa, Geraden, these are complex times. I suspect that all stories are remarkable. Nevertheless your arrival here suggests questions to which I must have answers.'

'Forgive me, my lord Prince,' Geraden put it as if he hadn't heard Kragen. 'So much has happened – The last we knew, Cadwal was marching. A vast army. Where *is* it? What's happened to the Perdon? How has Orison been able to hold you back so long?'

'Geraden, I am in command of this siege.' The Prince's voice became a soft purr, a threat. 'This army is mine. I wish to understand how you come to be here.'

'Of course' – Geraden allowed himself a slight, suggestive pause – 'my lord Prince. On the other hand, I wish to be able to measure the consequences of what I tell you. I'm talking to an honorable enemy and a dishonorable friend.' He ignored the way Elega stiffened, the violet flare of her gaze. 'Knowledge is power. I don't want to place a weapon in the wrong hands.'

'You will not.' Prince Kragen might have been a cat pretending that he wasn't about to spring. 'You will place it in *my* hands.'

Geraden didn't blink. 'Or else?'

The Prince shrugged delicately. 'There is no "or else." I simply state a fact. You *will* tell me your remarkable story.'

His tone left Terisa's stomach in knots. When she looked in her goblet, she found that it was already empty.

'Geraden,' Elega put in, 'why did you come here? You have never been stupid. You knew that this situation would arise. You knew that both the Prince and I desire the defeat of Orison. And you knew' – she seemed to falter, but only for an instant – 'that we cannot afford to let you keep your knowledge secret. We are too much at risk. My life is perhaps a little thing, but the Prince is responsible for the whole Alend army. In the end, he is responsible for the survival of all his father's realm.

'And for that,' Elega added firmly, 'I have my own responsibility. Like the King, I have brought us to this place.

'Why did you put yourself and the lady Terisa in our hands, if you do not intend to tell us what you know?'

'Because we are unable to reenter Orison without your consent.' Geraden didn't elaborate.

'That is what you want?' demanded Prince Kragen softly. 'You wish to be allowed to enter Orison, so that you can tell King Joyse the story you mean to withhold from me?'

Geraden contemplated this view of the situation. 'That's essentially true, my lord Prince.'

'I suspected as much.' The Prince held his hands together on his thighs, the tips of his fingers touching each other lightly as if his self-command had become perfect. 'My mind is not like my lady Elega's. When you entered my camp, I did not say, Here are Imagers. I said, Here are scouts who wish to report to their lord.

'If you believe that I will let you pass my siege in order to take assistance or information of any kind to King Joyse, you are seriously deranged.'

Geraden shrugged. Judging by the blandness of his expression, he had no idea how seriously he was being threatened.

Terisa was too full of anxiety to sit still. Without asking permission, she stood up and went to the wine decanter. 'Why don't we trade?' she said impulsively. Fatigue and the first effects of the wine might have been speaking for her. She had played the game of trading information with King Joyse: she knew it was dangerous. But it was the best she had to offer. Her goblet full, she returned to her seat. 'You tell us something. We'll tell you something. Fair exchange. That way we don't have to trust each other.'

'Who will speak first?' asked Elega in a carefully neutral tone.

'You will.' Terisa didn't hesitate. 'We're in your power. You can do anything you want to us anytime you want. What have you got to lose?'

She sat down.

Geraden kept his reaction hidden. The lady Elega looked at Prince Kragen.

The Prince thought for a while; he didn't appear to be aware that he was chewing his moustache. Two of his fingertips tapped soundlessly against each other, measuring the menace in the foretent. Then he said with steady nonchalance, 'I think not.

'My lady Elega,' he continued before Terisa was sure that she had heard him right, 'you have not heard the details of our guests' arrival. You will be interested, I am sure.

'Geraden and the lady Terisa made no attempt at stealth. They confronted one of my patrols' – he paused ominously – 'but they did not request an audience with me. They did not request permission to approach Orison. No, my lady, they demanded the right to speak with you.'

Involuntarily, Elega caught her breath.

While she stared at Geraden and Terisa, Prince Kragen added, 'It is clear that whatever device or policy they have prepared to get them into Orison is directed at you. They believe that they have the means to persuade you.' Again, he paused; then he remarked cryptically, 'It is even conceivable that they are aware of the existence of a precedent.'

In response, Elega's eyes widened with pain and anger. 'That is unfair, my lord.' Almost instantly, however, she seemed to catch the implications of what he said. In a rush, she asked, 'Geraden, have you seen—?'

So suddenly, so loudly that the sound made Terisa's heart lurch, Prince Kragen slapped his hands together, interrupting Elega; stopping her.

'My lady,' he articulated, 'I have said that I do not wish to trade stories with them. When they have told us what they know, I will decide what they may hear.'

Elega held her tongue; yet her face showed the difficulty of restraint. Abruptly, Terisa became aware that she wanted to hear Elega's story: the Elega she remembered wouldn't have suffered a command to *shut up* so compliantly. What had happened to change the lady, to make her acquiescent? What kind of contest was going on between her and the Prince? Was it just a question of blame because her attack on the reservoir had misfired? Or had she done something else to earn Kragen's distrust?

Because her heart was still racing and she wanted to be calm, Terisa went to get some more wine.

As if they were being polite, the other people in the fore-tent waited until she had seated herself again. She had the impression that they were all watching her.

'You serve a heady wine, my lord Prince,' Geraden murmured softly. 'I haven't tasted anything like it for a long time.'

In Terisa's opinion, that was an odd thing to say at a time like this.

Apparently, Prince Kragen agreed with her. He ignored Geraden's comment. Still speaking to Elega as if she were the true subject of his scrutiny, he said, 'In any case, my lady, I have not yet told you everything you must hear. When Geraden and the lady Terisa demanded to speak to you, they gave a most interesting explanation. They said that they had messages for you from Queen Madin, your mother.'

At once, Elega was on her feet. 'The Queen?' She didn't appear to realize that she was standing. 'You have spoken with the Queen? She sent messages for me?' Her eyes shone with excitement and anguish; her voice held a visceral tremor. 'Doubtless you told her of my part in the siege. What does my mother wish to say to me now?'

Terisa was bemused to find that she had slipped down in her chair. The wine seemed to have made her top-heavy.

Pushing herself upright, she said, 'We can tell you who the traitors are inside Orison. Who the renegade Imagers are. We can tell you how they planned all this with Cadwal. Together, we might be able to guess what kind of trap they plan to spring.'

Prince Kragen's gaze burned darkly at her. For no particular reason, she added, 'If you want to trade, we can even tell you what Domne and Termigan and Fayle are going to do about it.'

As far as she could tell, Geraden and Elega and Kragen were all speaking at once. Geraden asked, 'Do you know what you're doing? You look like you've had too much wine.' He sounded like a man who had lost his sense of humor.

At the same time, Elega protested, 'No! I will hear my mother's messages!'

Prince Kragen was saying, 'Continue, my lady Terisa.' Despite his self-control, he looked eager. 'I am sure that we will be able to achieve an equitable exchange when you are done.'

Grinning, Terisa wagged her finger at him. 'Oh, no, my lord Prince.' She actually wagged her finger at him. 'Be fair. That isn't the way the game is played.'

Geraden stood facing Elega; his voice was pitched to cover Terisa's. His tone didn't hold any authority, however. It didn't even convey confidence. Instead, it hinted at hysteria.

'The fact is,' he said, 'we don't have any messages from the Queen. She didn't have time to give us any. She was planning to come here herself. She wanted to stand beside the King. But she didn't get the chance.'

In spite of the pressure to speak, he faltered. Elega's gaze was fastened to his face; her whole body concentrated toward him.

'Go on,' she said with her throat clenched.

'Continue, my lady!' Prince Kragen snapped, apparently trying to startle words out of Terisa.

Just in time, Terisa put her finger to her lips and made a shushing noise.

'Elega, I'm sorry,' Geraden said miserably. 'While we were there, the Queen was taken. Ambushed. Imagery and soldiers. She was abducted.'

Slowly, as if she could barely lift them, Elega raised her hands to her mouth.

'We know who the Imager was.'

Her breath came hard, straining between her teeth.

'The soldiers were Alends.'

Prince Kragen was so startled that he sprang to his feet and barked, 'You lie!' before he could stop himself.

Terisa studied the three of them. 'No.' It was wonderful how clearly she could speak, despite the weight in her head. 'He's not lying. We were there. That's why we want to go into Orison. That's what we want to tell King Joyse. Your men kidnapped Queen Madin.'

From Terisa's perspective, the lady Elega went up like a candleflame. Without moving, she seemed to burst into passion; it swept through her toward the ceiling, hot enough to scorch. Confronting the Prince as if Terisa and Geraden were forgotten, she whispered like a cry, 'What have you done?'

Kragen's face twisted; his teeth showed under his moustache. 'They lie. I tell you, it is a lie.'

She didn't flicker. 'Geraden has never told a lie in his life – never one of such hurt. *What have you done?*'

'Nothing!' he shouted at her, trying to drive back her fury. 'Geraden does not lie? Perhaps not. *I* do not lift my hand against lonely and harmless women! Never in my life.'

Perhaps she didn't hear him: perhaps she couldn't. Her hands clenched into fists against her cheeks; blazing, she lifted her voice into a wail.

'Where is my mother? What have you done to my mother?'

In that outcry, she burned up too brightly to sustain herself. She was too vulnerable: her strength failed, and she fainted. Delicately, like heated wax, she slumped toward the floor.

Geraden caught her.

Holding her in his arms, he faced the Prince. Now he was the one breathing hard, panting for air as if he had caught fire from her. Her distress made him savage, heedless. Prince Kragen came to him in dismay, tried to take her from him. He wrenched her away as if he didn't care that the Prince could have him killed.

'There are only two possibilities. My lord Prince. Isn't that right? Either you did it. So you're going to tie me and Terisa up and start torturing us. Or it was done to you. So you're going to let us go see the King.

'Which is it?'

But Prince Kragen wasn't listening. 'Release her, Geraden,' he murmured, almost pleading. 'She is only your friend. I love her. If all of Cadwal and the wide sea itself come between us, I will wed her before I die. Give her to me.'

He held out his arms.

Terisa saw Geraden burning the way Elega had burned; she saw him on the verge of hurling something he wouldn't be able to retract into the teeth of the Prince's regret. Fortunately, she was already on her feet, pulled erect by his fury. Otherwise she couldn't have reached him in time. She put a hand on his shoulder, then slipped her arm around his neck and hugged him.

'I believe him,' she said softly. 'You called him an honorable enemy. He wouldn't do something like that. And if he did, he would have done it long ago.

'He's going to let us into Orison.'

She felt Geraden's muscles pull tight, as rigid as Elega's cry.

After a moment, she felt them relax.

Gently, he shifted Elega into Prince Kragen's embrace.

At once, Kragen sank to the floor, holding Elega close while he checked her pulse and respiration, made her comfortable. He bowed his head over her, ignoring Terisa and Geraden.

They stood near him and waited. The sides of the fore-tent were lined with servants and soldiers, summoned by the lady Elega's wail. They had no instructions, however, and didn't move.

Then Elega's eyes fluttered open. When she saw where she was, a slight smile curved her mouth. Gently, as if she didn't want to hurt him, she put up her hand to touch the Prince's cheek.

He let out a stiff sigh and raised his head.

His voice had to struggle out of his chest. 'Why am I going to let you into Orison?'

Geraden cleared his throat. Constricted with emotion, he rasped, 'Because if the men who took Queen Madin were Cadwals or mercenaries disguised as Alends, the attack is aimed at you as well as King Joyse. Part of the point is to keep anybody from trusting you. And part of it is to keep you and King Joyse from trusting each other, from forming an alliance.

'You're being manipulated. By High King Festten. And the traitors. And the only way you can save yourself is to let us talk to the King.'

'And if I do not let them into Orison' – the Prince was speaking to Elega – 'you will believe that I am responsible for your mother's abduction.'

Elega didn't nod or shake her head. The small smile stayed on her lips; her hand cupped Kragen's cheek. 'You want an alliance, my lord. You have always wanted an alliance, not this misconceived and aimless siege. Perhaps that is possible now. Perhaps it would be worth the attempt.'

Prince Kragen made a harsh noise like an attempted laugh. 'The last time I proposed that, he humiliated me. He went to considerable lengths to humiliate me.'

'He didn't—' Terisa began. Her legs were unsteady, however, and she had to support herself on Geraden's shoulder. For a moment, she forgot what she was saying.

Then she remembered.

'He was testing you. He thought you were his enemy. He didn't know who the traitor was. He didn't know what alliances had already been made. Now we can tell him.'

Prince Kragen's head turned; his eyes held an obsidian smolder which would have frightened her if she had been able to concentrate on it. Softly, he commanded, 'Tell me.'

Geraden took a deep breath, straightened his back. 'I'll tell you this much, my lord. The traitor is Master Eremis. We can guess how he does the translations that let him attack anywhere in Mordant – that let him and Gart and Master Gilbur move through flat glass without losing their minds. And we know where his power is located, where he keeps his mirrors.'

With an intensity Terisa didn't quite understand, Prince Kragen demanded, 'Where is that?'

When Geraden had described Esmerel and its location, the Prince lowered his head.

'My lady,' he asked Elega, 'can you stand?'

She nodded.

A flick of his fingers brought two servants running forward. They eased the lady out of his arms, assisted her to her feet. At once, Prince Kragen surged upright. He kept his face averted, so that Terisa and Geraden couldn't see his expression. Under his breath, he murmured, 'I must speak to the Alend Monarch.'

Without offering an explanation or waiting for an answer, he entered the darkness of the main tent and closed the flap behind him.

While Geraden and Elega studied each other with uncertainty and some embarrassment, Terisa went to refill her goblet.

She was stretched out on the floor, sound asleep and snoring gently, when the Alend Contender returned.

In a subtle way, his manner had changed. He looked less angry, less sick to the teeth with frustration; the prospect of immediate battle or danger came as a palpable relief to him. Despite his efforts to sound neutral, his voice was several shades lighter as he announced, 'The Alend Monarch has decided that you will be allowed to enter Orison tomorrow morning.'

When he said that, Elega's face shone at him.

Geraden let the air out of his tight chest with a burst like a laugh. 'Thanks, my lord Prince. I'm glad we were right about you. And I'm glad you don't hold a grudge against me for stopping Nyle.' He glanced affectionately at Terisa. 'She'll be glad, too – when she wakes up.'

The Prince nodded brusquely and continued, 'I will accompany you, both to demonstrate my good faith and to pursue the Alend Monarch's desire for an alliance.'

'Good idea,' Geraden remarked.

'The lady Elega will remain here to ensure that King Joyse does not abuse my good faith.'

Elega dropped her eyes, but didn't try to argue.

'In the meantime,' Prince Kragen concluded, commanding the attention of his soldiers with a gesture, 'it might be advisable to discontinue our assault on the gates.' He looked at one of his men. 'Give the order.'

The man saluted and left. The rest of the servants and soldiers also filed out of the fore-tent.

To his own surprise, Geraden found that he felt suddenly giddy, in the mood for jokes and foolishness. 'With your permission, my lord,' he said, 'I'll have some more of that strong wine. Then, if you're interested in the trade Terisa mentioned, I'll tell you a story that will curl your hair.'

Grinning like a predator, the Prince refilled Geraden's goblet himself.

THIRTY-NINE

THE FINAL
PIECE OF BAIT

𝓮

By midnight, Prince Kragen and the lady Elega knew most of Geraden's secrets.

The Alend Contender was an honorable man, however, and he kept his word.

While Terisa and Geraden slept the heavy sleep of too much wine, servants carried them to another tent, and put them to bed. At dawn more servants awakened them, offered them baths and food and clean clothes. According to the servants, Prince Kragen wished his guests to take full advantage of his hospitality. When they were entirely ready, he would approach the castle with them.

Terisa felt loggy with sleep, thick-headed with the wine's aftereffects. She wanted a bath so badly that she could hardly contain herself.

She was also considerably embarrassed.

When she realized that she couldn't quite meet Geraden's eyes, she asked awkwardly, 'Are you still speaking to me?'

'Of course.' There was a watchful air behind his smile, but no discernible irritation. 'If you want me to stop speaking to you, you're going to have to do something worse than that.'

At least he didn't pretend he didn't know what she was talking about. She covered her face with her hands. 'Did I make a complete idiot out of myself?'

He chuckled easily. 'That's the amazing part. You scared me, all right. I thought you were going to get us in terrible trouble. But everything you did turned out fine. Even drinking as much as you did may have helped. It made you believable. I don't think I could have handled either Elega or the Prince without you.'

She pulled down her hands. Deliberately, she glared at him. 'Stop being so nice to me. I was irresponsible. You ought to be furious.'

Geraden gaped like a clown. 'You're right. I'm sorry. Oh, I'm sorry, I'm sorry. Please forgive me. I'm so ashamed.'

She made a grim but halfhearted effort to kick his shins.

Laughing, he caught hold of her, held her, hugged her. After a while, a strange desire to weep came over her, and she found herself clinging to him hard. Fortunately, the desire only lasted a moment. As soon as it faded, she felt better.

She had to let go of him to wipe her nose. 'Thanks,' she said softly. 'Someday I'll do something nice for you.'

It surprised her to see that he was leering. 'If we had time, I'd get you to do it right now.'

That brought a smile out of her. 'No, you wouldn't.' She was definitely feeling better. 'I stink like a pig. I think I've got cockroaches living in my hair.'

He stuck out his tongue in mock-nausea.

She went to take a bath.

When they were clean, and dressed in the new clothes Prince Kragen had provided for them – comfortable traveling clothes sewn of leather as supple as kidskin – they ate breakfast. The impression that they were keeping the Alend Contender waiting nagged at the back of Terisa's mind; nevertheless she let him wait so that she would have a last chance to talk to Geraden. She had to prepare herself for Orison.

'We're aren't likely to get much of a welcome, you know,' she said between bites of honeyed bread and souffléd eggs – an unexpectedly rich sample of the Alend Monarch's hospitality. 'I tried to make the Castellan think I might be innocent, but Master Gilbur did a pretty good job of wiping that out.' She didn't mention Artagel. 'Everybody there has spent the whole time thinking you killed Nyle and I'm in league with the arch-Imager.'

Geraden nodded. 'It won't be much fun. But I'm not too worried. We'll have Prince Kragen with us. We'll be under a flag of truce. No matter what Lebbick and everybody else thinks of us, they'll leave us alone.'

He chewed for a moment in silence, then added, 'What I'm worried about is that mirror – the one that attacked the Perdon when he came here to get King Joyse's help.'

Suddenly, Terisa found a sick taste in her mouth. 'Didn't Eremis change all that? He used those creatures to try to kill us outside Sternwall. He may have used them to kill Underwell. What can he still do?'

'Well, he must have switched flat mirrors in the Image of the world where those creatures come from. Otherwise he couldn't have attacked us. But he's had plenty of time since then. He could have switched the mirrors back.

'In any case, the point is that he has a glass that shows the approach to Orison, the road. He'll be able to see us go in. He'll be forewarned.'

She thought about that while the taste in her mouth changed to an old, settled anger. Then she muttered, 'At least he'll be surprised. He won't have any idea how we managed to talk Prince Kragen into this.'

It did her good to be angry. Facing down Castellan Lebbick – or the Tor and Artagel, who had turned against her – would be hard enough. But confronting Master Eremis would be worse. The more she loved Geraden, the more her skin crawled at the memory of the things Master Eremis had done to her.

She could see Geraden's eagerness in his eyes, in the way he moved: he was starting to hurry. She had never been as confident or as clear as he was;

but she, too, felt a need for haste. By tacit agreement, they left the remains of their meal. They had nothing to pack, nothing to carry. They kissed each other once, like a promise; then they went out of the tent.

Prince Kragen was waiting for them. They caught him in the act of pacing back and forth across the open area among the luxurious tents.

He was dressed in his ceremonial garb: a black silk doublet and pantaloons covered by a brass breastplate with a high polish; a sword in a gleaming brass scabbard on his hip; a spiked brass helmet on his curling hair. The sheen of the metal emphasized his swarthy skin; it made his black eyes glitter and his moustache shine. And his impatience only increased the self-assertion of his bearing, emphasizing his habit of command.

Three horses were held ready beyond the tents. They, too, were dressed for show, with satin and silk streaming from their saddles and tack, gilt cords knotted into their manes and tails. Around them, an honor guard was already mounted: ten men to carry the Prince's pennon, and his dignity.

Terisa didn't see Elega anywhere.

Prince Kragen nodded to Geraden, bowed to Terisa. In a tightly reined voice, he explained, 'The lady Elega sends her goodwill to you – and to her father – but she cannot bid you farewell. She has already been placed under guard. The Alend Monarch intends to assure that no mistakes are made with us, and the lady Elega is his only means to that end. Even I do not know where she is held. Therefore I cannot enable the King's men – or his Imagers – to find her.'

Terisa swallowed hard. The sun was up, but it didn't seem to be enjoying its work. The light over the encampment and against the walls of Orison was thin, unconvincing; the air had a cold taste, more like a residue of winter than a part of spring. The castle's battlements looked bleak, as if they had been abandoned. If anything happened to her and Geraden there – but especially if anything happened to Prince Kragen – Elega would be in serious trouble.

'My lord Prince' – Geraden changed the subject awkwardly – 'you must have heard about the mirror that attacked the Perdon. If he didn't tell you about it himself, surely Elega did?'

'Yes.' A subtle shift in his expression suggested that Prince Kragen was glad to discuss something other than Elega. 'But I must confess that I am baffled. Our siege engines have no approach to the gates, except along the road. Our rams must pass through the Image which struck at the Perdon. Yet nothing has been translated against us.

'You have told me that Master Eremis is in league with Cadwal to destroy Mordant – and Alend as well. For that reason, his power has been used to defend Orison against us. Yet we are now within hours – within a day at most – of breaking down the gates, and he has done nothing to hinder us.'

Breaking down the gates. Terisa's stomach twisted. So it was now or never. If she and Geraden couldn't get King Joyse to accept an alliance, Orison would fall almost immediately.

The muscles along Geraden's jaw bunched; but if he was worried about Orison's vulnerability to Prince Kragen he didn't admit it. 'He probably hasn't given you trouble,' he said, 'because you haven't been attacking very hard. If you're about to break in, and he still isn't using Imagery, I'd guess his trap is just about ready to spring.'

Prince Kragen nodded darkly. Without a word, he beckoned for the horses and his honor guard.

In a moment, Terisa found herself being offered a charger so big that she couldn't see over its back. Oh, shit, she muttered to herself. That was one thing she had learned in Mordant, anyway: after some practice, she was now able to say *oh, shit* without sounding like she expected to have her mouth washed out with soap. If she fell off that beast, she might take days to hit the ground.

Unfortunately, Prince Kragen had already mounted; Geraden was swinging up into the saddle of his horse. This probably wouldn't be a good time to ask for something smaller.

Somehow, she climbed onto the charger's back.

The reins carried so many streamers that they looked like the lines of a maypole. She was afraid to move them: they might make her horse shy. But Prince Kragen and Geraden weren't having any trouble. Apparently, these beasts were trained for ceremonial occasions. Nothing embarrassing happened as she guided her mount to Geraden's side.

'Simply as a precaution,' the Prince announced, 'we will avoid the road. We will ride to the walls directly, and around them to the gates.'

Geraden seemed to think that made sense.

Prince Kragen nodded to his honor guard. His standard-bearer raised the green-and-red pennon of Alend, then affixed a flag of truce below it. The soldiers took their formal positions around their Prince and his companions.

In formation, the riders left the encampment.

The charger's strides made the distance shorter than it had any right to be. Before she had time to accustom herself to the beast's gait, Terisa found herself moving into what looked like arrow-range of the castle. She could see men on the walls now, watching, pointing; some of them hurried from place to place. She tried to stifle the fear that they would ignore the flag of truce and start firing, but it refused to go away.

Luckily, there was still some common sense left in Orison. None of the men on the battlements bent their bows. None of them made any threatening gestures.

Instead, the castle's trumpeter winded his horn, sending a forlorn call like a wail of defiance into the skeptical sunlight. As the riders rounded the corner of Orison and neared the entrance, they heard the great winches squeal against the strain of raising the battered and deformed gates up into the architrave.

Terisa felt nothing to indicate that a translation had ever taken place near here.

In formation, Prince Kragen and his company crossed the bare ground to the road in front of the gates.

Castellan Lebbick and ten of his men came out on horseback to meet them.

Seeing the Castellan filled Terisa's stomach with a watery panic. His men were nervous; the horses fretted because they hadn't had enough exercise. In contrast, he looked too obsessed and single-minded for nervousness. His eyes were red and raw, dangerously aggrieved; he moved as if the violence coiled in his muscles might burst out at any moment. His features were sharp with anticipation – almost with yearning.

'My lord Prince.' He bared his teeth: maybe he was trying to smile. 'You've got strange friends. A fratricide and a traitor. I never thought I was going to see either of *them* again.'

'Castellan Lebbick.' Prince Kragen lacked Lebbick's air of madness, but he matched the Castellan's tone. 'Geraden and the lady Terisa accompany me under a flag of truce. I have no interest in your opinion of them. You will respect the flag.'

'Oh, of course. They're as safe as babies. Especially since they're with *you*. You're the man who intends to break down my gates. I wouldn't lift a finger against any of you.'

Prince Kragen clenched his jaws. Before he could speak, however, Geraden said hotly, 'Castellan, I didn't kill my brother.' His face was flushed; anger glinted from his eyes. Hints of authority echoed in his voice. 'Terisa isn't a traitor. It's time for you to start believing us. You're doomed if you don't.'

The Castellan actually laughed – a rough sound like a piece of stone being crushed. 'Believe you? *I* believe you. I don't need you to tell me I'm doomed. That's not the problem.'

Prince Kragen contained himself. 'What *is* the problem, Castellan?'

'The problem, my lord Prince,' retorted Lebbick fiercely, 'is that I'm the only one. Nobody else here cares enough. Nobody else is *desperate* enough.'

Terisa recoiled from his vehemence. She didn't want to know what he was talking about: she wanted to get away from him. Geraden leaned forward in his saddle, however; he was almost panting. 'Did I hear you right, Castellan?' he demanded. 'Did I just hear you admit Terisa and I are innocent?'

'No.' The Castellan bared his teeth again. 'You heard me say I believe you. They all think I'm insane. If I said the sun is shining today, the people in there' – he indicated Orison with a twitch of his head – 'would run to get out of the rain.

'Nobody cares what a crazy man believes. Besides' – he shrugged maliciously – 'I might be wrong.'

'Castellan Lebbick.' Prince Kragen spoke harshly, trying to gain control of the situation. 'We will discuss the question of your sanity at another time. As you may guess, Geraden and the lady Terisa have traveled widely since they departed Orison. They bring news. I must have an audience with King Joyse.'

'An audience?' Lebbick snapped back at once, 'you? The Alend Contender? Any news you want King Joyse to hear is either false or dangerous. They're going to scream for your heart's blood when I let you in. Of course you can have an audience.'

Wheeling his horse as if the matter were settled, he faced his men. Counting off four of them, he ordered, 'Tell King Joyse. I'm going to take Kragen and these two to the hall of audiences. Tell him there are going to be riots unless he backs me up. We'll have to kill people to keep the Prince and his friends alive if King Joyse doesn't come to the hall.'

At once, Prince Kragen put in grimly, 'And tell him also that the lady Elega is being kept hostage. Until now, she has been an honored guest and friend of the Alend Monarch. To ensure my safety, however, she has been deprived of her freedom.' He spoke as if he intended to make someone pay for the necessity which compelled him to let Elega be used in this way. 'If any harm comes to me, or to my companions, she will be hurt as well.

'Tell King Joyse *that*.'

'Oh, of course, my lord Prince,' the Castellan grated without looking at Kragen. 'I burn to do everything you command. My men will keep you alive. Somehow.'

His four guards rode back into the courtyard. Terisa saw them dismount, saw them head at a run for one of the inner doorways.

'Come on,' added Lebbick. He might have been speaking to the wall stretching high above his head over the gates. 'Or ride back to Margonal and admit you haven't got the bare courage to do whatever it is you've got in mind.'

With his remaining men, he reentered the mouth of Orison.

Prince Kragen stared at the Castellan's back. He made no effort to lower his voice. 'That man has lost his mind.'

Still aching inside, Terisa murmured, 'King Joyse cut the ground out from under him. His wife died, and he didn't have anything else to live for except his loyalty, and the King made him look like a fool for being loyal.'

'A pitiful tale,' rasped the Prince. Obviously, he had no patience for Lebbick's problems. 'Sadly, it does not tell us whether or not he can be trusted. Will he not have us killed as soon as we cross that threshold?'

'Suit yourself.' Abruptly, Geraden jerked up his charger's head. 'I trust him. I'm going in.'

Breaking formation, he started for the gates.

Prince Kragen swore at him, ordered him back. Terisa was already following him, however, urging her mount almost onto his horse's heels. The Prince and his guard had no choice but to enter Orison behind Geraden and Terisa.

As she passed through the thick stone wall into the protected rectangle of the courtyard, her pulse went up a beat. In spite of her numerous anxieties – or perhaps because of them – she had the strange sensation that she was coming home.

The interior faces of the castle loomed above her, crowded with spectators, punctuated with clotheslines. Castellan Lebbick had dismounted in the mud. When the Alend party approached him, he saluted with withering sarcasm. At once, his guards took the heads of the horses and held them so that Prince Kragen and his people could dismount in an orderly fashion.

Pulling her leg hesitantly off the back of the charger, Terisa found herself caught and lifted down in Artagel's grasp.

He embraced her as if she were dear to him.

'Artagel!' He had hurt her once, badly. On the other hand, he was

725

Geraden's brother; she knew most of his family. And his hug was as eloquent as an apology. Instinctively, she flung her arms around his neck.

After a moment, he pushed her away and gave her a lopsided, rather embarrassed grin. 'Be careful, my lady.' He rolled his eyes at Geraden. 'We don't want to make him jealous.'

'*Artagel.*' Geraden practically jumped on his brother; he grabbed Artagel, shook him, hugged him, thumped his back. 'How are you, how's your side, are you all right, what's going on here, what's the matter with Lebbick?' Geraden's face shone with joy. 'Do you realize how long it's been since I saw you *well*? I can tell you, the Domne had some stern things to say about letting yourself get hurt like that.'

'"Da,"' Terisa put in happily. 'You promised to call him "Da."' Artagel's smile told her everything she needed to know. Now she was just glad that she had never told Geraden about Artagel's distrust.

Nevertheless Artagel's next words reassured her further. Instead of trying to answer Geraden's questions, he commented half casually, 'I heard what he said.' He nodded toward the Castellan. 'We all heard him. Actually, he isn't the *only* one who believes you. But I have to admit we're in the minority.'

Terisa beamed with pleasure and relief.

'Don't worry about it,' said Geraden. 'We'll get that straightened out as soon as we see King Joyse. Tell me something important. *How's your side?*'

Artagel laughed easily. 'Terrible. All this rest is giving me the twitches.' Humorously, he whispered, 'If I don't get to fight somebody soon, I'm going to end up like Lebbick.'

'My lady Terisa. Geraden.' Prince Kragen addressed them coldly, but his expression was one of bemusement rather than irritation. 'It might be wise to conduct this reunion later. The present circumstances are less than cordial. We must meet with King Joyse promptly.'

Artagel laughed again. 'He's right. First things first. I'll follow you to the hall. When you're done there, we'll talk.'

Waving his hand cheerfully, he retreated among the horses and guards.

When Terisa looked at Geraden, she saw that his eyes were full of tears.

He was happy: she knew he was happy. He loved Artagel. For that reason, she was surprised by the pain on his face.

Until she noticed Geraden's pain, she didn't absorb the fact that Artagel moved with a slight limp, as if he had an unhealed stiffness in his side.

And he wasn't carrying a sword.

Oh, Artagel!

Had Gart hurt him that badly? Or had his long sequence of overexertions and relapses aggravated the damage enough to cripple him? A swordsman of Artagel's prowess didn't have to be maimed or broken to be crippled. A few muscles which didn't heal properly in his side could do it.

'It's too much, Terisa,' Geraden gritted between his teeth. 'Too many people have been hurt. Too much harm has been done. This has got to stop. We've got to stop him.'

She put her arm through his and squeezed it: she knew whom he was talking about.

Unfortunately, she couldn't get the feeling out of her stomach that a lot more people were going to be hurt soon.

'Come on,' she murmured so that Prince Kragen wouldn't summon them again. 'If we're going to stop him, this is the way to do it.'

Geraden nodded; he scrubbed the expression of sorrow off his face.

Together, he and Terisa joined the Prince and Castellan Lebbick.

Lebbick considered them balefully. He didn't look like a man who believed them. He also didn't sound like a man who believed them. Without preamble, he asserted, 'You'll leave your men here, my lord Prince.'

Prince Kragen stiffened. 'What an odd idea, Castellan. Why would I do such a thing?'

The Castellan's mouth twisted. 'I understand your problem. You don't think you're safe here. Well, I have a problem, too. I could be wrong about you. You could be plotting treachery.

'If you're honest, I can tell you one thing for certain. I'll die before you do. But if you aren't—' He shrugged. 'You'll leave your men in the courtyard.'

Prince Kragen's fingers stroked the hilt of his sword lightly. His demeanor was unruffled, but Terisa could sense his ire. Softly, he asked, 'Are you so unconcerned about the lady Elega's position, Castellan?'

Castellan Lebbick returned a snort. 'She isn't *my* daughter. I don't care what happens to her. I'm in command of Orison. If you make me cut you down, King Joyse will never know the difference. I'll report it any way I like.'

He faced the Prince, daring the Alend Contender to doubt him.

The darkness in Prince Kragen's eyes scared Terisa. She thought she ought to do something, intervene somehow. But Geraden was holding her arm now; he kept her still.

After a moment, the Prince said, 'If you had come to me, Castellan, you would have received better treatment.'

'Swineswater,' remarked Lebbick succinctly.

Prince Kragen's jaws bunched; blood deepened the hue of his skin. After a moment, however, he nodded.

'My guard will wait outside the gates. If we do not return in an hour, they will ride to the Alend Monarch. The lady Elega will be killed. Tell King Joyse what you will.'

Castellan Lebbick gave another of his crushed-rock laughs. 'Let the Alends wait outside the gates,' he told one of his men. 'Be civil about it. Keep the gates open.'

Without waiting for a reply, he headed toward the nearest doorway.

Prince Kragen glanced at Terisa, at Geraden. She chewed her lip; but Geraden assented promptly. 'It's the best chance we've got. He's never stabbed anybody in the back.'

'You are a bad influence,' murmured Prince Kragen, 'both of you. You urge me to accept horrifying risks as if they were entirely plausible. If I am ever crowned the Alend Monarch, I will have to become more cautious.'

Smiling ominously, he led Terisa and Geraden after the Castellan.

Inside the castle, past the guards at the door, the halls were deserted. The spectators who packed the inner windows and balconies were nowhere to be seen; every indication of Orison's overcrowding was gone. 'Curfew,'

Castellan Lebbick explained as he strode along the echoing passage. 'I thought you were going to break through the gates today. I ordered everybody out of the way. Nobody's allowed to use the halls except the King's guard.'

He may have intended his explanation to be reassuring. Nevertheless the unnatural silence of the place plucked at Terisa's nerves. She seemed to feel vast numbers of people crouched out of sight, waiting—

Rumors would travel fast in a besieged castle. When enough people heard that Nyle's murderer and Master Quillon's murderer and the Alend Contender were in Orison, the curfew wouldn't hold. No curfew would hold.

And when it broke, what would Lebbick do?

King Joyse had to listen to them. That was all there was to it. He had to listen. He had to believe them.

Otherwise she and Geraden and even Prince Kragen might not live long enough to find out what Master Eremis' trap actually was.

They were obviously being watched. She didn't see anybody, but she could hear voices. Just a murmur at first, an impression of whispering which filled the corridors with hints of menace. Then the voices grew louder, bolder. One of them said, 'Killer.' Another called out clearly, 'Butcher!'

Castellan Lebbick didn't glance aside. He didn't seem to hear the voices. Or maybe he approved of them. He waited until they faded behind him. Then, to no one in particular, he commented, 'They don't mean you. They mean me.'

The way he walked was so tightly controlled that it made his whole body appear brittle.

He took Terisa, Geraden, and Prince Kragen directly to the audience hall.

Across a high, formal space marked with windows and pennons, they approached a set of peaked doors. Like the ones to the courtyard, those doors were guarded. Terisa took that as a good sign. She held Geraden's arm and tried to keep her respiration steady as the guards opened the doors into the hall of audiences.

She remembered it vividly – its cathedral-like height and length; the walls covered by carved wooden screens, their finials reaching twenty or thirty feet toward the vaulted ceiling; the two narrow windows high in the far wall. Working on short notice, a flustered old servant hurried along the rows of candles, past the batteries of lamps, trying to light them all as fast as he could. He still had a long way to go; yet he – and the windows – already gave enough illumination to show King Joyse's ornate mahogany throne on its pediment. A run of rich carpet led from the doors to the pediment; the rest of the wide area in front of the throne was open, surrounded by benches like pews. From each side of the pediment, a row of chairs reached toward the benches.

Because the light was so dim, the balcony surrounding the hall above the screens was shrouded in darkness. Terisa could see well enough, however, to note that the Castellan already had guards in position. Archers ranged there along the walls of the hall, four on each side.

Two pikemen closed the doors and stood to hold them. Four more were at attention beside the King's seat. She counted them again: fourteen guards. Sourly, she supposed that Lebbick's refusal to permit the attendance of

Prince Kragen's honor guard made sense. If the Castellan could only produce fourteen guards, Kragen's ten soldiers might have been sufficient to protect him from the consequences of treachery.

Then, as the old servant continued to do his job, and the light improved, she realized that the benches and chairs weren't empty.

The gathering was small, compared to the one which had greeted Prince Kragen's first visit. Terisa suspected, however, that the people here were the ones who mattered. No courtiers were present, no lords or ladies whose sole claim to significance arose from birth or wealth. Around the benches were several more guards, each wearing the insignia of a captain: Lebbick's seconds-in-command. Artagel sat among them, grinning encouragement. She saw some of King Joyse's counselors, men she had met only once before: the Lord of Commerce, for example; the Home Ambassador; the Lord of the Privy Purse. And in the chairs—

To the right of the throne sat the Tor, sprawling his bulk over at least two chairs. To all appearances, he hadn't changed his robe since Terisa had last seen him: it was crumpled and filthy, so badly stained that it looked like it would never come clean. The dull red in his eyes and the way his flesh sagged from the bones of his face gave the impression that he was drunk. If he recognized either Terisa or Geraden, he didn't show it.

As if to avoid him – as if he stank or had lost continence – everyone else was seated on the left.

The men there were Masters. Terisa knew Barsonage, of course: the mediator was scowling at her as if she had betrayed everything he valued. And most of the Imagers with him she had seen before. But at least one of them looked so unfamiliar – and so young – that she thought he must be an Apt who had just recently earned his chasuble.

Two of the three of them were breathing hard. They must have come at a run. After all, the Castellan's men hadn't had much time to summon people to this audience.

The reason for the attendance of the Masters was obvious. King Joyse had threatened to defend Orison with Imagery. To do that, he needed the support of the Congery.

The Imagers made her think of Master Quillon, and her heart twisted.

Then she realized that Adept Havelock was missing. The High King's Dastard wasn't in the hall anywhere.

Neither was Master Eremis, however. That was a relief.

Soundless on the carpet, Castellan Lebbick strode toward the chairs on the right and sat down a few places away from the Tor, leaving Prince Kragen, Geraden, and Terisa in the open space before the throne. Inconsequently, she noticed the burned spot on the rug, where Havelock had once dropped his censer. No one had bothered to mend it. King Joyse hadn't had much use for his audience hall in recent years.

He didn't have much use for it now, apparently. He wasn't present.

Prince Kragen surveyed the hall; he scanned the balconies. The corner of his moustache lifted as if he were sneering. When he had completed his study of the King's defenses, he said clearly, 'Remarkable. Is this the best audience King Joyse can produce? If an ambassador came to the Alend Monarch, at least a hundred nobles would commemorate the occasion, regardless of the hour – or the urgency.' A moment later, however, he remarked politely, 'Most impressive, Castellan. For the first time, I truly believe that you do not intend to harm us. You would not need so many men – and so many witnesses – to procure our deaths.

'What *do* you intend? Where is King Joyse?'

Castellan Lebbick remained sitting. In a voice which resembled his laugh, he barked, 'Norge!'

Slowly, almost casually, one of the captains stood and came to attention. He saluted the Castellan calmly. In fact, everything about him seemed calm. He sounded like he was talking in his sleep.

'My lord Castellan?'

'Norge, where is King Joyse?' demanded Lebbick.

Norge shrugged comfortably. 'I spoke to him myself, my lord Castellan. I told him what you said. I even told him what the Prince said. He said, "Then you'd better get the audience hall ready."'

Apparently, the captain didn't think any other comment was necessary. He sat down.

Terisa heard a door open and close as the servant left, his job done.

Castellan Lebbick faced the Prince. 'Now,' he said, 'you know as much as I do. Are you satisfied?'

'No, Castellan,' put in King Joyse. 'I doubt that he knows as much as you do. And I'm sure he isn't satisfied.'

Somehow, Terisa had missed the King's arrival. He must have entered from a door hidden behind his seat: she jumped to that conclusion because he was beside the pediment now, with one hand braced on the base of the throne as if he were about to go up the four or five steps and sit down. Nevertheless she hadn't seen him come in. For all she knew, he had appeared by Imagery.

He was wearing what she took to be his formal attire: a robe of purple velvet, not especially clean; a circlet of gold to keep his white hair off his forehead. And from a brocade strap over his right shoulder hung a tooled sheath which held a longsword with a jeweled pommel. His blue eyes were as watery and vague as she remembered them; his hands appeared arthritic, swollen and inflexible. The way he moved conveyed the impression that he was frail under his robe, barely able to support his own weight; too frail for dignity or decision.

Only his beard had changed. It had been trimmed short and neatly combed. Under his white whiskers, his cheeks showed a flush of exertion or wine.

At once, everyone stood. A bit too slowly for decorum, Lebbick stood also and bowed. 'Attend,' he drawled by way of announcement. 'This audience is granted to Prince Kragen, the Alend Contender, by Joyse, Lord of the Demesne and King of Mordant. It's a private audience. Everyone here is commanded to speak freely – and to say nothing when they have left the hall. To speak outside of what is said here is treason.'

Bitterly, as if he had no use for the King's permission, he sat down.

No one else sat. Even Lebbick's captains remained on their feet while King Joyse looked up and down the hall as if he were making a mental note of everyone present. Meeting Terisa's gaze, and Geraden's, he scowled so dramatically that she was tempted to think he didn't mean it; tempted to think he was scowling to conceal a leap of joy. She had no way of knowing the truth, however. Instead of addressing her or Geraden – or the audience generally – he turned abruptly and ascended his seat, dragging his sword upward like a millstone. When he reached his throne, he collapsed into it; he had to pause and breathe deeply for a moment before he was able to tell the gathering to sit.

The assembled captains and counselors and Imagers obeyed.

Of course, Prince Kragen, Terisa, and Geraden had to remain standing.

Her reaction to the sight of King Joyse was more complex than she had expected: she was at once gladder and more distressed. He had a strange power which always surprised her, an attraction of personality that made her want to believe he was still as strong and idealistic and dedicated and, yes, heroic as he had ever been. That was why his appearance upset her. He was simply too weak. There on his throne, with Mordant in shambles, and Eremis poised to strike the last, crushing blow, he was too close to his grave – the burial ground as much of his spirit as of his decaying frame. She understood why Geraden loved him. Oh, she *understood*. Everything in her chest ached because he wasn't equal to the love people gave him anymore.

Somebody else would have to save Orison and Mordant.

He seemed to share her opinion. In a dry, querulous tone that made him sound nearly decrepit, he said without preamble, 'You first, Kragen. And be quick about it. I don't have much patience for men who threaten my daughters.'

Prince Kragen's fists knotted on his anger; he held his voice steady. 'Then you must have no patience at all for yourself, my lord King. I have come because I have news which you must hear. Thanks in part to Apt Geraden and the lady Terisa – and in part to other sources of knowledge – I have an astonishing range of threats to lay before you. But they are all of your own making, not mine. Even the lady Elega is entirely safe – unless you have lost even the small honesty necessary to respect a flag of truce.'

Unexpectedly, the Tor let out a snorting noise like a snore. His eyes seemed to be falling closed; his head began to loll on his thick neck.

'Whoreslime,' commented Castellan Lebbick unceremoniously. 'You must have noticed that we're besieged. Maybe you've even noticed that you're the one besieging us.'

When King Joyse didn't intervene to silence the Castellan, Terisa's heart sank. The King had to listen, *had* to. He had to understand. Nevertheless he didn't look capable of understanding – and he didn't seem to be listening. He only stared at Prince Kragen as if the Alend Contender's presence were no more pleasant – and no more interesting – than a bad smell.

'No, my lord King.' Prince Kragen did what he could, under the circumstances: he treated Lebbick's words as if they came from King Joyse. 'Even that threat you have brought upon yourself. When I first came to you seeking an alliance, you humiliated me deliberately. And since that time your only ambition has been to destroy your realm before you die. You forget that Alend also is bound up in Mordant's need. You created the Congery, my lord King, and now you must face the consequences. If the power of all Imagery falls to High King Festten, our ruin is certain. We must fight for our survival. Even dogs will do as much. If you are determined to let the Congery fall to Cadwal, then we have no choice but to prevent you as best we can.'

The Prince had moved a step closer to King Joyse. Terisa and Geraden were on either side of him, a bit behind. Across Prince Kragen's back, she whispered to Geraden, 'This isn't going to work. We've got to do something.'

A clenched glitter filled Geraden's gaze. 'My lord King—' he murmured as if the words stuck in his throat. 'My lord King, please. Give us a chance.'

King Joyse paid no attention to him.

'No, my lord Prince.' Master Barsonage glared from under his shrubbery eyebrows. He didn't stand. On the other hand, he did speak courteously. 'Your view of the situation is persuasive, but not entirely fair. You forget that the Congery is composed of Imagers – and Imagers are also men. Like yourself, we must fight for our survival. Unlike you, however, we are men who have accepted the King's ideals, the King's purposes. Oh, there are some among us who serve the Congery only because they dislike the alternatives available to them. But they are few, my lord Prince – only a minority. The rest of us value what we are.

'Do you think we will calmly resign ourselves to High King Festten when Mordant collapses?

'You say you must keep the Congery from falling into Cadwal's hands, and that is a worthy endeavor, I am sure. But the assumption on which your actions are based is that the Congery is a thing, not men – that we do not choose, or believe, or have worth as men.

'Why do you believe you have the right to determine our survival – and our allegiance – for us?'

Prince Kragen received this argument with a closed face. Once again, he treated what was said as if it came from King Joyse. Only the sweat at his temples betrayed the pressure he felt.

'A fascinating debate, my lord King,' he said grimly, 'but irrelevant. We cannot leave Alend's future in the hands of men who are so confused – either by Imagery itself, or by the necessity of achieving decisions through debate – that they believed the translation of an uncontrollable battle-champion to be a sensible action.

'No, my lord King. Your people will defend you, as they must. Nevertheless the responsibility for this siege is yours.'

King Joyse shrugged. At least he was listening well enough to know that Prince Kragen had paused. He gave the Prince a chance to go on, then said abruptly, 'I know all this. Tell me something I don't know. Tell me about your "astonishing range of threats."'

The Tor snorted again, softly, and opened one eye. 'So Terisa and Geraden are traitors after all,' he rumbled. He was lost in a world of wine. 'How sad.' At once, he closed his eye again, dismissing whatever happened around him.

'In any case, my lord Prince,' the Castellan grated as if King Joyse hadn't spoken, 'you do have choices. We've already told you what they are. Withdraw to a safe position. Wait and see what happens. If you do that, King

Joyse is willing to meet Margonal under a flag of truce and discuss an alliance.'

When she heard that, a small flame of hope leaped up in Terisa.

And was quenched immediately. Before Prince Kragen could reply, King Joyse muttered shakily, 'No, Castellan. It's too late for that. It's too late for anything.

'It's time for the truth.'

His swollen hands gripped the arms of his seat; he had trouble holding himself upright. Almost whining, he said to the Prince, 'Tell me about your threats. Tell me what Terisa and Geraden know. Tell me why you stopped beating on my gates.' Under his whining, however, lay an iron blade, too well whetted and keen to be mistaken. All the light in the hall seemed to shine on him. 'Tell me now.'

A tight silence closed around the onlookers. Terisa couldn't bear to look at King Joyse any longer. She glanced at Geraden, saw him chewing the inside of his cheek; his eyes were wide and white, as if he were thinking desperately. Because Prince Kragen stood closer to the throne than she did, she couldn't see most of his face; but she could see a twitch run down the long muscle of his jaw, a bead of sweat trail from his temple across his cheekbone. Ignoring the proprieties of a royal audience, she turned her head and caught Artagel's eye; she was looking for inspiration. He didn't have any to give her, however. He looked stretched and pale, as if he were stifling nausea.

Still avoiding the King, she faced Master Barsonage. You're wrong about us. That was what she ought to say to him. All the assumptions here are wrong. Geraden didn't kill Nyle. I didn't kill Master Quillon.

But she didn't say anything. The silence held her.

Why were Geraden and Prince Kragen sweating? Surely the air was cooler than that?

Prince Kragen's fist sprang involuntarily from his side; he forced it down again. 'No,' he said through his teeth, 'I will not.'

A grin split Castellan Lebbick's face. He was going to laugh. Or wail. 'Why not, Prince? Why else did you come?'

Kragen ignored the Castellan. 'I will not suffer this senseless treatment. I will not trade my only hopes to a King so contemptible that he respects no one else.' Despite his efforts to speak quietly, his voice grew thick with passion until he was nearly shouting. 'The lady Elega persuaded me to come. Apt Geraden and the lady Terisa persuaded me. They are all deluded by the idea that their lord remains possessed of some vestige of wisdom – or of courage – or of bare decency.'

To Terisa, every word sounded like a nail being driven into the lid of Mordant's coffin.

'Do you hear me, Joyse?' Prince Kragen raged. 'You are deaf to everything else. You are deaf to the misery of your people, locked in a useless siege – caught in Cadwal's path – slaughtered by renegade Imagers. You are deaf to the simplest requirements of kingship, the wisdom and the *necessity* of dealing fairly with other monarchs. You are deaf to love, deaf to the loyalty which destroys your friends and family.'

'Enough, my lord Prince.' King Joyse raised one hand. 'I have heard you.'

Now he didn't sound querulous. And he didn't sound angry. He sounded oddly like a man who was experiencing a personal vindication. 'You have said enough.'

But Prince Kragen had gone too far to stop. For a second, he let his fists pound the air. 'By the stars, Joyse, it is not enough. You will not pull Alend down in Mordant's ruin. I will not allow it.'

'I will tell you *nothing!*'

Abruptly, he wheeled away from the throne.

Catching hold of Terisa and Geraden, he pulled them with him toward the doors.

Instinctively, she wrenched her arm out of his grasp.

She hadn't made a conscious decision, either against him or for King Joyse. She was simply so torn, so hurt by the difference between what was needed and what was happening, so urgent for another outcome that she couldn't bear to give up.

Geraden was clearer. He, too, jerked free of Prince Kragen. Swinging toward the throne, he cried out like a trumpet, 'My lord King— ! Houseldon is destroyed. Sternwall is falling. The people of Fayle are butchered by ghouls. *Your* people, my lord King, everywhere!'

King Joyse was on his feet. Terisa hadn't seen him stand: she only saw him standing now, towering over her on the pediment with his beard thrust forward and his hair full of light.

'*And?*' he demanded. '*And?*'

As if he left her no choice, she replied, 'And the Queen is gone. She's been abducted.'

Then her stomach knotted as if she were about to be sick.

The idea that he would crumple now, that she had hurt the King hard enough to break him, was too much for her. Prince Kragen was shouting, 'You fools! He will have me killed!' Too late. She turned her back on King Joyse, hugged her arms over her belly.

A movement on the balcony caught her eye. She cast a glance upward in time to see one of the archers fold to the floor.

Hands grabbed her, spun her. King Joyse had come down from his seat so fast that she didn't have time to think, to react; he clenched his fists in her soft shirt. Shouting the King's name, Geraden tried to intervene. King Joyse thrust him away.

'Who took her?' The king seemed to swell over Terisa. His eyes were blue fire; his teeth flashed; he shook her as if her heart were an empty sack. 'I'll have that man's head! *Who took her?*'

Terisa struggled to turn her head, look back up at the balcony. But King Joyse was shaking her too hard; she couldn't get her gaze into focus.

'Alends!' cried Geraden. 'She was taken by Alends!'

So suddenly that Terisa nearly fell, King Joyse dropped her. His sword came into his hands swiftly, catching the light like a whip of fire.

She stumbled around to scan the balcony.

Three of the archers were down.

The rest were so engrossed in the scene below them that they hadn't realized what was happening.

King Joyse and Prince Kragen confronted each other. The Prince had drawn his own blade: the tips of their swords danced at each other in the glow of the lamps and candles.

'Where is she?' demanded the King.

Wildly, Geraden pushed himself between the blades. 'They were dressed like Alends!' he panted. 'We think it's a trick! Prince Kragen came here to prove his good faith!' Before his King could cut him down, he added, 'Torrent went after her. She's going to leave a trail for help to follow.'

'The balcony,' Terisa said. She was hardly able to hear herself.

Shielded by Geraden, Prince Kragen lowered his sword. Facing King Joyse regally over Geraden's shoulder, he avowed, 'My lord King, I spit on the men who did this to you. And I spit on the cheap ploy which made them appear Alend. I would rather die than become a man who can only gain his ends by violence against women.'

He was too late: the blow which felled him was already in motion. Too quickly for any reaction – even from King Joyse – Artagel reared up behind the Prince and chopped him so hard across the back of the neck that he went down as if he had been hit with an axe.

At the same time, Castellan Lebbick cried like a howl of glee, *'Gart!'*

Terisa could see the High King's Monomach now. As the fourth archer went down, Gart rounded the balcony to attack those on the other side. He was black and swift, a slash of midnight, and his sword seemed to splash blood in all directions.

The remaining archers had their bows ready to protect King Joyse from Prince Kragen. Instantly, they shifted their aim toward Gart and let fly.

Unfortunately, he wasn't alone. He had a number of his Apts with him. Swooping like shadows, they caught the archers from behind, hacking the guards down, spoiling their aim. Only one of the arrows went true.

Gart knocked the shaft aside with the flat of his blade.

His return stroke beheaded the nearest archer. The head flopped lopsidedly over the balcony railing and fell among the benches with a thud.

Men yelled everywhere. Castellan Lebbick roared, 'I'm coming, you bastard! *I'm coming!*' and sprinted toward a door hidden behind one of the screens. Most of the Imagers started to flee. Master Barsonage lashed them back to his side with curses.

Geraden cried at Artagel uselessly, 'You idiot!'

'I didn't know!' retorted Artagel. Looking frantic and self-disgusted, he flung a glance up at the balcony, at Gart, then scanned the hall; he couldn't decide what to do. In spite of his uncertainty, however, he didn't hesitate to help himself to Prince Kragen's sword.

Laconic in the tumult, Norge demanded reinforcements. Two of the captains headed out of the hall to rally Orison; the rest of Lebbick's men followed him toward the stairwell to the balcony.

The noise awakened the Tor. He opened his eyes with a snuffle and gazed around blearily.

Terisa felt that she was still watching the severed head flop off the balcony and fall. The sound when it hit the bench was unmistakable: she would remember it for the rest of her life. She had to get out of the way, but for some reason she couldn't move. Geraden turned toward the Masters: she thought she heard him ask, 'Can you fight? Have you got mirrors with you?' The strain around Artagel's eyes was clear as he hefted the Prince's blade; he moved stiffly. She knew as if he had explained his dilemma at length that he yearned to go after Gart – that he feared to go because he was no match for the High King's Monomach. Distinctly, she heard a Master snap, 'We brought none. How could we know that mirrors would be needed in the audience hall?' She really ought to get moving. Before Gart or his Apts had a chance to come after her.

Instead of moving, she waited until she felt *a touch of cold as thin as a feather and as sharp as steel slide straight through the center of her abdomen.*

Then she flipped forward, dove to the floor, rolled away. When she got her feet under her again, she ran toward Geraden and the Masters.

Out of the air where she had been standing stepped Master Gilbur and Master Eremis.

Master Gilbur gripped his dagger in one fist. The hunch of his back and the thickness of his arms made his hands look as powerful as battering rams.

Master Eremis carried a sword in a scabbard belted around his jet cloak. His chief weapon was already in his hands, however.

A mirror the size and shape of a roofing tile.

With a precision that seemed like lunacy, she noticed that both men still wore their chasubles.

Immediately, Master Gilbur leaped to attack Prince Kragen.

Grinning happily, Master Eremis came toward Terisa and Geraden.

There were no guards to oppose them. Norge's reinforcements hadn't arrived. And the rest of the men had followed Castellan Lebbick.

Lebbick burst out onto the balcony with his sword in both hands, snarling for blood. And he almost caught Gart. Unfamiliar with the stairwell, Gart couldn't know where it opened; out of ignorance, he had placed himself in an awkward position. Nevertheless he countered Lebbick's first cut, blocked it against the railing so hard that chips flew. Retreating nimbly, he countered the backstroke.

That gave him all the time he needed to recover his balance.

Behind the Castellan, six guards and as many captains led by Norge rushed from the stairwell one at a time to engage the Monomach's Apts.

Gart had only four men with him: they were badly outnumbered. But the balcony was too narrow for any two men to stand and fight abreast. Gart blocked Lebbick on one side; on the other, an Apt battled the first pikeman to come at him. The rest of the defenders were caught in the middle, helpless.

Gart struck furiously, trying to jam his opponents against each other; he almost succeeded at driving the Castellan backward. Lebbick slipped one blow, blocked a second which hit hard enough to jar his joints and leave a notch on his blade. But he was happy at last, nearly ecstatic at the chance to fight without restraint. Savage joy lit his face as he held Gart's attack.

'Bastard!' he panted. 'I'll teach you to think you can do what you want in my castle!'

Behind him, unfortunately, the first pikeman didn't fare as well. The guard probably hadn't had a fraction of the training given to Gart's Apts. He stumbled; and his black-armored opponent gutted him almost without effort, then used the moment of surprise while he fell to cut halfway through the nearest captain's chest.

Norge stooped, snatched up one of the bows. So placidly that he didn't seem to be hurrying, he flipped a shaft into the Apt's throat.

Across the hall, one of Gart's men recklessly flung a dagger. It should have missed from that distance: its target should have seen it coming. Unluckily, he didn't. The guard went down with the blade buried in his left eye.

Norge shot the Apt cleanly in the chest.

Gart's gaze swept the balcony. He took in the positions of the people below him. Instead of ripping Castellan Lebbick's parries aside, the High King's Monomach began to give ground.

Artagel watched what was happening above him for one more moment, then turned his attention to Master Gilbur.

Plainly, Gilbur intended to kill the Alend Contender.

It was also plain that he wasn't going to succeed. Artagel's side was sore and tight; in some sense, he was a cripple. Nevertheless he could have handled a lone Imager armed with only a dagger in his sleep.

'Guard the Prince!' shouted the Tor for no discernible reason. He was on his feet, his legs splayed, swaying under the influence of too much wine.

Smiling pleasantly, Artagel aimed Prince Kragen's sword – and barely saved himself when Master Gilbur turned suddenly, picked up one of the benches, and hurled it at his head.

A corner of the bench punched his shoulder, and he went down; he hit the floor heavily, lost his direction. The Master's strength was prodigious. How was it possible to fight somebody who could throw benches around with one hand? Shock numbed Artagel's shoulder, but he ignored it. He ignored his side. Suppressing any kind of pain, he surged upright again as smoothly as he could—

Facing in the wrong direction.

He wheeled back to the Prince's sprawling body just in time to block Master Gilbur's dagger.

Roaring, Gilbur hit Artagel's blade so hard that Artagel nearly dropped it.

Nearly: not quite.

Mustering his balance, his poise, his old skill, Artagel pointed his sword at the base of Master Gilbur's throat and dared the Imager to move again.

The struggle over Prince Kragen apparently held no interest for Master Eremis. He approached Geraden and Terisa and the knot of Masters as if he were on the verge of an epiphany. His smile was so keen it seemed to cut the air. When Geraden cried in frustration, 'Doesn't anyone have a mirror?' Eremis began to laugh.

He tightened his fingers, murmured something Terisa couldn't hear.

Instantly, a creature the size and shape of a fruit-bat swept out of the glass, flapped forward, and fastened itself to the nearest Imager's cheek.

The man toppled backward, screaming.

'*Eremis!*' Geraden yelled as if that were the worst obscenity he knew. From under his jerkin, he produced a knife – an eating utensil he must have appropriated at breakfast – and threw it with all his strength.

For once in his life, he did something right. He had never trained with a knife; but by chance his blade shattered the glass in Eremis' hand as neatly as if that was what he had intended all along. Splinters sprayed out of Eremis' grasp, glittering like jewels in the light.

The Master's laugh turned to a snarl.

While he ripped out his sword, the doors of the hall slammed open and twenty guards charged inward.

Norge's reinforcements.

The guards were too late to save Geraden or Terisa. Their backs were to the wallscreens: they had no escape from the easy action of Eremis' blade. He plainly knew what to do with a sword. It seemed to flex like a live thing in his hands.

In contrast, Artagel didn't need any help. This was the work he had been born to do. First he slapped the dagger out of Master Gilbur's fist. Then he began to make small, delicate cuts in the Imager's thick neck, as if he were marking the spot at which Gilbur's head would be hacked away. All his movements were taut and precise.

Up on the balcony, Gart lost another Apt. Gart himself hadn't killed anyone: Lebbick kept him back. Lebbick's fury appeared almost equal to Gart's skill. The Apts had accounted for five of the defenders. Surveying the situation, Gart judged that one more pikeman would die before his last student fell. He prepared himself to dispatch Lebbick, perhaps eviscerate him; then he glanced downward, saw the arrival of the reinforcements, and changed his mind.

Before anyone could grasp his intent, he sprang away from Castellan Lebbick and vaulted over the railing.

A drop like that could have killed him; it should have snapped his legs. But he had been jumping from high places ever since he began his training under the previous Monomach: he knew how to do it.

When he hit the rug, he collapsed into himself and rolled to absorb the impact. Then, despite the fact that his feet and legs had gone numb as if his spine were broken, he launched himself at Artagel's back.

The only warning Artagel got was the thump when Gart landed. He turned just in time to keep the Monomach's sword out of his ribs.

Swiftly, he launched a second parry, a counterstroke. He knew he couldn't beat Gart, but in the rush of action, the heady flow of battle, he didn't care.

Unfortunately, he never finished his riposte. Gilbur's quickness was like his strength: prodigious. In an instant, he sprang after Artagel and clubbed him to the floor with both fists.

Prince Kragen was still unconscious. He could have been killed almost without effort.

Now, however, Master Gilbur and the High King's Monomach had other priorities. The charging guards had already covered half the distance from the doors. Master Eremis' allies only had a few seconds left.

Behind them, Castellan Lebbick came down on the rug with a smashing impact. He had tried Gart's jump, had landed badly. Pain ripped a gasp out of him; it muffled the sound of breaking bones.

Together, Gilbur and Gart raced to help Eremis.

He was fighting for his life.

No one had opposed his advance on the Masters, on Terisa and Geraden. The Masters were as useless and cowardly as he had always believed them to be; they wouldn't be worth the trouble of killing. Even Master Barsonage wasn't worth killing.

Geraden, on the other hand—

But at the last moment, Master Eremis had paused. He saw something in Geraden's eyes – an unexpected threat; some kind of fatal promise.

It caused the Master to check his swing.

Terisa didn't look dangerous. She didn't even look desirable. She had turned inward with her back against the wall as if she were trying to faint.

Eremis raised his sword to fend Geraden away while he grabbed at her.

Suddenly, a mountain of flesh slapped against him with such force that he nearly went sprawling.

The Tor—! Eremis got his blade up just in time to keep the fat, old lord from splitting his head open.

Considering the Tor's skill and age and drunkenness, his sword might as well have been a cudgel. Nevertheless it had *weight* behind it, and a mad, blubbering fury. Master Eremis parried as hard as he could, and again, and *again;* yet he was driven backward. He would have to disembowel that old slob to stop him.

'My lord!' Geraden yelled. 'Look out!'

The Tor didn't seem to hear the warning. He was still swinging his sword like a club when Gart kicked him in the stomach hard enough to rupture his guts.

Retching, he collapsed to his knees and presented his exposed neck to Gart's blade.

Geraden jumped at Eremis.

Gilbur intercepted him, however, and flung him aside like a handful of rags. Like Prince Kragen, Geraden wasn't important enough to risk death over. Terisa was the one who mattered. Eremis closed a hand around her arm. Gart braced himself for the quick satisfaction of beheading the Tor.

Fuming curses and agony, one knee crushed, an ankle cracked, Castellan Lebbick came up behind the High King's Monomach. He was barely able to stand; every movement ground splinters of bone against each other. His sword hung in his hands, too heavy to lift through the pain.

Yet he kept Gart from killing the Tor.

To save himself, Gart whirled and drove his sword straight through the Castellan's heart.

Lebbick's eyes flew wide, as if he had just seen an astonishing sight. Blood burst from his mouth, gushed down the front of his mail. He dropped his weapon. For a moment, his hands clutched at Gart's blade as if he wanted to wrench it out of his chest. Then, like a man who had decided to let go, he released the iron.

'Bastard,' he breathed between gouts of blood as if he were talking to someone else, not Gart at all. 'Now I'm free. You can't hurt me anymore.'

Slowly, as if performing at last the only graceful action of his life, he slid backward off Gart's sword.

In that way, Lebbick finished mourning for his wife.

Full of horror, Terisa tried to break Master Eremis' grip; but she couldn't do it. She had never been strong enough with him. Geraden lay on the floor without moving. Helplessly, she watched as Eremis made a strange, familiar gesture, a signal she had seen once before.

Only a heartbeat ahead of the charging guards, she and Eremis, Gilbur and Gart were translated out of the hall.

In the resulting confusion, a long time passed before anyone noticed that King Joyse had also disappeared.

Book Four

FORTY

THE LORD OF
LAST RESORT

Norge ordered everyone to stay in the hall; but he was already too late. Most of King Joyse's counselors had scattered, fled like their lord. And the Imagers were no better. Even Master Barsonage, who might in a reasonable world have been expected to set a good example – even the mediator of the Congery was gone. Apparently, he had taken Geraden with him. The only Master left was the man Eremis had killed; the creature which had actually slain him was still chewing on his head, oblivious to everything except food.

'Perfect,' Norge muttered generally. This was as close as he ever came to despair. All those Imagers and old men who could hardly hold their water for fear, already loose in Orison; already spreading panic. They would tell their friends, their wives, their children, their servants; some of them would tell total strangers. And when the story got out – when people heard that King Joyse was gone, and Lebbick was dead, and the 'hero of Orison,' Eremis, was in league with Cadwal – Norge sighed to think about it. Orison was going to come apart at the joints.

The siege was going to succeed after all.

Doing what he could, he sent one of the captains to take command of the gates, control the courtyard; make sure nobody did anything wild. That was the crucial place, the point at which panic could spill outward – the point at which Alend could be made aware that Orison was in chaos.

He ordered two more men to dispatch Eremis' vicious fruitbat. He detailed guards to locate the counselors and the Masters, so that decisions could be made. For no particular reason except thoroughness, he organized a search for the King. He made sure that Prince Kragen and Artagel were still alive.

Then he went to help the Tor get up.

The old lord was on his hands and knees, staring at Castellan Lebbick's face.

The Tor was in terrible pain. No, that wasn't true: he was *going* to be in terrible pain; he knew he was going to be in terrible pain as soon as the shock of Gart's kick faded a bit. At the moment, however, he was still stunned, protected from agony by surprise and wine.

743

He wanted to raise his head, but the effort was too much for him. He couldn't do anything except stare at Lebbick's ruined and happy face.

People looked like that, he thought, when their kings betrayed them. When they let something as simple and fallible as an ordinary human monarch cut the strings which held their lives together, the cords of purpose. When they drank too much – And then were lucky enough to die without having to watch everything else come apart around them.

It would be better to die. Better to think Gart's boot had torn something vital inside him and surrender to excruciation in advance. Better to let wine and loss carry him away. The alternatives—

The alternatives were distinctly unpleasant.

Unfortunately, the expression on Lebbick's face wouldn't let him go. Lebbick's blood wouldn't let him go. The first twinge of pain rumbled through his guts, and he nearly groaned aloud, Oh, Castellan. Mordant and Orison and you, he betrayed us all, abandoned us all – and you fought for him to the end. What did he ever do to deserve such service?

As soon as the Tor asked the question, however, he found that he knew the answer. Despite his tears, he could see it in Lebbick's twisted face, his wounds and blood. What King Joyse had done was to create something larger than any one man, something which deserved loyalty and service no matter how fallible and even treacherous the King himself proved to be.

Mordant. A buffer between the constant, bloody warring of Cadwal and Alend.

The Congery. An end to the ravages of Imagery when mirrors were used for nothing but power.

Pain pushed against the back of the Tor's throat, and his stomach knotted; but he clung to the cold stone with his hands and knees, kept his balance. When that captain, what was his name? Norge, when Norge came to him and tried to help him erect, he managed somehow to knot his fat fist in the captain's mail and pull him down, so that Norge had to meet him face-to-face.

'The King—' he gasped. His voice was a sick whisper, lost in the hurt clench of his abdomen.

'Gone, my lord Tor. I've sent men to look for him, but I don't expect any results.'

'Why not?'

Norge shrugged. 'Men who vanish like that usually don't want to be found.'

His immunity to distress was remarkable. Peering into the captain's face, the Tor began to remember him better. It was possible that Castellan Lebbick had promoted Norge simply because Norge was the only man under him who never flinched.

A man like that was hard to talk to. What did he care about? What were his convictions, his commitments?

'Help me up.' The Tor made no effort to move. The pain squeezed his voice to a husk. 'I will take his place.'

The Tor wasn't trying to stand, and Norge didn't try to lift him. Instead, the captain asked calmly, 'You, my lord?'

'Me.' For all the strength the Tor could muster, he might as well have been whispering deliberately. Maybe Gart really had ruptured something vital. 'Who else? I am the King's oldest friend. Apart from Adept Havelock – and you will not offer him the rule of Orison and Mordant.'

No question about it: the hurt in his bowels was going to be stupendous. Already it seemed to cut off his supply of air. Sweat or tears ran from him as if he were a sodden towel being twisted. There were too many candles glaring in his eyes. Yet he kept his grip on the captain.

'And I am the only lord here. King Joyse suffered me to remain when the others rode away. I have acted as his chancellor and advisor. Something must be done about the panic. Power must be assumed by someone who will be believed. Who else would you have?

'Who else is there?'

Norge blinked at this question as if he didn't think it was worth answering.

'I have no hereditary claim, no official standing.' The Tor wanted to wail or weep, but he couldn't get that much voice past the pain. 'But if you support me in this, Castellan Lebbick's second, a man with the King's guard behind him—' A gasp came up from his kneecaps, nearly blinding him. 'If you support me, I will be accepted.'

'My lord Tor,' the captain remarked dispassionately, 'even if I support you, you'll scarcely be able to stand.' After a moment, he added, 'If I can say so without offense, my lord, you aren't the king I would have chosen.'

'A fat old man sodden with wine and unable to stand.' It was embarrassing to be in tears at a time like this, but the Tor's hurt had to have some outlet. 'I understand. Do you?'

'My lord' – Norge's calm was maddening, really – 'you need a physician. Let people in better condition worry about Orison.'

'Fool,' the lord moaned. 'You do not understand.' Pulling on Norge's mail, heaving against the pain, he got one leg under him; that enabled him to shift his other hand from the floor to Norge's shoulder. He felt like he had Eremis' fruitbat gnawing on his guts. Nevertheless he panted through his tears and sweat, 'Someone must take command. Orison must be led. And I am *here*. Prince Kragen is *here*. For the first time, we know our enemies. We must not miss this opportunity.'

'Opportunity?' Norge asked noncommittally.

Oh, for the strength to scream! The Tor's stomach and throat seemed to be filling up with blood. 'An alliance with Alend,' he croaked out. 'Against Cadwal. A chance to end this siege and fight.'

The captain said nothing; his reaction was unreadable.

'Norge.' Peering through a blur of pain, the lord leaned closer to whisper straight into the captain's face. 'If I can make an alliance with Prince Kragen, will you support me?'

Norge spent an astonishing amount of time lost in thought. He took forever to arrive at a decision. Or maybe he just seemed to take forever.

Then he said, 'All right, my lord Tor,' as if he had never hesitated in his life.

The Tor groaned thickly – relief and anguish. A desire to lie down and hug his belly nearly overwhelmed him. Somehow, however, he forced himself to ask, 'How is the Prince?'

Norge glanced away, then answered, 'Rousing.'

Hoarse with stress, the Tor breathed, 'Reports. I need reports. I must know what is happening.'

Ponderously, as if Norge weren't carrying most of his weight, the old lord struggled to his feet.

For a moment, pain rose like vomit into his mouth. He couldn't see, couldn't breathe; if Norge hadn't held him, he would have fallen. But that was intolerable. So much weakness was intolerable. If he let himself fail now, Castellan Lebbick would probably get up from the dead and go do his job for him.

With a gasp that went through him like a blade, he pulled air into his chest. Almost at once, his vision cleared.

Prince Kragen was rousing, no question about it. Artagel still sprawled on the floor as if Master Gilbur had broken his neck; but the Prince was crawling stupidly toward his sword.

A guard who didn't know any better and probably hated Alends stepped forward to kick the sword out of Kragen's reach.

'Stop,' coughed the Tor.

Norge ordered the guard to stop.

Still barely conscious, Prince Kragen got a hand on his sword and at once began climbing to his feet.

Each movement helped bring him back to himself; the weight of his weapon seemed to make him stronger. By degrees, he came upright, planted his legs, clenched both fists on the hilt of his longsword. His eyes lost their glazed dullness and began to smolder with a murderous rage.

Instinctively, he sank into a fighter's crouch. The tip of his blade searched for the nearest enemy. He was going to swing— The Tor nearly wept at the thought that Prince Kragen might do something which would force the guards to kill him.

But the Prince didn't swing. Slowly, he turned toward the doors; he saw that men blocked his way. 'Dastards!' he spat as he wheeled back.

'Who struck me?' he demanded softly. 'Where is King Joyse?'

'My lord Prince.' Trembling, the Tor released one of his hands from Norge, then the other. Alone, he took two tottering steps toward Prince Kragen, as if he were presenting his belly to the Prince's blade. Fire seemed to run like water out of his guts and down the nerves of his legs; nevertheless he kept his head up. 'Forgive my weakness. I am unwell.

'You were struck by Artagel.' He nodded toward Artagel's supine form. 'You see the outcome.

'King Joyse is gone. He disappeared shortly after you fell – when Gart attacked.'

'Gart?' Prince Kragen's eyes widened; his rage receded slightly. His mind was beginning to function. He shifted his grip on his sword. 'The High King's Monomach was here?'

The Tor nodded, conserving his strength.

At once, Prince Kragen scanned the hall, plainly searching for confirmation. He noticed the archers and pikemen dead on the balcony, the slain Apts; he absorbed the absence of the King's counselors, the absence of the Masters. He saw Castellan Lebbick stretched out behind the Tor, and his mouth twisted under his moustache as if he were suddenly sick.

'My lord Tor,' he said in a bitter snarl, 'where are my companions, Geraden and the lady Terisa? They also were *protected* under a flag of truce.'

Still whispering because he didn't have any choice, the old lord replied, 'Gart had allies. Master Eremis. Master Gilbur.' He saw from Prince Kragen's face that the Prince wasn't particularly surprised by the names he mentioned.

'They took the lady Terisa, my lord Prince,' Norge put in casually. 'As for Geraden, he went with Master Barsonage. Or maybe it would be more accurate to say the mediator carried him off.'

Took the lady Terisa. The Tor blinked stupidly. He hadn't seen her go, hadn't known – But he couldn't afford to think about that now. He had to deal with Kragen.

'So you see,' he said as well as he could, 'we have nowhere else to turn for answers. My lord Prince, I think you should tell us the things you came to tell King Joyse.'

'*Why?*' Prince Kragen's question cut the air. 'Your King accused me of an atrocity. Although I was protected under a flag of truce, I was struck down before I could defend myself.' He bit into the words to control his passion. 'Apparently, it is amazing that I am still alive. Even your King's *audiences* are not safe. And now he has "disappeared."'

'Why should I say one word to you, my lord Tor?'

The Tor had to suppress a yearning for sleep. '*Because* King Joyse has disappeared, my lord Prince.' The damage to his stomach dragged at him. If he were horizontal, it might hurt less. And if he were asleep, it might stop hurting entirely.

On the other hand, Orison had been kicked in the gut as well. He was needed. He had to do whatever he was capable of doing.

'He is gone. And the Castellan is dead. He died saving my life when Gart was ready to kill me. There is no power left in Orison.

'None except Captain Norge, Lebbick's second. And Master Barsonage, the mediator of the Congery. And me.

'Master Barsonage is not present, but I will speak for him. If you deal openly with us, we are prepared to offer you an alliance. Orison's strength, and the Congery's, against Cadwal.'

That brought Prince Kragen's fury up short. He stared for a moment; his mouth hung open. Then, in a tone of fierce care, he asked, 'Do I understand you, my lord Tor? Have you just proclaimed yourself King of Mordant? Have you murdered Joyse? Have you and Norge been plotting revolt?'

'Of course not,' the Tor groaned. 'I claim only the position of a chancellor.' Really, this was too much. How could he possibly be expected to stand here and argue when he was probably bleeding to death inside? 'If I were a younger man, I would teach you to regret that accusation.' If Lebbick hadn't saved his life, he would have given up the whole business and let himself collapse. 'The King is only gone, not deposed. Not murdered. In his absence – and in his name – and with Captain Norge's support,' he added, hoping that Norge wouldn't contradict him, 'I will make decisions.

'We are prepared to offer you an alliance,' he repeated. 'If you will deal openly with us.'

Prince Kragen continued to hesitate, caught – the Tor supposed – between suspicion, curiosity, need. And he probably didn't trust the wine-soaked old lord in front of him. Who would? A guard came into the hall and crossed toward Norge, but the Tor ignored him. In addition, Artagel began to fumble toward consciousness. The Tor ignored that as well. He concentrated on Prince Kragen's silence.

'Come, my lord Prince,' he wheezed. 'I am not well. I will not be on my feet long. You have said that you desire an alliance. And your desire is demonstrably sincere. With the rupture' – poor choice of words – 'of Orison's gates nearly accomplished, you desisted when Terisa and Geraden came into your hands. But you did not keep them and their knowledge for yourself. You brought them here, risking them and your own person for the sake of what you hoped to gain.

'The blow which struck you down under a flag of truce was a mistake. Artagel will admit as much.' The Tor saw no reason to refrain from extravagant promises. 'Will you sacrifice your own needs and desires merely to punish us for a mistake?

'My lord Prince, tell us the things you came to say to King Joyse.'

Artagel levered himself off the floor, lurched to his feet; one hand clasped the back of his neck, trying too late to protect it from Gilbur's attack. When he saw Prince Kragen facing him, sword poised, he took a step backward and looked around urgently, searching to comprehend what had happened.

'A report, my lord Tor,' Norge announced tranquilly. 'You asked for reports.

'There's panic in Orison, and it's spreading, but we've been able to keep it out of the courtyard – away from the gates. The Prince's honor guard is waiting as patiently as possible. No sign of King Joyse. Geraden is definitely with Master Barsonage. The mediator's quarters.

'Two of the duty guards say they saw Adept Havelock's brown cloud lift off the King's tower.' Nonchalantly, Norge avoided Prince Kragen's sharp gaze. 'If they're right, it didn't attack the encampment. It just floated out of sight.'

The Tor suffered this interruption as well as he could, but he hardly heard what Norge was saying. At the moment, all he really wanted in life was the ability to cry out; scream his pain at the ceiling. And not just the pain of his brutalized abdomen. He had other hurts as well. Lebbick's death. King Joyse's abandonment, when he, the Tor, had staked his heart on the belief that Joyse still deserved trust. And the humiliation of being distrusted because he had drunk too much wine.

His eyes ran again. Stupid, stupid. Through the blur, he croaked, 'Artagel.'

'Is this certain?' Prince Kragen snapped at Norge. 'The report is to be trusted? The King's Dastard has not attacked us?'

'Lebbick?' Artagel demanded like a man who still wasn't entirely conscious. 'Lebbick?'

'You struck Prince Kragen under a flag of truce. That was a mistake. Tell him you know it was a mistake.'

Both Prince Kragen and Norge stared at the Tor as if the old lord had lost his mind.

'*Lebbick!*' Artagel cried through a clenched throat. 'What have they done to you?'

The Tor tried again. 'Artagel.'

'Terisa? Geraden?' Artagel jerked his head from side to side, scanning the hall, the guards, the bodies. 'Where are they?' A flush of blood and pain filled his face. 'Did Gart get them? Somebody give me a sword! *Where are they?*'

'Artagel!' Norge put an inflection of command into his easy tone. 'Eremis and Gart took the lady. Geraden is all right. Pay attention. The Tor gave you an order.'

'Gave me a *what?*' Artagel rasped as if he were about to begin howling. But then, abruptly, he froze; his eyes widened. Almost matching Norge's casualness, he asked, 'Where is King Joyse?'

'That,' said Prince Kragen in heavy sarcasm, 'is a question we would all like answered.'

Slowly, Artagel's jaw dropped.

The Tor made one more effort. 'Artagel, you struck Prince Kragen under a flag of truce. I want you to apologize.'

Then, deliberately, the old lord closed his eyes and held his breath.

He didn't look or breathe again until he heard Artagel say, 'My lord Prince, I was wrong.'

Artagel was smiling like a whetted axe. His voice held an edge he might have used against Gart. And yet—

And yet he did what the Tor needed.

'It's inexcusable to violate a flag of truce. And you saved my life once – you and the Perdon. I just didn't have time to think. I was afraid of what King Joyse might do. Everybody in Orison knows he's been practicing his swordsmanship. The Castellan said he was probably going to challenge you to a duel. I thought he was crazy enough to try it.'

Prince Kragen couldn't hide his surprise at this information, but the Tor clung to his pain and let everything else pass over his head. Unexpectedly, his spirits lifted a bit. There was good reason why everybody in Orison liked Artagel.

'I've seen you fight,' Artagel concluded. 'King Joyse didn't stand a chance. I was just trying to save him.'

Artagel had the Prince's attention now. Kragen thought intently for a moment, then said, 'Artagel, you have the reputation of a fighter. You understand warfare. What is your opinion? Who has the most to gain from an alliance, Orison or Alend?'

Without hesitation, Artagel answered, 'You do, my lord Prince. We've got the Congery.'

The Tor couldn't be sure of what he saw any longer. His eyes kept running, and the damage to his stomach seemed to throb up into his head; his brain felt like a balloon about to burst. Nevertheless he had the impression that the Prince was sagging, letting go of his fury.

'My lord Tor' – Prince Kragen's voice came from somewhere on the other side of a veil of pressure – 'Geraden and the lady Terisa approached me from the Care of Fayle, where they had witnessed Queen Madin's abduction. But that was by no means their only news. Among a number of other things, they informed me of Master Eremis' treachery.

'Simply for that – to warn King Joyse of his enemies – I might have been willing to risk myself here. But I have other information as well, knowledge which both confirms and worsens the things Geraden and the lady Terisa revealed.

'I know where High King Festten's army is.'

The Tor felt himself about to fall. Really, somebody ought to teach Gart to treat old men with more respect. Nevertheless he was determined to do what he could.

'Norge, announce in Orison that I have taken command during the King's absence. You are appointed Castellan. Make it heard. It is our only defense against panic. The people must believe that we still stand, regardless of treachery.'

Norge saluted equably, but the Tor ignored him. 'My lord Prince,' he wheezed as if his wounds were going to kill him, 'we must leave this hall before Master Eremis sees fit to attack again. Come with me to King Joyse's rooms. We have much to discuss.

'I must discuss it sitting down.'

FORTY-ONE

THE USES
OF TALENT

When Geraden actually recovered consciousness, he was sitting in one of Master Barsonage's handmade chair.

He had opened his eyes before the mediator got him out of the hall of audiences; he had forced his legs under him, despite their awkward tendency to flop in all directions, and had carried most of his own weight during the walk from the hall to Master Barsonage's private quarters; he had received the news of Terisa's capture as if he understood it. Nevertheless he had no effective idea of where he was or what he was doing until Barsonage shut the door on Orison's problems, positioned him in a sturdy armchair, and handed him a flagon of ale.

This room was familiar. And almost comfortable, like a restoration of old relationships, old truths. Master Barsonage was the mediator of the Congery. Geraden was an Apt – part servant, part student. That made everything simple. He had no worries, no responsibilities, unless the mediator assigned them to him. Unless the mediator explained them to him.

Simple.

Moving slowly because of the way his head throbbed, he accepted an automatic swallow from the flagon; then he drank deeply.

And then he remembered so hard that he nearly gasped.

Terisa. Eremis had *Terisa*.

'We've got to help her.'

Perhaps he wasn't entirely conscious after all. He wasn't aware that he had spoken aloud; he certainly didn't realize that he had dropped his flagon on the floor. He only knew that he was trying to get out of the chair, trying with all his strength, and Master Barsonage held him back. Braced over him, the mediator's bulk was implacable: he couldn't shift it.

Terisa!

'Let me go. We've got to help her.'

'How?' demanded the Master bluntly. 'How will you help her?'

'The mirror I made.' Geraden wanted to fret like a child, slap at Barsonage's hands, wail; somehow, he restrained himself. 'The one like

Gilbur's – the one I used to bring her here. I can shift it. I made it take me to Domne.'

'What will that accomplish?' The mediator continued to block Geraden's escape from the chair. 'Surely she was not taken to Domne?'

'No.' Geraden found it almost impossible not to yell or weep. 'He took her to Esmerel. That's where he's been working all this time. I've seen Esmerel. I can make my mirror show that Image. I can use it to look for her. If I find her, I can translate her back.'

Let me go!

'No. Forgive me.' Suddenly, the mediator didn't sound firm or implacable. He sounded grieved, almost wounded. 'That will be impossible.'

Maybe Master Barsonage had stepped back. Or maybe Geraden felt authority rise in him like fire, giving him strength no one could oppose. He was no Apt, not anymore. Eremis' enmity had transformed him.

Don't you understand? He's going to rape her. She's an arch-Imager. He's going to find some way to rape her talent.

Almost without effort, Geraden surged to his feet, pushed the older man back, cleared his own way to the door.

Yet the change in the mediator's tone stopped him; it had more effect on him than a shout of rage or protest. Now that he could have left, he stayed where he was, caught.

'What do you mean? Why is it impossible?'

'Geraden, forgive me,' Barsonage repeated. His grief was plain on his face. 'In this, I have failed you badly.'

Just for an instant, Geraden hung on the verge of an explosion: he was going to spit outrage, batter the mediator into talking sense, do something violent. Almost at once, however, he pulled himself back from the edge. 'Apologize later,' he said between his teeth. 'Just tell me what's wrong.'

'The truth was obvious.' Master Barsonage wasn't able to meet his hot gaze. 'A child could have seen it. Of course you were able to work wonders with that glass. You brought the lady Terisa among us. You escaped into it, leaving no trace of yourself. We all knew of your talent at last—

'But I did not think of your talent. I thought only of your guilt – or your innocence. And so I missed the obvious implication of the obvious truth. There I failed you.'

Geraden beat his fists against his thighs to keep himself from shouting, Get to the point!

'I did not see,' the mediator explained sadly, 'that your mirror required special protection, either to keep it from you if you were guilty, or to preserve it for you if you were innocent.' At last, he forced himself to look into Geraden's face. 'Some days ago, a riot took place. It appeared to be an outbreak against the Castellan – but by an astonishing series of coincidences its worst violence occurred in the laborium. During the tumult, several mirrors were shattered.

'The only one of importance was yours.'

Distinctly, as if the admission were an act of valor, Master Barsonage concluded, 'I have cost you the means to help the lady Terisa. You have no glass with which to search for her.'

Geraden found himself staring at nothing. For some reason, the mediator no longer seemed present in the room. Which was nonsense, of course, he was right there, with his chasuble hanging down his vast chest, with his face twisted in difficult honesty. Nevertheless the older man was gone in some way, erased from Geraden's attention.

A riot had taken place. In the laborium. Against Castellan Lebbick. And mirrors had been destroyed. The only whole, perfect mirror which he, Geraden, had ever made—

He would need at least a day to make another glass. Eremis had Terisa. At least a day.

A riot against Castellan Lebbick?

'You must understand how confused matters were to us in your absence.' Master Barsonage was speaking earnestly, trying to explain. Maybe he thought an explanation would help. 'First you were accused of Nyle's murder. Then Nyle's body was mutilated by means of Imagery, and the physician Underwell disappeared. Then Master Quillon was killed. That was clear evidence of the lady Terisa's guilt – evidence which demonstrated your own guilt by association. The Castellan himself witnessed her power, as well as her alliance with Master Gilbur.'

No, this wasn't working. Geraden didn't need an explanation. Or he didn't need *this* explanation. At least a day. Eremis had Terisa. If he could somehow have focused his attention on the mediator, he would have demanded, A riot against *Castellan Lebbick?*

'And then,' Barsonage was saying, 'the Castellan himself began to insist on your innocence – on the lady Terisa's innocence. Plainly, he had lost his reason. The King's madness had at last driven Lebbick mad. And yet he insisted, when all Orison except the guard had turned against him. He insisted – but privately, privately, so that few could hear him – upon accusing Master Eremis, who had single-handedly saved us from an Alend victory by thirst.

'What were we to think? Without doubt, the lady Terisa's talent – and your own – gave us back our purpose. The meaning of the Congery had been restored. But what were we to do? Had she come to save us, or destroy us? Had you in fact murdered your brother, or were you innocent? Such questions consumed us. We were not concerned for the safety of our mirrors. Men who covet the power of Imagery do not destroy mirrors.'

Geraden had the impression that if he moved – if he so much as opened his mouth to breathe – he would at once fall into a pit of blackness. It filled the room all around him, lurking behind the illusory images of Master Barsonage and the furniture. Everything he had ever done had gone wrong. Wasn't that true? For all practical purposes, he had brought Terisa here simply so that Master Eremis could have her at the peak of his power, at the moment of her greatest vulnerability. What a triumph. The climax of a brilliant life. Everything had gone wrong since the day his mother had died, and he had sworn, *sworn*, that he was never again going to let that happen to anyone he loved.

Nevertheless he couldn't stop trying. The bare idea of surrendering to Eremis made him sick. There had to be something he could do—

A riot against *Castellan Lebbick?*

Deliberately, he opened his mouth. Gritting his teeth, he forced himself to take a deep breath, focus his eyes on the mediator.

'Why Lebbick?' That wasn't exactly the question he wanted to ask, but it was close enough. 'Why did they turn against Lebbick?'

Master Barsonage shrugged his massive shoulders. 'The maid Saddith.' This subject was considerably less personal for him. 'He beat her – beat her nearly to death. She was maimed by it.

'She incited the riot to gain revenge.'

Suddenly, as if Barsonage had murmured the words and made the gestures to perform a translation, Geraden's weakness was gone, banished. There wasn't any pit of blackness around him: there was only a room he knew fairly well; a room which on this occasion didn't have enough lamps lit, with the result that the corners were obscure, like hiding places.

'Master Barsonage' – Geraden was mildly astonished by his own calm – 'why did he beat her? That's where it started – the "series of coincidences." What did she do?'

Geraden's interest obviously took the mediator aback. He hesitated for a moment, as if he thought he ought to steer the discussion in a more useful direction. Whatever he saw in Geraden's face, however, persuaded him to answer.

'The story is that she went to his bed, the night after the lady Terisa's disappearance. She said that she grieved for him in his distress and wished to comfort him. Those who were willing to doubt her – and they were few after the extent of her injuries became known – said that she offered herself to him so that he would elevate her above the position of a chambermaid.'

Again, Geraden wanted to explode. 'And *that* didn't warn you?' he snapped. 'It didn't make you suspicious at all? Didn't you remember she was Eremis' lover? I told you that. I *told* you he's been using her. Didn't it ever occur to you that he might have sent her to Lebbick? What have you done with your *mind?*'

'Geraden.' Master Barsonage's face turned hard; his eyes glittered. 'You are no longer an Apt. No one could deny that you have become an Imager. Yet I remain the mediator of the Congery. I expect your respect.

'I have admitted my fault. I did not foresee the danger to your glass. In other matters, however, I have not earned your anger.'

With difficulty, Geraden restrained himself. 'I'm sorry,' he gritted, unable to unclench his jaws. 'I didn't mean to offend you. I'm just terrified for Terisa.' At once, he went on, 'Do you mean you *were* suspicious of Eremis? What did you do?'

The mediator studied Geraden for a moment, then apparently decided to let himself be mollified. Shrugging again, he replied, 'The relationship between Master Eremis and the maid was of interest to me, naturally. But it was a matter of inference only – hardly a demonstration of treachery. And his public display of loyalty was impressive. I might,' he admitted wryly, 'have dismissed my suspicions, inevitable though they were.

'However, your brother Artagel came to speak with me—'

Geraden held himself still, waiting.

'After the lady Terisa's show of talent,' Master Barsonage explained, 'the Congery at last went to work with a will, showing the kind of dedication King Joyse has always wanted. Respecting the strictures he had placed upon us from the first, we began to search for tools of defense, ways in which we might preserve Orison, or even Mordant – methods to oppose or assist you and the lady Terisa when we learned the truth about you.'

Half-smiling, the mediator digressed to say, 'Prince Kragen seemed on the verge of breaking Orison's gates when you distracted him. I can assure you, however, that he would not have been able to enter this castle without my consent.'

Then he resumed, 'In this work, Master Eremis at first took no part. He was assumed to be resting after the exertion of refilling the reservoir.'

Geraden held his breath.

'The day after the riot, however, he came to me to announce that he was ready to take up his duties among the Congery.

'He could not know that I had had a long conversation with Artagel several days previously.   .

'Artagel informed me that – despite his own evidence – Castellan Lebbick was now convinced of your innocence. He was convinced of Master Eremis' guilt. And his reasoning was persuasive. From Artagel, it was very persuasive.'

Master Barsonage signed. 'Unfortunately, Geraden, there was no proof. There was no basis on which Master Eremis could be accused, no way it could be shown that the man who had saved us from Alend had done so for Cadwal's benefit rather than our own.

'Therefore I could not turn against him. I could not so much as deny him his place in the Congery, for fear that he would be alerted to my distrust. And yet I also could not further expose the Congery to his betrayal.

'Geraden, I have not served you well – but I have served the King better. I concealed the Congery's true work from Master Eremis. I lied to him about it. I allowed him to see no sign of it, play no part in it. He does not know how well prepared we are to assist in the defense of Orison.'

Geraden cleared his lungs slowly. His head was clear, and a number of things seemed to be growing clearer around him. After all, there was really no way Master Barsonage could have predicted that Eremis would use Saddith to start a riot in order to cover up an attack on his, Geraden's mirror. But to keep the Congery's work secret – to do practical labor on Orison's behalf without allowing the knowledge to fall into Eremis' hands— That was well done.

And Artagel trusted him, trusted Terisa. Even Castellan Lebbick had trusted both of them, despite Master Eremis' manipulations.

There was hope. He didn't know what it was yet, but he had the strongest feeling—

'What did you tell him?' he asked the mediator softly. 'What kind of lie did he believe?'

Unexpectedly, Master Barsonage smiled – a grin so sharp it seemed almost bloodthirsty. 'I told him that we have dedicated all our resources to discovering how our enemies are able to make use of flat mirrors without going mad.'

A muscle twitched in Geraden's cheek. Yes, that was a lie which would be believed by anyone who was convinced of the Congery's fundamental ineffectuality. 'Wasn't that true?' he asked.

The lift of the mediator's shoulders was like his grin. 'There was truth in it. I have asked two of the Masters to concentrate on that question. The rest of us, however, have been laboring for more immediate results.'

Geraden felt his courage coming back to him, his hope growing stronger. 'Good,' he pronounced.

'How did Eremis react?'

'He offered his help.' As he spoke, Barsonage lost his look of fierceness; it faded into a more familiar bafflement. 'In fact, he proposed the most plausible theory I have ever heard. He suggested that the translations are done, not with one mirror, but with two. A flat glass is placed in the Image of another mirror, and then both translations are enacted simultaneously, so that the flat mirror functions like a curved one and therefore doesn't exact the usual penalty.'

'He told you *that*?' Geraden was startled; his still-fragile self-confidence flinched. 'Then it must be wrong.' His own theory must be wrong.

'It is,' sighed Master Barsonage. 'Did you know that translation pulverizes glass? I did not. Yet it is true. We have attempted Master Eremis' suggestion three times, and each time the flat mirror was reduced to powder as it passed into the Image of the curved mirror.'

'Glass and splinters!' Geraden groaned. This was too much: he was wrong again; everything he thought he understood was wrong; Eremis was too far ahead of him. Hope was nonsense. He couldn't hold his head up, face the older Imager. There was nothing he could do to save Terisa.

'This surprises you,' observed the mediator thoughtfully. 'Not Master Eremis' suggestion, but rather its failure surprises you. Geraden, you amaze me. You had already considered this idea for yourself, when no other member of the Congery had so much as imagined it.'

Eremis was playing with him, playing with all of them, using them in an elaborate and insidious game they couldn't win, a game from which they couldn't even escape because they didn't know the rules. Like Prince Kragen in his audience with King Joyse, forced to play hop-board. At the mercy of his opponent.

But Master Barsonage was still speaking. 'You have disguised yourself for years as Geraden fumblefoot,' he said in a tone of admiration, 'and now at last I learn that your talent is prodigious. You are able to do translations which diverge from the Image in your mirror. Ideas which astonish us are familiar to you.

'Is there more, Geraden? Does your talent encompass other wonders as well?'

Geraden hardly heard the mediator. He was thinking, Oh, prodigious. Absolutely. They tremble when I walk into the room.

He was thinking, A riot against Castellan Lebbick.

Eremis wanted to preserve Orison for Cadwal. And no man could defend the castle better than Lebbick. And yet Eremis had sent his own lover to get beaten nearly to death, simply to generate a grievance against Lebbick, simply to make a riot possible, simply to make it possible for a riot to enter the laborium, so that Geraden's mirror could be destroyed. All that risk for nothing except to dispose of Geraden's only weapon.

Were Eremis and Gilbur and Vagel really that badly afraid of him?

It sounded ridiculous. But—

He took hold of himself, did his best to steady his heart.

But they knew his talent better than he did. Why else had they gone to such lengths to distract him, confuse him, demean him, kill him? Master Gilbur had guided – and studied – every moment of his mirror-making.

They knew his talent better than he did.

They feared it for reasons he didn't yet understand.

The same kind of argument had helped move him into action while Houseldon burned – and yet he had made no progress toward understanding it. Why had Eremis needed to attack Houseldon? Or Sternwall, for that matter? Why wasn't the destruction of Geraden's only mirror enough?

Suddenly – so suddenly that he couldn't pretend he had been listening to the mediator – Geraden said, 'Havelock.'

Master Barsonage blinked. 'Havelock?'

'He's got all those mirrors.' Geraden was already on his way toward the door. 'Come on.'

Mirrors which had helped Terisa escape from Gilbur. Mirrors which didn't belong to any Imager except the Adept – mirrors Geraden could take chances with.

Outside the mediator's quarters, he began to hurry; in a moment, he was almost running. Nevertheless Master Barsonage caught him, got a heavy hand on his arm and slowed him to a fast walk.

'What do you hope to accomplish with the Adept's mirrors? Will he permit you to touch them?'

A manic laugh burst from Geraden. 'Oh, he'll let me touch them. He is certainly going to let me touch them.'

Moving as rapidly as he could with Master Barsonage clasped on his arm, and refusing to answer the mediator's first question, refusing even to think about it for fear that the possibilities would evaporate if he did, he headed toward the lower levels of Orison, down toward the only entrance he knew of to Adept Havelock's personal domain.

During his one previous visit there, the circumstances had been very different. For one thing, Orison's extra inhabitants hadn't arrived yet; the depths of the castle had been deserted. And for another, he hadn't been paying particularly close attention: most of his mind had been focused on Artagel, suffering from a chestful of corrosive black vapor. As a result, he was momentarily flustered by the realization that he now didn't know how to get where he was going.

Fortunately, Master Barsonage knew.

At least some of the Adept's secrets had been exposed when Castellan Lebbick had followed Master Gilbur and Terisa into the room where

Havelock kept his mirrors. As a matter of course, the Castellan's discovery had eventually been reported to the mediator of the Congery. And Master Barsonage had gone so far as to visit that room full of mirrors himself, in part to see it with his own eyes, in part to make one more painful and ultimately futile effort to communicate with the Adept – specifically, to persuade Havelock that the Congery as a whole should be given access to these mirrors.

The memory caused Master Barsonage to shudder whenever he thought of it. Adept Havelock had responded with a gracious bow, had taken his hand as if to congratulate him, had kissed each of his fingers like a lover – and while Barsonage was distracted by this odd performance, Havelock had urinated on his feet.

Occasionally, Master Barsonage dreamed of beating the Adept senseless. Although he would never have admitted having them, he enjoyed those dreams.

Nevertheless he didn't hesitate to take Geraden to the Adept's quarters.

He and Geraden approached through the storeroom full of empty crates – crates, apparently, in which Havelock's mirrors had been brought to Orison. A door in a niche at the back of the room let them into a short passage. Unexpectedly, Geraden stopped.

Pointing at the impressive array of bolts and bars inside the door, he asked, 'Doesn't he ever lock this place? Does he let people just walk in whenever they want?'

Master Barsonage sniffed in distaste. 'I cannot say. I have come here three times. Twice the door was sealed, and he would not open it to me. Perhaps he did not hear me. The third time, the door was open. I found him snoring in his bed. And when I roused him, he was' – Barsonage grimaced – 'unpleasant.'

After a moment, he added, 'For my own peace of mind, however, I have insisted on guards in the outer hall. Men dressed as ordinary merchants and farmers marked us before we entered the storeroom. If you had not been in my company – or if you had not been recognized – you would have been halted.'

Geraden was scowling. 'Does Havelock know anything about that?'

'Perhaps. Who can say what the Adept knows? Perhaps he neither knows nor cares.'

Geraden was thinking about Terisa. Maybe she could have been saved – maybe everything would have been different – if guards had been placed outside the storeroom earlier. If Adept Havelock had had any idea what he was doing.

Snarling to himself, Geraden headed down the passage.

Almost immediately, he and Barsonage reached the room where Havelock's mirrors were kept.

It had been dramatically changed.

The difference was unmistakable: the room was tidy. Someone had dusted the tables and floor, the mirrors; swept the broken glass from the stone; arranged the full-length mirrors around the walls, displaying them as well as possible in the relatively constricted space. Someone had set up the small and medium-sized mirrors on the tables and adjusted them so that they caught the light of the few lamps and gleamed like promises.

That someone must have been Adept Havelock. Geraden and the mediator spotted him as soon as they entered the room: he was in one corner with a featherduster, crooning over a glass which had been restored to pristine clarity after decades of neglect.

He had made the chamber into a shrine. Or a mausoleum.

Just for a moment while Geraden and Master Barsonage stared at him, he failed to acknowledge their arrival. Then, however, he wheeled to give them a bow, flourishing his duster as though it were a scepter. His eyes gaped in different directions; his fat lips leered. 'Barsonage!' he cackled. 'You honor me. What a thrill. Who's the puppy with you?'

Simply because he couldn't resist staring, Geraden noticed a detail which might have escaped him otherwise: Havelock's surcoat was clean. In fact, it had been scrubbed spotless. Havelock wore it as if he were dressed for a celebration.

Master Barsonage kept his distance. 'Adept Havelock,' he said with formal distaste, 'I am certain that you remember Apt Geraden. He is an Imager now, and has an urgent interest in your mirrors.'

As if to tease the mediator, Havelock advanced toward him, smiling maliciously. 'What, "Apt Geraden"?' he cried in mock protest. 'This boy? How has that figure of augury and power been reduced to such doggishness? No, you're mistaken, it's impossible.'

Swooping suddenly away from Barsonage, he pounced on Geraden. With his hands clapped to Geraden's cheeks, he shook Geraden's head from side to side.

'Impossible, I tell you. Look, Barsonage. He's alive. He came back alive. Without her. She risked everything for him, and he came back without her.' Bitterly, the Adept began to laugh. 'Oh, no, Barsonage, you can't fool me. Geraden would never have done such a thing.'

Geraden seemed to hear the Adept through an abrupt roaring in his ears, a tumult of anger and distress. The suggestion that he might have come back without Terisa by choice, that he had turned his back on her in some way, was more than he could bear.

Harshly, struggling to control his passion, he demanded, 'Let me go, Havelock. I need your mirrors.'

As if he had been stung, the Adept let out a wail.

He dropped his hands, plunged himself to the floor; before Geraden could react, he kissed the toes of Geraden's boots. Then he scuttled backward. When he hit the leg of a table, he bounded to his feet.

Crouching in the intense stance of a man about to do battle, he commented casually, almost playfully, 'If you ever talk to Joyse like that, he'll cut your heart out. Or force you to marry all his daughters. With him it's hard to tell the difference.'

Shocked and disconcerted, Geraden turned a plea for help toward Master Barsonage.

Grimly, the mediator nodded. Swallowing to hold down a bellyful of

759

uneasiness, he stepped forward, edged his bulk a bit between the Adept and Geraden.

Geraden took that opportunity to turn his back on both of them.

Deliberately, he placed himself before the first full-length flat mirror he could find.

It was an especially elegant piece of work: he noticed its beauty in spite of his concentration on other things, because he loved mirrors. Its rosewood frame was nearly as tall as he was, and the wood had a deep, burnished glow which only long hours of care and polish could produce. The surface of the glass was meticulous, both in its flatness and in its craftsmanship. The glass itself held an evanescent suggestion of pink – a color which now appeared to complement the frame, although of course the frame had actually been chosen to suit the glass.

And the Image—

Bare sand. Nothing else.

Wind had whipped the sand into a dune with a keen, curled edge, like a breaker frozen in motion; but there was no wind now. The color of the sky was a dry, dusty blue that he associated almost automatically with Cadwal.

In some ways, this landscape was the purest he had ever seen, too clean even for bleached bones. No one and nothing alive had ever set foot on that dune.

Only urgency kept him from studying every inch of the mirror, simply to understand the Image – and to appreciate the workmanship.

He had no idea how Terisa worked with flat glass. And he had no particular reason to believe he could do the same thing. In fact, he hardly knew how he had contrived to translate himself from the laborium to the Closed Fist. He certainly hadn't done anything to prove himself an arch-Imager.

Nevertheless he didn't hesitate.

He came back alive. Without her. Geraden would never have done such a thing.

Facing the glass, he closed his eyes; he swept his thoughts clear. Master Barsonage and Adept Havelock were watching him, and Terisa was lost, and he had never tried anything like this before. Yet he had the strongest feeling—

He pulled his concentration together, firmly wiped panic and confusion and anguish out of his heart.

In the mirror of his mind, he began to construct an Image of Esmerel.

Still trying to intervene between Geraden and Havelock, the mediator asked the Adept carefully, 'You mentioned King Joyse. Do you know where he is?'

'He has flown,' spat back Havelock, his mouth full of vitriol. 'Like a bird, ha-ha. You think he has abandoned you, but it is a lie, a lie, a lie. When everything else is lost, he breaks my heart and gives me nothing.'

Geraden ignored both of them.

He found it easy to ignore distractions now. Something luminous was taking place. He had no training in Image-building; no Imager practiced that skill. He was working with an entirely new concept: that the Image of a mirror could be chosen; that translations could be done which ignored the apparent Image of a mirror. As new to the world as Terisa herself. And yet the process of creating the Image he wanted in his mind excited him; it enabled him to close his attention to anything which interfered.

Line by line, feature by feature, he put together a picture of Eremis' 'ancestral Seat.'

He had only seen it once, of course – and only from the outside. He had no notion what it looked like inside. But that didn't worry him. He believed that the scenes and landscapes in mirrors were real, that Images were reflections rather than inventions. So if he could induce the glass to show Esmerel from the outside, the manor's true interior would be included automatically.

'What do you mean,' asked Master Barsonage, '"flown"?' He didn't seem to expect an answer, however. He may not have been listening to himself at all.

Esmerel was a relatively low building in a deep, wedge-shaped valley with a brook bubbling picturesquely over its stones and out-croppings of rock like ramparts all along the walls – not low because of any lack of sweep or grace in its design, but because it was constructed on only one rambling, aboveground level. According to rumor, some of the best features of the house were belowground, dug down into the rock of the valley: an enviable wine cellar; a gallery for weavings, paintings, and small sculptures; a vast library; several research halls. But naturally Geraden knew nothing about those things. He knew, however, that a portico defined the entrance – a portico with massive redwood pillars for columns. The entrance, as he remembered it, was plain, only one lamp in a leaded glass frame on either side, no carving on the panels of the doors. The house's walls were layered planks – waxed rather than painted against Tor's weather – but all the corners and intersections were stone, with the result that Esmerel's face had a pleasingly varied texture.

Unless something had happened since he had seen it – or unless his memory or his imagination had gone wrong – Master Eremis' home looked precisely like *that*.

Master Barsonage let out a stifled gasp. His respiration was labored, as if he had stuffed his fist into his mouth and was trying to breathe around it.

To commemorate the occasion, Adept Havelock began whistling thinly through his teeth.

Geraden opened his eyes.

The mirror in front of him showed a sand dune under a calm sky, almost certainly somewhere in Cadwal.

The pang of his disappointment was so acute that he nearly groaned aloud.

'I would not have believed it,' whispered Barsonage. 'When I was first told that such things could happen, I did not believe it.'

'Are you out of your mind?' inquired the Adept politely. 'That's how I know this isn't Apt Geraden. Even if he did talk to me that way. A man who can do this wouldn't have to come back without her.'

Geraden blinked hard, shook his head. No, he wasn't going blind. The Image he was staring at hadn't changed at all.

Distressed and baffled, he turned toward Master Barsonage—

—and saw Esmerel, as clear as sunlight, exactly as he had envisioned it, in the curved mirror standing beside the flat glass he had chosen to work with.

'By the pure sand of dreams,' he murmured, 'that's incredible.' A curved mirror, a curved mirror. Excitement leaped up in him; he could hardly restrain a yell. 'I wouldn't have believed it myself.' A curved mirror, of *course*! Flat glass was Terisa's talent, not his. If he had tried to translate himself through a flat glass, he would have gone mad. Like Havelock.

'Don't flatter yourself,' Havelock advised sententiously. 'If you think I'm going to kiss your boots again, just because you can do a little trick like that, you're full of shit.'

But *curved* glass—! Like the only mirror he had ever been able to make for himself, the mirror which had reached Terisa behind the Image of the champion. He could shift the Images in curved mirrors.

Quickly, before he had time to be overwhelmed by his discovery, he approached the glass and began to adjust the focus.

'Now I'll find her.' The pressure of hope and need cramped his lungs. 'I'll get her away from you, you bastard. If I find you, I'll even get *you*. Just try to stop me. Just try.'

Fighting the tremors in his hands, the long shivers which made his fingers twitch, he tipped the mirror's frame to bring the Image of Esmerel closer.

Distance was the problem, distance. He knew that – and tried to keep it out of his mind, tried not to let it terrify him. If the focus of the Image was too far from the place where Terisa was being held, he wouldn't be able to adjust the mirror enough to reach her. Every glass had a limited range: it couldn't be focused more than a certain distance from its natural Image. If he couldn't reach Terisa, he would have to start over again from the beginning: based on what he learned now, he would have to build the Image of Esmerel again, re-create it in his mind – but closer this time, closer.

In his present turmoil, that kind of concentration might be impossible.

No, don't fail, he exhorted the glass, don't fail now, you've never done anything right in your life except love her, she's all there is for you and Orison and Mordant and even Alend, *don't fail now*.

With a jerk because his hand was unsteady, the Image moved to a near view of the entrance under the portico.

Another jerk.

The Image moved into the forehall of the manor.

Geraden stopped breathing.

Like the exterior walls, the floor was formed of fitted planks anchored with stone. Years of use and wax made the boards gleam, but couldn't conceal the fact that men who didn't care what damage they did had been there in nailed boots – had been there recently. Mud, footprints, gouged spots, splinters: they were all distinct in the Image.

Nevertheless the forehall was empty.

Sweat streamed into Geraden's eyes. He scrubbed at it with the back of his hand. Dimly, he was aware that both Master Barsonage and Adept Havelock were standing over him, watching his search; but he had no attention to spare for them.

More smoothly, he moved the Image into the first room which opened off the forehall.

A large sitting room: the kind of room in which formal guests sipped sweet wines before dinner. Tracked with mud and bootmarks.

Bloodstains.

Deserted.

'Why is no one there?' asked the mediator softly. 'Where is Master Eremis? Where are his mirrors – his power?'

Geraden's heart constricted. Nausea rose in his throat as he moved the Image through the house.

A cavernous dining room. More mud and bootmarks, more bloodstains. The edges of the table were ragged with swordcuts.

Deserted.

Oh, Terisa, please, where are you?

Geraden scanned two more fouled rooms, both empty, then located a wide staircase sweeping downward.

'The cellars,' murmured Master Barsonage. 'That is where they would imprison her.'

Of course. The cellars. Esmerel's equivalent of a dungeon. Eremis wouldn't keep his mirrors or his apparatus or any of his secrets where passersby or even tradesmen might catch sight of them. Everything would be belowground.

Who was responsible for all this mud, all these bootmarks?

Geraden nudged the Image downward.

For the first few steps, he was so absorbed in what he was doing – so caught up in the focus of the glass, the search for Terisa, the need to succeed – that he didn't understand what was about to happen to him, didn't realize the truth at all, even though it was perfectly plain in front of him, so obvious that any farmer or stonemason, any ordinary man or woman, would have grasped it automatically.

But then the Image began to dim, began to grow palpably dim in the glass, and Master Barsonage croaked, 'Light.'

Light.

Geraden's hands froze on the frame. His whole body lost movement, as if the breath and blood had been swept out of him. The stairs loomed below him darkly, treads descending into an immeasurable black.

There was no light. No lamps or lanterns or torches or candles. They had been extinguished.

The Image still existed, of course; but without light there was nothing to see.

He had no answer to that defense. By that one stroke, any attempt to rescue Terisa was instantly and effectively prevented. He couldn't help her if he couldn't find her – and how could he find her if he couldn't see her?

'Maybe—' The air seemed to thicken in his lungs; he felt like he was suffocating. 'Maybe there's light farther down. Maybe only the stairs are dark.'

At once, Master Barsonage clamped a warning hand onto his shoulder. 'Geraden,' he hissed as if the former Apt were far away, lost in urgency, almost out of reach, 'how will you find it? If there *is* light, how will you find it? You cannot focus an Image you cannot *see*. You may shift it into the foundations of the house, where no light will ever reach.'

'I've got to try.' Geraden was choking. The mediator's hand on his shoulder was choking him. 'Don't you understand? I've got to find her.'

'No!' Master Barsonage insisted. Geraden's passion appeared to affect him like anguish. *'You cannot focus an Image you cannot see.'*

That was true. Of course. Any idiot could have told him that. Even a failed Apt who had never done anything right in his life could recognize the truth. Darkness made all the mirrors blind – and all Imagers.

Somehow, Geraden stepped back against the pressure of Barsonage's grip. Facing the Image as it blurred into the obscure depths, he said harshly, 'Then I'll have to go myself.'

With a look of iron on his face, and no hope in his heart, he made the mental adjustment of translation and stepped into the glass.

As his face crossed into the Image, he cried out, 'Terisa!'

Master Barsonage wrenched him back so hard that he sprawled among the tables.

Before he could regain his feet – or curse or fight – Adept Havelock sat down on his chest, straddling his neck.

'Listen to me,' the Adept snarled, savage with strain. 'I can't do this for long.' His eyes rolled as if he were going into a seizure. 'You can make us let you go. Just use that voice. We'll obey. But we won't be able to get you back.'

Geraden bucked against the Adept, tried to pitch Havelock off him. Havelock braced his legs on either side, clutched at Geraden's jerkin with both hands, hung on.

'Listen to me, you fool! Your power sustains the shift! When you translate yourself, that glass will revert to its natural Image. You'll be cut off! – you and the lady Terisa both! You'll *both* be lost!'

It was too much. Geraden flung Adept Havelock aside. He surged to his feet. With all his strength, he punched Master Barsonage in the chest – a blow which nearly made the massive Imager take a step backward.

Then he faced the mirror and began to howl.

'Eremis! Don't touch her!'

FORTY-TWO

UNEXPECTED TRANSLATIONS

Eremis was touching her. He was certainly touching her.

She had never been strong enough against him. Her concentration had never been strong enough. While he had approached her in the audience hall, while he had threatened Geraden, while he had fought with the Tor, she had attempted something she didn't know how to do, something she had never heard of before: wild with anger and desperation, she had tried to reach out to the mirror which had brought him here and change it.

On some level, she knew that was impossible. She was on the wrong side of the glass, the side of the Image, not the side of the Imager. But the knowledge meant nothing to her. If she could feel a translation taking place, surely that gave her a link, a channel? And she didn't have any other way to fight. Her need was that extreme: she didn't care that what she was trying was probably insane. Her strange and unmeasured talent was her only weapon. If she could fade, if she could go far enough away to reach his mirror—

His hands made that impossible. They forced her to the surface of herself when she most needed to sink away.

First there was his grip on her arm. He flung her toward the translation point as if it were a wall against which he intended to break her bones. But he didn't let her go.

Then there was the bottomless instant of translation, the eternal dissolution.

Then there was a completely different kind of light.

It was orange and hot, part furnace, part torches – and full of smoke, rankly scented. Another man was there, someone she hadn't seen before, a blur as Eremis impelled her past him, kept her spinning. Gilbur and Gart were right behind her, as blurred as everything else.

And Eremis was shouting, 'The lights! Put out the lights!'

Before she could get her eyes into focus, see anything clearly, the torches dove into buckets of sand; a clang closed the door of the furnace. Darkness slammed against her like a wave of heat.

'What went wrong?' someone demanded in a rattling voice.

'Geraden,' snapped Master Eremis. 'He remains alive. We must not let him see this place.'

'I tried to kill him,' Gilbur snarled. 'I hit him hard. But that puppy is stronger than he appears.'

'*She* must not see it,' continued Eremis. 'She is his creation. Who knows what bonds exist between them? Perhaps they are able to share Images in their minds.'

The first voice, the man she didn't know, made an assenting noise. 'Then it is good that we were prepared for this eventuality. If we were in the Image-room—' A moment later, he added, 'It would be interesting to learn what he does when he regains consciousness.'

'As long as he cannot find us,' muttered Master Gilbur.

'In the dark?' Master Eremis laughed. 'Have no fear of that.' He sounded exultant, almost happy. His grip on Terisa shifted; with one hand, he held both her arms behind her back. 'She is mine now – and they are ours. No matter that Geraden still lives, and Kragen. That will only add spice to the sauce. They will do exactly what we wish.'

'And Joyse?' asked the rattling voice.

'You saw,' rasped Gilbur. 'He fled when we appeared. No doubt he is cowering in some hidey-hole, hoping for mad Havelock to save him.'

The tone of Eremis' laughter suggested that he doubted Gilbur's assessment. He didn't argue, however. Instead, he said, 'It will be safe to renew the lights when the door is closed.'

Firmly, irresistibly, he pushed Terisa ahead of him into the dark.

And all the time, she was still trying to concentrate, still trying to fade.

Now, of course, she wasn't reaching toward the glass Eremis had used; she was struggling to find Adept Havelock's supply of mirrors, striving to feel the potential for translation across the distance. She could sense translations as they occurred. She was sensitive to the opening of the gap between places. That must mean *something*. There must be some way she could use it.

But Eremis' grasp made everything impossible.

He held her too roughly, so that her arms hurt; he pushed her too far ahead of him into the blind dark. Through a doorway, along a lightless passage, through another door: the visceral fear of running into something kept her from being able to pull her heart and mind away. The way he chuckled between his teeth filled her with rage and despair.

I'm not yours. Never. I'll find some way to kill you. No matter what happens. I swear it.

It was impossible to fade while she was so full of fury.

And then the way he held her changed.

Through the second doorway and across a rough floor, he suddenly thrust her down. She couldn't catch herself because he didn't free her arms: she landed heavily on a pillow, a bed. Deftly, he turned her so that she lay on her back, with her wrists now clamped above her head by one of his hands. Then he clasped something iron around her left wrist; she heard a click, a faint rattle of chain. In spite of the fetter, however, he continued to hold her arms pinned.

He went on chuckling while his other hand undid the hooks of her soft, leather shirt, exposing her breasts, her vulnerable belly.

'I must chain you,' he murmured pleasantly, 'a small precaution against

766

your strange talents – and Geraden's. But it will not prevent me from satisfying my claim on you. You will find that I am not easily satisfied. On the other hand, we have plenty of time.

'If you are compliant, I will keep you bound as little as possible.'

In the dark, she struggled; she wanted to smash his face, wanted to feel his blood on her hands. He pinned her easily, however; he knew how to keep women from getting away from him. When she paused to gather her strength so that she wouldn't weep, he curled his tongue like a lick of wet fire around each of her nipples, and his hand slipped aside the sash of her trousers.

Gasping on the verge of tears, she tried to twist out of his hold; failed.

Abruptly, she stilled herself, let the resistance sag out of her muscles. She wasn't accomplishing anything; she was just contributing to her own defeat by making herself wild. She couldn't concentrate – Let him think her stillness was a form of surrender. If he was that arrogant.

'You will accept my manhood completely,' he murmured. 'I will take possession of you in all ways. And I will not be satisfied until you beg me to enter you wherever and whenever I desire.'

His mouth clung to her nipples, teasing them involuntarily erect, caressing and probing them. At the same time, his hand moved down into her open trousers to the place between her legs which only Geraden knew. His fingers stroked her there as if he believed that she was being seduced.

Far away in her mind, she was imagining his death.

When he began to pull her trousers off her hips, however, she returned to defend herself. Her eyes were starting to adjust – and this room wasn't absolutely lightless. Hints of illumination filtered into the air from what may have been an imperfectly sealed window in the wall above her. Eremis' head was a shape of deeper blackness poised to make her breasts ache. She couldn't fight him physically. But she could still fight.

Taking advantage of the fact that he had left her mouth free, she said, 'Gilbur thinks King Joyse is a coward, but you don't agree.' Her tone should have warned him: it wasn't unsteady enough, frightened enough, to indicate surrender. 'Why is that?'

'Because, my sweet lady' – he was too full of victory to refuse to answer her – 'you betrayed him to me.'

She could feel him grinning over her in the dark.

'I might have believed that he was a fool, or a coward, or a madman. But you came to me while Lebbick had me in his dungeon, and you opened my eyes. At a time when I might have remained innocent of the knowledge, you showed me that King Joyse understood his own actions – that he did what he did deliberately.'

Terisa's spirit squirmed at the thought; but she kept her body passive.

'This revelation enabled me to adjust my plans to accommodate the possibility that he may have been setting traps of his own. If I had been forced to wait until Quillon finally exposed himself and Joyse by rescuing you, I might have found myself in difficulty. But you' – Eremis entered her maliciously with his fingers, making her flinch – 'gave me time to prepare a more personal snare – time to arrange for Queen Madin's abduction, to cut the ground out from under Joyse at precisely the moment when I might be most exposed to counterattack.

'You made that possible, my lady.' His head was turned toward her now, momentarily sparing her breasts. He was gloating, hardly able to contain his triumph. At that moment, he might have been willing to tell her anything. 'You allowed me to perfect my plans against an opponent who may have proved worthier than he appeared.'

As he spoke, her mind turned cold and sick. It was true: she had given King Joyse to his enemies.

'You deserve Saddith's fate for attempting to thwart me. But because I am grateful I will use only as much force as you require.'

He laughed again – a snort of pleasure and contempt. Her senses were full of him. He smelled of sweat and confidence. 'Gart wished to kill you when you left Vale House, but I did not allow it. Doubtless your death and Geraden's would have been to our benefit. But then who would have taken the news of the Queen to King Joyse? How else could I arrange to master both you and Joyse at the same time, except by letting you live?

'You have served me perfectly, despite your opposition.' His fingers continued to work between her legs. 'My only regret is that I do not yet have Geraden in my power. That will come, however. I have said that I must think of something truly special to reward him for his interference, his dunder-headed enmity, and I will do it.

'If you are compliant, my lady, you will live a life which many women would envy. But *him*' – Eremis' fingers hurt her, nearly made her gasp – 'him I will destroy.'

'I doubt it,' she said, breathing hard to diffuse the pain. She was going to kill him. All she had to do was stay alive long enough. 'He can do translations you don't understand. Translations you didn't even know were possible until he brought me to Orison.'

For a moment, Eremis' laugh sounded more like a snarl. 'That is true. And it offends me. But again I have been abundantly forewarned. The Congery's augury made me suspicious of Geraden. And Gilbur learned much while teaching him to shape his mirror. That allowed me to set in motion all the dangers and distractions which prevented both him and you from exploring your talents, learning what they were. And it allowed me to preserve the disregard in which he was held by the Masters, so that the Congery did not try to help you.

'In that way, we gained a great deal of necessary time.

'And now, of course, he is helpless. You cannot threaten me with his power. He can translate nothing he cannot see.'

'I know that,' Terisa replied harshly – too harshly. She hadn't intended to let so much of her fury show. 'But you can't see, either. You need light sometime – unless you're planning to give up on Orison and Mordant and Alend, and spend the rest of your life just raping me.' She felt him grin over her. 'And when you go out into the light' – she did her best to lodge each word like a knife in his vitals – 'you'll find that he knows too much about you. He knows how you use flat mirrors without going mad.'

Eremis' reaction was stronger than she was expecting. He stiffened; his

768

breath hissed between his teeth; his hand raked across her belly as if to hurt her breasts or strike her face.

'How is that, my lady?'

Lying still, expressing defiance with her voice alone, she said, 'You put the flat glass inside a curved one and work both translations at the same time.'

As quickly as she had gained it, she lost her advantage. The Master relaxed tangibly; his fingers stroked her nipples while the tension ran out of him. 'That is quite accurate,' he commented. 'And I must say that I am impressed by Geraden's ability to reason his way so near the truth. By now, however, Barsonage has discovered that the technique you describe is impossible. Glass translated through glass only shatters.

'The true secret, my lady, lies in the oxidate which prepares the curved mirror. That is *my* discovery, the result of *my* sweat and study. *I* learned how to make a mirror into which other mirrors could be translated.'

At the moment, her determination to kill him was all that kept her from despair. There simply wasn't room in her for so much anger *and* the horror of seeing her last hope collapse.

'Most of my fellow Masters,' Eremis continued, 'would laugh themselves sick if they knew how I have spent my years as an Imager. And yet on my small discovery the world hinges. When I am done, all Mordant and Alend and Cadwal will be at my service, and even High King Festten will acknowledge me supreme.'

The prospect filled him with passion. He began kissing Terisa again, and this time she could feel his hunger in the way his mouth nipped and sucked her nipples, the way his tongue thrust against them. His free hand was back inside her trousers, pulling them down, making her ready for him.

If he had let her arms go – just for a second – she would have done her best to put his eyes out. In spite of his triumph, however, he didn't shift the grip that kept her under control.

She had no way to make him stop.

She didn't need to make him stop. Out of the dark, the unfamiliar, rattling voice said sourly, 'Festten wants you.'

Nearly choking with anger, Master Eremis sprang to his feet and wheeled away from Terisa. 'Am I to be interrupted with her forever? She is *mine*, I tell you, and I have earned her. Festten does not command *me!*'

The other voice conveyed a shrug. 'He has twenty thousand men who believe otherwise. And he desires a report.'

Her arms were free. She pulled them down, swung her legs off the bed, sat up; she tested the chain. It wasn't long enough to let her reach Eremis. The cold cuff on her wrist held.

'Report to him yourself,' Eremis countered. 'Send Gilbur to report. Send *Gart*. I do not come and go to suit the High King.'

'Eremis,' the rattling voice warned, 'think. The High King trusts me. He has always trusted me. But he does not trust you. He accepts your leadership – he does as you wish – only because you obtain results which please him. You bring him nearer to victory than he has ever been.

'But now you have risked a foray into the heart of Orison itself, and have accomplished nothing except Lebbick's death and her capture. High King

Festten considers that so far all his actions under your guidance have come to nothing. His only satisfaction has been the annihilation of the Perdon.

'He desires a report.'

'That sheepfucker,' growled Eremis in disgust. 'A man who has lost his interest in women – a man who can only find pleasure in animals – is not fit for kingship.'

Nevertheless his tone expressed acquiescence. Despite his anger and frustration, the Master left Terisa alone. Muttering obscenities to himself, he strode away through the dark.

Because she wasn't done – because she had never been further from surrender and wanted to know her enemy – she demanded after him sharply, 'Why are you doing this?'

He must have paused. His tone was at once hard and light; malign; jubilant.

'Because I can.'

Almost at once, she was sure that he was gone.

For what felt like a long moment, she didn't move. She had given King Joyse to his enemies. Queen Madin's abduction was her fault. She had gone to Eremis in the dungeon and told him what he needed to know and let him command her to betray Geraden and *how could she have been so stupid?* And Geraden didn't know the secret of the oxidate. He couldn't fight the Master. He couldn't find her in the dark.

Hope was out of the question, really.

Never mind that. She probably didn't have room for hope anyway. Her yearning for Eremis' blood was too big: it squeezed out everything else. It made the kind of concentration she needed impossible. She was powerless precisely because her ache for power was so intense.

The chain left her room to move around the bed. Grimly, she pulled up her trousers, tied the sash tightly, and began to rebutton her shirt.

'Unfortunate,' the rattling voice muttered.

She froze.

How many people were watching her – people she couldn't see?

'I see well without light. Darkness conceals no secrets from me. But opportunities to witness such nakedness have been rare in recent years.' The speaker's voice sounded like pebbles on glass. 'A woman with such proud breasts, and yet so full of fear. A tantalizing combination. And there is time. Eremis will be away for some little while. Festten will question him narrowly before allowing him to go ahead with his plans.'

Terisa wanted to finish buttoning her shirt, but she couldn't make her fingers work. How many people—? Until now, she had only been afraid of Eremis, not of the dark itself, not of the place where he had left her.

'Sadly, however, Eremis does not like used meat. And I do not like any meat enough to risk my alliance with him. Hide your breasts – or flaunt them – as you choose.' She heard relish as well as scorn in the rattle. 'They will not sway me.'

As if she had been waiting for his permission, she fumbled at the fastenings of the shirt.

At last, her eyes were adjusting to the dark. When she peered hard, she was able to discern the outlines of a figure near where she guessed the doorway to be. The voice came from that direction.

Clenching her teeth for courage, she stood up and tested the chain.

She was able to swing her arms before she came to its limit. Following it to its anchor, she found that it was stapled into the wall at the head of the bed – nearly ten feet of it, enough to let her perform almost any conceivable gymnastic feat on the bed, but not enough to let her evade the dim figure in the doorway. Nevertheless she was comforted to have that much range of motion. If everything else failed, she would at least have a chance to hit Master Eremis before he touched her again.

Deliberately, she wrapped some of the chain around her fist to give it weight. She placed her back against the wall. Then she faced the figure with the rattling voice.

'You're Vagel.' She didn't need confirmation: she was sure. 'The famous arch-Imager. The man who drove Havelock mad. Why do you do it?'

'Do what?'

'Put up with him. You call it an alliance, but he probably treats you like a servant. You're *the* arch-Imager. The most powerful man anybody has ever heard of. Why are you serving him? Why isn't it the other way around?'

The outlines of the figure suggested a shrug. 'Power,' he said like stones scattering against a mirror, 'is more often a matter of position than of talent. He told you the truth, in a way. The whole world hinges on the little discovery which enables him to translate glass through glass. But that is not his real power.'

'Really?' She couldn't stifle her impulse to goad Vagel. She was too frightened and furious for any other approach. Apparently, Vagel had been listening – *watching* – while Eremis had her naked. 'What *is*?'

'His real power,' rattled the arch-Imager, 'is that he is irreplaceable to all his allies – because of his talents, of course, but also because of his position, in the Congery, in Orison. What access do I have to his resources, his freedoms? Gilbur, I grant you, has also been favorably placed. But there it is his talent which is replaceable. He is only swift – uncommonly swift – rather than brilliant. And he hates everyone too much to form bonds – everyone except Eremis.

'No, Eremis' real power is that he can have his way with anyone.

'He has his way with me, although my Imagery far surpasses his – and although I am the link which allowed him to begin his dealings with Festten, years ago when he rescued me from renegade destitution among the Alend Lieges. He will have his way with Festten, despite the High King's taste for absolute authority. He will have his way with you' – Vagel let out a malign chuckle – 'until the only thing which prevents you from begging for death is that he does not let you speak.

'He will even have his way with King Joyse in the end.' Now Vagel's tone suggested hard things – broken things with sharp edges. 'For that reason I do not care how utterly I serve him.'

Unexpectedly, Terisa had stopped listening. The Alend Lieges. The way he said those words triggered a small leap of intuition, fitted on odd, minor detail into place. In surprise, she said, 'Carrier pigeons.'

Vagel was silent, as if she had startled him.

'You're the one who brought carrier pigeons here. You gave them to the Alend Lieges.'

'Those mucky barons,' growled the arch-Imager. 'Their squalor and their petty ambitions nearly drove me mad. They demanded – *demanded* – power. Imagery. I had to satisfy them to keep myself alive, *me*, the greatest Imager they had ever known. And yet they were *satisfied* with birds that could carry messages. I would have destroyed them long ago – I would have *required* that of Eremis – if they weren't such *little* men.

'For that also, for the humiliation they cost me, Joyse will suffer.'

'Revenge,' Terisa muttered. Her attention shifted back to Vagel. 'He and Havelock beat you back when you thought you were about to become the master of the world, and you can't live with it. Now you don't care who has the power. You don't care how much *Eremis* humiliates you. All you care about is hurting the people who showed you you were wrong about yourself.

'What Eremis is doing to you is worse than anything King Joyse ever did.'

'Is it?' Vagel's voice purred like a fall of small stones. 'How strangely you think. Your defeat becomes less and less surprising, despite all the nearly unguessable implications of your talent.

'Eremis' manner is demeaning, but the rewards he offers are not. Do you believe that either Joyse or Havelock proved themselves better men than I am – more able or deserving, more powerful? No. They only proved that they were more treacherous. And you have seen in the decline of Mordant and the collapse of Orison that there exists *nothing* so desirable, worthy, or powerful that it cannot be betrayed. I was beaten, not by a good Imager or a good king, but by a good *spy*.'

She expected the arch-Imager to advance, but he didn't. 'Do not despise revenge. Unless I am much mistaken' – he was sneering at her – 'you yourself have no other passion.

'In your case, however, revenge must fail. You do not *serve* any man who can make glass from the blood-soaked sand of your desires. Eremis will have his way with you, and then the truth of you will be proven absolutely.'

'It's the same for you,' she retorted, fighting back so that what he said wouldn't crush her. 'He's using you – having his way with you. And when he's done, he'll just discard you. You won't get your revenge after all. He wants all the fun for himself.'

Vagel made a sharp, hissing noise. After that, there was a long silence. Terisa tightened her grip on the chain, although the vague figure hadn't moved.

'No,' he said at last, as if she had provoked him to candor. 'All his allies must fear the same thing – but he will not discard *me*. Festten trusts me. Eremis' plotting would have come to nothing, if I had not stood with him before the High King. He needs Cadwal too much to risk that alliance by discarding me.

'And without me all the force of Imagery at his disposal will become a blunt instrument – able to strike hard, but unable to strike at will. Useless. I am the arch-Imager, as you have observed. The procedures by which we shape mirrors that show the Images we desire are mine. Did you believe that our successes could have been achieved randomly? That Gilbur for all his speed could have made the glass we need simply by mixing accidental combinations of tinct and oxidate, sand and surface? I tell you, he could have sweated until his heart burst without ever producing a mirror which gave us access to Vale House – or one which showed the audience hall of Orison. That victory is *mine*.

'Alone, I have overturned the tenets of Imagery, and no one on Joyse's foolish Congery can compare with me.'

Vagel's voice intensified. 'Eremis cannot do without me. His need for glass which only I can provide will never end. And because of that' – he seemed to be controlling an impulse to shout – '*before I am done I will roast Joyse's guts over a slow fire*. I will hear him *howl* until his mind goes, or by the stars! I will take my satisfaction from Eremis himself.'

A visceral tremor started up in Terisa's guts, so hard that she couldn't speak.

Abruptly, the arch-Imager turned to leave. 'Remember that,' he snapped while his voice faded. 'Perhaps it will inspire you to surrender to him prematurely, and then his pleasure in you will be made that much less.'

He left her with the chain wrapped around her fist and no one to strike.

She didn't trust his departure. Her senses strained into the dark, searching for evidence that she wasn't alone. But she heard nothing, felt nothing. As for sight— She could discern a hint of the doorway, but the corners of the room were as obscure as pits. When she turned her eyes to the wall behind the bed, however, she was able to make out the source of the scant illumination. Her first guess had been right: the light came from a window not quite perfectly sealed.

Dropping the chain to increase her range of motion, she climbed onto the bed and reached for the window. From that position, she could get her hands on the boards nailed over the frame. Unfortunately, her fingers found no purchase, either at the edges or in the cracks. She tried until her fingertips tore and her self-control threatened to crumble; then, so that she wouldn't start sobbing, she got down from the bed.

Calm. It was essential to remain calm. To preserve a semblance of calm until it became the real thing. So that she could concentrate *although of course it was impossible to translate herself out of here with a chain on her wrist* no, don't think about things like that, do not. Be calm. Concentrate.

Fade.

Pressing her hands over her face, she sat on the edge of the bed and tried to fade.

She couldn't do it: she was too angry and scared, deprived of hope. She had the shakes so badly that her heart itself quivered. She had betrayed King Joyse, and Vagel was going to make him *howl* – Geraden had no way to find her, rescue her. Too many people might still be watching her, concealed behind spyholes, hidden in the corners—

Eremis would come back as soon as he finished with High King Festten.

She needed time to pull herself together.

Searching for calm, she decided to explore the room as far as the chain allowed. What else could she do? Maybe if she failed to find anything she would recover some self-possession.

Shaking badly, and too angry to care whether she looked foolish to a spectator, she moved to the staple holding her chain and from there started to grope her way toward the corner, searching the cold, crude stone with her fingers.

When her hand touched iron in the wall, she nearly flinched.

Iron: another staple.

A short chain fixed to the staple. A manacle.

A wrist in the fetter.

That did make her flinch. She recoiled to the bed, sat down facing the dark. Her breath came in hard gasps.

She had felt a wrist. Skin. A hand that flexed away from her touch.

Another prisoner. Someone was chained in the corner.

Eremis had intended to rape her before witnesses.

Who are you? she panted. For a moment, the words refused to come out of her throat. Almost gagging, she forced them.

'Who are you?'

No answer. Maybe because she was breathing so hard herself, she couldn't hear any sigh or rustle of life.

'Are you hurt?' That was another possibility. Who could tell what Eremis or Vagel or Gilbur – or Gart – might do to their enemies? If she hadn't felt skin and movement, she would have been tempted to imagine a skeleton. Or a corpse.

'Can you hear me?' She got off the bed and started along the wall again, slowly, *slowly*, trying to control her alarm with caution. 'Are you all right?'

She found the staple, the short chain. The hand in the manacle tried to avoid her touch. Nevertheless she shifted from the fettered wrist to an arm. It was draped with loose cloth – the sleeve of a cloak? The fabric was rough and warm; worsted, perhaps.

She found a covered shoulder, a bare neck. The shoulder and neck twisted hard, but they couldn't get away; the other arm must be chained as well. Curse this dark. The prisoner was only a little taller than she was. Although she was near the limit of her own chain, she had no difficulty touching an unshaven face that strained away from her; terrified of her.

'Are you hurt?' she whispered. 'Who are you?'

Roughly, he wrenched his head up and sucked a strangled breath through his teeth.

'All right. You've found me. They told me not to make a sound, not to let you know I'm here, but this isn't my fault.'

His voice was familiar to her. His bitterness was familiar.

Nyle. Geraden's 'murdered' brother.

For a moment, she was so glad to find him alive that she could hardly stand. So it *was* Underwell who had been killed, disfigured; Eremis' plotting was just as vile as she had believed it must be.

And Nyle was *here;* had been kept prisoner for how long now? – held in case he were ever needed again against his brother.

'Oh, Nyle,' she whispered in relief and quick nausea, 'I'm so sorry. What have they done to you?'

'Same thing they're going to do to you.' His bitterness was worse than anger; he had gone too far beyond hope. 'A kind of rape. I'm just lucky Eremis still wants me alive. Gilbur likes what they call "male meat," but he has a tendency to kill his toys, so Eremis makes him leave me alone. Most of the time.

'They need me to make sure Geraden doesn't do something unpredictable. Or King Joyse either, for that matter.'

Oh, Nyle.

She couldn't stay on her feet. Nausea crowded all the relief out of her. Without thinking, she retreated to the bed, sat down again. For some reason, she wasn't trembling anymore. But she was going to be so sick— If she let go, she was going to puke her heart out.

'It's the same reason they've got you.' Now that Nyle had begun to talk, he seemed intent on continuing. 'Only the details are different. We're hostages. And bait. We're here to make sure Geraden and King Joyse do what Eremis wants.

'I actually thought somebody would try to rescue me.' His tone made her want to throw up. Gilbur liked *male meat*. 'But I was wrong. Maybe they'll forget about you, too. That's your only hope now – that Eremis made a mistake bringing you here.'

Fighting down bile, she forced herself to say, 'Nobody in Orison knew you needed rescuing. Don't you know what they did? They killed that physician, Underwell. They let monsters eat his face' – don't think about it, don't *think* about it – 'they dressed him up to look like you. Everybody thought you were dead.' Because it had to be said, she concluded, 'They thought Geraden killed you. You accomplished that, anyway.'

'I know all that.' Nyle coughed thinly, as if he were too weak and beaten to curse. 'They sent Gart and a couple of his Apts into the room to knock the guards and Underwell out. So there wouldn't be any noise. They translated me here. Then they sent some of their creatures to feed on the bodies. They told me all about it.

'Do you think that's what I wanted? Do you think I had a choice?'

No, it was cruel to accuse him, cruel, he had been Eremis' prisoner and Gilbur's for a long time now, and the decisions he had made which had put him here had all been based on King Joyse's policy of foolish passivity, it wasn't fair to include him in her anger. Nevertheless she said, 'Everybody has a choice.'

She had a choice, didn't she? She was chained to the wall in the dark, and Eremis intended to use her for his pleasure until her spirit broke, and there was no way she could possibly be rescued, and she still had a choice. Only dead people didn't make choices.

He coughed again, like a man whose lungs were full of dry rot. She could picture him in his fetters, with his mouth hanging open in his dirty beard and no strength. 'You're wrong,' he murmured when he was finished coughing. 'You're like Elega. You don't know. I haven't had a choice about anything since Geraden hit me with that club.'

Oh, great. Terisa barely swallowed a snarl. Now he was going to start blaming Geraden. Her stomach tried to come up; she had to force it down. She had already been harsher than she wanted to be. Instead of pursuing what Nyle said, she asked thickly, 'Do you know where we are? Do you know this place?'

'All I wanted to do was save Orison and Mordant.' Maybe he hadn't heard her. 'You can't say I deserve this. You can think I was wrong, but you can't say I was being malicious. I wasn't going to get anything out of it for myself. Not even Elega— Even if I was right, my family was still going to hate me. I was never going to be able to go home again. They all believed in King Joyse personally, not in the ideas that made him a good king – not in the Congery and Orison and Mordant. They were never going to forgive me for *betraying* their hero, even if everything I did turned out right.

'I didn't do it for myself.'

'Oh, Nyle,' she breathed softly. 'You don't understand. Of course they'll forgive you. They've already forgiven you.'

But maybe he wasn't able to hear her. Maybe he had spent too much time helpless, caught in an everlasting reiteration of what he had done and why – and what it had cost – without any way to break out. Instead of reacting to what she said, he continued explaining himself.

Trying to justify himself against the dark.

'But Geraden destroyed me. I know that wasn't what he wanted, but he set me up for all this. When he came after me, instead of concentrating on Prince Kragen – If he weren't so determined to have accidents—

'He got me locked up. Like an assassin. Like I was dangerous to all the decent people around me. If I were a farmer who went berserk and started slaughtering his friends and family with an axe, I would have been locked up, but I wouldn't have been sneered at. I wouldn't have been despised.

'Don't you understand? *I* love King Joyse, too. I always loved him, even though he didn't let me serve him – even though he didn't want me around. But some loves are more important than others. He wasn't interested in my loyalty – and that hurt, because he was so obviously interested in my brothers. Artagel. Geraden. But I could still love his victories, his ideals, his beliefs.

'What do you think I should have done?' For a moment, Nyle's voice brought a touch of passion into the dark. 'Abandon everything that made Mordant valuable for the sake of a failing old man who didn't care whether I lived or died?

'Then Geraden stopped me, and they threw me in the dungeon. Do you know what that means?' A coughing fit came over him, draining his intensity away. 'You should.

'It means I couldn't get away.

'Artagel came and flaunted his wounds at me. I couldn't get away. Castellan Lebbick practiced his obscenities on me for quite a while. I couldn't get away.

'And then Master Eremis came—'

'Nyle, stop.' Terisa didn't want to hear it. She knew what was coming, and she didn't want to hear it. 'This doesn't help. You're just tormenting yourself.' All she wanted was some way to contain the horror surging at the back of her throat so that she could concentrate, bring her fury and her dread and her ache for blood into focus. 'Do you know where we are?'

'Just like that,' Nyle went on as if she hadn't spoken. 'He just walked into the dungeon. He just unlocked my cell and took me out. I couldn't get away.' His tone frayed at the edges, worn ragged by bitterness and fatigue and coughing, by anger that didn't have anywhere else to go. 'He took me down the passage a little way. Then he made some kind of gesture, and we were translated here. Into his personal laborium. I couldn't get away from him.

'Do you know what he did to me?'

'Yes!' Fighting for a defense against pain, Terisa jumped to her feet. 'I *know*.' When she moved, her chain rang lightly against the wall. Quickly, she caught the chain in her fist and swung it harder, made the stone clang. 'I know what he *did* to you.'

Of course, she didn't truly *know*: she hadn't suffered the same experience. But she knew enough – more than she could stomach. Fiercely, she rushed on:

'He showed you a mirror with Houseldon in the Image.' She swung the chain. 'And he showed you other mirrors.' The iron links chimed on the wall. 'Mirrors with firecats. Mirrors with corrupt wolves. Mirrors with avalanches – mirrors with ghouls.' Each time, she swung the chain harder. 'And he made you believe he could bring them all down on your home and family without any warning of any kind if you didn't do what he wanted. If you didn't help him turn the Congery against Geraden.'

Panting, gasping, she stood still.

Nyle's silence was all the acknowledgment she needed.

'So you agreed because you thought you were saving most of the people you loved. And you figured somebody was bound to notice *eventually* that you weren't actually dead – which would save Geraden and recoil on Eremis. And somehow you managed to avoid the simple deduction that Eremis knew as much about the flaws in his plans as you did.

'Nyle, you made a *choice*. Geraden didn't do this to you. You did it to yourself.'

There. Now she had begun attacking people who were manacled to walls, accusing them of bad logic as well as weak moral fiber. As if they had caused the things their enemies did to them. What was she going to do next? Start beating up cripples?

And yet in her own case she had no one to blame but herself for the fact that she had been so slow to distrust Master Eremis, so poor at opposing him.

Out of the dark, Nyle asked in old pain, 'What choice did I have? What could I have done?'

Oh, shit. She forced her fingers to release the chain. 'You could have refused.'

'Weren't you listening to yourself?' He had some anger left in him after all. 'If I did that, he would have destroyed Houseldon. He would have killed my whole family – everybody I grew up with – my home, all of it.'

'No, Nyle,' she sighed. By degrees, she wrestled down her nausea, her racing pulse, her desire to hurt something. He was going to be hurt badly enough already. She didn't need to increase the force of the blow. 'You're the one who isn't listening. *He destroyed Houseldon anyway.* He burned it to the ground while Geraden and I were there, trying to kill us. Your cooperation didn't make any difference. You gave yourself away for nothing.'

There. It was said.

Far away from her, Nyle groaned softly, as if she had just slipped a knife between his ribs – as if she had just cut down the defenses, the self-justifications, which kept him alive in his fetters.

She went to him, feeling at once as brutal as a child molester and as vulnerable as a molested child. 'Nyle, I'm sorry.' Trying to comfort him, she stroked his face. Her hand came back wet with tears. 'We'll get out of here somehow. Sometime. I've talked to your whole family. I know they understand. They know *you.* They know you wouldn't betray Geraden unless you were trying to protect them. And it would have worked, if he hadn't escaped – if he and I hadn't gone to Houseldon.'

Then, aching like a prayer that no one could overhear her, use what she was about to say against her, she put her mouth close to his ear and whispered, 'They're safe. They all got away. They went to the Closed Fist and dug in. To defend themselves.

'Eremis doesn't know that.'

Trembling at the risk she had taken, she stepped back to the bed and waited.

Nyle didn't react. She had no way of knowing whether or not he heard her. But she had done what she could for him. She had needs of her own to take into account. After a while, she returned to her first question – the only one of her questions which he might be in any condition to answer.

'Nyle, do you know where we are?'

After a moment, he took a shuddering breath; he seemed to be raising his head. 'Esmerel, I guess. I don't know. I never saw this place until he brought me here – translated me. But he said it was Esmerel.'

'Nyle' – the casual threat in Master Eremis' voice was unmistakable – 'I told you not to speak to her.'

Stung and urgent, almost panicking, Terisa whirled to face the Master.

But not panicking: she was too angry and hurt and focused for panic.

'Why?' she demanded before she had time to think, time to falter. The Imager's shape, as vague as Vagel's, approached her out of the doorway's deeper black. 'You've got everything else you want. Why are you doing this to him? He can't do you any harm.'

'What, my lady?' Eremis drawled. 'Questions? Challenges? That is a poor start to our lovemaking.' He sounded confident, immaculately sure of himself – and sharper than he had earlier, as if he had spent his absence enduring petty vexations. 'I am surprised that you do not require to know what the High King and I said to each other.'

Terisa brushed his words away. 'I don't care about the High King. I'm talking about Nyle. Why do you need him? Why don't you let him go?'

Why have you got us chained here together? Why do you want him to know everything you do to me?

Focus. Concentration.

A blank space in the dark, a gap of existence.

Anger and blood.

'For the same reason I need you, my lady.' The Master's tone was full of mirth and scorn. 'To perfect my triumph. Your capture will require my enemies to march against me. They must attempt to rescue the lady Terisa of Morgan and her strange talents. They will form an alliance, or they will not. They will destroy each other, or they will not. Whatever happens, they must come to Esmerel in the end.

'Then I will release Nyle. I am not as harsh as you think me – I do not torment him gratuitously. He will witness what becomes of you while we await your rescuers.' The raw-edged pleasure in his voice went through her like a chill. 'And when I am ready, I will send him out to tell them what I have done to you.

'Then Geraden will begin to understand what a burden he has undertaken by opposing me.'

No. Never. Never.

Concentration. Focus.

'You bastard.'

He was near enough to touch her now. He could have hit her. She felt his presence, the pressure he emanated; she thought she could smell his lust. Yet he didn't hit her. 'Come, my lady,' he said as if he were sure of her. 'Is that how you speak to the man who will master you?' His hand reached out; one finger stroked the line of her cheek. When she didn't flinch, he cupped his hand around the base of her neck inside her shirt. Slowly, his grip tightened. 'Must I use force to teach you humility?'

A blank space; a gap between them. She was vanishing into the darkness, groping farther and farther away from him; groping— Her mind was full of Images, all of them insubstantial; wishful thinking.

'No,' she said from so far away that he would never be able to possess her. 'Take my chain off. Let me show you what I've learned from Geraden.'

She made no effort to sound seductive or helpless, to conceal her distance from him.

The trap she set for him was like the one he had prepared for his enemies. Obvious. And irresistible. How could he doubt that he was more than a match for her? that he could control her, coerce her, defeat her whenever he chose? Resistance would only make her final submission the more appalling to her.

Chuckling, he took hold of her arm and clicked the fetter off her wrist.

Because she was so far away, she did nothing to betray herself. And because she was so full of anger, she didn't hesitate.

Before he could secure his grip, she swung her leg with all her strength and kicked him in the crotch.

He gasped as much in surprise as in pain; recoiled violently from her.

Almost at once, he caught his balance, recovered from the shock and hurt. She wanted to hear him cursing in agony, frothing at the mouth; but he didn't oblige her. The oath he spat at her was simply vindictive, a promise that she had pushed him too far and was going to suffer for what she did.

Quickly, he jumped forward to capture her, punish her.

But not quickly enough. While he was still on his way toward her, she touched a moment of eternity.

It was hardly longer than the space between one frightened heartbeat and another – yet it was enough. Images coalesced, took on light and shape: dozens of them; chaos and fragments everywhere. She only needed one, however, the sharpest Image, the one with details so precise and unalienable that they might have been acidcut on her mind.

A sand dune poised in the timeless gap between high winds and nonexistence.

She had no idea where she might have seen that Image before. She didn't care. As soon as she saw it, she knew it was hers—

—*and a touch of cold as thin as a feather and as sharp as steel slid straight through the center of her abdomen.*

Eremis was grappling for her, trying to catch her by the shoulders and strike her at the same time. Only an intuitive reflexive leap enabled him to pull himself out of danger as she faded from him and fell backward into the wall.

Into the light of lamps; onto the floor so heavily that she knocked the breath out of herself.

For a long moment, she couldn't speak. She couldn't do anything except gape back up at Adept Havelock, Master Barsonage, and Geraden, who were staring at her as if she had tumbled out of a coffin.

FORTY-THREE

THE ONLY REASONABLE THING TO DO

The light was extraordinary, as life-giving as sunshine. While she waited to breathe, she was content to simply lie where she was and accept the glow of her escape.

Then Geraden let out a whoop and seemed to pounce on her. Oblivious to the fact that she couldn't inhale, he swept her up into his arms and began to whirl her, crying and laughing, 'Terisa! *Terisa!*' spinning her into a dance of wild joy. His happiness burned so brightly that she clung to his neck and didn't care whether she was able to breathe or not. If Master Barsonage hadn't immediately clamped a massive hug around both of them, forced Geraden to stop, he would have carried her careening into the mirrors, shattering glass in all directions.

'Stop,' the mediator panted. 'Are you mad? Stop.' He sounded half-delirious himself.

For a moment, her relief and exaltation turned into a convulsive retch for air.

At once, Geraden halted, put her down, held her tightly. 'Are you all right? Terisa, are you all right? I couldn't find you. I couldn't reach you. I changed a mirror to go looking for you, but I couldn't find you. I was afraid he had you for good. Oh, love, are you all right?'

She did her best to nod while the knot in her chest loosened enough to let air leak past it. Then she returned his hug, gasping in his ear, clasping him almost savagely because she was still full of impossible translations and promises of murder. After her encounter with Master Eremis, Geraden was so dear to her that she held him as if her heart depended on it.

Geraden. Help me.

He was going to rape me. Just for the fun of it. And to hurt you.

Geraden.

I'm going to kill him.

'My lady,' Adept Havelock said judiciously, as if he had become a completely different person, 'that was a very pretty trick. If you can truly do such things, then every action he has taken against you is plainly justified. In his place, I would have done the same.'

'Proof,' murmured Master Barsonage now that he no longer had to protect the Adept's mirrors. 'I would not have believed it. *Proof.*' He seemed lost in the wonder of his thoughts. 'Images *are* real, independent of their mirrors – independent of Imagery itself. King Joyse has been right all along.'

'Fornicate that uxorious bastard,' replied Havelock, relapsing to normalcy. 'A fine time to go kiting off. He should have seen this.'

I'm going to—

Nyle!

'Geraden.' Terisa jerked back, pulled away far enough to meet Geraden's gaze. He moved to kiss her; the look on her face stopped him. Quickly, so that he would understand, she said, 'He's got Nyle.'

He frowned, instantly sympathetic to her urgency. 'We knew that,' he muttered. 'Or we guessed it—'

'I've *seen* him.' Well, not *seen*, exactly; but she was in too much of a hurry to explain. 'I've talked to him. Eremis has him prisoner. The same place he took me. In Esmerel.' Eremis wanted him to watch what he did to me. So you would be hurt as much as possible. 'We've got to get him out of there. He's—'

She almost said, He's being destroyed. Eremis is breaking his spirit.

'She changed the Image,' Master Barsonage went on, caught in a kind of rapture. 'Across that distance, she took a glass with an Image which did not contain her, and she shifted it until the Image *did* contain her. Geraden could not have done it. Flat mirrors are not his talent. And she could not have done such a thing if she were not independently real. It is inconceivable that a woman created in a mirror could have power greater than the mirror – and the Image – that created her.'

'Who cares?' retorted the Adept happily. 'She's female. That's the point. We can't trust her. We can't trust *him*.' He sounded like a doting uncle. 'Look at him. He's as bad as Joyse. He's ready to die for her. If things get dangerous, he'll save her instead of us.'

She and Geraden weren't listening. As she caught herself, they both turned automatically to look at the mirror which had brought her back to Adept Havelock's rooms.

Its Image was dark, almost impenetrably black. Maybe she could have discerned a shape or two – the bed? the doorway? – if she had been given time; but before she could study the Image it began to melt away. Light bled into the darkness; the potential for obscure shapes became mounded sand. In a moment, the glass had resumed its natural scene, the desertscape for which it had been formed. A breeze was starting to blow, lifting delicate curls of sand from the rim of the dune.

'Nyle!' A new pain shot through her, a loss she hadn't anticipated. 'He was there. In that room. We could have reached him – rescued him—'

Holding himself steady, Geraden murmured, 'It takes effort to make that shift. As soon as you relaxed, as soon as you let go, the fundamental Image came back.

'That must have been what happened the second day you were here, when

782

you saw the Closed Fist in a flat glass.' It was obvious now that he was talking simply to help her, give her something to think about until she grew calmer. 'You were so surprised to find the Closed Fist in my glass that you instinctively recreated the Image in the nearest flat mirror. But as soon as Eremis and I distracted you, you let go, and the fundamental Image came back.'

Came back. She remembered, in spite of her distress. That Image had come back in time to let her see the Perdon's men being attacked by rapacious black spots which chewed their hearts out.

And Vagel had said that so far High King Festten's *only satisfaction has been the annihilation of the Perdon.*

Curse them all. Damn every one of them.

'A simple matter,' commented Havelock. He sounded as lunatic as ever, but somehow he clung to a pragmatic grasp on the situation. 'Restore the change. You've been in that room. Bring the Image back, and we'll rescue Nyle.'

He's chained, Terisa protested inwardly. They aren't going to just stand there and let us cut him loose.

Nevertheless she faced the flat glass at once, tried to push panic and doubt and urgency out of her mind, tried to recapture the particular dark where Eremis had held her prisoner—

She couldn't do it. She was too frantic; her concentration was too badly frayed. She couldn't so much as remember what the bed was like, how far away the doorway was, where the staples which had held her chain and Nyle's were in relation to each other. And without a precise Image in her mind—

Geraden put an arm around her. 'It isn't your fault. It's just impossible.' His tone was soft, soothing; it had an undercurrent of misery and yearning, which he suppressed. He must have been through horror of his own while she was away – he must be frantic to rescue Nyle – but he put himself aside for her sake. 'That's why he keeps the important parts of Esmerel dark. That's why I wasn't able to come after you. If you shift the mirror now, you won't know if you've got exactly the right piece of darkness. And if you're wrong we might all be killed. You might produce an Image that's actually inside a mountain somewhere, and as soon as you do any kind of translation we'll have a few million tons of rock to deal with. You need light.'

Hugging her, he repeated, 'It isn't your fault. We'll get him out some other way.'

There was no authority in his voice, no unexpected strength. All he was trying to do at the moment was comfort her. And yet she found that she believed him. *We'll get him out some other way.* He meant it, the same way she meant, I'm going to kill him.

Slowly, the panic in her muscles receded, and she slumped against him, mutely asking him to hold her until she had time to recover.

'Geraden is right, I think.' Apparently, Master Barsonage had returned from his exaltation. 'Master Eremis is cunning. Darkness is a ploy to which no Imager has ever found an answer. Even the crudest translations require light. Do not blame yourself, my lady. Already your achievements seem quite miraculous.'

All right. All right. She could never fight if she let herself collapse like this. She couldn't reach Nyle: all right. She could still think. Eremis had violated her with his hands. *Think*. He had come close to doing much worse things – but she got away. It was possible to think; choose; act. Just start somewhere. Geraden still held her. The way his arms supported her was more miraculous than any translation. He had no more intention of abandoning Nyle than she did. All right.

Start somewhere.

She took a shuddering breath. 'I don't understand. How did I do it? I was on the wrong side of the glass. I didn't think it was possible for something in an Image to translate itself out.'

Geraden tightened his hug. It was the mediator who answered, however.

'The Adept did that, my lady. The idea was Geraden's, but he can do nothing with flat glass.

'You are right. We know of no way for what is in an Image to translate itself out. Even for us – for Imagers of talent who have shaped the mirrors – entering a glass is nearly effortless, but bringing what is in the Image out requires gestures, invocations – a particular way of concentrating the Imager's talent. After all, the mirror itself is *here*, not where you were.

'Yet when the Image in this glass shifted from sand to darkness, we could hardly fail to notice the fact. And Geraden guessed that the shift was your doing. And Havelock is an Adept. We are fortunate' – Barsonage smiled sourly – 'that he is in a mood which allows him to react to events reasonably. After Geraden had made himself understood, the Adept performed the translation which rescued you.'

With startling clarity, Terisa felt Master Eremis springing toward her through the dark, remembered his attack. As if she were panicking, she broke away from Geraden. But she wasn't panicking; she may have lost the capacity for panic altogether.

Before Havelock could try to avoid her, she caught her arms around his neck and kissed him.

Just for a second, the mad old Imager's eyes came together; he grinned at her like an ecstatic boy. It was amazing, really, how easily she was able to forgive him for failing to help her against Master Gilbur.

Almost at once, however, his gaze split again; his nose jutted fiercely, like a promise of violence. Fortunately, he didn't try to say anything.

He didn't try to stop her when she turned back to Geraden.

Geraden was watching her hungrily. For the first time, she realized that he had tears streaming down his face.

This clear sight of him made her stop. He had known the danger she was in. While she was Eremis' prisoner, he had been here – cut off— She could picture him desperately trying to bridge the gap—

Abruptly, she locked an embrace around him. 'Oh, love,' she breathed, aching for him. 'You changed a mirror. You must have gone crazy trying to reach me.'

Geraden held her hard; but again it was Master Barsonage who answered.

'Our Geraden has proved to be nearly as great a source of wonders as you are, my lady.' He sounded steady, but behind his self-control she could hear a tremor of pride and vindication. 'Of course, we knew of his ability to perform astonishing things with his own glass. For that reason, in some sense we were not surprised when Orison's enemies contrived the destruction of his mirror.'

In shock, Terisa stiffened. *The destruction—?* Her link with her home was gone.

Then how—?

'Without his glass,' the mediator continued, 'we believed he would be helpless. But he has shown himself an Adept in his own right, at least where normal mirrors are concerned.' Barsonage indicated a curved glass beside the flat desertscape. 'He imposed an Image of Esmerel there and used it to search for you. Only the ploy of darkness prevented him from reaching you.'

As she absorbed the mediator's words, her dismay lifted. 'You can do that?' She was so pleased that she pushed back again to look into Geraden's anguish. 'You're an Adept as well as an Imager? That's wonderful!' Suddenly, she was so furious that it felt like ecstasy. 'Heaven help that bastard. *We'll tear him to pieces.*'

Her passion seemed to give him what he needed. She could see him shrug away his failure to rescue her, his helplessness to rescue Nyle. The lines of his face grew sharper; his eyes cast hints of fire.

'It won't be easy. Esmerel is two days away on a good horse. Prince Kragen thinks High King Festten has at least twenty thousand men. Not to mention all the abominations Eremis can translate. They can still use flat glass whenever they want – and we don't know how they do it.' He wasn't trying to daunt her. He was simply bringing up problems in order to solve them.

'I don't care about any of that,' she replied in the same spirit. 'They've got Nyle. They've got the Queen. High King Festten is there. Eremis talked to him this morning. They've destroyed the Perdon. *Annihilated* is the word Vagel used. They're destroying Sternwall and Fayle. And it's just going to get worse.' Tersely, she explained what the arch-Imager and Master Eremis had revealed about the speed, precision, and flexibility they had achieved with mirrors. While Geraden scowled at the information, and Master Barsonage blinked in consternation, she concluded, 'We've got to stop him before he goes any further.'

The mediator started to ask a question, then subsided. But Geraden accepted her explanation without wincing. When she was done, he said, 'There's one more thing. King Joyse is gone.'

Gone—?

'I mean really gone. Adept Havelock says he flew away.' Geraden glanced dubiously at the mad old Imager. 'I don't know what that means. But the last we heard no one's been able to find him.'

'Then who's in charge?' Orison without King Joyse: the concept was strangely appalling. His absence was a pit yawning at her feet. 'This whole thing was his idea. *He* wanted to fight Eremis this way. Who's giving the orders now?'

Geraden didn't flinch: he had regained his feet; felt as combative as she did. 'We don't know. We've been down here most of the time. Probably nobody knows where to find us.' He hesitated, then said, 'With King Joyse gone and Castellan Lebbick dead, the whole place may be collapsing.' Another flicker of hesitation. 'They may have turned on the Prince.'

That was true. Terisa imagined riots storming through the upper levels of the castle; panic and bloodshed. It was conceivable that Orison might destroy itself.

She wheeled on Adept Havelock.

'Where is he? This was *his* idea. *Your* idea. Curse that old man, we need him.'

A sick feeling rose in her stomach as she saw Havelock hunch forward with conspiratorial glee; his eyes nearly gyrated in opposite directions, rapacious and loony. He crooked a finger at her, summoning her near, as if he wanted to tell her a secret.

She didn't move; nevertheless he reacted as if she had come closer to hear him.

'I have seen an Image,' he whispered, 'an Image, an Image. In which the women are peculiar. Their tits are on their backs. Because of this, they look very strange. But it must be delightful to embrace them.'

Grinning, he concluded, 'He came to me and commanded. *Commanded.* What could I do? I don't know how to beg.' His manner didn't change, yet without transition his tone turned fierce. 'I have said it and said it. Hop-board pieces are *men.* Women make everything impossible.'

Terisa wanted to swear at him – and give him a hug as if he needed comforting. Torn between anger and pity, she faced Geraden and Master Barsonage again. She included the mediator in what she was saying, but all of her attention and intensity were focused on Geraden.

'We've got to find out what's going on.'

Both men nodded, Barsonage willingly, Geraden in passion and approval.

'Somebody has got to figure out what King Joyse intended to do now and make sure it gets done.'

Master Barsonage hesitated. Geraden nodded again.

To the Master, she said, 'We'll explain as soon as we get the chance. King Joyse set this all up. It's all deliberate.' Then she took hold of Geraden's arm.

Clasping each other hard, they strode away into the passage which led to the storeroom, out of Adept Havelock's quarters.

Master Barsonage followed them quickly. The bristling of his eyebrows and the frown of his concentration gave him a look of unfamiliar certainty.

Behind them, Havelock picked up his featherduster and went back to cleaning his already immaculate mirrors. The particular glass he chose to work on now happened to show the Image in which he had found the flying brown cloud that he had used against Prince Kragen's catapults.

Like Castellan Lebbick, he had been abandoned.

He didn't seem to be aware that he was weeping like a child.

Terisa, Geraden, and Master Barsonage heard weeping, especially in the lower levels of the castle, where most of Orison's newer occupants had been crowded: small children; frightened women; helpless oldsters and invalids. They heard shouts of alarm and fear, cries of protest and distrust. They heard blows. Once they saw several guards raise the butts of their pikes to strike at men who wanted to break out of a closed corridor. The men cursed and pleaded as they were forced back; the rumor of Gart's attack had reached them, and they wanted to clear a path for their families out of Orison before Cadwal's army arrived from nowhere to butcher them all.

But there was no sign of a riot.

Instead of rioting, the castle was full of guards. They were everywhere, blocking the movement of people and panic, controlling access to crucial passages or stairs or doors, facing down farmers and merchants and servants and stonemasons who wanted to attack or flee with their loved ones because Orison had been penetrated.

'Who is in command?' Master Barsonage demanded of the guards. 'Where is King Joyse?'

The answer was, Pissed if I know. Or the equivalent.

'Where did you get your orders?' asked Geraden.

That was easier. Norge. Castellan Lebbick's second.

For the moment, the fact that Norge was actually only one of the Castellan's seconds-in-command seemed unimportant. The point was that power still existed in Orison. It was being held together by someone from whom the guards were willing to take orders. Someone with enough credibility to be obeyed during an emergency.

Norge himself? What gave him precedence over the other captains? *Who* gave him precedence?

A Master of the Congery? Impossible. Never in the mediator's absence.

One of King Joyse's counselors? One of Orison's lords? Unlikely.

Prince Kragen himself? Inconceivable.

Artagel?

Was the situation so bad that no one could be found to take charge except Geraden's independent-minded and slightly crippled brother?

Terisa wanted to run. She would have run if Geraden hadn't held her back.

As she and her companions left the castle's lower levels, however, Orison's mood improved. Here the halls were under better control; less frightened by the possibility of an attack by Imagery. Soon a guard appeared who saluted the mediator. 'Master Barsonage,' he panted. Apparently, he had come running from the Imager's quarters. 'Geraden. The lady Terisa?' He knew enough about the day's events to be surprised. 'You're wanted in the King's rooms.'

The King's rooms? Terisa and Geraden and Master Barsonage stopped in their tracks.

'The audience hall is no longer safe,' explained the guard.

'*Who* wants us?' demanded Barsonage instantly.

Breathing hard, the guard replied, 'My lord Tor. He says he's taken command. In the King's absence. He and Norge. Norge is the new Castellan.'

The *Tor*. Terisa felt a surge of energy. Bless that old man!

'What about Prince Kragen?' she asked.

The guard hesitated as if he were unsure of how much he should say. After a moment, however, he answered, 'It's just a rumor. I was told my lord Tor offered him an alliance.'

Geraden let out a fierce cheer.

Together, he and Terisa started into a run.

Master Barsonage took time to pursue the question. 'What was the Prince's reply?'

The guard said, 'I don't know.'

Barsonage did his best to catch up with Terisa and Geraden.

In the King's tower, more guards joined them, escorted them upward. Guards swept the King's doors open; Terisa, Geraden, and the mediator went in. For the sake of dignity – not to mention caution – they slowed their pace as they entered.

The King's formal apartment was just the way she remembered it – richly appointed, paneled blond, carpeted in blue and red. She hardly noticed the furnishings, however. Although there were only eight or ten men – most of them captains – in the room, it seemed crowded; too full of anxiety and passion, conflict.

Before the door closed, she heard Prince Kragen's voice blare like a trumpet, *'I will not do it!'*

Her chest tightened. She found suddenly that she was breathing harder than she had realized. The Prince's shout seemed to throb around her, and the hope she had felt at the idea of an alliance began to curdle.

On one side of Prince Kragen stood Artagel, close enough to react to what the Prince did, far enough away to dissociate himself from the Alend Contender. On the other side was a captain Terisa didn't know. Norge?

All three of them had their backs to the doors. Each in his separate way, they confronted the chair where King Joyse used to sit when he played hop-board.

There sat the Tor, slumping over his great belly as if he were barely able to keep himself from oozing out of the position he had assumed.

'The alternatives you propose,' the old lord was saying as if he were in a kind of pain which had nothing to do with Prince Kragen, 'are intolerable.' He had a hand over his face. 'I will not permit you to occupy Orison, making us little more than a hostage population. I do not call that an *alliance*.'

'And I do not call it an *alliance* to wait outside in danger while you sit here in safety,' retorted the Prince hotly. 'If – no, *when* High King Festten marches against us – we will be helpless while you remain secure, watching the outcome. *We must be allowed to enter Orison. I will not* remain where I am, waiting for King Joyse to return – if he ever does return – and tell me his pleasure – if his pleasure involves anything more productive than a game of hop-board.'

The Tor didn't look strong enough to raise his head. 'I understand your dilemma, my lord Prince. Of course I do. But you cannot believe that Orison's people – or Orison's defenders – will sit quietly on their hams while *Alend* takes power over them. I have already said that I will open the gates to you if you—'

'No!' Prince Kragen barked. 'Do you take me for a fool? I have no intention of making Orison's people hostage. I will grant them precisely as

788

much freedom and respect as the necessary crowding of so many bodies permits. But I will *not* submit my forces to your authority.'

Orison's captains muttered restively. Some of them were viscerally incensed at the idea of an alliance with Alend. And some of them had noticed Geraden and Master Barsonage – had noticed Terisa—

'My lords!' Geraden cut in sharply. His voice carried potential authority across the room; and a thrill prickled suddenly down Terisa's back. 'There's no need to argue about *waiting*. We're done *waiting*. It's time to march!'

The Tor snatched his hand down from his face, peered bleary pain and desire at Terisa and Geraden. Artagel wheeled with joy already catching fire across his features. Norge turned more cautiously; but Prince Kragen spun like Artagel, his swarthy face congested with conflicting needs.

'Terisa! My lady!' Artagel crowed. 'Geraden! By the stars, you did it!' As if he had never been injured in his life, he caught Geraden in an exuberant bearhug, lifted him off his feet, then dropped him to snatch up Terisa's hand and kiss it hugely. 'Every time I see you, you're even more wonderful!'

She wanted to hug him, but she was distracted; there were too many other things going on. The captains were shouting encouragement to each other, or demanding silence. And the Tor had risen to his feet. Unsteadily, almost inaudibly, he murmured her name, Geraden's. 'You are indeed wondrous.' He spoke huskily, as if he were dragging his voice along the bottom of a cave. 'There must be hope for us after all, if such blows can be struck against our enemies.'

Prince Kragen was right behind Artagel; he grabbed Geraden by the shoulders when Artagel dropped him. 'How did you do it?' the Prince demanded. 'How did you rescue her? What has changed? Where is King Joyse? Did you say *march*?'

Somehow, Norge made himself heard through the hubbub. His laconic tone sounded so incongruous that it had to be heeded.

'You got away, my lady. What did you learn from him?

'What did you do to him?'

In the stark silence which followed, a moment passed before she understood the point of his question.

With her chin jutting unconsciously, she met the hot and eager and worried stares of the men around her. 'I didn't do anything to him.' I didn't kill him. I didn't even hurt him. 'But I learned enough.'

Too quickly for anyone to interrupt her, she added, 'Before Gilbur killed him, I had a long talk with Master Quillon. He told me what King Joyse has been doing all this time. Why he's been acting like a passive fool. What he wanted to accomplish. Geraden is right. It's time to march.'

In response, the room burst into tumult. Only Prince Kragen had been given any hint of the things she knew; and he had only heard pieces of the story from Geraden under the influence of too much wine, not from her. For a man like the Tor, who had spent so many miserable days praying that his besotted and stubborn loyalty would prove valuable in the end, her words must have struck as heavily as a blow. Norge and Prince Kragen and Artagel were surprised; Master Barsonage and the captains, astonished. But the Tor's cheeks turned the color of wet flour, and he sank down in King Joyse's chair as if his heart were being torn out.

Urgently, Terisa pushed between Artagel and Prince Kragen, hurried to the lord. 'Get him some wine!' she called. 'Oh, shit. He's having a heart attack.

'My lord Tor. Are you all right?'

His hands fluttered against the arms of the chair. For a moment, he gagged as if he were choking; under his lowered eyelids, his eyes rolled wildly. Then, however, he took a breath that made all his fat quiver. He raised one hand to his chest, knotted it in his robe; and his head lifted as if he were pulling it up by main strength.

'Do not be alarmed, my lady,' he wheezed thinly. 'The difficulty is only that I have pawned all I am for him. I have made myself contemptible for the belief that my King would at last prove worthy of service.' With remarkable celerity, one of the captains brought forward a flagon of wine. Then Tor accepted it and gulped a drink. Then torment clenched his features. 'Did you truly mean to suggest that he has been acting according to a plan – that the things he has done have had a purpose?'

'Yes,' she avowed at once, despite the fact that at the moment she would cheerfully have wrung King Joyse's neck. 'He didn't know you would come here. You heard him say you defy prediction.' The explanation Master Quillon had given her wasn't good enough to justify the cost King Joyse had exacted from men like Castellan Lebbick and the Tor, from his daughters, from Geraden and everybody else who loved him. 'His plans didn't include you. He didn't mean to hurt you.' For the time being, she supported the King, not because she approved of what he had done, but because he had left her no alternative.

'All this time, he's been working to save Mordant.'

Until now. That thought was enough to turn the edges of her vision black with bitterness. King Joyse put his people through the anguish of the doomed. And just when events arrived at the point when he could have safely explained his policy, safely given at least that much meaning or justification to the people he had hurt, he chose to disappear. *To go kiting off*, as Adept Havelock had said.

Nevertheless she took his side as if she had never doubted him.

'He didn't know who the renegades were – the Imagers who were willing to translate abominations against people who couldn't defend themselves. He didn't know where they made their mirrors, where they built their power.'

When she began, she was speaking to the Tor alone; she hadn't intended to address the entire gathering. But King Joyse's intentions carried her further than her own. As she spoke, her voice rose, and she turned partly away from the Tor to include everyone in the room.

'He knew they needed soldiers to back up their Imagery. Imagery can destroy, but *rule* requires manpower. But he didn't know what alliances they might have made, with Cadwal or Alend. There was only one thing he could be sure of. As long as he was the strongest ruler here – as long as Mordant was strong enough to fight back both Cadwal and Alend – the renegades would leave him alone. They would chip away at the Alend Lieges, or find a way to swallow Cadwal – but they would leave him alone. Until they were too strong to be stopped.'

She had to raise her voice more, until she was nearly shouting. That was the only way she could control her frustration and grief. He had smiled at her so gloriously that she would have done anything for him. And he had caused so much pain—

'The only way he could find out who they were, how they worked, where their power was before they grew too strong – the only way he could bring them out into the open – was to make himself weak. He had to convince everybody, *everybody*, that he had lost his will, his sense, his determination. He had to make himself the only reasonable target.

'*So that they would attack here.*

'So that he would have a chance to stop them. A chance to surprise them by turning their own traps against them.'

She had ruined that, of course. She had warned Eremis. Her bitterness included herself: she hadn't earned the right to be self-righteous. Yet her culpability only made her more determined.

'That's what we have to do. I don't know why he isn't here. He's been working toward this moment for years. I don't know why he's abandoned us now.' If he went to rescue Queen Madin – That was understandable, but it didn't help. At that distance, he wouldn't be able to return until long after the battle was decided. Terisa made an effort to steady herself, calm her raw anger. 'It doesn't matter. We're still here. We still have to save Orison and Mordant.

'We don't have any choice. He hasn't left us any choice. The only thing we can do is what he would do if he were here. We've got to march.'

The room was still; the men around her listened with all their senses, avidly. Geraden's face shone as if nothing could stop him now. Artagel nodded to himself happily. Prince Kragen's eyes were dark with dismay and calculation – and with something else, which might have been eagerness. Master Barsonage gaped, his mouth hanging open; he gave the impression that he was reeling inside.

'March,' muttered the Tor, struggling to straighten his spine against the back of his chair. '"So that they would attack here." My old friend. How I must have hurt you.'

Finally, however, it was Norge who asked the obvious question.

'March where, my lady?'

She was so full of pressure that she could hardly articulate the word: 'Esmerel.'

At once, Geraden supported her. 'That's Eremis' family Seat. Apparently, that's where he has his laborium. That's where he and Gilbur took her. And Vagel is there. Gart is there. *Cadwal* is there. Eremis consulted with the High King there this morning.

'That's where we need to strike.'

Terisa was thinking, In the Care of Tor. Where those riders with the red fur and the hate-filled eyes had come from to attack her and Geraden. No wonder they had been mounted on horses with tack from the Tor's Care.

The old lord's mind was running in a completely different direction, however. 'That explains it, then,' he rumbled.

He braced himself upright with an arm on one side, an elbow on the other. Canted in this posture as if his weight were about to overturn the chair, he muttered, 'That is why he told Lebbick to do whatever he wanted to her. He had to appear weak – had to seem like he had lost his reason. He had to persuade *me*. If I had failed to believe him, I could have betrayed him to Eremis.

'At the same time, he sent Master Quillon to remove her from the dungeon, so that no one would suffer from his feigned weakness – so that Lebbick would not have a crime on his heart – so that she would not be harmed.

'At last I understand.'

The Tor looked like a man whose hands had just been released from thumbscrews.

'And we have another reason to march now,' Geraden went on in a tone which Terisa would have found impossible to refuse. 'In Esmerel, the lady Terisa discovered Nyle alive.'

That announcement snatched most of the eyes in the room to him. Something in Artagel leaped up: his expression was as keen as a honed blade.

'I didn't kill him.' Geraden spoke through his teeth, restraining outrage. Now he didn't need the strange authority which sometimes came to him: his bone-bred passion was enough. 'I never lifted a hand against him. Eremis forced his help by threatening my family. *Our* family,' he said to the sharpness in Artagel's face. 'Nyle pretended I stabbed him. Then Eremis carried him off. He called for the physician Underwell, who was almost exactly Nyle's size and coloring. He had Underwell butchered by creatures of Imagery. Then he dressed Underwell in Nyle's clothes to make it look like I came back to finish what I started.'

This was news to the Tor, as well as to the captains. They stared at Geraden in undisguised astonishment.

'But Nyle is still alive. Eremis has him chained to a wall in Esmerel. To use against me if I ever try to fight him.

'I'm a son of the Domne.' Geraden held himself powerfully still. 'My family have been dear and loyal friends to King Joyse and Mordant from the beginning, and I want my brother rescued!'

Yes! Terisa said with the way she lifted her head, the way she carried herself. *Yes.*

'It's a simple question, really,' Artagel drawled into the silence when Geraden was finished. His nonchalant manner contrasted dramatically with the flame of combat in his eyes. 'As my lady Terisa says, we don't have any choice. We've already let the Perdon be destroyed.' His stance was casual, but his hands curled as if they ached to hold a sword. 'If we don't return to King Joyse's policy of supporting his lords – and do it soon – we'll lose everything that holds Mordant together, whether Eremis and Festten beat us or not. Everything that made Mordant worthwhile will be gone.'

Terisa smiled at him. She was trying to express thanks, gratitude; but the tension in her muscles made her grin too fierce for that.

The Tor took a deep breath, then gasped. The flagon dropped from his hand, spilling wine across the rug; but he didn't notice it. He looked at Norge, nearly squinting to get his eyes into focus; he looked at Prince Kragen.

'I am content.' His voice was flat, curiously unresonant. Apparently, Gart's kick still pained him. 'Let us call the matter settled. Tomorrow we will march against Master Eremis in Esmerel.'

Terisa wanted to applaud until she heard Prince Kragen rasp, 'No.'

'My lord Prince?' A fine dew of sweat covered the Tor's forehead.

'I am not *content*.' Kragen chewed the words under his moustache as if they were gristle and gall. 'I do not call the matter settled. You have proposed an *alliance* – on which we have been utterly unable to agree. Now you announce your intention to march away on a fool's mission. Is it your intention that Alend should march with you?' His tone sounded oddly conflicted to Terisa, at once furious and hungry, as if his passion had another name than the one he chose to give it. 'Is that what an *alliance* means to you now? Do you believe that the Alend Monarch will be *content* to let all his strength commit suicide beside you, for no other reason than because you have decided to die insanely?'

Artagel started to retort; Geraden stopped him.

'You have a better idea, my lord Prince?' Geraden asked. His voice made Terisa shiver: it was thick with hinted promises or threats.

'Of course!' the Prince snapped. 'An alliance here. In Orison. Let the High King come against us here and do his worst. Together, we will withstand him.'

'What about Nyle?' demanded Artagel, unable to restrain himself.

Geraden ignored his brother. 'I don't think so,' he answered Prince Kragen. 'Eremis doesn't need to come here. He can attack us anywhere by Imagery. While we stay in one place, *any* place, we're powerless, vulnerable. Without risking one Cadwal, he can fill Orison with enough horrors to leave even you screaming, my lord Prince. The only reason he hasn't done it so far is that he isn't ready. *Wasn't* ready. All he needed is time. He's ready now. If we don't carry the fight to him *now*, High King Festten and his twenty thousand men won't have to do anything except come here at their leisure and clean out the ruins. We'll all be dead or scattered.'

As well as she could, Terisa controlled her frustration at Prince Kragen, her fear of the things she remembered. 'Eremis—' she said, then swallowed hard to steady herself. 'Eremis knows how to use flat glass safely. He's discovered an oxidate which lets him translate a flat glass into a curved one, so that whatever is in the curved Image can be translated straight to whatever is in the flat Image.'

Master Barsonage and Geraden had had time to absorb this information. They didn't flinch. And they didn't interrupt her.

'Didn't Geraden tell you?' she asked the Prince. 'Eremis dropped an *avalanche* out of nowhere onto Vale House. That's how he was able to kidnap Queen Madin. And he has a flat mirror with *the audience hall* in the Image. He could bring an avalanche in there right now if he wanted to. And we know he has at least two other mirrors that show parts of Orison. His rooms. That place in the lower levels – near the dungeons. Maybe he has more.

'But that's not all. Vagel – the *arch-Imager* Vagel – has devised a system that allows him to create specific Images deliberately, instead of by trial and error.'

Despite the fact that she had already told Master Barsonage this, the mediator looked like he was on the brink of apoplexy.

'And Gilbur has the talent to make mirrors quickly,' Terisa continued. 'Together, they can shape enough Images to attack Orison anywhere, anytime.

'Eremis is ready now. It isn't suicide to march. It's suicide to stay here.'

A murmur rose from the captains – agreement, worry, caution.

'Perhaps.' For a moment, Prince Kragen's eagerness seemed to outweigh his outrage. 'Perhaps in that, you are right.' As if by an act of will, however, he brought back his indignation. 'Yet if it is madness to remain here, it is not therefore sane to march against Esmerel.'

He glanced at the Tor. Briefly, he appeared to consider addressing his challenge to Terisa. But at last he turned to Geraden and Artagel, drawn to them by the blood-claim of Nyle's imprisonment – and by Geraden's new stature.

Dangerously calm, he inquired, 'You have some acquaintance with Esmerel, I suppose?'

Artagel nodded without hesitation. Geraden said distinctly, 'Some.'

'I have heard reports of the terrain. Who will be favored in a battle there?'

'Good question,' Norge observed equably.

Artagel grinned. 'Whoever gets there first. The entrenched forces can pick their ground. It's a trap for whoever arrives second.'

Geraden shook his head, dismissing the issue. 'Why do you think Eremis chose that place, my lord Prince? You didn't think it was an accident. You didn't think High King Festten drove twenty thousand men there just for the pleasure of *annihilating* the Perdon.'

'No, Geraden' – Prince Kragen allowed himself a snarl of sarcasm – 'I did not think it was an accident. It is *your* thinking I question, not my own. Did you not hear Artagel use the word *trap*? You say that Nyle is intended as a hostage against you. Is he not also intended as *bait*? A march to Esmerel is precisely the action Eremis wishes us to take.'

'Of course,' Geraden retorted.

'That's one reason I was captured,' commented Terisa. 'More bait. Eremis wanted to have me where I couldn't hurt him.' He wanted to rape me. He wanted to break Geraden. 'But he also wanted to make sure you went to Esmerel. All of you.'

'Everything he's ever done us to us is a trap,' Geraden continued. 'That's his great strength – and his great weakness.'

'And you still believe we should go?' Prince Kragen's protest was an inextricable mixture of excitement and fury. '*Knowing* he has set this trap to destroy us, you believe that we should accommodate him – that we should rush to put our necks in his noose for him? Geraden, you *are* mad.' Wheeling toward the Tor, he unleashed a shout. 'My lord, *this is madness!*'

The Tor sat in his chair like a lump of stale dough and waited for Geraden's answer.

To Terisa's surprise, Geraden started laughing.

His laughter was like Artagel's grin: bloody-minded; ready for battle.

'That's King Joyse's method. His policy. Don't you understand? He sets his traps inside Eremis'. If he were here to spring them himself, it would make your head reel. But he isn't here, so we've got to do it for him. We've got to put our necks in Eremis' noose – and then take it away from him. We've got to walk into his trap and turn it against him.'

Prince Kragen stared as if Geraden were breaking out in boils. So flabbergasted that his sarcasm deserted him, he asked, 'How—? How do you think we can do that? He has at least twenty thousand men. He has Imagery. He has the terrain. He has at least one hostage. How can we possibly turn his trap against him?'

No longer laughing, Geraden replied, 'By being stronger than he expects.'

When Geraden said that, Terisa permitted herself a sigh of relief. Master Barsonage jerked up his head, listening intently. The Tor brushed a hand through the sweat on his forehead, then rubbed his fingers on his robe.

'How?' Prince Kragen pursued, nearly whispering. 'In what way are we stronger than he expects?'

Geraden shrugged. 'For one thing, there's no way he could have planned for Terisa's talent – or mine either. That's why he's worked so hard to distract us, confuse us, keep us guessing. He didn't know what he was up against – and he didn't want us to find out what we can do. He couldn't possibly know I'm an Adept, of a certain kind. I can shift the Images in normal mirrors, whether I made them or not.'

'That is true,' Master Barsonage averred. 'I have witnessed it.'

'And Terisa is even more powerful,' Geraden went on. 'What I do with curved glass, she can do with flat mirrors. *And* she's an arch-Imager. She can pass through flat glass without losing her mind. *And* she can use her talent across incredible distances. That's how she escaped. From as far away as Esmerel, she shifted a mirror *here* until she was in the Image. Then Adept Havelock translated her out of danger.'

'That also is true.' The mediator of the Congery seemed to be taking bulk with every passing moment, growing larger or more substantial as the tenets of Imagery were altered. 'I have witnessed it.'

'And I am another way in which we are stronger than Master Eremis expects.'

Prince Kragen swung to face Master Barsonage. Geraden and Artagel turned. Terisa studied the Tor to be sure he was holding himself together, then directed her attention to the mediator.

'I mean that the Congery is stronger,' Barsonage amended as if his own certainty surprised him. 'We have not been held in much esteem. Why should we be? Generally, we are little more than a body of discontented ditherers. And all our actions in defense of Mordant – and of ourselves – went awry. Oh, the augury we cast for Mordant's future was well done. On the other hand, the summoning of our champion was a disaster. Why should anyone esteem us? We did not esteem ourselves enough to preserve our own usefulness after we saw how badly we had gone wrong with our champion.

'But then we learned of Geraden's talent – and of the lady Terisa's. That restored us immeasurably. We did not know whether these new talents would be used to harm or benefit us. No, Artagel,' he digressed, 'even after your explanations, we still had room for doubt. But we knew now that our work was vital – that we had unleashed forces which only we could support or oppose – that the Congery had at last come into its own significance.

'Therefore we set to work as we had never worked before.

'And now we have been vindicated.' That was the linchpin of Master Barsonage's new sureness. 'We have been given proof that King Joyse was always in the right – that Images possess their own full independent reality, that the things we see in mirrors are not created by Imagery. The Congery's establishment has been justified.' He was elevated by clarity; his face shone. 'The translations of Master Eremis and Master Gilbur and the arch-Imager Vagel are not merely evil in their *consequences*, but also in their *means*.'

'The point,' growled Prince Kragen. 'Come to the point.'

'My lord Prince,' the mediator announced, 'my lord Tor, Master Eremis is ready. That is evident. The Congery is ready also. In the name of King Joyse – and of Mordant's need – we are prepared to do battle at your side against Esmerel.'

'How?' The Prince had an unflagging interest in that question. 'What can you do?'

Master Barsonage's smile bore an unfamiliar resemblance to a smirk. 'My lord Prince, you have not agreed to an alliance. For that reason, I will not discuss our weapons with you. But two things I will tell you. First, our weapons violate none of the strictures which King Joyse has placed upon the Congery. And second' – he paused for a moment of frank self-congratulation – 'until weapons are necessary, we can *supply* the march to Esmerel.'

Prince Kragen's mouth formed the word *supply* without a sound.

'We cannot translate men, of course,' the mediator explained, 'but we are prepared to move food, swords, bedding, or tents in whatever quantity you require. You will be able to travel without supply-wains, without the vast entourage of camp followers and porters which slows you. You will be able to reach Esmerel more swiftly than Master Eremis can possibly guess.

'My lord Prince, does that not make us stronger?'

'And then there's the matter of an alliance,' Geraden put in before Prince Kragen could recover from his surprise. 'Eremis must know it's a possibility, but he can't *expect* it. What do you have, my lord Prince? Roughly ten thousand men?'

The Prince nodded dumbly.

'And what about us, Castellan Norge?'

Norge consulted the ceiling. 'Near eight thousand altogether. We can put six thousand on the road and still leave enough here to keep the defenses going for a while.'

'My lord Prince' – Geraden spoke carefully, controlling his emotion – 'Eremis doesn't expect to face an army of sixteen thousand. High King Festten doesn't expect it. They don't want to fight us. They want to overwhelm us.' He didn't need to say the word, *annihilate:* it was implicit in his tone. 'And they don't have the strength to overwhelm sixteen thousand men.'

For a few moments, Prince Kragen didn't answer; he chewed his moustache and glowered at his thoughts. Geraden kept himself still. Terisa held her breath. Norge appeared to be wondering whether this might be an opportune time for a nap. In contrast, Artagel was barely able to refrain from hopping from foot to foot like an excited boy. The Tor clamped both arms over his belly as if he feared that something inside him might burst.

Abruptly, the Prince turned to face the old lord.

He cocked his fists on his hips. Terisa couldn't tell which took precedence in him, his eagerness or his anger; but he didn't prolong the suspense.

'My lord Tor,' he said clearly, 'you ask too much.'

The Tor raised an inquiring hand, lifted an eyebrow. The effort brought sweat rolling down the bridge of his nose.

'If this alliance you propose fails,' Kragen articulated, 'you can retreat to Orison. You have two thousand men for a final defense. I have nothing. *All* the Alend Monarch's might will be destroyed, and my people will have no defense left between the Pestil River and the mountains. I can *not* risk my father's entire monarchy on this business of necks and nooses.

'I will not go. I advise you not to go.'

Terisa wanted to yell at him; she wanted to hit him with her fists. Don't you understand? *We've got to try.* She contained herself, however, because Geraden was clenched still, unprotesting, and Artagel had gone ominously quiet.

In a dull rumble, the Tor asked, 'What *do* you advise, my lord Prince?'

'Fight for Orison as long as you can,' replied the Prince. 'Then join me across the Pestil. Bring the Fayle and the Termigan – bring the Armigite, if you can bear him – and add your forces to mine. With the Alend Lieges behind us, we will make Eremis and Festten pay dearly for every foot of ground they take.'

To himself, the Tor made a muttering noise, as if he were considering the idea. But before Terisa could panic – before Geraden could intervene – he heaved himself to his feet.

He tottered. Afraid he might fall, she reached out to support him. What was left of his hair straggled with sweat; his skin had a gray underhue, as if his heart pumped ashes rather than blood; his eyes were glazed, nearly opaque.

Nevertheless he spoke as if no one could doubt that he would be obeyed.

'Castellan Norge, do you hear me?'

'I hear you, my lord Tor.' Norge sounded vaguely somnolent: detached; impervious to argument.

'Escort my lord Prince out of Orison. I want him returned safely to his father. Safely and politely. Do you hear me?'

'I hear you, my lord Tor.'

'We march against Esmerel at dawn. Be ready. Confer with the Congery on the matter of supplies.'

Master Barsonage nodded assent.

'Yes, my lord Tor.' This time, there was a small bite in Norge's tone, a touch of grim happiness.

Prince Kragen threw up his hands.

'Wait a minute.' Artagel wore his battle grin. He was unarmed, but at the moment he didn't look like he needed a weapon. 'You're talking about marching into the teeth of the siege. Is that wise, my lord Tor? Shouldn't we keep Prince Kragen with us? A hostage of our own? If we let him go, he can cut us down as soon as we ride out of here.'

'No,' the Tor said at once. The flatness in his tone was turning to nausea. '*That* the Alend Contender will not do. He knows where we go, and why. He may well resume his attack on Orison when we are gone. For that reason, we will leave two thousand men behind us, and someone reliable to lead them. But he will not harm or hinder us.'

Terisa wanted to ask, Are you sure? The mix of emotions on Prince Kragen's face was too complex to give her much confidence. Maybe that was what he planned: a killing attack as soon as the guard left Orison? Unexpectedly, however, the Prince's excitement seemed to gain the upper hand for a moment.

'Thank you, my lord Tor.' He spoke softly; yet his voice carried a hint of trumpets. 'Rely on my respect. If my father's friends were as honorable as King Joyse's, Alend would have no need of Contenders to win the Seat.'

Kragen turned to go. Norge sent two captains to accompany him until more guards could be mustered. Nevertheless Terisa didn't see his departure. She was busy trying to catch the Tor's great weight as it tumbled to the floor.

The old lord had fainted.

FORTY-FOUR

MEN GO FORTH

ℰ

Terisa and Geraden wanted to talk to Artagel – they wanted to know in detail what had happened in Orison during their absence – but for most of the day he had no time. He was busy with Norge, supporting the new Castellan's authority, and the Tor's, against anyone who doubted it, distrusted it. Of course, he had no official standing, no authority of his own. That, however, only increased his credibility. He was Artagel, the best swordsman in Mordant – and a son of the Domne. Since King Joyse's decline, he was the closest thing Orison had to a popular hero. And he wasn't actually a member of the guard – wasn't actually under Norge's command. His word, his simple presence at Norge's side, threw more weight than half a dozen catapults.

Failing Artagel, Terisa and Geraden would have been content with Master Barsonage. But the mediator was busy as well. He had to ready the Congery for battle. And he had to make all the arrangements for supplying the guard. In practice, this meant determining with Norge's seconds what supplies were necessary, in what quantities, and then issuing explicit instructions for the placement of those supplies in manageable piles in the vast disused ballroom outside the laborium.

Since the Congery had rediscovered its sense of purpose, the Masters had been busy. Working from the formula Barsonage had used to create the mirror of his augury, one of them had chanced to shape a flat glass which showed the ballroom. With as much haste as possible, two other Masters had succeeded at duplicating that new mirror; one glass alone would have been too slow – and would have placed too much strain on the Master who had made it. Along with its other weapons, the Congery intended to carry these mirrors on the march. Then the supplies which had been piled in the ballroom could be translated to Orison's army at need.

Because the mediator had to put these plans into effect, Terisa and Geraden were left with no comfortable source of information.

Ribuld was almost gleefully glad to see them. Especially after Lebbick's death – which he had been unable to prevent – the scarred veteran was eager to assign himself the job of protecting them. And he was happy to talk. From him, they heard about Saddith's fate. On the other hand, he couldn't answer the pertinent questions – couldn't explain, for instance, how the maid had come to serve as a diversion for the breaking of Geraden's mirror. He didn't know the things Terisa and Geraden most wanted to hear.

For most of the day – what was left of it, at any rate – they had to rely on each other's company.

This didn't particularly distress them.

They had given the Tor over into the care of a physician, who had assured them that the old lord had the constitution of a stoat and would almost certainly recover as soon as he began to consume a diet more nourishing than wine alone – with the proviso, of course, that Gart's kick hadn't produced any interior bleeding. After the physician had reassured them, Terisa and Geraden went to her former rooms in the tower, the peacock rooms.

They explained to Ribuld that they were waiting to talk to either Artagel or Master Barsonage; and Ribuld promised to hound Artagel and the mediator with reminders. Then they closed the door and bolted it.

Suddenly giddy with relief and suppressed hysteria, they wedged a chair into the wardrobe – where her clothes still hung – to block the entrance from the passage inside the wall. 'Anybody who tries to sneak in here,' he said, 'is going to crack his shins.'

Laughing so that they wouldn't weep, they welcomed each other back as if they had been apart for months.

'Ah, love,' he murmured some time later, when he had become calm, 'I came so close to reaching you. That was worse than being helpless, I think. There I was, doing something so amazing that it turns everything we know about Imagery upside down, and Eremis made it all useless just by putting out the lights.' He paused, then admitted, 'Havelock had to sit on me to keep me from going after you anyway.'

'But you weren't really helpless, were you.' This was important to her.

As always, what she said was more interesting to him than his own pain. 'What do you mean?'

'You couldn't reach me,' she explained, 'you couldn't rescue me directly. But with that power there must have been dozens of things you could have done. You could have translated guards into Esmerel to look for me. Hundreds of them.'

He peered at her in a way that made her want to hug him again because he so obviously wasn't hurt, didn't interpret what she said as criticism. All he said was, 'I didn't have time.'

'I know that, you idiot.' Instead of hugging him, she tickled his ribs. 'That's not the point.'

He caught her hand by the wrist and punished her attack by nibbling gently on the tips of her fingers. Between nips, he asked, 'What *is* the point?'

'The point is' – it was amazing, really, just how much difficulty she had concentrating while he sucked her fingers – 'You weren't helpless. If I hadn't done that shift, you could have found a way to strike back. You would have found a way.' Determined to be serious, she repeated, 'You weren't helpless.'

'Of course I'm helpless,' he replied around her fingers. 'I'm completely at your mercy.'

'Idiot,' she said again.

But she didn't have any trouble thinking of something to do for him while he was at her mercy.

Still later, when her own sense of postponed fright had receded, she murmured softly into his shoulder, 'What would we have done?'

He analyzed that for a while before he remarked, 'I have no idea what you're talking about.'

'If the Tor hadn't agreed with us,' she explained. 'If Norge hadn't agreed with him. If they hadn't put themselves in charge of Orison. What would we have done?'

He stared up at one of the peacock-feather decorations on the wall. 'Well, *somebody* had to take command. We would have persuaded *him*.'

'And what if he turned us down?'

Geraden considered the question. 'I guess we would have left with Prince Kragen. We would have tried to persuade him – or Elega – or maybe even Margonal himself – to back us up.

'I know,' he added when she started to object, 'Prince Kragen is the one who wants to stay here. But that's only because the Tor wants to go. If he didn't have any hope of an alliance with Orison – if he knew he couldn't get in here without spending all the lives that would take, making himself that much weaker – he might have been persuaded to march. If Elega took our side. If he thought he didn't have anything else to try.'

'And what,' she continued, 'if we couldn't persuade him.'

He shrugged under her head. 'Then we probably would have to get back into Orison. We'd have to get anybody who agreed with us – Artagel, maybe some of the Masters, maybe some friends of Ribuld's – and use one of Adept Havelock's mirrors to translate ourselves to Esmerel. Try a surprise raid.'

She reached across his chest to hug him. 'So we wouldn't have given up.'

He held her hard. Through his teeth, he muttered, 'You suit yourself. I wouldn't give up if I had to walk there alone and take Esmerel apart with my fingernails.'

That was what she wanted to hear. Feeling at once more relaxed and readier for battle, she asked casually, 'Has it occurred to you that we're luckier than we look?'

'"Luckier"?' he inquired.

'Or King Joyse is. If it weren't for Elega, we probably wouldn't have been able to talk our way in here. If it weren't for the Castellan' – she felt a pang whenever she remembered Lebbick – 'Gart would probably have killed you and Artagel and Prince Kragen and the Tor. If it weren't for the Tor, Orison might be in chaos by now. Eremis hasn't won yet. We're still able to lay here and make love and talk about fighting.' Geraden kissed her, but she didn't stop. 'We've been *lucky*.'

In an unexpectedly somber tone, he returned, 'Or King Joyse is better at this game than anybody realizes.'

She nodded. After a moment, she said, 'I wonder why he can't beat Havelock at hop-board.'

Geraden looked at her sharply. 'That's an interesting question. Do you suppose it's just because Havelock is out of his mind most of the time?'

That sounded plausible. Terisa started to say, I guess so. But then, unaccountably, she remembered the time Adept Havelock had come to her rooms – had sneaked in through the secret passage and taken her to Master Quillon, so that Quillon could give her the raw materials with which to think about Mordant's need. He hadn't exactly been in one of his lucid phases. And yet he had said—

She groped for the memory momentarily; then it came to her, as clear as the note of a well-made chime.

No one understands hop-board. The King tries to protect his pieces.

King Joyse had protected her, protected Geraden. Had tried to protect the Tor. At some personal cost, he had done what he could to protect his wife and daughters. It was even conceivable that he had tried to protect Castellan Lebbick.

Individuals. What good are they? Worthless. It's all strategy. Sacrifice the right men to trap your opponent.

Maybe that was the truth. Maybe King Joyse couldn't outplay the Adept because he couldn't match Havelock's ruthlessness.

Maybe that was why he was gone now. Maybe he was out on a mad chase after Torrent and Queen Madin, driven by a need to protect individuals without regard to his overall strategy

Did that fundamental flaw cripple everything? Was his policy fatally marred by his inability to sacrifice individuals for the sake of something larger?

Geraden must have felt her shivering: he tightened his arms around her suddenly. 'Terisa,' he murmured, 'love. What's the matter?'

She couldn't explain, not directly; the idea scaring her was too elusive, almost metaphysical. Instead, she said, 'Do you remember the time King Joyse asked me to find a way out of a stalemate? It was the day after Master Gilbur translated his champion.' That memory did little to improve her morale. 'You rescued me from the Castellan by persuading the Tor to send for me in King Joyse's name.'

Geraden nodded. 'I remember.'

'After you got me to the King's rooms,' she continued for her own sake rather than for his, strengthening her grip on what she meant, 'he showed me a hop-board problem. A stalemate. He said Havelock set it up for him. He said there was a way out, but he couldn't find it.'

Her shivers mounted. 'So I tipped all the men off the board. No more stalemate.'

'I remember,' Geraden repeated, trying to steady her.

'I think I almost made him sick. He was almost in tears.'

He had said, *To you, it's just a game. To me, it's the difference between life and ruin.*

And he had said, *I suggest that you give the matter more consideration before you once again attempt to end a stalemate by tilting the board.*

'Geraden, what if that's what we're doing? Tilting the board?'

Instead of doing what King Joyse wants. Protecting his pieces. Or what Havelock wants. Sacrificing the right men.

'Do you think we should go alone?' Geraden countered. 'Against Eremis and Gilbur and Vagel and terrible Imagery and twenty thousand men?'

Abruptly, her trembling stopped; it fell away from her like an old panic fading into the dark.

'No,' she said distinctly. That would be sacrificing men for no reason. 'We wouldn't stand a chance. Even if we could fight all that Imagery, we couldn't stop High King Festten.

'It's just that I agree with King Joyse. Somehow, he persuaded me he's right by leaving us in the lurch. At first, I was angry. But now I think I'm starting to understand.'

Geraden studied her face. 'Terisa, you aren't making any sense.'

'I know.' She mustered another indirect effort to explain herself. 'Did I ever tell you about Reverend Thatcher?'

'The man who ran the "mission" where you served before I came to you.'

She kissed Geraden's nose quickly. 'I probably told you he was futile. Sad – hopeless. He must have felt that way. But he taught me something— Something I didn't understand for a long time.

'He was trying to help the most miserable people in the city. Indigents. Street people. Crazies. Drunks. Trying to give them food and clothing and maybe shelter. And that was hard because nobody wanted to pay for it. If you feed and clothe and shelter them today, what have you accomplished? All you've done is save their lives, so they'll need more food and clothing and shelter tomorrow. So if you have money and want to do some good, giving it to that mission is like throwing it away. There must be hundreds of things you can use your money for that would do more good for the city as a whole.'

'Yes, but—' began Geraden.

'Yes, but,' she agreed. 'Doing good for the city as a whole wouldn't make those poor people go away. It wouldn't make their misery go away. And Reverend Thatcher couldn't stop caring about them. If you gave him a choice between' – she searched for an example – 'I don't know, between free education for the whole city and helping one drunk get through another day with a hot meal, he'd choose to help the drunk. Not because he didn't think education is important, but because he couldn't help caring about the drunk.

'Maybe that's sad. Maybe it's even stupid. It's certainly hopeless.

'But it's also wonderful.'

She stopped as if she had made herself clear.

Geraden had to struggle for a couple of minutes, but eventually he reached the conclusion she hadn't been able to articulate. 'King Joyse,' he said slowly, 'persuaded you he was right by abandoning us. You think he went after Torrent – after Queen Madin. When somebody he loves is in danger, he forgets all about Mordant – all about his plans for saving his kingdom. He leaves that to us. Not because he doesn't think Mordant is important, but because he can't help caring about her.'

Terisa's spirit lifted. 'He isn't an idealist – not really. If anyone here is an idealist, it's Havelock. King Joyse didn't create Mordant and the Congery out of an abstract set of beliefs. He did it because people he knew and cared about were being hurt in the wars – hurt by Imagery. He wanted to save the world, a world made up of individual farmers and merchants and children who couldn't defend themselves.

'Don't forget that he risked a lot to protect *us*. Treating us the way he did, he confused us – even hurt us. But that gave Eremis a reason not to kill us. And we were left free to make our own choices. Just to keep us alive, King Joyse took the risk that we might go against him completely. Just to protect our lives and our choices.

'And,' she concluded, 'he trusts us to do the same thing for him. He trusts us to defend Mordant for him while he's out trying to rescue his wife.'

As if a knot of tension had been released in him, Geraden collapsed back on the bed. Happily, he said, 'I knew there was *some* good reason why I love that old man.'

'Besides,' she went on, now that she was sure of herself; 'we aren't the ones who want to tilt the board. That's what Eremis is doing. What we're doing may not be right, but we aren't making that mistake.'

'No,' he assented. Eagerness brightened his eyes and animated his features, making him inexpressibly precious to her. 'We aren't making *that* mistake.'

For the time being, she was content.

Just when it seemed, however, that she had reached the point where she no longer worried about what anybody else in Orison did, Master Barsonage arrived in answer to Ribuld's messages. She and Geraden kept the mediator waiting only long enough to put on some clothes; then they admitted him to her sitting room.

'Sleeping all day while Orison bustles, I see,' the Imager commented pleasantly while he closed the door. He looked happier than she had ever seen him: activity and a clear sense of purpose agreed with him. 'Well, doubtless you need the rest. I can only imagine the exertions and perils which you have endured.

'Since my imagination has not been all it should be, as you know' – he seated himself, frowned into the empty wine decanter, then shrugged his thick shoulders – 'I am eager to hear what has happened to the rest of Mordant. The siege has cut us off completely,' he explained. 'We know nothing but what we have learned from you and Prince Kragen.'

Terisa blew a sigh. 'That's going to take a while,' she said; and Geraden went to the door, chuckling. Outside, he asked Ribuld for wine and food.

Ribuld made some retort she didn't catch; then Geraden returned. 'Ribuld says we can have anything we want, if we don't mind waiting. Apparently, there's no end of servants available, but the kitchens are in chaos, trying to get supplies' – he glowered humorously at Master Barsonage – 'ready for tomorrow.'

'That is true,' replied the mediator with a nod. 'An appalling situation, in fact. No one knows what to do. Norge or one of his captains has to make every decision. It seems that Castellan Lebbick established plans and procedures for every conceivable eventuality – except a march.

'And, of course, every man who carries a sack of meal or a keg of water or a bale of hay to the ballroom goes in terror of his life, expecting to be translated away into madness at any moment.' Master Barsonage permitted himself a growl of disgust. 'If Norge were not so phlegmatic – and if Artagel were less supportive – we would be in worse danger of riots now than at any other time today.'

Terisa and Geraden glanced at each other. 'As Terisa says,' Geraden remarked to the mediator, 'our story is going to take a while. Why don't we wait for supper?' He set two chairs facing Master Barsonage and sat down in one of them; following his example, Terisa took the other. 'Maybe by then Artagel will join us, and we won't have to go over the same things twice.

'In the meantime, you can tell us how the preparations are going.'

Just for a moment, the Imager looked doubtfully at Geraden's proposal; he seemed to think Geraden intended to avoid answering him. Almost at once, however, he inhaled deeply, shook his head as if to rearrange his thoughts, and smiled in acquiescence.

While Terisa and Geraden listened intently, storing up information they might need, Master Barsonage described how the Congery planned to transport their mirrors – no simple problem, considering that the mirrors would have to be moved over hard road and uneven ground by horse cart. With deliberate frankness – perhaps reproaching Geraden's evasion – he discussed the chief weapon the Masters had devised, as well as the secondary actions they were equipped to take. That brought a shine to Geraden's eyes, made Terisa grip herself hard to keep her excitement in perspective; but neither of them interrupted as the mediator went on to explain the arrangements he had designed for the supplies in the ballroom, so that Orison's people could replenish the piles of stores without any risk of being inadvertently taken by a translation.

When he was done with his particular responsibilities, he gave the best report he could on the state of the castle. So far, the Tor's authority and Norge's were being accepted without much resistance: eagerly by most of the guard, men who favored almost any change which promised action; and eagerly as well by the servants, for whom the departure of six thousand guards would mean that much less work; more stoically by Orison's visiting population, people who felt King Joyse's absence keenly in theory, but in practice found Artagel's assurances persuasive; with ill grace and no little suspicion by many of King Joyse's minor lords and functionaries – excise-tax assessors, for example, or storeroom accountants, or secretaries to the Home Ambassador – men whose entire existence depended on the King, on his style of kingship. And without any active opposition to the Tor or Norge, most of Orison's social machinery continued to function. Meals were cooked, despite the chaos Ribuld had described. Halls were patrolled, guarding against unrest – and against attacks of Imagery. Duty rosters were maintained, the walls and gates manned.

In short, thanks to the Tor's quick assumption of authority, and to Norge's demonstrated acceptance, and to Artagel's grinning support, Orison remained almost miraculously intact after King Joyse's disappearance.

'Thank the stars,' Geraden breathed when Master Barsonage was done. 'You're right, Terisa. We're luckier than we look.' Then his eyes narrowed, and his lips pulled tight over his teeth. 'I wonder how many times Eremis has thought he could get away with laughing at the Tor. If he can see us now, he isn't laughing anymore.'

'And he isn't laughing at the Congery,' Terisa put in, partly to please Master Barsonage, and partly because the mediator had impressed her. 'Or he won't be, when he finds out what he's up against.'

'Thank you, my lady,' Barsonage replied quietly. 'We have been useless for a long time, while we distrusted both our King and ourselves. It is a pleasure to think that we will be effective at last.'

'If only Prince Kragen had listened to us,' Geraden mused.

'Or if he changes his mind—' added Terisa, remembering the strange conflict she had seen in the Prince's face.

Master Barsonage looked back and forth between them. Geraden knotted his fists as if to control an irrational hope.

Terisa started to say something about Elega and Margonal, then stopped because she heard voices at the door.

Someone – Ribuld? – guffawed at an unexpected joke.

Without knocking, Artagel swung the door open and entered the room.

He was grinning; his eyes flashed steel fire. If there hadn't been a thin sheen of sweat on his forehead, or a slight pallor of old pain in his cheeks, or a barely discernible hitch in his stride, he would have looked ready and able to carry the whole castle on his shoulders into battle. He was primed for action, packed full of necessity by long days of recuperation, by emotional stresses he couldn't relieve, by betrayals and self-doubt and grief. As soon as she saw him, Terisa knew that he wouldn't hesitate to tackle an entire platoon of Gart's Apts.

The mere sight of him did her good.

And it scared her. It reminded her that if eagerness went too far it could become a form of suicide.

For some reason, she noticed that the sunlight slanting in through her windows was tinged with red, approaching dusk.

Leaving the door for Ribuld to close, Artagel approached Geraden. Geraden surged upright, and Artagel clasped him in a hug which gave no sign of weakness or injury. Then Artagel came to Terisa and dropped to his knees, actually dropped to his knees, in order to capture both her hands and kiss them. Before she could protest or respond, however, he retreated to his feet again, glared at the empty wine decanter, humorously muttered a soldier's obscenity, then dropped himself half-sprawling into the nearest chair.

'Mirrors preserve us,' he drawled in a joking tone. 'Seeing you two makes me weak in the head. I don't think I can do much more of this dance between hope and despair. First you're gone forever. Then you show up – with Prince Kragen, may his skull ache for the rest of his life. Then he provokes a fight with King Joyse, and Gart appears, and the King disappears, and you're abducted' – he indicated Terisa – 'and you' – Geraden – 'run off with the mediator. Then the Tor tries to make an alliance with Prince Kragen, and it looks like the only reason that isn't going to work is because I hit him. And suddenly you both come back, and everything starts to go right, and I don't *care* what that pig-brained Alend decides to do about it. I don't even care where King Joyse is. I'm sure it'll all make sense eventually.

'Incidentally, I haven't exactly been cautious in the things I've said to keep people from worrying.' By *worrying* he obviously meant *questioning Norge and the Tor*. 'What scares them most is the idea of translations into Orison. Terrible Imagery, monsters, fire, a few hundred thousand Cadwals – that kind of thing.' He faced Terisa frankly. 'I've been telling everybody you can solve that problem. I've been saying you can shift Eremis' mirrors so they won't translate here. If that's not true, you might want to keep it to yourself.'

Shift Eremis' mirrors, Terisa thought while her stomach twisted. Oh, shit.

'Just tell me one thing.' Artagel hauled himself erect, nearly laughing. 'What in the name of sanity *is* going on here?'

'I'll be glad to explain it,' Geraden replied, grinning like his brother's reflection. 'All you have to do is *shut up*.'

With a gleam of joy, Artagel collapsed back into his sprawed posture.

At once, however, he jerked his spine straight, squared his shoulders. 'No,' he said, and all the mirth fell out of him. His expression turned to sweat and pallor. 'Tell me what happened at home. You said Houseldon was destroyed.'

Geraden made a warding gesture, warning his brother back from an explosion.

As if on summons, there was a knock at the door.

Ribuld pushed the door open, and two servingmen entered, carrying trays loaded with food and wine.

Artagel contained himself; but his eyes burned like fuses while the servingmen set out the food, poured the wine, handed around goblets. Master Barsonage accepted his goblet gratefully, emptied it in one long pull, and held it out to be refilled. Geraden and Artagel gripped their goblets without drinking, without looking anywhere except at each other.

Until one of the servingmen knelt to light a fire in the hearth, Terisa didn't realize that the air was turning cooler.

'No lamps tonight,' Ribuld commented generally. 'No oil. We used up what we had protecting the gates. There's just enough left to keep King Joyse's quarters and the public halls lit for a few more days. Don't let your fire go out.'

Ushering the servingmen out of the room, he paused to add, 'The Tor wants to talk to you. Before we march. The Castellan will send somebody to get you in the morning. Early.'

On that cheerful note, he closed the door.

At once, Master Barsonage articulated, 'You said, "Houseldon is destroyed,"' speaking steadily so that Artagel wouldn't have to shout. '"Sternwall is falling. The people of Fayle are butchered by ghouls." Everyone who heard you wants an explanation, Geraden.'

Geraden didn't hesitate; he had had time to marshall a reply. 'The Domne is all right,' he said promptly. 'At least he was when we left. Our family is safe. Most of the people we know survived. Under the circumstances, our losses were small.

'But Houseldon was burned to the ground.'

Holding his hands together because he didn't have a sword, Artagel listened to every word as if he were studying his enemies to learn how to fight them.

Grimly, Geraden described the salient features of his arrival at the Closed Fist, and Terisa's; he described the consequences for Houseldon. Then he explained, 'That's what made Nyle do it. That's why he cooperated with Eremis. The threat of an attack like that.

'But when we left, the Domne and all our people were going to dig themselves into the Closed Fist. If Eremis tries the same threat again, our father wants us to ignore it.'

At the moment, Terisa didn't care that Geraden had promised to call the Domne *Da*.

Slowly, Artagel sighed, letting violence out of his lungs. 'Tholden must be a lot tougher than he thinks.'

'So is the Tor,' Geraden muttered.

'But you did not return to Orison by translation,' prompted Master Barsonage. 'I gather the lady Terisa did not know then that her talent could reach across such distances.'

Terisa nodded; and Geraden said, 'But it might not have helped, even if she *had* known. She can translate herself through flat glass. If she translated me, I'd lose my mind.'

'I understand,' said the mediator. 'For that reason, you were required to cross Mordant on horseback. And you chose a road which took you to Sternwall and Romish.'

'Yes,' Geraden replied. 'That's how we happened to be at Vale House when the Queen was taken. We were trying to gather support for King Joyse – trying to get the Termigan and the Fayle to ride against Eremis.'

As briefly as possible, he told the story of the journey back to Orison, controlling his outrage at Eremis' tactics as well as he could. Terisa listened to him for a while; gradually, however, her attention drifted. The room was growing darker as the sun set. A few hints of crimson still clung to the plumage on the walls, but most of the light was gone. Darkness accumulated against Orison. She didn't want to remember pits of fire in the ground, or ghouls. She wanted to remember the Fayle.

The evening after the battle to save Naybel, sitting with her and Geraden in his camp, Queen Madin's father had talked about King Joyse. With one hand clenched into a fist he couldn't sustain, he had said, *In all his years of warfare against Cadwal and Alend and Imagery, he has never asked a lord for aid when that lord's Care was under attack. He came to me, freed my people. He did not ask me for any help until my Care was safe.*

He will not ask me now. He has no wish to break my heart.

Terisa understood the Fayle better now. She grieved for him – for his losses, his inadequacy in the face of the ghouls – but she understood him. And she wanted to believe that he and the Termigan were doing the right thing by not riding to King Joyse's support. By protecting their pieces.

I will not leave my people to die undefended.

She also wanted to believe that King Joyse wasn't making a horrible mistake.

Then Geraden was done. He drank some of his wine and began to pick at his food as if his story had left a bad taste in his mouth.

'Well,' Master Barsonage muttered morosely. 'Well. You have worked wonders to bring us this news, Geraden – my lady. But I am like other men in Orison, I suppose. I must admit that I had hoped to hear a more encouraging tale. We have all dreamed of the Perdon in vain. *Annihilated,* you said.' The mediator scowled. 'And now we learn that any dreams we may have had of the Termigan or the Fayle are also in vain.

'King Joyse has chosen a bad time to disappear.'

'He didn't choose it,' Artagel countered. 'There aren't any good times to have your wife abducted.'

'Do you believe,' Master Barsonage asked carefully, 'that is where the King has gone? To rescue Queen Madin?'

Artagel's confidence was greater than Terisa's or Geraden's. He said, 'Of course.'

The mediator considered that for a moment. Then he said, 'I hope you are right. I hope he is not simply cowering somewhere, overwhelmed by the consequences of his actions. To pursue the Queen at such a time may be foolish, but it is certainly understandable.'

Without waiting to debate the point, Barsonage rose to his feet. 'I will leave you to your supper. I have no urgent need of food' – he slapped his girth – 'and many other things to do. With your permission, Geraden, I will tell your story to the Congery.' Geraden nodded. 'And to Castellan Norge.' Geraden nodded again. 'And to the Tor. It will do us no good to march with false expectations of help.'

Geraden shrugged his assent.

'One other small matter,' the Master added before he reached the door. 'Do you want a chasuble, Geraden? Do you, my lady? I am prepared to initiate you to the Congery whenever you wish.'

The proposal seemed curiously irrelevant to Terisa. When Geraden heard it, however, his face turned as crimson as the sunset. Master Barsonage had just offered him his life's dream. The fact that he had tears in his eyes embarrassed him acutely.

'Later—' he murmured. 'Maybe later.' Roughly, he rubbed his hands into his eyes; then he met the mediator's gaze. 'All I want right now is to stop Eremis.'

Master Barsonage accepted that answer. 'My lady?'

Terisa shook her head. She had no desire to become a member of the Congery.

Still, she was glad to see that the mediator didn't take her refusal as a reproach. He had too many other things on his mind. Saying only, 'As you wish. We will see each other in the morning,' he let himself out of the room.

Terisa and Geraden and Artagel looked at each other.

She was starting to feel hungry, but that could wait a little longer. Reflections from the hearth continued to cast a red hue into Geraden's face. Rising to her feet, she moved around behind his chair and put her hands on his shoulders. His muscles were hard, knotted like iron. A chasuble: his life's dream. And now it didn't make any difference. He didn't need it. Deliberately, she dug her fingers into the knots, trying to massage them loose.

Artagel opened his mouth like a man who intended to say something facetious, perhaps at the mediator's expense; but his brother forestalled him. 'Now it's your turn,' Geraden said, still struggling to regain his composure. 'I want you to tell us *everything* that happened while we were away.'

'"Everything"?'

Terisa felt a tremor under her hands which wasn't audible in Geraden's voice. Acerbically, he returned, 'Leave out the part where you refused to eat all your vegetables and drank too much wine. And terrorized the serving girls. Tell us the rest.'

For a moment, Artagel chuckled, but there was no mirth in him now. Drawling to soften his tone, he warned, 'You aren't going to like it.'

'I know that already.' Slowly, Geraden's trembling eased. 'If I thought I was going to like it, I'd eat first. But I don't think I can stand it on a full stomach.'

Terisa rumpled his hair, kissed the top of his head. Then she went back to her chair.

'Castellan Lebbick,' she said, as if she had the strength to mention his name without panic or outrage; without sorrow. 'Tell us what happened to him.'

Artagel nodded stiffly in the gloom. He refilled his goblet as if he needed courage; however, he didn't drink.

As well as he could, he told Lebbick's story.

Along the way, of course, he mentioned Saddith. He discussed his own efforts to persuade Master Barsonage that Eremis was a traitor. He sketched the extent of Eremis' popularity after the refilling of the reservoir. He described the Tor's long drunkenness, as well as King Joyse's sudden interest in swordsmanship. He detailed the progress of the siege – and of the defense of Orison, by Adept Havelock as well as by the guard.

But mostly he talked about Castellan Lebbick. From his perspective, Orison's story had become the tale of Lebbick's wild and doomed struggle against disintegration. The Castellan had been driven to such desperation, and at last to such lorn heroism – the heroism, not of fighting Gart, but of keeping at least some grasp on sanity – by the fact that he stood almost alone for the castle and its people against Master Eremis' betrayals. And against King Joyse's abdication of responsibility.

And Artagel, who valued heroism, had watched Lebbick's story unfold, and had tried to affect its outcome. Now he didn't know whether he had helped or failed.

Listening to him, Terisa found her anger at King Joyse returning. To cut a man like Lebbick adrift, merely for the sake of a stratagem – merely because the Castellan had no duplicity in him and couldn't be trusted to tell lies—

Maybe the King wasn't particularly interested in preserving his pieces after all. Maybe Master Quillon's account of his actions was false. Maybe his disappearance – and everything else he did – had a completely different meaning.

Terisa wondered how Artagel had been able to retain his faith in King Joyse.

Geraden's thoughts, however, had taken a different turn. When Artagel was finished, Geraden muttered into the inaccurate light of the flames, 'It's hard to feel sorry for him. After what he did to Saddith. What he meant to do to Terisa.'

'No,' Terisa said at once, 'it's easy. His wife died. She and Orison and King Joyse were his reasons for living.' Curse that old man anyway, *curse* him. 'King Joyse would have been kinder to cut him off at the knees.'

'I know what you mean,' murmured Artagel, while Geraden studied Terisa bleakly. 'It was hard to watch. I just couldn't get him to look at things the way I did.'

'How did you look at them?' Geraden asked.

Artagel shifted in his chair, a bit embarrassed. 'Well, take you two, for example.' Terisa supposed he was thinking of the bad days during which he had believed the worst of his brother. 'All the evidence was against you. Eremis did a good job of making you look terrible. We only had two things to go on. Lebbick saw you' – he faced Terisa – 'disappear into a mirror *without* Master Gilbur. Whatever you did together, you escaped separately. And it was easy to guess Saddith got the idea of going to Lebbick's bed from Eremis. But that was enough. Because we *knew* you. We knew you weren't the kind of people Eremis made you look like. We didn't need much to make us question the whole situation.

'So I tried to tell him' – Artagel swallowed at the emotion in his throat – 'to look at King Joyse the same way. We *knew* the King. We *knew* he wasn't what he looked like. All we needed was some reason to believe in him.'

'What reason?' Geraden demanded. He sounded hungry.

'You two,' repeated Artagel. 'Why was Eremis afraid of your talent, my lady? Why was he afraid of yours, Geraden? Well, why else? He knew you were his enemies. He knew you were loyal to King Joyse.

'*Why* were you loyal? *We* didn't know. But you must have had a reason. I was sure of that. And it was enough. You know me. You know I don't exactly have a towering mind. There are probably lots of things I'll never understand. But *you* had a reason.' He made a sweeping gesture, at once vague and vehement in the dim light. 'That was enough for me.

'But Lebbick couldn't do it. I think he took it all too personally. The hurt' – Artagel stumbled over the word – 'went too deep. I know he tried. He held himself together because he didn't have anything else to hope for. But in the end—' Abruptly, Artagel shrugged; he picked up his goblet and drank it dry. 'In the end I guess he was glad to find a way to get killed.'

After a while, Terisa breathed to Geraden, 'You see? It's easy.'

Geraden nodded once, roughly. His gaze burned back at the embers of the fire.

The unexpected cold in the air made her pull her chair closer to the hearth.

Artagel stayed and talked for some time after supper. He wanted detailed news from Domne: he wanted to know about the Domne's health, and how tall Ruesha was now, and if Tholden and Quiss were likely to have more children; he wanted to know whether any irate husbands had succeeded at beating sense into Stead, or whether Minick's wife had lost any of her shyness. And talking about things like that did Geraden good. It eased Terisa, bringing back to her memories she treasured, memories which reminded her what the battles ahead would be fought *for*, as well as what they would be fought *against*. Nevertheless the day had been long – not to mention difficult. At last, she grew too tired to stifle her yawns.

Artagel took the hint, such as it was. Promising to see them early the next morning, he left her and Geraden alone.

They didn't have any trouble persuading each other that they needed to go to bed.

She felt safe in the peacock rooms. If Eremis had the means to attack here, he might hesitate, concerned by the impossibility of estimating what she or Geraden could do in retaliation. And she seemed to have left panic a long way behind her.

As soon as she was sure that Geraden was drowsy enough to sleep – that he wouldn't get out of bed to sit up and brood all night – she let herself slide away into dreams.

At first they were easy dreams, full of rest: in them, she watched herself sleep soundly. But gradually they took on rhythm – the slow labor of blow and rebound, repeated again and again. The rhythm grew faster. Out of the dark, she kicked at Eremis as hard as she could, felt her foot strike; then she recoiled, plunged backward to get away from his fury, backward against the wall, through the mirror. This time, however, there was no mirror, no translation. Her heart was too full of rage for fading, and the wall admitted nothing, allowed nothing; it only held her where he could reach her. So she kicked again, recoiled again; and he sprang at her again and again, violent, ultimately irresistible, a man who knew how to have his way with anyone; and horror rose in her throat like sobs because there was nothing she could do to fight him, no way she could beat him—

—until Geraden shook her shoulder, hissed, 'Terisa! You're having a nightmare!' and she heard the flat, wooden sound she made when she kicked against the blankets, the knock which seemed to pitch her back into the mattress.

The knock—

Abruptly, she locked herself still, sweating in runnels; and the sound went on, a wooden sound, not her feet belaboring the bed.

Someone was pounding on the door hidden inside one of the wardrobes. She could feel her pulse hammer against the bones of her skull.

She jerked upright.

At once, the sweat seemed to freeze on her skin.

The dim glow from the embers in the hearth lit Geraden as he leaped past her. He grabbed his underclothes and breeches, pulled them on; tossed a couple of logs into the fire. Then he went into the sitting room, unbolted the door, warned the guard outside.

The knocking was steadier than the rhythm of her heart.

A small crackle of flame caught at the new wood. As if that small sound, that little jump of light, released her, she swung her legs out of bed.

Luckily, her robe was in the other wardrobe, the safe one. Shivering as if her limbs were crusted with ice, she snatched out the garment, got her arms into the sleeves, sashed the velvet around her.

The knocking went on. Whoever was in the secret passage was apparently determined to pound there all night if necessary.

'You all right?' Geraden whispered.

She nodded. 'Just a bad dream.' She faced the wardrobe. 'Let's open it.'

The door of the wardrobe was already slightly ajar. Geraden swung it out of the way, then reached in and unblocked the chair from the hidden entrance.

As the secret door opened, light filtered through the clothes like sunshine through a forest.

Adept Havelock.

The light came from his hand-sized mirror, his piece of translated sun – the same mirror he had used to incinerate the red-furred creature which had attacked Geraden.

Seeing the Adept, Geraden let out a slow breath. At once, he turned away, left the bedroom. Terisa heard him tell the guard to relax, heard him bolt the door.

Havelock held his light with an unsteady hand. Its shifting illumination, and the dance of the flames in the hearth, cast wild shadows across his features – winks and leers; deathmasks; contortions of sorrow. His insanity looked irreparable.

'Take off your clothes,' he commanded her, grinning like a dog. 'I haven't seen a good pair of teats for a long time. Don't ask me any questions.'

Don't ask— To herself, she groaned bitterly.

Just to be on the safe side, she clenched one hand in the v of her robe, holding it closed.

Then Geraden rejoined her. 'You heard,' she said, afraid that any question might upset the Adept.

'I heard,' Geraden muttered. 'No questions. This is going to be such fun.'

'Have you been rutting?' demanded Havelock. He was incensed for a moment, full of righteous indignation. 'Naked as animals? Avid as goats?' Without transition, his self-righteousness became self-pity. 'Why didn't you invite me?'

Terisa hardly noticed what he said. She was watching the way his light weaved and wavered – the way it moved through the illumination from the hearth; the darkness across the back of his hand. Until she saw black drops spatter to the floor, she didn't understand that his hand was bleeding.

Knocking on the door inside the wardrobe, he had damaged his knuckles.

'Havelock—' She faltered momentarily, then took hold of herself, straightened her shoulders. 'You had a reason for coming here. It was a good reason. You hurt yourself to make us notice you. Tell us what it was.'

'A *reason*?' he cackled, laughing instantly. 'A madman like me?' And just as quickly, his mirth vanished. He extinguished his light, put his mirror away in a pocket somewhere, then raised his hand to his mouth to lick the blood. Red smeared his lips, his chin; a spot of blood appeared on his fierce nose.

Between licks, he said casually, 'Trust me.'

813

Terisa stared at him, waiting for him to explain. When he didn't say anything else, she shook her head. The air was *cold* – too cold for the time of year. Even the stones under her bare feet were warmer. And she was angry.

'I went to you for help. Master Gilbur was after me, and I didn't have anywhere else to go. You refused.

'Tell me how to trust you.'

To her chagrin, his eyes suddenly filled with tears, and his face twisted until he looked like a damaged schoolboy. His voice ached and cracked.

'I know it's hard. I'm crazy, aren't I? Vagel took my mind away. He showed me how to understand everything. Most of the time, I can't tell shit from shallots.

'But Joyse does it.' Trying to rub the tears from his eyes, he wiped blood across his face. 'Joyse does it.'

'Tell us—' Geraden put in softly, carefully, 'tell us where he is.'

One of Havelock's eyes turned toward Geraden; the other seemed to plead with Terisa. 'He told me not to.'

'Havelock—' Terisa was never able to sustain her anger against him. His dilemma moved her. As far as she was concerned, there was no real reason why she hadn't emerged in a condition like this from the closet where her parents had locked her. And maybe a certain kind of madness was required to play hop-board successfully with human beings as pieces.

'Havelock, you killed that creature in the dungeon.' Behind bars, helpless; burned down to tallow and stink. 'The one that attacked Geraden. With your mirror. But when Gart tried to kill me, you let him live. You didn't even damage him. You just blinded him temporarily.

'I want to trust you. He was trying to kill me. Tell me why you didn't even damage him.'

Geraden drew a breath between his teeth, held it hard.

'Oh, *that.*' Somehow, the Adept passed from distress to scorn without any discernible effort. 'You disappoint me. You should have figured that out long ago. How many times has Joyse told you to *think*?'

Terisa clamped her mouth shut and waited.

'It's obvious.' Havelock fluttered his hands as if he meant to start dancing. 'If I hurt him – if I really blinded him – he would have been caught. We'd lose the chance that he might lead us to his allies. If I killed him, we'd have the same problem, only worse.' Sharply, the Adept giggled. 'If you think things are bad *now*, try to guess how much trouble you'd be in if Gart hadn't accidentally betrayed Eremis by charging in here.

'*And,*' he went on, 'if I killed him, everybody would think *you* did it. Try to guess how long they would have let you live if they thought' – he giggled again – 'thought you were Imager enough to charcoal the High King's Monomach.

'No, you're being stupid.' From scorn and humor, he lapsed into vexation. 'You're wasting my time. If you aren't going to let me fondle your female beauties, at least learn something *useful.*'

In a rough voice, Geraden demanded, 'Tell us what you want us to know.'

For a moment, the Adept faced Geraden as if he couldn't bring the younger man into focus with either eye; then he muttered, 'Idiot. It's not that simple,' and headed back into the wardrobe.

Desperately, Terisa called after him, 'You said you saw the King's daughters in an augury,' because she didn't have any better ideas. 'Tell us what Elega was doing.'

Slapping at clothes, with a gown wrapped over his head and both fists full of fabric, he replied, 'Spreading her legs for Prince Kragen.'

That shocked Terisa; for a moment, it paralyzed her brain. Helplessly, she echoed Geraden. 'Tell us what you want.'

The Adept ripped the gown off his head. With both arms, he flung a bundle of clothes to the floor.

'*I want you to trust me!*'

Banging the hidden door after him, he vanished into the darkness of the passage.

She stared after him, dumbfounded.

Spreading her legs. For Prince Kragen.

So King Joyse had known. Before the Prince ever came to Orison as the Alend Monarch's ambassador, King Joyse had known that the Contender and his eldest daughter would become lovers. And he had let it happen. He had practically driven Elega into Kragen's arms.

Suddenly, the test King Joyse had arranged for Prince Kragen, the strange game of checkers in the audience hall, became poignant to her – poignant and awful. By that test, King Joyse had learned that his daughter would betray him.

By that test, he had forced her to betray him.

Now his last message to her made sense. *She carries my pride with her wherever she goes.* He had chosen to put her where she was. And Terisa's nagging sense that Elega had a vital role to play in his plans was confirmed.

And yet, despite what she had just learned, she knew she had missed the point of Havelock's visit.

Left weak by what had happened, what she was thinking, she murmured, 'What was *that* all about?'

Glowering darkly, Geraden thought for a moment. Then, to her surprise, his expression lightened, and he smiled like a son of the Domne.

'I think he wants us to trust him.'

Trust him. The man who advocates sacrificing pieces to win the game.

Oh, shit.

Really, she needed to increase her range of expletives. Thinking *oh, shit* over and over again just wasn't an adequate way to express herself.

Eventually, she and Geraden went back to bed.

The summons of the guard came much too early.

When Geraden stumbled into the sitting room to answer the door, the guard handed him a breakfast tray and said, 'The Tor wants you in an hour. In the King's rooms.'

Outside, the sky was still dark, too full of night to give any hint of dawn.

Today, the march would begin.

The air was unconscionably cold.

Blearily, Terisa asked, 'Is there any chance we can get some bathwater?'

'Use all the water you want, my lady.' She didn't recognize the guard's voice: he must have come during the night to relieve Ribuld. 'No rationing this morning. But you'll have to heat it yourself. Nobody has time to do it for you.'

'Thanks,' muttered Geraden.

After he had closed the door and put down the tray, he came into the bedroom. 'I'll put a bucket on the hearth,' he offered. 'We don't have time to let it get hot, but at least we won't freeze to death.'

Pulling a blanket around her, she forced her tired limbs out of bed. Off the rugs, the floorstones were still warmer than the air. On her way to help put more wood on the fires, she asked, 'What's happened to the weather?'

Geraden's tone conveyed a shrug. 'We had an early thaw. Now it looks like we're having a late freeze.'

Good. Perfect. I love being cold.

When she had put three more logs on the coals in the bedroom fireplace, she nearly climbed into the hearth in an effort to absorb some of the new heat.

Once the logs had begun to burn warmly, however, she went to look for some clothes.

Apparently undaunted by the cold – or maybe simply saving as much warmer water for her as he could – Geraden splashed around in the bathroom for a while; he came out toweling himself urgently. Still wrapped in her blanket, with a pile of the clothes Mindlin had made for her nearby, she set out the breakfast and began to gulp down hot tea, warm porridge. Then, when she and Geraden were done eating, she took the bucket from the hearth and retreated into the bathroom.

She didn't notice until she had given herself the best sponge bath she could manage, and had started to get dressed, that all her clothes carried a faint smell of blood.

Every garment she had – everything she could possibly wear on horseback, on a march – was stained with a few drops or a small smear of Havelock's blood.

For a moment, she wanted to break down and cry. The night seemed to have taken the courage out of her, cost her her immunity to panic. But the Adept's visit meant *something*. He wanted to be trusted. Or he had promised that he could be trusted. And King Joyse had known all along that Elega and Prince Kragen would become lovers.

Roughly, Terisa washed the fear off her face with the coldest water available. Then she put on a sturdy twill riding habit over some of Myste's silk undergarments.

Havelock's vehemence had left a crescent smear on the fabric over the curve of her left breast; but there wasn't anything she could do about that. As soon as she stopped thinking about it, the smell of blood receded.

Geraden grinned as she emerged from the bathroom. He had found her sheepskin coat and boots.

'What're you going to wear?' she asked.

He wasn't worried. 'I'll get something from the guards.'

Sooner than she was expecting, someone knocked on the door again. This time, it was Ribuld. He brought with him a mail shirt and a longsword in a shoulder scabbard for Geraden, in addition to a winter cloak. Something about the way he avoided looking at Terisa made her wonder why he hadn't brought any protection or weapons for her; but he started talking about the march, and she forgot her question.

'Six thousand men,' he said as he pulled the mail over Geraden's head. 'Two thousand horse. Four thousand foot. Castellan says we can make it to Esmerel in three days. Only sixty miles across the Broadwine, and the terrain isn't bad. But we couldn't do it carting supplies. If this translation business works, it's going to be the biggest thing in warfare since crossbows. Traveling light and fast.'

'Is the guard ready?' asked Geraden.

Ribuld nodded. 'But that isn't the hard part. Armies march on food. If we had to wait for it, we wouldn't get out of here for two or three more days. That's another way we save time, having our supplies translated. Orison can keep cooking for us long after we're gone.'

Getting as much information as he could, Geraden inquired, 'How's the Tor?'

'His physician says he should stay in bed. But he's got more guts than the rest of us put together.' Ribuld chuckled. 'He's up yelling at everybody.'

A sudden thought alarmed Terisa. 'He's staying here, isn't he? Somebody has to defend Orison. And he's in no condition to ride a horse.'

Deliberately, Ribuld continued not meeting her gaze. '*You* tell him that, my lady. Ever since Lebbick took my hide off for saving you from Gart without orders, I've given up arguing with lords and Castellans.'

Geraden's features seemed to grow sharper. 'Who's he going to leave in command?'

Ribuld shrugged. 'Better ask him yourself. That way, he'll end up yelling at you instead of me.'

Geraden looked at Terisa hard. 'I don't think I like the way this is starting to sound.'

'Come on.' She moved toward the door. 'Let's go see him.'

Geraden followed her with his sword dangling against his hip as if he had no idea what it was for.

Ribuld brought up the rear, brandishing his scar cheerfully.

Outside the peacock rooms, four more guards joined them, an escort to protect them from Master Eremis' unpredictable resources – creatures of Imagery, the High King's Monomach, flat mirrors. Terisa found, however, that she wasn't particularly concerned about a surprise attack here. If that was what Eremis wanted, he could have done it at any time. She felt sure that his real intentions were considerably nastier.

And she was worried about the Tor—

When she and Geraden reached the King's formal apartment, she noticed the fire blazing in the hearth. Apparently, the lord of Tor felt the cold as badly as she did.

There were four men already in the room: the Tor himself, Castellan

Norge, Master Barsonage, and Artagel. Norge stood with his back to one wall, casually at attention: he looked like a man who never needed sleep because he was always napping. In contrast, Master Barsonage seemed to be actually wringing his hands; he faced the Tor and Artagel alternately with a discomfited expression, as if he wanted to intervene but didn't know what to say.

The Tor and Artagel confronted each other like combatants. The old lord thrust his belly forward assertively; his cheeks were red with wine or exertion. Artagel stood in a fighter's balanced stance, his hands ready to go for either his longsword or his dagger.

As Terisa and Geraden entered the room, Artagel turned toward them. His grin twisted her stomach. He looked primed for battle, as fatal as his weapons – and yet in some way lost, like a man who needed help he wasn't going to get against impossible odds.

'Just in time,' he said, denying the Tor the bare courtesy of a chance to speak first. 'My lord Tor is a bit confused this morning. He doesn't realize I'm your bodyguard. You better tell him. I'm your *personal* bodyguard.'

Master Barsonage cast an unhappy look at Terisa and Geraden, then retreated to give them room in front of the Tor and Artagel.

'Artagel,' the Tor rumbled to them as if he were on the verge of an outburst, 'refuses a direct command. He refuses to obey me.'

Terisa looked at Geraden, baffled by the hostility in the room and the knot in her stomach. Geraden's gaze shifted to Artagel, then back to the Tor. 'Don't tell me, my lord Tor,' he said with a bitterness of his own. 'Let me guess. You want him to stay here.'

'I want him' – the Tor contained himself with difficulty – 'to rule Orison in my absence.'

Rule Orison—?

Artagel snarled an obscenity. 'It comes to the same thing. He thinks I'm a cripple.'

Terisa stared at him, at the Tor; she was simultaneously surprised, relieved, and appalled. The idea of putting Artagel in charge of Orison had never occurred to her.

'No!' the Tor retorted, almost retching, 'it does not come to the same thing. I do not ask you to remain behind because you are unfit to go. I command you to stay here because you are needed!

'I must leave Orison with less than two thousand men to defend it. And I have no alliance with the Alend Monarch. He will let us depart, of that I am sure. But when we are gone, he will not hesitate to renew his siege. Prince Kragen considers this castle to be the best safety available.

'If Orison is not defended – *well* defended – it will be lost.'

Artagel was in no condition for fighting. And yet the cost of having to stay behind – the price he would pay for remaining in Orison while Mordant's fate was decided without him – would be severe.

'After King Joyse,' the Tor concluded, 'you are the only man who can hope to hold these walls against the Alend army.'

'How?' Artagel snapped back. 'I don't have any authority. I don't even belong to the guard. I've never been able to take orders. How do you expect me to give them?'

'By being who you are,' the Tor answered heavily. 'The best-liked man in Orison.'

The old lord was right, Terisa thought. The guards would fight to the death for Artagel, of course. But so would half the population of the castle. He was the best swordsman in Mordant; his feats were legendary. And he was a son of the Domne. By simple likability, he might be able to rule Orison even more effectively than Castellan Lebbick.

Cursing, Artagel returned to his brother. 'Tell him,' he demanded. 'I'm going with you. You need me. When you go up against Eremis, you'll need somebody to watch your back. I want—'

The look on Geraden's face stopped him.

'You want to try Gart again,' Geraden said softly, 'is that it?'

Anger and distress pulled Artagel's expression in several directions at once.

'With muscles in your side that haven't finished healing?' Geraden continued: soft; relentless. 'You want to tackle a man who's already beaten you twice, when you can't even lift that sword without a twinge?'

Artagel flinched in helpless fury or frustration; he took a step backward. 'I'm coming with you somehow,' he said between his teeth. 'I won't stay here.'

'Yes, you will,' rasped the Tor. 'You may succeed in refusing to obey me, but I assure you that you will stay here.'

Artagel flung a glare like a challenge at the old lord. 'Are you going to make me, my lord Tor?'

'No, Artagel. *I* will not "make" you. Norge will do that. He will support me in this.'

From his place against the wall, the new Castellan nodded amiably. His bland calm was more convincing than a shout.

'Your choices,' the Tor finished, 'are to remain in command of Orison – or to remain in the dungeon.'

Artagel studied the Tor and Norge; he directed a last appeal at Geraden.

In response, Geraden muttered miserably, 'Don't you understand, you halfwit? You're too valuable to waste on a senseless contest with Gart. The Tor wants you to do the hardest job there is. King Joyse needs someplace to come back to. If everything else fails, he needs a castle and some men for the last defense of Mordant. He needs someone to give him that. He can't do it for himself. He needs someone like you, who can make old men and serving girls and children fight for him just by smiling at them.'

For a moment, Terisa feared that Artagel would break out in protest, do something wild. He was a fighter, by temperament and training unsuited to sit still for sieges. But then his face took on a smile she had never seen before – a grimace bloodier and more bitter than his fighting grin; a look that chilled her heart.

To Norge, he said, 'I want Lebbick's mail – I want all the things he was wearing when Gart got him. I want his insignia – his sash and that headband. The more blood on them, the better. Anybody who looks at me is *by the stars* going to know what I stand for.'

Norge glanced at the Tor. The Tor nodded; his eyes were glazed with pain. Phlegmatically, Norge said, 'Come,' and left the wall.

Artagel didn't look at either Geraden or Terisa as he followed the new Castellan out of the room.

Simply because she hated to see Artagel hurt like that, she groaned to herself. But what was the use of being upset? The Tor had found a better answer to Orison's problem – and to Artagel's – than she had been able to imagine for herself. Geraden had told his brother the truth. She could understand how Artagel felt – but so what? He—

'You also, my lady,' the Tor said as if he had boulders rolling around in his gut, 'will remain here.'

What—?

She looked around her. Geraden was gaping at the old lord, frankly dumbfounded. Master Barsonage's expression was white with consternation.

She had heard right. The Tor intended to leave her in Orison.

Which was why Ribuld hadn't brought any protective clothing or weapons for her. And why he had evaded her eyes, her inquiries. Of course.

Unexpectedly calm, she faced the lord. Her gaze was steady; even her pulse didn't flutter. Geraden started to speak for her; but when he noticed her demeanor, he bit his mouth closed. 'My lord Tor,' she said gently, as if he were as mad as Havelock, unable to be questioned, 'you don't want me to go with you.'

The tone of her reaction seemed to weaken his resolve. Speaking loudly in an apparent effort to shore up his position, he retorted, 'You are a woman.'

Because he had raised his voice, she lowered hers. 'And that makes a difference to you.'

'I am the lord of the Care of Tor.' His face grew redder, goaded toward passion by the fact that she wasn't yelling at him. 'And I am the King's chancellor in Orison. His honor is in my hands, as is my own. You are a *woman*.'

Deliberately rejecting sarcasm, she replied quietly, 'Please be plain, my lord Tor. I want to understand you.'

As if she were driving him to distraction, he shouted, 'By the heavens, my lady, *I do not take women into battle!*'

In spite of her determination to be kind, Terisa smiled. 'Then don't think of me as a woman, my lord. Think of me as an Imager. Ask Master Barsonage. He offered to make me a Master. I'm not going with you. I'm going with the Congery.'

The Tor took a deep breath, preparing to bellow.

At once, Master Barsonage put in, 'My lady Terisa is quite correct, my lord Tor,' speaking in the most placating voice he could manage. 'You have not forgotten that she is an Imager – in effect, a member of the Congery. It is possible that she is the most powerful Imager we have ever known. I do not believe that we can confront Master Eremis and Master Gilbur and the arch-Imager Vagel without her.'

Livid with anger – or perhaps with the pain of holding his damaged belly upright – the Tor demanded, '*Do you defy me, mediator?*'

Master Barsonage spread his hands. 'Of course not, my lord Tor. I merely observe that the lady Terisa is a question which belongs to the Congery. Regardless of the role we assign to her in the support of Orison and Mordant, she casts no aspersion on your honor – or the King's.'

Carefully, Geraden commented, 'And King Joyse doesn't hesitate to use women when he needs them. Adept Havelock told us last night that King Joyse knew years ago the lady Elega and Prince Kragen would become lovers. He consented to his own betrayal – he practically drove her into the Prince's arms. I don't think the Prince would ever have let Terisa and me into Orison if she hadn't been there. And she may do other things for us yet.

'My lord Tor, we need Terisa with us.'

The Tor looked back and forth between Master Barsonage and Geraden, his eyes swollen and baleful as a pig's. His face was crimson with stress.

Nevertheless he acquiesced.

Slowly, he slumped into a chair; his hands made weak gestures of dismissal. Terisa had to remind herself that she wasn't his only – or even his primary – reason for appearing so defeated. 'Leave me,' he muttered. 'We march at full dawn. I must have a moment's peace.'

She felt that somebody ought to stay with him. He seemed to be in need of comforting. He had suffered so long, and to so little purpose. From the day when he had arrived in Orison with his eldest son dead in his arms until now, he had been groping like a doomed man, struggling against his own heart and King Joyse's machinations for some way to heal his grief. Surely there were things he needed more than 'a moment's peace.'

But Master Barsonage moved to leave, and Geraden put a hand on her arm, urging her toward the door. 'Come on,' he breathed, 'before he changes his mind.'

Dumbly, she accompanied Geraden and the mediator.

Outside, trying to articulate her own sorrow, she said, 'Gart must have hurt him pretty badly. He doesn't look like he can stay on his feet much longer.'

Away from the Tor, Geraden's expression turned bleak, unconsoled. 'That doesn't matter. King Joyse hurt him worse than Gart did.' To Master Barsonage, he explained, 'Artagel told us the Tor spent most of the time we were away blind drunk.'

The mediator nodded grimly.

'What's holding him together,' Geraden continued, 'is feeling needed. As long as he knows he's necessary, he can stand being kicked. That's why it hurts him so much when we argue with him – even when he's wrong. He hasn't got the strength or the resolution or the *hope* left to survive doubting himself.'

Terisa hugged Geraden's hand where it held her arm; she was grateful that he understood.

Master Barsonage thought for a while as they descended from the King's tower. Then, speaking wryly as if to distance himself from what he felt, he said, 'I, on the other hand, have a passion for doubt. I cannot resist it. That is why I try to surround myself with so much solidity.' He made a mocking reference to his girth. 'Is he right, do you think? Are you certain of what we do? Are we on the path King Joyse would have chosen for us, if he were here?'

'And if we are,' Geraden growled, at least partially serious, 'did King Joyse know what he was doing? Did he ever know what he was doing? Do any of us have even the vaguest conception of the consequences of our actions?

'No, I'm sorry, Master Barsonage. I don't have any wisdom for you. We're doing the only thing that makes sense to me.'

Terisa nodded once, grimly.

The mediator sighed. 'We must be content with that, I suppose.'

More quickly than the circumstances required, they moved downward. The air took on a sharper edge as they neared one of the main public exits to the courtyard. No question about it, Mordant was having a late freeze. Terisa's breath began steaming well before she reached the high doorway. She could feel cold prickling along her scalp like an omen of some kind.

The halls of Orison had been nearly deserted; but there was nothing deserted about the courtyard. She could hear shouts and movement, hundreds – no, thousands – of boots hurrying in different directions. And from the doorway she saw a dark, torchlit seething of men and horses, as troubled in the early gloom as the contents of a witch's cauldron, brewed for destruction and bloodshed. From the cavernous stables under Orison, horses by the score had been led into the courtyard and readied for mounting. And more torches lit the passage which led like a throat down to the stables; in the passage more horses crowded, with more behind them. Most of the mounts were already tended by the men who would ride them, the men whose lives might depend on them.

And around the inner walls of the castle, around Orison's benighted inward face, the guards who would travel on foot were gathering in squads and platoons; ordinary individuals uprooted from their lives in order to endure a forced march for three days so that they could be hurled against an army which outnumbered them nearly four-to-one. And for what? Well, Terisa knew the answer to that. So that men like Master Eremis and High King Festten wouldn't have their way with the innocent of Mordant. To say such things, however, she had to believe that what the Congery and the guard, what she and Geraden were doing might work.

Failure meant *annihilation*. For all these people.

Clutching her coat against the cold, she followed Master Barsonage and Geraden, with Ribuld behind her, across the ice-crusted mud among the horses to the place near Orison's gates where the Congery assembled with its beasts and wagons.

The Masters nodded and muttered to the mediator. Some of them greeted Geraden with salutations or smiles which seemed sincere in the erratic light of the torches; others were too embarrassed by their old scorn for him to say anything; one or two of them made it clear that they still didn't believe what they had heard about his demonstrations of power. They all, however, acknowledged Terisa with as much courtesy as the circumstances allowed. Then they went back to the job of securing their cargo in the wagons.

She counted nine large bundles as big as crates: the Congery's mirrors. Each glass had been wrapped in blankets, then lashed into a protective wooden frame, then wrapped in more blankets and tied tightly before being bound to the side of the wagon. And the wagons themselves were unusual: a new bed had been built to fit on padded supports inside each of the original ones, so that over particularly rough terrain the new bed holding the mirrors could be lifted out and carried by men on foot.

Wiggling her toes against the cold that seeped into her boots, Terisa looked up at the sky.

It was gray with dawn, and cloudless, at once translucent and obscure, like a mirror on which cobwebs and dust had accumulated for years.

The march would begin soon.

Curse this freeze. Yesterday she was ready to set out on a moment's notice. But today, in the cold – She wondered if anyone was ever truly ready.

More men. More horses. Shouts rang hoarsely off the walls: questions; commands; messages. The bazaar was crowded with guards and their mounts. Gart had attacked her there once; Prince Kragen had used the bazaar to cover his meetings with Nyle. Now, at least temporarily, the whole place was unfit for business. But of course it had probably been unfit for days, cut off by the siege from any way to replenish its wares.

Grooms led horses forward for Terisa and Geraden. She glared suspiciously at the colorless old nag assigned to her, a beast clearly too decrepit for any rider except one who didn't know what she was doing. Geraden's mount, in contrast, was a spirited gelding with an odd white spot like a target on either side of its barrel.

Seeing her expression, he asked teasingly, 'Want to trade?'

'This thing's almost dead already,' she snorted. 'After what we've already been through, I think I could ride a firecat.'

Ribuld grinned around his scar.

But she didn't want to trade. She had an instinctive sense that she was in danger of overestimating her abilities.

As full dawn approached, and the level of noise in the courtyard increased, lights began to show in the windows around Orison's inner face – children dragging their parents out of bed to see what was happening; lords or ladies rousing themselves to witness events; wives and children and loved ones wanting some way to say goodbye to the guards.

By stages Terisa couldn't measure, the turmoil of men and horses seemed to resolve itself. More and more guards climbed onto their beasts. The Masters began to mount – except for those who intended to drive the wagons, or to ride on them to watch over the mirrors. The frost from the horses' nostrils was gray now, as pearly as mist, lit by the dawn rather than by torches. Geraden nudged Terisa's arm, indicated the horses; but she didn't move until she saw the Tor emerge from one of the main doors and waddle toward his charger.

She mounted when he did.

Slowly, accompanied by his personal guard – the men who had come with him from his Care – as well as by the Castellan Norge and Artagel, he rode to the gates so that when they were raised he would be the first to face the Alend army, the first to face the march. For some reason, his black cloak and hood – the mourning garb which he had worn to bring his son to Orison – made him appear smaller. Or maybe her horseback perspective deemphasized his bulk.

823

He didn't look large enough to take King Joyse's place, imposing enough to threaten King Joyse's enemies.

Yet when he lifted his voice he lifted her heart as well, like the remembered call of horns.

'It is a dangerous thing we do.' Somehow, the old lord made his words carry across the courtyard, made them echo around the face of Orison. 'Barely six thousand of us go to meet Cadwal and vile Imagery on the ground they have chosen for battle. And we will have the Alend army at our backs – if I cannot persuade the Alend Monarch to see reason at last. An attempt may be made to take Orison in our absence. King Joyse is not with us, and the power against us is staggering.

'It is a *dangerous* thing we do.

'*But it is the best we can.*

'The Congery rides with us. We have powers which our enemies cannot suspect. Artagel will preserve Orison for us – and High King Festten is weaker than he knows, helpless to supply his forces by any means which cannot be cut off. King Joyse has planned and labored for years to reach this moment. It will not fail.

'It is a dangerous and *desirable* thing we do. I am proud to take part in it.'

The Tor signalled with one hand. At once, the castle's trumpeter blew a fanfare which echoed against the walls, rang into the sky. Groaning, the great winches began to crank the gate open.

While the gate went up, the Tor pulled his charger around to face the opening and the future as if he had never been afraid in his life.

Artagel withdrew. Castellan Norge called the guard to order.

When the gate was up, the trumpeter sounded another fanfare.

With the Congery and six thousand men behind him, the Tor rode out of Orison.

FORTY-FIVE

THE ALEND
MONARCH'S GAMBLE

Out in the dawn, the Alend army waited.

Prince Kragen had withdrawn all his forces – his patrols and scouts, his siege engines, his battering rams – to the great circle of his encampment. Beyond the gates, none of his men came closer than the tree-lined roads from Tor and Perdon and Armigite. But his foot soldiers stood ready, holding their weapons. His mounted troops were on their horses. Past the intervening guards, past the Tor and Norge, Terisa could see the Alend strength among the trees like a black wall wrapped around the castle.

One of the riders who held the roads was a standard-bearer with the Alend Monarch's green-and-red pennon.

A cold wind came up out of the south, out of Tor, making the pennon flutter and snap like a challenge.

The standard-bearer held no flag of truce.

As always, however, Prince Kragen's men avoided the intersection where the roads came together. This created a gap in the Alend line, as if Kragen intended to let Orison's guard through.

The Tor spoke to Norge; Norge muttered a command Terisa didn't hear. At the head of the guard, King Joyse's plain purple insignia was raised.

Maybe Prince Kragen would think the King had returned.

Maybe he would reconsider.

Terisa gripped her reins with icy hands and prepared to nudge her nag into motion. Geraden held his head up as though he were waiting for sunrise. Ribuld scratched at his scar as if it itched in the chill, an old wound remembering pain.

Snorting steam, shaking their heads, rattling their tack, crunching the crusted mud, the horses began to follow the Tor and Castellan Norge.

Artagel still had his back to the Alends. By holding his mount stationary, he sifted through the vanguard until he was directly in front of Terisa and Geraden – until he came between them, forcing them to stop. As she had feared, he was wearing Lebbick's old, bloody mail over his shirt and leggings,

Lebbick's purple sash and headband. The sword belted to his hip looked so dark and grim that it must have belonged to the dead Castellan.

When he was dressed like that, she was afraid of what he might do.

At the moment, however, he didn't do anything fearful. He clasped his brother's shoulder; without quite managing to smile, he said, 'Take care of yourself. Take care of her. Rescue Nyle. This family has already suffered enough.'

Geraden replied with a grin that looked like it belonged to Artagel.

Artagel turned to Terisa. Striving to appear ready and whole – perhaps for her benefit, perhaps for his own – he said stiffly, 'Don't make a liar out of me now, my lady.'

'A liar—' she repeated as if the cold numbed her mouth. She had no idea what he was talking about.

'I've told half the men and women in Orison you can shift Eremis' mirrors so they won't translate here.' He watched her, studied her, like a man who didn't want to get caught pleading. 'The Tor is heading straight for the place where the Perdon and his men were attacked.'

Terisa thought her heart was going to stop.

The mirror which had brought those ravening black spots down on the Perdon and his men out of nowhere— Shapes no bigger than puppies, and yet as fatal as wolves—

She had forgotten it. Forgotten, forgotten.

Geraden winced. 'Terisa—' he started to say. 'Terisa—'

'Stop him,' she said, gasping gouts of steam. '*Stop him*. I need time to think.'

Instantly, Artagel wheeled his mount and plunged through the press of horses, chasing after the Tor.

—gnarled, round shapes with four limbs outstretched like grappling hooks and terrible jaws that occupied more than half the body—

The idea shocked her to the marrow, revolted her. The same creatures had attacked her and Geraden outside Sternwall – but that was different; then they had attacked completely by surprise, without time for panic or nausea. This time— The Tor and Castellan Norge were effectively defenseless. If they met Prince Kragen in the intersection, all the leaders of the armies could be struck at once. How had she *forgotten*?

Artagel had told everyone that she could *shift Eremis' mirrors*.

Outside the gates, Artagel caught up with the Tor and Norge, spoke to them urgently. Master Barsonage brought his horse up between Terisa and Geraden. 'What is amiss?' he asked. 'I was unable to hear.'

Geraden overrode the mediator. 'Why hasn't he used it already? If he still has that mirror set up – if it's ready – why hasn't he used it before this? He could bring anything through. Even if he didn't hurt us, he could cripple the Alends, maybe even kill Prince Kragen – or the Alend Monarch.'

'Because he didn't need it then.' Terisa wasn't thinking about what she said; the words seemed to come out by themselves, reasoned into clarity by a separate part of her mind. 'He needed time to set his traps, time to spring them. He needed time to get Festten's army in position, time to get rid of the Perdon, time to make all his mirrors.' The rest of her brain blundered helplessly around the edges of the promise Artagel had made in her name. 'But we let him do all that safely. Prince Kragen held off – he *held off* from trying to take Orison. Nobody interfered with what Eremis was doing. So he didn't need to use this mirror. He could afford to leave Alend alone.'

Geraden nodded harshly. 'I understand. *Now* it's time. *Now* he needs it. We're moving. His traps are ready. He's got everything he wanted except you. He can't beat us with just one mirror. Even a few hundred of those black spots can't beat an army this size. An avalanche can't. Firecats can't. But if he can hurt us now – if he can kill the Tor, or Norge, or Prince Kragen – he can damage us terribly.'

'Then we will foil him simply,' put in Master Barsonage. 'We will turn from the road. We will pass outside his mirror's range of focus.'

Geraden nodded again, rose up in his stirrups to shout to Artagel. But Terisa said at once, 'No!'

Master Barsonage and Geraden stared at her.

No. Oh, curse it. What was she *thinking*? This was insane.

'Artagel told everyone I can shift Eremis' mirrors.' But that wasn't what she meant to say, that wasn't the point. She tried again. 'This is a trap. We need to stick our heads in it. We need to spring it the other way. Isn't that why we're marching in the first place? Isn't that what we decided?'

Ahead of the guard, the Tor and Norge had stopped. Artagel had finished explaining what was on his mind. In the gray dawn, the Tor looked strangely sunken, irresolute, as if he were torn between the desire to flee and the necessity of marching. Kicking his mount, Artagel started back toward Terisa and Geraden.

'Eremis wants to scare us,' she said while her thoughts throbbed like her heart. 'He wants to make us doubt ourselves.

'We should try doing the same thing to him.'

'What do you mean, my lady?' asked Master Barsonage, nearly whispering.

'She means,' Geraden snarled back as though she appalled him, 'she thinks she ought to do it. Stick her head in the trap.' He had to swallow fiercely to clear his throat. 'Shift Eremis' mirror so he can't use it.'

'Impossible,' protested the mediator. 'Is it not true that she has never seen the mirror which shows the place where those fatal creatures are found? And how can we be sure that Master Eremis does not intend to translate some other evil against us? And—?'

'Not that mirror,' Geraden snapped, controlling his alarm with anger. 'The flat one. The one that shows the intersection.

'No.' Now he was speaking to Terisa, speaking so intensely that his words seemed to burn. 'What makes it impossible is the vantage, the direction. We know what the Image is, but we don't know what side it's seen from, what the perspective is. You can't shift an Image if you can't identify it first, see it exactly in your mind.'

He was saying, Don't do this, *don't do this.*

'I've got to try.' As if that were an explanation, she said, 'Artagel promised.' But the stricken look on Geraden's face demanded better. She made another effort. 'I don't really know how far my talent goes. I haven't had very many chances to explore it. We're counting on the idea that I have power we can use, but we don't really know what we're counting on. And the closer we get to Esmerel, the more dangerous everything is. I've got to try.'

Geraden clearly wanted to argue, shout. Deliberately, she went on, 'We're staking everything on the hope that King Joyse didn't abandon us. He *trusted* us – he *trusts* us to make his plans work while he's away.' She had the distinct impression that she was completely out of her mind. 'If we aren't going to at least make the attempt, we might as well stay here.'

For one painful moment, Geraden's expression turned to bleak, bitter iron. But then his lips pulled back into a fighting grimace. 'I'm coming with you.'

'No, you aren't,' Terisa countered before Master Barsonage could object. 'We can't afford to risk both of us.'

'If you think I'm going to let you do this alone—' Geraden began.

She wasn't listening to him: she had already hauled on her reins, dug her heels into the nag's sides. As if she were unaware of her own quickness and had never considered the possibility that she wouldn't be obeyed, she commanded, 'Stop him, Ribuld. Keep him here,' and started to forge among the riders toward Artagel, the Tor, and Castellan Norge.

Ribuld caught Geraden by the strap of his swordbelt and neatly plucked him off his horse. While Geraden sputtered in outrage, Ribuld wrestled with him. Geraden was tougher than he appeared, nearly frantic as well: he managed to unseat Ribuld. They fell together into the mud. But Geraden couldn't break away.

Terisa reached Artagel.

'I need protection,' she panted; her own strange audacity took her breath away. 'Eremis won't miss a chance to attack when he sees me in his mirror. Somebody's got to keep me alive so I can work.'

Artagel's excitement shone as brightly as Geraden's frenzy. Calling men after him, he wheeled his mount and began clearing a path for her.

They reached the Tor and Norge and rode past with six more guards behind them, hurrying now so that she wouldn't have time to lose her nerve – so that she wouldn't be infected by the Tor's slumped irresolution.

While she rushed toward the intersection, she tried to clear her mind, make herself ready.

This decisive urgency was different than the rage which sometimes blocked her. It was full of fear – and fear lead to fading – and fading led to translation. The first thing she needed was an alternative Image, a place she could shift Eremis' glass to. As soon as she recognized that necessity, however, her mind filled up with scenes which couldn't bear attack: the Closed Fist; rooms and halls in Orison; Sternwall; Vale House. She had to thrust them away, get them out of her thoughts before she did something terrible unintentionally. If only she had seen any part of Esmerel accurately, she could have used it – or tried to use it – to hurl Eremis' attack back against him.

He had cleverly avoided that danger.

Was his foresight really that good? Was he ready for her now?

A squad of Alend horse rode into the intersection, intending either to meet or to stop her. Artagel stretched his mount a few strides ahead and began yelling at the Alends, warning them away. She caught a glimpse of Prince Kragen, saw him react without hesitation, shout his men back.

Around her, the trees seemed to skid into focus past the bare ground leading from Orison. She had only been here on one previous occasion: the day Geraden had caught Nyle, dooming him to Master Eremis. And the ground then had been still covered with snow, the trees still black, leafless. And beyond the intersection had been cold, ice-caked snow, not an army of Alends.

Sawing inexpertly on the reins, she brought her horse to a halt. At once, Artagel and his companions formed a defensive cordon around her; instinctively, they faced the Alends with their swords drawn, as if the danger came from Prince Kragen's soldiers.

Her pulse straining and her head giddy, she did her best to ignore the men, the horses, the swords. A number of the Alends sat their mounts with their spears levelled – *ignore* that. She needed *time*, time to see the place vividly as it was now, time to consider it from as many different angles as possible; time to prepare herself for the Image which had to be shifted.

Unfortunately, her enemies weren't stupid. And her disappearance from Eremis' cell had given them at least a hint of her true talents. Either she had effected her escape herself, or she possessed some kind of link with Geraden which had enabled him to locate and translate her in the dark. In either case, she was a dangerous opponent.

Before she had a chance to calm herself, before she finished turning wildly, trying to see the intersection from every side at once, before she knew what she was going to do, *a touch of cold as thin as a feather and as sharp as steel slid straight through the center of her abdomen—*

—and a black shape full of teeth came down on the shoulders of one of the guards.

With a single, tearing bite, it ripped out the base of his neck.

By the time his body toppled to the ground, the creature had already gobbled its way into his chest.

More shapes: five, ten, fifteen. Shouts hit the trees. Swords flared in the cold sunrise. Prince Kragen and a dozen Alends charged into the fray. Artagel seemed to be dancing on the back of his mount, pirouetting, as he slashed an attacker out of the air above Terisa's head. Then he dove at her, carried her off her horse to the ground where he could control her movements, keep his sword between her and the creatures.

And still through the chaos of whirling vision, whirling blades, of horses and teeth and blood, she felt that *touch of cold* as the mirror stayed open, the translation continued, launching black raveners at her as fast as they could come.

She tried to use the sensation, cling to it, make it lead her to its Image; she had to see that Image in her mind before she could change it. But it eluded her.

Geraden was right. It was impossible.

Another guard went down. All the guards seemed to be down, with gnarled shapes no bigger than puppies feasting on them. But some of them must have been Alends, because she had guards around her yet, protecting her like Artagel, hacking their swords madly at the open air.

Artagel had to fling her aside, had to use both hands on his sword in order to cut away three beasts at once. The catch in his side slowed him, nearly cost him his life. With a wrench of effort and pain, he hauled his blade around.

She sprawled toward the hooves of a panicked horse. That *touch of cold* was driven through the center of her belly like a spike, nailing her to the ground. She was so afraid that she forgot everything – forgot to dodge the horse, the creatures, forgot to ward herself – forgot everything except the feather-and-steel sensation of Eremis' glass.

There she found it: on the edge of fading, the verge of the blind dark. *Above* her – higher than her own vantage. That was how it had eluded her: she hadn't taken into account the way the black shapes came *down* onto her defenders.

As if she were leaping up inside herself, carrying the cold of translation with her, she looked into its moment of temporary eternity, its flat abyss, and saw the Image.

She saw the bloodied ground from nearly fifteen feet in the air, saw the frantic and squealing horses, saw her defenders, the corpses, the dead or feeding creatures—

Fast and hard, desperately, like slamming a door, she turned what she saw opaque, gave it an Image as blank as frosted glass.

Inside her, the *touch of cold* snapped and vanished as if she had shattered something.

At the same instant, the rush of gnarled bodies and teeth was cut off. In fact, it was cut off in midcreature. Two of the beasts flopped to the ground without the rest of their bodies: they had been sliced in half as neatly as with a cleaver.

The attack was over.

'Terisa,' Artagel gasped, 'my lady.' He got his hands under her arms, lifted her to her feet. 'Are you all right?'

'I think I broke it.' She couldn't find a point of balance anywhere in the intersection. The ground tilted; men veered from side to side; Artagel's face swam in and out of view. She had no idea how she was able to speak, when it was obvious that she had lost the ability to breathe or think or hold up her head. 'The mirror. I think we're safe.'

Prince Kragen appeared: he seemed to heave over the horizon from somewhere far away. 'You like risks, my lady,' he said through his teeth. 'I have lost seven men.'

'And Eremis lost a mirror,' Artagel retorted over his shoulder, panting and angry. 'Maybe *you* don't like the trade, but *he's* going to think hard before he tries it again. My lord Prince.'

Terisa had no attention to spare for Kragen. Clinging to Artagel, she asked, 'How many did we lose?'

He looked around. 'Three.'

Three. Ten men altogether. Ten men dead because she took a risk she didn't know how to handle, *ten*. And if she hadn't finally shifted the mirror when she did, the carnage would have been worse. Maybe much worse. Because she took the risk—

Trembling like a child, she sank to the ground and clamped her hands over her face to shut out the sight of death.

Artagel stood over her and glared at Prince Kragen as if daring the Prince to blame her for anything. When Kragen shrugged and withdrew, Artagel sent his guards back to Orison. 'Tell my lord Tor the intersection is safe. And tell Geraden she's all right. She broke the mirror.'

Terisa didn't hear the men leave.

'My lady,' Artagel said thickly, 'you did the right thing. If we only lose ten men for every mirror Eremis has, he doesn't stand a chance.'

She couldn't raise her head, even for Artagel.

What about High King Festten and his twenty thousand Cadwals?

The Tor and Norge and their escort were the first riders to arrive from Orison. The Tor didn't dismount – maybe he couldn't, and still be sure of being able to get back up on his horse. But he addressed her in a voice she remembered, a voice with cunning and resolution hidden in its subterranean rumble.

'My lady Terisa of Morgan, it would have been a grave mistake if I had required you to remain behind.'

She tried to nod without looking up. Apparently, he had recovered some measure of assurance. She had accomplished that, if nothing else: she had given the old lord a bit of hope by demonstrating that it was possible to fight Eremis' Imagery.

Then Geraden reached her. Muddy and bedraggled, almost delirious with anger and relief, he flung himself off his mount in front of her as if he meant to snatch her from the ground. Instead of picking her up, however, he hunkered down to her, gripped her shoulders hard, shook her gently. 'Don't ever do that to me again,' he demanded. 'Don't you *dare*. Can't you get it through your thick skull that I love you? We're *together* in this. I'd rather walk through fire until I drop than be a spectator while you live or die.'

Oh, Geraden.

She put out her arms to him, and he caught her in a fierce hug. 'Together,' she murmured so that he wouldn't let her go. 'I promise.'

After a while, he helped her to her feet.

Until she wiped her eyes and looked around, she didn't realize that all the forces of Orison and Alend were waiting for her.

Prince Kragen was there, mounted before the Tor, with a new squad of men behind him. Artagel had gone back to his duty in Orison; but Castellan Norge and his escort supported the Tor, with a road full of guards issuing from the castle at his back. The old lord faced Prince Kragen squarely; however, the Prince didn't speak until Terisa met his gaze.

To her surprise, she saw unmistakably that some conflict in him had been resolved. The clenched bitterness, the suggestion of savagery, was gone from his expression; his black eyes shone with excitement. She had no idea what decision he had achieved – but she could see beyond question that he liked it.

After holding her gaze for a moment, he turned to the Tor.

'Should I conclude from this display of force, my lord Tor,' he asked acerbically, 'that your intention to march against High King Festten and Master Eremis in Esmerel is unchanged?'

'Assuredly, my lord Prince,' the Tor replied in a corresponding tone. 'If I had the slightest desire to do battle with you, I would not go about it in this fashion.'

Kragen indicated the purple pennon. 'Has King Joyse returned?'

'He has not.'

'In that case' – Prince Kragen straightened his shoulders – 'the Alend Monarch wishes to speak with you. He asks you to accept the hospitality of his tent, with Geraden, the lady Terisa, and Master Barsonage – and Castellan Norge, of course.'

Terisa and Geraden stared. Norge clenched his jaws as if he were stifling a yawn. The Tor's eyes showed an undisguised gleam of hope. Nevertheless he didn't ask what Margonal wanted to talk about. Instead, he inquired firmly, 'What guarantee of safety does the Alend Monarch offer us? As his guests, we will be deeply honored – and completely vulnerable.'

Prince Kragen shrugged slightly. 'My lord Tor, the Alend Monarch is a man of honor. He neither insults nor betrays his guests. On this occasion, however, he is prepared to match your vulnerability with his own. You may bring with you a hundred horsemen, who will be permitted to surround his tent. Surely no treachery on our part will succeed at killing a hundred men before they can threaten or kill the Alend Monarch himself.'

'A remarkable gesture,' Master Barsonage whispered to Terisa and Geraden. 'The Alend Monarch is not notoriously complaisant about hazards to his person. Perhaps there is hope for an alliance yet.'

Terisa and Geraden didn't reply. They were waiting to hear what the Tor would say.

'My lord Prince,' drawled the old lord as if nothing surprised him, 'the Alend Monarch is unexpectedly considerate. I am prepared to rely on his honor entirely. I will accompany you at once, with Master Geraden and the lady Terisa of Morgan.'

The Tor held up his hand to forestall movement. 'Castellan Norge will remain among his men – as will the mediator of the Congery. They will keep their strength ready to march at the earliest possible moment.'

Norge nodded amiably. Master Barsonage started to object, but subsided at once. The point of the Tor's decision was obvious: if the old lord was betrayed, most of Orison's fighting force would remain intact.

Prince Kragen permitted himself a bleak smile. 'As you wish, my lord Tor.' With a look toward Terisa and Geraden, he asked, 'Will you mount and join us?'

Trying not to hurry – trying not to look like people who desperately wanted an alliance – Terisa and Geraden found their horses, swung themselves up, and rode to the Tor's side.

Without discernible anxiety, Castellan Norge withdrew his escort; he retreated a short distance down the road and immediately sorted his men into a defensive shield around the Congery and its wagons. At his orders, what remained of the mounted guard emerged from Orison, fanning out into a formation ready either to commence battle or to resume marching. Then

Norge followed the men on foot, while Master Barsonage told the other Masters what had happened and prepared them for the possibility that they might have to defend themselves.

At the same time, Terisa and Geraden – with Ribuld trailing after them as if he thought no one would notice him – rode beside the Tor and Prince Kragen toward the tent where they had talked with the Prince and Elega less than two days ago.

As they moved, Geraden tried discreetly to wipe some of the mud off his clothing.

Terisa was distantly surprised to discover that her own clothes weren't especially dirty. The mud in the intersection had been frozen hard. And somehow she had escaped all that blood – even the gnarled creatures had died without marking her.

In the open area surrounded by luxurious living tents, the riders dismounted. Refusing the Prince's offer of help, the Tor got down by himself; but he had to hold his breath and hug his gut until his face turned black in order to do it. Gasping thinly, with his legs wedged to keep him upright, he murmured as an explanation, 'My lord Prince, I hope the Alend Monarch does not require his guests to be in good health. The blow I received from the High King's Monomach troubles me' – his face twisted – 'considerably.'

'My lord Tor,' replied the Prince evenly, 'the Alend Monarch will require only that you be seated comfortably, that you enjoy a flagon of wine' – Kragen bowed his guests toward the most sumptuous of the tents – 'and that you consent to see him without light.'

Allowing Terisa, Geraden, and the Tor no opportunity for questions, Prince Kragen approached the tentflaps and told the soldiers on duty to announce him.

Terisa and Geraden glanced at each other; but the Tor ignored both of them. Struggling as if he were up to his thighs in mire, he followed Kragen into the tent.

'Oh, well,' Geraden whispered. He had recovered his sense of humor. 'If we aren't allowed any light, at least I don't have to worry about appearing before the Alend Monarch looking like a pig wallow.'

Terisa wanted to smile for him, but she was too busy trying to control her sense that the defenders of Mordant urgently needed some good to come of this meeting with the Alend Monarch.

They entered the tent behind the Tor.

Ribuld tried to go with them. Kragen's soldiers stopped him.

As on the occasion of their previous visit, the fore-tent was illuminated only by braziers which had been set for warmth: apparently, Margonal suffered from an old man's sensitivity to cold. Now, however, Prince Kragen summoned no lamps to augment the glowing embers. In the gloom, slightly tinged with red, the chairs and furnishings were hard to see – imprecise; vaguely suggestive. Tent poles loomed out of the dark like obstacles.

A moment passed before Terisa realized that she and Geraden, the Tor and Prince Kragen weren't alone. Two soldiers held the tentflaps tightly closed. Servants waited around the walls.

And the dark shape of a man sat in a chair across the expanse of the fore-tent.

'My lord Tor.' The voice issuing from the dark shape was old and thin. 'I like courtesy, but I will dispense with it today, so that your march will not be delayed. Yet I must take time to give you my thanks for not bringing the hundred men I offered to permit. Even if I meant you ill – which I do not – your decision made you safe with me. A man of Mordant must be valorous to trust the honor of an Alend.'

'My lord Monarch,' replied the Tor, 'I also like courtesy. It would please me to give you the formal salutations and gratitude which custom and humility suggest. Unfortunately, I have been injured. I confess that I am hardly able to stand. Forgive me, my lord – I must sit.'

Prince Kragen had moved to stand beside his father. From that position, he made a sharp gesture. At once, a servant hurried forward with a broad stool for the Tor.

Groaning involuntarily, the Tor lowered his weight to the seat.

'You are injured, my lord Tor,' said the Alend Monarch, 'and yet you propose a hard march of three days in order to confront High King Festten and his new cabal of Imagers. Is that wise?'

Behind the age in Margonal's voice, Terisa heard another quality. Perhaps because the gloom in the tent gave every shape and tone an ominous cast, she thought that the Alend Monarch sounded haunted; harried by doubt.

He had invited – no, *summoned* – her and Geraden and the Tor here in order to test them in some way. Because he was afraid.

'My lord Monarch' – the Tor seemed to lift his voice by main strength off the floor of his belly – 'I am sincerely unsure that it is wise. King Joyse would never permit me to do such a thing in his place, if he were here to forbid it. But he is not here, and so I determine the nature of my own service to my King.

'The question is not one of wisdom, my lord. It is one of necessity. I go to fight the High King and his Imagers simply because they must be opposed.'

For a moment, no one spoke. Abruptly, Prince Kragen made another gesture. As if a ritual had been correctly completed, servants now came forward with chairs for Terisa and Geraden. Silently, they were urged to seat themselves.

Then a tray was brought around; it held four wine goblets, one each for Terisa, Geraden, and the Tor, one for the Alend Monarch himself. Margonal drank briefly before inviting his guests to do the same.

Prince Kragen abstained as if he were only a servant in his father's presence.

Terisa peered at the Alend Monarch until her temples throbbed, but she couldn't make out any details of his face or posture or clothes. Maybe the braziers weren't intended to warm him after all. He sat as far away from them as possible.

Why did he insist on darkness? What was he hiding – strength or frailty?

'So,' he said without preamble. 'I have heard rumors of violence and Imagery from the intersection.' Strangely, his suddenness didn't convey decision. Speaking quickly only made the note of anxiety in his voice more obvious. 'What transpired there this morning, my lord Tor?'

'An unexpected and hopeful thing, my lord Monarch.' For reasons of his own, the Tor made no effort to project optimism. 'Master Eremis translated vileness against us – and the lady Terisa of Morgan defeated him. Some men were lost defending her,' the old lord added. 'Prince Kragen gallantly aided her, and so some of the men lost were yours, my lord. Yet the attack was turned against our enemies. Across the miles, Master Eremis' mirror was broken.'

The Alend Monarch seemed to be fond of long silences. Eventually, he asked Terisa, 'How was that possible, my lady?'

With difficulty, she forced herself to sound steady. 'I guess I have a talent for flat glass, my lord. If I can see the mirror's Image – see it in my mind – I can make it change.' She spread her hands as if to show the blood on them. 'When I saw the Image Eremis was using, I made it go blank.

'Some of his creatures were caught in translation. I think the stress broke the mirror.'

'An unprecedented display of power,' remarked the Monarch, this time without pausing. 'And you, Master Geraden? Do you also have a talent which this Eremis cannot equal?'

Prince Kragen stood at his father's side without moving, without offering Terisa or Geraden or the Tor any help.

Slowly, Geraden replied, 'My lord Monarch, I can do roughly the same thing with normal mirrors – make them change their Images. But I haven't tried it across distance. I suspect my talent doesn't go that far. I think I have to have the glass in front of me to work with it.'

Again, the Alend Monarch lapsed into silence.

To ease the strain on her vision, Terisa turned her head away, glanced around the tent. Except in the immediate proximity of the braziers, the light was only enough to let her see the servants and soldiers as concentrations of gloom. Like Prince Kragen, they all stood against the walls, waiting for their sovereign's commands—

No. Almost directly behind her, in a corner she couldn't scrutinize without craning her neck ostentatiously – a corner as dark as the spot where Margonal sat – she glimpsed another seated figure. This audience had at least one spectator who was permitted to sit in the Alend Monarch's presence.

'My lord Tor.' Margonal seemed to be making an effort to key his voice to a firmer pitch. 'We are old enemies – although to my recollection most of your personal warfare has been waged against Cadwal rather than Alend. You know enough of my history to understand my caution where King Joyse is concerned.

'Where is he?'

'My lord Monarch?' asked the Tor as if he didn't understand the question – or hadn't expected it to be stated so bluntly.

'King Joyse.' The Monarch's enunciation hinted at anger and fear. 'Where is he?'

The Tor lifted his goblet, took what was for him a modest swig. 'My lord, I do not know.'

Stillness spread out around him. No one moved – and yet Terisa had the impression that every Alend in the tent had gone stiff. Margonal's posture filled the dim air with warnings.

As if the pressure of the silence had become too much for him, the Tor said huskily, 'Please believe me, my lord Monarch. He disappeared without consultation, without explanation. If I knew where he is – or why he has gone there – it is unlikely that I would be before you now. I would prefer to await his return, so that he could preside over our saving or destruction as he saw fit. This war is his doing and his duty, my lord, not mine.'

'Yet surely you speculate,' snapped the Alend Monarch promptly. 'You must have some conception of his actions, some guess as to his purpose.'

Carefully, the Tor replied, 'Does it matter, my lord Monarch? We must do what we do, regardless of his whereabouts – or his reasons.'

'It matters to me.' Margonal's voice conveyed the impression that he was sweating profusely. 'While I have held my Seat in Scarab, he has twice overturned the order of the world, once for peace and prosperity, for an end to bloodshed and the depredations of Imagery, and once for the ruin of everything he has created. He has *power*, that man, the power to plunge all our lives into chaos as surely as he once raised us to peace.

'Where is he?'

Terisa looked at Geraden. She could see him a little better than anyone else; the red tinge on his features made him appear fervid, a little mad – and a little hopeless.

The Tor sighed painfully. 'My lord, my only *guess* is that he has gone somehow in search of Queen Madin.'

Terisa thought that the Alend Monarch was going to fall silent again. Almost at once, however, he retorted, 'And Queen Madin has been abducted by Alends – or by men who appeared to be Alends. What will he do, my lord Tor, when he has rescued her?' Despite its thinness, his voice gathered passion. 'I do not doubt that he will rescue her. That man fails at nothing. And when he has restored her to safety, what will he do?'

As if he were in the presence of an ambush, the Tor answered, 'My lord Monarch, I only *guess* at where King Joyse has gone. Years have passed since I felt able to predict his actions.'

The Alend Monarch shifted suddenly, straightened himself in his chair. 'You have not studied him as I have, my lord Tor. *I* know what he will do. He will fall on me like the hammer of doom!'

Shocked, Terisa peered into the gloom, tried to penetrate it to read Margonal's face. But she could see nothing useful.

'My lord Monarch,' Geraden ventured cautiously, 'those men weren't Alends. Master Eremis admitted as much to the lady Terisa. King Joyse vanished before we could tell him everything we knew. That's a problem. But surely he'll find out the truth for himself. Surely when he's questioned' – tortured? – 'those men, he'll realize why she was taken. To disrupt his plans for Mordant's defense. And drive a wedge between us, so we don't join forces.

'When he comes back – Surely it isn't inevitable that he'll attack you.'

'Master Geraden.' Slowly, Margonal's voice lost its vehemence. 'I am the

836

Alend Monarch, responsible for all my lands and all my people – as well as for a rather unruly union with the Alend Lieges. In my place, would you be prepared to risk your entire kingdom on the naked hope that an apparent madman will recognize the truth – and respect it?'

The Monarch appeared to be shaking his head. To the Tor, he said, 'You wish an alliance. But if I unite my force with yours, I will lose most of my ability to defend myself and my realm. Against King Joyse. And against the possibility that High King Festten will strike behind you when you have left Orison.

'What you wish is impossible.'

Now it was the Tor's turn to be quiet for a long time. When he spoke, he sounded disappointed, even sad – but also untouched, as if nothing the Alend Monarch could do would weaken his determination.

'Then there is no more to be said, my lord. I thank you for the courtesy of this audience. With your permission, we will resume our march.'

The Tor made a move to rise from his seat.

'Why?' the Alend Monarch demanded suddenly, almost desperately. 'Can you deny that King Joyse appears to have gone mad? Can you deny that his purposes and policies have brought you to the verge of destruction? Why do you still serve him?'

For a moment, Terisa thought she sensed a fiery retort rushing up in the old lord, a subterranean blast. When his answer came, it surprised her with its gentleness. He might have been speaking to an old friend.

'My lord, Master Eremis and his Imagery have cost me my eldest son. In time, the High King will cost me all my family. Such men must be opposed.'

Prince Kragen didn't change his stance at all. None of the servants or soldiers moved. The figure seated behind Terisa made no sound. Geraden seemed to be holding his breath.

With a rustle of rich fabric, the Alend Monarch slumped back in his chair.

Thinly, he murmured, 'You are blessed with several sons, my lord Tor. I have but one. And by no act of mine can I assure his accession to my Seat. I must be careful of my risks.'

Then his tone sharpened. 'My lord, we would be safe in Orison. At worst, we would be safer than we are now. It is your fixed in tention to march against Esmerel. What is to prevent us from taking possession of Orison as soon as you are gone?'

Apparently, the Tor had come prepared for that question. 'Adept Havelock,' he replied without hesitation – a bolder bluff than Terisa had expected from him. 'Artagel and two thousand guards. And several thousand men and women who would rather lose their lives than be taken by Alend.'

'I see,' breathed the Alend Monarch as if he were sinking to the floor.

Through the dimness, Terisa barely saw him reach out and touch Prince Kragen's arm.

The Prince made a commanding gesture. At once, servants hurried forward to hold the chairs so that the Tor, Terisa, and Geraden could stand.

The audience was over.

The Tor braced a heavy hand on Geraden's shoulder and started toward the tentflaps.

Terisa turned the other way so that she could take a closer look at the person sitting behind her.

The flare of light as the tentflaps were opened confused her vision momentarily, made her squint, filled the corners of the tent with darkness. Before the soldier at the exit ushered her outward, however, she saw the mute figure in the chair clearly enough to recognize her.

The lady Elega.

At the last moment, Elega met Terisa's gaze deliberately and smiled.

Then Terisa found herself blinking in the cold sunshine outside the tent. The Tor and Geraden were already moving toward the horses.

Prince Kragen didn't emerge from his father's presence to accompany them.

Ribuld brought her nag and offered to help her mount. Apparently, no one had troubled him while he waited with the horses. For no clear reason, the fact that he also was smiling disturbed her. When had the scarred veteran learned to enjoy being alone and unprotected in an enemy camp?

She wanted to tell Geraden and the Tor about Elega – especially Geraden, who might be able to imagine what the lady's silent presence in the Alend Monarch's tent meant. Obviously, however, she had to contain herself until she and her companions had rejoined Orison's army.

The forces under Castellan Norge's command readied themselves to move again. Horsemen corrected their formations; guards on foot strode doggedly out of the castle by the dozens, the hundreds. Terisa's news perplexed and fascinated Geraden; but the Tor and Norge and even Master Barsonage didn't seem particularly interested in it. It changed nothing: they had still lost their last hope of an alliance with Alend. At the Tor's side, Castellan Norge gave the order which set the army in motion, then led it toward the intersection – toward the road which branched south in the direction of the Tor's Care.

Before the Tor and Norge, with Terisa and Geraden, Master Barsonage and the Congery behind them, reached the intersection, they began to receive reports which made them hesitate.

On the far side of Orison, the Alends had started to roll back the perimeter of their siege. Mounted soldiers took to their horses; foot soldiers formed squads.

Like King Joyse's guard, the Alend troops were moving.

Men spat obscenities and curses into the cold wind. Trying to match his Castellan's calm, the Tor asked, 'What do you suppose this means, Norge?'

Impenetrably phlegmatic, Norge shrugged. 'The Prince doesn't want to keep Orison cut off. Not anymore. What's left?

'As soon as we're gone, he's going to hit the gates headlong and drive his whole strength inside as fast as he can.'

The Tor nodded once, stiffly. His lips had a blue color in the chill; Terisa saw them trembling. To himself, he murmured, 'So the Alend Monarch masters Orison at last. And we must let it happen. My King, forgive me.'

Geraden looked like he was chewing a mouthful of glass, but he didn't say anything. Master Barsonage's expression was bleak and grim. Only Ribuld kept grinning, like a man with secret sources of gratification. Terisa didn't have any attention to spare for him, however. She was too busy trying to evaluate the new clarity she had seen in Prince Kragen's face.

Would it make him happy to take Orison?

Would Elega let him be happy about it?

In a mood that resembled defeat, despite Terisa's recent victory, the vanguard of Orison's army passed through the intersection and headed south, toward the Broadwine Ford and the Care of Tor.

Unencumbered by supplies or unnecessary equipment and weapons, they set a brisk pace. Soon the last of the riders were in the intersection; the last of the unmounted guards were emerging from Orison. Southward, the ground rose slightly – not enough to block the sight of the Broadwine from the high towers of the castle, but enough to give the vanguard a view down the length of the army. Now Terisa and everyone with her could see what Prince Kragen's men were doing.

Peeling away from Orison on both sides, they formed themselves into two masses: one larger, which took shape on the road northwest of the intersection; one considerably smaller apparently positioning itself to approach the gates.

The vast number of Alend servants and camp followers had already begun to strike the tents, break down the encampment.

The Prince must have been very sure that he would be settled inside Orison before dark.

Scanning the nausea on the faces of his companions, Ribuld chuckled maliciously.

At the crest of the slow, southward rise, the Tor left Castellan Norge to lead the army. With Terisa, Geraden, Master Barsonage, and a handful of guards, he moved to a vantage off the road from which he could watch the progress of his forces – and the fall of the castle.

'How long can Artagel hold out?' Terisa asked Geraden quietly.

'A lot longer than Prince Kragen thinks,' he replied, biting down hard on each word before he released it. 'He knows how important this is. If he fails, the Prince can cut off our supplies.'

Oh, good, Terisa groaned. Wonderful.

She could feel that her face was red, chafed by the cold. She wished the Tor looked the same, but he didn't. His cheeks were too pale; his mouth and eyes, too blue. He didn't seem to have enough blood left in him to bear what he was about to see.

Or perhaps he did. 'Now, Prince Kragen,' he muttered as the last of the guard reached the intersection and turned south, 'do your worst. Preserve yourself and your father if you can, and remember you were warned that this would never save you.'

While the lord and his companions watched, the smaller mass of the Alend army placed itself across the road in front of Orison's gates, just beyond effective bowshot from the walls.

At the head of the larger body, Prince Kragen rode into the intersection. With his standard-bearer carrying the Alend Monarch's pennon before him, Prince Kragen led at least six and perhaps seven thousand of his soldiers south along the road Orison's army took.

'You knew about this,' Geraden said severely to Ribuld.

Ribuld grinned. 'They shouted a lot of orders while I was waiting for you. I didn't have much trouble figuring out what they meant.'

'And you didn't think it was worth mentioning to us?' demanded Terisa. She wanted to hit the scarred veteran. She also wanted to shout for joy.

Enjoying his own joke, Ribuld replied piously, 'I could have been wrong, my lady. I didn't want to mislead you.'

'They were getting this ready while we talked to the Alend Monarch,' Geraden muttered with fire rising in his eyes. 'The decision was already made.' Which explained the excitement Terisa had seen in Prince Kragen. 'They were just waiting for a final word from Margonal.'

'Then why didn't they tell us?' asked Terisa.

'They don't want an alliance.' Geraden sounded wonderfully sure. 'They want to be ready to help if they think we're right. Prince Kragen *does* think we're right. But they also want to be free to abandon us – or even turn against us – if we're wrong.

'I told you the Prince is an honorable enemy.'

The Tor didn't say anything. While Prince Kragen led his forces up the rise after Orison's army, the old lord sat on his mount with tears in his eyes and a look like a promise on his broad face.

FORTY-SIX

A PLACE
OF DEATH

The wind continued to blow out of the south – not hard now, but steadily, and full of cold, rattling through the trees and along the ground like a rumor of icicles – and Orison's army marched into the teeth of it. The men went almost boisterously at first, when the word was passed down the lines that Prince Kragen and his troops were coming toward Esmerel instead of attacking the castle; then slowly the guards' mood turned grimmer, more painful, as the wind wore down hope, drove both men and horses to duck their heads and brunt a way forward with the tops of their skulls. The unseasonable chill stung the eyes, rubbed at the spots where tack or mail galled the skin; it searched out the gaps in winter cloaks and made the air hurtful for sore lungs and caused earaches. By the time the Tor and his forces had crossed Broadwine Ford and halted to make their first camp, they had lost whatever optimism they had carried with them from the Demesne. Disspirited and worried, the army turned its back on the wind, huddled into itself, and cursed the cold.

The men already looked beaten.

By Castellan Norge's reckoning, however, they had pulled nearly four miles ahead of the Alends.

'That disturbs me,' muttered the Tor while Master Barsonage and the other Imagers chose an open patch of ground and began to unpack their mirrors. 'I do not wish to be separated from the Prince – and I do not wish to wait for him.'

Norge shrugged as if the movement were a twitch in his sleep. 'They're carrying all their food and equipment and bedding and tents – everything they need. They're lucky they can come this close to our pace. If Prince Kragen tries to drive them this fast tomorrow, some of them will start to break.'

'And that will benefit no one,' fretted the Tor. Abruptly, he called, 'Master Barsonage!'

'My lord Tor?' the mediator answered.

'Do I understand correctly? This evening you will translate our necessities from Orison – and tomorrow before we march you will return everything to the castle for the day?'

Master Barsonage nodded. He was impatient to get to work. One of the Congery's three supply-mirrors was his.

The Tor kept him standing for a moment, then said, 'I will wager the Alends carry enough food and water to sustain them for eight or ten days. If their supplies were added to ours, could you manage so much translation?'

That got the mediator's attention. 'My lord, you propose a vast amount of material to be translated. All Imagery is taxing. And we have only three mirrors.'

'I understand,' the Tor replied rather sharply. 'Can you do it?'

Master Barsonage glared at the ground. 'We can make the attempt.'

'Good.' The old lord turned away. 'Castellan Norge.'

'My lord Tor?'

'Send a messenger to my lord Prince. Say that I wish to consult with him – that I wish to consult with him *urgently* – on the subject of his supplies.'

'Yes, my lord.' If Norge had any qualms about the Tor's idea, he didn't show them. Instead, he gave the necessary orders to one of his captains.

Muttering under his breath, Barsonage went back to work.

'He's right, you know,' Geraden commented to Terisa as they hugged their coats and watched the Masters prepare. 'That's a lot of translation for only three mirrors – three Imagers. It's going to be hard.'

Terisa didn't want to think about it. In fact, she didn't want to think. Men had died to keep her alive. That was what war meant: some men died to keep others alive. The bloodshed had hardly begun. Numbly, she asked, 'What do you suggest?'

He studied her. 'We could help.'

She blinked at him. She could see that he was cold, but he didn't seem to feel it as badly as she did. He was still able to be worried about her.

'The practice might be good for us,' he said casually. 'And you look like it wouldn't hurt you to be reminded that Imagery has a few' – he searched for a description – 'less bloody uses.'

She grimaced. 'I don't think I have the strength.'

'Terisa,' he said at once, 'listen to me. You didn't kill anybody. You were trying to stop the killing.'

He touched the sore place in her, the ache of responsibility. Stiffly, she said, 'They died protecting me.'

'But you didn't *kill* them. Their blood is on Eremis' head, not yours.'

'No,' she retorted. 'Don't you understand? I didn't have to give him the chance to attack me. We could have gone around the intersection. Nobody had to die. *I* made that decision.'

Like Lebbick, the men protecting her had died for nothing more than a ploy, a gambit – a move at checkers.

'That's true.' Geraden practically smiled at her. 'You struck back. You took the risk of striking back – and all risks are dangerous. Next time, you might want to choose your risks more carefully, so nobody has to face them except you. Us.

'But you were right. That's why we're here, *we*, all of us. Including those men who got killed. To strike back. If we aren't going to strike back, we should have stayed in Orison.'

Choose your risks more carefully.

'In the meantime,' he said as if he knew what her answer would be, 'we can make ourselves useful. The Congery has curved mirrors they aren't going to need tonight. I can tackle one of them. And there's probably a flat glass to spare. If there isn't, you can try your hand at a regular translation, where you don't have to shift the Image.'

As well as she could, she met his gaze. Sometimes she forgot how handsome he was. He had a boy's eyes, a lover's mouth, a king's forehead; the lines of his face were capable of iron and humor almost simultaneously. He lacked Eremis' magnetism – he was too vulnerable for that kind of attraction – but his vulnerability only made his strength more precious to her, just as his strength made his vulnerability dear. And he was so good at turning his attention to her when she needed it—

With one cold hand, she touched his cheek, ran a fingertip down the length of his nose. 'I hope Master Barsonage is in a tolerant mood,' she muttered. 'I might make some pretty dramatic mistakes.'

'Nonsense,' scoffed Geraden happily. 'After the mistakes I've already made, anything you can do wrong is going to be paltry by comparison.'

Chuckling, he led her toward the open ground where the Masters were unpacking their mirrors.

When he explained what he had in mind to the mediator, Master Barsonage's harried look eased noticeably. 'This is too good to be true,' Barsonage said as he assessed the possibilities. 'Something *must* go amiss. If neither of you cracks a glass – and I feel constrained to remind you that nothing of what we have can be replaced – perhaps Prince Kragen's Alends will be overwhelmed by sentiment against Imagery, and will feel compelled to throw a few propitious stones.

'Master Vixix.' This was a middle-aged Imager with hair like roofing thatch and a face as bland as a millstone. 'We require your glass.' To Terisa, the mediator explained, 'Master Vixix has shaped a flat mirror which shows a scene lost somewhere in the Fen of Cadwal. We brought it because a fen can be a useful place to drop trash and corpses. As a weapon, however, it has little value. Perhaps it would serve for you?'

Without waiting for an answer, he instructed another Master to unpack one of the Congery's normal mirrors for Geraden.

Soon the ground was cleared, the mirrors were set, and guards stood ready to carry away translated equipment and supplies. Nodding in satisfaction, Master Barsonage approached his own glass and said, 'Very well. Let us begin.'

Standing more beside the mirror than before it, he gave its focus a last touch, then began to stroke the edge of the frame with one hand while muttering words Terisa couldn't distinguish.

From the Image of Orison's ballroom, two sacks of flour and a side of cured beef flopped to the ground at Master Barsonage's feet.

Another Imager produced a cask of wine, which was greeted with a rough cheer by the nearby guards. The third began to spill a steady stream of bedrolls through his glass.

'You realize, don't you?' Terisa said to Geraden under her breath, 'that I don't have any idea how to do this. I don't know what words to say, or how to move my hands, or anything.'

His eyes sparkled as he faced the mirror which the Masters had unpacked for him. It showed an arid landscape under a hot sun, so dry that it seemed incapable of sustaining any kind of life, so hard-baked that the ground was split by a crack as deep as a chasm and wide enough to swallow men and horses. Despite his past, the Congery – or at least Master Barsonage – trusted him with that glass. Touching the convoluted mimosa wood frame delicately with the tips of his fingers, he smiled and said, 'This may sound strange, but that isn't exactly a secret. It's one of the first things Apts learn – as soon as the Congery knows them well enough to be sure they're serious. Imagery doesn't depend on waving your hands the right way, or making the right sounds. It depends on talent. The rest—'

Interrupting himself, he came to look at Master Vixix's glass with her. In the gloom of evening, the Fen of Cadwal looked forbidding: dark and wet; unpredictable.

'Here,' he said. 'Move your left hand on the frame – like this.' He showed her. 'Gesture with your right hand – like this.' He showed her. Then, without allowing her any opportunity for practice, he said, 'While you're doing that, mumble these sounds.' In her ear, he murmured a complex string of nonsense syllables.

'Most Apts,' he commented, 'work on things like this for a year, off and on. You ought to be able to handle it' – he gazed at her innocently – 'almost immediately.'

She stared back at him, unwilling to believe that he was making fun of her – and unable to think of any other interpretation.

'Try it,' he urged, as if half a hundred guards and most of the Congery weren't watching her. 'Go on.'

His smile seemed to promise that nothing would harm her.

Quickly, so that she wouldn't be paralyzed by self-consciousness, she approached the flat mirror.

Move your left hand on the frame – like this. No, more *like this. Gesture with your right –* that was wrong, try again – *with your right hand – like this.* At the same time. And *mumble.*

Working hard to remember the syllables Geraden had told her, she forgot for a moment what she was trying to accomplish.

With a roar like a cataract, rank swampwater began to rush over the edge of the frame onto her feet.

Startled, she jumped back.

Instantly, the translation stopped.

The Masters and most of the guards were laughing; but Geraden's grin was too full of approval to hurt her. 'I'm sorry.' He chuckled. 'I didn't mean to embarrass you. This is just one of those situations where if you know what you're trying to do it gets harder.'

Terisa looked down at the muck on her boots. Croaking in hoarse astonishment, a frog hopped away across the hard dirt. Despite the chill, her cheeks and ears were hot from the laughter of the spectators. Balanced between indignation and mirth, she rasped, 'I hope you can give me a better explanation than that.'

Her tone made him serious at once. 'The words and gestures don't have anything to do with translation. They're for your benefit – to help you concentrate in a particular way. When you're first learning, they help by forcing you to think about them instead of translation. And when you've learned, they help – sort of by force of habit. After enough repetition, they put you in the right frame of mind almost automatically.

'But if I told you all that first, you would think about *how* you were concentrating, instead of actually concentrating. It would be harder. Now that you know what the right frame of mind is, you'll have an easier time getting yourself back there.'

He made sense. She knew him well enough to know that he wasn't trying to make fun of her. She ought to laugh—

But she had seen men die today. And she had every intention of killing Master Eremis. She was in no mood to laugh at anything.

Deliberately, she went back to the mirror and began to clear her mind so that she could shift the Image, transform the Fen of Cadwal into the ballroom of Orison.

Before long, Prince Kragen arrived in person to discuss the question of his supplies with the Tor. By that time Terisa had already succeeded at bringing a stack of groundsheets through from the ballroom – and no one was laughing. The guards and the Masters were all hard at work, preparing to feed and shelter six thousand men for the night.

Prince Kragen observed that he had no alliance with Mordant. And without an alliance he certainly couldn't entrust his army's supplies – in effect, his army's ability to function – to a group of men who were historically his enemies, in addition to being notoriously crazy.

The Tor observed that if the Alend army continued to carry its own supplies, and continued to try to keep up with the forces of Orison, it would reach Esmerel no better able to function than if it had lost all its supplies.

Prince Kragen observed that it would not hurt Alend to let Orison meet Cadwal first and test the High King's mettle.

The Tor observed that two separate armies of six thousand men each would pose a trivial problem for High King Festten's twenty thousand, compared to a united force of twelve thousand.

Prince Kragen acquiesced. He also accepted the Tor's invitation to supper. Behind his tone of doubt and his dark glower, he looked positively happy.

That night, wrapped in their blankets and an oiled groundsheet, Terisa allowed Geraden to apologize again. 'I know you were right,' she sighed eventually. 'I just don't seem to be very resilient. All those men laughing – That's something else Master Eremis and my father have in common. They like to jeer.'

'But you showed them they were wrong,' Geraden countered. 'None of them has ever seen a woman with talent before. Most of them have never taken a woman seriously before. Until this evening, there was a chance they wouldn't back you up, if you ever needed them.

'Now you've got their attention. The whole camp is talking about you. What you did in the intersection was good. The only problem with it is, it was too abstract to have much impact. Nobody could *see* what you accomplished. Here—' He hugged her. 'Here you've got hundreds of witnesses. You're a Master. And the Masters are doing something useful, something vital. For a change.

'Terisa' – in the dark, he sounded like Artagel, eager for battle – 'we're going to beat that bastard.'

She hoped he was right. But she seemed to have lost the ability to laugh. For that reason, she wasn't sure.

The next morning, she and Geraden, with Master Barsonage and the other two Imagers, worked like mill-slaves to return Orison's equipment and virtually everything the Alend soldiers had carried to the ballroom. Then, guarded by a detachment of fifty horsemen, they had to drive the Congery's wagons furiously to catch up with the armies.

In some ways, that drive was harder than the translation. So much translation was a mind-numbing exertion: it sapped her strength until she felt too weak to stand; it ground her spirit down to the nub. But it wasn't dangerous. All she had to do was maintain the Image-shift, and be sure that none of Orison's inhabitants wandered into the ballroom at a bad time, and keep the glass open while guards pitched bedrolls and food sacks and cooking utensils through it.

On the other hand, the drive to rejoin the armies was distinctly dangerous.

The obvious danger was to the wagons themselves, to the mirrors they carried. From Broadwine Ford, the armies left the relatively smooth Marshalt road to turn west-southwest toward Esmerel, and the way to Esmerel wasn't particularly well maintained because it wasn't particularly well used. As soon as the wagons passed the small, clustered village around the inn which served the Ford (from a sensible distance, to avoid the danger of floods), the roadbed became much rougher.

In addition, the terrain rapidly grew more challenging. According to Geraden, what was in effect the only flatland in the Care of Tor lay along the road toward Marshalt. The rest of the Tor's Care was at best hilly; more often rugged than not; in places nearly mountainous. Despite the best efforts of the drivers, the wagons had to lumber over knobs of exposed rock, along gullies cobbled to jar bones apart, up hillsides barely packed hard enough for the horses' hooves to find purchase. And each jolt against an obstacle, each tilt over a boulder, each thud into a hole threatened the Congery's precious glass.

When the drive first began, Terisa thought that she would rest – and avoid the stiff-jointed gait of her nag – by riding on one of the wagons for a while. She soon found, however, that its ride made her nag's saddle look like a sedan chair by comparison.

If anything, the weather was getting colder. In the ravines and gullies, the wind swirled from all sides, chilling skin and bones like invisible ice; on the rises and crests, it swept straight down off the southern mountains, remorseless and keen. As tired as she was, as empty-hearted as she felt, there didn't seem to be anything Terisa could do to make herself warm.

'What do you suppose,' she asked Geraden in an effort to keep her mind occupied, 'those twenty thousand Cadwals are doing all this time?'

'*Resting,*' Geraden snapped with uncharacteristic bitterness. 'Building fortifications. Getting traps ready. Learning how to coordinate their movements with whatever Eremis and Gilbur and Vagel plan to do. Resting.'

'Looks like we have all the advantages,' she murmured. 'By the time we get there, we'll be exhausted.'

He nodded; then he added, 'Which reminds me. We've had so many other things to think about, I forgot to mention it. I've got the strongest feeling this isn't what we're supposed to be doing.'

She found that idea so upsetting that she stared at him in spite of her fatigue and the raw cold.

'Say that again.'

'I've got the strongest feeling—'

Their road was little more than a dirt track trodden hard by several thousand men. It lurched over a ridge and angled down into an erosion gully. 'Do you mean,' she interrupted, 'we shouldn't be going to Esmerel like this? We shouldn't be sticking our necks in the noose like this? It's all wrong?'

Why didn't you say so before we got started?

'No,' he replied at once. 'I'm sorry. I'm not being clear. I don't mean the Tor, or the army, or the Congery – or even Prince Kragen. I mean you and me. Personally. There's something else we should be doing.'

The advantage of an erosion gully was that the rocks were padded with sand. The disadvantage was that the wheels tended to cut in, making the wagons harder to pull. The teams began to snort and struggle in the traces.

Hardly able to contain herself, Terisa demanded, 'Like what?'

Geraden grimaced sheepishly. 'I don't have the vaguest notion. That's why we aren't doing it. You know me. I always take these feelings seriously, even when they don't make sense. If I understood it this time, I wouldn't be able to stop myself.'

The bed of the gully was wide enough for the wagons and riders. The walls quickly grew sheer, however; the gully became a ravine twisting among heavy hills. With an effort, she resisted a vehement urge to argue with him. Sourly, she muttered, 'You and your "strongest feelings."'

He spread his hands. 'I'm sorry. I shouldn't have brought it up. I just thought you ought to know.'

She should have reassured him that he had done no harm – that he was right to tell her what he was feeling. In addition, she should have kicked him for apologizing so often. Unfortunately, she was too frightened.

Like the voice of her fear, a shout rose from one of the guards at the front of the group.

The cry was so consistent with her mood that it didn't seem to need any other explanation. For a moment, she didn't even raise her head to see what was happening.

Then there were more shouts. The walls of the ravine caught the cries and flung them into chaos along the wind. Ahead of the wagons, horsemen snatched out their swords, brandished their pikes. Guards surged past the wagons on both sides, yelling at Terisa and Geraden and the Congery to stay back.

Ribuld spurred after them furiously.

For no reason except instinct, Terisa jammed her heels into the sides of her nag.

'No!' Geraden caught at her reins.

Recovering her balance, she heard a throaty snarl among the shouts as if the ravine itself were growling for blood.

Through the press of riders, she saw a guard plunge off his mount, unseated by a wolf strong enough to leap as high as his chest, big enough to topple him.

At the same time, more wolves came off the edge of the ravine: dozens of them; leaping onto the men and horses below as if they were in no danger of breaking their own legs and backs, or didn't care; wolves with spines jutting down their back's and double rows of fangs in their jaws, and malign eyes.

Those that were close enough launched themselves at the wagons. At Terisa and the Masters.

At Geraden.

The same kind of wolves which had attacked Houseldon. Predators with his spoor in their nostrils and no fear left at all.

Screaming, one horse in the traces pitched to the ground with its shoulder torn open. Its weight pulled its fellow over on top of it, nearly upset the wagon.

A wolf crashed like a hammer into the wagon, hit it so hard that the wagonbed recoiled as if its axles were springs. Despite the tumult of shouts and pain and wolves, Terisa distinctly heard glass shatter.

The wagoner jumped from the bench, scuttled under the wagon for shelter.

Ignoring a Master who yelled at it frantically, flapped his arms at it as if it were nothing more than an tomcat, the wolf lunged off the wagon toward Geraden.

Apparently, Geraden had forgotten his sword. Instead of trying to fight, he wrenched his mount out of the way, drove his horse bucking against Terisa's nag so that both horses stumbled to the wall of the ravine away from the attack.

A guard buried the head of his pike in the wolf's skull – then couldn't work the blade free in time to defend himself from another beast which seemed to sail entirely over the wagons at him. He fell with his fists knotted in the wolf's ruff, straining to keep the fangs from his face.

The fall broke his back before the wolf had a chance to kill him.

From horseback, Master Barsonage jumped awkwardly into the bed of the other wagon. Lashing the leads, the wagoner forced his team over against the wall directly under the wolves. In that position, the leaping wolves carried over the mediator's head toward the wagon with the broken glass.

While Master Vixix and the wagoner cowered on the bench, the mediator blocked the rails with his girth, swinging his fists like mallets at every wolf within reach, using his furnituremaker's strength to batter beasts away from his mirrors.

The guards milled in the ravine, thwarting each other, striking ineffectively; the walls crowded them, blocked them. And a number of them had gone ahead of the wagons to meet the attack, with the result that now most of the wolves were behind them. Nearly shrieking in fright, Terisa cried, 'Protect Geraden! They're after Geraden!'

Men shouted, raged; blades flashed; horses collided, knocked each other to the dirt. Nevertheless Terisa's shout pierced the confusion. The captain of the company roared orders she couldn't understand through the din.

The nearest riders wheeled back toward the wagons.

A wolf shot past the horses, slavering like a rabid thing. At the same time, two more picked themselves up off the ground behind the wagons, hurtled to the attack. And another sprang from the ravine's rim, hurling itself at the wagon between it and Geraden.

With a demented wail, the Master who had tried to shoo the first wolf away leaped off the wagonbench and attempted to catch this beast in middive.

Its weight and his leap carried the two of them over the rail among the horses.

Now Geraden remembered his sword. Still forcing his mount between Terisa and the wolves, driving her nag against the wall, he fumbled behind him, got a hand on his swordhilt, struggled to wrench the blade out of its scabbard over his shoulder.

The sword seemed to be stuck. Terisa could see a wolf already lifting from the ground as if it could fly. Wildly, almost unseating herself, she reached for Geraden's back and caught hold of the scabbard.

The blade rushed free, split the beast's head open from eye-socket to throat. Geraden was swinging so hard that only the jolt of impact kept him from being pulled off his mount by his own blow.

Out of the chaos, Ribuld's pike took another wolf by the chest and gutted it. That gave Geraden time to recover his balance – but not enough time for his lack of expertise to mislead him. Unable to haul the heavy blade back and swing it again before the next wolf sprang at him, he simply jammed his swordpoint into the beast's maw.

In case the wolf wasn't dead yet, Ribuld hacked its head off.

Without warning, the attack was over.

Men brandished their swords, shouting across the cries of the wounded; horses wheeled and stamped; the captain yelled warnings, instructions. But no more wolves appeared, either in the ravine or along its rim.

Terisa felt that she was about to fall over from holding her breath too long. Why hadn't she felt the translation? 'Watch out!' she called with as much strength as she had. Maybe it took place too far away. 'Eremis still has the mirror.' She had the impression that she was barely audible. Maybe Eremis didn't have exactly the mirror he needed, so he had to simply release his wolves among these hills and let them hunt for Geraden in their own way. The actual translation may have happened miles or hours ago. 'He can translate more whenever he wants.'

'I doubt it,' Geraden muttered, apparently speaking to himself. He held his sword erect in front of him and stared at it as if it appalled him. 'Wolves travel in packs.' Blood ran down the blade onto his hands, his forearms; the front of his cloak was splashed with red. 'And mirrors have a relatively small range. There isn't likely to be another pack living that near this one.' As he gripped the hilt, his arms began to shake. 'After his attack on Houseldon, Eremis probably had to wait all this time just to get these wolves.'

Abruptly, as if every movement hurt him, Geraden wiped the blade on his cloak and drove it back into its scabbard.

'Eremis can drop an avalanche on us whenever we're near one of his flat mirrors. But he can't force a wolf pack on another world into his reach.'

The captain nodded grimly, then announced, 'We're going to take precautions anyway.' He sent five men ahead to catch up with the Tor and report what had happened. Ten more men were assigned scouting duties.

Somehow, Terisa had come through the attack untouched. No blood had marked her. The only stain she bore was the one Adept Havelock had left on her shirt.

This time, no more than six of the people around her were dead. Two horses were dead. Two more had to be put out of their misery. One Master was dead: Cuebard. Until she saw his body, Terisa had never heard his name spoken. The captain counted nineteen dead wolves. 'Curse this terrain,' he rasped. 'On open ground, we could have chopped them into dogmeat – and suffered nothing but scratches.'

Trying not to hurry, Barsonage and the rest of the Masters unpacked all the mirrors.

Luckily, only one was broken: Master Vixix's flat glass, with its Image of the Fen of Cadwal.

'Thank the stars.' Despite the cold, Master Barsonage was sweating thickly. 'We are more fortunate than we deserve.'

'It's my fault,' said the captain, growling obscenities at himself. 'Castellan Norge is going to hang my balls on a stick. I should have had scouts around us right from the beginning.'

'Don't worry about it, captain,' Ribuld muttered sardonically. 'He needs you too much. He won't actually unman you unless we win this war and end up safe in Orison again.

'But if that happens, watch your groin.'

Several of the guards laughed, more in reaction to the fight than because they thought Ribuld was funny.

'Are you all right?' Terisa asked Geraden privately.

He shook his head; contradicted himself with a nod; shrugged his shoulders. To the cold wind and the ravine's wall, he said, 'I've got another strong feeling.'

'Oh, good.' She tried to help him by sounding wry rather than troubled. 'Somehow, I just know I'm going to love this one.'

'I've got the strongest feeling—' The muscles at the corners of his jaw knotted, released. 'When the fighting really starts, we'd better be sure we've got somebody with us who handles a sword better than I do.'

Terisa assented bleakly. And better than Ribuld, too, she thought to herself, remembering Gart, who had beaten Ribuld and his dead friend Argus simultaneously.

Choose your risks more carefully. She intended to do that. If she could just figure out how.

Well before noon, she and Geraden, with Master Barsonage, the Congery, and the guards, rejoined Orison's army. When the Tor had assured himself that their news was no worse than the report he had received, he rumbled, 'Tomorrow you will have five hundred men with you. Master Eremis may strike at you again. And tomorrow there will be a clear danger of encountering High King Festten's scouts and outriders.'

That made Terisa feel neither worse nor better. Caution was sensible. On the other hand, she felt sure that Mordant's fate wouldn't be decided by a chance encounter with scouts or outriders. And she had a distinct sense that Eremis wasn't going to attack again. With his enemies so close to him now, he would wait until they came all the way into his trap, put themselves completely in his power. He wasn't interested in anything as relatively straightforward as victory. He wanted to crush and humiliate, to *annihilate* everyone who opposed him. Whatever he did when his enemies reached Esmerel would be intended to hurt them spiritually as much as physically.

When she thought about Nyle, her insides contracted until she could scarcely breathe.

Throughout the afternoon, across the complex and dangerous terrain, Orison's army and Prince Kragen's marched into the unseasonable cold. Impatient and apprehensive young men demanded a return of spring; grizzled veterans with bunions or arthritis predicted snow. Horses stamped restively, pulled against their reins, shied at nothing. Orison and encouragement seemed painfully far away, despite the magic of mirrors. Mile after mile, the defenders of Mordant shortened the distance to Esmerel.

That evening, the men stopped to make camp on the high ground of a cluster of hilltops, where the wind could get at them with all its ice, and where their lights and cooking fires would be visible in all directions – and where it would be almost impossible for enemy troops to surprise them. Prince Kragen's commanders deployed their soldiers; Castellan Norge organized the guard. Master Barsonage and the Congery unpacked the mirrors.

When the mediator uncovered his glass, the first thing he and everyone else saw in the Image was Artagel sitting atop a particularly high pile of bedrolls and groundsheets.

He still wore Lebbick's clothes, Lebbick's blood. His expression was a strange combination of excitement and boredom.

'What is that idiot doing?' demanded the Prince. 'Is he not in danger of translation?'

Then: 'What has he done with our supplies?'

Kragen was right: none of the Alend supplies which had been translated to Orison that morning were visible in the Image.

Before anyone else could speak, however, Artagel made his purpose clear. With the air of a man repeating an action he had already performed to the point of tedium, he held up a large sheet of parchment and turned it slowly so that it could be seen from all sides around him.

There was writing on the parchment. Across the hillside where the mirror stood, the sun was setting, and the light wasn't especially good. But Artagel was prepared for that difficulty. Around him, the ballroom blazed with torches.

His message was easily read.

What do you want done with Kragen's supplies?

The Prince stiffened; his hand fingered his sword. He watched narrowly as the Tor called for a piece of parchment and a charcoal stylus.

The old lord wrote:

Prince Kragen treats us honorably. Return his supplies.

He showed his message to Prince Kragen, then handed the parchment to Master Barsonage.

Deftly, Barsonage deposited the message in Artagel's lap.

Artagel read it, glanced around him, shrugged. He looked disappointed; nevertheless he didn't balk. He waved his arms, shouted something; and at once men and women – conscripted villagers, apparently – began running stacks and piles of Alend possessions back into the center of the ballroom.

Noticing the congested look on Prince Kragen's face, Terisa gave a small, silent sigh of relief. He would have had little or no trouble believing that he had been betrayed – and then he would have had no choice but to attack the forces of Orison.

Shortly, everything was ready. Saluting the empty air casually, Artagel left the Image so that the process of translation could begin.

While guards and Alends gathered to distribute utensils and food and drink and bedding around the camp, Master Barsonage and his fellow Imagers went to work.

Geraden joined them, using the curved glass he was accustomed to. Terisa, on the other hand, had no contribution to make. Master Vixix's was the only flat glass of any size which the Congery had brought to supplement the three supply-mirrors. So, after watching the work for a while, she went to the most obviously weary of the three Masters – a frail, nearly antique individual named Harpool, who hadn't borne the attack of the wolves especially well – and offered to take his place so that he could rest.

He accepted gratefully and tottered away at once in the direction of a cup of wine and a nap before supper. When she faced his mirror, however, Terisa found to her chagrin that she could do nothing with it. She gestured and mumbled as Geraden had taught her; she reached toward the special frame of mind, the particular concentration, which had become familiar to her the previous evening and this morning. But now nothing happened.

Geraden, Master Barsonage, and the other Imager were unaware of her problem – they were straining like cart-horses over their own translations – but everyone else in the vicinity noticed her difficulty and stopped to observe.

'She's lost it,' a guard muttered. 'Scared out of her.'

'Give her time,' snapped Ribuld loyally.

This was too much – *really* too much. Two hard days on the road. Two bloody attacks on her life, or Geraden's. Hours of mind-draining labor at

Master Vixix's mirror. And now her talent disappeared as if it had been switched off inside her.

If King Joyse thought she could bear *this* on top of everything else, he was out of his mind.

For no reason except that she absolutely couldn't endure the shame of turning away, of showing off her failure in front of all those men, she tried to shift the Image.

Almost without effort, the ballroom of Orison became the Fen of Cadwal – not because she chose that scene consciously, but because it happened to be present in her thoughts.

Oh. She stared at it. The Fen of Cadwal. Her talent hadn't disappeared. Then why—?

She touched the frame of the glass; gestured; mumbled. Like a fool, she brought a second gush of swampwater pouring onto her boots. This time, there were no frogs.

Oh.

Then she understood. She couldn't use a mirror unless she shifted the Image. Her power only functioned with Images she had placed in the glass herself.

No, that didn't make any sense. Why had she been able to use Master Vixix's mirror yesterday without shifting it?

Concentrating fiercely now, ignoring the men carrying supplies away, the men watching her, she let Master Harpool's glass resume its natural Image. Then, with the brightly lit ballroom squarely in focus, she tried again to translate a hogshead of water.

This time, it came through the mirror so promptly that she had to jump aside to avoid being crushed.

Perfect. I love this. Who says Imagery is hard?

Grinding her teeth to stifle a yell, Terisa continued translating supplies out of the ballroom until Castellan Norge announced that the Alends and the guard had everything they needed for the night. At once, she stamped away from the mirror, demanded wine from Ribuld, and drank two cups so quickly that they made her head spin.

Nearly staggering with fatigue, Geraden moved to join her. At the moment, she considered it a blessing that he was too tired to notice her knotted state; too tired even to ask how her translations had gone. But later, after a hot supper had restored him somewhat, and they went to bed together, she forced herself to tell him what had happened. She needed an explanation, if he had one to give her.

Her tone made him open his eyes to look at her sharply. He listened hard until she was finished; then he rolled onto his back and stared up at the cold stars.

'Have you got any ideas?' she asked.

He took a long moment to think before he murmured, 'I'm not sure.

'This is all unmapped territory. Havelock is the only Adept the Congery has ever had – and he hasn't contributed much to our general knowledge of Imagery in recent years. We don't really understand people who can use mirrors they didn't make. For most of us, the way it usually works – you already know this – is that there's some kind of interaction between an Imager's talent and his mirror while he's shaping it. So no one can use that mirror except the man who made it.

'As an experiment years ago, the Congery took several men who wanted to be Apts, but who obviously had no talent of any kind, and let them try to make mirrors. It didn't work. Something always went wrong. You have to be an Imager to shape a mirror. And you have to be that particular Imager to shape that particular mirror.

'I'm not sure why you couldn't use Master Harpool's glass, and then you could. But we know he has a special relationship with it. No ordinary Imager could use it at all, except him. My guess is, his hold on it was too recent. You had to replace his talent with yours, impose your power on it, and you couldn't do that without shifting it first.

'If I'm right, the reason you didn't have any trouble with Master Vixix's glass is, he hadn't used it recently. In fact, he may never have done any translations with it at all. His interaction with it wasn't fresh enough to get in your way.'

Terisa had no way of knowing whether this explanation made sense or not. Softly, she said, 'You make it sound like the glass is actually alive.'

Geraden kissed her forehead. 'I don't know about that. But talent is certainly alive. The relationship between an Imager and his mirror must be alive in some way.'

She thought about that for a long time after he went to sleep. *Choose your risks more carefully.* If she wanted to help fight Master Eremis – if she really intended to kill him – she needed to understand her own limitations.

The next morning, before she and the Masters had finished returning supplies to Orison, the wind brought clouds up out of the south.

The rack was thin at first, dull gray rather than oppressive; it cut off the sunlight without making the air noticeably colder. But as the morning and the march wore on, the clouds thickened, turning the sky dull, bleeding away the colors of the landscape. A solid mass covered the Care from horizon to horizon; it weighed on the morale of the armies, pressing expectation into worry, worry into dread.

At the same time, the wind became a few significant degrees warmer.

Apprehensively, Terisa asked Geraden, 'You don't think Eremis has the power to translate *weather* against us, do you?'

Geraden snorted. 'If he could do translations on that scale, he wouldn't need to fight us at all. He could just send out tornadoes until we collapsed.'

That was a relief – of a sort. Eremis, also, had his limits. 'In other words, he's just lucky to get a cold spell like this when he needs it most.'

'Or we are.' Geraden looked at her, grinning with his teeth. 'The worse things get, the more we know we're doing what King Joyse wants. At the moment when Eremis looks most unbeatable, that's when he's most vulnerable.'

Now it was her turn to snort. 'Aren't you the one who accused *me* of having a morbid imagination?'

Geraden laughed, but he didn't sound especially amused.

854

Shortly after noon, the armies of Orison and Alend began to meet blood on the ground.

Old bloodstains: weatherworn, gone black; some across broad swaths of hard dirt; some in sheltered crannies; some clinging like lichen to rough rocks. They mottled stones and soil like the marks of a disease – infrequent at first; but soon more common, showing in open ravines or accessible hillsides all over the complex terrain, in pieces of earth where men could have fought for their lives.

'The Perdon,' Prince Kragen pronounced grimly. 'His men fought alone here against High King Festten. They were trapped here, hunted down in this' – he swallowed an obscenity – 'this maze, and massacred.

'They could have saved themselves. They could have fled to Orison. If we understand the High King rightly, he never intended to bring his force anywhere but here. But the Perdon did not know that. He knew only that he must fight for Mordant – and that he could not trust his King. So he led Cadwal here, where High King Festten most wished to go.

'He was a valiant man,' the Prince rasped, 'badly betrayed. I hope that he did not learn the truth before he died. It would have been unutterably bitter.'

But there were no bodies.

No remnants of weapons and gear.

No bones.

The entire region had been cleaned.

Carrion eaters might have emptied the mail, picked the iron clean; some of them might have dragged bones away to gnaw. Nevertheless the dead should have left more behind than just their blood.

Scouts brought back no word of Cadwal. Everywhere the men rode, they met old blood. In gullies protected from wind or rain, they found the marks of boots and hooves, running in all directions, trampled everywhere. But none of them encountered any evidence of High King Festten's army anywhere.

The Tor voiced the opinion that this was impossible. Castellan Norge and Prince Kragen sent out more scouts, doubled and tripled the number of men scouring the hillsides, the dry waterbeds, the stands of stubborn thicket. Yet the scouts discovered nothing, learned nothing.

And an hour or two before evening the vanguard of Orison's army and Alend's arrived in sight of Esmerel.

Master Eremis' 'ancestral seat' sat at the head of a wedge-shaped valley, almost directly against the sheer defile which brought a brook running into the valley. A bowman on the roof of the manor could have hit the valleysides in three directions. From the defile, however, the valley spread wide until it was more than broad enough to accommodate the armies approaching it. Its brook, and the expanse of its floor, gave the impression that it must be one of the most pleasant places in the Care of Tor.

Its walls, on the other hand, were high and rugged; impassable more than not. Blunt outcroppings of rock supported them like ramparts. And they didn't decline as the wedge spread wider. Instead, they reared their black stones against the sky until they ended abruptly, hooking inward before they stopped as if to constrict the wide foot of the valley.

There was no blood here. Nearly a mile outside the valley, all evidence of the Perdon's life and death disappeared.

The valley itself was empty.

Esmerel was a low building, for reasons which were obvious to the eye: even in this dull, cloud-locked light, the manor's flat-roofed, rambling profile suited its surroundings, providing enough contrast to be distinctive, enough self-effacement to be harmonious. Terisa had heard from Geraden that much of the house was belowground, anchored in the rock of the valley. Instinctively, she believed that – although she couldn't forget the sealed window and the faint light in the room where Eremis had chained her. Maybe Nyle's cell was on the aboveground level. Certainly the window was. It shouldn't be hard to locate.

With Prince Kragen and his captains, the Tor and Castellan Norge, Geraden and Master Barsonage, she studied Esmerel's front up the length of the valley. From this distance, she couldn't make out what gave the walls their texture; but she could see the portico clearly, supported over the main entrance by sturdy pillars.

The door was closed. All the windows were shuttered and dark. No one moved around the building, or in the neat horseyard on one side of the house, or along the brook. Under the dark clouds, the whole place had an air of desertion, as if it had been forgotten a long time ago.

The ground, however, still held the scars of hundreds of horses, hundreds of men.

After a while, Prince Kragen asked, 'What do you think, my lord Tor?'

'I think,' the Tor muttered as if his confidence were ebbing, 'we must look inside.'

'It's a trap, my lord,' commented Norge.

'Of course,' the Tor sighed. 'Is that not why we have come, Geraden, my lady Terisa?' He glanced at them morosely. 'To place our heads in the trap?'

For some reason, Geraden's mount distrusted the valley and tried to shy away. Reining his horse uncomfortably, he said, 'The only way we can find out what we're up against is to go look at it, my lord.'

Terisa couldn't take her eyes off Esmerel. It held her as Master Eremis himself did, full of promises and destruction. She had been a prisoner there. Had met Vagel; seen Nyle. Eremis had almost had his way with her—

'Let's go,' she said without meaning to speak aloud. 'Let's go look at it.'

Castellan Norge shrugged. The Tor blew his nose on the hem of his cloak.

Prince Kragen gave Terisa a bow which suggested either mockery or respect.

As if no one had actually given any commands, orders began to sift back to the main body of the armies. While the vanguard advanced on Esmerel, the Alend soldiers and the guard followed until they were well within the relative shelter of the valley, nearly halfway to the defile; then, with a company of five hundred horsemen, the vanguard pulled ahead, and the two armies – Alend on one side of the brook, Orison on the other – began to ready themselves for camp or battle. The men closest to the foot of the valley started throwing up a precautionary earthen breastwork from wall to wall.

In silence, the vanguard approached Esmerel.

'Do you know?' Master Barsonage said to no one in particular, talking simply to steady himself, 'I had never seen this manor until Geraden made an Image of it in Adept Havelock's glass. I am astonished now to observe how accurately he was able to envision it.'

No one in particular listened to the mediator.

The riders continued to advance. Now Terisa could tell that the pillars of the portico were redwood; that the sides of the manor were built of waxed boards supported by stone ribs and columns. A beautiful design – but the place was still vacant. Esmerel's air of abandonment grew deeper as the riders moved farther into the gloom of the valley walls.

All the horses became restive: prancing; stamping; sawing against their reins.

Prince Kragen's standard-bearer winded a call on his battle-horn, a fierce run of notes which nevertheless sounded forlorn and maybe doomed as it echoed back from the ramparts. Nothing shifted in Esmerel. None of the windows winked or opened. Under its portico, the door looked heavy enough to withstand anybody.

Abruptly, Geraden winced; Prince Kragen spat a curse; and all at once Terisa could smell what was disturbing the horses.

The sweet, rank, nauseating reek of blood and old rot, neglected death, flesh gone to carrion.

'What's *in* there?' one of the captains asked as if he had forgotten that everyone could hear him.

'Lucky you,' Ribuld muttered in response. 'Lucky us. We're going to find out.'

As soon as she recognized the stench, however, Terisa lost her fear. She had been expecting something like this. A spiritual attack as much as physical. Adrenaline pumped through her; energy filled her muscles. This was Master Eremis' domain: he was in his element here. Everything that happened now would happen because he intended it.

First she said, 'It wasn't like this four days ago. I couldn't smell any of this.' Then she said, 'This is where I saw Nyle. Inside.'

His face twisting, Geraden surged toward the door.

'*Geraden!*'

The Tor's shout snapped like a whip, jerked Geraden back. Fierce and pale, he wheeled to face the old lord.

'Come on,' he whispered. 'We've got to find him.'

The Tor didn't drop Geraden's gaze. 'Castellan Norge,' he coughed, 'open that door. Secure the rooms inside. We will enter when you signal for us.'

Norge saluted. At least three hundred guards rode away to form a protective perimeter around the manor and the vanguard. Some men dismounted to tend the horses. The rest followed Castellan Norge on foot.

In combat formation, swords ready, they approached the door.

It wasn't bolted. When Norge lifted the latch, the door swung inward, opening on darkness.

He and his men entered the house.

Terisa scanned the harsh rims of the valley. For no clear reason, she expected to see men there: Cadwals clutching their weapons; an army moving to surround the forces of Orison and Alend. Esmerel was a trap. But that didn't make any sense. She had been a prisoner here just a few days ago. Master Eremis had his own laborium here, his furnaces and glassworks. He had spoken to High King Festten here. It was inconceivable that he would surrender the Seat of his power to his enemies.

Sure. Of course. So where *was* he?

Where had she gone wrong?

Abruptly, the Castellan reappeared.

The gloom – and the fact that he was a few dozen yards away – confused Terisa's sight. She had the distinct impression that he had gone white. He held his arms stiffly at his sides; he moved as if he carried something breakable in his chest.

'My lord Tor—' His voice caught.

Peering at the portico and the door and Norge, the Tor asked, 'Is it safe?'

Norge shook his head, nodded. His throat worked. 'You need to see this. They're all here.'

No, Terisa thought blindly, don't go in there, don't go, it's too dangerous. But Geraden had already flung himself off his mount, was already running—

The Castellan stopped him, made him wait.

The Tor glanced wearily up at the sky. 'The truth is,' he rumbled, 'that three days in the saddle have done little to heal my belly.' The stubborn resolution which had brought him here appeared to be eroding. 'I fear that once I dismount I will never get up onto my horse again.'

Prince Kragen's gaze shone darkly. 'I will go, my lord Tor.'

The Tor passed a hand over his face. The skin of his cheeks seemed to pull away from the bones, giving him a skeletal aspect for a moment despite his fat.

'We will all go, my lord Prince,' he sighed.

No, Terisa thought as if she were panicking, it's a trap, Eremis is in there, he's already killed all Norge's men. Yet what she felt wasn't panic. Instead of crying out against Norge's pallor, Norge's distress, she swung off her nag and went after Geraden.

'Nyle,' he muttered urgently when she joined him – the only explanation she needed.

Heaving against his mortal weight, the Tor got his leg over the saddle, stumbled to the ground. For a moment, he sagged there as if his capacity to support himself were crumbling. But then he called up his fading strength and lumbered into motion.

With Prince Kragen, half a dozen Alend soldiers, Master Barsonage, and Ribuld, the Tor approached Esmerel on foot.

Terisa was right about Norge: his face had turned the color of old ash. He didn't say anything, didn't try to account for himself. When the Tor and Prince Kragen neared him, he pivoted harshly and stalked back into the manor.

They're all here.

Holding Geraden's hand to steady herself – and to restrain him from anything wild – Terisa entered Esmerel behind the old lord and the Prince.

Inside, the smell of blood and rot grew worse. Much worse.

Instead of fainting, Terisa tightened her grip on herself and went ahead.

The forehall was empty except for Castellan Norge and his men. They lined the walls, pale and grim, mirroring his distress. No one else was there – no one to account for the damage which nailed boots and mud had done to the once-fine floor. Some of the marks in the woodwork looked like swordcuts.

Full of misery, the Tor started for the nearest doorway off the forehall.

'Empty,' Norge croaked to stop him. 'Damage like this.' He gestured at the floor. 'And blood. There was a fight here. But there's nobody left.'

'It was like this,' Geraden breathed. 'In the Image I made.'

Master Barsonage nodded confirmation. 'I saw it.'

'What do you want me to see?' the Tor demanded of Norge.

The Castellan pointed toward a wide staircase sweeping downward. His arm shook until he snatched it back to his side.

'The cellars!' Geraden spat.

Norge and the Tor, Prince Kragen and Master Barsonage, Terisa and Geraden followed a line of guards to the stairs.

The staircase blazed with light: the Castellan's men had lit lamps down the walls. From the head of the stairs, the whole descent was visible until it reached bottom and spread out into the complex underground levels of Esmerel.

The stairs were like the floors: marked, stained, scarred. From below rose the reek of death, as palpable as a fist.

On both sides of the passage at the foot of the descent, corpses had been stacked like cordwood.

Under the dried blood, among the stiff, gaping wounds, the bodies wore the armor and insignia of the Perdon's men.

Forgetting caution – forgetting sanity – Geraden sprang down the stairs three at a time. Headlong into a storehouse of the dead, he rushed to find his brother.

Terisa and Ribuld went after him, with Prince Kragen close behind them.

Norge's men were already in the cellars, lighting more lamps, opening new rooms to look for signs of life. Most of them fought grimly against nausea; quite a few had already succumbed, adding a patina of bile to the general stench. Rats ran everywhere, so busy feasting that they hardly noticed the intrusion of light and boots. As soon as she reached the foot of the stairs, Terisa noticed one stack of bodies that obviously hadn't been soldiers. They looked more like servants – the men, women, and children who belonged to Esmerel.

Trying to keep up with Geraden, she hurried on.

Corpses were piled everywhere, neatly, deliberately. High King Festten had *annihilated* the Perdon. And he had brought the Perdon's dead here. Stacked them here, left them to rot. Where the defenders of Mordant might find them.

'*Nyle!*'

Geraden's yell died without echo in the halls, absorbed by flesh and maggots and rot.

The belowground rooms were much larger than she would have guessed.

One had obviously been a library – but all the books were gone. One might have been intended to display artwork – but all the paintings or sculptures were gone. There were workshops without tools, kitchens gutted of equipment. The people who had broken into Esmerel and slaughtered the manor's retainers had stripped it of everything valuable.

Ahead of her, Geraden faced a closed door. 'What's in there?'

'Wine cellar,' a guard answered as if he had just finished puking. 'Doesn't have any lamps, so we left it. Looks empty.'

No lamps, Terisa thought. That made sense. Wine needed to be kept cool. Lamps put out heat.

Geraden hauled the heavy door open.

Striding hard behind Terisa, Prince Kragen snapped, 'Bring light!'

With her and Ribuld, he followed Geraden into the cellar.

The air was colder here – much colder – therefore less foul. In this unseasonable chill, with no one to care what happened, the temperature had dropped below freezing. She was bitterly sure that Eremis hadn't left any wine behind to be ruined.

Using the reflected illumination from the doorway, Geraden moved among the wineracks.

Guards arrived carrying lamps; they entered the cellar.

When she saw what Eremis *had* left behind here, Terisa stopped to consider the advantages of passing out.

Preserved by the cold, more bodies had been stacked on the wineracks. Judging by the sigils on their mail, they were the Perdon's captains. Here, however, they hadn't been simply piled up like lumber. Instead, the bodies had been arranged in grotesque and degrading postures, as if death had caught them in a devils' dance, abusing themselves, copulating with each other, performing intricate atrocities. The shadows cast by the motion of the lamps gave the impression that the men were still alive, yearning toward a last taste of pleasure or pain.

On the corkage table in the middle of the cellar lay the Perdon himself.

Terisa recognized his bald pate, his red, thick eyebrows, his stained and shaggy moustache, his hairy ears; she recognized the passion in his glazed, staring eyes. It would have been impossible for her to mistake the man who had once helped Prince Kragen and Artagel save her from Gart.

The way he had died sickened her to the bottom of her heart.

His limbs and torso were cross-hatched with cuts, but none of them had caused his death. No, an honest end in battle apparently wasn't satisfactory for an enemy of Cadwal, a man who had pitted himself against High King Festten all his life. The Perdon had been killed by a corkscrew driven between his teeth through the back of his throat into the wooden table, so that he lay pinned there until he drowned on his own blood.

Passing out had advantages, no question about it. Oblivion might give Terisa the comfort she craved, if she could fade into it and never come back.

At the same time, she was so angry that when she bit down her lip to keep herself quiet she drew blood.

White with strain and horror, Geraden wheeled on the nearest guard. 'Where's Nyle?'

'Not here,' the guard answered thickly. 'Unless he's one of the bodies. No one's here.' A moment later, he added, 'None of the rooms down here was used for a cell.'

Then someone bumped Terisa so hard that she stumbled. The Tor brushed past without noticing her, shouldered Prince Kragen aside to approach the corkage table.

For a long moment while everyone watched him, he slumped against the edge of the table; the courage and determination seemed to leak out of him, as if he were sinking in on himself like a deflated bladder.

'Oh, my old friend. My old friend.'

In a constricted voice, Geraden muttered, 'He was never here. You were never here.' Apparently, he was talking to Terisa. 'We all made the same assumption, but we were wrong. When High King Festten came here, he had to kill Esmerel's servants and maybe even Eremis' relatives to get into the house. Eremis hasn't used this place for years.'

Abruptly, the Tor raised his head and brought up a wail like the cry of his damaged guts. Terisa was behind him: she couldn't see what he was doing. She didn't realize what he had done until a terrible convulsion shook him from head to foot and then his right fist sprang into the air, brandishing the corkscrew which had killed the Perdon.

As if he had no idea what was going on around him, Geraden muttered, 'We've come to the wrong place. This is just a trap. It doesn't even give us a chance to strike back.'

With a tearing groan, the Tor lifted the Perdon's rigid corpse. When he turned, Terisa saw that his face was streaked with tears. In the lamplight, he looked as pallid as the dead.

'And you wanted to make an alliance with that monster,' he cried to his friend's body. But he didn't expect an answer. Jerking his head at the ceiling, he shouted suddenly, 'Are you laughing at him now, Eremis? Does it amuse you to do this to a man who believed you?'

Oh, Eremis was laughing, all right. Terisa was sure of it.

Dumbly, she went to the Tor's side and helped support his quivering arms until Ribuld and some of the other guards came to take the Perdon away.

When she and Geraden went back outside, they found that the weather had turned to snow.

The air was as dark as evening, prematurely dim: the snow fell so thickly that it swallowed the light. Swirling inside the walls of the valley, it blanketed the atmosphere until she couldn't see five feet past the edge of the portico – a snowfall as heavy and thorough as a torrent, and yet composed of delicate, dry flakes, bits of powder so fine they stung the skin. The guards at the door had lit torches which the snow smothered as soon as they left the shelter of the portico. Everyone else in the valley, twelve thousand fighting men, had been erased from sight. Already the white cold accumulating on the ground was two or three inches thick.

Terisa shivered with a chill that felt almost metaphysical. She had dreamed once of snow; and because of that dream she had accepted Geraden's invitation to leave her old life behind.

With Castellan Norge and Master Barsonage, Prince Kragen came out of the house, gusting curses. 'By the stars,' he growled, 'if this snow does not blind our enemies as it does us, we are dead men. As matters stand, we will be hard pressed to locate our own encampment.'

Norge struggled to recover his essential equanimity. 'I think we should do that right away, my lord Prince. If we don't, we might get stuck here for the night. The armies need us. And I can't ask my guards to stay with that many corpses.'

The Prince nodded. 'I will instruct men to string lines to keep the horses together.' Followed by his soldiers, he strode away into the snowfall and disappeared as if the flakes swept his reality away.

Rather aimlessly, Norge commented, 'The Tor is resting. I'll go get him. But I don't think he'll be able to ride.'

No one answered. Scowling uncharacteristically, the Castellan went back into the manor.

Master Barsonage cleared his throat. 'It was a natural mistake, Geraden. We all made it. What do we know of Master Eremis, but that Esmerel is his ancestral home? What is more reasonable than the assumption that he built his power here – held his prisoners here?'

'Yes, it was reasonable,' Geraden said in a bleak tone.

'No, it wasn't.' Terisa hadn't intended to speak; she didn't know what she was going to say until she said it. 'King Joyse told me to think.' Her mind was full of the Perdon and the Tor, and the implications of snow. 'Esmerel was too obvious.

'We had to come here. We didn't know where else to go. But we should have known he wouldn't be here.'

'And now we're stuck,' Geraden finished.

No one argued with him.

Guards brought horses up to the portico. The mounts already had snow caked in their manes, on their withers; the flakes were so thick and cold that the horses' heat turned it to ice as it melted. But the wind kept the hoods and shoulders of the guards clear.

Men began to file out of the house. After a while, Castellan Norge and Ribuld brought the Tor to the portico. Physically, the old lord had never looked worse. His limbs were as frail as a child's; his hands shook as if the chill had already reached his bones; his skin was the color of moldy potatoes.

Nevertheless the glare in his eyes was unquenchable. His outrage at what had been done to the Perdon sustained him when his body and his ordinary courage failed.

As long as she ignored the rest of him and watched only his eyes, Terisa was able to keep her grasp on hope.

Norge was right: the Tor couldn't bear to be mounted again. But Ribuld stayed with him, and the Castellan assigned other guards to his side; shuffling heavily, he moved away into the snow. Like Prince Kragen, he seemed to vanish from the world almost immediately.

At a word from Norge, Terisa, Geraden, and Master Barsonage climbed onto their beasts. Led by guards who were connected with lines to other guards, invisible in the impenetrable snowfall, they rode away from Esmerel to search for their encampment.

Swirling snowflakes burned her eyes. They prickled on her cheeks like bits of premonition; hints sharp enough to cut, cold enough to numb the damage they did.

Despite the caution of the riders, they reached their part of the camp sooner than she would have believed possible. The men of Orison and the Alend soldiers had laid out a protected position for their commanders near Esmerel and the head of the valley, away from the exposed foot of the wedge; so Terisa and Geraden, Master Barsonage and Castellan Norge didn't have as far to go as the rest of the guards. And tents had already been set up for them: Master Harpool and his companion had apparently been at work with their mirrors for some time, translating equipment and supplies from Orison.

Master Barsonage and Geraden hurried to join them.

From horseback, Terisa saw bonfires and torches around her, some of them as much as twenty or thirty feet away. Maybe the snowfall was thinning. Even so, it was at least four or five inches deep. And – unless her sense of time had failed completely – sunset was still an hour or so away. Even if the snowfall *was* thinning, there might be a foot or more on the ground before night.

A guard urged her to dismount and enter a large tent which had been raised for the Tor and Castellan Norge; but she stayed where she was, trying to read the suggestions in the snow, until the Tor himself reached the camp. Then she got down and went with him into shelter.

A servant took his cloak, then brought food and wine, which the old lord rejected with a grimace. Supported by Ribuld and another guard, he lowered himself into a camp chair. He had snow in his eyebrows, snow on his head. His cheeks were the color of worn out ice. Ribuld knelt in front of him, offered to pull off his boots; he declined that comfort as well. 'I must go out again soon,' he murmured. 'There is no escaping it.'

'My lord Tor,' Ribuld said in a tone Terisa hadn't heard him use since Argus' death, 'you don't need to go out. Prince Kragen and Castellan Norge will come to you.'

'Ah, true,' sighed the Tor. 'But if I remain here, who will give the King's guard my blessing? I must visit every campfire tonight, every squadron, so that every man will know his bravery is valued and his loyalty, precious.

'No, Ribuld, I will wear my boots. I do not mean to take them off again.'

Ribuld bowed and withdrew to stand with Terisa. Around his scar, the veteran's face was tight with unexpected grief.

'Ribuld—?' she tried to ask; but she couldn't find the words she wanted. All she knew about him was that he had been Argus' friend; he liked and served Artagel; he seemed to enjoy suggestive conversation. And he had killed Saddith to save Lebbick. He would have saved Lebbick from Gart, if he could.

'My lady,' he said, almost snarling to control himself, 'my home's in the Care of Tor. Not far from Marshalt. I fought for the Tor – that's how he knows my name – and for the Perdon, too, before I joined the King's guard.' He looked at her as if, like her, he couldn't find the right words.

Maybe she understood. 'Take good care of him,' she replied softly. 'He needs you more than Geraden and I do.'

The twist of Ribuld's expression could have meant anything.

Terisa left the tent and went to see if Master Harpool required help.

As she and the Masters finished translating the last of the tents and bedrolls, the snowfall abruptly lessened. She felt cold to the bone; her face was wet and numb; her fingertips left trails of moisture down the frame of Master Harpool's glass. Nevertheless the easing of the snow caught at her attention like a call of horns—

—the call for which her heart had always been waiting.

She jerked her back straight, lifted her head, spun around before anyone else noticed the change.

Yes. Blowing down from the head of the valley, the wind parted the snow like curtains, let the gray light of early evening through the clouds. As if without transition, Esmerel and the valley became a winter landscape before twilight, a scene which needed only sunshine to reveal its surprising beauty.

Perhaps the horns – and those who sounded them – were on the far side: the far side of the manor, where the defile brought the brook gamboling over its ice into the valley.

Now Geraden joined her, looked around. Several of the Masters breathed thanks that the snow was stopping. Guards expressed the same sentiment less delicately. None of them could hear the premonition in the air *whetted with cold,* the implication *as penetrating as splinters.*

'Get the Tor,' she said as if the horns had lifted her out of herself, despite the fact that she couldn't hear them, could hardly remember them; maybe she had never heard them. 'Get Prince Kragen. Tell them to hurry.'

'Terisa?' Geraden asked. 'Terisa?'

She ignored him. She didn't need reason: intuition was enough. She was fixed on Esmerel and couldn't look away.

Master Barsonage sent Imagers into motion. Someone shouted for the Castellan. Infected by an urgency they couldn't explain, guards began to obey, began to run. She had that much credibility with them, anyway.

Then past the snow-clogged side of the manor *came charging men on horseback. As the horses fought for speed, their nostrils gusted steam, and their legs churned the snow until the dry, light flakes seemed to boil.* The sides of the valley and the snow muffled every sound, but each movement was distinct, *as edged as a shard of glass.*

Three riders with longswords held up in their fists and keen hate in the strides of their fierce mounts. The riders she had seen in the Congery's augury. The riders of her dream.

'Bowmen!' Norge snapped from somewhere nearby. 'Be ready! We'll pick them off as soon as they get in range.'

'No!' coughed the Tor. He had come out of his tent; he stood with his legs splayed in the snow, supported by Ribuld. 'That is a traitor's deed. Let them approach. We kill no one unless we must!'

'Well said, my lord Tor!' Prince Kragen arrived at a run, with his sword in

864

both hands. Using the blade as a pointer, he commanded, 'Look more closely!'

The light wasn't good: at first, she couldn't see what the Prince was pointing at. But after a moment she realized that each of the riders had a white cloth tied to the tip of his sword.

Flags of truce.

A *truce*, Eremis? With *you*?

One of the riders was certainly Master Eremis: that was unmistakable. He drove his mount plunging forward with an air of jaunty peril, as if he were in the grip of an exquisite and unutterable joy.

Beside him came Master Gilbur, hunchbacked and murderous.

The third man she didn't know by sight. Nevertheless she was sure of him. The arch-Imager Vagel. A relatively small man, at least compared to Eremis and Gilbur; dwarfed by his charger. Lank gray hair fluttered from his skull. He rode with his toothless mouth open like the entrance to a pit.

The riders of her dream.

'The gall of those bastards,' someone whispered. Ribuld? 'The *gall*.'

Abruptly, Gilbur and Vagel hauled on their reins, wrenched their horses to a halt. Just beyond reliable bow-range, they wheeled and stamped, waiting.

Master Eremis came forward as if he feared nothing. Intensely nonchalant, he approached his enemies.

There he stopped.

'My lord Prince.' His tone was full of secret laughter. 'My lord Tor. Master Barsonage. Terisa and Geraden. How fortuitous that you are all here together.'

The Tor leaned on Ribuld as if he had lost the power of speech. Geraden scowled intently, concentrating not on anger but on the ramifications of Master Eremis' presence. Terisa faced the tall Imager and felt the blood congeal in her chest.

'We are not patient with traitors,' snapped Prince Kragen: he was the Alend Contender, accustomed to authority. 'Tell us what you want and be done with it.'

Master Eremis paid no attention to that demand. 'My companions fear you,' he said. 'They believe you will kill them if they come near, despite our flags of truce.'

Prince Kragen snorted. 'That would be an action worthy of you, Eremis. We are not such men.'

In response, Master Eremis laughed along the wind, sent mirth and scorn across the snow. 'Do you hear?' he called over his shoulder. 'The Alend Contender thinks he is not such a man as we are.'

'You're lucky Lebbick isn't here,' muttered Norge. 'He'd castrate you first and worry about honor later.' But no one listened to him.

Spurring their horses, Master Gilbur and the arch-Imager came forward to join Master Eremis.

'Tell us what you want,' Prince Kragen repeated harshly.

'As I say,' gloated Master Eremis, 'it is fortuitous that you are all here together. Because you *are* all here, you will be able to give me what I want. I have a requirement for each of you. Each of you except the Congery' – he sneered at Master Barsonage – 'which has my permission to go sodomize itself whenever it chooses.'

Instead of retorting with threats, the mediator folded his arms on his thick chest and produced a grim smile. 'Be careful what you say, Master Eremis,' he articulated. 'Your insults only betray your fear.'

'Fear!' Master Gilbur waggled his sword mockingly. 'The day you teach me to fear you, Barsonage, I will walk into this camp naked and let you use me however you wish.'

The Tor made a weak gesture, requesting silence. In a thin voice, he said, 'You mentioned requirements, Master Eremis.'

'Indeed,' Eremis replied with a grin. 'And if you satisfy me, I am willing to let you all live.'

Norge pronounced an obscenity. No one else spoke.

'By now,' the tall Imager explained, 'even the thickest-headed among you must realize that we have an alliance with High King Festten. By force of Imagery and arms, we are prepared to crush you completely. We will wash the ground with your blood until you beg to share the Perdon's fate.'

'Try it,' grated Ribuld. Again, no one else spoke.

'As it happens, however,' Master Eremis continued humorously, 'the High King is not a comfortable ally. He wants to rule the world – and I intend that mastery for myself. Our ambitions are not well mated.'

'Doubtless,' the Tor sighed. 'What are your requirements?'

Master Eremis straightened his legs, raised himself high in his saddle. 'My lord Tor, my lord Prince, I require you to surrender.'

This time, it was Prince Kragen who laughed – a bloody and mirthless guffaw.

'If you do so,' Eremis went on smoothly, 'if you will pledge your precious honor and your lives to me, we will turn against Festten. Our Imagery and your arms will break him here, far from his sources of supply, his reinforcements. Then it will be Mordant which rules the world, not Cadwal.

'From the first,' he commented while everyone stared at him, 'my plans have cut in two directions. We are prepared to *annihilate* you, my lords. You are too paltry – you have no hope against us. At the same time, however, I have maneuvered Festten and his strength into a position of vulnerability – here, my lords, *here* – so that he, too, can be annihilated.

'Your choice is simple. Serve me and live. Refuse me and die.'

Geraden held himself still. Terisa glanced at him and saw that he wasn't looking at Master Eremis. He was watching the Tor with a dangerous brightness in his eyes.

Growling curses through his moustache, Prince Kragen also turned toward the Tor.

For a long moment, the Tor said nothing. In fact, the way he stood, his slumped and dependent posture, suggested that he didn't know what was going on. Nevertheless, before the Prince could lose patience with him, the old lord found his voice.

'You mentioned requirements for each of us. Except the Congery. What do you want from Master Geraden and the lady Terisa?'

Terisa caught her breath while the knot of anger and fear inside her pulled tighter.

Master Eremis shrugged, grinning as if only an iron will kept him from laughing his heart out. 'A small sacrifice, my lord. It will cost you little. I require them for myself.'

Master Gilbur snickered.

No, Terisa ached inside herself. No.

Geraden watched the Tor as if he expected something wonderful or terrible from the old lord.

'As a condition of your surrender,' Eremis explained. 'When you have pledged your honor to me – and when Terisa and Geraden have been given into my hands – at that moment, High King Festten's doom is assured.'

No.

Prince Kragen started to retort; but the Tor stopped him with another weak gesture. 'An interesting suggestion, Master Eremis.' The old lord's frailty made him sound mild. 'Unfortunately, you are a demonstrated traitor. What assurance is there that you can be trusted?'

'You need none,' Master Eremis shot back hotly, happily. 'Your choice is too simple for assurances. If you do not satisfy me, you will be destroyed.'

'My lord Tor,' Prince Kragen put in fiercely, 'he wants the lady Terisa and Geraden because he fears them. Their power is our assurance that he cannot destroy us.'

Again, the Tor gestured for silence, asking Kragen to bear with him.

'Master Eremis, you are overconfident,' he said softly, 'so sure of your strength and your *superiority* that you insult us. You insult our honor – but that does not surprise us.' His voice sank as he spoke – and yet gathered force at the same time, so that his quietness carried like a shout. 'No one expects a man of your moral poverty to respect honor.

'You do wrong, however, to insult our intelligence.

'You have no interest in our surrender. You have no intention of turning against High King Festten. I doubt that the arch-Imager would permit such betrayal.' For some reason, Vagel shook his head. 'Gart certainly would not. Your only interest here, your only purpose in coming, is to take the lady Terisa and Master Geraden from us.'

Eremis had heard enough. 'My lord Tor,' he snapped, 'I have not yet begun to insult your intelligence – but now you demonstrate that you are mad. I fear no one. I covet Terisa's female flesh. And I have a score to settle with Geraden. My reasons for coming are exactly as I have explained them.'

No! Terisa protested, insisted, *no*.

And the Tor said, 'No.

'You are a fool, Master Eremis. In the end, you will die a fool's death. If you had the slightest wish for our service – if you had the slightest intention of turning against the High King' – his passion was too fundamental to be shouted – '*you would have treated the Perdon with more respect.*'

Dismissing Eremis, he moved with Ribuld's support toward his tent.

'My lord Tor.' Geraden's face shone; he looked ready now to tackle both Master Eremis and High King Festten single-handedly. He spoke to the old lord's back formally, and his voice seemed to defy the snow and the wind, as if he had the power to command them. 'King Joyse has been fortunate in his friends – but never as fortunate as when he won your loyalty.'

The Tor stumbled, but Ribuld caught him.

Prince Kragen also turned his back. Glowering bloodshed, he barked at Castellan Norge, 'Give these traitors a count of five. Then instruct your bowmen to kill them.'

He didn't stay to watch the riders as they lashed their mounts away from Norge's eager call, surged back in the direction of the manor and the defile, strained for speed as if they had been routed. Bowing first to Geraden, then to Terisa, the Prince strode off toward his own camp.

Terisa heard a few bowstrings thrum, a few arrows hiss in the air. Unluckily, none of the riders fell.

As if on signal, more snow came down the valley. Snow closed off the light, swarmed over the tents, drifted onto Terisa's head and shoulders. The riders of her dream – and the Congery's augury. Geraden was right: she belonged here. And King Joyse was fortunate in his friends.

She put her arms around Geraden, hugged him tightly. Holding each other close, they followed the Tor toward the shelter of his tent.

Before the snowfall became thick enough to blind the sky completely, two or three of the guards on sentry duty down at the foot of the valley thought they saw an imprecise puff of smoke overhead, riding against the wind. Then the sight was gone, and snow came down so thickly that it made everything dark.

FORTY-SEVEN

ON THE VERGE

The Tor's tent was large enough for eight or ten people to stand and shout at each other, but it was ascetically furnished – one bedroll for the lord, one for the guard at the tentflaps, a brazier for warmth, three lanterns hanging around the pole, the Tor's camp chair, a few other stools. Maybe he wanted it that way: maybe he feared that if he ever became comfortable he wouldn't be able to move again. Or maybe he wasn't willing to put any more strain than necessary on the Masters and their translations.

When Terisa and Geraden entered the tent, they found the Tor in his chair, leaning as far back as it would allow. His eyes were dull, and he was panting thinly, as if he needed somehow to get more air past an obstacle which hurt him whenever he inhaled. Ribuld and one of the guards' physicians had removed his cloak, his mail, his shirt. Ribuld was dumb with misery.

For the first time, Terisa saw the place under the lord's ribs where Gart had kicked him.

Involuntarily, she tightened her grip on Geraden.

The Tor's injury was swollen like a tumor, black-purple and angry; it bloated out from his belly as if his skin might burst.

'Oh, my lord,' Geraden breathed, nearly groaned. 'What are you doing to yourself?'

The Tor had been bleeding inside for days, killing himself with the effort to fill his King's place.

He made a dismissive gesture; he may have wanted Terisa and Geraden to go away. Nevertheless they stayed where they were. After a moment, Geraden asked the physician, 'How is he?'

'As you see,' the man muttered. 'I told him this would happen. We all told him.' He mixed some herbs in a goblet and handed it to the Tor. 'He's too old. He drinks too much wine. He shouldn't be alive.'

For some reason, Ribuld shot out his arm, knotted his fist in the physician's cloak, jerked the man silent. Almost at once, however, he seemed to realize the uselessness of his anger. Releasing the physician, he muttered an apology, then moved away to get a stool for the Tor's legs.

With his legs supported, the lord was able to sink down until he could rest his head on the back of the chair. His eyes were closed now, and a bit of the strain went out of his breathing; apparently, the physician's herbs did him some good. He looked like he might sleep.

He didn't, however. Without opening his eyes, he murmured, 'Where?'

The physician stopped to listen.

'"Where," my lord?' asked Ribuld.

The Tor's fat lips tightened around a spasm of pain. For a moment, he couldn't breathe. Then, tightly, he asked, 'Where is Nyle?'

Where is Nyle. Where are Eremis and Gilbur and Vagel. Where is their laborium. Where is the High King. Terisa resisted an impulse to curse herself.

Geraden squeezed her, then left her to approach the old lord. Controlling himself grimly, he said, 'We've been wrong, my lord. Terisa and I. He was never here. We just assumed he would use Esmerel.' Geraden glanced at Terisa. 'I guess Nyle made the same assumption. He told Terisa Eremis was here. But he wasn't.'

Clenching his courage, Geraden concluded, 'We've brought you into a trap we can't get out of.'

The Tor inhaled weakly around his hemorrhage. 'Where?' he repeated.

'Somewhere close.' Geraden seemed to be speaking to Terisa as well as to the lord. 'Close enough for High King Festten to attack us. Close enough for Eremis and Vagel and Gilbur to find their way here through the snow. If I had to guess, I'd say the first thing Eremis did after he decided he wanted to rule the world – maybe even before he found Vagel – was build a secret stronghold for himself. Somewhere in these hills.' Somewhere in this maze. 'But it could be anywhere. Even if it's just on the other side of the valley rim, we can't get to it.'

The Tor exhaled thinly, a constricted sigh. 'What will you do?'

'About what?'

'What will you do' – the Tor made an effort to be clear – 'when Master Eremis decides to use Nyle against you?'

Terisa was glad that the old lord couldn't see the flush of distress in Geraden's face, the flinch around his eyes.

'I don't know,' Geraden murmured.

'Maybe,' she said without thinking, 'maybe we can find them. The snow will cover us. It's almost night. Maybe we can sneak out through that ravine and find them.'

Geraden shook his head. 'Snow and night will cover him, too. They'll cover his guards. If we don't get lost and freeze to death, we'll probably be captured.'

All right. All right. It wasn't a good idea. But we've got to do *something*. We can't just sit here and watch – watch—

Watching the lord's struggle to breathe made Terisa feel sick and wild.

At that moment, she heard voices outside the tent: a bark of command, a muffled acknowledgment.

The tentflaps were swept aside, and King Joyse strode in.

He startled Terisa so badly that she nearly stumbled to her knees.

He was filthy. Clots of mud clung to his battle gear – his breastplate and mail leggings, the protective iron pallettes on his shoulders, the brassards strapped to his arms. His mail had been cut, hacked at by swords. Blows dented his breastplate. Blood stained his thick cloak and the leather under his armor; black streaks marked the tooled scabbard which held his longsword. Grime filled his beard, caked his hair to his scalp.

Nevertheless he entered the tent like a much younger man. He strode forward with strength in his legs, authority in his arms; and his eyes flashed a blue so deep that it was almost purple.

When he saw Terisa and Geraden, he grinned like a boy.

'Well met. Better to come late than not to come at all, I always say.'

'My lord King,' Geraden breathed, gaping. He was too surprised to bow, almost too surprised to speak. 'Are you hurt?'

'A few scratches.' The King's grin broadened into the smile Terisa remembered, the smile of innocence and pleasure, the sunrise which lit all his features and made him the kind of man for whom people were willing to die. 'Nothing my enemies can pride themselves for.'

He might have gone on, but the Tor stopped him.

Hearing King Joyse's voice, the old lord jerked up his head, snatched open his eyes. Urgently, almost frantically, he hauled his legs off the stool and blundered to his feet like a surfacing grampus. Around the vivid bulge of his hemorrhage, his bare skin looked as pale as disease, tarnished with frailty and need.

Tottering, he caught a hand on Ribuld's shoulder. 'Prince Kragen,' he gasped. 'Summon the Prince.'

Then he plunged to his knees as if the ground had been cut out from under him.

Ribuld started to help the lord, but King Joyse's presence daunted him.

Bowing his face to the canvas, retching for breath, the Tor panted, 'My lord King, I beg you.'

King Joyse's smile turned to ashes on his face.

'I beg you. I have brought your guard and your Congery and all your friends to destruction. Tell me I have not betrayed you.'

'*Betrayed* me?' The passion in the King's face was wonderful and dire. As if he had no arthritis and no years, no weakness of any kind to hamper him, he caught hold of the Tor's arms and raised him to his feet by main strength. 'My old friend! If you have put all I love and all my force in the path of ruin, you have not betrayed me. If you have sold my kingdom to the Alend Contender, so that I have nothing left to rule, you have not betrayed me. You are *here* – *here*, where the fate of the world hinges.' Tears trailed through the grime on his cheeks. 'My lord Tor, I have used you abominably. I considered you an obstacle, your loyalty a stumbling block. And you have served me better than my best hope.'

Hardly able to bear what he heard, the Tor clamped his hands over his face and shuddered as if he were sobbing.

King Joyse glanced up and down the Tor's frame; at once, his expression darkened. To the astonished physician, he snapped, 'How was he injured? How severe is his hurt?'

'A kick, my lord King,' the physician fumbled out quickly. 'The High

King's Monomach. He bleeds inwardly.' The man faltered, then forced himself to say, 'If he does not rest, he will die. And even if he does rest, I cannot vouch for his life. He has used himself' – the physician seemed unaware that he was aping the King's words – 'abominably.'

'Then he will rest,' King Joyse replied in a tone which no one could have ignored. 'You will give him your best care. If he dies, you will justify yourself to *me*.'

Without waiting for an answer, he eased the Tor back into his camp chair. The Tor collapsed against the chair back weakly.

Geraden put a hand on Ribuld's arm. 'Prince Kragen.' He spoke in a whisper; but his tone was like the King's, irrefusable. 'And Master Barsonage.'

Ribuld went out of the tent in a daze.

'Now.' King Joyse faced Terisa and Geraden. He stood slightly poised, as if he were ready to spring, and his eyes blazed blue. 'You have a great deal to tell me. Before Prince Kragen comes. Begin from Gart's attack in the hall of audiences.

'Where is Castellan Lebbick?'

His intensity was so compelling that Terisa almost started to answer. Geraden, however, had other ideas. He shifted a bit away from her, a bit ahead of her, placing himself between her and danger. Folding his arms on his chest, he said firmly – so firmly that Terisa was simultaneously amazed and proud and frightened – 'You've been fighting your enemies, my lord King. I can decide better what to tell you if you'll tell me who gave you your "scratches."'

The King's eyes narrowed. 'Geraden,' he said harshly, 'do you remember who I am?'

Geraden didn't flinch. 'Yes, my lord King. You're the man who abandoned the throne of Mordant when we needed you most. You're the man who brought us all to the edge of ruin without *once*' – his anger stung the air – 'having the decency to tell us the truth.'

Instead of retorting, King Joyse studied Geraden as if the younger man had become someone he didn't know, a completely different person. A moment later, he shrugged, and the peril in his gaze eased.

'Your father, the Domne,' he said evenly, 'has given me many gifts, both of friendship and of service. His greatest gift to me, however, is the loyalty of his sons. I trust you, Geraden. I have trusted you for a long time. And I have given you little reason to trust me. You will answer me when you are ready.

'I have been fighting, as you see' – he indicated his battle gear – 'to rescue Queen Madin.'

Rescue Queen Madin. Rescue the Queen. Terisa didn't understand how that was possible – the distances were too great, the time too short – but his mere statement filled her with so much relief that she could hardly keep her legs under her.

'Doubtless,' King Joyse explained, 'you have been told of the strange shapeless cloud of Imagery with which Havelock broke Prince Kragen's catapults. That shape is a creature, a being – a being with which Havelock has contrived an improbable friendship.

'I must confess that when you told me of the Queen's abduction I became' – he pursed his lips wryly – 'a trifle unreasonable. It was always my intention to lead whatever forces Orison could muster myself. I meant to beg or intimidate an alliance out of Margonal. I could coerce the Congery somehow. For that reason, my old friend' – he nodded toward the sprawling Tor – 'had no place in my plans. I did not know that I would need him.'

'That's my fault,' Terisa said abruptly, unexpectedly. Geraden had placed himself between her and the King for a reason, a reason she ought to respect. Nevertheless she couldn't keep still. 'You were doing what you had to do. You hurt the Tor and Castellan Lebbick and Elega and everyone else so they wouldn't realize your weakness was only a ploy. So they wouldn't betray you. But I already betrayed you. I told Eremis' – the thought of her own folly choked her – 'told Eremis you knew what you were doing. That's why he took the Queen.'

King Joyse looked at her hard, so hard that she blushed in chagrin. Yet his gaze held no recrimination. After a brief pause, he said, 'My lady, you were provoked,' and returned his attention to Geraden.

'As I say,' he continued, 'I became unreasonable. I abandoned you. Though he pleaded with me to reconsider, I forced Havelock to translate his strange friend for me, and that shape bore me to the Care of Fayle as swift as wings. At the debris of Vale House, I found the trail of a motley collection of the Fayle's old servants and soldiers attempting to pursue Torrent and the Queen. That trail led me eventually to Torrent's – eventually, I say, or I would have returned to you a day or more sooner – and so to Torrent herself and the Queen.

'At the cost of much hardship and privation and danger' – his eyes hinted at pride – 'my demure and retiring daughter saved her mother. She enabled me to find the Queen and set her free.

'Her abductors defended themselves as well as they could – well enough to prevent the Fayle's men and me from capturing or questioning them – but at last they fell.' The state of his gear testified that the battle hadn't been easy. 'When I had taken Queen Madin and Torrent to safety in Romish, Havelock's friend brought me here as quickly as possible.'

Geraden absorbed this account without obvious surprise or appreciation. When King Joyse had finished, Geraden asked noncommittally, 'And you didn't stop in Orison? You don't have any news from there?'

The King was losing patience. 'Do I look like a man who has spent time on social amenities and conversation? I knew that if I did not find you here I could return to Orison at my leisure. But if I had stopped there first and failed to find you, the delay might have made me too late to join you. I have learned nothing, heard nothing, since the moment I left the hall of audiences.

'Geraden,' he concluded warningly, 'I must know what has happened in my absence. I must hear the tale you brought to Orison with Prince Kragen. I cannot go into battle without that knowledge.'

'My lord King,' Geraden responded as if he were immune to Joyse's impatience, 'Eremis is holding my brother Nyle hostage somewhere near here – a stronghold of some kind, probably. Eremis is going to use him against us. Against me. And it's my doing. If I hadn't been so determined to stop him

873

from betraying you for Elega and Prince Kragen, he never would have been vulnerable to Eremis. He wouldn't have been locked up where Eremis could get at him.

'But it's your doing, too. You've always been such a friend of the Domne. You welcomed Artagel. You went out of your way to draw me to you. And yet you always ignored Nyle.

'His yearning was as great as mine. He has plenty of ability. And he was raised from the beginning on Artagel's stories about you, the Domne's stories. He would have been willing to kill for you by the time he was *six*.'

'Geraden,' King Joyse growled.

Nevertheless Geraden went on, 'Why didn't you value him at all? Why didn't you give him something to save him while he was still young enough to save?'

'You exceed yourself,' snapped the King. 'I have not come all this way to answer such questions.'

'But you're going to answer this one,' Geraden replied as if he were sure – as if he had the capacity to make King Joyse do what he wanted. The hint of authority in his voice was so subtle that Terisa scarcely heard it. He meant to wrest some kind of truth from his King.

And the King did answer. To her astonishment, he retreated visibly, with a crestfallen air, a look of embarrassment; Geraden had touched an odd shame. 'Yes,' he muttered, 'all right. You are right. I always did ignore him. There was always a quality in his dumb need which I disliked. He pitied himself before I could pity him – and so I had no desire to pity him.

'But that is not the reason.

'Artagel was another matter altogether. His talent with the sword was obvious. Anyone would have welcomed him. But you, Geraden—' The King's gaze was angry and hurt at once, as if his own sense of culpability baffled him. 'I did not choose you out of a desire to give you precedence over Nyle. I would not have done that to the son of a friend. No, I drew you to me because I had already seen your importance in Havelock's augury.'

Geraden hissed a breath; but King Joyse didn't stop.

'The glass which he broke when I was an infant showed you exactly as you appear in the Congery's augury' – for a moment, the King's voice sounded as raw as splintered wood – 'surrounded entirely by mirrors in which Images of violence reflected against you. How could I let you be? I had to save you, if that were possible. And if it were not, I had to give you the chance to save me.

'Geraden,' King Joyse admitted in frank pain, 'on your father's love, I swear to you that I slighted Nyle's yearning only because I was not wise enough to see where it would lead him. The Domne has given me nothing but love and loyalty. In the matter of his son Nyle I failed him.'

For a long moment, Geraden didn't speak. When he did, his throat was tight with emotion. 'We all failed, my lord King. For my part – I swear to you on my father's love that I'll save you if I can. No matter how many people you've hurt. You haven't been honest with us for a long time, and I *hate* that. But you're still my King. Nobody can fill that place but you.'

Terisa couldn't keep quiet any longer. 'Castellan Lebbick is dead,' she put

874

in cruelly to get the King's attention. She needed answers of her own. 'Gart killed him. All he managed to do before he died was save the Tor.'

That made Geraden turn toward her, made King Joyse face her again.

The two men looked unexpectedly like a match for each other, suited to meet each other's demands.

'I defended you,' she said with Lebbick's body vivid in her mind, and the Perdon's; with the Tor's hurt displayed under the light of the lanterns. 'I stood up in front of everybody and told them what Master Quillon told me. You made yourself the only reasonable target. So the enemies you hadn't been able to identify would attack you instead of someone else, somewhere else. I told them. That's why we're all here. We decided to trust you even after you abandoned us.

'But Master Quillon is dead. Castellan Lebbick is dead. The *Perdon* is dead. The Tor is dying.' Her distress accumulated as she spoke. She thought that she would never be reconciled to all the different kinds of pain King Joyse had exacted from his friends. 'Nyle is a hostage, and Houseldon has been burned to the ground, and Sternwall is sinking in lava, and the Fayle doesn't even have enough men left to rescue his own daughter, and now we're probably going to be slaughtered because we don't know where Eremis' stronghold is,' oh, curse you, curse you, you crazy old man, 'and I want to know how you stand it. How do you live with yourself? How do you expect us to trust you?

'You can't help us now!' Overwhelmed by unpremeditated bitterness, Terisa cried, 'You can't even beat Havelock at *hop-board*!'

Despite her outburst, however, King Joyse faced her gently. Her accusation hurt him less than Geraden's had: maybe he was readier for it. His face softened while she protested against him; his gaze was blurred by compassion. He waited until she was finished. Then, incongruously, he pulled an old handkerchief out of the seam of his breastplate and handed it to her so that she could wipe her eyes.

Geraden stood now at the King's shoulder as if he had been won over. 'Terisa—' he began; but King Joyse touched his arm, stopped him.

'No, Geraden. I must answer her.

'My lady, I have already proved myself to you, after a fashion. You have seen atrocities in Mordant. Yet it was not I who perpetrated them. If I had not, as you say, made myself a target, if I had not risked those I love most in the name of my weakness, those atrocities would be everywhere. Without the lure of my weakness, Eremis might have had great difficulty forging an alliance with High King Festten – and so he would have had no choice except to afflict Cadwal and Mordant and Alend with vile Imagery until all things were destroyed. At the cost of Quillon's life, and Lebbick's, and the Perdon's – at the cost, yes, of my own wife's indignation, my own daughter's betrayal, I have procured my enemy's name as well as his attention, so that for Cadwal and Mordant and Alend there is still hope. I have given us the opportunity to fight for our world.

'But that is not what you wish to know, is it?'

His voice searched her, and his eyes seemed to probe her bitterness. When he looked at her like that, she felt an unaccountable desire to tell him about being locked in the closet, as if it were his fault in some way, as if there were something he could have done about it. Until this moment, he had cut himself off from her – as her father had cut himself off. What made King Joyse a better man than her father?

'You dislike what I have done,' the King said, 'but you are able to grasp the necessity of it. Otherwise you would not have supported me. No, my lady, what you want from me is a more immediate hope. You wish me to be greater than you can imagine. You wish me to justify myself with power. You wish me to tell you that I have the means to save you.'

Involuntarily, she ducked her head, unable to meet his steady blue scrutiny.

'Terisa,' he said softly, 'my lady, I cannot save you. I do not have the means.

'You know that already,' he continued at once. 'As you have observed, I cannot so much as defeat the Adept at hop-board. It is only a game, of course, a mere exercise – but I cannot forget that the pieces live and breathe, with names and spouses, children and bravery and fear. I am an *unreasonable* man. When Quillon told me that Myste went to you before her disappearance, I risked myself and all my plans in order to challenge you, even though Havelock's augury had given me reason to think I knew where she had gone. When my wife is threatened, I do not ask whether any larger need should outweigh her peril in my mind. I lack Havelock's particular sanity.

'And the same unreason weakens me everywhere. Shall I tell you a thing which shames me? When I learned that you had fled to Havelock after Quillon's death, that you had gone to him for rescue with Master Gilbur hot behind you, and that he had refused you— My lady, Havelock is my oldest friend. It was he who put me on the path to become what I am. But when I learned that he had refused you, I struck him—'

Geraden's eyes widened at that revelation; but he said nothing.

'Nevertheless,' the King went on as if mere shame couldn't hold him back, 'I am here. When Quillon was killed – Quillon, who had served me so long with such courage and cunning – I knew that this battle was mine to wage, rather than only to command. The blood must be on my hands. I will not have my pieces so contemptuously used. I will not allow Master Eremis to tilt the board, to remake the world in his own image.' Terisa could have sworn that he was growing taller, rising to power in front of her. 'Do you believe I care nothing for Lebbick's suffering, or the Tor's? Do you believe I have not felt your distress – or Geraden's – or Elega's?

'My lady, you have not seen me fight.'

Curse you. Oh, curse you completely. I'll do anything you want. Just tell me what it is.

'I *have* seen you fight, however,' put in Prince Kragen as he came between the tentflaps. 'Though it galls me to say so, my lord King, I am glad that you have come.'

The Prince had Ribuld with him, and Castellan Norge. Master Barsonage entered the tent on the Castellan's heels. And with them came a slim figure cloaked from head to foot in dark satin, face and shape and even hands hidden. As Prince Kragen strode forward to confront the King, as both Master Barsonage and Norge stopped and stared as if they couldn't believe their eyes, the cloaked figure slipped back along the tent wall, trying to remain as unobtrusive as possible.

'My lord Prince.' King Joyse swung away from Terisa and Geraden; the keenness in his stance intensified. 'Master Barsonage.' He looked ready to leap in any direction, haul out his sword at a moment's notice. 'Captain Norge.

'I have said it before, but I will gladly say it again. We are well met.'

'My lord King.' The Tor tried to reach his feet against the physician's restraining hands. His voice sounded as thin as a light breeze in cornshucks. 'I must speak.'

At once, King Joyse turned toward the Tor; but he kept his back to the tent wall, away from Prince Kragen. 'Speak sitting, my lord,' he commanded. 'And speak as little as possible. Your life is precious to me.'

Muffling a groan, the Tor sagged.

'If we are here wrongly, the fault is mine alone,' he said in a deathbed whisper. 'Master Geraden and the lady Terisa have discovered their talents. Already they have worked miracles of Imagery. Norge has become your Castellan, at my command. He leads the forces of Orison.'

With a visceral shiver, Terisa realized that the Tor was struggling to prepare King Joyse for his encounter with the Prince.

'Master Barsonage and the Congery have devised means of supply and defense, in accordance with your strictures. We would not have come so far without them.

'Prince Kragen is here with six thousand Alend soldiers because he is an honorable man.'

King Joyse put a hand on the Tor's naked shoulder, mutely urging the old lord to conserve his strength. '"An honorable man,"' he echoed distinctly, as if he had doubts on that point. Almost without transition, he appeared to become someone different – a figure of barely suppressed anger, spoiling for conflict. Facing the Prince again, and speaking mildly, but with a bright threat in his eyes, he asked, 'Does my old friend mean that he and the Alend Monarch have formed an alliance?'

'No.' Prince Kragen studied the King warily. The excitement which had brought him here was alloyed with a long-standing distrust; but his posture made it clear that he wouldn't back down from his own desires. 'He means that he has explained to the Alend Monarch his intention to place his head on Eremis' cutting-block and die rather than submit to a war of attrition he cannot win. And the Alend Monarch sent me to accompany him with the bulk of our force because we have no other way to determine whether the Tor's intention is mad or brilliant. My instructions from my sovereign are to join the Tor or to flee, according to the things I learn here.'

'Margonal is crafty,' commented King Joyse with deceptive nonchalance, 'and apparently he has grown in courage. Well, now you are here, my lord Prince. What have you learned?'

Prince Kragen allowed himself a noncommittal shrug. 'I have learned that we are indeed trapped. All our heads are on the cutting-block, and Alend will stand or fall with Mordant, regardless of my instructions.'

'I think not,' King Joyse retorted with the air of a man pouncing. 'I think you will turn against us at the last and join Cadwal, to preserve your father's true cowardice.'

At that, Kragen's head jerked back; a flush of fury darkened his cheeks; he closed his fist on his swordhilt.

In response, both Ribuld and Norge braced themselves to draw their blades. The cloaked figure against the tent wall started forward, then retreated. Geraden edged closer to Terisa, moving to protect her from the danger of swords.

No, she thought urgently, you don't understand, Prince Kragen is here *with* us, *with* us.

The Tor repeated hoarsely, 'He is honorable. Honorable.'

'My lord King,' the Prince said between his teeth, 'because you *are* the King, and because I have been told at length why I must trust you, I will assume you have *reason* to accuse me of such a betrayal.'

'I have *reason*,' snapped King Joyse. 'During my absence, I saved Queen Madin from her abductors. It will not surprise you to hear that when at last I found her she was across the Pestil. In Alend, my lord Prince. Her abductors were Alends, and she was being taken by the most direct route toward Scarab.'

Prince Kragen's mouth tightened under his moustache. His dark eyes burned with old enmity, with decades of violence, generations of bloodshed. He looked willing to gut King Joyse on the spot.

Yet he contained his outrage. And he didn't draw his sword. 'And you persist,' he demanded, 'in the mad belief that I am capable of such a vile act?'

'No!' Terisa protested. 'Eremis did it. He told me so.' What was the matter with King Joyse? How could he suddenly be so wrong-headed? 'It's just a trick to keep you and the Prince from joining forces.'

Before she could go on, King Joyse pointed a forbidding finger at her. 'That proves nothing.' The command in his stance forced her to be still. 'Master Eremis has a pact with Cadwal. Why not with Alend?'

'Because,' the cloaked figure cried, '*he is honorable!*'

'You do not trust him.' Elega swept the hood back from her head as she advanced, and her vivid eyes flashed in the lantern-light. 'Is the Tor wrong? Are Terisa and Geraden?' She called every gaze to herself, a cynosure of indignation and passion. Bright as a flame, she challenged her father. 'He held Orison in the palm of his siege for days and *days*. He could have taken you apart stone from stone. Yet he withheld. Does that mean nothing to you? He allowed you *time* to prove yourself. And you *dare* accuse him of dishonor? *You dare that to my face?*'

King Joyse looked at her as if he were stunned.

'No, Father!' she raged. 'The only dishonor in this tent is *yours*! It was *you* who refused to support the Perdon, *you* who refused to hear the Fayle. It was *you* who humiliated Prince Kragen in the hall of audiences, *you* who allowed Terisa's attacker to roam Orison freely, *you* who drove Myste away. You have no *right* to doubt the Prince. There is no alliance between Alend and Mordant because no one is able to trust *you!*'

Emotions throbbed under the King's old skin: outrage; alarm; disbelief. And vindication? *She carries my pride with her wherever she goes.* For a moment, no one moved; he didn't move. Elega met his stare as if she were prepared to outface the world.

All at once, King Joyse burst out laughing.

'Oh, very well, my lord Prince,' he chortled while the people around him stared. 'You are honest, and your father is honest, and I must apologize. If I do not, she will take the skin from my bones.'

Geraden's mouth hung open. Prince Kragen clenched his jaws as if he didn't dare speak.

'It was not wise to bring her with you,' King Joyse went on, 'a woman in battle, a useful hostage if Eremis should capture her. But it was *honest*. If you intended treachery, you would have left her with Margonal. And she would not love you if you had such treachery in you. I know that about her.

'My lord Prince, please accept my regrets – and also my thanks. If we can be saved, it will be because of your courage, as well as your honor.'

As King Joyse spoke, the excitement came back to Prince Kragen, the strange new eagerness which had led him into risks no Alend had ever hazarded before. His mouth twisted up the tips of his moustache. Slowly, he produced a smile to match Joyse's humor.

'Why do you think the decision was mine? Have *you* ever been able to tell her what to do?'

In response, the King laughed again; kindly, happily. He grinned like a new day. 'Tell *her* what to do? *Me?*' Elega glared at him in confusion, but he didn't stop. 'I am only her father. Tell her what to *do*? Most of the time, I am hardly allowed to make suggestions.'

Then he sobered. 'One thing, however, I will tell *you*, my lord Prince. Heed me well. While this war lasts, you will obey my orders.' Now his tone admitted no argument: his command was as clear as a shout. 'If we do not work together, we are doomed.'

Prince Kragen only hesitated for a moment; then, still grinning, he nodded once, briefly.

Still ignoring the surprise and consternation and hope around him, King Joyse turned to Elega.

'As for you, my daughter,' he said gladly, 'you are pride and joy to me.' Taking her hands, he raised them to his mouth and kissed them. 'No one could have done better. The Queen herself could not have done better. Alone and without power or position, you have made an alliance where none existed.

'Oh, you please me!' Abruptly, he swept his gaze around the tent, swung his arms expansively. 'You all please me! If we cannot save our world now, it will be because I have failed you, not because any one of you has failed Mordant. You have all given me better than I deserve.'

In sheer joy, he kept on laughing; and after a moment Geraden joined him. Then, surprising even himself, Prince Kragen began to chuckle. Elega's smile grew softer and easier as it spread.

Master Barsonage shook his head, laughing as well. Terisa squeezed her eyes hard to keep herself from weeping foolishly; but she didn't start to laugh until she realized that the Tor was snoring as if nothing had happened.

★

They talked together for a long time, King Joyse and Prince Kragen, Terisa and Elega, Geraden and Master Barsonage, with Castellan Norge looking on as if he would have found a good night's sleep far more interesting. Guards brought supper, cleared it away when it was done. Ribuld helped the physician put the snoring Tor to bed. For the most part, King Joyse and Prince Kragen and Elega listened, asking an occasional question, while Terisa and Geraden and the mediator recounted and explained. Little of what was said was news to the Prince or Elega, but King Joyse listened intently, emitting concern and curiosity and approval like benefactions.

His friends and supporters had done well: he said that repeatedly. His unwilling allies had done well. His smile shone on everyone until the tent was full of warmth; he seemed to take every sad or hurtful thing onto himself, so that no one around him felt blamed or criticized for confusion or distrust or failure. The time passed in a glow, and Terisa understood at last why so many people had loved and served him for so long. She no longer wondered why the Perdon had sacrificed himself and all his men for a King who had abandoned him, or why the Tor had come to her in the dungeon to beg her to save herself for the King's sake, or why the Domne was able to view the destruction of Houseldon without recrimination against his old friend, or why Queen Madin's first reaction on hearing of her husband's peril was to rejoin him. Terisa felt that way herself now, would have done those things herself.

She felt that she had come through hate and defeat to something else, to a kind of settled commitment, a mood in which all things were possible. She wasn't exactly eager to face the coming day – but she wasn't afraid of it, either.

For his part, Geraden was eager. His eyes shone at his King, and he took every occasion he could find to look toward Terisa and smile, as if he wanted to say, See, I told you he's worth serving.

He didn't come down from happiness until the talk turned to battle plans.

Master Barsonage described the Congery's resources, and King Joyse gave him instructions for the Masters. The King and Prince Kragen devised chains of command, ways to convey messages; they made the best arrangements they could to treat the injured and feed the well; they deployed in their minds the forces of horse and foot. And gradually Geraden's expression turned somber.

'What troubles you, Geraden?' asked Prince Kragen eventually.

Geraden shook his head, staring at nothing.

'Say it, Geraden,' King Joyse urged mildly. 'Words will not hurt us.'

'I'm sorry, my lord King, my lord Prince.' Geraden tried to force a happier look onto his face, without much success. 'Nothing's wrong. I just can't get rid of the feeling that Terisa and I don't belong here.'

Oh, good, Terisa thought dimly. This again.

'Why?' inquired the King. 'Where else should you be?'

Geraden grimaced in exasperation. 'I have no idea.' Almost at once, however, he added, 'But it's obvious we're useless where we are. The Congery doesn't really have mirrors to spare for us. And if we had mirrors, what could we do? We don't know where Eremis' stronghold is. We don't know' – a more crucial point – 'what it looks like. We have all this talent –

and Eremis presumably thinks we can hurt him, or why would he try so hard to hurt us? – but there doesn't seem to be anything we can *do*.'

Prince Kragen frowned studiously; Elega nodded as if she understood the problem. But for some reason King Joyse seemed unable to take Geraden's concern seriously. 'Well, Geraden,' he said in a tone of confidence, 'you can hardly expect advice from *us*. Those talents are yours, not ours. You are the only judge of what you can and cannot do.'

'True,' put in Master Barsonage. He seemed glad that he wasn't responsible for whatever Geraden and Terisa did.

'You will think of something in good time,' concluded the King comfortably.

Before anyone could object, he began to dismiss his companions so that they all could get a few hours of sleep.

Terisa made sure that Geraden came with her when she left the Tor's tent. He wasn't actually reluctant to accompany her: he was simply so caught up in King Joyse that he had trouble tearing himself away. The King insisted, however; and she and Geraden went out into the snow to find their bedroll.

She had no intention of sleeping. In fact, she couldn't imagine sleeping, under the circumstances. She just wanted to have Geraden to herself for a while.

They found their bedroll at the edge of the light cast by the guards' lanterns outside the Tor's tent. The snow was still falling, although less heavily; but the bedroll was wrapped in a waterproof canvas sheet, with one large end propped up by sticks to form a kind of miniature tent, letting air into the bedroll while keeping snow off its occupants. The only trick, Terisa soon discovered, was to get *into* the bedroll without tracking too much snow—

Shivering, she and Geraden swaddled themselves in their blankets and hugged each other for warmth.

'Have you got any ideas?' he asked; his mind was still on King Joyse and battle.

'Yes,' she said, 'but they don't have anything to do with Imagery.'

With her hands and her lips, she persuaded him to think about her instead. She wanted her whole body and her heart to be full of him, as if he were an antidote to Master Eremis and violence.

After that, they found it easier to relax.

Nevertheless they got up a few hours later – a long time before dawn – when King Joyse emerged to begin readying his forces.

The snowfall had stopped. It covered the ground deeply, shrouded the tents and bedrolls of twelve thousand men; it melted off the backs of the horses; it muffled every sound, absorbed even voices, and kept the campfires all across the valley small. King Joyse himself looked small in the face of so much snow and darkness. The way he rubbed his hands together suggested that the cold had brought back his arthritis. Nevertheless his eyes gleamed with blue. Gusting steam into the lantern-light, he demanded of Castellan Norge in feigned vexation, 'Where's that slugabed Prince?'

Norge shrugged with so little show of enthusiasm that the King chuckled.

'Make an effort to stay awake today, Castellan,' he joked. 'Our lives may become quite stimulating.'

The Castellan allowed himself a wan smile.

Through the light, Prince Kragen appeared with several of his captains and the lady Elega.

Together, he and King Joyse moved away to visit as much of their combined army as possible, ostensibly to explain their plans and reassure their men, but primarily to make King Joyse's presence – and his alliance with Alend – as widely felt as possible; to give every soldier and guard as many reasons for hope as possible.

At the same time, Master Barsonage and the Congery began to unpack mirrors. The Imagers needed time to get into position – and to conceal themselves. Several hundred men went with them to defend them, and their mirrors.

At the tentflaps, Terisa and Geraden learned from Ribuld that the Tor was still sleeping. They left the old lord.

With Elega, they watched the army prepare.

The mediator and his comrades translated more food from Orison. Horsemen delivered supplies throughout the camp and brought bedrolls and tents by the thousands back to the Masters. Huge stacks of hay appeared and were carried away for the mounts. The entire valley seethed with motion – dimly seen by firelight from the higher ground where the Tor's tent had been pitched – as thousands of men visited the brook and the latrines and the cooking fires.

'What do you think our chances are?' Terisa asked to ease the cold anxiety gnawing inside her.

'We're well bottled in this valley,' Geraden muttered. 'That's bad. On the other hand, it looks like we can only be attacked from one direction. The defile is too narrow. They can't send enough men through it fast enough to hurt us seriously. That's good. So what they'll try to do is drive us toward the walls. If we get too close, they can drop all kinds of things on us.'

'If Eremis has a mirror with Esmerel in the Image,' Terisa said, 'or any part of this valley—'

'Then,' Geraden finished for her, 'he can attack us any way he wants.' Abruptly, he turned and looked at her hard. 'But he won't. He won't risk it. He'll be afraid of you. If you shattered his glass, he wouldn't be able to see what's going on. What you did back at the crossroads is going to save us. If you hadn't done that, we'd probably all be dead by now.'

She didn't know how true that was. Nevertheless the fact that he said it loosened a knot inside her. 'Thanks,' she murmured to him privately.

'And there are other hopes,' the lady Elega commented. While darkness still filled the valley, her indoor beauty clung to her, and in the lantern-light her eyes seemed luminous with knowledge. 'The world is full of strange things, which our enemies do not understand. Master Eremis comprehends only fear and power. He is blinded by his contempt. He does not grasp how far valor may go against him.'

Terisa hardly heard the King's daughter. She was thinking, *Choose your risks more carefully.* And she was thinking, *We're useless where we are.* Geraden had the strongest feeling—

Unfortunately, no flash of inspiration came to her.

The sky began to grow pale. Laboring urgently, Master Barsonage and his companions translated unnecessary food and bedding and encumbrances back to Orison. Scouts were sent to watch the foot of the valley. Shifting through the gloom, the army moved into its battle formation: wedge-shaped, like the valley, but reversed, so that an attack from the foot of the valley would meet the point of the wedge and split, be forced against the walls itself; a wedge with mounted troops at the edges for mobility and a core of foot soldiers for strength.

When the sky grew pale enough to cast the valley rim into stark relief, everyone saw that during the night siege engines had been pulled into place.

Catapults: black against the pearl heavens: six, seven – no, nine of them around the valley, ready to pitch rocks or boulders onto the heads of Mordant's defenders.

Terisa groaned uselessly.

A murmur rose from the army. At first, she thought it was a reaction to the catapults. But then she saw King Joyse striding toward her from among the troops, holding his standard high in his fists. On the hillside leading up to the Tor's tent, he fixed his plain purple pennon, drove the butt of the standard into the snow and the ground.

The flag rose and fluttered there as if he had brought it straight from the Masters' augury.

'Here we stand.'

Terisa had the impression that King Joyse wasn't shouting. Yet his voice carried as if it could reach every corner of the valley.

'Let them come against us if they dare.'

No one cheered. No one got the chance.

Without warning, the beat of a wardrum throbbed in the air. The sound came from far away, down below the foot of the valley; yet like the King's voice it carried, a flat, fatal pulse so visceral that Terisa seemed to hear it with her throat and chest rather than her ears.

And from below the foot of the valley the darkness gathered into motion.

FORTY-EIGHT

THE CONGERY
AT WORK

The beat of the drums didn't waver. It continued to labor up the valley like the march of doom.

During the night, the sky had blown clear. Now as the sun rose, the heavens modulated from pearl to an ineffable purple-blue, transforming to vastness the mere scrap of King Joyse's pennon. Although the valley remained in a clenched gloom, enshadowed by its walls, the effect of clear daylight around the ramparts was to make the catapults look smaller, less imposing. According to the sun, those siege engines were only sticks of wood lashed together, as capable as toys of throwing a few rocks at irregular intervals. And the snow gave the ramparts themselves an aspect of enchantment and play.

Terisa didn't believe it. King Joyse's men were vulnerable to toys which threw rocks.

King Joyse obviously didn't believe it, either. After he had set his standard and cast his defiance, he called together Castellan Norge, his captains, and Prince Kragen, as well as all the Masters who weren't already deployed. Terisa, Geraden, and the lady Elega joined him in time to hear him say, 'We are readier to meet the High King than he thinks – thanks to the forces of the Alend Monarch, and to the dedication of the Congery. Nevertheless he has sprung his trap well. We must find a reply to those catapults. Men who must dodge danger from the sky will not fight well on the ground.'

'The best thing,' Norge observed, 'would be to circle around behind them. But we can't do that. I'm willing to wager Festten has the defile sealed.'

'Find out,' commanded the King.

With a nod, Castellan Norge sent one of his captains to lead a scouting party.

'Do you have any ideas, my lord Prince?' King Joyse asked.

Prince Kragen squinted up at the walls. Slowly, he said, 'There are regions of Alend – especially among the Lieges – where the villagers cannot get to market without scaling cliffs as bad as these. I have men who are good with ropes and rock.'

'My lord Prince,' one of the captains objected, 'Cadwal isn't going to leave those catapults unprotected. Anybody who climbs those walls is going to be defenseless on the way up – and outnumbered at the top.'

'We must make the attempt in any case,' King Joyse pronounced. He wasn't looking at Prince Kragen or the captains. He was looking at the gathered Masters. 'Any harm we can do to those catapults will be worth the cost.'

Several of the Masters shuffled their feet. Some of them studied the ground. In their robes and chasubles, they seemed decidedly unadventure-some. Without the mediator to lead – or goad – them, they had the air of men who would have preferred to be at home doing research.

After a moment, however, Master Vixix cleared his throat. 'My lord King.' He rubbed a nervous hand through his thatch of hair. 'I have a small glass I shaped as an Apt. It shows little more than a puddle of dank water. But when I translated a bit of that water – purely as an experiment – it ate a hole in my worktable.

'I carry it to defend myself.'

King Joyse nodded sharply. 'Very good, Master Vixix. Can you climb?'

The Master shrugged, showing as much discomfort as his bland features allowed. 'I fear not, my lord King.'

'He can be carried,' said Prince Kragen.

Vixix faltered for a moment. Then he took a deep breath. After all, he was old enough to remember Joyse's years of glory.

'I will do whatever I can, my lord King.'

'Very good,' King Joyse repeated, and turned his attention to the other Masters.

Eventually, three more Imagers admitted that they carried personal mirrors which might be useful against a catapult – or a catapult's defenders. With Master Vixix, they were hustled away by one of Prince Kragen's captains.

Geraden met Terisa's gaze and shrugged ruefully.

Elega studied the lower end of the valley as if she expected some kind of alteration to take place when the sun rose high enough, changing the churned and clotted snow until it became a setting for wonders.

The mass of the Cadwal army below the valley was plainly visible now: sunlight blocked from the valley itself caught the standards and armor of High King Festten's forces and made them shine. Twenty thousand men? Terisa wondered. They looked like more than that – more than enough to crush King Joyse's mere twelve thousand. Of course, the High King had had plenty of time to bring up reinforcements during the siege of Orison—

When were the catapults going to start?

Was she going to spend the entire battle trying to run away from falling rocks?

Abruptly, the wardrums ceased.

The absence of the beat snatched at everyone's attention.

After the silence came the hoarse, bleating call of a sackbut.

A rider left the massed front of the Cadwal army. His armor burned with sunlight as if he were clad in gold.

At the end of his spear, he displayed a flag of truce.

'An emissary,' observed King Joyse. 'The High King wants to speak to us. He means to offer us an opportunity to surrender.'

Growling through his moustache, Prince Kragen asked, 'Why does he bother?'

'He hopes to see some evidence that we are frightened.'

'Will you meet him?'

'*We* will, my lord Prince,' the King said; his tone didn't encourage discussion. 'It may surprise you to hear this, but in all my years of warfare and contest, I have never had a chance to laugh in High King Festten's face.'

Elega's eyes shone at her father as if she were delighted.

The Cadwal emissary was stopped and held at Mordant's front line, and a horseman brought to the King the message that High King Festten did indeed wish to speak to him and Prince Kragen. In reply, Joyse sent back word that he and Kragen were willing to meet Festten midway between the two armies as soon as the High King wished.

Mounted on sturdy chargers which had been trained for combat, King Joyse and Prince Kragen rode down the valley, accompanied only by Castellan Norge. Before them stretched the Cadwal army, as unbreachable as a cliff. And above them on the ramparts, the catapults watched and waited, apparently oblivious to several hundred men with ropes and four Masters who were already attempting to scale the walls at a number of different points.

At the front of their army, the King and the Prince waited until they saw High King Festten emerge from his own forces.

'Watch for treachery,' Norge warned, stifling a yawn.

'Treachery?' King Joyse chuckled grimly. 'The High King only betrays those he fears. At the moment, I feel quite certain he does not fear us. That is his weakness.' At once, he amended, '*One* of his weaknesses.'

'My lord King,' Prince Kragen said like a salute, 'I admire your confidence.'

King Joyse gave his ally a fierce grin. 'You justify it, my lord Prince.'

When they saw the High King leave his guards behind, they rode out alone to meet him, crossing clean, white snow unmarked except by the emissary's passage.

At the agreed spot – a long bowshot from both armies – the three men came together. No one offered to dismount; and High King Festten kept some distance between himself and his enemies, as if he expected them to do something desperate. The stamping of the horses raised gusts of dry snow around the riders.

He was a short man – too short, really, for all the power he wielded. He compensated for his shortness, however, by wearing a golden helmet topped with a long spike and an elaborate plume. Between the cheekplates of his helmet, his eyes were stark, as if he had outlined them with kohl to give them force. His beard as it curled against the gold breastplate of his armor was dark and lustrous, probably dyed; only the lines and wrinkles hidden under his whiskers betrayed that he was older than King Joyse – and dedicated to his pleasures.

Ignoring Prince Kragen, he said, 'Well, Joyse,' as if he and the King were intimately familiar, despite the fact that they had never met, 'after years of success you have come to a sorry end.'

'Do you think so?' King Joyse smiled a smile which held no innocence at all. '*I* am rather pleased with myself. At last I have a chance to deal with all my enemies at once. It was only with the greatest reluctance that I allowed the Alend Contender to persuade me to offer you this one last chance for surrender.'

If this remark surprised Prince Kragen, he didn't show it.

'"Surrender"?' spat the High King. Clearly, King Joyse had caught him off balance. 'You wish *me* to surrender?'

King Joyse shrugged as if only his sense of humor kept him from losing interest in the conversation altogether. 'Why not? You cannot win this war. The best you can hope for is the chance to save your life by throwing yourself on my mercy.

'You may be unaware,' he went on before High King Festten could sputter a retort, 'that your Master Eremis has offered me an alliance against you – which I have accepted.'

'That is a lie!' the High King shouted, momentarily apoplectic. Quickly, however, he regained control of himself. In a colder voice, a tone unacquainted with pity, he said, 'Master Eremis is mendacious, of course. But I have not trusted him blindly. Gart is with him. And he knows that I have commanded Gart to gut him at the slightest hint of treachery. Also he is aware that I no longer need him. I can *crush* you now' – he knotted his fist in the air – 'without Imagery.

'You have no alliance with him. And the strength of Alend is as paltry as your own.

'No, Joyse, it is *you* who must surrender. And you must surrender *now*, or the chance will be lost. You have thwarted me for years, denied me for decades. The rule which is my *right* you have cut apart and dissipated and limited. You have opposed my will, killed my strength – *you have denied me Imagery*. There is no day of my life which you have not made less. If you do not capitulate to me *here*, I will exterminate you and all you have ever loved as easily as I exterminate *rats*!'

At that, King Joyse looked over at Prince Kragen. Mock-seriously, he said, 'Come, my lord Prince. This discussion is pointless. The High King insists on jesting with us. In all the world, no one has ever succeeded at exterminating rats.'

Casually, he turned his horse away.

His dark eyes gleaming, Prince Kragen did the same.

Together they rode back to their troops. The High King was left so furious that he seemed to froth at the mouth.

That was Joyse's way of laughing in his face.

Behind them, the sackbut blared again – and again. With a palpable thud, the wardrums resumed their labor.

Around the valley rim, all the catapults began to cock their arms.

'Now,' said King Joyse to the Prince and Castellan Norge, 'If Master Barsonage is ready, we are ready. I do not doubt that High King Festten and Master Eremis have a number of unpleasant surprises in store for us. For the present, however, we will stand or fall according to our success against those engines.'

Prince Kragen considered what could be seen of the men climbing the walls. Quite a few of them were out of sight, concealed among the complex rocks. That was a good sign: perhaps the men would also be hard to spot from above.

Grimly, the Prince reported, 'Each catapult will be able to throw at least twice before it is threatened.'

King Joyse nodded. 'Castellan, only the front lines are required for battle – say three thousand men. Unless Master Barsonage miscalculates. Instruct the rest of the men to watch the catapults and protect themselves as best they can.

'Oh, and ready the physicians,' he added before Norge could ride off. 'Provide horses for litters. Tell them we will use Esmerel as our infirmary. It is unpleasant, but we have no other shelter to offer the injured.'

'Yes, my lord King.' Castellan Norge spurred away.

The King and Prince Kragen returned to the pennon, where Terisa, Geraden, and Elega waited, fretting.

The massed front of the Cadwal army was in motion, marching to the insistence of the wardrums.

As that army approached the foot of the valley, it took on its attacking formation: a core of horsemen like the shaft and point of an arrow; flanks of foot soldiers on both sides to provide the cutting edges of the arrowhead.

The pulse of the drums quickened slightly. The army increased its pace. All the catapults were cocked; now they took on their loads. Apparently, High King Festten wanted to time his charge so that it coincided with the first throw of the engines.

King Joyse remained on his mount to improve his view down the valley. From horseback, he looked tall and sure, capable of anything. 'Sound my call,' he said to his standard-bearer, who stood guard at the pennon.

Putting his trumpet to his lips, the standard-bearer raised a blast like a shout into the morning.

The sackbut bleated in response: three hoarse bursts.

With their spears set, the Cadwal horsemen kicked their chargers into a controlled canter, an attacking stride.

The King's forces braced themselves to receive the assault. Castellan Norge had gone to join them, so that his orders wouldn't need to be relayed down the length of the valley.

'Now,' King Joyse commented to no one in particular, 'we shall see if Master Barsonage is as good as his word.'

Terisa's chest hurt as if she were holding her breath. Involuntarily, she clasped Geraden's hand, gripped it hard. He tried to murmur something reassuring, but she didn't hear him; she was focused on the drums and the horses, the coming thunder of hooves.

Over the heads of Mordant's defenders, she saw the Cadwal horse charge into the valley.

At that moment, all the catapults threw.

The brutal sound they made as their arms hit the stops caught at her, jerked her head up.

Boulders this time: nine of them, imponderably graceful as they arced against the sky's blue; stones as big as ponies, just to show what the engines could do.

A chaotic yell went up from the army – shouts of warning, cries of fear, urgent commands. Cadwal responded with a battle howl. The shock as the forces came together resounded from the walls, broke into bloodshed against the ramparts. Only the boulders seemed to make no sound as they hit the snow, scattering men in all directions, splashing white into the air – white streaked with red where the soldiers of Alend and the guards of Orison didn't dodge well enough.

At once, the cocking of the catapults began again.

The King's lines bent under the weight of the Cadwal charge. Men and horses recoiled, retreated, as if they could see Festten's full strength coming at them and knew they had no hope. Spears thrust forward and either hit or failed. Swords flailed against each other, against shields, against armor; a metal clamor among the cries and whinnies of the beasts. Mounts reared, blundered, trampled. Bodies were buried in the snow, marking their own graves with their blood. The Cadwal battle howl took on a note of triumph.

Then the Congery struck.

Hiding themselves as well as they could in the jumbled rocks at the ends of the valley walls, the Masters had set two tall mirrors facing each other – exactly facing each other across the foot of the valley. The positioning of the mirrors to face each other exactly was a problem with which the Congery had wrestled for days; but it had been resolved by the simple – if imprecise – expedient of memorizing the Images as they appeared from every side, so that the mirrors could be held at angles which complemented each other. Their alignment across the intervening ground was more easily achieved: from their hiding places, under cover of darkness, the Masters had used lamps to orient themselves.

As the horsemen of Cadwal broke into the valley, they passed between two mirrors which showed the same Image – but the same Image seen from opposite sides, and from positions nearly a hundred yards apart.

The Image of an arid landscape under a hot sun, so dry that it seemed incapable of sustaining any kind of life, so hard-baked that the ground was split by a crack as deep as a chasm and wide enough to swallow men and horses.

Master Barsonage flashed his signal, a strip of blue silk which he waved from a place high among the rocks so that it could be seen over the heads of the charging troops. At once, the two Masters who had shaped the mirrors began their translation.

With a noise like a cataclysm and a violent heave that seemed to crack the bedrock of the valley, a chasm appeared under the hooves of the horses. The ground shook; tremors ran into the distance, pulling loose rock from the ramparts, knocking men and horses off their legs. The sound shocked the valley, stunned the air. Dust sifted from the cleft as if the sky itself had shattered.

Riders slammed headlong into the rent snow and dirt, toppled from the edge; horses dropped screaming with their legs shattered. And more of the charge plunged into the cleft until the Cadwals had time to halt, rear back. Even then, dozens of soldiers were forced over the lip by the uncontrolled press behind them. A few horsemen tried to leap the chasm: a few of those succeeded. The rest were swallowed by the riven ground.

The Cadwals who had already ridden into the valley were cut off from the support of their army.

Instantly, Castellan Norge gave up the appearance of retreat and rallied his forces. His riders parted to let foot soldiers in among their enemies. Three thousand of King Joyse's men turned on scarcely a third that many Cadwals.

Outnumbered, trapped in confusion, with no escape possible except by a wild and unlikely leap across the chasm, High King Festten's soldiers fell without doing much damage.

As if nothing unpropitious had happened, the catapults threw again.

Scattershot this time, for variety; hundreds of fist-sized stones launched into the valley with the force of crossbows.

Smaller stones were more effective than boulders. They were harder to see coming, harder to dodge. And most of the King's army had involuntarily turned to watch the fighting – and the Imagery – at the valley foot. Alends and Mordants died because they weren't watching the sky.

Master Barsonage saw a sudden pocket of carnage appear among the troops as he scrambled down the rocks. Another – another – he couldn't look anymore. Reaching the young Master who held the mirror, he panted, 'Hold the translation. As we agreed. If you stop and he' – the Imager at the other mirror – 'does not, our own chasm will engulf us.'

The young Master nodded without lifting his head from his fixed concentration.

Thank the stars he was young. He would have stamina. The man at the other glass, however—

Urgently, Master Barsonage scrubbed the chilled sweat out of his eyebrows.

They were in a gap like a room hidden among the rocks – a gap in which three or four men could have hacked at each other, as long as they didn't swing their swords too widely – with packed snow underfoot, ragged black boulders for concealment. The mirror was set between two rocks facing the opposite wall; another opening allowed the mediator to see across the valley. He and his companions were a good ten feet above the valley floor, however, and had more rock curving outward to protect them from above.

'Now the true danger begins, as you were warned,' he muttered, more to himself than to his companions – the young Imager and Master Harpool. 'The High King will turn his attack against us. And we dare not release the chasm, or enough Cadwals will sweep inward to slaughter us, regardless of how we are defended. As matters stand, we can only be attacked over the rocks.' Stroking his glass, the flat mirror with the Image of Orison's ballroom, he added, 'I hope Artagel received the King's message.'

'I saw him pick up the parchment,' muttered Master Harpool, not for the first time.

Master Barsonage ignored Harpool. He wasn't talking because he wanted answers – or even reassurance. He was talking so that he wouldn't dither.

He didn't like danger. Philosophically, he didn't approve of it. Imagery was for research and experiment, for understanding and knowledge, not for bloodshed. For that very reason, however, he approved passionately of the creation of the Congery. And the conflicts inherent in his own position had made him an indecisive mediator – a man, as someone had once observed, who couldn't keep his feet out of the shit on either side because he couldn't get the fencepost out of his ass.

Well, he had made decisions at last. He had brought the Congery here, into this mess, because he believed that was the right thing to do. But he still needed to keep talking.

'What I would most like to do at this moment,' he continued for no one's benefit except his own, 'is design a new couch. I am not altogether satisfied with the backrest of my last attempt.'

'Oh, shut up, Barsonage,' said Master Harpool; but he obviously didn't expect the mediator to heed him.

The valley had become strangely quiet. The sackbut had called back the Cadwal troops; the wardrums were still. Undoubtedly, High King Festten was conferring with his captains. In the meantime, Castellan Norge had sent half a thousand foot soldiers to pitch the High King's dead into the chasm; get the bodies out of the way. Weapons were collected; uninjured horses were appropriated; wounded men were unceremoniously clubbed senseless and taken to the infirmary. Everything else had to go.

'If you were the High King, Master Harpool,' Master Barsonage asked pointlessly, 'how much time would you require to get five hundred men into the rocks above us?'

The two Imagers were old friends. 'Oh, shut up, Barsonage,' Harpool repeated.

Most of the catapults were ready to throw again.

Master Barsonage had a painfully clear view of the engine nearest to him across the valley – a painfully clear view of Prince Kragen's men as they were stripped from the wall by a shower of rocks. As far as he could see, none of them survived the fall.

In contrast, the next catapult – cocked ready to throw – abruptly twisted itself into a wreck and collapsed, as if some of its crucial lashings had been cut or burned away so that it was destroyed by its own force.

Consumed by vexation, the Cadwals around the wrecked engine hurled a number of bodies off the rampart. Master Barsonage distinctly saw a chasuble flutter to the valley floor.

'Vivix,' he muttered. 'May the stars have mercy on you, Master Eremis, for I will not – if I ever get the chance.'

He did his best to tally the next throw, but he wasn't sure of the results: he thought he saw seven boulders thud into the army. One of them smashed a squad of injured Cadwals on its way to the infirmary (no great loss), killing at least one physician (a serious blow).

Seven. Had some of Prince Kragen's climbers succeeded? They must have.

'The difficulty of backrests,' he said through his teeth, 'is that they must suit such a variety of backs.'

The young Master at the mirror was beginning to breathe like a poorly trained runner. Sweat trickled from his beardless chin to the ground at his feet, where it grew slowly into ice. Shaded from the sun, the air in the gap was cold. One of his hands was clenched too tightly on the frame; the other rubbed the mimosa wood too hard, threatening the focus of the Image.

Master Barsonage was absolutely sure that he heard boots and armor among the rocks above him.

The chasm was vital now, vital. The Masters were prepared to release it, if necessary; close it. If, for instance, the Cadwals threw a bridge across the cleft, the chasm could be erased and then replaced, destroying the bridge. Nevertheless for the sake of the mirrors themselves the translation had to remain steady. If the chasm wavered or failed, nothing could stop the Cadwals from shattering the mirrors – or killing the Imagers.

In theory, at least, King Joyse's men – and the Masters – were ready for any attack which came at them over the rocks.

'Gently,' the mediator breathed into the young Imager's ear, 'gently. You are a Master, a *Master*. Translation has become a simple matter for you, an easy matter. You do not require such effort. Only relax. Hold the translation in your mind. Let your arms rest.'

The young Master didn't nod or speak. His eyes were shut in strain. Nevertheless he managed to soften his grip, ease his rubbing; some of the exertion left his shoulders.

'Good,' Master Barsonage whispered. 'You are doing well. Very well indeed.'

He was *sure* he heard boots and armor in the rocks—

He was right. From a hiding place twenty yards away, one of Norge's bowmen loosed a shaft, and a Cadwal with an arrow in his throat dove headfirst down the wall, gurgling audibly as he fell.

Past the young Master's shoulder, Barsonage saw soldiers of all kinds clambering toward the opposite mirror.

'Be ready, Harpool,' he breathed. 'Cover yourself with your glass. Remember that a mirror open for translation cannot be broken from the front.'

For some reason, Master Harpool chose this moment to say, 'You know, Barsonage, my wife begged me to stay at home. Said I was too old for such goings-on. If I fail to return, she promised to curse me—' Without warning, his old eyes spilled tears.

'Look out!' yelled a guard. Arrows flew. Cadwals staggered down the rocks, spilling blood everywhere.

'*Cover yourself,* you old fool!' Master Barsonage cried in desperation.

He himself was set to protect the opening through which he watched the valley. The space behind the mirror, the space through which he and his companions had entered the room, was Master Harpool's responsibility. Harpool turned toward it with an old man's fumbling slowness, a teary husband's confusion.

As if from nowhere, a brawny Cadwal appeared. He wore a helmet spiked like a less assertive version of the High King's, a brass breastplate rubbed to resemble gold; the longsword in his hand looked heavy enough to behead cattle. 'Here!' he roared when he saw the Masters. 'Found 'em!'

So quickly that Master Barsonage had no chance to do anything except flinch, the Cadwal drove his sword straight at Master Harpool's glass.

Master Harpool may have been old and grieved, but he understood translation: he had been doing it for decades. Somehow, he seemed to put himself in the right frame of mind without transition, achieve the right kind of concentration as simply as striking a flint.

The sword passed into the glass.

Carried forward by his own momentum, the Cadwal stumbled into the Image and vanished—

—into the ballroom of Orison, where (the mediator devoutly hoped) Artagel was ready to receive such gifts.

Another Cadwal came after the first. He fell into the mirror with an arrow in his back; already dead.

Master Barsonage was too busy watching Harpool: he missed the rope as it uncoiled across the opening he was supposed to guard. But he heard a grunt of effort from the man on the rope, turned in time.

The swing of the man's descent brought him within reach. The mediator hugged his mirror, muttered his concentration ritual as well as he could. Unfortunately, he couldn't think while the Cadwal released one hand from the rope, pulled out a knife. He didn't have the right kind of nerves to face danger. For one stupid, necessary instant, he shut his eyes.

Another present for Artagel.

There he nearly made a mistake, nearly let his glass close. Luckily, the sudden pressure on the rope warned him. Artagel must have been ready, must have gotten the message Master Harpool sent. Someone in the ballroom had a grip on the rope, was hauling on it fiercely.

If Master Barsonage had stopped his translation, the rope would only have been cut. Or the mirror would have broken. But he kept the glass open—

Abruptly, the three men anchoring the rope in the rocks above were dragged off their perch. They fell screaming past the mediator's vantage.

More arrows: more shouts. From somewhere out of sight came the clash of swords.

Then silence.

The attack was over. Temporarily. Some of the Cadwals were probably hidden among the rocks, marking the mirror's position while they waited for reinforcements; others must have gone back to report. Barsonage risked a look out over the young Master's shoulder and saw men still fighting around the opposite end of the chasm. The forces of Orison and Alend, however, seemed to be winning.

'Harpool,' Master Barsonage panted, 'I told you to *cover* yourself. You stood beside your mirror *begging* them to cut you down.'

Master Harpool didn't say anything. He had his eyes closed. Maybe he was taking a nap. More likely he didn't want to witness his own peril.

From the distance of the pennon, of course, Terisa and Geraden, Elega and

King Joyse and Prince Kragen couldn't see the details; but they saw the threat to the mirrors approach, saw it beaten back. Terisa let out a sigh to ease her cramped lungs. 'How long can they keep that up?'

'A good question,' replied King Joyse calmly. 'All translation is arduous. The Masters are already weary. And as his frustration mounts, High King Festten will redouble his attacks.

'As a defense, however, that chasm has already exhausted most of its usefulness. Its chief purpose now is to protect the Masters themselves – and to give us a period of time during which we can try to counter the catapults. When we must, we will muster a charge of our own. The Masters will close the chasm – and while we ride to engage Cadwal outside the valley, they will retreat to prepare another unexpected crevice somewhere else.

'At the moment, we are as effectively besieged as we ever were in Orison. If the High King trusted to that and held back, we would eventually be defeated. But he will not. He wants our blood – and he wants it today. That is another of his weaknesses.

'As for the catapults—'

One party of Prince Kragen's assault on the walls brought back a Master with an arrow in his shoulder. They hadn't been able to find any way upward which wasn't exposed to the defenders of their target; and after the Master with them was hit, they were forced to retreat. So there were still seven engines.

All seven of them were already cocked.

Another series of hard wooden thuds, like the sound of bones being broken: another hail of scattershot. This stone deluge did less harm than the last because the soldiers and guards were more careful. Nevertheless Terisa thought she saw as many as a hundred men go down.

At once, physicians ran with horses and litters to do what they could for the wounded. The procession of injuries toward Esmerel and the infirmary seemed to go on continuously. The dead were left where they lay.

If this onslaught continued, the army would be forced to protect itself by leaving the center of the valley, moving closer to the walls – too close for the catapults to hit. And then the King's men would be vulnerable to rockfalls, avalanches—

'The next move will be Eremis',' Elega said softly to Terisa and Geraden. 'We have introduced Imagery to the conflict. He will attempt to counter it.'

'How?' asked Geraden anxiously.

The lady looked at him, a faint smile on her lips. Sunlight cost her much of her beauty, but couldn't weaken the color of her eyes. 'You know him better than I do. You understand Imagery better. What *can* he do?'

'*I* don't know,' Geraden muttered. 'I'm willing to bet he has a mirror he can see us in. In fact, if I were him – and if Gilbur and Vagel are as good as they think – I'd have two. One to watch with, one to use. But he has to be careful. Terisa has already shattered one glass for him. If he gives her the chance, she can do it again.'

Terisa had no idea whether or not this were true. It seemed irrelevant.

The gaze King Joyse sent toward her and Geraden was curiously bland, like a mask.

The air was warmer than it had been for several days, but it didn't warm her. Clenching herself inside her robe, she shivered and ached. No matter how often she turned to Geraden, no matter how she clung to him, he couldn't help her. Helplessness and watching made her frantic. He had the strongest feeling they were in the wrong place. But what choice did they have? Where else could they be?

For some reason, the Cadwals were massing again outside the valley. The sackbut bleated raucously: the wardrums commenced their labor: horsemen cleared the way. Foot soldiers drew forward, as if High King Festten had decided to drive them into the chasm for their failures.

King Joyse studied them hard, his blue eyes straining to pierce their intentions. Abruptly, he put out a hand to the Prince. 'Reinforcements,' he snapped. 'Where in all this rout is Norge? The Masters must be reinforced.'

Prince Kragen had apparently passed the point where he needed – or even expected – explanations from the King. Wheeling away, he headed for his horse, shouting to his captains as he ran.

When Terisa first heard the distant, throaty rumble, as if the earth were moving, she had no idea what was about to happen.

When the Tor woke up – gasping, as he always did these days, at the great, hot pain in his side – the rumble hadn't started yet. Outside his tent, the valley was strangely quiet. That disconcerted him: he was expecting combat. The relative silence sounded like an omen of disaster, an indication that bloodshed and death had lost their meaning.

Opening his eyes, he saw from the hue of the canvas overhead that day had dawned. He was alone in the tent, except for Ribuld, who dozed against the tentpole with his head nodding on his knees. An experienced veteran, Ribuld could probably sleep on a battlefield, if he were left alone.

Silence outside: only a few shouts from time to time; the mortal sound of catapult arms against their stops. And a few daring or oblivious birds, following their calls among the rocks. The Tor knew all the birds of his Care. He would be able to identify each call, if he listened closely enough. For the sake of his sons, who had grown up in more peaceful times than he had, he had become avid at birding.

But there should have been a battle going on. Strange—

The Congery. Of course. Master Barsonage had promised to translate that crevice somewhere.

Must be quite a sight – clefts in the ground out of nowhere; the fate of Mordant depending on Imagery as well as swords.

'Ribuld,' said the old lord, 'help me up.'

Not loud enough: Ribuld didn't move.

'Ribuld, help me up. I want to see what is happening.'

I want to strike a blow for my son and my Care and my King in this war.

Ribuld jerked up his head, blinked the sleep out of his eyes. Alert almost at once, he rose and came to the cot where the Tor sprawled. 'My lord,' he murmured, 'the King says you've got to rest. He *commands* you to rest.'

Speaking softly around his pain, the Tor replied, 'Ribuld, you know me. Did you believe I would obey such a command?'

The guard shifted his feet uncomfortably. 'I'm supposed to make sure you do.'

The Tor managed a thin chuckle. 'Then let him execute us both when this war is done. We will share the block with Master Eremis for our terrible crimes. Help me up.'

Slowly, a grin tightened Ribuld's scar. 'As you say, my lord. Disobeying the King is always a terrible crime. Anybody fool enough to do that deserves what he gets.'

Bracing himself on the sides of the cot, Ribuld helped the lord roll into a sitting position.

Agony threatened to burst the Tor's side. He took a moment to absorb the pain; then, hoping he didn't look as pale as he felt, he said, 'Some wine first, I think. After that, mail and my sword.'

May it please the stars that I am able to strike one blow for my son and my Care and my King.

Ribuld produced a flagon from somewhere. The sound of catapults came again, followed by cries and curses, yells for physicians. *May it please the stars—* Some time passed before the Tor realized that he was staring into the flagon without drinking.

Gritting his courage, he swallowed all the wine. Before he could lapse into another stupor, he motioned for his undershirt and mail.

With gruff care, Ribuld helped him to his feet, helped him into his leathers and mail and cloak, helped him belt his ponderous and unusable sword around his girth below the swelling in his side. Several times, the old lord feared that he would lose consciousness and fall; but each time Ribuld supported him until his weakness went away, then continued dressing him as if nothing had happened.

'If I had a daughter,' the Tor murmured, 'who obeyed me better than the lady Elega obeys her father, I would order her to marry you, Ribuld.'

Ribuld laughed shortly. 'Be serious, my lord. What would a boozing old wencher like me do with a lord's daughter?'

'Squander her inheritance, of course,' retorted the Tor. 'That would be the whole point of marrying her to you. To give you that opportunity.'

This time, Ribuld's laugh was longer; it sounded happier.

'Now,' grunted the lord when Ribuld was done with his belt, 'let us go out and have a look at the field of valor.'

He managed two steps toward the tentflaps before his knees failed.

'My lord,' Ribuld murmured repeatedly, 'my lord,' while the Tor's head filled up with black water and he lost his vision in the dark, 'give this up. You need rest. The King told you to rest. You'll kill yourself.'

Precisely what I have in mind, friend Ribuld.

'Nonsense.' Somehow, the Tor found his voice and used it to lift his mind above the water. 'I only want to watch King Joyse justify the trust we have placed in him. I want to watch him bring High King Festten and Master Eremis to the ruin they deserve.

'A horse to sit on. So I can see better. Nothing more.'

Ribuld's eyes were red, and his face seemed congested in some way, as if

896

he understood – and couldn't show it. 'Yes, my lord,' he said through his teeth. 'I'd like to watch that myself.'

Carefully, he helped the Tor upright again.

Together, they reached the tentflaps and went out into the shadowed morning.

From the tent, they could see most of the valley, including the slope where King Joyse had planted his pennon. That purple scrap looked especially frail in contrast to the bright sunlight beyond the valley, the massive strength of the ramparts, the active violence of the siege engines. Around the standard stood King Joyse and his daughter, Prince Kragen and Terisa and Geraden. They were all watching the foot of the valley, however, watching unmounted troops mass as if the Congery's chasm could be defeated by swords and spears; they didn't notice the Tor and Ribuld. And neither the Tor nor Ribuld called attention to themselves.

Ribuld moved the Tor a little to the side, a bit out of sight. Then the guard went looking for horses.

The Tor did his best to estimate the damage the catapults had done. As a younger man, he had fought his share of battles. He was accustomed to carnage. But King Joyse possessed a quality he himself had always lacked. Perhaps it was an instinct for risk. In his bones, he counted loss instead of gain. That, really, was why he had given Joyse only two hundred men, all those long years ago, when Joyse was hardly more than a boy, and Mordant was nothing more than a battlefield. Not cowardice. And certainly not deafness to Joyse's bright, hopeful promises. No, he had simply given his future King as many men as he could bear to lose.

The lord fell into reverie, thinking about loss. Friends of many years ago, valiant fighters, precious villagers and farmers and merchants who didn't deserve to be slaughtered. The old Armigite, who hadn't earned a foppish son. And now the Tor's own firstborn. His tough, good comrade, the Perdon. The tormented Castellan, sick and honorable Lebbick. Too many, all of them: the cost was too high.

He shook his head. As if his pain were an anchor, a gift from the High King's Monomach, he used it to steady himself so that he could watch what happened in the valley.

Why was the High King massing his men? An interesting question. Well, obviously he intended to attack something. Someone.

I need a mount.

The Tor looked around for Ribuld.

There, he was coming. He had two horses, his own roan and the Tor's familiar bay. Now all the lord had to do was surmount his hurt one last time—

Distinctly, he heard King Joyse speak.

In that carrying voice which required obedience, the King snapped, 'Reinforcements. Where in all this rout is Norge? The Masters must be reinforced.'

Frantic with pain, the Tor lunged at the bay and struggled into the saddle.

He could have fainted then; but he was desperate, and his desperation held the darkness back. He was already moving, already kicking the bay into a gallop, when the rumble began.

The sound was a distant, throaty growl, as if by translating their chasm the Masters had given the earth a mouth with which to utter its distress.

But this wasn't the earth protesting, oh, no, the Tor saw that almost immediately as he goaded his horse faster, away from people who wanted to stop him; out of the center of the valley to the less occupied ground closer to the wall. This rumble had another meaning entirely.

As if someone had opened a window in the empty air, rock began to thunder downward. Across the gap between worlds, an avalanche rushed roaring into the chasm.

Broken rock in tons; hundreds of thousands of tons; enough rock to build a castle, a mountain; all slamming down out of the sky directly above the chasm, all howling torrentially into the Masters' crevice.

Enough rock to fill the rift. Plug it. Make it passable.

And behind the translated collapse of the mountainside came High King Festten's men, pressing forward to breach the valley as soon as the rockfall ended.

The avalanche moved along the chasm, distributing rubble as evenly as possible.

Then, while the whole valley watched in shock, the plunge of stone began to thin. Quickly, too quickly, the tons of rock became dirt and pebbles; the dirt and pebbles changed to dust; the dust billowed everywhere, as light and swirling as snow.

Raising their battle howl, High King Festten's men charged.

The crevice wasn't perfectly filled: in some places, the rock piled too high; in others, the dirt sank too low. Nevertheless at least a third of the chasm could be crossed now. Cadwal's troops rushed forward while Castellan Norge and Prince Kragen were still straining to rally their forces.

Within the valley, Festten's men split into two groups, curving around the inside of the chasm to attack the Masters hidden in the ends of the walls.

The Tor saw the Cadwals come as he rode, lashing his horse for more speed than it could give him. He had forgotten his pain: he had forgotten loss. He only knew that he was too late to help break the first shock of the assault. Norge had hundreds of archers and bowmen hidden around the Masters. And the Masters had mirrors. That would have to be enough, until help could come.

It wasn't enough; it was never going to be enough. Already there were a thousand Cadwals in the valley, two thousand. More came as fast as they could cross the chasm.

Forgetting all the things he couldn't do, the Tor unsheathed his longsword.

In the rocks ahead, he saw Master Barsonage. The mediator had climbed to his signalling-place above the mirrors. He looked small and doomed there, his chasuble fluttering. As if he had lost his mind, he yelled through the Cadwal battle howl, waved a blue cloth wildly at the opposite wall.

The Tor didn't understand what happened next until it was over; but somehow, by luck or inspiration, Master Barsonage achieved his aim.

Both Masters ceased their translation at the same moment.

The chasm blinked out of existence.

Now there was solid ground where the avalanche had fallen. Stone and soil occupied the space which the rockfall had filled.

In the convulsion, the Tor's horse stumbled, nearly lost its footing. With a spasm like an eruption, the closed earth spat the entire rockfall straight into the air.

Without transition, the battle howl changed to screams and chaos. Hundreds of Cadwals died in the blast while they tried to cross the vanished chasm; hundreds more were crushed by the rejected rock as it plunged back to the ground, blocking the valley from wall to wall. Granite thunder and groaning swallowed the sound of wardrums.

Unfortunately, the High King still had as many as two thousand men inside the valley – men still charging to kill the Masters, shatter the mirrors. And King Joyse's reinforcements were still too far away.

The Castellan's archers recovered their wits enough to begin shooting. But their arrows were too few, and the Cadwals were well armored. Men with swords swarmed up into the rocks, fighting to reach the Masters.

Master Barsonage had scuttled downward, vanished into a gap the Tor couldn't see. That movement told the Cadwals exactly where their target was. Spared the necessity of searching, they surged ahead.

With Ribuld beside him, the Tor crashed against the rear of the Cadwal force.

His sword was heavy: his whole body was heavy, weighted with pain and bereavement. He hacked at the Cadwals from side to side, once on the left, once on the right, back and forth; and each blow seemed to shear helmets and heads, breastplates and leather. His horse plunged, stumbled, scrambled forward – somehow he kept his balance. His sword was his balance, his life: up and down, side to side, hacking with all its strength, while his belly filled up with blood.

Above him, the Cadwals who reached the Masters' position seemed to be disappearing.

In their gap among the rocks, the Imagers concentrated grimly, working their translations against impossible odds.

That is to say, Master Barsonage concentrated grimly, grinding his courage into focus with such urgency that sweat stood on his skin and a dangerous flush darkened his face. For all the distress Master Harpool showed, he might as well have been performing translations in his sleep. Standing mostly behind his glass, with his eyes closed and an old man's mumble on his lips, he kept his mirror open and simply let everything that came near it fall into the Image – trusting, no doubt, that the haste and frenzy of the Cadwals would spare him from a direct attack on his person.

The young Master wasn't doing anything at all. He had slumped to the snow-packed floor; his glass leaned over him, useless. Something in him, some essential fortitude or will, had snapped. He had kept his translation open for the chasm until Master Barsonage had called for him to let it go; then his eyes had rolled back in his head, and he had crumbled.

The mirrors were vital: the Congery had nothing else to contribute to

Mordant's defense. Ignoring the young Imager, Master Barsonage forced himself to translate and translate, on and on, when every nerve in his body wailed to flinch away from the swords and blows and curses coming at him.

Unhappily, from where he stood he could see clearly that reinforcements were still too far away. He could see that the Tor and Ribuld didn't stand a chance.

The Tor went on fighting anyway, long after he had lost his strength and his balance and even his reason. A blow for his son. A blow for his Care. And now a blow for King Joyse. Then back to the beginning again. A blow for everyone he had ever loved, everyone who had ever died.

For some reason, there was a knife stuck in his leg. It was a big knife; really, quite a big knife. He couldn't tell whether it hurt him or not, but it seemed to catch his leg in a way he couldn't escape, so that he had no choice except to fall off his horse.

He dreaded that fall. It was a long way to the ground, and his swollen side couldn't endure an impact like that. Luckily, however, he managed to land on the man who stuck him; that was one less Cadwal to worry about. Now all he had to do was roll onto his back. He knew he didn't have the strength to stand again; but from the ground he would be able to cut at the legs of the men around him.

He rolled onto his back.

Unluckily, he had lost his sword. He didn't have anything left to fight with.

Ribuld stood over him.

Gripping his own blade in both fists, the guard fought for both of them: blows on all sides; spurts and splashes of blood; chips of armor, iron sword-shards. Ribuld's scar burned as if his life were on fire in his face, and his teeth snapped at the air.

Someone shouted, *'My lord Tor! Watch out!'*

The voice was familiar, but the old lord couldn't place it. It was too recent: it belonged to someone he hadn't known long enough to remember.

Then a swordpoint came right through the center of Ribuld's chest, driven like a spear from behind.

Oh, well. The stars had granted the Tor his last wish. And King Joyse had said, *You have not betrayed me.* That was enough.

A moment later, someone slammed a rock down on his head and brought all his losses to an end.

But when Master Barsonage cried, *'My lord Tor! Watch out!'* the young Imager sprang to his feet as if he had been galvanized.

Like Ribuld's, the young Master's home was in the Care of Tor, in Marshalt. In fact, he was distantly related by marriage to the Tor himself. That familiar name – and the mediator's alarm – wrenched him out of his stupor, brought him to his feet crying madly, 'The Tor? The Tor? *Oh, my lord!'*

He had no idea what was going on: his eyes held nothing but exhaustion and distress. The broken part of him only made him urgent; it didn't make him sane.

Sobbing, 'Save the Tor!' he grabbed up his mirror.

Master Barsonage was too slow. He was watching the Tor, watching the reinforcements; he didn't react in time.

The young Imager was hardly more than a boy, pushed past his limits. Facing his mirror in the general direction of the opposite glass, he began translating his chasm straight into the huge ridge of rock left by the avalanche; the rock which sealed the valley.

But of course the Master holding the other mirror didn't know what was about to happen. In any case, the two mirrors were no longer properly aligned. There was nothing to stop the tremendous and convulsive tremor which split the ridge and the ground and went on until it hit the end of the other wall and tore apart all that old stone, reducing the opposite glass and everyone near it to rubble.

Under the circumstances, it was probably a good thing that the young Master didn't live long. There was no way to tell how much damage his chasm might have done, if the translation had continued unchecked. And there was no way to tell how he would have endured the consequences of his action.

As matters fell out, however, he was saved by a particularly stubborn Cadwal, who already had his sword up to chop open Master Harpool's oblivious face when an Alend arrow nailed him between the shoulder blades. Falling forward, his upraised arms hit the top of Harpool's mirror. That impact made his fingers release his sword.

As if it had been thrown deliberately, the hilt of the blade snapped the young Master's neck. He, in turn, fell forward onto his glass, shattering it completely.

Full of terrible defeat, Master Barsonage hardly noticed that Master Harpool had somehow contrived to keep his own mirror from being broken. And the mediator's was undamaged. That was less than no consolation; it was almost an insult in the face of the general ruin. Every other glass which the Congery had prepared for this battle was destroyed.

He half expected another violent recoil as the chasm ceased to exist for the second time; but that didn't happen. The previous convulsion had been caused by reversing the translation. This translation, on the other hand, was only stopped, not undone. Vast portions of the piled ridge were engulfed; most of the end-rock of the opposite wall disappeared into the new crevice. Then the rending and spitting of the earth was over.

As a result, the High King's forces once again had access to the valley – a ragged and constricted access, treacherous to cross, like the spaces between rotting teeth, but access nonetheless.

When he saw that there were already men riding at full career in through one of the farther gaps, he covered his face with his hands.

FORTY-NINE

THE KING'S
LAST HOPES

Standing near the King's pennon with Terisa, Geraden, and her father, the lady Elega didn't know where to look, or what to feel.

She could watch the struggle down at the end of the valley wall, off to her right, where the Tor had fallen, and where Castellan Norge and his men fought to save what they could of the Masters and their mirrors. Or she could watch the breach where the other Masters used to be, the gap which had been made in the piled ridge of the avalanche by translating the Congery's chasm from only one side.

Riders were coming in through that gap, driving their horses hard. And Prince Kragen was there. From this distance, he appeared to be doing everything at once: rallying his men; finishing off the incursion of Cadwals; searching over the new jumble of rocks for survivors. To her eyes, each of his actions seemed as quick as a thrust, as decisive as a sword; the precision with which he used his men made Norge look like a blundering lout by comparison.

He was worthy – oh, he was worthy! Surely King Joyse could see that. Surely her father in this new manifestation could see and appreciate the qualities which made the Alend Contender precious to her. Prince Kragen deserved—

He deserved to be right.

Almost as an act of self-mortification, to humble herself so that she wouldn't hope so hard, fear so much, Elega forced her eyes to stay on the right side of the valley foot, not the left.

The question of what to feel was more difficult. She couldn't resolve it by an act of will.

Pride and panic: vindication and alarm. Suddenly, as much 'out of nowhere' as if translation were involved, the King had proved himself. He had made real the interpretations of himself which until now had been only ideas – concepts put forward by people like Terisa and Geraden for reasons of their own. He had shown that he merited the risks she had taken in his name, arguing for him against reason, common sense; he had justified the forbearance she had won from Prince Kragen and the Alend Monarch. In the privacy of her own thoughts, she understood why he had found it necessary to use her like a hop-board piece in his plans, rather than to hazard the truth with her. She was *proud* of him, there beside his standard, blue eyes blazing; as ready as a hawk to strike or defend.

She was proud of him – and afraid that she had failed him.

In a sense, she was playing his own game against him. At her urging, Prince Kragen and the Alend Monarch had made decisions concerning this war on the basis of knowledge and speculation which they hadn't shared with any representative of Orison.

Her purpose – as distinct from Kragen's or Margonal's – had been twofold: to make the forces of Alend *wait*, withhold their siege, long enough for King Joyse's plans to ripen; and to put pressure on the King, pressure which would force him to accept an alliance with Alend. By keeping secrets from her father, she reinforced Prince Kragen's position.

Now, today, here, what she had done came to the test. She would be right, as the Prince deserved – if for no other reason than because he had trusted her. Or she would be wrong.

Mordant itself might stand or fall on the outcome.

She could choose to keep her eyes away from Prince Kragen, away from the riders boiling into the valley on the left; but she couldn't choose to ignore her fear. The more pride she felt in King Joyse and the Prince, the more she dreaded the possibility that she had helped bring them both to ruin.

Maybe that was why she looked her worst in sunlight. The sun couldn't expose her secrets, of course; but it seemed to lay bare the fact that she had them.

Under the circumstances, she considered it fortunate that no one was paying much attention to her.

Unconscious of himself, Geraden muttered, 'Get up. Get up.' Everyone had seen the Tor go down; no one had seen the old lord regain his feet. For that matter, no one had seen any of the Masters emerge from the rocks. 'Get *up*. We need you.'

Terisa held his arm with both hands, clung to him. Nevertheless she kept her eyes averted as if she couldn't bear to watch what he was seeing. Facing to the left of the valley's foot, she asked softly, 'Who is *that*?'

Geraden apparently had no idea what she meant. And Elega was determined not to look. She needed a way to live with her fear, a way to endure her failure when it came.

Abruptly, it became obvious that Castellan Norge was done with the Cadwals attacking the Masters. Shouts were raised, and some of the men relaxed. Bowmen hurried out of the rocks to retrieve their shafts; riders sped away, some to deliver messages, others to help the Prince. Master Barsonage appeared, holding a glass nearly as tall as himself. Behind him came Master Harpool, doddering painfully. Two guards carried the old Imager's mirror for him.

Together, five or six men picked up the Tor's corpse; as gently as they could, they set it in a rude litter. Then they lifted the litter to other men on horseback. Ribuld's body also was put in a litter to accompany the Tor's. Castellan Norge mounted his horse, placed himself at the head of his riders.

In procession, like a cortege, the Castellan and his men came up the valley toward King Joyse.

'My lord,' Geraden sighed – an exhalation with his teeth clenched down on it hard enough to draw blood. 'My poor lord.'

Terisa shook his arm; maybe she was trying to distract him. 'Geraden, look. Who *is* that?'

Involuntarily, the lady Elega turned.

At once, she saw that the horsemen attempting to enter the valley were fighting for their lives—

—fighting for their lives against the forces of Cadwal outside. She had assumed that they, too, were Cadwals; but she was wrong. High King Festten opposed them bitterly: seen through the breaches in the piled ridge, it appeared that he had sent his entire mounted strength to destroy them.

She saw Prince Kragen spur his charger into a gallop, leading several hundred Alends to the defense of the riders; headlong against thousands of Cadwals.

At the same time, King Joyse shouted to the nearest captain, 'Get archers down there! I want bows up in those rockpiles! I want an ambush in each of those gaps! We cannot keep Cadwal out, but we can make the High King cautious. We must not allow him to mass his men inside those piles!'

Cupping his hands on either side of his mouth to make his voice ring, he added, '*Support the Prince!*'

With her jaw hanging down like a madwoman's, Elega saw that one of the riders Prince Kragen was risking himself to help bore the dull grape-on-wheat colors of the Termigan.

The *Termigan?*

What in the name of all sanity was *he* doing here?

'The Termigan!' Geraden breathed to Terisa. 'I don't believe it. He came after all.'

Elega was too surprised to notice that the catapults were ready to throw again. And she certainly didn't notice that one of them behind her had been reaimed toward King Joyse's pennon. She hardly heard the flat thudding of the arms, or the thin, high scream of scattershot through the air. At the moment, her only concern was that none of the engines could strike at Prince Kragen or the Termigan.

She didn't know how lucky she was when the catapult behind her failed to throw.

Instead of attacking, it leaned forward and toppled crookedly off the rampart, tearing itself to scrap on the rocks as it fell. From the valley rim, a group of Prince Kragen's climbers raised an inaudible cheer, then turned to defend themselves from Cadwals arriving too late to save the engine.

King Joyse, however, seemed to notice that as he noticed everything else. With a glance upward, he said to himself, 'Six left. Progress is made, friend Festten. Be warned.'

Unfortunately, the siege engines had already cost him hundreds of men, dead or hurt.

Elega held her breath, watching Prince Kragen hurl himself against High King Festten's horsemen. Hadn't Geraden said that the Termigan refused to come? She gnawed the inside of her cheek. Yes, that was what Geraden had said. Yet he was here. She felt a chill, despite the air's relative warmth. What new disaster had he come to report?

Who were those people in the center of his formation, those cloaked figures that didn't fight, that didn't do anything except ride where the Termigan's men took them? One of them seemed ordinary enough. The other was huge—

Echoes brought the sounds of battle to her, the strife of swords and shields. Piled rock hid most of the fighting: Prince Kragen had ventured through the gap and was out of sight behind the debris of the avalanche. He didn't have enough men to oppose that many Cadwals, not nearly enough. Only the speed of his charge could save him, its unexpectedness. But a mixed group of guards and soldiers was almost in position to help him, two hundred horse in the lead, half a thousand foot pelting furiously behind. And when the Termigan had brought all his people into the valley, he wheeled his mount, called most of his strength after him, and returned to aid the Prince.

Together, nearly side-by-side, Prince Kragen and the man who had declared flatly, *I trust no Alend*, fought their way back toward the bulk of King Joyse's army.

The rough mounds close on either side saved them: all that broken stone constricted the Cadwal countercharge; an abundance of scattered rubble where the chasm used to be prevented riders from moving in tight ranks. And when the High King's forces tried to enter the valley again, archers began loosing their shafts from high up among the rocks.

Prince Kragen and the Termigan brought each other to safety as if they had never been anything except comrades.

'Who're those people with him,' asked Terisa, 'the ones in the cloaks – the ones who didn't fight?'

Elega's heart began to soar. Who dared to speak of failure, where King Joyse and his daughters were at work?

The men bearing the Tor's body, and Ribuld's, arrived at King Joyse's pennon before the Termigan did; and King Joyse met them as if he weren't in the midst of a war, with catapults and unexplained arrivals to worry about; met them as if for that moment at least nothing was more important to him than the burden they carried, his old friend's corpse.

'He saved us,' said Master Barsonage. The Imager seemed too weary to dismount; he looked too haggard to say, *my lord King*. 'He and Ribuld—' The mediator's voice lapsed into grief.

'That's true, my lord King,' Castellan Norge reported without his usual ease. 'They were just two, but they hit at the right time. They did just enough damage, caused just enough confusion—' Like Barsonage, Norge seemed to be losing his voice. 'Without them, we wouldn't have saved the mediator. Or Master Harpool, either.'

Dully, as if he had said the same thing a dozen times, Master Harpool murmured, 'My wife promised to curse me if I don't return. She was that angry—' His nose was running; but he didn't have anything to wipe it with, so he snuffled loudly.

King Joyse looked at the Tor's body; he started to speak. Nevertheless he couldn't: he was breathing too hard. As if the sight of his friend's crushed head hit him harder than he was expecting, dealt him a blow for which he had thought he was braced and now found he wasn't, not braced at all despite the fact that he must have seen this moment coming, his chest began to heave, and he fought for air urgently, in great gasps. To stifle the sound, he clamped his hands over his mouth, against the sides of his nose; but he couldn't restrain his harsh respiration, his labor against grief.

After all, he wasn't young anymore. He had been alone for a long time; comforted – or at least understood – by only mad Havelock and lost Quillon. And the cost of his efforts to save Mordant kept growing. Without the Tor, there would have been no Mordant, no kingdom to defend; no King to be so profligate with the blood of those who loved him.

Fiercely, he pulled his hands down from his face, gripped the side of the Tor's litter. He seemed to want to lift his old friend in his arms, pick the Tor's body up out of death. But of course the corpse was too heavy. Four men were needed simply to support its slack weight.

Involuntarily, King Joyse sank to his knees in the trampled slush.

Terisa and Geraden started toward him without thinking; their desire to console him somehow was obvious in their faces. The lady Elega stopped them, however. She put a finger to her lips. Then, smiling despite the Tor's end and her father's sorrow, she pointed toward the riders approaching the pennon.

Prince Kragen. The Termigan. And the two cloaked figures, with everything about them except their size wrapped and hidden, kept secret.

Prince Kragen had a few battlemarks on him: some blood, plainly not his own; lines like galls across his mail. He looked worthy to Elega, *worthy* beyond question, like a man who had met the consequences of his most hazardous decisions and deserved his victory. The Termigan was in worse condition, gaunt from hard travel, strained and bitter around his eyes. Yet he, too, had an air of worth, almost of triumph, as if he knew now that he had done the right thing. His hard, flinty face held no reproach.

'My lord King,' he said, 'I've come to help you. I've only got two hundred men – all I could spare. But they're enough.'

'Enough and more,' put in Prince Kragen, kinder toward the King's grief. 'Is it not true that Mordant itself began with only two hundred men?'

'Father.' Myste pushed her hood back from her face, raised her strong gaze and her scarred cheek into the sunlight reaching past the valley rim.

'Myste.'

Terisa was at once so surprised and so thrilled that she nearly shouted; her whole body seemed tight with pleasure.

'You're all right.'

Geraden nearly burst out laughing in delight. Men all around the King's pennon whispered Myste's name as if it were powerful and dangerous.

'With the Termigan's aid,' she said, 'I have brought your champion.'

While the reaction to her appearance spread, the huge figure beside her dropped his cloak, revealing bright, blank armor scorched black in several places, burned open twice, with a flat, impenetrable plate over his face. Strange guns hung on his hips; the rifle with which he had blasted his way out of Orison was strapped to his back.

The circle of guards and soldiers stared. A number of them grabbed at their swords; a few unslung bows.

But the champion didn't make any threatening moves. Slowly, he reached one hand to his head, touched a stud in the side of his helmet. Without a sound, his visor slid up and away, exposing his face.

It was a man's face, ordinary in its details: pale eyes; a large nose, crooked as if it had been broken more than once; tight lips above an assertive jaw. Only the strange way he moved his mouth when he spoke betrayed his origins.

'My lord King,' he said in an alien voice, a tone with an incongruous resemblance to birdsong, 'I'm lost on this God-rotting planet. Myste says it's not your fault I'm here. Says the only people who might be able to help me are your Imagers. But you can't help me while you're stuck in this mess.

'I'm willing to do what I can. For her. On the off-chance your Imagers can help me.'

'So that's what it meant,' Terisa breathed, her tone hushed with relief and wonder. But at the moment even Geraden didn't have any attention to spare for her.

Kneeling beside the Tor, King Joyse had jerked his head up at the sound of Myste's voice, had stared at her and the champion with joy dawning in his blue eyes. Now he rose to his feet as if all his courage had come back. At first, however, he didn't speak to her, or to Prince Kragen and the Termigan, or even to the champion. Instead, he addressed Norge briskly.

'Several things, Castellan. Provide for my lord Termigan's men. Get those that need care to the physicians. Those that do not, assign among our horsemen. If I judge rightly' – he glanced toward the foot of the valley – 'High King Festten is regrouping. He will attack again shortly. We need riders desperately.

'My dear friend the Tor,' he continued without pausing, 'must be given an honorable grave outside Esmerel. Command as many men as necessary, bury him well. And the Perdon beside him – two faithful and valorous lords who spent their lives so that we will have a chance to save our world. If we succeed, their names will be praised before any other.'

Then, in a rush, he left the Tor's litter, pulled Myste off her mount, and hugged her to his heart.

At once, the champion, Darsint, dismounted; he seemed to think Myste might need his protection. When he had pushed the horses out of his way, however, he stopped, apparently content to leave Myste and the King alone.

Watching her sister and her father, Elega's only regret was that she had never been able to smile the way they did, with that clarity, as if they were able to go through life with their innocence intact.

'Dear child,' King Joyse murmured thickly, 'my Myste, I'm so glad – Havelock told me to trust you, but I couldn't help being afraid. My little girl, in such danger – I wanted you to be safe. And yet I needed you to do what you did.' He tightened his embrace momentarily, then released it and stepped back. 'Your mother would break my pate if she knew how I risked you.'

'Father,' Myste replied like the sun, 'all children must be risked. Mother knows that. How else are we to discover ourselves?'

If anything, her smile became warmer, cleaner, as she turned toward Elega.

Elega wanted to say, You have saved us – meant to say, Oh, Myste, you have saved us – but her throat closed suddenly, and her vision ran with tears. Myste's smile still had the power to make everything worthwhile.

Myste came to stand close to her. They didn't embrace: the way they felt was too private for the occasion. Nevertheless Myste said softly, 'You did it. Everything I wanted – everything I couldn't say. I'm so proud of you.'

Elega looked up at Prince Kragen, still on his horse, and held his gaze happily while Myste went to hug both Terisa and Geraden, then moved back to King Joyse.

'Now that the truth is revealed, my lord King,' the Prince said, speaking dryly to cover his pleasure, 'I suppose I must admit that the Alend Monarch's motives – and my own – have not been entirely disinterested recently. We withheld the siege of Orison to give you time in which to mature your plans. We kept open the possibility of an alliance, even when we had refused it, so that we might be able to aid you at need. But we also did those things' – he grinned under his moustache – 'because the lady Myste threatened to bring the champion's fire down on us otherwise.'

There: it was acknowledged in front of everyone that he and Elega had known Myste was alive, known she was with Darsint. The information brought a speculative frown to Geraden's face as he drew inferences; it turned Terisa's cheeks alternately pale and hot – relief at Myste's safety, anger that Myste's safety had been kept secret.

King Joyse wasn't offended, however. 'In other words, my lord Prince,' he retorted, suppressing a desire to laugh, 'you decided to respect my position because you were given reason to believe it might be stronger than it appeared.' Away from Myste, he had resumed his more formal style of speech. 'That was wise – as well as courageous. While honest admissions are being made, I will admit in my turn that I have often suspected your father of wisdom.' His eyes glinted with momentary mischief. 'His courage, however, came as a pleasant surprise.

'Unfortunately,' he went on promptly, speaking now to the group around his standard, 'we will be in battle again at any moment, and before that moment comes I must say that my position is also weaker than it appears.'

Facing the champion, he asked, 'How should I address you?'

The champion frowned. 'You mean name or rank? I'm Darsint, First Battle-Officer, Unified Expeditionary Force cruiser *Scourge*.'

'Darsint,' King Joyse pronounced. 'Your offer of aid is very welcome. I need it badly. I doubt, however, that I will ever be able to help you.'

Darsint's frown deepened.

Instinctively, Elega caught her breath. What was her father doing now? Yet a glance at Myste reassured her: Myste appeared grave, but undistressed. Geraden was nodding slowly, as if to confirm what King Joyse said. Terisa seemed to be watching the foot of the valley distractedly, expecting harm.

'I am sure,' King Joyse explained, 'my daughter has told you that you were brought here by translation – by mirror. But the glass responsible for your presence was broken.' Perhaps tactfully, he didn't mention that Darsint himself had broken it. 'In addition, the only mirror we had which resembled that glass has also been shattered, by the enemies we now confront. As a result, I have no immediate aid to offer.

'I doubt that Master Gilbur can be persuaded to reveal how your mirror was made. Geraden is therefore our only hope.' King Joyse didn't look at Geraden. 'And I do not doubt that he will be able to reshape his mirror exactly, if we are victorious – if he is given time and peace.'

Geraden continued nodding.

'But that only raises another difficulty,' went on the King, 'which is time itself. Our mirrors show Images of place, not of person. And the Images can be adjusted only over relatively small distances. Once Geraden has reshaped his glass, we will have the power to return you, not to your people or your home, but only to the place where you were found.

'How many days have passed since you were forced among us? And how many more will pass before Geraden is given time and peace? Will your "cruiser" – will this *Scourge* – remain where it was, waiting for you?'

'Pythas,' Darsint muttered darkly. 'God-rotting piece of real estate. Should have left it alone while we had the chance. UEF needs a staging-area in that sector – but nobody needs a staging-area that bad.'

King Joyse pursued his point. 'Is it not more likely that your *Scourge* will be gone? that we will consign you to death among your enemies if we return you after so many days?'

'Shit, yes.' The champion appeared to be chewing his lip below the rim of his visor's opening. 'Pythians had us on the run when I got snatched. Plasma beams like I've never seen.' He indicated his damaged armor. '*Scourge*'ll be long gone.'

'So I can promise you nothing,' King Joyse concluded, 'except that I will use you as hard as I can – and serve you as faithfully as I am able.

'Will you help us?'

Elega's chest hurt for air, but she kept holding each breath as long as she could, hoping that her father's candor wouldn't drive Darsint away.

The champion didn't take long to make up his mind. 'Oh, well,' he sighed like a disappointed nightingale. 'Myste warned me. She's still the only friend I've got. And you're her father. She thinks you're worth saving.

'Too bad I can't do it.' The twisting of his face resembled a grin; he may have been indulging in a piece of UEF humor. Elega wasn't sure: his features were as hard to read as stone. 'Weaker than I look. Like you. Handguns don't have the range you need – or the capacity. There's a limit to the number of people I can strangle personally. Can't stop what you've got coming.' Inside his helmet, he nodded toward High King Festten's army. 'And my rifle's about discharged—'

The blaring of the sackbut interrupted him.

At once, six catapults started winding back their arms.

Simultaneously, the wardrums began to beat their rhythm into the valley.

With a sharp look in that direction, Elega saw the Cadwal front advancing, preparing itself to pour through the breaks in the ridge. Too soon: the King and his champion weren't ready. And she hadn't had a chance to learn how Myste and Darsint and the Termigan came to be here – how they came to be together.

'But I'm not helpless.' By degrees, it became more obvious that Darsint's expression was intended as a smile. 'Might have enough charge left to take care of those toys for you.' He gestured up at the siege engines. 'Might even put a little God-rotting fear into your God-rotting enemies.'

He stopped as if he were waiting for someone to catch the joke and laugh.

After a moment, King Joyse did laugh – a short, hard chuckle, not of humor, but of recognition. '"A little God-rotting fear." I like the sound of that. Someday you must explain "God-rotting" to me. I suspect it is a phrase Castellan Lebbick would have enjoyed, if he had known it.

'Please do "take care of" the catapults.' King Joyse considered the Cadwal position, the readiness of the engines. 'As soon as possible.'

Still grinning that twisted, beaky grin, Darsint pulled his rifle off his back.

Involuntarily, a number of the guards and soldiers retreated a step.

Elega wished that Prince Kragen had dismounted, that he stood beside her. Like the Termigan, however, he stayed on his horse so that he could ride into battle at an instant's notice.

The champion checked a blinking red light on his strange weapon, thumbed a button. 'Range isn't a problem.' When he spoke softly, his voice sounded more than ever like birdsong. 'Not against wood. But I'd have to get closer – if I weren't such a good shot.'

Elega distinctly saw him wink at Myste.

For some reason, his wink reminded her that he was responsible for the burn-scar on Myste's cheek, the mark which seemed to transform Myste's expression from dreamy romance to decisiveness.

The wardrums picked up their pace.

Abruptly, Darsint raised the rifle to his shoulder, sighted along it.

During the space between one heartbeat and the next, his weapon let out a straight burst of fire.

Elega and Terisa and Geraden and everyone anywhere near the pennon turned in time to see one of the catapults catch the burst and fly to pieces. Chunks of timber and strands of rope sailed soundlessly off the rampart, shedding flames as they fell.

Elega thought she heard the hammering of the wardrums falter. Maybe she had imagined it.

'One,' Darsint announced flatly.

He aimed again, fired again.

Its legs broken, his target leaned forward, started to topple; then its arm snapped under the stress.

'Two.'

With some difficulty, Elega restrained an impulse to cheer. Everyone else was silent, clenched in awe and suspense.

Frowning, Darsint rechecked his rifle; he fired again. A blazing line sped as straight as a die toward the next catapult.

Apparently, the team of Cadwals at the engine panicked. They tried to throw before their catapult was ready. A load of scattershot sprayed harmlessly down the wall as fire reduced the catapult to wreckage.

'Three.'

This time, there was no question about it: the wardrums faltered. A moment later, they stumbled into confusion as their drummers lost the beat. Instead of reorganizing themselves, resuming their insistent drive, they stopped altogether.

Several of the guards cleared their throats and began to cheer hoarsely. A ragged shout of approval, raucous with urgency and relief, spread out across the valley.

Well done, Darsint! Elega crowed to herself. By the stars, we will teach High King Festten what it means to oppose us!

The champion fired again; another engine collapsed.

'Four.'

Frowning harder, Darsint peered at his rifle, pushed buttons, thudded the stock with the heel of his hand.

Through the mounting cheers, Prince Kragen called, 'Darsint, is it wise to empty your weapon now? This battle has hardly begun. You will need your strength.'

The champion gave another twisted grin. 'It's never wise to take low ground and let enemies throw rocks at your head.'

He lifted his rifle; from its muzzle came another shot of flame.

'Five.'

Over the tumult came the sackbut's blare, sounding retreat. The Cadwal front began to withdraw. As if they were already victorious, the King's guard and Prince Kragen's soldiers cheered more ferociously.

Nevertheless everyone around the pennon had seen how Darsint's fifth shot sputtered and fizzled. When he shrugged, aimed at the last catapult, and tried to fire, his weapon produced nothing except a spray of sparks, quickly gone.

He shrugged again, tried again: nothing. Automatically, he reslung the rifle across his back. To no one in particular, he said, 'Anybody got a portable cyclotron I can adapt to charge this thing?'

Smiling, Myste moved close to him and put a hand on his armor as if to congratulate or console him.

By degrees, the cheering died as everyone realized that the last catapult wasn't going to fall.

If King Joyse felt any disappointment, however, he didn't show it. 'That was well done, Darsint,' he asserted, 'well done indeed. Let the High King beware. His fortunes have begun to turn. Now he and his allies will know that you are here, and that you are with us.'

'They will also know,' put in the Prince, 'that his weapon has no more force.'

'But they cannot know how many weapons he has,' Joyse retorted confidently, 'or what his capabilities are. They will wait now. They must. High King Festten and Master Eremis will consult together. When they strike again, they will attempt something extravagant – a sign of growing desperation.'

Her father was amazing, really, Elega thought. Trapped in this valley, hugely outnumbered, with Darsint's resources effectively exhausted, and the Congery's as well, he somehow made everyone who heard him feel that he couldn't be beaten.

'In the meantime, my lord Prince,' he continued, 'we have a good opportunity to strengthen our defenses. We must make the best use we can of every obstacle to the High King's advance.'

Prince Kragen nodded once, grimly ready. 'As you say, my lord King.' His manner was severe: only the particular brightness of his gaze betrayed his pleasure in the things he and Elega had planned and hoped for together, in the validation of the risks he had persuaded the Alend Monarch to accept. 'I will undertake the matter.'

Gripping his reins, he turned his horse.

'I'll come with you,' said the Termigan before anyone else could speak. His flat eyes and dour expression gave no hint that he had ever considered the Prince an enemy. 'I didn't ride all this way to sit around watching other people work.'

'My lord Termigan.' King Joyse's tone made both the lord and Prince Kragen stop. 'You have not yet told us how you happen to be here, or why. And I have not had a chance to thank you. For bringing two hundred men to my side, I am grateful. For bringing Darsint and my daughter here safely, I am forever in your debt.'

The Termigan jerked at his horse's head. 'Sternwall is lost,' he snapped. For the first time, Elega noticed the froth on the beast's mouth, the exhaustion in the beast's eyes. 'I had no intention of coming. Geraden told you that. I held on as long as I could. But when I lost Sternwall I didn't have anywhere else to go.

'You're the only hope my Care has left – you, and your Imagers' – he looked like he wanted to spit – 'and your alliance with Alend.' Forcibly, he seemed to recollect that he was talking to his King. 'My father practically built that city with his bare hands. I'm sorry I don't have better manners.'

His mount stumbled as he wrenched it around. Nevertheless by simple willpower he pulled the beast into a trot as he rode away toward the foot of the valley.

King Joyse and Prince Kragen met each other's eyes. 'Use him carefully,' murmured the King. 'I have lost two good lords already and have no wish to lose another.'

The Prince replied with a bleak smile. 'In Alend, old soldiers still talk about what a terrible thing it was to do battle against the lord of the Care of Termigan. I will use him carefully.'

Bowing to the King, waving to Elega, Prince Kragen followed the Termigan.

Elega wanted him back. The knowledge that he was in no immediate danger didn't comfort her. At the same time, however, she felt a small shiver of eagerness because she knew that now she would get to hear Myste's story.

While the forces of Cadwal waited, and Prince Kragen did what he could to shore up the King's defenses, Elega and Myste withdrew to the Tor's tent, looking for a quiet place to talk. Terisa and Geraden were with them – and King Joyse as well, which surprised Elega because she expected him to be busy with matters of battle, and pleased her because it demonstrated that he trusted the Alend Contender, son of an old foe.

Darsint accompanied them also. In a way that made the mere idea of refusing him seem unimaginable, he insisted on staying with Myste.

Outside, the remaining catapult threw at intervals: a stubborn assailant, and quite useless. For the most part, the King's men were able to stay out of the engine's range. Eventually, it became clear that the catapult's only real purpose was to remind the guards and soldiers that High King Festten intended to destroy them.

But Elega wasn't thinking about destruction at the moment. She was marvelling at her sister, who had somehow become a force to be reckoned with in the struggle between kingdoms. Like Torrent, she had found a way to make a difference.

Elega was keenly proud of her.

'Did you really threaten your sister?' King Joyse asked as soon as everyone was settled. 'Did you really threaten to unleash Darsint against the whole Alend army?'

The light of lanterns dimmed Myste's beauty. Inside the tent, she seemed less sure of herself, more easily embarrassed. A bit shamefacedly, she answered, 'I fear so. I made an effort to be careful – to say less than I meant, rather than more. But I am certain Elega understood me.'

Happily, Elega nodded. 'I was glad of it, however – when I recovered from the shock. I needed as many arguments as possible to set before the Alend Monarch.'

No doubt about it: Myste was definitely blushing. 'Still I am relieved you did not put me to the test. My threats became hollow almost at once. As soon as we parted – as soon as you helped me from the Alend camp – Darsint and I left. We were not there to take any action against you.'

'No?' Elega was surprised. 'I would have sworn you were watching everything I did for days afterward.'

'Where did you go?' Geraden put in. Like Terisa, he appeared to have some special reason to be pleased by Myste's presence. Perhaps it was because he loved families. Not for the first time, Elega noticed that he had changed enormously. The sense of *ability* in him was unmistakable. In retrospect, she was ashamed that she had ever treated him with scorn.

Myste glanced a bit awkwardly at her father. 'Elega told me what I needed to know,' she said slowly. 'When I heard the High King was marching, not to Orison, but into the Care of Tor, I felt that my way became clear. Darsint and I went to help the Perdon, if we could.'

The Perdon, who fought a suicidal battle against the forces of Cadwal because his King had abandoned him.

'"I have always believed that problems should be solved by those who see them,"' Terisa said, quoting softly. Her eyes shone as if she, too, were proud of Myste.

King Joyse didn't react to the implications of what Myste and Terisa said, however. He only smiled at them, and at Elega, basking in their company. 'That was well done, Myste,' he murmured. 'Go on.'

His attitude relieved Myste. 'There is little to tell, really,' she said more easily. 'We traveled as best we could, but the High King's army was between us and the Perdon. We were saving Darsint's fire, since we knew it would soon be depleted, so instead of attacking High King Festten from the rear we attempted to pass around him to the fore. By the time we succeeded, the Perdon had already been trapped and killed.

'That was a hard time for us. Seeing my distress' – her eyes were wide with fondness – 'Darsint wanted to assail the Cadwals, to hurt them as much as he could alone.' Darsint nodded. 'But I felt certain that his force must not be wasted, and I required him to withhold. Together, we waited and watched, gathering as much knowledge of the High King's movements as we could without betraying our presence.

'When your army came, we were once again on the wrong side, unable to reach you directly. This time, however, our position was fortuitous. Circling the High King's forces, first to the south, then to the west, we encountered the Termigan and his men.

'Without him, we would not have been able to join you, except by a ruinous expenditure of Darsint's fire.'

Geraden interrupted again. 'Did he explain himself? When Terisa and I asked him to come, he refused.' He looked to Terisa for confirmation. 'He was pretty convincing about it.'

Myste shook her head. 'He told us only what he has already suggested to you. He held to Sternwall as long as he could, but at last the pits of fire in the ground left him nothing of his father's Seat. With what fighting men he could spare from the care of his people, he set out across-country to Esmerel, intending' – she faltered momentarily, then resumed in a quiet, sad tone – 'intending, I think, to both use and end his hate in one swift blow against Master Eremis.

'I cannot truly vouch for the state of his mind,' she added. 'I can only say that he was not easily persuaded to join us, to join his purpose to ours.'

'I've seen that look before,' Darsint muttered. 'Had his death all planned – until he met us. Now, who knows?' The champion may have shrugged inside his armor.

'It was not Darsint's presence that persuaded him,' Myste continued. 'He is savage against all Imagery. And I do not think he was moved by the knowledge that you were here.' She faced her father frankly. 'He is another lord who believes he was abandoned by his King. But for some reason your alliance with Alend changed him. He finds— Father, I must say this. I fear he finds his old enemies easier to trust.'

A shadow passed across the King's face. 'Who can blame him?'

Awkwardly, Myste finished her story. 'Once he was persuaded, however, he did not hold back. Since then, we have spent our time searching for a way past the Cadwals which would spare Darsint's fire. Without the Termigan's aid, we could not have reached you as we did.'

As she spoke, King Joyse's expression cleared. 'That is well,' he said when she was done. 'If we are defeated, my lord Termigan will be able to do whatever he wishes with his hate. And if we are victorious, he will know that we could not have won without him. That may do much to heal him.

'In the meantime, daughter, you have brought us new hope. Did you know that your meeting with Darsint was augured?'

Elega looked at King Joyse sharply. *Augured?*

Both Terisa and Geraden were grinning.

'Havelock cast an augury,' Joyse explained, 'in which you appeared, on your knees before Darsint as if you were begging him not to kill you.'

Darsint shifted his weight uncomfortably. 'She did kneel. I was hurt – out of my head. Couldn't get my eyes in focus. Everything was changed, enemies everywhere. Someone came, I fired. Nearly God-rotting killed her.

'Then I heard her voice. A woman. On her knees. Felt like shooting myself when I saw what I did to her.'

Distinctly, as if he wanted no mistake on this point, he said, 'She saved my life.' There was a threat in his tone. He had no intention of letting Myste be harmed again.

For a moment, the King's blue eyes blurred. 'When you disappeared from Orison,' he continued to Myste, 'I knew in my heart where you had gone – and I was afraid. That is why,' he explained to Terisa, 'I was so harsh with you, when I asked you to account for her absence. I could not resolve my fear of the truth.

'In fact,' he went on, addressing Myste again, 'when I first realized that the champion in Master Gilbur's glass was the same as the figure in Havelock's augury, I almost decided to shatter that glass. To spare you. So that Darsint would not be translated. Havelock had great difficulty dissuading me. Allowing that translation to take place – trusting the risks I had chosen—' His smile was sad and relieved and strong all at the same time. 'That did not come easily. If I had let the Fayle urge me to stop the Congery, my determination might have faltered.'

Geraden cleared his throat. 'Adept Havelock tried to tell us about that augury – tried to tell Terisa. I'm still not sure why. All he managed to do at the time was scare us. But maybe he was trying to make us understand you better. As well as he could, in his condition—'

Dryly, King Joyse replied, 'Perhaps. Don't underestimate him. At his worst, he's still the best hop-board player I know.'

Without preamble, Terisa said, 'There's got to be something we can do.'

At once, the King shifted his attention to her. 'My lady?'

'They're all here.' She didn't seem to be speaking to him, or to anyone. Her eyes studied the air; her attention was inward. 'All the pieces are in place. Myste and the champion. Elega and Prince Kragen. The Masters. Lebbick's army. He and the Perdon and the Tor all did what they were supposed to do before they were lost – sacrificed so the rest of us would come to this position. Even Torrent did her part. Everyone is doing what you want them to do, what you gave them the chance to do.

'Except Geraden and me.'

Again, King Joyse asked softly, 'My lady?'

No one else spoke. Geraden studied Terisa intently; Myste watched her with shining eyes.

'We've done what we can,' Terisa said. 'We helped bring about this position. But now we're useless. We might as well be pushed off the board.'

Now she met King Joyse's gaze. 'What do you want from us?'

He smiled at her as if she were wonderful. 'My lady, I can beat the High King. I want you to defeat Master Eremis.'

Before she could react – before Geraden or Elega or anyone else could say anything – Castellan Norge strode through the tent-flaps, unannounced and hurrying.

'My lord King,' he said with as much urgency as his phlegmatic manner could convey, 'you'll want to see this. Something's going to happen.'

So quickly that he may have been trying to escape the questions Terisa and Geraden wanted to ask, King Joyse left his chair and followed the Castellan out of the tent.

Elega hesitated momentarily; she thought she ought to say something to Terisa and Geraden – or even to Myste and Darsint. But her heart was with her father, with the battle and Prince Kragen; she couldn't remain behind.

Outside, she hardly noticed that the rest of the people in the tent joined her only a moment later.

The valley was full of midmorning sunshine. Only midmorning, after all that had happened— Above the ramparts, the sky was immeasurably blue, as clean and complete as springtime. The air was turning subtly but unquestionably warmer, and under the sunlight the night's thick snowfall had gone slushy. Where the army had trampled the snow, a few small stretches of dark, wet dirt were beginning to appear. The stream down the center of the valley ran more loudly, taking in water from the snow-melt.

Like King Joyse and his companions around the pennon, every Mordant and Alend from the valley foot to Esmerel watched what could be seen of High King Festten's army.

The Cadwal forces appeared to be withdrawing.

No, not withdrawing: dividing. The High King parted his men into a new formation, half on either side with a space of clear ground between them as wide as the valley itself.

'Does he think he can lure us out there?' Norge inquired. 'Does he think we're crazy enough to let him hit us from both sides?'

'No,' King Joyse snapped, unintentionally brusque. 'He is making room.'

'Eremis is going to translate something,' Terisa breathed to Geraden. 'If I go down there, if I get close enough— If I can figure out the Image, the way I did at the crossroads, I might be able to break his mirror.'

She wasn't talking to the King, but he heard her anyway. 'You will not, my lady,' he said at once. 'If you fail, you will be the first victim. That risk is too great, even for me.'

Geraden put his arm around her. He may have been trying to reassure her. Or maybe he was making sure she didn't sneak away.

Anticipation and dread knotted the atmosphere. King Joyse had said, *They will attempt something extravagant*— Everyone who had ever heard stories of the old wars knew that Imagers were capable of atrocities which could freeze blood in the heart.

Nevertheless when the next attack came no one was ready for it.

Because she was expecting something, concentrating hard, Terisa felt just a suggestion of the visceral cold of translation. Eremis' mirror was focused too far away to touch her strongly. She tightened her grip on Geraden.

In the clear space between the sides of the Cadwal army, a monster appeared.

She had seen it before. Every member of the Congery was familiar with it.

Huge eyes, insatiable and raging. Teeth dripping poison in a maw big enough to swallow houses. A vast, sluglike body. Slime-streaked sides.

Once, during the old wars, that beast had destroyed an entire village, eaten it hut by hut. The worm was too big to be killed, too big even to be hurt. Given time, it could have consumed anything. But King Joyse had captured the mirror from which the monster came, and Adept Havelock had translated the beast back to its cave in the Image.

Now Master Eremis had the mirror, and the beast was furious.

The creature gave a roar of hideous outrage, howling so fiercely that the walls of the valley rang. Then it slithered forward and began devouring the rubble that blocked High King Festten's approach, attacking the mounds as if piled rock offended it.

In spite of training and experience, determination and courage, the King's army broke into panic.

The monster's teeth among the rubble were as loud as detonations, inescapably destructive. Already the archers hidden in the mounds had to leap and run, risk snapping their legs or backs to get away. And when the rock was gone, the creature would enter the valley—

It would consume the entire army itself. Or it would drive guards and soldiers to the walls, where High King Festten's men could crush them at leisure. Or it would force them out of the valley, where the Cadwal army could fall on them from both sides. *Something extravagant—* This was extravagant, all right. But it wasn't desperate. It was a masterstroke, completely unanswerable; defeat as stark and terrible as the creature's teeth.

Helpless to save themselves, the Alend and Mordant ranks came apart like water and began spilling in all directions. Their cries were everywhere; hoarse and frantic; doomed.

The sight set King Joyse afire. 'Death's hatchetman, Eremis!' he roared in a voice that seemed to match the monster's, 'this is foul!'

But he didn't waste time on indignation. Wheeling to Norge, he barked like a trumpet, 'Find Kragen! Rally the men! Retreat! That beast is no danger yet! We must stop this panic!

'Bring my horse!'

Galvanized by the King's shout, Norge raced for his own mount while two dumbstruck guards hauled Joyse's suddenly frightened charger forward.

In a moment, both men were gone, spurring their horses into the face of an army transformed to tumult and chaos. King Joyse didn't rage at his enemies; he didn't shout at his men. He simply rode hard, rode *conspicuously*, straight for the foot of the valley, with his sword bright in his hands, so that as many soldiers and guards as possible would see him and think he wasn't beaten.

'There's got to be *something* we can do,' Geraden repeated, fretting at his helplessness like a boy.

Terisa chewed her lip. 'I said that already.' She hardly heard him, however. She was listening to the sound of the monster's teeth in the rubble – a savage, crushing noise which seemed somehow louder than the army's panic – and trying to think about several different things at the same time.

Choose your risks more carefully.

I want you to defeat Master Eremis.

Problems should be solved by those who see them.

I've got the strongest feeling—

And something else; something that refused to come clear. There was too much noise, too many people were shouting around her, too many people were going to die—

Something so stupidly obvious that she was going to kick herself as soon as she figured it out.

Master Barsonage was at Geraden's side. His eyes had a wild and aimless stare; he looked like a man who had wandered here after having his brains baked out in the desert. 'Now I understand,' he said, not – apparently – because anyone was listening to him, but because he had to say something, needed to hear a reasonable voice. 'When we rescued you from the ruin of our meeting hall, Eremis used that glass to help clear away the stone. I thought his choice was odd, but now I understand. He was making his beast mad, teaching it to hate stone.'

Something—

'Why did none of us realize that he must be the maker of that glass? Or an Adept?'

In spite of herself, she stopped to absorb what the Master said. He was right: Eremis must be an Adept. Or he had been working against King Joyse longer than anyone realized; had conceived his ambitions at a younger age. Unexpected abilities—

'But how did he get possession of the mirror?' asked the mediator. 'I thought it was among those broken when he shattered Geraden's glass. He must have captured it then. That must have been one of the reasons for his attack on the laborium.'

'Why did none of us think to see whether all the mirrors we lost were among those broken?'

It was unexpected: that's why. What Eremis did was unexpected. His abilities were unexpected. No one could expect the unexpected. By definition.

Then she had it, had it so suddenly that she seemed to reach her conclusion without taking any of the steps which led to it.

Yes.

Oh, *yes*.

'Geraden.' She grabbed his arm, pulled him around to face her. 'We've got to get back to Orison.'

Geraden stared at her in shock; his jaw dropped. For one moment that felt sickening, like a fall from a bad height, she thought he was going to protest, Do you want to run away? Then that danger passed, and as quick as it was gone another took its place; she could see it in his face: What are you *talking* about?

Oh, Geraden, don't ask, we haven't got *time*!

But he was Geraden, the man she loved; instinctively, he had always put her needs ahead of his confusion. Instead of making protests or demanding explanations, he said, 'We don't have a mirror.'

'Master Barsonage does.' With the ballroom of Orison in the Image.

'Flat glass. You can use it. I'll go mad.'

That was right. Oh, shit. 'Are you sure there aren't any others? Didn't the Congery bring *any* other normal mirrors?'

Hurry. Please. The creature was going to come through the rubble at any moment. And both King Joyse and Prince Kragen were down at the foot of the valley, vulnerable to those teeth—

As if the fact that he didn't know what was going on only made him more resolute, Geraden wheeled toward the mediator.

'Master Barsonage. Do you have another mirror? Did the Congery bring any other mirrors?'

Barsonage blinked some of the wildness out of his eyes. 'Why?'

'Do you have one?'

'Why do you want it?'

Terisa pushed herself beside Geraden, tried to make the mediator notice her. 'We've got to get back to Orison.'

She was putting too much pressure on him; her demand seemed to increase his air of being lost. In a hoarse, dry tone, he asked, 'Will you abandon King Joyse to his doom?'

Geraden clenched his fists, breathed, '*No*,' as if he were defending her.

Unfortunately, that just put more pressure on Master Barsonage. Terisa shook herself, forced down her fear, tried to give the mediator a better answer.

'I need to use Havelock's mirrors.'

She had other reasons as well, but she couldn't take the time to think about them, much less explain them.

At least now she had the Master's attention. The effort to think clarified his expression, made his expression at once sharper and more human.

'What will you do?'

Hurrying past illogic, impossibility, uselessness, she replied, 'Find Master Eremis' stronghold. Stop him.'

Now Geraden stared at her the same way Master Barsonage did. At the same moment, they both asked, 'How?'

'Unexpected abilities—' she began, fumbling for words, 'unexpected actions— He can't expect the unexpected. You said so yourself.'

Strictly literal, Master Barsonage returned, 'I said nothing of the kind.'

No. Listen. Let me think. 'I mean me.' Why couldn't she think? The monster devouring the rubble might have been eating her mind away. 'I've done something unexpected. Twice.'

Abruptly, with the beast already halfway through the piled stone, and the valley in panic, and Geraden and Master Barsonage staring at her as if she were demented, her sense of urgency and horror became too great for confusion. She knew how to think; she knew how to survive. She knew how to fight.

As if she were calm, she said, 'When I got away from Master Gilbur, that wasn't really unexpected. By then we knew I had some kind of ability. But when I changed the Image in the flat glass in the laborium – the first day after I came to Orison – that was unexpected. And when I changed another Image to escape from Master Eremis, changed it across all these miles – that was unexpected. We've never even tried to explain it.'

'Talent—' suggested Master Barsonage thinly.

She shook her head. 'I don't mean that. I'm talking about something else.' She faced Geraden squarely. 'When you tried to translate me home, I ended up near the Closed Fist. That was your doing. You're the one who works with curved glass. But it was the Closed Fist in spring. It was augury. You changed the Image across time as well as distance.

'But when *I* changed the flat mirror,' in shock, by reflex rather than conscious choice, 'my Image showed the Closed Fist the way it really was at the time. In winter. How did I do that? How did I know what it looked like in winter?'

Geraden watched her as if she had staggered him and he was struggling to keep his balance. 'I never thought of that.'

'And when I escaped from Eremis—' Now she addressed Master Barsonage as well. 'I used the same mirror that got me away from Gilbur. That makes sense. I was familiar with the Image. But the Image itself had changed in the meantime. The only time I actually saw it, when I used it to get away from Gilbur, it was full of wind. But when I used it to get away from Eremis, there was no wind. The Image was different. How could I change the Image in that mirror when I didn't even know what that Image looked like – when the Image I remembered was gone?'

Master Barsonage gaped. He would have looked foolish if the situation weren't so desperate.

'You mean,' Geraden murmured softly, eagerly, on the verge of a revelation, 'that's part of your talent. You don't need exact knowledge to change Images exactly. Something in you compensates for the things you don't know.'

Right. Now she was focused entirely on the mediator, urging him to believe her, urging him to act. 'I'm familiar with at least one of Havelock's mirrors. And I can't concentrate here, with that thing coming to get us.' And she had at least one other reason. 'I need to get back to Orison. So I can make an Image – an approximate Image – that might take us to Master Eremis' stronghold. It was dark, I couldn't see. But I remember a lot of details anyway. Maybe they'll be enough.'

For a moment, Master Barsonage went on staring at her as if her ideas were inconceivable, imponderable. He had the soul of a fence-sitter: he didn't like hazardous decisions. Just when she was about to start yelling at him, however, he lifted his head and smiled, and all the wildness fell away from him.

'Why did you not say that from the first?'

920

Turning, he headed toward one of the Congery's wagons, shouting for other Masters to join him as he ran.

Terisa was about to follow when Geraden snatched her exuberantly into his arms, whirled her in a circle with her feet off the ground and her breath gasping. 'I knew it!' he shouted to the blue sky and the chaos and the slug-beast. 'I knew we weren't supposed to be here!'

Even though she couldn't resist kissing him, she was thinking, Put me down you idiot we've got to *go*.

He put her down. Together, they raced to the wagon.

The Masters were unpacking a mirror which showed a limitless sea glittering under hot sunlight.

'I brought it on a whim, really,' Master Barsonage explained as the other Imagers set the glass as securely as possible in the wet snow. 'It served us so well when we rescued you from the champion's destruction of our meeting hall, I thought perhaps it could serve us again. When you demanded a mirror, I was reluctant to risk it. I was trying to imagine how it might be used to drown that monster.'

'I won't break it,' Geraden promised. He was already beside the mirror, already stroking his fingertips along its beautiful woodwork. Despite the running and cries of the men, the desperate commands of the officers, the loud ruin of the monster's teeth, he seemed to have no difficulty concentrating. To Terisa's eyes, he shone with confidence and strength which made everything possible.

Nothing happened to the Image of the sea. Waves went on rolling their long, slow unrest from edge to edge of the frame; the heavens remained an immaculate blue unmatched by any color in the world except the sky's hue above the valley.

'Ready?' he asked Terisa over his shoulder. Without looking away from the glass, he extended his hand to her.

Where were Havelock's rooms, Havelock's mirrors? What had happened to Geraden's talent?

No, she told herself, he can do it this way, everything's all right. He had the ability to use mirrors for translations which had nothing to do with their Images. That was how he had come to her in the first place, how he had showed her the Closed Fist, how he had rescued himself from Orison. All she had to do was trust him.

Choose your risks—

She took his hand, started moving at once toward the glass so that she wouldn't falter.

But she was holding her breath as the Image opened to embrace her like the sea.

Of course she didn't fall into the sea: Geraden had too much control over his talent; he was in no danger of going that far wrong. Instead, she faded as if she had winked out of existence.

Holding his hand with all her strength, pulling him after her, she evaporated through the transition of mirrors, the instant, eternal plummet and soar between places of being; the vast redemptive and ruinous dark which her parents had taught her to know and fear and love by locking her in the closet.

When she came out of the translation, she lost her balance and collapsed in a heap, drawing Geraden helplessly after her – breaking his brief hold on the mirror's frame, his only attachment to the world of the valley.

For some strange reason, she landed on a thick carpet.

A synthetic carpet, running from wall to wall on both sides of her.

Adept Havelock didn't have a carpet like this in his rooms. No one had a carpet like this anywhere in Orison.

Across the deep, woven pile, she saw that she was surrounded by people: women in gowns; men in tuxedos. Some of them had yelled recently, dropped glasses full of ice and alcohol onto the carpet. They were all still now, however, motionless, staring frozen at Geraden and her with shock on their polished faces.

Until she recognized the angle of the hall leading to the bedrooms, and the shape of the entryway to the dining room and kitchen, she didn't realize that she was back in her old apartment.

Back in her old world.

FIFTY

CAREFUL RISKS

Geraden was sprawled halfway across her; his weight held her down. Instinctively, she arched her back, tried to shift him so that she could get her legs under her. He didn't move. Staring at the strange carpet, the chrome-and-wicker furniture, the astonished men and women in their inexplicable clothes, he murmured, 'Glass and splinters. What have I done?'

She thought the answer was obvious.

He had brought her back to her old condominium. And during her absence time had passed; *months* had passed. Never one to cling to a useless investment, her father must have sold her apartment as soon as he felt sure she wasn't coming back. And the new owners had redecorated it, of course—

All her mirrors were gone – every conceivable link to Mordant, every way back—

On the other hand, what imaginable reason could Geraden have for bringing her back *here*? for bringing her back here *now*? This wasn't just an accident: it was an absolute disaster.

There was no way back.

'Get up,' she urged as if his weight were suffocating her. 'Oh, God. Oh, shit. Get up.'

'Call the police,' a frightened woman pleaded.

'Call security,' suggested someone else.

'Who *are* they?'

Geraden got up.

As he rose to his feet, the people in the gowns and tuxedos flinched; some of them retreated farther. A shoe kicked a glass, sent it rolling across the tile on the kitchen floor. Terisa could hear ice being crunched underfoot, as if that noise were louder than the voices.

'Call *security*, I said.'

'How did they get *in* here?'

'I don't know. They just appeared, that's all.'

'What have we been *drinking*?'

Her heart beat so hard that she had trouble finding her balance, trouble making her legs lift her upright.

'What have I done?' Geraden repeated softly; he was appalled to the bone.

'Miss Morgan?'

No, she was wrong again, she had jumped once again to the wrong conclusions. The ice wasn't louder than the voices: she had no difficulty at all hearing Reverend Thatcher.

He was there, squirming his way out of the press of people, a small, old man in a shabby suit. His pulse beat in the veins under his pale skin. He came a few steps toward her, then stopped; his eyes watered with surprise and relief and embarrassment.

'Miss Morgan?'

Her father was right behind Reverend Thatcher. His expression made him look like a startled barracuda.

Terisa gaped at him while her pulse faltered and her heart quailed.

Geraden, please. Oh, please. Get us out of here.

'Miss Morgan.' Reverend Thatcher seemed to face her through a veil of tears. 'We thought you were dead. Kidnapped – lost – I went to your father.'

She had always considered her father mercilessly handsome in a tuxedo. His appearance was a weapon he knew how to use. And it made his anger more brutal; it implied that no one had the right to ruffle him.

He came out of the rich crowd as if he were stalking her.

She wanted to run. Dash into the bedroom. Hide under the bed.

It wasn't her bedroom anymore.

Oh, Geraden.

'He was going to sell your apartment anyway,' Reverend Thatcher explained, driven by a need to justify himself. 'I persuaded him to sell it for charity. For the mission. He's going to auction it tonight. To raise money for the mission.'

Without warning, she nearly lost her fear.

Reverend Thatcher had persuaded her father? He had gone to her father and *persuaded* him, confronted him? Lonely and pitiable as he was, the small, old man must have risen to something approaching heroism, in order to confront her father like that – in order to best him.

This time, she didn't need the call of horns to help her see the change in Reverend Thatcher, the valor underlying his superficial futility. She and Geraden had blundered into his night of triumph.

'You *know* these people?'

'Who *are* they?'

'I don't care. Get them out of here.'

Or else her father had relented in some way? He cared about her enough to be made vulnerable by losing her?

That idea changed everything. She believed in his unlove. It was fundamental to her. Could she have been wrong about him? Was there another part of him, a part she didn't understand, a part he didn't see himself when he looked in the mirror?

If he cared about her, how could she ever leave him?

No. He thrust Reverend Thatcher aside with such force that the old man stumbled. Chewing his anger, he demanded, 'Terisa Morgan, how *dare* you embarrass me like this?'

'Terisa,' Geraden asked as if he were panting, 'do these people *know* you? Where are we?'

'You disappear without telling anyone,' her father spat. 'You abandon your job, your apartment, you abandon *me*, you don't have the simple decency to ask permission, you don't tell anyone where you're going, and then you show up like this, in front of my friends, when I'm trying to get a good price out of them for this place. Dressed like *that*? How *dare* you?'

Geraden, *please*.

Her father looked like he was going to hit her. 'I'm *ashamed* of you.'

That was too much. Nothing was changed. She had found depths in herself which no glass could reflect; but her father was only what he appeared to be. Reverend Thatcher positively soared in her estimation. Instead of cowering or crying or pleading, she faced her father squarely.

But she didn't speak to him. Just for an instant, she wanted to hurt him somehow, say or do something which would repay him for his years of mistreatment. Almost immediately, however, she realized that there was no need. Simply not being afraid of him was enough.

'Geraden,' she said deliberately, 'this is my old apartment. Where you found me the first time.' She didn't care how badly her voice shook, or how near she came to tears. 'This is my father. That's Reverend Thatcher. I've told you about them.

'If there's any way you can get us out of here, you better do it now.'

'I don't care,' a strident voice repeated. '*I'm* calling security.'

'No!' both her father and Reverend Thatcher protested at the same time.

Nevertheless she heard the sound of the phone snatched off the hook, the sound of dialing—

'*Stop!*'

When Geraden stepped in front of her, he seemed taller than she remembered. Or perhaps her father had become shorter. Geraden's voice rang with authority, and everything about him was strong; his heart never quailed; even his mistakes hinted at glory.

'Do not call. Do not move. Do nothing. We will be gone in a moment.'

Everyone froze. The man holding the phone dropped it. Even her father lost the power of movement. Like his guests, he stared at Geraden and her with his mouth hanging open.

Casually, as if she weren't frantic inside, and had completely forgotten panic, Terisa remarked to Geraden, 'I thought you said you can't shift mirrors across distances.'

He didn't look at her. He didn't look at anyone: he closed his eyes, trusting his authority – or sheer surprise – to protect him while he concentrated. He had a king's face, and every line of it promised strength.

Quietly, he muttered, 'Well, I've got to *try*, don't I?'

Her father closed his mouth; he swallowed hard. Snarling deep in his throat, he said, 'I'm going to punish you for this—'

As if he were immensely far away, Reverend Thatcher retorted, 'Mr. Morgan, that's absurd. She's come back. We all thought she was dead, and now she's *come back*. We should be delighted.'

Before anyone could respond, Geraden abruptly flung his arms wide. For no good reason except his own urgency, he cried, '*Havelock, we trust you!*'

Then he vanished.

Someone let out a vague shriek. Several of her father's guests gasped or flinched. Others appeared to be on the verge of fainting.

Suddenly, Terisa wanted to sing. Oh, he was wonderful, Geraden was wonderful, and nobody was going to be able to stop her, never again, she was never going to be afraid of her father again.

While she still had the chance, she turned to Reverend Thatcher.

'You can have your auction. Make him give you every penny he gets. I want you to have the money. It's a good cause, the best. And I might not come back. If I do, I certainly won't live here.'

After that, without transition, she dropped into the quick, immeasurable plunge of translation.

Once again, Geraden had done the right thing.

As usual, she lost her balance; but he caught her as she stumbled out of the mirror, so that she didn't fall.

The change of light made her blink: electric illumination was gone, replaced by a few oil lamps. As her vision came into focus, she found that she was in the shrine or mausoleum which Adept Havelock had made out of the room where he stored his mirrors.

Where she needed to be.

What did he celebrate here? she wondered obliquely. What did he mourn?

But she had no time to spare for the Adept. Geraden held her hard, as if he had no intention of ever letting her go again.

'Glass and splinters, Terisa!' he breathed, pressing his face against her hair, 'I'm sorry, I don't know what went wrong, thank the stars Havelock was watching his mirrors, I didn't mean to take us *there*—'

Already the Image of her apartment in the mirror he and the Adept had used was fading.

She kissed him to make him stop. 'Don't apologize. You rescued us – that's what counts.' That, and Reverend Thatcher's ability to extract money from her father. And the fact that she was no longer afraid. Part of her still felt like singing. 'It was worth it.

'We've got to hurry. King Joyse doesn't have much time.'

He met her gaze. For a moment, she could see the characteristic struggle between chagrin and eagerness going on inside him; self-distrust and hope at each other's throats. Almost at once, however, he smiled, and his eyes cleared, as if the acceptance he met in her turned the tide of the conflict.

'Right,' he said like a man who couldn't think of any reason to be alarmed by the prospect of entering Master Eremis' stronghold. 'Let's get started.'

Together, they turned toward Havelock.

The Adept wasn't alone. He had Artagel with him.

Artagel was dressed for battle, and he was grinning.

Havelock had apparently been cleaning the room again. In one hand, he brandished a rather limp featherduster; he wore an apron several sizes too large for him to protect his still-spotless surcoat. Twisting his features as if he wanted to howl, he poked his duster at Terisa and Geraden, and said, 'I *told* you to trust me.

'Don't you realize yet that I'm the one who planned all this? I planned it *all*. Joyse is the only man alive who could have *done* it, but I *planned* it. No matter how crazy I get, I'm the best fornicating hop-board player in Orison, *bar none*.

'*Remember* that, for a change.'

Terisa couldn't resist: she asked, 'You mean you knew we were coming?'

For once, the Adept was tolerant of questions. 'Of course not. But I considered the possibility. What do you think planning *is*?'

'It's good to see the two of you again,' Artagel interrupted happily. 'I gather things have finally gotten desperate enough for some dramatic Imagery. A few of the Cadwals we've been taking prisoner in the ballroom look actively horrified.

'What're you trying to do?'

'Go to Eremis' stronghold, if we can get there,' answered Geraden. 'He isn't in Esmerel. Nyle isn't there. That was a trap. But Terisa thinks she can make an Image of the place Eremis took her. If she can, maybe we can find it and get in.'

'Good.' Facing his brother boldly, Artagel said, 'This time, you aren't going to get rid of me so easily. Whatever you have in mind, you're going to need a bodyguard. And I am sick to the teeth' – he flashed his grin – 'of being in command of this useless pile of rocks.'

Geraden started to protest, but Terisa stopped him. This was another of her reasons for returning to Orison. Two days ago – was it only two days ago? – he had said, *When the fighting really starts, we'd better be sure we've got somebody with us who handles a sword better than I do.* One of his 'strongest feelings.' Instead of trying to explain, however, she said, 'Let him do what he wants. We don't have time to argue with him.'

As if to demonstrate her point, she left Geraden's side and went to the mirror she wanted, the flat glass reflecting a sanddune in Cadwal.

'Besides,' Artagel whispered to Geraden behind her, 'Havelock says you need me. He got me down here. I didn't have any idea you were coming back.'

'What makes you think you're ready for Gart?' demanded Geraden hotly. 'He's already beaten you twice. And you're still hurt.'

Artagel chuckled. 'What makes you think the two of you are ready for Eremis and Gilbur and Vagel? We've all got to do what we can. And,' he added more soberly, 'you may not have time for Nyle. Maybe I'll be able to help him.'

Geraden apparently found that argument difficult to refute. As if to relieve a personal anxiety, he changed the subject. 'How's the siege?'

'No trouble,' Artagel replied. 'Margonal is a model enemy. Yesterday he sent me a dozen sides of beef. Sovereign's courtesy. I sent him a cask of the King's best wine. We're becoming friends. As long as Orison doesn't panic, I'm not needed here.'

Terisa set herself in front of the glass she had chosen and tried to relax. Now that she had assumed this responsibility, it promised to be more difficult than she had allowed herself to imagine. She needed to conceive an Image of a place she had never seen, a place she knew only in small pieces, by feel. And during the relatively short time she was there, she hadn't exactly been concentrating on exact, concrete details. It had been dark – dark – Master Eremis had chained her to the wall; he had talked to her, threatened her, touched her. The arch-Imager Vagel had visited her. She had found and spoken to Nyle. And all the time her attention, her talent, had been directed elsewhere, groping for an answer to her fear – reaching out to the room in which she stood now, rather than teaching itself to recognize her prison.

She could make the mirror's desert Image melt into darkness: that was easy. But there were many different kinds of darkness in the world, in many different places. How could she be sure that the Image she conceived wasn't buried away inside the heart of some mountain, or lost in the depths of the sea?

Light: she remembered a faint, ambient illumination, a glow from an imperfectly sealed window above the bed. That was a start. How large was the bed? What was it made of? She had no idea. But the chain— Roughly ten feet of it, long enough to permit the exercises Eremis intended; stapled to the wall at the head of the bed. What else did she know?

Vaguely, the location of the doorway.

The distance between her fetter and Nyle's.

And she could remember exactly what those two iron staples felt like. Nyle's short chain. His wrist in its manacle. The rough, warm fabric of his sleeve—

Wait a minute. Wait a minute.

Images focused on places, not on people. But Nyle had been chained to the wall; she assumed he was still chained to the wall. Didn't that make him part of the place, an essential component of the Image she needed?

If she could remember what he looked like—

That, too, was easy: he looked like Geraden; slightly shorter; Geraden aged or embittered by disappointment and pessimism. *Geraden reduced to despair by Eremis and Gilbur,* no, don't think about that now, don't be distracted, take a deep breath, concentrate. She even remembered what Nyle was wearing.

A brown worsted cloak which covered him from neck to ankles, to keep the blood and the knife Eremis had given him hidden.

If she put together an Image of Nyle chained in that position, in those clothes, that close to the bed and her chain and the window, about that far from the door— Would it be enough?

She wanted to ask Geraden, but she knew he didn't know the answer. No one had ever measured her talent; no one knew what she could do. And there was only one way to learn. She had to test herself and see what happened.

She had to do the same thing to herself that King Joyse had done to her.

She wondered where he got his courage.

But she had no time for doubt. Geraden and the Adept and Artagel were watching her silently; they may all have stopped breathing. And back in the Care of Tor, in the valley of Esmerel, more lives and hopes were lost with every moment she delayed.

One deliberate piece at a time, she began to construct the Image.

Fortunately, before she made a mistake, she felt a sting of recollection.

Clothes – clothes— There was something wrong with Nyle's clothes.

Of course. Nyle wasn't wearing the clothes she remembered. After the physician Underwell had been butchered, disfigured, he had been dressed in Nyle's clothes. Otherwise no one would have jumped to the conclusion that the dead man was actually Geraden's brother.

Her pulse beat in her throat so hard that she had trouble speaking.

'What did Underwell have on? When he went to treat Nyle?'

The three men behind her shifted their feet; she heard their boots distinctly on the stone floor. 'My lady?' Artagel responded uncomfortably, as if he thought she might be losing her wits.

'Don't ask,' she breathed. 'Just tell me. I've got to concentrate.'

'If I told Joyse once, I told him a dozen times,' remarked the Adept, 'don't trust women.' He sounded especially happy. 'They've got their hearts in their finery and their brains in their loins.'

'You've seen it,' Geraden put in at once. 'It's kind of a uniform. All the physicians wear it. So they're easy to spot when they're needed. A gray doublet. Cotton breeches.' His voice trailed off; he may not have had much confidence in his ability to describe clothing.

He had said enough, however. A gray doublet with long sleeves and rough-spun fabric; not the worsted cloak she remembered.

As if by an act of will, she added that detail to the Image in her mind.

All she needed, she kept reminding herself, all she needed was a close approximation. Her unexpected abilities would take care of the rest.

Gradually, the mirror's reflection dissolved from hot sunlight to an almost impenetrable blackness.

How dare you embarrass me like this?

I'm ashamed of you.

I'm going to punish you—

Ha! she snorted reflexively. Try it.

She had a cramp between her shoulder blades. Every muscle in her body was knotted around itself. There were too many different kinds of dark in the world, too many different kinds of pain.

Studying the lightless Image, she said, 'I need a lamp.'

'What for?' inquired Artagel.

She wanted to repeat, Don't ask. I've got to concentrate. This time, however, it was important to be understood. Geraden had to be ready.

'I can use flat glass. You can't. I'm going to translate myself – there.' Into a blackness she couldn't read, even though she peered at it until her temples throbbed. 'With a lamp. If I don't lose control over this mirror, you'll be able to see where I am. Geraden can make another Image. A normal Image.'

As she spoke, Geraden brought her a lamp. She risked a glance at him, risked losing her concentration— He was intent and keen, tight with determination; she couldn't imagine him losing heart. Nevertheless a shadow of fear darkened his gaze.

'Are you sure?' he whispered.

She shook her head. 'Being sure is a weakness. Let Eremis have it.'

Let her father have it.

Surprised by the steadiness of her hands, she accepted the lamp. Its flame seemed to come between her and the glass, changing the adjustment of her vision so that now she couldn't see anything.

An almost impenetrable blackness—

Oh, well.

Before she had time to think of any more reasons why she might fail, she opened the Image and stepped into it—

—into the disorienting, endless, momentary absence between existence and existence.

When she hit the floor, she nearly dropped the lamp.

The cramp in her back hampered her, kept her from moving her arms freely. As a result, she had to struggle for balance, and her jerky movements almost threw the lamp out of her hands.

She caught herself, caught the lamp, drew a gasping breath.

There was a door in front of her, a wooden door banded and barred like the entrance to a cell. Her lamp was the only light in the room; her small flame sent shadows dancing across the raftered ceiling, down the stone walls. Like every other part of the world, the room was chilly.

Immediately, she turned to look around, at the place where the bed and the window and the iron staples were supposed to be – at the place where Nyle was supposed to be—

The sight of him suspended there in his manacles filled her with such triumph that she nearly shouted.

Geraden, hurry, I did it, I did it!

She didn't realize that she was losing her grip on the mirror in Orison until the details of Nyle's appearance struck her.

His face was chalky, not physically battered, but nonetheless haggard and abused. His eyes stared at her, dark pits from which the intelligence had been burned out. In spite of her sudden arrival, he slumped against his chains, unable to lift his weight off the manacles. Old blood crusted his wrists. A small caked pool marked the stone between his feet. Master Gilbur had strange tastes. Nyle looked like a man who had been used until the only part of him left alive was his sense of horror.

And that was the fate Master Eremis had intended for her. He had planned to reduce her to that condition, in order to hurt both her and Geraden as much as possible.

'Oh, Nyle!'

No, *concentrate*, don't think about it! In swift fright, she flung her attention back to Adept Havelock's mirror room, back to the glass which had translated her here. *Keep the Image.* There was light in Nyle's prison now, she held the lamp up, Geraden could see the scene, he could copy it in a curved mirror – if he was fast, if he did it before Nyle's blank, dead stare made her start to weep and rage—

If he didn't end up someplace else entirely—

Without warning, Artagel came through at a run.

Unable to anticipate the floor underfoot after the plunge of translation, he stumbled as if he were hurling himself at the door. His reflexes saved him from a collision, however. Recovering his balance almost instantly, he spun toward Terisa and Nyle. He had lost his grin in shock and surprise.

When he saw Nyle, he froze momentarily. The eagerness in him, the readiness for battle, seemed to shatter. Then he sprang past her and began trying to tear Nyle's fetters out of the wall with his bare hands.

Geraden was already there.

She didn't see him arrive, didn't see how he emerged from his translation; she only saw him throw himself at the cot as if he had gone mad. Coughing curses, he picked up the cot and crashed it against the wall, hammered and belabored it against the stone until the frame and legs broke into pieces the size of clubs.

With one of the legs, he went at Artagel and Nyle as if he meant to beat them both senseless.

Shouldering Artagel aside, he jammed the end of the leg into the nearest staple and levered it savagely out of the wall.

The iron staple sang like a sword as it skittered across the floor.

Nyle collapsed into Artagel's grasp.

Panting, 'Bastards bastards bastards,' Geraden attacked the second staple. It let out a thin, metallic scream as it pulled loose.

He and Artagel hunched over Nyle. Clenched sounds came between their teeth, as if both of them were weeping.

Terisa thought for a moment that Nyle was unconscious, too badly abused to understand what was happening. But then, in a voice made hoarse and ragged by howls, he croaked, 'Geraden? Artagel? Is it really you?'

Fiercely, Geraden whispered, 'We're here. We're here. Terisa brought us. As soon as you can stand, I'll translate you back to Orison.'

Too late, Terisa heard the door open, saw light from the corridor outside wash against her and the Domne's sons.

She whirled frantically away as a voice like silk said, 'If you can do that, it will be miraculous. I am going to cut your heart out before you can make the attempt. In my experience, dead men make poor Imagers.'

Stark against the unexpected light, the man seemed to have no face, no features. The longsword he held looked black and fatal, a blade of darkness.

Terisa recognized him anyway.

Gart.

Crouched over Nyle, Geraden and Artagel were insignificant, pitiable, in the shadow of Gart's silhouetted strength.

Despite that, however, Artagel drawled without moving, 'Don't tell me Eremis knew we were coming. I won't believe it.'

'No,' conceded Gart, as smooth as his blade. 'Yet even coincidence conspires to help victors. I was sent to bring Nyle to the Image-room. Master Eremis considered that you might do something desperate – although seeing you I doubt that he grasps how truly desperate you have become – so he wished to have your brother made ready to use against you.

'He may not be delighted to hear that I have slain you. He wishes that pleasure for himself. But I will answer for your deaths to the High King.'

'I'm sure you will.' Slowly, keeping his hands away from his sword, Artagel rose to his feet, left Nyle in Geraden's arms. Light from the doorway burned along the tears on Artagel's cheeks, lit sparks in his eyes. His fighting grin was gone; he seemed to have no heart left for it. 'You're forgetting just one thing.'

'And what is that?' the Monomach inquired maliciously.

Artagel shrugged. 'We aren't dead yet.'

As hard as she could, Terisa flung her lamp at Gart's head.

His quickness was appalling. As if he had known what she would do, he batted the lamp away from his face with the flat of his blade.

Nevertheless the lamp struck his shoulder. Flaming oil splashed down his chest, bright on his black leather armor.

In that instant, Artagel attacked.

So swiftly that his leap and the sweeping pull with which he drew his sword looked like one movement, wildly, almost in a frenzy, crying out his rage and hurt, he hacked at the burning man.

His assault was too sudden, too furious; Gart had trouble countering it. The High King's Monomach beat at the fire with one hand, trying to put it out before it took hold of his armor; with the other, he parried Artagel's blow awkwardly, barely succeeded at blocking it away from his head.

His whole weight behind the blow, Artagel swung again.

And again, as fast as he could.

Gart seemed to erase the flame, as if his touch were enough to extinguish it. Nevertheless he couldn't meet Artagel's attack one-handed. He was driven backward, into the doorway. And the door was too narrow for his strokes. His sword took chips out of the doorpost; the impact slowed him, so that he almost failed to lift Artagel's cut over his shoulder.

That counter left him off balance.

At once, Artagel drove forward with one foot and booted Gart in the chest.

Gart slammed against the far wall of the corridor and recoiled to the side, reeling to get his legs braced under him.

Artagel went through the doorway after him, steel on steel, steel on stone, out of sight to the left.

Terisa was already at Geraden's side. 'Come on,' she gasped, 'come on.' With both hands, she heaved at him, trying to raise him to his feet.

Clutching Nyle, Geraden surged upright.

They staggered together; Geraden struggled to hold Nyle; Nyle fought to help himself. Still gripping the cot leg he had used as a lever, Geraden hauled his brother toward the door.

In the corridor, Artagel fought for his life.

Gart had recovered; he was beginning to return the attack. And the wildness of Artagel's first assault was useless for defense. As a result, the nature of their combat changed. He was forced to meet Gart's skill with his own, instead of with frenzy.

He was still hampered by the tightness in his side.

And Gart had already beaten him twice.

The corridor clanged with blows, swirled with sparks. Artagel barely prevented the Monomach from returning to the doorway.

'Come on,' Terisa urged.

Geraden cast one white, urgent look at Artagel's back, then dragged Nyle in the opposite direction.

Terisa followed, pushing Geraden and Nyle to move faster.

Through the clamor of steel, they reached a corner.

As soon as they rounded it, the noise diminished.

They passed more doors: storerooms, cells, guards' quarters. Terisa thought they must be near the chamber where Master Eremis had his glassworks. Unless it was in the opposite direction. What was the 'Image-room'? *Where* was it?

At the fourth door, Geraden stopped. He wrenched it open: a storeroom, apparently; bedding and pillows. More roughly than he intended, he thrust Nyle inside.

'Hide!' he hissed. 'Let us do the fighting! All you have to do is stay hidden, so they can't threaten you.'

Nyle gave his brother a look of dumb, helpless anguish. Then he stumbled into the dark, and Geraden jerked the door shut, catching it just in time to make it close softly.

Pale and extreme, he faced Terisa. 'I hope to the stars,' he panted, 'we know what we're doing.'

She grabbed at his hand and drew him into a run again, on down the corridor.

Know what we're doing.

I want you to defeat Master Eremis.

Artagel wouldn't last much longer: she knew that. Yet she and Geraden were still alive because of him. And Eremis didn't know they were coming. Maybe King Joyse and Prince Kragen had already been crushed. But she had promised in her heart that she would kill Master Eremis. The men who had treated Nyle like *that* were going to die.

The cot leg in Geraden's fist looked too short, too weightless, to do any good. Nevertheless he held it like a man who intended to find a use for it.

She needed a weapon of her own; she didn't have anything to fight with except her empty hands.

She had no idea how big the stronghold was, how to find her enemies. She and Geraden kept running anyway, beyond the range of Artagel's valiant struggle, around corners, along passageways. Geraden no longer seemed to be breathing hard: he had settled into a state of exertion where nothing could stop him. She saw suggestions of the Domne in him, hints of Tholden, as if he had all his family's strength. Her own lungs were being torn open, but she didn't care. Details like that had lost their importance; she had left them behind with her father.

Then the corridor opened into a place of more light; a room with many windows, full of sunshine.

A large, round room, as large as the Congery's former meeting hall in Orison; high, with its domed ceiling encircled by clerestories so that the bright morning shone in from all sides; reached by several entrances around the walls, as if this chamber were the center of the stronghold, the hub around which all Master Eremis' activities turned; and full of mirrors.

The Image-room.

Tall mirrors of many kinds stood in a wide circle around the center of the chamber, meticulously spaced ten or so feet apart, and facing inward, so that they could all be watched – so that they were all ready to be used – by the men in their midst.

Master Eremis.

Master Gilbur.

The arch-Imager Vagel.

Terisa thought that she and Geraden were running loudly, panting like engines. Apparently, however, their approach was relatively quiet. None of the men noticed them. Eremis and Gilbur and Vagel were all studying a flat glass which stood with them in the middle of the circle.

That mirror showed the great slug-beast as it entered the valley of Esmerel.

The mounds of rock which had blocked the creature's advance were gone, devoured; now the monster squirmed along its slime into the valley foot.

Almost directly under the beast's jaws rode King Joyse, holding his sword up like a banner. From this perspective, he seemed already in reach of the vast, venomous fangs. He was shouting commands or appeals which didn't convey anything through the glass. Small with distance, he looked at once extravagant and pathetic, like a weather vane dancing in the onset of a hurricane.

'Do your best, Joyse,' growled Master Gilbur. 'Withdraw your men. Rally them if you can. Then it will be Festten's power that actually destroys you, rather than ours.'

Terisa and Geraden had slowed, almost stopped. He raised a finger to his mouth, urging silence; she nodded. They crept forward behind the Imagers, into the ring of mirrors.

The first mirror they saw from the front showed the side of a rocky mountain. The slope had a dark scar across it, as if a landslide had recently taken place. This was the source of the avalanches Eremis had used against Vale House and the Congery's chasm.

Grinning like Artagel, Geraden issued his challenge to his enemies by swinging his cot leg at the glass.

The mirror shattered like a cry; glass sprayed singing to the stone.

At the sound, the three Imagers spun.

Only Master Eremis showed any surprise. He may have had a secret liking for surprises: they tested him, gave him new chances to exercise his abilities. His expression when he saw Terisa and Geraden bore an unmistakable resemblance to joy.

'Astonishing,' he murmured. 'I did not believe that such talent existed in all the world.'

Unlike Eremis, Master Gilbur had only one reaction to the unexpected. Clenched like his back, his features brandished their old scowl, their black and unalterable fury. One powerful fist dove into his robe, brought out a dagger as long as Terisa's forearm; the dagger which had killed Master Quillon. Deep in his contorted chest, he snarled curses like a hunting lion.

The arch-Imager's mouth hung open, but he didn't look surprised. He looked hungry, avid for some bloody sustenance he had been too long denied, insatiably destructive. His chin was wet with drool, and his eyes smoldered like the eyes of a lover lost in cruelty.

Before any of the Imagers had time to move, Terisa pushed the nearest mirror onto its back. As it fell, she saw a bitter landscape running with lava. Then the scene broke into splinters and ruin.

'If you do that again, my lady,' Master Eremis said amiably, 'I swear I will rip Geraden's balls off and make you eat them.'

'Try it,' retorted Geraden. He sprang to the next glass, clubbed it to shards.

Roaring, Master Gilbur charged at him.

Geraden dodged behind another mirror, pulled it over. Unfortunately, that left him open to Gilbur's attack. The dagger stabbed for his heart.

He saved himself by staggering to the side, slipping on chips of glass, crashing to the floor in a splash of slivers. Master Gilbur sprang after him, hammered the dagger at him. He rolled away, scrambled his legs under him, scuttled toward the wall – just out of reach. He had lost his club; he was weaponless against Gilbur's tremendous strength, the Imager's long blade.

'Stand still and die, dogshit!' Master Gilbur panted.

He drove Geraden backward.

Terisa faced Eremis and the arch-Imager alone.

She knew how to fight them: without thinking about it, without planning anything, she *knew*. She could never break enough of their mirrors to save King Joyse. They would kill her long before she did that much damage. And she would accomplish nothing if she shifted the Image which showed the King's peril. Nevertheless she had glass to oppose Eremis and Vagel with, mirrors at her disposal which they couldn't see. All she had to do was stay alive.

And concentrate—

I want you to trust me.

—concentrate on the flat glass in Havelock's rooms, the mirror with the Image of the sand dune. If she put this scene, this room, into that glass, the Adept could see it. He would see it, if he hadn't fallen completely victim to his insanity. And then he could translate both Eremis and Vagel to Orison.

Trust me.

Eremis would lose his mind. And Vagel would be in Orison, with no way back here. He might use one of Havelock's mirrors to avoid capture, but he would cease to be a threat.

All she had to do *was concentrate.*

She stood still. Instinctively, she raised her hands as if to show Master Eremis she was no longer a threat to his mirrors.

The way he looked at her made her blood labor like sludge in her veins.

To keep himself from being pinned to the wall, Geraden had to retreat toward one of the exits. Apparently hoping to draw Master Gilbur after him, he turned suddenly and fled, running hard down the corridor.

Cunning despite his rage, Master Gilbur stopped. There was no harm Geraden could do anywhere except in this room.

Clutching his dagger, Gilbur returned to the ring.

To the Image in Terisa's mind.

She held it steady, hoping now that Havelock would wait until Master Gilbur came within reach, within range of Eremis' destruction. She had no pity of any kind left in her.

At that moment, *a touch of cold as thin as a feather and as sharp as steel slid straight through the center of her abdomen.*

'Hee-hee!' a thin voice cackled. 'Wait for me, Vagel! I'm coming.'

Adept Havelock burst out of the air at a run.

'I'm *coming!*'

Oh, *no!*

He was a madman full of glee. His feet seemed to find the stone without any possibility of misstep, as if losing his mind made him immune to all the other hazards of translation. His apron flapped about his ankles as he ran.

As swift as joy, he sped for the arch-Imager.

In both fists he clutched his featherduster as if it made him mighty: a sword or scepter no one could oppose.

That surprised Vagel; it took him too suddenly for any reaction except panic. Once, in the past, Havelock had cost him everything but his life: now the mad Adept wanted his life as well.

Havelock was oblivious to everyone else. He didn't see Terisa. He didn't seem to notice that Master Eremis had stretched out a casual foot to trip him; he was only after the arch-Imager. Vagel, however, had flinched away; he headed for one of the exits with all the speed his old legs could produce.

Veering to follow, the Adept unconsciously avoided Eremis' foot.

'I'm *coming!*'

One after the other, they disappeared down the corridor, taking Terisa's only hope with them, her only way to fight.

'Ballocks and bull-puke!' rasped Master Gilbur. 'Does every Imager left in the world now do these impossible translations?'

'I think not,' Eremis replied, grinning ferally. 'I think that was our lady Terisa's doing. I doubt, however, that she intended to bring the Adept here. *Her* thought was that he would translate us away – to Orison and madness.' Rage and joy mounted in him as he spoke. 'We are fortunate that Havelock is himself already mad, inaccessible to such cleverness.'

Spitting obscenities, Gilbur started toward Terisa.

'No!' Master Eremis snapped at once. 'The lady Terisa is mine. I will attend to her.'

Gilbur stopped, facing Eremis.

'The destruction of King Joyse,' Master Eremis continued, nonchalant and brutal, 'I leave to you.' He gestured around the mirrors. 'Enjoy it as much as you wish. For me, there is more pleasure' – he showed his teeth – 'in *undoing* an Imager with her unprecedented capacities than in slaughtering a mere King.

'When Gart returns with Nyle, use them as you think best.

'My lady.' Raising one long arm, he pointed at a passageway behind her. 'Go there.'

Because she had nothing left, Terisa turned and did as she was told.

Out in the valley, the destruction of King Joyse was proceeding as planned.

He had no weapon to combat the monster his enemies had unleashed. It finished eating its way through the rubble of the avalanche, then came on into the valley, hungry for other prey. The last time someone – Eremis? – had translated this beast, it had been considerably less ravenous. And noticeably less irate. Master Eremis must have found the means to make it very angry.

How old would he have been at the time of that previous translation? Fifteen? *Ten?*

Was it possible for a boy so young to be that good an Imager? Or that full of malice?

King Joyse didn't know. And the answers didn't matter. What mattered was the army, his men and Prince Kragen's. They were going to die quickly and horribly if he couldn't wrestle them back under control, quench their panic. And they were going to die anyway, unless someone found a defense against this creature.

One thing at a time. Death later was preferable to death now. During the interval between now and later, anything might happen. Someone might think of a way to hurt the beast. Or it might accidentally get hit by a throw from the catapult, might change direction. Or it might die of old age and indigestion.

The army had to be saved *now.*

So he drove his charger as close to the monster as he dared; so close that his mount snorted foam and quivered; so close that he could feel the beast's breath sweep over him, could smell its intense, rank stink. And there he raised his voice like a trumpet against the hoarse screaming and the panic, the white-eyed and unreasoning dread.

'Retreat! *Retreat,* I say!' Retreat wasn't rout. 'Find your captains! Rally to your captains! This beast can't outrun you!' It cannot silence *me,* and I am nearer to it than you are.

Behind him, the creature lifted its maw and howled. Somehow, he sent his call through the roar, demanding and clarion.

'*You must retreat in order!*'

The scene in front of him still looked like chaos. The shouting went on, full of fear. But he had an experienced eye: he could see the state of the army changing. Some of the captains held their ground and yelled for their men; more and more men began struggling through the press toward their captains. The army was like an augury in reverse, an Image resolving toward coherence out of a swirl of prescient bits.

Then riders came toward the King, goading their horses hard.

Prince Kragen. Castellan Norge.

Almost under the teeth of the creature, they met, reined their mounts. Norge's horse was frantic: it wheeled in fright, snorting as if it were deranged. A moment later, however, he fought it under control.

King Joyse held his sword high, in salute and defiance.

The sight of the three leaders there as if they were impervious to Imagery and horror seemed to have a palpable impact. Suddenly, the surge of men was transformed: no longer a rout interrupted by islands of order, it became an army vigorously quelling its own chaos.

'Well done, my lord King!' panted the Alend Contender. 'I thought we had lost them.'

'What now?' put in the Castellan. 'How can we fight that thing?'

'We must not lose them again!' King Joyse returned. 'Keep them to the

937

center of the valley. Keep them moving steadily. We are bottled in this valley, but if we are pushed far enough we will attempt to win through the neck.'

Howling again, the monster heaved itself forward.

In a group, King Joyse, Prince Kragen, and the Castellan spurred thirty yards up the valley, then stopped once more.

'Retreating won't save us!' cried Norge. 'We can't get out the defile! Festten wouldn't do this if he didn't have an ambush ready. As soon as you try, we're lost.' As if as an afterthought, he added, 'My lord King.'

The King restrained a sarcastic retort. 'Then we must not let ourselves be pushed so far,' he said with more mildness than he felt. The flash in his blue eyes may have been urgency – or it may have been a wild love of risk. 'Get archers up the walls, as many as you can. If that beast has eyes, perhaps we can put them out.'

Castellan Norge didn't waste time saluting. He dug his spurs into his mount and sped away at a dead gallop.

'A thin hope, my lord King,' Prince Kragen commented tensely.

'I am aware of that,' King Joyse allowed himself to snap, 'my lord Prince.' Then, however, he moderated his tone. 'Suggestions are welcome.'

Prince Kragen scowled over his shoulder at the beast. 'If the Congery cannot save us, we cannot be saved.'

King Joyse nodded grimly. 'Then may the stars send Master Barsonage inspiration, or everything I have loved must perish.'

His eyes continued flashing.

After a moment, Prince Kragen caught the King's mood and smiled himself.

Watching their father and the Alend Contender from the distance of the pennon, the ladies Elega and Myste stood like reflections of each other, holding their breath together when the monster roared or moved, exhaling in shared appreciation of what King Joyse and the Prince accomplished.

As the army fought down its panic, Elega murmured, 'I did not believe that we would ever see him like this again.'

'I hoped for it,' replied Myste softly. 'I could not bear to give it up. That is the difference between us. I cannot live without old hopes. You are willing to let them go in order to conceive new ones.'

At the moment, Elega had no idea whether she considered this an accurate observation or not.

'Wouldn't catch me doing that,' Darsint commented sourly. He stood a step or two behind Myste, apparently watching for threats in all directions. 'Haven't got the guts. Fighting I can do. But stand like that so the men won't panic? Make myself a target?' He seemed to be talking primarily to himself; nevertheless Myste turned to hear him. 'Maybe that's what went wrong on Pythas,' he added. 'Couldn't rally my men.'

'It was a different situation,' said Myste, 'in a different place. You did everything any man could have done there.'

Darsint looked at Myste strangely. He took no discernible comfort in her words. Elega had the impression that Myste had unwittingly aggravated whatever troubled him.

'That's what you people do, isn't it,' he muttered like a distressed songbird. '*He* does it. Both of you. You do "everything."'

'We would if we could,' answered Elega, more for her own benefit than to argue with him. 'Unfortunately, we're women.'

Down the valley, the monster surged forward; she thought both the King and Prince Kragen would be taken by those appalling fangs. But they rode out of reach in time, keeping themselves like a bulwark between the beast and their army, a defense which had nothing to do with physical force.

'And even if we could fight like men,' Elega continued, 'even if we were allowed, we couldn't do anything against that creature. If it is to be stopped, the Masters must do it.'

Master Barsonage had already informed her, however, that he had no hope left. A short way below her on the hillside, he had set up the mirror which had translated Terisa and Geraden away, the glass full of ocean. Eventually, he would try to hinder the beast with a rush of water. But he didn't expect much success. And none of the other mirrors remaining to the Congery could do anything against a creature that size.

As for Terisa and Geraden—

Where they were concerned, Elega would have been glad to hope; but she didn't know what to hope *for*. Her lack of confidence in Geraden was lifelong, hard to change. And Terisa also was no fighter.

Darsint made an uncomfortable noise in his throat, as if she had offended him somehow. Or frightened him.

'It is not your burden,' Myste whispered to him gently. 'You have already done more than we could have asked – more than most of us would have believed possible. And your rifle is exhausted. Doubtless that is the reason Master Eremis decided to risk his monster.'

This observation didn't comfort the champion much, either.

Elega was watching her father and Prince Kragen so hard, focusing on them so exclusively, that she almost didn't see what was about to happen to them.

A shout of warning jerked her attention back a step, widened her angle of vision. With a cry she didn't hear herself utter, she saw riders come up both sides of the monster into the valley, dozens of them, hundreds; riders with red fur and alien faces, with four arms and two scimitars, their blades raised for blood; mounted creatures like the ones which had once attacked Terisa and Geraden, riding now to sweep around in front of the slug-beast against King Joyse and the Prince.

'Father!' Myste wailed into the turmoil.

But she only had one man to lose, only her father. Elega was going to lose Prince Kragen as well, and then the High King's victory would be assured regardless of whether or not the army relapsed to panic. Norge had men moving back down the valley, back toward the Prince and King Joyse, but they were too slow, too late. For a moment, Elega's vision went dark around the edges. She had the distinct impression that she was going to faint.

Then Darsint's metalled hand caught her by the shoulder, turned her. She couldn't see his face; she was trying to pull away, trying to watch the foot of the valley. Yet he held her.

'Protect her.' His voice sounded like a warble. 'You can do it better than any of this lot. Understand? I love her. Can't let her be hurt.'

Harder than he may have intended, he pushed Elega at Myste.

The sisters collided, hugged each other to keep themselves from falling.

Darsint set off at a run.

He headed for the stream and used it as a path: it was relatively clear; few of the men were milling in the cold water. Uneven ground and unsteady rocks made his armored feet slip and his strides lurch, so that he looked like a damaged machine hurrying toward a breakdown. Nevertheless the power still in his suit was enough to give him speed; he ran as fast a horse.

Not fast enough to save King Joyse and Prince Kragen, of course. At that pace, however, he might reach the foot of the valley in time to help avenge them.

Unfortunately, the Cadwals at the last catapult saw what he was doing. They threw scattershot at him as soon as he came within range.

Stones caught the sunlight, the bright metal; soundless amid the shouts and clamor, they hit hard. In spite of his armor, he went down on his face in the chuckling brook.

King Joyse and Prince Kragen wheeled when they heard the shout which had warned Elega. Kragen spat a curse at the sight of the red-furred creatures. Their hate was vivid, even through the monster's loud advance. And they were so many – He and King Joyse would never be able to get away. And the men Castellan Norge had already sent to rescue them had too far to come.

But the King smiled, and his eyes grew brighter. 'As I said,' he remarked in a voice only Prince Kragen could hear, 'the High King grows desperate. He dares not fail. And men who dare not fail cannot succeed.'

Prince Kragen considered this a foolish piece of philosophy – and gratuitous as well – but he had no time for it. He had no time to regret that he was about to die, or that he had failed his father, or that he would never hold Elega in his arms again. His hands snatched out his sword as he kicked his charger into a gallop, heading not toward the impossible safety of the army, too distant to do him any good, but rather straight at the nearest creatures, the front of the attack.

For the space of two or three heartbeats, he had a chance to be surprised and a bit relieved by the fact that King Joyse was right beside him, longsword ready, eyes bright for battle. Then the Alend Contender and the King of Mordant crashed alone into a vicious wall of scimitars and fought, trying to take as many of their enemies as possible with them when they died.

Once again, Elega was concentrating too exclusively on her father and Prince Kragen to see Darsint struggle back to his feet. She was holding Myste tightly: she only knew that something new had happened by the way Myste's body reacted.

Lumbering like a wreck, Darsint continued down the stream.

He couldn't run now. Myste had helped heal the wounds on his body, but nothing in this world could have helped him repair the holes which the Pythians had burned in his armor, and those holes made him vulnerable. He was hurt again now, listing to the side, stumbling occasionally; the power inside his suit may have been damaged.

He kept going anyway.

Prince Kragen and King Joyse kept going as well.

In fact, they kept going so well that the Prince felt a rush of joy at the way their swords rose and fell, the way their blows struck; the surge of their horses through the attack. The red-furred creatures had eyes in the wrong places, with whiskers sprouting all around them; they had too many arms, too many scimitars. And their hate was palpable in the fray, a consuming lust. Nevertheless they were flesh-and-blood: they could be killed. And they weren't especially skillful with their blades; they relied more on fury than on expertise.

The Prince and King Joyse cut into the heart of the attack and kept going, kept fighting shoulder to shoulder, as if between them they had discovered something indomitable.

It was amazing, really, how many cuts they ducked or parried or slipped aside; how far into the furred bodies they delivered their swords; how their crazy charge made the mounts of the creatures falter and shy. And it was amazing, too, how well the King fought. Prince Kragen himself was much younger – presumably much stronger. Yet King Joyse matched the Alend Contender blow for blow, swung and thrust his longsword as if the weight of steel transformed him, restored him to his prime. Now his beard was splashed with blood; cuts laced his mail; grue stained his arms. And yet he kept all harm away from his companion on that side.

For a few precious moments, they succeeded against unbeatable odds.

And while they succeeded, Prince Kragen found that King Joyse made sense to him at last. If everything else was lost, still no one would ever be able to change the fact that the King of Mordant and the Alend Contender had died side by side instead of at each other's throats.

Their success had to end. Two men simply couldn't survive against so much mounted and murderous savagery. And yet they did survive. The momentum of the battle changed suddenly, and Prince Kragen felt another singing rush of joy at the realization that he and King Joyse were no longer alone.

The Termigan had appeared in the midst of the fray.

He had all his men with him.

The look on his face was as keen as a cleaver; he had the hands of a butcher. The way he slaughtered his enemies justified every story the Prince had ever heard of him. And his men were beyond panic. They had seen Sternwall eaten alive by Imagery, and nothing could frighten them. During the first attack of the slug-beast, they had waited with their grim lord down near the foot of the valley, readied themselves to strike. They may have intended to strike at the monster itself. The red-furred creatures were a more possible enemy, however, and the last force of Termigan had hurled itself into the fighting without hesitation.

The lord and his men kept Prince Kragen and King Joyse alive until Norge's reinforcements arrived.

There were nearly a thousand of the creatures. Castellan Norge had sent less than half that many men to the rescue. The thought that King Joyse and Prince Kragen were already lost had filled the valley with alarm again, paralyzing a large portion of the army. And the men who sprang to Norge's call had to contend with horses that were wild with fear, terrified by the slug-beast and the alien creatures. In one sense, the Castellan was lucky to send as much help as he did to his King. In another, he was unlucky that he couldn't muster enough strength to turn the battle.

Nevertheless he achieved a goal which had never crossed his mind: he thinned out the combat directly in front of the monster; thinned it sufficiently to let Darsint through.

In the middle of the fray, Darsint shambled, hardly able to force one foot ahead of the next. He must have been in better condition than he looked, however. Every creature which attacked him, he shot with one of his handguns, aiming and firing almost negligently, as if he could do this kind of fighting in his sleep. When he missed, scimitars rang off his armor without hindering him; he appeared unconscious that he was struck. He wasn't interested in mere blades and horses.

His target was the slug-beast.

Guns ready, he paused before the monster's gaping maw. But he wasn't hesitating: he may have been afraid to hesitate. Instead, he was making some kind of adjustment inside his suit.

Before anyone except Myste realized what he meant to do, his suit produced a burst of power that enabled him to leap past the dire fangs straight down the beast's throat.

FIFTY-ONE

THE THINGS MEN
DO WITH MIRRORS

Facing Gart's sword in the stone-walled corridor, Artagel felt that he was looking down the throat of death.

The High King's Monomach had recovered from the fire of the lamp, and from the first extremity of Artagel's attack; now he had his balance again, his command of steel and weight. Moment by moment, he seemed to grow stronger.

The lanterns which lit the passage made his eyes yellow; they gleamed like a beast's. His hatchet-nose faced his opponent, keen for blood. The scars on his cheeks, the initiation-marks of his craft, were pale streaks against the bronze hue of his skin. Though he was assailed by the best swordsman in Mordant, he wasn't even sweating. His blade moved like a live thing: as protective as a lover, it caught and countered every blow for him, as if to spare him the effort of defending himself.

His teeth showed, white and malign, between his lips; loathing stretched all the mercy out of his features. Yet Artagel felt sure that Gart's abhorrence had nothing personal to do with him. It involved no resentment of Artagel's reputation, no envy of his position, no particular desire to see him dead. In Gart, the lust for killing was a professional characteristic untainted by individual emotions.

Artagel had heard rumors about the training undergone by Apts of the High King's Monomach, the privations and hurts and dangers imposed on small boys to make them sure of what they were doing, sure of themselves; to harden their loathing. That was what gave Gart strength: his detachment; the impersonality of his passion. His heart held nothing which might confuse him.

Artagel, on the other hand, *was* sweating.

His hands were slick with moisture; under his mail, his jerkin clung to his skin. His sword had gone dead in his grasp, and his chest heaved with the exertion of swinging the blade. The tightness in his side had become a band of hot iron, fired to agony, and that pain seemed to sap the resilience from his legs, the quick tension from his wrists, the life from his weapon.

A flurry of blows, as loud as forgework, bright with sparks. A measuring pause. Another flurry.

There was no question about it: Gart was going to kill him.

Artagel didn't face this prospect with quite the same approval Lebbick had felt.

He couldn't afford to be beaten, absolutely could not afford to fail. If he went down, Gart would go after Terisa and Geraden. He would go after Nyle. They would all die, and King Joyse himself wouldn't stand a chance—

But when he thought about Nyle, remembered what had been done to his brother, his heart filled up with darkness, and he flung himself at Gart wildly, inexpertly. Only the sheer fury of his attack saved him from immediate death. Fury was all that kept him going; nothing but fury gave strength to his limbs, air to his lungs, life to his steel.

A quick, slicing pain brought him back to himself – a cut along the bunched muscle of his left shoulder. He recoiled from suicide as blood welled out of the wound. A minor injury: he knew that instinctively. Nevertheless it *hurt*— It hurt enough to restore his reason.

Not this way. He was never going to beat Gart this way. The truth was obvious in the effortless action of Gart's blade, the feral smirk on his face; it was unmistakable in the glint of his yellow eyes.

In fact, Artagel was barely able to keep Gart's swordpoint out of his chest as he retreated down the corridor, gasping for breath, battling to recover his balance. The Monomach's blade wove gleams and flashes of lantern-light as if his steel were somehow miraculous, like a mirror.

All right. Artagel couldn't beat Gart this way. Actually, he couldn't beat Gart at all. But he had to prolong the struggle as much as possible, had to buy time. Time was vital. So he needed some other way to fight. He had to start thinking like Geraden or Terisa, *but not about Nyle, no, don't think about Nyle, don't give in to the darkness.* He had to do something unexpected.

Something to ruffle Gart's detachment.

Down in the depths of Artagel's belly, a knot loosened, and he began to grin.

Geraden wasn't grinning.

When Master Gilbur didn't follow him, he wasn't surprised. Just disappointed. He had no idea in the world what he would have done if the Master had chased him. Gilbur knew the stronghold, after all, and Geraden could never hope to beat him in a test of violence. But at least the hunchbacked Imager would have been away from the mirrors, unable for the moment to do King Joyse any more damage.

That hope had failed, of course. Instead of drawing Master Gilbur away, Geraden had in effect abandoned Terisa, left her to contend with Master Gilbur and Master Eremis and the arch-Imager alone.

Wonderful. The perfect climax to a perfect life. Now all he had to do was blunder into a squad of guards somewhere and get himself uselessly killed, and the story of his life would be complete.

Now it's your turn, the Domne had said. *Make us proud of you. Make what we're doing worthwhile.*

944

Geraden had succeeded brilliantly.

He couldn't resist thinking like that. He had suffered too many accidents; the logic of mishap seemed irrefutable. Nevertheless he was too stubborn to accept defeat. He loved Terisa too much, and his brothers, and the King—

In the name of sanity, remember to call me 'Da.'

As soon as he was sure Master Gilbur had given up the chase, he turned down a side passage and began to double back toward the Image-room.

Unacquainted with the stronghold, he spent several maddening moments hunting his way. Where were the guards? Surely Master Eremis had guards, servants of the High King if not of Eremis himself? Why hadn't he encountered them already? At last, however, he reached another of the entrances to the Image-room.

From the entryway, he saw that Master Gilbur was the only one there.

Just for a moment, while his heart lurched in his chest and a cry struggled in his throat, he thought, Terisa *Terisa!* Master Eremis and Vagel had taken her to rape and torture her, just like Nyle, *just like Nyle.* He had to go after her, he had to find her, help her, he absolutely and utterly could not bear to let them destroy her.

At the same time, unfortunately, he noticed what Master Gilbur was doing.

The Imager had his back to Geraden. That was fortuitous. Plainly, he didn't know or care what Geraden might do. He was carrying a glass out of the center of the ring of mirrors.

The flat mirror which showed Esmerel's valley.

He was carrying it toward a mirror which stood in the direct, clean light from one of the windows. Sunshine illuminated the Image vividly.

The scene which the glass reflected swarmed with cockroaches.

Geraden remembered those creatures. They had nearly killed him, and Terisa, and Artagel. Nevertheless the horror of that memory gave way at once to a new dismay when Master Gilbur set the flat glass down before the other mirror and stepped back to consider his intentions.

In the flat mirror, Geraden saw King Joyse and Prince Kragen directly under the rearing jaws of the slug-beast.

They were engaged in a desperate struggle against huge numbers of red-furred creatures with too many arms holding too many scimitars.

The King and Prince Kragen weren't alone: the Termigan was with them, and his men. They were covered with blood, battling furiously. Yet they couldn't expect to survive against so many alien warriors. And if the red-furred creatures didn't get them, the slug-beast would.

And Master Gilbur planned to translate a new threat into the fray. He was considering the focus of his mirrors so that he could move his flat glass in among the swarming cockroaches and translate them straight onto King Joyse's head.

Lord of the Demesne. Sovereign of Mordant. And Geraden's father's friend.

Remember to call me 'Da.'

Terisa needed him. He let her go. Once, hard, with both fists, he punched himself in the forehead.

Then he moved.

Swallowing panic and love and regret, he left the entryway and crept toward the ring of mirrors.

If Terisa could have seen him then, she would have recognized the iron in his face, the look of despair – and of brutal determination.

He was quiet; but he went quickly. To the mirrors he and Terisa had broken, to the cotleg he had dropped. Snatching up the club from a pool of splinters, he threw it with all his strength at the flat glass.

Unluckily, his boots crunched a warning among the shards and slivers; and Master Gilbur heard it. With astonishing swiftness, the Imager spun around, flung up his arm—

—deflected the cotleg.

It skimmed past the top of the mirror's frame and skittered away across the stone, out of reach.

'Balls of a dog!' Gilbur spat. Already, he had his dagger in his fist; his face was a clench of darkness. 'Do you never give up?'

Geraden heard the cotleg knock against the wall as if that sound were the last thud of his heart. Another failure: his last chance gone wrong. Now he wouldn't be able to help King Joyse *or* Terisa, and they would both be lost. And if he didn't escape now, his own death was inevitable. No matter what happened, he would never be able to outfight Master Gilbur.

Nevertheless the augury drew him. This was his fate, his doom. Instead of fleeing, he stepped forward, into the ring of mirrors, until he was *surrounded entirely by mirrors, all of them reflecting scenes of violence and destruction against him.*

There he stopped.

'Why should I give up?' he asked as if he were just making conversation. 'Why should I want to make it easy for you?'

Master Gilbur snarled an obscenity. Cocking his dagger, he prepared to charge.

At once, Geraden barked, 'I wouldn't do that if I were you.'

In surprise, the Master paused.

'I don't have anywhere else to go,' Geraden explained. 'I don't have anything else to hope for. Oh, I suppose I could run away. I could try to hide somewhere. You don't seem to have any guards. I might be able to stay alive for a while. But I'll never escape. I'll never find Terisa.

'If you chase me, I'll just break as many mirrors as I can before I die. You've already lost four. How many more are you willing to risk? Do you think there's a chance I might be able to get them all?'

Obviously, Gilbur's first impulse was to attack: that was plain in the way his teeth showed through his beard, the way his knuckles whitened on his dagger. Almost immediately, however, he appeared to grasp the other side of the situation. Someone was bound to come soon, and then Geraden was lost. In the meantime, why risk damage to years of powerful work?

Instead of charging, he lowered his blade.

'You are wrong, puppy,' he rasped. 'We have guards. They will be here in a moment.'

'Oh, I don't think so.' Geraden fought to keep any hint of relief out of his voice. Time: that was all he wanted. A respite for King Joyse. A chance for something to happen. 'I'm sure you have them, plenty of them. But I'll bet they're all outside, protecting this place just in case someone tries a sneak attack. Watching the defile. You and Eremis and Vagel are so stupidly sure of yourselves, you never expected to be attacked from inside.'

Then, because he wanted to see how far he could goad the Imager, he asked, 'Where's Gart?'

Master Gilbur's eyebrows knotted involuntarily. 'Do not look behind you, pigshit boy. He may be there already. He has gone to fetch your dear brother Nyle – who, I may say, has given me considerable pleasure during his visit here.'

The flat mirror's Image showed the great monster writhing in a paroxysm of rage and hunger.

'I don't think so,' Geraden repeated. *Nyle.* He wanted to laugh so that he wouldn't do anything foolish, wouldn't go mad and try to attack the Imager; but he could barely keep himself from snarling. 'Terisa and I already rescued Nyle. We did that first. If Gart isn't here, the men we brought with us must have got him.' If Gart isn't here, Artagel must still be alive, still be fighting. 'Or else High King Festten has plans he hasn't told you about. You must have noticed that his reputation for treachery is older than you are.'

Unfortunately, Master Gilbur *was* able to laugh. 'Pure vapor,' he rasped with a guttural chuckle. 'Mist and moonshine.' He took a couple of nonthreatening steps, not toward Geraden, but to the side, away from the flat glass and the cockroaches. 'You have not rescued Nyle – you do not know where he *is*. The room where I have enjoyed him is kept dark. You have never seen it. Therefore you could not find it, or translate him away.

'Gart will join us soon.'

'Believe that if you can,' retorted Geraden. *He* believed it; and the thought made all his muscles feel as weak as water. Yet he kept his gaze and his voice steady. 'Just tell me one thing. Those redfurred creatures.' They continued pouring around King Joyse and the Prince, hacking savagely. The Termigan's men and Norge's appeared vastly outnumbered. And the slug-beast–'You didn't just translate them this morning, did you? How did you get them mounted? How did you get them to serve you?'

The slug-beast had reared up as if it strove to stand on its tail.

'No, we did not,' conceded Master Gilbur maliciously. 'In that, at least, you are right. Those things – they call themselves *callat*. Eremis has worked with them at some length. They have become what you might consider his "personal guard." A complex and difficult negotiation was required before he agreed to commit his callat to Festten's support.'

Too late, Geraden realized what the Imager was doing.

In the flat mirror, the rearing monster came down like a tower, crashed straight and limp to the ground. Its maw seemed to miss King Joyse and Prince Kragen; some of the callat were caught by its weight and crushed. But through the glass the reverberation of impact had no sound. And the beast made no effort to surge forward, devour more prey. It lay still with a strange curl of smoke rising between its teeth.

Master Gilbur reached one of the other mirrors in the ring.

He grasped its frame with his free hand, began snarling nonsense.

Out of the glass, like shot from a catapult, came hurtling a gnarled, black shape, no larger than a small dog, with claws like hooks at the ends of its four limbs and terrible jaws which filled half its body.

Master Eremis did like surprises. In a sense, he even liked unpleasant surprises. They raised the stakes, increased the challenge: they made him show what he could do. But there was nothing unpleasant about Terisa's unexpected arrival – or Geraden's either, for that matter. Master Gilbur could handle Geraden. And Terisa was beaten. He had seen her defeat in her eyes, had seen the light of intelligence and determination start to fade. She was his at last, *his,* and every spark of resistance left to her would only increase the fun of possessing her.

As he directed her toward his private quarters, watching from behind the way her hips moved inside her uncomplimentary garments, remembering the sweet shape and curve of her breasts, and the particular silken sensation between her legs, he thought that she would be more satisfying than any woman he had ever destroyed.

Saddith's death had been satisfying, of course: deft, inescapable, and almost infinitely clever. Nevertheless it had lacked the personal touch. He hadn't destroyed her himself; he had only arranged events so that she would suffer and die. On the unfortunately frequent occasions when he had found it necessary to make love to her, the exigencies of his plans had required him to treat her gently, almost kindly, so that she would believe he might help further her social ambitions. He was man enough, however, to meet even her boring tastes in fornication. And with Terisa there would be no limits— Nothing would inhibit the extravagant flavors of pain and debasement he meant to elicit from her.

He felt so primed and poised that he could hardly refrain from dancing as he followed her toward his rooms.

Obedient to his will, she entered his quarters and stopped in the center of the one, big chamber where he had his bed, his instruments of enjoyment, and his copy of the flat mirror which showed how matters progressed in the valley of Esmerel.

There King Joyse and Prince Kragen were about to go down under a tide of callat. Or they would be driven within reach of the monster rearing impressively over them.

Good. In fact, perfect. Eremis would like watching his enemies die while Terisa wept and wailed.

'Remove your clothes,' he told her, enjoying the harshness of his tone. 'You have evaded me too long, and the recompense I demand has grown correspondingly large.' If he took off his own clothes, she would see just how large it was. 'Nakedness is the very least of the gifts your fine body will give me today.'

Sunlight came from a series of windows along one wall, where he occasionally let men stand to observe his exercises. Today, of course, everyone was busy with battle or guard duty; but he was glad to have his victory to himself. Outside was only a rugged hillside, a freedom Terisa would never reach. The whole stronghold was austere, and he hadn't had time to procure rugs. But the sun warmed the chill of the stone floors, shedding brightness over his victim and the mirror.

She didn't obey. And she didn't pay any attention to the windows; as far as he could tell, she didn't notice them at all. Instead, she turned to the glass, as if it had more power over her than anything else did.

For the first time since they had left the Image-room, he saw her face.

Perhaps she wasn't beaten after all. Something in her conveyed a definite sense of evaporation, as if she were on the borderline of disappearing. Her expression was slack; her eyes, vaguely focused. And yet he also seemed to see something else, something secretive and wonderfully enticing. It may have been a covert hope: the hope, perhaps, that she could shift the Image in the mirror (but of course that wouldn't do anything to help either her or King Joyse); or the hope that Eremis would foolishly give her the chance to translate him away (but to do that she would have to physically thrust him toward the glass, and he was stronger than she was, much stronger); or the hope that she could use the mirror to escape herself (but he had no intention of giving her the opportunity).

Or maybe she was nourishing a hidden and hopeless desire to do him harm.

Whatever she concealed, it was exactly the spice he coveted. For a moment, he let her disobey him simply because he couldn't decide whether to kiss her gently or tear her clothes apart.

Studying the mirror, she asked in a thin, disinterested tone, 'Where did you get those creatures? The ones that attacked Geraden and me. How did you get them to serve you?'

Master Eremis was happy to answer her. 'The callat. They were a fortuitous discovery – as all things are fortuitous for men who can master life. They were first discovered among Vagel's Imagers in Cadwal, but no use was made of them. Apparently, every faction in Carmag feared that they might prove to be a decisive force – for someone else. However, after I had redeemed Vagel from his tenuous exile among the Alend Lieges, he remembered the formula and shaped a new mirror.

'The callat are indeed a powerful force, as you can see' – Eremis enjoyed a glance at the glass himself, although most of his mind was fixed on Terisa – 'but not as powerful as the Cadwals feared. Their numbers are not great enough to make an army.

'They are renegades in their own world. Actually, they are in danger of extermination by what I can only describe as a race of groundhogs. Very large groundhogs. And the callat are too bloody-minded to make peace. They can only fight or die.

'Witnessing their danger, I translated one or two of them and began bargaining. In exchange for escape from their enemies' – Eremis shrugged aside the fact that he had never intended to let the callat live, had meant from the start to use them in a way which would destroy them – 'they agreed to serve me.'

Slowly, Terisa nodded. He wondered if she understood: she seemed to be thinking about something else.

'They come from a completely different world,' she said. 'They have a history of their own, motives of their own. Do you still claim they didn't exist until Vagel shaped the mirror?'

Her question drew a chortle from the Master. He made no effort to conceal that he was inexpressibly pleased with himself. 'My lady, did you ever truly credit that piece of sophism?'

She regarded him gravely, as if she wanted to hear what he would say – and didn't care what it was.

Still chuckling, he continued, 'No man of any intelligence – of whom there are only a few, I admit – has ever thought that the Images we see in mirrors do not exist. That position, with all the arguments supporting it, was forced on us by King Joyse, by his demand that the Congery should define a "right" use of Imagery. Because he took it as proven that *if* Images were real in themselves *then* they must be treated with respect, forbearance – in effect, must be left alone – he allowed those who disagreed with him no ground on which to stand except that those Images have no independent existence.

'But of course his central tenet is so foolish that it is also unanswerable. He might as well claim that we must not breathe because we should not interfere with the air, or that we must not eat because we should not interfere with plants and cattle. The truth is that we have the *right* to interfere with Images because we have the *power* to interfere. It is *necessary* to interfere. Otherwise the power has no use, and it dies, and Imagery is lost.

'That is the law of life. Like every other thing which breathes and desires and chooses, we must *do what we can*.'

Eremis licked his lips. 'Terisa, I have sampled your breasts, and they are delectable. You must have an exceptionally vacuous mind, if you ever believed that you do not exist. I told you you were unreal only to make it as difficult as possible for you to discover your talent.'

As he spoke, he studied her, looking for her secret reaction, the truth she wished to conceal. Her eyes were too dark, too lost: they didn't betray anything. As far as they were concerned, she was already gone.

But her pretty, cleft chin tightened as if she were clenching her teeth.

Delighted by this evidence of anger, he reached out and bunched his fists in her unflattering leather shirt. He regretted, really, that she hadn't had a chance to wash her hair; but everything else about her was perfect. He was going to tear the shirt away. Then, before he began to hurt her, he would do things to her breasts which would make her ache for him in spite of her secrets. He would surprise her with the pain, as she had surprised him.

For some reason, however, she had turned her face away. She wasn't even afraid enough of him to watch what he was doing. Instead, she gazed darkly at the mirror.

Unintentionally, he glanced there in time to see the slug-beast come down from its full height, collapse like soundless thunder in the valley and lie still. Involuntarily, he held his breath, waiting to see the monster move again, waiting to see it pounce forward and devour King Joyse and the arrogant Alend Contender. But the beast remained as limp as a carcass. Odd smoke curled briefly out of its maw and drifted away along the breeze.

'Excrement of a pig!' Eremis breathed. Forgetting Terisa, he turned to the mirror, gripped the frame with both hands, studied the Image intently. 'That is impossible. You doddering old fool, that is *impossible.*'

'Interesting,' Terisa remarked as if she had never been less interested in her life. 'Maybe "all things" aren't as "fortuitous" as you think.'

Eremis thought he saw the Image of the valley begin to waver around the edges, thought he saw the rampart walls and the last catapult start to melt—

That also was impossible. He wasn't sure of what he was seeing.

He didn't delay to be sure. Swinging at once, he backhanded her across the side of the head so hard that she fell like a broken doll. She lay on one side in the warm sunshine, huddling around herself, with her hair spread out on the stone, and one hand cupped weakly over the place where she had been hit; she may have been weeping.

'If you try that again,' he spat, 'if you touch that glass with one more hint of your talent, I swear I will call Gilbur here and let him rape you with that dagger of his.'

Perhaps she wasn't weeping: she didn't make a sound. After a moment, however, she nodded her head – one small, frail jerk, like a twitch of defeat.

Despite his monster's unexpected demise, Master Eremis recovered his grin.

Artagel, too, was grinning, but for an entirely different reason.

Despite the blood which streamed from his cut shoulder, he beat back the hot, steel lightning and force of Gart's next attack. That defense cost him an exertion which seemed to shred his wounded side. Twice he only saved himself because the corridor was too narrow for perfect swordwork, and he was able to block Gart's blade away against the stone. But at last he managed to disengage.

Before the High King's Monomach could come at him again, he retreated several quick strides, then relaxed his stance and dropped the point of his sword.

Gart paused to scrutinize him curiously.

Trying not to breathe in whooping gasps that would betray his weakness, Artagel asked, 'Why do you do it?'

Gart cocked an eyebrow; he advanced a step.

Artagel put up a hand to ward off the Monomach. 'You're going to kill me anyway. You know that. You can afford to send me to my grave with my ignorance satisfied. Why do you do it?'

Swayed, perhaps, by the admission of defeat, Gart paused again. 'Why do I do what?'

With an effort which felt desperately heroic, Artagel tried to laugh. He failed, of course. Nevertheless he did contrive to sound cheerful as he said, 'Serve.'

The tip of Gart's blade watched Artagel warily as the Monomach waited.

'You're the best,' Artagel panted, 'the best. You lead and train a cadre of Apts who all want to be as good as you, and some of them may even have almost that much talent. You could be a power in the world. I'll wager you could unseat Festten anytime you want. You could be the one who decides, instead of the one who serves. Why do you do it?'

Gart considered the question for a moment. 'That is who I am,' he pronounced finally.

'But why?' demanded Artagel, fighting for a chance to regain his breath, his strength. 'What does Festten give you that you can't get anywhere else? What does being the High King's Monomach get you that isn't already yours by right? You could *choose* who you're going to kill. If I were you, I'd be embarrassed by the amount of time you've spent recently trying to kill a woman. Whose decision was that? Why did you have to demean yourself like that?'

A snarl pulled tighter across Gart's teeth.

'I tell you, you could be a *power*. Don't you have any self-respect?'

The Monomach came at him like a gale in the constricted passage, suddenly, without warning; and the only thing that saved him was that he wasn't surprised. He got his longsword up, parried hard, tried to riposte. Gart slipped the blow aside and swung again. Artagel felt steel ruffle his hair as he ducked; Gart's blade rang off the wall; Artagel hacked at the Monomach's legs fast enough to make him jump.

Somehow not stumbling, not clutching at his torn side, Artagel disengaged again, retreated down the corridor.

'That,' said Gart as if he had never been out of breath in his life, 'is who I am.'

'But the point is, you *serve*,' protested Artagel. 'You're nothing more than a servant, a *weapon*.'

'Listen to me,' Gart articulated dangerously. 'I will not say it again. *That is who I* am.'

'With *your* abilities?' Artagel's voice nearly rose to a cry. 'I don't believe it. You're content to be a *servant*? You're content to be *used* like a thing with no mind, no pride? Aren't you a man? Don't you dream? Haven't you got ambitions?'

It was probably madness to goad the Monomach like this; but Artagel didn't care. For the first time since their contest began, he was having fun.

'No wonder you're so hard to kill. Inside, where it counts, you're already dead.'

In response, Gart whirled his blade with such speed that the steel blurred into streaks of lantern-light. 'Oh, I have dreams, you fool,' he rasped. 'I have dreams.

'I dream of *blood*.'

So fiercely that nothing could stop him, he hurled himself at Artagel.

Now Gart was the mad one, the frenzied attacker, swinging as if he were out of control; Artagel was the one who couldn't do anything except parry and block – and try to keep his balance.

Unfortunately, the Monomach's fury only made their struggle more uneven. *He* wasn't wounded; *he* hadn't been weakened by a long convalescence. And at his worst he never forgot his skill.

As if by translation, cuts appeared on Artagel's mail, his leggings. A lick along his forehead sent blood dripping into his eyes. Reeling, almost falling, he slammed into the corner where the corridor turned, hit so hard that the last air was knocked out of his lungs.

He barely saved himself, *barely*, by diving out of the corner, rolling to his feet and running, his lungs on fire, his eyes full of sweat and blood, no life in his limbs, running until he gained enough ground to turn and plant his feet and stand there wobbling and face Gart for the last time.

The fun part of the fight was over.

Moved by instincts he didn't know he had, Geraden went down as if he had been clubbed.

The first vicious black shape missed him; its own momentum carried it beyond him, momentarily out of reach. And the second—

But Master Gilbur was bringing a whole stream of the beasts into the Image-room, translating them at Geraden as fast as they could leap. The Master's teeth gnashed the air, and his face burned, as if he were on his way to ecstasy.

A whole world of creatures like that. Of course. Ravening as if they had already eaten their way through all their natural prey. Terisa had shattered a mirror to end an attack like this; but that mirror wasn't this one. No, she had broken the flat glass which showed the intersection outside Orison. The original mirror, the source of the creatures, remained intact.

Obviously.

Flipping to the side, scrambling his legs under him, stumbling as if he would never regain his balance, Geraden struggled out of the direct spring of the creatures.

Three, five, nine of them, he lost count. Sliding in his boots as if the sunlit stone were ice, he rounded the edge of a mirror, wheeled behind it.

He was too frantic to think. And he had no chance against Master Gilbur anyway. All he knew was that he had to hurt the King's enemies as much as he could before he died. Gilbur clearly believed the gnarled shapes would get him before he did much harm. No doubt the Master was right. But every bit of damage might help. Any mirror Geraden could break might be the crucial one, the one that made sense of the Congery's augury – the one that gave King Joyse a chance against his doom.

The slug-beast had been killed. Surely anything was possible—

From behind, without knowing or caring what its Image was, *Geraden took hold of the mirror and wrenched it onto its back.*

And caught it before it hit the floor.

Inspiration: unexpected insight. As if the mere touch of the mirror's frame had shocked him, everything inside his head seemed to take fire and become new.

Not damage. If damage was all he tried to do, Gilbur had no reason to fear him. He would be dead in moments.

Imagery, on the other hand—

The first black shapes were already scrabbling over the stone to fling themselves on him. And more came furiously, avid for flesh. Master Gilbur turned his mirror in order to translate the creatures straight at Geraden.

Burning with inspiration, Geraden heaved the mirror upright again and opened it just as the nearest creature hit the glass.

Gone. As if the shape had never existed. Translated somewhere, he had no idea where, he still hadn't had a chance to so much as glance at the scene in the mirror.

Another and another, in rapid succession: gone. The gnarled creatures seemed to have no minds – or at least no sense of danger. Their hunger overwhelmed all other instincts; maybe they were starving to death in their own world. They hurled themselves into the glass as if it were Geraden's flesh.

The fire blazing up inside him felt like joy and triumph.

Four five six—

Master Gilbur bellowed something savage and sprang to a different mirror.

The last few shapes came at Geraden madly, their jaws stretched open, and Master Gilbur brought wolves rushing into the Image-room, wolves with spines along their curved backs and malign purpose in their eyes, wolves that were too big for Geraden's shield and would be forced by their sheer size to attack him over or around the mirror; and at that moment Geraden made the mistake of realizing what he was doing.

He was doing something worse than the translation of alien evils into his own world: he was translating them somewhere else, into a place completely unready for them, completely innocent. Whatever lived and moved in the Image he held was now being assaulted by vicious and entirely unexpected creatures for no good reason except to save his life.

No, this was wrong, it was *wrong*, he had no right to do it. These creatures, and the wolves, and anything else Gilbur might produce were only malignant because they had been translated, only because they were out of place. In their own worlds, they didn't deserve to be slaughtered. And no one else deserved to be slaughtered simply because Geraden was desperate.

Shoving the mirror away, he dove to the side.

The last black shapes struck the glass hard and slammed it onto its back. As they bounded up from the splinters to continue their attack, they left behind a shattered Image of their fellow creatures dying horribly in the acid of bitten ghouls.

A hunting snarl throbbed through the air; jaws slavered. Geraden scrambled across the ring of mirrors, trying to stay ahead of the gnarled shapes and the wolves.

Strange things were happening in the Image of Esmerel's valley. The slug-beast was definitely dead, no mistake about that. And its death altered the terms of the conflict. High King Festten committed all his forces to a killing charge. In two thrusts, seven or eight thousand men on each side of the supine monster, he sent his army to catch King Joyse while there was no escape, while the confused and lesser strength of Alend and Mordant was trapped between the defile at one end of the valley and the tremendous corpse blocking the other.

King Joyse should already have been crushed under the weight of the callat. He was still up and fighting, however. Prince Kragen was with him, and the Termigan, and Castellan Norge; but they weren't enough to keep him alive. No, he endured because the monster's death had galvanized his army: that impossible rescue from certain destruction had transformed panic into hope and fury. As fast as their horses or their legs could move them, his men came to support their King; the first several hundred of them had already charged in among the callat.

The Cadwals hadn't yet had time to catch up with the red-furred creatures. The callat had to face the recovered force of King Joyse's army alone.

Geraden dashed past the flat glass with black shapes on his heels. Master Gilbur seemed to be having trouble finding wolves. He had translated three, no, four into the Image-room; but now he was studying the Image, scanning its focus rapidly in search of more predators. The use he and Eremis had made of the wolves previously must have depleted their population.

Four would be enough, of course. The gnarled shapes would be enough. Geraden couldn't keep ahead of them, couldn't fight—

Not this way.

The first wolf appeared to rear straight up in front of him, springing for his head. Urgently, he wrenched himself aside. His boots skidded out from under him; he thumped down on his back, sliding beneath the attack.

The wolf landed among the black creatures.

They didn't care what they ate; they only wanted food. Swiftly, they all pounced on the wolf.

At once, their struggle became a whirl, a snarling dervish, a mad ball of claws and fangs. The wolf was big, powerful; the shapes sank their hooks and teeth in and clung.

With the air knocked out of his lungs, Geraden lay still.

As if they recognized a mortal enemy, the other wolves sped to help their fellow.

Master Gilbur spat curses, then crowed obscenely as he located more wolves.

Geraden couldn't breathe. He could hardly move his limbs. Nevertheless he had to act now, had to grab this brief chance. He might never get another one.

Talent was a remarkable thing: he was learning more about it all the time. He was an Adept of some kind; he could use other people's mirrors. And he had rescued himself and Terisa out of her former apartment, out of a world which had no Imagery. All he had to do was concentrate, take Master Gilbur by surprise.

In a way, it helped that he couldn't breathe. It almost helped that the struggle between the wolves and the gnarled creatures was only ten feet away, and that the wolves were winning, crunching the bones of the smaller beasts. The extremity of his plight left no room for doubt or hesitation.

He turned his head toward the mirror and studied the Image, fixed it in his mind: a forest full of harsh shadows, slashed by light *there* and *there*; boughs angling upward; underbrush of a kind he had never seen before. During the spaces between his heartbeats, he memorized the scene.

Master Gilbur hunched beside the mirror, clutching the frame with one fist, crooning to the glass. A feral ecstasy lit his features, as bright as fire, as consuming as lava.

When the first of the new wolves started through the mirror, Geraden closed his eyes and shifted the Image in his mind.

And the Image in the mirror shifted.

He didn't know what he shifted it to, and he didn't care. Instinctively, he must have selected some place or vista to fill the mirror: he couldn't imagine a blank glass. But that detail was unimportant. What mattered was that he could reach out with his talent, that by surprise if not by strength he could break Master Gilbur's hold on the glass.

It worked. The Image melted while the wolf was still caught in the prolonged instant of translation.

The wolf was cut in half.

The mirror shattered.

Gilbur wheeled to confront Geraden. For a moment, the brutal Imager actually gaped. Then rage knotted his face, and he let out a roar which seemed to strike the air dumb, leaving the battle of the wolves without a sound.

He turned to the next mirror in the ring.

From its dark depths, he brought out a burst of lightning so hot that it scorched the stone floor; a blast of thunder so loud that it thudded in Geraden's tight lungs; a wind so hard that it seemed to hammer him down even though he hadn't tried to rise, hadn't tried to move.

The Imager was translating a storm into the chamber.

Using it to buffet and confuse and overwhelm Geraden until Master Gilbur could get to him and drive a dagger into his heart.

Now that he had Terisa down on the floor and hurt, Master Eremis thought he would begin to take advantage of her. He found, however, that he had trouble pulling his attention away from the mirror.

He liked surprises: they were tests, opportunities. Yet the death of the slug-beast nagged at him. That was an unforeseen development. Of course, the creature could have collapsed for any number of reasons which had nothing to do with the battle. Nevertheless its demise suggested that he had underestimated his enemy's capabilities.

And King Joyse's forces were rallying now. That was perfectly predictable – but still frustrating to watch. Festten had made the right decision: to launch a full-scale assault while the armies of Mordant and Alend were still in disarray. Unfortunately, his men were too far away to save the callat. And King Joyse and Prince Kragen were doing entirely too good a job of pulling their forces into order to meet the Cadwal charge.

Soon the battle would degenerate into a simple contest of steel and determination.

King Joyse would lose, of course. Festten had him heavily out-numbered. And Gilbur had an impressive array of mirrors at hand. Yet Master Eremis wasn't pleased. On the scale of armies, Gilbur's remaining resources were relatively minor. And if the Cadwal victory weren't ultimately achieved by Imagery, the High King would become more difficult to rule in future. He would trust his own strength more, Eremis' less. He might begin to think he could dispense with Master Eremis altogether. And Gart was somewhere in the stronghold—

The Master was prepared for all these eventualities. Nevertheless he didn't find them especially attractive.

Carefully, Terisa got to her feet, so that she, too, could look at the mirror. She had the smudge of a growing bruise on her cheekbone, but it only made her lovelier. When she had been hurt enough, she would be intolerably beautiful.

Master Eremis considered hitting her again. But that was too crude, really. He expected better of himself: more imagination, greater subtlety. And he wanted to see what his enemies were going to do.

He wanted to see what Gilbur was going to do.

It would be something violent, something effective. Considering Gilbur's susceptibility to rage of all kinds, however, it might also be something premature. Master Eremis didn't want to see Joyse die too soon, too easily.

At the moment, there was no danger of that. The callat were beaten: Joyse was able to disengage, with Kragen, Norge, and the unanticipated Termigan. They rode a short way up the valley, conferred with each other briefly, then began shouting orders which conveyed nothing through the glass. And their army seemed to come into order around them almost magically.

None too soon, Kragen spurred away to command the defense to the right of the monster's corpse. Norge went to the left, with the Termigan beside him. Well, Joyse was an old man. No doubt he needed rest. He didn't appear to be resting, however. Instead, he rode everywhere, organizing his men.

For some reason, he divided them into three forces: one to support Kragen; one for Norge and the Termigan; one for himself.

'I don't understand,' said Terisa thinly, in that impersonal, disinterested tone.

Master Eremis felt that he was beginning to comprehend her. That tone didn't indicate defeat. It was a sign of withdrawal: not of retreat, but of hiding, of covert intentions. Perhaps she thought that if she could go far enough away in her mind, he wouldn't be able to hurt her. Or perhaps she hid so that she could take him by surprise.

A small thrill of anticipation ran through his veins, and he shifted his weight slightly onto the balls of his feet.

'Have you ever understood anything?' he countered with amiable sarcasm.

His scorn didn't seem to touch her. She may have been too distant to hear it accurately. In the same tone, she said, 'You have all these flat mirrors, but you don't use them very well.'

Another surprise: one with exciting possibilities. What was she thinking?

'Do we not?' he asked casually.

'You have a glass that shows Vale House.' Despite her dullness, her voice was strangely distinct. 'You could have taken Queen Madin yourself. You could have brought her here as a hostage. She would have been more use to you than Nyle.'

Oh, that. Master Eremis was mildly disappointed; he had hoped for something a bit more interesting. 'A predictable idea,' he commented acidly, 'and not precisely brilliant. If I had done that, I would have given up the wedge I wished to drive between Joyse and Margonal. I would have given up the obstacles I wished to place in your path.

'I must confess I am still somewhat surprised that Margonal let you into Orison. That was not a reasonable decision, in view of the news you carried.'

He paused to let Terisa volunteer an explanation, but she didn't speak. No matter. He would get all the answers he wanted from her eventually. 'I am sure,' he resumed, 'I came very close to achieving exactly what I desired with the Queen.

'If, on the other hand, I had done as you – and Festten – advise, I might have gained nothing. The Queen would have been in my hands – and the translation would have made her mad. Damaging hostages is a blade with two edges. Her madness might have hurt Joyse enough to weaken him. Or it might have incensed him enough to disregard her. Then the effort of attacking her would have been wasted.'

There remained the question of what had happened to the Queen. And the question of how Joyse had contrived to rejoin his army, after his disappearance from Orison. But those answers could wait as well. Thinking about his own tactics brought new joy to the Master's loins. The satisfaction he wanted from Terisa was long overdue.

'But you have this mirror now,' she said as if she couldn't see her peril in his eyes. 'Why don't you just translate King Joyse and Prince Kragen? Make them mad? Then you can't lose. Without them, the army will collapse. And you can lock them up the way you did Nyle. You can laugh at them until they die.'

Oh, how she pleased him! She made him laugh. 'I will do that, I assure you,' he promised. 'At the right moment, I will do it, and it will give me more pleasure than you can conceive.'

In the mirror, along the sides of the monster, the forces of Cadwal and Mordant and Alend met for their last battle.

'At first, of course,' Eremis explained, 'I had to be cautious. You taught me to respect your talents. If I had given you the chance, you might have broken my mirror. But that danger ended when you came here. When you gave yourself into my power.'

Initially, the fight was even. The walls of the valley and the bulk of the slug-beast narrowed the ground, restricted the number of Cadwals able to advance together. And Joyse's men fought as if they were inspired. Even Kragen and that dour loon the Termigan seemed inspired. For a time, at least, Festten lost a lot of men and gained nothing.

'Now I wait only to let these armies do each other as much harm as possible. Joyse cannot win, but before he dies he may give Festten a victory as costly as any defeat. That will humble even the High King's arrogance. It will make him too weak to think he can command or refuse me.'

Then, inevitably, the defenders on the left began to crumble. Norge went down; he disappeared under a rush of Cadwal hooves. In spite of his native grimness, the Termigan was forced backward. Their men tried to retreat in some semblance of order, but the Cadwals surged after them, overtook them, hacked them apart. Festten's strength started flooding into the valley.

'So I will let the battle progress a while. I will wish Joyse all the success he can manage. And then' – Eremis was so delighted that he wanted applause – 'at the crucial moment I will translate him away to the madness and ruin he deserves.'

He wasn't particularly surprised to see Festten himself lead the second wave of the assault. The High King had an old and overwhelming desire to see Joyse die; he would have been ecstatic to kill his nemesis himself. Eremis considered, however, that Festten was taking a useless risk. The Master had no intention of allowing the High King the gratification he craved.

There was something odd in the way Terisa regarded Master Eremis, something that resembled hunger. Softly, she asked, 'Have you hated him all your life? Even when you were just a kid? the first time you translated that monster? Did you hate him even then?'

'Hate him?' Eremis laughed again. 'Terisa, you mistake me. You always mistake me.' The pressure inside him was rising, rising. 'I do not hate him. I hate no one. I only despise weakness and folly. As a youth, when I shaped the mirror which showed what you call "that monster," I translated it merely as an experiment. To learn what I could do. Later I was forced to abandon my glass in order to avoid being captured with it, and that vexed me. I promised then I would retaliate.

'But I do not waste my time' – he was growing deliciously ready for her – 'I *assure* you that I do not waste my time on hate.'

She continued to gaze at him with her curious blend of absence and hunger. She had her back to the windows and the sunlight; perhaps that was what made her eyes look so dark, her beauty seem so fatal.

Huskily, bringing the words up from far down her throat, she said, 'Let me show you what I can do.'

With one hand, she reached out and gently touched her fingertips to the unmistakable bulge in the front of his cloak.

He felt like crowing.

Frantically, Artagel fought to prolong his life, keep himself on his feet for one more moment, just one, then another if he could do it. He was the best swordsman in Mordant, wasn't he? Surely he could keep himself alive one more moment at a time?

Maybe not. The pain in his side had become a fire that filled his lungs, so that he seemed to snatch each raw breath through a conflagration. His sword kept turning in his hands; blood and sweat ruined his grip. His legs had lost their spring; he had no more strength to do anything except shuffle his boots over the stone. Sometimes his heavy lurching from side to side dashed water and blood off his brows, cleared his vision; most of the time, however, he had trouble seeing.

How had the corridor become so narrow? He couldn't seem to get a full swing, no matter what he did.

Gart, on the other hand, didn't appear to be experiencing any difficulty. His brief, wild fury had faded. In fact, the pace of his attacks was slower now, more deliberate; more malicious. He was toying with his opponent. Yellow glee shone in his eyes, and he grinned as if he were crowing inside.

What a way to die. No, worse than that: what a way to be beaten. Artagel was a fighter; he had lived most of his life in the vicinity of death. For him, it was at once so familiar and so unimaginable that he couldn't be afraid of it. But to be beaten like this, utterly, miserably—

Oh, Geraden, forgive me.

959

If only, he thought dumbly, if only he hadn't been hurt the last time. If only he hadn't spent so much time in bed.

Terisa, forgive me.

But it was stupid to wish for things like that. Foolish regret: a waste of time and energy and life. Gart had beaten him the last time, too. And the time before that.

I will regret nothing.

He retreated down the passage, past more doors than he could count; stumbling, barely on his feet. By bare will, he kept his sword up for Gart to play with.

If anybody thinks he can do better than this, let him try.

That was enough. As unsteady as a drunk, he stopped; he locked both hands around his wet swordhilt.

I will regret nothing.

Almost retching for air, he jerked forward and did his absolute best to split Gart's head open.

Negligently, Gart blocked the blow.

Artagel's eyes were full of blood: he couldn't see what happened. But he knew from the sound, the familiar echoing clang after his swing, and from the sudden shift of balance, that he had broken his sword.

One jagged half remained in his fists; the other rang away across the floor, singing metallically of failure.

'Now,' Gart breathed like silk. 'Now, you fool.'

Involuntarily, Artagel went down on one knee, as if he couldn't stay on his feet without an intact weapon.

The High King's Monomach raised his sword. Between streaks of Artagel's blood, the steel gleamed.

For some reason, a door behind Gart opened.

Nyle came into the passage.

He looked like Artagel felt: abused to the bone; exhausted beyond bearing. But he held the chains of his manacles clenched in his fists, and he swung the heavy rings on the ends of the chains at Gart's head.

The instincts which had made Gart the High King's Monomach saved him. Warned by some visceral intuition, some impalpable tremor in the air, he wrenched himself aside and started turning.

The rings missed his head, came down on his left shoulder.

They hit him hard enough to strike that arm away from his sword. But he did most of his fighting one-handed anyway, despite his weapon's weight. While his left arm fell numb – maybe broken – his right was already in motion, bringing his blade around to sever Nyle's neck.

Nyle!

In that moment, a piece of time as quick and eternal as a translation, Artagel brought up the last strength from the bottom of his heart and lunged forward.

With his whole body, he drove his broken sword through the armhole of Gart's armor.

Then he and Nyle collapsed on Gart's corpse as if they had become kindred spirits at last.

He had the peculiar conviction that he needed to prevent Gart from rising up after death and shedding more blood. A long time seemed to pass before he recovered enough sanity to wonder whether Nyle was still alive.

The crash and burn of Master Gilbur's storm seemed to blot out Geraden's senses, smother his will. He couldn't remember the last time he had taken a breath. On the other hand, air wasn't especially important to him at the moment. Lightning struck the stone so close-by that it nearly scorched him; he could feel the shock like a tingle in the floor. Darkness swept the sunlight away: thunder tried to crush him.

Well, the storm daunted the wolves, held them at bay. That was some consolation. And if it continued to mount in this enclosed space, it would begin to topple the mirrors.

Master Gilbur didn't appear to care any longer what might happen to his mirrors. He was roaring like the blast, and his hunched back strained to lift his head as high as possible, gnash his jaws at the ceiling.

With a massive concussion, all the windows blew out. At once, the pressure around Geraden eased, and he started breathing again.

Too bad: the loss of the windows might save the mirrors. Unless the roof came down.

Gilbur had to be stopped. Geraden had the distinct impression that the Imager was going mad, transported by power. A storm like this, constricted like this, could conceivably level the whole building.

Geraden had done it once. Could he do it again?

Forget the thunder that deafened him, stunned his mind. Forget the lightning, the near-miss of fire hot enough to incinerate his bones. Forget wind and wolves and violence.

Think about glass.

Despite the storm, Gilbur's only real weapon was the mirror itself, a piece of normal glass. It had a particular hue blended of sand and tinct; a particular shape created by molds and rollers and heat. His talent had made it what it was. His talent opened it like a blown-out window between worlds. But Geraden also had talent. He could feel the mirror, see its Image in his mind as if by the simple intensity of his perception, his imagination, he made it real.

He didn't know how to halt the translation. But he could shift the Image.

No. Gilbur was resisting him. Forewarned by what had happened to the mirror of the wolves, the Imager clung to this glass grimly, forced the translation.

Don't give up. Don't get confused. No matter how it felt, this wasn't a contest between lightning and flesh, thunder and hearing, wind and muscle. Those things were irrelevant. The struggle was one of will and talent. Gilbur may have been mad, exalted by hate, but he had no experience with this kind of battle; none of the Masters had ever been trained to fight for control of their translations in this way.

And Geraden had gone wrong so often in his life that it had become intolerable. He loved too many people, and they had been too badly hurt.

In one moment briefer than a heartbeat, the Image shifted.

Severed in midpassage, the storm blasted the glass to powder.

Geraden couldn't hear anything: the abrupt silence seemed louder than thunder. He saw Master Gilbur cursing him, spitting apoplectic fury at him, but the oaths made no noise. The sprinkling fall of glass-dust was mute. The wolves bared their fangs, and their chests heaved, but their snarling was voiceless.

While Geraden struggled to his feet, Gilbur moved to another mirror.

For one stunned instant, Geraden gaped at the Image and didn't understand. What power did Gilbur see there? The glass showed an empty landscape, nothing more: a barren stretch of ground riddled with cracks, tossed with boulders, but devoid of anything that breathed or moved or could attack.

Then, as Master Gilbur got his hands on the frame and began to snarl his concentration-chant as if it were fundamentally obscene, Geraden saw the ground in the Image jumping.

The boulders rocked and heaved, lifted from the dirt; the edges of the landscape vibrated.

Earthquake.

Gilbur's mirror showed a place in a state of ongoing cataclysm, of almost perpetual orogenic crisis – the kind of crisis that built and broke mountains, shouldered oceans aside, shattered continents.

He was translating an earthquake.

'No!' Geraden cried through the mounting tectonic rumble. 'You will not do this!'

'Stop me!' bellowed back the Imager, impervious to authority, or reason, or self-destruction. '*Stop me,* you puny bastard!'

The stronghold would go down in moments: it hadn't been built to withstand an earthquake. That would end the translation. As soon as the ceiling fell, Gilbur would be crushed; his mirror would be crushed.

But in the meantime everyone else inside would die. Terisa and Eremis. Artagel and Gart. Nyle. Geraden himself. And the tremor might trigger the collapse of the surrounding hills. The devastation might spread for miles before it faded.

Yes! Geraden had no idea whether or not he shouted aloud. I will *stop* you! He ignored the accelerating tremble under his boots, the deepening, rocky groan in the air; he accepted Gilbur's challenge. *You will not do this!*

With all the force he possessed, he took control of the glass, arrested the translation.

This time, Master Gilbur was ready for him; braced and powerful; completely insane. The virulence of the Imager's will to open the mirror shocked through Geraden, burned him like fire, nauseated him like poison. The mirror itself was merely held, locked between opposing talents; but everything Gilbur brought to the battle seemed to strike straight into Geraden.

Rages he had never felt, needs he had never understood, lusts he had never imagined; loathsome things, destructive things; fears so inarticulate and consuming that they deformed the Master's essential being.

Long years ago, before King Joyse brought him to the Congery, Gilbur had been an Imager living alone in the Armigite hills, interested only in his own researches. But he had been attacked; and in the struggle the roof of his cave had fallen on him, pinning him under a block of stone. He had lain there for hours or days until Eremis had rescued him.

During that time, he had suffered like the damned.

Excruciating pain in the long, lonely dark; a horror of death elevated to agony by every terrible fear he could imagine; screams no one would ever hear, even though they went on for the rest of his life.

He had come through that experience mangled in spirit as well as in body. It had made him who he was: hungry and violent; eager for power; devoted to Eremis. Many times since joining the Congery, he would have gone amok, if he hadn't been restrained by Eremis' presence – or crippled by the suspicion that it was Eremis who had attacked him in the first place. Now he hurled all his twisted needs and desires into his translation; hurled them all at Geraden.

They should have been enough to make Geraden quail. But they weren't. In an odd, unforeseen way, he was prepared for them.

He, too, had once been buried alive, under the rubble of Darsint's escape from Orison. He had tasted pain and horror, hopeless suffocation. And now, as then, other people's needs were more important to him than his own.

If Gilbur's translation succeeded, Terisa and Artagel and Nyle would die. Everyone in and around the stronghold would probably die. Without the help Geraden and Terisa could give, King Joyse might die, taking Mordant and eventually Alend with him.

So Geraden ignored the harsh anguish Gilbur sent at him. He closed his mind to his visceral fear of trembling stone. He shut the wolves out of his awareness.

Will-to-will, he met Master Gilbur's madness and held the mirror, sealing the glass in the onset of translation, keeping the earthquake back.

That was Gilbur's chance. If he had let go of the mirror then and used his dagger, he could have killed Geraden almost without effort.

But he didn't let go. Maybe he couldn't. Or maybe somewhere down at the bottom of his heart he wanted to be stopped. Whatever the reason, he clung to the glass frame, clung to his translation, and tried to make his hate stronger than Geraden's determination.

In the end, it wasn't his hate that failed him: it was his body. Without warning, while he strained and raged, a pain as heavy as a spear drove through the center of his chest.

He blanched; his hands slipped from the mirror; involuntarily, he clutched at his heart. Slowly, his jaw dropped, and his eyes began to gape. Reaching for air he could no longer find, he stumbled to his knees as if the ground had been cut out from under him.

His whole face twisted as if he wanted to curse Geraden before he died. But he had lost his chance. He was already dead as he toppled to the stone.

The wolves would have killed Geraden then. He was too shaken to defend himself, too deeply shocked. Artagel and Nyle arrived in time to save him, however. Artagel was exhausted, of course, hardly able to lift his arms; but he had Gart's sword, and it seemed to give him strength. And Nyle swung his chains crazily, which made one or two of the wolves hesitate, giving Artagel the opportunity to dispatch them.

The three brothers hugged each other long and hard before they went to look for Terisa.

'No.' Master Eremis caught her by the wrist and pulled her hand away from him. 'Not yet. I am not ready to trust you.' But he was ready to do everything else to her. 'I have not forgotten that you once kicked me.'

She continued to gaze at him as if he hadn't spoken. The combination of hunger and absence in her eyes didn't change.

Again, he wondered what she had hidden away in the secret places of her heart. Was that where she kept her fear? Or did she still have surprises left in her?

He was ready for everything about her, ready to take away everything she had. Before he was done, she would confess her secrets, all of them, she would give him everything about herself, hoping that it would save her. But nothing would save her. He was going to take all she had and leave her empty.

Now, however, she wasn't looking at him any longer. Her attention had returned to the mirror.

Kragen still held his ground, blocked the right side of the valley with more success than Eremis had expected from him; but the defense to the left continued crumbling. The forces of Alend and Mordant seemed to dissolve under the Cadwal charge. Hurrying to take advantage of this opportunity, the Cadwals gathered speed.

High King Festten followed them, bringing all his reinforcements to that side. In moments, Festten himself rode past the dead length of the slug-beast, entering the valley at a hard canter.

As soon as the High King was in reach, Joyse struck. With the third portion of his army, he came down the valley like a hammer and smashed into the front of the charge.

At the same time, Kragen abandoned his position. Leaving behind only enough men to keep his side of the valley closed for a short time, he brought the rest of his strength against the Cadwal incursion.

And the Termigan did the same from the other side.

He was retreating, his men were scrambling for their lives, they were already beaten – and suddenly they turned and became a coherent force again and attacked. Backed by the rampart wall, they drove into the Cadwals near the narrowest point of access to the valley—

— hit so hard, so unexpectedly, that they cut Festten off.

With four or five thousand of his men still outside the valley, out of reach, the High King found himself facing his old enemy in battle.

Here for a short time at any rate the conditions of combat were almost even: the numbers of the armies were nearly equal. Nevertheless there was nothing equal about the way the men fought.

The Cadwals had been taken by surprise, outmaneuvered; their greatest weapon, the slug-beast, was dead; they couldn't retreat. Their consternation was obvious through the mirror, as vivid as a shout. And the forces of Mordant and Alend struck as if they knew that while King Joyse led them they could never be defeated.

964

They didn't know that Joyse was as good as dead, that Eremis could translate him to madness at any time. They only knew that he was leading them again, and fighting mightily, that no one had ever seen him lose. His spirit seemed to sweep them with him, carry them all to power.

Almost immediately, what should have been an even fight began to look like a victory for the King.

Terisa cleared her throat. Softly, but precisely, so that each word was unmistakable, she asked, 'Do you hear horns?'

Horns?

Eremis studied her narrowly. He didn't care about the battle, not anymore; the fire in him needed a different outlet. No matter what happened in the valley, Joyse's doom was *here*: this mirror would ruin him. And if Festten was beaten first, so much the better. Eremis was done with that alliance. It had served its purpose.

But she wasn't looking at him.

He wanted her to look at him. He wanted to see fear in her eyes.

With his hands on her shoulders, he turned her.

Still she wasn't afraid. The hunger she had revealed earlier was gone. Blankness filled her gaze.

No, Terisa, he promised, there is no escape that way. There is no part of you so secret that I cannot find it and hurt it.

To get her attention, he unclasped his cloak and let it drop, then undid his trousers so that she could see the size of his passion against her.

Still her eyes showed no fear. She looked past him or through him as if she had gone blind.

Fiercely, he caught hold of her, closed his arms around her, sealed his mouth on hers. He meant to kiss her until she resisted – or melted—

But she was already limp. All her muscles had gone dead. Her lips felt cold, as if the blood in her heart had become ice.

He gripped her brutally, so furious at her for defying him this way that he wanted to break her back, punish her at once, absolutely. He was strong enough: he could do it. Crushing his forearms across her spine, he tried to find the place where she could still feel pain.

An unexpected movement caught the corner of his eye.

She turned her head toward it as if she knew what it meant.

Before he had time to think, he looked at the mirror.

The movement was there; but it wasn't the movement of armies, it wasn't in the Image. The Image itself was moving, modulating—

While he watched, the scene which the glass reflected became a large room with a bed and instruments of enjoyment; stone floors; sunshine.

At the center of the scene, facing Eremis, stood a tall, naked man with a nose that was too big, cheekbones that sloped too much toward his ears, a thatch of black hair too far back on his skull. Despite their usual intelligence and humor, the man's eyes were wide, almost gaping.

His arms held an unattractively dressed woman. Her body sagged against him as if the last of her strength had faded away.

Her eyes, on the other hand—

They were no longer blank. She had gone so far down inside herself that she had reached a place of unexpected power. Darkness seemed to spill from her gaze like a void overflowing, a black emptiness reaching out to gather him in.

He was seeing himself, and her; that was his own Image echoed in the flat mirror. It had a luminous quality, a precise perfection, which startled him like a revelation, as if it were all he needed to know.

Let me show you what I can do.

The last thing he felt before his mind vanished into eternal translation was a sense of complete astonishment.

FIFTY-TWO

NO MORE FIGHTING

Terisa seemed to hang limp there in Master Eremis' frozen embrace for a long time.

At one point, she thought she remembered a peculiar tremor under her feet, a trembling in the stone. It was gone before she noticed it, however, and her recollection of it was uncertain.

Nevertheless the effort of trying to think helped bring her back.

Now she remembered something else, something she couldn't be mistaken about: the sound of horns.

She had heard them plainly, winding through her heart: the music of hunting, the bold summons of music; the call to risk and beauty. Even though mirrors couldn't transmit sound, the horns had come to her while she watched King Joyse ride into battle; she had heard the horns as she had seen him fight. They had lifted her up—

The memory of them lifted her now, restored her to herself.

It was time to move.

She didn't know what had happened to Artagel and Geraden, but she wasn't afraid; not yet. Gart would have stopped Geraden if he could. And Master Gilbur would have attacked King Joyse by Imagery if he could. Since Gilbur had done nothing – except make the floor tremble? – Geraden and Artagel must still be alive. She wanted to see them, however, all three of the brothers. She wanted to feel Geraden's arms around her and look at Artagel's face and find out how Nyle was.

She took one last look at her Image, making sure of herself. Then she released her hold on the mirror, so that it could resume its natural reflection.

After that, she began to squirm out of Eremis' grasp.

He was as hard as stone, still erect and rigid; every part of him was tight with unsatisfied ambition and striving. As a result, she found it difficult to get away from him. Nevertheless, because he couldn't react to her movements, he couldn't keep her.

After a moment, she was free.

He went on standing as though she were his forever – as if he had only turned his head momentarily from her best kiss to glance at the mirror before consummating their embrace.

Vaguely, she wondered if he might be in pain, if he had enough of himself left to feel outrage or loss. She doubted it.

Then Geraden and Artagel and Nyle entered the room.

Despite their obvious exhaustion, they had all come to fight for her. Artagel held his sword poised; Nyle swung his chains; Geraden's face was full of threats. They all came forward to fling themselves at Master Eremis. But when they saw that he wasn't moving, that he couldn't move, and she was unharmed, Geraden gave a shout of joy, Artagel blinked in happy astonishment, and Nyle dropped his chains.

Oh, Geraden. Oh, love. Mute with relief and constricted weeping, she hugged him and hugged him while Artagel thumped her back boisterously and Nyle shed quiet tears of his own.

None of them asked any questions. They were all happy to wait a while to find out what had happened.

On the other hand, after a moment they all found themselves looking at the mirror.

Its focus had to be adjusted before they could see King Joyse. He had ridden so far down the valley, was so heavily engaged among the Cadwals, that he was momentarily out of view. When they located him, however, they saw almost at once that he might win this battle.

His forces and the High King's still seemed roughly equal in numbers. But the Termigan and his men continued to block the left side of the valley; the soldiers Prince Kragen had left in place sealed the right side. As a result, High King Festten wasn't receiving any reinforcements.

He needed reinforcements. The Cadwals simply weren't fighting as well or as hard as their opponents. King Joyse and the Prince attacked them from two sides, and the Termigan cut at their rear, and the rampart wall and the slug-beast's corpse hemmed them in: they had no room to maneuver, no avenue of escape. And the men of Alend and Mordant fought as if they couldn't be beaten.

At the sight, Artagel's face shone, and Geraden cheered, 'Look at him! Didn't I tell you he was worth serving?' He had apparently forgotten that Nyle might have a different reaction. 'Didn't I?'

Terisa still needed to weep. At the same time, a fierce exultation rose in her. She had to struggle to make her throat work. 'Something I want to do.'

Unable to explain, she waved Geraden and Artagel and Nyle back from the mirror. She moved it so that Master Eremis no longer blocked her way. Nearly in tears, nearly crowing, she adjusted the focus of the Image up to the rampart, to the last catapult.

The engine was ready to throw – and both King Joyse and Prince Kragen appeared to be within range.

Striking her only blow of the battle, Terisa translated a strut out of the catapult's frame. The timber was under such pressure that it came through the glass like a shot and slammed against the far wall.

Without the strut, the engine wrenched itself apart.

This time, both Geraden and Artagel cheered. Some of the men in the valley looked like they might be cheering.

That helped; but she still couldn't unknot her grief and joy. If she remained where she was, with Master Eremis like that in front of her, she might begin sobbing wildly.

'Let's go,' she said.

Artagel nodded at once and turned to support Nyle. But Geraden looked at the erect Imager, and at the cloak on the floor, as if he were embarrassed by pity.

'Shouldn't we cover him?'

Terisa shook her head. 'Leave him alone. He's probably happy that way.'

In surprise and relief, Geraden gave a shout of laughter.

Artagel laughed, too, a loud, long hoot of mirth. Even Nyle managed a wan smile.

Suddenly, the knot inside Terisa loosened, and she started laughing as well.

Happy that way. Ready and capable and full of himself until he died. Giggling and chuckling, she and the Domne's sons laughed all the way back to the Image-room.

In the center of the damaged ring of mirrors, they found Adept Havelock. He sat on the bare stone as if he had appeared there by translation. His eyes were strangely focused, and his face wore lines of sorrow; he looked like a man who had lost an old friend.

His arms held the arch-Imager.

Vagel had what looked like a tree limb driven through his belly. He was covered with blood, obviously dead.

Havelock was singing to him softly.

'I understand,' the mad, old Imager crooned as if he were comforting a child. 'I understand everything. Everything.'

Terisa felt a renewed desire to weep, but it didn't last long.

The flat glass showed King Joyse surging through the press of Cadwals toward High King Festten. He wasn't using his sword anymore: he didn't seem to need it. His charge alone was enough to make the Cadwals give ground. They were being routed.

The destruction of the last catapult had struck them like an announcement from the stronghold that Master Eremis and Master Gilbur and the arch-Imager Vagel were defeated. And the forces of Mordant and Alend gave the Cadwals no space or time in which to rally. The High King appeared to be screaming furiously, but he couldn't make the wall of men around him hold.

'He's going to do it,' Artagel breathed happily. 'He's going to beat Festten.'

'With Prince Kragen,' Terisa said for Nyle's benefit, pointing out the alliance between Mordant and Alend. 'They're doing it together.'

Nyle stared as if he couldn't trust his eyes.

For a moment, Terisa thought that someone should talk to him. There was a great deal he didn't know, a number of things he needed to hear. But she still didn't have the heart for explanations; not yet.

'Can we go there?' she asked Geraden. 'To the valley?'

The only man she could think of who might have the power to do Nyle some real good was King Joyse.

'We don't know where it is from here,' Geraden replied thoughtfully. 'And there have *got* to be guards around here somewhere. We're bound to run into them, if we try to go on foot.' His smile came to him easily. 'Of course, we've got plenty of mirrors.'

Nyle looked apprehensive. In a tone of mock-boredom, Artagel said, 'Don't worry. There's really nothing to this translation business, once you get used to it.'

Terisa found herself laughing again. Geraden laughed as well, and Artagel chuckled.

She feared that she wouldn't be able to stop laughing if they didn't go soon. The things she had endured and suffered in the past few days required some kind of outlet. But Geraden sobered when he looked at Adept Havelock. After a moment of uncertainty, he went to stand near the Adept.

'Vagel is dead,' he said carefully. 'You finally beat him. We're going to join King Joyse. Will you come with us?'

Havelock didn't raise his head. Briefly, however, he stopped crooning. In a surprisingly lucid voice, he said, 'You go ahead. I'll stay here for a while. If things go badly at the last minute, I can use these mirrors to take care of Festten. That should guarantee Joyse's victory.'

Almost at once, he added, 'Not that he needs me to guarantee anything for him.'

Softly, he began singing again.

Geraden shrugged. With a bemused expression on his face, he returned to Terisa, Artagel, and Nyle.

He was becoming more familiar with his talent, more practiced. He needed only a few seconds to take one of the curved mirrors and shift it until its Image showed the hillside in the valley where King Joyse had set his pennon – the hillside where Myste and Elega, Master Barsonage and the Congery stood to watch the battle. When he was ready, he bowed sententiously to Terisa and his brothers, and gestured for one of them to go first.

Activity was a kind of outlet. Promptly, Terisa moved to face the glass.

Before she stepped into it, however, she met Geraden's intent, glad gaze and said, 'If you go wrong this time, you are really and truly going to owe me an apology.'

While he was still laughing, she accepted the translation.

As usual, she lost her footing when the quick, infinite passage was over. Ingloriously, she stumbled and fell to her knees in the slush of melting snow.

Myste and Elega cried out when she appeared; but Master Barsonage reached her first. Choking on solicitude, astonishment, and hope until he was completely unable to speak, he helped her to her feet.

She had time to see the fierce triumph on Elega's features, the vindication and the dark loss in Myste's eyes. Then Nyle and Artagel appeared beside her and had to be helped out of the muck.

At once, Artagel whipped out Gart's sword and held it high. 'The blade of the High King's Monomach!' he shouted.

The guards around the pennon started cheering.

To the accompaniment of hoarse cries, fervent applause, Geraden arrived.

He fell flat on his face as if the slush were a pig wallow. This time, however, the lady Elega helped him regain his feet; she beamed at him. At last, she had learned how to ignore his minor mishaps.

For some reason, the chagrin in his smile seemed wonderful to Terisa. It seemed to suggest that he had come through his experiences with a whole heart.

Then other cheers echoed up from the valley foot. King Joyse had reached the High King; he had knocked Festten's sword aside, pulled the Cadwal tyrant off his mount.

Frantically, the High King's men began to surrender as fast as they could.

They had good cause: outside the valley, their reinforcements were scattering. Maybe the destruction of the last catapult had taken the resolve out of them. Or maybe Havelock had performed some other translation to frighten them. Whatever the explanation, thousands of men stopped trying to batter their way into the valley and headed instead for the maze of the hills.

Without reinforcements, the Cadwal position became hopeless. High King Festten's men gave up to save their lives.

King Joyse had won what should have been an impossible victory.

Cheering spread up the valley, resounded from the ramparts into the clean sky. Abruptly, Master Barsonage let out an uncharacteristic yell, and the Imagers began congratulating each other delightedly. Elega's eyes spilled happy tears; Artagel flourished Gart's sword; Geraden hugged Terisa until she thought her ribs might crack. For a moment, the only unhappy people on the hillside were Myste, who had lost Darsint, and Nyle, who had helped bring King Joyse to the brink of defeat.

Almost at once, however, an unexpected silence followed the shouting up from the foot of the valley. Terisa and Geraden craned their necks without letting go of each other; for a moment, their view was blocked by the press of men. Fortuitously, a gap appeared just in time to let them see the slug-beast open its maw as if it had come back to life.

Struggling mightily, the champion forced open the monster's evil teeth and staggered between them.

Immediately, he wrenched off his helmet and flung it aside. For a while, he stood gasping as if he had come close to suffocation. Then he pressed several studs down the sides of his armor, and all the metal folded away and fell to the ground, leaving him dressed in what may have been his underwear.

'God-rotting suit,' he panted harshly. 'Ox-supply gave out. Like everything else.'

'Do you mean,' Artagel asked in amazement, 'he actually let that thing *eat* him?'

Several of the guards nodded.

The cheering started again, louder this time.

Myste's face seemed to flare with joy. She left the hillside at a run, racing to rejoin Darsint.

Gradually, the tumult gave way to a new kind of order. The surrendering Cadwals were organized and guarded, marched aside. High King Festten was put on another horse with his hands tied behind him. He had lost his golden helmet; without it, he appeared much smaller. Between King Joyse and Prince Kragen, with the Termigan beside them, he was brought up the valley to the hillside and the King's pennon.

Terisa had never seen King Joyse seem more like a man who deserved horns. He wasn't alone in his triumph, however. Prince Kragen had come through his personal doubts and risks to a look of achievement nearly as sharp-edged as the King's. And the Termigan positively glowered with satisfaction. In fact, the battle and its outcome had done him so much good that he couldn't contain himself. As soon as he and his companions reached the hillside, he ignored protocol and common sense by surging ahead of King Joyse and Prince Kragen.

He brought his charger directly to Terisa and Geraden, did a curvet that nearly knocked them down; then he settled his mount. 'You gave me good advice,' he said loudly, so that everyone could hear the lord of Termigan approach as close as he was able to an apology. 'I should have listened sooner.'

Geraden laughed again. 'You listened soon enough, my lord Termigan.'

The lord's flinty features almost grinned as he withdrew to let King Joyse and Prince Kragen speak.

The Prince didn't seem particularly interested in speaking. He had already jumped off his horse to embrace Elega; he was too busy hugging her to think about anything else for a while.

From horseback, regally, King Joyse faced Terisa and Geraden, Artagel and Nyle.

'You have a story,' he said, 'which I am eager to hear. For the moment, however, tell me only the result. What have you accomplished?'

'My lord King,' replied Artagel at once, 'the High King's Monomach is dead.'

'And Master Gilbur is dead,' Geraden said.

A moment later, he added, 'Adept Havelock has killed the arch-Imager Vagel.'

Terisa cleared her throat. She wanted to say, What about Nyle? Can't you see what happened to him? He needs help.

But the King's blue gaze held her; the memory of horns held her. As well as she could, she said, 'Master Eremis looked at his own Image in a flat mirror. I don't think he's going to bother you anymore.'

King Joyse's smile was as bright and cleansing as the warm sunlight and the ineffable sky.

When he looked at Nyle, however, his smile went away.

He dismounted; he strode toward Nyle sternly, like a sovereign with a traitor to punish.

Then he stopped.

Instead of speaking harshly, he murmured, 'Nyle, forgive me.'

Nyle's face twisted helplessly. 'Forgive—? My lord King, I betrayed you.'

'Yes!' King Joyse retorted at once. 'You betrayed me – as my daughter Elega betrayed me – as the Congery betrayed me. And because I was betrayed this victory became possible. Everything you did against me, you did out of love and honor. And for that reason everything you did played its part in the saving of my realm. You betrayed me to do Mordant good, Nyle. *I* failed you. I failed to see your importance, your *worth*, when my esteem would have been to your benefit.

'I could not have protected you from hurt. But I could have helped you place a higher value on yourself.'

Nyle tried to answer; there may have been a number of things he wanted to say. But he couldn't control his weeping.

Both Artagel and Geraden put their arms around him.

King Joyse turned away to address everyone within earshot.

'Nyle has suffered,' he announced in tone both grim and elated, sorry and glad. 'Do you hear me? He is not a traitor. He has suffered as the Perdon suffered, and as the Tor suffered, and Castellan Lebbick, because his love is strong and he did not understand.'

As he spoke, his voice carried farther and farther, until it reached the walls and the armies, the men of Mordant and Alend and Cadwal throughout the valley.

'A great many good men have suffered and died, among them Master Quillon, who served my purposes when I could risk them with no one else, and Castellan Norge, who served Orison and Mordant and all of you with his life. And with their pain they have purchased a victory which we could not have gained otherwise.

'Remember that they were hurt for us! Remember that we have freedom and victory and *life* because of them!

'And because all of you fought like heroes!

'Now the world is ours, and we must heal it. From this day, let us make our world a place of peace.'

When he finished, the cheering went on for a long time.

After the wounded had been cared for as well as the circumstances allowed, and the men of the three armies had been fed by supplies translated from Orison, King Joyse ordered all of High King Festten's captains, in addition to his own and Prince Kragen's, to join him while he heard the tales Terisa and Geraden, Artagel and Nyle had to tell. He asked the Prince and Elega, Myste and Darsint to describe what they had done. He told his own story again, so that his actions would be as widely understood as possible. Then he returned the Cadwal captains to their men.

He sent several hundred of his guards to find and subdue Master Eremis' stronghold. And he sent other riders to go among the hills, announcing to any hidden or belligerent Cadwals the same amnesty he offered the men who had surrendered: return to their homes or not, join him or not, as they chose, without fear of being hunted down or coerced. King Joyse feared no one and intended to shed no more blood.

Then the Congery began producing hogsheads of ale and casks of wine, and everyone who remained in the valley of Esmerel was invited to the King's celebration.

That night in the Care of Tor there was no more fighting.

CROWNING THE PIECES

Some time later, as spring turned toward summer, Terisa and Geraden rode out of Orison to the stand of trees among the hills where they had first been attacked by callat – where the horsemen of her dream had first appeared to her in the wrong guise, just as they had later come to her in the wrong place, doing the wrong things.

The late cold and snow which had hampered the march to Esmerel had done considerable damage to fruit trees and flowers and early vegetables across the Demesne and the Care of Tor; but there were no signs of chill-blight here. The trees were rich green and elegant, shading the long grass beneath them with easy sweetness; and through the grass wildflowers peeped like delicate and unexpected possibilities. A low breeze ruffled the foliage enough to make the trees murmur, keep the air cool; not enough to disturb the tranquility of the place.

Terisa had brought Geraden there because she wanted to hear horns again. She had a decision to make, and she thought that the keen music which had once lifted her out of herself in a dream, opening her heart to him and King Joyse and Mordant, would help her.

That dream had been a strange kind of augury, at once accurate and misleading: false on both occasions when it had been fulfilled, and somehow true in conflation, as if each occasion had contributed a piece of the truth.

Nevertheless she would have liked to have another dream to go by, an Image reflected in a mirror made of the pure sand of dreams. She needed a sense of direction, of purpose; a hint to guide her.

She had to decide whether to stay where she was. Or to return to her former life.

Geraden was being studiously, almost grimly noncommittal. She would have liked to hear him ask her to stay: that, too, might have helped. But he was determined to respect her wishes, bring no pressure to bear on her decision. Oh, he wanted her to stay; she knew that. But he also wanted her to be happy. He had always been that way, caught up in what she needed or wanted, instinctively willing to let her lead him. And the stronger he became, the more confidence he gained, the less he demanded for himself.

Her happiness wasn't something he could achieve by asking her to subordinate her desires to his own.

Unfortunately, his determination to let her reach her own decision only seemed to make the decision itself more difficult.

She wanted to hear horns.

The woods held a gentle music of their own, but it wasn't the call which thrilled her spirit, the potent blend of melody and hunting. The wildflowers bobbed their heads in the light breeze, nodding to her as if they understood, but revealing nothing. She thought of her former life as a struggle between Reverend Thatcher and her father – a battle to help the ruined and destitute of the world against rapacity and unconcern, against men who inflicted misery for their own benefit simply because they were able to do so. And the more strength Reverend Thatcher showed, the more she wanted to help him.

There were things she could do in her old world.

Mordant, on the other hand, was at peace. And likely to remain so for a long time.

She loved it anyway. She didn't want to give it up.

Geraden, help me.

Even though she knew he didn't want to answer, she asked, 'What should I do?'

He had reached a point where he apparently found it impossible to meet her gaze. Looking away through the trees as if he were searching for the place where the callat had first shown themselves – a place hard to recognize in a scene full of leaves and grass and wildflowers – he murmured, 'I get the impression Darsint is content to stay.'

'He might as well be,' she replied with more asperity than she intended. 'He doesn't have a way back. You can return him to the Image where you found him – to Pythas – but you can't return him to his people. And his suit doesn't have any power. He couldn't defend himself.

'I don't have that problem. You could send *me* back.'

Glumly, Geraden nodded.

Without warning, loneliness welled up inside her, and her eyes brimmed with tears. Oh, Geraden, love, can't you help me? Softly, so that he wouldn't hear how she felt, she asked, 'What are my choices?'

He shrugged. 'I can translate you home. Your father must have sold the apartment by now. You'll have to start your life over again.' Almost at once, however, he added, 'But it might not be so bad. I could visit you sometimes. You could visit me. We know how to do that.'

His voice faded into the rustle of leaves.

'Or?' she insisted.

'Or you can stay here.' For a moment longer, he held his face away, refused to look at her. But then, like a man who couldn't stop himself, he turned toward her. 'You can stay here and marry me.'

Through her tears, his eyes looked abashed and brave, accessible to joy or pain; troubled, sweet, and precious. And when he gazed at her like that, she heard the unmistakable sound of horns.

So they were married in high summer, in the great ballroom of Orison, the hollow hall which had seen no use for years until the Masters had turned it into a staging-area for supplies during the march to Esmerel.

As if regretting the neglect of those joyless years, King Joyse made the ballroom festive for the occasion: the walls were decked with banners and streamers; fragrant rushes were strewn upon the floor; fires in fine braziers gave the air a sheen of gold, while flames in the huge hearths took the old chill out of the stones; musicians arrayed themselves along the balconies, practicing flourishes and dances until every corner of the place seemed to sing and tremble.

All this was organized by the lady Torrent. She was still shy – the dangers and privations she had endured to help rescue her mother hadn't changed that – but she had discovered in herself a reflection of her mother's firm will, as well as the organizational skill to make people and objects come together at the right time. Like her sister Myste, she had rapidly become Terisa's friend, and they had spent many happy hours planning the wedding, to Geraden's alternating chagrin, amusement and delight.

Nonetheless she was still baffled by her new status: she hardly knew what to do with the fact that King Joyse had proclaimed her his heir and successor. Her talents, he declared, were the ones Mordant would need most when he was gone. Publically, she demurred, claiming that she only wished he would live forever. Privately, however, she found that she had a number of ideas about how Orison and Mordant should be ruled.

But even more impressive than the color and music and celebration which Torrent produced was the list of personages who came to the wedding.

Naturally, King Joyse and Queen Madin presided. From time to time, they held hands; and the Queen seemed to dote on Terisa and Geraden as if one of her own children were getting married. According to rumor, however, their reunion had been a stormy one for a long time after her return to Orison. She was said to have been furious at his treatment of her, his refusal to share his secrets with her, to involve her in his plans; and all his protestations and explanations had just made her angrier. This was only rumor, of course. It was true, however, that he had sometimes emerged from their private rooms looking like a man who would have preferred almost any warfare to this peace.

Nevertheless by the time of the wedding they had resolved or accepted their differences, and had begun to enjoy each other's company again. Perhaps he had aided their reconciliation by naming Torrent to succeed him. From their raised seats at one end of the ballroom, they smiled approval at the assembly, and at each other, and were satisfied.

First among the guests – not in nominal rank, but in actual status – were Prince Kragen, the High Regent of Cadwal, and his Consort, the lady Elega. As a couple, they were the basis on which King Joyse and the Alend Monarch had built their new alliance, their new peace. In an effort to insure that no new tyrant came to power in Cadwal, and that the three kingdoms would be held together by bonds of authority and family as well as of common interest, the Monarch's son and the King's daughter had been set on Festten's former Seat in Carmag.

This arrangement had been Joyse's idea, but Margonal had accepted it readily enough. He was learning to understand the way his old enemy thought. And he had ideas of his own—

Blind, weary, content – and unwilling to face the rigors of a second journey to Orison – the Alend Monarch had sent his new Contender to stand in his place at the wedding: a man who now could claim precedence over everyone in Orison except King Joyse and Queen Madin, because of his position as Margonal's representative and potential successor.

The new Alend Contender was Nyle.

Arriving for the ceremony, he still appeared perplexed and a bit daunted by his circumstances. But when Kragen had been installed as High Regent in Carmag, Margonal had needed another Contender; and the Alend Monarch had sensed in Nyle a man with a newborn but almost ferocious instinct for caution. Caution, the Monarch had declared, was the fundamental requirement for anyone who meant to rule over Scarab and the Alend Lieges. Kragen had shown himself altogether too prone to risks, and Margonal wished to replace him with someone who lacked that flaw.

Nyle had refused the honor – or the responsibility – at first. He didn't deserve it, he wasn't worthy. Eventually, however, King Joyse had confronted him with a royal command, and he had felt himself forced to acquiesce.

The reports which King Joyse had since received from the Alend Monarch indicated that Nyle was proving to be exactly the Contender Margonal wanted, despite his self-distrust.

Behind the Alend Contender, and behind the High Regent and his Consort, stood Castellan Darsint and his new bride, the lady Myste.

King Joyse and Queen Madin would have gladly combined the marriage of Darsint and Myste with that of Terisa and Geraden; but Darsint had flatly declined a public ceremony. On the other hand, he hadn't hesitated to accept the place of Castellan.

Chains of command, the procurement of supplies, the movement and housing of men and animals, discipline and defense: these were things the Congery's champion understood in his bones. And his role in the battle of Esmerel gave him an enormous personal credibility which carried him past the uncertain days while he was learning his new job. In addition, he had Myste's advice and support; and despite (or perhaps because of) her 'romantic notions' she had a sense of practical ethics which tempered and guided his authoritarian instincts.

After the Castellan and his lady, the lords of the Cares were arranged in an order of precedence which depended solely on the parts they – or their predecessors – had played in the King's war. First were the Tor, the Perdon, and the Termigan; next, the Fayle and the Domne; last, the Armigite.

The new Tor was one of the old lord's younger sons – in fact, the only one of his sons who wanted the position. But the old Perdon had died without children; and his widow had positively refused to look at the prospect of being the first female lord in Mordant's history as anything except a cruel burden. 'You have lost me my husband and my friends, my lord King,' she had protested harshly. 'Will you now deprive me of quiet as well?' So King Joyse, with a glint in his eyes which occasionally suggested humor, and occasionally malice, had named Artagel as the Perdon.

Artagel's protests had been considerably louder than those of the old lord's widow; but King Joyse had only smiled and insisted, glinting. And at last, in exasperation, he had snapped, 'Be reasonable, Artagel. You can't be the best swordsman in Mordant for the rest of your life. The years won't let you. And those scars are never going to be as resilient as whole flesh and muscle. It's about time you had something else to do.'

So Artagel had relented with an ill grace which had gradually faded as he realized that his new position in Scarping made it possible for him to have a home – and maybe even a family? – of his own at last.

As for the Termigan, everyone had expected him to refuse to attend the wedding, not out of any animosity, but simply because he was too busy rebuilding Sternwall. Nevertheless he had not only come, but he had come politely. Furthermore, he had brought with him an entire wainload of Rostrum wine as a marriage present: a gift which some people considered fit for a King; altogether too fine for mere Geraden and Terisa.

The Domne and the Fayle came next, old friends pleased in each other's company. But of Geraden's family no one else had made the trip to Orison: Tholden was consumed with the task of laying out and constructing a new Houseldon; Wester didn't enjoy travel; Minick couldn't leave his shy wife; Stead couldn't spare the time from his other pursuits. No one had accompanied the Domne except Quiss. Forthright and irrefusable as always, she had claimed that he couldn't hope to make the journey without someone to take care of him. Upon arriving in Orison, however, she had made it clear that her real reason for coming was to see Terisa and Geraden again, and to hear about everything they had done, and to give them the benefit of her advice.

The Domne himself didn't seem to feel compelled to give anyone advice. On the other hand, he was so happy and proud that he made Geraden's face shine and gave Terisa the glad impression that the whole family was present in the old lord's person.

Last of the lords came the Armigite, remarkably subdued in his manner and dress, miserable in his isolation. After the battle of Esmerel, everyone who spoke to King Joyse – in fact, everyone in Orison – had an opinion concerning how the Armigite should be treated. Among them, the Alend Monarch had counseled leniency: after all, the Armigite's imprecise loyalties had allowed the Alend army to reach Orison intact, with obvious (if unforeseen) benefits for both Alend and Mordant. In contrast, Darsint had recommended beheading: treachery deserved death. At last, however, King Joyse had settled on the worst punishment of all: he had decided to do nothing; to treat the Armigite as if his worse offenses were so trivial that they weren't worth noticing.

The Armigite spent most of his time before and after the festivities trying to get someone to talk to him; but no one was willing to be bothered.

Below and beside King Joyse sat Adept Havelock, in a place of honor – and of discretion, as well, a place from which he could withdraw easily if necessary. Since the battle of Esmerel, he seemed to have settled comfortably into his role as the madman of Orison. No longer obsessed by the need for lucidity, he had become able to relax and enjoy himself in odd ways. As a result, his madness appeared to grow more benign, driving him to fewer extremes, permitting him more satisfaction.

He never spoke of his struggle with the arch-Imager, never told how he had beaten Vagel. And he never explained why he had chosen to risk everything in personal combat with Vagel, instead of simply translating his old enemy and Eremis and Gilbur to Orison, as Terisa had intended. If anyone asked him a question, however, any question at all, he often replied with a complete, clear, and quite inappropriate description of everything he and King Joyse had done to meet Mordant's need.

So the celebration went forward, full of music and orations, dancing and wine, vows and homage. On the Congery's behalf, Master Barsonage rejected any unseemly ostentation for the Masters. For himself, however, he claimed the right to stand as Terisa's father during the ceremony. Happy and fustian in a remarkably red robe, he accompanied Terisa through the formalities, and made speeches on her behalf, and generally behaved as if he were as proud as the Domne.

Thus the arch-Imager Terisa of Morgan and Adept Geraden of Domne were married like the princess and the hero in a fable: grandly (some said gloriously) surrounded by family and friends and honor and respect, in a world which they had helped bring to safety. She had lost her father's wealth in order to gain her own power, and the enchantment which had held her was gone. And he had inherited something better than Cares or kingdoms, which was himself: his courage and his willing heart had come into their true birthright.

In the ceremony of marriage, they made a number of vows, all of which added up to the same thing: they promised to help each other hear horns.